W9-BHR-903

ESCUADRÓN
DE LA SOMBRA

OPERACIÓN
ÁGUILA

2015.671

STONE ARCH BOOKS
a capstone imprint

ESCUADRÓN
DE LA SOMBRA

OPERACIÓN ÁGUILA

ESCRITO POR
CARL BOWEN

ILUSTRADO POR
WILSON TORTOSA

COLOREADO POR
BENNY FUENTES

2012.241

AUTORIZANDO

El escuadrón de la sombra es publicado por
Stone Arch Books,
una imprenta de Capstone,
1710 Roe Crest Drive
North Mankato, MN 56003
www.capstonepub.com

Datos de catalogación en publicación
de la Biblioteca del Congreso

ISBN: 978-1-4965-8549-3

Resumen: Edgar Brighton se despierta
con un dolor de cabeza punzante. Al tratar
de enfocar la mirada, ve a una mujer
desconocida que lo observa fijamente. Trata
de hablar, pero lo han amordazado. Intenta
pararse, pero sus manos y pies han sido atados.
En ese momento, Edgar se da cuenta
de que sus problemas apenas han comenzado.

Diseñado por Brann Garvey.
Translated into the Spanish language by
Aparicio Publishing

ZOI9.681

Impreso y encuadernado en los Estados
Unidos de América.
PA70

CONTENIDO

1316.981

ESCUADRÓN DE LA SOMBRA............6

INFORME DE LA MISIÓN............8

CAPÍTULO UNO
ATERRIZÓ EL ÁGUILA............**11**

CAPÍTULO DOS
ENJAULADO............**31**

CAPÍTULO TRES
ALAS............**57**

CAPÍTULO CUATRO
PRESA............**73**

CAPÍTULO CINCO
VOLAR............**93**

REPORTE DE LA MISIÓN............96

2012.101

ACCESO PERMITIDO

CLASIFICADO

EXPEDIENTE DEL ESCUADRÓN DE LA SOMBRA

CROSS, RYAN

RANGO: Mayor
RAMA: Armada (SEAL)
PERFIL: Líder del Escuadrón
de la Sombra. Hombre leal
y enfocado en el control,
Cross insistió en seleccionar
personalmente a su equipo.

WALKER, ALONSO

RANGO: Suboficial jefe
RAMA: Armada (SEAL)
PERFIL: Segundo al mando
del Escuadrón de la Sombra.
Su experiencia en combate,
escepticismo y desconfianza
natural lo convierten en un buen
contrapeso al liderazgo de Cross.

YAMASHITA, KIMIYO

RANGO: Teniente
RAMA: Rangers del Ejército
PERFIL: Francotirador experto
y estoico. No demuestra
emociones y no vacila al disparar.

6

BRIGHTON, EDGAR

RANGO: Sargento
RAMA: Controlador de Combate
de la Fuerza Aérea
PERFIL: Técnico y especialista
en combates en zonas reducidas.
Popular entre sus compañeros,
pero suele perturbar
a sus superiores.

LARSSEN, NEIL

FOTO NO
DISPONIBLE

RANGO: Subteniente
RAMA: Rangers del Ejército
PERFIL: Se jacta de poder
hacer de todo. Su versatilidad
le permite desempeñar diversas
tareas en el Escuadrón.

SHEPHERD, MARK

FOTO NO
DISPONIBLE

RANGO: Teniente
RAMA: Ejército (Boinas Verdes)
PERFIL: Experto en artillería.
Su pasión por el combate
excede los límites.

2019.681

INFORME DE LA MISIÓN

OPERACIÓN

ÁGUILA

1234

Esta será una misión solitaria para el Sargento Edgar Brighton. Él encabezará el esfuerzo conjunto del gobierno para desarticular una red colombiana de tráfico de drogas, o nexo, que introduce drogas ilegales en territorio de Estados Unidos. El blanco es un astillero a lo largo de la costa del Pacífico en la selva colombiana. Brighton se reunirá con soldados colombianos, hará una evaluación del lugar y coordinará por radio un ataque aéreo para acabar con la red de drogas de una vez por todas.

El resto del Escuadrón de la Sombra asistirá a Brighton a distancia y esperarán su señal para recogerlo una vez que termine la misión.

3245.98 ●●●

– Mayor Ryan Cross

COLOMBIA

OBJETIVO(S) PRIMARIO(S)

- Incursionar de manera
  encubierta usando paracaídas

- Reunirse con fuerza especial
  colombiana

- Localizar astillero

- Proveer coordenadas para
  ataque aéreo certero

OBJETIVO(S) SECUNDARIO(S)

- Minimizar bajas

- Establecer relación positiva
  con fuerza especial colombiana

- Permanecer encubierto

1932.789

0412.981

TÉRMINOS TÁCTICOS

- CONTROLADOR DE COMBATE
  - soldado de la Fuerza Aérea
  especializado en apoyo aéreo,
  comunicación y organización

- FUERZA ESPECIAL - grupo temporal
  de unidades de combate bajo las
  órdenes de un comandante

- NEXO - núcleo o centro, o los medios
  de conexión entre varios elementos
  individuales; una organización

- RECONOCIMIENTO - búsqueda hecha
  para obtener información militar útil
  en el campo de combate

3245.98 ✳ ✳ ✳

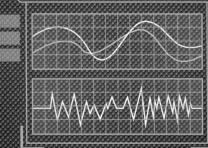

ATERRIZÓ EL ÁGUILA

1324.014

Todavía hasta el momento en que tocó tierra en la selva, el análisis de Brighton sobre la misión era que la Operación: Nexo iba muy bien.

Esta misión era un esfuerzo conjunto de Estados Unidos y Colombia centrado en asestar un duro golpe a la red de drogas ilegales colombianas, o nexo. Su objetivo primario era un astillero poco sofisticado escondido en alguna parte de la selva en la costa colombiana del Pacífico.

En algún lugar, entre los ríos sinuosos y árboles de manglar, había una instalación que fabricaba naves capaces de contrabandear hasta diez toneladas de cocaína a la vez. Y eran virtualmente indetectables.

Estos transportes, apodados "narcosubmarinos", eran pequeños vehículos de fibra de vidrio capaces de navegar justo debajo de la superficie del océano, guiados por periscopio y GPS. Una pequeña tripulación podía llevar una de estas naves desde el astillero, escabullirse por los ríos hasta la costa y llegar al océano fácilmente. Desde ahí, los narcosubmarinos tomaban rumbo norte hacia la costa de México. Luego, atracaban en diferentes puertos clandestinos para descargar las drogas ilegales y entregarlas a los distribuidores que las esperaban.

En años recientes, este sistema causó un marcado aumento en la cocaína proveniente de Colombia que entraba a México y luego a Estados Unidos. El cartel mexicano de Sinaloa cortaba, distribuía y vendía la cocaína. Elementos del ejército de rebeldes guerrilleros de las Fuerzas Armadas Revolucionarias de Colombia (o FARC) producían la cocaína. Las FARC también equipaban los narcosubmarinos y reclutaban a los aterrorizados pescadores que los pilotaban.

Cuando el cartel de Sinaloa vendía la cocaína en el extranjero, les daban un porcentaje de las ganancias a las guerrillas de las FARC. Con ese dinero las guerrillas compraban armas, equipo y suministros para continuar sus intentos de derrocar al gobierno legítimo de Colombia.

Después de hablar mucho acerca del problema y planificar mucho sobre qué hacer al respecto, Estados Unidos y Colombia habían decidido poner en marcha una estrategia que rompería el arreglo de tráfico de drogas FARC/Sinaloa. Los colombianos tenían información general sobre el lugar donde pensaban que estaba escondido el astillero de narcosubmarinos. Sin embargo, habían perdido cada soldado y oficial de policía que habían enviado a la selva. Peor aún, ninguno de ellos pudo confirmar la supuesta localización del astillero.

Los colombianos aseguraban estar dispuestos a atacar y destruir el astillero clandestino. No obstante, necesitaban la ayuda de los norteamericanos para hallar la base y reunir información confiable del astillero. No querían ni un gran número de tropas estadounidenses ni maquinaria militar metida de lleno en su territorio para pelear las batallas que les correspondían a ellos. En cambio, solo querían un poco de ayuda para empezar la pelea.

Esa ayuda llegó en la persona del sargento Edgar Brighton, un controlador de combate

de la Fuerza Aérea de Estados Unidos.
Y miembro fundador del equipo del Escuadrón
de la Sombra, algo que pocos sabían.

Junto con Brighton, el Escuadrón de la Sombra
estaba integrado por miembros de los Rangers
del Ejército, los Boinas Verdes, la Fuerza de
Reconocimiento de la Marina, y la Armada (SEAL).
Los colombianos aceptaron que el Escuadrón
de la Sombra usara la pequeña base militar
en la deshabitada isla Malpelo. Luego los colombianos
organizaron una fuerza especial conjunta de militares
y policías de su propia gente para coordinarla
con los norteamericanos excelentemente capacitados.

Todos habían estado trabajando y entrenando
juntos por varias semanas, y ya estaban listos para
poner en marcha la Operación: Nexo. La primera
etapa era mejorar la información de los colombianos
sobre el astillero antes de que un ataque aéreo iniciara
la etapa final.

Por sus destrezas únicas y su dominio del español,
el sargento Brighton fue elegido por el mayor Cross
para esta tarea.

Como controlador de combate, el trabajo

de Brighton sería incursionar solo en territorio hostil y llevar a cabo reconocimiento especial de la zona. Luego le reportaría sus hallazgos a Cross en los cuarteles generales improvisados. En el campo de combate, su trabajo sería mantener contacto con cualquier unidad aérea que estuviera disponible. Eso significaba que Brighton tendría que organizar aviones de combate rápidos, bombarderos y transportación aérea de emergencia. Tendría que mantenerlos enfocados en la misión, en el blanco y alejados unos de otros.

Brighton también sería responsable de la acción directa. Pelearía hombro con hombro con sus compañeros soldados cuando enfrentaran al enemigo.

Había más que suficiente apoyo aéreo para la Operación: Nexo, así que era responsabilidad de Brighton llegar primero. Dependía de él preparar todo para el resto de su equipo. Pero no estaría solo.

Para ayudarlo en su tarea, le habían ordenado que estableciera contacto en la selva con un equipo de avanzada de militares y policías colombianos de la fuerza especial. Ellos le indicarían la dirección exacta adónde ir una vez que pisara tierra. Le cubrirían

la espalda mientras él reuniría información
y la reportaría al mayor Cross y al resto del Escuadrón
de la Sombra.

El recorrido en bote y luego en auto desde la isla
Malpelo hasta la siguiente base de operaciones
en Popayán había sido suficientemente placentero.
Brighton tuvo la oportunidad de pasar el rato con
su superior, el mayor Ryan Cross. También pudo
conversar con los soldados colombianos que habían ido
a recogerlo.

Por ser miembros de un grupo de élite
de operaciones encubiertas especiales, Cross y Brighton
no podían decir nada personal acerca de ellos
ni de sus misiones pasadas a los colombianos.
Pero al parecer, a los policías del lugar y los soldados
de la fuerza especial les encantaba hablar de cosas
triviales.

La sesión del informe de la misión entre Brighton,
Cross y el mayor Timoleón Gaitán (el líder de la fuerza
especial), había ido a la perfección. Sin embargo,
Brighton se dio cuenta de que el militar colombiano
estaba nervioso de lo joven que era Brighton.

Pero Gaitán se guardó su opinión para sí mismo,

y Brighton no se vio forzado a enumerar la lista
de escuelas de capacitación especializada en cuyos
programas había obtenido la máxima calificación
después de la Escuela de Control de Combate. Él sabía
que lo habían seleccionado para el Escuadrón
de la Sombra siendo tan joven por una muy buena
razón. Pero el mayor Gaitán no preguntó cuáles eran
esas razones. Probablemente, eso fue lo mejor,
ya que Brighton no quería avergonzar a su anfitrión.

El vuelo sobre la selva había sido igual que docenas
de otros en los que Brighton había participado alrededor
del mundo. La cabina de pasajeros del Cessna 206
que la policía colombiana proporcionó como transporte,
era un tanto estrecha. O al menos así lo parecía,
con la tripulación, el maestro paracaidista y Brighton
con su equipo apiñados adentro.

Fue una pena que Brighton no tuviera tiempo
de conversar con el equipo de Popayán debido
a la revisión de último minuto de su equipo
y el paracaídas. Sin embargo, unas cuantas bromas
y su simpatía hicieron que todos se sintieran a gusto.
Es decir, lo a gusto que se puede estar en una cabina
de avión estrecha y oscura volando sobre territorio
hostil en horas de la madrugada.

Pero si alguien podía hacerlos sentir bien, Brighton sabía que él era el indicado. Le encantaba conocer gente nueva y disfrutaba de hacer nuevos amigos.

* * *

Justo antes del amanecer, el piloto dijo por el interfono que el avión estaba sobre la zona de salto. Brighton se colocó su máscara de visión nocturna, luego se aceró a la puerta lateral del Cessna junto al maestro paracaidista. Con varios tubos de intensificación de imagen de 16mm sobresaliendo de su máscara, como dedos alrededor de los ojos, Brighton tenía un escalofriante aspecto de insecto. Y notó que el maestro paracaidista lo tuvo que mirar dos veces a medida que se le acercaba.

Más allá del aspecto extraño, Brighton prefería el campo de visión amplio de su máscara panorámica en lugar de las que usaba el resto del Escuadrón de la Sombra. Las otras máscaras le hacían sentir que su campo de visión estaba limitado.

Viendo dónde apuntaba el dedo del maestro paracaidista, Brighton localizó un pequeño claro a unos cuantos cientos de yardas de la ribera de un río fangoso. En el centro del claro, un pequeño faro infrarrojo parpadeaba. Esa era la señal que el equipo de avanzada colombiano había colocado para guiar a Brighton hacia donde estaban ellos. Por fortuna, era visible solo desde el aire por medio de equipo de visión nocturna. Brighton no quería tocar tierra en medio de un equipo de enemigos armados.

Brighton aclaró su mente y se preparó para saltar. Desde esa altura, iba a ser difícil aterrizar en el centro del claro, pero no estaba preocupado. Saltar y aterrizar con precisión en la selva espesa antes del amanecer no era nada comparado con tener que lidiar con guerrilleros traficantes de drogas disparando contra él. Así que con una mente bien capacitada y plenamente confiada, él esperó la señal del maestro paracaidista.

—¡Salta! —gritó el maestro paracaidista.

Un momento después, Brighton se lanzó por la puerta y se zambulló en las tinieblas

¡FUUUUUUU!

La euforia de los primeros segundos de caída libre lo hizo sentirse mareado. El paracaidismo siempre le había encantado, desde aquel primer salto en tándem con su padre cuando tenía quince años. Le fascinó dejarse llevar por la emoción del descenso a medida que la Tierra se iba haciendo cada vez más grande frente a él.

Pero esta vez, se permitió sentir solo unos momentos fugaces de alegría antes de dejar que su mente entrenada tomara el control de la situación.

Brighton extendió sus brazos y piernas para enderezarse en el aire y maximizar la resistencia del viento. Luego verificó el altímetro y el aparato GPS que llevaba en la muñeca. Finalmente, se movió en el aire hasta que una vez más localizó el faro con sus gafas.

El giro suave y gradual le dio una buena oportunidad de observar la topografía del terreno. Con sus ojos trazó las muchas ensenadas y desembocaduras de ríos, memorizando unos cuantos de los puntos de referencia que podía distinguir con su máscara de visión nocturna. Cuando estaba a la altura apropiada, abrió su paracaídas.

¡FUUUUUUU!

Brighton entró en una amplia espiral descendente.
Estaba seguro de que eso lo pondría a diez yardas
de distancia del claro o incluso en el centro exacto.
De hecho, fácilmente.

Sin embargo, la parte más difícil era el aterrizaje
mismo. Todo el equipo que Brighton cargaba lo hacía
más pesado para el paracaídas. Como se esperaba,
Brighton logró aterrizar en el centro del pequeño claro.
Pero cuando pisó el suelo fangoso, el peso extra lo hizo
tropezar. Una ráfaga de viento empujó el paracaídas
contra las ramas. Brighton tuvo que dejarlo colgando
por un momento para colocar en el suelo la segunda
mochila de equipo y zafarse del arnés.

El procedimiento estándar era enterrar
el paracaídas y los aparejos después de aterrizar
para minimizar la posibilidad de que fuerzas enemigas
descubrieran la incursión. Acababa de abrir su mochila
para sacar su pala cuando escuchó varios pares
de botas chapoteando en el fango.

Brighton vio salir de entre las sombras de la selva
a un grupo de ocho hombres en uniforme de camuflaje
anticuado. Se veían rudos y robustos.

A Brighton le parecieron más una fuerza especial de aguerridos soldados que policías. Y todos se veían de bastante más edad que Brighton, aunque eso podía ser por el desgaste de los años de combate.

—Hola, amigos —los saludó Brighton—. ¿No pudieron elegir un claro más pequeño para aterrizar? Casi lo podía ver desde el aire.

—¿Es usted el que mandó Gaitán? —preguntó uno de los hombres más cerca de Brighton. Tenía la voz ronca de fumador empedernido.

Brighton asintió con la cabeza. El hombre no dijo nada, pero en cambio señaló a otro soldado detrás de Brighton.

—Denme un segundo para preparar mi radio —dijo Brighton—. Si alguno de ustedes puede descolgar ese paracaídas y enterrarlo, se los voy a agradecer.

Brighton se arrodilló a un lado de su mochila. Justo acababa de abrir la cubierta a prueba de agua y de tomar la antena, cuando un hombre se colocó detrás de él. Sin pensarlo, Brighton le pasó la pala doblada que tenía sobre el hombro.

—Ahí la tiene —dijo Brighton—. Gracias
por la ayuda.

¡ZZZAAAAAP!

Cincuenta mil voltios de electricidad penetraron
el cuerpo de Brighton por su espalda, en medio
omóplatos. Cada nervio y músculo le quemaban
de dolor.

Brighton se desplomó encorvado. Sentía
que había perdido el control de su cuerpo.
Ya había soportado esta misma sensación durante
su entrenamiento. De lo contrario, no hubiese sabido
lo que acababa de pasar.

En un escondite de su mente, alejado del dolor,
Brighton entendió que lo habían electrocutado
con una pistola eléctrica. Tan pronto se percató de esto,
recibió otra descarga.

¡ZZZAAAAAP!

Brighton trató de gritar, pero no pudo abrir la boca.
Sus dientes estaban apretados debido a los espasmos
musculares en todo su cuerpo.

Mientras Brighton yacía en el suelo respirando con dificultad, uno de los colombianos lo colocó sobre su espalda. El resto de los soldados lo rodearon para verlo. Uno de ellos sostenía en su mano el faro infrarrojo centelleante. A distancia tan corta, el intenso resplandor cegó los ojos de Brighton a través de su máscara de visión nocturna.

Un hombre se arrodilló frente a él. Alzó la pistola eléctrica donde Brighton pudiera verla.

—Todavía está consciente —dijo el hombre, en tono burlón. Bajó la pistola eléctrica hacia Brighton de nuevo.

"No es una varita mágica para aturdir", pensó en decir Brighton. Pero estaba demasiado adolorido para moverse, y menos aún para hablar. Por fortuna, otro de los soldados le quitó el arma de electrochoque al hombre antes de que electrocutara a Brighton otra vez.

—Ya basta de juguetear —se oyó decir. Brighton miró hacia arriba y vio la culata de un rifle de asalto M16 golpeando durísimo su máscara de visión nocturna.

¡PLONC!

Al mismo tiempo, Brighton vio estrellas y oyó
el repugnante sonido de vidrio haciéndose añicos.
Y entonces, todo se tornó oscuro.

* * *

Cuando Brighton recobró la consciencia, no tenía
idea de cuánto tiempo había estado inconsciente.
Podían haber sido horas, o incluso días.

Probablemente no habían sido días, pero Brighton
no tenía manera de saberlo. Lo único que sabía
con certeza era la sensación de que le habían partido
la cabeza por la mitad. Una palpitación pesada
y cegadora que emanaba de arriba de su ojo derecho,
latía al mismo tiempo que su pulso. "Es donde
el colombiano me golpeó con la culata del M16",
pensó.

A medida que recuperaba sus sentidos, miró
el área para analizar la situación. Al voltear la cabeza
cuidadosamente con su cuello tenso, vio que estaba
dentro de una habitación de 10 pies por 10 pies y sobre
una placa de concreto. El techo y las paredes eran
de metal corrugado.

El aire estaba cargado de la humedad de la selva,
y no había ventilación. Lo que si había eran luces

brillantes en el techo y en el muro frente a él.
Le brillaban justo frente al rostro y también podía oír
el estrepitoso ruido de un generador detrás de una
de las paredes.

Brighton trató de levantar la mano para escudar
sus ojos adoloridos del resplandor. Pero al no poder
mover la mano, se dio cuenta de que sus muñecas
habían sido esposadas a la silla en la que estaba
sentado.

La vieja silla de dentista estaba tapizada de vinilo
agrietado y descolorido. Al bajar la mirada para ver sus
tobillos, notó que estaban esposados en el reposapiés
que sobresalía frente a él. Sus botas y calcetines
habían desaparecido.

—FARC —refunfuñó Brighton.

No cabía la menor duda de que había
sido capturado por las FARC, los mismos rebeldes
por los que el Escuadrón de la Sombra y el gobierno
colombiano estaban trabajando juntos para eliminar.

La verdadera pregunta era qué había hecho
la guerrilla que lo capturó con la fuerza especial
conjunta de militares y policías. Se suponía que se iban
a encontrar en el punto de aterrizaje. El hecho

de que las guerrillas de las FARC hayan estado esperando cerca del faro infrarrojo implicaba eso.

Y el hecho de que hayan mencionado al mayor Gaitán por su nombre probaba que la captura de Brighton no era resultado de la mala suerte.

Brighton supuso que alguien en el equipo de avanzada era un traidor. Esa persona pudo haber advertido fácilmente a los rebeldes sobre la Operación: Nexo. Pero la sensación siniestra que provocaba la habitación en la que Brighton se encontraba, sugería que las FARC probablemente habían usado la tortura para obtener la información.

Y Brighton sabía con toda certeza que él sería el siguiente.

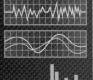

INTELIGENCIA

DESCIFRANDO
|||||||| ||||||||||||| ||||

12345

TÉRMINOS TÁCTICOS

- GARRAFÓN – recipiente grande
que se usa para guardar diferentes
líquidos, incluso agua

- CARTEL DE DROGAS – una
organización criminal enfocada
en el tráfico de drogas

- TRAJE DE FAENA – uniforme
de soldado

- AHOGAMIENTO SIMULADO – método
de tortura que consiste en verter
agua sobre el rostro de una persona
causándole una sensación de ahogo

3245.98 ▪ ▪ ▪

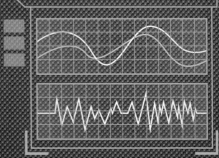

ENJAULADO

1324.014

¡CLINC!

Brighton escuchó abrir una puerta detrás de él.
Un colombiano caminó lentamente alrededor
de Brighton hasta estar a la vista. Vestía un traje
de faena limpio color verde olivo, guantes de hule
y una máscara azul de cirugía. Solo se le veían los ojos
debajo del ala de su sombrero. Escribía una nota
en una pequeña libreta de espiral y en eso se dio
cuenta de que Brighton estaba despierto.

El hombre guardó su libreta y bolígrafo
en el bolsillo de la cadera y le tomó el pulso a Brighton.
Luego oprimió delicadamente la protuberancia arriba
del ojo derecho de Brighton quien lo vigiló con recelo
durante el examen. El hombre no dijo nada.

—¿Me puede dar un poco de agua? —preguntó
Brighton.

El colombiano seguía sin decir nada.

—¿O mejor un sándwich? Ahora mismo le revelaría
algunos nombres a cambio de uno de queso y carne
estilo *Philly*.

El colombiano se detuvo, luego caminó por detrás
de Brighton hacia la entrada.

—Y consígame una aspirina cuando regrese
—exclamó Brighton—. El dolor de cabeza me está
matando.

La puerta se abrió y se cerró rápidamente detrás de él.

—Muy bien, tómese su tiempo —dijo Brighton—.
Píenselo un poquito.

Pasaron más o menos diez minutos. Entonces
la puerta se abrió y varias personas entraron arrastrando
los pies. Al principio, nadie se puso a la vista de Brighton,
pero los escuchaba moviéndose detrás de él. Alguien
seguía entrando y saliendo. Por su respiración, se deducía
que cargaba algo pesado. A Brighton le tomó un par de
repeticiones para percatarse de lo que era. Alguien estaba
metiendo pesados garrafones llenos de agua, como los

que se colocan en las fuentes de agua fría
de las oficinas. Según sus cálculos, habían traído
un total de seis garrafones.

Cuando eso terminó, alguien arrastró
a la habitación un carro con ruedas y luego cerró
la puerta. Fue entonces que los visitantes se pusieron
a la vista de Brighton.

A su derecha estaba el mismo colombiano
que Brighton había visto antes. Ahora ya no tenía
los guantes ni la máscara, pero la libreta y el bolígrafo
aún estaban en su bolsillo. Traía un estetoscopio
alrededor del cuello, y un oftalmoscopio en una mano.

El hombre se inclinó sobre Brighton y usó
el oftalmoscopio para revisarle los ojos. Después,
con el estetoscopio chequeó la frecuencia cardíaca
y la respiración de Brighton. En ningún momento
los ojos del hombre se encontraron con los de Brighton.

Detrás del "doctor", vestidos con trajes de faena
camuflados, estaban dos colombianos más. Brighton
los reconoció del claro en la selva. Uno de ellos fue
el que lo electrocutó con la pistola eléctrica. El otro fue
el que lo noqueó con el rifle.

—Oiga, amigo —le dijo Brighton al hombre que

lo examinaba—. ¿Dónde está mi aspirina?

Alguien más se paró al lado izquierdo de Brighton.

—*Good morning* —dijo una voz melodiosamente.

Brighton estaba sumamente sorprendido por la voz. Para empezar, era una mujer que hablaba inglés con acento español. Brighton no era muy bueno con los idiomas, pero estaba muy seguro de que la mujer era mexicana, no colombiana. Con plena seguridad, eso quería decir que era del cartel de drogas de Sinaloa de México, y estaba en préstamo con las guerrillas de las FARC.

"Más buenas noticias", pensó Brighton sarcásticamente. "Eso quiere decir que es una profesional a sueldo".

Brighton estaba muy sorprendido de que fuera una mujer. Cuando se puso a la vista, Brighton vio que vestía una blusa suelta de algodón abotonada sobre una camiseta negra. Los extremos de las perneras de su pantalón café oscuro estaban metidas en botas de combate camufladas. Parecía tener unos treinta y tantos años y estaba en excelente condición física.

—Mi nombre es Morgan Sáenz. Represento al cartel

de Sinaloa —dijo la mujer.

Brighton hizo una mueca. "Me fastidia tener la razón todo el tiempo", pensó él.

La mujer empujó hasta un lado de la silla de Brighton un carrito de metal con una bandeja de acero encima. Después se colocó junto al carrito. Una toalla blanca, como la de los hoteles, cubría un montón de misteriosos bultos sobre la bandeja. La mujer miraba a Brighton a los ojos, mientras pasaba los dedos juguetonamente sobre los bultos.

—No me importa que sepa mi nombre, jovencito —dijo Sáenz—. Déjeme que le explique la situación en la que está metido. No importa cuánta información obtenga sobre mí o nuestras operaciones en este lugar, sencillamente porque nunca tendrá oportunidad de revelársela a nadie.

—¿Y eso por qué? —preguntó Brighton, pese a que sabía perfectamente la respuesta.

—Porque lo vamos a matar —dijo Sáenz tajantemente—. Ahora, las circunstancias de su muerte dependen de usted. Si contesta mis preguntas voluntaria y detalladamente, me encargaré de que se quede dormido plácidamente y no despierte jamás. Si al principio ofrece resistencia, pero acaba por rendirse y coopera, lo premiaré disparándole en la cabeza una bala de grueso calibre. Una muerte igual de rápida, pero no tan placentera.

Para intimidarlo, Sáenz hizo una pausa y se colocó frente a la silla de Brighton. Las intensas luces en la pared detrás de ella hacían que su rostro se viera como una sombra y que un halo de luz brillara entre su larga y resplandeciente cabellera negra. Brighton tuvo que admitir que era una vista amenazante.

"Ya veo", pensó Brighton. "Definitivamente no es nueva en esto".

—Como sea, escuche con atención lo que pasará si pone a prueba mi paciencia —le dijo Sáenz. Entonces, se inclinó y apretó con las manos la silla de Brighton. Puso su rostro frente al de él—. Yo espero que al principio se resista. No lo respetaría si no lo hiciera. Pero si se resiste mucho tiempo, lo voy a castigar. Y si aún se rehúsa a cooperar, su castigo será peor. Y llegará el momento en que ya no me interese su cooperación.

Sáenz se enderezó e hizo otra pausa. Colocó las manos en sus caderas y dijo:

—Cuando eso pase, me voy a asegurar de que muera con más dolor del que se pueda siquiera imaginar. Nada que diga o haga en ese momento lo va a salvar. Aún si coopera, no cambiaré de parecer. ¿Entendió?

—Me lo ha dejado muy claro —dijo Brighton en voz baja.

—Muy bien —dijo Sáenz y se irguió—. Ahora será su mejor oportunidad de empezar a hablar. ¿Tiene algo que decir?

—La verdad es que sí —respondió Brighton—. Para ser una mujer mayor que yo, se ve muy bien.

Decepcionada, Sáenz sacudió la cabeza.

—Ah, de acuerdo —dijo ella con un suspiro—. Era su oportunidad y la desperdició.

Brighton hizo lo mejor que pudo para encoger los hombros.

—No puedo dejar de ser yo mismo —dijo Brighton con una sonrisa.

Sáenz miró al doctor y a dos de los guerrilleros de las FARC detrás de Brighton. Cuando ella asintió con la cabeza, el doctor bajó el respaldo de la silla de Brighton.

¡PLAM!

Brighton yacía sobre su espalda mirando a las intensas luces del techo. Se esforzó para librarse de las esposas e intentó incorporarse, pero no podía moverse. Sin esperanza alguna, lo único que podía hacer era ver cómo los guerrilleros de uniforme camuflado se acomodaban detrás de él.

Sáenz quitó la toalla sobre la bandeja y se la entregó al doctor, quien se puso en la cabecera de la silla de Brighton. El doctor le envolvió el rostro con la toalla. Amarró la toalla y retrocedió. Los guerrilleros avanzaron.

Cuando Brighton escuchó el chapoteo del agua, se dio cuenta de lo que estaba a punto de ocurrir. Respiró hondo. Un segundo después, los guerrilleros rompieron la tapa de plástico del garrafón que cargaban entre ellos y le vaciaron todo su contenido sobre el rostro.

¡CHAAASSSS!

El agua estaba increíblemente fría y pronto
la toalla estaba empapada sobre el rostro de Brighton,
convirtiéndola en una mano helada que sujetaba
con fuerza su boca y nariz.

¡CHAS! ¡CHAAASSSS!

El agua caía y caía, Brighton no sabía cuánto
podría contener la respiración. Le entró por la nariz,
y hubiera entrado en pánico de no haber sido porque
esperaba que sucediera así.

Por fortuna, el agua del garrafón se acabó antes
de que necesitara retomar el aire. Le ardían
los pulmones, pero logró soportar el primer torrente
sin aterrorizarse y sin que se le llenaran de agua
los pulmones.

—¿Qué? ¿Es la primera vez que hacen esto?
—preguntó Brighton, escupiendo agua y tratando
de no jadear muy fuerte—. Se supone que me tienen
que hacer algunas preguntas antes de torturarme.

—Esto no es más que una demostración —dijo
Sáenz, mientras tomaba con la mano algo
de la bandeja de metal junto a la silla—. Quiero
que entienda que no nos oponemos a lastimarlo.

—Me voy a acordar de eso si de verdad llegan a lastimarme —bromeó Brighton.

Ese comentario hizo reír a Sáenz, lo cual Brighton consideró como una pequeña victoria.

—Nuestra intención es obtener información —dijo Sáenz—. El soldado que trajimos aquí antes de usted, de hecho con el que se suponía que se iba a encontrar, no fue de mucha ayuda antes de morir.

—No entiendo cómo me atraparon tan rápido —dijo Brighton. Detrás de él, oyó que unos guerrilleros levantaban y abrían otro garrafón de agua. Todavía de espaldas, Brighton buscaba escuchar sonidos que le indicaran que estaban a punto de ahogarlo para saber cuándo tenía que aguantar la respiración.

—Sabe que no voy a hablar, ¿verdad? —dijo Brighton.

—Al principio no —dijo Sáenz—. Pero recuerde lo que dije acerca de resistirse. Una obstinada pérdida de mi tiempo será castigada severamente. Así que vamos a empezar muy fácil con algunas preguntas de control. ¿Cuál es su nombre? ¿Cuál rama del ejército representa? Y, ¿cuál es su rango?

Brighton se tomó un momento para ordenar sus pensamientos y prepararse para lo que venía. En su entrenamiento de resistencia de tortura, su instructor le había enseñado a pensar en algo que le gustara mucho y lo hiciera feliz. Al enfocarse en ese recuerdo, era más fácil aguantar el dolor. Para Brighton, ese recuerdo eran los comics de superhéroes que leía cada vez que tenía oportunidad de hacerlo.

Brighton sonrió. —Mi nombre es Bruce Banner — dijo él—. Y están empezando a hacerme enojar. Y no les va a gustar verme enojado.

Sáenz frunció el ceño e hizo un ademán a los hombres detrás de Brighton. Al instante, un galón de agua le cayó encima. Por fortuna, escuchó el chapoteo del agua dentro del garrafón, así que pudo tomar un poco de aire antes de que se la vaciaran encima. Esperaba lo mismo de antes, pero, de repente, los guerrilleros se detuvieron y se hicieron para atrás.

Brighton esperaba que le hicieran las preguntas de nuevo, pero Sáenz tenía otra idea. Apretó el gatillo de una pistola eléctrica y dejó que la electricidad chisporroteara por un segundo para que Brighton identificara el sonido. Él no tuvo ni tiempo de resistirse antes de que Sáenz le dirigiera el arma chispeante y la colocara en su muslo izquierdo, justo arriba de la rodilla.

¡ZZZZIIIIP!

Fue solo un segundo, pero fue más que suficiente. Apenas se detuvo, los guerrilleros derramaron agua otra vez.

¡SPLASH!

Esta vez, Brighton no pudo contener la respiración. Estremecido por el dolor que le causó la pistola eléctrica, instintivamente trató de respirar. En lugar de eso, tragó agua. Su cuerpo de inmediato entró en estado de pánico. Su mente comenzó a gritar que se estaba ahogando, ¡ahogando, ahogando!

Era todo lo que Brighton podía hacer para forzarse a no respirar. Solo endureció los músculos de su pecho y tuvo la voluntad de no toser, no sentir náuseas, no gritar. Se forzó a sí mismo a no rendirse y soportar el dolor lo mejor posible.

Afortunadamente, el segundo torrente de agua duró poco como el primero. Aguantó la respiración un par de segundos más para asegurarse, luego tragó una bocanada de helada que lo hizo toser y atragantarse.

—Tal vez no entendió la pregunta —dijo Sáenz.

El corazón de Brighton latía tan fuerte en sus oídos que apenas podía oírla.

—¿Cuál es su nombre? ¿Cuál rama del ejército representa? Y, ¿cuál es su rango?

Brighton recordó su segunda historieta favorita. Tosió y dijo:

—¡Ok, ok, se lo diré! —sonando tan serio como era posible—. Trabajo para el gobierno de Estados Unidos. De hecho, soy parte de un equipo secreto llamado "Los vengadores". Mi nombre real es Steve Rogers.

Brighton se calló por un momento para recuperar el aliento, y luego dijo:

—Pero el mundo me conoce como Capitán América.

¡ZZZZIIIIP!

Otra descarga de electricidad estremeció a Brighton, obligándolo a callar. Esta vez fue más larga. Luego más agua.

Brighton luchó contra sus instintos de pánico
lo mejor que pudo, pero su cabeza se había inclinado
hacia atrás por la descarga, y le entró agua
por la nariz. Por un rato, sintió que su mundo entero
era como estar atrapado bajo las olas del mar.
Tosió tan fuerte que detrás de sus párpados cerrados
cruzaron relámpagos blancos.

En eso se había terminado y podía respirar
de nuevo... a duras penas.

—Su nombre, su rama, su rango —dijo Sáenz
con naturalidad—. No son preguntas difíciles.

—Mi nombre es... —Brighton gimió—... Batman.

* * *

Después de los primeros interrogatorios, Brighton
perdió la habilidad de contar el tiempo. Parecía que
habían pasado horas. Al menos medio día. Tal vez
más. La incesante iluminación y la variación mínima
de temperatura desdibujaron todo en una neblina
sin sentido mientras su torturadora lo atormentaba.

A lo largo de la dura prueba, Brighton se convenció
a sí mismo de que estaba ganando una pequeña
victoria a fuerza de su obstinación. Él sabía que

en una sesión como esta, todo se basaba
en el equilibrio de poder entre torturador y víctima,
y estaba decidido a aferrarse a cualquier fragmento
de poder que pudiera. Si podía resistir dar información
al enemigo, fantástico. Pero si podía incomodar
al enemigo en el proceso, al menos estaba jugando
el juego con sus propias reglas.

El entrenamiento SERE (Supervivencia, Escape,
Resistencia, Evasión) de la Escuela de Control
de Combate de la Fuerza Aérea le había ayudado
a preparar a Brighton de alguna manera para este tipo
de situación. Parte del entrenamiento consistía
en fortalecerse a uno mismo ante los rigores
de la tortura, como aferrarse a los recuerdos favoritos.

Pero no existían técnicas secretas para hacer que
alguien fuera inmune al dolor, al miedo
o al agotamiento. No, la parte más extensa
del entrenamiento de resistencia había sido
la de describir formas comunes de tortura y demostrar
las sensaciones que esas técnicas infligen en el cuerpo
humano.

Eliminar de la ecuación el elemento
de lo desconocido hacía la idea de la tortura menos
intimidante. Entonces los instructores podían trabajar

con los estudiantes uno a uno para tratar de ayudarlos
a encontrar la fortaleza individual interior
que los ayudaría a sobrevivir el enemigo
en los momentos más duros.

Dicho esto, había una marcada diferencia
entre enseñarle a alguien lo que se puede esperar
de un "interrogatorio reforzado" y ser víctima
de tortura en la vida real. Una de las lecciones que
Brighton recordó más claramente de su primer día
en el entrenamiento SERE era a su instructor canoso
y experimentado diciéndole a la clase que tarde
o temprano la tortura destroza la voluntad
de cualquiera. El cuerpo llega hasta cierto límite antes
de que la mente colapse. Hasta el Capitán América
terminaría por convertirse en un colaborador dispuesto.

Pero no, lo mejor que un soldado capturado podía
hacer era mantener sus ojos y oídos abiertos para
hallar los medios para escapar cuando se presentara
la oportunidad. Brighton ya había tomado un paso
hacia esa meta, pero los medios no valían nada
sin la oportunidad.

Esto quería decir que tenía que soportar todo lo que
Sáenz y sus esbirros le hicieran hasta que se frustraran

lo suficiente para dejarlo solo por un tiempo.

Así que Brighton se concentró profundamente
y se rehusó a darse por vencido por el miedo
y la desesperación en que se sumía cada vez que
la pistola eléctrica de Sáenz lo estremecía y el agua
le caía de golpe. Se permitió toser, atragantar y escupir,
pero siguió diciéndose a sí mismo que no importaba
lo difícil que fuera, era demasiado pronto para que
Sáenz realmente lo quisiera muerto. Por lo que ella
sabía, Brighton tenía información valiosa. Él no creía
que ella estuviera lista para dejarlo morir, así que no
tenía miedo —bueno, no tanto al menos— de lo que
le pudiera hacer.

En cierto momento de esa primera sesión, Sáenz
se detuvo. Brighton sabía que su comportamiento
obstinado la estaba desesperando. Después de la
quinceava vez de hacerle la misma pregunta de quién
era y obtener como respuesta nombres de superhéroes,
ella cambió la táctica.

Comenzó a hacerle preguntas más amplias.
¿Cuántos estadounidenses estaban trabajando con
los colombianos en la Operación: Nexo? ¿Cuánto
tiempo les habían ordenado que permanecieran

en Colombia? ¿Qué sabían específicamente sobre la operación de contrabando de Sinaloa y las FARC? ¿Quién era el comandante en jefe de Brighton?

Sáenz le daba a Brighton bastante tiempo antes de hacer cada pregunta, luego cuando él la decepcionaba, Sáenz llamaba a sus matones con un ademán.

Durante esta fase del interrogatorio, ella le dio a Brighton una idea básica de qué le preocupaba al liderazgo de la operación Sinaloa-FARC sobre la presencia estadounidense. A Brighton le pareció una pequeña victoria el hecho de estar obteniendo más información de su torturadora, de la que ella podía obtener de él.

Finalmente, mientras esta fase estaba por concluir, y se agotaba el agua de los garrafones, Brighton se dio cuenta de que estaba debilitándose. No se sentía más cerca de colaborar que antes, pero su cuerpo estaba extenuado por el abuso.

Hubo tres preguntas que no pudo responder porque no se le ocurrió ninguna historieta para dar como respuesta en lugar de una respuesta sincera. Había llegado al punto donde Sáenz lo estaba castigando por su silencio en lugar de su desobediencia voluntaria. Por fin, el tono de su voz sugirió que ella se había dado cuenta de que estaba contra la pared.

—Supongo que estará contento de saber que es todo, por ahora —dijo Sáenz.

El doctor en verde olivo levantó la toalla empapada de la cara de Brighton y se inclinó sobre él para comprobar sus signos vitales de nuevo.

—Probablemente debí darle una pausa hace rato —dijo Sáenz—, pero quedé muy impresionada por su conocimiento tan amplio de las historietas. Parece que usted y yo tenemos un gusto sorprendentemente similar en la lectura.

—Genial —trató de decir Brighton, pero su garganta estaba muy lastimada para hablar fuerte—. ¿Qué le parece si salimos a comer algo juntos?

—Paso —dijo Sáenz—. Otra razón por la que nos tardamos tanto hoy fue porque quise determinar si este método de interrogación le afectaría en el largo plazo. Estará orgulloso de saber que no parece ser muy eficaz. Por lo tanto, la próxima vez que nos encontremos, mejoraré los castigos que se ha ganado.

—Tal vez la próxima vez podría tratar algo de reafirmación positiva —dijo Brighton, con un tono sarcástico —. Me puede traer un pastel de helado o un filete de ternera. Por cierto, no he visto la nueva película de Batman.

—Ya tengo algo pensado —dijo Sáenz—. Permítame que lo demuestre.

Tomó algo de la bandeja de acero junto a la silla de Brighton y movió la muñeca como si estuviera azotando con un látigo.

¡CHINC!

Brighton reconoció el sonido distintivo que hizo el objeto. Sáenz acababa de desplegar un bastón extensible.

—No suena como pastel de helado —dijo Brighton.

Sáenz no dijo nada. Con una expresión fría y severa, caminó hasta el extremo de la silla y alzó el bastón para dar un golpe de revés. Brighton comenzó a decir algo para que cambiara de opinión, pero ella rápidamente lo golpeó en ambas plantas de los pies descalzos.

¡ZAS!

¡ZAS!

¡ZAS!

Sáenz no asestó el golpe con mucha fuerza.
Pero eso no importó. Brighton aullaba mientras sus
piernas estallaban de dolor.

¡CHINC!

Sáenz plegó el bastón. Con cuidado lo colocó
de vuelta en la bandeja. Brighton hizo todo lo posible
para permanecer callado, pero no podía detener
su cuerpo que temblaba de dolor.

—Algo para que piense mientras estoy fuera
—dijo Sáenz. Su voz estaba llena de autosatisfacción
por el sufrimiento obvio de Brighton—. Así es como
lo castigaré durante nuestra próxima sesión
por las respuestas inútiles. A partir de ahora, cada
sesión que me obligue a tener con usted será peor que
la anterior.

Se inclinó sobre Brighton, luego enderezó el respaldo de la silla para que volviera a quedar sentado. Sáenz bajó la voz hasta susurrar.

—Hasta ahora, no estoy ni aburrida ni impresionada con usted, jovencito

—dijo Sáenz—. Muchos soldados de su edad pueden resistir al menos dos sesiones conmigo con su dignidad aún intacta. Sin embargo, algo más que eso y... ya verá cómo me pongo cuando estoy enojada. Y créame, no le va a gustar verme enojada.

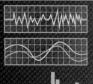

5514.108

INTELIGENCIA

DESCIFRANDO

12345

TÉRMINOS TÁCTICOS

- ATAQUE AÉREO – ataque con bombas llevado a cabo con un avión
- NUDILLO DE ACERO – cualquier tipo de metal colocado sobre los dedos para aumentar el daño causado por golpes
- M16 – rifle de asalto también conocido como AR-15 con capacidad de disparar en ráfaga
- PRIVACIÓN DEL SUEÑO – una forma de tortura psicológica que causa daño al mantener a la víctima despierta por un periodo prolongado de tiempo

3245.98

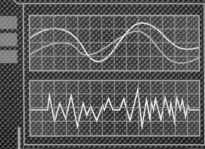

ALAS

1324.014

Ahora que Brighton estaba solo, a su cuerpo
golpeado le hubiese hecho muy bien un poco de
descanso. Desafortunadamente, dormir quedaba
descartado.

Para empezar, hacía demasiado calor. El sol
quemante sobre la selva húmeda sudamericana
convirtió la habitación de metal y concreto
en un horno sofocante. Además, las luces
lo encandilaban desde cualquier ángulo, lo que hacía
imposible un descanso aún en circunstancias apacibles.
Era como estar mirando el sol.

Por supuesto, ese era el punto. Las luces cegadoras
y las temperaturas incómodas evitan que un hombre

duerma, y la privación del sueño contribuye al colapso de la capacidad de juicio y la voluntad de un hombre. Esa era la tortura propiamente dicha.

De cualquier manera, Brighton no podía permitirse dormir ahora. No tenía idea cuánto pasaría antes de que Sáenz y sus matones regresaran. Lo último que él quería era que lo sorprendieran en medio de lo que estaba a punto de hacer. Se imaginó que serían más violentos con él si lo descubrían tratando de escapar.

Brighton había robado el medio para su escape en el momento en que Sáenz se presentó. Cuando el doctor de la guerrilla de las FARC se inclinó sobre él para revisarle los ojos, Brighton tomó el bolígrafo retráctil del bolsillo del hombre y lo empujó dentro del relleno del descansabrazos de su silla a través de una grieta en el vinilo viejo que la cubría.

Durante el interrogatorio, Brighton mantuvo su antebrazo sobre la abertura y el abultamiento que creaba el bolígrafo. No importó cuánto dolor sintió, no se había movido. De lo contrario, sus captores lo habrían visto.

Ahora que estaba solo, Brighton tomó el bolígrafo de su escondite. Ante sus ojos cansados y enrojecidos, la baratija de plástico se veía como un tesoro hecho de oro por una simple razón: tenía un clip plano de metal.

Con mucho cuidado, asegurándose de no dejar caer el bolígrafo, Brighton deslizó su uña debajo del clip y lo dobló hacia atrás hasta lograr un ángulo recto. Luego, colocó el bolígrafo al revés. Apenas respirando, insertó el extremo del clip dentro de la cerradura de las esposas en su mano derecha.

Cuando estaba firmemente en su lugar, usó el bolígrafo como palanca y dobló la punta del clip en un ángulo recto.

Brighton tomó el clip y en su mano le dio la vuelta al bolígrafo. Entonces reinsertó el clip doblado y lo dobló de nuevo haciéndole otro ángulo recto, pero en sentido contrario.

Pese a la urgencia de lo que estaba haciendo, Brighton manipulaba el objeto lentamente, como si tuviera todo el tiempo del mundo. Sabía que, tan cansado como estaba, si se apresuraba, muy probablemente arruinaría todo. Y luego, cuando

Sáenz regresara y se diera cuenta de lo que Brighton había estado haciendo, tendría que rendirle cuentas al mismo diablo.

Cuando terminó de doblar el clip del bolígrafo para hacer una ganzúa muy básica, Brighton hizo una pausa para calmarse y estabilizar sus manos.

Ahora venía el momento de la verdad. Apretando los dientes y respirando a un ritmo constante, colocó la ganzúa dentro de la cerradura de la esposa. Paciente y lentamente, giró el bolígrafo y aplicó presión en el mecanismo dentro de la cerradura. Milímetro a milímetro, giró, giró y giró...

¡CLIC!

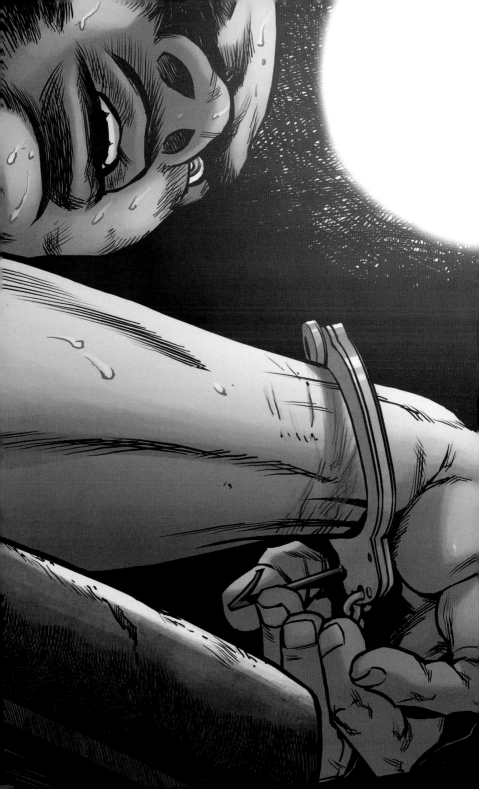

Brighton ahogó su grito de triunfo cuando
la cerradura se desenganchó y la esposa se abrió.
Sin perder tiempo para celebrar, abrió la esposa y luego
comenzó a usar la ganzúa en las cerraduras
de las esposas en su otra mano.

¡CLIC!

Brighton requirió de toda su concentración
para mantener la calma. Todavía no estaba libre.
Sus pies aún estaban esposados.

Lenta y calmadamente, Brighton dobló su espalda
rígida y alcanzó sus pies. Usó la ganzúa en las esposas
en su pie izquierdo.

¡CLIC!

Manteniendo la concentración, usó su peso
para apoyarse en el otro pie. Comenzó a manipular
las últimas ataduras de metal.

¡CLIC!

Brighton ya estaba suelto, pero aún lejos
de estar libre. Se dio suficiente tiempo para dar
un profundo suspiro.

Entonces, rápidamente recogió y guardó en sus bolsillos los cuatro pares de esposas. Se alzó lentamente.

Las muñecas y tobillos le picaban y ardían alternativamente justo donde los aros de metal le habían rozado. Pero esos pequeños dolores eran nada comparados con los de las plantas de los pies. Sáenz los había golpeado durísimo. Escapar a pie sin botas sería muy difícil, especialmente porque estaba cautivo en algún lugar de la selva.

Pero no había nada que él pudiera hacer al respecto, excepto aguantar. No se podía quedar ahí, menos aún si Sáenz se proponía enfocar su próxima sesión de castigo en sus pies, tal y como había amenazado. Los pies le ardían de dolor, dudaba que incluso pudiera caminar después de un día de golpizas.

Armándose de valor, Brighton caminó hasta la pared junto a la puerta. Podía oír que afuera dos personas murmuraban en español, así que tomó dos pares de las esposas que había recogido. Con manos firmes, puso un par de aros juntos y colocó los dedos entremedio para tomarlos como si fueran nudillos de acero.

Brighton hizo saltar el otro par de esposas en su mano.
Luego las arrojó al otro lado de la habitación.

¡CRAAAASS!

Las esposas golpearon una de las luces
y la destrozaron. Inmediatamente, la puerta se abrió
por completo y dos guerrilleros de las FARC irrumpieron
en la habitación.

Los guerrilleros tenían en sus rostros una expresión
casi cómica al ver la silla vacía. Ver esto hizo que
Brighton sonriera.

Aprovechando su confusión, Brighton saltó
de donde estaba escondido. Con sus improvisados
nudillos de acero golpeó en el cuello al hombre
más cercano a él.

¡PUUMM!

El guerrillero se tambaleó. En ese momento, soltó
el M16 que sostenía. Brighton tomó el arma en el aire
por la parte del cañón. Entonces se agachó y giró
hacia el segundo hombre que estaba por apuntar
su rifle. Brighton arremetió con la culata del rifle
como si fuera a dar un batazo de jonrón.

¡PUUMM!

Con la culata del rifle golpeó el estómago del segundo guerrillero. Con un segundo culatazo derribó al guerrillero que cayó de espaldas desmayado. Rápidamente, Brighton le hizo lo mismo al otro guerrillero.

Con dos guerrilleros menos en la cuenta, Brighton le quitó la camisa camuflada a uno de ellos y usó el cuchillo del otro para cortarla en dos tiras.

Brighton los esposó juntos, luego los esposó a ambos a la silla. Envolvió las tiras de tela alrededor de sus bocas para mantenerlos callados en caso de que recobraran el sentido pronto.

Brighton se colocó los cuchillos de los guerrilleros en su cinturón, luego le quitó las botas al hombre más alto para colocárselas. Guardó en su bolsillo el cargador del M16 del primer hombre y tomó el rifle del otro en su mano.

Armado y seguro de que los hombres no irían a ningún lado, Brighton decidió que era tiempo de irse. Lenta y cautelosamente, abrió la puerta y salió.

Al salir de la habitación de metal y concreto, finalmente tuvo oportunidad de orientarse. Estaba oscuro; era temprano por la mañana o tarde por la noche, y estaba mucho más fresco afuera que dentro del "sauna" donde estuvo prisionero.

Brighton miró el horizonte y vio que el área completa se hallaba rodeada de selva muy densa. El sonido de los pájaros y los insectos, y de agua en movimiento provenía de algún lugar a la distancia.

No muy lejos, Brighton oyó el sonido de herramientas eléctricas. También podía oír voces, pero no tan bien como para saber qué estaban diciendo.

Brighton sabía que tenía dos opciones. La primera era adentrarse en la selva aprovechando la oscuridad y hallar un río. Una vez que lo encontrara, podía seguir su cauce hasta una vía fluvial más grande o directo a la civilización, donde llegara primero. Desde ahí, podría encontrar un teléfono y llamar al Escuadrón de la Sombra para que lo recogieran.

La primera opción, desde luego, era la más fácil, segura y atractiva. Después de un día como el que pasó con Morgan Sáenz, la idea de que lo atraparan de nuevo le daba escalofríos.

Su segunda opción era completar la misión.

Agotado, apaleado y solo, Brighton estaba
en desventaja. De todos modos, decidió terminar
el trabajo. Después de todo, los colombianos
—y el Escuadrón de la Sombra— contaban con él.
La misión era más importante que su comodidad,
e incluso su seguridad. Y al ser el miembro más joven
del escuadrón, siempre tenía algo que probar.

Además, después de lo que las FARC le habían
hecho, le encantó la idea de sabotear sus planes.
Con suerte, el ataque aéreo acabaría con su operación.
Quizás para siempre.

Respiró profundo y cerró la puerta detrás de él.
Por delante tenía un camino estrecho y pisoteado
a través de la selva. Iba en dirección del sonido de las
herramientas eléctricas y gente hablando. Comenzó
a dirigirse hacia allí, aunque prefirió cortar por la selva
y moverse sigilosamente.

Resultó ser una buena elección. Al llegar al final
del sendero, vio que se abría en un complejo repleto
de guerrilleros de las FARC. En grupos de dos o tres,
patrullaban o estaban parados cerca de un extenso
edificio de una planta que abarcaba un amplio
estrecho de río fangoso. Los sonidos de construcción

venían de adentro del edificio. Los árboles cubrían
las paredes del edificio; sus ramas lo camuflaban visto
desde el aire. Las paredes habían sido pintadas
con un patrón de camuflaje en colores café y verde.
No había luces exteriores visibles.

Después de todo, parecía que Brighton
había descubierto el astillero clandestino de las FARC.

—Qué suerte tengo —murmuró.

Al menos los guerrilleros habían sido lo
suficientemente considerados para traerlo hasta aquí.
Ahora, si tan solo supiera en qué parte del mundo
estaba...

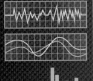

5514.108

INTELIGENCIA

DESCIFRANDO

12345

TÉRMINOS TÁCTICOS

- RADIO SINCGARS – sistema de radio terrestre y aéreo de un solo canal que los soldados usan en el campo de combate
- CARABINA M4 – rifle de asalto ligero y corto de fuego selectivo
- RACIONES DE COMIDA (MRE) – comidas precocinadas y empacadas listas para comer que usan los soldados en las Fuerzas Armadas de Estados Unidos

3245.98

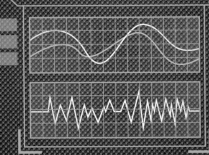

PRESA

Brighton bordeó la línea de árboles en forma
de arco alrededor del edificio central. Descubrió que
el astillero consistía en cuatro estructuras distintas,
excepto por el cobertizo de una habitación
en el que había pasado las horas anteriores. Había
una instalación principal dedicada a la construcción,
unas barracas de madera para los soldados
y los trabajadores, un edificio del tamaño
de un granero repleto de materiales de construcción
y un pequeño lugar con antena en la parte superior
con su propio generador.

"Ese edificio tiene que ser el centro de mando
del campamento de la guerrilla", pensó Brighton.

El edificio no era más grande que la pequeña base en la isla Malpelo donde estaba escondido el resto del Escuadrón de la Sombra. Además de esas instalaciones, también había una hilera de mesas para picnic debajo de una tienda hecha con red camuflada.

También había un muelle de madera para botes con lanchas rápidas atracadas allí. Un guardia lo vigilaba. Otro guardia estaba sentado en un banco junto al sendero sin pavimentar que conducía a la selva. Veinte o treinta pies detrás de ese guardia, una motocicleta todo terreno yacía sobre su soporte.

Moviéndose lentamente y medio agachado, Brighton se encaminó hacia el centro de mando. Atravesó la selva y se acercó al edificio bajo de madera fuera de la vista del guardia. No había ventanas en este lado, así que todo lo que podía hacer era presionar su oreja contra la pared exterior y oír. No oyó ni voces ni el sonido de gente moviéndose dentro. Sin embargo, no sabía si era porque no había nadie, o porque las paredes eran muy gruesas.

De cualquier modo, tenía que entrar.

Brighton se arrastró alrededor del edificio hasta la puerta lateral que daba a las barracas. Cuando se

aseguró de que nadie estuviera mirando, dio la vuelta a la esquina y entró.

Brighton cerró la puerta lo más cuidadosamente que pudo, pero las bisagras crujieron. Le preocupaba que su entusiasmo delatara su posición. Era probable que el sonido del generador retumbando al otro lado del edificio hubiera ahogado el ruido, pero Brighton se quedó congelado en la puerta por si acaso.

Aferró fuerte el rifle robado por si pasaba el guardia. Solo después de dos tensos minutos de silencio, Brighton se relajó y siguió adelante.

Adentro, el comando central no decía mucho. Era poco más que un largo pasillo con pequeñas habitaciones a cada lado y una sala de reuniones más grande al otro extremo. El suelo era una losa de concreto, y las paredes y las puertas estaban hechas de madera delgada. Era húmedo, sofocante y olía a sudor rancio. Sin embargo, no estaba mal para ser un escondite en la selva.

Delante de él había cuatro puertas: dos a la izquierda, una al final del pasillo, y una a la derecha.

La del final del pasillo estaba abierta, dejaba ver una habitación oscura con una mesa grande en el centro. En la paredes había toda clase de papeles pegados.

A la derecha de Brighton estaba el frente del edificio que daba al centro del campamento. Pensó que la puerta en ese lado probablemente condujera a una sala. Una de las puertas a la izquierda era más grande que la otra. Un borde de luz brillaba a su alrededor.

Brighton caminó por el pasillo dando pasos muy cortos. Se detuvo fuera de esa puerta para escuchar. Por suerte, no había luces encendidas en el pasillo, entonces su sombra no se reflejaba debajo de la puerta. Apuntó su rifle a la puerta y acercó el oído a la jamba. Lo primero que escuchó hizo que su sangre se enfriara.

Era la voz de Sáenz.

—Todavía es demasiado difícil de predecir —decía en español—. Él definitivamente pertenece a las fuerzas de operaciones especiales estadounidenses de algún tipo. Todo su equipo era de lo mejor, y ha tenido algún entrenamiento de resistencia a la tortura. No es ningún cobarde. Ablandarlo va a tomar tiempo.

A juzgar por el silencio después, Sáenz tuvo que

estar hablando por teléfono con alguien.

Brighton se dio cuenta de que temblaba un poco cuando Sáenz hablaba. Su cabeza se vio inundada de rabia descontrolada ante el sonido de la voz de su torturadora relatando calmadamente cómo había abusado de él.

Por un momento, consideró simplemente patear la puerta y entrar disparando con su rifle en automático. Eso daría a Sáenz tiempo suficiente para reconocerlo y darse cuenta de lo que estaba a punto de pasar antes de apretar el gatillo.

Pero no... no podía. Por un lado, abrir fuego atraería a todos los guerrilleros armados en el campamento. Si eso sucediera, Brighton terminaría tan muerto como Sáenz. Cabe añadir que Brighton nunca le había disparado a nadie. Claro, había causado la muerte de gente muy malvada, pero solo indirectamente, solicitando apoyo de bombardeo aéreo. Incluso cuando se unió a sus compañeros de equipo del Escuadrón de la Sombra en misiones de combate directo, en realidad nunca había participado en ningún enfrentamiento armado.

Pero lo más importante aún era que Brighton

no quería que su primer asesinato oficial implicara dispararle a una mujer desarmada a sangre fría, sin importar lo que le hubiera hecho a él.

Así que siguió caminando hacia el final del pasillo. La segunda puerta del mismo lado de la habitación de Sáenz resultó ser un pequeño clóset lleno de suministros de oficina y medicamentos. La puerta del otro lado del pasillo que daba al frente del edificio, conducía a una pequeña enfermería con una cama individual. La puerta principal del edificio llevaba directamente a la enfermería. Brighton continuó por el pasillo hasta la última habitación, con la mesa en el centro y los papeles pegados en las paredes.

Una vez adentro, Brighton sonrió. "¡Bingo!", pensó. Los papeles pegados en las paredes resultaron ser mapas. No tenía suficiente luz para leerlos. La única luz en la habitación era un suave resplandor anaranjado que emitía el interruptor eléctrico de un enchufe, pero al menos podía percatarse de que eran mapas. También había un reloj en la pared que indicaba 2:15, lo cual era útil.

Cuando reconoció una mochila de camuflaje digital en la esquina, los ojos de Brighton se llenaron

de enorme alegría. Era su equipo, o al menos parte.
Olvidando los mapas por un momento, se arrodilló
al lado de su mochila y abrió la solapa. Allí estaba su
vía de escape para reencontrarse con el Escuadrón
de la Sombra: su radio SINCGARS de combate.

Algunas otras cosas esenciales estaban intactas
en la mochila, incluyendo raciones de comida
precocinada, un botiquín de primeros auxilios,
una brújula y una libreta de notas. Pero la radio era
crucial. Prácticamente compensaba la pérdida de sus
gafas de visión nocturna, su carabina M4, toda su
munición, su granada paralizante de luz M84
y su granada de humo.

Al menos a esta misión no había traído su escopeta
de combate AA-12. Se habría deprimido si hubiera
perdido a su "bebé".

Después de hacer un rápido inventario, tomó
de la mochila una linterna de reserva y volvió
a meter todo lo demás. Se colgó la mochila y encendió
la linterna. Con el estrecho rayo de luz, podía leer
un mapa sin mucho riesgo de que el enemigo lo
descubriera de lejos.

Brighton encendió la linterna por un segundo

para mirar algunos de los mapas en las paredes. Después de un momento, eligió llevarse consigo dos mapas. El primero era un mapa bastante nuevo que mostraba el contorno de esa parte de la selva, con la ubicación del astillero convenientemente marcada. También mostraba las rutas terrestres para traer suministros y rutas fluviales para que los narcosubmarinos escaparan río abajo hasta el océano.

El segundo mapa mostraba las rutas marítimas frente a la costa colombiana que los pilotos de los narcosubmarinos tomaban para llegar a México. Brighton sacó las tachuelas, dobló el mapa lo más silenciosamente que pudo y lo metió en un bolsillo de su pantalón militar. Estudió el mapa del contorno de la selva por unos momentos más antes de guardarlo junto con la linterna.

Finalmente, tomó su M16 y volvió por el pasillo hacia la puerta por donde había entrado al edificio.

Hasta ese momento había tenido la suerte de que no lo detectaran. Pero cuando se acercó a la puerta donde había oído hablar a Morgan Sáenz, la puerta se abrió de repente.

Sáenz se echó para atrás y quedó de espaldas frente a Brighton.

Sáenz llevaba una linterna en una mano y un libro bajo un brazo. Cuando jaló de la puerta para cerrarla, se volteó y miró a Brighton directo a los ojos.

Sus ojos negros destellaban miedo y furia. Abrió la boca para gritar. Brighton apuntó su rifle al cuello de Sáenz y negó con la cabeza. Sáenz de inmediato cerró la boca.

Brighton sacudió la cabeza hacia un lado, indicando a Sáenz que regresara a la habitación. Sáenz lo obedeció y él la siguió adentro en lo que resultó ser la habitación de la mujer. Había un casillero, un escritorio con una computadora portátil y una cama doble bajo un mosquitero. Había una pila de libros en la esquina al lado del escritorio. Un par de velas de cidronela proporcionaban una luz tenue. Sáenz se volvió hacia Brighton.

—Nunca escapará —dijo ella.

—Siéntese —dijo Brighton enfáticamente, indicando con la cabeza a la cama. Ella lo hizo, sin apartar sus ojos de los de Brighton. Él tomó el par restante de esposas y lo arrojó sobre la cama junto a Sáenz.

—Espósese el tobillo al marco de la cama —le ordenó Brighton. Sáenz entrecerró los ojos, pero hizo lo que dijo.

—Solo tengo que gritar, jovencito —dijo ella—, y cada uno de los soldados de las FARC en este campamento vendrá en mi ayuda. Puede que me mate por ello, pero no vivirá lo suficiente para disfrutarlo.

Brighton le sonrió, mientras la miraba fijo a través de la mira de acero del M16.

—Vamos, atrévase, mi amiga —dijo Brighton retándola—. Grite tan fuerte como pueda.

Sáenz lo volvió a mirar y luego bajó los ojos.

—¿Y ahora qué? —preguntó ella.

—Me voy —dijo Brighton—. Debería tomarla prisionera, pero no vale la pena tanto problema. Probablemente, saltará del barco en cuanto le quite los ojos de encima. Así que puede quedarse aquí, pero no piense que la olvidaré, Sra. Sáenz.

Brighton retrocedió hacia el pasillo y se detuvo. Su rifle no vacilaría, pero su mente no estaba del todo estable. Tenía unas ganas enormes de apretar el gatillo y borrar a Sáenz de la faz de la Tierra. Quién sabe cuántos más sufrirían a manos de ella. Y sabía que ella daría la voz de alarma y vendrían todos corriendo

apenas Brighton se fuera. También podría tener
la satisfacción de matarla ahora mismo que tenía
la oportunidad...

Aunque pudiera darle satisfacción destruir a quien
lo había torturado a él y a quién sabe cuántos otros
más, Brighton simplemente no tuvo el ánimo
de hacerlo. Tenía que dominar esos impulsos si quería
ser capaz de mirarse en el espejo el día de mañana.
Tenía que ser mejor que el enemigo si deseaba estar
entre los buenos. No había nada más
que pudiera hacer.

Sin decir otra palabra, se giró y salió a toda prisa
por la puerta lateral. La abrió de un golpe y dio
la vuelta a la esquina del edificio, esperando con gran
nerviosismo que nadie lo estuviera mirando. Eso fue
todo lo que tardó Sáenz para llenarse de valor y gritar.

—¡El americano ha escapado! —gritó— ¡Va para
los botes! ¡Atrápenlo!

Oír a Sáenz gritar hizo sonreír a Brighton. "Idiota",
pensó.

Brighton siguió moviéndose por la parte trasera
del edificio hasta llegar a la motocicleta. Sáenz siguió
gritando dentro, y el guardia que había sido apostado

en el sendero que conducía la selva —presumiblemente Javier— corrió hacia el muelle. El hombre gritó para alertar a los demás. Todos los guerrilleros que estaban cerca entraron en acción y se dispersaron para hacer la búsqueda. Pero estaban mirando en la dirección equivocada.

Brighton llegó a la moto y encontró las llaves en el arranque, como esperaba. Pasó el rifle sobre un hombro, se subió a la moto y aceleró el motor al máximo. Como un imán, el sonido del motor atrajo la atención de los guerrilleros y silenció los gritos de Sáenz por un segundo. Pero nadie estaba lo suficientemente cerca para detenerlo.

Encendió el faro delantero y salió disparado por el camino de suministros. Algunos de los guardias llegaron corriendo y le dispararon unos cuantos tiros, pero las balas rebotaron inofensivamente desde los árboles cercanos.

¡BRRRRRUUUUUM!

Nadie podía detenerlo ahora.

INTELIGENCIA

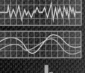

DESCIFRANDO
IIIIIIIIIII IIIIIIIIIIIIIIIIIIIIIII

12345

TÉRMINOS TÁCTICOS

- AEROTRANSPORTE – sistema para transportar personas o carga por medio de aviones, especialmente en una emergencia

- NOMBRE CLAVE – apodo secreto usado por los militares en comunicaciones por radio para preservar su anonimato de oyentes externos

- OSPREY – (águila pescadora, en español) aeronave estadounidense con rotores basculantes capaz de despegar o aterrizar verticalmente

3245.98 ■ ■ ■

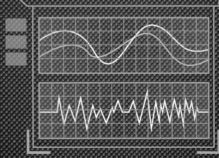

VOLAR

1324.014

La luz del sol matinal iluminaba las copas de los árboles de selva. Hacía rato que Brighton había abandonado la motocicleta robada. Ahora, se encaminaba por tierra con su mapa para hallar un terreno elevado y tener a la vista el terreno.

Acostado sobre su vientre en una cresta, con el mapa de la guerrilla a su lado, miró abajo hacia el río que pasaba por el centro del campamento de las FARC. No podía ver el astillero camuflado desde ahí, pero conocía la geografía y los puntos de referencia lo suficientemente bien, como para saber exactamente dónde se encontraba. Colocó su radio de combate en la frecuencia de emergencia del Escuadrón de la Sombra y apretó el botón del transmisor.

—Nido de águila, este es Águila —dijo Brighton, usando sus nombres clave—. Nido de águila, este es Águila. ¿Me copia?

—¡Águila! —el mayor Ryan Cross respondió
de inmediato. Su voz estaba llena de sorpresa, deleite
y alivio—. Águila, este es Nido de águila. Deme
un informe de su condición. ¿Está bien?

—He estado mucho mejor, mayor —dijo Brighton—.
Y voy a necesitar aerotransporte muy pronto.

—El Osprey ya está en el aire, Águila —dijo Cross—.
Hemos estado buscándolo.

—Es bueno oírlo, Nido de águila —dijo Brighton—.
Pero si le parece, primero tengo que conectar
con el mayor Gaitán. Es un pequeño asunto sobre
ataque aéreo que le prometí.

—Me parece bien, Águila —respondió Cross,
claramente impresionado—. Haga su llamada.
Aquí estaremos.

—Copiado —Brighton dijo muy animado—.
Nos vemos pronto, mayor. Águila fuera.

—Muy buen trabajo, Águila —dijo Cross—. Sabía
que podíamos contar con usted. Nido de águila fuera.

Brighton metió su radio en un bolsillo.

—Ni se imagina—dijo Brighton en voz baja—.
Ni se imagina.

CARGANDO...

2012.101

CLASIFICADO

REPORTE DE LA MISIÓN

OPERACIÓN

ÁGUILA 1234

OBJETIVOS PRIMARIOS

- Incursionar de manera encubierta usando paracaídas
- Reunirse con fuerza especial colombiana
- Localizar astillero
- Proveer coordenadas para ataque aéreo certero

ESTADO

5/7 COMPLETO

OBJETIVOS SECUNDARIOS

- Minimizar bajas

X Establecer relación positiva con fuerza especial colombiana

X Permanecer encubierto

BRIGHTON, EDGAR

RANGO: Sargento
RAMA: Controlador de combate
de la Fuerza Aérea
PERFIL: Técnico y especialista en
combates en zonas reducidas. Popular
entre sus compañeros, pero suele
perturbar a sus superiores.

He estado posponiendo escribir este informe, sobre todo
porque todavía estoy tratando de ordenar mentalmente
todo lo que me pasó durante la Operación: Nexo. Entre
el ahogamiento simulado, la pistola eléctrica y el pésimo
sentido del humor de mi interrogadora, llegué a un punto
en que casi me desmorono, o algo peor. Pero confiaba
en mi entrenamiento, que es la única razón por la que sigo
vivo… Bueno, eso y el bolígrafo. En cuanto a Morgan Sáenz,
la atrapó hace unos días la fuerza especial colombiana.
Es fácil adivinar quién les avisó que ella regresaba a México.

– Sargento Edgar Brighton

2019.681

CLASIFICADO

BIOGRAFÍAS DE LOS CREADORES

AUTOR

CARL BOWEN

Carl Bowen es padre, esposo y escritor y vive en Lawrenceville, Georgia. Nació en Louisiana, vivió brevemente en Inglaterra y se crio en Georgia, donde asistió a la escuela. Publicó un buen número de novelas, cuentos e historietas. Para Stone Arch Books volvió a narrar *20,000 leguas de viaje submarino*, *El extraño caso del Dr. Jekyll y Mr. Hyde*, *El libro de la selva*, *Aladino y la lámpara maravillosa*, *Julio César* y *Los crímenes de la calle Morgue*. Es el autor original de *BMX Breakthrough* y de la serie Escuadrón de la sombra.

INTELIGENCIA

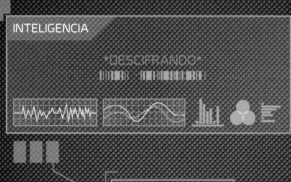

ILUSTRADOR

WILSON TORTOSA

Wilson "Wunan" Tortosa es un ilustrador de historietas
filipino, conocido principalmente por sus trabajos
en *Tomb Raider* y la versión estadounidense
de *Batalla de los planetas* para Top Cow Productions.
Wilson asistió a la Philippine Cultural High School
y luego a la Universidad de Santo Tomás,
donde cursó una licenciatura
en Bellas artes y una especialización en publicidad.

COLORISTA

BENNY FUENTES

Benny Fuentes vive en Villa Hermosa, Tabasco,
México, donde la temperatura es ardiente como
la salsa. Estudió diseño gráfico en la universidad.
Ahora trabaja como colorista a tiempo completo
en la industria de la historieta y la novela gráfica,
para compañías como Marvel, DC Comics y Top Cow
Productions. Comparte su casa con Chelo y Kitty, dos
gatos locos que se creen los dueños del lugar.

2019.681

REPORTE DEL AUTOR

ACCESO PERMITIDO

CARL BOWEN

P: ¿Cuándo y por qué decidió ser escritor?

R: Me gusta escribir desde que estaba en la escuela
primaria. Escribía todo lo que podía, esperando llegar
a ser el nuevo Lloyd Alexander o Stephen King,
pero vendí la primera historia cuando estuve
en la universidad. Fue una larga espera, pero el día
que vi mi historia publicada fue uno de los mejores días
de mi vida.

P: ¿Qué lo impulsó a escribir *Escuadrón de la sombra*?

R: De niño, mis héroes eran caballeros valientes o ermitaños
nobles que luchaban por su deber y no por fama o gloria.
Creo que los soldados de Operaciones especiales
del ejército de EE. UU. encarnan esos ideales. Su trabajo
es difícil y por lo general no reconocido, por eso quise
mostrar lo interesante que es su labor y expresar mi
gratitud hacia nuestros valientes guerreros.

P: ¿Qué lo inspira a escribir?

R: Mi mayor inspiración es mi familia. El amor y el apoyo
de mi esposa me animan cuando el trabajo se hace
cuesta arriba. Mi otra gran inspiración es mi hijo. Tiene

tres años y quiero que cuando lea mis libros sienta
lo mismo que yo cuando leía mis libros favoritos
de pequeño. Y si resulta que después quiere ser
un soldado de élite del ejército de EE. UU.,
me parecería genial.

P: Describa cómo fue escribir estos libros.
R: La única experiencia militar que tengo es el año que
pasé en el Entrenamiento de Oficiales de Reserva
del Ejército. Me hizo sentir mucho respeto hacia el
ejército y sus soldados, pero rápidamente me di cuenta
de que yo habría sido un terrible soldado.
Recientemente pude probar el arsenal de armas
de fuego de un amigo, incluyendo una escopeta
de combate, un rifle AR-15 y un rifle de francotirador
Barrett M82. Hicimos estallar una vieja máquina de fax.

P: ¿Cuál es su libro, película y juego favoritos?
R: Mi libro favorito de todos los tiempos es *Don Quijote*.
Es divertido y me hace reír. Tengo dos películas
favoritas: *Casablanca* y *Pacto de sangre*, ambas
en blanco y negro, filmadas antes de que yo naciera.
Mi juego favorito es, sin duda, *Skyrim*, donde juegas
a ser un heroico cazador de dragones. Pero ni siquiera
Skyrim puede evitar que escriba más historias
Escuadrón de la sombra, así que no tendrán
que esperar mucho tiempo para leer más sobre
Ryan Cross y su equipo. Prometido.

2019.681

INTELIGENCIA

DESCIFRANDO

12345

TÉRMINOS TÁCTICOS

-ADELANTO DE LA MISIÓN: OPERACIÓN ESCUDO
Heshem Shadid, un exterrorista convertido
en político, ha solicitado la ayuda del ejército
estadounidense. Los antiguos amigos de Shadid
están enfurecidos porque ha cambiado de bando
y harán lo que sea para eliminarlo. La información
que Shadid ha proporcionado hasta ahora
ha demostrado ser invaluable para las tareas
en la guerra en Iraq. Él debe ser protegido.

3245.58

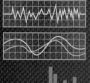

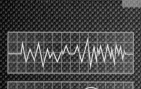

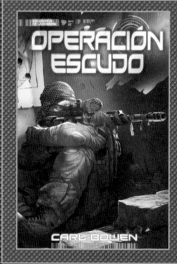

OPERACIÓN ESCUDO

CARL BOWEN

OPERACIÓN ESCUDO

1324.014

El helicóptero Seahawk negro del Escuadrón
de la Sombra rugía suavemente sobre el horizonte. Se
detuvo brevemente sobre el edificio del apartamento
abandonado. Prácticamente de inmediato,
seis miembros del Escuadrón de la Sombra bajaron
por una cuerda al tejado. Luego, el helicóptero se
trasladó a otro edificio al otro lado de la calle. Otros
dos miembros del equipo bajaron allí, entre ellos
Kimiyo Yamashita, el francotirador del equipo.
Estos dos harían la guardia para el resto del equipo,
eliminando cualquier insurgente que tratara
de escapar.

De momento, la operación se desenvolvía
sin problemas. Cross y su segundo al mando,
el suboficial jefe Alonso Walker, guiaron al escuadrón
de seis hombres hacia la parte de abajo del edificio.
Se abrieron camino lentamente a través

de la estructura, comprobando los puntos ciegos
y cubriéndose las espaldas los unos a los otros.
No encontraron resistencia, hasta que llegaron
a la planta baja. Cross y sus hombres se encontraron
con los insurgentes mientras estos almorzaban. Decir
que fueron sorprendidos totalmente desprevenidos sería
un eufemismo en toda regla.

Cross sonrió y apretó el gatillo de su carabina M4.

¡BANG!

Cross disparó una única bala hacia el techo a modo
de advertencia. Uno de los iraquíes salió corriendo
de la sala. El resto de los insurgentes cayeron
desesperados tratando de rendirse.

Cross hizo una señal a Walker y al sargento
Mark Shepherd para que se unieran a él
en la persecución del hostil que estaba tratando
de huir.

Los otros tres miembros del Escuadrón de la Sombra
se quedaron al cuidado de los no combatientes.

Cross persiguió al insurgente que huía
por un pasillo y dio la vuelta en una esquina.
De pronto, el insurgente apareció con un AK-47
en mano. **¡RA-TA-TA-TA-TA!**

El iraquí disparaba balas salvajemente
por el pasillo hacia Cross y sus hombres. Esquivando
el peligro, Cross alcanzó la vuelta de la esquina
con su rifle para disparar fuego de supresión. El espray
obligó al iraquí a entrar de nuevo en su escondite y eso
les dio tiempo a Walker y Shepherd para apresurarse
a dar la vuelta a la esquina y colocarse a cubierto
al final del pasillo.

Cuando el insurgente asomó la cabeza de nuevo,
se sorprendió al ver a los tres estadounidenses abriendo
fuego. El suboficial jefe Walker se las arregló para herir
al iraquí en el costado disparando directamente a
través de la precaria pared de yeso, al lado del marco
de la puerta. Al mismo tiempo, un afortunado disparo
de Cross le dio al iraquí en la muñeca.

El rifle del hombre se deslizó por el pasillo.

El hombre herido regresó a la habitación. Antes
de que Walker pudiera acercarse a él, le dio una patada
a la puerta y la cerró. Luego pasó el seguro.

Cross, Walker y Shepherd se apiñaron justo fuera
de la puerta cerrada. Walker y Shepherd miraron
a Cross esperando órdenes. Cross tomó posición
a la izquierda de la puerta y le hizo un gesto a Walker
para que se colocara en el lado opuesto y le hizo una

señal a Shepherd para que se preparara para patear la puerta.

Cross tocó el pequeño botón del intraauricular de doble dirección que tenía en su oreja derecha. —Equipo de fuego dos, informe —dijo Cross, susurrando lo suficientemente fuerte para que el diminuto auricular captara su voz.

—Despejado, señor —respondió el sargento Adam Paxton—. El único hombre no considerado es el que ustedes están buscando.

—Bien, lo traeremos —contestó Cross en voz baja—. Fuera—. Se detuvo un momento para dejar la línea despejada, luego tocó su intraauricular de nuevo. — Guardia, informe.

—No hay ratas, señor —reportó el sargento Edgar Brighton. El controlador de combate de la Fuerza Aérea de EE. UU. estaba situado en el tejado de enfrente con el teniente Kimiyo Yamashita, el francotirador del equipo. Mientras Yamashita escaneaba el edificio y la calle a través de la mira Leupold de su rifle de francotirador M110, Brighton escaneaba el área a través de su cámara de alta resolución por control remoto de reconocimiento de cuadricóptero VANT.
—No hay señal de refuerzos, tampoco.

—Bien —contestó Cross—. Fuera.

—Espere —dijo Yamashita—. Su fugitivo está escondido en una habitación en la cara sur del edificio, ¿verdad?

Cross se tomó un momento para comprobar en qué posición estaba respecto al edificio. —Afirmativo —dijo Cross—. ¿Visualizan ustedes a nuestro objetivo?

—Podría decirle en qué cuarto entró, pero no puedo verlo desde esta posición —dijo Yamashita—. Me estoy reubicando.

—Entendido —dijo Cross—. Fuera.

—Señor —dijo el suboficial jefe Walker cuando la comunicación por canal terminó. Señaló a la puerta cerrada entre ellos y el insurgente de Al Qaeda herido—. Déjeme tratar de hablar con él. Puedo conseguir hacerlo salir.

Shepherd parecía escéptico, pero no dijo nada. Cross también dudaba.

—No puede tener más de dieciocho años, señor —dijo Walker, leyendo sus expresiones—. Tiene dos disparos y probablemente esté muerto de miedo. Déjeme darle la oportunidad de rendirse

con la dignidad intacta. Aceptará.

Cross conocía a la perfección la fe en la humanidad que tenía el suboficial jefe y cómo de vez en cuando esta le nublaba el juicio. Sin embargo, a Cross tampoco le gustaba la idea de patear la puerta y disparar a un adolescente asustado. Así que, con un movimiento de cabeza, Cross hizo un gesto señalando la puerta, pero con su M4 listo, al igual que Shepherd.

—Hijo, quiero que me escuches —dijo Walker en árabe, inclinándose hacia la puerta—. Sé que estás sufriendo y que estás perdiendo sangre. Sé que estás asustado. Pero si colaboras conmigo, puedo sacarte de aquí sin...

—¡Tengo una salida! —gritó el insurgente— ¡Ya verán!

La desesperación en la voz del muchacho hizo que Cross se pusiera nervioso, pero al menos le dio una idea de su ubicación. Cross intercambió miradas con Shepherd, asegurándose de que el boina verde estaría listo para entrar por la puerta. Shepherd asintió.

—Hablemos —dijo Walker, su voz sonaba tranquila y estable, como si estuviera hablando con alguno de sus hijos—. ¿Cómo te llamas?

—No finjas que te importa quién soy —gruñó el insurgente en árabe—. Todo lo que te importa es...

Las palabras del muchacho se detuvieron al mismo tiempo que un golpe sordo sonó desde dentro de la habitación. Cross pensó haber escuchado un vidrio rompiéndose, pero sin hacerse añicos. Después, todo quedó en silencio. Cross no parecía contento.

En eso le hizo una señal a Shepherd para que abriera la puerta. Ignorando la frustración en el rostro de Walker, se movió rápidamente por el pasillo.

¡PAF!

Golpeó la puerta con una fuerte patada, rompiendo las bisagras. Cross y Walker le pisaban los talones mientras los tres se extendían por toda la habitación y cubrían todas las direcciones.

Apenas entraron por la puerta, escucharon la voz de Yamashita por el intraauricular. —Despejado —dijo el francotirador.

—Despejado —confirmó Cross. Al mirar alrededor de la habitación, vio que en una mesa cercana había una pila de explosivos; y el insurgente caído sostenía el detonador en la mano...

* ERROR DE TRANSMISIÓN *

PARA MAYOR INFORMACIÓN, CONTACTE
A SU BIBLIOTECA O LIBRERÍA LOCAL...

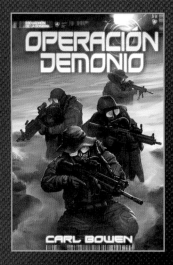

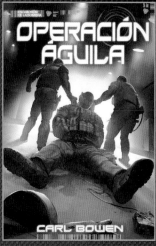

QUANTUM THEORY
OF MANY-PARTICLE
SYSTEMS

INTERNATIONAL SERIES IN PURE AND APPLIED PHYSICS

LEONARD I. SCHIFF, CONSULTING EDITOR

ADLER, BAZIN, AND SCHIFFER   Introduction to General Relativity
ALLIS AND HERLIN   Thermodynamics and Statistical Mechanics
BECKER   Introduction to Theoretical Mechanics
BJORKEN AND DRELL   Relativistic Quantum Fields
BJORKEN AND DRELL   Relativistic Quantum Mechanics
CHODOROW AND SUSSKIND   Fundamentals of Microwave Electronics
CLARK   Applied X-rays
COLLIN   Field Theory of Guided Waves
EVANS   The Atomic Nucleus
FETTER AND WALECKA   Quantum Theory of Many-Particle Systems
FEYNMAN AND HIBBS   Quantum Mechanics and Path Integrals
GINZTON   Microwave Measurements
HALL   Introduction to Electron Microscopy
HARDY AND PERRIN   The Principles of Optics
HARNWELL   Electricity and Electromagnetism
HARNWELL AND LIVINGOOD   Experimental Atomic Physics
HARRISON   Solid State Theory
HENLEY AND THIRRING   Elementary Quantum Field Theory
HOUSTON   Principles of Mathematical Physics
JAMMER   The Conceptual Development of Quantum Mechanics
KENNARD   Kinetic Theory of Gases
LEIGHTON   Principles of Modern Physics
LINDSAY   Mechanical Radiation
LIVINGSTON AND BLEWETT   Particle Accelerators
MIDDLETON   An Introduction to Statistical Communication Theory
MORSE   Vibration and Sound
MORSE AND FESHBACH   Methods of Theoretical Physics
MORSE AND INGARD   Theoretical Acoustics
MUSKAT   Physical Principles of Oil Production
NEWTON   Scattering Theory of Waves and Particles
PRESENT   Kinetic Theory of Gases
READ   Dislocations in Crystals
RICHTMYER, KENNARD, AND COOPER   Introduction to Modern Physics
ROSSI AND ALBERT   Introduction to the Physics of Space
SCHIFF   Quantum Mechanics
SCHWARTZ   Introduction to Special Relativity
SEITZ   The Modern Theory of Solids
SLATER   Quantum Theory of Atomic Structure, Vol. I
SLATER   Quantum Theory of Atomic Structure, Vol. II
SLATER   Quantum Theory of Matter
SLATER   Electronic Structure of Molecules: Quantum Theory of Molecules and Solids, Vol. 1
SLATER   Symmetry and Energy Bands in Crystals: Quantum Theory of Molecules and Solids, Vol. 2
SLATER   Insulators, Semiconductors, and Metals: Quantum Theory of Molecules and Solids, Vol. 3
SLATER AND FRANK   Introduction to Theoretical Physics
SLATER AND FRANK   Mechanics
SMYTHE   Static and Dynamic Electricity
STRATTON   Electromagnetic Theory
TINKHAM   Group Theory and Quantum Mechanics
TOWNES AND SCHAWLOW   Microwave Spectroscopy
WANG   Solid-State Electronics
WHITE   Introduction to Atomic Spectra

The late F. K. Richtmyer was Consulting Editor of the series from its inception in 1929 to his death in 1939. Lee A. DuBridge was Consulting Editor from 1939 to 1946; and G. P. Harnwell from 1947 to 1954.

QUANTUM THEORY OF MANY-PARTICLE SYSTEMS

ALEXANDER L. FETTER
Associate Professor of Physics
Stanford University

JOHN DIRK WALECKA
Professor of Physics
Stanford University

McGRAW-HILL BOOK COMPANY   New York
San Francisco   Mexico
St. Louis   Panama
Düsseldorf   Sydney
London   Toronto

**QUANTUM THEORY
OF MANY-PARTICLE
SYSTEMS**

TO JEAN AND KAY

PREFACE

This book grew from a one-year graduate course that we have taught at Stanford since 1964. The course was generally divided into three parts: the first third on many-body theory and the remaining two-thirds on applications to nuclear and low-temperature physics. Although these areas of physics have grown rapidly during the past 20 years and are now becoming a standard part of the graduate curriculum, we found no suitable introductory graduate-level textbook. The present book attempts to fill the gap between a first-year graduate course in quantum mechanics, and monographs and original research on the quantum theory of many interacting particles.

Our two basic aims are to present a unified treatment of nonrelativistic many-particle systems, and to have the text self-contained in the sense that the relevant material is developed without constant reference to outside sources. The first aim is especially important for students, since the literature contains a great variety of approaches. Throughout the book, the discussion relies on second quantization and the methods of quantum field theory. In

large part, these techniques were chosen for their power and flexibility; they form the basis for current theoretical work in such diverse fields as solid-state, low-temperature, nuclear, atomic, and molecular physics. As far as possible, we have tried to exhibit the essential unity of these subjects, hopefully combating the trend toward increased specialization.

The book is divided into five major parts. Second quantization is introduced in Part one, where some elementary concepts in thermodynamics and statistical mechanics are also reviewed. Part two uses Green's functions to discuss the ground state and low-lying excited states of interacting assemblies and develops the Feynman-Dyson perturbation theory for both Fermi and Bose systems. This analysis is extended to finite temperatures in Part three, where the measured quantities represent ensemble averages. Part four contains a discussion of the method of canonical transformations. Throughout these four parts, the electron gas serves as the primary illustrative example, but we also consider model systems such as hard-sphere Fermi and Bose gases. In Part five, these techniques are applied to several other physical systems: nuclear matter, interacting electrons and phonons, super-conductors, superfluid helium, and finite nuclei. Each of the five chapters of Part five starts with a brief review of the basic experimental and theoretical facts that assumes no specialized background knowledge. Each is intended to be self-contained and largely independent of the others so that the particular applications discussed can be left to the discretion of the instructor. For this reason, the book is somewhat too long for a one-year course.

We believe that the solution of problems forms an integral part of learning, and we have tried to include interesting exercises of varying degrees of difficulty. There are over 175 problems, some at the end of each chapter.

A comprehensive bibliography has not been attempted since it is impossible to include all developments in many-particle physics within a single text. The references quoted are only those directly relevant to the discussion.

It is assumed that the reader has studied quantum mechanics at the level of Schiff, Quantum Mechanics, Third Edition, McGraw-Hill Book Company, and has a working knowledge of complex variables and contour integration. Some familiarity with thermodynamics, statistical mechanics, and Maxwell's equations is helpful, while an elementary acquaintance with solid-state physics and nuclear physics will make the book more meaningful.

Two short appendixes have been included: a tabulation of definite integrals and a review of the theory of angular momentum.

We would like to thank Professor L. I. Schiff for his valuable help in this project and Mrs. B. Fowlie for her careful typing.

ALEXANDER L. FETTER
JOHN DIRK WALECKA

CONTENTS

PREFACE   vii

PART ONE☐INTRODUCTION   **1**

CHAPTER 1   SECOND QUANTIZATION   **3**

      1   THE SCHRÖDINGER EQUATION IN FIRST AND SECOND
         QUANTIZATION   4
         Bosons   7
         Many-particle Hilbert space and creation and destruction operators   12
         Fermions   15
      2   FIELDS   19
      3   EXAMPLE: DEGENERATE ELECTRON GAS   21

CHAPTER 2   STATISTICAL MECHANICS   **33**

      4   REVIEW OF THERMODYNAMICS AND STATISTICAL MECHANICS   34
      5   IDEAL GAS   36
         Bosons   38
         Fermions   45

                                                               ix

PART TWO □ GROUND-STATE (ZERO-TEMPERATURE) FORMALISM   51

CHAPTER 3   GREEN'S FUNCTIONS AND FIELD THEORY (FERMIONS)   53

    6   PICTURES   53
        Schrödinger picture   53
        Interaction picture   54
        Heisenberg picture   58
        Adiabatic "switching on"   59
        Gell-Mann and Low theorem on the ground state in quantum field
            theory   61
    7   GREEN'S FUNCTIONS   64
        Definition   64
        Relation to observables   66
        Example: free fermions   70
        The Lehmann representation   72
        Physical interpretation of the Green's function   79
    8   WICK'S THEOREM   83
    9   DIAGRAMMATIC ANALYSIS OF PERTURBATION THEORY   92
        Feynman diagrams in coordinate space   92
        Feynman diagrams in momentum space   100
        Dyson's equations   105
        Goldstone's theorem   111

CHAPTER 4   FERMI SYSTEMS   120

    10 HARTREE-FOCK APPROXIMATION   121
    11 IMPERFECT FERMI GAS   128
        Scattering from a hard sphere   128
        Scattering theory in momentum space   130
        Ladder diagrams and the Bethe-Salpeter equation   131
        Galitskii's integral equations   139
        The proper self-energy   142
        Physical quantities   146
        Justification of terms retained   149
    12 DEGENERATE ELECTRON GAS   151
        Ground-state energy and the dielectric constant   151
        Ring diagrams   154
        Evaluation of Π^0 158
        Correlation energy   163
        Effective interaction   166

CHAPTER 5   LINEAR RESPONSE AND COLLECTIVE MODES   171

    13 GENERAL THEORY OF LINEAR RESPONSE TO AN EXTERNAL
        PERTURBATION   172
    14 SCREENING IN AN ELECTRON GAS   175
    15 PLASMA OSCILLATIONS IN AN ELECTRON GAS   180
    16 ZERO SOUND IN AN IMPERFECT FERMI GAS   183
    17 INELASTIC ELECTRON SCATTERING   188

CHAPTER 6   BOSE SYSTEMS   198

    18 FORMULATION OF THE PROBLEM   199
    19 GREEN'S FUNCTIONS   203

20   PERTURBATION THEORY AND FEYNMAN RULES   207
Interaction picture   207
Feynman rules in coordinate space   208
Feynman rules in momentum space   209
Dyson's equations   211
Lehmann representation   214
21   WEAKLY INTERACTING BOSE GAS   215
22   DILUTE BOSE GAS WITH REPULSIVE CORES   218

PART THREE□FINITE-TEMPERATURE FORMALISM   225

CHAPTER 7   FIELD THEORY AT FINITE TEMPERATURE   227

23   TEMPERATURE GREEN'S FUNCTIONS   227
Definition   228
Relation to observables   229
Example : noninteracting system   232
24   PERTURBATION THEORY AND WICK'S THEOREM FOR FINITE
TEMPERATURES   234
Interaction picture   234
Periodicity of $\mathscr{G}$ 236
Proof of Wick's theorem   237
25   DIAGRAMMATIC ANALYSIS   241
Feynman rules in coordinate space   242
Feynman rules in momentum space   244
Evaluation of frequency sums   248
26   DYSON'S EQUATIONS   250

CHAPTER 8   PHYSICAL SYSTEMS AT FINITE TEMPERATURE   255

27   HARTREE-FOCK APPROXIMATION   255
28   IMPERFECT BOSE GAS NEAR T_c 259
29   SPECIFIC HEAT OF AN IMPERFECT FERMI GAS AT LOW
TEMPERATURE   261
Low-temperature expansion of $\mathscr{G}$ 262
Hartree-Fock approximation   262
Evaluation of the entropy   265
30   ELECTRON GAS   267
Approximate proper self-energy   268
Summation of ring diagrams   271
Approximate thermodynamic potential   273
Classical limit   275
Zero-temperature limit   281

CHAPTER 9   REAL-TIME GREEN'S FUNCTIONS AND LINEAR RESPONSE   291

31   GENERALIZED LEHMANN REPRESENTATION   292
Definition of $\bar{G}$ 292
Retarded and advanced functions   294
Temperature Green's functions and analytic continuation   297
32   LINEAR RESPONSE AT FINITE TEMPERATURE   298
General theory   298
Density correlation function   300
33   SCREENING IN AN ELECTRON GAS   303
34   PLASMA OSCILLATIONS IN AN ELECTRON GAS   307

PART FOUR☐CANONICAL TRANSFORMATIONS   311

CHAPTER 10 CANONICAL TRANSFORMATIONS   313

     35 INTERACTING BOSE GAS   314
     36 COOPER PAIRS   320
     37 INTERACTING FERMI GAS   326

PART FIVE☐APPLICATIONS TO PHYSICAL SYSTEMS   339

CHAPTER 11 NUCLEAR MATTER   341

     38 NUCLEAR FORCES: A REVIEW   341
     39 NUCLEAR MATTER   348
         Nuclear radii and charge distributions   348
         The semiempirical mass formula   349
     40 INDEPENDENT-PARTICLE (FERMI-GAS) MODEL   352
     41 INDEPENDENT-PAIR APPROXIMATION (BRUECKNER'S THEORY)   357
         Self-consistent Bethe-Goldstone equation   358
         Solution for a nonsingular square-well potential   360
         Solution for a pure hard-core potential   363
         Properties of nuclear matter with a "realistic" potential   366
     42 RELATION TO GREEN'S FUNCTIONS AND BETHE-SALPETER EQUATION   377
     43 THE ENERGY GAP IN NUCLEAR MATTER   383

CHAPTER 12 PHONONS AND ELECTRONS   389

     44 THE NONINTERACTING PHONON SYSTEM   390
         Lagrangian and hamiltonian   391
         Debye theory of the specific heat   393
     45 THE ELECTRON-PHONON INTERACTION   396
     46 THE COUPLED-FIELD THEORY   399
         Feynman rules for $T = 0$ 399
         The equivalent electron-electron interaction   401
         Vertex parts and Dyson's equations   402
     47 MIGDAL'S THEOREM   406

CHAPTER 13 SUPERCONDUCTIVITY   413

     48 FUNDAMENTAL PROPERTIES OF SUPERCONDUCTORS   414
         Basic experimental facts   414
         Thermodynamic relations   417
     49 LONDON-PIPPARD PHENOMENOLOGICAL THEORY   420
         Derivation of London equations   420
         Solution for halfspace and slab   421
         Conservation and quantization of fluxoid   423
         Pippard's generalized equation   425
     50 GINZBURG-LANDAU PHENOMENOLOGICAL THEORY   430
         Expansion of the free energy   430
         Solution in simple cases   432
         Flux quantization   435
         Surface energy   436

51 MICROSCOPIC (BCS) THEORY   439
    General formulation   439
    Solution for uniform medium   444
    Determination of the gap function $\Delta(T)$ 447
    Thermodynamic functions   449
52 LINEAR RESPONSE TO A WEAK MAGNETIC FIELD   454
    Derivation of the general kernel   455
    Meissner effect   459
    Penetration depth in Pippard (nonlocal) limit   461
    Nonlocal integral relation   463
53 MICROSCOPIC DERIVATION OF GINZBURG-LANDAU
    EQUATIONS   466

CHAPTER 14 SUPERFLUID HELIUM   479

54 FUNDAMENTAL PROPERTIES OF He II   481
    Basic experimental facts   481
    Landau's quasiparticle model   484
55 WEAKLY INTERACTING BOSE GAS   488
    General formulation   489
    Uniform condensate   492
    Nonuniform condensate   495

CHAPTER 15 APPLICATIONS TO FINITE SYSTEMS: THE ATOMIC NUCLEUS   503

56 GENERAL CANONICAL TRANSFORMATION TO PARTICLES AND
    HOLES   504
57 THE SINGLE-PARTICLE SHELL MODEL   508
    Approximate Hartree-Fock wave functions and level orderings in a
        central potential   508
    Spin-orbit splitting   511
    Single-particle matrix elements   512
58 MANY PARTICLES IN A SHELL   515
    Two valence particles: general interaction and $\delta(\mathbf{x})$ force   515
    Several particles: normal coupling   519
    The pairing-force problem   523
    The boson approximation   526
    The Bogoliubov transformation   527
59 EXCITED STATES: LINEARIZATION OF THE EQUATIONS OF
    MOTION   538
    Tamm-Dancoff approximation (TDA)   538
    Random-phase approximation (RPA)   540
    Reduction of the basis   543
    Solution for the [15]-dimensional supermultiplet with a $\delta(\mathbf{x})$ force   547
    An application to nuclei: O^{16} 555
60 EXCITED STATES: GREEN'S FUNCTION METHODS   558
    The polarization propagator   558
    Random-phase approximation   564
    Tamm-Dancoff approximation   565
    Construction of $\Pi(\omega)$ in the RPA   566
61 REALISTIC NUCLEAR FORCES   567
    Two nucleons outside closed shells: the independent-pair approxi-
        mation   567
    Bethe-Goldstone equation   568
    Harmonic-oscillator approximation   570
    Pauli principle correction   574
    Extensions and calculations of other quantities   574

APPENDIXES   **579**

A   DEFINITE INTEGRALS   579
B   REVIEW OF THE THEORY OF ANGULAR MOMENTUM   581
     Basic commutation relations   581
     Coupling of two angular momenta: Clebsch-Gordan coefficients   582
     Coupling of three angular momenta: the 6-j coefficients   585
     Irreducible tensor operators and the Wigner-Eckart theorem   586
     Tensor operators in coupled schemes   587

INDEX   589

QUANTUM THEORY
OF MANY-PARTICLE
SYSTEMS

part one

Introduction

1
Second Quantization

The physical world consists of interacting many-particle systems. An accurate description of such systems requires the inclusion of the interparticle potentials in the many-particle Schrödinger equation, and this problem forms the basic subject of the present book. In principle, the N-body wave function in configuration space contains all possible information, but a direct solution of the Schrödinger equation is impractical. It is therefore necessary to resort to other techniques, and we shall rely on second quantization, quantum-field theory, and the use of Green's functions. In a relativistic theory, the concept of second quantization is essential to describe the creation and destruction of particles.[1] Even in a nonrelativistic theory, however, second quantization greatly simplifies the discussion of many identical interacting particles.[2] This approach merely

---

[1] P. A. M. Dirac, *Proc. Roy. Soc.* (*London*), **114A**:243 (1927).
[2] P. Jordan and O. Klein, *Z. Physik*, **45**:751 (1927); P. Jordan and E. P. Wigner, *Z. Physik*, **47**:631 (1928); V. Fock, *Z. Physik*, **75**:622 (1932). Although different in detail, the approach presented here follows the spirit of this last paper.

reformulates the original Schrödinger equation. Nevertheless, it has several distinct advantages: the second-quantized operators incorporate the statistics (Bose or Fermi) at each step, which contrasts with the more cumbersome approach of using symmetrized or antisymmetrized products of single-particle wave functions. The methods of quantum field theory also allow us to concentrate on the few matrix elements of interest, thus avoiding the need for dealing directly with the many-particle wave function and the coordinates of all the remaining particles. Finally, the Green's functions contain the most important physical information such as the ground-state energy and other thermodynamic functions, the energy and lifetime of excited states, and the linear response to external perturbations.

Unfortunately, the exact Green's functions are no easier to determine than the original wave function, and we therefore make use of perturbation theory, which is here presented in the concise and systematic language of Feynman rules and diagrams.[1] These rules allow us to evaluate physical quantities to any order in perturbation theory. We shall also show, as first observed by Feynman, that the disconnected diagrams cancel exactly. This cancellation leads to linked-cluster expansions and makes explicit the volume dependence of all physical quantities. It is possible to formulate a set of integral equations (Dyson's equations) whose iterations yield the Feynman-Dyson perturbation theory to any arbitrary order in the perturbation parameter and which are independent of the original perturbation series.[2] Since the properties of many-particle systems frequently involve expressions that are nonanalytic in the coupling constant, the possibility of nonperturbative approximations is very important.

In addition, it is frequently possible to make physical approximations that reduce the second-quantized hamiltonian to a quadratic form. The resulting problem is then exactly solvable either by making a canonical transformation or by examining the linear equations of motion.

1□THE SCHRÖDINGER EQUATION IN FIRST AND SECOND QUANTIZATION

We shall start our discussion by merely reformulating the Schrödinger equation in the language of second quantization. In almost all cases of interest, the hamiltonian takes the form

$$H = \sum_{k=1}^{N} T(x_k) + \tfrac{1}{2} \sum_{k \neq l=1}^{N} V(x_k, x_l) \tag{1.1}$$

where T is the kinetic energy and V is the potential energy of interaction between the particles. The quantity x_k denotes the coordinates of the kth particle,

---

[1] R. P. Feynman, *Phys. Rev.*, **76**:749 (1949); **76**:769 (1949).
[2] F. J. Dyson, *Phys. Rev.*, **75**:486 (1949); **75**:1736 (1949).

including the spatial coordinate x_k and any discrete variables such as the z component of spin for a system of fermions or the z component of isotopic spin for a system of nucleons. The potential-energy term represents the interaction between every pair of particles, *counted once*, which accounts for the factor of $\frac{1}{2}$, and the double sum runs over the indices k and l separately, excluding the value k equal to l. With this hamiltonian, the time-dependent Schrödinger equation is given by

$$i\hbar \frac{\partial}{\partial t} \Psi(x_1 \cdots x_N, t) = H\Psi(x_1 \cdots x_N, t) \tag{1.2}$$

together with an appropriate set of boundary conditions for the wave function Ψ.

We start by expanding the many-particle wave function Ψ in a complete set of time-independent single-particle wave functions that incorporate the boundary conditions. For example, if we have a large homogeneous system, it is natural to expand in a set of plane waves in a large box with periodic boundary conditions; alternatively, if we have a system of interacting electrons in an atom, a complete set of single-particle coulomb wave functions is commonly used; finally, if we have particles moving in a crystal lattice, a convenient choice is the complete set of Bloch wave functions in the appropriate periodic potential. We shall use the general notation for the single-particle wave function

$$\psi_{E_k}(x_k)$$

where E_k represents a complete set of single-particle quantum numbers. For example, E_k denotes $\mathbf{p}$ for a system of spinless bosons in a box, or E, J, and M for a set of spinless particles in a central field, or $\mathbf{p}$, s_z for a homogeneous system of fermions, and so on. It is convenient to imagine that this infinite set of single-particle quantum numbers is ordered $(1, 2, 3, \ldots, r, s, t, \ldots, \infty)$ and that E_k runs over this set of eigenvalues. We can now expand the many-body wave function as follows:

$$\Psi(x_1 \cdots x_N, t) = \sum_{E_1' \cdots E_N'} C(E_1' \cdots E_N', t)\psi_{E_1'}(x_1) \cdots \psi_{E_N'}(x_N) \tag{1.3}$$

This expression is completely general and is simply the expansion of the many-particle wave function in a complete set of states. Since the $\psi_E(x)$ are time independent, all of the time dependence of the wave function appears in the coefficients $C(E_1 \cdots E_N, t)$.

Let us now insert Eq. (1.3) into the Schrödinger equation and then multiply by the expression $\psi_{E_1}(x_1)^\dagger \cdots \psi_{E_N}(x_N)^\dagger$, which is the product of the adjoint wave functions corresponding to a *fixed set of quantum numbers* $E_1 \cdots E_N$. Integrate over all the appropriate coordinates (this may include a sum over spin coordinates if the particles have spin). On the left-hand side, this procedure

projects out the coefficient C corresponding to the given set of quantum numbers $E_1 \cdots E_N$, and we therefore arrive at the equation

$$
i\hbar \frac{\partial}{\partial t} C(E_1 \cdots E_N, t) = \sum_{k=1}^{N} \sum_{W} \int dx_k \, \psi_{E_k}(x_k)^{\dagger} \, T(x_k) \, \psi_W(x_k)
$$
$$
\times \, C(E_1 \cdots E_{k-1} \, W E_{k+1} \cdots E_N, t)
$$
$$
+ \tfrac{1}{2} \sum_{\substack{k \neq l=1}}^{N} \sum_{W} \sum_{W'} \int\!\!\int dx_k \, dx_l \, \psi_{E_k}(x_k)^{\dagger} \, \psi_{E_l}(x_l)^{\dagger}
$$
$$
\times \, V(x_k, x_l) \, \psi_W(x_k) \, \psi_{W'}(x_l)
$$
$$
\times \, C(E_1 \cdots E_{k-1} \, W E_{k+1} \cdots E_{l-1} \, W' E_{l+1} \cdots E_N, t) \quad (1.4)
$$

Since the kinetic energy is a single-particle operator involving the coordinates of the particles one at a time, it can change only one of the single-particle wave functions. The orthonormality of the single-particle wave functions ensures that all but the kth particle must have the original given quantum numbers, but the wave function of the kth particle can still run over the infinite set of quantum numbers. To be very explicit, we have denoted this variable index by W in the above equation. A similar result holds for the potential energy. The situation is a little more complicated, however, because the potential energy involves the coordinates of two particles. At most, it can change the wave functions of two particles, the kth and lth particles for example, while all the other quantum numbers must be the same as those we have projected out. The quantum numbers of the kth particle still run over an infinite set of values, denoted by W, and the quantum numbers of the lth particle still run over an infinite set of values, denoted by W'. Each given set of quantum numbers $E_1 \cdots E_N$ leads to a different equation, yielding an infinite set of coupled differential equations for the time-dependent coefficients of the many-particle wave function.

We now incorporate the statistics of the particles. The many-particle wave function is assumed to have the following property

$$
\Psi(\cdots x_i \cdots x_j \cdots, t) = \pm \Psi(\cdots x_j \cdots x_i \cdots, t) \quad (1.5)
$$

where, as discussed above, the coordinate x_k includes the spin for an assembly of fermions. Equation (1.5) shows that the wave function must be either symmetric or antisymmetric under the interchange of the coordinates of any two particles. A necessary and sufficient condition for Eq. (1.5) is that the expansion coefficients themselves be either symmetric or antisymmetric under the interchange of the corresponding quantum numbers

$$
C(\cdots E_i \cdots E_j \cdots, t) = \pm C(\cdots E_j \cdots E_i \cdots, t) \quad (1.6)
$$

The sufficiency of Eq. (1.6) is easily seen by first carrying out the particle interchange on the wave function and then carrying out the appropriate interchange

of dummy summation variables. The necessity is shown by projecting a given coefficient out of the wave function with the orthonormality of the single-particle wave functions and then using property (1.5) of the total wave function. Thus we can put all the symmetry of the wave function into the set of coefficients C.

BOSONS

Particles that require the plus sign are called *bosons*, and we temporarily concentrate on such systems. The symmetry of the coefficients under interchange of quantum numbers allows us to regroup the quantum numbers appearing in any coefficient. Out of the given set of quantum numbers $E_1 \cdots E_N$, suppose that the state 1 occurs n_1 times, the state 2 occurs n_2 times, and so on, for example,

$$C(121324 \cdots, t) = C(\underbrace{111 \cdots}_{n_1} \quad \underbrace{222 \cdots}_{n_2} \cdots \cdots, t)$$

All of those terms in the expansion of the wave function with n_1 particles in the state 1, n_2 particles in the state 2, and so on, have the same *coefficient* in the wave function. It is convenient to give this coefficient a new name

$$\bar{C}(n_1 n_2 \cdots n_\infty, t) \equiv C(\underbrace{111 \cdots}_{n_1} \quad \underbrace{222 \cdots}_{n_2} \cdots \cdots, t) \tag{1.7}$$

Consider the normalization of the many-particle wave function. The normalization condition can be represented symbolically as

$$\int |\Psi|^2 (d\tau) = 1 \tag{1.8}$$

which means: take the wave function, multiply it by its adjoint, and integrate over all the appropriate coordinates. The resulting normalization guarantees that the total probability of finding the system somewhere in configuration space is unity. The orthonormality of the single-particle wave functions immediately yields a corresponding condition on our expansion coefficients C

$$\sum_{E_1 \cdots E_N} |C(E_1 \cdots E_N, t)|^2 = 1 \tag{1.9}$$

We now make use of the equality of all coefficients containing the same number of particles in the same states to rewrite this condition in terms of the coefficient $\bar{C}$

$$\sum_{n_1 n_2 \cdots n_\infty} |\bar{C}(n_1 n_2 \cdots n_\infty, t)|^2 \sum_{\substack{E_1 \cdots E_N \\ (n_1 n_2 \cdots n_\infty)}} 1 = 1 \tag{1.10}$$

Here the sum is split into two pieces: first, sum over all values of the quantum numbers $E_1 E_2 \cdots E_N$ consistent with the given set of occupation numbers $(n_1 n_2 n_3 \cdots n_\infty)$, and then sum over all sets of occupation numbers. It is clear that this procedure is merely a way of regrouping all the terms in the sum. The problem of summing over all sets of quantum numbers consistent with a given set of occupation numbers is equivalent to the problem of putting

N objects into boxes with n_1 objects in the first box, n_2 objects in the second box, and so on, which can be done in $N!/n_1!n_2! \cdots n_\infty!$ ways. We thus obtain the modified normalization statement

$$\sum_{n_1 n_2 \cdots n_\infty} |\bar{C}(n_1 n_2 \cdots n_\infty, t)|^2 \frac{N!}{n_1!n_2! \cdots n_\infty!} = 1 \tag{1.11}$$

In this relation, most of the n_i will be zero, since their total is finite

$$\sum_{i=1}^{\infty} n_i = N \tag{1.12}$$

By definition, however, 0! is equal to 1, and Eq. (1.11) is well defined as written. Our results can be expressed more elegantly if we define still another coefficient

$$f(n_1 n_2 \cdots n_\infty, t) \equiv \left(\frac{N!}{n_1!n_2! \cdots n_\infty!} \right)^{\pm} \bar{C}(n_1 n_2 \cdots n_\infty, t) \tag{1.13}$$

and the corresponding normalization statement for this set of coefficients is

$$\sum_{n_1 n_2 \cdots n_\infty} |f(n_1 n_2 \cdots n_\infty, t)|^2 = 1 \tag{1.14}$$

where the set $\{n_i\}$ must satisfy Eq. (1.12).

The original wave function can now be rewritten as follows:

$$\Psi(x_1 \cdots x_N, t) = \sum_{E_1 \cdots E_N} C(E_1 \cdots E_N, t) \psi_{E_1}(x_1) \cdots \psi_{E_N}(x_N)$$

$$= \sum_{E_1 \cdots E_N} \bar{C}(n_1 n_2 \cdots n_\infty, t) \psi_{E_1}(x_1) \cdots \psi_{E_N}(x_N)$$

$$= \sum_{n_1 n_2 \cdots n_\infty} f(n_1 n_2 \cdots n_\infty, t) \left(\frac{n_1!n_2! \cdots n_\infty!}{N!} \right)^{\pm}$$

$$\times \sum_{\substack{E_1 \cdots E_N \\ (n_1 n_2 \cdots n_\infty)}} \psi_{E_1}(x_1) \cdots \psi_{E_N}(x_N)$$

$$= \sum_{\substack{n_1 n_2 \cdots n_\infty \\ \left(\sum_i n_i = N \right)}} f(n_1 n_2 \cdots n_\infty, t)$$

$$\times \Phi_{n_1 n_2 \cdots n_\infty}(x_1 x_2 \cdots x_N) \tag{1.15}$$

where we have defined

$$\Phi_{n_1 n_2 \cdots n_\infty}(x_1 \cdots x_N)$$
$$\equiv \left(\frac{n_1!n_2! \cdots n_\infty!}{N!} \right)^{\pm} \sum_{\substack{E_1 \cdots E_N \\ (n_1 n_2 \cdots n_\infty)}} \psi_{E_1}(x_1) \cdots \psi_{E_N}(x_N) \tag{1.16}$$

Equation (1.15) is an important result, and it simply says that a totally symmetric wave function can be expanded in terms of a complete orthonormal basis of completely symmetrized wave functions $\Phi_{n_1 \cdots n_\infty}(x_1 \cdots x_N)$. Furthermore,

the coefficients in this expansion are just the set of f's. Note the following properties of the Φ's

$$\Phi(\cdots x_i \cdots x_j \cdots) = \Phi(\cdots x_j \cdots x_i \cdots) \tag{1.17}$$

$$\int dx_1 \cdots dx_N \, \Phi_{n_1' n_2' \cdots n_\infty'}(x_1 \cdots x_N)^\dagger \, \Phi_{n_1 n_2 \cdots n_\infty}(x_1 \cdots x_N)$$
$$= \delta_{n_1' n_1} \cdots \delta_{n_\infty' n_\infty} \tag{1.18}$$

The first result follows immediately from interchanging particle coordinates, and then, correspondingly, dummy variables in the defining equation (1.16); the second result follows from the orthonormality of the single-particle wave functions. As an explicit example, we shall write out the wave function for three spinless bosons, two of which occupy the ground state (denoted by the subscript 1) and one of which occupies the first excited state (denoted by the subscript 2):

$$\Phi_{210 \cdots 0}(x_1 \, x_2 \, x_3)$$
$$= \frac{1}{\sqrt{3}} [\psi_1(1) \psi_1(2) \psi_2(3) + \psi_1(1) \psi_2(2) \psi_1(3) + \psi_2(1) \psi_1(2) \psi_1(3)]$$

We return to the analysis of Eq. (1.4), where it is important to remember that $E_1 \cdots E_N$ *is a given set of quantum numbers in this expression.* Consider first the kinetic-energy term, which can be rewritten in an obvious shorthand

$$\sum_{k=1}^{N} \sum_{W} \langle E_k|T|W \rangle \, C(E_1 \cdots E_{k-1} \, W E_{k+1} \cdots E_N, t) = \sum_{k=1}^{N} \sum_{W} \langle E_k|T|W \rangle$$
$$\times \bar{C}(n_1 n_2 \cdots n_{E_k} - 1 \cdots n_W + 1 \cdots n_\infty, t) \tag{1.19}$$

Here, the right side makes explicit the observation that the quantum number E_k occurs one less time and the quantum number W occurs one more time. Now every time E_k takes the same value in the summation over k, let us say E (this occurs n_E times), it makes the same contribution to the sum. Therefore, and *this is the crucial point in the whole treatment,* instead of performing a sum over k from 1 to N, we can equally well sum over E and write

$$\sum_E n_E$$

That is, a sum over particles is equivalent to a sum over states, and Eq. (1.19) becomes

$$\sum_{k=1}^{N} \sum_{W} \langle E_k|T|W \rangle \, C(E_1 \cdots E_{k-1} \, W E_{k+1} \cdots E_N, t)$$
$$= \sum_{E} \sum_{W} \langle E|T|W \rangle \, n_E$$
$$\times \bar{C}(n_1 n_2 \cdots n_E - 1 \cdots n_W + 1 \cdots n_\infty, t) \tag{1.20}$$

The sum on E is now infinite, running over all of the single-particle quantum numbers, but most of the n_E are zero since those states are not occupied in the original given set of quantum numbers $E_1 \cdots E_N$. Finally, it is convenient to simplify the notation, which yields

$$\sum_{k=1}^{N} \sum_{W} \langle E_k | T | W \rangle C(E_1 \cdots E_{k-1} W E_{k+1} \cdots E_N, t) = \sum_{i} \sum_{j} n_i \langle i | T | j \rangle$$
$$\times \bar{C}(n_1 n_2 \cdots n_i - 1 \cdots n_j + 1 \cdots n_\infty, t) \quad (1.21)$$

Exactly the same manipulations apply to the potential energy term:

$$\tfrac{1}{2} \sum_{k \neq l=1}^{N} \sum_{W} \sum_{W'} \langle E_k E_l | V | W W' \rangle$$
$$\times C(E_1 \cdots E_{k-1} W E_{k+1} \cdots E_{l-1} W' E_{l+1} \cdots E_N, t)$$
$$= \tfrac{1}{2} \sum_{k \neq l=1}^{N} \sum_{W} \sum_{W'} \langle E_k E_l | V | W W' \rangle$$
$$\times \bar{C}(n_1 \cdots n_{E_k} - 1 \cdots n_W + 1 \cdots n_{E_l} - 1 \cdots$$
$$n_{W'} + 1 \cdots n_\infty, t) \quad (1.22)$$

As in the preceding discussion, the states E_k and E_l are each occupied one less time, and the states W and W' are each occupied one more time in this sum. Again, every time E_k takes the same value, say E (this occurs n_E times), and E_l takes the same value, say E' (this occurs $n_{E'}$ times), it makes the same contribution to the sum. There is only one slight further complication here, owing to the restriction $k \neq l$ in the double sum. Thus it is necessary to use the following counting for the number of terms appearing in this sum

$$\tfrac{1}{2} n_E n_{E'} \text{ if } E \neq E' \qquad \tfrac{1}{2} n_E (n_E - 1) \text{ if } E = E'$$

because the restriction $k \neq l$ does not affect the counting if $E \neq E'$, while the eigenvalue E is counted one less time in the second sum if $E = E'$. The potential energy now becomes a doubly infinite sum, but most of the factors n_E and $n_{E'}$ are zero. Thus, just as before, we can write Eq. (1.22) as

$$\tfrac{1}{2} \sum_{k \neq l=1}^{N} \sum_{W} \sum_{W'} \langle E_k E_l | V | W W' \rangle$$
$$\times C(E_1 \cdots E_{k-1} W E_{k+1} \cdots E_{l-1} W' E_{l+1} \cdots E_N, t)$$
$$= \sum_{E} \sum_{E'} \sum_{W} \sum_{W'} \tfrac{1}{2} n_E (n_{E'} - \delta_{EE'}) \langle EE' | V | W W' \rangle$$
$$\times \bar{C}(n_1 \cdots n_E - 1 \cdots n_W + 1 \cdots n_{E'} - 1 \cdots$$
$$n_{W'} + 1 \cdots n_\infty, t)$$
$$= \sum_{i} \sum_{j} \sum_{k} \sum_{l} \tfrac{1}{2} n_i (n_j - \delta_{ij}) \langle ij | V | kl \rangle$$
$$\times \bar{C}(n_1 \cdots n_i - 1 \cdots n_k + 1 \cdots n_j - 1 \cdots$$
$$n_l + 1 \cdots n_\infty, t) \quad (1.23)$$

If the coefficients f defined in Eq. (1.13) are substituted into Eqs. (1.21) and (1.23), we arrive at the following infinite set of coupled differential equations

$$i\hbar \left[\frac{n_1! \cdots n_\infty!}{N!}\right]^{\pm} \frac{\partial}{\partial t} f(n_1 \cdots n_\infty, t)$$

$$= \sum_i \langle i|T|i\rangle n_i \left[\frac{\cdots n_i! \cdots}{N!}\right]^{\pm} f(n_1 \cdots n_i \cdots n_\infty, t)$$

$$+ \sum_{i \neq j} \langle i|T|j\rangle n_i \left[\frac{\cdots (n_i - 1)! \cdots (n_j + 1)! \cdots}{N!}\right]^{\pm}$$

$$\times f(n_1 \cdots n_i - 1 \cdots n_j + 1 \cdots n_\infty, t)$$

$$+ \sum_{i \neq j \neq k \neq l} \langle ij|V|kl\rangle \tfrac{1}{2} n_i n_j$$

$$\times \left[\frac{\cdots (n_i - 1)! \cdots (n_j - 1)! \cdots (n_k + 1)! \cdots (n_l + 1)! \cdots}{N!}\right]^{\pm}$$

$$\times f(\cdots n_i - 1 \cdots n_j - 1 \cdots n_k + 1 \cdots n_l + 1 \cdots n_\infty, t)$$

$$+ \sum_{i = j \neq k \neq l} \langle ii|V|kl\rangle \tfrac{1}{2} n_i(n_i - 1)$$

$$\times \left[\frac{\cdots (n_i - 2)! \cdots (n_k + 1)! \cdots (n_l + 1)! \cdots}{N!}\right]^{\pm}$$

$$\times f(\cdots n_i - 2 \cdots n_k + 1 \cdots n_l + 1 \cdots n_\infty, t) + \text{etc.} \quad (1.24)$$

where "etc." stands for the remaining 13 possible enumerations of the equalities and inequalities between the indices i, j, k, and l. Multiplication by the factor $(N!/n_1! n_2! \cdots n_\infty!)^{\pm}$ on both sides of the equation finally yields the coupled set of equations

$$i\hbar \frac{\partial}{\partial t} f(n_1 \cdots n_\infty, t) = \sum_i \langle i|T|i\rangle n_i f(n_1 \cdots n_i \cdots n_\infty, t)$$

$$+ \sum_{i \neq j} \langle i|T|j\rangle (n_i)^{\pm} (n_j + 1)^{\pm} f(n_1 \cdots n_i - 1 \cdots n_j + 1 \cdots n_\infty, t)$$

$$+ \sum_{i \neq j \neq k \neq l} \langle ij|V|kl\rangle \tfrac{1}{2} (n_i)^{\pm} (n_j)^{\pm} (n_k + 1)^{\pm} (n_l + 1)^{\pm}$$

$$\times f(n_1 \cdots n_i - 1 \cdots n_j - 1 \cdots n_k + 1 \cdots n_l + 1 \cdots n_\infty, t)$$

$$+ \sum_{i = j \neq k \neq l} \langle ii|V|kl\rangle \tfrac{1}{2} (n_i)^{\pm} (n_i - 1)^{\pm} (n_k + 1)^{\pm} (n_l + 1)^{\pm}$$

$$\times f(n_1 \cdots n_i - 2 \cdots n_k + 1 \cdots n_l + 1 \cdots n_\infty, t) + \text{etc.} \quad (1.25)$$

There is such an equation for each set of values of the occupation numbers $n_1 n_2 \cdots n_\infty$; in this form, the equations are very complicated. As shown in the following discussion, however, it is possible to recast these equations in an extremely compact and elegant form.

MANY-PARTICLE HILBERT SPACE AND CREATION AND DESTRUCTION OPERATORS

We shall temporarily forget the previous analysis and instead seek a completely different quantum-mechanical basis that describes the number of particles occupying each state in a complete set of single-particle states. For this reason we introduce the *time-independent abstract state vectors*

$$|n_1 n_2 \cdots n_\infty\rangle$$

where the notation means that there are n_1 particles in the eigenstate 1, n_2 particles in the eigenstate 2, etc. We want this basis to be complete and orthonormal, which requires that these states satisfy the conditions

$$\langle n_1' n_2' \cdots n_\infty' | n_1 n_2 \cdots n_\infty \rangle$$

$$= \delta_{n_1' n_1} \delta_{n_2' n_2} \cdots \delta_{n_\infty' n_\infty} \qquad \text{orthogonality}$$

(1.26)

$$\sum_{n_1 n_2 \cdots n_\infty} |n_1 n_2 \cdots n_\infty\rangle\langle n_1 n_2 \cdots n_\infty|$$

$$= 1 \qquad \text{completeness}$$

Note that the completeness sum is over all possible occupation numbers, with no restriction. To make this basis more concrete, introduce *time-independent* operators b_k, $b_k^\dagger$ that satisfy the commutation rules

$$[b_k, b_{k'}^\dagger] = \delta_{kk'} \qquad \text{bosons}$$

$$[b_k, b_{k'}] = [b_k^\dagger, b_{k'}^\dagger] = 0$$

(1.27)

These are just the commutation rules for the creation and destruction operators of the harmonic oscillator. *All of the properties* of these operators follow directly from the commutation rules, for example[1]

$$b_k^\dagger b_k |n_k\rangle = n_k |n_k\rangle \qquad n_k = 0, 1, 2, \ldots, \infty$$

$$b_k |n_k\rangle = (n_k)^{\frac{1}{2}} |n_k - 1\rangle$$

(1.28)

$$b_k^\dagger |n_k\rangle = (n_k + 1)^{\frac{1}{2}} |n_k + 1\rangle$$

The number operator $b_k^\dagger b_k$ has a spectrum of eigenvalues that includes all the positive integers and zero. b_k is a destruction operator that decreases the occupation number by 1 and multiplies the state by $n_k^{\frac{1}{2}}$; $b_k^\dagger$ is a creation operator that increases the eigenvalue by one and multiplies the state by $(n_k + 1)^{\frac{1}{2}}$. The proof of these relations appears in any standard book on quantum mechanics; since it is crucial that all of these results follow directly from the commutation rules, we here include a proof of Eqs. (1.28).

[1] Compare L. I. Schiff, "Quantum Mechanics," 3d ed., pp. 182–183, McGraw-Hill Book Company, New York, 1968.

The operator $b^\dagger b$ is a hermitian operator and therefore has real eigenvalues; call this operator the *number operator*. The eigenvalues of the number operator are greater than or equal to zero, as seen from the relation

$$n = \langle n|b^\dagger b|n\rangle = \sum_m \langle n|b^\dagger|m\rangle\langle m|b|n\rangle = \sum_m |\langle m|b|n\rangle|^2 \geqslant 0 \qquad (1.29)$$

Now consider the commutation relation, which follows from Eq. (1.27).

$$[b^\dagger b, b] = -b \qquad (1.30)$$

With Eq. (1.30), it is easy to see that the operator b acting on an eigenstate with eigenvalue n produces a new eigenstate of the number operator but with eigenvalue reduced by one unit. This result is proved with the following relations

$$b^\dagger b(b|n\rangle) = b(b^\dagger b)|n\rangle + [b^\dagger b, b]|n\rangle$$
$$= (n-1)(b|n\rangle) \qquad (1.31)$$

Repeated applications of b to any eigenstate must eventually give zero, since otherwise Eq. (1.31) could produce a state with a negative eigenvalue of the number operator, in contradiction to Eq. (1.29). Hence zero is one possible eigenvalue of the number operator. In exactly the same way, the adjoint commutation rule

$$[b^\dagger b, b^\dagger] = b^\dagger \qquad (1.32)$$

shows that $b^\dagger$ is the creation operator and increases the eigenvalue of the number operator by one unit. The first of Eqs. (1.28) is thus proved. Furthermore, a combination of Eqs. (1.29) and (1.31) yields the second of Eqs. (1.28), apart from an overall phase which can be chosen to be unity with no loss of generality. Finally the last of Eqs. (1.28) is proved in exactly similar fashion.[1]

The preceding discussion has been restricted to a single mode. It is, however, readily verified that the number operators for different modes commute, which means that the eigenstates of the total system can be simultaneous eigenstates of the set $\{b_k^\dagger b_k\} \equiv \{n_k\}$. In particular, our desired occupation-number basis states are simply the direct product of eigenstates of the number operator for each mode

$$|n_1 n_2 \cdots n_\infty\rangle = |n_1\rangle|n_2\rangle \cdots |n_\infty\rangle \qquad (1.33)$$

Consider now the question, can we rewrite the Schrödinger equation in terms of these more abstract state vectors? Form the following state

$$|\Psi(t)\rangle = \sum_{n_1 n_2 \cdots n_\infty} f(n_1 n_2 \cdots n_\infty, t)|n_1 n_2 \cdots n_\infty\rangle \qquad (1.34)$$

---

[1] If the no-particle state (or vacuum) is required to be one of our states, then the results of Eqs. (1.28) are unique.

where the f's are taken to be the set of expansion coefficients of Eq. (1.15) and satisfy the coupled partial differential equations (1.25). This state vector in the abstract Hilbert space satisfies the differential equation

$$i\hbar \frac{\partial}{\partial t}|\Psi(t)\rangle = \sum_{n_1 n_2 \cdots n_\infty} i\hbar \frac{\partial}{\partial t} f(n_1 n_2 \cdots n_\infty, t)|n_1 n_2 \cdots n_\infty\rangle \qquad (1.35)$$

Since the basis state vectors are assumed to be time independent, the entire time dependence of the equation is contained in the coefficients f. As an example, look at the second kinetic-energy term in Eqs. (1.25).

$$i\hbar \frac{\partial}{\partial t}|\Psi(t)\rangle = \cdots + \sum_{\substack{n_1 n_2 \cdots n_\infty \\ \left(\sum_i n_i = N\right)}} \sum_{i \neq j} \langle i|T|j\rangle f(\cdots n_i - 1 \cdots$$

$$n_j + 1 \cdots, t)(n_i)^{\pm}(n_j + 1)^{\pm}|n_1 n_2 \cdots n_\infty\rangle + \cdots \qquad (1.36)$$

The dummy indices in this summation may be relabeled with the substitution

$$n_i - 1 \equiv n_i' \qquad n_j + 1 \equiv n_j' \qquad n_k \equiv n_k' \qquad (k \neq i \text{ or } j)$$

$$\sum_l n_l = \sum_l n_l' \qquad\qquad\qquad\qquad\qquad\qquad\qquad\qquad (1.37)$$

Furthermore, it is possible to sum the primed occupation numbers over exactly the same values as the original unprimed occupation numbers, because the coefficient $(n_i)^{\pm}(n_j + 1)^{\pm}$ vanishes for $n_j' = 0$ and for $n_i' = -1$. Thus Eq. (1.36) may be rewritten as

$$i\hbar \frac{\partial}{\partial t}|\Psi(t)\rangle = \cdots + \sum_{\substack{n_1' n_2' \cdots n_\infty' \\ \left(\sum_i n_i' = N\right)}} \sum_{i \neq j} \langle i|T|j\rangle f(\cdots n_i' \cdots n_j' \cdots, t)$$

$$\times (n_i' + 1)^{\pm}(n_j')^{\pm}|\cdots n_i' + 1 \cdots n_j' - 1 \cdots\rangle + \cdots \qquad (1.38)$$

Now observe that the state vector with the value of n_i' raised by one and the value n_j' lowered by one, together with the multiplicative statistical weight factor, can be simply rewritten in terms of the creation and destruction operators acting on the state vector with n_i' and n_j'

$$(n_i' + 1)^{\pm}(n_j')^{\pm}|n_1' \cdots n_i' + 1 \cdots n_j' - 1 \cdots n_\infty'\rangle$$

$$= b_i^\dagger b_j |n_1' n_2' \cdots n_\infty'\rangle \qquad (1.39)$$

The only dependence on the occupation number left in this expression is contained in the coefficients f and in the state vector; hence the summation can be carried out and gives our original abstract state vector $|\Psi(t)\rangle$ defined by Eq. (1.34). Thus this term in the energy reduces to the following expression

$$i\hbar \frac{\partial}{\partial t}|\Psi(t)\rangle = \cdots + \sum_{i \neq j} \langle i|T|j\rangle b_i^\dagger b_j |\Psi(t)\rangle + \cdots \qquad (1.40)$$

The other terms in the hamiltonian can be treated in exactly the same fashion; as a consequence, this abstract state vector $|\Psi(t)\rangle$ satisfies the Schrödinger equation

$$ i\hbar \frac{\partial}{\partial t} |\Psi(t)\rangle = \hat{H} |\Psi(t)\rangle \tag{1.41} $$

where the circumflex denotes an operator in the abstract occupation-number Hilbert space (except where this is obvious, as in the creation and destruction operators) and the hamiltonian $\hat{H}$ is given by the expression

$$ \hat{H} = \sum_{ij} b_i^\dagger \langle i|T|j\rangle b_j + \tfrac{1}{2} \sum_{ijkl} b_i^\dagger b_j^\dagger \langle ij|V|kl\rangle b_l b_k \tag{1.42} $$

It is important to distinguish between the operators and c numbers in Eq. (1.42). Thus $\hat{H}$ is an operator in this abstract occupation-number space because it depends on the creation and destruction operators. In contrast, the matrix elements of the kinetic energy and the potential energy taken between the single-particle eigenstates of the Schrödinger equation in first quantization are merely complex numbers multiplying the operators. Equations (1.41) and (1.42) together restate the Schrödinger equation in second quantization, and all of the statistics and operator properties are contained in the creation and destruction operators $b^\dagger$ and b. The physical problem is clearly unchanged by the new formulation. In particular the coefficients f specify the connection between first and second quantization.

For every solution to the original time-dependent many-particle Schrödinger equation there exists a set of expansion coefficients f. Given this set of expansion coefficients f, it is possible to construct a solution to the problem in second quantization, as shown above. Conversely, if the problem is solved in second quantization, we can determine a set of expansion coefficients f, which then yield a solution to the original time-dependent many-particle Schrödinger equation.

FERMIONS

If the negative sign in Eq. (1.6) is used, the particles are called *fermions*. The same general analysis applies, but the details are a little more complicated because of the minus signs involved in the antisymmetry of the coefficient C.

$$ C(\cdots E_i \cdots E_j \cdots, t) = -C(\cdots E_j \cdots E_i \cdots, t) \tag{1.43} $$

The C's are antisymmetric in the interchange of any two quantum numbers, which implies that the quantum number E_i must be different from the quantum number E_j or the coefficient vanishes. This result shows that the occupation number n_i must be either zero or one, which is the statement of the Pauli exclusion principle. Any coefficients that have the same states occupied are equal within a minus sign, and it is possible to define a coefficient $\bar{C}$

$$ \bar{C}(n_1 n_2 \cdots n_\infty, t) \equiv C(\cdots E_i < E_j < E_k \cdots, t) \tag{1.44} $$

where we first arrange all the quantum numbers in the coefficient C in an increasing sequence. Exactly as before, the many-particle wave function Ψ can be expanded as

$$\Psi(x_1 \cdots x_N, t) = \sum_{n_1 \cdots n_\infty = 0}^{1} f(n_1 \cdots n_\infty, t) \Phi_{n_1 \cdots n_\infty}(x_1 \cdots x_N) \tag{1.45}$$

where the basis wave functions Φ are given by a normalized determinant

$$\Phi_{n_1 \cdots n_\infty}(x_1 \cdots x_N) = \left(\frac{n_1! \cdots n_\infty!}{N!}\right)^{\pm} \begin{vmatrix} \psi_{E_1^0}(x_1) & \cdots & \psi_{E_1^0}(x_N) \\ & \cdot & \\ & \cdot & \\ & \cdot & \\ \psi_{E_N^0}(x_1) & \cdots & \psi_{E_N^0}(x_N) \end{vmatrix} \tag{1.46}$$

The single-particle quantum numbers of the occupied states are now assumed to be ordered $E_1^0 < E_2^0 \cdots < E_N^0$. These functions form a complete set of orthonormal antisymmetric time-independent many-particle wave functions and are usually referred to as the *Slater determinants*.[1]

It is once more convenient to introduce the abstract occupation-number space and define

$$|\Psi(t)\rangle = \sum_{n_1 n_2 \cdots n_\infty} f(n_1 n_2 \cdots n_\infty, t) |n_1 n_2 \cdots n_\infty\rangle \tag{1.47}$$

Here the coefficients f obey equations which differ from (1.25) only by phase factors [see Eq. (1.57)] and the restrictions that $n_i = 0,1$. This restriction, which reflects the particle statistics, must be incorporated into the operators in the abstract occupation-number space. As a convenient procedure, we shall follow the method of Jordan and Wigner[2] and work with *anticommutation* rules

$$\{a_r, a_s^\dagger\} = \delta_{rs} \qquad \text{fermions}$$

$$\{a_r, a_s\} = \{a_r^\dagger, a_s^\dagger\} = 0 \tag{1.48}$$

where the anticommutator is defined by the following relation

$$\{A, B\} \equiv [A, B]_+ \equiv AB + BA \tag{1.49}$$

It is easily seen that this different set of commutation rules produces the correct statistics:

1. $a_s^2 = a_s^{\dagger 2} = 0$; therefore $a_s^\dagger a_s^\dagger |0\rangle = 0$, which prevents two particles from occupying the same state.

[1] J. C. Slater, *Phys. Rev.*, **34**:1293 (1929).
[2] P. Jordan and E. P. Wigner, *loc. cit.*

2. $a^\dagger a = 1 - aa^\dagger$ (where we take the operators referring to the same mode); therefore

$$(a^\dagger a)^2 = 1 - 2aa^\dagger + aa^\dagger aa^\dagger = 1 - 2aa^\dagger + a(1 - aa^\dagger)a^\dagger = 1 - aa^\dagger = a^\dagger a$$

or

$$a^\dagger a(1 - a^\dagger a) = 0 \tag{1.50}$$

This last relation implies that the number operator for the sth mode $\hat{n}_s = a_s^\dagger a_s$ has the eigenvalues zero and one, as required. Furthermore, it is straight-forward to prove that the *commutator* $[\hat{n}_r, \hat{n}_s]$ vanishes, even though the individual creation and destruction operators anticommute. This result permits the simultaneous diagonalization of the set $\{\hat{n}_r\}$, in agreement with the definition of the occupation-number state vectors.

3. The anticommutation rules themselves, along with an overall choice of phase, therefore yield the following relations for the raising and lowering operators

$$a^\dagger|0\rangle = |1\rangle \qquad a|1\rangle = |0\rangle$$
$$\tag{1.51}$$
$$a^\dagger|1\rangle = 0 \qquad a|0\rangle = 0$$

The anticommutation rules slightly complicate the direct-product state $|n_1 n_2 \cdots n_\infty\rangle$, because it becomes essential to keep track of *signs*. With the definition

$$|n_1 n_2 \cdots n_\infty\rangle = (a_1^\dagger)^{n_1} (a_2^\dagger)^{n_2} \cdots (a_\infty^\dagger)^{n_\infty}|0\rangle \tag{1.52}$$

we can compute directly the effect of the destruction operator a_s on this state; if $n_s = 1$, we find

$$a_s|n_1 n_2 \cdots n_\infty\rangle = (-1)^{S_s}(a_1^\dagger)^{n_1} \cdots (a_s a_s^\dagger) \cdots (a_\infty^\dagger)^{n_\infty}|0\rangle \tag{1.53}$$

where the phase factor S_s is defined by

$$S_s = n_1 + n_2 + \cdots + n_{s-1} \tag{1.54}$$

Note that if $n_s = 0$, the operator a_s can be moved all the way to the vacuum, yielding zero. If there is one particle in the state n_s, it is convenient first to use the anticommutation relation $a_s a_s^\dagger = 1 - a_s^\dagger a_s$ and then to take the a_s of the second term to the vacuum where it gives zero. Thus we finally arrive at the three relations

$$a_s|\cdots n_s \cdots\rangle = \begin{cases} (-1)^{S_s}(n_s)^{\frac{1}{2}}|\cdots n_s - 1 \cdots\rangle & \text{if } n_s = 1 \\ 0 & \text{otherwise} \end{cases}$$

$$a_s^\dagger|\cdots n_s \cdots\rangle = \begin{cases} (-1)^{S_s}(n_s + 1)^{\frac{1}{2}}|\cdots n_s + 1 \cdots\rangle & \text{if } n_s = 0 \\ 0 & \text{otherwise} \end{cases} \tag{1.55}$$

$$a_s^\dagger a_s|\cdots n_s \cdots\rangle = n_s|\cdots n_s \cdots\rangle \qquad n_s = 0,1$$

The third relation is the most useful, for it shows that the number operator introduces no extra phases. The reason for writing the first two equations with the factor $(n_s)^{\pm}$ and $(n_s + 1)^{\pm}$ instead of the more familiar notation using n_s and $1 - n_s$ is that they now assume *exactly the same form as before, or vanish, except for the extra phase factor* $(-1)^{S_s}$.

As an example of the role played by this factor in the case of fermions, consider the kinetic-energy term in Eq. (1.4)

$$i\hbar \frac{\partial}{\partial t} C(E_1 \cdots E_N, t) = \sum_{k=1}^{N} \sum_{W} \langle E_k | T | W \rangle$$

$$\times C(E_1 \cdots E_{k-1} W E_{k+1} \cdots E_N, t) + \cdots \quad (1.56)$$

where $E_1 \cdots E_N$ is a given set of quantum numbers. These quantum numbers can be reordered simultaneously on *both sides of this equation* into the proper sequence. One problem remains, however, because the quantum number W appears on the right, where E_k appears on the left. If W is moved to its proper place in the ordered form, an extra phase factor

$$\begin{aligned} (-1)^{n_{W+1}+n_{W+2}+ \cdots +n_{E_k-1}} \quad & W < E_k \\ (-1)^{n_{E_k+1}+n_{E_k+2}+ \cdots +n_{W-1}} \quad & W > E_k \end{aligned} \quad (1.57)$$

is needed, representing the number of interchanges to put W in its proper place. Just as before, we now go over to the f coefficients and again change variables. For example, consider part of the kinetic-energy term

$$i\hbar \frac{\partial}{\partial t} |\Psi(t)\rangle = \cdots + \sum_{n_1' n_2' \cdots n_\infty'} \sum_{i < j} \langle i | T | j \rangle$$

$$\times f(\cdots n_i' \cdots n_j' \cdots, t)(n_i' + 1)^{\pm} (n_j')^{\pm} \delta_{n_i' 0} \delta_{n_j' 1}$$

$$\times (-1)^{n_i'+1+n_i'+2+ \cdots +n_j'-1} |\cdots n_i' + 1 \cdots n_j' - 1 \cdots \rangle + \cdots \quad (1.58)$$

Note that the phase factor appearing in this expression is equivalent to $(-1)^{S_j - S_i - n_i'}$; furthermore, this term contributes only if n_i' is equal to 0 and n_j' is equal to 1, so that this phase factor is just $(-1)^{S_j - S_i}$. Equations (1.55) now allow us to rewrite the relevant factor as

$$\delta_{n_i' 0} \delta_{n_j' 1}(n_i' + 1)^{\pm} (n_j')^{\pm} (-1)^{S_j - S_i} |\cdots n_i' + 1 \cdots n_j' - 1 \cdots \rangle$$

$$= a_i^\dagger a_j |n_1' \cdots n_\infty'\rangle \quad (1.59)$$

which demonstrates that the creation and destruction operators *defined with the anticommutation rules* indeed have the required properties. In this way the Schrödinger equation again assumes the following form in second quantization

$$i\hbar \frac{\partial}{\partial t} |\Psi(t)\rangle = \hat{H} |\Psi(t)\rangle$$

$$\hat{H} = \sum_{rs} a_r^\dagger \langle r | T | s \rangle a_s + \tfrac{1}{2} \sum_{rstu} a_r^\dagger a_s^\dagger \langle rs | V | tu \rangle a_u a_t$$

$$(1.60)$$

Note particularly the ordering of the final two destruction operators in the hamiltonian, which is opposite that of the last two single-particle wave functions in the matrix elements of the potential (the reader is urged to verify this in detail for himself). In the case of bosons, of course, this ordering is irrelevant because the final two destruction operators commute with each other, but for fermions the order affects the overall sign. Exactly as before, Eq. (1.60) is wholly equivalent to the Schrödinger equation in first quantization, but the phases arising from the antisymmetry of the expansion coefficients have been incorporated into the hamiltonian and the direct-product state vectors.

2□FIELDS

It is often convenient to form the linear combinations of the creation and destruction operators (denoted $c^\dagger$ and c for generality)

$$\hat{\psi}(\mathbf{x}) \equiv \sum_k \psi_k(\mathbf{x})\, c_k$$

$$\hat{\psi}^\dagger(\mathbf{x}) \equiv \sum_k \psi_k(\mathbf{x})^\dagger\, c_k^\dagger \tag{2.1}$$

where the coefficients are the single-particle wave functions and the sum is over the complete set of single-particle quantum numbers. In particular, the index k for spin-$\frac{1}{2}$ fermions may denote the set of quantum numbers $\{\mathbf{k}, s_z\}$ or $\{E, L, J, M\}$ and the corresponding wave functions have two components

$$\psi_k(\mathbf{x}) = \begin{bmatrix} \psi_k(\mathbf{x})_1 \\ \psi_k(\mathbf{x})_2 \end{bmatrix} \equiv \psi_k(\mathbf{x})_\alpha \qquad \alpha = 1,2 \tag{2.2}$$

These quantities $\hat{\psi}$ and $\hat{\psi}^\dagger$ are called *field operators*. They are operators in this abstract occupation-number Hilbert space because they depend on the creation and destruction operators. The field operators satisfy simple commutation or anticommutation relations depending on the statistics

$$[\hat{\psi}_\alpha(\mathbf{x}), \hat{\psi}_\beta^\dagger(\mathbf{x}')]_\mp = \sum_k \psi_k(\mathbf{x})_\alpha\, \psi_k(\mathbf{x}')_\beta^* = \delta_{\alpha\beta}\, \delta(\mathbf{x} - \mathbf{x}') \tag{2.3a}$$

$$[\hat{\psi}_\alpha(\mathbf{x}), \hat{\psi}_\beta(\mathbf{x}')]_\mp = [\hat{\psi}_\alpha^\dagger(\mathbf{x}), \hat{\psi}_\beta^\dagger(\mathbf{x}')]_\mp = 0 \tag{2.3b}$$

where the upper (lower) sign refers to bosons (fermions). Here the first equality in Eq. (2.3a) follows from the commutation or anticommutation relations for the creation and destruction operators, and the second follows from the completeness of the single-particle wave functions.

The hamiltonian operator can be rewritten in terms of these field operators as follows:

$$\hat{H} = \int d^3x\, \hat{\psi}^\dagger(\mathbf{x})\, T(\mathbf{x})\, \hat{\psi}(\mathbf{x}) + \tfrac{1}{2} \iint d^3x\, d^3x'\, \hat{\psi}^\dagger(\mathbf{x})\, \hat{\psi}^\dagger(\mathbf{x}')\, V(\mathbf{x},\mathbf{x}')\, \hat{\psi}(\mathbf{x}')\, \hat{\psi}(\mathbf{x}) \tag{2.4}$$

This expression is readily verified since the integration over spatial coordinates produces the single-particle matrix elements of the kinetic energy and potential

energy, leaving a sum of these matrix elements multiplied by the appropriate creation and destruction operators. An additional matrix element in spin space is implied if the particles have spin-$\frac{1}{2}$. Note carefully the ordering of the last two field operators in the potential energy, which agrees with our previous remarks and ensures that $\hat{H}$ is hermitian. In this form, the hamiltonian suggests the name *second quantization*, for the above expression looks like the expectation value of the hamiltonian taken between wave functions. The quantities $\hat{\psi}$ and $\hat{\psi}^\dagger$ are not wave functions, however, but field operators; thus in second quantization the fields are the operators and the potential and kinetic energy are just complex coefficients.

The extension to any other operator is now clear from the foregoing analysis. For example, consider a general one-body operator

$$J = \sum_{i=1}^{N} J(\mathbf{x}_i) \tag{2.5}$$

written in first-quantized form. The corresponding second-quantized operator is given by

$$\hat{J} = \sum_{rs} \langle r|J|s \rangle c_r^\dagger c_s$$
$$= \int d^3x \sum_{rs} \psi_r(\mathbf{x})^\dagger J(\mathbf{x}) \psi_s(\mathbf{x}) c_r^\dagger c_s$$
$$= \int d^3x \, \hat{\psi}^\dagger(\mathbf{x}) J(\mathbf{x}) \hat{\psi}(\mathbf{x}) \tag{2.6}$$

where the last form is especially useful. In particular, the number-density operator

$$n(\mathbf{x}) = \sum_{i=1}^{N} \delta(\mathbf{x} - \mathbf{x}_i) \tag{2.7}$$

becomes

$$\hat{n}(\mathbf{x}) = \sum_{rs} \psi_r(\mathbf{x})^\dagger \psi_s(\mathbf{x}) c_r^\dagger c_s = \hat{\psi}^\dagger(\mathbf{x}) \hat{\psi}(\mathbf{x}) \tag{2.8}$$

while the total-number operator assumes the simple form

$$\hat{N} = \int d^3x \, \hat{n}(\mathbf{x}) = \sum_r c_r^\dagger c_r = \sum_r \hat{n}_r$$
$$= \int d^3x \, \hat{\psi}^\dagger(\mathbf{x}) \hat{\psi}(\mathbf{x}) \tag{2.9}$$

because of the orthonormality of the single-particle wave functions. The number operator commutes with the hamiltonian of Eq. (2.4), as can be verified by using either the commutation rules for the creation and destruction operators or those of the field operators. This result is physically obvious since the ordinary Schrödinger hamiltonian does not change the total number of particles. We infer that $\hat{N}$ is a constant of the motion and can be diagonalized simultaneously with the hamiltonian. Thus the problem in the abstract Hilbert

space separates into a sequence of problems in the subspaces corresponding to a fixed total number of particles. Nevertheless, *the abstract Hilbert space contains states with any number of particles.*

3□EXAMPLE: DEGENERATE ELECTRON GAS

To illustrate the utility of second quantization, we consider a simple model that provides a first approximation to a metal or a plasma. This system is an interacting electron gas placed in a uniformly distributed positive background chosen to ensure that the total system is neutral. In a real metal or plasma, of course, the positive charge is localized in the ionic cores, whose dynamical motion must also be included in the calculation. These positive ions are much heavier than the electrons, however, and it is permissible to neglect the ionic motion entirely. In contrast, the assumption of a uniform background is more drastic; for this reason, the present model can provide only a qualitative account of real metals.

We are interested in the properties of the bulk medium. It therefore is convenient to enclose the system in a large cubical box with sides of length L; the limit $L \to \infty$ will be taken at the end of the calculation. In a uniform infinite medium, all physical properties must be invariant under spatial translation; this observation suggests the use of periodic boundary conditions on the single-particle wave functions, which then become plane-wave states

$$\psi_{\mathbf{k}\lambda}(\mathbf{x}) = V^{-\frac{1}{2}} e^{i\mathbf{k}\cdot\mathbf{x}} \eta_\lambda \tag{3.1}$$

Here $V (\equiv L^3)$ is the volume of the box, and η_λ are the two spin functions for spin-up and spin-down along a chosen z axis,

$$\eta_\uparrow = \begin{bmatrix} 1 \\ 0 \end{bmatrix} \qquad \eta_\downarrow = \begin{bmatrix} 0 \\ 1 \end{bmatrix}$$

The periodic boundary conditions determine the allowed wavenumbers as

$$k_i = \frac{2\pi n_i}{L} \qquad i = x, y, z \qquad n_i = 0, \pm 1, \pm 2, \ldots \tag{3.2}$$

The total hamiltonian can be written as the sum of three terms

$$H = H_{el} + H_b + H_{el-b} \tag{3.3}$$

where

$$H_{el} = \sum_{i=1}^{N} \frac{p_i^2}{2m} + \frac{1}{2} e^2 \sum_{i \neq j}^{N} \frac{e^{-\mu|\mathbf{r}_i - \mathbf{r}_j|}}{|\mathbf{r}_i - \mathbf{r}_j|} \tag{3.4}$$

is the hamiltonian for the electrons,

$$H_b = \tfrac{1}{2} e^2 \iint d^3x\, d^3x' \frac{n(\mathbf{x})\, n(\mathbf{x}')\, e^{-\mu|\mathbf{x}-\mathbf{x}'|}}{|\mathbf{x} - \mathbf{x}'|} \tag{3.5}$$

is the energy of the positive background whose particle density is $n(\mathbf{x})$, and

$$H_{el-b} = -e^2 \sum_{i=1}^{N} \int d^3x \, \frac{n(\mathbf{x}) e^{-\mu|\mathbf{x}-\mathbf{r}_i|}}{|\mathbf{x}-\mathbf{r}_i|} \tag{3.6}$$

is the interaction energy between the electrons and the positive background. We have inserted an exponential convergence factor to define the integrals, and μ will eventually be allowed to vanish. Because of the long-range nature of the coulomb interaction, the three terms in Eq. (3.3) individually diverge in the "thermodynamic limit" $N \to \infty$, $V \to \infty$, but $n = N/V$ constant. The entire system is neutral, however, and the sum of these terms must remain meaningful in this limit. The presence of the convergence factor μ ensures that the expressions are mathematically well defined at every step and allows us to make this cancellation explicit. Since we are interested in the bulk properties of the neutral medium, for example E/N (which depends only on n), our limiting procedure will be first $L \to \infty$ and then $\mu \to 0$. Equivalently, we can assume $\mu^{-1} \ll L$ at each step in our calculation; this allows us to shift the origin of integration at will, apart from surface corrections, which are negligible in this limit.

In Eq. (3.3) the only dynamical variables are those referring to the electrons, because the positive background is inert. Thus H_b is a pure c number and is readily evaluated for a uniform distribution $n(\mathbf{x}) = N/V$:

$$\begin{aligned}
H_b &= \tfrac{1}{2}e^2 \left(\frac{N}{V}\right)^2 \iint d^3x \, d^3x' \frac{e^{-\mu|\mathbf{x}-\mathbf{x}'|}}{|\mathbf{x}-\mathbf{x}'|} \\
&= \tfrac{1}{2}e^2 \left(\frac{N}{V}\right)^2 \int d^3x \int d^3z \, \frac{e^{-\mu z}}{z} \\
&= \tfrac{1}{2}e^2 \frac{N^2}{V} \frac{4\pi}{\mu^2}
\end{aligned} \tag{3.7}$$

Here the translational invariance has been used to shift the origin of integration in the second line. The quantity $N^{-1}H_b$ diverges in the limit $\mu \to 0$, because the long range of the coulomb potential allows every element of charge to interact with every other one.

In principle, H_{el-b} is a one-particle operator since it acts on each electron. For the present system, however, we may again use the translational invariance to write

$$\begin{aligned}
H_{el-b} &= -e^2 \sum_{i=1}^{N} \frac{N}{V} \int d^3x \, \frac{e^{-\mu|\mathbf{x}-\mathbf{r}_i|}}{|\mathbf{x}-\mathbf{r}_i|} \\
&= -e^2 \sum_{i=1}^{N} \frac{N}{V} \int d^3z \, \frac{e^{-\mu z}}{z} \\
&= -e^2 \frac{N^2}{V} \frac{4\pi}{\mu^2}
\end{aligned} \tag{3.8}$$

showing that H_{el-b} is in fact a c number. The total hamiltonian thus reduces to

$$H = -\tfrac{1}{2}e^2\, N^2\, V^{-1}\, 4\pi\mu^{-2} + H_{el} \tag{3.9}$$

and all of the interesting physical effects are contained in H_{el}. We shall now rewrite Eq. (3.9) in second quantization. The kinetic-energy term requires the matrix element

$$\langle k_1\,\lambda_1 | T | k_2\,\lambda_2 \rangle = (2mV)^{-1} \int d^3x\, e^{-ik_1\cdot x}\, \eta_{\lambda_1}^\dagger (-\hbar^2\,\nabla^2)\, e^{ik_2\cdot x}\, \eta_{\lambda_2}$$

$$= \frac{\hbar^2 k_2^2}{2mV}\, \delta_{\lambda_1\lambda_2} \int d^3x\, e^{i(k_2-k_1)\cdot x}$$

$$= \frac{\hbar^2 k_2^2}{2m}\, \delta_{\lambda_1\lambda_2}\, \delta_{k_1 k_2} \tag{3.10}$$

where the usual definition of the Kronecker delta

$$\int d^3x\, e^{i(k_2-k_1)\cdot x} = V\delta_{k_1 k_2} \tag{3.11}$$

has been used. The kinetic-energy operator becomes

$$\hat{T} = \sum_{k\lambda} \frac{\hbar^2 k^2}{2m}\, a_{k\lambda}^\dagger a_{k\lambda} \tag{3.12}$$

which can be interpreted as the kinetic energy of each mode multiplied by the corresponding number operator. For the potential energy it is necessary to evaluate the following more complicated matrix element

$$\langle k_1\,\lambda_1\, k_2\,\lambda_2 | V | k_3\,\lambda_3\, k_4\,\lambda_4 \rangle = \frac{e^2}{V^2} \int\!\!\int d^3x_1\, d^3x_2\, e^{-ik_1\cdot x_1}\, \eta_{\lambda_1}(1)^\dagger$$

$$\times\, e^{-ik_2\cdot x_2}\, \eta_{\lambda_2}(2)^\dagger \frac{e^{-\mu|x_1-x_2|}}{|x_1-x_2|}$$

$$\times\, e^{ik_3\cdot x_1}\, \eta_{\lambda_3}(1)\, e^{ik_4\cdot x_2}\, \eta_{\lambda_4}(2) \tag{3.13}$$

With the substitution $x = x_2$ and $y = x_1 - x_2$, this expression reduces to

$$\langle k_1\,\lambda_1\, k_2\,\lambda_2 | V | k_3\,\lambda_3\, k_4\,\lambda_4 \rangle = \frac{e^2}{V^2} \int d^3x\, e^{-i(k_1+k_2-k_3-k_4)\cdot x}$$

$$\times \int d^3y\, e^{i(k_3-k_1)\cdot y} \frac{e^{-\mu y}}{y}\, \delta_{\lambda_1\lambda_3}\, \delta_{\lambda_2\lambda_4}$$

$$= \frac{e^2}{V}\, \delta_{\lambda_1\lambda_3}\, \delta_{\lambda_2\lambda_4}\, \delta_{k_1+k_2,\, k_3+k_4} \frac{4\pi}{(k_1-k_3)^2 + \mu^2} \tag{3.14}$$

where the Kronecker deltas in the spin indices arise from the orthogonality of the spin wave functions. Once again, we have shifted the origin of integration, and

the final Kronecker delta represents the conservation of momentum in a uniform system.   The total hamiltonian can now be written as

$$\hat{H} = -\frac{1}{2}\frac{e^2 N^2}{V}\frac{4\pi}{\mu^2} + \sum_{k\lambda}\frac{\hbar^2 k^2}{2m}a_{k\lambda}^\dagger a_{k\lambda} + \frac{e^2}{2V}$$

$$\times \sum_{k_1\lambda_1}\sum_{k_2\lambda_2}\sum_{k_3\lambda_3}\sum_{k_4\lambda_4}\delta_{\lambda_1\lambda_3}\delta_{\lambda_2\lambda_4}\delta_{k_1+k_2,\,k_3+k_4}$$

$$\times \frac{4\pi}{(k_1-k_3)^2+\mu^2}a_{k_1\lambda_1}^\dagger a_{k_2\lambda_2}^\dagger a_{k_4\lambda_4}a_{k_3\lambda_3} \qquad (3.15)$$

The electrical neutrality of our system makes it possible to eliminate μ from the hamiltonian, as we shall now show.   The conservation of momentum really limits the summation over $\{k_i\}$ to three independent variables instead of four.   The change of variables

$$\mathbf{k}_1 = \mathbf{k} + \mathbf{q} \qquad \mathbf{k}_3 = \mathbf{k}$$

$$\mathbf{k}_2 = \mathbf{p} - \mathbf{q} \qquad \mathbf{k}_4 = \mathbf{p}$$

guarantees that $\mathbf{k}_1 + \mathbf{k}_2 = \mathbf{k}_3 + \mathbf{k}_4$, and furthermore identifies $\hbar(\mathbf{k}_1 - \mathbf{k}_3) = \hbar\mathbf{q}$ as the momentum transferred in the two-particle interaction.   With these new variables, the last term of Eq. (3.15) becomes

$$\frac{e^2}{2V}\sum_{kpq}\sum_{\lambda_1\lambda_2}\frac{4\pi}{q^2+\mu^2}a_{k+q,\,\lambda_1}^\dagger a_{p-q,\,\lambda_2}^\dagger a_{p\lambda_2}a_{k\lambda_1} \qquad (3.16)$$

where two of the spin summations have been evaluated with the Kronecker deltas. It is convenient to separate Eq. (3.16) into two terms, referring to $\mathbf{q} \neq 0$ and $\mathbf{q} = 0$, respectively,

$$\frac{e^2}{2V}{\sum_{kpq}}'\sum_{\lambda_1\lambda_2}\frac{4\pi}{q^2+\mu^2}a_{k+q,\,\lambda_1}^\dagger a_{p-q,\,\lambda_2}^\dagger a_{p\lambda_2}a_{k\lambda_1}$$

$$+\frac{e^2}{2V}\sum_{kp}\sum_{\lambda_1\lambda_2}\frac{4\pi}{\mu^2}a_{k\lambda_1}^\dagger a_{p\lambda_2}^\dagger a_{p\lambda_2}a_{k\lambda_1} \qquad (3.17)$$

where the prime on the first summation means: omit the term $\mathbf{q} = 0$.   The second summation may be rewritten with the anticommutation relation as

$$\frac{e^2}{2V}\frac{4\pi}{\mu^2}\sum_{k\lambda_1}\sum_{p\lambda_2}a_{k\lambda_1}^\dagger a_{k\lambda_1}(a_{p\lambda_2}^\dagger a_{p\lambda_2}-\delta_{kp}\delta_{\lambda_1\lambda_2}) = \frac{e^2}{2V}\frac{4\pi}{\mu^2}(\hat{N}^2-\hat{N})$$

where Eq. (2.9) has been used to identify $\hat{N}$.   Since we shall always deal with states of fixed N, the operator $\hat{N}$ may be replaced by its eigenvalue N, thereby yielding a c-number contribution to the hamiltonian

$$\frac{e^2}{2}\frac{N^2}{V}\frac{4\pi}{\mu^2} - \frac{e^2}{2}\frac{N}{V}\frac{4\pi}{\mu^2} \qquad (3.18)$$

It is clear that the first term of Eq. (3.18) cancels the first term of Eq. (3.15). The second term of Eq. (3.18) represents an energy $-\frac{1}{4} 4\pi e^2 (V\mu^2)^{-1}$ per particle and vanishes in the proper physical limit discussed previously: first $L \to \infty$ and then $\mu \to 0$ (always keeping $\mu^{-1} \ll L$). Thus the explicit μ^{-2} divergence cancels identically in the thermodynamic limit, which reflects the electrical neutrality of the total system; furthermore, it is now permissible to set $\mu = 0$ in the first term of Eq. (3.17), since the resulting expression is well defined. We therefore obtain the final hamiltonian for a bulk electron gas in a uniform positive background

$$\hat{H} = \sum_{\mathbf{k}\lambda} \frac{\hbar^2 k^2}{2m} a_{\mathbf{k}\lambda}^\dagger a_{\mathbf{k}\lambda} + \frac{e^2}{2V} \sum_{\mathbf{kpq}}' \sum_{\lambda_1 \lambda_2} \frac{4\pi}{q^2} a_{\mathbf{k}+\mathbf{q},\lambda_1}^\dagger a_{\mathbf{p}-\mathbf{q},\lambda_2}^\dagger a_{\mathbf{p}\lambda_2} a_{\mathbf{k}\lambda_1} \tag{3.19}$$

where it is understood that the limit $N \to \infty$, $V \to \infty$, $N/V = n = $ constant is implicitly assumed.

It is now convenient to introduce dimensionless variables. We define a length r_0 in terms of the volume per particle:

$$V \equiv \tfrac{4}{3}\pi r_0^3 N \tag{3.20}$$

r_0 is essentially the interparticle spacing. The coulomb interaction provides a second length, given by the Bohr radius

$$a_0 = \frac{\hbar^2}{me^2} \tag{3.21}$$

and the (dimensionless) ratio between these two quantities

$$r_s \equiv \frac{r_0}{a_0} \tag{3.22}$$

evidently characterizes the density of the system. With r_0 as the unit of length, we define the following quantities

$$\bar{V} = r_0^{-3}\,V \qquad \bar{\mathbf{k}} = r_0\mathbf{k} \qquad \bar{\mathbf{p}} = r_0\mathbf{p} \qquad \bar{\mathbf{q}} = r_0\mathbf{q} \tag{3.23}$$

and thus obtain the following dimensionless form of Eq. (3.19)

$$\hat{H} = \frac{e^2}{a_0 r_s^2} \left(\sum_{\bar{\mathbf{k}}\lambda} \frac{1}{2} \bar{k}^2 a_{\bar{\mathbf{k}}\lambda}^\dagger a_{\bar{\mathbf{k}}\lambda} + \frac{r_s}{2\bar{V}} \sum_{\bar{\mathbf{k}}\bar{\mathbf{p}}\bar{\mathbf{q}}}' \sum_{\lambda_1 \lambda_2} \frac{4\pi}{\bar{q}^2} a_{\bar{\mathbf{k}}+\bar{\mathbf{q}},\lambda_1}^\dagger a_{\bar{\mathbf{p}}-\bar{\mathbf{q}},\lambda_2}^\dagger a_{\bar{\mathbf{p}}\lambda_2} a_{\bar{\mathbf{k}}\lambda_1} \right) \tag{3.24}$$

This is an important result, for it shows that the potential energy becomes a small perturbation as $r_s \to 0$, corresponding to the high-density limit ($r_0 \to 0$). Thus the leading term in the interaction energy of a high-density electron gas can be obtained with first-order perturbation theory, even though the potential is neither weak nor short range. One might expect that the ground-state energy has a power-series expansion in the small parameter r_s, but, in fact, the second-

order term diverges logarithmically (see Probs. 1.4 and 1.5). Instead, the series takes the form

$$E = \frac{Ne^2}{a_0 r_s^2}(a + br_s + cr_s^2 \ln r_s + dr_s^2 + \cdots)$$

where $a, b, c, d \cdots$ are numerical constants. We shall now evaluate a and b, while c may be inferred from the calculation in Prob. 1.5. The proper calculation of c and higher coefficients is very difficult, however, and requires the more elaborate techniques developed in Chaps. 3 to 5.

In the high-density limit, the preceding discussion enables us to separate the original dimensional form of the hamiltonian [Eq. (3.19)] into two parts:

$$\hat{H}_0 = \sum_{k\lambda} \frac{\hbar^2 k^2}{2m} a_{k\lambda}^\dagger a_{k\lambda} \tag{3.25a}$$

$$\hat{H}_1 = \frac{e^2}{2V} \sum_{kpq}{}' \sum_{\lambda_1\lambda_2} \frac{4\pi}{q^2} a_{k+q,\lambda_1}^\dagger a_{p-q,\lambda_2}^\dagger a_{p\lambda_2} a_{k\lambda_1} \tag{3.25b}$$

where $\hat{H}_0$ is the unperturbed hamiltonian, representing a noninteracting Fermi system, and $\hat{H}_1$ is the (small) perturbation. Correspondingly, the ground-state energy E may be written as $E^{(0)} + E^{(1)} + \cdots$, where $E^{(0)}$ is the ground-state energy of a free Fermi gas, while $E^{(1)}$ is the first-order energy shift. Since the Pauli exclusion principle allows only two fermions in each momentum eigenstate, one with spin-up and one with spin-down, the normalized ground-state $|F\rangle$ is obtained by filling the momentum states up to a maximum value, the Fermi momentum $p_F = \hbar k_F$. In the limit that the volume of the system becomes infinite, we can replace sums over states by integrals with the following familiar relation

$$\sum_{k\lambda} f_\lambda(\mathbf{k}) = \sum_{n_x n_y n_z} \sum_\lambda f_\lambda\left(\frac{2\pi\mathbf{n}}{L}\right) \xrightarrow[L\to\infty]{} \iiint dn_x\, dn_y\, dn_z \sum_\lambda f_\lambda\left(\frac{2\pi\mathbf{n}}{L}\right)$$

$$= V(2\pi)^{-3} \sum_\lambda \int d^3k\, f_\lambda(\mathbf{k}) \tag{3.26}$$

Here, Eq. (3.2) has been used to convert the sum over momenta into a sum over the integers characterizing the wavenumbers. For very large L, the function f varies slowly when the integers change by unity so that n_x, n_y and n_z may be considered continuous variables. Finally, Eq. (3.2) again allows us to replace the variables $\{n_i\}$ by $\{k_i\}$, leaving an integral over wavenumbers.

The maximum wavenumber k_F is determined by computing the expectation value of the number operator in the ground state $|F\rangle$

$$N = \langle F|\hat{N}|F\rangle = \sum_{k\lambda} \langle F|\hat{n}_{k\lambda}|F\rangle = \sum_{k\lambda} \theta(k_F - k)$$

$$= V(2\pi)^{-3} \sum_\lambda \int d^3k\, \theta(k_F - k) = (3\pi^2)^{-1} V k_F^3 = N \tag{3.27}$$

where $\theta(x)$ denotes the step function

$$\theta(x) = \begin{cases} 1 & x > 0 \\ 0 & x < 0 \end{cases} \qquad (3.28)$$

This important relation between the Fermi wavenumber k_F and the particle density $n \equiv N/V$ will be used repeatedly in subsequent work; an alternative form

$$k_F = \left(\frac{3\pi^2 N}{V}\right)^{\frac{1}{3}} = \left(\frac{9\pi}{4}\right)^{\frac{1}{3}} r_0^{-1} \approx 1.92 r_0^{-1} \qquad (3.29)$$

shows that k_F^{-1} is comparable with the interparticle spacing. The expectation value of $\hat{H}_0$ may be evaluated in the same fashion

$$E^{(0)} = \langle F|\hat{H}_0|F\rangle = \frac{\hbar^2}{2m} \sum_{k\lambda} k^2 \langle F|\hat{n}_{\mathbf{k}\lambda}|F\rangle$$

$$= \frac{\hbar^2}{2m} \sum_{k\lambda} k^2 \,\theta(k_F - k)$$

$$= \frac{\hbar^2}{2m} \sum_{\lambda} V(2\pi)^{-3} \int d^3k \, k^2 \,\theta(k_F - k)$$

$$= \frac{3}{5}\frac{\hbar^2 k_F^2}{2m} N = \frac{e^2}{2a_0}\frac{N}{r_s^2}\frac{3}{5}\left(\frac{9\pi}{4}\right)^{\frac{1}{3}} = \frac{e^2}{2a_0} N \frac{2.21}{r_s^2}. \qquad (3.30)$$

In a free Fermi gas, the ground-state energy per particle $E^{(0)}/N$ is $\frac{3}{5}$ of the Fermi energy $\epsilon_F^0 = \hbar^2 k_F^2/2m$; alternatively $E^{(0)}/N$ may be expressed as $2.21 r_s^{-2}$ ry(ryd-berg), where 1 ry $= e^2/2a_0 \approx 13.6$ eV is the ground-state binding energy of a hydrogen atom.

We shall now compute the first-order energy shift

$$E^{(1)} = \langle F|\hat{H}_1|F\rangle$$

$$= \frac{e^2}{2V} \sum_{\mathbf{kpq}}' \sum_{\lambda_1\lambda_2} \frac{4\pi}{q^2} \langle F|a_{\mathbf{k}+\mathbf{q},\lambda_1}^\dagger a_{\mathbf{p}-\mathbf{q},\lambda_2}^\dagger a_{\mathbf{p}\lambda_2} a_{\mathbf{k}\lambda_1}|F\rangle \qquad (3.31)$$

The matrix element is readily analyzed as follows: the states $\mathbf{p}\lambda_2$ and $\mathbf{k}\lambda_1$ must be occupied in the ground state $|F\rangle$, since the destruction operators acting to the right would otherwise give zero. Similarly the states $\mathbf{k}+\mathbf{q},\lambda_1$ and $\mathbf{p}-\mathbf{q},\lambda_2$ must also be occupied in $|F\rangle$, since the operators $a^\dagger$ acting to the *left* would otherwise give zero. Finally, the same state appears on each side of the matrix element, which requires the two creation operators to fill up the holes made by the two destruction operators. The operators must therefore be paired off, and there are only two possibilities:

$$\begin{array}{ccc} \mathbf{k}+\mathbf{q},\lambda_1 = \mathbf{k}\lambda_1 & & \mathbf{k}+\mathbf{q},\lambda_1 = \mathbf{p}\lambda_2 \\ & \text{or} & \\ \mathbf{p}-\mathbf{q},\lambda_2 = \mathbf{p}\lambda_2 & & \mathbf{p}-\mathbf{q},\lambda_2 = \mathbf{k}\lambda_1 \end{array} \qquad (3.32)$$

The first pairing is here forbidden because the term $\mathbf{q} = 0$ is excluded from the sum, and the matrix element becomes

$$\delta_{\mathbf{k}+\mathbf{q},\mathbf{p}}\,\delta_{\lambda_1\lambda_2}\langle F|a^{\dagger}_{\mathbf{k}+\mathbf{q},\lambda_1}\,a^{\dagger}_{\mathbf{k}\lambda_1}\,a_{\mathbf{k}+\mathbf{q},\lambda_1}\,a_{\mathbf{k}\lambda_1}|F\rangle$$

$$= -\delta_{\mathbf{k}+\mathbf{q},\mathbf{p}}\,\delta_{\lambda_1\lambda_2}\langle F|\hat{n}_{\mathbf{k}+\mathbf{q},\lambda_1}\,\hat{n}_{\mathbf{k}\lambda_1}|F\rangle$$

$$= -\delta_{\mathbf{k}+\mathbf{q},\mathbf{p}}\,\delta_{\lambda_1\lambda_2}\,\theta(k_F - |\mathbf{k} + \mathbf{q}|)\,\theta(k_F - k) \quad (3.33)$$

A combination of Eqs. (3.31) and (3.33) yields

$$E^{(1)} = -\frac{e^2}{2V}\sum_{\lambda_1}\sum_{\mathbf{k}\mathbf{q}}{}'\,\frac{4\pi}{q^2}\,\theta(k_F - |\mathbf{k} + \mathbf{q}|)\,\theta(k_F - k)$$

$$= -\frac{e^2}{2}\frac{4\pi V}{(2\pi)^6}2\int d^3k\,d^3q\,q^{-2}\,\theta(k_F - |\mathbf{k} + \mathbf{q}|)\,\theta(k_F - k) \quad (3.34)$$

where the factor 2 arises from the spin sum, and the restriction $\mathbf{q} \neq 0$ may now be omitted since it affects the integrand at only a single point. It is convenient to change variables from $\mathbf{k}$ to $\mathbf{P} = \mathbf{k} + \tfrac{1}{2}\mathbf{q}$, which reduces Eq. (3.34) to the symmetrical form

$$E^{(1)} = -4\pi e^2\,V(2\pi)^{-6}\int d^3q\,q^{-2}\int d^3P\,\theta(k_F - |\mathbf{P} + \tfrac{1}{2}\mathbf{q}|)\,\theta(k_F - |\mathbf{P} - \tfrac{1}{2}\mathbf{q}|)$$

The region of integration over $\mathbf{P}$ is shown in Fig. 3.1. Both particles lie inside the Fermi sea, so that $|\mathbf{P} + \tfrac{1}{2}\mathbf{q}|$ and $|\mathbf{P} - \tfrac{1}{2}\mathbf{q}|$ must both be smaller than k_F.

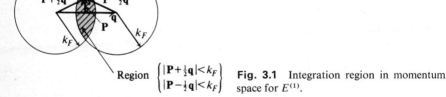

Region $\begin{Bmatrix} |\mathbf{P}+\tfrac{1}{2}\mathbf{q}|<k_F \\ |\mathbf{P}-\tfrac{1}{2}\mathbf{q}|<k_F \end{Bmatrix}$ **Fig. 3.1** Integration region in momentum space for $E^{(1)}$.

The evaluation of this volume is a simple problem in geometry, with the result

$$\int d^3P\,\theta(k_F - |\mathbf{P} + \tfrac{1}{2}\mathbf{q}|)\,\theta(k_F - |\mathbf{P} - \tfrac{1}{2}\mathbf{q}|) = \frac{4\pi}{3}k_F^3(1 - \tfrac{3}{2}x + \tfrac{1}{2}x^3)\,\theta(1 - x)$$

$$x \equiv \frac{q}{2k_F} \quad (3.35)$$

The remaining calculation is elementary, and we find

$$E^{(1)} = -4\pi e^2\,V(2\pi)^{-6}\tfrac{4}{3}\pi k_F^3\,2k_F\int_0^1 dx\,4\pi(1 - \tfrac{3}{2}x + \tfrac{1}{2}x^3)$$

$$= -\frac{e^2}{2a_0}\frac{N}{r_s}\left(\frac{9\pi}{4}\right)^{\frac{1}{3}}\frac{3}{2\pi} = -\frac{e^2}{2a_0}N\frac{0.916}{r_s} \quad (3.36)$$

Thus the ground-state energy per particle in the high-density limit is given approximately as

$$\frac{E}{N}_{r_s \to 0} = \frac{e^2}{2a_0}\left[\frac{2.21}{r_s^2} - \frac{0.916}{r_s} + \cdots\right] \tag{3.37}$$

Note that the energy per particle is finite, which shows that the total energy is an extensive quantity. The first term in Eq. (3.37) is simply the kinetic energy of the Fermi gas of electrons; it becomes the dominant term as $r_s \to 0$, that is, in the limit of very high densities. The second term is known as the *exchange energy* and is negative. It arises because the evaluation of the matrix element in Eq. (3.31) involves two terms [Eq. (3.32)], direct and exchange, owing to the antisymmetry of the wave functions. As we have seen, the direct term arises from the $\mathbf{q} = 0$ part of the interaction and serves to cancel $H_b + H_{el-b}$. This

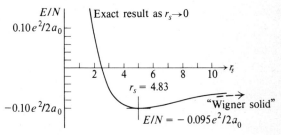

Fig. 3.2 Approximate ground-state energy [first two terms in Eq. (3.37)] of an electron gas in a uniform positive background.

cancellation leads to the restriction $\mathbf{q} \neq 0$ and reflects the electrical neutrality of the system. All that remains is the (negative) exchange energy. The remaining terms in this series (indicated by dots) are called the *correlation energy*;[1] we shall return to this problem in Secs. 12 and 30, where the leading term in the correlation energy will be evaluated explicitly.

For the present, however, it is interesting to consider the first two terms of Eq. (3.37) as a function of r_s (Fig. 3.2). The attractive sign of the exchange energy ensures that the curve has a minimum occurring for negative values of the energy; the system is therefore bound. As $r_s \to 0$ (the high-density limit), Eq. (3.37) represents the exact solution to the problem. For larger values of r_s, our solution is only approximate, but we can now use the familiar Rayleigh-Ritz variational principle, which asserts that the *exact* ground state of a quantum-mechanical system always has a lower energy than that evaluated by taking the expectation value of the total hamiltonian in any normalized state. The conditions of this principle are clearly satisfied, since we have merely computed the expectation value of the hamiltonian $\hat{H}$ in the state $|F\rangle$. It follows that the

[1] E. P. Wigner, *Phys. Rev.*, **46**:1002 (1934).

exact solution to our model problem must also represent a bound system with energy lying below the curve in Fig. 3.2. The minimum of Eq. (3.37) occurs at the values

$$(r_s)_{min} = 4.83 \qquad \left(\frac{E}{N}\right)_{min} = -0.095\frac{e^2}{2a_0} \tag{3.38}$$

Although there is no reason to expect that our solution is correct in this region, it is interesting to observe that these values

$$r_s = 4.83 \qquad \frac{E}{N} = -1.29 \text{ eV} \qquad \text{at minimum} \tag{3.39}$$

compare favorably with the experimental values for metallic sodium under laboratory conditions[1]

$$r_s = 3.96 \qquad \frac{E}{N} = -1.13 \text{ eV} \qquad \text{Na (experiment)} \tag{3.40}$$

where the binding energy is the heat of vaporization of the metal. Thus this very simple model is able to explain the largest part of the binding energy of metals. In real metals, one must further localize the positive background of charge on the crystal lattice sites, as first discussed by Wigner and Seitz.[2,3]

It is also interesting to use Eq. (3.37) to evaluate the thermodynamic properties of the electron gas. The pressure is given by

$$P = -\left(\frac{\partial E}{\partial V}\right)_N = -\frac{dE}{dr_s}\frac{dr_s}{dV} = \frac{Ne^2}{2a_0}\frac{r_s}{3V}\left[\frac{2(2.21)}{r_s^3} - \frac{0.916}{r_s^2}\right] \tag{3.41}$$

The pressure vanishes at the point $r_s = 4.83$, where the system is in equilibrium. Furthermore, the bulk modulus

$$B = -V\left(\frac{\partial P}{\partial V}\right)_N = \frac{Ne^2}{2a_0}\frac{2}{9V}\left[\frac{5(2.21)}{r_s^2} - \frac{2(0.916)}{r_s}\right] \tag{3.42}$$

vanishes at the higher value $r_s = 6.03$, where the system ceases to be metastable in this approximation.

In the low-density limit ($r_s \to \infty$) Wigner[4] has shown that one can obtain a lower energy of the system by allowing the electrons to "crystallize" in a "Wigner solid." This situation occurs because the zero-point kinetic energy associated with localizing the electrons eventually becomes negligible in comparison to the electrostatic energy of a classical lattice. Wigner has shown that

---

[1] See, for example, C. Kittel, "Quantum Theory of Solids," p. 115, John Wiley and Sons, Inc., New York, 1963.
[2] E. P. Wigner and F. Seitz, *Phys. Rev.*, **43**:804 (1933); **46**:509 (1934).
[3] A modern account of the relevant corrections may be found in C. Kittel, *op. cit.*, pp. 93–94, 115.
[4] E. P. Wigner, *Trans. Farad. Soc.*, **34**:678 (1938); W. J. Carr, Jr., *Phys. Rev.*, **122**:1437 (1961).

the energy per particle in this solid is given asymptotically by

$$\frac{E}{N}_{r_s \to \infty} = \frac{e^2}{2a_0}\left[-\frac{1.79}{r_s} + \frac{2.66}{r_s^{\frac{3}{2}}} + \cdots\right] \qquad \text{``Wigner solid''} \qquad (3.43)$$

and it is clear that this expression gives a lower value of the energy than that of Eq. (3.37). The low-density limit [Eq. (3.43)] is sketched as the dotted line in Fig. 3.2. The variational principle guarantees that this Wigner solid represents a better wave function as $r_s \to \infty$, because it has a lower energy.

PROBLEMS

1.1. Prove that the number operator $\hat{N} = \int \hat{\psi}^\dagger(x)\hat{\psi}(x)d^3x$ commutes with the hamiltonians of Eqs. (1.42) and (1.60).

1.2. Given a homogeneous system of spin-$\frac{1}{2}$ particles interacting through a potential V

(a) show that the expectation value of the hamiltonian in the noninteracting ground state is

$$E^{(0)} + E^{(1)} = 2\sum_k^{k_F} \frac{\hbar^2 k^2}{2m} + \frac{1}{2}\sum_{k\lambda}^{k_F}\sum_{k'\lambda'}^{k_F} \{\langle k\lambda k'\lambda'|V|k\lambda k'\lambda'\rangle$$
$$- \langle k\lambda k'\lambda'|V|k'\lambda' k\lambda\rangle\}$$

where λ is the z component of the spin.

(b) Assume V is central and spin independent. If $V(|x_1 - x_2|) < 0$ for all $|x_1 - x_2|$ and $\int |V(x)|d^3x < \infty$, prove that the system will collapse (*Hint*: start from $(E^{(0)} + E^{(1)})/N$ as a function of density).

1.3. Given a homogeneous system of spin-zero particles interacting through a potential V

(a) show that the expectation value of the hamiltonian in the noninteracting ground state is $E^{(1)}/N = (N-1)V(0)/2V \approx \frac{1}{2}nV(0)$, where

$$V(q) = \int d^3x\, V(x)e^{-iq\cdot x} \qquad \text{and} \qquad V(0) \text{ means } V(q=0)$$

(b) Repeat Prob. 1.2b.

(c)‡ Show that the second-order contribution to the ground-state energy is

$$\frac{E^{(2)}}{N} = -\frac{N-1}{2V}\int \frac{d^3q}{(2\pi)^3}\frac{|V(q)|^2}{\hbar^2 q^2/m} \approx -\frac{n}{2}\int \frac{d^3q}{(2\pi)^3}\frac{|V(q)|^2}{\hbar^2 q^2/m}$$

‡ Use standard second-order perturbation theory: If $H = H_0 + H_1$ and the unperturbed eigenvectors $|j\rangle$ satisfy $H_0|j\rangle = E_j|j\rangle$, then

$$E^{(2)} = \sum_{j\neq 0} \frac{|\langle 0|H_1|j\rangle|^2}{E_0 - E_j} = \langle 0|H_1 \frac{P}{E_0 - H_0}H_1|0\rangle$$

where $|0\rangle$ is the ground-state eigenvector of H_0 with energy E_0, and $P = 1 - |0\rangle\langle 0|$ is a projection operator on the excited states.

1.4.‡ Show that the second-order contribution to the ground-state energy of an electron gas is given by $E^{(2)} = (Ne^2/2a_0)(\epsilon_2^r + \epsilon_2^b)$, where

$$\epsilon_2^r = -\frac{3}{8\pi^5} \int \frac{d^3q}{q^4} \int_{|k+q|>1} d^3k \int_{|p+q|>1} d^3p \, \frac{\theta(1-k)\,\theta(1-p)}{q^2 + q \cdot (k+p)}$$

$$\epsilon_2^b = \frac{3}{16\pi^5} \int \frac{d^3q}{q^2} \int_{|k+q|>1} d^3k \int_{|p+q|>1} d^3p \, \frac{\theta(1-k)\,\theta(1-p)}{(q+k+p)^2 \, [q^2 + q \cdot (k+p)]}$$

1.5. The exchange term ϵ_2^b in Prob. 1.4 is finite, while the direct term ϵ_2^r diverges.
(a) Consider the function $f(q)$ defined as

$$f(q) = \int_{|k+q|>1} d^3k \int_{|p+q|>1} d^3p \, \frac{\theta(1-k)\,\theta(1-p)}{q^2 + q \cdot (k+p)}$$

Show that $f(q) \approx (4\pi/3)^2 q^{-2}$ as $q \to \infty$ and $f(q) \approx \frac{2}{3}(2\pi)^2(1 - \ln 2)q$ as $q \to 0$. Hence conclude that $\epsilon_2^r = -(3/8\pi^5) \int d^3q \, f(q) q^{-4}$ diverges logarithmically for small q.
(b) The polarizability of the intervening medium modifies the effective interaction between two electrons at long wavelength, where it behaves as

$$V(q)_{\text{eff}} \approx 4\pi e^2 [q^2 + (4r_s/\pi)k_F^2(4/9\pi)^{\frac{1}{3}}]^{-1}$$

for $q \to 0$. [See Eq. (12,65).] In the limit $r_s \to 0$, use this result to demonstrate that

$$\epsilon_2^r = 2\pi^{-2}(1 - \ln 2)\ln r_s + \text{const} = 0.0622 \ln r_s + \text{const}$$

(c) How does ϵ_2^r of part b affect the equation of state? Find the density at which the compressibility becomes negative.

1.6. Consider a polarized electron gas in which $N_\pm$ denotes the number of electrons with spin-up (-down).[1]
(a) Find the ground-state energy to first order in the interaction potential as a function of $N = N_+ + N_-$ and the polarization $\zeta = (N_+ - N_-)/N$.
(b) Prove that the ferromagnetic state ($\zeta = 1$) represents a lower energy than the unmagnetized state ($\zeta = 0$) if $r_s > (2\pi/5)(9\pi/4)^{\frac{1}{3}}(2^{\frac{1}{3}} + 1) = 5.45$. Explain why this is so.
(c) Show that $\partial^2(E/N)/\partial\zeta^2|_{\zeta=0}$ becomes negative for $r_s > (3\pi^2/2)^{\frac{2}{3}} = 6.03$.
(d) Discuss the physical significance of the two critical densities. What happens for $5.45 < r_s < 6.03$?

1.7. Repeat Prob. 1.6 for a potential $V(|x - y|) = g\delta^{(3)}(x - y)$. Show that the system is partially magnetized for $20/9 < gN/V\bar{T} < (5/3)2^{\frac{2}{3}} = 2.64$, where $\bar{T}$ is the mean kinetic energy per particle in the unmagnetized state, and N/V is the corresponding particle density. What happens outside of these limits?

‡ See footnote on p. 31.
[1] F. Bloch, Z. Physik, 57:545 (1929).

2
Statistical Mechanics

Before formulating the quantum-mechanical description of many-particle assemblies, it is useful to review some thermodynamic relations. The elementary discussions usually consider assemblies containing a fixed number of particles, but such a description is too restricted for the present purposes. We must therefore generalize the treatment to include the possibility of variable number of particles N. This approach is most simply expressed in the grand canonical ensemble, which is generally more tractable than the canonical ensemble (N fixed). In addition, there are physical systems where the variable number of particles is an essential feature, rather than a mathematical convenience; for example, the macroscopic condensate in superfluid helium and in superconductors acts as a particle bath that can exchange particles with the remainder of the system. Indeed, these systems are best described with model hamiltonians that do not even conserve N, and the more general description must be used.

4□REVIEW OF THERMODYNAMICS AND STATISTICAL MECHANICS

Although it is possible to treat systems containing several different kinds of particles, the added generality is not needed for most physical applications, and we shall consider only single-component systems. The fundamental thermodynamic identity

$$dE = T\,dS - P\,dV + \mu\,dN \tag{4.1}$$

specifies the change in the internal energy E arising from small independent changes in the entropy S, the volume V, and the number of particles N. Equation (4.1) shows that the internal energy is a thermodynamic function of these three variables, $E = E(S,V,N)$, and that the temperature T, the pressure P, and the chemical potential μ are related to the partial derivatives of E:

$$T = \left(\frac{\partial E}{\partial S}\right)_{VN} \qquad -P = \left(\frac{\partial E}{\partial V}\right)_{SN} \qquad \mu = \left(\frac{\partial E}{\partial N}\right)_{SV} \tag{4.2}$$

In the particular case of a quantum-mechanical system in its ground state, the entropy vanishes, and the chemical potential reduces to

$$\mu = \left(\frac{\partial E}{\partial N}\right)_{V} \qquad S = 0 \tag{4.3}$$

where E is the ground-state energy. More generally, Eqs. (4.1) and (4.2) may be interpreted as defining the chemical potential.

The internal energy is useful for studying isentropic processes; in practice, however, experiments are usually performed at fixed T, and it is convenient to make a Legendre transformation to the variables (T,V,N) or (T,P,N). The resulting functions are known as the *Helmholtz free energy* $F(T,V,N)$ and the *Gibbs free energy* $G(T,P,N)$, defined by

$$F = E - TS \qquad G = E - TS + PV \tag{4.4}$$

The differential of these two equations may be combined with Eq. (4.1) to yield

$$dF = -S\,dT - P\,dV + \mu\,dN \qquad dG = -S\,dT + V\,dP + \mu\,dN \tag{4.5}$$

which demonstrates that F and G are indeed thermodynamic functions of the specified variables. In particular, the chemical potential may be defined as

$$\mu = \left(\frac{\partial F}{\partial N}\right)_{TV} = \left(\frac{\partial G}{\partial N}\right)_{TP} \tag{4.6}$$

Furthermore, it is often important to consider the set of independent variables (T,V,μ), which is appropriate for variable N. A further Legendre transformation leads to the *thermodynamic potential*

$$\Omega(T,V,\mu) = F - \mu N = E - TS - \mu N \tag{4.7}$$

with the corresponding differential

$$d\Omega = -S\,dT - P\,dV - N\,d\mu \tag{4.8}$$

The coefficients are immediately given by

$$S = -\left(\frac{\partial\Omega}{\partial T}\right)_{V\mu} \qquad P = -\left(\frac{\partial\Omega}{\partial V}\right)_{T\mu} \qquad N = -\left(\frac{\partial\Omega}{\partial\mu}\right)_{TV} \tag{4.9}$$

which will be particularly useful in subsequent applications.

Although E, F, G, and Ω represent formally equivalent ways of describing the same system, their natural independent variables differ in one important way. In particular, the set (S,V,N) consists entirely of extensive variables, proportional to the actual amount of matter present. The transformation to F and then to G or Ω may be interpreted as reducing the number of extensive variables in favor of intensive ones that are independent of the total amount of matter. This distinction between extensive and intensive variables leads to an important result. Consider a scale change in which all extensive quantities (including E, F, G, and Ω) are multiplied by a factor λ. For definiteness, we shall study the internal energy, which becomes

$$\lambda E = E(\lambda S, \lambda V, \lambda N)$$

Differentiate with respect to λ and set $\lambda = 1$:

$$E = S\left(\frac{\partial E}{\partial S}\right)_{VN} + V\left(\frac{\partial E}{\partial V}\right)_{SN} + N\left(\frac{\partial E}{\partial N}\right)_{SV} = TS - PV + \mu N \tag{4.10}$$

where Eq. (4.2) has been used. Equation (4.10), which here arises from physical arguments, is a special case of Euler's theorem on homogeneous functions. The remaining thermodynamic functions are immediately found as

$$F = -PV + \mu N \qquad G = \mu N \qquad \Omega = -PV \tag{4.11}$$

which shows that the chemical potential in a one-component system is the Gibbs free energy per particle $\mu = N^{-1}G(T,P,N)$ and that $P = -V^{-1}\Omega(T,V,\mu)$. This last result is also an obvious consequence of Eq. (4.9), because Ω and V are extensive, whereas T and μ are intensive.

To this point, we have used only macroscopic thermodynamics, which merely correlates bulk properties of the system. The microscopic content of the theory must be added separately through statistical mechanics, which relates the thermodynamic functions to the hamiltonian of the many-particle assembly. In the grand canonical ensemble at chemical potential μ and temperature

$$T \equiv \frac{1}{k_B\beta} \tag{4.12}$$

where k_B is Boltzmann's constant, $k_B = 1.381 \times 10^{-16}$ erg/degree, the grand partition function Z_G is defined as

$$
\begin{aligned}
Z_G &\equiv \sum_N \sum_j e^{-\beta(E_j - \mu N)} \\
&= \sum_N \sum_j \langle Nj | e^{-\beta(\hat{H} - \mu \hat{N})} | Nj \rangle \\
&= \mathrm{Tr}\,(e^{-\beta(\hat{H} - \mu \hat{N})})
\end{aligned}
\tag{4.13}
$$

where j denotes the set of all states for a fixed number of particles N, and the sum implied in the trace is over both j and N.   A fundamental result from statistical mechanics then asserts that

$$
\Omega(T, V, \mu) = -k_B T \ln Z_G
\tag{4.14}
$$

which allows us to compute all the macroscopic equilibrium thermodynamics from the grand partition function.

The statistical operator $\hat{\rho}_G$ corresponding to Eq. (4.13) is given by

$$
\hat{\rho}_G = Z_G^{-1} e^{-\beta(\hat{H} - \mu \hat{N})}
\tag{4.15}
$$

With the aid of Eq. (4.14), $\hat{\rho}_G$ may be rewritten compactly as

$$
\hat{\rho}_G = e^{\beta(\Omega - \hat{H} + \mu \hat{N})}
\tag{4.16}
$$

For any operator $\hat{O}$, the ensemble average $\langle \hat{O} \rangle$ is obtained with the prescription

$$
\begin{aligned}
\langle \hat{O} \rangle &= \mathrm{Tr}\,(\hat{\rho}_G \hat{O}) \\
&= \mathrm{Tr}\,(e^{\beta(\Omega - \hat{H} + \mu \hat{N})} \hat{O}) \\
&= \frac{\mathrm{Tr}\,(e^{-\beta(\hat{H} - \mu \hat{N})} \hat{O})}{\mathrm{Tr}\, e^{-\beta(\hat{H} - \mu \hat{N})}}
\end{aligned}
\tag{4.17}
$$

The utility of these expressions will be illustrated in Sec. 5, which reviews the thermodynamic behavior of ideal Bose and Fermi gases.

5☐IDEAL GAS[1]

We now apply these results by reviewing the properties of noninteracting Bose and Fermi gases.   Throughout our discussion we use the notational simplification

$$
\beta = (k_B T)^{-1}
\tag{5.1}
$$

---

[1] The arguments in this section are contained in any good book on statistical mechanics, for example, L. D. Landau and E. M. Lifshitz, "Statistical Physics," chap. V, Pergamon Press, London, 1958.

If Eq. (4.13) is written out in detail with the complete set of states in the abstract occupation-number Hilbert space, we have

$$Z_G = \text{Tr}\,(e^{-\beta(\hat{H}_0 - \mu \hat{N})})$$
$$= \sum_{n_1 \cdots n_\infty} \langle n_1 \cdots n_\infty | e^{\beta(\mu \hat{N} - \hat{H}_0)} | n_1 \cdots n_\infty \rangle$$
$$= e^{-\beta \Omega_0(T,V,\mu)} \tag{5.2}$$

Since these states are eigenstates of the hamiltonian $\hat{H}_0$ and the number operator $\hat{N}$, both operators can be replaced by their eigenvalues

$$Z_G = \sum_{n_1 \cdots n_\infty} \langle n_1 \cdots n_\infty | \exp\left[\beta \left(\mu \sum_i n_i - \sum_i \epsilon_i n_i \right) \right] | n_1 \cdots n_\infty \rangle \tag{5.3}$$

The exponential is now a c number and is equivalent to a product of exponentials; hence the sum over expectation values factors into a product of traces, one referring to each mode,

$$Z_G = \sum_{n_1} \langle n_1 | e^{\beta(\mu n_1 - \epsilon_1 n_1)} | n_1 \rangle \cdots \sum_{n_m} \langle n_\infty | e^{\beta(\mu n_\infty - \epsilon_\infty n_\infty)} | n_\infty \rangle \tag{5.4}$$

which may be written compactly as

$$Z_G = \prod_{i=1}^{\infty} \text{Tr}_i \, e^{-\beta(\epsilon_i - \mu)\hat{n}_i} \tag{5.5}$$

For bosons the occupation numbers are unrestricted so that we must sum n_i over all integers in Eq. (5.5)

$$Z_G = \prod_{i=1}^{\infty} \sum_{n=0}^{\infty} (e^{\beta(\mu - \epsilon_i)})^n = \prod_{i=1}^{\infty} (1 - e^{\beta(\mu - \epsilon_i)})^{-1} \tag{5.6}$$

The logarithm of Eq. (5.6) yields the thermodynamic potential

$$\Omega_0(T,V,\mu) = -k_B T \ln \prod_{i=1}^{\infty} (1 - e^{\beta(\mu - \epsilon_i)})^{-1} \tag{5.7}$$

$$\Omega_0(T,V,\mu) = k_B T \sum_{i=1}^{\infty} \ln (1 - e^{\beta(\mu - \epsilon_i)}) \qquad Bose \tag{5.8}$$

The mean number of particles is obtained from Ω_0 by differentiating with respect to the chemical potential, as in Eq. (4.9), keeping T and V (equivalently the ϵ_i) fixed:

$$\langle N \rangle \equiv \sum_{i=1}^{\infty} n_i^0 = \sum_{i=1}^{\infty} \frac{1}{e^{\beta(\epsilon_i - \mu)} - 1} \qquad Bose \tag{5.9}$$

where n_i^0 is the mean occupation number in the ith state.

For fermions, the occupation numbers are either 0 or 1, and the sum in Eq. (5.5) is restricted to these values

$$Z_G = \prod_{i=1}^{\infty} \sum_{n=0}^{1} (e^{\beta(\mu-\epsilon_i)})^n = \prod_{i=1}^{\infty} (1 + e^{\beta(\mu-\epsilon_i)}) \tag{5.10}$$

Taking the logarithm of both sides, we have

$$\Omega_0(T,V,\mu) = -k_B T \sum_{i=1}^{\infty} \ln(1 + e^{\beta(\mu-\epsilon_i)}) \qquad Fermi \tag{5.11}$$

while the number of particles becomes

$$\langle N \rangle \equiv \sum_{i=1}^{\infty} n_i^0 = \sum_{i=1}^{\infty} \frac{1}{e^{\beta(\epsilon_i-\mu)} + 1} \qquad Fermi \tag{5.12}$$

Although bosons and fermions differ only by the sign in the denominator in Eqs. (5.9) and (5.12), this sign leads to rather remarkable differences in the behavior of these assemblies.

BOSONS

We shall first consider a collection of noninteracting bosons, where the energy spectrum is given by

$$\epsilon_p = \frac{p^2}{2m} = \frac{\hbar^2 k^2}{2m} \tag{5.13}$$

We assume that the assembly is contained in a large volume V and apply periodic boundary conditions on the single-particle wave functions. Just as in Eq. (3.26), sums over single-particle levels can be replaced by an integral over wavenumbers according to

$$\sum_i \rightarrow g \int d^3n = gV(2\pi)^{-3} \int d^3k \tag{5.14}$$

where g is the degeneracy of each single-particle momentum state. For example, $g = 1$ for spinless particles. With Eq. (5.13), the density of states in Eq. (5.14) can be rewritten as

$$\frac{gV}{(2\pi)^3} 4\pi k^2 \, dk = \frac{gV}{2\pi^2} \left(\frac{2m}{\hbar^2}\right)^{\frac{3}{2}} \frac{\epsilon \, d\epsilon}{2\epsilon^{\frac{1}{2}}} = \frac{gV}{4\pi^2} \left(\frac{2m}{\hbar^2}\right)^{\frac{3}{2}} \epsilon^{\frac{1}{2}} \, d\epsilon \tag{5.15}$$

and the thermodynamic potential Eq. (5.8) for an ideal Bose gas becomes

$$-\frac{\Omega_0}{k_B T} = \frac{PV}{k_B T} = -\frac{gV}{4\pi^2} \left(\frac{2m}{\hbar^2}\right)^{\frac{3}{2}} \int_0^{\infty} d\epsilon \, \epsilon^{\frac{1}{2}} \ln(1 - e^{\beta(\mu-\epsilon)}) \tag{5.16}$$

A simple partial integration then yields

$$PV = \frac{gV}{4\pi^2} \left(\frac{2m}{\hbar^2}\right)^{\frac{3}{2}} \frac{2}{3} \int_0^{\infty} d\epsilon \, \frac{\epsilon^{\frac{3}{2}}}{e^{\beta(\epsilon-\mu)} - 1} \tag{5.17}$$

Alternatively, a combination of Eqs. (4.9), (4.10), and (5.8) allows us to write

$$E = \sum_i n_i^0 \, \epsilon_i = \frac{gV}{4\pi^2} \left(\frac{2m}{\hbar^2}\right)^{\frac{3}{2}} \int_0^\infty d\epsilon \frac{\epsilon^{\frac{3}{2}}}{e^{\beta(\epsilon-\mu)} - 1} \tag{5.18}$$

showing that the equation of state of an ideal Bose gas is given by

$$PV = \tfrac{2}{3}E \tag{5.19}$$

In a similar way, the number of particles becomes

$$\frac{N}{V} = \frac{g}{4\pi^2} \left(\frac{2m}{\hbar^2}\right)^{\frac{3}{2}} \int_0^\infty d\epsilon \frac{\epsilon^{\frac{1}{2}}}{e^{\beta(\epsilon-\mu)} - 1} \tag{5.20}$$

Although Eqs. (5.17) and (5.20) determine the thermodynamic variables of an ideal Bose gas as functions of T, V, and μ, Eq. (5.20) can in principle be inverted to obtain the chemical potential as a function of the number of particles.   Substitution into Eq. (5.17) then yields the thermodynamic variables as a function of T, V, and N.

Equation (5.20) is meaningful only if

$$\epsilon - \mu \geqslant 0$$

Otherwise the mean occupation number n^0 would be less than zero for some values of ϵ.   In particular, ϵ can vanish so that the chemical potential of an ideal Bose gas must satisfy the condition

$$\mu \leqslant 0 \tag{5.21}$$

To understand this relation, we recall the classical limit of the chemical potential for fixed N:[‡]

$$\frac{\mu}{k_B T} \to -\infty \qquad T \to \infty \tag{5.22}$$

In this limit we see that Bose and Fermi gases give the same expression

$$N \to \sum_i e^{\beta(\mu-\epsilon_i)} \qquad T \to \infty \tag{5.23}$$

which is just the familiar Boltzmann distribution, and

$$\Omega_0 = -PV = -k_B T \sum_i e^{\beta(\mu-\epsilon_i)} = -Nk_B T \qquad T \to \infty \tag{5.24}$$

which is the equation of state of an ideal classical gas.   The sum may be evaluated approximately as an integral

$$\sum_i e^{-\beta\epsilon_i} = g(2\pi)^{-3} V \int d^3k \, e^{-\hbar^2 k^2/2mk_B T}$$

$$= gV \left(\frac{mk_B T}{2\pi\hbar^2}\right)^{\frac{3}{2}} \tag{5.25}$$

[‡] L. D. Landau and E. M. Lifshitz, *op. cit.*, sec. 45.

and Eq. (5.23) then yields the classical expression μ_c for the chemical potential

$$\frac{\mu_c}{k_B T} = \ln\left[\frac{N}{gV}\left(\frac{2\pi\hbar^2}{mk_B T}\right)^{\frac{3}{2}}\right] \tag{5.26}$$

in terms of T, V, N. Note that Eq. (5.22) is indeed satisfied as $T \to \infty$. Furthermore, it is clear that Fermi, Bose, and Boltzmann statistics now coincide, since the particles are distributed over many states. Thus the mean occupation number of any one state is much less than one, and quantum restrictions play no role.

The classical chemical potential of Eq. (5.26) is sketched in Fig. 5.1. As the temperature is reduced at fixed density, $\mu_c/k_B T$ passes through zero and

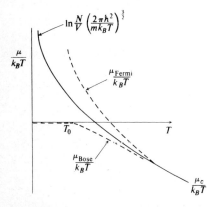

Fig. 5.1 The chemical potential of ideal classical, Fermi, and Bose gases for fixed N and V.

becomes positive, diverging to $+\infty$ at $T=0$. Since this behavior violates Eq. (5.21), the chemical potential for an ideal Bose gas must lie below the classical value, staying negative or zero. Let T_0 be the temperature where the chemical potential of an ideal Bose gas vanishes. This critical temperature is readily determined with Eq. (5.20)

$$\frac{N}{V} = \frac{g}{4\pi^2}\left(\frac{2m}{\hbar^2}\right)^{\frac{3}{2}} \int_0^\infty d\epsilon \frac{\epsilon^{\frac{1}{2}}}{e^{\epsilon/k_B T_0} - 1} \tag{5.27}$$

which may be rewritten with the new variable $x \equiv \epsilon/k_B T_0$ as

$$\frac{N}{V} = \frac{g}{4\pi^2}\left(\frac{2mk_B T_0}{\hbar^2}\right)^{\frac{3}{2}} \int_0^\infty dx \frac{x^{\frac{1}{2}}}{e^x - 1} \tag{5.28}$$

The integral is evaluated in Appendix A

$$\frac{N}{V} = \frac{g}{4\pi^2}\left(\frac{2mk_B T_0}{\hbar^2}\right)^{\frac{3}{2}} \zeta(\tfrac{3}{2})\,\Gamma(\tfrac{3}{2}) \tag{5.29}$$

and Eq. (5.29) may be inverted to give

$$T_0 = \frac{\hbar^2}{2mk_B}\left(\frac{4\pi^2}{g\Gamma(\tfrac{3}{2})\,\zeta(\tfrac{3}{2})}\right)^{\frac{2}{3}}\left(\frac{N}{V}\right)^{\frac{2}{3}} = \frac{3.31}{g^{\frac{2}{3}}}\frac{\hbar^2}{mk_B}\left(\frac{N}{V}\right)^{\frac{2}{3}} \tag{5.30}$$

as the temperature at which the chemical potential of an ideal Bose gas reaches zero. This value has the simple physical interpretation that the thermal energy $k_B T_0$ is comparable with the only other intensive energy for a perfect gas, the zero-point energy $(\hbar^2/m)(N/V)^{\frac{2}{3}}$ associated with localizing a particle in a volume V/N.

What happens as we lower the temperature below T_0? It is clear physically that many bosons will start to occupy the lowest available single-particle state, namely the ground state. For $\mu = 0$ and $T < T_0$, however, the integral in Eq. (5.20) is less than N/V because these conditions increase the denominator relative to its value at T_0. Thus the theory appears to break down because Eq. (5.20) will not reproduce the full density N/V. This difficulty can be traced to the replacement of the sum by an integral in Eq. (5.14), and we therefore examine the original sum

$$N = \sum_i (e^{\beta(\epsilon_i - \mu)} - 1)^{-1}$$

As $\mu \to 0$, all of the terms except the first approach a finite limit; the sum of these finite terms is just that given by the integral evaluated above.[1] In contrast, the first term has been lost in passing to the integral because the $\epsilon^{\frac{1}{2}}$ in the density of states vanishes at $\epsilon = 0$. We see, however, that this first term becomes arbitrarily large as $\mu \to 0$ and can therefore make up the rest of the particles. This behavior reflects the macroscopic occupation of the single quantum state $\epsilon = 0$.

For temperatures $T < T_0$, we conclude that the chemical potential μ must be infinitesimally small and negative

$$\mu = 0^- \qquad \text{for } T \leqslant T_0 \tag{5.31}$$

In this temperature range, the density of particles with energies $\epsilon > 0$ becomes

$$\frac{dN_\epsilon}{V} = \frac{g}{4\pi^2} \left(\frac{2m}{\hbar^2}\right)^{\frac{3}{2}} \frac{\epsilon^{\frac{1}{2}} \, d\epsilon}{e^{\beta\epsilon} - 1} \tag{5.32}$$

with the integrated value

$$\frac{N_{\epsilon>0}}{V} = \frac{g}{4\pi^2} \left(\frac{2mk_B T}{\hbar^2}\right)^{\frac{3}{2}} \int_0^\infty dx \, \frac{x^{\frac{1}{2}}}{e^x - 1} = \frac{N}{V}\left(\frac{T}{T_0}\right)^{\frac{3}{2}} \tag{5.33}$$

The remaining particles are then in the lowest energy state with $\epsilon = 0$

$$\frac{N_{\epsilon=0}}{V} = \frac{N}{V}\left[1 - \left(\frac{T}{T_0}\right)^{\frac{3}{2}}\right] \tag{5.34}$$

---

[1] Strictly speaking, the occupation number of the low-lying excited states is of order $N^{\frac{1}{3}}$, which becomes negligible only in the thermodynamic limit. A rigorous discussion of the Bose-Einstein condensation may be found in R. H. Fowler and H. Jones, *Proc. Cambridge Phil. Soc.*, **34**:573 (1938).

In the degenerate region ($T < T_0$) where the chemical potential is given by Eq. (5.31), the energy of the Bose gas arises entirely from those particles not in the condensate

$$\frac{E}{V} = \frac{g}{4\pi^2} \left(\frac{2mk_B T}{\hbar^2}\right)^{\frac{3}{2}} k_B T \int_0^\infty dx \, \frac{x^{\frac{3}{2}}}{e^x - 1}$$

This integral is again treated in Appendix A, and we find

$$\frac{E}{V} = \frac{g}{4\pi^2} \left(\frac{2mk_B T}{\hbar^2}\right)^{\frac{3}{2}} k_B T \zeta(\tfrac{5}{2}) \, \Gamma(\tfrac{5}{2}) \tag{5.35}$$

which may be rewritten in terms of T_0 from Eq. (5.29) as

$$E = \frac{\zeta(\tfrac{5}{2}) \, \Gamma(\tfrac{5}{2})}{\zeta(\tfrac{3}{2}) \, \Gamma(\tfrac{3}{2})} Nk_B T \left(\frac{T}{T_0}\right)^{\frac{3}{2}} = 0.770 Nk_B T \left(\frac{T}{T_0}\right)^{\frac{3}{2}} \qquad T \leqslant T_0 \tag{5.36}$$

The constant-volume heat capacity then becomes

$$C_V = \frac{5}{2}\left[0.770 Nk_B \left(\frac{T}{T_0}\right)^{\frac{3}{2}}\right] \qquad T \leqslant T_0 \tag{5.37}$$

which varies as $T^{\frac{3}{2}}$ and vanishes at $T = 0$. Equation (5.35) also can be used to rewrite the equation of state:

$$P = \frac{2}{3}\frac{E}{V} = \frac{2}{3}\frac{2\sqrt{2}}{4\pi^2} \zeta(\tfrac{5}{2}) \, \Gamma(\tfrac{5}{2}) \frac{m^{\frac{3}{2}}(k_B T)^{\frac{5}{2}} g}{\hbar^3}$$

$$= 0.0851 m^{\frac{3}{2}}(k_B T)^{\frac{5}{2}} \hbar^{-3} g \qquad T \leqslant T_0 \tag{5.38}$$

The pressure vanishes at zero temperature because all of the particles are in the zero-momentum state and therefore exert no force on the walls of the container. Furthermore, the pressure is independent of the density N/V, depending only on the temperature $T \leqslant T_0$.

We have seen that the ideal Bose gas has a critical temperature T_0 where the chemical potential changes its analytic form. Since $\mu(T,V,N)$ is related to the free energy by Eq. (4.6), it is natural to expect similar discontinuities in other thermodynamic functions, and we now show that the heat capacity at constant volume C_V has a discontinuous slope at T_0. The behavior for $T < T_0$ is given in Eq. (5.37); the corresponding quantity for $T > T_0$ can be found as follows: Define the (fictitious) number of particles computed for $\mu = 0$ and $T > T_0$ by

$$N_0(T) \equiv \frac{gV}{4\pi^2} \left(\frac{2m}{\hbar^2}\right)^{\frac{3}{2}} \int_0^\infty d\epsilon \, \frac{\epsilon^{\frac{1}{2}}}{e^{\epsilon/k_B T} - 1}$$

This expression clearly implies

$$\frac{N_0(T)}{N_0(T_0)} = \frac{N_0(T)}{N} = \left(\frac{T}{T_0}\right)^{\frac{3}{2}} \qquad T > T_0$$

Equation (5.20), which determines the actual $\mu(T,V,N)$ for $T > T_0$, can now be rewritten

$$N - N_0(T) = \frac{gV}{4\pi^2}\left(\frac{2m}{\hbar^2}\right)^{\frac{3}{2}}\int_0^\infty d\epsilon\, \epsilon^{\frac{1}{2}}\left\{\frac{1}{e^{(\epsilon-\mu)/k_BT}-1} - \frac{1}{e^{\epsilon/k_BT}-1}\right\}$$

The dominant contribution to this integral arises from small values of ϵ because μ/k_BT is small and negative for $0 < T - T_0 \ll T_0$. Thus we shall expand the integrand to give

$$N - N_0(T) \approx \frac{gV}{4\pi^2}\left(\frac{2m}{\hbar^2}\right)^{\frac{3}{2}}\mu k_B T \int_0^\infty d\epsilon \frac{1}{\epsilon^{\frac{1}{2}}(\epsilon + |\mu|)}$$

$$\approx -\frac{gV}{4\pi^2}\left(\frac{2m}{\hbar^2}\right)^{\frac{3}{2}}\pi k_B T_0 |\mu|^{\frac{1}{2}}$$

where we have set $T = T_0$ to leading order in $T - T_0$. A combination with Eq. (5.29) leads to

$$\mu \approx -\left[\frac{\zeta(\frac{3}{2})\,\Gamma(\frac{3}{2})}{\pi}\right]^2 k_B T_0 \left[\frac{N_0(T)}{N} - 1\right]^2$$

$$= -\left[\frac{\zeta(\frac{3}{2})\,\Gamma(\frac{3}{2})}{\pi}\right]^2 k_B T_0 \left[\left(\frac{T}{T_0}\right)^{\frac{3}{2}} - 1\right]^2 \qquad T \gtrsim T_0$$

Note that μ vanishes quadratically as $T \to T_0^+$ so that $\mu(T,V,N)$ has a discontinuous second derivative at T_0 (see Fig. 5.1).

The remaining calculation can be carried out by differentiating the equation of state (5.19)

$$\left(\frac{\partial E}{\partial \mu}\right)_{TV} = \frac{3}{2}\left[\frac{\partial(PV)}{\partial \mu}\right]_{TV} = \frac{3}{2}N$$

where the last equality follows from Eqs. (4.9) and (4.11). This result allows us to find the change in energy arising from a small change in μ at constant T and V. If $E(T,V)$ is the energy for zero chemical potential [Eq. (5.35)], then the actual energy is given approximately as

$$E = \begin{cases} E(T,V) & T < T_0 \\ E(T,V) + \frac{3}{2}N\mu & T > T_0 \end{cases}$$

We now change variables to T, V, and N using the expression obtained above for $\mu(T,V,N)$. The jump in the slope of C_V is then given by[1]

$$\Delta\left[\frac{\partial C_V}{\partial T}\right]_{T_0} = -\frac{3}{2}Nk_B T_0\left[\frac{\zeta(\frac{3}{2})\,\Gamma(\frac{3}{2})}{\pi}\right]^2\left\{\frac{\partial^2}{\partial T^2}\left[\left(\frac{T}{T_0}\right)^{\frac{3}{2}} - 1\right]^2\right\}_{T_0}$$

$$= -\frac{27}{4}\left[\frac{\zeta(\frac{3}{2})\,\Gamma(\frac{3}{2})}{\pi}\right]^2 \frac{Nk_B}{T_0} = -3.66\frac{Nk_B}{T_0} \tag{5.39}$$

[1] F. London, "Superfluids," vol. II, sec. 7, Dover, New York, 1964; we here follow the approach of L. D. Landau and E. M. Lifshitz, *op. cit.*, p. 170.

The full curve is sketched in Fig. 5.2. Such discontinuities imply that an ideal Bose gas exhibits a *phase transition* at a temperature T_0. This temperature has a physical interpretation as the point where a finite fraction of all the particles begins to occupy the zero-momentum state. Below T_0 the occupation number n_0^0 of the lowest single-particle state is of order N, rather than of order 1. As emphasized by F. London,[1] the assembly is ordered in *momentum* space and not in coordinate space; this phenomenon is called *Bose-Einstein condensation*.

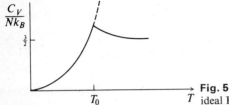

Fig. 5.2 Constant-volume heat capacity C_V of an ideal Bose gas.

To estimate the magnitude of the quantities involved, we recall that the density of liquid He^4 at low temperature is

$$\rho_4 = 0.145 \text{ g cm}^{-3}$$

Inserting this quantity into Eq. (5.30), we find the value

$$T_0 = 3.14°\text{K} \tag{5.40}$$

as the transition temperature of an ideal Bose gas with the parameters appropriate to liquid helium. Below this temperature, the foregoing discussion indicates that the assembly consists of two different components, one corresponding to the particles that occupy the zero-momentum state and therefore have no energy, and the other corresponding to the particles in the excited states. Indeed, it is an experimental fact that liquid He^4 has a transition at 2.2°K (the λ point) between the two phases He I and He II. Below this temperature He^4 acts like a mixture of a superfluid and a normal fluid, and the superfluid has no heat capacity or viscosity. It is also true that the fraction of normal component vanishes as the temperature goes to zero. The Bose-Einstein condensation of the ideal Bose gas therefore provides a qualitative description of actual He^4. In detail, however, the ideal Bose gas is an oversimplified model. For example, the actual specific heat varies as T^3 at low temperature and becomes logarithmically infinite at the λ point for liquid He^4. In addition, it is incorrect to identify the superfluid component of He II with the particles in the zero-momentum state. Indeed, the excitation spectrum of the ideal Bose gas precludes superfluidity at any finite velocity. These questions are discussed in detail in Chaps. 6, 10, and 14, where we show that the interparticle interactions play a crucial role in understanding the properties of quantum fluids such as liquid He^4.

[1] F. London, *op. cit.*, pp. 39, 143.

FERMIONS

We now discuss Eqs. (5.11) and (5.12) referring to an assembly of fermions, which serves as a model for many physical systems. The basic equation is the mean occupation number

$$n_i^0 = (e^{\beta(\epsilon_i - \mu)} + 1)^{-1} \tag{5.41}$$

With the nonrelativistic energy spectrum [Eq. (5.13)], the same analysis as for bosons gives

$$PV = \tfrac{2}{3}E = \frac{2}{3}\frac{gV}{4\pi^2}\left(\frac{2m}{\hbar^2}\right)^{\frac{3}{2}}\int_0^\infty d\epsilon\,\frac{\epsilon^{\frac{3}{2}}}{e^{\beta(\epsilon-\mu)}+1} \tag{5.42}$$

$$\frac{N}{V} = \frac{g}{4\pi^2}\left(\frac{2m}{\hbar^2}\right)^{\frac{3}{2}}\int_0^\infty d\epsilon\,\frac{\epsilon^{\frac{1}{2}}}{e^{\beta(\epsilon-\mu)}+1} \tag{5.43}$$

where g is the degeneracy factor ($g = 2$ for a spin-$\frac{1}{2}$ Fermi gas). As noted previously, the only difference between bosons and fermions is the minus or plus sign in the denominators of Eqs. (5.42) and (5.43).

Consider the distribution function n^0. Equation (5.41) shows that the condition

$$n^0 \leqslant 1$$

is guaranteed for all values of μ and T. It is interesting to invert Eq. (5.43) and determine the chemical potential for fixed N; this function is sketched in Fig. 5.1. In the high-temperature or classical limit, we again find

$$n^0 = e^{\beta(\mu-\epsilon)} \qquad T \to \infty$$

which is just the familiar Boltzmann distribution. Unlike the situation for bosons, however, there is nothing to prevent the chemical potential from becoming positive as the temperature is reduced; in particular, we have

$$n^0 = \tfrac{1}{2} \qquad \text{when } \epsilon = \mu$$

In the zero-temperature limit, the Fermi distribution reduces to a step function

$$\frac{1}{e^{(\epsilon-\mu)/k_B T}+1} \xrightarrow[T\to 0]{} \begin{cases} 0 & \epsilon > \mu \\ 1 & \epsilon < \mu \end{cases} = \theta(\mu - \epsilon) \tag{5.44}$$

This behavior is readily understood, because the lowest energy state of the system is obtained by filling the energy levels up to

$$\mu = \epsilon_F \qquad \text{at } T = 0$$

Hence the chemical potential of an ideal Fermi gas at zero temperature is a finite positive number, equal to the Fermi energy. The equilibrium distribution numbers in three representative cases are sketched in Fig. 5.3.

We shall first evaluate the properties of an ideal Fermi gas at $T = 0$.   From Eqs. (5.43) and (5.44), the density is given by

$$\frac{N}{V} = \frac{g}{4\pi^2}\left(\frac{2m}{\hbar^2}\right)^{\frac{3}{2}}\int_0^\mu d\epsilon\,\epsilon^{\frac{1}{2}}$$

because the distribution number is then a step function.   This integral is easily evaluated as

$$\frac{N}{V} = \frac{g}{4\pi^2}\left(\frac{2m}{\hbar^2}\right)^{\frac{3}{2}}\frac{2}{3}\mu^{\frac{3}{2}} \tag{5.45}$$

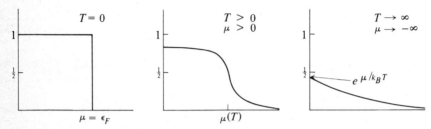

Fig. 5.3 Schematic distribution functions $n(\epsilon)$ for an ideal Fermi gas at various temperatures.

which may be inverted to find the Fermi energy

$$\epsilon_F \equiv \mu(T = 0) = \left(\frac{6\pi^2}{g}\right)^{\frac{2}{3}}\frac{\hbar^2}{2m}\left(\frac{N}{V}\right)^{\frac{2}{3}} \equiv \frac{\hbar^2 k_F^2}{2m} \tag{5.46}$$

or the Fermi wavenumber

$$k_F = \left(\frac{6\pi^2\,N}{gV}\right)^{\frac{1}{3}} \tag{5.47}$$

Similarly, the energy is obtained from

$$\frac{E}{V} = \frac{g}{4\pi^2}\left(\frac{2m}{\hbar^2}\right)^{\frac{3}{2}}\int_0^\mu d\epsilon\,\epsilon^{\frac{3}{2}} = \frac{g}{4\pi^2}\left(\frac{2m}{\hbar^2}\right)^{\frac{3}{2}}\frac{2}{5}\mu^{\frac{5}{2}}$$

A combination with Eq. (5.45) yields

$$\frac{E}{N} = \tfrac{3}{5}\mu = \tfrac{3}{5}\epsilon_F \tag{5.48}$$

Finally, the equation of state (5.42) becomes

$$PV = \tfrac{2}{3}E = \tfrac{2}{5}N\epsilon_F \tag{5.49a}$$

$$P = \frac{2}{5}\left(\frac{6\pi^2}{g}\right)^{\frac{2}{3}}\frac{\hbar^2}{2m}\left(\frac{N}{V}\right)^{\frac{5}{3}} \tag{5.49b}$$

which shows that a Fermi gas exerts a finite pressure at zero temperature. This result arises because the Pauli principle requires that the momentum states be filled up to the Fermi momentum, and these higher momentum states exert a pressure on the walls of any container.

We now turn to small but finite temperature, where the difficult part is the inversion of Eq. (5.43) to determine the chemical potential in terms of the total number of particles. Define the variable $x \equiv (\epsilon - \mu)/k_B T$. Equation (5.42) may then be rewritten as

$$PV = \frac{2}{3}\frac{gV}{4\pi^2}\left(\frac{2m}{\hbar^2}\right)^{\frac{3}{2}}(k_B T)^{\frac{5}{2}}\int_{-\mu/k_B T}^{\infty} dx \frac{(x + \mu/k_B T)^{\frac{3}{2}}}{e^x + 1} \tag{5.50}$$

It is also convenient to introduce $\alpha \equiv \mu/k_B T$; since μ is finite as $T \to 0$, we are interested in the limit $\alpha \to \infty$. Consider the integral

$$I(\alpha) \equiv \int_{-\alpha}^{\infty} dx \frac{(x + \alpha)^{\frac{3}{2}}}{e^x + 1} = \int_{-\alpha}^{0} dx \frac{(\alpha + x)^{\frac{3}{2}}}{e^x + 1} + \int_{0}^{\infty} dx \frac{(\alpha + x)^{\frac{3}{2}}}{e^x + 1} \tag{5.51}$$

The change of variable $x \to -x$ in the first integral and use of the identity $(e^{-x} + 1)^{-1} \equiv 1 - (e^x + 1)^{-1}$ yield

$$I(\alpha) = \int_{0}^{\alpha} dx (\alpha - x)^{\frac{3}{2}} + \int_{0}^{\infty} dx \frac{(\alpha + x)^{\frac{3}{2}} - (\alpha - x)^{\frac{3}{2}}}{e^x + 1} + \int_{\alpha}^{\infty} dx \frac{(\alpha - x)^{\frac{3}{2}}}{e^x + 1}$$

The last term is exponentially small in the limit of large α, and we can approximate the numerator in the second integral as

$$(\alpha + x)^{\frac{3}{2}} - (\alpha - x)^{\frac{3}{2}} = 3x\alpha^{\frac{1}{2}} + O(\alpha^{-\frac{1}{2}}) \qquad \alpha \to \infty$$

A straightforward calculation (see Appendix A) therefore gives the asymptotic expansion

$$I(\alpha) = \frac{2}{5}\alpha^{\frac{5}{2}} + \frac{\pi^2}{4}\alpha^{\frac{1}{2}} + \cdots = \left(\frac{1}{k_B T}\right)^{\frac{5}{2}}\left[\frac{2}{5}\mu^{\frac{5}{2}} + (k_B T)^2\frac{\pi^2}{4}\mu^{\frac{1}{2}} + \cdots\right] \tag{5.52}$$

Thus Eq. (5.50) can be written to order T^2 or $1/\alpha^2$ as

$$PV \underset{T \to 0}{=} \frac{gV}{4\pi^2}\left(\frac{2m}{\hbar^2}\right)^{\frac{3}{2}}\frac{2}{3}\left[\frac{2}{5}\mu^{\frac{5}{2}} + (k_B T)^2\frac{\pi^2}{4}\mu^{\frac{1}{2}} + \cdots\right] \tag{5.53}$$

Note that this result gives $PV(T,V,\mu)$, which are the proper thermodynamic variables for the thermodynamic potential. The correction terms in this equation (indicated by dots) are of higher order in T^2 and thus negligible to the present order.

The number of particles can be determined immediately from this expression:

$$N = \left[\frac{\partial(PV)}{\partial\mu}\right]_{TV} = \frac{gV}{4\pi^2}\left(\frac{2m}{\hbar^2}\right)^{\frac{3}{2}}\frac{2}{3}\left[\mu^{\frac{3}{2}} + (k_B T)^2\frac{\pi^2}{8\mu^{\frac{1}{2}}} + \cdots\right] \tag{5.54}$$

If N/V is rewritten in terms of the Fermi energy ϵ_F using Eq. (5.46) we have

$$\mu = \epsilon_F\left[1 + \frac{\pi^2}{8}\left(\frac{k_B T}{\mu}\right)^2 + \cdots\right]^{-\frac{3}{2}} \tag{5.55}$$

which may be solved for μ as a power series in T^2

$$\mu = \epsilon_F\left[1 - \frac{\pi^2}{12}\left(\frac{k_B T}{\epsilon_F}\right)^2 + \cdots\right] \tag{5.56}$$

The entropy can be determined from Eq. (5.53) by differentiating at *fixed V and μ*

$$S(T,V,\mu) = \left[\frac{\partial(PV)}{\partial T}\right]_{V\mu} = \frac{gV}{4\pi^2}\left(\frac{2m}{\hbar^2}\right)^{\frac{3}{2}}\frac{2}{3}\left[\frac{2\pi^2}{4}k_B^2 T\mu^{\frac{1}{2}} + \cdots\right] \tag{5.57}$$

Since S is a thermodynamic function, it may be expressed in any variables; in particular, substitution of Eq. (5.56) yields

$$S(T,V,N) = Nk_B\frac{k_B T}{\epsilon_F}\frac{\pi^2}{2} \tag{5.58}$$

to lowest order in T.   We can thus compute the heat capacity from the relation

$$C_V = T\left(\frac{\partial S}{\partial T}\right)_{VN} = \frac{\pi^2}{2}Nk_B\frac{k_B T}{\epsilon_F} \tag{5.59}$$

which gives

$$C_V = S = \frac{mk_B^2}{\hbar^2}\left(\frac{g\pi}{6}\right)^{\frac{2}{3}}NT\left(\frac{V}{N}\right)^{\frac{2}{3}} \qquad T \to 0 \tag{5.60}$$

Note that the heat capacity for a Fermi gas at low temperature is linear in the temperature.   In contrast, at high temperature, where Boltzmann statistics apply, the heat capacity of a perfect (Bose or Fermi) gas is

$$C_V \to \tfrac{3}{2}Nk_B \qquad T \to \infty \tag{5.61}$$

and the heat capacity of an ideal Fermi gas at all temperatures is indicated in Fig. 5.4.   Note that a Fermi gas has no discontinuities in the thermodynamic variables at any temperature.

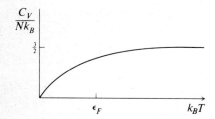

Fig. **5.4** Constant-volume heat capacity of an ideal Fermi gas.

The noninteracting Fermi gas forms a useful first approximation in the theory of metals, in the theory of liquid He^3, in studies of nuclear structure, and even for understanding such diverse phenomena as the structure of white-dwarf and neutron stars. For a detailed understanding of the behavior of these many-body assemblies, however, we must include the interactions between the particles, which forms the central problem of this book.

PROBLEMS

2.1. Prove that the entropy of an ideal quantum gas is given by

$$S = -k_B \sum_i [n_i^0 \ln n_i^0 \mp (1 \pm n_i^0) \ln (1 \pm n_i^0)]$$

where the upper (lower) signs refer to bosons (fermions). Find the corresponding expression for Boltzmann statistics. Prove that the internal energy is given by $E = \sum_i \epsilon_i n_i^0$ for all three cases.

2.2. Given the energy spectrum $\epsilon_p = [(pc)^2 + m_0^2 c^4]^{\frac{1}{2}} \to pc$ ($p \to \infty$), prove that an ultrarelativistic ideal gas satisfies the equation of state $PV = E/3$ where E is the total energy. [Compare with Eqs. (5.19) and (5.42).]

2.3. Show that there is no Bose-Einstein condensation at any finite temperature for a two-dimensional ideal Bose gas.

2.4. Consider an ideal gas in a cubical box ($V = L^3$) with the boundary condition that the single-particle wave function vanish at the walls.
(a) Find the density of states. In the thermodynamic limit, show that the thermodynamic functions for both bosons and fermions reduce to those obtained in Sec. 5.
(b) Discuss the onset of Bose condensation and compute the properties for $T < T_0$.

2.5. When a metal is heated to a sufficiently high temperature, electrons are emitted from the metal surface and can be collected as thermionic current. Assuming the electrons form a noninteracting Fermi gas, derive the Richardson-Dushman equation[1] for the current $i = (4\pi e m k_B^2 T^2/h^3) e^{-W/k_B T}$, where W is the work function for the metal (i.e., the energy necessary to remove an electron).

2.6. Prove that the paramagnetic spin susceptibility of a free Fermi gas of spin-$\frac{1}{2}$ particles at $T = 0$ is given by $\chi(T = 0) = \frac{3}{2}(2m/\hbar^2 k_F^2)\mu_0^2 N/V$ where μ_0 is the magnetic moment of one of the particles. Derive the corresponding high-temperature result $\chi(T \to \infty) = \mu_0^2 N/k_B TV$.

[1] S. Dushman, *Rev. Mod. Phys.*, **2**:381 (1930).

2.7. For a first approximation to atomic nuclei, consider the nucleus as a degenerate noninteracting Fermi gas of neutrons and protons.

(*a*) What is the degeneracy factor for each level?

(*b*) If the radius of a nucleus with A nucleons is given by $R = r_0 A^{\frac{1}{3}}$ with $r_0 \approx$ 1.2×10^{-13} cm, what are k_F and ϵ_F? How do they vary with A?

(*c*) What is the pressure exerted by this Fermi gas?

(*d*) If each nucleon is considered to be moving in a constant potential of depth V_0, how large must V_0 be?

(*e*) At what temperature will the nucleus act like a collection of particles described by Boltzmann statistics?

2.8. As a model of a white-dwarf star, consider an electrically neutral gas composed of fully ionized He (α particles) and degenerate electrons.

(*a*) Write the equation of *local hydrostatic equilibrium* in the low-density (non-relativistic electron gas) and high-density (relativistic electron gas) limits assuming an ideal Fermi system.

(*b*) Hence find expressions for the density $\rho(r)$ and the relation $M = M(R)$ between the total mass M and the radius R of the star.

(*c*) Show there exists a maximum mass M_{max} comparable with the solar mass $M_\odot$. Explain the physics of why this is so.

(*d*) Check the initial model using the typical parameters of a white dwarf $\rho \approx 10^7$ g/cm$^3 \approx 10^7 \rho_\odot$, $M \approx 10^{33}$ g $\approx M_\odot$, central temperature $\approx 10^7°$K $\approx T_\odot$. Note the following results obtained by numerical integration:[1]

1. $\left. \begin{array}{l} \dfrac{1}{\xi^2} \dfrac{d}{d\xi} \left(\xi^2 \dfrac{df}{d\xi} \right) = -f^{\frac{3}{2}} \\[2mm] f'(0) = 0; \; f(1) = 0 \end{array} \right\}$ implies $\begin{array}{l} f(0) = 178.2 \\ f'(1) = -132.4 \end{array}$

2. $\left. \begin{array}{l} \dfrac{1}{\xi^2} \dfrac{d}{d\xi} \left(\xi^2 \dfrac{df}{d\xi} \right) = -f^{3} \\[2mm] f'(0) = 0; \; f(1) = 0 \end{array} \right\}$ implies $\begin{array}{l} f(0) = 6.897 \\ f'(1) = -2.018 \end{array}$

[1] L. D. Landau and E. M. Lifshitz, *op. cit.*, sec. 106.

Ground-state (Zero-temperature) Formalism

3
Green's Functions and Field Theory (Fermions)

In most cases of interest, the first few orders of perturbation theory cannot provide an adequate description of an interacting many-particle system. For this reason, it becomes essential to develop systematic methods for solving the Schrödinger equation to all orders in perturbation theory.

6□PICTURES

As a preliminary step, we shall introduce three important pictures (Schrödinger, interaction, and Heisenberg) that are useful in analyzing the second-quantized form of the Schrödinger equation [Eqs. (1.41) and (1.60)].

SCHRÖDINGER PICTURE

The usual elementary description of quantum mechanics assumes that the state vectors are time dependent, whereas the operators are time independent and are

constructed by the familiar rules from the corresponding classical quantities. The Schrödinger equation therefore takes the form

$$ i\hbar \frac{\partial}{\partial t} |\Psi_S(t)\rangle = \hat{H} |\Psi_S(t)\rangle \tag{6.1} $$

where $\hat{H}$ is assumed to have no explicit time dependence. Since Eq. (6.1) is a first-order differential equation, the initial state at t_0 determines the subsequent behavior, and a formal solution is readily obtained by writing

$$ |\Psi_S(t)\rangle = e^{-i\hat{H}(t-t_0)/\hbar} |\Psi_S(t_0)\rangle \tag{6.2} $$

Here the exponential of an operator is defined in terms of its power-series expansion. Furthermore, $\hat{H}$ is hermitian so that the exponential represents a unitary operator. Given the solution to the Schrödinger equation at the time t_0, the unitary transformation in Eq. (6.2) generates the solution at time t.

INTERACTION PICTURE

Assume, as is usually the case, that the hamiltonian is time independent and can be expressed as the sum of two terms

$$ \hat{H} = \hat{H}_0 + \hat{H}_1 \tag{6.3} $$

where $\hat{H}_0$ acting alone yields a soluble problem. How can we now include *all* the effects of $\hat{H}_1$? Define the interaction state vector in the following way

$$ |\Psi_I(t)\rangle \equiv e^{i\hat{H}_0 t/\hbar} |\Psi_S(t)\rangle \tag{6.4} $$

which is merely a unitary transformation carried out at the time t. The equation of motion of this state vector is easily found by carrying out the time derivative

$$ i\hbar \frac{\partial}{\partial t} |\Psi_I(t)\rangle = -\hat{H}_0 e^{i\hat{H}_0 t/\hbar} |\Psi_S(t)\rangle + e^{i\hat{H}_0 t/\hbar} i\hbar \frac{\partial}{\partial t} |\Psi_S(t)\rangle $$

$$ = e^{i\hat{H}_0 t/\hbar} [-\hat{H}_0 + \hat{H}_0 + \hat{H}_1] e^{-i\hat{H}_0 t/\hbar} |\Psi_I(t)\rangle $$

and we therefore obtain the following set of equations in the interaction picture

$$ i\hbar \frac{\partial}{\partial t} |\Psi_I(t)\rangle = \hat{H}_1(t) |\Psi_I(t)\rangle $$

$$ \hat{H}_1(t) \equiv e^{i\hat{H}_0 t/\hbar} \hat{H}_1 e^{-i\hat{H}_0 t/\hbar} \tag{6.5} $$

In general, $\hat{H}_0$ does not commute with $\hat{H}_1$, so that the proper order of these operators is very important. An arbitrary matrix element in the Schrödinger picture may be written as

$$ \langle \Psi_S(t) | \hat{O}_S | \Psi_S(t) \rangle = \langle \Psi_I(t) | e^{i\hat{H}_0 t/\hbar} \hat{O}_S e^{-i\hat{H}_0 t/\hbar} | \Psi_I(t) \rangle \tag{6.6} $$

which suggests the following definition of an operator in the interaction picture

$$\hat{O}_I(t) \equiv e^{i\hat{H}_0 t/\hbar} \hat{O}_S e^{-i\hat{H}_0 t/\hbar} \tag{6.7}$$

Equations (6.4) and (6.7) show that the operators $\hat{O}_I(t)$ and the state vectors $|\Psi_I(t)\rangle$ *both* depend on time in the interaction picture. The important point here is that the time dependence of the operators is particularly simple. Differentiate Eq. (6.7) with respect to time.

$$i\hbar \frac{\partial}{\partial t} \hat{O}_I(t) = e^{i\hat{H}_0 t/\hbar}(\hat{O}_S \hat{H}_0 - \hat{H}_0 \hat{O}_S) e^{-i\hat{H}_0 t/\hbar}$$

$$= [\hat{O}_I(t), \hat{H}_0] \tag{6.8}$$

Here the time independence of the Schrödinger operator has been used along with the observation that any function of an operator commutes with the operator itself. Consider a representation in which $\hat{H}_0$ is diagonal.

$$\hat{H}_0 = \sum_k \hbar\omega_k c_k^\dagger c_k \tag{6.9}$$

The time dependence of the creation and destruction operators in the interaction picture can be determined from the differential equation

$$i\hbar \frac{\partial}{\partial t} c_{kI}(t) = e^{i\hat{H}_0 t/\hbar}[c_{kS}, \hat{H}_0] e^{-i\hat{H}_0 t/\hbar} = \hbar\omega_k c_{kI}(t)$$

which is easily solved to yield

$$c_{kI}(t) = c_k e^{-i\omega_k t} \tag{6.10a}$$

along with its adjoint

$$c_{kI}^\dagger(t) = c_k^\dagger e^{i\omega_k t} \tag{6.10b}$$

Thus the time occurs only in a complex phase factor, which means that the operator properties of $c_I(t)$ and $c_I^\dagger(t)$ are just the same as in the Schrödinger picture. In particular, the commutation relations of c_k and $c_k^\dagger$ are simply the canonical ones from Chap. 1. Furthermore, *any* operator in the Schrödinger picture may be expressed in terms of the complete set c_k and $c_k^\dagger$, and the corresponding operator in the interaction picture is obtained with the substitution $c_k \rightarrow c_{kI}(t)$, $c_k^\dagger \rightarrow c_{kI}^\dagger(t)$. This last result follows from the identity

$$1 = e^{-i\hat{H}_0 t/\hbar} e^{i\hat{H}_0 t/\hbar}$$

which may be inserted between each operator in the Schrödinger picture.

We shall now try to solve the equations of motion in the interaction picture. Define a unitary operator $\hat{U}(t, t_0)$ that determines the state vector at time t in terms of the state vector at the time t_0.

$$|\Psi_I(t)\rangle = \hat{U}(t, t_0)|\Psi_I(t_0)\rangle \tag{6.11}$$

Evidently, $\hat{U}$ must satisfy the relation

$$\hat{U}(t_0,t_0) = 1 \qquad (6.12)$$

For finite times $\hat{U}(t,t_0)$ can be constructed explicitly by using the Schrödinger picture:

$$|\Psi_I(t)\rangle = e^{i\hat{H}_0 t/\hbar}|\Psi_S(t)\rangle = e^{i\hat{H}_0 t/\hbar} e^{-i\hat{H}(t-t_0)/\hbar}|\Psi_S(t_0)\rangle$$

$$= e^{i\hat{H}_0 t/\hbar} e^{-i\hat{H}(t-t_0)/\hbar} e^{-i\hat{H}_0 t_0/\hbar}|\Psi_I(t_0)\rangle$$

which therefore identifies

$$\hat{U}(t,t_0) = e^{i\hat{H}_0 t/\hbar} e^{-i\hat{H}(t-t_0)/\hbar} e^{-i\hat{H}_0 t_0/\hbar} \qquad \text{(finite times)} \qquad (6.13)$$

Since $\hat{H}$ and $\hat{H}_0$ do not commute with each other, the order of the operators must be carefully maintained. Equation (6.13) immediately yields several general properties of $\hat{U}$

1. $\quad \hat{U}^\dagger(t,t_0)\,\hat{U}(t,t_0) = \hat{U}(t,t_0)\,\hat{U}^\dagger(t,t_0) = 1$

which implies that $\hat{U}$ is unitary:

$$\hat{U}^\dagger(t,t_0) = \hat{U}^{-1}(t,t_0) \qquad (6.14)$$

2. $\quad \hat{U}(t_1,t_2)\,\hat{U}(t_2,t_3) = \hat{U}(t_1,t_3) \qquad (6.15)$

which shows that $\hat{U}$ has the group property, and

3. $\quad \hat{U}(t,t_0)\,\hat{U}(t_0,t) = 1$

which implies that

$$\hat{U}(t_0,t) = \hat{U}^\dagger(t,t_0) \qquad (6.16)$$

Although Eq. (6.13) is the formal solution to the problem posed by Eq. (6.11), it is not very useful for computational purposes. Instead we shall construct an integral equation for $\hat{U}$, which can then be solved by iteration. It is clear from Eqs. (6.5) and (6.11) that $\hat{U}$ satisfies a differential equation

$$i\hbar \frac{\partial}{\partial t}\hat{U}(t,t_0) = \hat{H}_1(t)\,\hat{U}(t,t_0) \qquad (6.17)$$

Integrate this equation from t_0 to t

$$\hat{U}(t,t_0) - \hat{U}(t_0,t_0) = -\frac{i}{\hbar} \int_{t_0}^{t} dt'\, \hat{H}_1(t')\,\hat{U}(t',t_0)$$

This result, combined with the boundary condition (6.12), yields an integral equation

$$\hat{U}(t,t_0) = 1 - \frac{i}{\hbar} \int_{t_0}^{t} dt'\, \hat{H}_1(t')\,\hat{U}(t',t_0) \qquad (6.18)$$

If $\hat{U}$ were a c-number function, Eq. (6.18) would be a Volterra integral equation, because the independent variable t appears as the upper limit of the integral. Under very broad conditions Volterra equations may be solved by iteration, and the solution is guaranteed to converge, no matter how large the kernel.[1] There is no assurance that the present operator equation has the same properties; nevertheless we shall attempt to solve Eq. (6.18) by iteration, always maintaining the proper ordering of the operators.   The solution thus takes the form

$$\hat{U}(t,t_0) = 1 + \left(\frac{-i}{\hbar}\right) \int_{t_0}^{t} dt' \, \hat{H}_1(t') + \left(\frac{-i}{\hbar}\right)^2 \int_{t_0}^{t} dt'$$
$$\int_{t_0}^{t'} dt'' \, \hat{H}_1(t') \, \hat{H}_1(t'') + \cdots \quad (6.19)$$

Consider the third term in this expansion.   It may be rewritten as

$$\int_{t_0}^{t} dt' \int_{t_0}^{t'} dt'' \, \hat{H}_1(t') \, \hat{H}_1(t'')$$
$$= \tfrac{1}{2} \int_{t_0}^{t} dt' \int_{t_0}^{t'} dt'' \, \hat{H}_1(t') \, \hat{H}_1(t'') + \tfrac{1}{2} \int_{t_0}^{t} dt'' \int_{t''}^{t} dt' \, \hat{H}_1(t') \, \hat{H}_1(t'') \quad (6.20)$$

since the last term on the right is just obtained by reversing the order of the integrations, as illustrated in Fig. 6.1.   We now change dummy variables in this

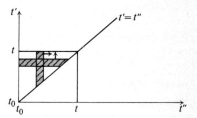

Fig. 6.1   Integration regions for second-order term in $\hat{U}(t, t_0)$.

second term, interchanging the labels t' and t'', and the second term of Eq. (6.20) therefore becomes

$$\tfrac{1}{2} \int_{t_0}^{t} dt'' \int_{t''}^{t} dt' \, \hat{H}_1(t') \, \hat{H}_1(t'') = \tfrac{1}{2} \int_{t_0}^{t} dt' \int_{t'}^{t} dt'' \, \hat{H}_1(t'') \, \hat{H}_1(t')$$

These two terms may now be recombined to give

$$\int_{t_0}^{t} dt' \int_{t_0}^{t'} dt'' \, \hat{H}_1(t') \, \hat{H}_1(t'') = \tfrac{1}{2} \int_{t_0}^{t} dt' \int_{t_0}^{t} dt''$$
$$\times [\hat{H}_1(t') \, \hat{H}_1(t'') \, \theta(t' - t'') + \hat{H}_1(t'') \, \hat{H}_1(t') \, \theta(t'' - t')] \quad (6.21)$$

---

[1] See, for example, F. Smithies, "Integral Equations," p. 31, Cambridge University Press, Cambridge, 1962.

where the step function [Eq. (3.28)] is essential because the operators $\hat{H}_1$ do not necessarily commute at different times. Equation (6.21) has the characteristic feature that the operator containing the latest time stands farthest to the left. We call this a *time-ordered product of operators*, denoted by the symbol T. Thus Eq. (6.21) can be rewritten as

$$\int_{t_0}^{t} dt' \int_{t_0}^{t'} dt'' \, \hat{H}_1(t') \, \hat{H}_1(t'') \equiv \tfrac{1}{2} \int_{t_0}^{t} dt' \int_{t_0}^{t} dt'' \, T[\hat{H}_1(t') \, \hat{H}_1(t'')] \qquad (6.22)$$

This result is readily generalized, and the resulting expansion for $\hat{U}$ becomes

$$\hat{U}(t,t_0) = \sum_{n=0}^{\infty} \left(\frac{-i}{\hbar}\right)^n \frac{1}{n!} \int_{t_0}^{t} dt_1 \, \cdots \, \int_{t_0}^{t} dt_n \, T[\hat{H}_1(t_1) \, \cdots \, \hat{H}_1(t_n)] \qquad (6.23)$$

where the $n = 0$ term is just the unit operator.[1] The proof of Eq. (6.23) is as follows. Consider the nth term in this series. There are $n!$ possible time orderings of the labels $t_1 \cdots t_n$. Pick a particular one, say, $t_1 > t_2 > t_3 \cdots > t_n$. Any other time ordering gives the same contribution to $\hat{U}$. This result is easily seen by relabeling the dummy integration variables t_i to agree with the previous ordering, and then using the symmetry of the T product under interchange of its arguments:

$$T[\cdot \, \cdot \, \cdot \, \hat{H}_1(t_i) \, \cdots \, \hat{H}_1(t_j) \, \cdots \,]$$
$$= T[\cdot \, \cdot \, \cdot \, \hat{H}_1(t_j) \, \cdots \, \hat{H}_1(t_i) \, \cdots \,] \qquad (6.24)$$

Equation (6.24) follows from the definition of the T product, which puts the operator at the latest time farthest to the left, the operator at the next latest time next, and so on, since the prescription holds equally well for both sides of Eq. (6.24). In this way, Eq. (6.23) reproduces the iterated series of Eq. (6.19).

HEISENBERG PICTURE

The state vector in the Heisenberg picture is defined as

$$|\Psi_H(t)\rangle \equiv e^{i\hat{H}t/\hbar}|\Psi_S(t)\rangle \qquad (6.25)$$

Its time derivative may be combined with the Schrödinger equation (6.1) to yield

$$i\hbar \frac{\partial}{\partial t} |\Psi_H(t)\rangle = 0 \qquad (6.26)$$

which shows that $|\Psi_H\rangle$ is time independent. Since an arbitrary matrix element in the Schrödinger picture can be written as

$$\langle \Psi_S(t)|\hat{O}_S|\Psi_S(t)\rangle = \langle \Psi_H|e^{i\hat{H}t/\hbar} \, \hat{O}_S \, e^{-i\hat{H}t/\hbar}|\Psi_H\rangle \qquad (6.27)$$

---

[1] Equation (6.23) is sometimes written as a formal time-ordered exponential

$$\hat{U}(t,t_0) = T\left\{\exp\left[-i\hbar^{-1} \int_{t_0}^{t} dt' \, \hat{H}_1(t')\right]\right\}$$

since the power-series expansion reproduces Eq. (6.23) term by term.

a general operator in the Heisenberg picture is given by

$$\hat{O}_H(t) \equiv e^{i\hat{H}t/\hbar}\,\hat{O}_S\,e^{-i\hat{H}t/\hbar} \tag{6.28}$$

Note that $\hat{O}_H(t)$ is a complicated object since $\hat{H}$ and $\hat{O}_S$ in general do not commute. We see that the Heisenberg picture ascribes all the time dependence to the operators, whereas the corresponding state vectors are time independent. In contrast, the operator $\hat{O}_S$ in the Schrödinger picture is time independent, and the time derivative of Eq. (6.28) yields

$$i\hbar\frac{\partial}{\partial t}\hat{O}_H(t) = e^{i\hat{H}t/\hbar}[\hat{O}_S,\hat{H}]\,e^{-i\hat{H}t/\hbar} = [\hat{O}_H(t),\hat{H}] \tag{6.29}$$

This important result determines the equation of motion of any operator in the Heisenberg picture. In particular, if $\hat{O}_S$ commutes with $\hat{H}$, the right side vanishes identically, and $\hat{O}_H$ is a constant of the motion.

Equation (6.28) can be rewritten in terms of interaction-picture operators [Eq. (6.7)]

$$\hat{O}_H(t) = e^{i\hat{H}t/\hbar}\,e^{-i\hat{H}_0 t/\hbar}\,\hat{O}_I(t)\,e^{i\hat{H}_0 t/\hbar}\,e^{-i\hat{H}t/\hbar} \tag{6.30}$$

and the formal solution for the operator $\hat{U}$ [Eq. (6.13)] yields

$$\hat{O}_H(t) = \hat{U}(0,t)\,\hat{O}_I(t)\,\hat{U}(t,0) \tag{6.31}$$

In addition, the various definitions show that

$$|\Psi_H\rangle = |\Psi_S(0)\rangle = |\Psi_I(0)\rangle$$
$$\hat{O}_S = \hat{O}_H(0) = \hat{O}_I(0) \tag{6.32}$$

so that all three pictures coincide at the time $t = 0$. The stationary solutions to the Schrödinger equation have a definite energy, and the corresponding state vectors in the Heisenberg picture satisfy the time-independent form of the Schrödinger equation

$$\hat{H}|\Psi_H\rangle = E|\Psi_H\rangle \tag{6.33}$$

These state vectors are therefore the *exact eigenstates* of the system and are naturally very complicated for an interacting system. Equation (6.32) and the definition of the operator $\hat{U}$ together lead to the relation

$$|\Psi_H\rangle = |\Psi_I(0)\rangle = \hat{U}(0,t_0)|\Psi_I(t_0)\rangle \tag{6.34}$$

which allows us to construct these exact eigenstates from the interaction state vectors at the time t_0 with the unitary operator $\hat{U}$.

ADIABATIC "SWITCHING ON"

The notion of switching on the interaction adiabatically represents a mathematical device that generates exact eigenstates of the interacting system from those of the

noninteracting system. Since we presumably know all about the noninteracting system, for example, the ground state, the excited states, etc., this procedure lets us follow the development of each eigenstate as the interaction between the particles is switched on. Specifically, we introduce a new time-dependent hamiltonian

$$\hat{H} = \hat{H}_0 + e^{-\epsilon|t|}\,\hat{H}_1 \tag{6.35}$$

where ϵ is a small positive quantity. At very large times, both in the past and in the future, the hamiltonian reduces to $\hat{H}_0$, which presents a soluble problem. At the time $t = 0$, $\hat{H}$ becomes the full hamiltonian of the interacting system. If ϵ tends to zero at the end of the calculation, the perturbation is turned on and off infinitely slowly, or adiabatically, and any meaningful result must be *independent* of the quantity ϵ.

The hamiltonian (6.35) presents a time-dependent problem that depends on the parameter ϵ, and we shall seek a solution in the interaction picture. It is readily verified that Eqs. (6.17) and (6.23) remain correct even when $\hat{H}_1$ is time dependent in the Schrödinger picture, and we immediately obtain

$$|\Psi_I(t)\rangle = \hat{U}_\epsilon(t,t_0)|\Psi_I(t_0)\rangle \tag{6.36}$$

where the time-development operator depends explicitly on ϵ and is given by

$$\hat{U}_\epsilon(t,t_0) = \sum_{n=0}^{\infty} \left(\frac{-i}{\hbar}\right)^n \frac{1}{n!} \int_{t_0}^{t} dt_1 \cdots \int_{t_0}^{t} dt_n$$
$$\times\, e^{-\epsilon(|t_1|+\cdots+|t_n|)}\, T[\hat{H}_1(t_1) \cdots \hat{H}_1(t_n)] \tag{6.37}$$

Now let the time t_0 approach $-\infty$; Eq. (6.35) shows that $\hat{H}$ then approaches $\hat{H}_0$. In this limit, the Schrödinger-picture state vector reduces to

$$|\Psi_S(t_0)\rangle = e^{-iE_0 t_0/\hbar}|\Phi_0\rangle \tag{6.38}$$

where $|\Phi_0\rangle$ is some time-independent stationary eigenstate of the unperturbed hamiltonian $\hat{H}_0$

$$\hat{H}_0|\Phi_0\rangle = E_0|\Phi_0\rangle \tag{6.39}$$

and the corresponding interaction-picture state vector becomes

$$|\Psi_I(t_0)\rangle = e^{i\hat{H}_0 t_0/\hbar}|\Psi_S(t_0)\rangle = |\Phi_0\rangle \tag{6.40}$$

Thus $|\Psi_I(t_0)\rangle$ becomes time independent as $t_0 \to -\infty$; alternatively, the same conclusion follows from the equation

$$i\hbar\frac{\partial}{\partial t}|\Psi_I(t)\rangle = e^{-\epsilon|t|}\,\hat{H}_1(t)|\Psi_I(t)\rangle \to 0 \qquad t \to \pm\infty \tag{6.41}$$

If there were no perturbation, these eigenstates in the interaction picture would remain constant in time, being the stationary-state solutions to the unperturbed

Schrödinger equation. As t increases from $-\infty$, however, the interaction is turned on, and Eq. (6.36) determines how the state vector develops in time, all the way to the time $t = 0$, when the interaction is at full strength. For finite times $|t| \ll \epsilon^{-1}$, all of our previous results remain valid, in particular Eqs. (6.32) and (6.34). We thus obtain the basic relation

$$|\Psi_H\rangle = |\Psi_I(0)\rangle = \hat{U}_\epsilon(0, -\infty)|\Phi_0\rangle \tag{6.42}$$

which expresses an exact eigenstate of the interacting system in terms of an eigenstate of $\hat{H}_0$.

We must now ask what happens in the limit $\epsilon \to 0$. Do we get finite meaningful results? This question is answered by the Gell-Mann and Low theorem, which is proved in the next section.

GELL-MANN AND LOW THEOREM ON THE GROUND STATE IN QUANTUM FIELD THEORY[1]

The Gell-Mann and Low theorem is easily stated: If the following quantity exists to all orders in perturbation theory,

$$\lim_{\epsilon \to 0} \frac{\hat{U}_\epsilon(0, -\infty)|\Phi_0\rangle}{\langle \Phi_0|\hat{U}_\epsilon(0, -\infty)|\Phi_0\rangle} \equiv \frac{|\Psi_0\rangle}{\langle \Phi_0|\Psi_0\rangle} \tag{6.43}$$

then it is an eigenstate of $\hat{H}$,

$$\hat{H} \frac{|\Psi_0\rangle}{\langle \Phi_0|\Psi_0\rangle} = E \frac{|\Psi_0\rangle}{\langle \Phi_0|\Psi_0\rangle} \tag{6.44}$$

This prescription generates the eigenstate that *develops adiabatically* from $|\Phi_0\rangle$ as the interaction is turned on. If $|\Phi_0\rangle$ is the ground state of the noninteracting system, the corresponding eigenstate of $\hat{H}$ is usually the interacting ground state, but this is by no means necessary. For example, the ground-state energy of some systems does not have a perturbation series in the coupling constant. (For another example see Prob. 7.5.) Multiply Eq. (6.44) from the left by the state $\langle \Phi_0|$; since $\hat{H}_0|\Phi_0\rangle = E_0|\Phi_0\rangle$, we conclude

$$E - E_0 = \frac{\langle \Phi_0|\hat{H}_1|\Psi_0\rangle}{\langle \Phi_0|\Psi_0\rangle} \tag{6.45}$$

An essential point of the theorem is that the numerator and the denominator of Eq. (6.43) *do not separately exist* as $\epsilon \to 0$. An equivalent statement is that Eq. (6.42) becomes meaningless in the limit $\epsilon \to 0$; indeed, its phase diverges like ϵ^{-1} in this limit. The denominator in Eq. (6.43) serves precisely to cancel this infinite phase [see Eq. (6.51) and subsequent discussion]. The theorem thus asserts that if the ratio in Eq. (6.43) exists, the eigenstate is well defined and has the eigenvalue given in Eq. (6.45). We proceed to the proof given by Gell-Mann and Low.

[1] M. Gell-Mann and F. Low, *Phys. Rev.*, **84**:350 (1951).

Consider the expression

$$(\hat{H}_0 - E_0)|\Psi'_0(\epsilon)\rangle = (\hat{H}_0 - E_0)\,\hat{U}_\epsilon(0,-\infty)|\Phi_0\rangle - [\hat{H}_0, \hat{U}_\epsilon(0,-\infty)]|\Phi_0\rangle \quad (6.46)$$

We shall explicitly evaluate the commutator appearing on the right side. Consider the nth term in Eq. (6.37) for the operator $\hat{U}_\epsilon$, and pick an arbitrary time ordering of the n time indices. The associated commutator can be written identically as

$$[\hat{H}_0, \hat{H}_1(t_i)\,\hat{H}_1(t_j) \cdots \hat{H}_1(t_k)] \equiv [\hat{H}_0, \hat{H}_1(t_i)]\,\hat{H}_1(t_j) \cdots \hat{H}_1(t_k)$$
$$+ \hat{H}_1(t_i)\,[\hat{H}_0, \hat{H}_1(t_j)] \cdots \hat{H}_1(t_k) + \cdots$$
$$+ \hat{H}_1(t_i)\,\hat{H}_1(t_j) \cdots [\hat{H}_0, \hat{H}_1(t_k)]$$

Furthermore, Eq. (6.8) allows us to write

$$\frac{\hbar}{i}\frac{\partial \hat{H}_1(t)}{\partial t} = [\hat{H}_0, \hat{H}_1(t)] \tag{6.47}$$

In consequence, each of the commutators with $\hat{H}_0$ yields a time derivative of the interaction hamiltonian,

$$[\hat{H}_0, \hat{H}_1(t_i)\,\hat{H}_1(t_j) \cdots \hat{H}_1(t_k)]$$
$$= \frac{\hbar}{i}\left(\frac{\partial}{\partial t_1} + \frac{\partial}{\partial t_2} + \cdots + \frac{\partial}{\partial t_n}\right)\hat{H}_1(t_i)\,\hat{H}_1(t_j) \cdots \hat{H}_1(t_k)$$

for *all possible time orderings.* Equation (6.46) thus becomes

$$(\hat{H}_0 - E_0)|\Psi'_0(\epsilon)\rangle = -\sum_{n=1}^{\infty}\left(\frac{-i}{\hbar}\right)^{n-1}\frac{1}{n!}\int_{-\infty}^{0}dt_1 \cdots \int_{-\infty}^{0}dt_n$$
$$\times e^{\epsilon(t_1 + \cdots + t_n)}\left(\sum_{i=1}^{n}\frac{\partial}{\partial t_i}\right)T[\hat{H}_1(t_1) \cdots \hat{H}_1(t_n)]|\Phi_0\rangle \quad (6.48)$$

In deriving Eq. (6.48), all the time derivatives have been taken outside of the time-ordering symbol. The validity of this step can be seen from the identity

$$\left(\sum_{i=1}^{n}\frac{\partial}{\partial t_i}\right)\theta(t_p - t_q)\,\theta(t_q - t_r) \cdots \theta(t_u - t_v) \equiv 0$$

where $p, q, r, \ldots, u, v$ is any permutation of the indices $1, 2, \ldots, n$. The differentiation is most easily evaluated with the representation

$$\theta(t) = \int_{-\infty}^{t}dt'\,\delta(t')$$

which immediately yields $d\theta(t)/dt = \delta(t) = \delta(-t)$. Thus the integrand of Eq. (6.48) may be rewritten as

$$T\left[\left(\sum_{i=1}^{n} \frac{\partial}{\partial t_i}\right)\hat{H}_1(t_1) \cdots \hat{H}_1(t_n)\right] = \left(\sum_{i=1}^{n} \frac{\partial}{\partial t_i}\right)T[\hat{H}_1(t_1) \cdots \hat{H}_1(t_n)]$$

All the time-derivative terms in Eq. (6.48) make the same contribution to the integral, as shown by changing dummy variables; we therefore retain just one, say $\partial/\partial t_1$, and multiply by a factor n. Integrate by parts with respect to t_1: This procedure leads to two terms, one of which is simply the integrand evaluated at the end points, and the other arises from the derivative of the adiabatic factor. We therefore obtain

$$(\hat{H}_0 - E_0)|\Psi_0(\epsilon)\rangle = -\hat{H}_1|\Psi_0(\epsilon)\rangle + \epsilon i\hbar g \frac{\partial}{\partial g}|\Psi_0(\epsilon)\rangle \tag{6.49}$$

where $\hat{H}_1$ is assumed proportional to a coupling constant g in order to write

$$\left(\frac{-i}{\hbar}\right)^{n-1} \frac{1}{(n-1)!} g^n = i\hbar g \frac{\partial}{\partial g}\left(\frac{-i}{\hbar}\right)^n \frac{1}{n!} g^n$$

By this means, we obtain a series that reproduces the state vector $|\Psi_0(\epsilon)\rangle$ again. Equation (6.49) is readily rewritten as

$$(\hat{H} - E_0)|\Psi_0(\epsilon)\rangle = i\hbar\epsilon g \frac{\partial}{\partial g}|\Psi_0(\epsilon)\rangle \tag{6.50}$$

Multiply this equation on the left by $[\langle\Phi_0|\Psi_0(\epsilon)\rangle]^{-1}\langle\Phi_0|$; since $(\partial/\partial g)\langle\Phi_0| = 0$, we find

$$\frac{\langle\Phi_0|\hat{H}_1|\Psi_0(\epsilon)\rangle}{\langle\Phi_0|\Psi_0(\epsilon)\rangle} = i\hbar\epsilon g \frac{\partial}{\partial g} \ln \langle\Phi_0|\Psi_0(\epsilon)\rangle \equiv E - E_0 = \Delta E \tag{6.51}$$

If ϵ were allowed to vanish at this point, it would be tempting to conclude that $\Delta E = 0$, which is clearly absurd. In fact, the amplitude $\langle\Phi_0|\Psi_0(\epsilon)\rangle$ must acquire an infinite phase proportional to $i\epsilon^{-1}$ so that $\epsilon \ln\langle\Phi_0|\Psi_0(\epsilon)\rangle$ remains finite as $\epsilon \to 0$.‡ Equation (6.50) may be manipulated to give

$$\left(\hat{H} - E_0 - i\hbar\epsilon g \frac{\partial}{\partial g}\right)\frac{|\Psi_0(\epsilon)\rangle}{\langle\Phi_0|\Psi_0(\epsilon)\rangle} = \frac{|\Psi_0(\epsilon)\rangle}{\langle\Phi_0|\Psi_0(\epsilon)\rangle}\left[i\hbar\epsilon g \frac{\partial}{\partial g} \ln \langle\Phi_0|\Psi_0(\epsilon)\rangle\right]$$

and a combination with Eq. (6.51) finally yields

$$(\hat{H} - E)\frac{|\Psi_0(\epsilon)\rangle}{\langle\Phi_0|\Psi_0(\epsilon)\rangle} = i\hbar\epsilon g \frac{\partial}{\partial g}\left[\frac{|\Psi_0(\epsilon)\rangle}{\langle\Phi_0|\Psi_0(\epsilon)\rangle}\right] \tag{6.52}$$

We are now in a position to let ϵ go to zero. By assumption, the quantity in brackets on the right side of Eq. (6.52) is finite to all orders in perturbation

‡ See, for example, J. Hubbard, *Proc. Roy. Soc.* (*London*), **A240**:539 (1957).

theory, that is, in g, and the derivative with respect to g cannot change this property. Since the right side is multiplied by ϵ, it vanishes as ϵ tends to zero, which proves the basic theorem

$$(\hat{H} - E)\lim_{\epsilon \to 0} \frac{|\Psi_0(\epsilon)\rangle}{\langle \Phi_0|\Psi_0(\epsilon)\rangle} = 0 \qquad (6.53)$$

This proof applies equally well to the quantity

$$\frac{\hat{U}_\epsilon(0,+\infty)|\Phi_0\rangle}{\langle \Phi_0|\hat{U}_\epsilon(0,+\infty)|\Phi_0\rangle} \qquad (6.54)$$

where

$$\hat{U}_\epsilon(0,+\infty) = \hat{U}_\epsilon^\dagger(+\infty,0)$$

Here the system "comes back" from $t = +\infty$, where the eigenstate is $|\Phi_0\rangle$. If the state that develops out of $|\Phi_0\rangle$ is nondegenerate, then these two definitions must be the same. They could differ by a phase factor, but the common normalization condition

$$\langle \Phi_0|\left[\frac{|\Psi_0\rangle}{\langle \Phi_0|\Psi_0\rangle}\right] = 1 \qquad (6.55)$$

precludes even this possibility. Thus, for a *nondegenerate* eigenstate of $\hat{H}$

$$\lim_{\epsilon \to 0} \frac{\hat{U}_\epsilon(0,+\infty)|\Phi_0\rangle}{\langle \Phi_0|\hat{U}_\epsilon(0,+\infty)|\Phi_0\rangle} = \lim_{\epsilon \to 0} \frac{\hat{U}_\epsilon(0,-\infty)|\Phi_0\rangle}{\langle \Phi_0|\hat{U}_\epsilon(0,-\infty)|\Phi_0\rangle} \qquad (6.56)$$

As noted before, the state obtained from the adiabatic switching procedure need not be the true ground state, even if $|\Phi_0\rangle$ is the noninteracting ground state. The Gell-Mann and Low theorem merely asserts that it is an eigenstate; in addition, if it is a nondegenerate eigenstate, then both ways of constructing it [Eq. (6.56)] must yield the same result.

7□GREEN'S FUNCTIONS

This section introduces the concept of a Green's function[1] (or propagator, as it is sometimes called), which plays a fundamental role in our treatment of many-particle assemblies.

DEFINITION

The single-particle Green's function is defined by the equation

$$iG_{\alpha\beta}(\mathbf{x}t, \mathbf{x}'t') = \frac{\langle \Psi_0|T[\hat{\psi}_{H\alpha}(\mathbf{x}t)\,\hat{\psi}_{H\beta}^\dagger(\mathbf{x}'t')]|\Psi_0\rangle}{\langle \Psi_0|\Psi_0\rangle} \qquad (7.1)$$

[1] V. M. Galitskii and A. B. Migdal, *Sov. Phys.-JETP*, **7**:96 (1958); A. Klein and R. Prange, *Phys. Rev.*, **112**:994 (1958); P. C. Martin and J. Schwinger, *Phys. Rev.*, **115**:1342 (1959).

where $|\Psi_0\rangle$ is the *Heisenberg ground state* of the interacting system satisfying

$$\hat{H}|\Psi_0\rangle = E|\Psi_0\rangle \tag{7.2}$$

and $\hat{\psi}_{H\alpha}(\mathbf{x}t)$ is a *Heisenberg operator* with the time dependence

$$\hat{\psi}_{H\alpha}(\mathbf{x}t) = e^{i\hat{H}t/\hbar}\,\hat{\psi}_\alpha(\mathbf{x})\,e^{-i\hat{H}t/\hbar} \tag{7.3}$$

Here the indices α and β label the components of the field operators; α and β can take two values for spin-$\frac{1}{2}$ fermions, whereas there are no indices for spin-zero bosons, because such a system is described by a one-component field. The T product here represents a generalization of that in Eq. (6.22):

$$T[\hat{\psi}_{H\alpha}(\mathbf{x}t)\,\hat{\psi}^\dagger_{H\beta}(\mathbf{x}'\,t')] = \begin{cases} \hat{\psi}_{H\alpha}(\mathbf{x}t)\,\hat{\psi}^\dagger_{H\beta}(\mathbf{x}'\,t') & t > t' \\ \pm\hat{\psi}^\dagger_{H\beta}(\mathbf{x}'\,t')\,\hat{\psi}_{H\alpha}(\mathbf{x}t) & t' > t \end{cases} \tag{7.4}$$

where the upper (lower) sign refers to bosons (fermions). More generally, the T product of several operators orders them from right to left in ascending time order and adds a factor $(-1)^P$, where P is the number of interchanges of *fermion* operators from the original given order. This definition agrees with that in Eq. (6.22), because $\hat{H}_1$ always contains an *even* number of fermion fields. Equation (7.1) may now be written explicitly as

$$iG_{\alpha\beta}(\mathbf{x}t, \mathbf{x}'\,t') = \begin{cases} \dfrac{\langle\Psi_0|\hat{\psi}_{H\alpha}(\mathbf{x}t)\,\hat{\psi}^\dagger_{H\beta}(\mathbf{x}'\,t')|\Psi_0\rangle}{\langle\Psi_0|\Psi_0\rangle} & t > t' \\[3mm] \pm\dfrac{\langle\Psi_0|\hat{\psi}^\dagger_{H\beta}(\mathbf{x}'\,t')\,\hat{\psi}_{H\alpha}(\mathbf{x}t)|\Psi_0\rangle}{\langle\Psi_0|\Psi_0\rangle} & t' > t \end{cases} \tag{7.5}$$

The Green's function is an expectation value of field operators; as such, it is simply a function of the coordinate variables $\mathbf{x}t$ and $\mathbf{x}'t'$. If $\hat{H}$ is time independent, then G depends only on the time difference $t - t'$, which follows immediately from Eqs. (7.2) and (7.3):

$$iG_{\alpha\beta}(\mathbf{x}t, \mathbf{x}'\,t')$$

$$= \begin{cases} e^{iE(t-t')/\hbar}\dfrac{\langle\Psi_0|\hat{\psi}_\alpha(\mathbf{x})\,e^{-i\hat{H}(t-t')/\hbar}\,\hat{\psi}^\dagger_\beta(\mathbf{x}')|\Psi_0\rangle}{\langle\Psi_0|\Psi_0\rangle} & t > t' \\[3mm] \pm e^{-iE(t-t')/\hbar}\dfrac{\langle\Psi_0|\hat{\psi}^\dagger_\beta(\mathbf{x}')\,e^{i\hat{H}(t-t')/\hbar}\,\hat{\psi}_\alpha(\mathbf{x})|\Psi_0\rangle}{\langle\Psi_0|\Psi_0\rangle} & t' > t \end{cases} \tag{7.6}$$

Here the factor $\exp[\pm iE(t - t')/\hbar]$ is merely a complex c number and may be taken out of the matrix element; in contrast, the operator $\hat{H}$ between the field operators must remain as written.

RELATION TO OBSERVABLES

There are several reasons for studying the Green's functions. First, the Feynman rules for finding the contribution of nth order perturbation theory are simpler for G than for other combinations of field operators. This result is discussed in detail in Sec. 9. Second, although the ground-state expectation value in Eq. (7.1) implies the loss of much detailed information about the ground state, the single-particle Green's function still contains the observable properties of greatest interest:

1. The expectation value of any single-particle operator in the ground state of the system
2. The ground-state energy of the system
3. The excitation spectrum of the system

The first two points are demonstrated below, while the third follows from the Lehmann representation, which is discussed later in this section.

Consider the single-particle operator

$$\hat{J} = \int d^3x \, \hat{\mathscr{J}}(\mathbf{x})$$

where $\hat{\mathscr{J}}(\mathbf{x})$ is the second-quantized density for the first-quantized operator $J_{\beta\alpha}(\mathbf{x})$:

$$\hat{\mathscr{J}}(\mathbf{x}) = \sum_{\alpha\beta} \hat{\psi}_\beta^\dagger(\mathbf{x}) J_{\beta\alpha}(\mathbf{x}) \, \hat{\psi}_\alpha(\mathbf{x})$$

The ground-state expectation value of the operator density is given by

$$
\begin{aligned}
\langle \hat{\mathscr{J}}(\mathbf{x}) \rangle &\equiv \frac{\langle \Psi_0 | \hat{\mathscr{J}}(\mathbf{x}) | \Psi_0 \rangle}{\langle \Psi_0 | \Psi_0 \rangle} \\
&= \lim_{\mathbf{x}' \to \mathbf{x}} \sum_{\alpha\beta} J_{\beta\alpha}(\mathbf{x}) \frac{\langle \Psi_0 | \hat{\psi}_\beta^\dagger(\mathbf{x}') \, \hat{\psi}_\alpha(\mathbf{x}) | \Psi_0 \rangle}{\langle \Psi_0 | \Psi_0 \rangle} \\
&= \pm i \lim_{t' \to t^+} \lim_{\mathbf{x}' \to \mathbf{x}} \sum_{\alpha\beta} J_{\beta\alpha}(\mathbf{x}) \, G_{\alpha\beta}(\mathbf{x}t, \mathbf{x}'t') \\
&= \pm i \lim_{t' \to t^+} \lim_{\mathbf{x}' \to \mathbf{x}} \mathrm{tr}\left[J(\mathbf{x}) \, G(\mathbf{x}t, \mathbf{x}'t') \right]
\end{aligned}
\tag{7.7}
$$

Here the operator $J_{\beta\alpha}(\mathbf{x})$ must act before the limit $\mathbf{x}' \to \mathbf{x}$ is performed because J may contain spatial derivatives, as in the momentum operator. Furthermore, the symbol t^+ denotes a time infinitesimally later than t, which ensures that the field operators in the third line occur in the proper order [compare Eq. (7.5)]. Finally, the sum over spin indices may be recognized as a trace of the matrix product JG, which is here denoted by tr. For example, the number density $\langle \hat{n}(\mathbf{x}) \rangle$, the spin density $\langle \hat{\boldsymbol{\sigma}}(\mathbf{x}) \rangle$, and the total kinetic energy $\langle \hat{T} \rangle$ are readily found to be

$$\langle \hat{n}(\mathbf{x}) \rangle = \pm i \, \mathrm{tr} \, G(\mathbf{x}t, \mathbf{x}t^+) \tag{7.8}$$

$$\langle \hat{\mathbf{\sigma}}(\mathbf{x}) \rangle = \pm i \operatorname{tr}\left[\mathbf{\sigma} G(\mathbf{x}t, \mathbf{x}t^{+}) \right] \tag{7.9}$$

$$\langle \hat{T} \rangle = \pm i \int d^{3}x \lim_{\mathbf{x}' \to \mathbf{x}} \left[-\frac{\hbar^{2} \nabla^{2}}{2m} \operatorname{tr} G(\mathbf{x}t, \mathbf{x}'\,t^{+}) \right] \tag{7.10}$$

The interesting question now arises: Is it also possible to construct the potential energy

$$\langle \hat{V} \rangle = \tfrac{1}{2} \sum_{\substack{\alpha\alpha' \\ \beta\beta'}} \int d^{3}x \, d^{3}x' \frac{\langle \Psi_{0} | \hat{\psi}_{\alpha}^{\dagger}(\mathbf{x}) \, \hat{\psi}_{\beta}^{\dagger}(\mathbf{x}') \, V(\mathbf{x},\mathbf{x}')_{\alpha\alpha',\beta\beta'} \, \hat{\psi}_{\beta'}(\mathbf{x}') \, \hat{\psi}_{\alpha'}(\mathbf{x}) | \Psi_{0} \rangle}{\langle \Psi_{0} | \Psi_{0} \rangle}$$

$$\tag{7.11}$$

and thereby determine the total ground-state energy? Since Eq. (7.11) involves four field operators, we might expect to need the two-particle Green's function. The Schrödinger equation itself contains the potential energy, however, which allows us to find $\langle \hat{V} \rangle$ in terms of the single-particle Green's function. Consider the *Heisenberg* field operator $\hat{\psi}_{H\alpha}(\mathbf{x}t)$, with the hamiltonian

$$\hat{H} = \sum_{\alpha} \int d^{3}x \, \hat{\psi}_{\alpha}^{\dagger}(\mathbf{x}) \, T(\mathbf{x}) \, \hat{\psi}_{\alpha}(\mathbf{x})$$

$$+ \tfrac{1}{2} \sum_{\substack{\alpha\alpha' \\ \beta\beta'}} \int d^{3}x \, d^{3}x' \; \hat{\psi}_{\alpha}^{\dagger}(\mathbf{x}) \, \hat{\psi}_{\beta}^{\dagger}(\mathbf{x}') \, V(\mathbf{x},\mathbf{x}')_{\alpha\alpha',\beta\beta'} \, \hat{\psi}_{\beta'}(\mathbf{x}') \, \hat{\psi}_{\alpha'}(\mathbf{x}) \tag{7.12}$$

The identity of the particles in the assembly requires that the interaction be unchanged under particle interchange

$$V(\mathbf{x},\mathbf{x}')_{\alpha\alpha',\,\beta\beta'} = V(\mathbf{x}',\mathbf{x})_{\beta\beta',\,\alpha\alpha'} \tag{7.13}$$

[More formally, such a term is the only kind that gives a nonvanishing contribution in Eq. (7.12).] The Heisenberg equation of motion [Eq. (6.29)] relates the time derivative of $\hat{\psi}$ to the commutator of $\hat{\psi}$ with $\hat{H}$.

$$i\hbar \frac{\partial}{\partial t} \hat{\psi}_{H\alpha}(\mathbf{x}t) = e^{i\hat{H}t/\hbar} [\hat{\psi}_{\alpha}(\mathbf{x}), \hat{H}] \, e^{-i\hat{H}t/\hbar} \tag{7.14}$$

where

$$[\hat{\psi}_{\alpha}(\mathbf{x}), \hat{H}] = \sum_{\beta} \int d^{3}z \; [\hat{\psi}_{\alpha}(\mathbf{x}), \hat{\psi}_{\beta}^{\dagger}(\mathbf{z}) \, T(\mathbf{z}) \, \hat{\psi}_{\beta}(\mathbf{z})] + \tfrac{1}{2} \sum_{\substack{\beta\beta' \\ \gamma\gamma'}} \int d^{3}z \, d^{3}z'$$

$$\times \; [\hat{\psi}_{\alpha}(\mathbf{x}), \hat{\psi}_{\beta}^{\dagger}(\mathbf{z}) \, \hat{\psi}_{\gamma}^{\dagger}(\mathbf{z}') \, V(\mathbf{z},\mathbf{z}')_{\beta\beta',\,\gamma\gamma'} \, \hat{\psi}_{\gamma'}(\mathbf{z}') \, \hat{\psi}_{\beta'}(\mathbf{z})] \tag{7.15}$$

We now use the very important identity

$$[A,BC] = ABC - BCA = ABC - BAC + BAC - BCA$$

$$= \begin{cases} [A,B]C - B[C,A] \\ \{A,B\}C - B\{C,A\} \end{cases} \tag{7.16}$$

which allows us to express Eq. (7.15) in terms of either *commutators* or *anticommutators*. For definiteness, consider the fermion case, since this is more

complicated. With the canonical anticommutation relations [Eq. (2.3)] the commutator is readily evaluated, and we find

$$[\hat{\psi}_\alpha(\mathbf{x}),\hat{H}] = T(\mathbf{x})\,\hat{\psi}_\alpha(\mathbf{x}) - \tfrac{1}{2}\sum_{\beta\beta'\gamma'}\int d^3z\,\hat{\psi}_\beta^\dagger(\mathbf{z})\,V(\mathbf{z},\mathbf{x})_{\beta\beta',\,\alpha\gamma'}\,\hat{\psi}_{\gamma'}(\mathbf{x})\,\hat{\psi}_{\beta'}(\mathbf{z})$$

$$+ \tfrac{1}{2}\sum_{\beta'\gamma\gamma'}\int d^3z'\,\hat{\psi}_\gamma^\dagger(\mathbf{z}')\,V(\mathbf{x},\mathbf{z}')_{\alpha\beta',\,\gamma\gamma'}\,\hat{\psi}_{\gamma'}(\mathbf{z}')\,\hat{\psi}_{\beta'}(\mathbf{x}) \qquad (7.17)$$

In the first potential-energy term, change the dummy variables $\beta \to \gamma$, $\beta' \to \gamma'$, $\gamma' \to \beta'$, $\mathbf{z} \to \mathbf{z}'$. The symmetry of the potential [Eq. (7.13)] and the anticommutativity of the fields $\hat{\psi}$ then yield

$$[\hat{\psi}_\alpha(\mathbf{x}),\hat{H}] = T(\mathbf{x})\,\hat{\psi}_\alpha(\mathbf{x}) + \sum_{\beta'\gamma\gamma'}\int d^3z'\,\hat{\psi}_\gamma^\dagger(\mathbf{z}')\,V(\mathbf{x},\mathbf{z}')_{\alpha\beta',\,\gamma\gamma'}\,\hat{\psi}_{\gamma'}(\mathbf{z}')\,\hat{\psi}_{\beta'}(\mathbf{x})$$

$$\qquad\qquad (7.18)$$

while the field equation (7.14) becomes

$$\left[i\hbar\frac{\partial}{\partial t} - T(\mathbf{x})\right]\hat{\psi}_{H\alpha}(\mathbf{x}t)$$

$$= \sum_{\beta'\gamma\gamma'}\int d^3z'\,\hat{\psi}_{H\gamma}^\dagger(\mathbf{z}'\,t)\,V(\mathbf{x},\mathbf{z}')_{\alpha\beta',\,\gamma\gamma'}\,\hat{\psi}_{H\gamma'}(\mathbf{z}'\,t)\,\hat{\psi}_{H\beta'}(\mathbf{x}t) \qquad (7.19)$$

Equations (7.18) and (7.19) are also correct for bosons.

Multiply Eq. (7.19) by $\hat{\psi}_{H\alpha}^\dagger(\mathbf{x}'\,t')$ on the left, and then take the ground state expectation value

$$\left[i\hbar\frac{\partial}{\partial t} - T(\mathbf{x})\right]\frac{\langle\Psi_0|\hat{\psi}_{H\alpha}^\dagger(\mathbf{x}'\,t')\,\hat{\psi}_{H\alpha}(\mathbf{x}t)|\Psi_0\rangle}{\langle\Psi_0|\Psi_0\rangle} = \sum_{\beta'\gamma\gamma'}\int d^3z'$$

$$\times\frac{\langle\Psi_0|\hat{\psi}_{H\alpha}^\dagger(\mathbf{x}'\,t')\,\hat{\psi}_{H\gamma}^\dagger(\mathbf{z}'\,t)\,V(\mathbf{x},\mathbf{z}')_{\alpha\beta',\,\gamma\gamma'}\,\hat{\psi}_{H\gamma'}(\mathbf{z}'\,t)\,\hat{\psi}_{H\beta'}(\mathbf{x}t)|\Psi_0\rangle}{\langle\Psi_0|\Psi_0\rangle} \qquad (7.20)$$

In the limit $\mathbf{x}' \to \mathbf{x}$, $t' \to t^+$, the left side is equal to

$$\pm i\lim_{t'\to t^+}\lim_{\mathbf{x}'\to\mathbf{x}}\left[i\hbar\frac{\partial}{\partial t} - T(\mathbf{x})\right]G_{\alpha\alpha}(\mathbf{x}t,\mathbf{x}'\,t') \qquad (7.21)$$

We now sum over α and integrate over $\mathbf{x}$, which finally yields [compare Eq. (7.11)]

$$\langle\hat{V}\rangle = \pm\tfrac{1}{2}i\int d^3x\lim_{t'\to t^+}\lim_{\mathbf{x}'\to\mathbf{x}}\sum_\alpha\left[i\hbar\frac{\partial}{\partial t} - T(\mathbf{x})\right]G_{\alpha\alpha}(\mathbf{x}t,\mathbf{x}'\,t') \qquad (7.22)$$

A combination of Eqs. (7.10) and (7.22) then expresses the total ground-state energy solely in terms of the single-particle Green's function.

$$E = \langle\hat{T} + \hat{V}\rangle = \langle\hat{H}\rangle$$

$$= \pm\tfrac{1}{2}i\int d^3x\lim_{t'\to t^+}\lim_{\mathbf{x}'\to\mathbf{x}}\left[i\hbar\frac{\partial}{\partial t} + T(\mathbf{x})\right]\operatorname{tr}G(\mathbf{x}t,\mathbf{x}'\,t')$$

$$= \pm\tfrac{1}{2}i\int d^3x\lim_{t'\to t^+}\lim_{\mathbf{x}'\to\mathbf{x}}\left[i\hbar\frac{\partial}{\partial t} - \frac{\hbar^2\,\nabla^2}{2m}\right]\operatorname{tr}G(\mathbf{x}t,\mathbf{x}'\,t') \qquad (7.23)$$

These expressions assume a simpler form for a homogeneous system in a large box of volume V, where the single-particle Green's function may be written as [compare Eq. (3.1)][1]

$$G_{\alpha\beta}(\mathbf{x}t, \mathbf{x}'\,t') = \sum_{\mathbf{k}} \int_{-\infty}^{\infty} \frac{d\omega}{2\pi V} e^{i\mathbf{k}\cdot(\mathbf{x}-\mathbf{x}')} e^{-i\omega(t-t')} G_{\alpha\beta}(\mathbf{k},\omega) \qquad (7.24)$$

In the limit $V \to \infty$, the sum over wave vectors reduces to an integral [Eq. (3.26)]

$$G_{\alpha\beta}(\mathbf{x}t, \mathbf{x}'\,t') = (2\pi)^{-4} \int d^3k \int_{-\infty}^{\infty} d\omega\, e^{i\mathbf{k}\cdot(\mathbf{x}-\mathbf{x}')} e^{-i\omega(t-t')} G_{\alpha\beta}(\mathbf{k},\omega) \qquad (7.25)$$

and a combination of Eqs. (7.8), (7.23), and (7.25) gives

$$N = \int d^3x \, \langle \hat{n}(\mathbf{x}) \rangle = \pm i \frac{V}{(2\pi)^4} \lim_{\eta \to 0^+} \int d^3k \int_{-\infty}^{\infty} d\omega\, e^{i\omega\eta} \operatorname{tr} G(\mathbf{k},\omega) \qquad (7.26)$$

$$E = \pm \tfrac{1}{2} i \frac{V}{(2\pi)^4} \lim_{\eta \to 0^+} \int d^3k \int_{-\infty}^{\infty} d\omega\, e^{i\omega\eta} \left(\frac{\hbar^2 k^2}{2m} + \hbar\omega \right) \operatorname{tr} G(\mathbf{k},\omega) \qquad (7.27)$$

Here the convergence factor

$$\lim_{t' \to t^+} e^{i\omega(t'-t)} \equiv \lim_{\eta \to 0^+} e^{i\omega\eta}$$

defines the appropriate contour in the complex ω plane; henceforth, the limit $\eta \to 0^+$ will be implicit whenever such a factor appears.

For some purposes, it would be more convenient to have the difference $\hbar\omega - \hbar^2 k^2/2m$ appearing in Eq. (7.27). This result can be achieved with the following trick, apparently due to Pauli and since rediscovered many times.[2] The hamiltonian is written with a variable coupling constant λ as

$$\hat{H}(\lambda) = \hat{H}_0 + \lambda \hat{H}_1$$

then

$$\hat{H}(1) = \hat{H} \quad \text{and} \quad \hat{H}(0) = \hat{H}_0$$

and we attempt to solve the time-independent Schrödinger equation for an arbitrary value of λ:

$$\hat{H}(\lambda)|\Psi_0(\lambda)\rangle = E(\lambda)|\Psi_0(\lambda)\rangle \qquad (7.28)$$

where the state vector is assumed normalized

$$\langle \Psi_0(\lambda)|\Psi_0(\lambda)\rangle = 1$$

---

[1] For a proof that G depends only on the coordinate difference $\mathbf{x} - \mathbf{x}'$ in a uniform system, see the discussion preceding Eq. (7.53).

[2] See, for example, D. Pines, "The Many-Body Problem," p. 43, W. A. Benjamin, Inc., New York, 1961; T. D. Schultz, "Quantum Field Theory and the Many-Body Problem," p. 18, Gordon and Breach, Science Publishers, New York, 1964.

The scalar product of Eq. (7.28) with $\langle \Psi'_0(\lambda)|$ immediately yields

$$E(\lambda) = \langle \Psi'_0(\lambda)|\hat{H}(\lambda)|\Psi'_0(\lambda)\rangle$$

and its derivative with respect to the parameter λ reduces to

$$\frac{d}{d\lambda}E(\lambda) = \left\langle \frac{d\Psi'_0(\lambda)}{d\lambda}\middle|\hat{H}(\lambda)|\Psi'_0(\lambda)\right\rangle + \left\langle \Psi'_0(\lambda)|\hat{H}(\lambda)\middle|\frac{d\Psi'_0(\lambda)}{d\lambda}\right\rangle$$

$$+ \left\langle \Psi'_0(\lambda)\middle|\frac{d\hat{H}(\lambda)}{d\lambda}\middle|\Psi'_0(\lambda)\right\rangle$$

$$= E(\lambda)\frac{d}{d\lambda}\langle \Psi'_0(\lambda)|\Psi'_0(\lambda)\rangle + \langle \Psi'_0(\lambda)|\hat{H}_1|\Psi'_0(\lambda)\rangle$$

$$= \langle \Psi'_0(\lambda)|\hat{H}_1|\Psi'_0(\lambda)\rangle \tag{7.29}$$

where the normalization condition has been used in obtaining the last line. Integrate Eq. (7.29) with respect to λ from zero to one and note that $E(0) = E_0$ and $E(1) = E$

$$E - E_0 = \int_0^1 \frac{d\lambda}{\lambda}\langle \Psi'_0(\lambda)|\lambda\hat{H}_1|\Psi'_0(\lambda)\rangle \tag{7.30}$$

The shift in the ground-state energy is here expressed solely in terms of the matrix element of the interaction $\lambda\hat{H}_1$. Unfortunately, this matrix element is required for *all values* of the coupling constant $0 \leqslant \lambda \leqslant 1$. In the usual situation, where $\hat{H}_1$ represents the potential energy [Eq. (7.12)], a combination of Eqs. (7.22) and (7.30) gives

$$E - E_0 = \pm\tfrac{1}{2}i\int_0^1\frac{d\lambda}{\lambda}\int d^3x \lim_{t'\to t^+}\lim_{\mathbf{x}'\to\mathbf{x}}\left[i\hbar\frac{\partial}{\partial t} - T(\mathbf{x})\right]\mathrm{tr}\, G^\lambda(\mathbf{x}t, \mathbf{x}'\,t') \tag{7.31}$$

with the corresponding expression for a uniform system

$$E - E_0 = \pm\tfrac{1}{2}i\frac{V}{(2\pi)^4}\int_0^1\frac{d\lambda}{\lambda}\int d^3k \int_{-\infty}^\infty d\omega\, e^{i\omega\eta}\left(\hbar\omega - \frac{\hbar^2 k^2}{2m}\right)\mathrm{tr}\, G^\lambda(\mathbf{k},\omega) \tag{7.32}$$

EXAMPLE: FREE FERMIONS

As an example of the above formalism, consider the Green's function for a noninteracting homogeneous system of fermions. It is first convenient to perform a canonical transformation to *particles* and *holes*. In the definition of the field [compare Eqs. (2.1) and (3.1)]

$$\hat{\psi}(\mathbf{x}) = \sum_{\mathbf{k}\lambda} \psi_{\mathbf{k}\lambda}(\mathbf{x})\, c_{\mathbf{k}\lambda} \tag{7.33}$$

we redefine the fermion operator $c_{\mathbf{k}\lambda}$ as[1]

$$c_{\mathbf{k}\lambda} = \begin{cases} a_{\mathbf{k}\lambda} & k > k_F \quad \text{particles} \\ b^\dagger_{-\mathbf{k}\lambda} & k < k_F \quad \text{holes} \end{cases} \tag{7.34}$$

[1] The absence of a particle with momentum $+\mathbf{k}$ from the filled Fermi sea implies that the system possesses a momentum $-\mathbf{k}$. For a proper interpretation of the spin of the hole state, see Sec. 56.

which is a canonical transformation that preserves the anticommutation rules

$$\{a_k, a_{k'}^\dagger\} = \{b_k, b_{k'}^\dagger\} = \delta_{kk'} \tag{7.35}$$

and therefore leaves the physics unchanged. Here the a's and b's clearly anti-commute with each other because they refer to different modes. The $a^\dagger$ and a operators create and destroy particles above the Fermi sea, while the $b^\dagger$ and b operators create and destroy holes inside the Fermi sea, as is evident from Eq. (7.34). The fields may now be rewritten in terms of these new operators as

$$\hat{\psi}_S(\mathbf{x}) = \sum_{k\lambda > k_F} \psi_{k\lambda}(\mathbf{x}) a_{k\lambda} + \sum_{k\lambda < k_F} \psi_{k\lambda}(\mathbf{x}) b_{-k\lambda}^\dagger \tag{7.36}$$

$$\hat{\psi}_I(\mathbf{x}t) = \sum_{k\lambda > k_F} \psi_{k\lambda}(\mathbf{x}) e^{-i\omega_k t} a_{k\lambda} + \sum_{k\lambda < k_F} \psi_{k\lambda}(\mathbf{x}) e^{-i\omega_k t} b_{-k\lambda}^\dagger \tag{7.37}$$

where the first equation is in the Schrödinger picture and the second equation is in the interaction picture. Equations (7.36) and (7.37) differ only in that the interaction picture contains a complex time-dependent phase. Correspondingly, the hamiltonian becomes

$$\hat{H}_0 = \sum_{k\lambda} \hbar\omega_k c_{k\lambda}^\dagger c_{k\lambda}$$

$$= \underbrace{\sum_{k\lambda > k_F} \hbar\omega_k a_{k\lambda}^\dagger a_{k\lambda}}_{\text{(particles)}} - \underbrace{\sum_{k\lambda < k_F} \hbar\omega_k b_{k\lambda}^\dagger b_{k\lambda}}_{\text{(holes)}} + \underbrace{\sum_{k\lambda < k_F} \hbar\omega_k}_{\text{(filled Fermi sea)}} \tag{7.38}$$

In the absence of particles or holes, the energy is that of the filled Fermi sea. Creating a hole lowers the energy, whereas creating a particle raises the energy. If the total number of fermions is fixed, however, particles and holes necessarily occur in pairs. Each particle-hole pair then has a net positive energy, showing that the filled Fermi sea represents the ground state.

By definition, the noninteracting fermion Green's function is given by

$$iG_{\alpha\beta}^0(\mathbf{x}t, \mathbf{x}'t') = \langle \Phi_0 | T[\hat{\psi}_{I\alpha}(\mathbf{x}t) \hat{\psi}_{I\beta}^\dagger(\mathbf{x}'t')] | \Phi_0 \rangle \tag{7.39}$$

where the noninteracting ground state vector is assumed normalized, and the superscript zero indicates that this is a Green's function with no interactions. We now observe that the particle and hole destruction operators both annihilate the ground state

$$b_{k\lambda}|\Phi_0\rangle = a_{k\lambda}|\Phi_0\rangle = 0 \tag{7.40}$$

since there are no particles above or holes below the Fermi sea in the state $|\Phi_0\rangle$. Equation (7.40) shows the usefulness of the particle-hole notation. The remaining term for each time ordering is easily computed, and we find

$$iG_{\alpha\beta}^0(\mathbf{x}t, \mathbf{x}'t') = \delta_{\alpha\beta} V^{-1} \sum_k e^{i\mathbf{k}\cdot(\mathbf{x}-\mathbf{x}')} e^{-i\omega_k(t-t')}$$

$$\times [\theta(t-t')\theta(k-k_F) - \theta(t'-t)\theta(k_F-k)] \tag{7.41}$$

where the factor $\delta_{\alpha\beta}$ arises because the sum over spin states is complete. In the limit of an infinite volume, the summation over $\mathbf{k}$ becomes an integration

$$iG^0_{\alpha\beta}(\mathbf{x}t, \mathbf{x}'\,t') = \delta_{\alpha\beta}(2\pi)^{-3} \int d^3k\, e^{i\mathbf{k}\cdot(\mathbf{x}-\mathbf{x}')}\, e^{-i\omega_k(t-t')}$$

$$\times\, [\theta(t-t')\,\theta(k-k_F) - \theta(t'-t)\,\theta(k_F-k)] \quad (7.42)$$

It is now useful to introduce an integral representation for the step function

$$\theta(t-t') = -\int_{-\infty}^{\infty} \frac{d\omega}{2\pi i} \frac{e^{-i\omega(t-t')}}{\omega + i\eta} \quad (7.43)$$

Equation (7.43) is readily verified as follows: If $t > t'$, then the contour must be closed in the lower-half ω plane, including the simple pole at $\omega = -i\eta$ with residue -1. If $t < t'$, then the contour must be closed in the upper-half ω plane and gives zero, because the integrand has no singularities for $\mathrm{Im}\,\omega > 0$. Equation (7.43) may be combined with Eq. (7.42) to give

$$G^0_{\alpha\beta}(\mathbf{x}t, \mathbf{x}'\,t') = (2\pi)^{-4} \int d^3k \int_{-\infty}^{\infty} d\omega\, e^{i\mathbf{k}\cdot(\mathbf{x}-\mathbf{x}')}\, e^{-i\omega(t-t')}$$

$$\times\, \delta_{\alpha\beta}\left[\frac{\theta(k-k_F)}{\omega - \omega_k + i\eta} + \frac{\theta(k_F-k)}{\omega - \omega_k - i\eta}\right] \quad (7.44)$$

which immediately yields

$$G^0_{\alpha\beta}(\mathbf{k},\omega) = \delta_{\alpha\beta}\left[\frac{\theta(k-k_F)}{\omega - \omega_k + i\eta} + \frac{\theta(k_F-k)}{\omega - \omega_k - i\eta}\right] \quad (7.45)$$

It is instructive to verify explicitly that Eq. (7.44) indeed reproduces Eq. (7.42), and also that Eq. (7.45) gives the correct value for $\langle \hat{N} \rangle$ [Eq. (7.26)] and $E \equiv E_0$ [Eq. (7.27)]. Equation (7.45) also can be derived directly by evaluating the Fourier transform of Eq. (7.42), in which case the $\pm i\eta$ terms are required to render the time integrals convergent.

THE LEHMANN REPRESENTATION[1]

Certain features of the single-particle Green's function follow directly from fundamental quantum-mechanical principles and are therefore independent of the specific form of the interaction. This section is devoted to such general properties. Although our final expressions are *formally* applicable to both bosons and fermions, the existence of Bose condensation at $T = 0$ introduces additional complications (see Chap. 6), and we shall consider only fermions in the next two subsections. The exact Green's function is given by

$$iG_{\alpha\beta}(\mathbf{x}t, \mathbf{x}'\,t') = \langle \Psi_0 | T[\hat{\psi}_{H\alpha}(\mathbf{x}t)\, \hat{\psi}^\dagger_{H\beta}(\mathbf{x}'\,t')] | \Psi_0 \rangle \quad (7.46)$$

[1] H. Lehmann, *Nuovo Cimento*, **11**:342 (1954). Our treatment follows that of V. M. Galitskii and A. B. Migdal, *loc. cit.* and A. A. Abrikosov, L. P. Gorkov, and I. E. Dzyaloshinskii, "Methods of Quantum Field Theory in Statistical Physics," sec. 7, Prentice-Hall, Inc., Englewood Cliffs, N. J., 1963.

where the ground state is assumed normalized $[\langle \Psi_0 | \Psi_0 \rangle = 1]$. In general, the Heisenberg field operators and state vectors in this expression are very complicated. Nevertheless, it is possible to derive some interesting and general results. Insert a complete set of Heisenberg states between the field operators; these states are eigenstates of the full hamiltonian, and include all possible numbers of particles. The right side of Eq. (7.46) becomes

$$iG_{\alpha\beta}(\mathbf{x}t, \mathbf{x}'\,t') = \sum_n \left[\theta(t - t') \langle \Psi_0 | \hat{\psi}_{H\alpha}(\mathbf{x}t) | \Psi_n \rangle \langle \Psi_n | \hat{\psi}^\dagger_{H\beta}(\mathbf{x}'\,t') | \Psi_0 \rangle \right.$$
$$\left. - \theta(t' - t) \langle \Psi_0 | \hat{\psi}^\dagger_{H\beta}(\mathbf{x}'\,t') | \Psi_n \rangle \langle \Psi_n | \hat{\psi}_{H\alpha}(\mathbf{x}t) | \Psi_0 \rangle \right] \quad (7.47)$$

Each Heisenberg operator may be rewritten in the form

$$\hat{O}_H(t) = e^{i\hat{H}t/\hbar} \, \hat{O}_S \, e^{-i\hat{H}t/\hbar}$$

which allows us to make explicit the time dependence of these matrix elements

$$iG_{\alpha\beta}(\mathbf{x}t, \mathbf{x}'\,t') = \sum_n \left[\theta(t - t') e^{-i(E_n - E)(t - t')/\hbar} \langle \Psi_0 | \hat{\psi}_\alpha(\mathbf{x}) | \Psi_n \rangle \langle \Psi_n | \hat{\psi}^\dagger_\beta(\mathbf{x}') | \Psi_0 \rangle \right.$$
$$\left. - \theta(t' - t) e^{i(E_n - E)(t - t')/\hbar} \langle \Psi_0 | \hat{\psi}^\dagger_\beta(\mathbf{x}') | \Psi_n \rangle \langle \Psi_n | \hat{\psi}_\alpha(\mathbf{x}) | \Psi_0 \rangle \right] \quad (7.48)$$

As a preliminary step, we show that the states $|\Psi_n\rangle$ contain $N \pm 1$ particles if the state $|\Psi_0\rangle$ contains N particles. The number operator has the form

$$\hat{N} = \sum_\alpha \int d^3x \, \hat{\psi}^\dagger_\alpha(\mathbf{x}) \, \hat{\psi}_\alpha(\mathbf{x})$$

and its commutator with the field operator is easily evaluated (for both bosons and fermions) as

$$[\hat{N}, \hat{\psi}_\beta(\mathbf{z})] = -\hat{\psi}_\beta(\mathbf{z})$$

or, equivalently,

$$\hat{N}\hat{\psi}_\beta(\mathbf{z}) = \hat{\psi}_\beta(\mathbf{z})(\hat{N} - 1)$$

Apply this last operator relation to the state $|\Psi_0\rangle$:

$$\hat{N}[\hat{\psi}_\beta(\mathbf{z})|\Psi_0\rangle] = (N - 1)[\hat{\psi}_\beta(\mathbf{z})|\Psi_0\rangle] \quad (7.49)$$

where we have noted that $|\Psi_0\rangle$ is an eigenstate of the number operator with eigenvalue N. Thus the field $\hat{\psi}$ acting on the state $|\Psi_0\rangle$ yields an eigenstate of the number operator with one less particle. Similarly, the operator $\hat{\psi}^\dagger$ increases the number of particles by one. Equation (7.48) thus contains one new feature that does not occur in the ordinary Schrödinger equation, for we must now consider assemblies with different numbers of particles.

Until this point, the discussion has been completely general, assuming only that $\hat{H}$ is time independent. Although it is possible to continue this analysis without further restriction, we shall now consider only the simpler case of translational invariance. This implies that the momentum operator, which is the generator of spatial displacements, commutes with $\hat{H}$. It is natural to use the

plane-wave basis of Eq. (3.1) for such a system, and the momentum operator is given by

$$\hat{\mathbf{P}} = \sum_\alpha \int d^3x\, \hat{\psi}_\alpha^\dagger(\mathbf{x})(-i\hbar\boldsymbol{\nabla})\,\hat{\psi}_\alpha(\mathbf{x}) = \sum_{\mathbf{k}\lambda} \hbar\mathbf{k} c_{\mathbf{k}\lambda}^\dagger c_{\mathbf{k}\lambda} \tag{7.50}$$

The commutator of $\hat{\mathbf{P}}$ with the field operator $\hat{\psi}$ (for both bosons and fermions) is easily evaluated as

$$-i\hbar\boldsymbol{\nabla}\hat{\psi}_\alpha(\mathbf{x}) = [\hat{\psi}_\alpha(\mathbf{x}),\hat{\mathbf{P}}] \tag{7.51}$$

which can also be rewritten in integral form:

$$\hat{\psi}_\alpha(\mathbf{x}) = e^{-i\hat{\mathbf{P}}\cdot\mathbf{x}/\hbar}\,\hat{\psi}_\alpha(0)\,e^{i\hat{\mathbf{P}}\cdot\mathbf{x}/\hbar} \tag{7.52}$$

Since $\hat{\mathbf{P}}$ is a constant of the motion, the complete set of states also can be taken as eigenstates of momentum. We therefore extract the $\mathbf{x}$ dependence of the matrix elements in Eq. (7.48):

$$iG_{\alpha\beta}(\mathbf{x}t,\mathbf{x}'\,t') = \sum_n [\theta(t-t')\,e^{-i(E_n-E)(t-t')/\hbar}\,e^{i\mathbf{P}_n\cdot(\mathbf{x}-\mathbf{x}')/\hbar}$$

$$\times \langle\Psi_0|\hat{\psi}_\alpha(0)|\Psi_n\rangle\langle\Psi_n|\hat{\psi}_\beta^\dagger(0)|\Psi_0\rangle - \theta(t'-t)\,e^{i(E_n-E)(t-t')/\hbar}\,e^{-i\mathbf{P}_n\cdot(\mathbf{x}-\mathbf{x}')/\hbar}$$

$$\times \langle\Psi_0|\hat{\psi}_\beta^\dagger(0)|\Psi_n\rangle\langle\Psi_n|\hat{\psi}_\alpha(0)|\Psi_0\rangle] \tag{7.53}$$

where we have observed that $\hat{\mathbf{P}}|\Psi_0\rangle = 0$. Equation (7.53) makes explicit that G depends only on the variables $\mathbf{x}-\mathbf{x}'$ and $t-t'$.‡ The corresponding Fourier transform is

$$G_{\alpha\beta}(\mathbf{k},\omega) = \int d^3(\mathbf{x}-\mathbf{x}')\int d(t-t')\,e^{-i\mathbf{k}\cdot(\mathbf{x}-\mathbf{x}')}\,e^{i\omega(t-t')}\,G_{\alpha\beta}(\mathbf{x}t,\mathbf{x}'\,t')$$

$$= V\sum_n \delta_{\mathbf{k},\mathbf{P}_n/\hbar} \frac{\langle\Psi_0|\hat{\psi}_\alpha(0)|\Psi_n\rangle\langle\Psi_n|\hat{\psi}_\beta^\dagger(0)|\Psi_0\rangle}{\omega - \hbar^{-1}(E_n-E) + i\eta}$$

$$+ V\sum_n \delta_{\mathbf{k},-\mathbf{P}_n/\hbar} \frac{\langle\Psi_0|\hat{\psi}_\beta^\dagger(0)|\Psi_n\rangle\langle\Psi_n|\hat{\psi}_\alpha(0)|\Psi_0\rangle}{\omega + \hbar^{-1}(E_n-E) - i\eta} \tag{7.54}$$

where the $\pm i\eta$ is again necessary to ensure the convergence of the integral over $t - t'$. In the first (second) term, the contribution vanishes unless the momentum of the state $|\Psi_n\rangle$ corresponds to a wavenumber $\mathbf{k}(-\mathbf{k})$, which can be used to restrict the intermediate states:

$$G_{\alpha\beta}(\mathbf{k},\omega) = V\sum_n \left[\frac{\langle\Psi_0|\hat{\psi}_\alpha(0)|n\mathbf{k}\rangle\langle n\mathbf{k}|\hat{\psi}_\beta^\dagger(0)|\Psi_0\rangle}{\omega - \hbar^{-1}(E_n-E) + i\eta} \right.$$

$$\left. + \frac{\langle\Psi_0|\hat{\psi}_\beta^\dagger(0)|n,-\mathbf{k}\rangle\langle n,-\mathbf{k}|\hat{\psi}_\alpha(0)|\Psi_0\rangle}{\omega + \hbar^{-1}(E_n-E) - i\eta} \right] \tag{7.55}$$

‡ For many problems it is more convenient to assume that the interacting particles move relative to a fixed frame of reference. For example, in the problem of interacting electrons in crystalline solids and atoms, the crystalline lattice and heavy atomic nucleus provide such fixed frames. In this case the $\hat{\mathbf{P}}$ of the interacting particles no longer commutes with $\hat{H}$, and the Green's function may depend explicitly on $\mathbf{x}$ and $\mathbf{x}'$. This more complicated situation is discussed in Chap. 15.

Thus the general principles of quantum mechanics enable us to exhibit the frequency dependence of the Green's function, because ω *now appears only in the denominator of this sum.*

It is helpful to examine these denominators in a little more detail. In the first sum the intermediate state has $N + 1$ particles, and the denominator may be written as

$$\omega - \hbar^{-1}[E_n(N + 1) - E(N)] = \omega - \hbar^{-1}[E_n(N + 1) - E(N + 1)]$$
$$- \hbar^{-1}[E(N + 1) - E(N)] \quad (7.56)$$

Now $E(N + 1) - E(N)$ is the change in ground-state energy as one extra particle is added to the system. Since the volume of the system is kept constant, this change in energy is just the chemical potential [compare Eq. (4.3)]. Furthermore, the quantity $E_n(N + 1) - E(N + 1) \equiv \epsilon_n(N + 1)$ is the *excitation* energy of the $N + 1$ particle system; by definition, $\epsilon_n(N + 1)$ is greater than or equal to zero. Similarly, the denominator of the second term can be written

$$\omega + \hbar^{-1}[E_n(N - 1) - E(N)] = \omega - \hbar^{-1}[E(N) - E(N - 1)]$$
$$+ \hbar^{-1}[E_n(N - 1) - E(N - 1)]$$
$$= \omega - \hbar^{-1}\mu + \hbar^{-1}\epsilon_n(N - 1) \quad (7.57)$$

since $E(N) - E(N - 1)$ is again the chemical potential μ, apart from corrections of order N^{-1}. Indeed, the very definition of the thermodynamic limit ($N \to \infty$, $V \to \infty$, but N/V constant) implies

$$\mu(N + 1) = \mu(N) + O(N^{-1}) \quad (7.58)$$

Although we shall not attempt to prove this relation in general, it is readily demonstrated for a free Fermi gas at zero temperature, where the Pauli principle further ensures that $\mu = \epsilon_F^0$. Equations (7.56) and (7.57) can now be combined with Eq. (7.55) to give the Lehmann representation

$$G_{\alpha\beta}(\mathbf{k},\omega) = \hbar V \sum_n \left[\frac{\langle \Psi_0 | \hat{\psi}_\alpha(0) | n\mathbf{k} \rangle \langle n\mathbf{k} | \hat{\psi}_\beta^\dagger(0) | \Psi_0 \rangle}{\hbar\omega - \mu - \epsilon_{n\mathbf{k}}(N + 1) + i\eta} \right.$$
$$\left. + \frac{\langle \Psi_0 | \hat{\psi}_\beta^\dagger(0) | n, -\mathbf{k} \rangle \langle n, -\mathbf{k} | \hat{\psi}_\alpha(0) | \Psi_0 \rangle}{\hbar\omega - \mu + \epsilon_{n, -\mathbf{k}}(N - 1) - i\eta} \right] \quad (7.59)$$

It is possible to simplify the matrix structure of G in the special case of spin-$\frac{1}{2}$. Since G is a 2×2 matrix, it can be expanded in the complete set consisting of the unit matrix and the three Pauli spin matrices $\boldsymbol{\sigma}$. If there is no preferred direction in the problem, then G must be a scalar under spatial rotations. Since $\mathbf{k}$ is the only vector available to combine with $\boldsymbol{\sigma}$, G necessarily takes the form

$$G(\mathbf{k},\omega) = a\mathbf{1} + b\boldsymbol{\sigma} \cdot \mathbf{k}$$

where the invariance under rotations implies that a and b are functions of $\mathbf{k}^2$ and ω. If, in addition, the hamiltonian is invariant under spatial reflections, then G must also have this property; but $\boldsymbol{\sigma}\cdot\mathbf{k}$ is a pseudoscalar under spatial reflections, so that the coefficient b must vanish. Thus, if the hamiltonian and ground state are invariant under spatial rotations and reflections, the Green's function has the following matrix structure

$$G_{\alpha\beta}(\mathbf{k},\omega) = \delta_{\alpha\beta}\, G(\mathbf{k},\omega) = \delta_{\alpha\beta}\, G(|\mathbf{k}|,\omega) \tag{7.60}$$

proportional to the unit matrix.

It is instructive to use Eq. (7.59) to reproduce our previous expression for $G^0(\mathbf{k},\omega)$ [Eq. (7.45)] in a free Fermi system. For the first term of Eq. (7.59), the added particle must lie above the Fermi sea, and the matrix elements of the field operators become

$$\langle\Psi_0|\hat{\psi}_\alpha(0)|n\mathbf{k}\rangle\,\langle n\mathbf{k}|\hat{\psi}_\beta^\dagger(0)|\Psi_0\rangle \to V^{-1}\,\delta_{\alpha\beta}\,\theta(k - k_F) \tag{7.61}$$

In the denominator of this term, the excitation energy is the difference between the actual energy of the additional particle and the energy that it would have at the Fermi surface. Thus the energy difference is given by

$$E_{\mathbf{k}}(N+1) - E(N+1) \equiv \epsilon_{\mathbf{k}}(N+1) \to \epsilon_k^0 - \epsilon_F^0 = \frac{\hbar^2(k^2 - k_F^2)}{2m}$$

The second term of Eq. (7.59) clearly corresponds to a hole below the Fermi surface, and the matrix elements of the field operators become

$$\langle\Psi_0|\hat{\psi}_\beta^\dagger(0)|n,-\mathbf{k}\rangle\,\langle n,-\mathbf{k}|\hat{\psi}_\alpha(0)|\Psi_0\rangle \to V^{-1}\,\delta_{\alpha\beta}\,\theta(k_F - k)$$

The ground state of the $N-1$ particle system is reached by letting a particle from the Fermi surface come down and fill up the hole; hence the energy difference in the second denominator is given by

$$E_{-\mathbf{k}}(N-1) - E(N-1) \equiv \epsilon_{-\mathbf{k}}(N-1) \to \epsilon_F^0 - \epsilon_{-\mathbf{k}}^0 = \frac{\hbar^2(k_F^2 - k^2)}{2m}$$

Since $\mu = \epsilon_F^0$ for a noninteracting system, we obtain Eq. (7.45).

As noted above, Eq. (7.59) exhibits the dependence of the *exact* Green's function on the frequency ω, and it is interesting to consider the analytic properties of this function. The crucial observation is that *the function $G(\mathbf{k},\omega)$ is a meromorphic function of $\hbar\omega$, with simple poles at the exact excitation energies of the interacting system corresponding to a momentum $\hbar\mathbf{k}$.* For frequencies below $\mu/\hbar$, these singularities lie slightly above the real axis, and for frequencies above $\mu/\hbar$, these singularities lie slightly below the real axis (compare Fig. 7.1). In this way, the singularities of the Green's function immediately yield the energies of those excited states for which the numerator does not vanish. For an interacting system, the field operator connects the ground state with very many excited states of the system containing $N \pm 1$ particles. For the non-

interacting system, however, the field operator connects only one state to the ground state, so that $G^0(\mathbf{k},\omega)$ has only a single pole, slightly below the real axis at $\hbar\omega = \hbar^2 k^2/2m$ if $k > k_F$ and slightly above the real axis at the same value of $\hbar\omega$ if $k < k_F$.

It is clear from this discussion that the Green's function G is analytic in *neither* the upper *nor* the lower ω plane. For contour integrations, however, it is useful to consider functions that are analytic in one half plane or the other.

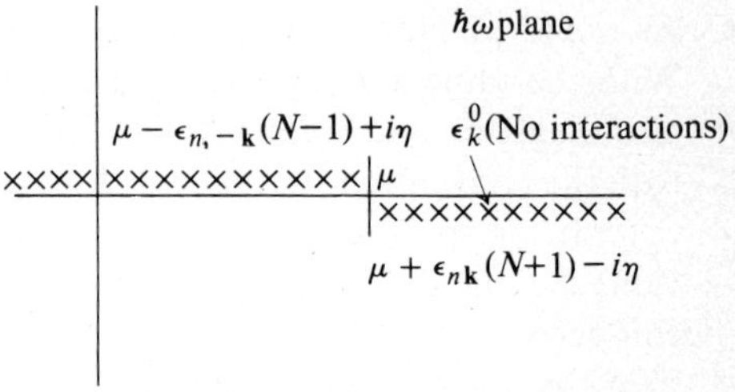

Fig. 7.1 Singularities of $G(\mathbf{k},\omega)$ in the complex $\hbar\omega$ plane.

We therefore define a new pair of functions, known as *retarded* and *advanced* Green's functions

$$iG^R_{\alpha\beta}(\mathbf{x}t, \mathbf{x}'\,t') = \langle \Psi_0|\{\hat{\psi}_{H\alpha}(\mathbf{x}t), \hat{\psi}^\dagger_{H\beta}(\mathbf{x}'\,t')\}|\Psi_0\rangle\, \theta(t - t')$$

$$iG^A_{\alpha\beta}(\mathbf{x}t, \mathbf{x}'\,t') = -\langle \Psi_0|\{\hat{\psi}_{H\alpha}(\mathbf{x}t), \hat{\psi}^\dagger_{H\beta}(\mathbf{x}'\,t')\}|\Psi_0\rangle\, \theta(t' - t)$$

$$(7.62)$$

where the braces denote an anticommutator. The analysis of these functions proceeds exactly as for the time-ordered Green's function. In a homogeneous system, we find the following Lehmann representation of their Fourier transforms:

$$G^{R,A}_{\alpha\beta}(\mathbf{k},\omega) = \hbar V \sum_n \left[\frac{\langle \Psi_0|\hat{\psi}_\alpha(0)|n\mathbf{k}\rangle \langle n\mathbf{k}|\hat{\psi}^\dagger_\beta(0)|\Psi_0\rangle}{\hbar\omega - \mu - \epsilon_{n\mathbf{k}}(N + 1) \pm i\eta} \right.$$

$$\left. + \frac{\langle \Psi_0|\hat{\psi}^\dagger_\beta(0)|n,-\mathbf{k}\rangle \langle n,-\mathbf{k}|\hat{\psi}_\alpha(0)|\Psi_0\rangle}{\hbar\omega - \mu + \epsilon_{n,-\mathbf{k}}(N - 1) \pm i\eta} \right] \quad (7.63)$$

Note that the Fourier transforms $G^R(\mathbf{k},\omega)$ and $G^A(\mathbf{k},\omega)$ are again meromorphic functions of ω. All the poles of $G^R(\mathbf{k},\omega)$ lie in the lower half plane, so that $G^R(\mathbf{k},\omega)$ is analytic for $\mathrm{Im}\,\omega > 0$; in contrast, all the poles of $G^A(\mathbf{k},\omega)$ lie in the upper half plane, so that $G^A(\mathbf{k},\omega)$ is analytic for $\mathrm{Im}\,\omega < 0$. For *real* ω, these functions are simply related by

$$[G^R_{\alpha\beta}(\mathbf{k},\omega)]^* = G^A_{\beta\alpha}(\mathbf{k},\omega) \quad (7.64)$$

where the asterisk denotes complex conjugation. The retarded and advanced Green's functions differ from each other and from the time-ordered Green's function only in the convergence factors $\pm i\eta$, which are important near the singularities. If ω is real and greater than $\hbar^{-1}\mu$, then the infinitesimal imaginary parts $\pm i\eta$

in the second term of Eqs. (7.59) and (7.63) play no role. We therefore conclude
that in this limited domain of the complex ω plane

$$G_{\alpha\beta}^R(\mathbf{k},\omega) = G_{\alpha\beta}(\mathbf{k},\omega) \qquad \hbar\omega \text{ real, } > \mu \tag{7.65a}$$

Similarly,

$$G_{\alpha\beta}^A(\mathbf{k},\omega) = G_{\alpha\beta}(\mathbf{k},\omega) \qquad \hbar\omega \text{ real, } < \mu \tag{7.65b}$$

As noted previously, $G_{\alpha\beta}$ is usually diagonal in the spin indices: $G_{\alpha\beta} = G\delta_{\alpha\beta}$.
With the same assumptions, the retarded and advanced Green's functions are
also diagonal, and we may solve for G as $G = (2s + 1)^{-1}\Sigma_\alpha G_{\alpha\alpha} \equiv (2s + 1)^{-1} G_{\alpha\alpha}$
with the convention that repeated indices are to be summed.

   If the spacing between adjacent energy levels is characterized by a typical
value $\Delta\epsilon$, the discrete level structure can be resolved only over time scales long
compared with $\hbar/\Delta\epsilon$. Conversely, if an observation lasts for a typical time τ,
then the corresponding energy resolution is of order $\hbar/\tau$. Since $\Delta\epsilon$ becomes
vanishingly small for a macroscopic sample, it generally satisfies the restriction
$\Delta\epsilon \ll \hbar/\tau$, and we therefore detect only the *level density*, averaged over an energy
interval $\hbar/\tau$. In the thermodynamic limit of a bulk system, it follows that the
discrete variable n can be replaced by a continuous one. If dn denotes the
number of levels in a small energy interval $\epsilon < \epsilon_{n\mathbf{k}} < \epsilon + d\epsilon$, then the summations
in Eqs. (7.59) and (7.63) can be rewritten as

$$(2s + 1)^{-1} V \sum_n |\langle n\mathbf{k}|\hat{\psi}_\alpha^\dagger(0)|\Psi_0\rangle|^2 \cdots$$

$$\approx (2s + 1)^{-1} V \int dn \, |\langle n\mathbf{k}|\hat{\psi}_\alpha^\dagger(0)|\Psi_0\rangle|^2 \cdots$$

$$= (2s + 1)^{-1} V \int d\epsilon \, |\langle n\mathbf{k}|\hat{\psi}_\alpha^\dagger(0)|\Psi_0\rangle|^2 \frac{dn}{d\epsilon} \cdots$$

$$\equiv \hbar^{-1} \int d\epsilon \, A(\mathbf{k},\epsilon\hbar^{-1}) \cdots \tag{7.66a}$$

and

$$(2s + 1)^{-1} V \sum_n |\langle n, -\mathbf{k}|\hat{\psi}_\alpha(0)|\Psi_0\rangle|^2 \cdots \equiv \hbar^{-1} \int d\epsilon \, B(\mathbf{k},\epsilon\hbar^{-1}) \cdots \tag{7.66b}$$

which define the positive-definite weight functions $A(\mathbf{k},\epsilon/\hbar)$ and $B(\mathbf{k},\epsilon/\hbar)$. The
corresponding Fourier transform of the single-particle Green's function becomes

$$G(\mathbf{k},\omega) = \int_0^\infty d\omega' \left[\frac{A(\mathbf{k},\omega')}{\omega - \hbar^{-1}\mu - \omega' + i\eta} + \frac{B(\mathbf{k},\omega')}{\omega - \hbar^{-1}\mu + \omega' - i\eta} \right] \tag{7.67}$$

which now has a *branch cut* in the complex ω plane *along the whole real axis*.
Thus the infinite-volume limit completely alters the analytic structure of $G(\mathbf{k},\omega)$,
because the discrete poles have merged to form a branch line. The same result
describes a finite system whenever the individual levels cannot be resolved.

A similar analysis for the retarded and advanced Green's functions yields

$$G^{R,A}(\mathbf{k},\omega) = \int_0^\infty d\omega' \left[\frac{A(\mathbf{k},\omega')}{\omega - \hbar^{-1}\mu - \omega' \pm i\eta} + \frac{B(\mathbf{k},\omega')}{\omega - \hbar^{-1}\mu + \omega' \pm i\eta} \right] \quad (7.68)$$

which shows that all three Green's functions can be constructed if A and B are known. In addition, the symbolic identity valid for real ω

$$\frac{1}{\omega \pm i\eta} = \mathscr{P}\frac{1}{\omega} \mp i\pi\delta(\omega) \quad (7.69)$$

shows that G^R and G^A satisfy dispersion relations

$$\operatorname{Re} G^{R,A}(\mathbf{k},\omega) = \mp\mathscr{P}\int_{-\infty}^{\infty} \frac{d\omega'}{\pi} \frac{\operatorname{Im} G^{R,A}(\mathbf{k},\omega')}{\omega - \omega'} \quad (7.70)$$

where $\mathscr{P}$ denotes a Cauchy principal value. This equation also holds for finite systems, where $\operatorname{Im} G$ is a sum of delta functions.

These Green's functions all have a simple asymptotic behavior for large $|\omega|$. Consider the ground-state expectation value of the anticommutator

$$\langle \Psi_0 | \{\hat{\psi}_\alpha(\mathbf{x}), \hat{\psi}_\beta^\dagger(\mathbf{x}')\} | \Psi_0 \rangle = \delta_{\alpha\beta}\,\delta(\mathbf{x} - \mathbf{x}') \quad (7.71)$$

An analysis similar to Eq. (7.53) shows that

$$\delta(\mathbf{x} - \mathbf{x}') = (2s + 1)^{-1} \sum_n \left[e^{i\mathbf{P}_n \cdot (\mathbf{x}-\mathbf{x}')/\hbar} |\langle \Psi_n | \hat{\psi}_\alpha^\dagger(0) | \Psi_0 \rangle|^2 \right.$$
$$\left. + e^{-i\mathbf{P}_n \cdot (\mathbf{x}-\mathbf{x}')/\hbar} |\langle \Psi_n | \hat{\psi}_\alpha(0) | \Psi_0 \rangle|^2 \right]$$

and its Fourier transform with respect to $\mathbf{x} - \mathbf{x}'$ yields

$$1 = (2s + 1)^{-1} V \sum_n \left[|\langle n\mathbf{k} | \hat{\psi}_\alpha^\dagger(0) | \Psi_0 \rangle|^2 + |\langle n, -\mathbf{k} | \hat{\psi}_\alpha(0) | \Psi_0 \rangle|^2 \right]$$

$$= \int_0^\infty d\omega \, [A(\mathbf{k},\omega) + B(\mathbf{k},\omega)]$$

where the last line follows from Eq. (7.66). For $|\omega| \to \infty$, Eqs. (7.67) and (7.68) yield

$$G(\mathbf{k},\omega) = G^R(\mathbf{k},\omega) = G^A(\mathbf{k},\omega) \sim \frac{1}{\omega} \int_0^\infty d\omega' \, [A(\mathbf{k},\omega') + B(\mathbf{k},\omega')]$$

$$\sim \frac{1}{\omega} \qquad |\omega| \to \infty \quad (7.72)$$

which remains correct for an arbitrary interacting system.

PHYSICAL INTERPRETATION OF THE GREEN'S FUNCTION

To understand the physical interpretation of the single-particle Green's function, consider the interaction-picture state $|\Psi_I(t')\rangle$, and add a particle at the point $(\mathbf{x}'\,t') : \hat{\psi}_{I\beta}^\dagger(\mathbf{x}'\,t') |\Psi_I(t')\rangle$. Although this state is not in general an eigenstate of

the hamiltonian, it still propagates in time according to $\hat{U}(t,t')\hat{\psi}^\dagger_{I\beta}(\mathbf{x}'\,t')|\Psi_I(t')\rangle$. For $t > t'$ what is the overlap of this state with the state $\hat{\psi}^\dagger_{I\alpha}(\mathbf{x}t)|\Psi_I(t)\rangle$?

$$\langle\Psi_I(t)|\hat{\psi}_{I\alpha}(\mathbf{x}t)\,\hat{U}(t,t')\,\hat{\psi}^\dagger_{I\beta}(\mathbf{x}'\,t')|\Psi_I(t')\rangle$$

$$= \langle\Phi_0|\hat{U}(\infty,t)\,[\hat{U}(t,0)\,\hat{\psi}_{H\alpha}(\mathbf{x}t)\,\hat{U}(0,t)]\,\hat{U}(t,t')$$
$$\times\,[\hat{U}(t',0)\,\hat{\psi}^\dagger_{H\beta}(\mathbf{x}'\,t')\,\hat{U}(0,t')]\,\hat{U}(t',-\infty)|\Phi_0\rangle$$

$$= \langle\Psi_0|\hat{\psi}_{H\alpha}(\mathbf{x}t)\,\hat{\psi}^\dagger_{H\beta}(\mathbf{x}'\,t')|\Psi_0\rangle$$

where we have used the results of Sec. 6. This quantity is just the Green's function for $t > t'$, which therefore characterizes the propagation of a state containing an additional particle. In a similar way, if $t < t'$, the field operator first creates a hole at time t, and the system then propagates according to the full hamiltonian. These holes can be interpreted as particles going backward in time, as discussed in the famous papers of Feynman.[1] The probability amplitude at a later time t' for finding a single hole in the ground state of the interacting system is again just the Green's function for $t < t'$.

We shall now study how this propagation in time is related to the function $G(\mathbf{k},\omega)$, and, for definiteness, we shall consider only the usual case where the time scale is too short to resolve the separate energy levels.[2] By the definition of the Fourier transform, the time dependence is given by

$$G(\mathbf{k},t) = \int_{-\infty}^{\infty}\frac{d\omega}{2\pi}e^{-i\omega t}G(\mathbf{k},\omega) \tag{7.73}$$

If $t > 0$, the integral may be evaluated by deforming the contour into the lower half ω plane. Since $G(\mathbf{k},\omega)$ has a rather complicated analytic structure, it is convenient to separate Eq. (7.73) into two parts:

$$G(\mathbf{k},t) = \int_{-\infty}^{\mu/\hbar}\frac{d\omega}{2\pi}e^{-i\omega t}G(\mathbf{k},\omega) + \int_{\mu/\hbar}^{\infty}\frac{d\omega}{2\pi}e^{-i\omega t}G(\mathbf{k},\omega) \tag{7.74}$$

In the first term (ω real and $< \hbar^{-1}\mu$), $G(\mathbf{k},\omega)$ coincides with the advanced Green's function $G^A(\mathbf{k},\omega)$ [Eq. (7.65b)], and the integral thus becomes

$$\int_{-\infty}^{\mu/\hbar}\frac{d\omega}{2\pi}e^{-i\omega t}G(\mathbf{k},\omega) = \int_{-\infty}^{\mu/\hbar}\frac{d\omega}{2\pi}e^{-i\omega t}G^A(\mathbf{k},\omega) \tag{7.75}$$

Now $G^A(\mathbf{k},\omega)$ is analytic in the lower half plane, and the contour can be deformed from C_1 to C_1' (Fig. 7.2a). Equation (7.72) shows that G^A (and G^R) behaves

---

[1] R. P. Feynman, *Phys. Rev.*, **76**:749 (1949); **76**:769 (1949).
[2] Our argument follows that of V. M. Galitskii and A. B. Migdal, *loc. cit.* and of A. A. Abrikosov, L. P. Gorkov, and I. E. Dzyaloshinskii, *loc. cit.*

like ω^{-1} for $|\omega| \to \infty$; Jordan's lemma[1] thus ensures that the contribution from the arc at infinity vanishes, and Eq. (7.75) reduces to

$$\int_{-\infty}^{\mu/\hbar} \frac{d\omega}{2\pi} e^{-i\omega t} G(\mathbf{k},\omega) = \int_{\mu/\hbar - i\infty}^{\mu/\hbar} \frac{d\omega}{2\pi} e^{-i\omega t} G^A(\mathbf{k},\omega) \tag{7.76}$$

The second term of Eq. (7.74) can be treated similarly, because $G(\mathbf{k},\omega)$ coincides with $G^R(\mathbf{k},\omega)$ for real $\omega > \mu/\hbar$. There is one important new feature, however,

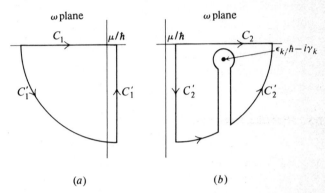

Fig. 7.2 Contours used in evaluating $G(\mathbf{k},t)$ for $t > 0$.

because $G^R(\mathbf{k},\omega)$ is *not* analytic in the lower half ω plane but instead has singularities. For definiteness we *make a very elementary model* of the interacting assembly and assume that $G^R(\mathbf{k},\omega)$ has a *simple pole close to the real axis* in the lower half plane at $\omega = \hbar^{-1}\epsilon_k - i\gamma_k$ with residue a, where $\epsilon_k > \mu$ and $\epsilon_k - \mu \gg \hbar\gamma_k \geqslant 0$. (If G^R has several poles, the same analysis applies to each one separately.) The contour C_2 can be deformed to C_2' (Fig. 7.2b), and the large arc at infinity again makes no contribution; the second term of Eq. (7.74) then becomes

$$\int_{\mu/\hbar}^{\infty} \frac{d\omega}{2\pi} e^{-i\omega t} G(\mathbf{k},\omega) = \int_{\mu/\hbar}^{\mu/\hbar - i\infty} \frac{d\omega}{2\pi} e^{-i\omega t} G^R(\mathbf{k},\omega) - ia\, e^{-i\epsilon_k t/\hbar} e^{-\gamma_k t} \tag{7.77}$$

A combination of Eqs. (7.76) and (7.77) yields

$$G(\mathbf{k},t) = \int_{\mu/\hbar - i\infty}^{\mu/\hbar} \frac{d\omega}{2\pi} e^{-i\omega t}[G^A(\mathbf{k},\omega) - G^R(\mathbf{k},\omega)] - ia\, e^{-i\epsilon_k t/\hbar} e^{-\gamma_k t} \tag{7.78}$$

If t is neither too large nor too small, the integral in Eq. (7.78) is negligible, and the state containing one additional particle propagates like an approximate eigenstate with a frequency $\epsilon_k/\hbar$ and damping constant γ_k. More precisely, we shall now show that if

1. $|t|(\epsilon_k - \mu) \gg \hbar$
2. $|t|\gamma_k \lesssim 1$

[1] See, for example, E. G. Phillips, "Functions of a Complex Variable," p. 122, Interscience Publishers, Inc., New York, 1958.

then[1]

$$G(\mathbf{k},t) \approx -ia\, e^{-i\epsilon_k t/\hbar}\, e^{-\gamma_k t} \tag{7.79}$$

Note that the condition $\epsilon_k - \mu \gg \hbar\gamma_k$ is assumed implicitly, so that the pole must lie very close to the real axis. In this case, Eq. (7.79) shows that the real and imaginary parts of the poles of the analytic continuation of $G^R(\mathbf{k},\omega)$ into the lower half plane determine the frequency and lifetime of the excited states obtained by adding a particle to an interacting ground state. Equation (7.79) is readily proved by noting that the integrand in Eq. (7.78) is *exponentially* small as $\mathrm{Im}\,\omega$ becomes large and negative, so that the dominant contributions come from the region near the real axis. On the real axis, in the vicinity of the pole we have

$$G^R(\mathbf{k},\omega) \approx \frac{a}{\omega - \epsilon_k/\hbar + i\gamma_k}$$

$$G^A(\mathbf{k},\omega) = [G^R(\mathbf{k},\omega)]^* \approx \frac{a}{\omega - \epsilon_k/\hbar - i\gamma_k}$$

where the second relation follows from Eq. (7.64). These relations allow us to analytically continue $G^R(\mathbf{k},\omega)$ and $G^A(\mathbf{k},\omega)$ into the complex ω plane, and the integral in Eq. (7.78) can therefore be written as

$$\int_{\mu/\hbar - i\infty}^{\mu/\hbar} \frac{d\omega}{2\pi} e^{-i\omega t}[G^A(\mathbf{k},\omega) - G^R(\mathbf{k},\omega)]$$

$$\approx 2i\gamma_k a \int_{\mu/\hbar - i\infty}^{\mu/\hbar} \frac{d\omega}{2\pi} \frac{e^{-i\omega t}}{(\omega - \hbar^{-1}\epsilon_k)^2 + \gamma_k^2}$$

$$= -\frac{\gamma_k a\, e^{-i\mu t/\hbar}}{\pi} \int_0^\infty du\, \frac{e^{-ut}}{\gamma_k^2 + [\hbar^{-1}(\mu - \epsilon_k) - iu]^2}$$

$$\approx -(\pi t)^{-1}\gamma_k a\hbar^2(\mu - \epsilon_k)^{-2} e^{-i\mu t/\hbar} \ll -ia\, e^{-i\epsilon_k t/\hbar} e^{-\gamma_k t} \tag{7.80}$$

where the third line is obtained with the substitution $u = i(\omega - \hbar^{-1}\mu)$. The final form follows by using assumptions 1 and 2, along with the condition $\gamma_k \ll \hbar^{-1}(\epsilon_k - \mu)$. Note that the last inequality in Eq. (7.80) fails if t is too large or too small. In a wholly analogous fashion, the poles of the analytic continuation of $G^A(\mathbf{k},\omega)$ into the upper half ω plane determine the frequency and lifetime of the state obtained by creating a hole (destroying a particle) in the interacting ground state.

---

[1] The apparent exponential decay is slightly misleading because condition 2 restricts us to the region where $e^{-\gamma t} \approx 1 - \gamma t$.

8□WICK'S THEOREM[1]

The preceding section defined the single-particle Green's function and exhibited its relation to observable properties. This analysis in no way solves the fundamental many-body problem, however, and we must still calculate G for nontrivial physical systems. As our general method of attack, we shall evaluate the Green's function with perturbation theory. This procedure is most easily carried out in the interaction picture, where the various terms can be enumerated with a theorem of Wick, derived in this section. The remainder of this chapter (Sec. 9) is devoted to the diagrammatic analysis of the perturbation series.

The Green's function consists of a matrix element of Heisenberg operators in the exact interacting ground state. This form is inconvenient for perturbation theory, and we now prove a basic theorem that relates the matrix element of a Heisenberg operator $\hat{O}_H(t)$ to the matrix element of the corresponding interaction operator $\hat{O}_I(t)$:

$$\frac{\langle \Psi_0 | \hat{O}_H(t) | \Psi_0 \rangle}{\langle \Psi_0 | \Psi_0 \rangle} = \frac{1}{\langle \Phi_0 | \hat{S} | \Phi_0 \rangle} \langle \Phi_0 | \sum_{\nu=0}^{\infty} \left(\frac{-i}{\hbar} \right)^{\nu} \frac{1}{\nu!} \int_{-\infty}^{\infty} dt_1 \cdots \int_{-\infty}^{\infty} dt_{\nu}$$

$$\times \, e^{-\epsilon(|t_1| + \cdots + |t_\nu|)} T[\hat{H}_1(t_1) \cdots \hat{H}_1(t_\nu) \hat{O}_I(t)] | \Phi_0 \rangle \quad (8.1)$$

Here the operator $\hat{S}$ is defined by

$$\hat{S} = \hat{U}_\epsilon(\infty, -\infty) \quad (8.2)$$

The proof is as follows: The Gell-Mann and Low theorem expresses the ground state of the interacting system in the interaction picture

$$\frac{|\Psi_0\rangle}{\langle \Phi_0 | \Psi_0 \rangle} = \frac{\hat{U}_\epsilon(0, \pm\infty) | \Phi_0 \rangle}{\langle \Phi_0 | \hat{U}_\epsilon(0, \pm\infty) | \Phi_0 \rangle}$$

The denominator on the left side of Eq. (8.1) can be calculated by writing $\hat{U}_\epsilon(0, -\infty) | \Phi_0 \rangle$ on the right and $\hat{U}_\epsilon(0, \infty) | \Phi_0 \rangle$ on the left

$$\frac{\langle \Psi_0 | \Psi_0 \rangle}{|\langle \Phi_0 | \Psi_0 \rangle|^2} = \frac{\langle \Phi_0 | \hat{U}_\epsilon(0, \infty)^\dagger \hat{U}_\epsilon(0, -\infty) | \Phi_0 \rangle}{|\langle \Phi_0 | \Psi_0 \rangle|^2}$$

$$= \frac{\langle \Phi_0 | \hat{U}_\epsilon(\infty, 0) \hat{U}_\epsilon(0, -\infty) | \Phi_0 \rangle}{|\langle \Phi_0 | \Psi_0 \rangle|^2}$$

$$= \frac{\langle \Phi_0 | \hat{S} | \Phi_0 \rangle}{|\langle \Phi_0 | \Psi_0 \rangle|^2} \quad (8.3)$$

where both Eqs. (6.15) and (6.16) have been used. In a similar way, the numerator on the left side of Eq. (8.1) becomes, with the aid of Eq. (6.31),

$$\frac{\langle \Phi_0 | \hat{U}_\epsilon(\infty, 0) \hat{U}_\epsilon(0, t) \hat{O}_I(t) \hat{U}_\epsilon(t, 0) \hat{U}_\epsilon(0, -\infty) | \Phi_0 \rangle}{|\langle \Phi_0 | \Psi_0 \rangle|^2}$$

$$= \frac{\langle \Phi_0 | \hat{U}_\epsilon(\infty, t) \hat{O}_I(t) \hat{U}_\epsilon(t, -\infty) | \Phi_0 \rangle}{|\langle \Phi_0 | \Psi_0 \rangle|^2} \quad (8.4)$$

[1] G. C. Wick, *Phys. Rev.*, **80**:268 (1950).

The common denominators of Eqs. (8.3) and (8.4) cancel in forming the ratio, and we find

$$\frac{\langle \Psi_0 | \hat{O}_H(t) | \Psi_0 \rangle}{\langle \Psi_0 | \Psi_0 \rangle} = \frac{\langle \Phi_0 | \hat{U}_\epsilon(\infty,t)\, \hat{O}_I(t)\, \hat{U}_\epsilon(t,-\infty) | \Phi_0 \rangle}{\langle \Phi_0 | \hat{S} | \Phi_0 \rangle} \tag{8.5}$$

The remaining problem is to rewrite the numerator of the right side of Eq. (8.5), containing the operator

$$\hat{U}_\epsilon(\infty,t)\, \hat{O}_I(t)\, \hat{U}_\epsilon(t,-\infty)$$

$$= \sum_{n=0}^{\infty} \left(\frac{-i}{\hbar} \right)^n \frac{1}{n!} \int_t^\infty dt_1 \cdots \int_t^\infty dt_n\, e^{-\epsilon(|t_1| + \cdots + |t_n|)}\, T[\hat{H}_1(t_1) \cdots \hat{H}_1(t_n)]$$

$$\times \hat{O}_I(t) \sum_{m=0}^{\infty} \left(\frac{-i}{\hbar} \right)^m \frac{1}{m!} \int_{-\infty}^t dt_1 \cdots \int_{-\infty}^t dt_m$$

$$\times e^{-\epsilon(|t_1| + \cdots + |t_m|)}\, T[\hat{H}_1(t_1) \cdots \hat{H}_1(t_m)] \tag{8.6}$$

where Eq. (6.37) has been used. The theorem will now be proved by demonstrating that the operator in the numerator on the right side of Eq. (8.1) is equal to Eq. (8.6). In the νth term of the sum in Eq. (8.1), divide the integration variables into n factors with $t_i > t$ and m factors with $t_i < t$, where $m + n = \nu$. There are $\nu!/m!n!$ ways to make this partition, and a summation over all values of m and n consistent with the restriction $\nu = m + n$ completely enumerates the regions of integration in this ν-fold multiple integral. The operator in Eq. (8.1) therefore becomes

$$\sum_{\nu=0}^{\infty} \left(\frac{-i}{\hbar} \right)^\nu \frac{1}{\nu!} \sum_{n=0}^{\infty} \sum_{m=0}^{\infty} \delta_{\nu, m+n} \frac{\nu!}{m!n!} \int_t^\infty dt_1 \cdots \int_t^\infty dt_n\, e^{-\epsilon(|t_1| + \cdots + |t_n|)}$$

$$\times T[\hat{H}_1(t_1) \cdots \hat{H}_1(t_n)]\, \hat{O}_I(t) \int_{-\infty}^t dt_1 \cdots \int_{-\infty}^t dt_m$$

$$\times e^{-\epsilon(|t_1| + \cdots + |t_m|)}\, T[\hat{H}_1(t_1) \cdots \hat{H}_1(t_m)] \tag{8.7}$$

The Kronecker delta here ensures that $m + n = \nu$, but it also can be used to perform the summation over ν, which proves the theorem because Eq. (8.7) then reduces to Eq. (8.6).

In a similar manner, the expectation value of time-ordered Heisenberg operators may be written as

$$\frac{\langle \Psi_0 | T[\hat{O}_H(t)\, \hat{O}_H(t')] | \Psi_0 \rangle}{\langle \Psi_0 | \Psi_0 \rangle} = \frac{1}{\langle \Phi_0 | \hat{S} | \Phi_0 \rangle} \langle \Phi_0 | \sum_{\nu=0}^{\infty} \left(\frac{-i}{\hbar} \right)^\nu \frac{1}{\nu!}$$

$$\times \int_{-\infty}^\infty dt_1 \cdots \int_{-\infty}^\infty dt_\nu\, e^{-\epsilon(|t_1| + \cdots + |t_\nu|)}$$

$$\times T[\hat{H}_1(t_1) \cdots \hat{H}_1(t_\nu)\, \hat{O}_I(t)\, \hat{O}_I(t')] | \Phi_0 \rangle \tag{8.8}$$

This result depends on the observation

$$\langle\Phi_0|\hat{U}_\epsilon(\infty,0)\,[\hat{U}_\epsilon(0,t)\,\hat{O}_I(t)\,\hat{U}_\epsilon(t,0)]\,[\hat{U}_\epsilon(0,t')\,\hat{O}_I(t')\,\hat{U}_\epsilon(t',0)]\,\hat{U}_\epsilon(0,-\infty)|\Phi_0\rangle$$
$$=\langle\Phi_0|\hat{U}_\epsilon(\infty,t)\,\hat{O}_I(t)\,\hat{U}_\epsilon(t,t')\,\hat{O}_I(t')\,\hat{U}_\epsilon(t',-\infty)|\Phi_0\rangle$$

and we must therefore partition the integration variables into three distinct groups. Otherwise, the proof is identical with that of Eq. (8.1). Since Eqs. (8.1) and (8.8) both consist of ratios, the divergent phase factors cancel, and it is permissible to take the limit $\epsilon \to 0$. In this last form, these theorems are among the most useful results of quantum field theory.

As an interesting example, the exact Green's function may be written as

$$iG_{\alpha\beta}(x,y) = \sum_{\nu=0}^{\infty}\left(\frac{-i}{\hbar}\right)^\nu \frac{1}{\nu!}\int_{-\infty}^{\infty}dt_1\cdots\int_{-\infty}^{\infty}dt_\nu$$

$$\times \frac{\langle\Phi_0|T[\hat{H}_1(t_1)\cdots\hat{H}_1(t_\nu)\,\hat{\psi}_\alpha(x)\,\hat{\psi}_\beta^\dagger(y)]|\Phi_0\rangle}{\langle\Phi_0|\hat{S}|\Phi_0\rangle} \quad (8.9)$$

where the notation $x \equiv (\mathbf{x},x_0) \equiv (\mathbf{x},t_x)$ has been introduced. Here and henceforth, the subscript I will be omitted, since we shall consistently work in the interaction picture. It is also convenient to rewrite the interparticle potential in $\hat{H}_1$ as

$$U(x_1,x_2) \equiv V(\mathbf{x}_1,\mathbf{x}_2)\,\delta(t_1 - t_2) \quad (8.10)$$

which allows us to write the integrations symmetrically.[1] For example, the numerator of Eq. (8.9), which we will denote by $i\tilde{G}$, becomes

$$i\tilde{G}_{\alpha\beta}(x,y) \equiv iG_{\alpha\beta}^0(x,y) + \left(\frac{-i}{\hbar}\right)\sum_{\substack{\lambda\lambda'\\\mu\mu'}}\frac{1}{2}\int d^4x_1\,d^4x_1'\,U(x_1,x_1')_{\lambda\lambda',\mu\mu'}$$

$$\times\langle\Phi_0|T[\hat{\psi}_\lambda^\dagger(x_1)\,\hat{\psi}_\mu^\dagger(x_1')\,\hat{\psi}_{\mu'}(x_1')\,\hat{\psi}_{\lambda'}(x_1)\,\hat{\psi}_\alpha(x)\,\hat{\psi}_\beta^\dagger(y)]|\Phi_0\rangle + \cdots \quad (8.11)$$

where $iG_{\alpha\beta}^0(x,y) = \langle\Phi_0|T[\hat{\psi}_\alpha(x)\,\hat{\psi}_\beta^\dagger(y)]|\Phi_0\rangle$ refers to the noninteracting system. This expression shows that we must evaluate the expectation value in the noninteracting ground state of T products of creation and destruction operators of the form

$$\langle\Phi_0|T[\hat{\psi}^\dagger\cdots\hat{\psi}\hat{\psi}_\alpha(x)\,\hat{\psi}_\beta^\dagger(y)]|\Phi_0\rangle \quad (8.12)$$

[1] The Green's function now assumes a covariant appearance and, indeed, is just that obtained in relativistic quantum electrodynamics, where the interaction of Eq. (8.10) is mediated by the exchange of virtual photons of the electromagnetic field. The only difference is that quantum electrodynamics involves the retarded electromagnetic interaction, whereas the present theory involves a static instantaneous potential proportional to a delta function $\delta(t_1 - t_2)$. It should be emphasized, however, that the *formalism* developed here applies equally well to relativistic quantum field theory, which is especially evident in Chap. 12, where we consider a nonrelativistic retarded interaction arising from phonon exchange.

It is clear that the creation and destruction operators must be paired or the expectation value vanishes; even in this lowest-order term, however, the straightforward approach of classifying all possible contributions by direct application of the commutation or anticommutation relations is very lengthy. Instead, we shall rely on Wick's theorem, which provides a general procedure for evaluating such matrix elements.

The essential idea is to move all destruction operators to the right, where they annihilate the noninteracting ground state. In so doing, we generate additional terms, proportional to the commutators or anticommutators of the operators involved in the interchanges of positions. For most purposes, it is more convenient to use the field operators directly rather than the operators $\{c_k\}$ referring to a single mode. In most systems of interest, $\hat{\psi}(x)$ can be uniquely separated into a destruction part $\hat{\psi}^{(+)}(x)$ that annihilates the noninteracting ground state and a creation part $\hat{\psi}^{(-)}(x)$.‡

$$\hat{\psi}(x) = \hat{\psi}^{(+)}(x) + \hat{\psi}^{(-)}(x) \tag{8.13}$$

$$\hat{\psi}^{(+)}(x)|\Phi_0\rangle = 0 \tag{8.14}$$

Correspondingly, the adjoint operator becomes

$$\hat{\psi}^\dagger(x) = \hat{\psi}^{(+)\dagger}(x) + \hat{\psi}^{(-)\dagger}(x) \tag{8.15}$$

where

$$\hat{\psi}^{(-)\dagger}(x)|\Phi_0\rangle = 0 \tag{8.16}$$

Thus $\hat{\psi}^{(+)}(x)$ and $\hat{\psi}^{(-)\dagger}(x)$ are both destruction parts, while $\hat{\psi}^{(-)}(x)$ and $\hat{\psi}^{(+)\dagger}(x)$ are both creation parts. The notation is a vestige of the original application of Wick's theorem to relativistic quantum field theory, where $(+)$ and $(-)$ signs refer to a Lorentz-invariant decomposition into positive and negative frequency parts. For our purposes, however, they can be considered superscripts denoting destruction and creation parts. As an explicit example of this decomposition, consider the free fermion field, rewritten with the canonical transformation of Eq. (7.34):

$$\hat{\psi}(x) = \sum_{k\lambda > k_F} V^{-\frac{1}{2}} e^{i(k\cdot x - \omega_k t)} \eta_\lambda a_{k\lambda} + \sum_{k\lambda < k_F} V^{-\frac{1}{2}} e^{i(k\cdot x - \omega_k t)} \eta_\lambda b^\dagger_{-k\lambda}$$

$$\equiv \hat{\psi}^{(+)}(x) + \hat{\psi}^{(-)}(x) \tag{8.17}$$

In this case, the symbols $(+)$ and $(-)$ may be interpreted as the sign of the frequencies of the field components *measured with respect to the Fermi energy*.

To present Wick's theorem in a concise and useful manner, it is necessary to introduce some new definitions.

1. *T product*: The T product of a collection of field operators has already been defined [Eq. (7.4)]. It orders the field operators with the latest time on

‡ For a discussion of the special problems inherent in the treatment of condensed Bose systems, see Chap. 6.

the left and includes an additional factor of -1 for each interchange of fermion operators.   By definition

$$T(\hat{A}\hat{B}\hat{C}\hat{D} \cdot \cdot \cdot) = (-1)^P T(\hat{C}\hat{A}\hat{D}\hat{B} \cdot \cdot \cdot) \tag{8.18}$$

where P is the number of permutations of fermion operators needed to rearrange the product as given on the left side of Eq. (8.18) to agree with the order on the right side.   It is clearly permissible to treat the boson fields as if they commute and the fermion fields as if they anticommute when reordering fields *within* a T product.

2.   *Normal ordering*: This term represents a different ordering of a product of field operators, in which all the annihilation operators are placed to the right of all the creation operators, again including a factor of -1 for every interchange of fermion operators.   By definition

$$N(\hat{A}\hat{B}\hat{C}\hat{D} \cdot \cdot \cdot) = (-1)^P N(\hat{C}\hat{A}\hat{D}\hat{B} \cdot \cdot \cdot) \tag{8.19}$$

so that the fields *within* a normal-ordered product can again be treated as if they commute (bosons) or anticommute (fermions).   For example, if we deal with fermion fields,

$$N[\hat{\psi}^{(+)}(x)\,\hat{\psi}^{(-)}(y)] = -\hat{\psi}^{(-)}(y)\,\hat{\psi}^{(+)}(x)$$

$$N[\hat{\psi}^{(+)}(x)\,\hat{\psi}^{(+)\dagger}(y)] = -\hat{\psi}^{(+)\dagger}(y)\,\hat{\psi}^{(+)}(x) \tag{8.20}$$

In both cases the creation part of the field is written to the left, and the factor -1 reflects the single interchange of fermion operators.   The reader is urged to write out several examples of each definition.

A normal-ordered product of field operators is especially convenient because *its expectation value in the unperturbed ground state* $|\Phi_0\rangle$ *vanishes identically* [see Eqs. (8.14) and (8.16)].   This result remains true even if the product consists entirely of creation parts, as is clear from the adjoint of the equations defining the destruction parts.   Thus the ground-state expectation value of a T product of operators [for example (8.12)] may be evaluated by reducing it to the corresponding N product; the fundamental problem is the enumeration of the additional terms introduced in the reduction.   This process is simplified by noting that *both the T product and the N product are distributive.* For example,

$$N[(\hat{A} + \hat{B})(\hat{C} + \hat{D}) \cdot \cdot \cdot] = N(\hat{A}\hat{C} \cdot \cdot \cdot) + N(\hat{A}\hat{D} \cdot \cdot \cdot) + N(\hat{B}\hat{C} \cdot \cdot \cdot)$$
$$+ N(\hat{B}\hat{D} \cdot \cdot \cdot) + \cdot \cdot \cdot$$

It is therefore sufficient to prove the theorems separately for creation or destruction parts.

3.   *Contractions*: The contraction of two operators $\hat{U}$ and $\hat{V}$ is denoted $\hat{U}^{\cdot}\,\hat{V}^{\cdot}$ and is equal to the difference between the T product and the N product.

$$\hat{U}^{\cdot}\,\hat{V}^{\cdot} \equiv T(\hat{U}\hat{V}) - N(\hat{U}\hat{V}) \tag{8.21}$$

It represents the additional term introduced by rearranging a time-ordered product into a normal-ordered product and is therefore different for different time orderings of the operators. As an example, all of the following contractions vanish

$$\hat{\psi}^{(+)\cdot}\,\hat{\psi}^{(-)\cdot} = \hat{\psi}^{(+)\dagger\cdot}\,\hat{\psi}^{(-)\dagger\cdot} = \hat{\psi}^{(+)\dagger\cdot}\,\hat{\psi}^{(-)\cdot} = \hat{\psi}^{(+)\cdot}\,\hat{\psi}^{(-)\dagger\cdot} = 0 \tag{8.22}$$

because the T product of these operators is identical with the N product of the same operators. To be more specific, consider the first pair of operators in Eq. (8.22). Their T product is given by

$$T[\hat{\psi}^{(+)}(x)\,\hat{\psi}^{(-)}(y)] \equiv \begin{cases} \hat{\psi}^{(+)}(x)\,\hat{\psi}^{(-)}(y) & t_x > t_y \\ \pm\hat{\psi}^{(-)}(y)\,\hat{\psi}^{(+)}(x) & t_y > t_x \end{cases} \tag{8.23}$$

where the $\pm$ in the second line refers to bosons or fermions. But the field operator $\hat{\psi}$ is a linear combination of interaction-picture operators of the form $c_k e^{-i\omega_k t}$ [compare Eq. (6.10a)]. Thus, for either statistics, Eq. (8.23) may be rewritten as

$$T[\hat{\psi}^{(+)}(x)\,\hat{\psi}^{(-)}(y)] = \pm\hat{\psi}^{(-)}(y)\,\hat{\psi}^{(+)}(x) \tag{8.24}$$

because $\hat{\psi}^{(-)}$ and $\hat{\psi}^{(+)}$ commute or anticommute *at any time*. Note that this result is true *only* in the interaction picture, where the operator properties are the same as in the Schrödinger picture. By the definition of a normal-ordered product, we have

$$N[\hat{\psi}^{(+)}(x)\,\hat{\psi}^{(-)}(y)] \equiv \pm\hat{\psi}^{(-)}(y)\,\hat{\psi}^{(+)}(x) \tag{8.25}$$

and their contraction therefore vanishes

$$\hat{\psi}^{(+)}(x)^{\cdot}\,\hat{\psi}^{(-)}(y)^{\cdot} \equiv T[\hat{\psi}^{(+)}(x)\,\hat{\psi}^{(-)}(y)] - N[\hat{\psi}^{(+)}(x)\,\hat{\psi}^{(-)}(y)] = 0 \tag{8.26}$$

The other contractions in Eq. (8.22) also vanish because all of the paired interaction-picture operators commute or anticommute with each other.

Equation (8.22) shows that *most contractions are zero*. In particular, a contraction of two creation parts or two destruction parts vanishes, and the only nonzero contractions are given by

$$\hat{\psi}^{(+)}(x)^{\cdot}\,\hat{\psi}^{(+)\dagger}(y)^{\cdot} = \begin{cases} iG^0(x,y) & t_x > t_y \\ 0 & t_y > t_x \end{cases}$$

$$\hat{\psi}^{(-)}(x)^{\cdot}\,\hat{\psi}^{(-)\dagger}(y)^{\cdot} = \begin{cases} 0 & t_x > t_y \\ iG^0(x,y) & t_y > t_x \end{cases} \tag{8.27}$$

For fermions, this result is derived with the canonical anticommutation relations of the creation and destruction operators [Eq. (1.48)] and the definition of the free Green's function given in Eq. (7.41). A similar derivation applies for noncondensed bosons (see, for example, Chap. 12). Note that the contractions

are *c numbers* in the occupation-number Hilbert space, not operators.   Equation (8.27) is more simply derived with the observation

$$\langle\Phi_0|T(\hat{U}\hat{V})|\Phi_0\rangle = \langle\Phi_0|\hat{U}^{\cdot}\,\hat{V}^{\cdot}|\Phi_0\rangle + \langle\Phi_0|N(\hat{U}\hat{V})|\Phi_0\rangle = \hat{U}^{\cdot}\,\hat{V}^{\cdot} \qquad (8.28)$$

since $\langle\Phi_0|N(\hat{U}\hat{V})|\Phi_0\rangle$ vanishes by definition.   The distributive properties then yield the contraction of the field operators themselves

$$\hat{\psi}_\alpha(x)^{\cdot}\,\hat{\psi}^{\dagger}_\beta(y)^{\cdot} = iG^0_{\alpha\beta}(x,y) \qquad (8.29)$$

4. *A convention*: We introduce a further sign convention. Normal-ordered products of field operators with more than one contraction will have the contractions denoted by pairs of superscripts with single dots, double dots, etc. Two factors that are contracted must be brought together by rearranging the order of the operators within the normal product, always keeping the standard sign convention for interchange of operators.   The contracted operators are then to be replaced by the value of the contraction given by Eq. (8.27).   Since this contraction is now just a function of the coordinate variables, it can be taken outside of the normal-ordered product.

$$N(\hat{A}^{\cdot}\,\hat{B}\hat{C}^{\cdot}\,\hat{D}\,\cdot\,\cdot\,\cdot) = \pm N(\hat{A}^{\cdot}\,\hat{C}^{\cdot}\,\hat{B}\hat{D}\,\cdot\,\cdot\,\cdot) = +\hat{A}^{\cdot}\,\hat{C}^{\cdot}\,N(\hat{B}\hat{D}\,\cdot\,\cdot\,\cdot) \qquad (8.30)$$

Finally, note that

$$\hat{U}^{\cdot}\,\hat{V}^{\cdot} = \pm\hat{V}^{\cdot}\,\hat{U}^{\cdot} \qquad (8.31)$$

which follows from Eq. (8.21) and the definition of T product and normal-ordered product.   It is now possible to state

5. *Wick's theorem*:

$$T(\hat{U}\hat{V}\hat{W}\,\cdot\,\cdot\,\cdot\,\hat{X}\hat{Y}\hat{Z}) = N(\hat{U}\hat{V}\hat{W}\,\cdot\,\cdot\,\cdot\,\hat{X}\hat{Y}\hat{Z}) + N(\hat{U}^{\cdot}\,\hat{V}^{\cdot}\,\hat{W}\,\cdot\,\cdot\,\cdot\,\hat{X}\hat{Y}\hat{Z})$$

$$+ N(\hat{U}^{\cdot}\,\hat{V}\hat{W}^{\cdot}\,\cdot\,\cdot\,\cdot\,\hat{X}\hat{Y}\hat{Z}) + \cdot\,\cdot\,\cdot$$

$$+ N(\hat{U}^{\cdot}\,\hat{V}^{\cdot\cdot}\,\hat{W}^{\cdot\cdot\cdot}\,\cdot\,\cdot\,\cdot\,\hat{X}^{\cdot\cdot\cdot}\,\hat{Y}^{\cdot\cdot}\,\hat{Z}^{\cdot})$$

$$= N(\hat{U}\hat{V}\hat{W}\,\cdot\,\cdot\,\cdot\,\hat{X}\hat{Y}\hat{Z})$$

$$+ N(\text{sum over all possible pairs of} \atop \text{contractions}) \qquad (8.32)$$

The basic idea of the theorem is as follows: Consider a given time ordering, and start moving the creation parts to the left within this product of field operators. Each time a creation part fails to commute or anticommute, it generates an additional term, which is just the contraction.   It is permissible to include *all* possible contractions, since the contraction vanishes if the creation part is already to the left of the destruction part (remember that *most contractions are zero*); hence the theorem clearly enumerates all the extra terms that occur in reordering a T product into a normal-ordered product.

To prove the theorem, we shall follow Wick's derivation and first prove the following.

6. *Basic lemma*: If $N(\hat{U}\hat{V} \cdots \hat{X}\hat{Y})$ is a normal-ordered product and $\hat{Z}$ is a factor *labeled with a time earlier* than the times for $\hat{U}$, $\hat{V} \cdots \hat{X}$, $\hat{Y}$, then

$$N(\hat{U}\hat{V} \cdots \hat{X}\hat{Y})\hat{Z} = N(\hat{U}\hat{V} \cdots \hat{X}\hat{Y}\cdot\overset{\cdot}{\hat{Z}}) + N(\hat{U}\hat{V} \cdots \overset{\cdot}{\hat{X}}\cdot \hat{Y}\hat{Z}\cdot)$$

$$+ \cdots + N(\hat{U}\cdot\overset{\cdot}{\hat{V}} \cdots \hat{X}\hat{Y}\hat{Z}\cdot) + N(\hat{U}\hat{V} \cdots \hat{X}\hat{Y}\hat{Z}) \quad (8.33)$$

Thus if a normal-ordered product is multiplied on the right with any operator at an earlier time, we obtain a sum of normal-ordered products containing the extra operator contracted in turn with all the operators standing in the original product, along with a term where the extra operator is included within the normal-ordered product. To prove the lemma, note the following points:

(*a*) If $\hat{Z}$ is a destruction operator, then all the contractions vanish since $T(\hat{A}\hat{Z}) = N(\hat{A}\hat{Z})$. Thus, only the last term in Eq. (8.33) contributes and the lemma is proved.

(*b*) The operator product $\hat{U}\hat{V} \cdots \hat{X}\hat{Y}$ can be assumed to be normal ordered, since otherwise the operators can be reordered on *both sides* of the equation. Our sign conventions ensure the same signature factor occurs in each term of Eq. (8.33) and therefore cancels identically.

(*c*) We can further assume that $\hat{Z}$ is a creation operator, and $\hat{U} \cdots \hat{Y}$ are all destruction operators. If the lemma is proved in this form, creation operators may be included by multiplying on the left; the additional contractions so introduced vanish identically and can therefore be added to the right side of Eq. (8.33) without changing the result.

Hence it is sufficient to prove Eq. (8.33) for $\hat{Z}$ a creation operator and $\hat{U} \cdots \hat{Y}$ destruction operators. The proof follows by induction. Equation (8.33) is evidently true for two operators by definition [Eq. (8.21)]

$$\hat{Y}\hat{Z} = T(\hat{Y}\hat{Z}) = \hat{Y}\cdot\hat{Z}\cdot + N(\hat{Y}\hat{Z}) \quad (8.34)$$

We now assume it is true for n operators and prove it for $n + 1$ operators. Multiply the lemma (8.33) on the left by another destruction operator $\hat{D}$ having a time later than that of $\hat{Z}$.

$$\hat{D}N(\hat{U}\hat{V} \cdots \hat{X}\hat{Y})\hat{Z}$$

$$= N(\hat{D}\hat{U}\hat{V} \cdots \hat{X}\hat{Y})\hat{Z}$$

$$= N(\hat{D}\hat{U}\hat{V} \cdots \hat{X}\hat{Y}\cdot\hat{Z}\cdot) + N(\hat{D}\hat{U}\hat{V} \cdots \overset{\cdot}{\hat{X}}\cdot \hat{Y}\hat{Z}\cdot) + \cdots$$

$$+ N(\hat{D}\hat{U}\cdot\overset{\cdot}{\hat{V}} \cdots \hat{X}\hat{Y}\hat{Z}\cdot) + \hat{D}N(\hat{U}\hat{V} \cdots \hat{X}\hat{Y}\hat{Z}) \quad (8.35)$$

Since $\hat{U}$, $\hat{V} \cdots \hat{X}$, $\hat{Y}$ are all destruction operators and the contraction of $\hat{Z}$ with any destruction operator is a c number, $\hat{D}$ has been taken inside the normal ordering except for the very last term in Eq. (8.35), where $\hat{Z}$ is still an operator.

Consider this last term, which, we assert, can be written as

$$\hat{D}N(\hat{U}\hat{V} \cdots \hat{X}\hat{Y}\hat{Z}) = N(\hat{D}^{\cdot}\,\hat{U}\hat{V} \cdots \hat{X}\hat{Y}\hat{Z}^{\cdot}) + N(\hat{D}\hat{U}\hat{V} \cdots \hat{X}\hat{Y}\hat{Z}) \tag{8.36}$$

This equation is readily verified.

$$\hat{D}N(\hat{U}\hat{V} \cdots \hat{X}\hat{Y}\hat{Z})$$

$$= (-1)^{P}\,\hat{D}\hat{Z}\hat{U}\hat{V} \cdots \hat{X}\hat{Y}$$

$$= (-1)^{P}\,T(\hat{D}\hat{Z})\,\hat{U}\hat{V} \cdots \hat{X}\hat{Y}$$

$$= (-1)^{P}\,\hat{D}^{\cdot}\hat{Z}^{\cdot}\,\hat{U}\hat{V} \cdots \hat{X}\hat{Y} + (-1)^{P+Q}\,N(\hat{Z}\hat{D})\,\hat{U}\hat{V} \cdots \hat{X}\hat{Y}$$

$$= [(-1)^{P}]^{2}\,\hat{D}^{\cdot}\,\hat{U}\hat{V} \cdots \hat{X}\hat{Y}\hat{Z}^{\cdot} + [(-1)^{P+Q}]^{2}\,N(\hat{D}\hat{U}\hat{V} \cdots \hat{X}\hat{Y}\hat{Z})$$

$$= N(\hat{D}^{\cdot}\,\hat{U}\hat{V} \cdots \hat{X}\hat{Y}\hat{Z}^{\cdot}) + N(\hat{D}\hat{U}\hat{V} \cdots \hat{X}\hat{Y}\hat{Z}) \tag{8.37}$$

In the second line $\hat{Z}$ is moved to the left within the normal-ordered product, introducing a signature factor $(-1)^{P}$. The factors now appear in normal order, and the N product can be removed. Furthermore, the product $\hat{D}\hat{Z}$ is already time ordered by assumption. The fourth line follows from the definition of a contraction, with a factor $(-1)^{Q}$ arising from the interchange of $\hat{D}$ and $\hat{Z}$. The last term in the fourth line is in normal order, because $\hat{U}\hat{V} \cdots \hat{X}\hat{Y}$ are all destruction operators. The sign conventions then allow us to reorder the operators to obtain the final form, which proves the basic lemma (8.33).

The result can be generalized to normal-ordered products already containing contractions of field operators. Multiply both sides of Eq. (8.33) by the contraction of two more operators, $\hat{R}^{\cdot\cdot}\hat{S}^{\cdot\cdot}$, say, and then interchange the operators on *both sides*. Each term has the same overall sign change which cancels identically. Thus we can rewrite the basic lemma (8.33) as

$$N(\hat{U}\hat{V}^{\cdot\cdot} \cdots \hat{X}^{\cdot\cdot}\hat{Y})\hat{Z} = N(\hat{U}\hat{V}^{\cdot\cdot} \cdots \hat{X}^{\cdot\cdot}\,\hat{Y}^{\cdot}\hat{Z}^{\cdot}) + \cdots$$

$$+ N(\hat{U}^{\cdot}\,\hat{V}^{\cdot\cdot} \cdots \hat{X}^{\cdot\cdot}\,\hat{Y}\hat{Z}^{\cdot}) + N(\hat{U}\hat{V}^{\cdot\cdot} \cdots \hat{X}^{\cdot\cdot}\hat{Y}\hat{Z}) \tag{8.38}$$

7. *Proof of Wick's theorem*: Again the theorem will be proved by induction. It is obviously true for two operators, by the definition of a contraction

$$T(\hat{U}\hat{V}) = N(\hat{U}\hat{V}) + \hat{U}^{\cdot}\,\hat{V}^{\cdot} \tag{8.39}$$

Assume it is true for n factors, and multiply on the right by an operator $\hat{\Omega}$ with a time *earlier* than that of any other factor.

$$T(\hat{U}\hat{V}\hat{W} \cdots \hat{X}\hat{Y}\hat{Z})\hat{\Omega}$$

$$= T(\hat{U}\hat{V}\hat{W} \cdots \hat{X}\hat{Y}\hat{Z}\hat{\Omega})$$

$$= N(\hat{U}\hat{V}\hat{W} \cdots \hat{X}\hat{Y}\hat{Z})\hat{\Omega} + N(\hat{U}^{\cdot}\,\hat{V}^{\cdot}\,\hat{W} \cdots \hat{X}\hat{Y}\hat{Z})\hat{\Omega} + \cdots$$

$$= N(\hat{U}\hat{V}\hat{W} \cdots \hat{X}\hat{Y}\hat{Z}\hat{\Omega})$$

$$+ N(\text{sum over all possible pairs of contractions}) \tag{8.40}$$

The operator $\hat{\Omega}$ can be included in the T product because it is at a time earlier than any of those already in the T product. On the right side, we use our basic lemma (8.33) to introduce the operator $\hat{\Omega}$ into the normal-ordered products. The restriction on the time of the operator $\hat{\Omega}$ can now be removed by simultaneously reordering the operators in each term of Eq. (8.40). Again the sign conventions give the same overall sign on both sides of the equation, which therefore remains correct. Wick's theorem has now been proved under the assumption that the operators are either creation or destruction parts of the field. The T product and the normal-ordered product are both distributive, however, and Wick's theorem thus applies to the fields themselves.

It must be emphasized that Wick's theorem is an *operator identity* that remains true for an arbitrary matrix element. Its real use, however, is for a ground-state average $\langle \Phi_0 | \cdots | \Phi_0 \rangle$, where all uncontracted normal-ordered products vanish. In particular, the exact Green's function [Eq. (8.9)] consists of all possible fully contracted terms.

9□DIAGRAMMATIC ANALYSIS OF PERTURBATION THEORY

Wick's theorem allows us to evaluate the exact Green's function (8.9) as a perturbation expansion involving only wholly contracted field operators in the interaction picture. These contractions are just the free-field Green's functions G^0 [Eq. (8.29)], and G is thereby expressed in a series containing U and G^0. This expansion can be analyzed directly in coordinate space, or (for a uniform system) in momentum space. As noted previously, the zero-temperature theory for condensed bosons requires a special treatment (Chap. 6), and we shall consider only fermions in this section.

FEYNMAN DIAGRAMS IN COORDINATE SPACE

As an example of the utility of Wick's theorem, we shall calculate the first-order contributions in Eq. (8.11). The expectation value of all the terms containing normal-ordered products of operators vanishes in the noninteracting ground state $|\Phi_0\rangle$, leaving only the fully contracted products of field operators. Wick's theorem then requires us to sum over all possible contractions, and Eq. (8.29) shows that the only nonvanishing contraction is between a field $\hat{\psi}_\alpha$ and an adjoint field $\hat{\psi}^\dagger_\beta$. In this way, the first-order term of Eq. (8.11) becomes

$$i\tilde{G}^{(1)}_{\alpha\beta}(x,y) = \frac{-i}{\hbar} \frac{1}{2} \sum_{\lambda\lambda'\mu\mu'} \int d^4x_1\, d^4x_1'\, U(x_1,x_1')_{\lambda\lambda',\mu\mu'}$$

$$\{iG^0_{\alpha\beta}(x,y)\,[iG^0_{\mu'\,\mu}(x_1',x_1')\,iG^0_{\lambda'\,\lambda}(x_1,x_1) - iG^0_{\mu'\,\lambda}(x_1',x_1)\,iG^0_{\lambda'\,\mu}(x_1,x_1')]$$
$$\quad\quad\quad\quad (A) \quad\quad\quad\quad\quad\quad\quad\quad\quad\quad\quad\quad\quad\quad\quad (B)$$

$$+ iG^0_{\alpha\lambda}(x,x_1)\,[iG^0_{\lambda'\,\mu}(x_1,x_1')\,iG^0_{\mu'\,\beta}(x_1',y) - iG^0_{\lambda'\,\beta}(x_1,y)\,iG^0_{\mu'\,\mu}(x_1',x_1')]$$
$$\quad\quad\quad\quad (C) \quad\quad\quad\quad\quad\quad\quad\quad\quad\quad\quad\quad\quad\quad\quad (D)$$

$$+ iG^0_{\alpha\mu}(x,x_1')\,[iG^0_{\mu'\,\lambda}(x_1',x_1)\,iG^0_{\lambda'\,\beta}(x_1,y) - iG^0_{\mu'\,\beta}(x_1',y)\,iG^0_{\lambda'\,\lambda}(x_1,x_1)]\} \quad (9.1)$$
$$\quad\quad\quad\quad (E) \quad\quad\quad\quad\quad\quad\quad\quad\quad\quad\quad\quad\quad\quad\quad (F)$$

The reader is urged to obtain Eq. (9.1) directly from Eq. (8.11) by enumerating all nonvanishing contributions for all possible time orderings. This procedure is very complicated, even in the first order, and Wick's theorem clearly provides a very powerful and simple tool.

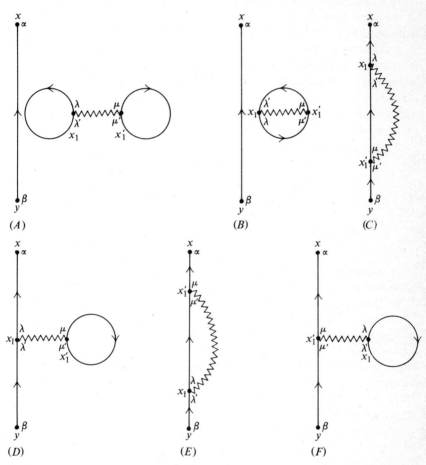

Fig. 9.1   First-order contributions to $\tilde{G}_{\alpha\beta}(x,y)$.

We can now associate a picture with each of the terms appearing in expression (9.1), as illustrated in Fig. 9.1.   The Green's function G^0 is denoted by a straight line with an arrow running from the second argument to the first, while the interaction potential is denoted by a wavy line.   These diagrams appearing in the perturbation analysis of G form a convenient way of classifying the terms obtained with Wick's theorem.   They are known as *Feynman diagrams* because the first diagrammatic expansion of this form was developed by Feynman in his

work on quantum electrodynamics.[1]   The precise relation with quantum field theory was first demonstrated by Dyson.[2]

The analytic expression in Eq. (9.1) and the corresponding diagrams (Fig. 9.1) have several interesting features.

1. The terms A, B, D, and F contain a Green's function with both arguments at the same time, which is indicated by a solid line closed on itself.   By the definition [Eq. (7.41)], the expression $iG^0_{\alpha\beta}(x,x)$ is ambiguous, and it is necessary to decide how to interpret it.   This quantity represents a contraction of $\hat{\psi}$ and $\hat{\psi}^\dagger$, but the time-ordered product is undefined at equal times.   Such a term, however, arises from a contraction of two fields *within* the interaction hamiltonian $\hat{H}_1$, where they appear in the form $\hat{\psi}^\dagger_\beta(x)\hat{\psi}_\alpha(x)$ with the adjoint field always occurring to the *left* of the field.   In consequence, the Green's function at equal times must be interpreted as

$$iG^0_{\alpha\beta}(x,x) = \lim_{t' \to t^+} \langle \Phi_0 | T[\hat{\psi}_\alpha(\mathbf{x}t)\,\hat{\psi}^\dagger_\beta(\mathbf{x}t')] | \Phi_0 \rangle$$

$$= -\langle \Phi_0 | \hat{\psi}^\dagger_\beta(\mathbf{x})\,\hat{\psi}_\alpha(\mathbf{x}) | \Phi_0 \rangle$$

$$= -(2s+1)^{-1}\,\delta_{\alpha\beta}\,n^0(\mathbf{x})$$

$$= -\frac{\delta_{\alpha\beta}\,N}{(2s+1)\,V} \qquad uniform \text{ system} \qquad (9.2)$$

for a system of spin-s fermions.   Here $n^0(\mathbf{x})$ is the particle density in the unperturbed ground state [compare Eq. (7.8)] and need not be identical with $n(\mathbf{x})$ in the interacting system because the interaction may redistribute the particles. For a uniform system, however, $n^0 = n = N/V$, because the interaction does not change the *total* number of particles.   The terms D and F thus represent the lowest-order direct interaction with all the particles that make up the non-interacting ground state (filled Fermi sea), while the terms C and E provide the corresponding lowest-order exchange interaction.   Here the terms "direct" and "exchange" arise from the original antisymmetrized Slater determinants, as discussed below Eq. (3.37).

2. The terms A and B are *disconnected diagrams*, containing subunits that are not connected to the rest of the diagram by any lines.   Equation (9.1) shows that such terms typically have Green's functions and interactions whose arguments close on themselves.   As a result, the contribution of this subunit can be factored out of the expression for $\tilde{G}$.   Thus, in the terms A and B above, $iG^0_{\alpha\beta}(x,y)$ represents one factor and the integral represents another factor.   To *first order in the interaction*, we assert that Eq. (8.11) can be rewritten as shown in Fig. 9.2.   Each diagram in this figure denotes a well-defined integral, given in Eq. (9.1).   The validity of Fig. 9.2 is readily verified by expanding the product and retaining only the first-order terms, which are just those in Fig. 9.1.   The

[1] R. P. Feynman, *loc. cit.*
[2] F. J. Dyson, *Phys. Rev.*, **75**:486 (1949); **75**:1736 (1949).

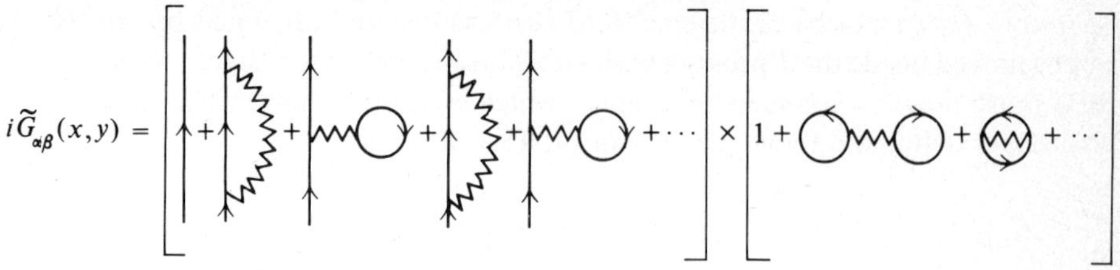

Fig. 9.2 Factorization of first-order contributions to $\tilde{G}_{\alpha\beta}(x,y)$.

additional terms of second order in the interaction are here unimportant because the present calculation is consistent only to *first* order in the interaction.

The denominator $\langle\Phi_0|\hat{S}|\Phi_0\rangle = \langle\Phi_0|\hat{U}(\infty,-\infty)|\Phi_0\rangle$ in Eq. (8.9) has been ignored to this point, and we shall now evaluate it to first order in the interaction potential. The operator $\hat{U}(\infty,-\infty)$ is the same as that in the numerator of Eq. (8.9), except that the operators $\hat{\psi}_\alpha(x)\hat{\psi}_\beta^\dagger(y)$ must be deleted. Thus the denominator can also be evaluated with Wick's theorem, and only the fully contracted terms contribute. The resulting calculation evidently yields the terms shown in Fig. 9.3, where each diagram again stands for a well-defined

Fig. 9.3 Disconnected diagrams in the denominator of $G_{\alpha\beta}(x,y)$.

$$\langle\Phi_0|\hat{S}|\Phi_0\rangle = 1 + + + \cdots$$

integral. These integrals are precisely the same as those appearing in the terms A and B of Eq. (9.1). We therefore conclude that *the contribution of the denominator in Eq. (8.9)* exactly *cancels the contribution of the disconnected diagrams in the numerator.* This important result has so far been verified only to lowest order in the interaction, but we shall now prove it to all orders.[1]

A disconnected diagram closes on itself; consequently, its contribution to $G_{\alpha\beta}(x,y)$ factors. Thus the νth-order term of the numerator of Eq. (8.9) can be written as

$$i\tilde{G}_{\alpha\beta}^{(\nu)}(x,y) = \sum_{n=0}^{\infty}\sum_{m=0}^{\infty}\left(\frac{-i}{\hbar}\right)^{n+m}\delta_{\nu,n+m}\frac{1}{\nu!}\frac{\nu!}{n!\,m!}\int_{-\infty}^{\infty}dt_1\cdots\int_{-\infty}^{\infty}dt_m$$

$$\times\langle\Phi_0|T[\hat{H}_1(t_1)\cdots\hat{H}_1(t_m)\hat{\psi}_\alpha(x)\hat{\psi}_\beta^\dagger(y)]|\Phi_0\rangle_{\text{connected}}$$

$$\times\int_{-\infty}^{\infty}dt_{m+1}\cdots\int_{-\infty}^{\infty}dt_\nu\langle\Phi_0|T[\hat{H}_1(t_{m+1})\cdots\hat{H}_1(t_\nu)]|\Phi_0\rangle$$

$$(9.3)$$

which can be seen by applying Wick's theorem on both sides of this expression. The second factor, containing n integrations, in general consists of many disconnected parts. The factor $\nu!/n!\,m!$ represents the number of ways that the ν

---

[1] Here we follow the proof given by A. A. Abrikosov, L. P. Gorkov, and I. E. Dzyaloshinskii, *op. cit.*, sec. 8.

operators $\hat{H}_1(t_i)$ can be partitioned into two groups, and, as noted before, $\hat{H}_1$ can be moved inside the T product with no additional changes of sign. Equation (9.3) must now be summed over all ν, which is trivially performed with the Kronecker delta, and the numerator of Eq. (8.9) becomes

$$
i\tilde{G}_{\alpha\beta}(x,y) = \sum_{m=0}^{\infty} \left(\frac{-i}{\hbar}\right)^m \frac{1}{m!} \int_{-\infty}^{\infty} dt_1 \cdots \int_{-\infty}^{\infty} dt_m
$$
$$
\times \langle \Phi_0 | T[\hat{H}_1(t_1) \cdots \hat{H}_1(t_m)\,\hat{\psi}_\alpha(x)\,\hat{\psi}_\beta^\dagger(y)] | \Phi_0 \rangle_{\text{connected}}
$$
$$
\times \sum_{n=0}^{\infty} \left(\frac{-i}{\hbar}\right)^n \frac{1}{n!} \int_{-\infty}^{\infty} dt_1 \cdots \int_{-\infty}^{\infty} dt_n
$$
$$
\times \langle \Phi_0 | T[\hat{H}_1(t_1) \cdots \hat{H}_1(t_n)] | \Phi_0 \rangle \tag{9.4}
$$

The first factor is the sum of all *connected* diagrams, while the second is identical with the denominator $\langle \Phi_0 | \hat{S} | \Phi_0 \rangle$. We therefore obtain the fundamental formula

$$
iG_{\alpha\beta}(x,y) = \sum_{m=0}^{\infty} \left(\frac{-i}{\hbar}\right)^m \frac{1}{m!} \int_{-\infty}^{\infty} dt_1 \cdots \int_{-\infty}^{\infty} dt_m
$$
$$
\times \langle \Phi_0 | T[\hat{H}_1(t_1) \cdots \hat{H}_1(t_m)\,\hat{\psi}_\alpha(x)\,\hat{\psi}_\beta^\dagger(y)] | \Phi_0 \rangle_{\text{connected}} \tag{9.5}
$$

which expresses the factorization of disconnected diagrams. A related "linked-cluster" expansion for the ground-state energy was first conjectured by Brueckner,[1] who verified the expansion to fourth order in the interaction potential; the proof to all orders was then given by Goldstone[2] with the techniques of quantum field theory. Equation (9.5) is important because it allows us to ignore all diagrams that contain parts not connected to the fermion line running from y to x.

The expansion of $G_{\alpha\beta}(x,y)$ into *connected* diagrams is wholly equivalent to the original perturbation series. These are the celebrated Feynman diagrams, and we shall now derive the precise rules that relate the diagrams to the terms of the perturbation series. It must be emphasized, however, that the detailed structure of the Feynman rules depends on the form of the interaction hamiltonian $\hat{H}_1$, and the present derivation applies *only* to a system of identical particles interacting through a two-body potential.

3. For any given diagram, there is an identical contribution from all similar diagrams that differ merely in the permutation of the labels $1 \cdots m$ in the interaction hamiltonian $\hat{H}_1$. For example, the two diagrams in Fig. 9.4 have the same numerical value because they differ merely in the labeling of the dummy integration variables. In addition, they have the same sign because

[1] K. A. Brueckner, *Phys. Rev.*, **100**:36 (1955).
[2] J. Goldstone, *Proc. Roy. Soc.* (*London*), **A239**:267 (1957).

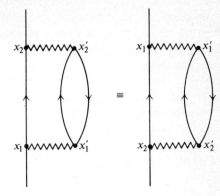

Fig. 9.4 Typical permutation of $\hat{H}_1$ in connected diagrams.

$\hat{H}_1$ contains an even number of fermion fields and may therefore be moved at will within the T product. In mth order there are $m!$ possible interchanges of this type corresponding to the $m!$ ways of choosing the interaction hamiltonian $\hat{H}_1$ in applying Wick's theorem. All of these terms make the same contribution to the Green's function, so that we can count each diagram just once and cancel the factor $(m!)^{-1}$ in Eq. (9.5). Note that this result is true only for the *connected* diagrams, where the external points x and y are fixed. In contrast, the *disconnected* diagram shown in Fig. 9.5 represents only a single term. This result is

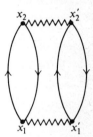

Fig. 9.5 Typical disconnected diagram.

easily seen by expanding $\langle \Phi_0 | \hat{S} | \Phi_0 \rangle$ with Wick's theorem. There is only one way to contract all of the fields, and the diagram obtained by the interchange $x_1 x_1' \rightleftarrows x_2 x_2'$ does not correspond to a new and different analytic term. This distinction between connected and disconnected diagrams is one of the basic reasons for studying the Green's function; the fixed external points greatly simplify the counting of diagrams in perturbation theory.

We therefore find the following rule for the nth-order contribution to the single-particle Green's function $G_{\alpha\beta}(x,y)$:

(*a*) Draw all *topologically distinct* connected diagrams with n interaction lines U and $2n + 1$ directed Green's functions G^0.

This procedure can be simplified with the observation that a fermion line either *closes on itself* or *runs continuously* from y to x. Each of these diagrams

represents all the n! different possibilities of choosing among the set of variables $(x_1 x_1') \cdots (x_n x_n')$. If there is a question as to the precise meaning of topo-logically distinct diagrams, Wick's theorem can always be used to verify the enumeration.

4. In our first-order example [Eq. (9.1)] we note that the terms C and E are equal, as are the terms D and F; they differ only in that x and x' (and the corresponding matrix indices) are interchanged, whereas the potential is sym-metric under this substitution [Eq. (7.13)]. It is therefore sufficient to retain just one diagram of each type, simultaneously omitting the factor $\frac{1}{2}$ in front of Eq. (9.1), which reflects the factor $\frac{1}{2}$ in the interaction potential [Eq. (2.4)].[1]

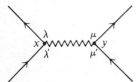

Fig. 9.6   Matrix indices for $U(x,y)_{\lambda\lambda',\mu\mu'}$.

We therefore obtain the additional rules:

(b) Label each vertex with a four-dimensional space-time point x_i.
(c) Each solid line represents a Green's function $G^0_{\alpha\beta}(x,y)$ running from y to x.
(d) Each wavy line represents an interaction

$$U(x,y)_{\lambda\lambda',\mu\mu'} = V(\mathbf{x},\mathbf{y})_{\lambda\lambda',\mu\mu'} \, \delta(t_x - t_y)$$

where the association of matrix indices is shown in Fig. 9.6.
(e) Integrate all internal variables over space and time.

5. We note that the summations appearing in the subscript indices on the Green's functions and interaction potentials in Eq. (9.1) are precisely in the form of a matrix product that runs along the fermion line.   Thus we state the rule:

(f) There is a spin matrix product along each continuous fermion line, including the potentials at each vertex.

6. The overall sign of the various contributions appearing in Eq. (9.1) or the diagrams appearing in Fig. 9.1 is determined as follows.   Every time a fermion line closes on itself, the term acquires an extra minus sign.   This is seen by noting that the fields contracted into a closed loop can be arranged in the order $[\hat{\psi}^\dagger(1)\,\hat{\psi}(1)\,][\hat{\psi}^\dagger(2)\,\hat{\psi}(2)\,] \cdots [\,\hat{\psi}(N)\,]$ with no change in sign.   An odd number of interchanges of fermion operators is now needed to move the last field operator over to its proper position at the left.   Thus we obtain the rule:

(g) Affix a sign factor $(-1)^F$ to each term, where F is the number of closed fermion loops in the diagram.

[1] Note that this result again applies only to connected diagrams, as is evident from Fig. 9.1A and B.

7. The nth-order term of Eq. (9.5) has an explicit numerical factor $(-i/\hbar)^n$, while the $2n + 1$ contractions of field operators contribute an additional factor i^{2n+1} [see Eq. (8.29)].   We therefore obtain the rule:

(h) To compute $G(x,y)$ assign a factor $(-i)(-i/\hbar)^n(i)^{2n+1} = (i/\hbar)^n$ to each nth-order term.

Finally, the earlier discussion of Eq. (9.2) yields the rule:

(i) A Green's function with equal time variables must be interpreted as

$G^0_{\alpha\beta}(\mathbf{x}t, \mathbf{x}'\, t^+)$

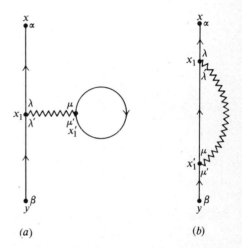

Fig. 9.7 All first-order Feynman diagrams for $G_{\alpha\beta}(x,y)$.

(a)   (b)

The foregoing arguments provide a unique prescription for drawing all Feynman diagrams that contribute to $G(x,y)$ in coordinate space.   Each diagram corresponds to an analytic expression that can now be written down explicitly with the Feynman rules.   The calculation of G thus becomes a relatively automatic process.

As an example of the Feynman rules, we shall now write out the complete first-order contribution to $G_{\alpha\beta}(x,y)$, shown in Fig. 9.7,

$$G^{(1)}_{\alpha\beta}(x,y) = i\hbar^{-1} \int d^4x_1 \int d^4x_1' \{(-1) G^0_{\alpha\lambda}(x,x_1) U(x_1,x_1')_{\lambda\lambda',\,\mu\mu'} G^0_{\lambda'\beta}(x_1,y)$$

$$\times\, G^0_{\mu'\mu}(x_1',x_1') + G^0_{\alpha\lambda}(x,x_1) U(x_1,x_1')_{\lambda\lambda',\,\mu\mu'} G^0_{\lambda'\mu}(x_1,x_1') G^0_{\mu'\beta}(x_1',y)\} \quad (9.6)$$

Here and henceforth, an implicit summation is to be carried out over all repeated spin indices.   The corresponding second-order contribution $G^{(2)}(x,y)$ requires more work, and we merely *assert* that there are 10 second-order Feynman diagrams (Fig. 9.8).   The reader is urged to convince himself that these diagrams exhaust the class of second-order topologically distinct connected diagrams, and to write down the analytic expression associated with each term.

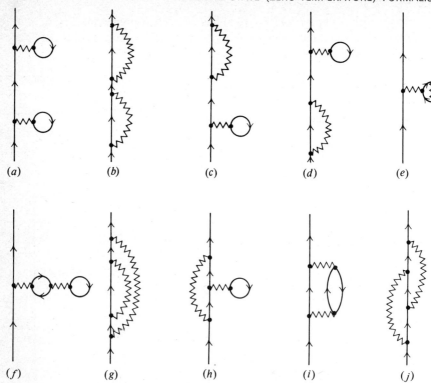

Fig. 9.8 All second-order Feynman diagrams for $G_{\alpha\beta}(x,y)$.

FEYNMAN DIAGRAMS IN MOMENTUM SPACE

In principle, the Feynman rules enable us to write down the exact Green's function to arbitrary order, but the actual evaluation of the terms can lead to formidable problems because *each* noninteracting Green's function $G^0(x,y)$ consists of two disjoint pieces. Thus even the first-order contribution [Eq. (9.6)] must be split into many separate pieces according to the relative values of the time variables. In contrast, the Fourier transform $G^0(\mathbf{x},\mathbf{y},\omega)$ with respect to time has a simple form, and it is convenient to incorporate this into the calculations. Although it is possible to consider a mixed representation $G_{\alpha\beta}(\mathbf{x},\mathbf{x}',\omega)$, which would apply to spatially inhomogeneous systems with a time-independent hamiltonian, we shall now restrict the discussion to uniform and isotropic systems, where the exact Green's function takes the form $\delta_{\alpha\beta}G(x-y)$. The spatial and temporal invariance then allows a full Fourier representation, and we write

$$G_{\alpha\beta}(x,y) = (2\pi)^{-4} \int d^4k\, e^{ik\cdot(x-y)}\, G_{\alpha\beta}(k) \tag{9.7a}$$

$$G_{\alpha\beta}^0(x,y) = (2\pi)^{-4} \int d^4k\, e^{ik\cdot(x-y)}\, G_{\alpha\beta}^0(k) \tag{9.7b}$$

where the limit $V \to \infty$ has already been taken. Here a convenient four-dimensional notation has been introduced

$$d^4k \equiv d^3k\, d\omega \qquad k \cdot x \equiv \mathbf{k} \cdot \mathbf{x} - \omega t \tag{9.8}$$

In addition, we assume that the interaction depends only on the coordinate difference

$$U(x,x') = V(\mathbf{x} - \mathbf{x}')\, \delta(t - t') \tag{9.9}$$

It may then be written as

$$
\begin{aligned}
U(x,x')_{\alpha\alpha',\,\beta\beta'} &= (2\pi)^{-4} \int d^4k\, e^{ik \cdot (x-x')}\, U(k)_{\alpha\alpha',\,\beta\beta'} \\
&= (2\pi)^{-3} \int d^3k\, e^{i\mathbf{k} \cdot (\mathbf{x}-\mathbf{x}')}\, V(\mathbf{k})_{\alpha\alpha',\,\beta\beta'}\, \delta(t - t')
\end{aligned} \tag{9.10}
$$

where

$$U(k)_{\alpha\alpha',\,\beta\beta'} = V(\mathbf{k})_{\alpha\alpha',\,\beta\beta'} \tag{9.11a}$$

$$= \int d^3x\, e^{-i\mathbf{k} \cdot \mathbf{x}}\, V(\mathbf{x})_{\alpha\alpha',\,\beta\beta'} \tag{9.11b}$$

is the spatial Fourier transform of the interparticle potential.

As an example of the transformation to momentum space, consider the diagram shown in Fig. 9.7b

$$
\begin{aligned}
G^{(1b)}_{\alpha\beta}(x,y) &= i\hbar^{-1} \int d^4x_1\, d^4x_1'\, (2\pi)^{-16} \int d^4k\, d^4p\, d^4p_1\, d^4q \\
&\quad \times G^0_{\alpha\lambda}(k)\, U(q)_{\lambda\lambda',\,\mu\mu'}\, G^0_{\lambda'\mu}(p)\, G^0_{\mu'\beta}(p_1) \\
&\quad \times e^{ik \cdot (x-x_1)}\, e^{iq \cdot (x_1-x_1')}\, e^{ip \cdot (x_1-x_1')}\, e^{ip_1 \cdot (x_1'-y)} \\
&= i\hbar^{-1} (2\pi)^{-8} \int d^4k\, d^4p\, d^4p_1\, d^4q\, G^0_{\alpha\lambda}(k)\, U(q)_{\lambda\lambda',\,\mu\mu'} \\
&\quad \times G^0_{\lambda'\mu}(p)\, G^0_{\mu'\beta}(p_1)\, e^{ik \cdot x}\, e^{-ip_1 \cdot y}\, \delta^{(4)}(p+q-k)\, \delta^{(4)}(p_1-q-p) \\
&= (2\pi)^{-4} \int d^4k\, e^{ik \cdot (x-y)} [i\hbar^{-1}\, G^0_{\alpha\lambda}(k)\, (2\pi)^{-4} \int d^4p \\
&\quad \times U(k-p)_{\lambda\lambda',\,\mu\mu'}\, G^0_{\lambda'\mu}(p)\, G^0_{\mu'\beta}(k)]
\end{aligned} \tag{9.12}
$$

where the four-dimensional Dirac delta function has the usual integral representation

$$\delta^{(4)}(p) = (2\pi)^{-4} \int d^4x\, e^{ip \cdot x}$$

Note that Eq. (9.12) indeed has the expected form, and comparison with Eq. (9.7a) identifies the quantity in square brackets as the corresponding contribution to $G_{\alpha\beta}(k) \equiv G_{\alpha\beta}(\mathbf{k},\omega)$.

This approach is readily generalized. Consider the typical internal vertex shown in Fig. 9.9. In accordance with our definitions of Fourier transforms in Eqs. (9.10) and (9.7b), we can also assign a conventional direction $x' \to x$ to the interaction $U(x - x')$. [This convention cannot alter the problem since the potential is symmetric $U(x - x')_{\lambda\lambda',\,\mu\mu'} = U(x' - x)_{\mu\mu',\,\lambda\lambda'}$.] The coordinate x

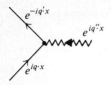

Fig. 9.9   Typical internal vertex in a Feynman diagram.

now appears *only* in the plane-wave exponential, and there is a factor $e^{+iq \cdot x}$ for each incoming line and $e^{-iq \cdot x}$ for each outgoing line.   The integration over x therefore yields

$$\int d^4x \, e^{i(q - q' + q'') \cdot x} = (2\pi)^4 \, \delta^{(4)}(q - q' + q'') \tag{9.13}$$

which conserves *energy and momentum at each internal vertex*.   The only remaining question is the end points, where the typical structure is shown in Fig. 9.10.

Fig. 9.10   Typical structure of Feynman diagrams for $G_{\alpha\beta}(x - y)$.

The translational invariance ensures that $q' = q''$, as seen explicitly in Eq. (9.12); the remaining factor $e^{iq' \cdot (x-y)}$ is just that needed in the definition of the Fourier transform of $G_{\alpha\beta}(q')$.

We can now state the Feynman rules for the nth-order contribution to $G_{\alpha\beta}(\mathbf{k},\omega) \equiv G_{\alpha\beta}(k)$:

1. Draw all topologically distinct connected diagrams with n interaction lines and $2n + 1$ directed Green's functions.
2. Assign a direction to each interaction line; associate a directed four-momentum with each line and conserve four-momentum at each vertex.
3. Each Green's function corresponds to a factor

$$G^0_{\alpha\beta}(\mathbf{k},\omega) = \delta_{\alpha\beta} \, G^0(\mathbf{k},\omega) = \delta_{\alpha\beta}\left[\frac{\theta(|\mathbf{k}| - k_F)}{\omega - \omega_{\mathbf{k}} + i\eta} + \frac{\theta(k_F - |\mathbf{k}|)}{\omega - \omega_{\mathbf{k}} - i\eta}\right] \tag{9.14}$$

4. Each interaction corresponds to a factor $U(q)_{\lambda\lambda', \mu\mu'} = V(\mathbf{q})_{\lambda\lambda', \mu\mu'}$ where the matrix indices are associated with the fermion lines as in Fig. 9.11.
5. Perform a spin summation along each continuous particle line including the potential at each vertex.
6. Integrate over the n independent internal four-momenta.

7. Affix a factor $(i/\hbar)^n (2\pi)^{-4n} (-1)^F$ where F is the number of closed fermion loops.

8. Any single-particle line that forms a closed loop as in Fig. 9.11a or that is linked by the same interaction line as in Fig. 9.11b is interpreted as $e^{i\omega\eta} G_{\alpha\beta}(\mathbf{k},\omega)$, where $\eta \to 0^+$ at the end of the calculation.

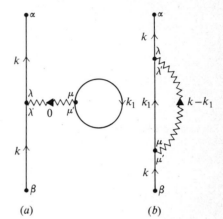

Fig. 9.11 All first-order Feynman diagrams for $G_{\alpha\beta}(k)$.

(a) (b)

As an example of the Feynman rules in momentum space, we compute the first-order contribution $G^{(1)}_{\alpha\beta}(\mathbf{k},\omega)$, shown in Fig. 9.11.   Although the topological structure is identical with the corresponding diagrams in coordinate space (Fig. 9.7), the labeling and interpretation are naturally quite different.   In Fig. 9.11a, the four-vector associated with the interaction vanishes because of the conservation requirement at each end. A straightforward identification yields

$$G^{(1)}_{\alpha\beta}(k) = i\hbar^{-1}(-1)(2\pi)^{-4} \int d^4k_1\, G^0_{\alpha\lambda}(k)\, U(0)_{\lambda\lambda',\,\mu\mu'}\, G^0_{\lambda'\beta}(k)\, G^0_{\mu'\mu}(k_1)\, e^{i\omega_1\eta}$$

$$+\, i\hbar^{-1}(2\pi)^{-4} \int d^4k_1\, G^0_{\alpha\lambda}(k)\, U(k-k_1)_{\lambda\lambda',\,\mu\mu'}$$

$$\times\, G^0_{\lambda'\mu}(k_1)\, G^0_{\mu'\beta}(k)\, e^{i\omega_1\eta}$$

$$= i\hbar^{-1}\, G^0(k)\{(2\pi)^{-4}\!\int d^4k_1\, [-U(0)_{\alpha\beta,\,\mu\mu}\, G^0(k_1)\, e^{i\omega_1\eta}$$

$$+\, U(k-k_1)_{\alpha\mu,\,\mu\beta}\, G^0(k_1)\, e^{i\omega_1\eta}]\}\, G^0(k) \tag{9.15}$$

where the spin summation has been simplified with the Kronecker delta for each factor G^0.   Here, and subsequently, we use the conventions that

$$U(0) \equiv U(k=0) \tag{9.16a}$$

$$V(0) \equiv V(\mathbf{k}=0) \tag{9.16b}$$

To make further progress, we shall consider spin-$\tfrac{1}{2}$ particles with two distinct possibilities for the interaction potential.

1. If the interaction is spin independent, then it has the form $\mathbf{1}(1)\,\mathbf{1}(2)$ in spin space, namely, the unit spin matrix with respect to both particles:

$$U(q)_{\alpha\beta,\lambda\mu} = U(q)\,\delta_{\alpha\beta}\,\delta_{\lambda\mu} \qquad (9.17)$$

The matrix elements then become

$$U_{\alpha\beta,\mu\mu} = 2U\delta_{\alpha\beta} \qquad U_{\alpha\mu,\mu\beta} = U\delta_{\alpha\beta} \qquad (9.18)$$

2. If the interaction is spin dependent of the form $\boldsymbol{\sigma}(1)\cdot\boldsymbol{\sigma}(2)$, then

$$U(q)_{\alpha\beta,\lambda\mu} = U(q)\,\boldsymbol{\sigma}(1)_{\alpha\beta}\cdot\boldsymbol{\sigma}(2)_{\lambda\mu} \qquad (9.19)$$

and the relevant quantities are

$$\boldsymbol{\sigma}_{\alpha\beta}\cdot\boldsymbol{\sigma}_{\mu\mu} = 0 \qquad \boldsymbol{\sigma}_{\alpha\mu}\cdot\boldsymbol{\sigma}_{\mu\beta} = [(\boldsymbol{\sigma})^2]_{\alpha\beta} = 3\delta_{\alpha\beta} \qquad (9.20)$$

These results have been obtained with the observations $\mathrm{tr}\,\boldsymbol{\sigma} = 0$ and $\mathrm{tr}\,\mathbf{1} = 2$. For interactions of the form

$$V(\mathbf{x}_1 - \mathbf{x}_2) = V_0(|\mathbf{x}_1 - \mathbf{x}_2|)\,\mathbf{1}(1)\,\mathbf{1}(2) + V_1(|\mathbf{x}_1 - \mathbf{x}_2|)\,\boldsymbol{\sigma}(1)\cdot\boldsymbol{\sigma}(2) \qquad (9.21)$$

Eqs. (9.15) to (9.20) show that $G^{(1)}$ is indeed diagonal in the matrix indices:

$$G^{(1)}_{\alpha\beta} = \delta_{\alpha\beta}\,G^{(1)}.$$

The exact Green's function can always be written in the form

$$G(k) = G^0(k) + G^0(k)\,\Sigma(k)\,G^0(k) \qquad (9.22)$$

which defines the self-energy $\Sigma(k)$. The first term is just the zero-order contribution, and the structure of the second term follows from that of Fig. 9.10. The same structure occurs in Eq. (9.15), which thus identifies the first-order self-energy as

$$\hbar\Sigma^{(1)}(k) = i(2\pi)^{-4} \int d^4k_1\,[-2V_0(0) + V_0(\mathbf{k} - \mathbf{k}_1)$$

$$+ 3V_1(\mathbf{k} - \mathbf{k}_1)]\,G^0(k_1)\,e^{i\omega_1\eta} \qquad (9.23)$$

The frequency integral can now be performed explicitly with Eq. (9.14)

$$\int_{-\infty}^{\infty} \frac{d\omega_1}{2\pi}\,e^{i\omega_1\eta}\left[\frac{\theta(|\mathbf{k}_1| - k_F)}{\omega_1 - \omega_{\mathbf{k}_1} + i\eta} + \frac{\theta(k_F - |\mathbf{k}_1|)}{\omega_1 - \omega_{\mathbf{k}_1} - i\eta}\right] = i\theta(k_F - |\mathbf{k}_1|)$$

where the convergence factor requires us to close the contour in the upper-half plane. The momentum integral in the first term of Eq. (9.23) then gives the particle density $n = N/V$ [compare Eq. (3.27)], and we find

$$\hbar\Sigma^{(1)}(k) \equiv \hbar\Sigma^{(1)}(\mathbf{k})$$

$$= nV_0(0) - (2\pi)^{-3} \int d^3k'\,[V_0(\mathbf{k} - \mathbf{k}') + 3V_1(\mathbf{k} - \mathbf{k}')]\,\theta(k_F - k')$$

$$(9.24)$$

Note that the first-order self-energy is frequency independent. The two terms appearing in Eq. (9.24) have the following physical interpretation. The first term represents the Born approximation for forward scattering from the particles in the medium (Fig. 9.11a), and the second represents the exchange scattering with the particles in the medium, again in Born approximation (Fig. 9.11b).

DYSON'S EQUATIONS[1]

We shall now classify the various contributions in an arbitrary Feynman diagram. This procedure yields Dyson's equations, which summarize the Feynman-Dyson perturbation theory in a particularly compact form.

   1. *Self-energy insertion*: Our graphical analysis makes clear that the exact Green's function consists of the unperturbed Green's function plus all connected

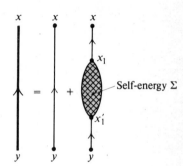

Fig. 9.12   General structure of $G_{\alpha\beta}(x,y)$.

terms with a free Green's function at each end. This structure is shown in Fig. 9.12, where the heavy line denotes G and the light line denotes G^0. The corresponding analytic expression is given by

$$G_{\alpha\beta}(x,y) = G^0_{\alpha\beta}(x,y) + \int d^4x_1 \int d^4x'_1\, G^0_{\alpha\lambda}(x,x_1)\, \Sigma(x_1,x'_1)_{\lambda\mu}\, G^0_{\mu\beta}(x'_1,y) \quad (9.25)$$

which defines the *self-energy* $\Sigma(x_1,x'_1)_{\lambda\mu}$.   A self-energy insertion is defined as any part of a diagram that is connected to the rest of the diagram by two particle lines (one in and one out).

   We next introduce the concept of a *proper* self-energy insertion, which is a self-energy insertion that cannot be separated into two pieces by cutting a single particle line.   For example, Figs. 9.8a, 9.8b, 9.8c, and 9.8d all contain improper self-energy insertions, while the remaining terms of Fig. 9.8 contain only *proper* self-energy insertions.   By definition, the proper self-energy is the sum of all proper self-energy insertions, and will be denoted $\Sigma^\star(x_1,x'_1)_{\alpha\beta}$.   It follows from

[1] F. J. Dyson, *loc. cit.*   (A discussion of the vertex part and the complete set of Dyson's equations is presented in Chap. 12 of this book.)

these definitions that the self-energy consists of a sum of all possible repetitions of the proper self-energy.

$$\Sigma(x_1,x_1') = \Sigma^\star(x_1,x_1') + \int d^4x_2\, d^4x_2'\, \Sigma^\star(x_1,x_2)\, G^0(x_2,x_2')\, \Sigma^\star(x_2',x_1')$$
$$+ \int d^4x_2\, d^4x_2' \int d^4x_3\, d^4x_3'\, \Sigma^\star(x_1,x_2)\, G^0(x_2,x_2')$$
$$\times \Sigma^\star(x_2',x_3)\, G^0(x_3,x_3')\, \Sigma^\star(x_3',x_1') + \cdots \quad (9.26)$$

Here each quantity denotes a matrix in the spinor indices, and the indices are therefore suppressed. The structure of Eq. (9.26) is shown in Fig. 9.13. Corre-

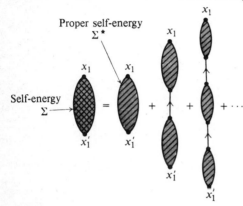

Fig. 9.13 Relation between self-energy Σ and proper self-energy $\Sigma^\star$.

spondingly, the single-particle Green's function [Eq. (9.25)] becomes (Fig. 9.14)

$$G(x,y) = G^0(x,y) + \int d^4x_1\, d^4x_1'\, G^0(x,x_1)\, \Sigma^\star(x_1,x_1')\, G^0(x_1',y)$$
$$+ \int d^4x_1\, d^4x_1' \int d^4x_2\, d^4x_2'\, G^0(x,x_1)\, \Sigma^\star(x_1,x_1')$$
$$\times G^0(x_1',x_2)\, \Sigma^\star(x_2,x_2')\, G^0(x_2',y) + \cdots \quad (9.27)$$

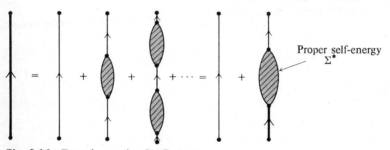

Fig. 9.14 Dyson's equation for $G_{\alpha\beta}(x,y)$.

which can be summed formally to yield an *integral equation* (Dyson's equation) for the exact G.

$$G_{\alpha\beta}(x,y) = G^0_{\alpha\beta}(x,y) + \int d^4x_1\, d^4x_1'\, G^0_{\alpha\lambda}(x,x_1)\, \Sigma^\star(x_1,x_1')_{\lambda\mu}\, G_{\mu\beta}(x_1',y) \quad (9.28)$$

The validity of Eq. (9.28) can be verified by iterating the right side, which reproduces Eq. (9.27) term by term.

Dyson's equation naturally becomes much simpler if the interaction is invariant under translations and the system is spatially uniform. In this case the quantities appearing in Eq. (9.27) depend only on the coordinate differences, and it is possible to introduce four-dimensional Fourier transforms in these differences. With the definition

$$\Sigma^\star(x,y)_{\alpha\beta} = (2\pi)^{-4} \int d^4k \, e^{ik\cdot(x-y)} \, \Sigma^\star(k)_{\alpha\beta} \tag{9.29}$$

and Eq. (9.7), the space-time integrations in Eq. (9.28) are readily evaluated, and we find an *algebraic* equation in momentum space [compare Eq. (9.22)]

$$G_{\alpha\beta}(k) = G^0_{\alpha\beta}(k) + G^0_{\alpha\lambda}(k) \, \Sigma^\star(k)_{\lambda\mu} \, G_{\mu\beta}(k) \tag{9.30}$$

In the usual case, G, G^0, and $\Sigma^\star$ are all diagonal in the matrix indices, and Dyson's equation can then be solved explicitly as

$$G(k) = \frac{1}{[G^0(k)]^{-1} - \Sigma^\star(k)} \tag{9.31}$$

The inverse of G^0 is given by

$$[G^0(k)]^{-1} \equiv [G^0(\mathbf{k},\omega)]^{-1} = \omega - \omega_\mathbf{k} \equiv \omega - \hbar^{-1}\epsilon^0_\mathbf{k} \tag{9.32}$$

because the $\pm i\eta$ in Eq. (9.14) is now irrelevant, and we find

$$G_{\alpha\beta}(k) \equiv G_{\alpha\beta}(\mathbf{k},\omega) = \frac{1}{\omega - \hbar^{-1}\epsilon^0_\mathbf{k} - \Sigma^\star(\mathbf{k},\omega)} \delta_{\alpha\beta} \tag{9.33}$$

In the general case, this expression must be replaced by an inverse matrix that solves the *matrix* equation (9.30). As shown in Sec. 7, the singularities of the exact Green's function $G(\mathbf{k},\omega)$, considered as a function of ω, determine both the excitation energies $\epsilon_\mathbf{k}$ of the system and their damping $\gamma_\mathbf{k}$. Furthermore, the Lehmann representation ensures that for real ω

$$\operatorname{Im} \Sigma^\star(\mathbf{k},\omega) \geqslant 0 \qquad \omega < \mu/\hbar$$
$$\tag{9.34}$$
$$\operatorname{Im} \Sigma^\star(\mathbf{k},\omega) \leqslant 0 \qquad \omega > \mu/\hbar$$

so that the chemical potential can be determined as the point where $\operatorname{Im}\Sigma^\star(\mathbf{k},\omega)$ changes sign.

As an example of the present analysis, we shall consider all the first- and second-order diagrams, shown in Figs. 9.7 and 9.8. It is evident that both first-order terms represent proper self-energy insertions; as a result the first-order proper self-energy $\Sigma^\star_{(1)}$ is given by the diagrams in Fig. 9.15. Here the small arrows at the ends specify how the Green's functions are to be connected, and the diagrams can be interpreted either in coordinate space or in momentum space. The situation is considerably more complicated in second order. In particular, the diagrams in Fig. 9.8a to d represent all possible second-order iterations of $\Sigma^\star_{(1)}$ and therefore correspond to improper self-energy insertions.

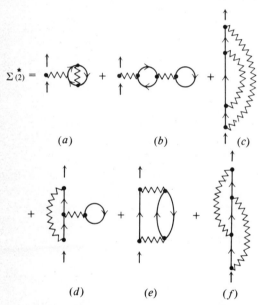

Fig. 9.15 First-order proper self-energy $\Sigma^{\star}_{(1)}$.

On the other hand, the remaining terms (Fig. 9.8e to j) all contain proper self-energy insertions, and we now exhibit *all* contributions to $\Sigma^{\star}_{(2)}$ in Fig. 9.16.

A particularly simple approximation is to write $\Sigma^{\star}(\mathbf{k},\omega) \approx \Sigma^{\star}_{(1)}(\mathbf{k},\omega) \equiv \Sigma^{\star}_{(1)}(\mathbf{k})$ [see Eq. (9.24)] in the solution of Dyson's equation (9.33). This approximation corresponds to summing an *infinite* class of diagrams containing arbitrary

Fig. 9.16 Second-order proper self-energy $\Sigma^{\star}_{(2)}$.

iterations of $\Sigma^{\star}_{(1)}$ (Fig. 9.17). The poles of the approximate Green's function occur at the energy

$$\epsilon^{(1)}_{k} = \epsilon^{0}_{k} + \hbar\Sigma^{\star}_{(1)}(\mathbf{k})$$

$$= \frac{\hbar^2 k^2}{2m} + nV_0(0) - (2\pi)^{-3} \int d^3k'\, [V_0(\mathbf{k} - \mathbf{k}') + 3V_1(\mathbf{k} - \mathbf{k}')]\,\theta(k_F - k')$$

$$(9.35)$$

which determines the energy $\epsilon^{(1)}_{k}$ of a state with momentum $\hbar\mathbf{k}$ containing an additional particle. Here the term $nV_0(0)$ is a *constant* energy shift; it arises from the "tadpole" diagram Fig. 9.15a and represents the forward scattering

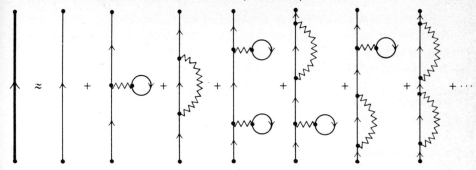

Fig. 9.17 Approximate G obtained with the substitution $\Sigma^{\star} \approx \Sigma^{\star}_{(1)}$.

off all the other particles. The integral term depends on $\mathbf{k}$ and arises from Fig. 9.15b. In the present (first-order) approximation, the proper self-energy is *real*, and the system propagates forever without damping. This example clearly demonstrates the power of Dyson's equation, because *any* approximation for $\Sigma^{\star}$ generates an *infinite-order* approximate series for the Green's function. Dyson's equation thus enables us to sum an infinite class of perturbation terms in a compact form.

The explicit solution for G [Eq. (9.33)] allows us to rewrite the ground-state energy of a uniform system [Eqs. (7.27) and (7.32)] in a particularly simple form. Consider Eq. (7.27) for spin-s fermions with $\Sigma^{\star}$ and G diagonal in the matrix indices. A combination with Eq. (9.33) yields

$$
\begin{aligned}
E &= -iV(2s+1)\int \frac{d^4k}{(2\pi)^4}\,e^{i\omega\eta}\tfrac{1}{2}\hbar\left[\frac{\hbar\omega+\epsilon_{\mathbf{k}}^0}{\hbar\omega-\epsilon_{\mathbf{k}}^0-\hbar\Sigma^{\star}(\mathbf{k},\omega)}\right] \\
&= -iV(2s+1)(2\pi)^{-4}\int d^4k\,e^{i\omega\eta}\{[\epsilon_{\mathbf{k}}^0+\tfrac{1}{2}\hbar\Sigma^{\star}(\mathbf{k},\omega)]\,G(\mathbf{k},\omega)+\tfrac{1}{2}\hbar\} \\
&= -iV(2s+1)(2\pi)^{-4}\int d^4k\,e^{i\omega\eta}[\epsilon_{\mathbf{k}}^0+\tfrac{1}{2}\hbar\Sigma^{\star}(\mathbf{k},\omega)]\,G(\mathbf{k},\omega)
\end{aligned}
\tag{9.36}
$$

where the last line is obtained with the limiting procedure

$$
\begin{aligned}
\lim_{\eta\to 0^+}\int_{-\infty}^{\infty}\frac{d\omega}{2\pi}\,e^{i\omega\eta} &\equiv \lim_{\eta\to 0^+}\left[\lim_{\epsilon\to 0^+}\int_{-\infty}^{\infty}e^{-\epsilon|\omega|}\,e^{i\omega\eta}\,\frac{d\omega}{2\pi}\right] \\
&= \lim_{\eta\to 0^+}\left[\lim_{\epsilon\to 0^+}\frac{1}{\pi}\frac{\epsilon}{\eta^2+\epsilon^2}\right]=0
\end{aligned}
\tag{9.37}
$$

It is readily verified that this is the correct limiting process by applying Eq. (9.36) to a noninteracting Fermi system. In the same way, Eq. (7.32) can be rewritten as

$$
\begin{aligned}
E-E_0 &= -\tfrac{1}{2}iV(2s+1)\int_0^1\frac{d\lambda}{\lambda}\int\frac{d^4k}{(2\pi)^4}\,e^{i\omega\eta}\hbar\left[\frac{\hbar\omega-\epsilon_{\mathbf{k}}^0}{\hbar\omega-\epsilon_{\mathbf{k}}^0-\hbar\Sigma^{\star\lambda}(\mathbf{k},\omega)}\right] \\
&= -\tfrac{1}{2}iV(2s+1)(2\pi)^{-4}\int_0^1 d\lambda\lambda^{-1}\int d^4k\,e^{i\omega\eta}\hbar\Sigma^{\star\lambda}(\mathbf{k},\omega)\,G^\lambda(\mathbf{k},\omega)
\end{aligned}
\tag{9.38}
$$

where *both* $\Sigma^{\star\lambda}$ and G^λ must be evaluated for all λ between 0 and 1.

2. *Polarization insertion*: A similar analysis can be carried out for the interaction between two particles, which always consists of the lowest-order interaction plus a series of connected diagrams with lowest-order interactions coming in and out (Fig. 9.18). We can evidently write an integral equation for

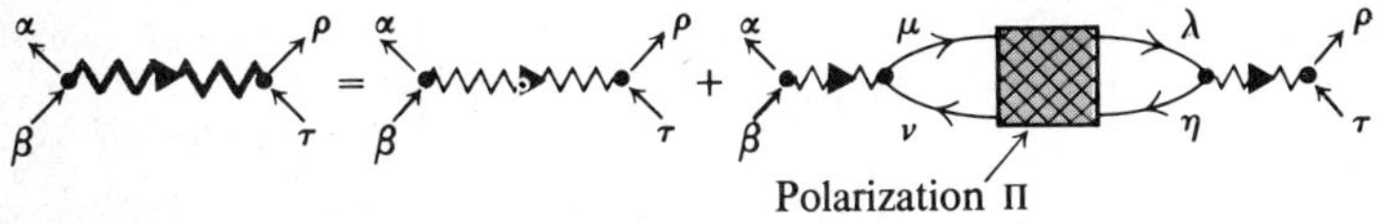

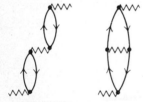

Polarization Π

Fig. 9.18   General structure of the effective interaction $U_{\alpha\beta,\rho\tau}$.

the exact interaction; this equation again becomes simpler for a uniform system, where it is possible to work in momentum space. If $U(q)_{\alpha\beta,\rho\tau}$ and $U_0(q)_{\alpha\beta,\rho\tau}$ denote the exact and lowest-order interactions, the corresponding equation takes the form

$$U(q)_{\alpha\beta,\rho\tau} = U_0(q)_{\alpha\beta,\rho\tau} + U_0(q)_{\alpha\beta,\mu\nu}\,\Pi_{\mu\nu,\eta\lambda}(q)\,U_0(q)_{\eta\lambda,\rho\tau} \qquad (9.39)$$

which defines the *polarization insertion* $\Pi_{\mu\nu,\eta\lambda}(q)$. It is also convenient to introduce the concept of a proper polarization Π^*, which is a polarization part that cannot be separated into two polarization parts by cutting a single interaction line (Fig. 9.19). Equation (9.39) can then be rewritten as an equation between

Improper   Proper   **Fig. 9.19**   Typical improper and proper polarization insertions.

the exact interaction and the proper polarization (Fig. 9.20). For a homogeneous system this equation becomes an algebraic equation

$$U(q)_{\alpha\beta,\rho\tau} = U_0(q)_{\alpha\beta,\rho\tau} + U_0(q)_{\alpha\beta,\mu\nu}\,\Pi^{\star}_{\mu\nu,\eta\lambda}(q)\,U(q)_{\eta\lambda,\rho\tau} \qquad (9.40)$$

In general, Eqs. (9.39) and (9.40) have a complicated matrix structure, and we shall usually consider only spin-independent potentials

$$U_0(q)_{\alpha\beta,\rho\tau} = U_0(q)\,\delta_{\alpha\beta}\,\delta_{\rho\tau} \qquad (9.41)$$

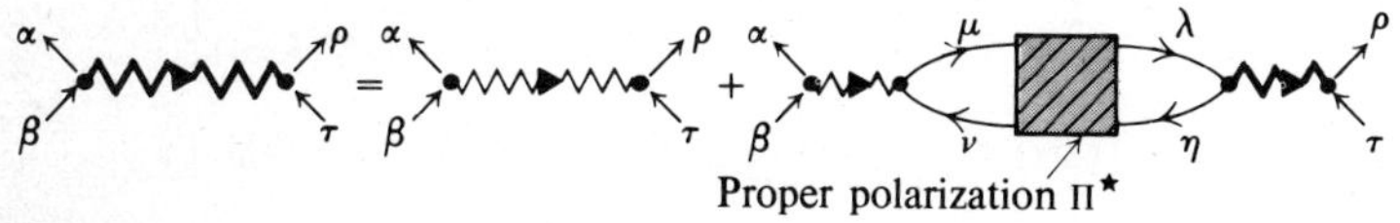

Proper polarization Π*

Fig. 9.20   Dyson's equation for $U_{\alpha\beta,\rho\tau}$.

It then follows immediately that the exact interaction has the same structure

$$U(q)_{\alpha\beta,\rho\tau} = U(q)\delta_{\alpha\beta}\delta_{\rho\tau} \tag{9.42}$$

where the function $U(q)$ is determined by the simpler equations

$$U(q) = U_0(q) + U_0(q)\Pi(q)U_0(q) \tag{9.43a}$$

$$U(q) = U_0(q) + U_0(q)\Pi^*(q)U(q) \tag{9.43b}$$

Here we have introduced the abbreviations

$$\Pi(q) \equiv \Pi_{\alpha\alpha,\lambda\lambda}(q) \tag{9.44a}$$

$$\Pi^*(q) \equiv \Pi^*_{\alpha\alpha,\lambda\lambda}(q) \tag{9.44b}$$

and a direct solution of Eq. (9.43b) yields

$$U(q) = \frac{U_0(q)}{1 - \Pi^*(q)U_0(q)} \tag{9.45}$$

This result can be used to define a generalized dielectric function $\kappa(q)$

$$U(q) = \frac{U_0(q)}{\kappa(q)} \tag{9.46}$$

which characterizes the modification of the lowest-order interaction by the polarization of the medium. Comparison of Eqs. (9.45) and (9.46) yields

$$\kappa(q) = 1 - U_0(q)\Pi^*(q) \tag{9.47}$$

GOLDSTONE'S THEOREM

The application of quantum field theory to the many-body problem was initiated by Goldstone in 1957.[1] He proved the cancellation of the disconnected diagrams to all orders, and derived the following expression for the energy shift of the ground state

$$E - E_0 = \langle\Phi_0|\hat{H}_1 \sum_{n=0}^{\infty} \left(\frac{1}{E_0 - \hat{H}_0}\hat{H}_1\right)^n |\Phi_0\rangle_{\text{connected}} \tag{9.48}$$

where $\hat{H}_0$ and $\hat{H}_1$ are the time-independent operators in the Schrödinger representation. This result can be interpreted by inserting a complete set of eigenstates of $\hat{H}_0$ between each interaction $\hat{H}_1$. The $\hat{H}_0$ in the denominator can then be replaced by the corresponding eigenvalue. All matrix elements of the operator in Eq. (9.48) that start from the ground state $|\Phi_0\rangle$ and end with the ground state $|\Phi_0\rangle$ are to be included. We can visualize these matrix elements in the following way: the operator $\hat{H}_1$ acting on the state $|\Phi_0\rangle$ creates two particles and two holes. This state then *propagates* with $(E_0 - \hat{H}_0)^{-1}$, and the next $\hat{H}_1$

[1] J. Goldstone, *loc. cit.*

can then create more particles and holes or scatter the existing particles or holes. The resulting intermediate state again propagates with $(E_0 - \hat{H}_0)^{-1}$, and so on. The final $\hat{H}_1$ must then return the system to the ground state $|\Phi_0\rangle$. A typical process may be pictured as shown in Fig. 9.21, where an arrow running upward

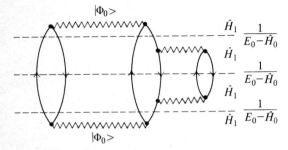

Fig. 9.21 Typical Goldstone diagram in the expansion of $E - E_0$.

represents the presence of a particle, an arrow running downward represents the presence of a hole, and a horizontal wavy line represents the application of an $\hat{H}_1$. Thus the sequence of events starts at the bottom of the diagram and proceeds upward. These diagrams are known as *Goldstone diagrams* and merely keep track of all the matrix elements that contribute in evaluating Eq. (9.48). The subscript "connected" means that only those diagrams that are connected to the final interaction are to be included. In particular, the state $|\Phi_0\rangle$, which has no particles or holes present, can never occur as an intermediate state in Eq. (9.48), for the resulting matrix element would necessarily consist of disconnected parts.

Goldstone's theorem (9.48) is an exact restatement (to all orders) of the familiar time-independent perturbation expression for the ground-state energy. This equivalence is readily verified in the first few terms by inserting a complete set of eigenstates of $\hat{H}_0$ between each interaction $\hat{H}_1$.

$$E - E_0 = \langle\Phi_0|\hat{H}_1|\Phi_0\rangle + \sum_{n \neq 0} \frac{\langle\Phi_0|\hat{H}_1|\Phi_n\rangle\langle\Phi_n|\hat{H}_1|\Phi_0\rangle}{E_0 - E_n} + \cdots \qquad (9.49)$$

The corresponding Goldstone diagrams for a homogeneous medium (see Prob. 3.13) are shown in Fig. 9.22. The first two diagrams represent the usual direct and exchange contributions in $\langle\Phi_0|\hat{H}_1|\Phi_0\rangle$.

In applying Goldstone's theorem to a uniform system, we observe that the *momentum* will be conserved at every interaction because the matrix elements in $\hat{H}_1$ involve an integration over all space. Furthermore, the particles in the intermediate states have *physical* unperturbed energies ϵ_q^0 related to their momentum $\mathbf{q}$, and the virtual nature of the intermediate state is summarized in the energy denominators. In contrast, the Feynman-Dyson perturbation theory for the

Green's function, from which we can also compute $E - E_0$, conserves *both energy and momentum* at every vertex, but the intermediate particles can propagate with any frequency ω, independent of $\mathbf{q}$. For this reason, the Feynman-Dyson approach has the advantage of being manifestly covariant, which is essential in any relativistic theory. *Nevertheless, the two approaches merely represent two different ways of grouping and interpreting the terms in the perturbation expansion, and all physical results must be identical.*

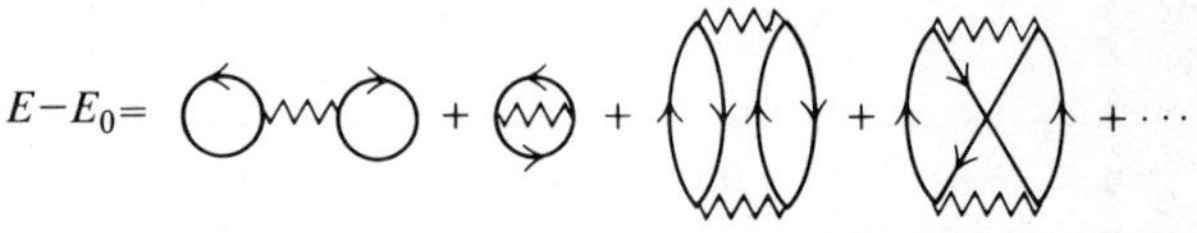

$$E - E_0 = \text{(diagram)} + \text{(diagram)} + \text{(diagram)} + \text{(diagram)} + \cdots$$

Fig. 9.22 All first- and second-order Goldstone diagrams for $E - E_0$ in a uniform system.

We now prove Goldstone's theorem [Eq. (9.48)]. If the ground state of the interacting system is obtained adiabatically from that of the noninteracting system, the Gell-Mann and Low theorem [Eq. (6.45)] expresses the energy shift of the ground state as

$$E - E_0 = \frac{\langle\Phi_0|\hat{H}_1\,\hat{U}(0,-\infty)|\Phi_0\rangle}{\langle\Phi_0|\hat{U}(0,-\infty)|\Phi_0\rangle} \tag{9.50}$$

The numerator can be evaluated by writing

$$\langle\Phi_0|\hat{H}_1\,\hat{U}(0,-\infty)|\Phi_0\rangle = \sum_{\nu=0}^{\infty}\left(\frac{-i}{\hbar}\right)^{\nu}\frac{1}{\nu!}\int_{-\infty}^{0}dt_1\cdots\int_{-\infty}^{0}dt_\nu$$

$$\times\,\langle\Phi_0|T[\hat{H}_1\,\hat{H}_1(t_1)\cdots\hat{H}_1(t_\nu)]|\Phi_0\rangle \tag{9.51}$$

Here the factor $\hat{H}_1$ appearing on the left has been incorporated in the T product since $\hat{H}_1 \equiv \hat{H}_1(0)$ corresponds to a later time than all the other factors in the integrand. Use Wick's theorem to evaluate all the contractions that contribute to the matrix element in Eq. (9.51). The factor $\hat{H}_1(0)$ provides a fixed external point that enables us to distinguish between connected and disconnected diagrams; a connected diagram is one that is contracted into $\hat{H}_1(0)$. The distinction is illustrated in Fig. 9.23. Suppose that there are n connected $\hat{H}_1$'s

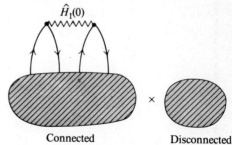

$\hat{H}_1(0)$

Fig. 9.23 Typical connected and disconnected Goldstone diagrams.

Connected   ×   Disconnected

and m disconnected $\hat{H}_1$'s where $v = n + m$; this partition can be performed in $v!/n!m!$ ways. The summation over v in Eq. (9.51) can therefore be rewritten

$$\sum_n \sum_m \left(\frac{-i}{\hbar}\right)^{n+m} \frac{v!}{n!m!} \frac{1}{v!} \int_{-\infty}^{0} dt_1 \cdots \int_{-\infty}^{0} dt_n$$

$$\times \langle \Phi_0 | T[\hat{H}_1 \hat{H}_1(t_1) \cdots \hat{H}_1(t_n)] | \Phi_0 \rangle_C \int_{-\infty}^{0} dt_{n+1} \cdots \int_{-\infty}^{0} dt_{n+m}$$

$$\times \langle \Phi_0 | T[\hat{H}_1(t_{n+1}) \cdots \hat{H}_1(t_{n+m})] | \Phi_0 \rangle \qquad (9.52)$$

just as in Eq. (9.4). (For simplicity, we now use a subscript C to indicate connected.) The summation over m reproduces the denominator of Eq. (9.50), and we thus obtain

$$E - E_0 = \sum_{n=0}^{\infty} \left(\frac{-i}{\hbar}\right)^n \frac{1}{n!} \int_{-\infty}^{0} dt_1 \cdots \int_{-\infty}^{0} dt_n$$

$$\times \langle \Phi_0 | T[\hat{H}_1 \hat{H}_1(t_1) \cdots \hat{H}_1(t_n)] | \Phi_0 \rangle_C \qquad (9.53)$$

which demonstrates the cancellation of the disconnected diagrams in this expression.

We now proceed to *carry out the time integrations in Eq. (9.53) explicitly.* Consider the nth-order contribution and insert the relation between $\hat{H}_1(t)$ and $\hat{H}_1$ from Eq. (6.5)

$$[E - E_0]^{(n)} = \left(\frac{-i}{\hbar}\right)^n \int_{-\infty}^{0} dt_1 \int_{-\infty}^{t_1} dt_2 \cdots \int_{-\infty}^{t_{n-1}} dt_n \, e^{\epsilon(t_1 + t_2 + \cdots + t_n)}$$

$$\times \langle \Phi_0 | \hat{H}_1 e^{i\hat{H}_0 t_1/\hbar} \hat{H}_1 e^{-i\hat{H}_0 t_1/\hbar} e^{i\hat{H}_0 t_2/\hbar} \hat{H}_1 e^{-\hat{H}_0 t_2/\hbar} \cdots$$

$$\hat{H}_1 e^{-i\hat{H}_0 t_{n-1}/\hbar} e^{i\hat{H}_0 t_n/\hbar} \hat{H}_1 e^{-i\hat{H}_0 t_n/\hbar} | \Phi_0 \rangle_C$$

Here we have observed that all $n!$ possible time orderings make identical contributions (see Sec. 6) and therefore work with one definite time ordering of the operators in this matrix element. The adiabatic damping factor has also been explicitly restored. Change variables to *relative* times

$$
\begin{aligned}
&x_1 = t_1 && t_1 = x_1 \\
&x_2 = t_2 - t_1 && t_2 = x_2 + x_1 \\
&x_3 = t_3 - t_2 \qquad \text{or} \qquad && t_3 = x_3 + x_2 + x_1 \\
&\quad\vdots && \quad\vdots \\
&x_n = t_n - t_{n-1} && t_n = x_n + x_{n-1} + \cdots + x_1
\end{aligned}
$$

and use

$$\hat{H}_0 | \Phi_0 \rangle = E_0 | \Phi_0 \rangle$$

This transformation yields

$$[E - E_0]^{(n)} = \left(\frac{-i}{\hbar}\right)^n \langle \Phi_0 | \hat{H}_1 \int_{-\infty}^0 e^{n\epsilon x_1} e^{i(\hat{H}_0 - E_0) x_1/\hbar} dx_1 \hat{H}_1$$

$$\times \int_{-\infty}^0 e^{(n-1)\epsilon x_2} e^{i(\hat{H}_0 - E_0) x_2/\hbar} dx_2 \hat{H}_1 \cdots$$

$$\int_{-\infty}^0 e^{\epsilon x_n} e^{i(\hat{H}_0 - E_0) x_n/\hbar} dx_n \hat{H}_1 | \Phi_0 \rangle_c$$

The integrations can now all be carried out explicitly, and we find

$$[E - E_0]^{(n)} = \langle \Phi_0 | \hat{H}_1 \frac{1}{E_0 - \hat{H}_0 + i\epsilon n\hbar} \hat{H}_1 \frac{1}{E_0 - \hat{H}_0 + i\epsilon(n-1)\hbar} \hat{H}_1 \cdots$$

$$\hat{H}_1 \frac{1}{E_0 - \hat{H}_0 + i\epsilon\hbar} \hat{H}_1 | \Phi_0 \rangle_c$$

This result immediately yields Goldstone's theorem Eq. (9.48) because the limitation to connected diagrams ensures that $|\Phi_0\rangle$ cannot appear as an intermediate state, and the state $|\Phi_0\rangle$ is nondegenerate. It follows that $E_0 - \hat{H}_0 + i\epsilon\hbar$ can never vanish, so that the convergence factor $+i\epsilon$ becomes irrelevant, and we can use the propagator $[E_0 - \hat{H}_0]^{-1}$, as in Eq. (9.48).

This formal proof can be made more concrete by explicitly considering all nth-order Feynman diagrams that contribute to Eq. (9.53). Each diagram consists of unperturbed Green's functions G^0, which evidently contain both particle and hole propagation [compare Eq. (7.41)]. These diagrams can be grouped into sets containing $n!$ equivalent diagrams that differ only by permuting the time variables. The symmetry of the integrand again allows the replacement

$$\frac{1}{n!} \int_{-\infty}^0 dt_1 \cdots \int_{-\infty}^0 dt_n = \int_{-\infty}^0 dt_1 \int_{-\infty}^{t_1} dt_2 \cdots \int_{-\infty}^{t_{n-1}} dt_n$$

With the choice of a definite time ordering, each of the $n!$ diagrams now represents a distinct process. The integral over relative times $(0 \geqslant x_i \geqslant -\infty)$ then yields $n!$ distinct Goldstone diagrams corresponding to the $n!$ possible time orderings of the original Feynman diagram. Thus the set of all possible time-ordered connected Feynman diagrams gives the complete set of connected Goldstone diagrams. The Feynman-Dyson and Goldstone approaches are clearly equivalent to every order in perturbation theory, but the *Feynman-Dyson analysis has the fundamental advantage of combining many terms of time-independent perturbation theory into a single Feynman diagram.* We may note that a similar analysis applies to *any* ground-state expectation value of Heisenberg field operators, for example, the single-particle Green's function $G(\mathbf{x}, \mathbf{y}, \omega)$, which is the Fourier transform of Eq. (9.5). If the integration over all times is carried out explicitly, the resulting perturbation expansion may be classified according to the intermediate states, just as in Fig. 9.21. In this way we can obtain a unique correspondence between a given Feynman diagram and a set of Goldstone diagrams (or diagrams of time-independent perturbation theory).

Goldstone's theorem (9.48) was originally stimulated by Brueckner's theory of strongly interacting Fermi systems. This Brueckner-Goldstone approach has formed the basis for extensive work on the ground-state properties of nuclear matter,[1] He³,[2] and atoms.[3]

PROBLEMS

3.1. Show that when $t < t_0$ the integral equation for $\hat{U}(t,t_0)$ can be written as

$$\hat{U}(t,t_0) = 1 + \frac{i}{\hbar} \int_t^{t_0} dt' \, \hat{H}_1(t') \, \hat{U}(t',t_0)$$

Hence show that

$$\hat{U}(t,t_0) = \sum_{n=0}^{\infty} \left(\frac{i}{\hbar}\right)^n \frac{1}{n!} \int_t^{t_0} dt_1 \cdots \int_t^{t_0} dt_n \, \tilde{T}[\hat{H}_1(t_1) \cdots \hat{H}_1(t_n)]$$

where $\tilde{T}$ denotes the anti-time-ordering (latest times to the right). Derive this result from Eqs. (6.16) and (6.23).

3.2. One of the most useful relations in quantum field theory is

$$e^{i\hat{S}} \hat{O} e^{-i\hat{S}} = \hat{O} + i[\hat{S},\hat{O}] + \frac{i^2}{2!}[\hat{S},[\hat{S},\hat{O}]] + \frac{i^3}{3!}[\hat{S},[\hat{S},[\hat{S},\hat{O}]]] + \cdots$$

Verify this result to the order indicated. Evaluate the commutators explicitly and re-sum the series to derive Eqs. (6.10) from Eqs. (6.7) and (6.9).

3.3. Define the two-particle Green's function by

$$G_{\alpha\beta;\gamma\delta}(\mathbf{x}_1 t_1, \mathbf{x}_2 t_2; \mathbf{x}_1' t_1', \mathbf{x}_2' t_2')$$
$$= (-i)^2 \frac{\langle \Psi_0 | T[\hat{\psi}_\alpha(\mathbf{x}_1 t_1) \, \hat{\psi}_\beta(\mathbf{x}_2 t_2) \, \hat{\psi}_\delta^\dagger(\mathbf{x}_2' t_2') \, \hat{\psi}_\gamma^\dagger(\mathbf{x}_1' t_1')] | \Psi_0 \rangle}{\langle \Psi_0 | \Psi_0 \rangle}$$

Prove that the expectation value of the two-body interaction in the exact ground state is given by

$$\langle \hat{V} \rangle = -\tfrac{1}{2} \int d^3x \int d^3x' \, V(\mathbf{x},\mathbf{x}')_{\mu'\lambda',\mu\lambda} \, G_{\lambda\lambda';\mu\mu'}(\mathbf{x}' t, \mathbf{x}t; \mathbf{x}' t^+, \mathbf{x}t^+)$$

---

[1] K. A. Brueckner, C. A. Levinson, and H. M. Mahmoud, *Phys. Rev.*, **95**:217 (1954); H. A. Bethe, *Phys. Rev.*, **103**:1353 (1956); K. A. Brueckner and J. L. Gammel, *Phys. Rev.*, **109**:1023 (1958); K. A. Brueckner, Theory of Nuclear Structure, in C. DeWitt (ed.), "The Many-Body Problem," p. 47, John Wiley and Sons, Inc., New York, 1959; H. A. Bethe, B. H. Brandow, and A. G. Petschek, *Phys. Rev.*, **129**:225 (1963); see also Chap. 11.

[2] K. A. Brueckner and J. L. Gammel, *Phys. Rev.*, **109**:1040 (1958); T. W. Burkhardt, *Ann. Phys. (N.Y.)*, **47**:516 (1968); E. Østgaard, *Phys. Rev.*, **170**:257 (1968).

[3] See, for example, H. P. Kelly, Correlation Structure in Atoms, in K. A. Brueckner (ed.), "Advances in Theoretical Physics," vol. 2, p. 75, Academic Press Inc., New York, 1968. A review of this topic is also given in Correlation Effects in Atoms and Molecules, R. Lefebvre and C. Moser (eds.), "Advances in Chemical Physics," vol. XIV, Interscience Publishers, New York, 1969.

3.4. Consider a many-body system in the presence of an external potential $U(\mathbf{x})$ with a spin-independent interaction potential $V(\mathbf{x} - \mathbf{x}')$. Show that the exact one-particle Green's function obeys the equation of motion

$$\left[i\hbar \frac{\partial}{\partial t_1} + \frac{\hbar^2 \nabla_1^2}{2m} - U(\mathbf{x}_1) \right] G_{\alpha\beta}(\mathbf{x}_1 t_1, \mathbf{x}_1' t_1')$$

$$\mp i \int d^3 x_2 \, V(\mathbf{x}_1 - \mathbf{x}_2) \, G_{\alpha\gamma;\beta\gamma}(\mathbf{x}_1 t_1, \mathbf{x}_2 t_1; \mathbf{x}_1' t_1', \mathbf{x}_2 t_1^+)$$

$$= \hbar\delta(\mathbf{x}_1 - \mathbf{x}_1') \, \delta(t_1 - t_1') \, \delta_{\alpha\beta}$$

where the upper (lower) sign refers to bosons (fermions) and the two-particle Green's function is defined in Prob. 3.3.

3.5. Use Eqs. (3.29) and (3.30) to verify Eq. (7.58) for an ideal Fermi gas, and show that $\mu = \epsilon_F^0$.

3.6. Consider the function

$$F_\alpha(z) = \frac{2}{\pi\alpha} \sum_{n=0}^{\infty} \frac{1}{n^2 + z/\alpha^2}$$

and discuss its analytic structure in the complex z plane.
(a) Show that the series can be summed to give $F_\alpha(z) = z^{-\frac{1}{2}} \coth(\pi z^{\frac{1}{2}}/\alpha) + (\alpha/\pi z)$, which has the *same* analytic structure.
(b) Examine the limit $\alpha \to 0$ and compare with the discussion of Eq. (7.67).

3.7. (a) If $\int_{-\infty}^{\infty} dx \, |\rho(x)| < \infty$, show that $f(z) \equiv \int_{-\infty}^{\infty} dx \, \rho(x)(z - x)^{-1}$ is bounded and analytic for $\mathrm{Im}\, z \neq 0$. Prove that $f(z)$ is discontinuous across the real axis whenever $\rho(x) \neq 0$, and thus $f(z)$ has a branch cut in this region.
(b) Assume the following simple form $\rho(x) = \gamma(\gamma^2 + x^2)^{-1}$. Evaluate $f(z)$ explicitly for $\mathrm{Im}\, z > 0$ and find its analytic continuation to $\mathrm{Im}\, z < 0$.
(c) Repeat part (b) for $\mathrm{Im}\, z < 0$. Compare and discuss.

3.8. Derive the Lehmann representation for $D(\mathbf{k},\omega)$, which is the Fourier transform of

$$iD(x,y) \equiv \frac{\langle \Psi_0' | T[\tilde{n}_H(x)\, \tilde{n}_H(y)] | \Psi_0' \rangle}{\langle \Psi_0' | \Psi_0' \rangle}$$

with the *density fluctuation operator* defined by

$$\tilde{n}(\mathbf{x}) \equiv \hat{\psi}_\alpha^\dagger(\mathbf{x})\, \hat{\psi}_\alpha(\mathbf{x}) - \frac{\langle \Psi_0' | \hat{\psi}_\alpha^\dagger(\mathbf{x})\, \hat{\psi}_\alpha(\mathbf{x}) | \Psi_0' \rangle}{\langle \Psi_0' | \Psi_0' \rangle}$$

Show that $D(\mathbf{k},\omega)$ is a meromorphic function with poles in the second and fourth quadrant of the complex ω plane. Introduce the corresponding retarded and advanced functions, and construct a Lehmann representation for their Fourier transforms. Discuss the analytic properties and derive the *dispersion relations* analogous to Eq. (7.70).

3.9. Make the canonical transformation to particles and holes for fermions $c_{k\lambda} = \theta(k - k_F)a_{k\lambda} + \theta(k_F - k)b^{\dagger}_{-k\lambda}$. By applying Wick's theorem, prove the relation

$$c_1^{\dagger} c_2^{\dagger} c_4 c_3 = N(c_1^{\dagger} c_2^{\dagger} c_4 c_3) + \theta(k_F - k_2)[\delta_{24} N(c_1^{\dagger} c_3) - \delta_{23} N(c_1^{\dagger} c_4)]$$

$$+ \theta(k_F - k_1)[\delta_{13} N(c_2^{\dagger} c_4) - \delta_{14} N(c_2^{\dagger} c_3)]$$

$$+ \theta(k_F - k_1) \theta(k_F - k_2)[\delta_{13} \delta_{24} - \delta_{14} \delta_{23}]$$

where the normal-ordered products on the right side now refer to the new particle and hole operators, and the subscripts indicate the quantum numbers $(\mathbf{k}, \lambda)$.

3.10. Verify the cancellation of disconnected diagrams [Eqs. (8.11), (9.3), and (9.4)] explicitly to second order in the interaction potential.

3.11. Consider a system of noninteracting spin-$\frac{1}{2}$ fermions in an external static potential with a hamiltonian $\hat{H}^{ex} = \int d^3x \, \hat{\psi}^{\dagger}_{\alpha}(\mathbf{x}) V_{\alpha\beta}(\mathbf{x}) \hat{\psi}_{\beta}(\mathbf{x})$.
(a) Use Wick's theorem to find the Feynman rules for the single-particle Green's function in the presence of the external potential.
(b) Show that Dyson's equation becomes

$$G^{ex}_{\alpha\beta}(x, y) = G^0_{\alpha\beta}(x - y) + \hbar^{-1} \int d^3z \, G^0_{\alpha\lambda}(x - z) V_{\lambda\lambda'}(\mathbf{z}) G^{ex}_{\lambda'\beta}(z, y)$$

(c) Express the ground-state energy in a form analogous to Eqs. (7.23) and (7.31). What happens if the particles also interact?

3.12. Consider a uniform system of spin-$\frac{1}{2}$ fermions with spin-independent interactions.
(a) Use the Feynman rules in momentum space to write out the second-order contributions to the proper self-energy; evaluate the frequency integrals (some of them will vanish).
(b) Hence show that the second-order contribution to the ground-state energy can be written

$$\frac{E^{(2)}}{V} = 2m\hbar^{-2} \int \cdots \int (2\pi)^{-9} d^3k \, d^3p \, d^3l \, d^3n \, \delta^{(3)}(\mathbf{k} + \mathbf{p} - \mathbf{l} - \mathbf{n})$$

$$\times [2V(\mathbf{l} - \mathbf{k})^2 - V(\mathbf{l} - \mathbf{k}) V(\mathbf{p} - \mathbf{l})] \theta(k_F - p) \theta(k_F - k)$$

$$\times \theta(n - k_F) \theta(l - k_F)(p^2 + k^2 - l^2 - n^2 + i\eta)^{-1}$$

(c) Specialize to an electron gas and rederive the results of Prob. 1.4.

3.13. Derive the expression for $E^{(2)}$ given in Prob. 3.12 from Goldstone's theorem (9.48). From this result, give the rules for evaluating those Goldstone diagrams shown in Fig. 9.22.

3.14.   Use Eq. (9.33) to show that the energy ϵ_k and damping $|\gamma_k|$ of long-lived single-particle excitations are given by

$$\epsilon_k = \epsilon_k^0 + \operatorname{Re} \hbar \Sigma^\star(\mathbf{k}, \epsilon_k/\hbar)$$

$$\gamma_k = \left[1 - \frac{\partial \operatorname{Re} \Sigma^\star(\mathbf{k}, \omega)}{\partial \omega}\bigg|_{\epsilon_k/\hbar}\right]^{-1} \operatorname{Im} \Sigma^\star(\mathbf{k}, \epsilon_k/\hbar)$$

3.15.   Consider a uniform system of spin-$\frac{1}{2}$ fermions with the spin-dependent interaction potential of Eq. (9.21), and assume that $\Pi^\star_{\mu\nu,\kappa\lambda}(q)$ may be approximated by $\frac{1}{2}\Pi^0(q)\delta_{\nu\kappa}\delta_{\lambda\mu}$.
(*a*) Solve Eq. (9.40) to find

$$U(q)_{\alpha\beta,\rho\tau} = \frac{V_0(q)\delta_{\alpha\beta}\delta_{\rho\tau}}{1 - V_0(q)\Pi^0(q)} + \frac{V_1(q)\boldsymbol{\sigma}_{\alpha\beta}\cdot\boldsymbol{\sigma}_{\rho\tau}}{1 - V_1(q)\Pi^0(q)}$$

(*b*) Combine Eqs. (9.39) and (9.40) to obtain Dyson's equation for Π in terms of $\Pi^\star$ and U_0. Solve this equation with the above approximation for $\Pi^\star$, and prove that

$$\Pi_{\mu\nu,\eta\lambda}(q) = \tfrac{1}{2}\Pi^0(q)\delta_{\nu\eta}\delta_{\lambda\mu} + \tfrac{1}{2}\Pi^0(q)U(q)_{\nu\mu,\lambda\eta}\tfrac{1}{2}\Pi^0(q)$$

where $U(q)$ is taken from (*a*).

4
Fermi Systems

In principle, the perturbation theory and Feynman diagrams developed in Chap. 3 enable us to evaluate the Green's function G to all orders in the interaction potential. Such a procedure is impractical, however, and we must instead resort to approximation schemes. For example, the simplest approximation consists in retaining only the first-order contributions $\Sigma_{(1)}^{\star}$ to the proper self-energy, as discussed in Eqs. (9.24) and (9.35). Unfortunately, this approximation is inadequate for most systems of interest, and it becomes necessary to include certain classes of higher-order terms. Two approaches have been especially successful; both include infinite orders in perturbation theory, but they are otherwise quite distinct. In the first, a small set of proper self-energy insertions is *reinterpreted*, so that the particle lines represent *exact* Green's functions G instead of noninteracting Green's functions G^0. These approximations are therefore *self-consistent*, because G both determines and is determined by the

proper self-energy $\Sigma^\star$. In contrast, the second approach retains a selected (infinite) class of proper self-energy insertions, expressed in terms of G^0. The details of the many-particle hamiltonian determine which procedure is suitable, and we shall consider three examples that illustrate how this choice can be made: The (self-consistent) Hartree-Fock approximation (Sec. 10), the summation of *ladder* diagrams, appropriate for repulsive hard-core potentials (Sec. 11), and the summation of *ring* diagrams, appropriate for long-range coulomb potentials (Sec. 12).

10□HARTREE-FOCK APPROXIMATION

The starting point for our discussion of interacting quantum mechanical assemblies has been the state $|\Phi_0\rangle$, which is the ground state of the hamiltonian $\hat{H}_0$

$$\hat{H}_0 = \sum_k \hbar\omega_k\, c_k^\dagger c_k$$

In $|\Phi_0\rangle$, each of the N particles occupies a definite single-particle state, so that its motion is independent of the presence of the other particles. This situation will be clearly modified by the interactions between the particles; nevertheless, it is an experimental fact that a single-particle description forms a surprisingly good approximation in many different systems, for example, metals, atoms, and nuclei. Hence a natural approach is to retain the single-particle picture and assume that *each particle moves in a single-particle potential that comes from its average interaction with all of the other particles.* The single-particle energy should then be the unperturbed energy plus the potential energy of interaction averaged over the states occupied by all of the other particles. This is the result obtained in Eq. (9.35); thus as a first approximation we can keep just the first-order contribution to the proper self-energy $\Sigma^\star_{(1)}$. The corresponding Feynman diagrams are shown in Fig. 10.1. This calculation is not fully consistent,

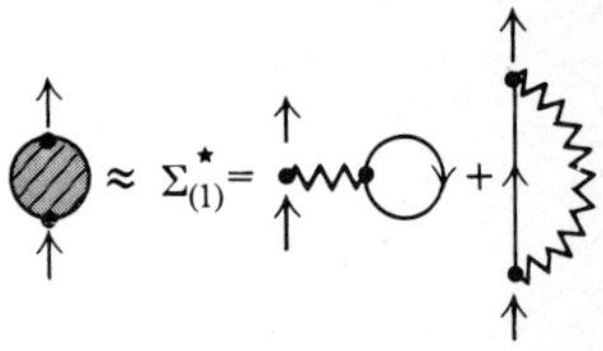

Fig. 10.1   Lowest-order proper self-energy.

however, since the background particles contributing to $\Sigma^\star_{(1)}$ are treated as non-interacting. In reality, of course, these particles also move in an average potential coming from the presence of all the other particles. Thus instead of just the two self-energy terms shown in Fig. 10.1 we should include all the graphs shown in Fig. 10.2. The shaded circles again denote the proper self-energy, which is the quantity we are trying to compute. Since the exact Green's function can be expressed as a series containing the proper self-energy [Eq. (9.27)] all the

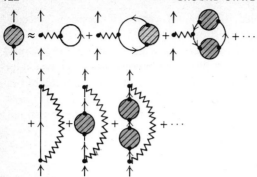

Fig. 10.2 Series for proper self-energy in Hartree-Fock approximation.

terms of Fig. 10.2 can be summed in the pair of diagrams shown in Fig. 10.3, where the heavy line denotes the exact G, which is itself determined from the proper self-energy as indicated in Fig. 10.4. We proceed to examine these equations in detail.

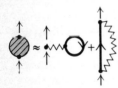

Fig. 10.3 Self-consistent proper self-energy in Hartree-Fock approximation.

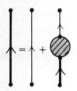

Fig. 10.4 Dyson's equation for G.

We shall consider a system in a static spin-independent external potential $U(\mathbf{x})$, which destroys the spatial uniformity—for example, electrons in a metal or an atom. The total hamiltonian then becomes

$$\hat{H}_0 = \int d^3x \, \hat{\psi}_\alpha^\dagger(\mathbf{x}) \left[-\frac{\hbar^2 \nabla^2}{2m} + U(\mathbf{x}) \right] \hat{\psi}_\alpha(\mathbf{x}) \tag{10.1a}$$

$$\hat{H}_1 = \tfrac{1}{2} \int d^3x \, d^3x' \, \hat{\psi}_\alpha^\dagger(\mathbf{x}) \, \hat{\psi}_\beta^\dagger(\mathbf{x}') \, V(\mathbf{x} - \mathbf{x}') \, \hat{\psi}_\beta(\mathbf{x}') \, \hat{\psi}_\alpha(\mathbf{x}) \tag{10.1b}$$

where for simplicity the interparticle potential has been assumed spin independent

$$V(\mathbf{x},\mathbf{x}')_{\lambda\lambda', \mu\mu'} = V(\mathbf{x} - \mathbf{x}') \, \delta_{\lambda\lambda'} \, \delta_{\mu\mu'} \tag{10.2}$$

In the present approximation, Dyson's equation takes the form shown in Fig. 10.5 where the light line denotes G^0 (the noninteracting Green's function corre-

sponding to $\hat{H}_0$), and the heavy line denotes the self-consistent G. The corresponding analytic equation is given by

$$G(x,y) = G^0(x,y) + \int d^4x_1 \, d^4x_1' \, G^0(x,x_1) \, \Sigma^\star(x_1,x_1') \, G(x_1',y) \tag{10.3}$$

where the Kronecker delta in the matrix indices has been factored out.   Exactly as in Chap. 3, the Feynman rules yield an explicit expression for the proper self-energy

$$\hbar\Sigma^\star(x_1,x_1') = -i\delta(t_1 - t_1') \, [\delta(\mathbf{x}_1 - \mathbf{x}_1')(2s + 1) \int d^3x_2 \, G(\mathbf{x}_2 t_2, \mathbf{x}_2 t_2^+)$$
$$\times \, V(\mathbf{x}_1 - \mathbf{x}_2) - V(\mathbf{x}_1 - \mathbf{x}_1') \, G(\mathbf{x}_1 t_1, \mathbf{x}_1' t_1^+)] \tag{10.4}$$

which is valid for spin-s fermions.   Note that the first term has an extra factor $(2s + 1)$ relative to the second term; this arises from the spin sums [compare Eq. (9.18)].

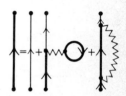

Fig. 10.5   Dyson's equation for G in Hartree-Fock approximation.

In the present example, both $\hat{H}$ and $\hat{H}_0$ are time independent, and it is therefore convenient to use a Fourier representation

$$G(\mathbf{x}t, \mathbf{x}' t') = (2\pi)^{-1} \int d\omega \, e^{-i\omega(t-t')} \, G(\mathbf{x},\mathbf{x}',\omega) \tag{10.5a}$$

$$G^0(\mathbf{x}t, \mathbf{x}' t') = (2\pi)^{-1} \int d\omega \, e^{-i\omega(t-t')} \, G^0(\mathbf{x},\mathbf{x}',\omega) \tag{10.5b}$$

$$\Sigma^\star(\mathbf{x}t, \mathbf{x}' t') = \Sigma^\star(\mathbf{x},\mathbf{x}') \, \delta(t - t') = (2\pi)^{-1} \int d\omega \, e^{-i\omega(t-t')} \, \Sigma^\star(\mathbf{x},\mathbf{x}') \tag{10.5c}$$

As in the first-order approximation [Eq. (9.24)], the proper self-energy is here independent of frequency.   The time integrations in Eq. (10.3) can now be performed explicitly, and we find

$$G(\mathbf{x},\mathbf{y},\omega) = G^0(\mathbf{x},\mathbf{y},\omega) + \int d^3x_1 \, d^3x_1' \, G^0(\mathbf{x},\mathbf{x}_1,\omega) \, \Sigma^\star(\mathbf{x}_1,\mathbf{x}_1') \, G(\mathbf{x}_1',\mathbf{y},\omega) \tag{10.6}$$

Correspondingly, Eq. (10.4) reduces to

$$\hbar\Sigma^\star(\mathbf{x}_1,\mathbf{x}_1') = -i(2s + 1) \, \delta(\mathbf{x}_1 - \mathbf{x}_1') \int d^3x_2 \, V(\mathbf{x}_1 - \mathbf{x}_2)(2\pi)^{-1} \int d\omega \, e^{i\omega\eta}$$
$$\times \, G(\mathbf{x}_2,\mathbf{x}_2,\omega) + iV(\mathbf{x}_1 - \mathbf{x}_1')(2\pi)^{-1} \int d\omega \, e^{i\omega\eta} \, G(\mathbf{x}_1,\mathbf{x}_1',\omega) \tag{10.7}$$

It is convenient to introduce the complete set of orthonormal eigenfunctions of H_0:

$$H_0 \varphi_j^0(\mathbf{x}) = \left[-\frac{\hbar^2 \nabla^2}{2m} + U(\mathbf{x}) \right] \varphi_j^0(\mathbf{x}) = \epsilon_j^0 \, \varphi_j^0(\mathbf{x}) \tag{10.8}$$

These single-particle states form a natural basis for the field operators $\hat{\psi}_\alpha(\mathbf{x}t)$ in the interaction picture, and the noninteracting Green's function then becomes

$$iG^0(\mathbf{x}t, \mathbf{x}'\,t') = \sum_j \varphi_j^0(\mathbf{x})\,\varphi_j^0(\mathbf{x}')^* \exp\left[\frac{-i\epsilon_j^0(t-t')}{\hbar}\right]$$

$$\times \left[\theta(t-t')\langle\Phi_0|a_j a_j^\dagger|\Phi_0\rangle - \theta(t'-t)\langle\Phi_0|a_j^\dagger a_j|\Phi_0\rangle\right]$$

$$= \sum_j \varphi_j^0(\mathbf{x})\,\varphi_j^0(\mathbf{x}')^* \exp\left[\frac{-i\epsilon_j^0(t-t')}{\hbar}\right]$$

$$\times \left[\theta(t-t')\,\theta(\epsilon_j^0 - \epsilon_F^0) - \theta(t'-t)\,\theta(\epsilon_F^0 - \epsilon_j^0)\right] \quad (10.9)$$

where ϵ_F^0 is the energy of the last filled state. The Fourier transform can be computed exactly as in Eq. (7.44), which yields

$$G^0(\mathbf{x},\mathbf{x}',\omega) = \sum_j \varphi_j^0(\mathbf{x})\,\varphi_j^0(\mathbf{x}')^* \left[\frac{\theta(\epsilon_j^0 - \epsilon_F^0)}{\omega - \hbar^{-1}\epsilon_j^0 + i\eta} + \frac{\theta(\epsilon_F^0 - \epsilon_j^0)}{\omega - \hbar^{-1}\epsilon_j^0 - i\eta}\right] \quad (10.10)$$

We can now evaluate the particle density $n^0(\mathbf{x})$ in the unperturbed ground state $|\Phi_0\rangle$

$$n^0(\mathbf{x}) = -i(2s+1)(2\pi)^{-1}\int d\omega\, e^{i\omega\eta}\, G^0(\mathbf{x},\mathbf{x},\omega)$$

$$= (2s+1)\sum_j |\varphi_j^0(\mathbf{x})|^2\,\theta(\epsilon_F^0 - \epsilon_j^0) \quad (10.11)$$

while the total number of particles is given by

$$N^0 = \int d^3x\, n^0(\mathbf{x}) = (2s+1)\sum_j \theta(\epsilon_F^0 - \epsilon_j^0) \quad (10.12)$$

because the single-particle wave functions are assumed normalized.

Equations (10.6) to (10.8) and Eq. (10.10) define a set of coupled equations for the self-consistent Green's function G. Since Σ^* is independent of frequency, it is natural to seek a solution for G in the same form as G^0:

$$G(\mathbf{x},\mathbf{x}',\omega) = \sum_j \varphi_j(\mathbf{x})\,\varphi_j(\mathbf{x}')^* \left[\frac{\theta(\epsilon_j - \epsilon_F)}{\omega - \hbar^{-1}\epsilon_j + i\eta} + \frac{\theta(\epsilon_F - \epsilon_j)}{\omega - \hbar^{-1}\epsilon_j - i\eta}\right] \quad (10.13)$$

where $\{\varphi_j(\mathbf{x})\}$ denotes a complete set of single-particle wave functions with energies ϵ_j, and ϵ_F is the energy of the last filled state. The associated particle density in the interacting system becomes [compare Eq. (10.11)]

$$n(\mathbf{x}) = (2s+1)\sum_j |\varphi_j(\mathbf{x})|^2\,\theta(\epsilon_F - \epsilon_j) \quad (10.14)$$

while

$$N = N^0 = (2s+1)\sum_j \theta(\epsilon_F - \epsilon_j) \quad (10.15)$$

because the perturbation $\hat{H}_1$ conserves the total number of particles. Thus the interaction merely shifts the single-particle levels, which are still filled according

to their energy up to the Fermi level ϵ_F. The frequency integral in Eq. (10.7) can now be evaluated directly, and we find

$$\hbar\Sigma^\star(\mathbf{x}_1,\mathbf{x}_1') = (2s+1)\,\delta(\mathbf{x}_1 - \mathbf{x}_1')\int d^3x_2\, V(\mathbf{x}_1 - \mathbf{x}_2)\sum_j |\varphi_j(\mathbf{x}_2)|^2\,\theta(\epsilon_F - \epsilon_j)$$

$$- V(\mathbf{x}_1 - \mathbf{x}_1')\sum_j \varphi_j(\mathbf{x}_1)\varphi_j(\mathbf{x}_1')^*\,\theta(\epsilon_F - \epsilon_j)$$

$$= \delta(\mathbf{x}_1 - \mathbf{x}_1')\int d^3x_2\, V(\mathbf{x}_1 - \mathbf{x}_2)\,n(\mathbf{x}_2)$$

$$- V(\mathbf{x}_1 - \mathbf{x}_1')\sum_j \varphi_j(\mathbf{x}_1)\varphi_j(\mathbf{x}_1')^*\,\theta(\epsilon_F - \epsilon_j) \quad (10.16)$$

Note that $\Sigma^\star$ depends on φ_j; a combination of Eqs. (10.6) and (10.16) then yields a *nonlinear* integral equation for φ_j in terms of (the assumed known) φ_j^0.

This equation may be simplified with the differential operator

$$L_1 = \hbar\omega + \frac{\hbar^2\nabla_1^2}{2m} - U(\mathbf{x}_1) = \hbar\omega - H_0$$

If L_1 is applied to $G^0(\mathbf{x}_1,\mathbf{x}_1',\omega)$ we obtain

$$L_1 G^0(\mathbf{x}_1,\mathbf{x}_1',\omega) = \sum_j (\hbar\omega - \epsilon_j^0)\,\varphi_j^0(\mathbf{x}_1)\,\varphi_j^0(\mathbf{x}_1')^* \left[\frac{\theta(\epsilon_j^0 - \epsilon_F^0)}{\omega - \epsilon_j^0/\hbar + i\eta} + \frac{\theta(\epsilon_F^0 - \epsilon_j^0)}{\omega - \epsilon_j^0/\hbar - i\eta}\right]$$

$$= \hbar\sum_j \varphi_j^0(\mathbf{x}_1)\,\varphi_j^0(\mathbf{x}_1')^*$$

$$= \hbar\delta(\mathbf{x}_1 - \mathbf{x}_1')$$

where the last line follows from the assumed completeness of the set $\{\varphi_j^0\}$. Thus $\hbar^{-1}L_1$ is the inverse operator $(G^0)^{-1}$, and application of L_1 to Eq. (10.6) yields

$$L_1 G(\mathbf{x}_1,\mathbf{x}_1',\omega) = \hbar\delta(\mathbf{x}_1 - \mathbf{x}_1') + \int d^3x_2\,\hbar\Sigma^\star(\mathbf{x}_1,\mathbf{x}_2)\,G(\mathbf{x}_2,\mathbf{x}_1',\omega)$$

It is useful to insert the explicit forms of G and L_1:

$$\left[\hbar\omega + \frac{\hbar^2\nabla_1^2}{2m} - U(\mathbf{x}_1)\right]\sum_j \varphi_j(\mathbf{x}_1)\varphi_j(\mathbf{x}_1')^* \left[\frac{\theta(\epsilon_j - \epsilon_F)}{\omega - \hbar^{-1}\epsilon_j + i\eta} + \frac{\theta(\epsilon_F - \epsilon_j)}{\omega - \hbar^{-1}\epsilon_j - i\eta}\right]$$

$$- \int d^3x_2\,\hbar\Sigma^\star(\mathbf{x}_1,\mathbf{x}_2)\sum_j \varphi_j(\mathbf{x}_2)\varphi_j(\mathbf{x}_1')^* \left[\frac{\theta(\epsilon_j - \epsilon_F)}{\omega - \hbar^{-1}\epsilon_j + i\eta} + \frac{\theta(\epsilon_F - \epsilon_j)}{\omega - \hbar^{-1}\epsilon_j - i\eta}\right]$$

$$= \hbar\delta(\mathbf{x}_1 - \mathbf{x}_1')$$

Multiply by $\varphi_k(\mathbf{x}_1')$ and integrate over $\mathbf{x}_1'$. The orthogonality of $\{\varphi_j\}$ leads to a simple Schrödinger-like equation for $\varphi_j(\mathbf{x}_1)$

$$\left[-\frac{\hbar^2\nabla_1^2}{2m} + U(\mathbf{x}_1)\right]\varphi_j(\mathbf{x}_1) + \int d^3x_2\,\hbar\Sigma^\star(\mathbf{x}_1,\mathbf{x}_2)\varphi_j(\mathbf{x}_2) = \epsilon_j\varphi_j(\mathbf{x}_1) \quad (10.17)$$

where the proper self-energy $\hbar\Sigma^\star$ acts as a static *nonlocal* potential. Since $\Sigma^\star$ is hermitian and independent of j, the usual proof of orthogonality remains

unchanged, thereby justifying our initial assumption.   Equation (10.16) shows
that $\Sigma^\star$ consists of two terms: a local (direct) term proportional to the particle
density and a nonlocal (exchange) term.   These equations are just the Hartree-
Fock equations[1] familiar from atomic theory.

It is apparent that these equations constitute a very complicated problem:
An initial set of single-particle wave functions and energies is assumed known,
and the corresponding $\Sigma^\star$ is calculated from Eq. (10.16).   Equation (10.17) then
becomes a one-body eigenvalue equation that determines a new set of eigenfunctions and eigenvalues, which are used to recompute $\Sigma^\star$.   This process is
continued until a self-consistent solution is obtained for *both* $\{\varphi_j\}$ and $\{\epsilon_j\}$.
The ground-state energy can then be evaluated with Eq. (7.23), suitably generalized to include the external potential $U(\mathbf{x}_1)$

$$
E = -\tfrac{1}{2}i(2s+1)\int d^3x_1 \int \frac{d\omega}{2\pi} e^{i\omega\eta} \lim_{\mathbf{x}_1'\to\mathbf{x}_1}\left[\hbar\omega - \frac{\hbar^2\nabla_1^2}{2m} + U(\mathbf{x}_1)\right]G(\mathbf{x}_1,\mathbf{x}_1',\omega)
$$

$$
= -i(2s+1)\int d^3x_1 \sum_j \varphi_j(\mathbf{x}_1)^* \int \frac{d\omega}{2\pi} e^{i\omega\eta}\left\{\tfrac{1}{2}\hbar\varphi_j(\mathbf{x}_1) + [\epsilon_j\varphi_j(\mathbf{x}_1)\right.
$$

$$
\left. - \tfrac{1}{2}\int d^3x_2\, \hbar\Sigma^\star(\mathbf{x}_1,\mathbf{x}_2)\varphi_j(\mathbf{x}_2)]\left[\frac{\theta(\epsilon_j-\epsilon_F)}{\omega - \hbar^{-1}\epsilon_j + i\eta} + \frac{\theta(\epsilon_F-\epsilon_j)}{\omega - \hbar^{-1}\epsilon_j - i\eta}\right]\right\}
$$

$$
- (2s+1)\sum_j \epsilon_j\theta(\epsilon_F-\epsilon_j) - \tfrac{1}{2}(2s+1)\int d^3x_1\, d^3x_2 \sum_j \varphi_j(\mathbf{x}_1)^*
$$

$$
\times \hbar\Sigma^\star(\mathbf{x}_1,\mathbf{x}_2)\varphi_j(\mathbf{x}_2)\theta(\epsilon_F-\epsilon_j) \quad (10.18)
$$

where the second line has been obtained with Eq. (10.17) and the last with Eq.
(9.37) and a contour integration.   The first term of this expression has a simple
interpretation as the sum of the energies of all occupied states.   Each single-
particle state incorporates the effect of the other particles through the nonlocal
self-consistent potential $\hbar\Sigma^\star$.   In computing the ground-state energy, however,
the first term of Eq. (10.18) by itself includes the interaction energy twice; this
double counting is then compensated by the second term.   A combination of
Eqs. (10.16) and (10.18) yields

$$
E = (2s+1)\sum_j \epsilon_j\theta(\epsilon_F-\epsilon_j) - \tfrac{1}{2}(2s+1)\sum_{jk}\theta(\epsilon_F-\epsilon_j)\theta(\epsilon_F-\epsilon_k)\int d^3x_1
$$

$$
\times \int d^3x_2\, V(\mathbf{x}_1-\mathbf{x}_2)[(2s+1)|\varphi_j(\mathbf{x}_1)|^2|\varphi_k(\mathbf{x}_2)|^2
$$

$$
- \varphi_j(\mathbf{x}_1)^*\varphi_k(\mathbf{x}_1)\varphi_k(\mathbf{x}_2)^*\varphi_j(\mathbf{x}_2)] \quad (10.19)
$$

which is the usual Hartree-Fock result.

The two terms in brackets in Eq. (10.19) yield the direct and exchange
energies, respectively.   For a short-range interparticle potential (as in nuclear
physics), the direct and exchange terms are comparable in magnitude; for a

[1] D. R. Hartree, *Proc. Cambridge Phil. Soc.*, **24**:89; 111 (1928); J. C. Slater, *Phys. Rev.*, **35**:210 (1930); V. Fock, *Z. Physik*, **61**:126 (1930).

long-range interparticle potential (as in atomic physics), the exchange contribution is usually much smaller than the direct one. Indeed, the exchange term is occasionally neglected entirely in determining the self-consistent energy levels of atoms, and the corresponding equations are known as the self-consistent Hartree equations. The physical basis for the distinction between short- and long-range potentials is the following. The exclusion principle prevents two particles of the same spin from occupying the same single-particle state. As a result, the two-particle density correlation function for parallel spins vanishes throughout a region comparable with the interparticle spacing. If the range of the potential is less than the interparticle spacing, then this exclusion hole is crucial in determining the ground-state energy. In contrast, a long-range potential extends far beyond the interparticle spacing, and the exclusion hole then plays only a minor role (compare Probs. 4.1 and 5.10, which exhibit this distinction explicitly).

For a general external potential $U(\mathbf{x})$, the Hartree-Fock equations are very difficult to solve, because the single-particle wave functions $\varphi_j(\mathbf{x})$ and energies ϵ_j must both be determined self-consistently. These equations become much simpler for a uniform system, where $U(\mathbf{x})$ vanishes and the proper self-energy takes the form $\Sigma^\star(\mathbf{x} - \mathbf{x}')$. It is readily verified that a plane wave $\varphi_{\mathbf{k}}(\mathbf{x}) = V^{-\frac{1}{2}} e^{i\mathbf{k}\cdot\mathbf{x}}$ satisfies the self-consistency requirements, since it is a solution of Eq. (10.17). The corresponding self-consistent single-particle energy becomes

$$\epsilon_{\mathbf{k}} = \epsilon_{\mathbf{k}}^0 + \hbar\Sigma^\star(\mathbf{k}) \tag{10.20}$$

where

$$
\begin{aligned}
\hbar\Sigma^\star(\mathbf{k}) &= \int d^3(x - x')\, e^{-i\mathbf{k}\cdot(\mathbf{x}-\mathbf{x}')}\, \hbar\Sigma^\star(\mathbf{x} - \mathbf{x}') \\
&= (2s + 1)\, V(0)\,(2\pi)^{-3} \int d^3k'\, \theta(k_F - k') \\
&\qquad\qquad - (2\pi)^{-3} \int d^3k'\, V(\mathbf{k} - \mathbf{k}')\, \theta(k_F - k') \\
&= nV(0) - (2\pi)^{-3} \int d^3k'\, V(\mathbf{k} - \mathbf{k}')\, \theta(k_F - k') \tag{10.21}
\end{aligned}
$$

The ground-state energy (10.18) reduces to the simple form

$$
\begin{aligned}
E &= (2s + 1)\, V(2\pi)^{-3} \int d^3k\, [\epsilon_{\mathbf{k}} - \tfrac{1}{2}\hbar\Sigma^\star(\mathbf{k})]\, \theta(k_F - k) \\
&= (2s + 1)\, V(2\pi)^{-3} \int d^3k\, [\epsilon_{\mathbf{k}}^0 + \tfrac{1}{2}\hbar\Sigma^\star(\mathbf{k})]\, \theta(k_F - k) \tag{10.22}
\end{aligned}
$$

which shows how the self-energy modifies the ground-state energy of the non-interacting system. It is interesting that these self-consistent expressions for a *uniform* medium are identical with the contributions evaluated in first-order perturbation theory [Eqs. (9.35) and (9.36)]. This equality arises only because the unperturbed (plane-wave) eigenfunctions in a uniform system are also the self-consistent ones; for a nonuniform system, however, the self-consistent calculation clearly goes far beyond the first-order expression.

11□IMPERFECT FERMI GAS

We shall now consider in detail a dilute Fermi gas with strong short-range repulsive potentials ("hard cores").[1] This system is of considerable intrinsic interest, and it also forms the basis for studies of nuclear matter and He^3, as initiated by Brueckner.[2] The fundamental observation is the following. Although the *potential* may be strong and singular, the *scattering amplitude* can be small for such interactions. For definiteness, the potential will be taken as purely repulsive with a strong short-range core, thereby neglecting any possibility of a self-bound liquid. Any realistic potential must clearly have such a repulsive core; otherwise there would be no equilibrium density and the system would collapse. (See Prob. 1.2.) In particular, the nucleon-nucleon potential has a repulsive core arising from the strongly interacting meson cloud, and the He^3–He^3 potential has a repulsive core arising from the interaction between the electrons.

SCATTERING FROM A HARD SPHERE

To illustrate these remarks, consider the scattering of two particles interacting through a strong repulsive potential of strength $V_0 > 0$ and range a (Fig. 11.1). An infinite hard core clearly corresponds to the limit $V_0 \to \infty$. The spatial Fourier transform of the potential is just the Born approximation for the scattering amplitude; it is proportional to V_0 and therefore diverges for a hard core.

$$V(\mathbf{q}) = \int e^{-i\mathbf{q}\cdot\mathbf{x}} V(\mathbf{x}) d^3x \to \infty \qquad V_0 \to \infty \tag{11.1}$$

In fact, the true scattering amplitude is given by the partial-wave expansion[3]

$$f(k,\theta) = \sum_{l=0}^{\infty} \frac{2l+1}{k} e^{i\delta_l} \sin \delta_l P_l(\cos \theta) \tag{11.2}$$

Since the Schrödinger equation is trivially soluble in the region outside the potential, each phase shift can be obtained explicitly with the boundary condition

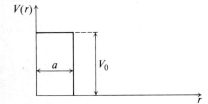

Fig. 11.1   Repulsive square-well potential.

[1] We follow the analysis of V. M. Galitskii, *Sov. Phys.-JETP*, **7**:104 (1958).
[2] K. A. Brueckner, Theory of Nuclear Structure, in C. DeWitt (ed.), "The Many Body Problem," p. 47, John Wiley and Sons, Inc., New York, 1959.
[3] For the basic elements of scattering theory used in this section, the reader is referred to any standard textbook on quantum mechanics, for example, L. I. Schiff, "Quantum Mechanics," 3d ed., sec. 19, McGraw-Hill Book Company, New York, 1968.

that the wave function vanish at $r = a$, and we find the well-known expression

$$\delta_l(k) = -\frac{(ka)^{2l+1}}{(2l+1)!!\,(2l-1)!!} \qquad ka \to 0,\, l > 0$$

$$\delta_0(k) = -ka \qquad ka \to 0 \tag{11.3}$$

where $(2l+1)!! = 1\cdot3\cdot5\,\cdots\,(2l-1)\cdot(2l+1)$. Hence the scattering amplitude vanishes in the limit of vanishing hard-core range, as is physically obvious. In contrast, the Fourier transform of the potential [Eq. (11.1)] is infinite for *all* values of the hard-core range.

This conclusion can be verified in another way. Consider the Schrödinger equation for two particles of mass m interacting with a potential V. The Schrödinger equation in the center-of-mass coordinate system is given by

$$(\nabla^2 + k^2)\,\psi(\mathbf{x}) = v(\mathbf{x})\,\psi(\mathbf{x}) \tag{11.4}$$

where $\mathbf{x}$ is the separation of the two particles,

$$v(\mathbf{x}) \equiv \frac{2m_{\mathrm{red}}\,V(\mathbf{x})}{\hbar^2} \equiv \frac{mV(\mathbf{x})}{\hbar^2} \tag{11.5}$$

and $m_{\mathrm{red}} = \tfrac{1}{2}m$ is the reduced mass. In scattering problems, it is generally convenient to rewrite Eq. (11.4) as an integral equation, using the outgoing-wave Green's function

$$G^{(+)}(\mathbf{x} - \mathbf{y}) = \int \frac{d^3p}{(2\pi)^3}\,\frac{e^{i\mathbf{p}\cdot(\mathbf{x}-\mathbf{y})}}{p^2 - k^2 - i\eta} = \frac{1}{4\pi}\frac{e^{ik|\mathbf{x}-\mathbf{y}|}}{|\mathbf{x} - \mathbf{y}|} \tag{11.6}$$

The function $G^{(+)}$ satisfies the differential equation

$$(\nabla_{\mathbf{x}}^2 + k^2)\,G^{(+)}(\mathbf{x} - \mathbf{y}) = -\delta(\mathbf{x} - \mathbf{y}) \tag{11.7}$$

and Green's theorem then yields the following equation for the scattering wave function $\psi_{\mathbf{k}}^{(+)}(\mathbf{x})$ representing an incident plane wave with wave vector $\mathbf{k}$ plus an outgoing scattered wave:

$$\psi_{\mathbf{k}}^{(+)}(\mathbf{x}) = e^{i\mathbf{k}\cdot\mathbf{x}} - \int d^3y\, G^{(+)}(\mathbf{x} - \mathbf{y})\,v(\mathbf{y})\,\psi_{\mathbf{k}}^{(+)}(\mathbf{y}) \tag{11.8}$$

The asymptotic form of $\psi_{\mathbf{k}}^{(+)}(\mathbf{x})$ is equal to

$$\psi_{\mathbf{k}}^{(+)}(\mathbf{x}) \sim e^{i\mathbf{k}\cdot\mathbf{x}} + f(\mathbf{k}',\mathbf{k})\frac{e^{ikx}}{x} \qquad x \to \infty$$

which defines the scattering amplitude for a transition from an incident wave vector $\mathbf{k}$ to a final wave vector $\mathbf{k}'$

$$f(\mathbf{k}',\mathbf{k}) = -(4\pi)^{-1} \int d^3y\, e^{-i\mathbf{k}'\cdot\mathbf{y}}\,v(\mathbf{y})\,\psi_{\mathbf{k}}^{(+)}(\mathbf{y}) \tag{11.9}$$

Equation (11.9) is correct for any finite-range potential $v(\mathbf{x})$, and we can now examine its behavior for a hard core. In this limit $\psi_{\mathbf{k}}^{(+)}$ vanishes wherever v becomes infinite, so that the scattering amplitude remains finite. Thus the

potential drastically alters the wave function from its unperturbed form, and this effect is entirely absent in the Born approximation [Eq. (11.1)]. Any perturbation expansion of Eq. (11.9) for such singular potentials will at best converge slowly, and it is therefore essential to *solve the integral equation* exactly if the modifications of the wave function are to be properly included. This exact solution evidently contains all orders in perturbation theory.

SCATTERING THEORY IN MOMENTUM SPACE

The preceding discussion has been confined to the coordinate representation, but it is more useful for the present analysis to express all quantities in momentum space. Since the resulting Schrödinger equation is less familiar, we shall derive the expressions in some detail. With the definitions

$$\psi_{\mathbf{k}}(\mathbf{p}) = \int d^3x \, e^{-i\mathbf{p}\cdot\mathbf{x}} \psi_{\mathbf{k}}^{(+)}(\mathbf{x}) \tag{11.10a}$$

$$v(\mathbf{p}) = \int d^3x \, e^{-i\mathbf{p}\cdot\mathbf{x}} v(\mathbf{x}) \tag{11.10b}$$

the Schrödinger equation (11.8) may be rewritten in momentum space

$$\psi_{\mathbf{k}}(\mathbf{p}) = (2\pi)^3 \, \delta(\mathbf{p} - \mathbf{k}) - \frac{1}{p^2 - k^2 - i\eta} \int \frac{d^3q}{(2\pi)^3} v(\mathbf{q}) \psi_{\mathbf{k}}(\mathbf{p} - \mathbf{q}) \tag{11.11}$$

where Eq. (11.6) has been used on the right side. Furthermore, it is useful to introduce a modified scattering amplitude written in momentum space

$$\tilde{f}(\mathbf{k}',\mathbf{k}) \equiv -4\pi f(\mathbf{k}',\mathbf{k}) = (2\pi)^{-3} \int d^3q \, v(\mathbf{q}) \psi_{\mathbf{k}}(\mathbf{k}' - \mathbf{q}) \tag{11.12}$$

and Eq. (11.11) then becomes

$$\psi_{\mathbf{k}}(\mathbf{p}) = (2\pi)^3 \, \delta(\mathbf{p} - \mathbf{k}) + \frac{\tilde{f}(\mathbf{p},\mathbf{k})}{k^2 - p^2 + i\eta} \tag{11.13}$$

Multiply Eq. (11.13) by $v(\mathbf{q} - \mathbf{p})$ and integrate $(2\pi)^{-3} \int d^3p$; an elementary substitution then yields

$$\tilde{f}(\mathbf{p},\mathbf{k}) = v(\mathbf{p} - \mathbf{k}) + \int \frac{d^3q}{(2\pi)^3} \frac{v(\mathbf{p} - \mathbf{q}) \tilde{f}(\mathbf{q},\mathbf{k})}{k^2 - q^2 + i\eta} \tag{11.14}$$

which is an *integral* equation for $\tilde{f}$ in terms of v. As noted before, the scattering amplitude $\tilde{f}$ is well defined even for a singular potential ($v \to \infty$). If Eq. (11.14) were expanded in a perturbation series, each term would separately diverge; nevertheless, the sum of all the terms necessarily remains finite. Note that the solution of Eq. (11.14) requires the function $\tilde{f}(\mathbf{q},\mathbf{k})$ for all $q^2 > 0$, not just for $q^2 = k^2$; this is expressed by saying that $\tilde{f}$ is needed "off the energy shell" as well as "on the energy shell."

If the potential has no bound states, as will be assumed throughout this section, then the exact scattering solutions with a given boundary condition form a complete set of states and satisfy the relation

$$(2\pi)^{-3} \int d^3k \, \psi_{\mathbf{k}}^{(+)}(\mathbf{x}) \psi_{\mathbf{k}}^{(+)}(\mathbf{x}')^* = \delta(\mathbf{x} - \mathbf{x}') \tag{11.15}$$

The numerical factors here may be checked by noting that the exact wave function obeys the same completeness relation as the unperturbed wave function $e^{i\mathbf{k}\cdot\mathbf{x}}$ [compare the first term in Eq. (11.8)]. A combination of Eqs. (11.10a) and (11.15) yields the corresponding completeness relation in momentum space:

$$(2\pi)^{-3} \int d^3k \, \psi_{\mathbf{k}}(\mathbf{p}) \, \psi_{\mathbf{k}}(\mathbf{p}')^* = (2\pi)^3 \, \delta(\mathbf{p} - \mathbf{p}') \tag{11.16}$$

Multiply Eq. (11.12) by $\psi_{\mathbf{k}}(\mathbf{p}')^*$ and integrate over $\mathbf{k}$; the above completeness relation leads to

$$(2\pi)^{-3} \int d^3k \, \tilde{f}(\mathbf{p},\mathbf{k}) \, \psi_{\mathbf{k}}(\mathbf{p}')^* = v(\mathbf{p} - \mathbf{p}')$$

which merely represents a complicated way of writing v. The complex conjugate of Eq. (11.13) may now be substituted into this relation:

$$v(\mathbf{p} - \mathbf{p}') = \tilde{f}(\mathbf{p},\mathbf{p}') + \int \frac{d^3k}{(2\pi)^3} \, \tilde{f}(\mathbf{p},\mathbf{k}) \, \tilde{f}(\mathbf{p}',\mathbf{k})^* \, \frac{1}{k^2 - p'^2 - i\eta}$$

But the potential is hermitian and therefore satisfies

$$v(\mathbf{p} - \mathbf{p}')^* = v(\mathbf{p}' - \mathbf{p})$$

which finally yields

$$\tilde{f}(\mathbf{p},\mathbf{p}') - \tilde{f}(\mathbf{p}',\mathbf{p})^* = \int \frac{d^3k}{(2\pi)^3} \, \tilde{f}(\mathbf{p},\mathbf{k}) \, \tilde{f}(\mathbf{p}',\mathbf{k})^* \left(\frac{1}{k^2 - p^2 + i\eta} - \frac{1}{k^2 - p'^2 - i\eta} \right) \tag{11.17}$$

If the magnitude of $\mathbf{p}$ is equal to the magnitude of $\mathbf{p}'$, the principal parts in Eq. (11.17) vanish, and we obtain

$$\tilde{f}(\mathbf{p},\mathbf{p}') - \tilde{f}(\mathbf{p}',\mathbf{p})^* = -2\pi i (2\pi)^{-3} \int d^3k \, \tilde{f}(\mathbf{p},\mathbf{k}) \, \tilde{f}(\mathbf{p}',\mathbf{k})^* \, \delta(p^2 - k^2)$$
$$|\mathbf{p}| = |\mathbf{p}'| \quad (11.18)$$

where the radial k integral is easily evaluated. If, in addition, the potential is spherically symmetric, then the scattering amplitude $\tilde{f}$ is a function only of p^2 and $\hat{\mathbf{p}}\cdot\hat{\mathbf{p}}'$, and the left side of this relation becomes $2i\,\mathrm{Im}\,\tilde{f}$. The resulting expression

$$\mathrm{Im}\,\tilde{f}(\mathbf{p},\mathbf{p}') = \frac{-p}{16\pi^2} \int d\Omega_k \, \tilde{f}(\mathbf{p},\mathbf{k}) \, \tilde{f}(\mathbf{p}',\mathbf{k})^* \qquad \begin{array}{l} |\mathbf{k}| = |\mathbf{p}| = |\mathbf{p}'| \\ v = v(|\mathbf{x}|) \end{array} \tag{11.19}$$

is a generalization of the ordinary optical theorem for the scattering amplitude.

LADDER DIAGRAMS AND THE BETHE-SALPETER EQUATION

The previous discussion has been restricted to the scattering of two particles in free space, and we now turn to the much more complicated problem of a dilute many-particle assembly interacting with singular repulsive potentials. The hard core clearly precludes any straightforward perturbation expansion in the strength of the interparticle potential. Instead, it is essential first to incorporate

the effect of the repulsive potential on the wave function of two particles in the medium; only then can we consider how the many-particle background affects the interacting pair.

Although the potential is singular, a *dilute* Fermi gas still contains one small parameter, namely $k_F a$, where k_F is the Fermi wavenumber, and a is the scattering length (equal to the particle diameter for a hard-sphere gas). We therefore expect the ground-state energy to have a series expansion of the form

$$\frac{E}{N} = \frac{\hbar^2 k_F^2}{2m} [A + B k_F a + C(k_F a)^2 + \cdots]$$ (11.20)

which should be meaningful either for small scattering length ($a \to 0$) or for low density ($k_F \to 0$). In this section we calculate the first three coefficients in this series. In addition, the techniques developed here can be used as a basis for realistic theories of Fermi systems at physical densities.

A truly infinite repulsive core introduces certain artificial complications, because every term of any perturbation expansion diverges. We shall instead consider a strong but finite potential [Fig. 11.1, with $V_0 < \infty$] and pass to the limit $V_0 \to \infty$ only at the end of the calculation. As shown in the following calculations, this procedure yields finite answers that are independent of V_0. For such a finite potential, the two-particle scattering equations (11.8) and (11.9) in free space can be expanded as

$$\psi_k^{(+)}(x) = e^{ik \cdot x} - \int d^3y \, G^{(+)}(x - y) v(y) e^{ik \cdot y}$$
$$+ \int d^3y \, d^3z \, G^{(+)}(x - y) v(y) G^{(+)}(y - z) v(z) e^{ik \cdot z} + \cdots \quad (11.21a)$$

$$f(k', k) = -(4\pi)^{-1} \int d^3y \, e^{-ik' \cdot y} v(y) \psi_k^{(+)}(y)$$ (11.21b)

The terms in the wave function have a simple interpretation as the unperturbed solution plus propagation with one or more repeated interactions. We may evidently represent the terms in the perturbation series (Born series) for $-4\pi f(k', k)$ diagrammatically as indicated in Fig. 11.2 (the rules for constructing these diagrams follow by inspection). These are not Feynman diagrams but

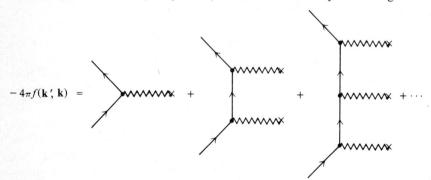

Fig. 11.2 Perturbation expansion for two-body scattering amplitude in free space.

are again just a way of keeping track of the terms that contribute to the time-independent perturbation series for the scattering amplitude.   A weak repulsive potential can be adequately described with the first few terms of Eq. (11.21), but a *strong* repulsive potential requires all the terms.   As is evident from Eq. (11.21a) the higher-order terms represent the modification of the wave function by the potential, and the sum of the series gives the exact wave function.

In a similar way, the first-order proper self-energy $\hbar\Sigma^{\star}_{(1)}$ (Fig. 10.1) is totally inadequate for a strong repulsive potential, and we must retain a selected class of higher-order Feynman diagrams.   From the present discussion it is quite clear which diagrams must be kept; every time the interaction appears, it must be allowed to act repeatedly so as to include the effect of the potential on the wave

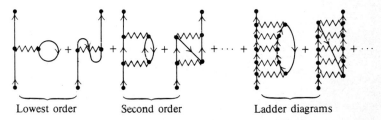

Lowest order   Second order   Ladder diagrams

Fig. 11.3 Sum of ladder Feynman diagrams for proper self-energy.

function, thereby yielding a well-defined product $v\psi$.   In other words, the relevant quantity in a two-particle collision is the two-body scattering amplitude in the presence of the medium, which remains well defined even for a singular two-body potential.   We therefore retain all the *ladder diagrams* indicated in Fig. 11.3; this choice clearly represents a generalization of the above discussion because the terms in Fig. 11.3 denote Feynman diagrams and hence contain both hole and particle propagation.   In particular, we sum only the ladders between Green's functions with arrows running in the same direction.   Since the two-particle interaction is instantaneous, this set of diagrams includes as a subset all those processes where both intermediate fermions are *particles* above the Fermi sea at every step.   Such particle-particle contributions come from the particle part of the Feynman propagator, which propagates forward in time.

As shown below, the diagrams in Fig. 11.3 suffice to obtain the first three terms in Eq. (11.20) for a hard-sphere Fermi gas.   This result has a direct physical interpretation: the first term in the expansion is the energy of a noninteracting Fermi system.   The second term, which is linear in the scattering length, represents the forward scattering (both direct and exchange) from the other particles in the medium.   This identification follows because the low density $(k_F \to 0)$ allows us to consider only low-energy collisions, where the free-particle scattering amplitude reduces to a constant

$$f(\mathbf{k},\mathbf{k}') \to -a \qquad k = k' \to 0 \tag{11.22}$$

Although Eq. (11.22) may be derived directly from Eqs. (11.2) and (11.3) in the case of hard spheres, it also serves as a general definition of the s-wave scattering length a. In the presence of the medium, however, the actual scattering amplitude differs from f because the other particles limit the intermediate states available to the interacting pair. The Pauli principle restriction first appears when a particle is excited above the Fermi sea and is then de-excited; if the sum of ladder diagrams in Fig. 11.3 is reexpressed in terms of the *free* scattering length, this effect gives a correction of order $(k_F a)^2$ to the ground-state energy.

Any other process that contributes to the ground-state energy involves at least three distinct collisions and thus yields a contribution of order $(k_F a)^3$ to Eq. (11.20). In particular, consider the Feynman diagrams shown in Fig. 11.4,

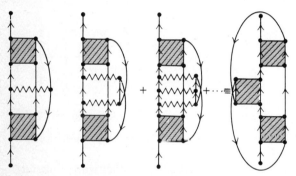

Fig. 11.4 A class of additional contributions to Σ^*, neglected in the ladder approximation.

where the shaded box denotes the sum of ladder diagrams. These processes clearly include the scattering of an intermediate particle and hole, which really represents the transfer of an additional particle inside the Fermi sea, filling the original hole and leaving a new one in its place. Thus a collision between a particle and a hole always involves an extra particle and introduces an extra power of $k_F a$. It is evident from Eqs. (11.2) and (11.3) that two-body collisions in relative p states also lead to corrections of order $(k_F a)^3$, which is again negligible in our approximation. We shall justify our choice of diagrams in more detail at the end of this section.

Before proceeding with the detailed analysis of the sum of ladder diagrams, we now show that the foregoing discussion immediately yields the first two terms in the series (11.20). Consider a uniform system of spin-$\frac{1}{2}$ fermions interacting through a spin-independent nonsingular potential. Then the lowest-order ground-state energy is obtained from Eqs. (10.21) and (10.22)

$$\frac{E}{V} = \frac{3}{5}\frac{\hbar^2 k_F^2}{2m}\frac{N}{V} + \frac{1}{2}2\int^{k_F}\frac{d^3k}{(2\pi)^3}\int^{k_F}\frac{d^3k'}{(2\pi)^3}[2V(0) - V(\mathbf{k} - \mathbf{k}')] \qquad (11.23)$$

For a nonsingular potential, however, Eqs. (11.9) and (11.22) show that

$$V(0) \equiv \int d^3x \, V(x) = -\frac{4\pi\hbar^2}{m} f_B(\mathbf{k},\mathbf{k}) \xrightarrow[k\to 0]{} \frac{4\pi\hbar^2}{m} a_B \qquad (11.24)$$

where the subscript B indicates the Born approximation obtained with the substitution $\psi_{\mathbf{k}}^{(+)}(\mathbf{x}) \to e^{i\mathbf{k}\cdot\mathbf{x}}$. It is clear that our description of scattering from the particles in the medium can be improved by the simple replacement

$$a_B \to a \qquad (11.25)$$

Here a *is the actual scattering length for free two-particle scattering*, which remains well defined even for singular potentials. In the low-density limit where $k_F \to 0$, we can furthermore approximate

$$V(\mathbf{k} - \mathbf{k}') \approx V(0)$$

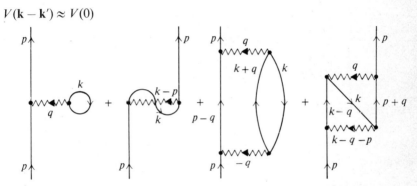

Fig. 11.5 First two orders in ladder approximation to $\Sigma^\star$.

under the integral, and Eq. (11.23) thus becomes

$$E = \frac{3}{5}\frac{\hbar^2 k_F^2}{2m} N + \frac{1}{2}\frac{N}{V}\frac{4\pi\hbar^2 a}{m}\frac{N}{2}$$

The standard relation (3.29) between the density and the Fermi wavenumber $N/V = k_F^3/3\pi^2$ therefore gives

$$\frac{E}{N} = \frac{\hbar^2 k_F^2}{2m}\left(\frac{3}{5} + \frac{2}{3\pi} k_F a + \cdots\right) \qquad (11.26)$$

An equivalent result was derived by Lenz[1] from the relation between the index of refraction and the forward-scattering amplitude.

With these remarks in mind, we turn to our basic approximation, which is to retain *only* the Feynman diagrams of Fig. 11.3 in evaluating the proper self-energy $\Sigma^\star$. To clarify the various factors, we shall initially concentrate on the first- and second-order contributions shown in Fig. 11.5 in momentum space.

[1] W. Lenz, *Z. Physik*, **56**:778 (1929).

It is straightforward to calculate $\Sigma^\star$ using the Feynman rules of Sec. 9, and the first-order contribution is given by [compare Eq. (9.23)]

$$\hbar\Sigma^\star_{(1)}(p) = -2iU_0(0)(2\pi)^{-4} \int d^4k\, G^0(k)\, e^{ik_0\eta}$$
$$+ i(2\pi)^{-4} \int d^4k G^0(k)\, U_0(k-p)\, e^{ik_0\eta} \quad (11.27)$$

where a spin-independent interaction has been assumed. The second-order contribution introduces the following additional elements:

1. Two extra factors G^0
2. One extra interaction line U_0
3. One extra independent four-momentum (compare Fig. 11.5)
4. One extra factor $(i/\hbar)(2\pi)^{-4}$

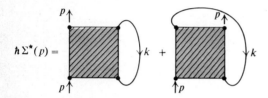

Fig. 11.6   Proper self-energy in ladder approximation.

These factors can be combined with the Feynman rules to yield the second-order contribution

$$\hbar\Sigma^\star_{(2)}(p) = 2\hbar^{-1}(2\pi)^{-8} \int d^4k\, G^0(k) \int d^4q\, U_0(q)\, G^0(p-q)\, G^0(k+q)\, U_0(-q)$$
$$- \hbar^{-1}(2\pi)^{-8} \int d^4k\, G^0(k) \int d^4q\, U_0(q)\, G^0(p+q)\, G^0(k-q)\, U_0(k-q-p)$$

It is clear that this procedure can be carried out to all orders and the general form of $\Sigma^\star(p)$ will be (see Fig. 11.6)

$$\hbar\Sigma^\star(p) = -2i(2\pi)^{-4} \int d^4k\, G^0(k)\, \Gamma(pk;pk) + i(2\pi)^{-4} \int d^4k\, G^0(k)\, \Gamma(kp;pk) \quad (11.28)$$

where we have defined an *effective* two-particle interaction $\Gamma(p_1 p_2; p_3 p_4)$ that may be interpreted as a generalized scattering amplitude in the medium. In

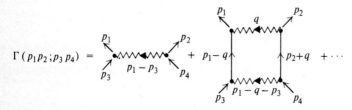

Fig. 11.7   Series expansion for effective interaction in ladder approximation.

this particular example, Γ includes the sum of repeated (ladder) interactions (Fig. 11.7) and has the form

$$\Gamma(p_1 p_2; p_3 p_4) = U_0(p_1 - p_3) + i\hbar^{-1}(2\pi)^{-4} \int d^4q\, U_0(q)\, G^0(p_1 - q)$$
$$\times\, G^0(p_2 + q)\, U_0(p_1 - q - p_3) + \cdots \quad (11.29)$$

This sum of ladder diagrams now can be rewritten as an integral equation for Γ that automatically includes all orders [Fig. 11.8 and Eq. (11.30)]

$$\Gamma(p_1 p_2; p_3 p_4) = U_0(p_1 - p_3) + i\hbar^{-1}(2\pi)^{-4} \int d^4q\, U_0(q)$$
$$\times\, G^0(p_1 - q)\, G^0(p_2 + q)\, \Gamma(p_1 - q, p_2 + q; p_3 p_4) \quad (11.30)$$

In analogy with similar equations in relativistic field theory, Eq. (11.30) is known as the Bethe-Salpeter equation[1] (more precisely, the *ladder approximation* to the

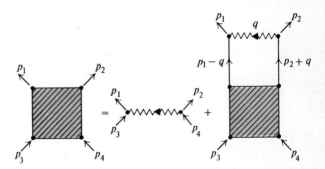

Fig. 11.8 Bethe-Salpeter equation for effective interaction.

Bethe-Salpeter equation). If this equation is expanded in perturbation theory, assuming U_0 is small, we obtain the sum of all ladder diagrams (Fig. 11.7). The first two terms precisely reproduce those of Eq. (11.29), which ensures that the signs and numerical factors are also correct; in particular, the factor $i/\hbar$ is just that associated with the extra order in the perturbation U_0.

The calculation of $\Sigma^\star$ is now reduced to that of finding the solution Γ to Eq. (11.30). Although Γ is related to a two-particle Green's function, it is more useful to exploit the similarity between Γ and the scattering amplitude $\tilde{f}$ in free space. Indeed, to lowest order in the potential, Γ is just equal to the Fourier transform U_0. We shall now pursue this analogy and introduce an effective wave function Q for two particles in the medium [compare Eqs. (11.12) and (11.13)]:

$$\Gamma(p_1 p_2; p_3 p_4) \equiv (2\pi)^{-4} \int d^4q\, U_0(q)\, Q(p_1 - q, p_2 + q; p_3 p_4) \quad (11.31)$$

[1] E. E. Salpeter and H. A. Bethe, *Phys. Rev.*, **84**:1232 (1951).

This representation for Γ agrees with Eq. (11.30) only if Q satisfies the integral equation

$$Q(p_1p_2;p_3p_4) = (2\pi)^4\,\delta^{(4)}(p_1 - p_3) + i\hbar^{-1}\,G^0(p_1)\,G^0(p_2)(2\pi)^{-4}$$
$$\times \int d^4q\, U_0(q)\, Q(p_1 - q, p_2 + q; p_3 p_4) \quad (11.32)$$

The labeling and ordering of the momentum variables requires considerable care, and the reader is urged to verify these equations in detail.

It is convenient to introduce the total center of mass wave vector

$$P = p_1 + p_2 = p_3 + p_4$$

where the last equality follows from the conservation of total four-momentum in a homogeneous system, and the relative wave vectors

$$p = \tfrac{1}{2}(p_1 - p_2) \qquad p' = \tfrac{1}{2}(p_3 - p_4)$$

In addition, the instantaneous interaction means that $U_0(q) \equiv U_0(\mathbf{q})$ is *independent of frequency* q_0, and we can perform the frequency integral in Eq. (11.32) for a fixed center of mass four-momentum $\hbar P$ of the interacting pair. Integrate Eq. (11.32) over the relative frequency $(2\pi)^{-1} \int dp_0$ and define the quantity

$$\chi(\mathbf{p},\mathbf{p}',P) \equiv (2\pi)^{-1} \int_P dp_0\, Q(\tfrac{1}{2}P + p, \tfrac{1}{2}P - p; \tfrac{1}{2}P + p', \tfrac{1}{2}P - p')$$

$$= (2\pi)^{-1} \int_P dp_0\, Q(p_1 p_2; p_3 p_4) \quad (11.33)$$

A simple rearrangement then yields an integral equation for χ

$$\chi(\mathbf{p},\mathbf{p}',P) = (2\pi)^3\,\delta(\mathbf{p} - \mathbf{p}') + i\hbar^{-1}(2\pi)^{-1} \int dp_0\, G^0(\tfrac{1}{2}P + p)\, G^0(\tfrac{1}{2}P - p)(2\pi)^{-3}$$
$$\times \int d^3q\, U_0(\mathbf{q})\,\chi(\mathbf{p} - \mathbf{q}, \mathbf{p}', P) \quad (11.34)$$

which, as shown in Eq. (11.39), is very similar to the scattering equation in free space [Eq. (11.11)]. If this equation is iterated as an expansion in U_0, each term depends explicitly on the variables $(\mathbf{p},\mathbf{p}',P)$, thus justifying our notation in Eq. (11.33).

It is now necessary to evaluate the coefficient of the last term in Eq. (11.34). Since each G^0 has two terms [Eq. (9.14)], the integrand has four terms in all. Two of these terms have both poles on the same side of the real p_0 axis; in this case, we close the contour in the opposite half plane, showing that these terms make no contribution. In contrast, each of the remaining two terms has one pole above and one pole below the real axis. These contributions are readily evaluated with a contour integral, and we find

$$\frac{i}{\hbar} \int \frac{dp_0}{2\pi}\, G^0(\tfrac{1}{2}P + p)\, G^0(\tfrac{1}{2}P - p) = \frac{\theta(|\tfrac{1}{2}\mathbf{P} + \mathbf{p}| - k_F)\,\theta(|\tfrac{1}{2}\mathbf{P} - \mathbf{p}| - k_F)}{\hbar P_0 - \epsilon^0_{\frac{1}{2}\mathbf{P}+\mathbf{p}} - \epsilon^0_{\frac{1}{2}\mathbf{P}-\mathbf{p}} + i\eta}$$

$$- \frac{\theta(k_F - |\tfrac{1}{2}\mathbf{P} + \mathbf{p}|)\,\theta(k_F - |\tfrac{1}{2}\mathbf{P} - \mathbf{p}|)}{\hbar P_0 - \epsilon^0_{\frac{1}{2}\mathbf{P}+\mathbf{p}} - \epsilon^0_{\frac{1}{2}\mathbf{P}-\mathbf{p}} - i\eta} \quad (11.35)$$

This expression has the physical interpretation that the pair of interacting particles in the intermediate states of Fig. 11.3 can propagate either as a pair of particles above the Fermi sea [the first term in Eq. (11.35)] or as a pair of holes below the Fermi sea [the second term in Eq. (11.35)]. Since *Feynman* diagrams contain all possible time orderings, both modes of propagation are included in the diagram of Fig. 11.8.

The form of Eq. (11.35) can be simplified by introducing the total energy

$$E \equiv \hbar P_0 - \frac{\hbar^2 \mathbf{P}^2}{4m} \tag{11.36}$$

of the interacting pair in the center of mass frame and the function

$$N(\mathbf{P,p}) \equiv 1 - n^0_{\frac{1}{2}\mathbf{P}+\mathbf{p}} - n^0_{\frac{1}{2}\mathbf{P}-\mathbf{p}} \tag{11.37}$$

where $n^0_{\mathbf{p}} = \theta(k_F - p)$ is the occupation number in the unperturbed ground state. Thus $N(\mathbf{P,p}) = 1$ if both states $\frac{1}{2}\mathbf{P} \pm \mathbf{p}$ are outside the Fermi sea, $N(\mathbf{P,p}) = -1$ if both are inside, and $N(\mathbf{P,p}) = 0$ otherwise. With this notation, Eq. (11.35) assumes the compact form

$$\frac{i}{\hbar} \int \frac{dp_0}{2\pi} G^0(\tfrac{1}{2}P + p) G^0(\tfrac{1}{2}P - p) = \frac{N(\mathbf{P,p})}{E - \hbar^2 \mathbf{p}^2/m + i\eta N(\mathbf{P,p})} \tag{11.38}$$

and Eq. (11.34) reduces to

$$\chi(\mathbf{p,p'},P) = (2\pi)^3 \delta(\mathbf{p} - \mathbf{p'}) + \frac{N(\mathbf{P,p})}{E - \hbar^2 \mathbf{p}^2/m + i\eta N(\mathbf{P,p})} \int \frac{d^3q}{(2\pi)^3}$$
$$\times U_0(\mathbf{q}) \chi(\mathbf{p} - \mathbf{q}, \mathbf{p'}, P) \tag{11.39}$$

Correspondingly, Γ may be reexpressed in terms of center of mass and relative wave vectors using Eqs. (11.31) and (11.33):

$$\Gamma(\mathbf{p,p'},P) \equiv \Gamma(\tfrac{1}{2}P + p, \tfrac{1}{2}P - p; \tfrac{1}{2}P + p', \tfrac{1}{2}P - p')$$
$$= (2\pi)^{-3} \int d^3q \, U_0(\mathbf{q}) \chi(\mathbf{p} - \mathbf{q}, \mathbf{p'}, P) \tag{11.40}$$

We have already noted that Eq. (11.39) is similar to the scattering equation for the wave function $\psi_{\mathbf{p'}}(\mathbf{p})$ of two particles in free space [Eq. (11.11)]. The present equation is more complicated, however, because the exclusion principle restricts the available intermediate states through the factor N, and also because the function Γ must be evaluated for all values of the frequency P_0 [compare Eq. (11.28)].

GALITSKII'S INTEGRAL EQUATIONS

Until this point, the equations have been written in terms of the interparticle potential U_0. Such an approach can never describe an infinite repulsive core, and we now follow Galitskii by rewriting Eqs. (11.39) and (11.40) in terms of the scattering amplitude $\tilde{f}$ for two particles in free space. Indeed, the lowest approxi-

mation to Γ is proportional to $\tilde{f}$, and the higher-order corrections arise explicitly from the many-particle background. It is convenient to define the reduced variables

$$v \equiv mU_0 \hbar^{-2} \qquad \epsilon \equiv mE\hbar^{-2} \tag{11.41}$$

and to consider a simplified version of Eq. (11.39) obtained by replacing the exclusion-principle factor N by 1. Note that this substitution becomes exact as $k_F \to 0$ and thus describes the low-density limit. If χ_0 denotes the corresponding solution to Eq. (11.39) with $N = 1$, multiplication by $\epsilon - p^2 + i\eta$ yields the equation

$$
\begin{aligned}
(\epsilon - p^2 + i\eta)\chi_0(\mathbf{p},\mathbf{p}',P) - (2\pi)^{-3} \int d^3q \, v(\mathbf{q})\chi_0(\mathbf{p} - \mathbf{q}, \mathbf{p}', P) \\
= (2\pi)^3 (\epsilon - p^2 + i\eta)\,\delta(\mathbf{p} - \mathbf{p}') \\
= (2\pi)^3 (\epsilon - p'^2 + i\eta)\,\delta(\mathbf{p} - \mathbf{p}') \quad (11.42)
\end{aligned}
$$

where the redundant $i\eta$ keeps track of the boundary conditions. For comparison, the free Schrödinger equation (11.11) may be written as

$$(k^2 - p^2 + i\eta)\psi_{\mathbf{k}}(\mathbf{p}) - (2\pi)^{-3} \int d^3q \, v(\mathbf{q})\psi_{\mathbf{k}}(\mathbf{p} - \mathbf{q}) = 0 \tag{11.43}$$

since $(k^2 - p^2 + i\eta)\,\delta(\mathbf{p} - \mathbf{k})$ vanishes identically.

The quantity χ_0 can now be expressed *solely* in terms of the solutions to the free Schrödinger equation (11.43) as follows:

$$\chi_0(\mathbf{p},\mathbf{p}',P) = (\epsilon - p'^2 + i\eta) \int \frac{d^3k}{(2\pi)^3} \frac{\psi_{\mathbf{k}}(\mathbf{p})\psi_{\mathbf{k}}(\mathbf{p}')^*}{\epsilon - k^2 + i\eta} \tag{11.44}$$

This representation is easily verified by substituting Eq. (11.44) into Eq. (11.42), and using Eq. (11.43) and the completeness relation [Eq. (11.16)]. A combination with the complex conjugate of Eq. (11.13) then yields

$$\chi_0(\mathbf{p},\mathbf{p}',P) = \psi_{\mathbf{p}'}(\mathbf{p}) + \int \frac{d^3k}{(2\pi)^3}\psi_{\mathbf{k}}(\mathbf{p}) \left(\frac{1}{\epsilon - k^2 + i\eta} + \frac{1}{k^2 - p'^2 - i\eta} \right) \tilde{f}(\mathbf{p}',\mathbf{k})^*$$

We finally define Γ_0 in analogy with Eq. (11.40)

$$
\begin{aligned}
\Gamma_0(\mathbf{p},\mathbf{p}',P) &= (2\pi)^{-3} \int d^3q \, U_0(\mathbf{q})\chi_0(\mathbf{p} - \mathbf{q}, \mathbf{p}', P) \\
&= (2\pi)^{-3} \hbar^2 m^{-1} \int d^3q \, v(\mathbf{q})\chi_0(\mathbf{p} - \mathbf{q}, \mathbf{p}', P)
\end{aligned}
$$

and it follows immediately that Γ_0 has the integral representation

$$
\frac{m}{\hbar^2}\Gamma_0(\mathbf{p},\mathbf{p}',P) = \tilde{f}(\mathbf{p},\mathbf{p}') + \int \frac{d^3k}{(2\pi)^3}\tilde{f}(\mathbf{p},\mathbf{k}) \left(\frac{1}{\epsilon - k^2 + i\eta} + \frac{1}{k^2 - p'^2 - i\eta} \right)
$$
$$\times \tilde{f}(\mathbf{p}',\mathbf{k})^* \quad (11.45)$$

where Eqs. (11.12) and (11.41) have been used. This expression has the important feature that it contains only the free-particle scattering amplitudes and thus remains meaningful even for a *singular* repulsive potential.

The function Γ_0 depends on the parameter ϵ.   If we set $\epsilon = p'^2$, then

$$m\Gamma_0 \hbar^{-2} = \tilde{f}(\mathbf{p},\mathbf{p}') \qquad \epsilon = p'^2 \tag{11.46}$$

which is just the free scattering amplitude.   More generally, Eq. (11.45) determines Γ_0 for scattering off the energy shell, namely, for values of $p'^2 \neq \epsilon$.   Note that we also need the quantity $\tilde{f}$ off the energy shell, for *all* values of its two momentum arguments.   In a free scattering experiment, however, the scattering amplitude $\tilde{f}$ is measured only for equal magnitudes of the two momentum arguments $|\mathbf{p}| = |\mathbf{p}'|$ (we here consider only elastic scattering).   Thus the simplicity of Eq. (11.45) is slightly deceptive, for the evaluation of $\tilde{f}$ off the energy shell requires a detailed model, such as a potential $V(\mathbf{x})$.   Nevertheless, Eq. (11.45) is very useful.

We now try to solve for the full scattering function χ in the medium. With the reduced variables of Eq. (11.41), the exact Eq. (11.39) becomes

$$\chi(\mathbf{p},\mathbf{p}',P) - \frac{N(\mathbf{P},\mathbf{p})}{\epsilon - p^2 + i\eta N(\mathbf{P},\mathbf{p})} \int \frac{d^3q}{(2\pi)^3} v(\mathbf{q})\chi(\mathbf{p}-\mathbf{q},\mathbf{p}',P) = (2\pi)^3 \delta(\mathbf{p}-\mathbf{p}')$$

and a slight rearrangement yields

$$\chi(\mathbf{p},\mathbf{p}',P) - \frac{1}{\epsilon - p^2 + i\eta} \int \frac{d^3q}{(2\pi)^3} v(\mathbf{q})\chi(\mathbf{p}-\mathbf{q},\mathbf{p}',P)$$

$$= (2\pi)^3 \delta(\mathbf{p}-\mathbf{p}') + \left(\frac{N(\mathbf{P},\mathbf{p})}{\epsilon - p^2 + i\eta N(\mathbf{P},\mathbf{p})} - \frac{1}{\epsilon - p^2 + i\eta} \right) \frac{m}{\hbar^2} \Gamma(\mathbf{p},\mathbf{p}',P) \tag{11.47}$$

Comparison with Eq. (11.42) divided by $\epsilon - p^2 + i\eta$ shows that the operator on the left side of Eq. (11.47) is just the inverse of χ_0, which means that χ can be expressed in terms of χ_0 as follows:

$$\chi(\mathbf{p},\mathbf{p}',P) = \chi_0(\mathbf{p},\mathbf{p}',P) + \int \frac{d^3k}{(2\pi)^3} \chi_0(\mathbf{p},\mathbf{k},P)$$

$$\times \left[\frac{N(\mathbf{P},\mathbf{k})}{\epsilon - k^2 + i\eta N(\mathbf{P},\mathbf{k})} - \frac{1}{\epsilon - k^2 + i\eta} \right] \frac{m}{\hbar^2} \Gamma(\mathbf{k},\mathbf{p}',P)$$

This equation can be verified by carrying out the operation indicated on the left side of Eq. (11.47) and by using Eq. (11.42).   We now take the convolution with v [see Eq. (11.40)], which yields our final equation for the scattering amplitude in the medium

$$\Gamma(\mathbf{p},\mathbf{p}',P) = \Gamma_0(\mathbf{p},\mathbf{p}',P) + \int \frac{d^3k}{(2\pi)^3} \Gamma_0(\mathbf{p},\mathbf{k},P)$$

$$\times \left[\frac{N(\mathbf{P},\mathbf{k})}{\epsilon - k^2 + i\eta N(\mathbf{P},\mathbf{k})} - \frac{1}{\epsilon - k^2 + i\eta} \right] \frac{m}{\hbar^2} \Gamma(\mathbf{k},\mathbf{p}',P) \tag{11.48}$$

Since Eqs. (11.45) and (11.48) are expressed in terms of the *free scattering amplitudes*, we may pass to the limit of an infinite hard-core potential ($V_0 \to \infty$).

As noted before, however, $\tilde{f}(\mathbf{p},\mathbf{p}')$ must be known for all values of $\mathbf{p}$ and $\mathbf{p}'$ (*off* the energy shell), while it can be measured only *on* the energy shell. Roughly speaking, the quantity Γ_0 [Eq. (11.45)] contains the effects of scattering off the energy shell, while Eq. (11.48), which is still an integral equation for Γ, incorporates the exclusion principle in intermediate states. We shall refer to these equations as *Galitskii's integral equations*.[1] (These equations were derived jointly with Beliaev,[2] who studied similar problems in an imperfect Bose gas.)

THE PROPER SELF-ENERGY

For a low-density Fermi gas, Eq. (11.48) can be solved iteratively as a power series in $k_F a \ll 1$. This expansion is possible because the integrand vanishes when the vectors $\frac{1}{2}\mathbf{P} \pm \mathbf{k}$ both lie outside the Fermi sea; since we are interested in energies of the order ϵ_F, the last term of Eq. (11.48) can be estimated (apart from numerical factors) as $\Gamma_0 k_F m \Gamma / \hbar^2$. Thus the order of magnitude of the correction will be given by $(\Gamma - \Gamma_0)/\Gamma \approx k_F m \Gamma_0/\hbar^2 \approx k_F \tilde{f} \approx k_F a \ll 1$, where Eqs. (11.46) and (11.22) have been used.

Before attempting a careful expansion of Eq. (11.48), we notice that the full set of variables $(\mathbf{p}, \mathbf{p}', P)$ is never needed in any calculation. Indeed, all that is required is the proper self-energy [Eq. (11.28)]:

$$\hbar \Sigma^\star(p) = -2i(2\pi)^{-4} \int d^4 k\, G^0(k)\, \Gamma(pk; pk) + i(2\pi)^{-4} \int d^4 k\, G^0(k)\, \Gamma(kp; pk)$$

$$(11.49)$$

Define the relative and total wave vectors and frequency

$$\tfrac{1}{2}(\mathbf{p} - \mathbf{k}) = \mathbf{q} \qquad \mathbf{p} + \mathbf{k} = \mathbf{P} \qquad p_0 + k_0 = P_0 \qquad (11.50)$$

Since Γ depends only on the variables shown in Eq. (11.40), the proper self-energy can be rewritten as

$$\hbar \Sigma^\star(p) = -2i(2\pi)^{-4} \int d^4 k\, G^0(k)\, \Gamma(\mathbf{q},\mathbf{q},P) + i(2\pi)^{-4} \int d^4 k\, G^0(k)\, \Gamma(-\mathbf{q},\mathbf{q},P)$$

$$(11.51)$$

We now expand Γ to second order in $k_F a$. By the definition of the *s*-wave scattering length a, the *s*-wave phase shift has the long-wavelength expansion

$$\delta_0 \approx -ka + O[(ka)^3]$$

Furthermore, the leading term of the *l*th partial wave is given by $\delta_l \approx O[(ka)^{2l+1}]$.

[1] V. M. Galitskii, *loc. cit.*
[2] S. T. Beliaev, *Sov. Phys.-JETP,* **7**:299 (1958).

Thus the scattering amplitude has the limiting value

$$f(\mathbf{k},\mathbf{k}') = \sum_{l=0}^{\infty} \frac{2l+1}{k} e^{i\delta_l} \sin \delta_l P_l(\cos\theta)$$

$$= k^{-1}(1+i\delta_0)\delta_0 + O(k^2 a^3)$$

$$= -a + ika^2 + O(k^2 a^3) \qquad |\mathbf{k}| = |\mathbf{k}'| \to 0 \qquad (11.52)$$

It is remarkable that this long-wavelength limit depends *only* on the s-wave scattering length; for a hard-sphere gas, a is just the diameter of the sphere, but Eq. (11.52) is clearly more general. In particular, the scattering amplitude always reduces to a constant as $\mathbf{k}$ and $\mathbf{k}'$ vanish, which enables us to take the leading contribution to $f(\mathbf{k},\mathbf{k}')$ off the energy shell in the long-wavelength limit. The second term in Eq. (11.52) is pure imaginary, and ensures that the generalized unitarity equation (11.19) is satisfied to order a^2. To this order, the corresponding amplitude $\tilde{f}$ [Eq. (11.12)] becomes

$$\tilde{f} \approx 4\pi a - 4\pi i a^2 k \qquad |\mathbf{k}| = |\mathbf{k}'| \to 0 \qquad (11.53)$$

As noted at the beginning of this section, the expansion parameter for an imperfect Fermi gas is $k_F a$, which is small for either low density ($k_F \to 0$) or small scattering length ($a \to 0$). In this limit, Galitskii's equations can be used to evaluate the scattering amplitude in the medium $\Gamma(\mathbf{q},\mathbf{q},P)$ to order $(k_F a)^2$. Equations (11.45) and (11.53) together give

$$\frac{m}{\hbar^2}\Gamma_0(\mathbf{q},\mathbf{q},P)$$

$$= 4\pi a - 4\pi i q a^2 + (4\pi a)^2 \int \frac{d^3 k'}{(2\pi)^3} \left(\frac{1}{\epsilon - k'^2 + i\eta} + \frac{1}{k'^2 - q^2 - i\eta} \right) + \cdots$$

$$= 4\pi a + (4\pi a)^2 \int \frac{d^3 k'}{(2\pi)^3} \left(\frac{1}{\epsilon - k'^2 + i\eta} + \frac{\mathscr{P}}{k'^2 - q^2} \right) + \cdots$$

where $\mathscr{P}$ denotes the principal value and the imaginary part cancels the term $-4\pi i q a^2$. This expansion to order a^2 now can be combined with Eq. (11.48) to obtain

$$\frac{m}{\hbar^2}\Gamma(\mathbf{q},\mathbf{q},P) = 4\pi a + (4\pi a)^2 \int \frac{d^3 k'}{(2\pi)^3} \left[\frac{N(\mathbf{P},\mathbf{k}')}{\epsilon - k'^2 + i\eta N(\mathbf{P},\mathbf{k}')} + \frac{\mathscr{P}}{k'^2 - q^2} \right] + \cdots$$

$$(11.54)$$

since the terms containing $(\epsilon - k'^2 + i\eta)^{-1}$ in the integrand cancel identically. Note that Eq. (11.54) is an *explicit* representation for $\Gamma(\mathbf{q},\mathbf{q},P)$ in terms of known quantities; furthermore, it is easily seen that

$$\Gamma(\mathbf{q},\mathbf{q},P) = \Gamma(-\mathbf{q},\mathbf{q},P) \qquad (11.55)$$

to this order. Thus the second term of Eq. (11.51) cancels one-half of the first, and we obtain

$$\hbar\Sigma^\star(p) = -i(2\pi)^{-4} \int d^4k \, G^0(k) \, \Gamma(\mathbf{q},\mathbf{q},P) \tag{11.56}$$

which is valid through order a^2. This cancellation typifies the general result noted in Sec. 10 that the direct and exchange terms are comparable in magnitude for a short-range potential.

The expansion of Γ in Eq. (11.54) leads to a corresponding expansion of the self-energy in powers of a

$$\hbar\Sigma^\star(p) = \hbar\Sigma^\star_{(1)}(p) + \hbar\Sigma^\star_{(2)}(p) + \cdots$$

where

$$\hbar\Sigma^\star_{(1)}(p) = -i \int \frac{d^4k}{(2\pi)^4} G^0(k) \frac{4\pi a\hbar^2}{m} e^{ik_0\eta'}$$

$$\hbar\Sigma^\star_{(2)}(p) = -i \int \frac{d^4k}{(2\pi)^4} G^0(k) e^{ik_0\eta'} (4\pi a)^2 \frac{\hbar^2}{m} \int \frac{d^3k'}{(2\pi)^3}$$

$$\times \left[\frac{N(\mathbf{P},\mathbf{k}')}{\epsilon - k'^2 + i\eta N(\mathbf{P},\mathbf{k}')} + \frac{\mathscr{P}}{k'^2 - q^2} \right]$$

and the subscripts here denote powers of a, *not* orders in perturbation theory. The first term is easily evaluated by closing the contour in the upper half plane [the convergence factor $e^{ik_0\eta'}$ plays the same role as in Eq. (11.27)]

$$\hbar\Sigma^\star_{(1)}(p) = -i \int \frac{d^3k}{(2\pi)^3} \frac{4\pi a\hbar^2}{m} \int \frac{dk_0}{2\pi} e^{ik_0\eta'} \left[\frac{\theta(k - k_F)}{k_0 - \omega_k + i\eta} + \frac{\theta(k_F - k)}{k_0 - \omega_k - i\eta} \right]$$

$$= \frac{4\pi a\hbar^2}{m} \int \frac{d^3k}{(2\pi)^3} \theta(k_F - k)$$

$$= \frac{\hbar^2 k_F^2}{m} \frac{2k_F a}{3\pi} \tag{11.57}$$

The second term is considerably more complicated, because the frequency k_0 appears in the denominator through the combination $\epsilon = mP_0/\hbar - \tfrac{1}{4}\mathbf{P}^2 = mp_0/\hbar + mk_0/\hbar - \tfrac{1}{4}\mathbf{P}^2$. It is precisely this dependence that necessitated the solution for Γ off the energy shell. The evaluation of the k_0 integral is very similar to that of Eq. (11.35), and we find

$$\hbar\Sigma^\star_{(2)}(\mathbf{p},p_0)$$

$$= \frac{\hbar^2}{m} 16\pi^2 a^2 \int \frac{d^3k \, d^3k'}{(2\pi)^6} \left[\frac{\theta(k_F - k)\,\theta(|\tfrac{1}{2}\mathbf{P} + \mathbf{k}'| - k_F)\,\theta(|\tfrac{1}{2}\mathbf{P} - \mathbf{k}'| - k_F)}{mp_0/\hbar - \tfrac{1}{2}p^2 + q^2 - k'^2 + i\eta} \right.$$

$$\left. + \frac{\theta(k - k_F)\,\theta(k_F - |\tfrac{1}{2}\mathbf{P} + \mathbf{k}'|)\,\theta(k_F - |\tfrac{1}{2}\mathbf{P} - \mathbf{k}'|)}{mp_0/\hbar - \tfrac{1}{2}p^2 + q^2 - k'^2 - i\eta} - \frac{\mathscr{P}\theta(k_F - k)}{q^2 - k'^2} \right]$$

$$\tag{11.58}$$

which has been simplified by writing [compare Eq. (11.50)]

$$\frac{\hbar k^2}{2m} - \frac{\hbar P^2}{4m} = \frac{\hbar q^2}{m} - \frac{\hbar p^2}{2m}$$

Equations (11.57) and (11.58) together express $\Sigma^\star$ as a series, including all terms of order $(k_F a)^2$.

The single-particle Green's function for a dilute Fermi gas now takes the approximate form

$$G(\mathbf{p}, p_0) \approx \left[p_0 - \frac{\hbar p^2}{2m} - \Sigma^\star_{(1)}(\mathbf{p}, p_0) - \Sigma^\star_{(2)}(\mathbf{p}, p_0) \right]^{-1} \tag{11.59}$$

and the excitation spectrum $p_0 = \hbar^{-1} \epsilon_\mathbf{p} + i\gamma_\mathbf{p}$ is determined by the solution of the equation

$$p_0 - \frac{\hbar p^2}{2m} - \Sigma^\star_{(1)}(\mathbf{p}, p_0) - \Sigma^\star_{(2)}(\mathbf{p}, p_0) = 0 \tag{11.60}$$

Since $\Sigma^\star_{(1)}$ is a *constant* of order $k_F a$, the spectrum must have the following expansion

$$p_0 = \frac{\hbar p^2}{2m} [1 + O(k_F a)] \tag{11.61}$$

We can therefore set $p_0 \approx \hbar p^2 / 2m$ in the last term of Eq. (11.60), which is *already* of order $(k_F a)^2$; this constitutes a major simplification, and the *explicit* solution then becomes

$$
\begin{aligned}
\epsilon_\mathbf{p} + i\hbar\gamma_\mathbf{p} &= \frac{\hbar^2 p^2}{2m} + \hbar\Sigma^\star_{(1)} + \hbar\Sigma^\star_{(2)}(\mathbf{p}, \omega_\mathbf{p}) \\
&= \frac{\hbar^2 p^2}{2m} + \frac{\hbar^2 k_F^2}{m} \Bigg\{ \frac{2}{3\pi} k_F a + 16\pi^2 (k_F a)^2 \int \frac{d^3 k \, d^3 k'}{(2\pi)^6} \\
&\quad \times \Bigg[\frac{\theta(1-k)\,\theta(|\tfrac{1}{2}\mathbf{P} + \mathbf{k}'| - 1)\,\theta(|\tfrac{1}{2}\mathbf{P} - \mathbf{k}'| - 1)}{q^2 - k'^2 + i\eta} \\
&\quad + \frac{\theta(k-1)\,\theta(1 - |\tfrac{1}{2}\mathbf{P} + \mathbf{k}'|)\,\theta(1 - |\tfrac{1}{2}\mathbf{P} - \mathbf{k}'|)}{q^2 - k'^2 - i\eta} \\
&\quad - \frac{\mathscr{P}\theta(1-k)}{q^2 - k'^2} \Bigg] + O(k_F^3 a^3) \Bigg\} \qquad \mathbf{P} = \mathbf{p} + \mathbf{k}, \ \mathbf{q} = \tfrac{1}{2}(\mathbf{p} - \mathbf{k}) \quad (11.62)
\end{aligned}
$$

where the integral has been rendered dimensionless by expressing all wave vectors in terms of k_F.

This equation resembles a second-order expansion obtained with time-independent perturbation theory for an interparticle potential $4\pi\hbar^2 a/m$ in momentum space that is chosen to reproduce the correct s-wave scattering

amplitude. The quantity in braces is proportional to the proper self-energy and has the physical interpretation shown schematically in Fig. 11.9. (These are now meant to be diagrams of time-independent perturbation theory, the analog of the Goldstone diagrams. An arrow running upward denotes a particle, while an arrow running downward denotes a hole.) The term of order $k_F a$ in Eq. (11.62) and in Fig. 11.9a represents the forward scattering from the other particles in the medium with an effective potential $4\pi\hbar^2 a/m$. The second-order corrections in Eq. (11.62) incorporate the effect of the medium on the intermediate states. Of these latter terms, the first two represent the processes indicated in Fig. 11.9b and c, while the last term $[\mathscr{P}(q^2 - k'^2)^{-1}]$ must be subtracted explicitly because the real part of the *exact scattering amplitude* would

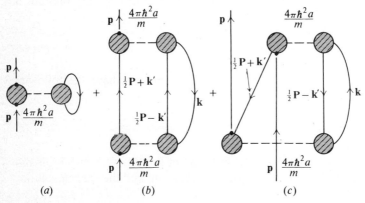

Fig. 11.9 Schematic expansion of proper self-energy.

be given by $-a$ to this order if there were no filled Fermi sea as a background. The terms in Fig. 11.9b and c denote the following physical processes. In the first case, the incident particle collides with a particle in the medium, exciting it to some state above the Fermi sea, thereby leaving the hole in the medium; the same two particles then collide a second time, bringing the system back to its initial state of a Fermi sea and the incident particle. The second case is an exchange process. Two particles in the medium interact; they are both excited above the Fermi sea, thereby leaving two holes in the medium. The incident particle collides with one of the excited particles, and these two particles then fill the two holes. The system thus returns to its initial state, the only alteration being the exchange of the initial incident particle with one of the excited particles.

PHYSICAL QUANTITIES

We now examine the implications of Eq. (11.62).

1. *Lifetime of single-particle excitations*: It is evident that the real part ϵ_p contains a shift in the single-particle energies for particles with wave vector **p**,

whereas the imaginary part γ_p leads to a finite lifetime [compare Eq. (7.79)]. When the indicated integration in Eq. (11.62) is carried out, we find[1]

$$\hbar\gamma_p = \frac{\hbar^2 k_F^2}{2m} \frac{2}{\pi} (k_F a)^2 \left(\frac{k_F - p}{k_F}\right)^2 \operatorname{sgn}(k_F - p) \tag{11.63}$$

which is valid for $|p - k_F| \ll k_F$. In accordance with the general Lehmann representation (Fig. 7.1) the pole lies below (above) the real axis for $p > k_F$ ($p < k_F$). Since γ_p vanishes like $(p - k_F)^2$, the lifetime becomes infinite as $p \to k_F$, and the condition $\epsilon_p - \mu \gg \hbar\gamma_p$ is satisfied [compare the discussion leading to Eq. (7.79)].[2] These long-lived single-particle excitations are often known as *quasiparticles*. Note that γ_p is proportional to $(k_F a)^2$, because the finite lifetime reflects the possibility of real transitions and thus involves $|f|^2 \propto a^2$.

2. *Single-particle excitation spectrum*: The present quasiparticle approximation

$$G(\mathbf{p}, p_0) \approx (p_0 - \epsilon_p \hbar^{-1} - i\gamma_p)^{-1} \tag{11.64}$$

implies that the ground state remains a Fermi sea filled up to wavenumber k_F,‡ but with a different dispersion relation ϵ_p. Since γ_p changes sign at k_F, the Lehmann representation shows that the chemical potential is given by $\mu = \epsilon_{k_F}$. It is therefore necessary to evaluate ϵ_p at the Fermi surface. A lengthy integration with Eq. (11.62) gives

$$\mu = \epsilon_{k_F} = \frac{\hbar^2 k_F^2}{2m} \left[1 + \frac{4}{3\pi} k_F a + \frac{4}{15\pi^2}(11 - 2\ln 2)(k_F a)^2\right] \tag{11.65}$$

which was first obtained by Galitskii.[1]

Close to the Fermi surface, the energy spectrum can be expanded in a Taylor series

$$\epsilon_p = \epsilon_{k_F} + \left.\frac{\partial\epsilon_p}{\partial p}\right|_{k_F} (p - k_F) + \cdots$$

$$\equiv \epsilon_{k_F} + \frac{\hbar^2 k_F}{m^*}(p - k_F) + \cdots \tag{11.66}$$

---

[1] V. M. Galitskii, *loc. cit.*

[2] This detailed result typifies a general theorem of J. M. Luttinger [*Phys. Rev.*, **121**:942 (1961)] that $\operatorname{Im}\Sigma^\star$ vanishes like $(\omega - \mu/\hbar)^2$ near the Fermi surface, which holds to all orders of perturbation theory.

‡ A more detailed evaluation based on Eq. (11.59) shows that distribution function n_p is slightly altered, but this does not affect our subsequent results [V. A. Belyakov, *Sov. Phys.-JETP*, **13**:850 (1961)].

which defines the effective mass

$$m^* = \hbar^2 k_F \left(\frac{\partial \epsilon_p}{\partial p}\bigg|_{k_F}\right)^{-1} \tag{11.67}$$

in terms of the slope of ϵ_p at the Fermi surface.   A detailed calculation with Eq. (11.62) yields

$$\frac{m^*}{m} = 1 + \frac{8}{15\pi^2}(7\ln 2 - 1)(k_F a)^2 \tag{11.68}$$

correct to order $(k_F a)^2$.   Note the following features of Eq. (11.68):

(a) m^* has no terms linear in $k_F a$, which reflects the constant value of $\Sigma_{(1)}^*$ in Eq. (11.57).

(b) m^* determines the heat capacity of the system in the zero-temperature limit because the heat capacity depends on the density of states near the Fermi surface and thus on the effective mass.   As is shown in Sec. 29, the precise relation is given by [compare Eq. (5.60)]

$$\frac{C_V}{V} \approx \frac{k_B^2 T m^* k_F}{3\hbar^2} \qquad T \to 0 \tag{11.69}$$

and Eq. (11.68) shows that the interactions enhance C_V.   Although the present model applies only for $k_F a \ll 1$, it is interesting that experiments[1] on pure He^3 suggest $(m^*/m)_{He^3} \approx 2.9$ in qualitative agreement with Eq. (11.68).   Unfortunately, the large numerical value precludes a simple perturbation expansion, and a more sophisticated approach is required.[2]

3. *Ground-state energy*: The ground-state energy can be readily obtained with thermodynamic identities, as noted by Galitskii.   It could, of course, be calculated directly from $\Sigma^*(\mathbf{p}, p_0)$ with Eq. (9.36), but the following approach is much simpler.   By definition, the chemical potential at $S = 0$ is related to the exact ground-state energy E by the equation (4.3)

$$\mu = \left(\frac{\partial E}{\partial N}\right)_V \qquad S = 0 \tag{11.70}$$

Integrate Eq. (11.70) at constant V (and $S = 0$)

$$E = \int_0^N dN' \, \mu(S = 0, V, N') \qquad \text{const } V, S = 0$$

Since N appears in Eq. (11.65) only through $k_F = (3\pi^2 N/V)^{\frac{1}{3}}$, the integral is easily evaluated with the relation

$$\int_0^N dN' [k_F(N')]^\lambda = \frac{3}{3+\lambda} k_F^\lambda N$$

---

[1] An excellent survey may be found in J. Wilks, "The Properties of Liquid and Solid Helium," chap. 17, Oxford University Press, Oxford, 1967.
[2] See for example, L. D. Landau, *Sov. Phys.-JETP*, **3**:920 (1957).

and we find

$$\frac{E}{N} = \frac{\hbar^2 k_F^2}{2m} \left[\frac{3}{5} + \frac{2}{3\pi} k_F a + \frac{4}{35\pi^2} (11 - 2\ln 2)(k_F a)^2 + 0.23(k_F a)^3 + \cdots \right]$$

(11.71)

The first term is the familiar kinetic energy of a free Fermi gas [Eq. (3.30)], whereas the second term was discussed following Eq. (11.26). The third term arises from the modification of the intermediate states by the exclusion principle and was first obtained by Huang and Yang.[1] The final term, which we have not discussed here, was obtained by DeDominicis and Martin.[2] It requires a study of three-particle correlations, and also depends on the precise shape of the potential through the s-wave effective range and p-wave scattering length. As written here, Eq. (11.71) describes a hard-sphere Fermi gas with two degrees of freedom; the corresponding expression for nuclear matter (four degrees of freedom, neutron and proton, spin-up and spin-down) is

$$\left. \frac{E}{N} \right|_{\substack{\text{nuclear} \\ \text{matter}}} = \frac{\hbar^2 k_F^2}{2m}$$

$$\times \left[\frac{3}{5} + \frac{2}{\pi} k_F a + \frac{12}{35\pi^2} (11 - 2\ln 2)(k_F a)^2 + 0.78(k_F a)^3 + \cdots \right] \quad (11.72)$$

JUSTIFICATION OF TERMS RETAINED

We shall now further justify our basic approximation of retaining only the self-energy of Fig. 11.3, in which two particles or two holes interact repeatedly. One of these terms is shown in Fig. 11.10a, along with a typical omitted one

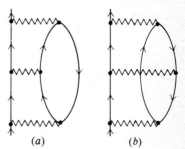

Fig. 11.10 Comparison of diagrams (a) retained and (b) omitted in ladder approximation.

(a)　　　　(b)

[1] K. Huang and C. N. Yang, *Phys. Rev.*, **105**:767 (1957); T. D. Lee and C. N. Yang, *Phys. Rev.*, **105**:1119 (1957).

[2] Strictly speaking, C. DeDominicis and P. C. Martin [*Phys. Rev.*, **105**:1417 (1957)] obtained the $(k_F a)^3$ correction for nuclear matter [Eq. (11.72)], and the general expression was subsequently derived by V. N. Efimov and M. Ya. Amusya, *Sov. Phys.-JETP*, **20**:388 (1965).

(Fig. 11.10b). The basic point is that only *one* line in Fig. 11.10a runs in the reverse direction, whereas *two* lines in Fig. 11.10b run in the reverse direction. To show precisely how the direction of the lines affects the term, we consider the following two pieces of the respective graphs shown in Fig. 11.11 [compare the discussion following Eq. (11.27)]. The corresponding integrations over q are given, respectively, by

$$i\hbar^{-1}(2\pi)^{-4}\int d^4q\, U_0(q)\, G^0(p_1+q)\, G^0(p_2-q) \tag{11.73a}$$

$$i\hbar^{-1}(2\pi)^{-4}\int d^4q\, U_0(q)\, G^0(p_1+q)\, G^0(p_2+q) \tag{11.73b}$$

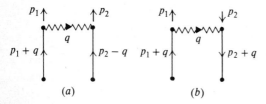

(a)   (b)

Fig. 11.11 Pieces of graphs (a) retained and (b) omitted in ladder approximation.

In case (a), the two Green's functions contain q with opposite signs, whereas in (b), they have the same sign. This difference has a crucial effect on the frequency integrals, as is readily verified by carrying out the q_0 integration. In particular, Eq. (11.73a) contains two terms, with the factors $(1 - n^0_{\mathbf{p}_1+\mathbf{q}})(1 - n^0_{\mathbf{p}_2-\mathbf{q}})$ and $n^0_{\mathbf{p}_1+\mathbf{q}}n^0_{\mathbf{p}_2-\mathbf{q}}$, while the corresponding terms in Eq. (11.73b) contain $(1 - n^0_{\mathbf{p}_1+\mathbf{q}})n^0_{\mathbf{p}_2+\mathbf{q}}$ and $n^0_{\mathbf{p}_1+\mathbf{q}}(1 - n^0_{\mathbf{p}_2+\mathbf{q}})$ [compare the calculation leading to Eq. (11.35)]. For the present low-density system, momentum integrations inside the Fermi sea have *very restricted* phase space because $k_F \propto (N/V)^{\frac{1}{3}}$ is small, while those outside are essentially unbounded. Thus the presence of a factor n^0 (a hole) reduces the term relative to one containing only particles. This calculation explicitly illustrates the distinction made between particles and holes in the discussion of Figs. 11.3 and 11.4.

It is interesting to ask how the present theory can be improved. The most obvious flaw is the lack of self-consistency, because $\Sigma^\star$ is evaluated with *free* Green's functions G^0, while $\Sigma^\star$ determines the fully *interacting* G. The calculation can be made self-consistent (in the sense of Sec. 10) by changing all factors of G^0 into G in Eqs. (11.28) and (11.30); in effect, this changes the free-particle energies $\epsilon^0_k = \hbar^2 k^2/2m$ appearing in Eq. (11.58) into interacting energies ϵ_k and introduces additional frequency dependence. In this approach, $\Sigma^\star$ thus depends on the *exact* single-particle energies, which, in turn, depend on $\Sigma^\star$. Although different in detail, this modified theory is very similar to Brueckner's theory of nuclear matter and He^3.[‡] These questions are discussed further in Chap. 11.[1]

‡ K. A. Brueckner, *loc. cit.*
[1] See also A. L. Fetter and K. M. Watson, The Optical Model, secs. V and VI, in K. A. Brueckner (ed.), "Advances in Theoretical Physics," vol. I, p. 115, Academic Press, Inc., New York, 1965.

12□DEGENERATE ELECTRON GAS

For the final example in this chapter, we return to the degenerate (high-density) electron gas treated in Sec. 3. The most straightforward approach is to analyze the higher-order terms in the proper self-energy; just as in Sec. 11, the dominant contribution arises from a particular class of diagrams that may be summed explicitly. This procedure is studied in detail in Sec. 30, where we consider the electron gas at finite temperature. For variety, we here describe an alternative formulation, in which the ground-state energy is expressed in terms of the polarization insertions Π and generalized dielectric constant.

GROUND-STATE ENERGY AND THE DIELECTRIC CONSTANT

To simplify our treatment, the present section is restricted to a spatially homogeneous system of particles with a *spin-independent* static potential

$$V(\mathbf{x},\mathbf{x}')_{\lambda\lambda',\,\mu\mu'} = V(\mathbf{x} - \mathbf{x}')\,\delta_{\lambda\lambda'}\,\delta_{\mu\mu'} \tag{12.1a}$$

$$\begin{aligned} U_0(x,x')_{\lambda\lambda',\,\mu\mu'} &= U_0(x - x')\,\delta_{\lambda\lambda'}\,\delta_{\mu\mu'} \\ &= V(\mathbf{x} - \mathbf{x}')\,\delta(t - t')\,\delta_{\lambda\lambda'}\,\delta_{\mu\mu'} \end{aligned} \tag{12.1b}$$

The interaction energy for both bosons and fermions [Eq. (7.11)] then reduces to

$$\begin{aligned} \langle \hat{V} \rangle &= \tfrac{1}{2} \int d^3x\, d^3x'\, V(\mathbf{x} - \mathbf{x}') \langle \hat{\psi}^{\dagger}_{\alpha}(\mathbf{x})\, \hat{\psi}^{\dagger}_{\beta}(\mathbf{x}')\, \hat{\psi}_{\beta}(\mathbf{x}')\, \hat{\psi}_{\alpha}(\mathbf{x}) \rangle \\ &= \tfrac{1}{2} \int d^3x\, d^3x'\, V(\mathbf{x} - \mathbf{x}')\, [\langle \hat{n}(\mathbf{x})\, \hat{n}(\mathbf{x}') \rangle - \delta(\mathbf{x} - \mathbf{x}')\langle \hat{n}(\mathbf{x}) \rangle] \end{aligned} \tag{12.2}$$

where the second line has been rewritten with the canonical commutation or anticommutation relations [Eq. (2.3)], and the angular brackets denote the ground-state expectation value. It is convenient to introduce the *deviation* operator

$$\tilde{n}(\mathbf{x}) \equiv \hat{n}(\mathbf{x}) - \langle \hat{n}(\mathbf{x}) \rangle \tag{12.3}$$

in which case Eq. (12.2) becomes

$$\begin{aligned} \langle \hat{V} \rangle = \tfrac{1}{2} \int d^3x\, d^3x'\, V(\mathbf{x} - \mathbf{x}')\, [\langle \tilde{n}(\mathbf{x})\, \tilde{n}(\mathbf{x}') \rangle + \langle \hat{n}(\mathbf{x}) \rangle \langle \hat{n}(\mathbf{x}') \rangle \\ - \delta(\mathbf{x} - \mathbf{x}')\langle \hat{n}(\mathbf{x}) \rangle] \end{aligned} \tag{12.4}$$

This equation describes an arbitrary interacting system and is therefore quite complicated. Its real usefulness, however, is for a uniform system, where $\langle \hat{n}(\mathbf{x}) \rangle$ is a constant equal to $n = N/V$. The last two terms of Eq. (12.4) are then trivial, and we may concentrate on the density correlation function $\langle \tilde{n}(\mathbf{x})\tilde{n}(\mathbf{x}') \rangle$, which contains all of the interesting physical effects.

To make use of the diagrammatic analysis of Chap. 3, we introduce a *time-ordered* correlation function

$$iD(x,x') = \frac{\langle \Psi_0 | T[\tilde{n}_H(x)\, \tilde{n}_H(x')]|\Psi_0 \rangle}{\langle \Psi_0 | \Psi_0 \rangle} \tag{12.5}$$

which is clearly symmetric in its arguments:

$$D(x,x') = D(x',x) \tag{12.6}$$

For reasons that are made clear in the subsequent discussion, D is frequently called the *polarization propagator*. In the usual case of a uniform medium with time-independent $\hat{H}$, D depends only on $x - x'$. The interaction energy [Eq. (12.4)] can now be rewritten as

$$\langle \hat{V} \rangle = \tfrac{1}{2} \int d^3x \, d^3x' \, V(\mathbf{x} - \mathbf{x}') \, [iD(\mathbf{x}' \, t, \mathbf{x}t) + n^2 - \delta(\mathbf{x} - \mathbf{x}')n] \tag{12.7}$$

where the symmetry of D enables us to set $t = t'$ directly. If D^0 denotes the corresponding correlation function for a noninteracting system

$$iD^0(x',x) = \langle \Phi_0 | T[\tilde{n}_I(x') \, \tilde{n}_I(x)] | \Phi_0 \rangle \tag{12.8}$$

then the interaction energy can be separated into a first-order contribution and all the higher-order contributions

$$\langle \hat{V} \rangle = \tfrac{1}{2} \int d^3x \, d^3x' \, V(\mathbf{x} - \mathbf{x}') \, [iD^0(\mathbf{x}' \, t, \mathbf{x}t) + n^2 - \delta(\mathbf{x} - \mathbf{x}')n]$$
$$+ \tfrac{1}{2} \int d^3x \, d^3x' \, V(\mathbf{x} - \mathbf{x}') \, [iD(\mathbf{x}' \, t, \mathbf{x}t) - iD^0(\mathbf{x}' \, t, \mathbf{x}t)] \tag{12.9a}$$

$$\langle \hat{V} \rangle = \langle \Phi_0 | \hat{V} | \Phi_0 \rangle + \tfrac{1}{2} \int d^3x \, d^3x' \, V(\mathbf{x} - \mathbf{x}') \, [iD(\mathbf{x}' \, t, \mathbf{x}t)$$
$$- iD^0(\mathbf{x}' \, t, \mathbf{x}t)] \tag{12.9b}$$

This separation is very convenient, for we have already evaluated the first term in Sec. 3. Note that Eq. (12.9*b*) applies only to a homogeneous system, where $\langle \hat{n}(\mathbf{x}) \rangle = N/V$ is independent of the interaction between particles. In an *inhomogeneous* system, the interparticle potential alters the density, and $\langle \hat{n}(\mathbf{x}) \rangle$ therefore contains contributions from all orders in perturbation theory. A simple example are the electrons in an atom, where the coulomb repulsion modifies the unperturbed hydrogenic orbitals.

Equation (12.9*b*) can be combined with Eq. (7.30) to yield the total ground-state energy and the correlation energy defined in Sec. 3

$$E = \langle \Phi_0 | \hat{H} | \Phi_0 \rangle + \tfrac{1}{2} \int_0^1 d\lambda \, \lambda^{-1} \int d^3x \, d^3x' \, \lambda V(\mathbf{x} - \mathbf{x}')$$
$$\times [iD^\lambda(\mathbf{x}' \, t, \mathbf{x}t) - iD^0(\mathbf{x}' \, t, \mathbf{x}t)]$$
$$= \langle \Phi_0 | \hat{H} | \Phi_0 \rangle + E_{\text{corr}} \tag{12.10}$$

where the integral over the variable coupling constant λ has been evaluated explicitly in the first-order term. For the present uniform system, this expression becomes much simpler in momentum space, where we find

$$E_{\text{corr}} = \tfrac{1}{2} V(2\pi)^{-4} \int_0^1 d\lambda \, \lambda^{-1} \int d^4q \, \lambda V(\mathbf{q}) \, [iD^\lambda(\mathbf{q},\omega) - iD^0(\mathbf{q},\omega)] \tag{12.11}$$

Here $V(\mathbf{q})$ denotes the Fourier transform of $V(\mathbf{x})$, and

$$D^\lambda(x,x') = D^\lambda(\mathbf{x} - \mathbf{x}', t - t')$$
$$= (2\pi)^{-4} \int d^4q \, e^{i\mathbf{q}\cdot(\mathbf{x}-\mathbf{x}')} \, e^{-i\omega(t-t')} \, D^\lambda(\mathbf{q},\omega) \tag{12.12}$$

The symmetry of $D(x,x')$ [Eq. (12.6)] allows us to write Eq. (12.11) without a convergence factor $e^{\pm i\omega\eta}$, which thus differs from Eq. (7.32).

We have now expressed the ground-state energy of an interacting system in terms of the time-ordered density correlation function D^λ for an arbitrary value of the coupling constant. As an introduction to this function, it is useful to evaluate $D^0(x,x')$ which describes a noninteracting system

$$iD^0(x,x') = \langle\Phi_0|T[\hat{\psi}^\dagger_\alpha(x)\,\hat{\psi}_\alpha(x)\,\hat{\psi}^\dagger_\beta(x')\,\hat{\psi}_\beta(x')]|\Phi_0\rangle$$
$$- \langle\Phi_0|\hat{\psi}^\dagger_\alpha(x)\,\hat{\psi}_\alpha(x)|\Phi_0\rangle\langle\Phi_0|\hat{\psi}^\dagger_\beta(x')\,\hat{\psi}_\beta(x')|\Phi_0\rangle$$

This expression is easily evaluated with Wick's theorem

$$iD^0(x,x') = iG^0_{\alpha\alpha}(x,x^+)\,iG^0_{\beta\beta}(x',x'^+) - iG^0_{\alpha\beta}(x,x')\,iG^0_{\beta\alpha}(x',x) - \langle\hat{n}(\mathbf{x})\rangle\langle\hat{n}(\mathbf{x}')\rangle$$
$$= (2s+1)\,G^0(x,x')\,G^0(x',x)$$

where we now restrict the discussion to a uniform Fermi system with spin s. This product of noninteracting Green's functions has the form shown in Fig.

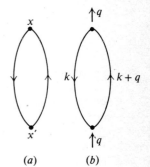

Fig. 12.1 Lowest-order contribution D^0 to density correlation function (a) in coordinate space, (b) in momentum space.

12.1a and is typical of a polarization insertion. Indeed, the lowest-order contributions to $U(x,x')$ are shown in Fig. 12.2, and may be written as

$$U(x,x') = U_0(x,x') - i\hbar^{-1} \int d^4x_1\,d^4x_1'\,U_0(x,x_1)\,G^0_{\alpha\beta}(x_1,x_1')$$
$$\times\,G^0_{\beta\alpha}(x_1',x_1)\,U_0(x_1',x') + \cdots$$
$$= U_0(x,x') + \int d^4x_1\,d^4x_1'\,U_0(x,x_1)\,\Pi^0(x_1,x_1')\,U_0(x_1',x') + \cdots$$

We therefore identify [compare (9.44)]

$$D^0(x,x') = -iG^0_{\alpha\beta}(x,x')\,G^0_{\beta\alpha}(x',x)$$
$$= \hbar\Pi^0(x,x') \tag{12.13}$$

It is easily verified that this structure persists to all orders, so that $D(x,x')$ is $\hbar$ times the *total* polarization insertion

$$D(x,x') = \hbar\Pi(x,x') = \hbar\Pi(x',x) \tag{12.14}$$

Furthermore, Dyson's equation allows us to rewrite $\int d^4x_1 \, U_0(x,x_1)\Pi(x_1,x')$ as $\int d^4x_1 \, U(x,x_1)\Pi^\star(x_1,x')$, where $\Pi^\star$ is the proper polarization. The corresponding relation in momentum space is given by $U_0(q)\Pi(q) = U(q)\Pi^\star(q)$, and the correlation energy [Eq. (12.11)] becomes

$$E_{\text{corr}} = +\tfrac{1}{2} i V \hbar (2\pi)^{-4} \int_0^1 d\lambda \, \lambda^{-1} \int d^4q \, [U^\lambda(q)\Pi^{\star\lambda}(q) - \lambda U_0(q)\Pi^0(q)] \quad (12.15)$$

Note that

$$\Pi^0(q) \equiv \Pi^\star_{(0)}(q) \tag{12.16}$$

where $\Pi^\star_{(0)}(q)$ is the lowest-order proper polarization propagator.

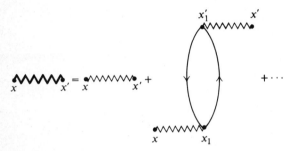

Fig. 12.2　Expansion of effective interaction.

Equation (12.15) can also be expressed in terms of the generalized dielectric constant $\kappa(\mathbf{q},\omega) = \kappa(q)$, defined by Eqs. (9.46) and (9.47). Thus the integrand of Eq. (12.15) may be rewritten with the relation

$$U(q)\Pi^\star(q) = \frac{U_0(q)\Pi^\star(q)}{1 - U_0(q)\Pi^\star(q)}$$

$$= \frac{1 - \kappa(q)}{\kappa(q)} = \frac{1}{\kappa(q)} - 1 \tag{12.17}$$

which yields

$$E_{\text{corr}} = +\tfrac{1}{2} i V \hbar (2\pi)^{-4} \int_0^1 d\lambda \, \lambda^{-1} \int d^4q \, \{[\kappa^\lambda(q)]^{-1} - 1 - \lambda U_0(q)\Pi^0(q)\} \quad (12.18)$$

RING DIAGRAMS

Equation (12.15) applies to any uniform system, and we now specialize to a degenerate electron gas, described by the hamiltonian in Eq. (3.19). As shown in Sec. 3, the uniform positive background precisely cancels the $\mathbf{q}=0$ term in the potential, so that $V(0)$ vanishes identically. This reflects the physical observation that there is no forward scattering from a neutral medium. In consequence, all "tadpole" diagrams (Figs. 9.7a, 9.8a, c, d, etc.) disappear from the theory, which simplifies the perturbation analysis considerably.

To understand the structure of Eq. (12.15), we shall *temporarily* expand $U\Pi^\star$ in a perturbation series, as follows:

$$U\Pi^\star = U_0\Pi^\star + U_0\Pi^\star U_0\Pi^\star + \cdots$$
$$= U_0\Pi^\star_{(0)} + U_0\Pi^\star_{(1)} + U_0\Pi^\star_{(0)}U_0\Pi^\star_{(0)} + \cdots$$

where $\Pi^\star_{(0)}$ is given by Eq. (12.16), and $\Pi^\star_{(1)}$ is the first-order proper polarization with the contributions shown in Fig. 12.3. The first and last terms (Fig. 12.3*a*

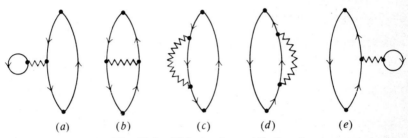

$(a) \qquad (b) \qquad (c) \qquad (d) \qquad (e)$

Fig. 12.3   All first-order contributions to proper polarization.

and *e*) vanish in the present example $[V(0) - 0]$, and we are left with the middle three. Correspondingly, the correlation energy has the expansion

$$E_{\text{corr}} = E_2^r + E_2^b + E_2^c + E_2^d + \cdots \tag{12.19}$$

where the various second-order contributions are given by

$$E_2^r = \tfrac{1}{2}iV\hbar(2\pi)^{-4}\int_0^1 d\lambda\lambda^{-1}\int d^4q\,[\lambda U_0(q)\Pi^0(q)]^2 \tag{12.20}$$

$$E_2^{b,c,d} = \tfrac{1}{2}iV\hbar(2\pi)^{-4}\int_0^1 d\lambda\lambda^{-1}\int d^4q\,[\lambda U_0(q)\Pi^\star_{(1)b,c,d}(q)] \tag{12.21}$$

Here $\Pi^\star_{(1)b}$, $\Pi^\star_{(1)c}$, and $\Pi^\star_{(1)d}$ denote the proper polarizations in Fig. 12.3*b* to *d*.

It is easily shown that the contributions in (12.21) are finite (Prob. 4.13). In contrast, E_2^r diverges logarithmically (we explicitly exhibit this divergence later in the discussion; see also Prob. 1.5), and the present expansion through second order is clearly insufficient. The source of this divergence is the singular behavior of the coulomb potential $U_0(q) = V(\mathbf{q}) = 4\pi e^2/\mathbf{q}^2$ at long wavelengths; in particular, E_2^r has two factors of $U_0(q)$, leading to a $(\mathbf{q})^{-4}$ behavior. A similar behavior occurs in all orders, because there is always a single nth-order term with the integrand $[U_0(q)\Pi^0(q)]^n$. Fortunately, these singular terms are readily included to all orders in perturbation theory by introducing the *effective interaction* $U_r(q)$ [compare Eq. (9.45)]

$$U_r(q) = U_0(q) + U_0(q)\Pi^0(q)U_0(q) + \cdots$$
$$= \frac{U_0(q)}{1 - \Pi^0(q)U_0(q)} \tag{12.22}$$

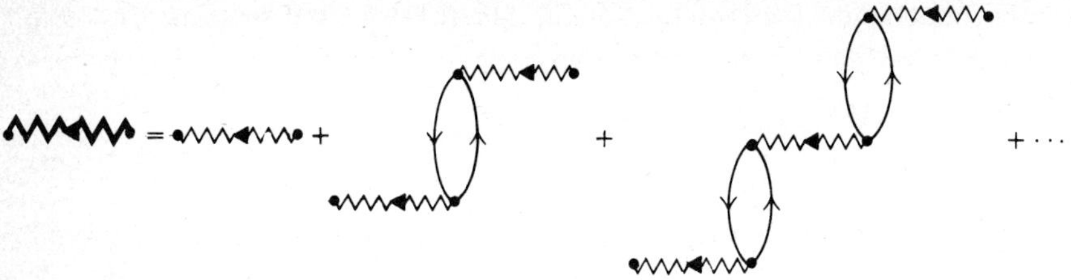

$$U_r = U_0 + \cdots$$

Fig. 12.4 Ring approximation for effective interaction.

which is an approximation to the true interaction in the medium $U(q)$ obtained by retaining only the zero-order proper polarization $\Pi^\star_{(0)} \equiv \Pi^0$ in Eq. (9.45). Equation (12.22) contains the diagrams shown in Fig. 12.4 and is known as the sum of *ring diagrams*. For historical reasons, it is also known as the *random-phase approximation*, although this name is not especially illuminating here.[1] This selected class of higher-order ring diagrams makes the following contribution to the ground-state energy:

$$E_r = \sum_{n=2}^{\infty} E_n^r$$

$$= \tfrac{1}{2} i V \hbar (2\pi)^{-4} \int_0^1 d\lambda \, \lambda^{-1} \int d^4q \sum_{n=2}^{\infty} [\lambda U_0(q) \Pi^0(q)]^n$$

$$= \tfrac{1}{2} i V \hbar (2\pi)^{-4} \int_0^1 d\lambda \, \lambda^{-1} \int d^4q \, \frac{[\lambda U_0(q) \Pi^0(q)]^2}{1 - \lambda U_0(q) \Pi^0(q)}$$

$$= \tfrac{1}{2} i V \hbar (2\pi)^{-4} \int_0^1 d\lambda \, \lambda^{-1} \int d^4q \, \lambda U_0(q) \Pi^0(q) \, U_r^\lambda(q) \Pi^0(q) \tag{12.23}$$

The physical interpretation of E_r is clear from the last line, because one of the "bare" interactions $U_0(q)$ in Eq. (12.20) has been replaced by the (less singular) effective interaction $U_r(q)$. Although the first term of E_r is formally of second order in the potential, we see in the following calculation that the sum has a wholly different analytic structure that cannot be obtained in any finite order of perturbation theory.

The effective interaction $U_r(q)$ [Eq. (12.22)] can be rewritten in terms of a dielectric constant $\kappa_r(q)$ by the relation [compare Eqs. (9.46) and (9.47)]

$$\kappa_r(q) = 1 - U_0(q) \Pi^0(q) = \frac{U_0(q)}{U_r(q)} \tag{12.24}$$

where $\kappa_r(q)$ may be considered the ring-diagram approximation to the exact dielectric constant. The energy E_r then becomes

$$E_r = \tfrac{1}{2} i V \hbar (2\pi)^{-4} \int_0^1 d\lambda \, \lambda^{-1} \int d^4q \, \frac{[\lambda U_0(q) \Pi^0(q)]^2}{\kappa_r^\lambda(q)} \tag{12.25}$$

[1] D. Bohm and D. Pines, *Phys. Rev.*, **92**:609 (1953); D. Pines, *Phys. Rev.*, **92**:626 (1953).

In the present approximation, the correlation energy of a degenerate electron gas reduces to[1]

$$E_{\text{corr}} = E_r + E_2^b + E_2^c + E_2^d + \cdots \tag{12.26}$$

In each term [compare Eqs. (12.20) and (12.21)], the two ends of a polarization insertion are joined with a bare interaction $U_0(q)$, and the contributions to the energy are drawn in terms of the equivalent Feynman diagrams in Fig. 12.5.

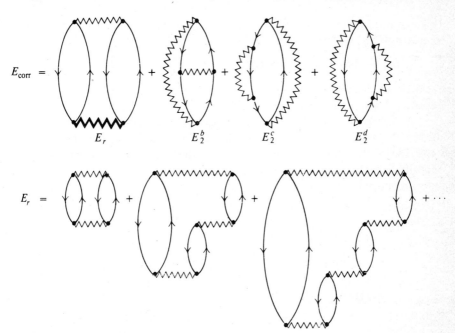

Fig. 12.5 Leading contributions to correlation energy.

It must be emphasized that these disconnected diagrams cannot be obtained directly from the Feynman rules of Chap. 3, because the counting of independent contributions differs from that of the connected parts as is evident in Fig. 12.5 (E_2^c and E_2^d are the same Feynman diagram).   Although it is possible to introduce a diagrammatic analysis of E_{corr}, we prefer to study only quantities with *fixed* external points, such as Π, Σ, G, and so forth, since a single set of Feynman rules then applies to all cases.   This restriction causes no difficulty, because E is readily expressed in terms of Σ (Sec. 11) or Π (Sec. 12).

---

[1] This contribution was first evaluated by M. Gell-Mann and K. A. Brueckner, *Phys. Rev.*, **106**:364 (1957).   We here follow the approach of J. Hubbard, *Proc. Roy. Soc. (London)*, **A243**:336 (1957); see also T. D. Schultz, "Quantum Field Theory and the Many-Body Problem," secs. III.H to III.J, Gordon and Breach, Science Publishers, New York, 1964.

EVALUATION OF Π^0

For further detailed analysis, we must evaluate the lowest-order polarization insertion Π^0, given in Eq. (12.13).[1] This quantity is independent of the interparticle potential and is therefore determined solely by the properties of a noninteracting Fermi system. The sum over α and β yields a factor 2 for spin-$\frac{1}{2}$ fermions so that

$$\Pi^0(x,x') = -2i\hbar^{-1} G^0(x,x') G^0(x',x) \tag{12.27}$$

This expression is most simply evaluated in momentum space, and the Fourier transform $\Pi^0(q) \equiv i\Pi^0(\mathbf{q},q_0)$ is given by

$$\Pi^0(q) = -2i\hbar^{-1}(2\pi)^{-4} \int d^4k\, G^0(k) G^0(k+q) \tag{12.28}$$

as can be verified either by an explicit calculation with Eq. (12.27) or by using the Feynman rules of Sec. 9 with Fig. 12.1b.

As a first step, it is convenient to perform the frequency integral in Eq. (12.28); the integrand contains four terms, of which two have their poles on the same side of the real axis. In these terms, the contour can be closed in the opposite half plane, and the contribution vanishes. The other two terms have poles on opposite sides of the real axis, and a straightforward contour integration yields

$$\Pi^0(q) = \frac{2}{(2\pi)^3\,\hbar} \int d^3k$$

$$\times \left[\frac{\theta(|\mathbf{q}+\mathbf{k}| - k_F)\,\theta(k_F - k)}{q_0 + \omega_{\mathbf{k}} - \omega_{\mathbf{q}+\mathbf{k}} + i\eta} - \frac{\theta(k_F - |\mathbf{q}+\mathbf{k}|)\,\theta(k - k_F)}{q_0 + \omega_{\mathbf{k}} - \omega_{\mathbf{q}+\mathbf{k}} - i\eta} \right] \tag{12.29}$$

where, as before, $\omega_{\mathbf{k}} = \hbar^{-1}\epsilon_k^0 = \hbar k^2/2m$. The second term can be rewritten with the change of variables $\mathbf{k}' = -\mathbf{k} - \mathbf{q}$; this transformation leads to

$$\Pi^0(\mathbf{q},q_0) = \frac{2}{\hbar} \int \frac{d^3k}{(2\pi)^3}\, \theta(|\mathbf{q}+\mathbf{k}| - k_F)\,\theta(k_F - k)$$

$$\times \left(\frac{1}{q_0 + \omega_{\mathbf{k}} - \omega_{\mathbf{q}+\mathbf{k}} + i\eta} - \frac{1}{q_0 + \omega_{\mathbf{q}+\mathbf{k}} - \omega_{\mathbf{k}} - i\eta} \right) \tag{12.30}$$

where the superfluous prime has now been omitted. By inspection, the integrand is an even function of q_0, and we conclude that

$$\Pi^0(\mathbf{q},q_0) \sim O(q_0^{-2}) \qquad |q_0| \to \infty$$

This symmetry allows us to study only positive q_0.

If the frequency difference in the denominators is denoted

$$\omega_{\mathbf{q}\mathbf{k}} \equiv \omega_{\mathbf{q}+\mathbf{k}} - \omega_{\mathbf{k}} = \frac{\hbar}{2m}[(\mathbf{k}+\mathbf{q})^2 - k^2] = \frac{\hbar}{m}(\mathbf{q}\cdot\mathbf{k} + \tfrac{1}{2}q^2) \tag{12.31}$$

[1] J. Lindhard, *Kgl. Danske Videnskab. Selskab, Mat.-Fys. Medd.*, **28**, no. 8 (1954).

then the symbolic identity (7.69) immediately yields

$$\operatorname{Re}\Pi^0(\mathbf{q},q_0) = \frac{2\mathscr{P}}{\hbar} \int \frac{d^3k}{(2\pi)^3} [1 - \theta(k_F - |\mathbf{k} + \mathbf{q}|)]\,\theta(k_F - k)\frac{2\omega_{\mathbf{qk}}}{q_0^2 - (\omega_{\mathbf{qk}})^2}$$

(12.32)

where the first step function has been rewritten with the relation

$$\theta(x) = 1 - \theta(-x)$$

(12.33)

The second term of Eq. (12.32) vanishes identically, because the product of step functions is even under the interchange $\mathbf{k} \rightleftarrows \mathbf{k} + \mathbf{q}$, while $\omega_{\mathbf{qk}}$ is odd; consequently, $\operatorname{Re}\Pi^0$ reduces to

$$\operatorname{Re}\Pi^0(\mathbf{q},q_0) = \frac{2\mathscr{P}}{\hbar} \int \frac{d^3k}{(2\pi)^3}\,\theta(k_F - k)$$

$$\times \left[\frac{1}{q_0 - \hbar m^{-1}(\mathbf{q}\cdot\mathbf{k} + \tfrac{1}{2}q^2)} - \frac{1}{q_0 + \hbar m^{-1}(\mathbf{q}\cdot\mathbf{k} + \tfrac{1}{2}q^2)} \right] \quad (12.34)$$

We now introduce the dimensionless frequency variable

$$\nu = \hbar q_0 \frac{m}{\hbar^2 k_F^2}$$

(12.35)

and measure all wave vectors in terms of k_F. With these dimensionless variables, Eq. (12.34) becomes

$$\operatorname{Re}\Pi^0(\mathbf{q},\nu) = \frac{2mk_F}{\hbar^2}\,\mathscr{P} \int \frac{d^3k}{(2\pi)^3}\,\theta(1 - k)$$

$$\times \left(\frac{1}{\nu - qk\cos\theta - \tfrac{1}{2}q^2} - \frac{1}{\nu + qk\cos\theta + \tfrac{1}{2}q^2} \right)$$

This integral is elementary and yields

$$\operatorname{Re}\Pi^0(\mathbf{q},\nu) = \frac{2mk_F}{\hbar^2}\,\frac{1}{4\pi^2}\left\{ -1 + \frac{1}{2q}\left[1 - \left(\frac{\nu}{q} - \frac{q}{2}\right)^2\right]\ln\left|\frac{1 + (\nu/q - \tfrac{1}{2}q)}{1 - (\nu/q - \tfrac{1}{2}q)}\right| \right.$$

$$\left. - \frac{1}{2q}\left[1 - \left(\frac{\nu}{q} + \frac{q}{2}\right)^2\right]\ln\left|\frac{1 + (\nu/q + \tfrac{1}{2}q)}{1 - (\nu/q + \tfrac{1}{2}q)}\right| \right\} \quad (12.36)$$

The imaginary part of Π^0 can also be evaluated with Eqs. (12.30) and (7.69)

$$\operatorname{Im}\Pi^0(\mathbf{q},q_0) = -\hbar^{-1}(2\pi)^{-2} \int d^3k\,\theta(|\mathbf{q} + \mathbf{k}| - k_F)\,\theta(k_F - k)$$

$$\times [\delta(q_0 - \omega_{\mathbf{qk}}) + \delta(q_0 + \omega_{\mathbf{qk}})] \quad (12.37)$$

It is again sufficient to consider only $q_0 > 0$, and the pair of step functions ensures that $\omega_{\mathbf{qk}}$ is also positive. We note that $\operatorname{Im}\Pi^0(\mathbf{q},q_0)$ has a direct physical interpretation, for it is proportional to the absorption probability for transferring

four-momentum $(\mathbf{q}, q_0)$ to a free Fermi gas; the process moves a particle from inside the Fermi sea ($k < k_F$) to outside ($|\mathbf{k} + \mathbf{q}| > k_F$), while the delta function guarantees that energy is conserved. This application of Π^0 is discussed at length in Sec. 17.

With the same dimensionless variables as in Eq. (12.36), the identity

$$\delta(ax) = |a|^{-1}\,\delta(x) \tag{12.38}$$

can be used to rewrite the only relevant delta function in Eq. (12.37) as

$$\delta(q_0 - \omega_{\mathbf{qk}}) = \frac{m}{\hbar k_F^2}\,\delta(\nu - \mathbf{q}\cdot\mathbf{k} - \tfrac{1}{2}q^2)$$

and we therefore need to evaluate

$$\operatorname{Im}\Pi^0(\mathbf{q}, \nu > 0) = -mk_F(2\pi\hbar)^{-2} \int d^3k\,\theta(|\mathbf{q}+\mathbf{k}|-1)\,\theta(1-k)$$
$$\times\,\delta(\nu - \mathbf{q}\cdot\mathbf{k} - \tfrac{1}{2}q^2) \tag{12.39}$$

The integration is restricted to the interior of the Fermi sphere ($k < 1$), while the vector $\mathbf{k} + \mathbf{q}$ must simultaneously lie outside the Fermi sphere. Furthermore, the conservation of energy requires that

$$\tfrac{1}{2}q + \hat{q}\cdot\mathbf{k} = \frac{\nu}{q}$$

which defines a plane in the three-dimensional $\mathbf{k}$ space. The integral in Eq. (12.39) represents the area of intersection of this plane with the allowed portion of the Fermi sphere, as shown in Fig. 12.6. There are three distinct possibilities:

1. $q > 2$ $\tfrac{1}{2}q^2 + q \geqslant \nu \geqslant \tfrac{1}{2}q^2 - q$ (12.40)

If $q > 2$, then the two Fermi spheres in Fig. 12.6 do not intersect, and we need only the area of intersection of the plane and the upper sphere. This area clearly vanishes if the energy transfer ν is too large or too small, and the condition that

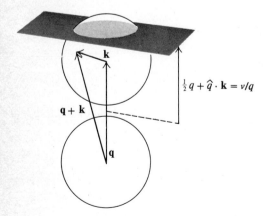

$$\tfrac{1}{2}q + \hat{q}\cdot\mathbf{k} = \nu/q$$

Fig. 12.6 Integration region for $\operatorname{Im}\Pi^0$ for $q > 2$. (The Fermi spheres are of unit radius.)

they intersect is just the second condition in Eq. (12.40).   The integration can
be performed with the substitution $t = \cos\theta$

$$\text{Im}\,\Pi^0(\mathbf{q},\nu) = -\frac{mk_F}{4\pi^2\hbar^2}\,2\pi\int_{\nu/q-\frac{1}{2}q}^{1}k^2\,dk\int_{-1}^{1}dt\,\frac{1}{qk}\,\delta\!\left(\frac{\nu}{qk}-\frac{1}{2}\frac{q}{k}-t\right)$$

and an elementary calculation yields

$$\text{Im}\,\Pi^0(\mathbf{q},\nu) = -\frac{mk_F}{\hbar^2}\frac{1}{4\pi q}\left[1-\left(\frac{\nu}{q}-\frac{1}{2}q\right)^2\right]\tag{12.41}$$

under the restrictions on the variables set in Eq. (12.40).   If ν lies outside the
regions defined in Eq. (12.40), the integral is zero.

2. $q < 2$ $q + \tfrac{1}{2}q^2 \geqslant \nu \geqslant q - \tfrac{1}{2}q^2$ $\tag{12.42}$

If $q < 2$, then the spheres defined by the conditions $k < 1$ and $|\mathbf{q} + \mathbf{k}| > 1$ intersect,
with the typical configuration shown in Fig. 12.7.   The plane will not intersect

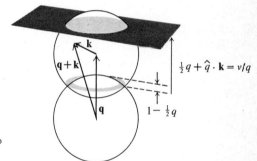

Fig. 12.7   Integration regions for Im Π^0
for $q < 2$.

the upper sphere if the energy transfer ν is too large, and Im Π^0 vanishes in this
case.   As ν decreases, the intersection is a circle until ν becomes sufficiently
small that the plane begins to intersect the *forbidden* Fermi sphere at the bottom.
This limited domain in which the intersection remains circular is just that defined
in Eq. (12.42); the integration is performed exactly as before with the result

$$\text{Im}\,\Pi^0(\mathbf{q},\nu) = -\frac{mk_F}{\hbar^2}\frac{1}{4\pi q}\left[1-\left(\frac{\nu}{q}-\frac{1}{2}q\right)^2\right]\tag{12.43}$$

3. $q < 2$ $0 \leqslant \nu \leqslant q - \tfrac{1}{2}q^2$ $\tag{12.44}$

In this case, the intersecting plane passes through the forbidden Fermi sphere
at the bottom, and the allowed region of intersection becomes an annulus, as
indicated in Fig. 12.7.   The area of this annulus can be evaluated with the
geometric relations in Fig. 12.8, which show that the minimum value of k is
given by

$$k_{\text{min}}^2 = (\tfrac{1}{2}q - \nu q^{-1})^2 + [1 - (\tfrac{1}{2}q + \nu q^{-1})^2] = 1 - 2\nu$$

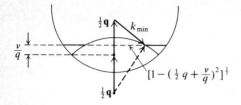

Fig. 12.8   Geometry in momentum space used in obtaining Eq. (12.45).

while the maximum value is the Fermi momentum ($k_{max} = 1$ in the present system of units).   The integral can now be evaluated directly:

$$\operatorname{Im}\Pi^0(\mathbf{q},\nu) = -\frac{mk_F}{\hbar^2}\frac{1}{4\pi^2}2\pi\int_{(1-2\nu)^{\frac{1}{2}}}^{1}\frac{k\,dk}{q}\int_{-1}^{1}dt\,\delta\left(\frac{\nu}{qk}-\frac{1}{2}\frac{q}{k}-t\right)$$

$$= -\frac{mk_F}{\hbar^2}\frac{1}{4\pi q}[1-(1-2\nu)]$$

$$= -\frac{mk_F}{\hbar^2}\frac{1}{4\pi q}2\nu \tag{12.45}$$

Equations (12.41), (12.43), and (12.45) determine $\operatorname{Im}\Pi^0(\mathbf{q},\nu)$ for all $\mathbf{q}$ and ν. We sketch $-(4\pi\hbar^2/mk_F)\operatorname{Im}\Pi^0(\mathbf{q},\nu)$ for fixed $|\mathbf{q}|$ in two cases of interest in Figs. 12.9a and 12.9b.

For many applications it is useful to list some limiting forms of the zero-order polarization part:

1. Fix the momentum q and let the energy transfer ν approach zero:

$$\operatorname{Im}\Pi^0(q,0) = 0 \tag{12.46a}$$

$$\operatorname{Re}\Pi^0(q,0) = \frac{mk_F}{\hbar^2}\frac{1}{2\pi^2}\left[-1+\frac{1}{q}(1-\tfrac{1}{4}q^2)\ln\left|\frac{1-\tfrac{1}{2}q}{1+\tfrac{1}{2}q}\right|\right] \tag{12.46b}$$

2. Fix the energy transfer ν and let the momentum transfer q approach zero:

$$\operatorname{Im}\Pi^0(0,\nu) = 0 \tag{12.47a}$$

$$\operatorname{Re}\Pi^0(q,\nu) \approx \frac{mk_F}{\hbar^2}\frac{1}{2\pi^2}\frac{2q^2}{3}\frac{q^2}{\nu^2} \qquad q\to 0 \tag{12.47b}$$

3. Finally, fix the ratio of energy transfer to momentum transfer $\nu/q \equiv x$, and let the momentum transfer q approach zero:

$$\operatorname{Im}\Pi^0(q,qx) = \begin{cases} -\dfrac{mk_F}{\hbar^2}\dfrac{x}{2\pi} & q\to 0,\ 0\leqslant x\leqslant 1 \\[2mm] 0 & q\to 0,\ x>1 \end{cases} \tag{12.48a}$$

$$\operatorname{Re}\Pi^0(q,qx) = -\frac{mk_F}{\hbar^2}\frac{1}{2\pi^2}\left(2-x\ln\left|\frac{1+x}{1-x}\right|\right) \qquad q\to 0 \tag{12.48b}$$

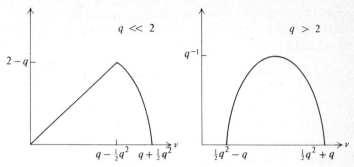

Fig. 12.9 Sketch of $-(4\pi\hbar^2/mk_F)\,\mathrm{Im}\,\Pi^0(\mathbf{q},\nu)$ for typical values of q.

The expressions for $\Pi^0(q,\nu)$ can now be used to find the corresponding dielectric constant $\kappa_r(q,\nu) = 1 - U_0(q)\Pi^0(q,\nu)$ in the ring approximation. The zero-order polarization has been expressed as $mk_F/\hbar^2$ times a dimensionless function; consequently, the dimensionless quantity $U_0\Pi^0$ has the typical value $(mk_F/\hbar^2)(4\pi e^2/k_F^2) = 4\pi(k_F a_0)^{-1} = 4\pi(4/9\pi)^{\frac{1}{3}} r_s$ [compare Eqs. (3.20) to (3.22) and (3.29)]. In fact, we shall require only the three limiting cases just discussed, and we find

1. Fix q, let $\nu \to 0$:

$$\kappa_r(q,0) = 1 + \frac{2\alpha r_s}{\pi q^2}\left[1 - \frac{1}{q}(1 - \tfrac{1}{4}q^2)\ln\left|\frac{1 - \tfrac{1}{2}q}{1 + \tfrac{1}{2}q}\right|\right] \qquad (12.49)$$

2. Fix ν, let $q \to 0$:

$$\kappa_r(0,\nu) = 1 - \frac{4\alpha r_s}{3\pi\nu^2} \qquad (12.50)$$

3. Fix $\nu/q \equiv x > 0$, let $q \to 0$:

$$\kappa_r(q,qx) = 1 + \frac{4\alpha r_s}{\pi q^2}\left[1 - \frac{x}{2}\ln\left|\frac{1 + x}{1 - x}\right|\right] + \frac{2i\alpha r_s x}{q^2}\theta(1 - x) \qquad (12.51)$$

where q and ν are both dimensionless and α is a numerical constant[1]

$$\alpha \equiv \left(\frac{4}{9\pi}\right)^{\frac{1}{3}} \qquad (12.52)$$

CORRELATION ENERGY

We now return to the evaluation of the correlation energy of a degenerate electron gas. Although it is possible to evaluate all the terms in Eq. (12.26), such a calculation would largely duplicate that of Sec. 30. Hence we here consider only E_r, which contains a proper treatment of the logarithmic divergence appear-

---

[1] We follow this historical but unfortunate notation; α is *not the fine-structure constant* in this problem.

ing in E_2^r and therefore gives the dominant contribution to the correlation energy. The integration over λ can be carried out explicitly in Eq. (12.23) and yields [see Eq. (12.24)]

$$
\begin{aligned}
E_r &= \tfrac{1}{2} i V \hbar (2\pi)^{-4} \int d^4q \int_0^1 d\lambda\, \lambda [U_0(q) \Pi^0(q)]^2 [1 - \lambda U_0(q) \Pi^0(q)]^{-1} \\
&= -\tfrac{1}{2} i V \hbar (2\pi)^{-4} \int d^4q \{\log [1 - U_0(q) \Pi^0(q)] + U_0(q) \Pi^0(q)\} \\
&= -\tfrac{1}{2} i V \hbar (2\pi)^{-4} \int d^4q \{\log [\kappa_r(q)] + 1 - \kappa_r(q)\}
\end{aligned}
\tag{12.53}
$$

It is again helpful to introduce the dimensionless variables $v = mq_0/\hbar k_F^2$ and $\mathbf{q}' = \mathbf{q}/k_F$. The ring energy then becomes—with the aid of Eqs. (3.21), (3.22), (3.29), and (12.52)—

$$
E_r = \frac{Ne^2}{2a_0}\, \epsilon_r
\tag{12.54}
$$

where

$$
\epsilon_r = -\frac{3i}{16\pi^2 \alpha^2 r_s^2} \int d^3q' \int_{-\infty}^{\infty} dv\, \{\log [\kappa_r(q',v)] + 1 - \kappa_r(q',v)\}
\tag{12.55}
$$

The energy ϵ_r must be real, and we shall consider only the real part of Eq. (12.55). In addition, κ_r is an even function of v, which allows us to simplify the limits of integration (we now omit the prime on q).

$$
\epsilon_r = \frac{3}{2\pi\alpha^2 r_s^2} \int_0^{\infty} q^2\, dq \int_0^{\infty} dv \left\{ \tan^{-1} \left[\frac{\kappa_{r2}(q,v)}{\kappa_{r1}(q,v)} \right] - \kappa_{r2}(q,v) \right\}
\tag{12.56}
$$

where the dielectric function has been separated into its real and imaginary parts

$$
\kappa_r = \kappa_{r1} + i\kappa_{r2}
$$

and we have used the relation

$$
\log (\kappa_{r1} + i\kappa_{r2}) = \tfrac{1}{2} \ln (\kappa_{r1}^2 + \kappa_{r2}^2) + i \tan^{-1} \frac{\kappa_{r2}}{\kappa_{r1}}
$$

As noted previously, the singular behavior of the electron gas arises at *small* wave vectors ($q \ll 1$), and we shall therefore divide the q integration into two parts, $q < q_c$ and $q > q_c$

$$
\epsilon_{r1} \equiv \frac{3}{2\pi\alpha^2 r_s^2} \int_0^{q_c} q^2\, dq \int_0^{\infty} dv \left\{ \tan^{-1} \left[\frac{\kappa_{r2}(q,v)}{\kappa_{r1}(q,v)} \right] - \kappa_{r2}(q,v) \right\}
$$

$$
\epsilon_{r2} \equiv \frac{3}{2\pi\alpha^2 r_s^2} \int_{q_c}^{\infty} q^2\, dq \int_0^{\infty} dv \left\{ \tan^{-1} \left[\frac{\kappa_{r2}(q,v)}{\kappa_{r1}(q,v)} \right] - \kappa_{r2}(q,v) \right\}
$$

This separation isolates the divergence, which occurs only in the first term ϵ_{r1}; for this reason, ϵ_{r2} is finite and can be expanded in powers of r_s. Furthermore, if q_c is chosen to be much less than 1, then κ_r may be approximated by its limiting form [Eq. (12.51)] in evaluating ϵ_{r1}, thereby giving a tractable integral. The

imaginary part of κ_r is proportional to $-V(q)\,\text{Im}\,\Pi^0(q,\nu)$, which is positive or zero [see Eq. (12.39)]. Thus $\tan^{-1}(\kappa_{r2}/\kappa_{r1})$ varies from 0 to π. In particular, $\tan^{-1}(\kappa_{r2}/\kappa_{r1}) = 0$ if $\kappa_{r2} = 0$ and $\kappa_{r1} > 0$, while $\tan^{-1}(\kappa_{r2}/\kappa_{r1}) = \pi$ if $\kappa_{r2} = 0$ and $\kappa_{r1} < 0$. In the region $0 \leqslant q \leqslant q_c \ll 1$, the approximate expression in Eq. (12.51) may be used, and we find

$$
\begin{aligned}
\epsilon_{r1} &= \frac{3}{2\pi\alpha^2 r_s^2} \int_0^{q_c} q^3\,dq \int_0^\infty dx \left\{ \tan^{-1}\left[\frac{2\alpha r_s\, x\theta(1-x)}{q^2 + 2\alpha r_s f(x)}\right] - \frac{2\alpha r_s\, x\theta(1-x)}{q^2} \right\} \\
&= \frac{6}{\pi\lambda^2} \int_0^{q_c} q^3\,dq \left\{ \int_0^1 dx\left[\tan^{-1}\left(\frac{\lambda x}{q^2 + \lambda f(x)}\right) - \frac{\lambda x}{q^2}\right] \right. \\
&\qquad\qquad\qquad\qquad\qquad\qquad \left. + \int_1^\infty dx\,\pi\theta[-q^2 - \lambda f(x)]\right\} \\
&\equiv I_1 + I_2
\end{aligned}
\tag{12.57}
$$

where

$$
f(x) \equiv \frac{2}{\pi}\left(1 - \tfrac{1}{2}x\ln\left|\frac{1+x}{1-x}\right|\right)
\tag{12.58}
$$

and

$$
\lambda \equiv 2\alpha r_s
\tag{12.59}
$$

The two terms in Eq. (12.57) arise from the regions of the $q\nu$ plane where $\kappa_{r2} > 0$ and $\kappa_{r2} = 0$, respectively.

If we now expand ϵ_r as a power series in the coupling constant $\lambda \propto e^2$, the leading term must reproduce the second-order term $(2a_0/Ne^2)E_2^r$. In particular, the singularity for small q has been isolated in I_1, and we find

$$
\begin{aligned}
I_1 &\approx \frac{6}{\pi\lambda^2}\int_0^{q_c} q^3\,dq \int_0^1 dx\left[\frac{\lambda x}{q^2} - \frac{\lambda^2 x f(x)}{q^4} + \cdots - \frac{\lambda x}{q^2}\right] \\
&= -\frac{6}{\pi}\int_0^{q_c}\frac{dq}{q}\int_0^1 dx\, x f(x) + O(\lambda)
\end{aligned}
$$

The first term of this perturbation expansion diverges logarithmically at the origin because of the q^{-2} behavior of the coulomb potential $V(q)$. Thus we see explicitly the logarithmic divergence of E_2^r mentioned at the beginning of this section. The exact integral I_1, however, contains terms of all orders in λ, and its integrand is finite as $q \to 0$. More precisely, the q^{-4} dependence of the integrand is cut off for $q^2 < \lambda f(x)$. In consequence, I_1 can be evaluated *with logarithmic accuracy* as follows:

$$
\begin{aligned}
I_1 &\approx -\frac{6}{\pi}\int_{\lambda^{\frac{1}{2}}}^{q_c}\frac{dq}{q}\int_0^1 dx\, x f(x) \\
&= \frac{6}{\pi^2}\ln\left(\frac{\lambda}{q_c^2}\right)\int_0^1 dx\, x\left(1 - \tfrac{1}{2}x\ln\frac{1+x}{1-x}\right) \\
&= \frac{2}{\pi^2}(1 - \ln 2)\ln\frac{\lambda}{q_c^2}
\end{aligned}
\tag{12.60}
$$

which means

$$\epsilon_{corr} = 2\pi^{-2}(1 - \ln 2)\ln r_s + \text{const} \qquad r_s \to 0 \qquad (12.61)$$

This result is originally due to Macke.[1] Note that this expression is nonanalytic in r_s and has no power series around $r_s = 0$.

The constant term in the correlation energy requires the evaluation of all the remaining terms in Eq. (12.26). In particular, it is essential to prove that the arbitrary wavenumber q_c drops out of the final answer for ϵ_r. This calculation is very similar to that in Sec. 30 and will not be repeated here. Furthermore, it is easy to see that E_2^c and E_2^d vanish identically, while

$$E_2^b = \frac{Ne^2}{2a_0}\,\epsilon_2^b$$

is just the second-order exchange energy studied in Prob. 1.4. The final expression can only be obtained numerically, and the correlation energy becomes

$$\frac{E_{corr}}{N} = \frac{e^2}{2a_0}\left[\frac{2}{\pi^2}(1 - \ln 2)\ln r_s - 0.094 + O(r_s \ln r_s)\right]$$

$$= \frac{e^2}{2a_0}[0.0622\ln r_s - 0.094 + O(r_s \ln r_s)] \qquad (12.62)$$

correct through order $\ln r_s$ and r_s^0.[‡] By an extension of the arguments presented here, DuBois[2] shows that the sum of the next most divergent terms in each order in perturbation theory [those terms with one less power of $U_0(q)$] gives a correction of $O(r_s \ln r_s)$ to Eq. (12.62).

EFFECTIVE INTERACTION

We have already mentioned that the perturbation expansion fails because of the singular $(\mathbf{q})^{-2}$ behavior of $U_0(\mathbf{q})$. In contrast, the ring approximation to the effective interaction $U_r(\mathbf{q},q_0)$ has a very different behavior at long wavelengths. For simplicity, we shall consider only the static limit ($q_0 = 0$), and a combination of Eqs. (12.24) and (12.49) yields

$$U_r(\mathbf{q},0) = \frac{4\pi e^2}{q^2 + (4\alpha r_s/\pi)\,k_F^2\,g(q/k_F)} \qquad (12.63)$$

---

[1] W. Macke, *Z. Naturforsch.*, **5a**:192 (1950).
[‡] The logarithmic term was first obtained by W. Macke, *loc. cit.*, and the complete expression was then derived by M. Gell-Mann and K. A. Brueckner, *loc. cit.* See also L. Onsager, L. Mittag, and M. J. Stephen, *Ann. Physik*, **18**:71 (1966).
[2] D. F. DuBois, *Ann. Phys.* (*N.Y.*), **7**:174, appendix C, (1959). DuBois' calculation was repeated and corrected by W. J. Carr, Jr., and A. A. Maradudin, *Phys. Rev.*, **133**:A371 (1964), who find $0.018r_s \ln r_s$ as the next correction to ϵ_{corr}.

where

$$g(x) = \frac{1}{2} - \frac{1}{2x}(1 - \tfrac{1}{4}x^2)\ln\left|\frac{1 - \tfrac{1}{2}x}{1 + \tfrac{1}{2}x}\right| \tag{12.64}$$

Thus the medium composed of the electrons and the positive background modifies Coulomb's law. It is clear from Eq. (12.63) that this modification is important only for wavelengths $(q/k_F)^2 \lesssim r_s$; in the high-density limit where $r_s \to 0$, we can therefore approximate $g(q/k_F)$ by $g(0) = 1$, so that

$$U_r(\mathbf{q},0) \underset{r_s \to 0}{\approx} \frac{4\pi e^2}{q^2 + (4\alpha r_s/\pi)\,k_F^2} \tag{12.65}$$

Hence the effective potential is cut off for $q^2 \lesssim r_s k_F^2$ and is *finite* at $q = 0$, which confirms the assertions below Eq. (12.23). This behavior provides a physical basis for the cutoff used to find ϵ_{corr} in Eq. (12.60) and in Prob. 1.5.

Although Eq. (12.65) is only an approximation to the exact $U_r(\mathbf{q},0)$ given in Eq. (12.63), it is very easy to take the Fourier transform of this approximate expression, which gives a Yukawa potential. We thereby obtain a qualitative picture of the effective interaction in coordinate space

$$V_r(\mathbf{x}) \approx e^2 e^{-q_{TF}x}x^{-1} \tag{12.66}$$

Hence the simple e^2/x Coulomb's law between two charges is "shielded" with the Thomas-Fermi[1] screening length q_{TF}^{-1} defined by

$$q_{TF}^2 = \frac{4\alpha r_s}{\pi}k_F^2 = \frac{4}{\pi}\left(\frac{4}{9\pi}\right)^{\frac{1}{3}}r_s k_F^2 = 0.66 r_s k_F^2 \tag{12.67}$$

In fact, the nonanalytic structure of (12.63) complicates the actual expression for $V_r(\mathbf{x})$ considerably, as is discussed in detail in Sec. 14.

In the present section, $U_r(\mathbf{q},q_0)$ has been used only to evaluate the correlation energy, which is an equilibrium property. As shown in the preceding paragraph, however, U_r contains much additional physical information because it determines the effective static and dynamic interparticle potential. This behavior is really a particular example of the response to an external perturbation. For this reason, we shall first develop the general theory of linear response (Chap. 5) and then return to the nonequilibrium properties of the degenerate electron gas.

PROBLEMS

4.1. A uniform spin-s Fermi system has a spin-independent interaction potential $V(\mathbf{x}) = V_0 x^{-1} e^{-x/a}$.
(a) Evaluate the proper self-energy in the Hartree-Fock approximation. Hence find the excitation spectrum ϵ_k and the Fermi energy $\epsilon_F = \mu$.

---

[1] The Thomas-Fermi theory is described in Sec. 14.

(*b*) Show that the exchange contribution to ϵ_F is negligible for a long-range interaction ($k_F a \gg 1$) but that the direct and exchange terms are comparable for a short-range interaction ($k_F a \ll 1$).

(*c*) In this approximation prove that the effective mass m^* is determined solely *by the exchange contribution.* Compute m^*, and discuss the limiting cases $k_F a \gg 1$ and $k_F a \ll 1$.

(*d*) What is the relation between the limit $a \to \infty$ of this model and the electron gas in a uniform positive background?

4.2. Use Eq. (11.70) to determine the first-order shift in the ground-state energy for the system considered in Prob. 4.1. Compare this calculation with a direct approach.

4.3. Using $1S$ coulomb wave functions as approximate Hartree-Fock wave functions, compute the ionization energies of atomic He, and compare with the experimental values He $\to$ He$^+$ + e^- (24.48 eV) and He $\to$ He^{++} + 2e^- (78.88 eV). Show that this approach is actually a variational calculation and use this observation to improve your results. How would you further improve these calculations?

4.4. The equation of Prob. 3.4 can be considered the first of an infinite hierarchy of equations in which the n particle G is coupled to the $n - 1$ and $n + 1$ particle G's. A common calculational scheme is to "decouple" these equations by approximating the n particle G in terms of lower-order (in n) Green's functions. For example, use Wick's theorem to show that the noninteracting 2 particle G satisfies

$$G_{\alpha\beta;\gamma\delta}(\mathbf{x}_1 t_1, \mathbf{x}_2 t_2; \mathbf{x}_1' t_1', \mathbf{x}_2' t_2')$$
$$= G_{\alpha\gamma}(\mathbf{x}_1 t_1, \mathbf{x}_1' t_1') G_{\beta\delta}(\mathbf{x}_2 t_2, \mathbf{x}_2' t_2') \pm G_{\alpha\delta}(\mathbf{x}_1 t_1, \mathbf{x}_2' t_2') G_{\beta\gamma}(\mathbf{x}_2 t_2, \mathbf{x}_1' t_1')$$

Approximate the *interacting* 2 particle G with the same expression and verify that the resulting self-consistent approximation for the 1 particle G reproduces the Hartree-Fock approximation.

4.5. How are the Hartree-Fock equations for spin-$\frac{1}{2}$ particles modified for spin-dependent potentials of the form given in Eq. (9.21)?

4.6. A uniform spin-$\frac{1}{2}$ Fermi gas interacts only through a p-wave hard-core potential of range a so that $\delta_1 \to -(ka)^3/3$ for $ka \to 0$.

(*a*) Show from Galitskii's equation that the proper self-energy is given to order $(k_F a)^3$ by

$$\hbar\Sigma^\star(\mathbf{k}) = \frac{\hbar^2 k_F^2}{2m} \frac{(k_F a)^3}{\pi} \left[\frac{3}{5} + \left(\frac{k}{k_F} \right)^2 \right]$$

(b) Show that the first two terms in the expansion of the ground-state energy as a power series in $k_F a$ are

$$\frac{E}{N} = \frac{\hbar^2 k_F^2}{2m}\left[\frac{3}{5} + \frac{3}{5\pi}(k_F a)^3\right]$$

(c) Show that the spectrum is strictly quadratic with an effective mass given by $m^*/m = 1 - (k_F a)^3/\pi$, correct to order $(k_F a)^3$.

4.7. Given a uniform Fermi gas with a degeneracy factor of g, show that (a) the ground-state energy expansion for a hard-core potential of range a becomes

$$\frac{E}{N} = \frac{\hbar^2 k_F^2}{2m}\left\{\frac{3}{5} + (g-1)\left[\frac{2k_F a}{3\pi} + \frac{4}{35\pi^2}(11 - 2\ln 2)(k_F a)^2\right] + O[(k_F a)^3]\right\}$$

(b) the result in Prob. 4.6 becomes

$$\frac{E}{N} = \frac{\hbar^2 k_F^2}{2m}\left[\frac{3}{5} + (g+1)\frac{(k_F a)^3}{5\pi}\right]$$

4.8. Verify Eqs. (11.63), (11.65), and (11.68).

4.9. For a degenerate electron gas show that $\Sigma^\star(\mathbf{q})$ is given to first order in the interaction by

$$\hbar\Sigma^\star_{(1)}(\mathbf{q}) = -\frac{e^2}{2\pi}\left(\frac{k_F^2 - q^2}{q}\ln\left|\frac{k_F + q}{k_F - q}\right| + 2k_F\right)$$

Sketch the resulting single-particle spectrum. Discuss the effective mass $m^*(q)$ defined by $m^*(q) \equiv (\hbar^2 q)(\partial\epsilon_q/\partial q)^{-1}$.

4.10. Apply Prob. 1.7 to an imperfect spin-$\frac{1}{2}$ Fermi gas, and show that the ground state becomes partially magnetized for $k_F a > \pi/2$.

4.11. Verify Eq. (12.36).

4.12. A system of spin-s fermions interacts through a spin-independent static potential $V(\mathbf{q})$.
(a) Analyze the Feynman diagrams for the proper polarization, and show that $\Pi^\star_{\alpha\beta,\lambda\mu}(q) = \Pi^\star_\sigma(q)(2s+1)^{-1}\delta_{\beta\lambda}\delta_{\alpha\mu} + [\Pi^\star(q) - \Pi^\star_\sigma(q)](2s+1)^{-2}\delta_{\alpha\beta}\delta_{\lambda\mu}$ [see Eq. (9.44b)].
(b) Solve Dyson's equation for $\Pi_{\alpha\beta,\lambda\mu}(q)$ (compare Prob. 3.15).
(c) Show that $D(q)$ [Eq. (12.12)] is equal to $\hbar\Pi_{\alpha\alpha,\lambda\lambda}(q)$, and hence rederive the expression $D(q) = \hbar\Pi^\star(q)[1 - V(\mathbf{q})\Pi^\star(q)]^{-1}$.

4.13. Consider the diagrams in Fig. 12.3 for an arbitrary potential $V(\mathbf{q})$, and show that only $\Pi^\star_{(1)b}$ contributes to E_2 in Eq. (12.21). Use Eq. (12.21) to evaluate E_2^b, and show that it agrees with that in Prob. 1.4.

4.14. (a) Evaluate ϵ_{r1} in Eq. (12.57) by first performing the q integral and then expanding in powers of r_s.

(b) Evaluate ϵ_{r2} defined below Eq. (12.56) by expanding in powers of r_s directly.

(c) Show that $\epsilon_{r1} + \epsilon_{r2}$ is independent of q_c, and compare your expression for the constant term in ϵ_{corr} with that obtained by K. Sawada, *Phys. Rev.*, **106**:372 (1957) and by K. Sawada, K. A. Brueckner, N. Fukuda, and R. Brout, *Phys. Rev.*, **108**:507 (1957).

5
Linear Response and
Collective Modes

The preceding chapter concentrated on the equilibrium properties of a Fermi system at zero temperature, along with the spectrum of single-particle excitations following the addition or removal of one particle. These fermion excitations can be directly observed through such processes as positron annihilation in metals, nuclear reactions, etc. In addition, most physical systems also have long-lived excited states that do not change the number of particles. These excitations (phonons, spin waves, etc.) have a boson character and are frequently known as *collective modes*. They can be detected with experimental probes that couple directly to the particle density, spin density, or other particle-conserving operators. Typical experiments scatter electromagnetic waves or electrons from metals and nuclei, or neutrons from crystals and liquid He^4. These probes all interact weakly with the system of interest and therefore can be treated in Born approximation. To provide a general background, we shall first discuss the theory of linear response to a weak external perturbation.

13□GENERAL THEORY OF LINEAR RESPONSE TO AN EXTERNAL PERTURBATION

Consider an interacting many-particle system with a time-independent hamiltonian $\hat{H}$. The exact state vector in the Schrödinger picture $|\Psi_S(t)\rangle$ satisfies the Schrödinger equation

$$i\hbar\frac{\partial|\Psi_S(t)\rangle}{\partial t} = \hat{H}\,|\Psi_S(t)\rangle \tag{13.1}$$

with the explicit solution

$$|\Psi_S(t)\rangle = e^{-i\hat{H}t/\hbar}|\Psi_S(0)\rangle \tag{13.2}$$

Suppose that the system is perturbed at $t = t_0$ by turning on an additional time-dependent hamiltonian $\hat{H}^{ex}(t)$. The new Schrödinger state vector $|\bar{\Psi}_S(t)\rangle$ satisfies the modified equation $(t > t_0)$

$$i\hbar\frac{\partial|\bar{\Psi}_S(t)\rangle}{\partial t} = [\hat{H} + \hat{H}^{ex}(t)]|\bar{\Psi}_S(t)\rangle \tag{13.3}$$

and we shall seek a solution in the form

$$|\bar{\Psi}_S(t)\rangle = e^{-i\hat{H}t/\hbar}\,\hat{A}(t)|\Psi_S(0)\rangle \tag{13.4}$$

where the operator $\hat{A}(t)$ obeys the causal boundary condition

$$\hat{A}(t) = 1 \qquad t \leqslant t_0 \tag{13.5}$$

A combination of Eqs. (13.3) and (13.4) yields the operator equation for $\hat{A}(t)$:

$$i\hbar\frac{\partial\hat{A}(t)}{\partial t} = e^{i\hat{H}t/\hbar}\,\hat{H}^{ex}(t)\,e^{-i\hat{H}t/\hbar}\,\hat{A}(t)$$

$$\equiv \hat{H}_H^{ex}(t)\,\hat{A}(t) \tag{13.6}$$

where $\hat{H}_H^{ex}(t)$ is in the usual Heisenberg picture that makes use of the full interacting $\hat{H}$.

Equation (13.6) may be solved iteratively for $t > t_0$

$$\hat{A}(t) = 1 - i\hbar^{-1}\int_{t_0}^{t} dt'\,\hat{H}_H^{ex}(t') + \cdots \tag{13.7}$$

where the causal boundary condition [Eq. (13.5)] is automatically satisfied because $\hat{H}^{ex}(t) = 0$ if $t < t_0$. The corresponding state vector is given by

$$|\bar{\Psi}_S(t)\rangle = e^{-i\hat{H}t/\hbar}|\Psi_S(0)\rangle - i\hbar^{-1}e^{-i\hat{H}t/\hbar}\int_{t_0}^{t} dt'\,\hat{H}_H^{ex}(t')|\Psi_S(0)\rangle + \cdots \tag{13.8}$$

All physical information of interest is contained in matrix elements of Schrödinger picture operators $\hat{O}_S(t)$ (which may depend explicitly on time)

$$
\begin{aligned}
\langle \hat{O}(t) \rangle_{\text{ex}} &\equiv \langle \bar{\Psi}'_S(t) | \hat{O}_S(t) | \Psi'_S(t) \rangle \\
&= \langle \Psi'_S(0) | \left[1 + i\hbar^{-1} \int_{t_0}^t dt' \, \hat{H}_H^{\text{ex}}(t') + \cdots \right] e^{i\hat{H}t/\hbar} \hat{O}_S(t) \, e^{-i\hat{H}t/\hbar} \\
&\qquad\qquad\qquad \times \left[1 - i\hbar^{-1} \int_{t_0}^t dt' \, \hat{H}_H^{\text{ex}}(t') + \cdots \right] | \Psi'_S(0) \rangle \\
&= \langle \Psi'_H(0) | \hat{O}_H(t) | \Psi'_H(0) \rangle + i\hbar^{-1} \langle \Psi'_H(0) | \int_{t_0}^t dt' \\
&\qquad\qquad\qquad \times [\hat{H}_H^{\text{ex}}(t'), \hat{O}_H(t)] | \Psi'_H(0) \rangle + \cdots \quad (13.9)
\end{aligned}
$$

Only the linear terms in $\hat{H}^{\text{ex}}$ have been retained, and the subscript H denotes the Heisenberg picture with respect to the time-independent hamiltonian $\hat{H}$ [compare Eqs. (6.28) and (6.32)].   The first-order change in a matrix element arising from an external perturbation is here expressed in terms of the exact Heisenberg operators of the interacting but unperturbed system.   In particular, if $|\Psi_H\rangle$ and $|\Psi'_H\rangle$ both denote the normalized ground state $|\Psi_0\rangle$, the linear response of the ground-state expectation value of an operator is given by

$$
\begin{aligned}
\delta\langle \hat{O}(t) \rangle &\equiv \langle \hat{O}(t) \rangle_{\text{ex}} - \langle \hat{O}(t) \rangle \\
&= i\hbar^{-1} \int_{t_0}^t dt' \, \langle \Psi_0 | [\hat{H}_H^{\text{ex}}(t'), \hat{O}_H(t)] | \Psi_0 \rangle \quad (13.10)
\end{aligned}
$$

As a specific example, consider a system with charge e per particle in the presence of an external scalar potential $\varphi^{\text{ex}}(\mathbf{x}t)$, which is turned on at $t = t_0$. The corresponding external perturbation is equal to

$$
\hat{H}_H^{\text{ex}}(t) = \int d^3x \, \hat{n}_H(\mathbf{x}t) \, e\varphi^{\text{ex}}(\mathbf{x}t) \quad (13.11)
$$

where $\hat{n}_H$ is the exact particle density operator in the unperturbed system.   The linear response may be characterized by the change in the density

$$
\begin{aligned}
\delta\langle \hat{n}(\mathbf{x}t) \rangle &= i\hbar^{-1} \int_{t_0}^t dt' \int d^3x' \, e\varphi^{\text{ex}}(\mathbf{x}'\,t') \langle \Psi_0 | [\hat{n}_H(\mathbf{x}'\,t'), \hat{n}_H(\mathbf{x}t)] | \Psi_0 \rangle \\
&= i\hbar^{-1} \int_{t_0}^t dt' \int d^3x' \, e\varphi^{\text{ex}}(\mathbf{x}'\,t') \langle \Psi_0 | [\tilde{n}_H(\mathbf{x}'\,t'), \tilde{n}_H(\mathbf{x}t)] | \Psi_0 \rangle \quad (13.12)
\end{aligned}
$$

where we have now introduced the deviation operators $\tilde{n}_H(\mathbf{x}t) \equiv \hat{n}_H(\mathbf{x}t) - \langle \hat{n}_H(\mathbf{x}t) \rangle$ [compare Eq. (12.3)].   (Note that the c numbers always commute.)   If the retarded density correlation function is defined in analogy with Eq. (12.5)

$$
iD^R(x,x') = \theta(t - t') \frac{\langle \Psi_0 | [\tilde{n}_H(x), \tilde{n}_H(x')] | \Psi_0 \rangle}{\langle \Psi_0 | \Psi_0 \rangle} \quad (13.13)
$$

then Eq. (13.12) may be rewritten as

$$
\delta\langle \hat{n}(\mathbf{x}t) \rangle = \hbar^{-1} \int_{-\infty}^\infty dt' \int d^3x' \, D^R(\mathbf{x}t, \mathbf{x}'\,t') \, e\varphi^{\text{ex}}(\mathbf{x}'\,t') \quad (13.14)
$$

where the causal behavior is enforced by the retarded nature of D^R, and we have used the fact that φ^{ex} vanishes for $t' < t_0$. Equation (13.14) typifies a general result that the linear response of an operator to an external perturbation is expressible as the space-time integral of a suitable retarded correlation function.

If the system is spatially homogeneous, then $D^R(x,x') = D^R(x - x')$, and it is useful to introduce Fourier transforms

$$\varphi^{ex}(\mathbf{k},\omega) \equiv \int d^3x \int dt\, e^{-i\mathbf{k}\cdot\mathbf{x}} e^{i\omega t} \varphi^{ex}(\mathbf{x}t) \tag{13.15}$$

$$\delta\langle \hat{n}(\mathbf{k},\omega)\rangle \equiv \int d^3x \int dt\, e^{-i\mathbf{k}\cdot\mathbf{x}} e^{i\omega t} \delta\langle \hat{n}(\mathbf{x}t)\rangle \tag{13.16}$$

$$D^R(\mathbf{k},\omega) \equiv \int d^3x \int dt\, e^{-i\mathbf{k}\cdot\mathbf{x}} e^{i\omega t} D^R(\mathbf{x}t) \tag{13.17}$$

Equation (13.14) immediately reduces to

$$\delta\langle \hat{n}(\mathbf{k},\omega)\rangle = \hbar^{-1} D^R(\mathbf{k},\omega)\, e\varphi^{ex}(\mathbf{k},\omega) \tag{13.18}$$

which shows that the system responds at the same wave vector and frequency as the perturbation. This relation is sometimes used to define a generalized susceptibility

$$\chi_{nn}(\mathbf{k},\omega) \equiv \frac{\delta\langle \hat{n}(\mathbf{k},\omega)\rangle}{e\varphi^{ex}(\mathbf{k},\omega)} = \hbar^{-1} D^R(\mathbf{k},\omega) \tag{13.19}$$

Such relations are especially useful in studying transport coefficients, which represent certain long-wavelength and low-frequency limits of the generalized susceptibilities (compare Prob. 9.7).

The foregoing analysis shows that the linear response is most simply expressed in terms of retarded correlation functions of exact Heisenberg operators. Unfortunately, such functions cannot be calculated directly with the Feynman-Dyson perturbation series because Wick's theorem applies only to a time-ordered product of operators. Consequently, it is generally convenient to define an associated time-ordered correlation function of the *same* operators, which necessarily has the form of Eq. (8.8). Wick's theorem can now be used to evaluate the time-ordered correlation function in perturbation theory. The remaining problem of relating the time-ordered and retarded functions can be solved with the Lehmann representation. A specific example has been given in Sec. 7, where $G(\mathbf{k},\omega)$ and $G^R(\mathbf{k},\omega)$ were shown to satisfy Eqs. (7.67) and (7.68). The method is clearly very general, and we state here the corresponding relations for the density correlation functions (Prob. 3.8)

$$\text{Re } D(\mathbf{q},\omega) = \text{Re } D^R(\mathbf{q},\omega)$$

$$\text{Im } D(\mathbf{q},\omega)\, \text{sgn } \omega = \text{Im } D^R(\mathbf{q},\omega) \tag{13.20}$$

which are valid for real ω. (In this expression, $\text{sgn}\,\omega \equiv \omega/|\omega|$.) Equations (13.20) are very important, because *any* approximation for $D(\mathbf{q},\omega)$ immediately yields an approximate $D^R(\mathbf{q},\omega)$ and hence the associated linear response. It is also clear from the Lehmann representation for $D(\mathbf{q},\omega)$ that the poles of this

function occur at the exact excitation energies of those states of the interacting assembly that are coupled to the ground state through the density operator.

14□SCREENING IN AN ELECTRON GAS

As our first example, we consider the response of a degenerate electron gas to a static impurity with positive charge Ze, where the external potential is given by

$$\varphi^{ex}(\mathbf{x}t) = Zex^{-1} \tag{14.1}$$

and

$$\varphi^{ex}(\mathbf{q},\omega) = 8\pi^2 Zeq^{-2}\,\delta(\omega) \tag{14.2}$$

Note that we have here let $t_0 \to -\infty$. This point charge alters the electron distribution in its vicinity, and Eqs. (13.16) and (13.18) together determine the induced particle density to be (for electrons, the interaction is $-e\varphi^{ex}$)

$$\delta\langle\hat{n}(\mathbf{x})\rangle = -(2\pi)^{-3}\int d^3q\, e^{i\mathbf{q}\cdot\mathbf{x}}\, D^R(\mathbf{q},0)\, 4\pi Ze^2(\hbar q^2)^{-1} \tag{14.3}$$

Equation (12.14) shows that the time-ordered density correlation function D is equal to $\hbar\Pi$, where Π is the time-ordered polarization part. If Π^R is defined as the corresponding retarded polarization, then Eq. (14.3) assumes the simple form

$$
\begin{aligned}
\delta\langle\hat{n}(\mathbf{x})\rangle &= -(2\pi)^{-3}\int d^3q\, e^{i\mathbf{q}\cdot\mathbf{x}}\,\Pi^R(\mathbf{q},0)\, 4\pi Ze^2 q^{-2}\\
&= -(2\pi)^{-3}\int d^3q\, e^{i\mathbf{q}\cdot\mathbf{x}}\,\Pi^R(\mathbf{q},0)\, ZU_0(\mathbf{q})\\
&= -(2\pi)^{-3}Z\int d^3q\, e^{i\mathbf{q}\cdot\mathbf{x}}[\Pi^\star(\mathbf{q},0)\,U(\mathbf{q},0)]^R\\
&= -(2\pi)^{-3}Z\int d^3q\, e^{i\mathbf{q}\cdot\mathbf{x}}\{[\kappa^R(\mathbf{q},0)]^{-1} - 1\}
\end{aligned}
\tag{14.4}
$$

where the third line has been obtained with Dyson's equation [see Eqs. (9.43) and (14.5)], and the fourth with the retarded version of Eq. (12.17). The previous perturbation analysis (Sec. 12) allows us to calculate the time-ordered functions Π and κ, and the Lehmann representation then yields [compare Eq. (13.20) for $D \equiv \hbar\Pi$]‡

$$
\begin{aligned}
\Pi^R(\mathbf{q},\omega) &\equiv (\mathrm{Re} + i\,\mathrm{sgn}\,\omega\,\mathrm{Im})\,\Pi(\mathbf{q},\omega)\\
&= \mathrm{Re}\,\Pi(\mathbf{q},\omega) + i\,\mathrm{sgn}\,\omega\,\mathrm{Im}\,\Pi(\mathbf{q},\omega)
\end{aligned}
\tag{14.5}
$$

$$\kappa^R(\mathbf{q},\omega) = \mathrm{Re}\,\kappa(\mathbf{q},\omega) + i\,\mathrm{sgn}\,\omega\,\mathrm{Im}\,\kappa(\mathbf{q},\omega) \tag{14.6}$$

A combination of Eqs. (14.4) and (14.6) then provides an exact description of the screening about a point charge.

In the approximation of retaining only ring diagrams, $\kappa_r(\mathbf{q},0)$ is purely real [Eq. (12.49)], and the retarded function becomes

$$\kappa_r^R(\mathbf{q},0) = \kappa_r(\mathbf{q},0) = 1 + 4\alpha r_s k_F^2(\pi q^2)^{-1} g\left(\frac{q}{k_F}\right) \tag{14.7}$$

‡ Note $[\mathrm{Re} + i\,\mathrm{sgn}\,\omega\,\mathrm{Im}][\mathrm{Re}\,\kappa + i\,\mathrm{Im}\,\kappa]^{-1} = [\mathrm{Re}\,\kappa - i\,\mathrm{sgn}\,\omega\,\mathrm{Im}\,\kappa][|\mathrm{Re}\,\kappa|^2 + |\mathrm{Im}\,\kappa|^2]^{-1} = [\mathrm{Re}\,\kappa + i\,\mathrm{sgn}\,\omega\,\mathrm{Im}\,\kappa]^{-1}$.

Here the function $g(x)$ [Eq. (12.64)] is given by

$$g(x) = \frac{1}{2} - \frac{1}{2x}(1 - \tfrac{1}{4}x^2)\ln\left|\frac{1 - \tfrac{1}{2}x}{1 + \tfrac{1}{2}x}\right| \tag{14.8}$$

and has the following limiting behavior

$$g(x) \approx 1 + O(x^2) \qquad\qquad\qquad x \ll 1 \tag{14.9a}$$
$$g(x) \approx \tfrac{1}{2} + \tfrac{1}{4}(x - 2)\ln\left[\tfrac{1}{4}|x - 2|\right] \quad |x - 2| \ll 1 \tag{14.9b}$$
$$g(x) \sim \tfrac{4}{3}\,x^{-2} \qquad\qquad\qquad\quad x \gg 1 \tag{14.9c}$$

Equation (14.7) may be substituted into Eq. (14.4); the induced *charge* density then reduces to

$$\delta\langle\hat{\rho}(\mathbf{x})\rangle_r = -e\delta\langle\hat{n}(\mathbf{x})\rangle_r$$
$$= -Ze\int\frac{d^3q}{(2\pi)^3}\,e^{i\mathbf{q}\cdot\mathbf{x}}\frac{4\alpha r_s\,\pi^{-1}g(q/k_F)}{(q/k_F)^2 + 4\alpha r_s\,\pi^{-1}g(q/k_F)} \tag{14.10}$$

This expression has several interesting features:

1. The total induced charge is easily determined as

$$\delta Q_r = \int d^3x\,\delta\langle\hat{\rho}(\mathbf{x})\rangle_r$$
$$= -Ze\int d^3q\,\delta(\mathbf{q})\frac{4\alpha r_s\,\pi^{-1}g(q/k_F)}{(q/k_F)^2 + 4\alpha r_s\,\pi^{-1}g(q/k_F)}$$
$$= -Ze \tag{14.11}$$

   which shows that the screening is complete at large distances.
2. The integrand of Eq. (14.10) is bounded for all $|q|$ and vanishes like q^{-4} as $q \to \infty$ [compare Eq. (14.9c)]. Hence the induced charge density is everywhere finite *including the origin* because

$$|\langle\delta\hat{\rho}(\mathbf{x})\rangle_r| \leqslant |\langle\delta\hat{\rho}(0)\rangle_r|$$
$$= Ze\int\frac{d^3q}{(2\pi)^3}\frac{4\alpha r_s\,\pi^{-1}g(q/k_F)}{(q/k_F)^2 + 4\alpha r_s\,\pi^{-1}g(q/k_F)} < \infty \tag{14.12}$$

   Here the first inequality arises from the oscillatory exponential which reduces the charge density for $x \neq 0$.
3. The singular q^{-2} dependence for small q^2 is cut off at

$$q_{min} = \left(\frac{4\alpha r_s}{\pi}\right)^{\frac{1}{2}}k_F = \left(\frac{4k_F}{\pi a_0}\right)^{\frac{1}{2}} = \left(\frac{6\pi ne^2}{\epsilon_F^0}\right)^{\frac{1}{2}} \equiv q_{TF} \tag{14.13}$$

[see Eqs. (3.20 to 3.22), (3.29), and (12.67)], where q_{TF} is the Thomas-Fermi[1]

---

[1] L. H. Thomas, *Proc. Cambridge Phil. Soc.*, **23**:542 (1927); E. Fermi, *Z. Physik*, **48**:73 (1928). An elementary account of its application to metals may be found in J. M. Ziman, "Principles of the Theory of Solids," secs. 5.1 to 5.3, Cambridge University Press, Cambridge, 1964.

wavenumber.   The induced charge density can now be rewritten as

$$\delta\langle\hat{\rho}(\mathbf{x})\rangle_r = -Ze \int \frac{d^3q}{(2\pi)^3} e^{i\mathbf{q}\cdot\mathbf{x}} \frac{q_{TF}^2 g(q/k_F)}{q^2 + q_{TF}^2 g(q/k_F)}$$

$$= -\frac{Ze}{2\pi^2 x} \int_0^\infty dq\, q \sin qx \frac{q_{TF}^2 g(q/k_F)}{q^2 + q_{TF}^2 g(q/k_F)} \qquad (14.14)$$

Since $g(0) = 1$, it is tempting to infer that the induced charge density has the following asymptotic form $(x \to \infty)$

$$\delta\langle\hat{\rho}(\mathbf{x})\rangle_r \sim \delta\rho_{TF}(x) \equiv -Zeq_{TF}^2(4\pi x)^{-1} e^{-q_{TF}x} \qquad (14.15)$$

where $\delta\rho_{TF}(x)$ is that obtained in the Thomas-Fermi approximation.

The Thomas-Fermi result can be understood very simply in the following way.   A noninteracting Fermi gas at $T = 0$ exerts a pressure given by Eq. (5.49b)

$$P = \frac{2}{5}\frac{\hbar^2}{2m}(3\pi^2)^{\frac{2}{3}} n^{\frac{5}{3}} \qquad (14.16)$$

If we put a charge Ze into a uniform electron gas (imposed on a uniform, positive fixed background of charge density en_0 that makes the unperturbed system neutral), then the condition of local hydrostatic equilibrium requires that the forces on a small (unit) volume element must balance

$$\sum_i \mathbf{F}_i = 0 = -\nabla P - en\mathscr{E} \qquad (14.17)$$

where $\mathscr{E}$ is the resulting electric field.   Poisson's equation becomes

$$\nabla\cdot\mathscr{E} = -\nabla^2\varphi = 4\pi[Ze\delta(\mathbf{x}) - e(n - n_0)] \qquad (14.18)$$

where φ is the electrostatic potential.   We can now write

$$n - n_0 = \delta n \qquad (14.19a)$$

$$\nabla n = \nabla\delta n \qquad (14.19b)$$

and a combination of Eqs. (14.16), (14.17), and (14.19b) yields

$$\frac{2}{3}\frac{\hbar^2}{2m}(3\pi^2)^{\frac{2}{3}}\frac{1}{n^{\frac{1}{3}}}\nabla\delta n = e\nabla\varphi \qquad (14.20)$$

Since the left side is already linear in small quantities, we can use Eq. (3.29) to write

$$\frac{2}{3}\frac{\hbar^2 k_F^2}{2m}\frac{1}{n_0}\nabla\delta n = e\nabla\varphi \qquad (14.21)$$

The divergence of this equation combined with Eq. (14.18) gives

$$(\nabla^2 - q_{TF}^2)\,\delta n(\mathbf{x}) = -Zq_{TF}^2\,\delta(\mathbf{x})$$

or equivalently

$$(\nabla^2 - q_{TF}^2)\,\delta\rho(\mathbf{x}) = Zeq_{TF}^2\,\delta(\mathbf{x}) \tag{14.22}$$

where the Thomas-Fermi wavenumber is defined in Eq. (14.13).   The solution to this equation is that quoted in Eq. (14.15)

$$\delta\rho_{TF}(x) = -Zeq_{TF}^2(4\pi x)^{-1}\,e^{-q_{TF}x} \tag{14.23}$$

The approximate result in Eq. (14.15) is *incorrect*, however, because $g(x)$ has a singularity at $x = 2$, where its first derivative becomes infinite.   The presence of this singularity in the range of integration $(0 < q < \infty)$ gives $\delta\langle\hat\rho(\mathbf{x})\rangle_r$ an *algebraic* asymptotic dependence on x in contrast to the apparent *exponential* behavior arising from the approximate simple pole at $q = \pm iq_{TF}$.   We may extract the correct asymptotic behavior of $\delta\langle\hat\rho(\mathbf{x})\rangle_r$ in the following manner: first rewrite the logarithm appearing in $g(q/k_F)$ as [see Eq. (14.8)]

$$\ln\left|\frac{q - 2k_F}{q + 2k_F}\right| = \lim_{\eta\to 0}\tfrac{1}{2}\ln\frac{(q - 2k_F)^2 + \eta^2}{(q + 2k_F)^2 + \eta^2}$$

Since g is an even function of its argument, the integral in Eq. (14.14) can be written as

$$\delta\langle\hat\rho(\mathbf{x})\rangle_r = \frac{Ze}{4\pi^2 ix}\int_{-\infty}^{\infty} q\,dq\,e^{iqx}\left[\frac{q^2}{q^2 + q_{TF}^2\,g(q/k_F)} - 1\right] \tag{14.24}$$

The integrand is now an analytic function of q with the singularity structure shown in Fig. 14.1, and the branch cuts of the logarithms have been chosen so that the logarithm is real along the real axis.   The contour can be deformed as indicated, and the pole at $q \approx iq_{TF}$ gives the contribution of Eq. (14.15), which vanishes exponentially for large x.   In contrast, the cuts extend down to (within η) the real axis.   The integrals along the two branch cuts depend on the difference of the function across the cut; this difference arises solely from the phase of the logarithm, and with the branch cuts as shown we have

$$\Delta\left[\frac{1}{2}\log\frac{(q - 2k_F)^2 + \eta^2}{(q + 2k_F)^2 + \eta^2}\right] = \begin{cases} \pi & \text{on } C_1 \\ -\pi & \text{on } C_2 \end{cases}$$

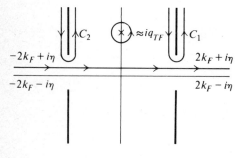

Fig. 14.1   Contour for asymptotic evaluation of $\delta\langle\hat\rho(\mathbf{x})\rangle_r$.

where Δ indicates the value of the phase on the right side of the cut minus the value of the phase on the left. Because of the decreasing exponential in the integrand, all the slowly varying functions in the integrand can then be replaced by their values at the start of the branch cut. Thus we have

$$\delta\langle\hat{\rho}(\mathbf{x})\rangle_r \underset{x\to\infty}{\sim} \frac{Ze}{4\pi^2\,ix} \lim_{\eta\to 0} \left(\int_{C_1} + \int_{C_2}\right) q\,dq\,e^{iqx} \left(q^2\left\{q^2 + q_{TF}^2\left[\frac{1}{2} - \frac{k_F}{2q}\right.\right.\right.$$

$$\times\left.\left.\left.\left(1 - \frac{q^2}{4k_F^2}\right)\frac{1}{2}\log\frac{(q-2k_F)^2 + \eta^2}{(q+2k_F)^2 + \eta^2}\right]\right\}^{-1} - 1\right)$$

$$\underset{x\to\infty}{\sim} \frac{Ze}{4\pi^2\,ix} \lim_{\eta\to 0} \left[\frac{\pi q_{TF}^2}{4k_F}\frac{8k_F^3}{(4k_F^2 + \tfrac{1}{2}q_{TF}^2)^2}\right.$$

$$\times\left.\left(e^{-2ik_F x}\,i\int_\eta^\infty ue^{-ux}\,du + e^{2ik_F x}\,i\int_\eta^\infty ve^{-vx}\,dv\right)\right] \qquad (14.25)$$

where we have introduced $q = 2k_F + iv$ along C_1 and $q = -2k_F + iu$ along C_2. The remaining integrals are elementary, and we find

$$\delta\langle\hat{\rho}(\mathbf{x})\rangle_r \underset{x\to\infty}{\sim} \frac{Ze}{\pi}\frac{2\xi}{(4+\xi)^2}\frac{\cos(2k_F x)}{x^3} \qquad (14.26a)$$

$$\xi \equiv \frac{q_{TF}^2}{2k_F^2} \qquad (14.26b)$$

which was first derived by Langer and Vosko.[1] The expression (14.26a) is qualitatively different from that predicted in Eq. (14.15) and exhibits long-range oscillations with a radial wavelength π/k_F and an envelope proportional to x^{-3}. It is clear that $\delta\langle\hat{\rho}(\mathbf{x})\rangle_r$ is an improvement over $\delta\rho_{TF}(\mathbf{x})$, since the former incorporates the distribution function of the interacting medium in computing the response to the external field.

From a physical point of view, the long-range oscillations in the screening charge arise from the sharp Fermi surface, because it is not possible to construct a smooth function out of the restricted set of wave vectors $q > k_F$. This effect was first suggested by Friedel,[2] and such *Friedel oscillations* have been observed as a broadening of nuclear magnetic resonance lines in dilute alloys.[3] A similar effect also occurs in dilute magnetic alloys; the conduction electrons induce an indirect interaction between magnetic impurities of the form $x_{ij}^{-3}\cos(2k_F x_{ij})$, where x_{ij} is the separation of the impurities.[4] At low but finite temperatures, the Fermi surface is smeared over a thickness $k_B T$ in energy, and it turns out that

---

[1] J. S. Langer and S. H. Vosko, *J. Phys. Chem. Solids*, **12**:196 (1960).

[2] J. Friedel, *Phil. Mag.*, **43**:153 (1952); *Nuovo Cimento*, **7**:287, *Suppl.* 2 (1958).

[3] N. Bloembergen and T. J. Rowland, *Acta Met.*, **1**:731 (1953); T. J. Rowland, *Phys. Rev.*, **119**:900 (1960); W. Kohn and S. H. Vosko, *Phys. Rev.*, **119**:912 (1960); see also, J. M. Ziman, *op. cit.*, secs. 5.4 and 5.5.

[4] M. A. Ruderman and C. Kittel, *Phys. Rev.*, **96**:99 (1954).

Eq. (14.26a) must be multiplied by the factor $\exp(-2\pi m k_B T x/\hbar^2 k_F)$. The importance of a sharp Fermi surface is confirmed by the behavior in a super-conductor, where the Fermi surface is smeared over an energy width $\Delta \ll \epsilon_F^0$ even at $T = 0$ (see Chap. 13). In this case, the asymptotic form of the screening density is proportional to $x^{-3}\cos(2k_F x)\exp(-k_F x\Delta/\epsilon_F^0)$, completely analogous to that for a normal metal at finite temperature.[1]

15□PLASMA OSCILLATIONS IN AN ELECTRON GAS

It has already been pointed out that $\Pi(\mathbf{q},\omega)$ has poles at the exact excitation energy of those collective states of the interacting system that are connected to the ground state through the density operator. Recalling Eqs. (9.43a) and (9.46)

$$\frac{U(q)}{U_0(\mathbf{q})} = \frac{1}{\kappa(\mathbf{q},\omega)} = 1 + U_0(\mathbf{q})\,\Pi(\mathbf{q},\omega) \tag{15.1}$$

we observe that $\kappa(\mathbf{q},\omega)$ vanishes at these same energies. In the ring approxi-mation, Eq. (12.50) shows that the dielectric constant κ_r has one obvious zero, occurring for fixed energy transfer ν and long wavelengths $q \to 0$

$$\kappa_r(\mathbf{q},\omega) = 1 - \frac{4\alpha r_s}{3\pi\nu^2} \tag{15.2}$$

This quantity vanishes at

$$\nu_{pl}^2 = 4\alpha r_s(3\pi)^{-1} \tag{15.3}$$

Rewriting this expression in dimensional units [see Eqs. (3.20) to (3.22), (12.35), and (12.52)] we find a collective excitation at the classical plasma frequency[2] given by

$$\Omega_{pl}^2 = \frac{4\pi n e^2}{m} \tag{15.4}$$

We shall investigate these plasma oscillations in more detail by considering the linear response of a degenerate electron gas to an impulsive perturbation

$$\varphi^{ex}(\mathbf{x}t) = e^{i\mathbf{q}\cdot\mathbf{x}}\varphi_0\,\delta(t) \tag{15.5}$$

whose Fourier transform is given by

$$\varphi^{ex}(\mathbf{k},\omega) = \varphi_0(2\pi)^3\,\delta(\mathbf{q} - \mathbf{k}) \tag{15.6}$$

The corresponding induced density perturbation becomes

$$\begin{aligned}
\delta\langle\hat{n}(\mathbf{x}t)\rangle &= -e(2\pi)^{-4}\int d^3k\,d\omega\,e^{i\mathbf{k}\cdot\mathbf{x}}\,e^{-i\omega t}\,\Pi^R(\mathbf{k},\omega)\,\varphi^{ex}(\mathbf{k},\omega)\\
&= -e\varphi_0\,e^{i\mathbf{q}\cdot\mathbf{x}}(2\pi)^{-1}\int d\omega\,e^{-i\omega t}\,\Pi^R(\mathbf{q},\omega)\\
&= -e\varphi_0\,e^{i\mathbf{q}\cdot\mathbf{x}}(2\pi)^{-1}\int d\omega\,e^{-i\omega t}\,U_0(\mathbf{q})^{-1}\{[\kappa^R(\mathbf{q},\omega)]^{-1} - 1\}
\end{aligned} \tag{15.7}$$

[1] A. L. Fetter, Phys. Rev., 140:A1921 (1965).
[2] The classical theory of plasma oscillations is discussed at the end of this section.

which shows that the singularities of Π^R in the complex ω plane also determine the resonant frequencies of the system.

Although Eq. (15.7) is exact, we shall consider only the approximation of retaining the ring diagrams. In this case $\kappa_r^R(\mathbf{q},\omega)$ is given by Eqs. (12.24) and (14.6) as

$$\kappa_r^R(\mathbf{q},\omega) = 1 - V(\mathbf{q})\,\Pi^{0R}(\mathbf{q},\omega) \tag{15.8}$$

where [compare Eqs. (12.29) and Eqs. (14.5)]

$$
\begin{aligned}
\Pi^{0R}(\mathbf{q},\omega) &= \mathrm{Re}\,\Pi^0(\mathbf{q},\omega) + i\,\mathrm{sgn}\,\omega\,\mathrm{Im}\,\Pi^0(\mathbf{q},\omega) \\
&= \frac{2}{\hbar}\int \frac{d^3k}{(2\pi)^3}\left[\frac{(1-n_{\mathbf{k}+\mathbf{q}}^0)\,n_{\mathbf{k}}^0}{\omega + \omega_{\mathbf{k}} - \omega_{\mathbf{q}+\mathbf{k}} + i\eta} - \frac{n_{\mathbf{k}+\mathbf{q}}^0(1-n_{\mathbf{k}}^0)}{\omega + \omega_{\mathbf{k}} - \omega_{\mathbf{k}+\mathbf{q}} + i\eta}\right] \\
&= -\frac{2}{\hbar}\int \frac{d^3k}{(2\pi)^3}\left[\frac{n_{\mathbf{k}+\mathbf{q}}^0 - n_{\mathbf{k}}^0}{\omega - (\omega_{\mathbf{k}+\mathbf{q}} - \omega_{\mathbf{k}}) + i\eta}\right]
\end{aligned}
\tag{15.9}
$$

where $n_{\mathbf{k}}^0 = \theta(k_F - k)$. Thus Π^{0R} differs from Π^0 only in the infinitesimals $\pm i\eta$. The frequency and lifetime of the collective modes are determined by the poles of the integrand in Eq. (15.7).[1] These occur at the values $\Omega_q - i\gamma_q$ that satisfy the equation

$$1 = V(\mathbf{q})\,\Pi^{0R}(\mathbf{q},\Omega_q - i\gamma_q) \tag{15.10}$$

In general, this equation can be solved only with numerical analysis; if the damping is small ($\gamma_q \ll \Omega_q$), however, then the real and imaginary parts separate, and we find

$$1 = V(\mathbf{q})\,\mathrm{Re}\,\Pi^{0R}(\mathbf{q},\Omega_q) = V(\mathbf{q})\,\mathrm{Re}\,\Pi^0(\mathbf{q},\Omega_q) \tag{15.11}$$

$$
\begin{aligned}
\gamma_q &= \mathrm{Im}\,\Pi^{0R}(\mathbf{q},\Omega_q)\left[\frac{\partial\,\mathrm{Re}\,\Pi^{0R}(\mathbf{q},\omega)}{\partial\omega}\bigg|_{\Omega_q}\right]^{-1} \\
&= \mathrm{sgn}\,\Omega_q\,\mathrm{Im}\,\Pi^0(\mathbf{q},\Omega_q)\left[\frac{\partial\,\mathrm{Re}\,\Pi^0(\mathbf{q},\omega)}{\partial\omega}\bigg|_{\Omega_q}\right]^{-1}
\end{aligned}
\tag{15.12}
$$

Equation (15.11) determines the dispersion relation Ω_q of the collective mode, while Eq. (15.12) then yields an explicit formula for the damping constant. This approximate separation of real and imaginary parts will be shown to be valid at long wavelengths, and we now consider the expansion of Π^{0R} for $q \to 0$.

Although it is possible to expand Eq. (12.36) for small q, we instead work directly with Eq. (15.9). A simple change of variables in the first term of this

---

[1] In general, Π^R also has a cut in the complex ω plane just below the real axis, with a discontinuity proportional to $\mathrm{Im}\,\Pi^R(\mathbf{q},\omega)$ (see, for example, Fig. 12.9). As $t \to \infty$, however, this cut makes a negligible contribution to Eq. (15.7); hence the dominant long-time behavior here arises from the collective mode, which is undamped in the present approximation.

expression reduces the integral to

$$\Pi^{0R}(\mathbf{q},\omega) = -\frac{2}{\hbar} \int \frac{d^3k}{(2\pi)^3} n_k^0 \left[\frac{1}{\omega - (\omega_k - \omega_{k-q}) + i\eta} - \frac{1}{\omega - (\omega_{k+q} - \omega_k) + i\eta} \right]$$

$$= \frac{2q^2}{m} \int \frac{d^3k}{(2\pi)^3} n_k^0 \frac{1}{(\omega - \hbar\mathbf{q}\cdot\mathbf{k}/m + i\eta)^2 - (\hbar q^2/2m)^2} \tag{15.13}$$

It is clear that $\mathrm{Im}\,\Pi^{0R} = 0$ if $|\omega| > \hbar k_F q/m + \hbar q^2/2m$; in this region of the $q - \omega$ plane, $\mathrm{Re}\,\Pi^{0R} = \mathrm{Re}\,\Pi^0$ may be evaluated as an ascending series in q. To order q^4 we have

$$\mathrm{Re}\,\Pi^{0R}(\mathbf{q},\omega) = \frac{2q^2}{m\omega^2} \int \frac{d^3k}{(2\pi)^3} n_k^0 \left[1 + \frac{2\hbar\mathbf{k}\cdot\mathbf{q}}{m\omega} + 3\left(\frac{\hbar\mathbf{k}\cdot\mathbf{q}}{m\omega}\right)^2 + \cdots \right]$$

$$= \frac{k_F^3}{3\pi^2} \frac{q^2}{m\omega^2} \left[1 + \frac{3}{5}\left(\frac{\hbar k_F q}{m\omega}\right)^2 + \cdots \right] \tag{15.14}$$

since

$$2 \int \frac{d^3k}{(2\pi)^3} n_k^0 = \frac{N}{V} = \frac{k_F^3}{3\pi^2} \tag{15.15}$$

and the mean value of k^2 for the Fermi distribution is $\frac{3}{5}k_F^2$. The dispersion relation [Eq. (15.11)] now becomes

$$1 = \frac{4\pi n e^2}{m\Omega_q^2} \left[1 + \frac{3}{5}\left(\frac{\hbar k_F q}{m\Omega_q}\right)^2 + \cdots \right] \tag{15.16}$$

which can be solved iteratively to yield

$$\Omega_q = \pm\Omega_{pl} \left[1 + \frac{9}{10}\left(\frac{q}{q_{TF}}\right)^2 + \cdots \right] \tag{15.17}$$

where

$$\Omega_{pl} = \left(\frac{4\pi n e^2}{m}\right)^{\frac{1}{2}} \tag{15.18}$$

is the *plasma frequency* and $q_{TF} = (6\pi n e^2/\epsilon_F^0)^{\frac{1}{2}}$ is the Thomas-Fermi wavenumber introduced in Sec. 14. Since $\mathrm{Im}\,\Pi^{0R}(q,\Omega_q)$ vanishes if $|\Omega_q| > \hbar q k_F/m + \hbar q^2/2m$, these collective modes are undamped at long wavelengths. This result arises from the approximations used in the present calculations; when higher-order corrections are included, the plasma oscillations are damped at all wavelengths.[1]

The resonant frequency at zero wavelength is the classical plasma frequency and is therefore independent of $\hbar$. To clarify the physics of these collective modes, we shall review the classical derivation of plasma oscillations.[2] Consider a uniform electron gas; the equilibrium particle density n_0 must equal that of the positive background n_b to ensure that the system is electrically neutral. If

[1] D. F. DuBois, *Ann. Phys. (N. Y.),* **7**:174 (1959); **8**:24 (1959).
[2] L. Tonks and I. Langmuir, *Phys. Rev.,* **33**:195 (1929).

the electron density is slightly perturbed to

$$n(\mathbf{x}t) = n_0 + \delta n(\mathbf{x}t) \tag{15.19}$$

the resulting uncompensated charge gives rise to an electric field $\mathscr{E}$ that satisfies Poisson's equation

$$\nabla \cdot \mathscr{E}(\mathbf{x}t) = -4\pi e[n(\mathbf{x}t) - n_b] = -4\pi e \delta n(\mathbf{x}t) \tag{15.20}$$

Newton's second law determines the force on the electrons in a small (unit) volume element

$$m\frac{d(n\mathbf{v})}{dt} = m\left[\frac{\partial(n\mathbf{v})}{\partial t} + (\mathbf{v} \cdot \nabla)(n\mathbf{v})\right] = -en\mathscr{E}$$

or

$$mn_0 \frac{\partial \mathbf{v}}{\partial t} \approx -en_0 \mathscr{E} \tag{15.21}$$

while the equation of continuity may be written as

$$\frac{\partial n}{\partial t} + \nabla \cdot (n\mathbf{v}) \approx \frac{\partial \delta n}{\partial t} + n_0 \nabla \cdot \mathbf{v} = 0 \tag{15.22}$$

Both Eqs. (15.21) and (15.22) have been linearized in the small quantities δn and $\mathbf{v}$. The time derivative of Eq. (15.22) may be combined with Poisson's equation and the divergence of Eq. (15.21) to yield

$$\frac{\partial^2 \delta n(\mathbf{x}t)}{\partial t^2} = -n_0 \frac{\partial}{\partial t}\nabla \cdot \mathbf{v}(\mathbf{x}t) = \frac{en_0}{m}\nabla \cdot \mathscr{E}(\mathbf{x}t) = -\frac{4\pi n_0 e^2}{m}\delta n(\mathbf{x}t)$$

or

$$\frac{\partial^2 \delta n(\mathbf{x}t)}{\partial t^2} = -\Omega_{pl}^2 \,\delta n(\mathbf{x}t) \tag{15.23}$$

Thus the perturbed charge density executes simple harmonic motion with a frequency Ω_{pl}. Note that Eq. (15.23) does not contain spatial derivatives, so that there is no mass transport. This result agrees with the specific form of Eq. (15.17), because the group velocity $\partial \Omega_q / \partial q$ vanishes at long wavelengths.

16☐ZERO SOUND IN AN IMPERFECT FERMI GAS

Section 15 shows that a charged system can support density oscillations with the long-wavelength dispersion relation $\omega \approx \Omega_{pl}$. This represents a true collective mode because the restoring force on the displaced particles arises from the self-consistent electric field generated by the local excess charges. It is interesting to ask whether a similar collective mode occurs in a neutral Fermi system at $T = 0$. As shown in the subsequent discussion, a repulsive short-range inter-particle potential is sufficient to guarantee such a mode, at least in a simple model. The resulting density oscillation turns out to have a *linear* dispersion

relation $\omega = c_0 q$ for $q \to 0$ and is known as zero sound.[1] Nevertheless, zero sound is physically very different from ordinary first sound, despite the similar dispersion relation $\omega = c_1 q$. The distinction between the two density oscillations depends on the role of collisions: ordinary sound can propagate only if the system is in local thermodynamic equilibrium; this condition requires that the mean interparticle collision time τ be short compared to the period of oscillation $2\pi/\omega$ (that is, $\omega\tau \ll 1$). In contrast, zero sound is a collective mode sustained by the coherent self-consistent interaction arising from neighboring particles; zero sound thus occurs only in a collisionless regime where $\omega\tau \gg 1$. The crucial observation is that the Pauli principle greatly limits the possible interparticle collisions at low temperature, and, indeed, τ becomes infinite like T^{-2} as $T \to 0$.‡ At a fixed frequency, there is a critical temperature below which ordinary sound is strongly attenuated, while zero sound propagates freely. At $T = 0$, ordinary sound ceases to propagate at *any* frequency, and only zero sound can occur.

In an electron gas, the plasma oscillations appeared as a resonant response to an impulsive perturbation. A very similar analysis applies to a neutral Fermi system, where the perturbing hamiltonian may be written quite generally as

$$\hat{H}^{\text{ex}}(t) = \int d^3x \, \hat{n}(\mathbf{x}t) \, U^{\text{ex}}(\mathbf{x}t) \tag{16.1}$$

Here $U^{\text{ex}}(\mathbf{x}t)$ is an external time-dependent potential that couples to the density. The subsequent analysis is identical with that of Sec. 13, and the linear response is given by

$$\delta\langle\hat{n}(\mathbf{x}t)\rangle = (2\pi)^{-4} \int d^3k \, d\omega \, e^{i\mathbf{k}\cdot\mathbf{x}} e^{-i\omega t} \, \Pi^R(\mathbf{k},\omega) \, U^{\text{ex}}(\mathbf{k},\omega) \tag{16.2}$$

For the special case of an impulsive perturbation

$$U^{\text{ex}}(\mathbf{x}t) = U_0^{\text{ex}} e^{i\mathbf{q}\cdot\mathbf{x}} \delta(t) \tag{16.3}$$

a simple calculation yields

$$\delta\langle\hat{n}(\mathbf{x}t)\rangle = U_0^{\text{ex}} e^{i\mathbf{q}\cdot\mathbf{x}} (2\pi)^{-1} \int d\omega \, e^{-i\omega t} \, U_0(\mathbf{q})^{-1} \{[\kappa^R(\mathbf{q},\omega)]^{-1} - 1\} \tag{16.4}$$

in complete analogy with Eq. (15.7). The resonant frequency for wave vector $\mathbf{q}$ is again determined by the poles of the integrand, which occur at the zeros of the retarded generalized dielectric function $\kappa^R(\mathbf{q},\omega)$.

The simplest approximation to $\kappa(\mathbf{q},\omega)$ consists in retaining only the zero-order proper polarization part Π^0; in this case, the pole occurs at the value $\Omega_q - i\gamma_q$ determined by

$$1 = V(\mathbf{q}) \, \Pi^{0R}(\mathbf{q}, \Omega_q - i\gamma_q) \tag{16.5}$$

We assume that Ω_q exhibits a phonon dispersion relation

$$\Omega_q = c_0 q \tag{16.6}$$

---

[1] L. D. Landau, *Sov. Phys.-JETP*, **3**:920 (1957); **5**:101 (1957).
‡ This result depends only on the available phase space and was first noted by I. Ia. Pomeranchuk, *Zh. Eksp. Teor. Fiz.*, **20**:919 (1950).

so that the ratio Ω_q/q remains fixed as $q \to 0$. The relevant limit of Π^0 has already been calculated in Eq. (12.48), and the associated retarded function may be written as ($q \to 0$)

$$\Pi^{0R}(q,\omega) = \frac{mk_F}{\pi^2 \hbar^2}\left[\frac{1}{2}x\ln\left|\frac{x+1}{x-1}\right| - 1 - \frac{i\pi}{2}x\theta(1-|x|)\right] \tag{16.7}$$

where $x = m\omega/\hbar k_F q$. The factor $x = |x|\,\mathrm{sgn}\,x$ in the imaginary part reflects the change from the time-ordered to the retarded function. An undamped mode

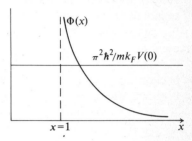

Fig. 16.1 Graphical determination of the dispersion relation for zero sound.

is possible only if $|x| > 1$. In this case, the long-wavelength dispersion relation is given by

$$\lim_{q\to 0}\frac{\pi^2 \hbar^2}{mk_F V(q)} = \tfrac{1}{2}x\ln\left(\frac{x+1}{x-1}\right) - 1 \equiv \Phi(x) \tag{16.8}$$

where

$$x = \lim_{q\to 0}\frac{m\Omega_q}{\hbar k_F q} = \frac{mc_0}{\hbar k_F} = \frac{c_0}{v_F} > 1 \tag{16.9}$$

and v_F is the Fermi velocity. We see that zero sound is possible only if $c_0 > v_F$.

The function on the right side of Eq. (16.8) will be denoted $\Phi(x)$; it is sketched in Fig. 16.1. The most interesting feature is the logarithmic singularity at $x = 1$. If we assume that $V(q)$ approaches a finite constant $V(0)$ as $q \to 0$, then the speed of zero sound is determined by the intersection of $\Phi(x)$ with the horizontal line $\pi^2 \hbar^2/mk_F V(0)$. It is clear that there is no intersection unless $V(0) > 0$, which implies a repulsive potential because $V(0) = \int d^3 x\, V(\mathbf{x})$. In this case, the explicit solution is readily found in the weak- and strong-coupling limits:

Weak coupling:

$$c_0 \approx v_F\left\{1 + 2\exp\left[-\frac{2\pi^2 \hbar^2}{mk_F V(0)} - 2\right]\right\} \qquad V(0) \ll \frac{\hbar^2}{mk_F} \tag{16.10}$$

Strong coupling:

$$c_0 \approx v_F \left[\frac{V(0)}{3\pi^2(\hbar^2/mk_F)} \right]^{\frac{1}{2}} \approx \left[\frac{k_F^3 \, V(0)}{3\pi^2 \, m} \right]^{\frac{1}{2}}$$

$$\approx [nV(0)m^{-1}]^{\frac{1}{2}} \qquad\qquad V(0) \gg \frac{\hbar^2}{mk_F} \qquad (16.11)$$

Equations (16.10) and (16.11) show that c_0 is *nonanalytic* in the interparticle potential and thus cannot be obtained with perturbation theory. Indeed, the present approximation of retaining only the lowest-order proper polarization cannot be justified on the basis of perturbation theory for a short-range potential. Instead, we expect that the logarithmic singularity of $\Phi(x)$ for $x \approx 1$ would also occur in more realistic approximations; an improved calculation would therefore *renormalize* the numerical value of c_0/v_F but not alter the qualitative physical phenomenon in the weak-coupling limit. This assumption is borne out by Prob. 5.8, where a selected class of higher-order polarization insertions is included.

It is interesting to rewrite Eq.(16.11) as

$$\Omega_q^2 = c_0^2 q^2 = \frac{nV(0)q^2}{m} \qquad\qquad (16.12)$$

which shows the importance of a short-range potential. If $V(q)$ were unbounded as $q \to 0$, the character of the dispersion relation would be *qualitatively* different; in the special case of a coulomb potential $[V(q) = 4\pi e^2/q^2]$, Eq. (16.12) reproduces the plasma frequency found in Sec. 15. From this viewpoint, zero sound and plasma oscillations are physically very similar; they differ only in the detailed form of the long-wavelength dispersion relation, which is fixed by the behavior of $q^2 V(q)$ as $q \to 0$.

For comparison, we shall briefly review the classical theory of sound waves in a gas, in which the equilibrium mass density $\rho_0 = mn_0$ is slightly perturbed

$$\rho(\mathbf{x}t) = \rho_0 + \delta\rho(\mathbf{x}t) \qquad\qquad (16.13)$$

The restoring force arises from the pressure gradient, and Newton's second law becomes

$$\frac{d(\rho\mathbf{v})}{dt} = \frac{\partial(\rho\mathbf{v})}{\partial t} + (\mathbf{v}\cdot\boldsymbol{\nabla})(\rho\mathbf{v}) \approx \rho_0 \frac{\partial\mathbf{v}}{\partial t} = -\boldsymbol{\nabla}P \qquad\qquad (16.14)$$

Correspondingly, the equation of continuity reduces to [compare Eq. (15.22)]

$$\frac{\partial\delta\rho}{\partial t} = -\boldsymbol{\nabla}\cdot(\rho\mathbf{v}) \approx -\rho_0 \boldsymbol{\nabla}\cdot\mathbf{v} \qquad\qquad (16.15)$$

where both Eqs. (16.14) and (16.15) have been linearized in the small quantities.

A combination of these equations yields

$$\frac{\partial^2 \delta\rho}{\partial t^2} = \nabla^2 P \tag{16.16}$$

The system has an equation of state $P(\rho,S)$ relating the pressure to the density and entropy. If this equation is expanded to first order in the density perturbation at constant entropy, we find

$$\nabla^2 P = \nabla^2 \left[P(\rho_0,S) + \left(\frac{\partial P}{\partial \rho}\right)_S \delta\rho + \cdots \right] \approx \left(\frac{\partial P}{\partial \rho}\right)_S \nabla^2 \delta\rho \tag{16.17}$$

Hence $\delta\rho$ obeys a wave equation

$$\frac{\partial^2 \delta\rho_m}{\partial t^2} = c_1^2 \nabla^2 \delta\rho_m \tag{16.18}$$

where the speed of sound is given by

$$c_1^2 = \left(\frac{\partial P}{\partial \rho_m}\right)_S \tag{16.19}$$

and the subscript m now explicitly denotes the mass density. Here the restriction to constant entropy means that the process is adiabatic and that no heat is transferred while the compressional wave propagates through the system. For a perfect Fermi gas in its ground state ($S = 0$), Eq. (14.16) gives

$$c_1 = \left(\frac{\partial P}{\partial \rho_m}\right)^{\frac{1}{2}} = \frac{\hbar k_F}{\sqrt{3}m} = \frac{v_F}{\sqrt{3}} \tag{16.20}$$

A comparison of Eqs. (16.10) and (16.20) shows that

$$c_0 = \sqrt{3}c_1 \tag{16.21}$$

in the weak-coupling limit. A more general analysis based on Landau's Fermi liquid theory[1] shows that c_0 lies between the speed of first sound and $\sqrt{3}$ times the speed of first sound for all coupling strengths and that the two speeds are approximately equal for strong coupling. There is now definite evidence for zero sound in liquid He³, which is a strongly interacting system. Experiments indicate that[2] $(c_0 - c_1)/c_1 \approx 0.03$, in good agreement with the theoretical estimates. Landau's theory also allows a detailed study of the attenuation of zero sound and first sound; experiments fully confirm these predictions.

---

[1] L. D. Landau, loc. cit.; A. A. Abrikosov and I. M. Khalatnikov, Rep. Prog. Phys., 22:329 (1959); J. Wilks, "The Properties of Liquid and Solid Helium," chap. 18, Oxford University Press, Oxford, 1967.

[2] B. E. Keen, P. W. Matthews, and J. Wilks, Proc. Roy. Soc. (London), A284:125 (1965); W. R. Abel, A. C. Anderson, and J. C. Wheatley, Phys. Rev. Letters, 17:74 (1966).

17□INELASTIC ELECTRON SCATTERING[1]

We next consider inelastic electron scattering from systems such as nuclei and metals. For simplicity we retain only the coulomb interaction between the electrons and the charged particles in the target

$$\hat{H}^{ex} = -e^2 \int\int \frac{\hat{\rho}_{el}(\mathbf{x}')\hat{\rho}(\mathbf{x})\, d^3x\, d^3x'}{|\mathbf{x}-\mathbf{x}'|} \tag{17.1}$$

Throughout this section, the charge density operator for the target is denoted $e\hat{\rho}(\mathbf{x})$, since, in principle, $\hat{\rho}(\mathbf{x})$ can differ from the particle density operator $\hat{n}(\mathbf{x})$ (for example, in heavy nuclei with a large neutron excess). The small value of the fine structure constant ($e^2/\hbar c \approx 1/137$) allows us to analyze the scattering process in Born approximation. The matrix element for the electron to scatter from an initial plane-wave state $|ks\rangle$ (s denotes the spin projection) to a final plane-wave state $|\mathbf{k}'s'\rangle$ is just the overlap of the initial and final electron wave functions [2]

$$\langle \mathbf{k}'s'|\hat{\rho}_{el}(\mathbf{x}')|ks\rangle = \frac{1}{\Omega} e^{i\mathbf{q}\cdot\mathbf{x}'} u_{s'}^{\dagger}(\mathbf{k}')\, u_s(\mathbf{k}) \tag{17.2}$$

where the u's are Dirac wave functions for the electrons, Ω is the normalization volume, and we have introduced the three-momentum transferred from the electron

$$\hbar\mathbf{q} \equiv \hbar(\mathbf{k}-\mathbf{k}') \tag{17.3}$$

In an inelastic electron scattering experiment, the three-momentum transfer and the (positive) energy loss

$$\hbar\omega \equiv (k-k')\hbar c \geqslant 0 \tag{17.4}$$

may be varied independently, the only restriction being that the four-momentum transfer be positive

$$k_{\mu}^2 \equiv (\mathbf{k}-\mathbf{k}')^2 - (k-k')^2 = 4kk'\sin^2(\tfrac{1}{2}\theta) \geqslant 0$$

or

$$\mathbf{q}^2 - \omega^2 c^{-2} \geqslant 0 \tag{17.5}$$

where we assume ultrarelativistic electrons with $\epsilon = \hbar k c$ and θ is the electron scattering angle. With the relations

$$\int e^{i\mathbf{q}\cdot\mathbf{x}'} \frac{1}{|\mathbf{x}-\mathbf{x}'|}\, \hat{\rho}(\mathbf{x})\, d^3x\, d^3x' = \frac{4\pi}{\mathbf{q}^2}\hat{\rho}(-\mathbf{q}) \tag{17.6}$$

$$\hat{\rho}(-\mathbf{q}) \equiv \int e^{i\mathbf{q}\cdot\mathbf{x}}\hat{\rho}(\mathbf{x})\, d^3x \tag{17.7}$$

---

[1] For a detailed account of electron scattering from nuclei, see T. deForest and J. D. Walecka, Electron Scattering and Nuclear Structure, in *Advan. Phys.*, **15**:1 (1966).

[2] See, for example, L. I. Schiff, "Quantum Mechanics," 3d ed., chap. 13, McGraw-Hill Book Company, New York, 1968.

the electron scattering cross section for an unpolarized target may be written as

$$d^2\sigma = \frac{2\pi}{\hbar}\frac{1}{2}\sum_s\sum_{s'}\sum_n \delta[\hbar\omega - (E_n - E_0)]|\langle\Psi_n|\hat{\rho}(-\mathbf{q})|\Psi_0\rangle|^2\frac{\Omega d^3k'}{(2\pi)^3}$$

$$\times\left(\frac{4\pi}{q^2}\right)^2\left(\frac{e^2}{\Omega}\right)^2|u_{s'}^\dagger(\mathbf{k}')u_s(\mathbf{k})|^2\left(\frac{c}{\Omega}\right)^{-1} \quad (17.8)$$

which follows from Fermi's "Golden Rule" along with the incident electron flux c/Ω. In Eq. (17.8) the states $|\Psi_0\rangle$ and $|\Psi_n\rangle$ are the exact Heisenberg eigenstates of the target particles. The spin sums are evaluated in the ultrarelativistic limit with the relation[1]

$$\tfrac{1}{2}\sum_s\sum_{s'}|u_{s'}^\dagger(\mathbf{k}')u_s(\mathbf{k})|^2 = \cos^2(\tfrac{1}{2}\theta)$$

and we find[2]

$$\frac{1}{\sigma_M}\frac{d^2\sigma}{d\Omega'\,d\epsilon'} = \sum_n|\langle\Psi_n|\hat{\rho}(-\mathbf{q})|\Psi_0\rangle|^2\,\delta[\hbar\omega - (E_n - E_0)] \quad (17.9)$$

$$\sigma_M \equiv \left(\frac{e^2}{\hbar c}\right)^2\frac{4k'^2}{q^4}\cos^2\left(\frac{\theta}{2}\right) \underset{q^2\gg\omega^2/c^2}{=} \left(\frac{e^2}{\hbar c}\right)^2\frac{\cos^2(\theta/2)}{4k^2\sin^4(\theta/2)} \quad (17.10)$$

For the remainder of this section we shall consider only *inelastic* scattering (that is, $\omega > 0$); in this case the operator $\hat{\rho}$ in Eq. (17.9) may be replaced by the fluctuation density

$$\tilde{\rho} \equiv \hat{\rho} - \langle\Psi_0|\hat{\rho}|\Psi_0\rangle \quad (17.11)$$

without changing the result. We can therefore rewrite the right side of Eq. (17.9) as

$$\sum_n|\langle\Psi_n|\tilde{\rho}(-\mathbf{q})|\Psi_0\rangle|^2\,\delta[\hbar\omega - (E_n - E_0)]$$

$$= \sum_n\langle\Psi_0|\tilde{\rho}^\dagger(-\mathbf{q})|\Psi_n\rangle\langle\Psi_n|\tilde{\rho}(-\mathbf{q})|\Psi_0\rangle\,\delta[\hbar\omega - (E_n - E_0)] \quad (17.12a)$$

$$= -\frac{1}{\pi}\text{Im}\sum_n\langle\Psi_0|\tilde{\rho}^\dagger(-\mathbf{q})|\Psi_n\rangle\langle\Psi_n|\tilde{\rho}(-\mathbf{q})|\Psi_0\rangle\frac{1}{\hbar\omega - (E_n - E_0) + i\eta} \quad (17.12b)$$

$$= -\frac{1}{\pi}\text{Im}\left\{\sum_n\left[\frac{\langle\Psi_0|\tilde{\rho}^\dagger(-\mathbf{q})|\Psi_n\rangle\langle\Psi_n|\tilde{\rho}(-\mathbf{q})|\Psi_0\rangle}{\hbar\omega - (E_n - E_0) + i\eta}\right.\right.$$

$$\left.\left. -\frac{\langle\Psi_0|\tilde{\rho}^\dagger(\mathbf{q})|\Psi_n\rangle\langle\Psi_n|\tilde{\rho}(\mathbf{q})|\Psi_0\rangle}{\hbar\omega + (E_n - E_0) \mp i\eta}\right]\right\} \quad (17.12c)$$

[1] This relation follows from the wave functions given in L. I. Schiff, *op. cit.*, eq. (52.17).
[2] The right side of Eq. (17.9) defines the *dynamic structure factor* $S(\mathbf{q},\omega)$, a commonly used notation.

Equation (17.12c) is equivalent to (17.12b) since the last term in brackets has no imaginary part if $\omega > 0$. The two numerators in Eq. (17.12c) are equal if the ground state is invariant under rotations, for then the sum over n at fixed E_n must yield just a function of $\mathbf{q}^2$. We shall henceforth assume this to be the case. Note that the right side of Eq. (17.12) vanishes at $\omega = 0$ and thus explicitly excludes the elastic contribution.

In this way we obtain the important result[1]

$$\frac{1}{\sigma_M} \frac{d^2\sigma}{d\Omega'\,d\epsilon'} = -\frac{1}{\pi} \operatorname{Im} \Pi(\mathbf{q},\mathbf{q};\omega) \tag{17.13a}$$

$$\frac{1}{\sigma_M} \frac{d^2\sigma}{d\Omega'\,d\epsilon'} = -\frac{1}{\pi} \operatorname{Im} \Pi^R(\mathbf{q},\mathbf{q};\omega) \tag{17.13b}$$

where we have defined a general polarization propagator for the target[2]

$$i\hbar\Pi(x,y) \equiv \langle \Psi_0 | T[\tilde{\rho}_H(x)\,\tilde{\rho}_H(y)] | \Psi_0 \rangle \tag{17.14a}$$

$$i\hbar\Pi(x,y) \equiv \int \frac{d^3q}{(2\pi)^3} \int \frac{d^3q'}{(2\pi)^3} \int \frac{d\omega}{2\pi} e^{i\mathbf{q}\cdot\mathbf{x}} e^{-i\omega(t_x - t_y)} e^{-i\mathbf{q}'\cdot\mathbf{y}} \, i\hbar\Pi(\mathbf{q},\mathbf{q}';\omega) \tag{17.14b}$$

appropriate to both uniform and nonuniform systems (e.g., finite nuclei), and corresponding retarded function

$$i\hbar\Pi^R(x,y) = \theta(t_x - t_y)\langle \Psi_0 | [\tilde{\rho}_H(x),\tilde{\rho}_H(y)] | \Psi_0 \rangle \tag{17.15}$$

Equation (17.13a) is immediately verified by inverting the Fourier transform in (17.14b) and then setting $\mathbf{q} = \mathbf{q}'$, which gives

$$\Pi(\mathbf{q},\mathbf{q};\omega) = \sum_n \left[\langle \Psi_0 | \tilde{\rho}^\dagger(-\mathbf{q}) | \Psi_n \rangle \langle \Psi_n | \tilde{\rho}(-\mathbf{q}) | \Psi_0 \rangle \right.$$

$$\left. \times \left(\frac{1}{\hbar\omega - (E_n - E_0) + i\eta} - \frac{1}{\hbar\omega + (E_n - E_0) - i\eta} \right) \right] \tag{17.16}$$

Equation (17.13b) follows because $\Pi^R(\mathbf{q},\mathbf{q};\omega)$ differs from Eq. (17.16) only by having a $+i\eta$ in the denominator of the last term. The momentum conservation in a uniform system simplifies these results; comparing Eq. (17.12) and the equivalent of Eq. (7.55), we find $\Pi(\mathbf{q},\mathbf{q}';\omega) = V\delta_{\mathbf{q}\mathbf{q}'}\Pi(\mathbf{q},\omega)$, where $\Pi(\mathbf{q},\omega)$ is the Fourier transform in the coordinate difference $\mathbf{x} - \mathbf{y}$ and V is the volume of the target. Therefore

$$\frac{1}{\sigma_M} \frac{d^2\sigma}{d\Omega'\,d\epsilon'} = -\frac{V}{\pi} \operatorname{Im} \Pi(\mathbf{q},\omega)$$

$$\text{uniform system} \tag{17.17}$$

$$= -\frac{V}{\pi} \operatorname{Im} \Pi^R(\mathbf{q},\omega)$$

[1] W. Czyż and K. Gottfried, *Ann. Phys. (N.Y.)*, **21**:47 (1963).
[2] We consistently suppress the normalization factor $[\langle \Psi_0 | \Psi_0 \rangle]^{-1}$ in this section.

Note that it is the cross section per unit volume (or per target particle) that is the meaningful quantity for an extended system.

Inelastic electron scattering therefore measures the imaginary part of the polarization propagator directly; complete knowledge of the imaginary part is sufficient, however, because the function itself follows immediately from Eq. (17.16)

$$\Pi(\mathbf{q},\mathbf{q};\omega) = \frac{1}{\pi} \int_0^\infty \text{Im}\,\Pi(\mathbf{q},\mathbf{q};\omega') \left(\frac{1}{\hbar\omega' - \hbar\omega - i\eta} + \frac{1}{\hbar\omega' + \hbar\omega - i\eta} \right) d(\hbar\omega')$$

(17.18)

$$\Pi^R(\mathbf{q},\mathbf{q};\omega) = \frac{1}{\pi} \int_0^\infty \text{Im}\,\Pi^R(\mathbf{q},\mathbf{q};\omega') \left(\frac{1}{\hbar\omega' - \hbar\omega - i\eta} + \frac{1}{\hbar\omega' + \hbar\omega + i\eta} \right) d(\hbar\omega')$$

It is possible to construct sum rules directly from Eqs. (17.9) and (17.13), for we observe that

$$\int_0^\infty \hbar\, d\omega \left(\frac{1}{\sigma_M} \frac{d^2\sigma}{d\Omega'\, d\epsilon'} \right) = -\frac{\hbar}{\pi} \int_0^\infty \text{Im}\,\Pi(\mathbf{q},\mathbf{q};\omega)\, d\omega$$

$$= \langle \Psi_0 | \hat{\rho}^\dagger(-\mathbf{q})\, \tilde{\rho}(-\mathbf{q}) | \Psi_0 \rangle$$

$$= \langle \Psi_0 | \hat{\rho}^\dagger(-\mathbf{q})\, \hat{\rho}(-\mathbf{q}) | \Psi_0 \rangle - |\langle \Psi_0 | \hat{\rho}(-\mathbf{q}) | \Psi_0 \rangle|^2 \quad (17.19)$$

It follows that the total integrated inelastic cross section directly determines the mean-square density fluctuations in the ground state. Writing out the operators of Eq. (17.19) in detail we have

$$\langle \Psi_0 | \hat{\rho}^\dagger(-\mathbf{q})\, \tilde{\rho}(-\mathbf{q}) | \Psi_0 \rangle$$

$$= \int e^{-i\mathbf{q}\cdot\mathbf{x}} \langle \Psi_0 | \hat{\psi}_\alpha^\dagger(\mathbf{x})\, \hat{\psi}_\alpha(\mathbf{x})\, \hat{\psi}_\beta^\dagger(\mathbf{y})\, \hat{\psi}_\beta(\mathbf{y}) | \Psi_0 \rangle\, e^{i\mathbf{q}\cdot\mathbf{y}}\, d^3x\, d^3y$$

$$- \int e^{-i\mathbf{q}\cdot\mathbf{x}} \langle \Psi_0 | \hat{\psi}_\alpha^\dagger(\mathbf{x})\, \hat{\psi}_\alpha(\mathbf{x}) | \Psi_0 \rangle\, \langle \Psi_0 | \hat{\psi}_\beta^\dagger(\mathbf{y})\, \hat{\psi}_\beta(\mathbf{y}) | \Psi_0 \rangle\, e^{i\mathbf{q}\cdot\mathbf{y}}\, d^3x\, d^3y \quad (17.20)$$

The canonical commutation relations immediately give

$$\hat{\psi}_\alpha^\dagger(\mathbf{x})\, \hat{\psi}_\alpha(\mathbf{x})\, \hat{\psi}_\beta^\dagger(\mathbf{y})\, \hat{\psi}_\beta(\mathbf{y}) = \delta_{\alpha\beta}\, \delta(\mathbf{x} - \mathbf{y})\, \hat{\psi}_\alpha^\dagger(\mathbf{x})\, \hat{\psi}_\beta(\mathbf{y}) + \hat{\psi}_\alpha^\dagger(\mathbf{x})\, \hat{\psi}_\beta^\dagger(\mathbf{y})\, \hat{\psi}_\beta(\mathbf{y})\, \hat{\psi}_\alpha(\mathbf{x})$$

(17.21)

and

$$\int d^3x\, \hat{\psi}_\alpha^\dagger(\mathbf{x})\, \hat{\psi}_\alpha(\mathbf{x}) = \hat{Z}$$

(17.22)

where the eigenvalue of $\hat{Z}$ is the total number of charged scatterers in the target. Thus we can write

$$-\frac{\hbar}{\pi} \int_0^\infty d\omega\, \text{Im}\,\Pi(\mathbf{q},\mathbf{q};\omega) = Z + \int e^{-i\mathbf{q}\cdot\mathbf{x}}\, g(\mathbf{x},\mathbf{y})\, e^{i\mathbf{q}\cdot\mathbf{y}}\, d^3x\, d^3y$$

(17.23a)

$$g(\mathbf{x},\mathbf{y}) \equiv \langle \Psi_0 | \hat{\psi}_\alpha^\dagger(\mathbf{x})\, \hat{\psi}_\beta^\dagger(\mathbf{y})\, \hat{\psi}_\beta(\mathbf{y})\, \hat{\psi}_\alpha(\mathbf{x}) | \Psi_0 \rangle$$

$$- \langle \Psi_0 | \hat{\psi}_\alpha^\dagger(\mathbf{x})\, \hat{\psi}_\alpha(\mathbf{x}) | \Psi_0 \rangle\, \langle \Psi_0 | \hat{\psi}_\beta^\dagger(\mathbf{y})\, \hat{\psi}_\beta(\mathbf{y}) | \Psi_0 \rangle \quad (17.23b)$$

The function $g(\mathbf{x},\mathbf{y})$ is a measure of two-particle correlations in the ground state.

In the special case of a uniform medium, where $g(\mathbf{x},\mathbf{y}) = g(|\mathbf{x} - \mathbf{y}|)$, we have

$$-\frac{V\hbar}{\pi} \int_0^\infty d\omega \, \mathrm{Im}\,\Pi(\mathbf{q},\omega) = Z + V \int e^{-i\mathbf{q}\cdot\mathbf{z}} g(z) \, d^3 z \qquad \text{uniform system}$$

(17.24)

The matrix elements in Eq. (17.23b) can be evaluated for a noninteracting Fermi gas (Prob. 5.10) and give

$$g^0(|\mathbf{x} - \mathbf{y}|) = -\tfrac{1}{2}\rho_0^2 \left[\frac{3 j_1(k_F|\mathbf{x} - \mathbf{y}|)}{k_F|\mathbf{x} - \mathbf{y}|}\right]^2$$

(17.25)

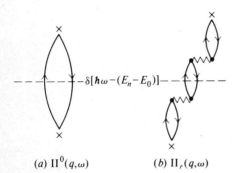

(a) $\Pi^0(q,\omega)$ (b) $\Pi_r(q,\omega)$

Fig. 17.1 Im Π in (a) perfect Fermi gas (b) ring approximation.

Thus the integral in Eq. (17.23a) will become small for large q because of the oscillations of the exponential. This same behavior is to be expected in the interacting system, and we can therefore write

$$\lim_{q\to\infty} \left[-\frac{\hbar}{\pi} \int_0^\infty \mathrm{Im}\,\Pi(\mathbf{q},\mathbf{q};\omega)\,d\omega \right] = Z$$

(17.26)

In this limit the scattering particle sees just the Z individual charges.[1] Note that this limit provides the only really meaningful expression because of the restriction in Eq. (17.5) [unless for some reason $\mathrm{Im}\,\Pi(\mathbf{q},\mathbf{q};\omega)$ is small for $\omega/c > q$].

We discuss three very brief applications of these results in the approximation that the target can be replaced by an equivalent uniform medium with the correct density and total number of charged scatterers determined from the relation

$$\frac{Z}{V} = \rho_0 = \frac{k_F^3}{3\pi^2}$$

(17.27)

The simplest approximation to Π is just Π^0 shown in Fig. 17.1a. The imaginary part of the diagram retains only the energy-conserving processes in the intermediate state [see Eq. (17.12a)]. Thus the inelastic scattering in this simple model is the creation of a particle-hole pair, or equivalently, the ejection of a

[1] Throughout this discussion we have assumed that the target particles have no intrinsic structure.

single particle from the Fermi sea.   In this case we can write

$$\frac{1}{\sigma_M}\frac{d^2\sigma}{d\epsilon'\,d\Omega'} = -\frac{V}{\pi}\,\text{Im}\,\Pi(\mathbf{q},\omega) = -\frac{3\pi Z}{k_F^3}\,\text{Im}\,\Pi(\mathbf{q},\omega)$$

$$\approx \frac{3Z}{8\epsilon_F^0}\left[-\frac{4\pi\hbar^2}{mk_F}\,\text{Im}\,\Pi^0(\mathbf{q},\omega)\right] \qquad (17.28)$$

which is given in Eqs. (12.40) to (12.48a) and shown in Fig. 12.9.   This feature of the spectrum is referred to as the *quasielastic peak*.   If $q/k_F > 2$, there is no Pauli principle restriction in the final state, and the maximum of the curve in Fig. 12.9 occurs at

$$\hbar\omega_{\text{max}} = \frac{\hbar^2\mathbf{q}^2}{2m} \qquad (17.29)$$

[see Eq. (12.41)].   Equation (17.29) is simply the kinematical relation between the energy and momentum transferred to a single target particle initially at rest. The spread of the quasielastic peak is due to the Fermi motion of the target nucleons and the half-width is a direct measure of the Fermi momentum.   Figure 17.2 shows a comparison of the theory with electron scattering data in Ca^{40}.

As a second example, consider the polarization propagator computed by summing the ring diagrams as in Fig. 17.1b.   In using the imaginary part of $\Pi_r(\mathbf{q},\omega)$, we include the propagation of the particle-hole pair through the interacting assembly

$$-\frac{1}{\pi}\,\text{Im}\,\Pi_r(\mathbf{q},\omega) = -\frac{1}{\pi}\,\text{Im}\left\{[U_0(\mathbf{q})]^{-1}\left[\frac{1}{\kappa_r(\mathbf{q},\omega)} - 1\right]\right\}$$

$$= -\frac{1}{\pi}\,\text{Im}\left\{[U_0(\mathbf{q})]^{-1}\left[\frac{1}{1 - U_0(\mathbf{q})\,\Pi^0(\mathbf{q},\omega)} - 1\right]\right\}$$

$$= \left[-\frac{1}{\pi}\,\text{Im}\,\Pi^0(\mathbf{q},\omega)\right]\{[1 - U_0(\mathbf{q})\,\text{Re}\,\Pi^0(\mathbf{q},\omega)]^2$$
$$+ [U_0(\mathbf{q})\,\text{Im}\,\Pi^0(\mathbf{q},\omega)]^2\}^{-1} \quad (17.30)$$

This improved approximation keeps the quasielastic peak within the same kinematical regions where $\text{Im}\,\Pi^0(\mathbf{q},\omega) \neq 0$ but redistributes the strength within the peak.

In addition to the quasielastic peak, there are also peaks at the discrete collective excitations of the system.   For an isolated resonant peak at energy $\hbar\omega = \hbar\omega_{\text{res}}$, the integrated strength gives the absolute value of the inelastic form factor

$$\hbar\int_{\substack{\text{over}\\ \text{resonance}}} d\omega\left(\frac{1}{\sigma_M}\frac{d^2\sigma}{d\Omega'\,d\epsilon'}\right) = |F_{n0}(\mathbf{q})|^2 \qquad (17.31)$$

where

$$F_{n0}(\mathbf{q}) \equiv \rho_{n0}(-\mathbf{q}) = \int e^{i\mathbf{q}\cdot\mathbf{x}}\langle\Psi_n|\hat{\rho}(\mathbf{x})|\Psi_0\rangle\,d^3x$$

At fixed energy loss $\hbar\omega_{res}$, the inelastic form factor can now be measured for all $\mathbf{q}^2$ (still with the restriction $\mathbf{q}^2 \geqslant \omega_{res}^2/c^2$), allowing us to map out the Fourier transform of the transition charge density. By inverting this relation, we can obtain the spatial distribution of the transition charge density itself.[1] For example, to the extent that the uniform electron gas is a good model, the cross

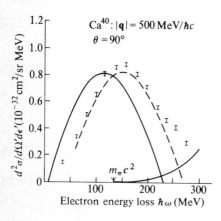

Fig. 17.2 Quasielastic peak in Ca^{40}. [P. Zimmerman, Stanford University Ph.D. Thesis, 1969 (unpublished).] The theoretical curves are calculated from a noninteracting Fermi-gas model using the experimental relativistic electromagnetic interaction with the nucleons. [E. Moniz, *Phys. Rev.*, **184**: 1154 (1969).] The dashed curve is obtained by assuming an average single-particle binding energy -35 MeV per nucleon. The Fermi wavenumber was taken as $k_F = 235$ MeV/$\hbar c = 1.19 \times 10^{13}$ cm^{-1}. The solid curve in the lower right is a theoretical estimate of pion production.

section for electron excitation[2] of the plasma oscillations in a metal is given by [see Eqs. (15.8), (15.10) to (15.12), and (17.17)]

$$\frac{1}{Z}\frac{1}{\sigma_M}\frac{d^2\sigma}{d\Omega'\,d\epsilon'} = \frac{4}{3\pi^3}\frac{(\epsilon_F^0)^3}{(\hbar\Omega_{pl})^4}\left(\frac{q}{k_F}\right)^4\left[-\frac{\hbar^2}{2mk_F}\frac{\partial\,\mathrm{Re}\,\Pi^0(\mathbf{q},\omega)}{\partial\omega}\bigg|_{\Omega_q}\right]^{-1}\frac{\gamma_q}{(\omega-\Omega_q)^2+\gamma_q^2}$$

$$(17.32)$$

where Z is the number of conduction electrons. The cross section is sharply peaked at an energy loss $\hbar\Omega_q$, with a width $\hbar\gamma_q$. Such effects have been observed in the transmission of electrons through thin metallic films.[3] A very similar treatment describes inelastic neutron scattering, as shown in Prob. 5.13.

PROBLEMS

5.1. Consider a uniform noninteracting system of spin-s fermions. Reduce the retarded density correlation function

$$iD^R(x,x') = \theta(t-t')\langle\Psi_0|[\tilde{n}_H(x),\tilde{n}_H(x')]|\Psi_0\rangle/\langle\Psi_0|\Psi_0\rangle$$

to definite integrals. Consider the following limits:

[1] For a transition between discrete states, the phase of $F_{n0}(\mathbf{q})$ can be determined from time-reversal invariance. (See T. deForest and J. D. Walecka, *op. cit.*, appendix B.)

[2] This result neglects the exchange scattering between the incident electron and the electrons in the metal. It also assumes a small damping of the plasma oscillations; however, the integrated strength $\gamma_q\int_0^\infty d\omega[(\omega-\Omega_q)^2+\gamma_q^2]^{-1} \approx \pi$ in Eq. (17.32) is independent of the damping.

[3] The comparison with experiments is described in D. Pines and P. Nozières, "The Theory of Quantum Liquids," vol. I, sec. 4.4, W. A. Benjamin, Inc., New York, 1966.

(a) $t = t'$ all $\mathbf{x}$ and $\mathbf{x}'$

(b) $\mathbf{x} = \mathbf{x}'$ $t - t' \ll \hbar \epsilon_F^{-1}$

(c) $\mathbf{x} = \mathbf{x}'$ $t - t' \gg \hbar \epsilon_F^{-1}$

and interpret the various terms.

5.2. Retain the first correction in Eq. (14.25) and derive the asymptotic expansion [compare Eq. (14.26)]

$$\delta\langle\hat{\rho}(\mathbf{x})\rangle_r \sim \frac{Ze}{\pi}\frac{2\xi}{(4+\xi)^2}\frac{k_F^2}{x}\left\{\frac{\cos 2k_F x}{(k_F x)^2} - \frac{\sin 2k_F x}{(k_F x)^3}\frac{2}{4+\xi}\right.$$

$$\left. \times [\xi \ln 4k_F x - 3 + \xi(\gamma - \tfrac{1}{4})]\right\}$$

where $\gamma = 0.577 \cdots$ is Euler's constant and the remaining contributions vanish faster than x^{-4} as $x \to \infty$.‡

5.3. Derive the Thomas-Fermi equations for the potential and electron charge distribution in a neutral atom of atomic number Z in the following way:
(a) Use the hydrodynamic equation of static equilibrium [Eq. (14.17)] and the boundary condition at $r \to \infty$ to show that $\varphi(r) = (1/e)(\hbar^2/2m)[3\pi^2 n(r)]^{\frac{2}{3}}$ where $\varphi(r)$ is the electrostatic potential.
(b) From Poisson's equation and the physics of the problem show that $\varphi(r)$ satisfies $\nabla^2 \varphi = \kappa \varphi^{\frac{3}{2}}$ with the boundary conditions $\varphi(0) \approx Ze/r$ and $r\varphi(r) \to 0$ as $r \to \infty$, where κ is a constant defined by $\kappa = (8\sqrt{2}/3\pi a_0^2)(e/a_0)^{-\frac{1}{2}}$. (Note: $a_0 = \hbar^2/me^2$ is the Bohr radius.)

5.4. Verify the dispersion relation for plasma oscillations [Eqs. (15.16) to (15.18)] directly from Eq. (12.36).

5.5. Show that the plasma oscillation is damped above a critical wave vector k_{max} determined by the equation $y^2 = (\alpha r_s/\pi)[(2+y)\ln(1+2y^{-1}) - 2]$, where $y = k_{max}/k_F$. Show that zero sound is also damped above a critical wavenumber, given in the weak-coupling limit by $y = 2e^{-1}\exp[-2\pi^2\hbar^2/mk_F V(0)]$.

5.6. Generalize the discussion of Sec. 16 to a hard-sphere Fermi gas at low density, and show that the dispersion relation for long-wavelength zero sound is given by [compare Eq. (16.8)] $\Phi(x) = \pi/4k_F a$ where $x = c_0/v_F$. What is the resulting velocity of zero sound?

‡ The contribution proportional to $\ln k_F x$ was obtained by J. S. Langer and S. H. Vosko, *J. Phys. Chem. Solids*, **12**:196 (1960), but they did not retain all the constant terms.

5.7. (a) Generalize the treatment of Sec. 12 to express $i\hbar\Pi_{\alpha\beta,\,\rho\tau}(x,x')$ in terms of Heisenberg field operators.

(b) Use Prob. 3.15 to prove that Eq. (16.5) with $V(q)$ replaced by $V_0(q)$ correctly describes zero-sound density oscillations for spin-dependent interactions of the form (9.21).

(c) Consider a perturbation $\hat{H}^{\,\mathrm{ex}}(t) = \int d^3x\,\hat{\mathbf{\sigma}}(\mathbf{x}t)\cdot\mathbf{U}^{\mathrm{ex}}(\mathbf{x}t)$, and prove that the same system can support spin waves, described by Eq. (16.5) with $V(q)$ replaced by $V_1(q)$.

5.8. (a) For a uniform spin-s Fermi system with a short-range potential $V(q) \approx V(0)$ ($=$ const), show that all proper polarization insertions with repeated horizontal interaction lines across the fermion loop can be summed to give $\Pi^\star(q) = \Pi^\star_{(0)} + \Pi^\star_{(1)b} + \cdots = \Pi^0(q)[1 + \Pi^0(q)\,V(0)/(2s+1)]^{-1}$ (see Figs. 12.1b and 12.3b).

(b) Show that zero sound is now described by the equation $\Phi(x) = \pi^2\hbar^2/smk_F\,V(0)$ where $x = c_0/v_F$ [see Eq. (16.8)].

(c) Find the corresponding expression for a dilute hard-sphere gas (compare Prob. 5.6).‡

5.9. Define a time-ordered Green's function

$$iD_\sigma(x,x') = \langle\Psi_0|T[\hat{\sigma}_{Hz}(\mathbf{x}t)\,\hat{\sigma}_{Hz}(\mathbf{x}'\,t')]|\Psi_0\rangle/\langle\Psi_0|\Psi_0\rangle$$

where $\hat{\sigma}_z(\mathbf{x}) = \hat{\psi}^\dagger_\alpha(\mathbf{x})(\sigma_z)_{\alpha\beta}\hat{\psi}_\beta(\mathbf{x})$, and relate $D_\sigma(x,x')$ to $\Pi_{\alpha\beta,\,\lambda\mu}(x,x')$. Use Prob. 4.12$a$ to obtain $D_\sigma(q) = \hbar\Pi^\star_\sigma(q)$ for a spin-$\frac{1}{2}$ Fermi system with spin-independent potentials. Why does D_σ differ from D?

5.10. Derive the expression (17.25)'for the two-particle correlation function of a noninteracting spin-$\frac{1}{2}$ Fermi gas.

5.11. Evaluate the sum rule of Eq. (17.24) for a noninteracting spin-$\frac{1}{2}$ Fermi gas.

5.12. How is the width at $\frac{1}{2}$-maximum of the high momentum transfer ($q \gg 2k_F$) quasielastic peak (see Fig. 12.9) related to the Fermi momentum?

5.13. Consider inelastic neutron scattering from an interacting assembly of atoms or molecules.

(a) The *nuclear* interaction between the neutron and a free target particle can be described with the aid of a *pseudopotential*§ $V(|\mathbf{x}_n - \mathbf{x}|) = (4\pi a\hbar^2/2m_{\mathrm{red}})\,\delta(\mathbf{x}_n - \mathbf{x})$.

‡ K. Gottfried and L. Pičman, *Kgl. Danske Videnskab. Selskab Mat.-Fys. Medd.*, **32**, no. 13 (1960).

§ E. Fermi, *Ricerca Sci.*, **7**:13 (1936); J. M. Blatt and V. F. Weisskopf, "Theoretical Nuclear Physics," p. 71, John Wiley and Sons, New York, 1952.

If this potential is treated in Born approximation, it gives the exact low-energy s-wave nuclear scattering of the neutron from one of the target particles.   In this expression m_{red} and $a(\approx 10^{-13}$ cm$)$ are the appropriate reduced mass and scattering length.   Show that this result follows immediately from Eqs. (11.5), (11.9), and (11.22).

(b) Hence show that the interaction of the neutron with the many-body assembly is $\hat{H}^{ex} = (4\pi a \hbar^2/2m_{red})\hat{n}(\mathbf{x}_n)$.   This hamiltonian must be treated in Born approximation.

(c) If the atomic interactions among the target particles are treated exactly, how must the discussion of Sec. 17 be modified to describe inelastic neutron scattering?

6
Bose Systems

In Sec. 5 we saw the drastic effect of statistics on the low-temperature properties of an ideal gas. Fermions obey the exclusion principle, and the ground state consists of a filled Fermi sea. In contrast, the ground state of an ideal Bose system has all the particles in the one single-particle mode with lowest energy. Since the ideal gas forms the basis for calculating the properties of interacting many-particle assemblies, it is natural that the perturbation theory for bosons has a very different structure from that previously discussed for fermions. Indeed, the macroscopic occupation of one single mode poses a fundamental difficulty, and it is essential to reformulate the problem in order to obtain a well-defined theory.

18☐FORMULATION OF THE PROBLEM

The usual form of perturbation theory cannot be applied to bosons for the following reason. The noninteracting ground state of N bosons is given by

$$|\Phi_0(N)\rangle = |N,0,0, \ \ldots\rangle \tag{18.1}$$

where all the particles are in the lowest energy mode. For definiteness, we here consider a large box of volume V with periodic boundary conditions, where this preferred state has zero momentum, but similar macroscopic occupation occurs in other situations (see Chap. 14). If the creation and destruction operators $a_0^\dagger$ and a_0 for the zero-momentum mode are applied to the ground state, Eq. (1.28) implies that

$$a_0|\Phi_0(N)\rangle = N^{\frac{1}{2}}|\Phi_0(N-1)\rangle$$

$$a_0^\dagger|\Phi_0(N)\rangle = (N+1)^{\frac{1}{2}}|\Phi_0(N+1)\rangle \tag{18.2}$$

Thus neither a_0 nor $a_0^\dagger$ annihilates the ground state, and the usual separation of operators into creation and destruction parts (Sec. 8) fails completely. Consequently, it is not possible to define normal-ordered products with vanishing ground-state expectation value, and the application of Wick's theorem becomes much more complicated.

It is interesting to compare Eq. (18.2) with the corresponding relations for fermions, where the occupation numbers cannot exceed 1, and any single mode at most contributes a term of order N^{-1} to the thermodynamic properties of the total system. On the other hand, the operators a_0 and $a_0^\dagger$ for a Bose system multiply the ground state by $N^{\frac{1}{2}}$ or $(N+1)^{\frac{1}{2}}$, which is evidently large. Since it is generally preferable to deal with intensive variables, we shall introduce the operators

$$\hat{\xi}_0 \equiv V^{-\frac{1}{2}} a_0 \qquad \hat{\xi}_0^\dagger \equiv V^{-\frac{1}{2}} a_0^\dagger \tag{18.3}$$

with the following properties

$$[\hat{\xi}_0,\hat{\xi}_0^\dagger] = V^{-1} \tag{18.4}$$

$$\hat{\xi}_0|\Phi_0(N)\rangle = \left(\frac{N}{V}\right)^{\frac{1}{2}}|\Phi_0(N-1)\rangle$$

$$\hat{\xi}_0^\dagger|\Phi_0(N)\rangle = \left(\frac{N+1}{V}\right)^{\frac{1}{2}}|\Phi_0(N+1)\rangle \tag{18.5}$$

Although $\hat{\xi}_0$ and $\hat{\xi}_0^\dagger$ each multiply $|\Phi_0\rangle$ by a finite factor, their *commutator* vanishes in the thermodynamic limit ($N \to \infty$, $V \to \infty$, $N/V \to$ const). Hence it is permissible to treat the operators $\hat{\xi}_0$ and $\hat{\xi}_0^\dagger$ as c numbers,[1] as long as we

[1] N. N. Bogoliubov, *J. Phys.* (*USSR*), **11**:23 (1947). See also P. A. M. Dirac, "The Principles of Quantum Mechanics," 2d ed., sec. 63, Oxford University Press, Oxford, 1935.

consider only states where a finite fraction of the particles occupies the $\mathbf{k}=0$ mode. This approximate procedure clearly neglects fluctuations in the occupation number of the condensate.

The preceding discussion has implicitly assumed a perfect Bose gas, where all the particles are in the zero-momentum state. In an interacting system, however, the interparticle potential energy reduces the occupation of the preferred mode, so that the ground-state expectation value

$$\langle \Psi_0 | \hat{\xi}_0^\dagger \hat{\xi}_0 | \Psi_0 \rangle = N_0 \, V^{-1} \equiv n_0 \tag{18.6}$$

is less than the total density $n = N/V$. Nevertheless, the Bogoliubov replacement of $\hat{\xi}_0$ and $\hat{\xi}_0^\dagger$ by c numbers correctly describes the interacting ground state in the thermodynamic limit whenever the number of particles in the zero-momentum state remains a finite fraction of N. We are therefore led to write the boson field operator as

$$\hat{\psi}(\mathbf{x}) = \xi_0 + \sum_{\mathbf{k}}' V^{-\frac{1}{2}} e^{i\mathbf{k}\cdot\mathbf{x}} a_{\mathbf{k}} = \xi_0 + \hat{\varphi}(\mathbf{x}) = n_0^{\frac{1}{2}} + \hat{\varphi}(\mathbf{x}) \tag{18.7}$$

where the prime means to omit the term $\mathbf{k}=0$. The operator $\hat{\varphi}(\mathbf{x})$ has no zero-momentum components, and ξ_0 is a constant c number.

The separation of $\hat{\psi}$ into two parts modifies the hamiltonian in a fundamental way. Consider the potential energy

$$\hat{V} = \tfrac{1}{2} \int d^3x \, d^3x' \, \hat{\psi}^\dagger(\mathbf{x}) \, \hat{\psi}^\dagger(\mathbf{x}') \, V(\mathbf{x}-\mathbf{x}') \, \hat{\psi}(\mathbf{x}') \, \hat{\psi}(\mathbf{x}) \tag{18.8}$$

If Eq. (18.7) is substituted into Eq. (18.8), the resulting terms can be classified according to the number of factors $n_0^{\frac{1}{2}}$. The interaction hamiltonian then separates into eight distinct parts

$$E_0 = \tfrac{1}{2} n_0^2 \int d^3x \, d^3x' \, V(\mathbf{x}-\mathbf{x}') \tag{18.9}$$

$$\hat{V}_1 = \tfrac{1}{2} n_0 \int d^3x \, d^3x' \, V(\mathbf{x}-\mathbf{x}') \, \hat{\varphi}(\mathbf{x}') \, \hat{\varphi}(\mathbf{x}) \tag{18.10}$$

$$\hat{V}_2 = \tfrac{1}{2} n_0 \int d^3x \, d^3x' \, \hat{\varphi}^\dagger(\mathbf{x}) \, \hat{\varphi}^\dagger(\mathbf{x}') \, V(\mathbf{x}-\mathbf{x}') \tag{18.11}$$

$$\hat{V}_3 = 2(\tfrac{1}{2} n_0) \int d^3x \, d^3x' \, \hat{\varphi}^\dagger(\mathbf{x}') \, V(\mathbf{x}-\mathbf{x}') \, \hat{\varphi}(\mathbf{x}) \tag{18.12}$$

$$\hat{V}_4 = 2(\tfrac{1}{2} n_0) \int d^3x \, d^3x' \, \hat{\varphi}^\dagger(\mathbf{x}) \, V(\mathbf{x}-\mathbf{x}') \, \hat{\varphi}(\mathbf{x}) \tag{18.13}$$

$$\hat{V}_5 = 2(\tfrac{1}{2} n_0^{\frac{1}{2}}) \int d^3x \, d^3x' \, \hat{\varphi}^\dagger(\mathbf{x}) \, \hat{\varphi}^\dagger(\mathbf{x}') \, V(\mathbf{x}-\mathbf{x}') \, \hat{\varphi}(\mathbf{x}) \tag{18.14}$$

$$\hat{V}_6 = 2(\tfrac{1}{2} n_0^{\frac{1}{2}}) \int d^3x \, d^3x' \, \hat{\varphi}^\dagger(\mathbf{x}) \, V(\mathbf{x}-\mathbf{x}') \, \hat{\varphi}(\mathbf{x}') \, \hat{\varphi}(\mathbf{x}) \tag{18.15}$$

$$\hat{V}_7 = \tfrac{1}{2} \int d^3x \, d^3x' \, \hat{\varphi}^\dagger(\mathbf{x}) \, \hat{\varphi}^\dagger(\mathbf{x}') \, V(\mathbf{x}-\mathbf{x}') \, \hat{\varphi}(\mathbf{x}') \, \hat{\varphi}(\mathbf{x}). \tag{18.16}$$

Figure 18.1 indicates the different processes contained in the interaction hamiltonian, where a solid line denotes a particle not in the condensate ($\hat{\varphi}$ or $\hat{\varphi}^\dagger$), a wavy line denotes the interaction potential V, and a dashed line denotes a particle

belonging to the condensate (ξ_0 or $\xi_0^\dagger \equiv n_0^{\frac{1}{2}}$).   In deriving Eqs. (18.9) to (18.16), we have used the relation

$$\int d^3x \, \hat{\varphi}(\mathbf{x}) = V^{-\frac{1}{2}} \sum_{\mathbf{k}}' a_{\mathbf{k}} \int d^3x \, e^{i\mathbf{k}\cdot\mathbf{x}} = V^{\frac{1}{2}} \sum_{\mathbf{k}}' a_{\mathbf{k}} \, \delta_{\mathbf{k}0} = 0 \qquad (18.17)$$

so that $\hat{V}$ contains no terms with only a single particle out of the condensate. The term E_0 in Eq. (18.9) is a c number

$$E_0 = \tfrac{1}{2} V^{-1} N_0^2 \, V(0) = \tfrac{1}{2} V n_0^2 \, V(0) \qquad (18.18)$$

that merely shifts the zero of energy but has no operator character.

In a noninteracting assembly, the ground state is given by Eq. (18.1) with $N_0 = N$.   Since the Bogoliubov prescription eliminates the operators a_0 and $a_0^\dagger$

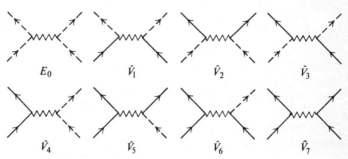

Fig. 18.1   Processes contained in $\hat{V}$ for bosons.

entirely, all remaining destruction operators annihilate the ground state, which thereby becomes the *vacuum*

$$|0\rangle \equiv |\Phi_0\rangle = |N, 0, 0, \ldots\rangle \qquad (18.19)$$

The vacuum expectation value of the total hamiltonian arises solely from Eq. (18.9)

$$\langle 0|\hat{H}|0\rangle = E_0 = \tfrac{1}{2} V^{-1} N^2 \, V(0) \qquad (18.20)$$

which is the first-order shift in the ground-state energy of an interacting Bose gas.

The use of Eq. (18.7) removes the problem associated with the zero-momentum state, but the following difficulty still remains.   Consider the number operator

$$\hat{N} = N_0 + \int d^3x \, \hat{\varphi}^\dagger(\mathbf{x}) \, \hat{\varphi}(\mathbf{x}) = N_0 + \sum_{\mathbf{k}}' a_{\mathbf{k}}^\dagger a_{\mathbf{k}} \qquad (18.21)$$

where N_0 is a c number.   It is evident that $\hat{N}$ no longer commutes with the total hamiltonian

$$[\hat{T} + E_0 + \hat{V}_1 + \cdots + \hat{V}_7, \hat{N}] \neq 0 \qquad (18.22)$$

since the various interaction terms alter the number of particles out of the condensate. As a result, the total number of particles is no longer a constant of the motion but must instead be determined through the subsidiary condition

$$N = N_0 + \sum_{\mathbf{k}}{}' \langle a_{\mathbf{k}}^\dagger a_{\mathbf{k}} \rangle \tag{18.23}$$

where the brackets denote the ground-state expectation value in the interacting system. In Chap. 10, we study an example of this procedure, but it is usually simpler to reformulate the entire problem from the beginning.

We therefore return to the original hamiltonian $\hat{H} = \hat{T} + \hat{V}$, in which a_0 and $a_0^\dagger$ are still operators. Introduce the hermitian operator

$$\hat{K} = \hat{H} - \mu \hat{N} \tag{18.24}$$

which has a complete set of eigenvectors and eigenvalues

$$\hat{K} |\Psi_j\rangle = K_j |\Psi_j\rangle \tag{18.25}$$

The operator $\hat{K}$ commutes with $\hat{N}$ so that the exact problem separates into subspaces of given total number N. Within a subspace, the ground state clearly corresponds to the lowest eigenvalue of $\hat{K}$

$$\hat{K} |\Psi_0(N)\rangle = K(\mu, V, N) |\Psi_0(N)\rangle = [E(V,N) - \mu N] |\Psi_0(N)\rangle \tag{18.26}$$

These relations hold for any value of μ. If we now choose to look for that subspace in which the thermodynamic relation (4.3) holds

$$\mu = \frac{\partial E(V,N)}{\partial N} \tag{18.27}$$

then we will have found the absolute minimum of K

$$\frac{\partial K(\mu, V, N)}{\partial N} = \frac{\partial E(V,N)}{\partial N} - \mu = 0 \tag{18.28}$$

Equation (18.27) may be considered a relation to eliminate N in terms of the variables μ and V. In this subspace, the expectation value $\langle \Psi_0 | \hat{K} | \Psi_0 \rangle$ is the minimum value of the thermodynamic potential at zero temperature [see Eq. (4.7)] and fixed μ and V

$$\langle \Psi_0(\mu) | \hat{K} | \Psi_0(\mu) \rangle = \Omega(T=0, V, \mu) = (E - \mu N)|_{T=0} \tag{18.29}$$

In accordance with general thermodynamic principles, $|\Psi_0(\mu)\rangle$ therefore represents the equilibrium state of the assembly at fixed $T = 0$, V, and μ. All of the thermodynamic relations from Sec. 4 now remain unchanged, for example,

$$\left[-\frac{\partial \Omega(T, V, \mu)}{\partial \mu} \right]_{T=0, V} = -\frac{\partial}{\partial \mu} \langle \Psi_0(\mu) | \hat{K} | \Psi_0(\mu) \rangle = \langle \Psi_0(\mu) | - \frac{\partial \hat{K}}{\partial \mu} | \Psi_0(\mu) \rangle$$

$$= \langle \Psi_0(\mu) | \hat{N} | \Psi_0(\mu) \rangle = N \tag{18.30}$$

where we have used the normalization condition $\langle \Psi_0 | \Psi_0 \rangle = 1$.

As long as a_0 and $a_0^\dagger$ represent operators, both $\hat{H}$ and $\hat{K}$ provide acceptable descriptions of the interacting assembly. When we use the Bogoliubov prescription, however, the thermodynamic potential offers a definite advantage, for it allows a consistent treatment of the nonconservation of particles.[1] Indeed, μ may be interpreted as a Lagrange multiplier that incorporates the subsidiary condition (18.23). We therefore carry out the following steps:

1. Replace $\hat{\xi}_0$ and $\hat{\xi}_0^\dagger$ by c numbers

$$\hat{\xi}_0 \to n_0^{\frac{1}{2}} \qquad \hat{\xi}_0^\dagger \to n_0^{\frac{1}{2}} \tag{18.31}$$

In this way, $\hat{N}$ and $\hat{K}$ become

$$\hat{N} \to N_0 + {\sum_{\mathbf{k}}}' a_{\mathbf{k}}^\dagger a_{\mathbf{k}} \equiv N_0 + \hat{N}' \tag{18.32}$$

$$\hat{K} \to E_0 - \mu N_0 + {\sum_{\mathbf{k}}}' (\epsilon_{\mathbf{k}}^0 - \mu) a_{\mathbf{k}}^\dagger a_{\mathbf{k}} + \sum_{j=1}^{7} \hat{V}_j$$

$$\equiv E_0 - \mu N_0 + \hat{K}' \tag{18.33}$$

which define $\hat{N}'$ and $\hat{K}'$.

2. Since all remaining destruction operators annihilate the noninteracting ground state $|\Phi_0\rangle$, it may again be considered the vacuum

$$|\Phi_0\rangle \to |0\rangle \tag{18.34}$$

Wick's theorem is now applicable, and we may use the previous theorems of quantum field theory.

3. All the final expressions contain the extra parameter N_0, which may be determined as follows. Since the equilibrium state of any assembly at constant (T, V, μ) minimizes the thermodynamic potential, the condition of thermodynamic equilibrium becomes

$$\left[\frac{\partial \Omega(T=0, V, \mu, N_0)}{\partial N_0} \right]_{V\mu} = 0 \tag{18.35}$$

which is an implicit relation for $N_0(V, \mu)$.

19□GREEN'S FUNCTIONS

Steps 1 and 2 described above are quite distinct, and it is convenient to treat them separately. In the present section, we introduce a Heisenberg picture based on $\hat{K}'$ and use the exact single-particle Green's function to determine the thermodynamic functions of the ground state. In Sec. 20, we introduce an interaction

---

[1] N. M. Hugenholtz and D. Pines, *Phys. Rev.*, **116**:489 (1959).

picture and derive the Feynman rules for evaluating the Green's function in perturbation theory.

The Bogoliubov prescription has led us to consider the operator

$$\hat{K} = E_0 - \mu N_0 + \hat{K}' \tag{19.1a}$$

where

$$\hat{K}' = \int d^3x \, \hat{\varphi}^\dagger(\mathbf{x}) \, [T - \mu] \, \hat{\varphi}(\mathbf{x}) + \sum_{j=1}^{7} \hat{V}_j \tag{19.1b}$$

Since $\hat{K}$ is hermitian, it has a complete set of eigenfunctions, and we shall let $|\mathbf{O}\rangle$ denote the ground state of the operator $\hat{K}$. It is essential to bear in mind that $|\mathbf{O}\rangle$ is *not* an eigenstate of $\hat{N}$ and thus differs from the state $|\Psi_0\rangle$ introduced in Eq. (18.26). The *Heisenberg picture* is defined as follows

$$\hat{O}_K(t) \equiv e^{i\hat{K}t/\hbar} \, \hat{O}_S \, e^{-i\hat{K}t/\hbar}$$
$$= e^{i\hat{K}'t/\hbar} \, \hat{O}_S \, e^{-i\hat{K}'t/\hbar} \tag{19.2}$$

where the c-number part of $\hat{K}$ does not affect the time dependence. In particular, the field operator $\hat{\psi}(\mathbf{x})$ becomes

$$\hat{\psi}_K(\mathbf{x}t) = e^{i\hat{K}'t/\hbar} \, \xi_0 \, e^{-i\hat{K}'t/\hbar} + e^{i\hat{K}'t/\hbar} \, \hat{\varphi}(\mathbf{x}) \, e^{-i\hat{K}'t/\hbar}$$
$$= \xi_0 + \hat{\varphi}_K(x) = n_0^{\frac{1}{2}} + \hat{\varphi}_K(x) \tag{19.3}$$

which shows that the condensate part of $\hat{\psi}_K$ is independent of space and time. The single-particle Green's function is defined exactly as in Sec. 7

$$iG(x,y) \equiv \frac{\langle \mathbf{O} | T\{[\xi_0 + \hat{\varphi}_K(x)][\xi_0^\dagger + \hat{\varphi}_K^\dagger(y)]\} | \mathbf{O}\rangle}{\langle \mathbf{O} | \mathbf{O}\rangle}$$
$$= n_0 + n_0^{\frac{1}{2}} \frac{\langle \mathbf{O} | \hat{\varphi}_K(x) + \hat{\varphi}_K^\dagger(y) | \mathbf{O}\rangle}{\langle \mathbf{O} | \mathbf{O}\rangle} + \frac{\langle \mathbf{O} | T[\hat{\varphi}_K(x)\,\hat{\varphi}_K^\dagger(y)] | \mathbf{O}\rangle}{\langle \mathbf{O} | \mathbf{O}\rangle} \tag{19.4}$$

where the signature factor is $+1$ for all time orderings.

We first prove that the second term on the right of Eq. (19.4) vanishes. This result does not follow from number conservation, since $|\mathbf{O}\rangle$ is not an eigenstate of $\hat{N}$; instead, the argument makes use of the translational invariance of the ground state. The quantity $\langle \mathbf{O} | \hat{\varphi}_K^\dagger(x) | \mathbf{O}\rangle$ is a linear combination of matrix elements $\langle \mathbf{O} | a_\mathbf{k}^\dagger | \mathbf{O}\rangle$ for $\mathbf{k} \neq 0$, each multiplied by a c-number function of x. By definition, the momentum operator

$$\hat{\mathbf{P}} = \sum_\mathbf{k} \hbar \mathbf{k} a_\mathbf{k}^\dagger a_\mathbf{k} = \sum_\mathbf{k}' \hbar \mathbf{k} a_\mathbf{k}^\dagger a_\mathbf{k} \tag{19.5}$$

has no zero-momentum component. Hence $\hat{\mathbf{P}}$ commutes with $\hat{K}$, which follows either by direct calculation or by noting that the original operator $\hat{a}_0$ itself commutes with $\hat{\mathbf{P}}$

$$[\hat{a}_0, \hat{\mathbf{P}}] = 0 \tag{19.6}$$

so that the Bogoliubov replacement does not alter the translational invariance of the assembly. Each eigenstate of $\hat{K}$ can therefore be labeled by a definite value of the momentum, and the ground state corresponds to $\mathbf{P} = 0$:

$$\hat{\mathbf{P}}|\mathbf{O}\rangle = 0 \tag{19.7}$$

The relation

$$[\hat{\mathbf{P}}, a_{\mathbf{k}}^{\dagger}] = \hbar \mathbf{k} a_{\mathbf{k}}^{\dagger} \tag{19.8}$$

implies that $a_{\mathbf{k}}^{\dagger}$ increases the momentum by $\hbar\mathbf{k}$, and the orthogonality of the momentum eigenstates shows that

$$\langle \mathbf{O}|a_{\mathbf{k}}^{\dagger}|\mathbf{O}\rangle = 0 \qquad \mathbf{k} \neq 0 \tag{19.9}$$

thereby proving the assertion that $G(x, y)$ takes the form

$$iG(x, y) = n_0 + iG'(x, y) \tag{19.10}$$

$$iG'(x, y) \equiv \frac{\langle \mathbf{O}|T[\hat{\varphi}_K(x)\,\hat{\varphi}_K^{\dagger}(y)]|\mathbf{O}\rangle}{\langle \mathbf{O}|\mathbf{O}\rangle} \tag{19.11}$$

As in Eqs. (18.32) and (18.33), the primed part refers to the noncondensate. With the usual definition of Fourier transforms, the expectation value of $\hat{N}$ may be written as

$$N = \langle \hat{N} \rangle = N_0 + V(2\pi)^{-4} \int d^4q \, iG'(q) \, e^{iq_0\eta} \tag{19.12}$$

where the limit $\eta \to 0^+$ is implicit. Since G' depends on μ and N_0 through the operator $\hat{K}'$ in the Heisenberg picture, Eq. (19.12) may be used to find $N(V,\mu,N_0)$; alternatively, this relation may be inverted to find $\mu(V,N,N_0)$.

The ground-state expectation value of any one-body operator can be expressed in terms of the single-particle Green's function. An interesting example is the kinetic energy

$$T = \langle \hat{T} \rangle = V \int \frac{d^4q}{(2\pi)^4} \frac{\hbar^2 \mathbf{q}^2}{2m} iG'(q) \, e^{iq_0\eta} \tag{19.13}$$

which shows that the stationary condensate makes no contribution to T. It is also possible to determine the potential energy, but the detailed proof is more complicated than in Sec. 7. Equation (19.2) may be rewritten as

$$i\hbar \frac{\partial \hat{\varphi}_K(x)}{\partial t} = [\hat{\varphi}_K(x), \hat{K}'] \tag{19.14}$$

In the thermodynamic limit, the fields $\hat{\varphi}$ and $\hat{\varphi}^{\dagger}$ obey the canonical commutation relations, and the commutator is readily evaluated with Eqs. (18.10) to (18.16) and (19.1). After some manipulation, we find

$$\int d^3x \, \hat{\varphi}_K^{\dagger}(x) \left(i\hbar \frac{\partial}{\partial t} - T + \mu \right) \hat{\varphi}_K(x) = 2\hat{V}_2 + \hat{V}_3 + \hat{V}_4 + 2\hat{V}_5 + \hat{V}_6 + 2\hat{V}_7$$

$$\tag{19.15}$$

where $\hat{V}_1$ commutes with $\hat{\phi}$ and thus cancels identically. The adjoint of Eq. (19.15) may be written as

$$\int d^3x \left[\left(-i\hbar \frac{\partial}{\partial t} - T + \mu \right) \hat{\phi}_\kappa^\dagger(x) \right] \hat{\phi}_\kappa(x)$$

$$= 2\hat{V}_1 + \hat{V}_3 + \hat{V}_4 + \hat{V}_5 + 2\hat{V}_6 + 2\hat{V}_7 \quad (19.16)$$

while their average becomes

$$\tfrac{1}{2} \int d^3x \left\{ \hat{\phi}_\kappa^\dagger(x) \left(i\hbar \frac{\partial}{\partial t} - T + \mu \right) \hat{\phi}_\kappa(x) + \left[\left(-i\hbar \frac{\partial}{\partial t} - T + \mu \right) \hat{\phi}_\kappa^\dagger(x) \right] \hat{\phi}_\kappa(x) \right\}$$

$$= (\hat{V}_1 + \hat{V}_2 + \hat{V}_3 + \hat{V}_4) + \tfrac{3}{2}(\hat{V}_5 + \hat{V}_6) + 2\hat{V}_7$$

$$= 2\hat{V} - n_0 \frac{\partial \hat{V}}{\partial n_0} \quad (19.17)$$

where $\hat{V}$ is the total interaction energy

$$\hat{V} = E_0 + \sum_{j=1}^{7} \hat{V}_j \quad (19.18)$$

The ground-state expectation value of (19.17) becomes

$$\int d^3x \lim_{\mathbf{x}' \to \mathbf{x}} \lim_{t' \to t^+} \tfrac{1}{2} \left[i\hbar \frac{\partial}{\partial t} - T(\mathbf{x}) + \mu - i\hbar \frac{\partial}{\partial t'} - T(\mathbf{x}') + \mu \right] iG'(\mathbf{x}t, \mathbf{x}'\,t')$$

$$= 2\langle \hat{V} \rangle - n_0 \left\langle \frac{\partial \hat{V}}{\partial n_0} \right\rangle \quad (19.19)$$

thereby expressing $\langle \hat{V} \rangle$ in terms of G'.

The thermodynamic potential at $T = 0$ is the ground-state expectation value of the operator $\hat{K}$

$$\Omega(T = 0, V, \mu, N_0) = \langle \mathbf{O} | \hat{K} | \mathbf{O} \rangle \quad (19.20)$$

where $|\mathbf{O}\rangle$ is assumed normalized. The condition (18.35) of thermodynamic equilibrium remains unaltered, and we find

$$\left(\frac{\partial \Omega}{\partial N_0} \right)_{V\mu} = \frac{\partial}{\partial N_0} \langle \mathbf{O} | \hat{K} | \mathbf{O} \rangle = \langle \mathbf{O} | \frac{\partial \hat{K}}{\partial N_0} | \mathbf{O} \rangle = \langle \mathbf{O} | \frac{\partial \hat{V}}{\partial N_0} - \mu | \mathbf{O} \rangle = 0 \quad (19.21)$$

This equation therefore provides a representation for the chemical potential

$$\mu = \langle \mathbf{O} | \frac{\partial \hat{V}}{\partial N_0} | \mathbf{O} \rangle \quad (19.22)$$

but it must be noted that the state vector $|\mathbf{O}\rangle$ itself depends on μ and N_0. A combination of Eqs. (19.12), (19.19), and (19.22) yields

$$E = \langle \hat{T} + \hat{V} \rangle = \tfrac{1}{2}\mu N + \tfrac{1}{2} \int d^3x \lim_{\mathbf{x}' \to \mathbf{x}} \lim_{t' \to t^+} \left[\tfrac{1}{2}i\hbar \left(\frac{\partial}{\partial t} - \frac{\partial}{\partial t'} \right) + T(\mathbf{x}) \right] iG'(x, x')$$

$$(19.23)$$

which may be rewritten with a Fourier transform

$$E = \tfrac{1}{2}\mu N + \tfrac{1}{2} V \int \frac{d^4 q}{(2\pi)^4} \left(\hbar q_0 + \frac{\hbar^2 \mathbf{q}^2}{2m} \right) i G'(q) e^{iq_0\eta} \qquad (19.24)$$

The thermodynamic potential

$$\Omega(T=0) = E - \mu N = -\tfrac{1}{2}\mu N + \tfrac{1}{2} V \int \frac{d^4 q}{(2\pi)^4} \left(\hbar q_0 + \frac{\hbar^2 \mathbf{q}^2}{2m} \right) i G'(q) e^{iq_0\eta} \qquad (19.25)$$

follows immediately. Since Eq. (18.35) [or Eq. (19.22)] determines $N_0(\mu)$, whereas Eq. (19.12) determines $N(\mu, N_0)$, we are now able to find the thermodynamic potential from (19.25) and thus obtain the physical quantities of interest. The remaining problem, of course, is the evaluation of $G'(x,y)$, which is considered in Sec. 20.

20☐PERTURBATION THEORY AND FEYNMAN RULES

We now use the techniques of quantum field theory to study the perturbation expansion of the boson Green's function defined in Eq. (19.11).

INTERACTION PICTURE

We first introduce the operator

$$\hat{K}_0 = E_0 - \mu N_0 + \hat{K}_0' \qquad (20.1)$$

where

$$\hat{K}_0' \equiv \hat{T} - \mu \hat{N}' = \int d^3 x \, \hat{\varphi}^\dagger(\mathbf{x}) [T - \mu] \, \hat{\varphi}(\mathbf{x}) \qquad (20.2)$$

and a corresponding interaction picture

$$\hat{O}_I(t) \equiv e^{i\hat{K}_0 t/\hbar} \hat{O}_S e^{-i\hat{K}_0 t/\hbar}$$
$$= e^{i\hat{K}_0' t/\hbar} \hat{O}_S e^{-i\hat{K}_0' t/\hbar} \qquad (20.3)$$

Just as in Sec. 6, the Heisenberg picture in (19.2) and the interaction picture are related by an operator

$$\hat{U}(t,t_0) = e^{i\hat{K}_0' t/\hbar} e^{-i\hat{K}'(t-t_0)/\hbar} e^{-i\hat{K}_0' t_0/\hbar} \qquad (20.4)$$

which obeys the following equation of motion

$$i\hbar \frac{\partial \hat{U}(t,t_0)}{\partial t} = e^{i\hat{K}_0' t/\hbar} (\hat{K}' - \hat{K}_0') e^{-i\hat{K}_0' t/\hbar} \hat{U}(t,t_0)$$
$$= e^{i\hat{K}_0' t/\hbar} \hat{K}_1 e^{-i\hat{K}_0' t/\hbar} \hat{U}(t,t_0)$$
$$= \hat{K}_1(t) \, \hat{U}(t,t_0) \qquad (20.5)$$

with

$$\hat{K}_1 = \sum_{j=1}^{7} \hat{V}_j \qquad \hat{K} = \hat{K}_0 + \hat{K}_1 \tag{20.6}$$

Note that

$$[\hat{K}_0, \hat{N}] = 0 \tag{20.7}$$

Thus the ground state $|0\rangle$ of the operator $\hat{K}_0$ can be considered a state of definite number of particles. It is evident that $|0\rangle$ is just the state introduced in Eq. (18.19) where the number N is determined from Eq. (19.12). Furthermore,

$$a_{\mathbf{k}}|0\rangle = 0 \tag{20.8}$$

for all $\mathbf{k}$, which means that all of the perturbation analysis of Sec. 9 remains correct with $|0\rangle$ as the noninteracting vacuum. In particular, we immediately conclude that[1]

$$iG'(x,y) = \sum_{m=0}^{\infty} \left(\frac{-i}{\hbar} \right)^m \frac{1}{m!} \int_{-\infty}^{\infty} dt_1 \cdots \int_{-\infty}^{\infty} dt_m$$
$$\times \langle 0|T[\hat{K}_1(t_1) \cdots \hat{K}_1(t_m) \, \hat{\varphi}_I(x) \, \hat{\varphi}_I^\dagger(y)]|0\rangle_{\text{connected}} \tag{20.9}$$

Since the operator $\hat{\varphi}_I(x)\hat{\varphi}_I^\dagger(y)$ also commutes with $\hat{N}$, the difficulty associated with the nonconservation of particles is isolated in the factors $\hat{K}_1(t_i)$ in Eq. (20.9). The zero-order term becomes

$$iG^0(x,y) = \langle 0|T[\hat{\varphi}_I(x) \, \hat{\varphi}_I^\dagger(y)]|0\rangle \tag{20.10}$$

which is the Green's function for a free Bose gas, and a simple calculation yields its Fourier transform

$$G^0(q) = [q_0 - \omega_{\mathbf{q}} + \mu\hbar^{-1} + i\eta]^{-1} \tag{20.11}$$

Equation (20.8) shows that $G^0(x,y)$ vanishes if $t_y > t_x$; thus $G^0(x,y)$ only *propagates forward in time*. In contrast to the fermion case [Eq. (7.45)], there is *no hole propagation* in Eq. (20.11).

FEYNMAN RULES IN COORDINATE SPACE

The analysis of Eq. (20.9) into Feynman diagrams is straightforward, and we only note the following features of the Feynman rules for $G'(x,y)$.

1. There is a factor $n_0^{\frac{1}{2}}$ for each dashed line entering or leaving a vertex. The total number of lines (solid and dashed) going into a Feynman diagram must equal the number coming out.

---

[1] The proof that

$$\frac{|\mathbf{O}\rangle}{\langle 0|\mathbf{O}\rangle} = \frac{\hat{U}(0, \pm\infty)|0\rangle}{\langle 0|\hat{U}(0, \pm\infty)|0\rangle}$$

is an eigenstate of $\hat{K}$ follows just as in the Gell-Mann and Low theorem.

2. In mth order, the m operators $\hat{K}_1$ can be chosen in $m!$ ways.   This factor $m!$ corresponds to the possible ways of relabeling the different interaction lines, and it cancels the explicit $(m!)^{-1}$ in Eq. (20.9).   As in Sec. 9, this cancellation occurs only for the connected diagrams.

3. The terms $\hat{V}_1$, $\hat{V}_2$, and $\hat{V}_7$ are symmetric under the interchange of dummy variables $x \leftrightarrow x'$, whereas the other terms $\hat{V}_3$, $\hat{V}_4$, $\hat{V}_5$, and $\hat{V}_6$ have no such symmetry.   In consequence, each time $\hat{V}_1$, $\hat{V}_2$, or $\hat{V}_7$ appears in a Feynman diagram, there is always another contribution that precisely cancels the factor $\frac{1}{2}$ in front of these terms.   Since $\hat{V}_3$, $\hat{V}_4$, $\hat{V}_5$, and $\hat{V}_6$ already have a factor 1, we conclude that every *distinct* Feynman diagram need be counted only once, and the potential enters with a factor unity, exactly as in Sec. 9.

4. Each mth-order diagram in the perturbation expansion of $G'(x,y)$ has a factor $(i/\hbar)^m(-i)^C$, where C is the number of condensate factors n_0 appearing in the diagram.

5. The absence of backward propagation in time, or hole propagation, allows us to eliminate large classes of diagrams at the outset.   For example, there are no contractions within the $\hat{V}_i$ since they are already normal ordered; thus there are no contributions in which the same particle line G^0 either closes on itself or has its ends joined by the same interaction.   In addition, we note that the Feynman diagram is integrated over all internal variables, which means that all possible time orderings of the interactions are included.   No diagram can contribute unless there is *some time ordering in which all its particle lines G^0 run forward in time*.   For example, Fig. 9.8i and j vanish identically because there are pairs of particle lines running in opposite directions.   Note that these restrictions eliminate every one of the first- and second-order diagrams in Figs. 9.7 and 9.8 that contribute to the fermion propagator.

FEYNMAN RULES IN MOMENTUM SPACE

The rules for $G'(q)$ in momentum space are the same as before, with a factor $n_0^{\frac{1}{2}}$ for every dashed line, an overall factor of $(i/\hbar)^m(-i)^C(2\pi)^{4(C-m)}$ in mth order, and the zero-order Green's function given by Eq. (20.11).   The basic vertices are shown in Fig. 20.1 and four-momentum is conserved at each vertex.   Since a condensate line carries vanishing four-momentum, whereas a particle line must have $\mathbf{k} \neq 0$, we again conclude that no interaction line can join one particle line and three condensate lines.

   As an example, consider the first-order correction $G'^{(1)}$.   The terms $\hat{V}_1$, $\hat{V}_2$, $\hat{V}_5$, $\hat{V}_6$ make no contribution to G' in first order because they do not conserve

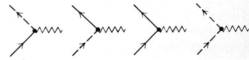

Fig. 20.1 Basic vertices for bosons.

the number of particles. The term containing $\hat{V}_7$ also vanishes because the only possible diagrams would involve holes. We are left with $\hat{V}_4$ and $\hat{V}_3$, which lead

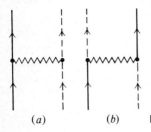

(a)   (b)   **Fig. 20.2**   All first-order contributions $G'^{(1)}$.

to the diagrams shown in Fig. 20.2a and b, respectively, and the Feynman rules immediately give

$$G'^{(1)}(q) = n_0 \hbar^{-1} G^0(q)\,[V(0) + V(\mathbf{q})]\,G^0(q) \tag{20.12}$$

The corresponding analysis in second order is substantially longer, and we shall only exhibit the diagrams (Fig. 20.3). Note that Fig. 20.3b and e represent

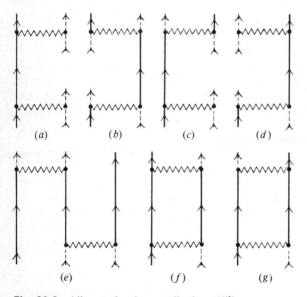

(a)   (b)   (c)   (d)

(e)   (f)   (g)

Fig. 20.3   All second-order contributions $G'^{(2)}$.

different contractions because the direction of propagation, or momentum flow, is different in the two cases. The diagrams of Fig. 20.3a through e are of order n_0^2, whereas 20.3f and g are of order n_0. As noted previously, the absence of holes means that no second-order diagrams involve only noncondensate lines.

DYSON'S EQUATIONS

The nonconservation of particles arises from the Bose condensation, which provides a source and sink for particles out of the condensate. As a result, the particle lines need not run continuously through a diagram, as opposed to the situation for fermions. Nevertheless, if a proper self-energy is defined as a part of a Feynman diagram connected to the rest of the diagram by two noncondensate particle lines, then it is still possible to analyze the contributions to the Green's function in a form similar to Dyson's equations for fermions. The structure is more complicated than indicated in Sec. 9, however, because there are three distinct proper self-energies, as indicated in Fig. 20.4. The first one $\Sigma_{11}^{\star}(p)$

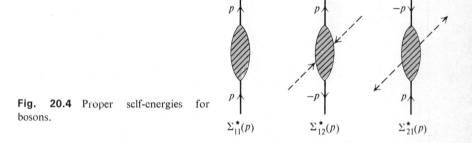

Fig. 20.4 Proper self-energies for bosons.

$$\Sigma_{11}^{\star}(p) \qquad \Sigma_{12}^{\star}(p) \qquad \Sigma_{21}^{\star}(p)$$

has one particle line going in and one coming out, similar to that for fermions. The other ones have two particle lines either coming out ($\Sigma_{12}^{\star}$) or going in ($\Sigma_{21}^{\star}$) and reflect the new features associated with Bose condensation; the lowest-order contributions to these new self-energies may be seen explicitly in Fig. 20.3e. [The choice of subscripts will become clear in Eq. (20.21).]

Correspondingly, we must introduce two new *exact* Green's function G_{12}' and G_{21}', representing the appearance and disappearance of two particles from the condensate. They are shown in Fig. 20.5, along with G', where the arrows indicate either the direction of propagation in coordinate space or the direction of momentum flow in momentum space. The Dyson's equations for this system

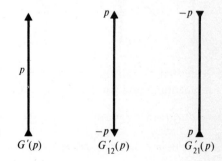

Fig. 20.5 Noncondensate Green's functions for bosons.

$$G'(p) \qquad G_{12}'(p) \qquad G_{21}'(p)$$

were first derived by Beliaev.[1]   They are shown in Fig. 20.6 and may be written in momentum space as follows:

$$G'(p) = G^0(p) + G^0(p)\, \Sigma_{11}^{\star}(p)\, G'(p) + G^0(p)\, \Sigma_{12}^{\star}(p)\, G_{21}'(p) \qquad (20.13a)$$

$$G_{12}'(p) = G^0(p)\, \Sigma_{12}^{\star}(p)\, G'(-p) + G^0(p)\, \Sigma_{11}^{\star}(p)\, G_{12}'(p) \qquad (20.13b)$$

$$G_{21}'(p) = G^0(-p)\, \Sigma_{21}^{\star}(p)\, G'(p) + G^0(-p)\, \Sigma_{11}^{\star}(-p)\, G_{21}'(p) \qquad (20.13c)$$

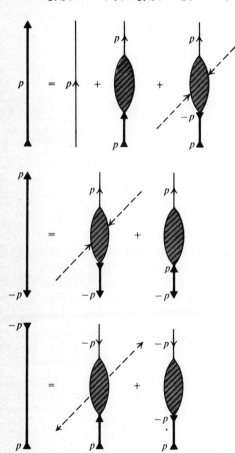

Fig. 20.6 Dyson's equations for bosons.

Note that overall four-momentum conservation determines the direction of the momentum flow in Fig. 20.6. An equivalent equation for $G'(p)$ is clearly

$$G'(-p) = G^0(-p) + G^0(-p)\, \Sigma_{11}^{\star}(-p)\, G'(-p) + G^0(-p)\, \Sigma_{21}^{\star}(p)\, G_{12}'(p) \quad (20.13d)$$

[1] S. T. Beliaev, *Sov. Phys.-JETP*, **7**:289 (1958).

When these equations are iterated consistently, we obtain all the improper self-energies and Green's functions to arbitrary order in perturbation theory.

The *anomalous* Green's functions introduced above have a precise definition in terms of Heisenberg field operators:

$$iG_{12}'(x,y) = \frac{\langle \mathbf{O}|T[\hat{\varphi}_K(x)\,\hat{\varphi}_K(y)]|\mathbf{O}\rangle}{\langle \mathbf{O}|\mathbf{O}\rangle} \tag{20.14a}$$

$$iG_{21}'(x,y) = \frac{\langle \mathbf{O}|T[\hat{\varphi}_K^\dagger(x)\,\hat{\varphi}_K^\dagger(y)]|\mathbf{O}\rangle}{\langle \mathbf{O}|\mathbf{O}\rangle} \tag{20.14b}$$

where the nonconservation of particle number is particularly evident. The definitions imply that

$$G_{12}'(x,y) = G_{12}'(y,x) \qquad G_{21}'(x,y) = G_{21}'(y,x) \tag{20.15}$$

so that their Fourier transforms are even functions of the four-momentum

$$G_{12}'(p) = G_{12}'(-p) \qquad G_{21}'(p) = G_{21}'(-p) \tag{20.16}$$

The structure of Dyson's equations can be clarified by introducing a matrix notation in which

$$\hat{\Phi}_K(x) = \begin{bmatrix} \hat{\varphi}_K(x) \\ \hat{\varphi}_K^\dagger(x) \end{bmatrix} \tag{20.17}$$

Correspondingly, we define a 2×2 matrix Green's function

$$i\mathbf{G}'(x,y) = \frac{\langle \mathbf{O}|T[\hat{\Phi}_K(x)\,\hat{\Phi}_K^\dagger(y)]|\mathbf{O}\rangle}{\langle \mathbf{O}|\mathbf{O}\rangle} \tag{20.18}$$

whose off-diagonal elements are just those in Eq. (20.14). With the identification

$$G_{11}'(x,y) = G'(x,y) \qquad G_{22}'(x,y) = G'(y,x) \tag{20.19}$$

Dyson's equation becomes a single matrix equation

$$\mathbf{G}'(x,y) = \mathbf{G}^0(x,y) + \int d^4x_1\, d^4x_1'\, \mathbf{G}^0(x,x_1)\,\boldsymbol{\Sigma}^\star(x_1,x_1')\,\mathbf{G}(x_1',y) \tag{20.20}$$

where

$$\boldsymbol{\Sigma}^\star(x,y) = \begin{bmatrix} \Sigma_{11}^\star(x,y) & \Sigma_{12}^\star(x,y) \\ \Sigma_{21}^\star(x,y) & \Sigma_{11}^\star(y,x) \end{bmatrix} \tag{20.21}$$

and

$$\mathbf{G}^0(x,y) = \begin{bmatrix} G^0(x,y) & 0 \\ 0 & G^0(y,x) \end{bmatrix} \tag{20.22}$$

We shall generally consider a uniform medium, where Eq. (20.20) may be simplified to

$$\mathbf{G}'(p) = \mathbf{G}^0(p) + \mathbf{G}^0(p)\,\mathbf{\Sigma}^\star(p)\,\mathbf{G}'(p)$$

$$\mathbf{G}'(p) = \begin{bmatrix} G'(p) & G'_{12}(p) \\ G'_{21}(p) & G'(-p) \end{bmatrix}$$

$$\mathbf{G}^0(p) = \begin{bmatrix} G^0(p) & 0 \\ 0 & G^0(-p) \end{bmatrix} \qquad (20.23)$$

$$\mathbf{\Sigma}^\star(p) = \begin{bmatrix} \Sigma^\star_{11}(p) & \Sigma^\star_{12}(p) \\ \Sigma^\star_{21}(p) & \Sigma^\star_{11}(-p) \end{bmatrix}$$

It is easily verified that this matrix equation reproduces Eq. (20.13). A matrix inversion then yields

$$G'(p) = \frac{p_0 + \omega_\mathbf{p} - \mu/\hbar + S(p) - A(p)}{D(p)}$$

$$\qquad (20.24)$$

$$G'_{12}(p) = -\frac{\Sigma^\star_{12}(p)}{D(p)} \qquad G'_{21}(p) = -\frac{\Sigma^\star_{21}(p)}{D(p)}$$

where

$$D(p) = [p_0 - A(p)]^2 - [\omega_\mathbf{p} - \mu\hbar^{-1} + S(p)]^2 + \Sigma^\star_{12}(p)\,\Sigma^\star_{21}(p) \qquad (20.25)$$

and

$$S(p) = \tfrac{1}{2}[\Sigma^\star_{11}(p) + \Sigma^\star_{11}(-p)] \qquad A(p) = \tfrac{1}{2}[\Sigma^\star_{11}(p) - \Sigma^\star_{11}(-p)] \qquad (20.26)$$

These equations express the various Green's functions in terms of the exact proper self-energies and are therefore entirely general.

LEHMANN REPRESENTATION

Before we study specific approximations for $\mathbf{\Sigma}^\star$, it is interesting to derive the Lehmann spectral representation for $\mathbf{G}'$. The proof proceeds exactly as in Sec. 7, and we find [compare Eq. (7.55)]

$$\mathbf{G}'(p) = V \sum_n \left[\frac{\langle \mathbf{O}|\hat{\Phi}(0)|n\mathbf{p}\rangle\langle n\mathbf{p}|\hat{\Phi}^\dagger(0)|\mathbf{O}\rangle}{p_0 - \hbar^{-1}(K_{n\mathbf{p}} - K_{00}) + i\eta} \right.$$

$$\left. - \frac{\langle \mathbf{O}|\hat{\Phi}^\dagger(0)|n,-\mathbf{p}\rangle\langle n,-\mathbf{p}|\hat{\Phi}(0)|\mathbf{O}\rangle}{p_0 + \hbar^{-1}(K_{n,-\mathbf{p}} - K_{00}) - i\eta} \right] \qquad (20.27)$$

where the complete set of states $|n\mathbf{p}\rangle$ satisfies the relations

$$\hat{\mathbf{P}}|n\mathbf{p}\rangle = \hbar\mathbf{p}|n\mathbf{p}\rangle \qquad \hat{K}|n\mathbf{p}\rangle = K_{n\mathbf{p}}|n\mathbf{p}\rangle \qquad (20.28)$$

and each residue is a 2×2 matrix. It is evident that all the Green's functions have the same singularities in the complex p_0 plane, occurring at the resonant

frequencies $\pm\hbar^{-1}(K_{n,\pm\mathbf{p}} - K_{00})$. The residues of $G'(p)$ are real, while those of $G'_{12}(p)$ and $G'_{21}(p)$ are complex conjugates of each other.

21□WEAKLY INTERACTING BOSE GAS

As our first application of this formalism, we consider a weakly interacting Bose gas whose potential $V(\mathbf{x})$ has a well-defined Fourier transform $V(\mathbf{p})$. The

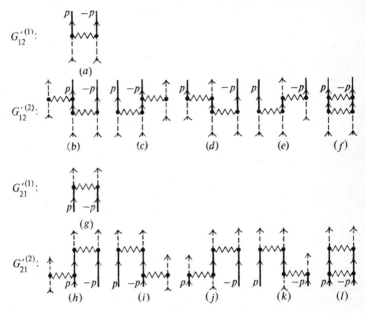

Fig. 21.1 All first- and second-order contributions to G'_{12} and G'_{21}.

proper self-energies need only be evaluated to lowest order, and Eq. (20.12) shows that

$$\hbar\Sigma^{\star}_{11}(p) = n_0[V(0) + V(\mathbf{p})] \qquad \text{lowest order} \tag{21.1}$$

which is independent of p_0. The Feynman rules of Sec. 20 also apply to G'_{12} and G'_{21}, and we exhibit all nonvanishing first- and second-order contributions in Fig. 21.1. We see by inspection that the first-order proper self-energies are

$$\hbar\Sigma^{\star}_{12}(p) = \hbar\Sigma^{\star}_{21}(p) = n_0\,V(\mathbf{p}) \qquad \text{lowest order} \tag{21.2}$$

again independent of frequency. This equality of $\Sigma^{\star}_{12}(p)$ and $\Sigma^{\star}_{21}(p)$ for a uniform Bose gas at rest can be proved to all orders by examining the diagrams. Since the arrows denote the direction of momentum flow, reversing the direction of all the arrows is equivalent to taking $p \leftrightarrow -p$. Thus $\Sigma^{\star}_{12}(p) = \Sigma^{\star}_{21}(-p)$. The symmetry of the diagrams, however, shows that both $\Sigma^{\star}_{12}$ and $\Sigma^{\star}_{21}$ must be even functions of p, which also follows from Eqs. (20.16) and (20.24).

Before the solution of Dyson's equation can be used, it is essential to determine the chemical potential, which can be done with Eq. (19.22). If this equation is rewritten in the interaction representation, we obtain

$$
\mu = \frac{\displaystyle\sum_{m=0}^{\infty} \left(\frac{-i}{\hbar}\right)^m \frac{1}{m!} \int_{-\infty}^{\infty} dt_1 \cdots \int_{-\infty}^{\infty} dt_m \langle 0|T\left[\hat{K}_1(t_1)\cdots\hat{K}_1(t_m)\frac{\partial\hat{V}}{\partial N_0}\right]|0\rangle}{\displaystyle\sum_{m=0}^{\infty} \left(\frac{-i}{\hbar}\right)^m \frac{1}{m!} \int_{-\infty}^{\infty} dt_1 \cdots \int_{-\infty}^{\infty} dt_m \langle 0|T[\hat{K}_1(t_1)\cdots\hat{K}_1(t_m)]|0\rangle}
$$

$$(21.3)$$

where the operator $\partial\hat{V}/\partial N_0$ is assigned the time $t = 0$. The denominator serves to cancel the disconnected diagrams, exactly as in our discussion of the proof of Goldstone's theorem in Sec. 9. Thus we find

$$
\mu = \sum_{m=0}^{\infty} \left(\frac{-i}{\hbar}\right)^m \frac{1}{m!} \int_{-\infty}^{\infty} dt_1 \cdots \int_{-\infty}^{\infty} dt_m
$$

$$
\times \langle 0|T\left[\hat{K}_1(t_1)\cdots\hat{K}_1(t_m)\frac{\partial\hat{V}}{\partial N_0}\right]|0\rangle_{\text{connected}} \quad (21.4)
$$

The lowest-order contribution is

$$
\mu = \langle 0|\frac{\partial\hat{V}}{\partial N_0}|0\rangle
$$

$$
= 2E_0 N_0^{-1} + N_0^{-1}\langle 0|\hat{V}_1 + \hat{V}_2 + \hat{V}_3 + \hat{V}_4|0\rangle + (2N_0)^{-1}\langle 0|\hat{V}_5 + \hat{V}_6|0\rangle
$$

$$
= n_0 V(0) \quad (21.5)
$$

where the matrix elements vanish because they are already normal ordered. Comparison of Eqs. (21.1), (21.2), and (21.5) shows that these first-order quantities satisfy the relation

$$
\mu = \hbar\Sigma_{11}^{\star}(0) - \hbar\Sigma_{12}^{\star}(0) \quad (21.6)
$$

This equation is in fact correct to all orders in perturbation theory and was first derived by Hugenholtz and Pines.[1]

The single-particle Green's function is now readily found from Eq. (20.24). We note that $A(p)$ vanishes identically, and a straightforward calculation yields

$$
G'(p) = \frac{p_0 + \hbar^{-1}[\epsilon_{\mathbf{p}}^0 + n_0 V(\mathbf{p})]}{p_0^2 - (E_{\mathbf{p}}/\hbar)^2}
$$

$$(21.7)$$

$$
G_{12}'(p) = G_{21}'(p) = \frac{-\hbar^{-1} n_0 V(\mathbf{p})}{p_0^2 - (E_{\mathbf{p}}/\hbar)^2}
$$

where

$$
E_{\mathbf{p}} = \{[\epsilon_{\mathbf{p}}^0 + n_0 V(\mathbf{p})]^2 - [n_0 V(\mathbf{p})]^2\}^{\frac{1}{2}}
$$

$$
= \{\epsilon_{\mathbf{p}}^{0^2} + 2\epsilon_{\mathbf{p}}^0 n_0 V(\mathbf{p})\}^{\frac{1}{2}} \quad (21.8)
$$

[1] N. M. Hugenholtz and D. Pines, *loc. cit.*

It is convenient to separate the two poles in Eq. (21.7):

$$G'(p) = \frac{u_{\mathbf{p}}^2}{p_0 - E_{\mathbf{p}}/\hbar + i\eta} - \frac{v_{\mathbf{p}}^2}{p_0 + E_{\mathbf{p}}/\hbar - i\eta} \tag{21.9a}$$

$$G'_{12}(p) = G'_{21}(p) = \frac{-u_{\mathbf{p}} v_{\mathbf{p}}}{p_0 - E_{\mathbf{p}}/\hbar + i\eta} + \frac{u_{\mathbf{p}} v_{\mathbf{p}}}{p_0 + E_{\mathbf{p}}/\hbar - i\eta} \tag{21.9b}$$

where

$$u_{\mathbf{p}} = \{\tfrac{1}{2} E_{\mathbf{p}}^{-1}[\epsilon_{\mathbf{p}}^0 + n_0 V(\mathbf{p})] + \tfrac{1}{2}\}^{\frac{1}{2}}$$

$$v_{\mathbf{p}} = \{\tfrac{1}{2} E_{\mathbf{p}}^{-1}[\epsilon_{\mathbf{p}}^0 + n_0 V(\mathbf{p})] - \tfrac{1}{2}\}^{\frac{1}{2}} \tag{21.10}$$

and the infinitesimals $\pm i\eta$ have been determined from the Lehmann representation.

The most striking feature of these expressions is the form of the excitation spectrum $E_{\mathbf{p}}$. In the long-wavelength limit, $E_{\mathbf{p}}$ reduces to a linear (phonon-like) dispersion relation

$$E_{\mathbf{p}} \approx \hbar|\mathbf{p}| \left[\frac{n_0 V(0)}{m}\right]^{\frac{1}{2}} \qquad |\mathbf{p}| \to 0 \tag{21.11}$$

with the characteristic velocity [compare Eq. (16.11)]

$$c = \left[\frac{n_0 V(0)}{m}\right]^{\frac{1}{2}} \tag{21.12}$$

This expression shows that the theory is well defined only if $V(0) > 0$. The present calculation does not allow us immediately to identify c as the speed of compressional waves, since $E_{\mathbf{p}}$ is here derived from the single-particle Green's function rather than the density correlation function. Nevertheless, a detailed calculation of the ground-state energy (Sec. 22) shows that c is indeed the true speed of sound. This question is discussed at the end of Sec. 22.

The behavior of $E_{\mathbf{p}}$ for large momenta depends on the potential $V(\mathbf{p})$, and we assume that $V(\mathbf{x})$ is repulsive with a range r_0. It follows that $V(\mathbf{p})$ is approximately constant for $|\mathbf{p}| < r_0^{-1}$, and we also assume that

$$n_0 V(0) \ll \frac{\hbar^2}{2mr_0^2} \tag{21.13}$$

which limits the allowed range of density. The dispersion relation $E_{\mathbf{p}}$ then changes from linear to quadratic in the vicinity of $|\mathbf{p}| \approx [2mn_0 V(0)/\hbar^2]^{\frac{1}{2}}$ and becomes

$$E_{\mathbf{p}} \approx \epsilon_{\mathbf{p}}^0 + n_0 V(\mathbf{p}) \qquad p^2 \gg 2mn_0 V(0)\hbar^{-2} \tag{21.14}$$

for large wave vectors. The last term represents an additional potential energy arising from the interaction with the particles in the condensate.

It is interesting to evaluate the total number of particles from Eq. (19.12). Only the pole at $p_0 = -E_\mathbf{p}/\hbar + i\eta$ contributes, and we obtain

$$n = n_0 + (2\pi)^{-3} \int d^3p \, v_\mathbf{p}^2 \tag{21.15}$$

Thus $v_\mathbf{p}^2$ may be interpreted as the ground-state momentum distribution function for particles out of the condensate. The most notable feature is the behavior of $v_\mathbf{p}^2$ at long wavelengths, where it varies as $|\mathbf{p}|^{-1}$. In addition, n_0 is definitely less than n because the integrand of Eq. (21.15) is positive definite. We see that the interaction alters the ground state by removing some particles from the condensate, exciting them to states of finite momentum. From this point of view, the increase of $v_\mathbf{p}^2$ as $|\mathbf{p}| \to 0$ reflects the macroscopic occupation of the zero-momentum state. In the limit $V(\mathbf{p}) \to 0$, the energy spectrum $E_\mathbf{p}$ reduces to $\epsilon_\mathbf{p}^0$, while $v_\mathbf{p}^2$ vanishes, properly reproducing the behavior of a perfect gas. An equivalent observation is that the second pole in Eq. (21.9a) arises solely from the interactions between particles, and $\mathbf{G}'(p)$ reduces to $\mathbf{G}^0(p)$ as $V(\mathbf{p}) \to 0$.

22□DILUTE BOSE GAS WITH REPULSIVE CORES

We now consider a dilute Bose gas, in which the potentials are repulsive but may be arbitrarily strong.[1] Just as in Sec. 11, the only small parameter is the ratio of the scattering length a to the interparticle spacing $n^{-\frac{1}{3}}$, and we therefore assume $na^3 \ll 1$. The potential $V(\mathbf{x})$ no longer has a well-defined Fourier transform,

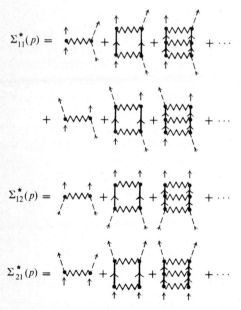

Fig. 22.1 Ladder summation for proper self-energies.

and it becomes essential to sum a selected class of diagrams to obtain the proper self-energy. In particular, note that Fig. 20.3f and g and Fig. 21.1f and l represent the second terms in a sum of ladder diagrams for $\Sigma^\star$ (Fig. 22.1). This summation may be evaluated with a Bethe-Salpeter equation, exactly as in a dilute Fermi gas (Sec. 11), which yields

$$\chi(\mathbf{p},\mathbf{p}',P) = (2\pi)^3\,\delta(\mathbf{p}-\mathbf{p}') + (\epsilon + 2m\mu\hbar^{-2} - p^2 + i\eta)^{-1}(2\pi)^{-3}$$
$$\times \int d^3q\,v(\mathbf{q})\,\chi(\mathbf{p}-\mathbf{q},\mathbf{p}',P) \quad (22.1)$$

$$m\hbar^{-2}\,\Gamma(\mathbf{p},\mathbf{p}',P) = (2\pi)^{-3}\int d^3q\,v(\mathbf{q})\,\chi(\mathbf{p}-\mathbf{q},\mathbf{p}',P) \quad (22.2)$$

The μ in the last term of Eq. (22.1) arises from the form of $G^0(p)$, which depends explicitly on the chemical potential. These equations are simpler than those for fermions because the theory has no hole propagation; for this reason, they are just those solved as χ_0 and Γ_0 in Sec. 11, and their solution may be written as [see Eq. (11.45)]

$$\frac{m}{\hbar^2}\,\Gamma(\mathbf{p},\mathbf{p}',P) = \tilde{f}(\mathbf{p},\mathbf{p}') + \int \frac{d^3k}{(2\pi)^3}\,\tilde{f}(\mathbf{p},\mathbf{k})$$
$$\times \left(\frac{1}{\epsilon + 2m\mu/\hbar^2 - k^2 + i\eta} + \frac{1}{k^2 - p'^2 - i\eta}\right)\tilde{f}(\mathbf{p}',\mathbf{k})^* \quad (22.3)$$

In the long-wavelength limit ($|\mathbf{p}| \to 0$), the leading term reduces to [see Eq. (11.53)]

$$\Gamma(\mathbf{p},\mathbf{p}',P) \to 4\pi a\hbar^2\,m^{-1} \qquad |\mathbf{p}|a \ll 1,\ |\mathbf{p}'|a \ll 1 \quad (22.4)$$

where a is the s-wave scattering length. Hence the corresponding proper self-energies become [compare Eqs. (11.30) and (11.40)]

$$\hbar\Sigma_{11}^\star(p) = n_0\,\Gamma(\tfrac{1}{2}\mathbf{p},\tfrac{1}{2}\mathbf{p},P) + n_0\,\Gamma(-\tfrac{1}{2}\mathbf{p},\tfrac{1}{2}\mathbf{p},P) \approx 8\pi n_0\,a\hbar^2\,m^{-1}$$
$$\hbar\Sigma_{12}^\star(p) = n_0\,\Gamma(\mathbf{p},0,0) \approx 4\pi n_0\,a\hbar^2\,m^{-1} \quad (22.5)$$
$$\hbar\Sigma_{21}^\star(p) = n_0\,\Gamma(0,\mathbf{p},0) \approx 4\pi n_0\,a\hbar^2\,m^{-1}$$

We again see that $\Sigma_{12}^\star(p) = \Sigma_{21}^\star(p)$.

It is interesting to compare these expressions with those for a weakly interacting Bose gas. For a short-range potential, the results of the previous section can be written

$$\hbar\Sigma_{11}^\star(p) = 2n_0\,V(0)$$
$$\hbar\Sigma_{12}^\star(p) = \hbar\Sigma_{21}^\star(p) = n_0\,V(0) \qquad |\mathbf{p}|r_0 \ll 1 \quad (22.6)$$

In Born approximation, the Bethe-Salpeter scattering amplitude reduces to

$$\Gamma_B(\mathbf{p},\mathbf{p}',P) \approx \hbar^2\,\tilde{f}_B(0,0)\,m^{-1} = V(0) = 4\pi a_B\,\hbar^2\,m^{-1} \qquad |\mathbf{p}|r_0 \ll 1 \quad (22.7)$$

and the summation of ladder diagrams therefore replaces the Born approximation a_B by the true scattering length a. [Compare Eqs. (11.24) and (11.25).]

The corresponding chemical potential is determined from Eq. (21.4). In the present approximation, the dominant terms arise from the excitation of two particles out of the condensate, where they interact repeatedly and then drop back into the condensate. This process is shown in Fig. 22.2, where the first term is just that studied in Sec. 21. The mth-order contribution must contain one factor $\hat{V}_2$ to excite the particles, $m - 1$ factors $\hat{V}_7$ to allow them to scatter, and a factor $\hat{V}_1$ to return them to the condensate. Since the operator $\partial\hat{V}/\partial N_0$ does not contain $\hat{V}_7$, it must furnish either the $\hat{V}_1$ or the $\hat{V}_2$. The precise

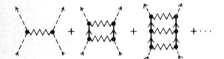

Fig. 22.2 Ladder approximation for chemical potential.

numerical factors can be determined by noting that the contributions in Fig. 22.2 are a subset of the following terms:

$$\mu - n_0 V(0) \approx N_0^{-1} \sum_{m=0}^{\infty} \left(\frac{-i}{\hbar}\right)^m \frac{1}{m!} \int_{-\infty}^{\infty} dt_1 \cdots \int_{-\infty}^{\infty} dt_m$$

$$\times \langle 0|T[\hat{K}_1(t_1) \cdots \hat{K}_1(t_m)\{\hat{V}_1(0) + \hat{V}_2(0)\}]|0\rangle_{\text{connected}}$$

$$= \tfrac{1}{2}i(2\pi)^{-4} \int d^4q\, V(\mathbf{q})\,[G'_{12}(q) + G'_{21}(q)] \tag{22.8}$$

where Eqs. (18.10), (18.11), and (20.14) have been used. Applying our Feynman rules to compute the contribution of the graphs in Fig. 22.2, we obtain the same ladder summation as in the proper self-energy; hence the approximate chemical potential becomes

$$\mu = n_0 \Gamma(0,0,0) \approx 4\pi n_0 a\hbar^2 m^{-1} \tag{22.9}$$

which again satisfies the Hugenholtz-Pines relation (21.6).

It is now possible to evaluate the single-particle Green's function in the region $|\mathbf{p}|a \ll 1$; the calculation is identical with that of Sec. 21 if we again make the replacement $V(0) = 4\pi a_B \hbar^2/m \to 4\pi a\hbar^2/m$ and yields

$$G'(p) = \frac{u_{\mathbf{p}}^2}{p_0 - E_{\mathbf{p}}/\hbar + i\eta} - \frac{v_{\mathbf{p}}^2}{p_0 + E_{\mathbf{p}}/\hbar - i\eta} \tag{22.10}$$

where

$$u_{\mathbf{p}}^2 = \tfrac{1}{2}[E_{\mathbf{p}}^{-1}(\epsilon_{\mathbf{p}}^0 + 4\pi n_0 a\hbar^2 m^{-1}) + 1]$$

$$v_{\mathbf{p}}^2 = \tfrac{1}{2}[E_{\mathbf{p}}^{-1}(\epsilon_{\mathbf{p}}^0 + 4\pi n_0 a\hbar^2 m^{-1}) - 1] \tag{22.11}$$

and

$$E_{\mathbf{p}} = (\epsilon_{\mathbf{p}}^{0^2} + 8\pi n_0 a\hbar^2 \epsilon_{\mathbf{p}}^0 m^{-1})^{\tfrac{1}{2}} \tag{22.12}$$

The total density n is readily found from Eq. (19.12):

$$n - n_0 = \tfrac{1}{2}(2\pi)^{-3} \int d^3q \, [E_q^{-1}(\epsilon_q^0 + 4\pi n_0 a\hbar^2 m^{-1}) - 1]$$
$$= (4\pi^2)^{-1} (8\pi n_0 a)^{\frac{3}{2}} \int_0^\infty y^2 \, dy \, [(y^4 + 2y^2)^{-\frac{1}{2}} (y^2 + 1) - 1]$$
$$= \tfrac{8}{3}\pi^{-\frac{1}{2}}(n_0 a)^{\frac{3}{2}} \approx \tfrac{8}{3}\pi^{-\frac{1}{2}}(na)^{\frac{3}{2}} \tag{22.13}$$

The fractional depletion of the zero-momentum state is given by

$$\frac{n - n_0}{n} = \frac{8}{3}\left(\frac{na^3}{\pi}\right)^{\frac{1}{2}} \tag{22.14}$$

which is small in the present limit. Note that we have used Eq. (22.10) for all $\mathbf{p}$, including the range $|\mathbf{p}|a \gg 1$; it is easily verified that this approximation introduces negligible error in the limit $na^3 \ll 1$ because the integral over $y = (qa)/(8\pi n_0 a^3)^{\frac{1}{2}}$ in Eq. (22.13) converges.

In a similar way, the energy is determined from Eq. (19.24):

$$EV^{-1} = \tfrac{1}{2}\mu n + (32\pi^3)^{-1} \int d^3q \, (\epsilon_q^0 - E_q) \, [E_q^{-1}(\epsilon_q^0 + 4\pi n_0 a\hbar^2 m^{-1}) - 1]$$
$$= \tfrac{1}{2}\mu n + \hbar^2 (8\pi n_0 a)^{\frac{5}{2}} (16\pi^2 m)^{-1} \int_0^\infty y^2 \, dy \, [(2y^3 + 3y)(y^2 + 2)^{-\frac{1}{2}} - 2y^2 - 1]$$
$$= \tfrac{1}{2}\mu n - \frac{64\pi^{\frac{1}{2}}(n_0 a)^{\frac{5}{2}} \hbar^2}{15m} \approx \tfrac{1}{2}\mu n - \frac{64\pi^{\frac{1}{2}}(na)^{\frac{5}{2}} \hbar^2}{15m} \tag{22.15}$$

In both Eqs. (22.13) and (22.15), the integral represents a small correction of order $(n_0 a^3)^{\frac{1}{2}}$ relative to the leading term, and we have therefore set $n_0 \approx n$. The final determination of E and μ is most simply performed with thermodynamics.[1] Assume that

$$\mu = 4\pi na\hbar^2 m^{-1}[1 + \alpha(na^3)^{\frac{1}{2}}] \tag{22.16}$$

where α is a numerical constant that will be determined below. Substitution into Eq. (22.15) yields

$$\frac{E}{V} = \frac{2\pi n^2 a\hbar^2}{m}\left[1 + \alpha(na^3)^{\frac{1}{2}} - \frac{32}{15}\left(\frac{na^3}{\pi}\right)^{\frac{1}{2}}\right] \tag{22.17}$$

The derivative with respect to n defines the chemical potential

$$\mu = \left(\frac{\partial E}{\partial N}\right)_V = \frac{1}{V}\frac{\partial E}{\partial n} = \frac{4\pi na\hbar^2}{m}\left[1 + \tfrac{5}{4}\alpha(na^3)^{\frac{1}{2}} - \frac{8}{3}\left(\frac{na^3}{\pi}\right)^{\frac{1}{2}}\right] \tag{22.18}$$

---

[1] N. M. Hugenholtz and D. Pines, *loc. cit.*

and comparison with Eq. (22.16) shows that $\alpha = 32/3\pi^{\frac{1}{2}}$. In this way we find

$$\frac{E}{V} = \frac{2\pi n^2 a \hbar^2}{m} \left[1 + \frac{128}{15} \left(\frac{na^3}{\pi} \right)^{\frac{1}{2}} \right] \tag{22.19}$$

$$\mu = \frac{4\pi n a \hbar^2}{m} \left[1 + \frac{32}{3} \left(\frac{na^3}{\pi} \right)^{\frac{1}{2}} \right] \tag{22.20}$$

Equation (22.19), which determines the leading correction to the ground-state energy, was first obtained by Lee and Yang.[1] Note that the correction is of order $(na^3)^{\frac{1}{2}}$ and is thus nonanalytic in the interaction. The next-order correction to the ground-state energy has been evaluated by Wu,[2] who finds

$$\frac{E}{V} = \frac{2\pi n^2 a \hbar^2}{m} \left[1 + \frac{128}{15} \left(\frac{na^3}{\pi} \right)^{\frac{1}{2}} + 8(\tfrac{4}{3}\pi - \sqrt{3})(na^3)\ln(na^3) + O(na^3) \right] \tag{22.21}$$

but the coefficient of the last term has never been determined.

The pressure P and compressibility c^2 [see Eq. (16.19)] are easily found from Eq. (22.19)

$$P = -\left(\frac{\partial E}{\partial V} \right)_N = \frac{2\pi n^2 a \hbar^2}{m} \left[1 + \frac{64}{5} \left(\frac{na^3}{\pi} \right)^{\frac{1}{2}} \right] \tag{22.22}$$

$$c^2 = \frac{\partial P}{\partial \rho_m} = \frac{1}{m} \frac{\partial P}{\partial n} = \frac{4\pi n a \hbar^2}{m^2} \left[1 + 16 \left(\frac{na^3}{\pi} \right)^{\frac{1}{2}} \right] \tag{22.23}$$

It is clear that we must have a repulsive potential ($a > 0$) to ensure that the system is stable against collapse. To leading order, the speed of sound agrees with the slope of E_p in Eq. (22.12) as $|\mathbf{p}| \to 0$; in addition, Eq. (22.23) also gives the first-order correction to c. Beliaev has evaluated $E_p/\hbar|\mathbf{p}|$ to next order in $(na^3)^{\frac{1}{2}}$ for small $|\mathbf{p}|$ and verified that it agrees with that found above, but his calculation is very lengthy. Indeed, it has been proved to all orders in perturbation theory that the single-particle excitation spectrum vanishes linearly as $|\mathbf{p}| \to 0$, with a slope equal to the macroscopic speed of sound.[3] This linear dependence can be obtained directly from Eqs. (20.24) to (20.26), the first equality in Eq. (21.2) and the Hugenholtz-Pines relation Eq. (21.6)

$$D(p) \to p_0^2 - 2\omega_p \Sigma_{12}^{\star}(0) \qquad p \to 0 \tag{22.24}$$

where we assume $\Sigma_{12}^{\star}(p)$ is well behaved as $p \to 0$.

[1] T. D. Lee and C. N. Yang, *Phys. Rev.*, **105**:1119 (1957); see also K. A. Brueckner and K. Sawada, *Phys. Rev.*, **106**:1117 (1957).
[2] T. T. Wu, *Phys. Rev.*, **115**:1390 (1959). This value has been verified by N. M. Hugenholtz and D. Pines, *loc. cit.*, who introduced the technique used in Eq. (22.16), and by K. Sawada, *Phys. Rev.*, **116**:1344 (1959).
[3] J. Gavoret and P. Nozières, *Ann. Phys.* (*N.Y.*), **28**:349 (1964); P. C. Hohenberg and P. C. Martin, *Ann. Phys.* (*N.Y.*), **34**:291 (1965).

The ladder approximation (Fig. 22.1) includes all first- and second-order contributions to the proper self-energy. As a result, the corresponding solution of Dyson's equation (20.13) contains all the first- and second-order diagrams for the single-particle Green's function (Figs. 20.2, 20.3, and 21.1). When the remaining third-order corrections to $\Sigma^\star$ are reexpressed in terms of a, the leading contributions contain the factors $n_0^2 a^3$ and do not affect Eqs. (22.14), (22.19), or (22.20). Hence we see that our method correctly treats a dilute Bose gas to order $(na^3)^{\frac{1}{2}}$.

PROBLEMS

6.1. Use Wick's theorem to evaluate $G'(p)$, $G'_{12}(p)$, and $G'_{21}(p)$ to second order in the interaction potential. Hence verify the numerical factors stated in the Feynman rules, and obtain the diagrams in Figs. 20.2, 20.3, and 21.1.

6.2. Iterate the Dyson Eqs. (20.13) consistently to second order in V, and thus reproduce the results of Prob. 6.1.

6.3. (a) Use the Bogoliubov prescription to express the leading contribution to the density correlation function $D(\mathbf{k},\omega)$ in terms of G', G'_{12}, and G'_{21}. Show that the resulting $D(\mathbf{k},\omega)$ has the same spectrum as the exact $G'(\mathbf{k},\omega)$.
(b) Evaluate $D(\mathbf{k},\omega)$ explicitly for a dilute Bose gas with repulsive cores.

6.4. Prove the Hugenholtz–Pines relation [Eq. (21.6)] to second order in V.

6.5. Consider a dense charged spinless Bose gas in a uniform incompressible background (for charge neutrality).
(a) Show that the excitation spectrum is given by $E_k \approx [(\hbar\Omega_{pl})^2 + (\epsilon_k^0)^2]^{\frac{1}{2}}$ where Ω_{pl} is the plasma frequency [Eq. (15.4)]; compare it with that derived in Sec. 22.
(b) Show that the depletion and ground state energy E are given to leading order by‡ $(n - n_0)/n = 0.211 r_s^{\frac{3}{4}}$ and $E/N = -0.803 r_s^{-\frac{3}{4}} e^2/2a_0$, respectively, where $r_s^3 = 3/4\pi na_0^3$, $a_0 = \hbar^2/m_B e^2$, and m_B is the mass of the boson.
(c) Deduce the chemical potential and the pressure in the ground state. Interpret your results.

6.6. Suppose Bose condensation occurs in a state with momentum $\hbar\mathbf{q}$, which describes a condensate in uniform motion with velocity $\mathbf{v} = \hbar\mathbf{q}/m$. Show that the condensate lines now include a factor $e^{\pm i\mathbf{q}\cdot\mathbf{x}}$. Derive the analogs of Eqs. (21.9) and (21.10). Find an expression for the depletion in a dilute hard-sphere gas as a function of $\mathbf{v}$, and compare with Eq. (22.14). Show that the total momentum density is $nm\mathbf{v}$ and not $n_0 m\mathbf{v}$. Explain this result.

‡ L. L. Foldy, *Phys. Rev.*, **124**:649 (1961); **125**:2208 (1962).

Finite-temperature Formalism

7
Field Theory at Finite Temperature

23□TEMPERATURE GREEN'S FUNCTIONS

Our theory of many-particle systems at zero temperature made extensive use of the single-particle Green's function. Knowledge of G provided *both* the complete equilibrium properties of the system *and* the excitation energies of the system containing one more or one less particle. Furthermore, G was readily expressed as a perturbation expansion in the interaction picture. At finite temperatures, however, the analogous single-particle Green's function is essentially more complicated, and it is necessary to separate the calculation into two parts. The first step, which is treated in Chaps. 7 and 8, is the introduction of a *temperature* Green's function $\mathscr{G}$. This function has a simple perturbation expansion similar to that for G at $T = 0$ and also enables us to evaluate the *equilibrium* thermodynamic properties of the system. The second step (Chap. 9)

then relates $\mathscr{G}$ to a *time-dependent* Green's function that describes the linear response of the system to an external perturbation; this last function provides the excitation energies of the system containing one more or one less particle.

DEFINITION

In treating systems at finite temperatures, it will be most convenient to use the grand canonical ensemble, which allows for the possibility of a variable number of particles. With the definition

$$\hat{K} = \hat{H} - \mu\hat{N} \tag{23.1}$$

the grand partition function and statistical operator (see Sec. 4) may be written as

$$Z_G = e^{-\beta\Omega} = \mathrm{Tr}\, e^{-\beta\hat{K}} \tag{23.2}$$

$$\hat{\rho}_G = Z_G^{-1} e^{-\beta\hat{K}} = e^{\beta(\Omega-\hat{K})} \tag{23.3}$$

where we again use the short-hand notation $\beta = 1/k_B T$. The operator $\hat{K}$ may be interpreted as a *grand canonical* hamiltonian; for any Schrödinger operator $\hat{O}_S(\mathbf{x})$, we then introduce the (modified) Heisenberg picture

$$\hat{O}_K(\mathbf{x}\tau) \equiv e^{\hat{K}\tau/\hbar}\, \hat{O}_S(\mathbf{x})\, e^{-\hat{K}\tau/\hbar} \tag{23.4}$$

In particular, the field operators assume the form

$$\hat{\psi}_{K\alpha}(\mathbf{x}\tau) = e^{\hat{K}\tau/\hbar}\, \hat{\psi}_\alpha(\mathbf{x})\, e^{-\hat{K}\tau/\hbar}$$
$$\hat{\psi}^\dagger_{K\alpha}(\mathbf{x}\tau) = e^{\hat{K}\tau/\hbar}\, \hat{\psi}^\dagger_\alpha(\mathbf{x})\, e^{-\hat{K}\tau/\hbar} \tag{23.5}$$

Note that $\hat{\psi}^\dagger_{K\alpha}(\mathbf{x}\tau)$ is *not* the adjoint of $\hat{\psi}_{K\alpha}(\mathbf{x}\tau)$ as long as τ is real.[1] If τ is interpreted as a complex variable, however, it may be analytically continued to a pure imaginary value $\tau = it$. The resulting expression $\hat{\psi}^\dagger_{K\alpha}(\mathbf{x},it)$ then becomes the true adjoint of $\hat{\psi}_{K\alpha}(\mathbf{x},it)$ and is formally identical with the original Heisenberg picture defined in Eq. (6.28), apart from the substitution of $\hat{K}$ for $\hat{H}$.‡ For this reason, Eq. (23.5) is sometimes called an *imaginary-time* operator.

The single-particle temperature Green's function is defined as

$$\mathscr{G}_{\alpha\beta}(\mathbf{x}\tau, \mathbf{x}'\,\tau') \equiv -\mathrm{Tr}\{\hat{\rho}_G\, T_\tau[\hat{\psi}_{K\alpha}(\mathbf{x}\tau)\, \hat{\psi}^\dagger_{K\beta}(\mathbf{x}'\,\tau')]\} \tag{23.6}$$

where $\hat{\rho}_G$ is given in Eq. (23.3). Here the symbol T_τ orders the operators according to their value of τ, with the smallest at the right; T_τ also includes the signature factor $(-1)^P$, where P is the number of permutations of fermion operators needed to restore the original ordering. We emphasize that the trace (Tr) implies that this Green's function $\mathscr{G}$ involves a sum over a complete set of states in the Hilbert space, each contribution being weighted with the operator $\hat{\rho}_G$ (see Sec. 4).

---

[1] To avoid confusion, the adjoint of an operator $\hat{O}$ is explicitly denoted by $[\hat{O}]^\dagger$ in this chapter.
‡ This connection was first pointed out by F. Bloch, *Z. Physik*, **74**:295 (1932).

RELATION TO OBSERVABLES

The temperature Green's function is useful because it enables us to calculate the thermodynamic behavior of the system. If the hamiltonian $\hat{H}$ is time independent, as is usually the case, then $\mathscr{G}$ depends only on the combination $\tau - \tau'$ and not on τ and τ' separately. The proof of this statement is identical with that at $T = 0$ [Eq. (7.6)] and will not be repeated here.

Consider the quantity

$$\sum_\alpha \mathscr{G}_{\alpha\alpha}(\mathbf{x}\tau,\mathbf{x}\tau^+) = \operatorname{tr} \mathscr{G}(\mathbf{x}\tau,\mathbf{x}\tau^+) \tag{23.7}$$

where τ^+ denotes the limiting value $\tau + \eta$ as η approaches zero from positive values, and tr represents the trace of the matrix indices. By definition,

$$
\begin{aligned}
\operatorname{tr} \mathscr{G}(\mathbf{x}\tau,\mathbf{x}\tau^+) &= \mp \sum_\alpha \operatorname{Tr}[\hat{\rho}_G \, \hat{\psi}^\dagger_{K\alpha}(\mathbf{x}\tau) \, \hat{\psi}_{K\alpha}(\mathbf{x}\tau)] \\
&= \mp e^{\beta\Omega} \sum_\alpha \operatorname{Tr}[e^{-\beta K} e^{K\tau/\hbar} \, \hat{\psi}^\dagger_\alpha(\mathbf{x}) \, \hat{\psi}_\alpha(\mathbf{x}) e^{-K\tau/\hbar}] \\
&= \mp e^{\beta\Omega} \sum_\alpha \operatorname{Tr}[e^{-\beta K} \, \hat{\psi}^\dagger_\alpha(\mathbf{x}) \, \hat{\psi}_\alpha(\mathbf{x})] \\
&= \mp \langle \hat{n}(\mathbf{x}) \rangle
\end{aligned}
\tag{23.8}
$$

where the cyclic property of the trace has been used $[\operatorname{Tr}(ABC) = \operatorname{Tr}(BCA) = \operatorname{Tr}(CAB)]$, along with the commutativity of any two functions of the same operator. As before, our convention is that upper (lower) signs refer to bosons (fermions). The mean number of particles in the system is given by

$$N(T,V,\mu) = \mp \int d^3x \operatorname{tr} \mathscr{G}(\mathbf{x}\tau,\mathbf{x}\tau^+) \tag{23.9}$$

and is an *explicit* function of the variables specified. Similarly, the ensemble average of any one-body operator is expressible in terms of $\mathscr{G}$. With the notation of Eq. (7.7), we have

$$
\begin{aligned}
\langle \hat{J} \rangle &= \operatorname{Tr}(\hat{\rho}_G \hat{J}) \\
&= \sum_{\alpha\beta} \int d^3x \lim_{\mathbf{x}'\to\mathbf{x}} J_{\beta\alpha}(\mathbf{x}) \operatorname{Tr}[\hat{\rho}_G \, \hat{\psi}^\dagger_\beta(\mathbf{x}') \, \hat{\psi}_\alpha(\mathbf{x})] \\
&= \mp \sum_{\alpha\beta} \int d^3x \lim_{\mathbf{x}'\to\mathbf{x}} \lim_{\tau'\to\tau^+} J_{\beta\alpha}(\mathbf{x}) \, \mathscr{G}_{\alpha\beta}(\mathbf{x}\tau, \mathbf{x}'\,\tau') \\
&= \mp \int d^3x \lim_{\mathbf{x}'\to\mathbf{x}} \lim_{\tau'\to\tau^+} \operatorname{tr}[J(\mathbf{x}) \, \mathscr{G}(\mathbf{x}\tau, \mathbf{x}'\,\tau')]
\end{aligned}
\tag{23.10}
$$

Particular examples of interest are

$$\langle \hat{\boldsymbol{\sigma}} \rangle = \mp \int d^3x \operatorname{tr}[\boldsymbol{\sigma} \mathscr{G}(\mathbf{x}\tau,\mathbf{x}\tau^+)] \tag{23.11a}$$

$$\langle \hat{T} \rangle = \mp \int d^3x \lim_{\mathbf{x}'\to\mathbf{x}} \frac{-\hbar^2 \nabla^2}{2m} \operatorname{tr} \mathscr{G}(\mathbf{x}\tau, \mathbf{x}'\,\tau^+) \tag{23.11b}$$

Two-body operators are also important, but the ensemble average of such an operator usually requires a two-particle temperature Green's function. In the special case that the hamiltonian consists of a sum of kinetic and two-body potential energies [Eq. (7.12)], however, the mean potential energy can be expressed solely in terms of $\mathscr{G}$, exactly as in Eq. (7.22). The calculation starts from the Heisenberg equation of motion

$$\hbar \frac{\partial}{\partial \tau} \hat{\psi}_{K\alpha}(\mathbf{x}\tau) = \hbar \frac{\partial}{\partial \tau} [e^{\hat{K}\tau/\hbar} \hat{\psi}_\alpha(\mathbf{x}) e^{-\hat{K}\tau/\hbar}]$$

$$= [\hat{K}, \hat{\psi}_{K\alpha}(\mathbf{x}\tau)] \tag{23.12}$$

For simplicity, we shall assume that the potential is spin independent [compare Eq. (10.2)], as is usually the case in applications of the finite-temperature theory. It is straightforward to evaluate the commutator in Eq. (23.12), which yields [compare Eq. (7.19)]

$$\hbar \frac{\partial}{\partial \tau} \hat{\psi}_{K\alpha}(\mathbf{x}\tau) = \frac{\hbar^2 \nabla^2}{2m} \hat{\psi}_{K\alpha}(\mathbf{x}\tau) + \mu \hat{\psi}_{K\alpha}(\mathbf{x}\tau)$$

$$- \int d^3x'' \, \hat{\psi}_{K\gamma}^\dagger(\mathbf{x}'' \tau) \hat{\psi}_{K\gamma}(\mathbf{x}'' \tau) V(\mathbf{x} - \mathbf{x}'') \hat{\psi}_{K\alpha}(\mathbf{x}\tau) \tag{23.13}$$

Thus the single-particle Green's function satisfies the relation

$$\lim_{\tau' \to \tau^+} \left[\hbar \frac{\partial}{\partial \tau} \mathscr{G}_{\alpha\beta}(\mathbf{x}\tau, \mathbf{x}' \tau') \right] = \mp \mathrm{Tr} \left[\hat{\rho}_G \, \hat{\psi}_{K\beta}^\dagger(\mathbf{x}' \tau) \hbar \frac{\partial}{\partial \tau} \hat{\psi}_{K\alpha}(\mathbf{x}\tau) \right]$$

$$= \mp \mathrm{Tr} \left\{ \hat{\rho}_G \, \hat{\psi}_{K\beta}^\dagger(\mathbf{x}' \tau) \left[\left(\frac{\hbar^2 \nabla^2}{2m} + \mu \right) \hat{\psi}_{K\alpha}(\mathbf{x}\tau) \right. \right.$$

$$\left. \left. - \int d^3x'' \, \hat{\psi}_{K\gamma}^\dagger(\mathbf{x}'' \tau) \hat{\psi}_{K\gamma}(\mathbf{x}'' \tau) V(\mathbf{x} - \mathbf{x}'') \hat{\psi}_{K\alpha}(\mathbf{x}\tau) \right] \right\}$$

The last term is essentially the quantity of interest, and we find

$$\langle \hat{V} \rangle \equiv \tfrac{1}{2} \int d^3x \, d^3x'' \, V(\mathbf{x} - \mathbf{x}'') \, \mathrm{Tr} \, [\hat{\rho}_G \, \hat{\psi}_\alpha^\dagger(\mathbf{x}) \hat{\psi}_\gamma^\dagger(\mathbf{x}'') \hat{\psi}_\gamma(\mathbf{x}'') \hat{\psi}_\alpha(\mathbf{x})]$$

$$= \mp \tfrac{1}{2} \int d^3x \lim_{\mathbf{x}' \to \mathbf{x}} \lim_{\tau' \to \tau^+} \left[-\hbar \frac{\partial}{\partial \tau} + \frac{\hbar^2 \nabla^2}{2m} + \mu \right] \mathrm{tr} \, \mathscr{G}(\mathbf{x}\tau, \mathbf{x}' \tau') \tag{23.14}$$

where the cyclic properties of the trace have been used to change from the Heisenberg to the Schrödinger picture. Equations (23.11b) and (23.14) may be combined to provide the ensemble average of the hamiltonian, which is just the internal energy E (see Sec. 4).

$$E = \langle \hat{H} \rangle = \langle \hat{T} + \hat{V} \rangle$$

$$= \mp \tfrac{1}{2} \int d^3x \lim_{\mathbf{x}' \to \mathbf{x}} \lim_{\tau' \to \tau^+} \left[-\hbar \frac{\partial}{\partial \tau} - \frac{\hbar^2 \nabla^2}{2m} + \mu \right] \mathrm{tr} \, \mathscr{G}(\mathbf{x}\tau, \mathbf{x}' \tau') \tag{23.15}$$

The mean interaction energy can also be used to obtain the thermodynamic potential Ω, by means of an integration over a variable coupling constant. If

the hamiltonian is written as

$$\hat{H}(\lambda) = \hat{H}_0 + \lambda \hat{H}_1 \qquad \hat{K}(\lambda) = \hat{K}_0 + \lambda \hat{K}_1 \tag{23.16}$$

where $\hat{K}_0 = \hat{H}_0 - \mu \hat{N}$ and $\hat{K}_1 = \hat{H}_1$, then the value $\lambda = 1$ describes the actual physical system, while $\lambda = 0$ describes some simpler system. For most applications, $\hat{H}_0$ will be the hamiltonian for noninteracting particles, but this is by no means necessary. Define the grand partition function for $K(\lambda)$:

$$Z_{G\lambda} = e^{-\beta \Omega_\lambda} = \mathrm{Tr}\, e^{-\beta \hat{K}(\lambda)} \tag{23.17}$$

The derivative with respect to λ is then given by

$$\frac{\partial \Omega_\lambda}{\partial \lambda} = -k_B T Z_{G\lambda}^{-1} \frac{\partial Z_{G\lambda}}{\partial \lambda} \tag{23.18}$$

The immediate problem is how to calculate the derivative. Expand the exponential operator in Eq. (23.17)

$$Z_{G\lambda} = \sum_{n=0}^{\infty} (n!)^{-1} (-\beta)^n \, \mathrm{Tr}\, (\hat{K}_0 + \lambda \hat{K}_1)^n$$

so that

$$\frac{\partial Z_{G\lambda}}{\partial \lambda} = \sum_{n=1}^{\infty} (n!)^{-1} (-\beta)^n \frac{\partial}{\partial \lambda} \mathrm{Tr}\, (\hat{K}_0 + \lambda \hat{K}_1)^n$$

In the nth term of the series, the derivative must be applied to each of the n factors $\hat{K}_0 + \lambda \hat{K}_1$ in turn, which yields n terms with the single factor $\hat{K}_1$ in all possible positions. The cyclic property of the trace allows each of these n terms to be reordered showing that they are identical. In this way, the derivative becomes

$$\frac{\partial Z_{G\lambda}}{\partial \lambda} = \sum_{n=1}^{\infty} (n!)^{-1} (-\beta)^n n \, \mathrm{Tr}\, [(\hat{K}_0 + \lambda \hat{K}_1)^{n-1} \hat{K}_1]$$

$$= -\beta \sum_{n=1}^{\infty} [(n-1)!]^{-1} (-\beta)^{n-1} \, \mathrm{Tr}\, [(\hat{K}_0 + \lambda \hat{K}_1)^{n-1} \hat{K}_1]$$

$$= -\beta \, \mathrm{Tr}\, (e^{-\beta \hat{K}(\lambda)} \hat{K}_1)$$

$$= -\frac{\beta}{\lambda} e^{-\beta \Omega_\lambda} \langle \lambda \hat{K}_1 \rangle_\lambda \tag{23.19}$$

where $\langle \cdots \rangle_\lambda$ denotes the ensemble average with the operator $\hat{K}(\lambda)$. A combination of Eqs. (23.18) and (23.19) yields

$$\frac{\partial \Omega_\lambda}{\partial \lambda} = \lambda^{-1} \langle \lambda \hat{K}_1 \rangle_\lambda = \lambda^{-1} \langle \lambda \hat{H}_1 \rangle_\lambda \tag{23.20}$$

Integrate from $\lambda = 0$ to $\lambda = 1$

$$\Omega - \Omega_0 = \int_0^1 \lambda^{-1} \, d\lambda \, \langle \lambda \hat{H}_1 \rangle_\lambda \tag{23.21}$$

The quantity Ω_0 is the thermodynamic potential for the hamiltonian $\hat{H}_0$ and is presumably easy to calculate; Eq. (23.21) therefore provides an expression for Ω in the interacting system in terms of the interaction energy for a system with variable coupling constant. This formula may be rewritten with Eq. (23.14) in terms of the single-particle Green's function $\mathscr{G}^\lambda$ for a system with hamiltonian $\hat{H}(\lambda)$

$$\Omega(T,V,\mu) = \Omega_0(T,V,\mu) + \int_0^1 \lambda^{-1}\, d\lambda \int d^3 x$$

$$\times \lim_{x'\to x}\lim_{\tau'\to\tau^+} \frac{1}{2}\left[-\hbar\frac{\partial}{\partial\tau} + \frac{\hbar^2\nabla^2}{2m} + \mu\right] \text{tr}\,\mathscr{G}^\lambda(x\tau, x'\,\tau') \quad (23.22)$$

which will be useful in studying the thermodynamics of an electron gas (Sec. 30). It is notable that Eqs. (23.15) and (23.22) represent different physical quantities at finite temperatures, in contrast with the situation at zero temperature [Eqs. (7.23) and (7.31)]. Furthermore, the thermodynamic potential at finite temperature requires a coupling-constant integration, as seen in Eq. (23.22).

EXAMPLE: NONINTERACTING SYSTEM

As a simple example, it is interesting to compute the temperature Green's function $\mathscr{G}^0_{\alpha\beta}(x\tau, x'\,\tau')$ for a noninteracting system. In the absence of external fields, the single-particle states are plane waves, so that [compare Eq. (7.33)]

$$\hat{\psi}(\mathbf{x}) = V^{-\frac{1}{2}} \sum_{\mathbf{k}\lambda} e^{i\mathbf{k}\cdot\mathbf{x}} \eta_\lambda a_{\mathbf{k}\lambda}$$

$$\hat{\psi}^\dagger(\mathbf{x}) = V^{-\frac{1}{2}} \sum_{\mathbf{k}\lambda} e^{-i\mathbf{k}\cdot\mathbf{x}} \eta_\lambda^\dagger a_{\mathbf{k}\lambda}^\dagger \qquad (23.23)$$

where the spin indices and spin wave functions are absent for spin-zero bosons. Since we now consider ensemble averages rather than ground-state expectation values, the canonical transformation to particles and holes for fermions offers no advantage, and the relations in Eq. (7.40) no longer stand on a special footing. The Heisenberg field operators for the noninteracting system are thus

$$\hat{\psi}_K(\mathbf{x}\tau) = V^{-\frac{1}{2}} \sum_{\mathbf{k}\lambda} e^{i\mathbf{k}\cdot\mathbf{x}} \eta_\lambda e^{\hat{K}_0\tau/\hbar} a_{\mathbf{k}\lambda} e^{-\hat{K}_0\tau/\hbar}$$

$$\hat{\psi}_K^\dagger(\mathbf{x}\tau) = V^{-\frac{1}{2}} \sum_{\mathbf{k}\lambda} e^{-i\mathbf{k}\cdot\mathbf{x}} \eta_\lambda^\dagger e^{\hat{K}_0\tau/\hbar} a_{\mathbf{k}\lambda}^\dagger e^{-\hat{K}_0\tau/\hbar} \qquad (23.24)$$

Although the operators on the right can be simplified by direct calculation, it is easier to use the equation of motion

$$\hbar\frac{\partial}{\partial\tau} a_{\mathbf{k}\lambda}(\tau) = e^{\hat{K}_0\tau/\hbar}[\hat{K}_0, a_{\mathbf{k}\lambda}] e^{-\hat{K}_0\tau/\hbar}$$

$$= -(\epsilon_k^0 - \mu) a_{\mathbf{k}\lambda}(\tau) \qquad (23.25)$$

where $\epsilon_k^0 = \hbar^2 k^2 / 2m$. This differential equation is easily integrated:

$$a_{k\lambda}(\tau) = a_{k\lambda} \exp \frac{-(\epsilon_k^0 - \mu)\tau}{\hbar} \qquad (23.26a)$$

and similarly

$$a_{k\lambda}^\dagger(\tau) = a_{k\lambda}^\dagger \exp \frac{(\epsilon_k^0 - \mu)\tau}{\hbar} \qquad (23.26b)$$

Note again that Eq. (23.26b) is not the adjoint of Eq. (23.26a).

The noninteracting temperature Green's function is defined as

$$\mathscr{G}_{\alpha\beta}^0(\mathbf{x}\tau, \mathbf{x}'\,\tau') = -e^{\beta\Omega_0} \operatorname{Tr}\{e^{-\beta \hat{K}_0} T_\tau[\hat{\psi}_{K\alpha}(\mathbf{x}\tau)\,\hat{\psi}_{K\beta}^\dagger(\mathbf{x}'\,\tau')]\} \qquad (23.27)$$

and, for definiteness, we first consider the case $\tau > \tau'$:

$$\mathscr{G}_{\alpha\beta}^0(\mathbf{x}\tau, \mathbf{x}'\,\tau') = -V^{-1} \sum_{\mathbf{k}\mathbf{k}'} \sum_{\lambda\lambda'} e^{i(\mathbf{k}\cdot\mathbf{x} - \mathbf{k}'\cdot\mathbf{x}')}(\eta_\lambda)_\alpha (\eta_{\lambda'}^\dagger)_\beta$$

$$\times \exp\left[\frac{-(\epsilon_k^0 - \mu)\tau}{\hbar} + \frac{(\epsilon_{k'}^0 - \mu)\tau'}{\hbar}\right]\langle a_{k\lambda} a_{k'\lambda'}^\dagger \rangle_0$$

$$= -V^{-1} \delta_{\alpha\beta} \sum_{\mathbf{k}} e^{i\mathbf{k}\cdot(\mathbf{x} - \mathbf{x}')} \exp\left[\frac{-(\epsilon_k^0 - \mu)(\tau - \tau')}{\hbar}\right]\langle a_{k\lambda} a_{k\lambda}^\dagger \rangle_0$$

which follows from the translational and rotational invariance of the non-interacting system. In addition, the ensemble average may be rewritten as

$$\langle a_{k\lambda} a_{k\lambda}^\dagger \rangle_0 = 1 \pm \langle a_{k\lambda}^\dagger a_{k\lambda} \rangle_0 = 1 \pm n_k^0 \qquad (23.28)$$

where the upper (lower) sign refers to bosons (fermions) and n_k^0 is known from statistical mechanics [Eqs. (5.9) and (5.12)] to be

$$n_k^0 = \{\exp[\beta(\epsilon_k^0 - \mu)] \mp 1\}^{-1} \qquad (23.29)$$

These equations may be combined to yield

$$\mathscr{G}_{\alpha\beta}^0(\mathbf{x}\tau, \mathbf{x}'\,\tau') = -\delta_{\alpha\beta} V^{-1} \sum_{\mathbf{k}} e^{i\mathbf{k}\cdot(\mathbf{x} - \mathbf{x}')} \exp\left[\frac{-(\epsilon_k^0 - \mu)(\tau - \tau')}{\hbar}\right](1 \pm n_k^0)$$

$$\tau > \tau' \quad (23.30a)$$

An identical calculation for $\tau < \tau'$ gives

$$\mathscr{G}_{\alpha\beta}^0(\mathbf{x}\tau, \mathbf{x}'\,\tau') = \mp \delta_{\alpha\beta} V^{-1} \sum_{\mathbf{k}} e^{i\mathbf{k}\cdot(\mathbf{x} - \mathbf{x}')} \exp\left[\frac{-(\epsilon_k^0 - \mu)(\tau - \tau')}{\hbar}\right]n_k^0$$

$$\tau < \tau' \quad (23.30b)$$

As expected, $\mathscr{G}^0$ is diagonal in the matrix indices and depends only on the combinations $(\mathbf{x} - \mathbf{x}', \tau - \tau')$. It is interesting to evaluate the mean number of

particles N_0 and mean energy E_0 with Eqs. (23.9) and (23.15); a straightforward calculation reproduces the results in Sec. 5.

$$N_0(T,V,\mu) = \sum_k n_k^0 = \sum_k \{\exp[\beta(\epsilon_k^0 - \mu)] \mp 1\}^{-1} \qquad (23.31a)$$

$$E_0(T,V,\mu) = \sum_k \epsilon_k^0 n_k^0 = \sum_k \epsilon_k^0 \{\exp[\beta(\epsilon_k^0 - \mu)] \mp 1\}^{-1} \qquad (23.31b)$$

24□PERTURBATION THEORY AND WICK'S THEOREM FOR FINITE TEMPERATURES

The temperature Green's function is useful only to the extent that it is calculable from the microscopic hamiltonian.   Just as in the zero-temperature formalism, it is convenient to introduce an interaction picture, which then serves as a useful basis for perturbation calculations.

INTERACTION PICTURE

For any operator $\hat{O}_S$ in the Schrödinger picture, we formally define the interaction picture $\hat{O}_I(\tau)$ and Heisenberg picture $\hat{O}_K(\tau)$ by the equations

$$\hat{O}_I(\tau) \equiv e^{\hat{K}_0 \tau/\hbar} \hat{O}_S e^{-\hat{K}_0 \tau/\hbar}$$
$$\hat{O}_K(\tau) \equiv e^{\hat{K}\tau/\hbar} \hat{O}_S e^{-\hat{K}\tau/\hbar} \qquad (24.1)$$

The two pictures are simply related [compare Eq. (6.31)]:

$$\hat{O}_K(\tau) = e^{\hat{K}\tau/\hbar} e^{-\hat{K}_0\tau/\hbar} \hat{O}_I(\tau) e^{\hat{K}_0\tau/\hbar} e^{-\hat{K}\tau/\hbar}$$
$$= \hat{\mathcal{U}}(0,\tau) \hat{O}_I(\tau) \hat{\mathcal{U}}(\tau,0) \qquad (24.2)$$

where the operator $\hat{\mathcal{U}}$ is defined by

$$\hat{\mathcal{U}}(\tau_1,\tau_2) \equiv e^{\hat{K}_0\tau_1/\hbar} e^{-\hat{K}(\tau_1-\tau_2)/\hbar} e^{-\hat{K}_0\tau_2/\hbar} \qquad (24.3)$$

Note that $\hat{\mathcal{U}}$ is *not* unitary, but it still satisfies the group property

$$\hat{\mathcal{U}}(\tau_1,\tau_2) \hat{\mathcal{U}}(\tau_2,\tau_3) = \hat{\mathcal{U}}(\tau_1,\tau_3) \qquad (24.4)$$

and the boundary condition

$$\hat{\mathcal{U}}(\tau_1,\tau_1) = 1 \qquad (24.5)$$

In addition, the "time" derivative of $\hat{\mathcal{U}}$ is easily calculated:

$$\hbar \frac{\partial}{\partial \tau} \hat{\mathcal{U}}(\tau,\tau') = e^{\hat{K}_0\tau/\hbar}(\hat{K}_0 - \hat{K}) e^{-\hat{K}(\tau-\tau')/\hbar} e^{-\hat{K}_0\tau'/\hbar}$$
$$= e^{\hat{K}_0\tau/\hbar}(\hat{K}_0 - \hat{K}) e^{-\hat{K}_0\tau/\hbar} \hat{\mathcal{U}}(\tau,\tau')$$
$$= -\hat{K}_1(\tau) \hat{\mathcal{U}}(\tau,\tau') \qquad (24.6)$$

where

$$\hat{K}_1(\tau) = e^{\hat{K}_0 \tau / \hbar} \, \hat{K}_1 e^{-\hat{K}_0 \tau / \hbar} \tag{24.7}$$

It follows that the operator $\mathscr{U}(\tau, \tau')$ obeys essentially the same differential equation as the unitary operator introduced in Eq. (6.11), and we may immediately write down the solution

$$\mathscr{U}(\tau, \tau') = \sum_{n=0}^{\infty} \left(-\frac{1}{\hbar}\right)^n \frac{1}{n!} \int_{\tau'}^{\tau} d\tau_1 \cdots \int_{\tau'}^{\tau} d\tau_n \, T_\tau [\hat{K}_1(\tau_1) \cdots \hat{K}_1(\tau_n)] \tag{24.8}$$

Finally, Eq. (24.3) may be rewritten as

$$e^{-\hat{K}\tau/\hbar} = e^{-\hat{K}_0 \tau/\hbar} \, \mathscr{U}(\tau, 0) \tag{24.9}$$

If τ is set equal to $\beta\hbar$, Eq. (24.9) provides a perturbation expansion for the grand partition function

$$
\begin{aligned}
e^{-\beta\Omega} &= \operatorname{Tr} e^{-\beta\hat{K}} \\
&= \operatorname{Tr} \left[e^{-\beta\hat{K}_0} \, \mathscr{U}(\beta\hbar, 0) \right] \\
&= \sum_{n=0}^{\infty} \left(-\frac{1}{\hbar}\right)^n \frac{1}{n!} \int_0^{\beta\hbar} d\tau_1 \cdots \int_0^{\beta\hbar} d\tau_n \, \operatorname{Tr} \{ e^{-\beta\hat{K}_0} \, T_\tau [\hat{K}_1(\tau_1) \cdots \hat{K}_1(\tau_n)] \}
\end{aligned}
\tag{24.10}
$$

where all of the integrals extend over a finite domain. In practice, this equation is less useful for diagrammatic analysis than Eq. (23.22) because of difficulties associated with counting the disconnected diagrams.

The exact temperature Green's function now may be rewritten in the interaction picture. If $\tau > \tau'$, we have

$$
\begin{aligned}
\mathscr{G}_{\alpha\beta}(\mathbf{x}\tau, \mathbf{x}'\,\tau') &= -e^{\beta\Omega} \operatorname{Tr} \left[e^{-\beta\hat{K}} \, \hat{\psi}_{K\alpha}(\mathbf{x}\tau) \, \hat{\psi}^\dagger_{K\beta}(\mathbf{x}'\,\tau') \right] \\
&= -e^{\beta\Omega} \operatorname{Tr} \{ e^{-\beta\hat{K}_0} \, \mathscr{U}(\beta\hbar, 0) \, [\mathscr{U}(0,\tau) \, \hat{\psi}_{I\alpha}(\mathbf{x}\tau) \, \mathscr{U}(\tau, 0)] \\
&\qquad\qquad \times [\mathscr{U}(0,\tau') \, \hat{\psi}^\dagger_{I\beta}(\mathbf{x}'\,\tau') \, \mathscr{U}(\tau', 0)] \} \\
&= \frac{ - \operatorname{Tr} \left[e^{-\beta\hat{K}_0} \, \mathscr{U}(\beta\hbar, \tau) \, \hat{\psi}_{I\alpha}(\mathbf{x}\tau) \, \mathscr{U}(\tau, \tau') \, \hat{\psi}^\dagger_{I\beta}(\mathbf{x}'\,\tau') \, \mathscr{U}(\tau', 0) \right] }{ \operatorname{Tr} \left[e^{-\beta\hat{K}_0} \, \mathscr{U}(\beta\hbar, 0) \right] }
\end{aligned}
\tag{24.11}
$$

where Eq. (24.9) has been used with $\tau = \beta\hbar$. A similar calculation for $\tau < \tau'$ yields

$$\mathscr{G}_{\alpha\beta}(\mathbf{x}\tau, \mathbf{x}'\,\tau') = \frac{\mp \operatorname{Tr} \left[e^{-\beta\hat{K}_0} \, \mathscr{U}(\beta\hbar, \tau') \, \hat{\psi}^\dagger_{I\beta}(\mathbf{x}'\,\tau') \, \mathscr{U}(\tau', \tau) \, \hat{\psi}_{I\alpha}(\mathbf{x}\tau) \, \mathscr{U}(\tau, 0) \right]}{\operatorname{Tr} \left[e^{-\beta\hat{K}_0} \, \mathscr{U}(\beta\hbar, 0) \right]} \tag{24.12}$$

Equations (24.11) and (24.12) have precisely the structure analyzed in Eq. (8.8), and it is evident that they may be combined in the form

$$\mathcal{G}_{\alpha\beta}(\mathbf{x}\tau,\mathbf{x}'\,\tau') =$$

$$-\operatorname{Tr}\left\{e^{-\beta \hat{K}_0}\sum_{n=0}^{\infty}(-\hbar)^{-n}(n!)^{-1}\int_0^{\beta\hbar}d\tau_1\cdots\int_0^{\beta\hbar}d\tau_n\,T_\tau[\hat{K}_1(\tau_1)\,\cdots \right.$$
$$\left. \hat{K}_1(\tau_n)\,\hat{\psi}_{I\alpha}(\mathbf{x}\tau)\,\hat{\psi}^\dagger_{I\beta}(\mathbf{x}'\,\tau')]\right\}$$

over

$$\operatorname{Tr}\left\{e^{-\beta \hat{K}_0}\sum_{n=0}^{\infty}(-\hbar)^{-n}(n!)^{-1}\int_0^{\beta\hbar}d\tau_1\cdots\int_0^{\beta\hbar}d\tau_n\,T_\tau[\hat{K}_1(\tau_1)\,\cdots\,\hat{K}_1(\tau_n)]\right\}$$

$$(24.13)$$

As noted in Eq. (24.10), the denominator is just the perturbation expansion of $e^{-\beta\Omega}$; in the present form, however, it serves to eliminate all disconnected diagrams, exactly as in the zero-temperature formalism [compare Eqs. (9.3) to (9.5)].

PERIODICITY OF $\mathcal{G}$

Equation (24.13) shows that the integrations over the dummy variables τ_i all extend from 0 to $\beta\hbar$. We shall see that it is also sufficient to restrict τ and τ' to this interval, so that the difference $\tau-\tau'$ satisfies the condition $-\beta\hbar < \tau-\tau' < \beta\hbar$. In this limited domain, the temperature Green's function displays a remarkable *periodicity*, which is fundamental to all of the subsequent work. For definiteness, suppose τ' fixed ($0 < \tau' < \beta\hbar$). A simple calculation shows that

$$\mathcal{G}_{\alpha\beta}(\mathbf{x}0,\mathbf{x}'\,\tau') = \mp e^{\beta\Omega}\operatorname{Tr}\{e^{-\beta \hat{K}}\,\hat{\psi}^\dagger_{K\beta}(\mathbf{x}'\,\tau')\,\hat{\psi}_{K\alpha}(\mathbf{x}0)\}$$
$$= \mp e^{\beta\Omega}\operatorname{Tr}\{\hat{\psi}_{K\alpha}(\mathbf{x}0)\,e^{-\beta \hat{K}}\,\hat{\psi}^\dagger_{K\beta}(\mathbf{x}'\,\tau')\}$$
$$= \mp e^{\beta\Omega}\operatorname{Tr}\{e^{-\beta \hat{K}}\,\hat{\psi}_{K\alpha}(\mathbf{x}\beta\hbar)\,\hat{\psi}^\dagger_{K\beta}(\mathbf{x}'\,\tau')\}$$
$$= \pm\mathcal{G}_{\alpha\beta}(\mathbf{x}\beta\hbar,\mathbf{x}'\,\tau') \qquad (24.14a)$$

where the cyclic property of the trace has been used in the second line. A similar analysis yields

$$\mathcal{G}_{\alpha\beta}(\mathbf{x}\tau,\mathbf{x}'\,0) = \pm\mathcal{G}_{\alpha\beta}(\mathbf{x}\tau,\mathbf{x}'\,\beta\hbar) \qquad (24.14b)$$

so that *the single-particle temperature Green's function for bosons (fermions) is periodic (antiperiodic) in each time variable with period $\beta\hbar$ in the range $0\leqslant\tau$, $\tau'\leqslant\beta\hbar$.* This relation is very important for the following analysis, and it incorporates the precise form of the statistical operator $\hat{\rho}_G$ in the grand canonical ensemble.

In the usual situation, $\hat{H}$ is time independent, and $\mathcal{G}$ depends only on the combination $\tau-\tau'$. Equation (24.14) may then be rewritten as

$$\mathcal{G}_{\alpha\beta}(\mathbf{x},\mathbf{x}',\tau-\tau' < 0) = \pm\mathcal{G}_{\alpha\beta}(\mathbf{x},\mathbf{x}',\tau-\tau'+\beta\hbar) \qquad (24.15)$$

The condition $\tau - \tau' < 0$ necessarily implies $\tau - \tau' + \beta\hbar > 0$ in the restricted range $0 \leqslant \tau, \tau' \leqslant \beta\hbar$. It is interesting to see how Eq. (24.15) is satisfied for the non-interacting Green's function $\mathscr{G}^0$. Comparison of Eqs. (23.30a) and (23.30b) yields the relation

$$n_k^0 \, e^{\beta(\epsilon_k^0 - \mu)} = 1 \pm n_k^0 \tag{24.16}$$

which may also be verified directly with Eq. (23.29).

PROOF OF WICK'S THEOREM

It is apparent that the perturbation expansion for the temperature Green's function $\mathscr{G}$ [Eq. (24.13)] is very similar to that for the zero-temperature Green's function G [Eq. (8.9)]. In that case, the expansion could be greatly simplified with Wick's theorem, which provided a prescription for relating a T product of interaction-picture operators to the normal-ordered product of the same operators. The ground-state expectation value of the normal products vanished identically, so that G contained *only* fully contracted terms. Unfortunately, no such simplification occurs at finite temperature, because the *ensemble* average of the normal product is zero only at zero temperature. Nevertheless, as first proved by Matsubara,[1] there exists a generalized Wick's theorem that allows a diagrammatic expansion of $\mathscr{G}$. This generalized Wick's theorem deals only with the ensemble average of operators and relies on the detailed form of the statistical operator $e^{-\beta \hat{K}_0}$. It therefore differs from the original Wick's theorem, which is an *operator identity* valid for arbitrary matrix elements.

Before we consider the general theorem, it is helpful to examine the first few terms of Eq. (24.13). The numerator may be written as

$$-\mathrm{Tr}\{e^{-\beta \hat{K}_0} T_\tau [\hat{\psi}_{I\alpha}(\mathbf{x}\tau) \, \hat{\psi}_{I\beta}^\dagger(\mathbf{x}' \, \tau')]\}$$
$$+ \hbar^{-1} \mathrm{Tr}\left\{e^{-\beta \hat{K}_0} \int_0^{\beta\hbar} d\tau_1 \, T_\tau \, [\hat{K}_1(\tau_1) \, \hat{\psi}_{I\alpha}(\mathbf{x}\tau) \, \hat{\psi}_{I\beta}^\dagger(\mathbf{x}' \, \tau')]\right\} + \cdots \tag{24.17}$$

Here the first term is $e^{-\beta \Omega_0} \mathscr{G}_{\alpha\beta}^0(\mathbf{x}\tau, \mathbf{x}' \tau')$ and is exact if $\hat{K}_1 = 0$. In the usual situation, $\hat{K}_1$ contains a spatial integral of four field operators in the interaction picture, and the second term of Eq. (24.17) involves the ensemble average of six field operators, evaluated with the statistical operator $e^{-\beta \hat{K}_0}$. This general structure occurs in all orders, and the generalized Wick's theorem is designed precisely to handle such problems.

Although the unperturbed system is frequently homogeneous, many examples of interest are inhomogeneous, and we shall therefore use a general single-particle basis $\{\varphi_j^0(\mathbf{x})\}$ for the interaction-picture operators. As in Sec. 2,

---

[1] T. Matsubara, *Prog. Theoret. Phys. (Kyoto)*, **14**:351 (1955); the present proof follows that of M. Gaudin, *Nucl. Phys.*, **15**:89 (1960).

the field operators are written as

$$\hat{\psi}(\mathbf{x}) = \sum_j \varphi_j^0(\mathbf{x}) \, a_j$$

$$\hat{\psi}^\dagger(\mathbf{x}) = \sum_j \varphi_j^0(\mathbf{x})^\dagger \, a_j^\dagger \qquad (24.18)$$

where the eigenfunctions satisfy the eigenvalue equation

$$K_0 \, \varphi_j^0(\mathbf{x}) = (\epsilon_j^0 - \mu) \, \varphi_j^0(\mathbf{x}) \qquad (24.19)$$

and the index j includes both spin and spatial quantum numbers. With the convenient abbreviation

$$e_j \equiv \epsilon_j^0 - \mu \qquad (24.20)$$

the interaction picture of Eq. (24.18) becomes

$$\hat{\psi}_I(\mathbf{x}\tau) = \sum_j \varphi_j^0(\mathbf{x}) \, a_j \, e^{-e_j \tau / \hbar}$$

$$\hat{\psi}_I^\dagger(\mathbf{x}\tau) = \sum_j \varphi_j^0(\mathbf{x})^\dagger \, a_j^\dagger \, e^{e_j \tau / \hbar} \qquad (24.21)$$

The corresponding single-particle Green's function is readily evaluated as

$$\mathscr{G}^0(\mathbf{x}\tau, \mathbf{x}'\tau') = -\sum_j \varphi_j^0(\mathbf{x}) \, \varphi_j^0(\mathbf{x}')^\dagger \, e^{-e_j(\tau-\tau')/\hbar} \times \begin{cases} 1 \pm n_j^0 & \tau > \tau' \\ \pm n_j^0 & \tau < \tau' \end{cases} \qquad (24.22)$$

where

$$n_j^0 = e^{\beta \, \Omega_0} \, \mathrm{Tr} \, (e^{-\beta \hat{K}_0} \, a_j^\dagger a_j)$$

$$= (e^{\beta e_j} \mp 1)^{-1} \qquad (24.23)$$

The general term in the perturbation expansion [Eq. (24.17)] typically contains the factor

$$\mathrm{Tr}\{\hat{\rho}_{G0} \, T_\tau[\hat{A}\hat{B}\hat{C} \, \cdots \, \hat{F}]\} \equiv \langle T_\tau[\hat{A}\hat{B}\hat{C} \, \cdots \, \hat{F}]\rangle_0 \qquad (24.24)$$

where $\hat{A}, \hat{B}, \hat{C}, \ldots, \hat{F}$ are field operators in the interaction picture, each with its own τ variable, and

$$\hat{\rho}_{G0} = e^{\beta(\Omega_0 - \hat{K}_0)} \qquad (24.25)$$

Define a *contraction*

$$\hat{A}^{\boldsymbol{\cdot}} \, \hat{B}^{\boldsymbol{\cdot}} = \langle T_\tau[\hat{A}\hat{B}]\rangle_0 = \mathrm{Tr}\{\hat{\rho}_{G0} \, T_\tau[\hat{A}\hat{B}]\} \qquad (24.26)$$

For example,

$$\hat{\psi}_{I\alpha}(\mathbf{x}\tau)^{\boldsymbol{\cdot}} \, \hat{\psi}_{I\beta}^\dagger(\mathbf{x}'\tau')^{\boldsymbol{\cdot}} = -\mathscr{G}_{\alpha\beta}^0(\mathbf{x}\tau, \mathbf{x}'\tau') \qquad (24.27)$$

The generalized Wick's theorem then asserts that Eq. (24.24) is equal to the sum over all possible fully contracted terms

$$\langle T_\tau[\hat{A}\hat{B}\hat{C} \cdots \hat{F}]\rangle_0 = [\hat{A}^. \hat{B}^. \hat{C}^{..} \cdots \hat{F}^{...}] + [\hat{A}^. \hat{B}^{..} \hat{C}^. \cdots \hat{F}^{...}] + \cdots \tag{24.28}$$

where $[\hat{A}^. \hat{B}^{..} \hat{C}^. \cdots \hat{F}^{...}]$ is interpreted as $\pm[\hat{A}^. \hat{C}^. \hat{B}^{..} \cdots \hat{F}^{...}]$. It is clearly sufficient to prove Eq. (24.28) for the case that the operators are already in the proper time (τ) order, because the operators may be reordered on both sides of the equation without introducing any additional changes of sign. We therefore want to prove the *algebraic* identity

$$\langle \hat{A}\hat{B}\hat{C} \cdots \hat{F}\rangle_0 = [\hat{A}^. \hat{B}^. \hat{C}^{..} \cdots \hat{F}^{...}] + [\hat{A}^. \hat{B}^{..} \hat{C}^. \cdots \hat{F}^{...}] + \cdots \tag{24.29}$$

subject to the restriction $\tau_A > \tau_B > \tau_C > \cdots > \tau_F$, which allows us to remove the T_τ sign on the left side of Eq. (24.28).

It is convenient to introduce a general notation for an operator in the interaction picture, and Eq. (24.21) will be written as

$$\hat{\psi}_I \text{ or } \hat{\psi}_I^\dagger = \sum_j \chi_j(\mathbf{x}\tau)\alpha_j \tag{24.30}$$

where α_j denotes a_j or $a_j^\dagger$ and $\chi_j(\mathbf{x}\tau)$ denotes $\varphi_j^0(\mathbf{x})e^{-e_j\tau/\hbar}$ or $\varphi_j^0(\mathbf{x})^\dagger e^{e_j\tau/\hbar}$. With this simplification, the left side of Eq. (24.29) becomes

$$\langle \hat{A}\hat{B}\hat{C} \cdots \hat{F}\rangle_0 = \sum_a \sum_b \sum_c \cdots \sum_f \chi_a\chi_b\chi_c \cdots \chi_f$$
$$\times \text{Tr}(\hat{\rho}_{G0}\alpha_a\alpha_b\alpha_c \cdots \alpha_f) \tag{24.31}$$

Since $\hat{K}_0$ commutes with $\hat{N}$, the trace vanishes unless the set $\{\alpha_a \cdots \alpha_f\}$ contains an equal number of creation and annihilation operators; as a corollary, the total number of operators must be even. Commute α_a successively to the right

$$\text{Tr}(\hat{\rho}_{G0}\alpha_a\alpha_b\alpha_c \cdots \alpha_f) = \text{Tr}\{\hat{\rho}_{G0}[\alpha_a,\alpha_b]_\mp \alpha_c \cdots \alpha_f\}$$
$$\pm \text{Tr}\{\hat{\rho}_{G0}\alpha_b[\alpha_a,\alpha_c]_\mp \cdots \alpha_f\} + \cdots + \text{Tr}\{\hat{\rho}_{G0}\alpha_b\alpha_c \cdots [\alpha_a,\alpha_f]_\mp\}$$
$$\pm \text{Tr}(\hat{\rho}_{G0}\alpha_b\alpha_c \cdots \alpha_f\alpha_a) \tag{24.32}$$

where, as usual, the upper (lower) signs refer to bosons (fermions). The commutators (anticommutators) are either 1, 0, or −1 [compare Eqs. (1.27) and (1.48)], depending on the precise operators involved, and may therefore be taken outside the trace. In addition, a simple generalization of Eq. (23.26) shows that

$$e^{\beta\hat{K}_0}\alpha_a e^{-\beta\hat{K}_0} = \alpha_a e^{\lambda_a\beta e_a} \tag{24.33}$$

where $\lambda_a = 1$ if α_a is a creation operator and $\lambda_a = -1$ if α_a is a destruction operator. This relation is equivalent to the equation

$$\alpha_a\hat{\rho}_{G0} = \hat{\rho}_{G0}\alpha_a e^{\lambda_a\beta e_a} \tag{24.34}$$

and the last term of Eq. (24.32) may be rewritten with the cyclic property as

$$\pm \mathrm{Tr}\,(\alpha_a \hat{\rho}_{G0}\, \alpha_b\, \alpha_c \, \cdots \, \alpha_f) = \pm e^{\lambda_a \beta e_a}\, \mathrm{Tr}\,(\hat{\rho}_{G0}\, \alpha_a\, \alpha_b\, \alpha_c \, \cdots \, \alpha_f) \tag{24.35}$$

In this way, Eqs. (24.32) and (24.35) lead to the important result

$$\mathrm{Tr}\,(\hat{\rho}_{G0}\, \alpha_a\, \alpha_b\, \alpha_c \, \cdots \, \alpha_f) = \frac{[\alpha_a, \alpha_b]_\mp}{1 \mp e^{\lambda_a \beta e_a}}\, \mathrm{Tr}\,(\hat{\rho}_{G0}\, \alpha_c \, \cdots \, \alpha_f)$$

$$\pm \frac{[\alpha_a, \alpha_c]_\mp}{1 \mp e^{\lambda_a \beta e_a}}\, \mathrm{Tr}\,(\hat{\rho}_{G0}\, \alpha_b \, \cdots \, \alpha_f) + \cdots + \frac{[\alpha_a, \alpha_f]_\mp}{1 \mp e^{\lambda_a \beta e_a}}\, \mathrm{Tr}\,(\hat{\rho}_{G0}\, \alpha_b\, \alpha_c \, \cdots) \tag{24.36}$$

Equation (24.36) assumes a more compact form with the following definition of a contraction

$$\overset{\cdot}{\alpha_a}\, \overset{\cdot}{\alpha_b} = \frac{[\alpha_a, \alpha_b]_\mp}{1 \mp e^{\lambda_a \beta e_a}} \tag{24.37}$$

and we find

$$\mathrm{Tr}\,(\hat{\rho}_{G0}\, \alpha_a\, \alpha_b\, \alpha_c \, \cdots \, \alpha_f) = \overset{\cdot}{\alpha_a}\, \overset{\cdot}{\alpha_b}\, \mathrm{Tr}\,(\hat{\rho}_{G0}\, \alpha_c \, \cdots \, \alpha_f)$$

$$\pm \overset{\cdot}{\alpha_a}\, \overset{\cdot}{\alpha_c}\, \mathrm{Tr}\,(\hat{\rho}_{G0}\, \alpha_b \, \cdots \, \alpha_f) + \cdots$$

$$+ \overset{\cdot}{\alpha_a}\, \overset{\cdot}{\alpha_f}\, \mathrm{Tr}\,(\hat{\rho}_{G0}\, \alpha_b\, \alpha_c \, \cdots)$$

$$= \mathrm{Tr}\,(\hat{\rho}_{G0}\, \overset{\cdot}{\alpha_a}\, \overset{\cdot}{\alpha_b}\, \alpha_c \, \cdots \, \alpha_f)$$

$$+ \mathrm{Tr}\,(\hat{\rho}_{G0}\, \overset{\cdot}{\alpha_a}\, \alpha_b\, \overset{\cdot}{\alpha_c} \, \cdots \, \alpha_f) + \cdots$$

$$+ \mathrm{Tr}\,(\hat{\rho}_{G0}\, \overset{\cdot}{\alpha_a}\, \alpha_b\, \alpha_c \, \cdots \, \overset{\cdot}{\alpha_f}) \tag{24.38}$$

which defines the trace of an operator expression containing a contraction. In practice, most of the terms vanish, and the only nonzero contractions between the time-ordered operators in Eq. (24.38) are

$$\overset{\cdot}{a_j^\dagger}\, \overset{\cdot}{a_j} = \frac{[a_j^\dagger, a_j]_\mp}{1 \mp e^{\beta e_j}} = \frac{\mp 1}{1 \mp e^{\beta e_j}} = \frac{1}{e^{\beta e_j} \mp 1} = n_j^0 \tag{24.39}$$

$$\overset{\cdot}{a_j}\, \overset{\cdot}{a_j^\dagger} = \frac{[a_j, a_j^\dagger]_\mp}{1 \mp e^{-\beta e_j}} = \frac{1}{1 \mp e^{-\beta e_j}} = 1 \pm n_j^0$$

Both of these contractions are also equal to the ensemble average of the same operators, and we conclude quite generally that

$$\overset{\cdot}{\alpha_a}\, \overset{\cdot}{\alpha_b} = \langle \alpha_a\, \alpha_b \rangle_0 = \langle T_\tau [\alpha_a\, \alpha_b] \rangle_0 \tag{24.40}$$

because $\tau_A > \tau_B > \tau_C > \cdot \cdot \cdot > \tau_F$. A combination of Eqs. (24.31) and (24.38) yields

$$\langle \hat{A}\hat{B}\hat{C} \cdot \cdot \cdot \hat{F} \rangle_0$$

$$= \sum_a \sum_b \sum_c \cdot \cdot \cdot \sum_f \chi_a \chi_b \chi_c \cdot \cdot \cdot \chi_f \{ \mathrm{Tr}\,[\hat{\rho}_{G0}\,\alpha_a^{\cdot}\,\alpha_b^{\cdot}\,\alpha_c \cdot \cdot \cdot \alpha_f]$$

$$+ \mathrm{Tr}\,[\hat{\rho}_{G0}\,\alpha_a^{\cdot}\,\alpha_b\,\alpha_c^{\cdot} \cdot \cdot \cdot \alpha_f] + \cdot \cdot \cdot + \mathrm{Tr}\,[\hat{\rho}_{G0}\,\alpha_a^{\cdot}\,\alpha_b\,\alpha_c \cdot \cdot \cdot \alpha_f^{\cdot}] \}$$

$$= \langle \hat{A}^{\cdot}\,\hat{B}^{\cdot}\,\hat{C} \cdot \cdot \cdot \hat{F} \rangle_0 + \langle \hat{A}^{\cdot}\,\hat{B}\hat{C}^{\cdot} \cdot \cdot \cdot \hat{F} \rangle_0 + \cdot \cdot \cdot + \langle \hat{A}^{\cdot}\,\hat{B}\hat{C} \cdot \cdot \cdot \hat{F}^{\cdot} \rangle_0$$

$$(24.41)$$

The contraction is a c number and may be taken out of the trace, leaving a structure similar to that originally considered. The same analysis again applies, and we therefore conclude

$$\langle \hat{A}\hat{B}\hat{C} \cdot \cdot \cdot \hat{F} \rangle_0 = \langle \hat{A}^{\cdot}\,\hat{B}^{\cdot}\,\hat{C}^{\cdot\cdot} \cdot \cdot \cdot \hat{F}^{\cdot\cdot\cdot} \rangle_0$$

$$+ \langle \hat{A}^{\cdot}\,\hat{B}^{\cdot\cdot}\,\hat{C}^{\cdot} \cdot \cdot \cdot \hat{F}^{\cdot\cdot\cdot} \rangle_0 + \cdot \cdot \cdot \quad (24.42)$$

where $\tau_A > \tau_B > \tau_C > \cdot \cdot \cdot > \tau_F$. By assumption, the left side is time ordered and may be written as $\langle T_\tau[\hat{A}\hat{B}\hat{C} \cdot \cdot \cdot \hat{F}] \rangle_0$, which proves Eq. (24.28).

The present proof shows that the finite-temperature form of Wick's theorem is very general; it describes a finite system in an external potential as well as an infinite translationally invariant system. The only assumption is the existence of a *time-independent* single-particle hamiltonian $\hat{H}_0$ that determines the statistical operator $e^{\beta(\Omega_0 - \hat{K}_0)}$. For definiteness, we have considered a self-coupled field in which $\hat{H}$ refers to a single species. A similar proof can be constructed for coupled fields, however, as long as $\hat{H}_0$ is a sum of quadratic terms referring to the separate fields. In this case, the trace factors into products, one for each field, and the contractions between operators referring to different fields vanish identically. The generalized Wick's theorem therefore allows us to study arbitrary interacting systems in thermodynamic equilibrium.

25□DIAGRAMMATIC ANALYSIS

The preceding analysis shows that the perturbation series for the temperature Green's function $\mathscr{G}_{\alpha\beta}(\mathbf{x}\tau, \mathbf{x}'\tau')$ is identical with that at zero temperature, the only difference being the substitution of $\mathscr{G}^0$ for G^0 and the finite domain of the time integrals over τ from 0 to $\beta\hbar$. As a concrete example, consider the quantity $\langle T_\tau[\hat{\psi}_\alpha(1)\,\hat{\psi}_\beta(2)\,\hat{\psi}_{\beta'}^\dagger(2')\,\hat{\psi}_{\alpha'}^\dagger(1')] \rangle_0$ where the number 1 denotes the variables $(\mathbf{x}_1, \tau_1)$, and the subscript I has been omitted because all subsequent work is in the interaction picture. The field operators can be contracted in two different ways, and Eq. (24.27) then gives

$$\langle T_\tau[\hat{\psi}_\alpha(1)\,\hat{\psi}_\beta(2)\,\hat{\psi}_{\beta'}^\dagger(2')\,\hat{\psi}_{\alpha'}^\dagger(1')] \rangle_0$$

$$= \langle \hat{\psi}_\alpha(1)^{\cdot}\,\hat{\psi}_\beta(2)^{\cdot\cdot}\,\hat{\psi}_{\beta'}^\dagger(2')^{\cdot\cdot}\,\hat{\psi}_{\alpha'}^\dagger(1')^{\cdot} \rangle_0 + \langle \hat{\psi}_\alpha(1)^{\cdot}\,\hat{\psi}_\beta(2)^{\cdot\cdot}\,\hat{\psi}_{\beta'}^\dagger(2')^{\cdot}\,\hat{\psi}_{\alpha'}^\dagger(1')^{\cdot\cdot} \rangle_0$$

$$= \mathscr{G}_{\alpha\alpha'}^0(1,1')\,\mathscr{G}_{\beta\beta'}^0(2,2') \pm \mathscr{G}_{\alpha\beta'}^0(1,2')\,\mathscr{G}_{\beta\alpha'}^0(2,1') \quad (25.1)$$

Each term in the numerator of Eq. (24.13) can be analyzed in a similar way. Since the *algebraic* structure of the finite-temperature Wick's theorem [Eq. (24.28)] is identical with that of the fully contracted terms in the zero-temperature form [Eq. (8.32)], the temperature Green's function $\mathscr{G}$ has the same set of all Feynman diagrams that G had at zero temperature. In particular, a given diagram is either connected or disconnected, and the denominator of Eq. (24.13) precisely cancels the contribution of the disconnected terms, exactly as in Sec. 9. As a result, the temperature Green's function has the same formal structure as Eq. (9.5)

$$\mathscr{G}_{\alpha\beta}(1,2) = -\sum_{n=0}^{\infty} \left(-\frac{1}{\hbar}\right)^n \frac{1}{n!} \int_0^{\beta\hbar} d\tau_1' \cdots \int_0^{\beta\hbar} d\tau_n'$$

$$\times \operatorname{Tr}\{\hat{\rho}_{G0} T_\tau [\hat{K}_1(\tau_1') \cdots \hat{K}_1(\tau_n') \hat{\psi}_\alpha(1) \hat{\psi}_\beta^\dagger(2)]\}_{\text{connected}} \quad (25.2)$$

where only connected diagrams are retained. For any particular choice of $\hat{K}_1 \equiv \hat{H}_1$, the detailed derivation of the Feynman rules is also unchanged, and we shall merely state the final results.

FEYNMAN RULES IN COORDINATE SPACE

The most common situation is a self-coupled field, in which $\hat{H}_1$ represents a two-particle interaction

$$\hat{K}_1 \equiv \hat{H}_1 = \tfrac{1}{2} \iint d^3x_1 \, d^3x_2 \, \hat{\psi}_\alpha^\dagger(\mathbf{x}_1) \hat{\psi}_\beta^\dagger(\mathbf{x}_2) V(\mathbf{x}_1 - \mathbf{x}_2) \hat{\psi}_\beta(\mathbf{x}_2) \hat{\psi}_\alpha(\mathbf{x}_1) \quad (25.3)$$

where $V(\mathbf{x})$ is taken as spin independent. The corresponding interaction-picture operator is easily obtained

$$\hat{K}_1(\tau_1) = \tfrac{1}{2} \iint d^3x_1 \, d^3x_2 \, \hat{\psi}_\alpha^\dagger(\mathbf{x}_1 \tau_1) \hat{\psi}_\beta^\dagger(\mathbf{x}_2 \tau_1) V(\mathbf{x}_1 - \mathbf{x}_2) \hat{\psi}_\beta(\mathbf{x}_2 \tau_1) \hat{\psi}_\alpha(\mathbf{x}_1 \tau_1)$$

$$= \tfrac{1}{2} \iint d^3x_1 \, d^3x_2 \int_0^{\beta\hbar} d\tau_2 \, \hat{\psi}_\alpha^\dagger(\mathbf{x}_1 \tau_1) \hat{\psi}_\beta^\dagger(\mathbf{x}_2 \tau_2) \mathscr{V}_0(\mathbf{x}_1 \tau_1, \mathbf{x}_2 \tau_2)$$

$$\times \hat{\psi}_\beta(\mathbf{x}_2 \tau_2) \hat{\psi}_\alpha(\mathbf{x}_1 \tau_1) \quad (25.4)$$

where the subscript I has again been omitted and the general potential

$$\mathscr{V}_0(\mathbf{x}_1 \tau_1, \mathbf{x}_2 \tau_2) = V(\mathbf{x}_1 - \mathbf{x}_2) \delta(\tau_1 - \tau_2) \quad (25.5)$$

has been introduced. The perturbation expansion of Eq. (25.2) includes precisely the same Feynman diagrams as in Sec. 9, and the only modification is the Feynman rules used to evaluate the nth-order contribution to $\mathscr{G}_{\alpha\beta}(1,2)$.

1. Draw all topologically distinct diagrams containing n interaction lines and $2n + 1$ directed particle lines.
2. Associate a factor $\mathscr{G}_{\alpha\beta}^0(1,2)$ with each directed particle line running from 2 to 1.
3. Associate a factor $\mathscr{V}_0(1,2)$ with each interaction line joining points 1 and 2.
4. Integrate all internal variables: $\int d^3x_i \int_0^{\beta\hbar} d\tau_i$.

5. The indices form a matrix product along any continuous particle line. Evaluate all spin sums.
6. Multiply each nth-order diagram by $(-1/\hbar)^n (-1)^F$, where F is the number of closed fermion loops.
7. Interpret any temperature Green's function at equal values of τ as

$$\mathcal{G}^0(\mathbf{x}_i \tau_i, \mathbf{x}_j \tau_i) = \lim_{\tau_j \to \tau_i^+} \mathcal{G}^0(\mathbf{x}_i \tau_i, \mathbf{x}_j \tau_j).$$

As a specific example, consider the set of all zero- and first-order terms (Fig. 25.1). The specific choice of labels for the internal lines is irrelevant

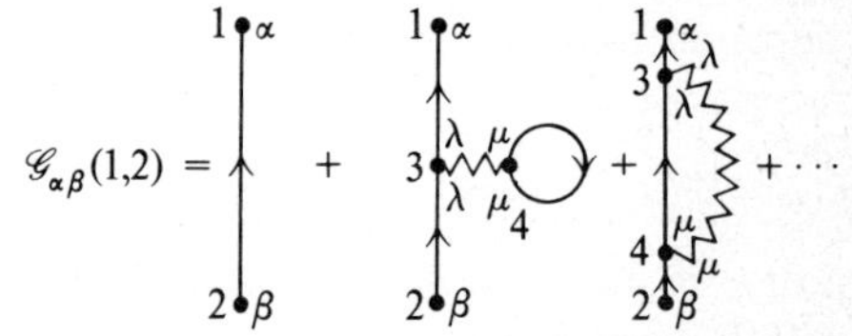

$$\mathcal{G}_{\alpha\beta}(1,2) =$$

Fig. 25.1 Zero- and first-order contributions to $\mathcal{G}_{\alpha\beta}(1,2)$ in coordinate space.

because they represent dummy variables. According to the rules just stated, Fig. 25.1 implies the following terms:

$$\mathcal{G}_{\alpha\beta}(1,2) = \mathcal{G}^0_{\alpha\beta}(1,2) - \hbar^{-1} \int d^3x_3 \, d^3x_4 \int_0^{\beta\hbar} d\tau_3 \, d\tau_4 \, [\pm \mathcal{G}^0_{\alpha\lambda}(1,3) \, \mathcal{G}^0_{\lambda\beta}(3,2)$$
$$\times \, \mathcal{G}^0_{\mu\mu}(4,4) \, \mathscr{V}_0(3,4) + \mathcal{G}^0_{\alpha\lambda}(1,3) \, \mathcal{G}^0_{\lambda\mu}(3,4) \, \mathcal{G}^0_{\mu\beta}(4,2) \, \mathscr{V}_0(3,4)] + \cdots$$

$$(25.6)$$

where the $\pm$ in the second term arises from the closed loop. If $\mathcal{G}^0_{\alpha\beta}$ is diagonal in the spin indices $[= \mathcal{G}^0 \delta_{\alpha\beta}]$, then $\mathcal{G}$ is also diagonal, and the spin sums are readily evaluated

$$\mathcal{G}(1,2) = \mathcal{G}^0(1,2) - \hbar^{-1} \int d^3x_3 \, d^3x_4 \int_0^{\beta\hbar} d\tau_3 \, d\tau_4 \, [\pm(2s+1) \, \mathcal{G}^0(1,3)$$
$$\times \, \mathcal{G}^0(3,2) \, \mathcal{G}^0(4,4) \, \mathscr{V}_0(3,4) + \mathcal{G}^0(1,3) \, \mathcal{G}^0(3,4) \, \mathcal{G}^0(4,2) \, \mathscr{V}_0(3,4)] + \cdots$$

$$(25.7)$$

Here the factor $(2s+1)$ represents the degeneracy associated with particles of spin s. As noted in rule 7, $\mathcal{G}^0(4,4)$ is interpreted as $\mathcal{G}^0(4,4^+)$. It may also be identified as a generalized particle density

$$\mathcal{G}^0(4,4^+) = \mp(2s+1)^{-1} \langle \hat{n}^0(\mathbf{x}_4) \rangle_0$$
$$= \mp(2s+1)^{-1} \sum_j |\varphi_j^0(\mathbf{x}_4)|^2 (e^{\beta(\epsilon_j^0 - \mu)} \mp 1)^{-1} \quad (25.8)$$

that depends on the parameter μ; it therefore differs from the unperturbed particle density unless μ is assigned the value appropriate to the noninteracting system.

FEYNMAN RULES IN MOMENTUM SPACE

There is no difficulty in writing out Eq. (25.7) in detail, but the different form of $\mathscr{G}^0(i, j)$ for $\tau_i \gtrless \tau_j$ soon leads to a proliferation of terms. For this reason, it is advantageous to introduce a Fourier representation in the variable τ, which automatically includes the different orderings. This step has been central to the development of many-body theory at finite temperature and was introduced independently by Abrikosov, Gorkov, and Dzyaloshinskii,[1] by Fradkin,[2] and by Martin and Schwinger.[3] It leads to the same simplification as in the zero-temperature formalism.

The crucial point is the periodicity (antiperiodicity) of $\mathscr{G}$ in each τ variable with period $\beta\hbar$ [Eqs. (24.14) and (24.15)]. For simplicity, we assume that $\mathscr{G}$ depends only on the difference $\tau_1 - \tau_2$, which represents the most common situation:

$$\mathscr{G}(\mathbf{x}_1 \tau_1, \mathbf{x}_2 \tau_2) = \mathscr{G}(\mathbf{x}_1, \mathbf{x}_2, \tau_1 - \tau_2) \tag{25.9}$$

For *both* statistics, $\mathscr{G}$ is *periodic* over the range $2\beta\hbar$ and may therefore be expanded in a Fourier *series*

$$\mathscr{G}(\mathbf{x}_1, \mathbf{x}_2, \tau) = (\beta\hbar)^{-1} \sum_n e^{-i\omega_n\tau} \mathscr{G}(\mathbf{x}_1, \mathbf{x}_2, \omega_n)$$

$$\tau \equiv \tau_1 - \tau_2 \tag{25.10}$$

where

$$\omega_n = \frac{n\pi}{\beta\hbar} \tag{25.11}$$

This representation ensures that $\mathscr{G}(\mathbf{x}_1, \mathbf{x}_2, \tau + 2\beta\hbar) = \mathscr{G}(\mathbf{x}_1, \mathbf{x}_2, \tau)$ and the associated Fourier coefficient is given by

$$\mathscr{G}(\mathbf{x}_1, \mathbf{x}_2, \omega_n) = \tfrac{1}{2} \int_{-\beta\hbar}^{\beta\hbar} d\tau\, e^{i\omega_n\tau} \mathscr{G}(\mathbf{x}_1, \mathbf{x}_2, \tau) \tag{25.12}$$

It is convenient to separate Eq. (25.12) into two parts

$$\mathscr{G}(\mathbf{x}_1, \mathbf{x}_2, \omega_n) = \tfrac{1}{2} \int_{-\beta\hbar}^{0} d\tau\, e^{i\omega_n\tau} \mathscr{G}(\mathbf{x}_1, \mathbf{x}_2, \tau) + \tfrac{1}{2} \int_{0}^{\beta\hbar} d\tau\, e^{i\omega_n\tau} \mathscr{G}(\mathbf{x}_1, \mathbf{x}_2, \tau)$$

$$= \pm\tfrac{1}{2} \int_{-\beta\hbar}^{0} d\tau\, e^{i\omega_n\tau} \mathscr{G}(\mathbf{x}_1, \mathbf{x}_2, \tau + \beta\hbar) + \tfrac{1}{2} \int_{0}^{\beta\hbar} d\tau\, e^{i\omega_n\tau} \mathscr{G}(\mathbf{x}_1, \mathbf{x}_2, \tau)$$

$$= \tfrac{1}{2}(1 \pm e^{-i\omega_n\beta\hbar}) \int_{0}^{\beta\hbar} d\tau\, e^{i\omega_n\tau} \mathscr{G}(\mathbf{x}_1, \mathbf{x}_2, \tau) \tag{25.13}$$

where the second and third lines are obtained respectively with Eqs. (24.15) and an elementary change of variables. Equation (25.11) shows that $e^{-i\omega_n\beta\hbar}$ is

---

[1] A. A. Abrikosov, L. P. Gorkov, and I. E. Dzyaloshinskii, *Sov. Phys.-JETP*, **9**:636 (1959).
[2] E. S. Fradkin, *Sov. Phys.-JETP*, **9**:912 (1959).
[3] P. C. Martin and J. Schwinger, *Phys. Rev.*, **115**:1342 (1959).

equal to $e^{-in\pi} = (-1)^n$, and the factor $\frac{1}{2}(1 \pm e^{-i\omega_n\beta\hbar})$ reduces to

$$\frac{1}{2}[1 \pm (-1)^n] = \begin{cases} 1 & n\ \text{even} \\ 0 & n\ \text{odd} \end{cases} \text{boson} \\ \begin{cases} 0 & n\ \text{even} \\ 1 & n\ \text{odd} \end{cases} \text{fermion}$$

We may therefore rewrite the Fourier coefficient [Eq. (25.12)] as

$$\mathcal{G}(\mathbf{x}_1,\mathbf{x}_2,\omega_n) = \int_0^{\beta\hbar} d\tau\, e^{i\omega_n\tau}\, \mathcal{G}(\mathbf{x}_1,\mathbf{x}_2,\tau) \tag{25.14}$$

where

$$\omega_n = \begin{cases} \dfrac{2n\pi}{\beta\hbar} & \text{boson} \\[2mm] \dfrac{(2n+1)\pi}{\beta\hbar} & \text{fermion} \end{cases} \tag{25.15}$$

Consequently, *the Fourier series in Eq. (25.10) is restricted to even (odd) terms for bosons (fermions)*.

The noninteracting Green's function [Eq. (24.22)] provides an interesting example of Eq. (25.14). It is simplest to treat bosons and fermions separately, and we first consider bosons

$$\mathcal{G}^0(\mathbf{x},\mathbf{x}',\omega_n) = -\sum_j \varphi_j^0(\mathbf{x})\, \varphi_j^0(\mathbf{x}')^\dagger \int_0^{\beta\hbar} d\tau\, e^{i\omega_n\tau}\, e^{-(\epsilon_j{}^0-\mu)\tau/\hbar}(1+n_j^0)$$

$$= -\sum_j \frac{\varphi_j^0(\mathbf{x})\, \varphi_j^0(\mathbf{x}')^\dagger\,(1+n_j^0)}{i\omega_n - \hbar^{-1}(\epsilon_j^0 - \mu)}\{\exp[i\omega_n\beta\hbar - \beta(\epsilon_j^0 - \mu)] - 1\}$$

$$\tag{25.16}$$

The condition $\omega_n = 2n\pi/\beta\hbar$ reduces the quantity in braces to

$$\{\exp[-\beta(\epsilon_j^0 - \mu)] - 1\} = -(1 + n_j^0)^{-1}$$

and Eq. (25.16) then becomes

$$\mathcal{G}^0(\mathbf{x},\mathbf{x}',\omega_n) = \sum_j \frac{\varphi_j^0(\mathbf{x})\, \varphi_j^0(\mathbf{x}')^\dagger}{i\omega_n - \hbar^{-1}(\epsilon_j^0 - \mu)} \tag{25.17}$$

The analysis for fermions is very similar:

$$\mathcal{G}^0(\mathbf{x},\mathbf{x}',\omega_n) = -\sum_j \frac{\varphi_j^0(\mathbf{x})\, \varphi_j^0(\mathbf{x}')^\dagger\,(1-n_j^0)}{i\omega_n - \hbar^{-1}(\epsilon_j^0 - \mu)}\{e^{i\omega_n\beta\hbar}\exp[-\beta(\epsilon_j^0 - \mu)] - 1\}$$

$$\tag{25.18}$$

where $\omega_n = (2n+1)\pi/\beta\hbar$. The quantity in braces again simplifies to

$$-\{\exp[-\beta(\epsilon_j^0 - \mu)] + 1\} = -(1 - n_j^0)^{-1}$$

and *Eq. (25.17) is seen to be correct for both statistics, the only distinction being the restriction to even or odd integers in Eq. (25.15).*

To develop the Feynman rules in momentum space, we consider an arbitrary vertex in a Feynman diagram contributing to Eq. (25.2). The static two-body potential has the trivial Fourier representation

$$\mathscr{V}_0(\mathbf{x}_1\tau_1,\mathbf{x}_2\tau_2) = (\beta\hbar)^{-1} \sum_{n \text{ even}} e^{-i\omega_n(\tau_1-\tau_2)} \mathscr{V}_0(\mathbf{x}_1,\mathbf{x}_2,\omega_n) \tag{25.19}$$

where

$$\mathscr{V}_0(\mathbf{x}_1,\mathbf{x}_2,\omega_n) \equiv V(\mathbf{x}_1 - \mathbf{x}_2) \tag{25.20}$$

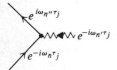

Fig. 25.2   Basic vertex in temperature formalism.

and we have used the identity

$$\delta(\tau) = (\beta\hbar)^{-1} \sum_{n \text{ even}} e^{-i\omega_n\tau} \tag{25.21}$$

valid in the range $-\beta\hbar < \tau < \beta\hbar$. Each internal vertex joins a single interaction line and two particle lines (one entering and one leaving), as in Fig. 25.2. The entire τ_j dependence is contained in the exponential factors shown in Fig. 25.2, and the integral over τ_j becomes

$$\int_0^{\beta\hbar} d\tau_j \exp\left[-i(\omega_n + \omega_{n'} - \omega_{n''})\tau_j\right] = \beta\hbar \,\delta_{\omega_n+\omega_{n'},\,\omega_{n''}} \tag{25.22}$$

Equation (25.22) shows that the *discrete frequency is conserved at each vertex*, exactly like the continuous frequency in Eq. (9.13). Note that this condition is independent of statistics, because both particle lines carry even or odd frequencies, whereas the interaction line always carries an even frequency.

It is now straightforward to derive the Feynman rules for the nth-order contribution to $\mathscr{G}_{\alpha\beta}(\mathbf{x}_1,\mathbf{x}_2,\omega_n)$, which would apply to an inhomogeneous system such as an electron gas in a periodic crystal potential. For most purposes, however, it is permissible to restrict ourselves to systems with translational invariance, where $\mathscr{G}$ depends only on the difference of the spatial variables $\mathbf{x}_1 - \mathbf{x}_2$. In this case, the Feynman diagrams can be evaluated in momentum space, which greatly simplifies the calculations. The transformation of the Feynman rules follows immediately from the analysis in Sec. 9, along with Eqs. (23.30). For simplicity, only the limit of an infinite volume ($V \to \infty$) is considered, and the temperature Green's functions can then be expanded as follows:

$$\mathscr{G}_{\alpha\beta}(\mathbf{x},\mathbf{x}',\tau) = (\beta\hbar)^{-1} (2\pi)^{-3} \int d^3k \, e^{i\mathbf{k}\cdot(\mathbf{x}-\mathbf{x}')} \sum_n e^{-i\omega_n\tau} \mathscr{G}_{\alpha\beta}(\mathbf{k},\omega_n) \tag{25.23}$$

$$\mathscr{G}^0_{\alpha\beta}(\mathbf{x},\mathbf{x}',\tau) = (\beta\hbar)^{-1}(2\pi)^{-3}\delta_{\alpha\beta}\int d^3k\, e^{i\mathbf{k}\cdot(\mathbf{x}-\mathbf{x}')}$$
$$\times \sum_n e^{-i\omega_n\tau}[i\omega_n - \hbar^{-1}(\epsilon_k^0 - \mu)]^{-1} \quad (25.24)$$

The physical quantities N, E, and Ω [see Eqs. (23.9), (23.15), and (23.22)] become

$$N = \mp V(2\pi)^{-3}(\beta\hbar)^{-1}\int d^3k \sum_n e^{i\omega_n\eta}\,\mathrm{tr}\,\mathscr{G}(\mathbf{k},\omega_n) \quad (25.25)$$

$$E = \langle\hat{H}\rangle = \mp V(2\pi)^{-3}(\beta\hbar)^{-1}\int d^3k \sum_n e^{i\omega_n\eta}\tfrac{1}{2}(i\hbar\omega_n + \epsilon_k^0 + \mu)\,\mathrm{tr}\,\mathscr{G}(\mathbf{k},\omega_n)$$
$$(25.26)$$

$$\Omega = \Omega_0 \mp V\int_0^1 \lambda^{-1}\,d\lambda\,(2\pi)^{-3}(\beta\hbar)^{-1}\int d^3k \sum_n e^{i\omega_n\eta}$$
$$\times \tfrac{1}{2}(i\hbar\omega_n - \epsilon_k^0 + \mu)\,\mathrm{tr}\,\mathscr{G}^\lambda(\mathbf{k},\omega_n) \quad (25.27)$$

and we shall now state the Feynman rules for evaluating the nth-order contribution to $\mathscr{G}(\mathbf{k},\omega_m)$.

1. Draw all topologically distinct connected graphs with n interaction lines and $2n+1$ directed particle lines.
2. Assign a direction to each interaction line. Associate a wave vector and discrete frequency with each line and conserve each quantity at every vertex.
3. With each particle line associate a factor

$$\mathscr{G}^0_{\alpha\beta}(\mathbf{k},\omega_m) = \frac{\delta_{\alpha\beta}}{i\omega_m - \hbar^{-1}(\epsilon_k^0 - \mu)} \quad (25.28)$$

where ω_m contains even (odd) integers for bosons (fermions).
4. Associate a factor $\mathscr{V}_0(\mathbf{k},\omega_m) \equiv V(\mathbf{k})$ with each interaction line.
5. Integrate over all n independent internal wave vectors and sum over all n independent internal frequencies.
6. The indices form a matrix product along any continuous particle line. Evaluate all matrix sums.
7. Multiply by $[-\beta\hbar^2(2\pi)^3]^{-n}(-1)^F$, where F is the number of closed fermion loops.
8. Whenever a particle line either closes on itself or is joined by the same interaction line, insert a convergence factor $e^{i\omega_m\eta}$.

As an example, we once again consider the zero- and first-order diagrams (Fig. 25.3). After the spin sums have been evaluated, we find

$$\mathscr{G}(\mathbf{k},\omega_n) = \mathscr{G}^0(\mathbf{k},\omega_n) - (\beta\hbar^2)^{-1}[\mathscr{G}^0(\mathbf{k},\omega_n)]^2(2\pi)^{-3}\sum_{n'}e^{i\omega_{n'}\eta}$$
$$\times \int d^3k'\,[\pm(2s+1)V(0)\mathscr{G}^0(\mathbf{k}',\omega_{n'}) + V(\mathbf{k}-\mathbf{k}')\mathscr{G}^0(\mathbf{k}',\omega_{n'})] + \cdots$$
$$(25.29)$$

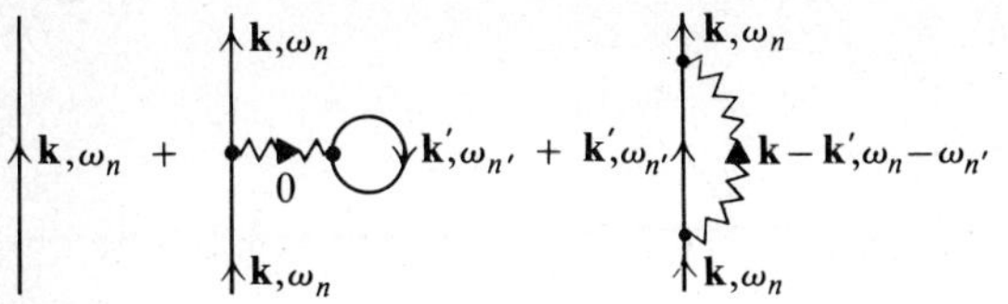

Fig. 25.3 Zero- and first-order contributions to $\mathscr{G}(\mathbf{k},\omega_n)$ in momentum space.

This expression has the expected form [compare Eq. (9.22)]

$$\mathscr{G}(\mathbf{k},\omega_n) = \mathscr{G}^0(\mathbf{k},\omega_n) + \mathscr{G}^0(\mathbf{k},\omega_n)\,\Sigma(\mathbf{k},\omega_n)\,\mathscr{G}^0(\mathbf{k},\omega_n) \qquad (25.30)$$

where $\Sigma(\mathbf{k},\omega_n)$ is the self-energy. In particular, the first-order self-energy is given by [compare Eq. (9.23)]

$$\Sigma_{(1)}(\mathbf{k},\omega_n) \equiv \Sigma_{(1)}(\mathbf{k})$$

$$= (-\hbar^2\beta)^{-1}\sum_{n'} e^{i\omega_{n'}\eta}\,(2\pi)^{-3}\int d^3k'\,\mathscr{G}^0(\mathbf{k'},\omega_{n'})$$

$$\times\,[\pm(2s+1)\,V(0) + V(\mathbf{k}-\mathbf{k'})]$$

$$= \frac{1}{\hbar}\int \frac{d^3k'}{(2\pi)^3}\,[\mp(2s+1)\,V(0) - V(\mathbf{k}-\mathbf{k'})]\frac{1}{\beta\hbar}$$

$$\times\,\sum_{n'} \frac{e^{i\omega_{n'}\eta}}{i\omega_{n'} - \hbar^{-1}(\epsilon_{k'}^0 - \mu)} \qquad (25.31)$$

It is clear that $\Sigma_{(1)}$ is independent of ω_n and may therefore be written as $\Sigma_{(1)}(\mathbf{k})$.

EVALUATION OF FREQUENCY SUMS

The frequency sum in Eq. (25.31) is typical of those occurring in many-body physics, and we therefore study it in detail. For definiteness, consider the case

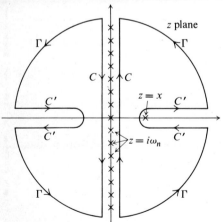

Fig. 25.4 Contour for evaluation of frequency sums.

of bosons, where the sum is of the form

$$\sum_n e^{i\omega_n \eta} (i\omega_n - x)^{-1} \qquad (25.32)$$

with $\omega_n = 2n\pi/\beta\hbar$. Equation (25.32) is not absolutely convergent, for it would diverge logarithmically without the convergence factor; η must therefore remain positive until after the sum is evaluated.

The most direct approach is to use contour integration, which requires a meromorphic function with poles at the even integers. One possible choice is $\beta\hbar(e^{\beta\hbar z} - 1)^{-1}$, whose poles occur at $z = 2n\pi i/\beta\hbar = i\omega_n$, each with unit residue. If C is a contour encircling the imaginary axis in the positive sense (Fig. 25.4), then the contour integral

$$\frac{\beta\hbar}{2\pi i} \int_C \frac{dz}{e^{\beta\hbar z} - 1} \frac{e^{\eta z}}{z - x} \qquad (25.33)$$

exactly reproduces the sum in Eq. (25.32), because the integrand has an infinite sequence of simple poles at $i\omega_n$ with residue $(\beta\hbar)^{-1} e^{i\omega_n \eta} (i\omega_n - x)^{-1}$. Deform the contour to C' and Γ shown in Fig. 25.4. If $|z| \to \infty$ along a ray with $\text{Re}\, z > 0$, then the integrand is of order $|z|^{-1} \exp[-(\beta\hbar - \eta)\text{Re}\, z]$; if $|z| \to \infty$ along a ray with $\text{Re}\, z < 0$, then the integrand is of order $|z|^{-1} \exp(\eta \,\text{Re}\, z)$. Since $\beta\hbar > \eta > 0$, Jordan's lemma shows that the contributions of the large arcs Γ vanish and we are left with the integrals along C'

$$\sum_n \frac{e^{i\omega_n \eta}}{i\omega_n - x} = \frac{\beta\hbar}{2\pi i} \int_{C'} \frac{dz}{e^{\beta\hbar z} - 1} \frac{e^{\eta z}}{z - x} \qquad (25.34)$$

The only singularity included in C' is a simple pole at $z = x$, and Cauchy's theorem yields

$$\lim_{\eta \to 0} \sum_{n \text{ even}} \frac{e^{i\omega_n \eta}}{i\omega_n - x} = \frac{-\beta\hbar}{e^{\beta\hbar x} - 1} \qquad (25.35)$$

where the minus sign arises from the negative sense of C', and it is now permissible to let $\eta \to 0$. This derivation exhibits the essential role of the convergence factor. Although the function $-\beta\hbar(e^{-\beta\hbar z} - 1)^{-1}$ also has simple poles at $z = i\omega_n$ with unit residue, the contributions from Γ would diverge in this case, thus preventing the deformation from C to C'.

A similar analysis may be given for fermions, where $\omega_n = (2n + 1)\pi/\beta\hbar$. The function $-\beta\hbar(e^{\beta\hbar z} + 1)^{-1}$ has simple poles at the odd integers $z = i\omega_n$ with unit residue, and the series can be rewritten as

$$\sum_{n \text{ odd}} \frac{e^{i\omega_n \eta}}{i\omega_n - x} = \frac{-\beta\hbar}{2\pi i} \int_C \frac{dz}{e^{\beta\hbar z} + 1} \frac{e^{\eta z}}{z - x} \qquad (25.36)$$

where C is the same contour as in Fig. 25.4. Jordan's lemma again allows the contour deformation from C to C' because $\beta\hbar > \eta > 0$, and the simple pole at $z = x$ yields

$$\lim_{\eta \to 0} \sum_{n \text{ odd}} \frac{e^{i\omega_n \eta}}{i\omega_n - x} = \frac{\beta\hbar}{e^{\beta\hbar x} + 1} \tag{25.37}$$

The two cases can be combined in the single expression

$$\lim_{\eta \to 0} \sum_{n} \frac{e^{i\omega_n \eta}}{i\omega_n - x} = \mp \frac{\beta\hbar}{e^{\beta\hbar x} \mp 1} \tag{25.38}$$

which will be used repeatedly in the subsequent chapters.

The first-order self-energy [Eq. (25.31)] can now be simplified with Eq. (25.38), and we find

$$\hbar\Sigma_{(1)}(\mathbf{k}) = \int \frac{d^3k'}{(2\pi)^3} \frac{[(2s+1)\,V(0) \pm V(\mathbf{k}-\mathbf{k}')]}{\exp\left[\beta(\epsilon_{k'}^0 - \mu)\right] \mp 1}$$
$$= V(0)(2s+1)(2\pi)^{-3} \int d^3k'\, n_{\mathbf{k}'}^0 \pm (2\pi)^{-3} \int d^3k'\, V(\mathbf{k}-\mathbf{k}')\, n_{\mathbf{k}'}^0 \tag{25.39}$$

This expression applies to fermions at all temperatures and to bosons at sufficiently high temperatures that the unperturbed system has no Bose-Einstein condensation. It is important to remember that $n_{\mathbf{k}}^0$ depends *explicitly* on the chemical potential μ. For this reason, $(2s+1)(2\pi)^{-3} \int d^3k\, n_{\mathbf{k}}^0$ is also a function of μ and cannot be identified with the particle density. Apart from this one difference, however, Eq. (25.39) is a direct generalization of that at zero temperature [Eq. (9.24)].

26□DYSON'S EQUATIONS

The structure of Dyson's equations at zero temperature was determined by the set of all Feynman diagrams. As shown in the previous section, the temperature Green's function leads to an identical set of diagrams, and it is therefore not surprising that Dyson's equations remain unaltered. Indeed, this represents the primary reason for introducing the temperature function, even though $\mathscr{G}$ is less directly related to physical quantities than the analogous zero-temperature function G. In coordinate space, the temperature Green's function always has the form [compare Sec. 9]

$$\mathscr{G}(1,2) = \mathscr{G}^0(1,2) + \int d3\,d4\, \mathscr{G}^0(1,3)\,\Sigma(3,4)\,\mathscr{G}^0(4,2) \tag{26.1}$$

where the integrals contain an implicit spin summation and the time integrations run over τ_i from 0 to $\beta\hbar$. Equation (26.1) defines the *total* self-energy $\Sigma(3,4)$; it is also convenient to introduce the *proper* self-energy $\Sigma^\star(3,4)$, which consists of all self-energy diagrams that cannot be separated into two parts by cutting

one particle line $\mathscr{G}^0$. As in the zero-temperature formalism [Eq. (9.26)], the self-energy is obtained by iterating the proper self-energy

$$\Sigma(1,2) = \Sigma^\star(1,2) + \int d3\,d4\,\Sigma^\star(1,3)\,\mathscr{G}^0(3,4)\,\Sigma^\star(4,2) + \cdots \tag{26.2}$$

and the corresponding temperature Green's function obeys the integral (Dyson's) equation

$$\mathscr{G}(1,2) = \mathscr{G}^0(1,2) + \int d3\,d4\,\mathscr{G}^0(1,3)\,\Sigma^\star(3,4)\,\mathscr{G}(4,2) \tag{26.3}$$

Iteration of Eq. (26.3) clearly reproduces Eqs. (26.1) and (26.2).

Dyson's equation becomes much simpler if the hamiltonian is time independent and if the system is uniform. Although it is easy to write down the expressions for spatially varying systems [corresponding to the Green's function $\mathscr{G}(\mathbf{x}_1,\mathbf{x}_2,\omega_n)$], we shall concentrate on the more usual situation where the full Fourier representation is possible [see Eqs. (25.23) and (25.24)]. The sums and integrals in Eq. (26.3) are then readily evaluated, leaving an algebraic equation

$$\mathscr{G}(\mathbf{k},\omega_n) = \mathscr{G}^0(\mathbf{k},\omega_n) + \mathscr{G}^0(\mathbf{k},\omega_n)\,\Sigma^\star(\mathbf{k},\omega_n)\,\mathscr{G}(\mathbf{k},\omega_n) \tag{26.4}$$

where all quantities are assumed diagonal in the matrix indices. Equation (26.4) has the explicit solution

$$\mathscr{G}(\mathbf{k},\omega_n) = [\mathscr{G}^0(\mathbf{k},\omega_n)^{-1} - \Sigma^\star(\mathbf{k},\omega_n)]^{-1}$$

$$\mathscr{G}_{\alpha\beta}(\mathbf{k},\omega_n) = \delta_{\alpha\beta}[i\omega_n - \hbar^{-1}(\epsilon_k^0 - \mu) - \Sigma^\star(\mathbf{k},\omega_n)]^{-1} \tag{26.5}$$

where the last form has been obtained with Eq. (25.28). This expression for $\mathscr{G}(\mathbf{k},\omega_n)$ is formally very similar to Eq. (9.33) for $G(k)$. There is one important difference, however, because ω_n is a *discrete* variable, instead of a true frequency or energy. For this reason, the determination of the excitation spectrum $\epsilon_{\mathbf{k}}$ for a system containing one more or one less particle is more complicated than at $T = 0$; we shall return to this important problem in Chap. 9.

The previous expressions for N, E, and Ω [Eqs. (25.25) to (25.27)] can be simplified with Dyson's equation:

$$N(T,V,\mu) = \mp V(2s+1)\int \frac{d^3k}{(2\pi)^3}\frac{1}{\beta\hbar}\sum_n \frac{e^{i\omega_n\eta}}{i\omega_n - \hbar^{-1}(\epsilon_k^0 - \mu) - \Sigma^\star(\mathbf{k},\omega_n)} \tag{26.6}$$

$$E(T,V,\mu) = \mp V(2s+1)\int \frac{d^3k}{(2\pi)^3}\frac{1}{\beta\hbar}\sum_n e^{i\omega_n\eta}$$

$$\times \tfrac{1}{2}\hbar\left[\frac{i\omega_n + \hbar^{-1}(\epsilon_k^0 + \mu)}{i\omega_n - \hbar^{-1}(\epsilon_k^0 - \mu) - \Sigma^\star(\mathbf{k},\omega_n)}\right]$$

$$= \mp V(2s+1)\int \frac{d^3k}{(2\pi)^3}\frac{1}{\beta\hbar}\sum_n e^{i\omega_n\eta}$$

$$\times\left[\tfrac{1}{2}\hbar + \frac{\epsilon_k^0 + \tfrac{1}{2}\hbar\Sigma^\star(\mathbf{k},\omega_n)}{i\omega_n - \hbar^{-1}(\epsilon_k^0 - \mu) - \Sigma^\star(\mathbf{k},\omega_n)}\right] \tag{26.7}$$

$$\Omega(T,V,\mu) = \Omega_0(T,V,\mu) \mp V(2s+1) \int_0^1 \frac{d\lambda}{\lambda} \int \frac{d^3k}{(2\pi)^3} \frac{1}{\beta\hbar} \sum_n e^{i\omega_n\eta}$$

$$\times \left[\tfrac{1}{2}\hbar + \frac{\tfrac{1}{2}\hbar\Sigma^{\star\lambda}(\mathbf{k},\omega_n)}{i\omega_n - \hbar^{-1}(\epsilon_k^0 - \mu) - \Sigma^{\star\lambda}(\mathbf{k},\omega_n)} \right] \quad (26.8)$$

The convergence factor again plays an important role, for it allows us to eliminate the constant term in the last two expressions.   For definiteness, consider bosons where

$$\sum_n e^{i\omega_n\eta} = \sum_n e^{2\pi i n\eta/\beta\hbar} = \sum_{n=0}^{\infty} (e^{2\pi i\eta/\beta\hbar})^n + \sum_{n=0}^{\infty} (e^{2\pi i\eta/\beta\hbar})^{-n} - 1$$

$$= (1 - e^{2\pi i\eta/\beta\hbar})^{-1} + (1 - e^{-2\pi i\eta/\beta\hbar})^{-1} - 1$$

$$= 0 \qquad\qquad\qquad\qquad\qquad\qquad\qquad\qquad\qquad\qquad (26.9)$$

The second line is merely the sum of a geometric series while the last line follows for $0 < \eta < \beta\hbar$.   [Compare the discussion following Eq. (9.36).]   The fermion summation differs only by a factor $e^{\pi i\eta/\beta\hbar}$, and Eqs. (26.7) and (26.8) therefore become

$$E = \mp V(2s+1)(2\pi)^{-3}(\beta\hbar)^{-1} \int d^3k \sum_n e^{i\omega_n\eta} [\epsilon_k^0 + \tfrac{1}{2}\hbar\Sigma^{\star}(\mathbf{k},\omega_n)] \mathcal{G}(\mathbf{k},\omega_n)$$

$$(26.10)$$

$$\Omega = \Omega_0 \mp V(2s+1) \int_0^1 \frac{d\lambda}{\lambda} \int \frac{d^3k}{(2\pi)^3} (\beta\hbar)^{-1} \sum_n e^{i\omega_n\eta} \tfrac{1}{2}\hbar\Sigma^{\star\lambda}(\mathbf{k},\omega_n) \mathcal{G}^\lambda(\mathbf{k},\omega_n)$$

$$(26.11)$$

where both $\Sigma^{\star\lambda}$ and G^λ must be evaluated for variable coupling constant λ.

It is also useful to introduce the polarization Π and effective interaction $\mathcal{V}$, exactly as in Eq. (9.39).   In the present case, where the interparticle potential is spin independent, $\mathcal{V}(\mathbf{q},\omega_n)$ for a uniform system satisfies the algebraic expression

$$\mathcal{V}(\mathbf{q},\omega_n) = \mathcal{V}_0(\mathbf{q},\omega_n) + \mathcal{V}_0(\mathbf{q},\omega_n) \Pi(\mathbf{q},\omega_n) \mathcal{V}_0(\mathbf{q},\omega_n) \qquad (26.12)$$

If the *proper* polarization $\Pi^\star$ is defined as the sum of all polarization insertions that cannot be separated into two parts by cutting a single interaction line $\mathcal{V}_0$, Eq. (26.12) can then be rewritten as [compare Eq. (9.43b)]

$$\mathcal{V}(\mathbf{q},\omega_n) = \mathcal{V}_0(\mathbf{q},\omega_n) + \mathcal{V}_0(\mathbf{q},\omega_n) \Pi^\star(\mathbf{q},\omega_n) \mathcal{V}(\mathbf{q},\omega_n) \qquad (26.13)$$

with the explicit solution

$$\mathcal{V}(\mathbf{q},\omega_n) = \mathcal{V}_0(\mathbf{q},\omega_n) [1 - \mathcal{V}_0(\mathbf{q},\omega_n) \Pi^\star(\mathbf{q},\omega_n)]^{-1} \qquad (26.14)$$

Although this equation is similar to that at $T = 0$ [Eq. (9.45)], the discrete frequency ω_n precludes a direct interpretation of $\mathcal{V}(\mathbf{q},\omega_n)$ as the effective physical

interaction for a given momentum and energy transfer. Thus the determination of the collective modes associated with density oscillations at finite temperature requires a more careful analysis, which is given in Chap. 9.

PROBLEMS

7.1. Define the two-particle temperature Green's function by

$$\mathscr{G}_{\alpha\beta;\gamma\delta}(\mathbf{x}_1 \tau_1, \mathbf{x}_2 \tau_2; \mathbf{x}_1' \tau_1', \mathbf{x}_2' \tau_2')$$
$$= \mathrm{Tr}\{\hat{\rho}_G T_\tau[\hat{\psi}_{K\alpha}(\mathbf{x}_1 \tau_1)\,\hat{\psi}_{K\beta}(\mathbf{x}_2 \tau_2)\,\hat{\psi}_{K\delta}^\dagger(\mathbf{x}_2' \tau_2')\,\hat{\psi}_{K\gamma}^\dagger(\mathbf{x}_1' \tau_1')]\}$$

Prove that the ensemble average of the two-body interaction energy is

$$\langle \hat{V} \rangle = \tfrac{1}{2} \int d^3x \int d^3x'\, V(\mathbf{x},\mathbf{x}')_{\mu'\,\lambda',\,\mu\lambda}\, \mathscr{G}_{\lambda\lambda';\,\mu\mu'}(\mathbf{x}'\,\tau, \mathbf{x}\tau; \mathbf{x}'\,\tau^+, \mathbf{x}\tau^+)$$

7.2. Consider a many-body system in the presence of an external potential $U(\mathbf{x})$ with a spin-independent interaction potential $V(\mathbf{x} - \mathbf{x}')$. Show that the exact one-particle temperature Green's function obeys the following equation of motion

$$\left[-\hbar\frac{\partial}{\partial\tau_1} + \frac{\hbar^2 \nabla_1^2}{2m} + \mu - U(\mathbf{x}_1)\right]\mathscr{G}_{\alpha\beta}(\mathbf{x}_1 \tau_1, \mathbf{x}_1' \tau_1') \pm \int d^3x_2\, V(\mathbf{x}_1 - \mathbf{x}_2)$$

$$\times\, \mathscr{G}_{\alpha\gamma;\beta\gamma}(\mathbf{x}_1 \tau_1, \mathbf{x}_2 \tau_1; \mathbf{x}_1' \tau_1', \mathbf{x}_2 \tau_1^+) = \hbar\delta(\mathbf{x}_1 - \mathbf{x}_1')\,\delta(\tau_1 - \tau_1')\,\delta_{\alpha\beta}$$

where the two-particle Green's function is defined in Prob. 7.1.

7.3. Assuming a uniform system of spin-$\tfrac{1}{2}$ fermions at temperature T, and using the Feynman rules in momentum space,
(a) write out the second-order contributions to the proper self-energy in the case of a spin-independent interaction;
(b) evaluate the frequency sums.

7.4. Consider a system of noninteracting particles in an external static potential with a hamiltonian $\hat{H}^{\mathrm{ex}} = \int d^3x\,\hat{\psi}_\alpha^\dagger(\mathbf{x})\,V_{\alpha\beta}(\mathbf{x})\,\hat{\psi}_\beta(\mathbf{x})$.
(a) Use Wick's theorem to evaluate the temperature Green's function to second order in $\hat{H}^{\mathrm{ex}}$. Hence deduce the Feynman rules for $\mathscr{G}_{\alpha\beta}^{\mathrm{ex}}(\mathbf{x}\tau, \mathbf{x}'\tau')$ to all orders.
(b) Define the Fourier transform

$$\mathscr{G}_{\alpha\beta}^{\mathrm{ex}}(\mathbf{x}\tau, \mathbf{x}'\tau') = (\beta\hbar)^{-1} \iint (2\pi)^{-6}\, d^3k\, d^3k'\, e^{i(\mathbf{k}\cdot\mathbf{x} - \mathbf{k}'\cdot\mathbf{x}')}$$

$$\times \sum_n e^{-i\omega_n(\tau - \tau')}\, \mathscr{G}_{\alpha\beta}^{\mathrm{ex}}(\mathbf{k},\mathbf{k}';\omega_n)$$

Find $\mathscr{G}_{\alpha\beta}^{\mathrm{ex}}(\mathbf{k},\mathbf{k}';\omega_n)$ to second order, and hence obtain the corresponding Feynman rules in momentum space.
(c) Show that Dyson's equation becomes

$$\mathscr{G}_{\alpha\beta}^{\mathrm{ex}}(\mathbf{k},\mathbf{k}';\omega_n) = \mathscr{G}_{\alpha\beta}^0(\mathbf{k},\omega_n)\,(2\pi)^3\,\delta(\mathbf{k} - \mathbf{k}')$$
$$+ (2\pi)^{-3}\,\hbar^{-1} \int d^3p\, \mathscr{G}_{\alpha\lambda}^0(\mathbf{k},\omega_n)\, V_{\lambda\lambda'}(\mathbf{k} - \mathbf{p})\, \mathscr{G}_{\lambda'\beta}^{\mathrm{ex}}(\mathbf{p},\mathbf{k}';\omega_n)$$

(d) Express the internal energy and thermodynamic potential in a form analogous to Eqs. (23.15) and (23.22).

7.5. Apply the theory of Prob. 7.4 to a system of spin-$\frac{1}{2}$ fermions in a uniform magnetic field, where $V_{\alpha\beta}(\mathbf{x}) = -\mu_0 \mathcal{H} \cdot \boldsymbol{\sigma}_{\alpha\beta}$.
(a) Express the magnetization $\mathbf{M}$ (magnetic moment per unit volume) in terms of G^{ex} (for $T = 0$) and $\mathcal{G}^{\text{ex}}$ (for $T \geqslant 0$).
(b) Solve Dyson's equation in each case and find $\mathbf{M}$; hence obtain the following limits $\chi_P = 3\mu_0^2 n/2\epsilon_F$ as $T \to 0$ (Pauli paramagnetism) and $\chi_C = \mu_0^2 n/k_B T$ as $T \to \infty$ (Curie's law), where n is the particle density.
(c) *Why does the zero-temperature formalism give the wrong answer?*

7.6. Prove

$$\frac{1}{2\pi i} \int_C f(z) \tanh z \, dz = \sum_{n=-\infty}^{\infty} f\left(\frac{2n+1}{2} i\pi\right)$$

$$\frac{1}{2\pi i} \int_C f(z) \coth z \, dz = \sum_{n=-\infty}^{\infty} f\left(\frac{2n}{2} i\pi\right)$$

where C is the contour shown in Fig. 25.4. State clearly any assumptions about the analytic structure of $f(z)$.

7.7. Use Eqs. (26.10) and (26.11) to compute the first-order correction to E and Ω for both bosons and fermions.

8
Physical Systems at Finite Temperature

27□HARTREE-FOCK APPROXIMATION

As discussed in Sec. 10, there are many physical systems where it is meaningful to talk about the motion of single particles in the average self-consistent field generated by all the other particles. The simplest of these self-consistent approximations is shown in Fig. 27.1 (compare Fig. 10.3), where the heavy lines denote $\mathscr{G}$ itself and not just $\mathscr{G}^0$. This approximate self-energy yields a finite-temperature

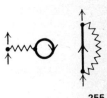

Fig. 27.1 Self-consistent Hartree-Fock approximation to the proper self-energy at finite temperature.

generalization of the Hartree-Fock equations that is valid for both bosons and fermions.

We again consider a system in a static spin-independent external potential $U(\mathbf{x})$. The *grand canonical hamiltonian* is then given by [compare Eqs. (10.1a) and (10.1b)]

$$\hat{K}_0 = \int d^3x\, \hat{\psi}_\alpha^\dagger(\mathbf{x}) \left[-\frac{\hbar^2 \nabla^2}{2m} + U(\mathbf{x}) - \mu \right] \hat{\psi}_\alpha(\mathbf{x}) \tag{27.1}$$

$$\hat{K}_1 = \tfrac{1}{2} \int d^3x\, d^3x'\, \hat{\psi}_\alpha^\dagger(\mathbf{x})\, \hat{\psi}_\beta^\dagger(\mathbf{x}')\, V(\mathbf{x} - \mathbf{x}')\, \hat{\psi}_\beta(\mathbf{x}')\, \hat{\psi}_\alpha(\mathbf{x}) \tag{27.2}$$

where the interparticle potential is again assumed to be spin independent., In the present approximation, Dyson's equation takes the form shown in Fig. 27.2,

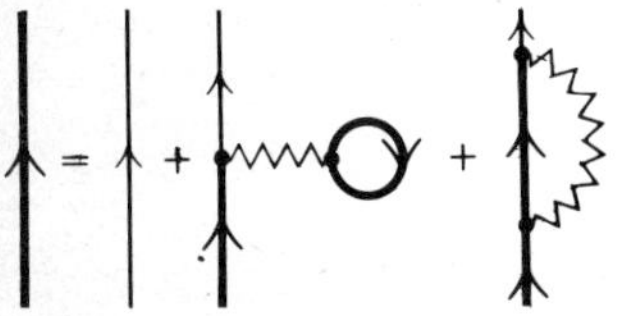

Fig. 27.2 Dyson's equation for $\mathscr{G}$ in Hartree-Fock approximation.

which is formally identical with that at zero temperature (Fig. 10.5). Since $\hat{K}$ is time independent, it is permissible to introduce a Fourier series with respect to the τ variables:

$$\mathscr{G}(\mathbf{x}\tau, \mathbf{x}'\,\tau') = (\beta\hbar)^{-1} \sum_n e^{-i\omega_n(\tau-\tau')}\, \mathscr{G}(\mathbf{x},\mathbf{x}',\omega_n) \tag{27.3}$$

$$\Sigma^\star(\mathbf{x}\tau, \mathbf{x}'\,\tau') = (\beta\hbar)^{-1} \sum_n e^{-i\omega_n(\tau-\tau')}\, \Sigma^\star(\mathbf{x},\mathbf{x}',\omega_n) \tag{27.4}$$

The analytic expressions corresponding to Figs. 27.1 and 27.2 are easily found to be [compare Eqs. (10.6) and (10.7)]

$$\hbar\Sigma^\star(\mathbf{x}_1,\mathbf{x}_1',\omega_n) \equiv \hbar\Sigma^\star(\mathbf{x}_1,\mathbf{x}_1')$$

$$= \mp(2s+1)\,\delta(\mathbf{x}_1 - \mathbf{x}_1')\int d^3x_2\, V(\mathbf{x}_1 - \mathbf{x}_2)(\beta\hbar)^{-1}$$

$$\times \sum_{n'} e^{i\omega_{n'}\eta}\, \mathscr{G}(\mathbf{x}_2,\mathbf{x}_2,\omega_{n'}) - V(\mathbf{x}_1 - \mathbf{x}_1')(\beta\hbar)^{-1}$$

$$\times \sum_{n'} e^{i\omega_{n'}\eta}\, \mathscr{G}(\mathbf{x}_1,\mathbf{x}_1',\omega_{n'}) \tag{27.5}$$

$$\mathscr{G}(\mathbf{x},\mathbf{y},\omega_n) = \mathscr{G}^0(\mathbf{x},\mathbf{y},\omega_n) + \int d^3x_1\, d^3x_1'\, \mathscr{G}^0(\mathbf{x},\mathbf{x}_1,\omega_n)\,\Sigma^\star(\mathbf{x}_1,\mathbf{x}_1')\,\mathscr{G}(\mathbf{x}_1',\mathbf{y},\omega_n) \tag{27.6}$$

where the self-energy $\Sigma^\star(\mathbf{x}_1,\mathbf{x}_1')$ is independent of the frequency ω_n.

The unperturbed temperature Green's function $\mathscr{G}^0$ can be expressed in terms of the orthonormal eigenfunctions of H_0 [Eq. (10.8)], and we find [compare Eqs. (10.10) and (25.17)]

$$\mathscr{G}^0(\mathbf{x},\mathbf{x}',\omega_n) = \sum_j \frac{\varphi_j^0(\mathbf{x})\,\varphi_j^0(\mathbf{x}')^*}{i\omega_n - \hbar^{-1}(\epsilon_j^0 - \mu)} \tag{27.7}$$

In a similar way, the interacting temperature Green's function $\mathscr{G}$ is assumed to have the expansion

$$\mathscr{G}(\mathbf{x},\mathbf{x}',\omega_n) = \sum_j \frac{\varphi_j(\mathbf{x})\,\varphi_j(\mathbf{x}')^*}{i\omega_n - \hbar^{-1}(\epsilon_j - \mu)} \tag{27.8}$$

where $\{\varphi_j\}$ denotes a complete orthonormal set of single-particle wave functions with energy ϵ_j. The mean number density can be evaluated with Eqs. (23.8) and (25.38):

$$\langle \hat{n}(\mathbf{x}) \rangle = \mp(2s+1)(\beta\hbar)^{-1} \sum_n e^{i\omega_n\eta}\,\mathscr{G}(\mathbf{x},\mathbf{x},\omega_n)$$

$$= (2s+1) \sum_j |\varphi_j(\mathbf{x})|^2\, n_j \tag{27.9}$$

where

$$n_j = (e^{\beta(\epsilon_j-\mu)} \mp 1)^{-1} \tag{27.10}$$

is the equilibrium distribution function for the jth state. Correspondingly, the mean number of particles is given by

$$N(T,V,\mu) = (2s+1) \sum_j n_j \tag{27.11}$$

which can (in principle) be inverted to find $\mu(T,V,N)$ if N is considered fixed. The frequency sums in Eq. (27.5) can now be evaluated immediately, with the result

$$\hbar\Sigma^\star(\mathbf{x}_1,\mathbf{x}_1') = (2s+1)\,\delta(\mathbf{x}_1-\mathbf{x}_1')\int d^3x_2\,V(\mathbf{x}_1-\mathbf{x}_2)\sum_j|\varphi_j(\mathbf{x}_2)|^2\,n_j$$

$$\pm V(\mathbf{x}_1-\mathbf{x}_1')\sum_j\varphi_j(\mathbf{x}_1)\,\varphi_j(\mathbf{x}_1')^*\,n_j$$

$$= \delta(\mathbf{x}_1-\mathbf{x}_1')\int d^3x_2\,V(\mathbf{x}_1-\mathbf{x}_2)\langle\hat{n}(\mathbf{x}_2)\rangle$$

$$\pm V(\mathbf{x}_1-\mathbf{x}_1')\sum_j\varphi_j(\mathbf{x}_1)\,\varphi_j(\mathbf{x}_1')^*\,n_j \tag{27.12}$$

A combination of Eqs. (27.6) and (27.12) yields a nonlinear equation for φ_j in terms of φ_j^0.

It is convenient to introduce a differential operator

$$\mathscr{L}_1 = i\hbar\omega_n + \frac{\hbar^2\,\nabla_1^2}{2m} + \mu - U(\mathbf{x}_1) = i\hbar\omega_n - K_0$$

which is the inverse of $\hbar^{-1}\mathscr{G}^0$. The subsequent analysis is identical with that of Sec. 10, and we shall only state the final equation for φ_j:

$$\left[-\frac{\hbar^2\,\nabla_1^2}{2m} + U(\mathbf{x}_1)\right]\varphi_j(\mathbf{x}_1) + \int d^3x_1'\,\hbar\Sigma^\star(\mathbf{x}_1,\mathbf{x}_1')\,\varphi_j(\mathbf{x}_1') = \epsilon_j\,\varphi_j(\mathbf{x}_1) \tag{27.13}$$

where $\hbar\Sigma^\star$ now depends *explicitly* on T and μ.   This set of self-consistent equations is a generalization of the Hartree-Fock theory to finite temperatures; the temperature affects the distribution function n_j directly and also modifies ϵ_j and φ_j through the self-consistent potential.   Although the theory loses its physical content for bosons below the condensation temperature, it remains valid for fermions at all temperatures.   In particular, the Fermi-Dirac function n_j reduces to a step function $\theta(\mu - \epsilon_j)$ at $T = 0$, so that all states with energy less than μ are filled.   As expected, this Hartree-Fock theory for fermions fixes the total number of particles at $T = 0$ by the number of occupied states [Eq. (27.11)].

The internal energy in the Hartree-Fock approximation can be evaluated with a generalization of Eq. (23.15)

$$E(T,V,\mu) = \mp(2s + 1) \int d^3x \lim_{\mathbf{x}' \to \mathbf{x}} (\beta\hbar)^{-1} \sum_n e^{i\omega_n \eta}$$

$$\times \tfrac{1}{2}[i\hbar\omega_n - \frac{\hbar^2 \nabla^2}{2m} + U(\mathbf{x}) + \mu]\, \mathcal{G}(\mathbf{x},\mathbf{x}',\omega_n)$$

$$= (2s + 1) \sum_j \epsilon_j n_j - \tfrac{1}{2}(2s + 1) \int d^3x\, d^3x'$$

$$\times \sum_j \varphi_j(\mathbf{x})^* \,\hbar\Sigma^\star(\mathbf{x},\mathbf{x}')\, \varphi_j(\mathbf{x}')\, n_j \quad (27.14)$$

where the final form has been obtained with Eqs. (27.13), (25.38), and (26.9). This expression can be interpreted as the ensemble average of the self-consistent single-particle energies ϵ_j determined from Eq. (27.13), while the second term explicitly removes the effect of double counting [see the discussion following Eq. (10.18)].   A combination of Eqs. (27.12) and (27.14) yields

$$E(T,V,\mu) = (2s + 1) \sum_j \epsilon_j n_j - \tfrac{1}{2}(2s + 1) \sum_{jk} n_j n_k \int d^3x\, d^3x'\, V(\mathbf{x} - \mathbf{x}')$$

$$\times [(2s + 1)|\varphi_j(\mathbf{x})|^2 |\varphi_k(\mathbf{x}')|^2 \pm \varphi_j(\mathbf{x})^* \varphi_k(\mathbf{x}) \varphi_k(\mathbf{x}')^* \varphi_j(\mathbf{x}')] \quad (27.15)$$

which (for fermions) reduces to the usual Hartree-Fock expression at zero temperature, apart from the dependence on μ instead of N.

It is interesting to consider the form of these equations for a uniform system, where $U(\mathbf{x}) = 0$ and $\Sigma^\star(\mathbf{x},\mathbf{x}') = \Sigma^\star(\mathbf{x} - \mathbf{x}')$.   The self-consistency conditions then become much simpler, since $\varphi_j(\mathbf{x})$ may be taken as a plane wave $V^{-\frac{1}{2}} e^{i\mathbf{k}\cdot\mathbf{x}}$ and only ϵ_k remains to be determined.   Direct substitution shows that $e^{i\mathbf{k}\cdot\mathbf{x}}$ indeed represents a solution of Eq. (27.13); furthermore, the self-consistent single-particle energy becomes

$$\epsilon_k = \epsilon_k^0 + \hbar\Sigma^\star(\mathbf{k}) \tag{27.16}$$

where $\Sigma^\star(\mathbf{k})$ is the Fourier transform of $\Sigma^\star(\mathbf{x})$ and is given by

$$\hbar\Sigma^\star(\mathbf{k}) = (2s + 1) V(0) (2\pi)^{-3} \int d^3k'\, n_{k'} \pm (2\pi)^{-3} \int d^3k'\, n_{k'}\, V(\mathbf{k} - \mathbf{k}')$$

$$\tag{27.17}$$

The self-consistency condition reduces to

$$n_k = \frac{1}{e^{(\epsilon_k - \mu)/k_B T} \mp 1} \tag{27.18}$$

in which ϵ_k both determines, and is determined by n_k. Note that n_k and ϵ_k both depend on μ, which may be fixed by the requirement

$$N(T,V,\mu) = (2s + 1) V (2\pi)^{-3} \int d^3 k \, n_k \tag{27.19}$$

Finally, the internal energy becomes

$$E = (2s + 1) V (2\pi)^{-3} \int d^3 k \, [\epsilon_k - \tfrac{1}{2}\hbar\Sigma^\star(\mathbf{k})] n_k$$

$$= (2s + 1) V (2\pi)^{-3} \int d^3 k \, [\epsilon_k^0 + \tfrac{1}{2}\hbar\Sigma^\star(\mathbf{k})] n_k \tag{27.20}$$

We emphasize that ϵ_k, n_k, and $\Sigma^\star(\mathbf{k})$ in these expressions all depend on T and μ through Eq. (27.18).

28□IMPERFECT BOSE GAS NEAR T_c

As an example of the self-consistent Hartree-Fock approximation, we consider a spin-zero imperfect Bose gas near its condensation temperature T_c. It is helpful first to recall the situation in a perfect gas, where there are only two characteristic energies: the thermal energy $k_B T$ and the zero-point energy $\hbar^2 n^{\frac{2}{3}}/m$ arising from the localization within a volume n^{-1}. The condensation temperature T_0 in an ideal Bose gas is determined by the condition $k_B T_0 \approx \hbar^2 n^{\frac{2}{3}}/m$ [see Eq. (5.30)], which is evident from dimensional considerations. In contrast, the introduction of interactions complicates the problem considerably, since the potential $V(\mathbf{x})$ has both a strength and a range a. As shown below, the present calculation is valid when

$$k_B T_c \approx k_B T_0 \approx \frac{\hbar^2 n^{\frac{2}{3}}}{m} \ll \frac{\hbar^2}{ma^2} \tag{28.1}$$

$$nV(0) \ll \frac{\hbar^2}{ma^2} \tag{28.2}$$

where $V(0) \equiv V(\mathbf{k} = 0)$. The first condition shows that this is a low-density approximation ($na^3 \ll 1$), while the second condition limits the strength of the potential. Note, however, that we do not require the usual condition for the Born approximation [$V(0) \ll \hbar^2 a/m$], which is more stringent by a factor $na^3 \ll 1$.

The mean particle density and self-consistent excitation spectrum are given by

$$n(T,V,\mu) = \int \frac{d^3 k}{(2\pi)^3} \frac{1}{e^{(\epsilon_k - \mu)/k_B T} - 1} \tag{28.3}$$

$$\epsilon_k = \frac{\hbar^2 k^2}{2m} + \int \frac{d^3 k'}{(2\pi)^3} \frac{V(0) + V(\mathbf{k} - \mathbf{k}')}{e^{(\epsilon_{k'} - \mu)/k_B T} - 1} \tag{28.4}$$

Equation (28.3) specifies the density as a function of T and μ, but it is more convenient to fix n and then invert to find $\mu(T,V,N)$. In this case, the chemical potential is large and negative at high temperatures [see Eq. (5.26)], but it increases toward positive values as T is lowered. Exactly as for a *perfect* Bose gas, the temperature T_c for the onset of condensation is determined by the condition $\epsilon_k - \mu = 0$ at $k = 0$, when a finite fraction of the particles starts to occupy the lowest energy state ϵ_0 [see the discussion following Eq. (5.30)]. The present calculation is more complicated, however, because both ϵ_k and μ depend on T.

We assume that $V(\mathbf{x})$ has a Fourier transform

$$V(\mathbf{k}) = \int d^3x\, V(\mathbf{x})\, e^{-i\mathbf{k}\cdot\mathbf{x}} \tag{28.5}$$

whose finite range allows an expansion of the form

$$V(\mathbf{k}) = \int d^3x\, V(\mathbf{x})\, [1 - i\mathbf{k}\cdot\mathbf{x} - \tfrac{1}{2}(\mathbf{k}\cdot\mathbf{x})^2 + \cdots] \tag{28.6}$$

For a spherically symmetric potential, the linear term vanishes. If the mean square radius a^2 is defined by the relation

$$a^2 = \frac{\int d^3x\, V(\mathbf{x})\, x^2}{\int d^3x\, V(\mathbf{x})} \tag{28.7}$$

Eq. (28.6) can then be written as

$$V(\mathbf{k}) = V(0)\, [1 - \tfrac{1}{6}(ka)^2 + \cdots] \tag{28.8}$$

where $V(0)$ and a^2 are both positive if $V(\mathbf{x})$ is everywhere repulsive. The energy spectrum can also be expanded in powers of k^2:

$$\epsilon_k = \epsilon_0 + \frac{\hbar^2 k^2}{2m^*} + \cdots \tag{28.9}$$

where, from Eqs. (28.3) and (28.4),

$$\epsilon_0 = 2nV(0) - \tfrac{1}{6}V(0)\, a^2 \int \frac{d^3k'}{(2\pi)^3} \frac{k'^2}{e^{(\epsilon_{k'}-\mu)/k_B T} - 1}$$

$$= 2nV(0)\left[1 + O\left(\frac{ma^2 k_B T}{\hbar^2}\right)\right] \tag{28.10}$$

and

$$\frac{1}{m^*} = \frac{1}{m}\left[1 - \frac{nV(0)\, ma^2}{3\hbar^2}\right] \tag{28.11}$$

The second term in both of these expressions represents a small correction because of conditions (28.1) and (28.2), respectively. Since the effective mass arises entirely from the exchange interaction in Eq. (28.4), it clearly represents a quantum-mechanical effect.

The transition temperature and corresponding chemical potential are determined by the pair of equations

$$n = \int \frac{d^3k}{(2\pi)^3} \frac{1}{\exp(\hbar^2 k^2/2m^* k_B T_c) - 1} \tag{28.12}$$

$$\mu(T_c) = \epsilon_0 \tag{28.13}$$

Equation (28.12) is identical with that for a perfect gas with mass m^*, and we find [see Eq. (5.30)]

$$k_B T_c = \frac{2\pi\hbar^2}{m^*} \left[\frac{n}{\zeta(\frac{3}{2})} \right]^{\frac{2}{3}} \tag{28.14}$$

If T_0 denotes the transition temperature for a noninteracting gas of the same density and mass m, the interparticle potential shifts the transition temperature by an amount[1]

$$\frac{\Delta T_c}{T_0} = \frac{T_c - T_0}{T_0} = \frac{m}{m^*} - 1 = -\frac{1}{3} \frac{ma^2 nV(0)}{\hbar^2} \tag{28.15}$$

Note that a purely repulsive potential lowers the transition temperature. The constants a^2 and $V(0)$ are readily evaluated for any specific choice of $V(\mathbf{x})$; in particular, $\Delta T_c = 0$ for a point potential $V(\mathbf{x}) = V_0 \delta(\mathbf{x})$.

29□SPECIFIC HEAT OF AN IMPERFECT FERMI GAS AT LOW TEMPERATURE

The Hartree-Fock approximation also represents a useful model for fermions; as a specific and nontrivial example, we shall evaluate the entropy and specific heat in the low-temperature limit.[2] One possible approach is to compute the thermodynamic potential $\Omega(T,V,\mu)$ from Eq. (26.11) but it is easier to work with Eqs. (25.25) and (25.26):

$$K = E - \mu N = \frac{1}{2} V (2\pi)^{-3} (\beta\hbar)^{-1} \int d^3k \sum_n e^{i\omega_n \eta} [i\hbar\omega_n + \epsilon_k^0 - \mu] \, \text{tr} \, \mathscr{G}(\mathbf{k},\omega_n) \tag{29.1}$$

The fundamental relation is the identity $K = \Omega + TS$ [Eq. (4.7)], so that

$$\left(\frac{\partial K}{\partial T}\right)_{V\mu} = \left(\frac{\partial \Omega}{\partial T}\right)_{V\mu} + S + T\left(\frac{\partial S}{\partial T}\right)_{V\mu} \tag{29.2}$$

---

[1] This result was obtained by M. Luban, *Phys. Rev.*, **128**: 965 (1962) and by V. K. Wong, Ph.D. Thesis, University of California, Berkeley, 1966 (unpublished).

[2] Some of the techniques used here were introduced by A. A. Abrikosov, L. P. Gorkov, and I. E. Dzyaloshinskii, "Methods of Quantum Field Theory in Statistical Physics," sec. 19, Prentice-Hall, Inc., Englewood Cliffs, N.J., 1963, but our calculation differs from theirs in several important ways.

The first two terms on the right cancel [Eq. (4.9)], leaving

$$\left(\frac{\partial K}{\partial T}\right)_{V\mu} = T\left(\frac{\partial S}{\partial T}\right)_{V\mu} \tag{29.3}$$

This expression differs from the usual specific heat because μ is held fixed, but it allows us to compute the entropy by integrating at constant V and μ.

LOW-TEMPERATURE EXPANSION OF $\mathscr{G}$

Equation (29.1) is completely general, but the present calculation can be simplified considerably by studying only the leading finite-temperature correction. The exact Green's function $\mathscr{G}$ depends on T *both* through the discrete frequency $\omega_n = (2n + 1)\pi/\beta\hbar$ *and* through the self-energy $\Sigma^\star(\mathbf{k},\omega_n,T)$ [see, for example, Eq. (27.17)]. This functional dependence may be made explicit by writing Dyson's equation as

$$\mathscr{G}(\mathbf{k},\omega_n,T) = \mathscr{G}^0(\mathbf{k},\omega_n) + \mathscr{G}^0(\mathbf{k},\omega_n)\,\Sigma^\star(\mathbf{k},\omega_n,T)\,\mathscr{G}(\mathbf{k},\omega_n,T) \tag{29.4}$$

where $\mathscr{G}^0$ depends on T only through ω_n and the matrix indices are suppressed. The inverse functions $\mathscr{G}(\mathbf{k},\omega_n,T)^{-1}$ and $\mathscr{G}(\mathbf{k},\omega_n,0)^{-1}$ satisfy the equations

$$\mathscr{G}(\mathbf{k},\omega_n,T)^{-1} = \mathscr{G}^0(\mathbf{k},\omega_n)^{-1} - \Sigma^\star(\mathbf{k},\omega_n,T)$$

$$\mathscr{G}(\mathbf{k},\omega_n,0)^{-1} = \mathscr{G}^0(\mathbf{k},\omega_n)^{-1} - \Sigma^\star(\mathbf{k},\omega_n,0) \tag{29.5}$$

whose difference yields

$$\mathscr{G}(\mathbf{k},\omega_n,T)^{-1} - \mathscr{G}(\mathbf{k},\omega_n,0)^{-1} = -\Sigma^\star(\mathbf{k},\omega_n,T) + \Sigma^\star(\mathbf{k},\omega_n,0) \tag{29.6}$$

Multiply by $\mathscr{G}(\mathbf{k},\omega_n,0)$ on the left and $\mathscr{G}(\mathbf{k},\omega_n,T)$ on the right:

$$\mathscr{G}(\mathbf{k},\omega_n,T) = \mathscr{G}(\mathbf{k},\omega_n,0) + \mathscr{G}(\mathbf{k},\omega_n,0)\,[\Sigma^\star(\mathbf{k},\omega_n,T) - \Sigma^\star(\mathbf{k},\omega_n,0)]\,\mathscr{G}(\mathbf{k},\omega_n,T) \tag{29.7}$$

Here the last term explicitly vanishes as $T \to 0$, and this exact equation can therefore be approximated at low temperature by

$$\mathscr{G}(\mathbf{k},\omega_n,T) \approx \mathscr{G}(\mathbf{k},\omega_n,0) + \mathscr{G}(\mathbf{k},\omega_n,0)\,[\Sigma^\star(\mathbf{k},\omega_n,T) - \Sigma^\star(\mathbf{k},\omega_n,0)]\,\mathscr{G}(\mathbf{k},\omega_n,0) \tag{29.8}$$

HARTREE-FOCK APPROXIMATION

The only assumption used in deriving Eq. (29.8) is that of low temperature. The subsequent analysis is less general, however, because we shall now restrict ourselves to the Hartree-Fock model, in which $\Sigma^\star$ is *independent of frequency* and is determined from the diagrams in Fig. 27.1. Assuming spin-$\tfrac{1}{2}$ fermions and spin-independent interactions, we have from the Feynman rules

$$\hbar\Sigma^\star(\mathbf{k},T) = (\beta\hbar)^{-1}(2\pi)^{-3} \int d^3q \sum_{n'} e^{i\omega_{n'}\eta}[2V(0) - V(\mathbf{k}-\mathbf{q})]\,\mathscr{G}(\mathbf{q},\omega_{n'},T) \tag{29.9}$$

where we now write $\mathscr{G}_{\alpha\beta} = \delta_{\alpha\beta}\mathscr{G}$. Equation (29.8) may be used to rewrite this expression as

$$\hbar\Sigma^\star(\mathbf{k},T) = (\beta\hbar)^{-1}(2\pi)^{-3}\int d^3q \sum_{n'} e^{i\omega_{n'}\eta}[2V(0) - V(\mathbf{k}-\mathbf{q})]$$

$$\times \{\mathscr{G}(\mathbf{q},\omega_{n'},0) + [\mathscr{G}(\mathbf{q},\omega_{n'},0)]^2[\Sigma^\star(\mathbf{q},T) - \Sigma^\star(\mathbf{q},0)]\} \quad (29.10)$$

Here the second term in braces apparently becomes negligible as $T \to 0$, and it is tempting to replace the discrete summation over $\omega_{n'}$ by an integral [see Eq. (25.15)]:

$$(\beta\hbar)^{-1}\sum_{n'} \to (2\pi)^{-1}\int_{-\infty}^{\infty} d\omega_{n'} \quad (29.11)$$

Such a procedure is permissible only if the sum and the integral both converge to the same limit. In the present case, however, the resulting integral is too singular to permit the substitution.[1]

To demonstrate this rather subtle distinction, we shall evaluate the sum explicitly and then compare it with the approximate integral. Consider the quantity occurring in Eq. (29.10):

$$(\beta\hbar)^{-1}\sum_{n'} e^{i\omega_{n'}\eta}[\mathscr{G}(\mathbf{q},\omega_{n'},0)]^2 = (\beta\hbar)^{-1}\sum_{n'} e^{i\omega_{n'}\eta}[i\omega_{n'} - \hbar^{-1}(\epsilon_q - \mu)]^{-2}$$

$$= \hbar\frac{\partial}{\partial\epsilon_q}\{(\beta\hbar)^{-1}\sum_{n'} e^{i\omega_{n'}\eta}[i\omega_{n'} - \hbar^{-1}(\epsilon_q - \mu)]^{-1}\}$$

$$= \hbar\frac{\partial n_q(T)}{\partial\epsilon_q} \quad (29.12)$$

where we have introduced the excitation spectrum at zero temperature

$$\epsilon_q = \epsilon_q^0 + \hbar\Sigma^\star(\mathbf{q},0) \quad (29.13)$$

and

$$n_q(T) = (e^{\beta(\epsilon_q - \mu)} + 1)^{-1} \quad (29.14)$$

depends on T only through the explicit appearance of β. Equation (29.12) does *not* vanish at $T = 0$; instead, it reduces to $-\hbar\delta(\mu - \epsilon_q)$. We now turn to the corresponding zero-temperature integral

$$\int_{-\infty}^{\infty} \frac{d\omega}{2\pi} \frac{e^{i\omega\eta}}{[i\omega - \hbar^{-1}(\epsilon_q - \mu)]^2} \quad (29.15)$$

The double pole at $\omega = i\hbar^{-1}(\mu - \epsilon_q)$ with residue $-i\eta e^{\eta\hbar^{-1}(\epsilon_q - \mu)}$ apparently ensures that the integral vanishes as $\eta \to 0$. Closer examination shows that the integral diverges at $\epsilon_q = \mu$. A limiting procedure is therefore required to define its value at that point, and the discrete summation of the finite-temperature theory examined in Eq. (29.12) serves just this purpose.[2]

---

[1] This point was first emphasized by J. M. Luttinger and J. C. Ward, *Phys. Rev.*, **118**:1417 (1960).
[2] Note that the adiabatic damping terms $\pm i\eta$ in the denominators of the corresponding real-frequency integrals in the zero-temperature theory serve exactly this same function.

The explicit form of the self-energy $\Sigma^\star(\mathbf{k},T)$ at low temperature can now be found

$$\hbar\Sigma^\star(\mathbf{k},T) = (2\pi)^{-3} \int d^3q \, [2V(0) - V(\mathbf{k} - \mathbf{q})] \, n_q(T) + (2\pi)^{-3} \int d^3q$$

$$\times \, [2V(0) - V(\mathbf{k} - \mathbf{q})] \, [\hbar\Sigma^\star(\mathbf{q},T) - \hbar\Sigma^\star(\mathbf{q},0)] \frac{\partial n_q(0)}{\partial \epsilon_q} \quad (29.16)$$

where it is permissible to replace $n_q(T)$ by $n_q(0)$ in the second (correction) term. At zero temperature, Eq. (29.16) reduces to the familiar form [compare Eq. (27.17)]

$$\hbar\Sigma^\star(\mathbf{k},0) = (2\pi)^{-3} \int d^3q \, [2V(0) - V(\mathbf{k} - \mathbf{q})] \, \theta(\mu - \epsilon_q) \quad (29.17)$$

because $n_q(0) = \theta(\mu - \epsilon_q)$. In the present approximation of retaining only the leading low-temperature corrections, Eqs. (29.16) and (29.17) together yield

$$\hbar\Sigma^\star(\mathbf{k},T) - \hbar\Sigma^\star(\mathbf{k},0) = (2\pi)^{-3} \int d^3q \, [2V(0) - V(\mathbf{k} - \mathbf{q})] \, \{n_q(T) - n_q(0)$$

$$+ \frac{\partial n_q(0)}{\partial \epsilon_q} [\hbar\Sigma^\star(\mathbf{q},T) - \hbar\Sigma^\star(\mathbf{q},0)]\} \quad (29.18)$$

which may be considered an integral equation for $\Sigma^\star(\mathbf{q},T) - \Sigma^\star(\mathbf{q},0)$.

The fundamental thermodynamic function $K(T,V,\mu)$ can now be rewritten by combining Eqs. (29.1) and (29.8)

$$K(T,V,\mu) = V(2\pi)^{-3} \int d^3k \, (\beta\hbar)^{-1} \sum_n e^{i\omega_n\eta}(i\hbar\omega_n + \epsilon_k^0 - \mu) \, \mathscr{G}(\mathbf{k},\omega_n,0)$$

$$+ V(2\pi)^{-3} \int d^3k \, (\beta\hbar)^{-1} \sum_n e^{i\omega_n\eta}(i\hbar\omega_n + \epsilon_k^0 - \mu) \, [\mathscr{G}(\mathbf{k},\omega_n,0)]^2$$

$$\times \, [\Sigma^\star(\mathbf{k},T) - \Sigma^\star(\mathbf{k},0)] \quad (29.19)$$

Here the summation in the first term is easily evaluated with Eqs. (25.38), (26.9), and (29.13):

$$(\beta\hbar)^{-1} \sum_n e^{i\omega_n\eta}(i\hbar\omega_n + \epsilon_k^0 - \mu) \, [i\omega_n - \hbar^{-1}(\epsilon_k^0 - \mu) - \Sigma^\star(\mathbf{k},0)]^{-1}$$

$$= [2(\epsilon_k - \mu) - \hbar\Sigma^\star(\mathbf{k},0)] \, n_k(T) \quad (29.20)$$

The second term in Eq. (29.19) formally vanishes as $T \to 0$, but the summation is again too singular to replace by an integral; a direct evaluation yields

$$(\beta\hbar)^{-1} \sum_n e^{i\omega_n\eta}(i\hbar\omega_n + \epsilon_k^0 - \mu) \, [\mathscr{G}(\mathbf{k},\omega_n,0)]^2$$

$$= \hbar n_k(T) + [2(\epsilon_k - \mu) - \hbar\Sigma^\star(\mathbf{k},0)] \, \hbar \frac{\partial n_k(T)}{\partial \epsilon_k} \quad (29.21)$$

and we may now take the limit $T \to 0$. A combination of Eqs. (29.19) to (29.21) gives

$$K(T,V,\mu) - K(0,V,\mu) = V(2\pi)^{-3} \int d^3k \, 2(\epsilon_k - \mu) \, [n_k(T) - n_k(0)]$$

$$+ V(2\pi)^{-3} \int d^3k \, 2(\epsilon_k - \mu) \frac{\partial n_k(0)}{\partial \epsilon_k} [\hbar\Sigma^\star(\mathbf{k},T) - \hbar\Sigma^\star(\mathbf{k},0)]$$

$$+ V(2\pi)^{-3} \int d^3k \, n_k(0) \, [\hbar\Sigma^\star(\mathbf{k},T) - \hbar\Sigma^\star(\mathbf{k},0)]$$

$$- V(2\pi)^{-3} \int d^3k \, \hbar\Sigma^\star(\mathbf{k},0) \{n_k(T) - n_k(0)$$

$$+ \frac{\partial n_k(0)}{\partial \epsilon_k} [\hbar\Sigma^\star(\mathbf{k},T) - \hbar\Sigma^\star(\mathbf{k},0)]\} \qquad (29.22)$$

The second term vanishes owing to the factor $\epsilon_k - \mu$ that multiplies the delta function $\partial n_k(0)/\partial \epsilon_k = -\delta(\epsilon_k - \mu)$. This cancellation occurs because all quantities have been expressed in terms of the exact spectrum ϵ_k, showing the necessity of retaining the full self-consistency in the Hartree-Fock theory. In addition, the last two terms of Eq. (29.22) also cancel, which can be seen by substituting Eq. (29.18) into the third term of Eq. (29.22) and then using Eq. (29.17). Equation (29.22) thus reduces to the extremely simple result

$$K(T,V,\mu) - K(0,V,\mu) = V(2\pi)^{-3} \int d^3k \, 2(\epsilon_k - \mu) \, [n_k(T) - n_k(0)] \qquad (29.23)$$

which is our final form. This result indicates that the only low-temperature corrections to $\langle \hat{H} - \mu\hat{N} \rangle_0$ arise from a statistical *redistribution* of the particles among the zero-temperature energy levels ϵ_k determined from the *interactions in the ground state*.

EVALUATION OF THE ENTROPY

The entropy can now be computed from the thermodynamic identity [Eq. (29.3)]

$$T\left(\frac{\partial S}{\partial T}\right)_{V\mu} = V \frac{\partial}{\partial T} \int \frac{d^3k}{(2\pi)^3} 2(\epsilon_k - \mu) n_k(T)$$

$$= V \frac{\partial}{\partial T} \int \frac{d^3k}{(2\pi)^3} (\epsilon_k - \mu)\left(1 - \tanh \frac{\epsilon_k - \mu}{2k_B T}\right)$$

$$= \frac{V}{2k_B T^2} \int \frac{d^3k}{(2\pi)^3} (\epsilon_k - \mu)^2 \operatorname{sech}^2 \frac{\epsilon_k - \mu}{2k_B T} \qquad (29.24)$$

which is an *explicit* function of (T,V,μ). The angular integrations are easily performed:

$$T\left(\frac{\partial S}{\partial T}\right)_{V\mu} = \frac{V}{4\pi^2 k_B T^2} \int_0^\infty k^2 \, dk \, (\epsilon_k - \mu)^2 \operatorname{sech}^2 \frac{\epsilon_k - \mu}{2k_B T} \qquad (29.25)$$

which leaves a single integral over k. At low temperatures, the integrand is peaked at the point $\epsilon_k = \mu$, with a width that vanishes as $T \to 0$. If we change

variables to $\xi \equiv (1/2k_B T)(\epsilon_k - \mu)$, the lower limit may be extended to $\xi = -\infty$ with negligible error:

$$T\left(\frac{\partial S}{\partial T}\right)_{V\mu} = Vk_B^2 T\left[k^2 \frac{dk}{d\epsilon_k}\right]_{\epsilon_k = \mu} \frac{2}{\pi^2} \int_{-\infty}^{\infty} d\xi \, \xi^2 \operatorname{sech}^2 \xi$$

$$= \tfrac{1}{3} Vk_B^2 T\left[k^2 \frac{dk}{d\epsilon_k}\right]_{\epsilon_k = \mu} \tag{29.26}$$

where the slowly varying factor $k^2 dk/d\epsilon_k$ has been taken outside the integral. The integration at constant V and μ is trivial, and we find

$$S(T,V,\mu) = \tfrac{1}{3} Vk_B^2 T\left[k^2 \left(\frac{d\epsilon_k}{dk}\right)^{-1}\right]_{\epsilon_k = \mu} \tag{29.27}$$

The entropy is a thermodynamic function of the state of the system, and it is now permissible to change variables from fixed μ to fixed N. To obtain the leading order in the low-temperature corrections, we may use the zero-temperature equation

$$N = 2V(2\pi)^{-3} \int d^3k \, \theta(\mu - \epsilon_k)$$
$$= 2V(2\pi)^{-3} \int d^3k \, \theta(k_F - k) = Vk_F^3(3\pi^2)^{-1} \tag{29.28}$$

where the Fermi energy is now defined by the relation [see Eqs. (29.13) and (29.17)]

$$\mu = \epsilon_{k_F} = \frac{\hbar^2 k_F^2}{2m} + \hbar\Sigma^\star(k_F, 0)$$

$$= \frac{\hbar^2 k_F^2}{2m} + \{(2\pi)^{-3} \int d^3q \, [2V(0) - V(\mathbf{k} - \mathbf{q})]\, \theta(k_F - q)\}|_{k=k_F} \tag{29.29}$$

The derivative $(d\epsilon_k/dk)|_{k_F}$ at the Fermi surface defines the effective mass

$$\frac{d\epsilon_k}{dk}\bigg|_{k_F} = \frac{\hbar^2 k_F}{m^*} \tag{29.30}$$

and the low-temperature entropy and heat capacity become

$$S(T,V,N) = C_V = T\left(\frac{\partial S}{\partial T}\right)_{VN} = Nk_B^2 T \frac{2m^*}{\hbar^2 k_F^2} \frac{\pi^2}{2} \tag{29.31}$$

These expressions are formally identical with those for a perfect Fermi gas, apart from the appearance of the effective mass m^* [see Eqs. (5.58) and (5.59)]. A simple calculation yields

$$\frac{1}{m^*} = \frac{1}{m} + \frac{1}{\hbar k_F} \frac{\partial \Sigma^\star(\mathbf{k}, 0)}{\partial k}\bigg|_{k_F} \tag{29.32}$$

It is notable that the low-temperature thermodynamic functions are determined solely by the zero-temperature excitation spectrum. This simple result, which

is in fact quite general,[1] arises here from the special form of the Hartree-Fock self-energy. Since $\Sigma^*(\mathbf{k},T)$ is independent of frequency, the spectrum ϵ_k merely shifts the energy of each single-particle level, and the interacting ground state still consists of a filled Fermi sea. The low-temperature heat capacity is determined by those particles within an energy shell of thickness $\approx k_B T$ around the Fermi energy $\epsilon_F \equiv \epsilon_{k_F}$. At a temperature T, the increase in the total energy ΔE is proportional to the energy change per particle $k_B T$ times the number of excited particles

$$\Delta E \propto (k_B T) V (2\pi)^{-3} \int_s d^3k \tag{29.33}$$

where the subscript s denotes the integration region $|\epsilon_k - \epsilon_F| \lesssim k_B T$. Since $k_B T \ll \epsilon_F$, we obtain

$$\Delta E \propto (k_B T)^2 \frac{V}{2\pi^2} \left[k^2 \frac{dk}{d\epsilon_k} \right]_{k_F} = (k_B T)^2 \left(\frac{3N}{2k_F^3} \frac{m^* k_F}{\hbar^2} \right) \tag{29.34}$$

where m^* is identified with the help of Eq. (29.30) and Eq. (29.28) has been used. Thus we see that

$$C_V = \frac{d(\Delta E)}{dT} \propto \frac{N k_B^2 T m^*}{\hbar^2 k_F^2} \tag{29.35}$$

and the constant of proportionality must clearly be the same as for a perfect Fermi gas with mass m^*.

30□ELECTRON GAS

In the previous sections, we studied the Hartree-Fock approximation at finite temperature, which applies to systems with simple two-body potentials. For example, the Fourier transform $V(\mathbf{q})$ must be well defined and bounded for all $\mathbf{q}$; these restrictions preclude both a hard core [$V(\mathbf{x}) \to \infty$ for $x < a$] and a long-range coulomb tail [$V(\mathbf{q}) \to \infty$ as $q \to 0$]. Most physical systems have more complicated interactions, however, which must be treated by summing selected classes of diagrams, exactly as in the zero-temperature formalism (Secs. 11 and 12). For definiteness, we study the thermodynamic properties of an electron gas in a uniform positive background; this system is particularly interesting, because the final expressions describe both the high-temperature classical limit and the zero-temperature quantum limit.[2]

---

[1] J. M. Luttinger, *Phys. Rev.*, **119**:1153(1960), has constructed a general proof valid to all orders in perturbation theory.

[2] This point was first noted by E. W. Montroll and J. C. Ward, *Phys. Fluids*, **1**:55 (1958), who derived the results presented in this section. Our treatment differs in detail, but not in spirit.

APPROXIMATE PROPER SELF-ENERGY

The hamiltonian is that studied previously in Secs. 3 and 12, in which the uniform positive background cancels the $\mathbf{q} = 0$ component of $V(\mathbf{q})$. Thus the diagrammatic expansion of $\mathscr{G}$ has no terms containing $\mathscr{V}_0(\mathbf{q} = 0, \omega_n) = V(0)$. The equilibrium behavior is most easily calculated from the thermodynamic potential [see Eq. (26.11)]

$$\Omega(T,V,\mu) = \Omega_0(T,V,\mu) + V \int_0^1 \frac{d\lambda}{\lambda} \int \frac{d^3k}{(2\pi)^3} \frac{1}{\beta\hbar} \sum_n e^{i\omega_n\eta} \hbar\Sigma^{\star\lambda}(\mathbf{k},\omega_n)\,\mathscr{G}^\lambda(\mathbf{k},\omega_n)$$

(30.1)

where $\Sigma^{\star\lambda}$ and $\mathscr{G}^\lambda$ are the appropriate functions for an interaction potential $\lambda V(\mathbf{x})$ and the spin sum gives rise to an added factor of 2. We would normally evaluate Ω as a power series in the coupling constant e^2, but the second-order term diverges, just as at $T = 0$ (see Prob. 8.4). It is therefore necessary to

$$\Sigma^{\star}_{(1)}(\mathbf{k},\omega_n) = \qquad$$

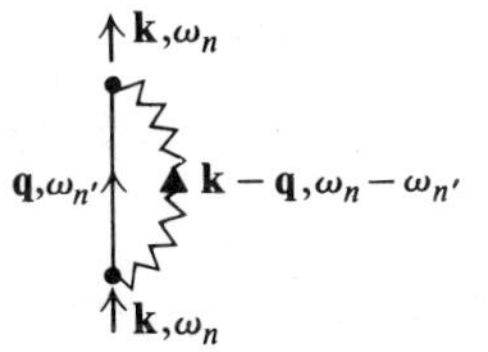

Fig. 30.1 First-order contribution to the proper self-energy for an electron gas.

include a selected class of higher-order diagrams, whose sum yields a finite contribution. The choice of diagrams can be made by examining the perturbation expansion, and we now turn to the Feynman series for $\Sigma^\star$ and $\mathscr{G}$. It is convenient to isolate the effect of the interaction in the proper self-energy; we shall write $\mathscr{G} = \mathscr{G}^0 + \mathscr{G}^0\Sigma^\star\mathscr{G}^0 + \cdots$, and the integrand of Eq. (30.1) becomes $\Sigma^\star\mathscr{G}^0 + \Sigma^\star\mathscr{G}^0\Sigma^\star\mathscr{G}^0 + \cdots$.

The condition $V(0) = 0$ means that all tadpole diagrams vanish. In particular, there is only one first-order proper self-energy (Fig. 30.1). This contribution is easily evaluated with the Feynman rules of Chap. 7:

$$\Sigma^\star_{(1)}(\mathbf{k},\omega_n)$$
$$= -\hbar^{-1}(2\pi)^{-3} \int d^3q \,(\beta\hbar)^{-1} \sum_{n'} e^{i\omega_{n'}\eta}\,\mathscr{V}_0(\mathbf{k} - \mathbf{q}, \omega_n - \omega_{n'})\,\mathscr{G}^0(\mathbf{q},\omega_{n'})$$
$$= -\hbar^{-1}(2\pi)^{-3} \int d^3q\, V(\mathbf{k} - \mathbf{q})\, n_q^0$$

(30.2)

where Eq. (25.38) has been used to evaluate the sum and $n_q^0 = (e^{\beta(\epsilon_q^0 - \mu)} + 1)^{-1}$ is a function of the chemical potential μ. Equation (30.2) differs from Eq. (25.39) because the uniform positive background cancels the direct contribution.

The corresponding first-order term in the thermodynamic potential is given by

$$\Omega_1(T,V,\mu) = V(2\pi)^{-3} \int d^3k\, (\beta\hbar)^{-1} \sum_n e^{i\omega_n\eta} \hbar\Sigma^\star_{(1)}(\mathbf{k},\omega_n)\,\mathscr{G}^0(\mathbf{k},\omega_n)$$

(30.3a)

$$\Omega_1(T,V,\mu) = -V(2\pi)^{-6} \int d^3k \, d^3q \, V(\mathbf{k} - \mathbf{q}) \, n_k^0 \, n_q^0 \qquad (30.3b)$$

where the λ integration has already been performed. Apart from the explicit dependence on μ instead of $N = Vk_F^3/3\pi^2$, which is discussed in detail in this section, this expression is a direct generalization of the first-order exchange contribution to the ground-state energy [Eq. (3.34)]. If Ω is approximated by $\Omega_0 + \Omega_1$, a direct calculation (see Prob. 8.1) predicts that the low-temperature specific heat behaves like $-T[\ln T]^{-1}$, which definitely disagrees with experiments on the electronic specific heat in metals.[1] The same divergence has already

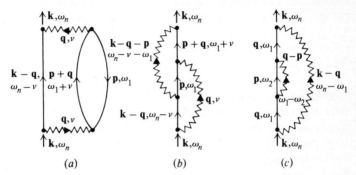

Fig. 30.2 Second-order contributions to the proper self-energy for an electron gas.

appeared in the Hartree-Fock theory of a shielded potential $V(\mathbf{x}) = V_0 x^{-1} e^{-x/a}$ where the effective mass m^* and low-temperature specific heat both vanish like $[\ln(k_F a)]^{-1}$ as $a \to \infty$ (see Probs. 4.1 and 8.2).

The unphysical behavior predicted by the first-order contribution necessitates an examination of the higher-order terms. At $T = 0$, the second-order proper self-energies have already been enumerated in Fig. 9.16, and the same diagrams occur in the finite-temperature formalism. In the present calculation however, three terms vanish identically [$V(0) = 0$], and the only second-order contributions to $\Sigma_{(2)}^{\star}$ are shown in Fig. 30.2. Here and throughout this section, we use ν and ω to denote even and odd frequencies, respectively. The corresponding analytic expressions are (the subscript r denotes the ring contribution of Fig. 30.2a)

$$\Sigma_{(2),r}^{\star}(\mathbf{k},\omega_n) = (-\hbar)^{-2}(-2)(\beta\hbar)^{-2} \sum_{\omega_1\nu} (2\pi)^{-6} \int d^3p \, d^3q \, [V(\mathbf{q})]^2$$

$$\times \, \mathcal{G}^0(\mathbf{p},\omega_1) \, \mathcal{G}^0(\mathbf{q}+\mathbf{p},\omega_1+\nu) \, \mathcal{G}^0(\mathbf{k}-\mathbf{q},\omega_n-\nu) \quad (30.4a)$$

$$\Sigma_{(2),b}^{\star}(\mathbf{k},\omega_n) = (-\hbar)^{-2}(\beta\hbar)^{-2} \sum_{\omega_1\nu} (2\pi)^{-6} \int d^3p \, d^3q \, V(\mathbf{q}) \, V(\mathbf{k}-\mathbf{q}-\mathbf{p})$$

$$\times \, \mathcal{G}^0(\mathbf{k}-\mathbf{q},\omega_n-\nu) \, \mathcal{G}^0(\mathbf{p},\omega_1) \, \mathcal{G}^0(\mathbf{p}+\mathbf{q},\omega_1+\nu) \quad (30.4b)$$

[1] J. Bardeen, *Phys. Rev.*, **50**:1098 (1936); E. P. Wohlfarth, *Phil. Mag.*, **41**:534 (1950).

$$\Sigma^\star_{(2)c}(\mathbf{k},\omega_n) = (-\hbar)^{-2}(\beta\hbar)^{-2} \sum_{\omega_1\omega_2} (2\pi)^{-6} \int d^3p\, d^3q\, V(\mathbf{k}-\mathbf{q})\, V(\mathbf{q}-\mathbf{p})$$

$$\times\, \mathscr{G}^0(\mathbf{q},\omega_1)\, \mathscr{G}^0(\mathbf{p},\omega_2)\, e^{i\omega_2\eta}\, \mathscr{G}^0(\mathbf{q},\omega_1) \quad (30.4c)$$

where the factor (-2) in $\Sigma^\star_{(2)r}$ arises from the spin sum and the closed loop, while the factor $e^{i\omega_2\eta}$ in $\Sigma^\star_{(2)c}$ arises because an instantaneous interaction line $V(\mathbf{q}-\mathbf{p})$ connects both ends of the same particle line $\mathscr{G}^0(\mathbf{p},\omega_2)$. Although all three terms are formally of order e^4, the first differs from the other two in the following way. In each term, the frequency sums yield various combinations of Fermi-Dirac distribution functions n^0 but do not qualitatively alter the momentum integrals for small $\mathbf{p}$ and $\mathbf{q}$. It is therefore clear that $\Sigma^\star_{(2)r}$ diverges as $q \to 0$ [$\propto e^4 \int d^3q\, q^{-4}$ $\cdots$], whereas $\Sigma^\star_{(2)b}$ and $\Sigma^\star_{(2)c}$ converge. For this reason, any calculation that includes only first- and second-order terms in $\Sigma^\star$ cannot be considered satisfactory, and it is essential to examine the higher-order diagrams.

The source of the divergence in $\Sigma^\star_{(2)r}$ is the occurrence of the *same* momentum transfer $\hbar\mathbf{q}$ on each interaction line; in contrast, the other diagrams transfer different momentum on the two interaction lines. A similar structure persists to all orders. For example, the third-order proper self-energy has one (and only one) diagram $\Sigma^\star_{(3)r}$, with the same momentum $\hbar\mathbf{q}$ transferred by all three interaction lines (Fig. 30.3a). This term contains the *most* divergent third-order

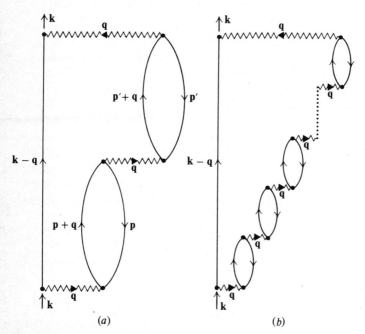

Fig. 30.3 Ring contribution to the proper self-energy in (*a*) third order (*b*) higher order.

term $\propto e^6 \int d^3q \, q^{-6}$; all other third-order terms are less divergent ($e^6 \int d^3q \, q^{-4}$ at most). Correspondingly in nth order, there is always a *single* diagram $\Sigma^{\star}_{(n)\,r} \propto \int d^3q \, [V(q)]^n$ that is more divergent (by a factor q^{-2}) than any other term (Fig. 30.3b). The fundamental approximation in the theory of the electron gas is to retain this selected class of *most* divergent higher-order diagrams along with the complete first- and second-order contributions

$$\Sigma^{\star} \approx \Sigma^{\star}_{(1)} + \Sigma^{\star}_{(2)\,b} + \Sigma^{\star}_{(2)\,c} + \sum_{n=2}^{\infty} \Sigma^{\star}_{(n)\,r}$$

$$= \Sigma^{\star}_{(1)} + \Sigma^{\star}_{(2)\,b} + \Sigma^{\star}_{(2)\,c} + \Sigma^{\star}_{r} \qquad (30.5)$$

where $\Sigma^{\star}_r$ is the sum of all self-energy diagrams with the structure of Fig. 30.3b (ring diagrams).

SUMMATION OF RING DIAGRAMS

The evaluation of $\Sigma^{\star}_r$ is most simply performed by introducing an approximate effective two-body interaction $\mathcal{V}_r$ that includes the polarization of the medium (compare Secs. 9, 12, and 26) associated with the closed loop in $\Sigma^{\star}_r$. Figure 30.4

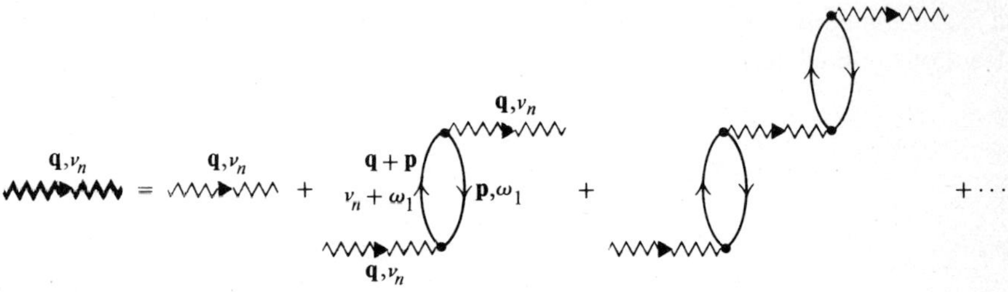

Fig. 30.4 Ring approximation to the effective two-body interaction.

shows the relevant diagrams and the corresponding analytic expressions are

$$\mathcal{V}_r(\mathbf{q},\nu_n) = \mathcal{V}_0(\mathbf{q},\nu_n) + \mathcal{V}_0(\mathbf{q},\nu_n)\,\Pi^0(\mathbf{q},\nu_n)\,\mathcal{V}_0(\mathbf{q},\nu_n) + \cdots$$

$$= \mathcal{V}_0(\mathbf{q},\nu_n) + \mathcal{V}_0(\mathbf{q},\nu_n)\,\Pi^0(\mathbf{q},\nu_n)\,\mathcal{V}_r(\mathbf{q},\nu_n) \qquad (30.6)$$

The function $\Pi^0(\mathbf{q},\nu_n)$ represents the lowest-order proper polarization insertion and will be evaluated in detail below. For the moment, however, it is sufficient to solve Dyson's equation

$$\mathcal{V}_r(\mathbf{q},\nu_n) = \mathcal{V}_0(\mathbf{q},\nu_n)\,[1 - \mathcal{V}_0(\mathbf{q},\nu_n)\,\Pi^0(\mathbf{q},\nu_n)]^{-1}$$

$$= V(\mathbf{q})\cdot[1 - V(\mathbf{q})\,\Pi^0(\mathbf{q},\nu_n)]^{-1} \qquad (30.7)$$

This solution is formally identical with that at zero temperature [Eq. (12.22)] except that $\mathcal{V}_r(\mathbf{q},\nu_n)$ depends on the discrete (even) frequency ν_n.

The analytic form of $\Pi^0(\mathbf{q},\nu_n)$ is easily determined by writing out the first two terms of Fig. 30.4

$$\mathscr{V}_r(\mathbf{q},\nu_n) = \mathscr{V}_0(\mathbf{q},\nu_n) + [\mathscr{V}_0(\mathbf{q},\nu_n)]^2 (-\hbar)^{-1}(\beta\hbar)^{-1}(-2)$$
$$\times \sum_{\omega_1} (2\pi)^{-3} \int d^3p \,\, \mathscr{G}^0(\mathbf{p},\omega_1)\,\mathscr{G}^0(\mathbf{p}+\mathbf{q},\omega_1+\nu_n) + \cdots$$

where the factors $(-\hbar)^{-1}$ and (-2) arise from the extra power of e^2 and the spin sum around the closed fermion loop. By comparing with Eq. (30.6), we identify

$$\Pi^0(\mathbf{q},\nu_n) = 2(\beta\hbar^2)^{-1} \sum_{\omega_1} (2\pi)^{-3} \int d^3p \,\, \mathscr{G}^0(\mathbf{p},\omega_1)\,\mathscr{G}^0(\mathbf{p}+\mathbf{q},\omega_1+\nu_n)$$

$$= \frac{2}{\hbar} \int \frac{d^3p}{(2\pi)^3} \frac{1}{\beta\hbar} \sum_{\omega_1} \left[\frac{1}{i\omega_1 - \hbar^{-1}(\epsilon_{\mathbf{p}}^0 - \mu)} \frac{1}{i\omega_1 + i\nu_n - \hbar^{-1}(\epsilon_{\mathbf{p}+\mathbf{q}}^0 - \mu)} \right]$$

$$\tag{30.8}$$

which is very similar to Eq. (12.28). A typical term of the frequency sum is of order $|\omega_1|^{-2}$ as $|\omega_1| \to \infty$, and the sum therefore converges absolutely. It can be evaluated directly with a contour integral, but a simpler approach is to insert a *redundant* convergence factor $e^{i\omega_1\eta}$, which permits a decomposition into partial fractions. Each term may then be summed separately with Eq. (25.38) and gives

$$\Pi^0(\mathbf{q},\nu_n) = \frac{2}{\hbar} \int \frac{d^3p}{(2\pi)^3} \frac{1}{i\nu_n - \hbar^{-1}(\epsilon_{\mathbf{p}+\mathbf{q}}^0 - \epsilon_{\mathbf{p}}^0)} \frac{1}{\beta\hbar} \sum_{\omega_1} e^{i\omega_1\eta}$$

$$\times \left[\frac{1}{i\omega_1 - \hbar^{-1}(\epsilon_{\mathbf{p}}^0 - \mu)} - \frac{1}{i\omega_1 + i\nu_n - \hbar^{-1}(\epsilon_{\mathbf{p}+\mathbf{q}}^0 - \mu)} \right]$$

$$= -2 \int \frac{d^3p}{(2\pi)^3} \frac{n_{\mathbf{p}+\mathbf{q}}^0 - n_{\mathbf{p}}^0}{i\hbar\nu_n - (\epsilon_{\mathbf{p}+\mathbf{q}}^0 - \epsilon_{\mathbf{p}}^0)} \tag{30.9}$$

where the identity $e^{i\beta\hbar\nu_n} = 1$ has been used. We emphasize again that $n_{\mathbf{p}}^0$ depends on the parameter μ, which can be related to the particle density N/V only at the *end* of the calculation.

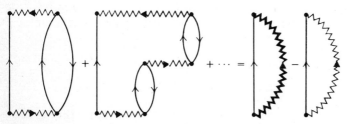

Fig. 30.5 Ring contribution to the proper self-energy.

The contribution $\Sigma_r^\star(\mathbf{k},\omega_n)$ to the proper self-energy can now be evaluated directly in terms of $\mathscr{V}_r$ (Fig. 30.5)

$$\Sigma_r^\star(\mathbf{k},\omega_n) = (-\hbar)^{-1}(2\pi)^{-3} \int d^3q\,(\beta\hbar)^{-1} \sum_{\nu_n} [\mathscr{V}_r(\mathbf{q},\nu_n)$$
$$- \mathscr{V}_0(\mathbf{q},\nu_n)]\,\mathscr{G}^0(\mathbf{k}-\mathbf{q},\omega_n-\nu_n) \quad (30.10)$$

Equation (30.9) shows that $\Pi^0(\mathbf{q},\nu_n)$ vanishes at least as fast as $|\nu_n|^{-1}$ for $|\nu_n| \to \infty$. In consequence, the difference $\mathscr{V}_r - \mathscr{V}_0$ also has this behavior, which ensures the absolute convergence of the frequency summation for $\Sigma_r^\star$. This convergence may be made explicit by rewriting the square bracket in Eq. (30.10) as follows:

$$\mathscr{V}_r(\mathbf{q},\nu_n) - \mathscr{V}_0(\mathbf{q},\nu_n) = \frac{V(\mathbf{q})}{1 - V(\mathbf{q})\,\Pi^0(\mathbf{q},\nu_n)} - V(\mathbf{q})$$
$$= \frac{[V(\mathbf{q})]^2\,\Pi^0(\mathbf{q},\nu_n)}{1 - V(\mathbf{q})\,\Pi^0(\mathbf{q},\nu_n)} \quad (30.11)$$

and $\Sigma_r^\star$ then reduces to

$$\Sigma_r^\star(\mathbf{k},\omega_n) = -\frac{1}{\beta\hbar^2} \int \frac{d^3q}{(2\pi)^3} \sum_{\nu_n} \frac{[V(\mathbf{q})]^2\,\Pi^0(\mathbf{q},\nu_n)}{1 - V(\mathbf{q})\,\Pi^0(\mathbf{q},\nu_n)}\,\mathscr{G}^0(\mathbf{k}-\mathbf{q},\omega_n-\nu_n) \quad (30.12)$$

APPROXIMATE THERMODYNAMIC POTENTIAL

It is now possible to evaluate the corrections to the thermodynamic potential arising from the terms in Eq. (30.5). The integrand of Eq. (30.1) corresponds to

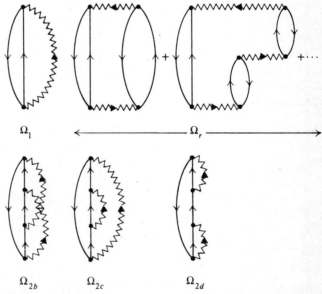

Fig. 30.6 Leading terms in thermodynamic potential for an electron gas.

adding a factor $\mathscr{G}^0$ joining the two ends of $\Sigma^\star + \Sigma^\star \mathscr{G}^0 \Sigma^\star + \cdots$, thereby making a closed loop. Thus $\Sigma^\star_{(1)}$, $\Sigma^\star_{(2)b}$, $\Sigma^\star_{(2)c}$, and $\Sigma^\star_r$ taken once lead to the terms Ω_1, Ω_{2b}, Ω_{2c}, and Ω_r shown in Fig. 30.6, where we have already evaluated Ω_1 with the correct convergence factors in Eq. (30.3). There is also an additional second-order contribution Ω_{2d} arising from the iteration of $\Sigma^\star_{(1)}$. The term Ω_r contains the most interesting physical effects and is studied in detail in the following discussion. The other (explicitly) second-order terms can be written out by combining Eqs. (30.1) and (30.4). It is evident from Fig. 30.6 that Ω_{2c} and Ω_{2d} are topologically equivalent, and a detailed evaluation shows that they are equal. A straightforward calculation yields

$$\Omega_{2b}(T,V,\mu) = V \int \frac{d^3k \, d^3p \, d^3q \, V(\mathbf{q}) \, V(\mathbf{k}+\mathbf{p}+\mathbf{q}) \, n_\mathbf{k}^0 n_\mathbf{p}^0 (1 - n_{\mathbf{k}+\mathbf{q}}^0)(1 - n_{\mathbf{p}+\mathbf{q}}^0)}{(2\pi)^9} \frac{}{\epsilon_{\mathbf{k}+\mathbf{q}}^0 + \epsilon_{\mathbf{p}+\mathbf{q}}^0 - \epsilon_\mathbf{k}^0 - \epsilon_\mathbf{p}^0}$$

$$(30.13a)$$

$$\Omega_{2c}(T,V,\mu) = \Omega_{2d}(T,V,\mu)$$
$$= -\tfrac{1}{2} V \beta (2\pi)^{-9} \int d^3k \, d^3p \, d^3q \, V(\mathbf{k}-\mathbf{q}) \, V(\mathbf{p}-\mathbf{q}) \, n_\mathbf{k}^0 n_\mathbf{p}^0 n_\mathbf{q}^0 (1 - n_\mathbf{q}^0)$$

$$(30.13b)$$

and the total contribution to the thermodynamic potential becomes

$$\Omega = \Omega_0 + \Omega_1 + \Omega_r + \Omega_{2b} + 2\Omega_{2c} \qquad (30.14)$$

Note that the coupling-constant integration in Eq. (30.1) leads to an additional factor n^{-1} for each nth-order contribution to Ω, which is automatically included in our calculational procedure based on the proper self-energy and the single-particle Green's function. As an alternative approach, Ω is sometimes evaluated directly from Fig. 30.6 with a set of *modified* Feynman rules, but the counting of topologically equivalent diagrams and the factor n^{-1} makes such a calculation quite intricate. Our procedure, however, requires only the Feynman rules and diagrams developed previously for $\mathscr{G}$.

The preceding expressions apply to an arbitrary two-body potential, and the special features of the electron gas become apparent only in the evaluation of

$$\Omega_r(T,V,\mu) = V\beta^{-1}(2\pi)^{-3} \int_0^1 \lambda^{-1} \, d\lambda \int d^3k \sum_{\omega_n} e^{i\omega_n \eta} \Sigma_r^{\star\lambda}(\mathbf{k},\omega_n) \, \mathscr{G}^0(\mathbf{k},\omega_n)$$

$$= -V \int_0^1 \frac{d\lambda}{\lambda} \int \frac{d^3q}{(2\pi)^3} \frac{1}{\beta\hbar} \sum_{\nu_n} \frac{\lambda^2 [V(\mathbf{q})]^2 \, \Pi^0(\mathbf{q},\nu_n)}{1 - \lambda V(\mathbf{q}) \, \Pi^0(\mathbf{q},\nu_n)}$$

$$\times \left[\int \frac{d^3k}{(2\pi)^3} \frac{1}{\beta\hbar} \sum_{\omega_n} e^{i\omega_n \eta} \, \mathscr{G}^0(\mathbf{k}-\mathbf{q}, \omega_n - \nu_n) \mathscr{G}^0(\mathbf{k},\omega_n) \right] \qquad (30.15)$$

where $\Sigma_r^\star$ has been taken from Eq. (30.12). The summation over ω_n converges even if $\eta = 0$, and comparison with Eq. (30.8) shows that the quantity in square brackets is $\tfrac{1}{2}\hbar\Pi^0(\mathbf{q},\nu_n)$. [We show in Eq. (30.18) that Π^0 is an even function of

its arguments.]   Since $\mathscr{G}^0$ is independent of λ, the integration over λ is easily carried out, and we find

$$\Omega_r = -\frac{V}{2\beta} \sum_{\nu_n} \int \frac{d^3q}{(2\pi)^3} \int_0^1 \frac{d\lambda}{\lambda} \frac{\lambda^2 [V(\mathbf{q})\,\Pi^0(\mathbf{q},\nu_n)]^2}{1 - \lambda V(\mathbf{q})\,\Pi^0(\mathbf{q},\nu_n)}$$

$$= V(2\beta)^{-1}(2\pi)^{-3} \int d^3q \sum_{\nu_n} \{\ln\,[1 - V(\mathbf{q})\,\Pi^0(\mathbf{q},\nu_n)] + V(\mathbf{q})\,\Pi^0(\mathbf{q},\nu_n)\}$$

$$(30.16)$$

If Eq. (30.16) is expanded in a power series in e^2, the leading contribution is formally of order e^4 owing to the explicit removal of the first-order term.   As shown below, however, the summation of the infinite series modifies this simple power-law dependence on e^2, and, indeed, $e^{-4}\Omega_r$ diverges as $e^2 \to 0$.

Further progress with Eq. (30.16) depends on the explicit form of $\Pi^0(\mathbf{q},\nu_n)$, and we first prove that

$$\Pi^0(\mathbf{q},\nu_n) = \Pi^0(\mathbf{q},-\nu_n) \tag{30.17}$$

Add and subtract $n^0_{\mathbf{p}+\mathbf{q}} n^0_{\mathbf{p}}$ in the numerator of Eq. (30.9)

$$\Pi^0(\mathbf{q},\nu_n) = -2 \int \frac{d^3p}{(2\pi)^3} \frac{n^0_{\mathbf{p}+\mathbf{q}}(1 - n^0_{\mathbf{p}}) - n^0_{\mathbf{p}}(1 - n^0_{\mathbf{p}+\mathbf{q}})}{i\hbar\nu_n - (\epsilon^0_{\mathbf{p}+\mathbf{q}} - \epsilon^0_{\mathbf{p}})}$$

The first term may be rewritten with the substitution $(\mathbf{p} + \mathbf{q} \to -\mathbf{p})$ along with the assumed isotropy of the distribution function (note that $\epsilon^0_{\mathbf{p}} = \epsilon^0_{-\mathbf{p}} = \epsilon^0_p$)

$$\Pi^0(\mathbf{q},\nu_n) = -2 \int \frac{d^3p}{(2\pi)^3} n^0_{\mathbf{p}}(1 - n^0_{\mathbf{p}+\mathbf{q}}) \left[\frac{1}{i\hbar\nu_n - (\epsilon^0_{\mathbf{p}} - \epsilon^0_{\mathbf{p}+\mathbf{q}})} - \frac{1}{i\hbar\nu_n - (\epsilon^0_{\mathbf{p}+\mathbf{q}} - \epsilon^0_{\mathbf{p}})} \right]$$

$$= -4 \int \frac{d^3p}{(2\pi)^3} n^0_{\mathbf{p}}(1 - n^0_{\mathbf{p}+\mathbf{q}}) \frac{\epsilon^0_{\mathbf{p}} - \epsilon^0_{\mathbf{p}+\mathbf{q}}}{(i\hbar\nu_n)^2 - (\epsilon^0_{\mathbf{p}} - \epsilon^0_{\mathbf{p}+\mathbf{q}})^2} \tag{30.18}$$

which proves Eq. (30.17).   It is also clear from the above calculations that Π^0 is an even function of $\mathbf{q}$ and of order ν_n^{-2} as $|\nu_n| \to \infty$:

$$\Pi^0(\mathbf{q},\nu_n) \underset{|\nu_n|\to\infty}{\sim} \frac{4}{(\hbar\nu_n)^2} \int \frac{d^3p}{(2\pi)^3} n^0_{\mathbf{p}}(1 - n^0_{\mathbf{p}+\mathbf{q}})(\epsilon^0_{\mathbf{p}} - \epsilon^0_{\mathbf{p}+\mathbf{q}}) \tag{30.19}$$

CLASSICAL LIMIT

The ring-diagram contribution to the thermodynamic potential Ω_r can now be used to study two limiting cases, and we first consider the behavior at high temperature and low density, when the quantum-mechanical Fermi-Dirac distribution may be approximated by the classical Boltzmann distribution [see Eq. (5.23)]

$$n^0_p = \exp\,[\beta(\mu - \epsilon^0_p)] = e^{\mu/k_B T} e^{-\hbar^2 p^2/2mk_B T} \qquad T \to \infty \tag{30.20}$$

This approximation is justified whenever $e^{\mu/k_B T} \ll 1$ or equivalently for $\mu/k_B T \to -\infty$. In this limit, Eq. (30.19) shows that $\Pi^0(q, \nu_l)$ vanishes as T^{-2} for $l \neq 0$. The frequency sum in Eq. (30.16) separates into two parts

$$\Omega_r = \tfrac{1}{2} V k_B T (2\pi)^{-3} \int d^3q \left\{ \ln\left[1 - V(q)\,\Pi^0(q,0)\right] + V(q)\,\Pi^0(q,0) \right\}$$

$$+ V k_B T (2\pi)^{-3} \int d^3q \sum_{l=1}^{\infty} \left\{ \ln\left[1 - V(q)\,\Pi^0(q, 2\pi l k_B T \hbar^{-1})\right]\right.$$

$$\left. + V(q)\,\Pi^0(q, 2\pi l k_B T \hbar^{-1}) \right\} \quad (30.21)$$

corresponding to $l = 0$ and $l \neq 0$, respectively, and the divergence at small q has now been isolated in the first term ($l = 0$). To verify this assertion, we look at the contribution to the second term from a small region around $q = 0$. In the high-temperature limit Eqs. (30.19) and (30.20) give

$$\Pi^0(q, 2\pi l k_B T \hbar^{-1}) \to 4(2\pi l k_B T)^{-2}(2\pi)^{-3} \int d^3p\,(\epsilon_p^0 - \epsilon_{p+q}^0)\, n_p^0$$

$$= -2\epsilon_q^0 n_0 (2\pi l k_B T)^{-2} \qquad T \to \infty$$

where we have defined

$$n_0 = 2(2\pi)^{-3} \int d^3p\, n_p^0$$

Furthermore, the product

$$V(q)\,\Pi^0(q, 2\pi l k_B T \hbar^{-1}) \to -4\pi e^2 (2\pi l k_B T)^{-2} \hbar^2 n_0 m^{-1} \qquad T \to \infty$$

remains bounded as $q \to 0$. The logarithm in the second term in Eq. (30.21) can now be expanded as a power series in e^2, and the integrand becomes

$$\sum_{l=1}^{\infty} \left\{ \ln\left[1 - V(q)\,\Pi^0\left(q, \frac{2\pi l k_B T}{\hbar}\right)\right] + V(q)\,\Pi^0\left(q, \frac{2\pi l k_B T}{\hbar}\right) \right\}$$

$$\underset{T \to \infty}{\to} -\frac{1}{2} \sum_{l=1}^{\infty} \frac{1}{l^4} \left(\frac{e}{k_B T}\right)^4 \left(\frac{\hbar^2 n_0}{m\pi}\right)^2$$

The sum over l converges, and the singular behavior at $q \approx 0$ has thus disappeared. Hence the second term on the right side of Eq. (30.21) contributes to the thermodynamic potential in Eq. (30.14) in order e^4, just like $\Omega_{2b} + 2\Omega_{2c}$.

The leading contribution to Ω_r therefore requires only $\Pi^0(q,0)$, which can be evaluated with the original definition

$$\Pi^0(q,0) = 2 \int \frac{d^3p}{(2\pi)^3} \frac{n_{p+q}^0 - n_p^0}{\epsilon_{p+q}^0 - \epsilon_p^0} \equiv 2\mathscr{P} \int \frac{d^3p}{(2\pi)^3} \frac{n_{p+q}^0 - n_p^0}{\epsilon_{p+q}^0 - \epsilon_p^0} \qquad (30.22)$$

Since the numerator vanishes at the same place as the denominator, we can keep track of the singularity by treating the integral as a Cauchy principal value. The

remaining integrations are elementary and give

$$\Pi^0(q,0) = 4\mathscr{P} \int \frac{d^3p}{(2\pi)^3} \frac{n_p^0}{\epsilon_p^0 - \epsilon_{p-q}^0}$$

$$= \frac{8m}{(2\pi\hbar)^2} \mathscr{P} \int_0^\infty p^2\, dp\, n_p^0 \int_{-1}^1 dz\, \frac{1}{2pqz - q^2}$$

$$= \frac{m}{q(\pi\hbar)^2} \int_0^\infty p\, dp\, n_p^0 \ln\left|\frac{2p - q}{2p + q}\right|$$

$$= -2\beta e^{\beta\mu}\lambda^{-3}\,\varphi(q\lambda) \tag{30.23}$$

where

$$\lambda \equiv \left(\frac{2\pi\beta\hbar^2}{m}\right)^{\frac{1}{2}} = \left(\frac{2\pi\hbar^2}{mk_B T}\right)^{\frac{1}{2}} \tag{30.24}$$

is the thermal wavelength. Here $\varphi(x)$ is a dimensionless function

$$\varphi(x) \equiv \frac{1}{\pi x} \int_0^\infty d\xi\, \xi e^{-\xi^2/4\pi} \ln\left|\frac{2\xi + x}{2\xi - x}\right| \tag{30.25a}$$

with the limiting behavior

$$\varphi(0) = 1 \tag{30.25b}$$

$$\varphi(x) \sim 8\pi x^{-2} \qquad x \gg 1 \tag{30.25c}$$

The dominant contribution to Ω_r in the high-temperature limit becomes

$$\Omega_r = V(2\beta)^{-1}(2\pi)^{-3} \int d^3q\, \{\ln[1 + 8\pi\beta\lambda^{-3}\,e^{\beta\mu}\,e^2 q^{-2}\,\varphi(q\lambda)]$$
$$- 8\pi\beta\lambda^{-3}\,e^{\beta\mu}\,e^2 q^{-2}\,\varphi(q\lambda)\}$$

$$= 2V\beta^{\frac{1}{2}}e^3\,\pi^{-\frac{1}{2}}(2e^{\beta\mu}\lambda^{-3})^{\frac{3}{2}} \int_0^\infty x^2\, dx\, \{\ln[1 + x^{-2}\varphi[2e(2\pi\beta e^{\beta\mu}\lambda^{-1})^{\frac{1}{2}}x]]$$
$$- x^{-2}\varphi[2e(2\pi\beta e^{\beta\mu}\lambda^{-1})^{\frac{1}{2}}x]\} \tag{30.26}$$

where the second line is obtained with the change of variables $q^2 = 8\pi\beta\lambda^{-3}\,e^{\beta\mu}e^2 x^2$. This equation contains the coupling constant e^2 both in an overall coefficient and in the argument of φ; we may obtain the leading contribution by setting $e = 0$ *in the integrand*, since the terms neglected are of higher order in e^2. A combination of Eqs. (30.25b) and (30.26) yields

$$\Omega_r(T,V,\mu) = 2V\beta^{\frac{1}{2}}\pi^{-\frac{1}{2}}e^3(2e^{\beta\mu}\lambda^{-3})^{\frac{3}{2}} \int_0^\infty dx\, x^2[\ln(1 + x^{-2}) - x^{-2}]$$
$$= -\tfrac{2}{3}V\beta^{\frac{1}{2}}e^3\,\pi^{\frac{1}{2}}(2e^{\beta\mu}\lambda^{-3})^{\frac{3}{2}} \tag{30.27}$$

where the convergent definite integral has been evaluated by partial integration.

It is notable that Ω_r is of order e^3, although the lowest-order term in $\Sigma_r^\star$ is formally of order e^4. This behavior can be understood by examining the

perturbation series for Ω_r, which is obtained by expanding Eq. (30.26)

$$\Omega_r \approx V(2\beta)^{-1}(2\pi)^{-3} \int d^3q \{ -\tfrac{1}{2}(8\pi\beta e^{\beta\mu}\lambda^{-3})^2 (eq^{-1})^4 [\varphi(q\lambda)]^2$$
$$+ \tfrac{1}{3}(8\pi\beta e^{\beta\mu}\lambda^{-3})^3 (eq^{-1})^6 [\varphi(q\lambda)]^3 + \cdots \} \quad (30.28)$$

The leading term (e^4) diverges linearly, the next (e^6) cubically, etc., and each integral must be cut off at a lower limit q_{min}. It is clear from Eq. (30.26) (see also Sec. 33) that the natural cutoff q_{min} is proportional to e, which means that each divergent term is really of order e^3 and must be retained in a consistent calculation. Our procedure for evaluating Ω_r provides a convenient way to include all of these terms.

The thermodynamic potential for a high-temperature electron gas can now be written as

$$\Omega(T,V,\mu) = \Omega_0 + \Omega_1 + \Omega_r + O(e^4) \quad (30.29)$$

because the remaining (finite) second-order terms are explicitly of order e^4. We show, in the following discussion, that the first-order exchange contribution Ω_1 is also negligible in the *classical* limit, and Eq. (30.29) reduces to

$$\Omega(T,V,\mu) = \Omega_0(T,V,\mu) + \Omega_r(T,V,\mu) \quad (30.30)$$

At high temperatures, the thermodynamic potential $\Omega_0(T,V,\mu)$ for a perfect (classical) gas is given by [Eqs. (5.24) and (5.25)]

$$\Omega_0(T,V,\mu) = -2V\beta^{-1} e^{\beta\mu} \lambda^{-3} \quad (30.31)$$

and a combination of Eqs. (30.27) and (30.31) yields

$$\Omega(T,V,\mu) = -\frac{2V}{\lambda^3} k_B T e^{\mu/k_B T}[1 + \tfrac{2}{3}(2\pi)^{\frac{1}{2}} \left(\frac{e^2/\lambda}{k_B T}\right)^{\frac{3}{2}} e^{\mu/2k_B T}] \quad (30.32)$$

The thermal wavelength λ is given in terms of T by Eq. (30.24); thus Ω is properly expressed in terms of (T,V,μ).

Only at this point is it possible to find the mean particle density as a function of μ

$$N(T,V,\mu) = -\left(\frac{\partial\Omega}{\partial\mu}\right)_{TV} = \frac{2V}{\lambda^3} e^{\mu/k_B T}[1 + (2\pi)^{\frac{1}{2}} \left(\frac{e^2/\lambda}{k_B T}\right)^{\frac{3}{2}} e^{\mu/2k_B T}] \quad (30.33)$$

As usual, however, we prefer to consider a system at fixed density; Eq. (30.33) is easily inverted to first order, which provides an equation for $\mu(N)$

$$\frac{\mu}{k_B T} \approx \ln \left\{ \frac{n\lambda^3}{2}\left[1 - \pi^{\frac{1}{2}}\left(\frac{e^2 n^{\frac{1}{3}}}{k_B T}\right)^{\frac{3}{2}}\right] \right\} \quad (30.34)$$

where the first term in brackets is the result for a classical ideal gas Eq. (5.26). The corresponding pressure is given by Eqs. (30.32) and (30.34)

$$P(T,V,N) = -\frac{\Omega(T,V,N)}{V} \approx nk_B T\left[1 - \frac{\pi^{\frac{1}{2}}}{3}\left(\frac{e^2 n^{\frac{1}{3}}}{k_B T}\right)^{\frac{3}{2}}\right] \quad (30.35)$$

which is the Debye-Hückel equation of state for a classical ionized gas.[1]   The leading term describes a perfect gas, while the correction term reduces the pressure slightly.   Our approximations require that $(e^2 n^{\frac{1}{3}}/k_B T)^{\frac{3}{2}} \ll 1$, which ensures that the average potential energy per particle $e^2 n^{\frac{1}{3}}$ is much smaller than the thermal energy per particle $k_B T$.   This condition restricts the present theory to high temperature and low density.   Note that the leading correction to the perfect-gas law is of order e^3 and cannot be obtained with any finite-order perturbation series in the parameter e^2.   Furthermore, Eq. (30.35) is independent of $\hbar$, as befits a classical expression.

The Debye-Hückel result is obtained classically by first examining the charge density and potential in the vicinity of a single electron [compare Eqs. (14.16) to (14.23)].   If the mean electron density is n_0 (exactly equal to that of the uniform positive background), then the Boltzmann distribution gives

$$\frac{n}{n_0} = e^{e\varphi/k_B T} \tag{30.36}$$

where φ is the electrostatic potential in the vicinity of the electron [note that $\varphi(x) \to 0$ as $x \to \infty$ because of the neutrality of the medium].   Furthermore, φ is related to the charge density through Poisson's equation

$$\nabla^2 \varphi = 4\pi e(n - n_0) + 4\pi e\delta(\mathbf{x}) = 4\pi e n_0 [e^{e\varphi/k_B T} - 1] + 4\pi e\delta(\mathbf{x})$$

$$\approx 4\pi e^2 \frac{n_0 \varphi}{k_B T} + 4\pi e\delta(\mathbf{x}) \tag{30.37}$$

when the last equality holds under the conditions discussed above, that is, $e\varphi \ll k_B T$.   This equation can be rewritten

$$(\nabla^2 - q_D^2)\varphi = 4\pi e\delta(\mathbf{x}) \tag{30.38}$$

where q_D is the reciprocal of the Debye shielding length

$$q_D^2 \equiv \frac{4\pi n_0 e^2}{k_B T} \tag{30.39}$$

Since Eq. (30.38) has the solution

$$\varphi(x) = -ex^{-1} e^{-q_D x} \tag{30.40}$$

the charge cloud around the electron is given by

$$\rho_{\text{cloud}} = \left[-\frac{1}{4\pi} \nabla^2 \varphi \right]_{x>0} = -\frac{e^2 n_0 \varphi}{k_B T} = \frac{e^3 n_0}{k_B T x} e^{-q_D x} \tag{30.41a}$$

or alternatively

$$\rho_{\text{cloud}} = e q_D^2 \frac{e^{-q_D x}}{4\pi x} \tag{30.41b}$$

[1] P. Debye and E. Hückel, *Physik. Z.*, **24**:185 (1923).

The work necessary to bring an infinitesimal charge element $-de$ from infinity to the center of this charge cloud is given by the electrostatic potential at the origin.   Thus if dW is the work done *by* the system when the charge on each of the N electrons is increased by $-de$, we find

$$dW = Nde\varphi_{\text{cloud}}(0) = Nde \int \rho_{\text{cloud}}(x)\, x^{-1}\, d^3x$$

$$= Nq_D\, ede = N\left(\frac{4\pi N}{k_B TV}\right)^{\frac{1}{2}} e^2\, de \qquad (30.42)$$

The work done by the system in building up the entire charge $-e$ on each electron is therefore

$$W_{\text{el}} = \int_0^e dW = \frac{Ne^3}{3}\left(\frac{4\pi N}{Vk_B T}\right)^{\frac{1}{2}} \qquad (30.43)$$

From Eq. (4.4) the change in Helmholtz free energy can be written

$$dF = dE - T\, dS - S\, dT = -dW - S\, dT \qquad (30.44a)$$

$$dF|_T = -dW|_T \qquad (30.44b)$$

where the last form of Eq. (30.44a) follows from the first law of thermodynamics. Thus the change in the Helmholtz free energy of the assembly due to electrical work is

$$F_{\text{el}} = -W_{\text{el}} = -\frac{Ne^3}{3}\left(\frac{4\pi N}{Vk_B T}\right)^{\frac{1}{2}} \qquad (30.45)$$

The corresponding change in pressure is obtained from Eq. (4.5)

$$P_{\text{el}} = -\left(\frac{\partial F_{\text{el}}}{\partial V}\right)_{TN} = \frac{F_{\text{el}}}{2V} \qquad (30.46)$$

$$\frac{P_{\text{el}}}{n_0 k_B T} = -\frac{\pi^{\frac{1}{2}}}{3}\left(\frac{e^2 n_0^{\frac{1}{3}}}{k_B T}\right)^{\frac{3}{2}} \qquad (30.47)$$

which is the result given in Eq. (30.35).

We can now verify that Ω_1 is indeed negligible in the classical limit.   When Boltzmann statistics apply, Eq. (30.3b) may be rewritten as

$$\Omega_1(T,V,\mu) = -4\pi e^2\, Ve^{2\beta\mu}(2\pi)^{-6} \int d^3p\, d^3q\, |\mathbf{p} - \mathbf{q}|^{-2} \exp\frac{-\beta\hbar^2(p^2 + q^2)}{2m}$$

$$= -\frac{V}{(\pi\lambda)^3}\frac{e^2}{\lambda}e^{2\mu/k_B T} \iint d^3x\, d^3y\, \frac{e^{-x^2-y^2}}{|\mathbf{x} - \mathbf{y}|^2} \qquad (30.48)$$

where the dimensionless definite integral converges.   A straightforward calculation shows that Ω_1/Ω_r is of order $(\hbar^2 n^{\frac{2}{3}}/m)(e^2 n^{\frac{1}{3}} k_B T)^{-\frac{1}{2}}$, which vanishes in the

classical limit ($\hbar \to 0$) or as $T \to \infty$. The quantity $\hbar^2 n^{\frac{2}{3}}/m$ is an average kinetic energy per particle, and Ω_1 thus becomes negligible if this energy is much smaller than the geometric mean of the average thermal and potential energy per particle.

Finally, we remark that the first quantum-mechanical correction to the classical equation of state for a *perfect* gas (Sec. 5) is of order

$$e^{\beta \mu} \approx \tfrac{1}{2} n \lambda^3 \approx \frac{1}{2} \left(\frac{2 \pi \hbar^2 n^{\frac{2}{3}}}{m k_B T} \right)^{\frac{3}{2}}$$

which is small at high temperatures and low densities. For comparison, the Debye-Hückel term included in Eq. (30.32) is of order $(e^2/\lambda k_B T)^{\frac{1}{2}} e^{\pm \frac{1}{2} \beta \mu} \approx 2(e^2 n^{\frac{1}{3}}/2k_B T)^{\frac{1}{2}}$, which is again small at high temperatures and low densities. It is evident that the quantum correction is negligible as long as $\hbar^2 n^{\frac{2}{3}}/m \ll e^2 n^{\frac{1}{3}}$, which guarantees that the mean kinetic energy is much smaller than the mean potential energy. In summary, the three relevant energies (kinetic, potential, and thermal) must satisfy the set of inequalities $\hbar^2 n^{\frac{2}{3}}/m \ll e^2 n^{\frac{1}{3}} \ll k_B T$; the first allows the use of Boltzmann statistics and renders Ω_1 negligible, while the second ensures that the Debye-Hückel term represents a small correction to the perfect-gas law.

ZERO-TEMPERATURE LIMIT

The preceding section considered only the classical limit, but the same ring diagrams must be retained at all temperatures to yield a convergent answer.[1] As an interesting example, we shall now turn to the opposite (zero-temperature) limit, when the distribution function becomes a step function $n_p^0 = \theta(\mu - \epsilon_p^0)$. Once again, it is important to remember that μ is an independent parameter. Thus the mean particle density and the Fermi wavenumber $k_F \equiv (3\pi^2 N/V)^{\frac{1}{3}}$ cannot be fixed until the end of the calculation, which differs considerably from the previous ground-state formalism (Chaps. 3 to 5).

The terms Ω_1 [Eq. (30.3)], Ω_{2b} [Eq. (30.13a)], and Ω_{2c} [Eq. (30.13b)] in the thermodynamic potential have already been evaluated in a form that is convenient at low temperature. The remaining difficulty is the evaluation of Ω_r, which gives the dominant correction to Ω_1 because it correctly incorporates the long-wavelength behavior. Since the integrand in $\Pi^0(q, \nu_n)$ has only a simple pole as a function of ν_n [Eq. (30.9)], it is permissible to replace the discrete frequency sum $(\beta \hbar)^{-1} \sum_{\nu_n}$ in Eq. (30.16) by a continuous integral $(2\pi)^{-1} \int d\nu$, because the difference vanishes at $T \to 0$ (see the discussion in Sec. 29):

$$\Omega_r(T = 0, V, \mu) = \tfrac{1}{2} V \hbar (2\pi)^{-4} \int_{-\infty}^{\infty} d\nu \int d^3 q \, \{ \ln[1 - V(q) \Pi^0(q, \nu)] $$
$$+ V(q) \Pi^0(q, \nu) \} \quad (30.49)$$

---

[1] M. Gell-Mann and K. A. Brueckner, *Phys. Rev.*, **106**:364 (1957).

Once again, it is most important to evaluate $\Pi^0(q,\nu)$ accurately for small q, and Eq. (30.9) immediately gives

$$
\Pi^0(q,\nu) = -2 \int \frac{d^3p}{(2\pi)^3} \frac{n^0_{\mathbf{p}+\mathbf{q}} - n^0_{\mathbf{p}}}{i\hbar\nu - (\hbar^2/m)(\mathbf{p}\cdot\mathbf{q} + \tfrac{1}{2}q^2)}
$$

$$
\underset{q\to 0}{\approx} -2 \int \frac{d^3p}{(2\pi)^3} \frac{\mathbf{q}\cdot\nabla_{\mathbf{p}} n^0_{\mathbf{p}}}{i\hbar\nu - (\hbar^2/m)\,\mathbf{p}\cdot\mathbf{q}} \tag{30.50}
$$

since the corrections of order q^2 in the denominator can be neglected as long as ν is finite. At zero temperature, $n^0_{\mathbf{p}}$ reduces to a step function, and its gradient becomes $\nabla_{\mathbf{p}} n^0_{\mathbf{p}} = -\hat{p}\delta(p - k_0)$, where k_0 is *defined* by the relation

$$
\hbar k_0 \equiv (2m\mu)^{\frac{1}{2}} \tag{30.51}
$$

The integrations in Eq. (30.50) are readily performed, and we find

$$
\Pi^0(q,\nu) = -\frac{k_0 m}{2\pi^2 \hbar^2} \int_{-1}^{1} \frac{dz\, z}{z - im\nu/\hbar q k_0}
$$

$$
= -\frac{k_0 m}{\pi^2 \hbar^2} R(x) \qquad q \to 0 \tag{30.52}
$$

where

$$
x = \frac{m\nu}{\hbar q k_0} \tag{30.53}
$$

and

$$
R(x) = \int_0^1 \frac{dz\, z^2}{z^2 + x^2} = 1 - x\arctan\frac{1}{x} \tag{30.54}
$$

We now return to Eq. (30.49) and introduce the dimensionless variables x [Eq. (30.53)] and $\zeta = q/k_0$

$$
\Omega_r = \frac{V\hbar^2 k_0^5 4\pi}{2m(2\pi)^4} \int_{-\infty}^{\infty} dx \int_0^{\infty} \zeta^3 \, d\zeta \left\{ \ln\left[1 - \frac{4\pi e^2}{k_0^2 \zeta^2} \Pi^0\left(k_0 \zeta, \frac{\hbar k_0^2 x\zeta}{m}\right) \right] \right.
$$

$$
\left. + \frac{4\pi e^2}{k_0^2 \zeta^2} \Pi^0\left(k_0 \zeta, \frac{\hbar k_0^2 x\zeta}{m}\right) \right\} \tag{30.55}
$$

Although we really want only the dominant term in Eq. (30.55) for small e^2, the divergent behavior of the integrand precludes a direct expansion in powers of e^2. Instead, the ζ integration will be split into two parts: from 0 to $\zeta_0 \ll 1$ and from ζ_0 to ∞. For $\zeta < \zeta_0$, it is permissible to approximate $\Pi^0(k_0\zeta, \hbar k_0^2 x\zeta/m)$ by $\Pi^0(0, \hbar k_0^2 x\zeta/m) = -(k_0 m/\hbar^2 \pi^2) R(x)$, while the full ζ dependence must be retained for $\zeta > \zeta_0$. As long as ζ_0 is finite, however, the integrand in the region $\zeta > \zeta_0$ can be expanded in powers of e^2, retaining the leading term of order e^4. This procedure yields [compare the treatment of Eq. (12.56)]

$$
\Omega_r = \Omega_{r1} + \Omega_{r2} \tag{30.56}
$$

where

$$\Omega_{r1} = \frac{V\hbar^2 k_0^5}{8\pi^3 m} \int_{-\infty}^{\infty} dx \int_0^{\zeta_0} \zeta^3 \, d\zeta \left\{ \ln\left[1 + \frac{4m}{k_0 \pi \hbar^2}\left(\frac{e}{\zeta}\right)^2 R(x)\right]\right.$$

$$\left. - \frac{4m}{k_0 \pi \hbar^2}\left(\frac{e}{\zeta}\right)^2 R(x)\right\} \quad (30.57a)$$

$$\Omega_{r2} \approx -\frac{1}{2}\frac{V\hbar^2 k_0^5}{8\pi^3 m} \int_{-\infty}^{\infty} dx \int_{\zeta_0}^{\infty} \zeta^3 \, d\zeta \left[\frac{4\pi e^2}{k_0^2 \zeta^2} \Pi^0\left(k_0 \zeta, \frac{\hbar k_0^2 x\zeta}{m}\right)\right]^2 \quad (30.57b)$$

The ζ integration in Eq. (30.57a) can now be evaluated explicitly:

$$\int_0^{\zeta_0} \zeta^3 \, d\zeta \left\{\ln\left[1 + \frac{Ae^2}{\zeta^2}\right] - \frac{Ae^2}{\zeta^2}\right\} = \tfrac{1}{4}A^2 e^4 \left\{\frac{\zeta_0^4}{A^2 e^4}\left[\ln\left(1 + \frac{Ae^2}{\zeta_0^2}\right) - \frac{Ae^2}{\zeta_0^2}\right]\right.$$

$$\left. - \ln\left(1 + \frac{\zeta_0^2}{Ae^2}\right)\right\}$$

$$\approx \tfrac{1}{4}A^2 e^4 [\ln(Ae^2) - \tfrac{1}{2} - 2\ln\zeta_0] + O(e^6)$$

$$(30.58)$$

where

$$A(x) = \frac{4mR(x)}{k_0 \pi \hbar^2} = \frac{4m}{k_0 \pi \hbar^2}\left(1 - x\arctan\frac{1}{x}\right) \quad (30.59)$$

This expression exhibits the nonanalytic behavior of Ω_r. Although the definite integral is finite for any $\zeta_0 > 0$, each term of the formal perturbation series diverges:

$$\int_0^{\zeta_0} \zeta^3 \, d\zeta \left\{\ln\left[1 + \frac{Ae^2}{\zeta^2}\right] - \frac{Ae^2}{\zeta^2}\right\}$$

$$= -\tfrac{1}{2}A^2 e^4 \int_0^{\zeta_0} \frac{d\zeta}{\zeta} + \tfrac{1}{3}A^3 e^6 \int_0^{\zeta_0} \frac{d\zeta}{\zeta^3} + \cdots \quad (30.60)$$

This behavior is similar to that of Eq. (30.28) describing a classical electron gas. The high- and low-temperature limits differ in one important way, however, because the leading term here diverges logarithmically rather than linearly. In consequence, when Eq. (30.60) is cut off at a lower limit $\zeta_{min} \propto e$, we see that the first term is of order $e^4 \ln e$ while the remaining ones are of order e^4, in contrast to the e^3 dependence of each term in Eq. (30.28). It is this isolation of the $e^4 \ln e$ behavior that allowed us to determine the leading term in the correlation energy directly from the second-order term in the ground-state energy (Prob. 1.5).

The contribution Ω_{r2} also exhibits a logarithmic singularity as $\zeta_0 \to 0$, because $\Pi^0(k_0\zeta, \hbar k_0^2 x\zeta/m)$ approaches a constant value as $\zeta \to 0$. It is easily verified from Eq. (30.52) that the divergence is identical with that in Eq. (30.58), and the quantity

$$I(x) \equiv -\frac{6}{\pi^3}\lim_{\zeta_0 \to 0}\left\{R^2(x)\ln\zeta_0 + \left(\frac{\hbar^2 \pi^2}{mk_0}\right)^2 \int_{\zeta_0}^{\infty} \frac{d\zeta}{\zeta}\left[\Pi^0\left(k_0\zeta, \frac{\hbar k_0^2 x\zeta}{m}\right)\right]^2\right\} \quad (30.61)$$

is finite.   A combination of Eqs. (30.56), (30.58), and (30.61) yields

$$\Omega_r \approx \frac{V \hbar^2 k_0^5}{8\pi^3 m} \int_{-\infty}^{\infty} dx \left\{ \tfrac{1}{4}[e^2 A(x)]^2 \ln [e^2 A(x)] - \tfrac{1}{8}[e^2 A(x)]^2 \right.$$
$$\left. + \frac{4\pi}{3} \left(\frac{me^2}{\hbar^2 k_0} \right)^2 I(x) \right\} \quad (30.62)$$

correct through order e^4.   The calculation has now been reduced to a one-dimensional integral containing the functions $A(x)$ and $I(x)$, given in Eqs. (30.59) and (30.61).

Before we complete the evaluation of Ω_r, it is useful to collect all the terms of Ω through order $e^4 \ln e$ and e^4:

$$\Omega(T,V,\mu) = \Omega_0 + \Omega_1 + \Omega_r + \Omega_{2b} + 2\Omega_{2c} \quad (30.63)$$

To the same order of approximation, the mean number of particles is given by

$$N(T,V,\mu) = -\left(\frac{\partial \Omega}{\partial \mu} \right)_{TV} = -\frac{\partial \Omega_0}{\partial \mu} - \frac{\partial \Omega_1}{\partial \mu} - \frac{\partial (\Omega_r + \Omega_{2b} + 2\Omega_{2c})}{\partial \mu} \quad (30.64)$$

which expresses N as a function of μ.   *These two equations* (30.63) and (30.64) *provide a valid and complete description of a degenerate electron gas*, for they constitute a parametric relation between N and Ω.   Nevertheless, it is frequently convenient to eliminate μ *explicitly*; this is readily performed by expanding μ as a perturbation series[1]

$$\mu = \mu_0 + \mu_1 + \mu_2 + \cdots \quad (30.65)$$

where the subscript denotes the corresponding order in e^2, and then by expanding each term on the right side of Eq. (30.64) as a Taylor series about the value $\mu = \mu_0$.   Equation (30.64) can now be inverted order by order in e^2, and the first two terms yield

$$N = -\left(\frac{\partial \Omega_0}{\partial \mu} \right)_{\mu=\mu_0} \quad (30.66)$$

$$\mu_1 = -\frac{(\partial \Omega_1/\partial \mu)_{\mu=\mu_0}}{(\partial^2 \Omega_0/\partial \mu^2)_{\mu=\mu_0}} \quad (30.67)$$

Here the first equation determines μ_0 as a function of N, while the second determines μ_1 in terms of μ_0 (and therefore N).   Note that μ_0 is just the chemical potential for an ideal Fermi gas at temperature T with density N/V.

The change of variable from μ to N indicates that the relevant thermodynamic function is the Helmholtz free energy [see Eq. (4.5)]

$$F(T,V,N) = E - TS = \Omega + \mu N$$

---

[1] The present treatment follows that of W. Kohn and J. M. Luttinger, *Phys. Rev.*, **118**:41 (1960).

which may be formally expanded through second order in powers of e^2:

$$F = \Omega_0(\mu_0) + (\mu_1 + \mu_2)\left(\frac{\partial \Omega_0}{\partial \mu}\right)_{\mu=\mu_0} + \tfrac{1}{2}\mu_1^2\left(\frac{\partial^2 \Omega_0}{\partial \mu^2}\right)_{\mu=\mu_0} + \Omega_1(\mu_0)$$

$$+ \mu_1\left(\frac{\partial \Omega_1}{\partial \mu}\right)_{\mu=\mu_0} + \Omega_r(\mu_0) + \Omega_{2b}(\mu_0) + 2\Omega_{2c}(\mu_0) + \mu_0 N + (\mu_1 + \mu_2)N$$

$$(30.68)$$

The second and last terms cancel because of Eq. (30.66) so that the explicit form of μ_2 is never needed. Equations (30.67) and (30.68) can be combined to give

$$F(T,V,N) = F_0(T,V,N) + \Omega_1(\mu_0) + \Omega_r(\mu_0) + \Omega_{2b}(\mu_0)$$

$$+ \left[2\Omega_{2c}(\mu_0) - \frac{1}{2}\frac{(\partial \Omega_1/\partial \mu)^2_{\mu=\mu_0}}{(\partial^2 \Omega_0/\partial \mu^2)_{\mu=\mu_0}}\right] \quad (30.69)$$

where μ_0 is a function of N, and $F_0(T,V,N) = \Omega_0(\mu_0) + \mu_0 N$ is the Helmholtz free energy of an ideal Fermi gas.

The present description becomes especially simple at zero temperature [see Eq. (5.53)]:

$$\Omega_0(0,V,\mu_0) = -\frac{2}{15\pi^2}V\left(\frac{2m}{\hbar^2}\right)^{\frac{3}{2}}\mu_0^{\frac{5}{2}}$$

$$\left(\frac{\partial \Omega_0(0,V,\mu)}{\partial \mu}\right)_{\mu=\mu_0} = -\frac{1}{3\pi^2}V\left(\frac{2m}{\hbar^2}\right)^{\frac{3}{2}}\mu_0^{\frac{3}{2}} \quad (30.70)$$

$$\left(\frac{\partial^2 \Omega_0(0,V,\mu)}{\partial \mu^2}\right)_{\mu=\mu_0} = -\frac{1}{2\pi^2}V\left(\frac{2m}{\hbar^2}\right)^{\frac{3}{2}}\mu_0^{\frac{1}{2}}$$

In this limit, the zero-order term μ_0 is given by

$$\mu_0(N) = \frac{\hbar^2}{2m}\left(\frac{3\pi^2 N}{V}\right)^{\frac{2}{3}} \equiv \frac{\hbar^2 k_F^2}{2m} = \epsilon_F^0 \quad (30.71)$$

where k_F is the usual Fermi wavenumber. The subsequent discussion shows that the last term of Eq. (30.69) (in square brackets) vanishes at $T = 0$. Consequently, the ground-state energy of the N-particle interacting system has the following expansion

$$E = E_0 + \Omega_1(\epsilon_F^0) + \Omega_r(\epsilon_F^0) + \Omega_{2b}(\epsilon_F^0) \quad (30.72)$$

because $F \equiv E - TS \to E$ as $T \to 0$. Here the first term E_0 is the ground-state energy of the corresponding perfect Fermi gas [$E_0 = \tfrac{3}{5}N\epsilon_F^0$], while $\Omega_1(\epsilon_F^0)$ is the first-order exchange energy [compare Eqs. (3.34) and (30.3b)]

$$\Omega_1(\epsilon_F^0) = -4\pi e^2 V(2\pi)^{-6} \int d^3p \, d^3q \, |\mathbf{p} - \mathbf{q}|^{-2} \, \theta(k_F - p)\,\theta(k_F - q) \quad (30.73)$$

The remaining terms of Eq. (30.72) clearly represent the leading contribution to the correlation energy

$$E_{\text{corr}} = \Omega_r(\epsilon_F^0) + \Omega_{2b}(\epsilon_F^0) \quad (30.74)$$

The dominant term in the correlation energy comes from the long-wave-length part of Ω_r. Introducing the usual dimensionless units (see Sec. 3) and identifying k_0 with k_F, we can write

$$E_{corr} = \frac{Ne^2}{2a_0} \epsilon_{corr} \tag{30.75}$$

where from Eqs. (30.59) and (30.62)

$$\epsilon_{corr} = \frac{3}{\pi^3} \ln r_s \int_{-\infty}^{\infty} [R(x)]^2 \, dx \qquad r_s \to 0 \tag{30.76}$$

The integral is most easily performed with the integral representation Eq. (30.54)

$$\int_{-\infty}^{\infty} dx \, [R(x)]^2 = \int_0^1 dy \int_0^1 dz \int_{-\infty}^{\infty} dx \frac{y^2 z^2}{(y^2 + x^2)(z^2 + x^2)}$$

$$= \pi \int_0^1 dy \int_0^1 dz \frac{yz}{y + z}$$

$$= \tfrac{2}{3}\pi(1 - \ln 2) \tag{30.77}$$

Thus

$$\epsilon_{corr} = \frac{2}{\pi^2} (1 - \ln 2) \ln r_s + \text{const} \qquad r_s \to 0 \tag{30.78}$$

which agrees with Eq. (12.61).

The constant term can also be obtained from Eq. (30.74), but the evaluation is considerably more difficult. Introducing the same dimensionless units into Eqs. (30.13a) and (30.62) gives

$$\Omega_{2b}(\epsilon_F^0) = \frac{Ne^2}{2a_0} \epsilon_2^b \tag{30.79a}$$

$$\Omega_r(\epsilon_F^0) = \frac{Ne^2}{2a_0} \left\{ 3\pi^{-3} \int_{-\infty}^{\infty} dx [R(x)]^2 \left[\ln (4\alpha r_s \pi^{-1}) + \ln R(x) - \tfrac{1}{2} \right] + \delta \right\} \tag{30.79b}$$

where $\alpha = (4/9\pi)^{\frac{1}{3}}$, ϵ_2^b is a definite integral given in Prob. 1.4, and

$$\delta \equiv \int_{-\infty}^{\infty} dx \, I(x) = \lim_{\zeta_0 \to 0} \left\{ -\frac{4}{\pi^2}(1 - \ln 2) \ln \zeta_0 - \frac{3}{2\pi^4} \int_{\zeta_0}^{\infty} \frac{dq}{q^2} \right.$$

$$\left. \times \int\int \frac{d^3k \, d^3p \, \theta(1 - k) \, \theta(1 - p) \, \theta(|\mathbf{p} + \mathbf{q}| - 1) \, \theta(|\mathbf{k} + \mathbf{q}| - 1)}{q^2 + \mathbf{q} \cdot (\mathbf{p} + \mathbf{k})} \right\} \tag{30.80}$$

is independent of r_s. The last expression for δ is just ϵ_2^r with the logarithmic singularity removed (see Probs. 1.4 and 1.5); its derivation is outlined in Prob.

8.7.   Substitution of Eqs. (30.77) and (30.79) into Eq. (30.74) yields

$$\epsilon_{\text{corr}} = \frac{2}{\pi^2}(1 - \ln 2)\left[\ln\left(\frac{4\alpha r_s}{\pi}\right) + \langle \ln R \rangle_{\text{av}} - \frac{1}{2}\right] + \delta + \epsilon_2^b \tag{30.81}$$

Here the numerical constants $\langle \ln R \rangle_{\text{av}}$ and δ must be found numerically[1]

$$\langle \ln R \rangle_{\text{av}} \equiv \frac{\int_{-\infty}^{\infty} dx\, R^2 \ln R}{\int_{-\infty}^{\infty} dx\, R^2} = -0.551 \tag{30.82a}$$

$$\delta = -0.0508 \tag{30.82b}$$

while the nine-dimensional integral ϵ_2^b has been evaluated analytically by Onsager[2]

$$\epsilon_2^b = \tfrac{1}{3}\ln 2 - \frac{3}{2\pi^2}\zeta(3) \approx 0.048 \tag{30.83}$$

The final expression for the correlation energy becomes

$$\epsilon_{\text{corr}} = 0.0622\ln r_s - 0.094 + O(r_s \ln r_s) \tag{30.84}$$

in complete agreement with Eq. (12.62) derived from the zero-temperature formalism.   It is interesting that the present zero-temperature approximation is valid at *high* densities ($n^{\frac{1}{3}} e^2 \ll \hbar^2 n^{\frac{2}{3}}/m$), in contrast to the previous classical calculation.   In both cases, however, the potential energy $n^{\frac{1}{3}} e^2$ is small compared to the other relevant energy ($\hbar^2 n^{\frac{2}{3}}/m$ at $T = 0$, $k_B T$ at $T \to \infty$).

To complete this calculation,[3] it is necessary to show that the last term in Eq. (30.69) indeed vanishes.   The second-order correction Ω_{2c} [Eq. (30.13b)] can be rewritten for *all* temperatures as

$$\Omega_{2c}(T,V,\mu) = \tfrac{1}{2}V \int \frac{d^3k\, d^3p\, d^3q}{(2\pi)^9}\, V(\mathbf{k} - \mathbf{q})\, V(\mathbf{p} - \mathbf{q})\, n_k^0 n_p^0 \frac{\partial n_q^0}{\partial \epsilon_q^0} \tag{30.85}$$

because

$$-\beta n_q^0(1 - n_q^0) = \frac{\partial n_q^0}{\partial \epsilon_q^0}$$

In the limit $T \to 0$, the factor $\partial n_q^0/\partial \epsilon_q^0$ reduces to $-\delta(\mu - \epsilon_q^0)$, and we can write

$$\Omega_{2c}(0,V,\mu_0) = -\tfrac{1}{2}V(2\pi)^{-3}\int d^3q\, \delta(\mu_0 - \epsilon_q^0)(f_q)^2 \tag{30.86}$$

Here

$$f_q \equiv (2\pi)^{-3}\int d^3k\, V(\mathbf{k} - \mathbf{q})\, n_k^0 \big|_{\mu=\mu_0,\, T=0}$$
$$= (2\pi)^{-3}\int d^3k\, V(\mathbf{k} - \mathbf{q})\, \theta(\mu_0 - \epsilon_k^0) \tag{30.87}$$

[1] M. Gell-Mann and K. A. Brueckner, *loc. cit.*
[2] L. Onsager, L. Mittag, and M. J. Stephen, *Ann. Physik,* **18:**71 (1966).
[3] This point was first emphasized by W. Kohn and J. M. Luttinger, *loc. cit.*

and μ has been set equal to μ_0, as required by Eq. (30.69). A similar calculation leads to [compare Eq. (30.3b) for $T = 0$]

$$
\left(\frac{\partial\Omega_1}{\partial\mu}\right)_{\mu=\mu_0} = -V \int \frac{d^3k\,d^3q}{(2\pi)^6} V(\mathbf{k} - \mathbf{q})\left[n_k^0 \frac{\partial n_q^0}{\partial\mu} + n_q^0 \frac{\partial n_k^0}{\partial\mu}\right]_{\mu=\mu_0,\,T\to0}
$$

$$
= -2V(2\pi)^{-3} \int d^3q\,\delta(\mu_0 - \epsilon_q^0)\,f_q \tag{30.88}
$$

Finally, a direct evaluation yields

$$
\left(\frac{\partial^2\Omega_0}{\partial\mu^2}\right)_{\mu=\mu_0} = -2V \int \frac{d^3q}{(2\pi)^3} \delta(\mu_0 - \epsilon_q^0) \tag{30.89}
$$

which is equivalent to the last line of Eq. (30.70). With the following definition of an average over the Fermi surface

$$
\langle \cdots \rangle_F = \frac{(2\pi)^{-3} \int d^3q \; \cdots \; \delta(\mu_0 - \epsilon_q^0)}{(2\pi)^{-3} \int d^3q\,\delta(\mu_0 - \epsilon_q^0)} \tag{30.90}
$$

the last term of Eq. (30.69) assumes the transparent form

$$
2\Omega_{2c}(\mu_0) - \frac{1}{2}\frac{(\partial\Omega_1/\partial\mu)^2_{\mu=\mu_0}}{(\partial^2\Omega_0/\partial\mu^2)_{\mu=\mu_0}}
$$

$$
= -V[\langle(f_q - \langle f_q\rangle_F)^2\rangle_F](2\pi)^{-3} \int d^3q\,\delta(\mu_0 - \epsilon_q^0)
$$

$$
\leqslant 0 \tag{30.91}
$$

This contribution to the ground-state energy is proportional to the mean square deviation of f_q over the *unperturbed* Fermi surface and can never raise the energy. Furthermore, the correction evidently vanishes for a spherical Fermi surface, which is the case for an electron gas in a uniform positive background.

The foregoing cancellation is a specific example of a general theorem[1] for spin-$\frac{1}{2}$ fermions that the $T \to 0$ limit of the finite temperature formalism always gives the same ground-state energy as that calculated with the $T = 0$ formalism (either in Feynman or in Brueckner-Goldstone form), as long as the unperturbed Fermi surface is spherically symmetric and the interactions are invariant under spatial rotations. This result is not at all obvious, because the two approaches describe the interacting system in very different ways. The $T \neq 0$ formalism computes the thermodynamic potential Ω as a function of the parameter μ, and its $T \to 0$ limit involves integrals over Fermi distribution functions that are singular where the energy is equal to μ. At the end of the calculation, μ may be eliminated in favor of the particle density N/V, and μ then defines the Fermi energy ϵ_F of the *interacting* ground state. On the other hand, the usual $T = 0$ formalism considers a fixed number of particles N from the start and evaluates the ground-state energy as a series in the coupling constant of the

[1] W. Kohn and J. M. Luttinger, *loc. cit.*; J. M. Luttinger and J. C. Ward, *loc. cit.*

two-body potential. Each term in this series involves integrals over the *unperturbed* Fermi distribution function, which has its discontinuity at the unperturbed Fermi energy $\epsilon_F^0 = (\hbar^2/2m)(3\pi^2 N/V)^{\frac{2}{3}}$.

In comparing the two formalisms, we immediately note that the $T \neq 0$ expansion contains terms that are never considered at $T = 0$. For example, the zero-temperature version of $\Sigma_{(2)c}^{\star}$ contains an integral over $\theta(k_F - q)\,\theta(q - k_F)$ and therefore vanishes [Prob. 3.12]. At finite temperature, however, the thermal width yields a nonzero value that remains finite even in the limit $T = 0$. All of these additional diagrams contain singular factors at zero temperature, such as $\delta(\epsilon_k^0 - \mu)$ or its derivatives, whereas the diagrams that are common to both formalisms contain only step functions at $T = 0$. Since the $T = 0$ formalism antedates the $T \neq 0$ one, these additional terms are conventionally described as *anomalous*. The two formalisms also differ because one uses the exact chemical potential $\mu \equiv \epsilon_F$, while the other uses the unperturbed Fermi energy $\epsilon_F^0 \equiv \mu_0$. The Taylor series for $\Omega(T = 0, \epsilon_F)$ about the value $\Omega(T = 0, \epsilon_F^0)$ involves an expansion of step functions at ϵ_F in terms of those at ϵ_F^0; this expansion leads to additional delta functions and derivatives of delta functions. The content of the Kohn-Luttinger-Ward theorem is that the extra contribution incurred in the shift in Fermi energy from ϵ_F to ϵ_F^0 precisely cancels the anomalous diagrams, leaving the Brueckner-Goldstone series for the ground-state energy.

If perturbation theory provides a valid description of an interacting system, then the $T = 0$ limit of the temperature formalism necessarily yields the *true* ground state for any value of the coupling constant. In contrast, the $T = 0$ formalism merely generates that eigenstate of the hamiltonian that develops adiabatically from the *noninteracting* ground state. For an arbitrary system, these two approaches may yield different eigenstates, as shown by the simple example of a perfect Fermi gas in a uniform magnetic field (Prob. 7.5). The Kohn-Luttinger-Ward theorem can therefore be interpreted as specifying sufficient conditions to ensure that the $T = 0$ formalism indeed yields the *true* ground state. Unfortunately, the very interesting question of *necessary* conditions remains unanswered.

PROBLEMS

8.1. Verify that C_V for an electron gas in the Hartree-Fock approximation behaves like $-T(\ln T)^{-1}$ as $T \to 0$. [Compare the discussion following Eq. (30.3).]

8.2. (*a*) Using the results of Prob. 4.9 for the lowest-order proper self-energy of an electron gas $\hbar\Sigma_{(1)}^{\star}(\mathbf{q})$ and effective mass m^*, show that the corresponding heat capacity at zero temperature satisfies $C_V/T = 0$.
(*b*) The long-wavelength coulomb interaction is modified by the presence of the medium according to Eq. (12.65). Show that the correct low-temperature

heat capacity is given by $C_V/C_V^F = \{1 - (\alpha r_s/2\pi)[\ln(\alpha r_s/\pi) + 2] + \cdots\}^{-1}$ as $r_s \to 0$, where C_V^F is the heat capacity of a noninteracting Fermi gas.‡

8.3. Repeat Prob. 4.4 with the finite-temperature Green's functions.

8.4. (a) Use the Feynman rules to evaluate the second-order self-energy contributions to the temperature Green's function shown in Fig. 30.2a and b for a uniform system of spin-$\frac{1}{2}$ fermions. Find the corresponding contributions to the thermodynamic potential and evaluate the necessary frequency sums (see Prob. 7.3) to obtain

$$\Omega_{2a} = -2V \iiint (2\pi)^{-9} d^3q\, d^3p\, d^3k\, |V(\mathbf{q})|^2 n_\mathbf{k}^0 n_\mathbf{p}^0 (1 - n_{\mathbf{k+q}}^0)$$
$$\times (1 - n_{\mathbf{p+q}}^0)\,[\epsilon_{\mathbf{k+q}}^0 + \epsilon_{\mathbf{p+q}}^0 - \epsilon_\mathbf{k}^0 - \epsilon_\mathbf{p}^0]^{-1}$$

and Eq. (30.13a).

(b) Consider an electron gas at high temperatures where $n_\mathbf{k}^0 = e^{\beta\mu}\exp(-\beta\epsilon_\mathbf{k}^0) \ll 1$. By using cylindrical polar coordinates $[\mathbf{k} = \hat{q}k_\parallel + \mathbf{k}_\perp]$ show that

$$\Omega_{2a} = -\frac{mVe^4}{\pi^3\hbar^2} e^{2\beta\mu}\left(\frac{m}{2\pi\beta\hbar^2}\right)^2 \int \frac{d^3q}{q^4} \mathcal{P}\int_{-\infty}^{\infty} dp_\parallel \int_{-\infty}^{\infty} dk_\parallel$$
$$\times \exp\left[-\frac{\beta\hbar^2(k_\parallel^2 + p_\parallel^2)}{2m}\right]\frac{1}{q(p_\parallel + k_\parallel) + q^2}$$

Hence conclude that Ω_{2a} is *linearly* divergent at small momentum transfer $(q \to 0)$.

8.5. (a) In the classical limit where $n_\mathbf{p}^0 = \exp(\beta\mu - \beta\epsilon_\mathbf{p}^0)$, show that $\Pi^0(\mathbf{q},\nu_l)$ has the asymptotic form $\Pi^0(\mathbf{q},\nu_l) \sim -16\pi\beta e^{\beta\mu}(q^2/\lambda)[(q\lambda)^4 + (8\pi^2 l)^2]^{-1}$ for large $q\lambda = q(2\pi\hbar^2/mk_BT)^{\frac{1}{2}}$ and $|l|$.
(b) If $\delta\Omega_r$ denotes the summation of terms for $l > 0$ in Eq. (30.21), verify that $\delta\Omega_r/\Omega_r = O[(e^2 n^{\frac{1}{3}})^{\frac{1}{2}}(n^{\frac{1}{3}}\hbar^2/m)^{\frac{1}{2}}(1/k_BT)]$ where Ω_r is taken from Eq. (30.27).

8.6. (a) Use Eq. (30.32) to compute the specific heat of an electron gas in the classical limit $C_V = \frac{3}{2}Nk_B[1 + \frac{1}{3}\pi^{\frac{1}{2}}(e^2 n^{\frac{1}{3}}/k_BT)^{\frac{3}{2}}]$.
(b) Derive this result from Eq. (30.45) in the Debye theory.

8.7. Evaluate $(1/\beta\hbar)\sum_\nu [\Pi^0(\mathbf{q},\nu)]^2$ with the integral representation (30.9). In the zero-temperature limit, this sum may be approximated by an integral over a continuous variable. Hence evaluate $\int_{-\infty}^{\infty} dx\, I(x)$, where $I(x)$ is given in Eq. (30.61), and verify Eq. (30.80).

‡ M. Gell-Mann, *Phys. Rev.*, **106**:369 (1957).

9
Real-time Green's Functions and Linear Response

In the zero-temperature formalism, the poles of the single-particle Green's function $G(\mathbf{k},\omega)$ yield the energy and lifetime of the excited states of a system containing one more or less particle. Similarly, the function $D^R(\mathbf{k},\omega)$ determines the screening of an impurity in an electron gas as well as the spectrum of collective density modes such as plasma oscillations or zero sound. Throughout Chap. 8, however, the temperature Green's function $\mathscr{G}$ was used only to calculate equilibrium thermodynamic properties. We shall now complete the description at finite temperature by introducing a real-time Green's function $\bar{G}$ that contains the frequencies and lifetimes of excited states at finite temperature.

31□GENERALIZED LEHMANN REPRESENTATION

We start our discussion by generalizing the notion of a Green's function from the ground-state expectation value of a time-ordered product of field operators to the ensemble average of this same quantity.

DEFINITION OF $\bar{G}$

The real-time Green's function is defined in direct analogy with Eq. (7.1) at $T = 0$:

$$i\bar{G}_{\alpha\beta}(\mathbf{x}t, \mathbf{x}'t') \equiv \text{Tr}\{\hat{\rho}_G \, T[\hat{\psi}_{K\alpha}(\mathbf{x}t) \, \hat{\psi}_{K\beta}^\dagger(\mathbf{x}'t')]\} \tag{31.1}$$

where $\hat{\rho}_G$ is the statistical operator for the grand canonical ensemble [Eq. (4.15)] and $\hat{\psi}_{K\alpha}(\mathbf{x}t)$ is a true Heisenberg operator

$$\hat{\psi}_{K\alpha}(\mathbf{x}t) \equiv e^{i\hat{K}t/\hbar} \, \hat{\psi}_\alpha(\mathbf{x}) \, e^{-i\hat{K}t/\hbar} \tag{31.2}$$

with respect to the hamiltonian $\hat{K}$. As in Chap. 3, the ordering operator T includes a factor $(-1)^P$ for fermions. Equation (31.1) has one important new feature because $\bar{G}$ depends explicitly on T and μ in addition to the usual space-time variables.

In most cases, the hamiltonian is time independent, and the resulting Green's function contains only the combination $t - t'$. Furthermore, we shall consider only homogeneous systems, and the Green's function assumes the simple form

$$\bar{G}_{\alpha\beta}(\mathbf{x}t, \mathbf{x}'t') = \bar{G}_{\alpha\beta}(\mathbf{x} - \mathbf{x}', t - t') \tag{31.3}$$

Finally, we exclude external magnetic fields and ferromagnetism so that $\bar{G}_{\alpha\beta}$ is diagonal in the matrix indices

$$\bar{G}_{\alpha\beta}(\mathbf{x},t) = \delta_{\alpha\beta} \, \bar{G}(\mathbf{x},t) \tag{31.4}$$

Each of these assumptions can be relaxed, but the subsequent analysis becomes considerably more cumbersome.

Assume that t is positive. Equation (31.1) then becomes

$$i\bar{G}^>(\mathbf{x},t) = (2s + 1)^{-1} \text{Tr}\{\hat{\rho}_G \, \hat{\psi}_{K\alpha}(\mathbf{x}t) \, \hat{\psi}_{K\alpha}^\dagger(0)\} \tag{31.5}$$

In the present homogeneous system, the Heisenberg operators may be rewritten as [compare Eq. (7.52)]

$$\hat{\psi}_{K\alpha}(\mathbf{x}t) = e^{-i\hat{\mathbf{P}}\cdot\mathbf{x}/\hbar} e^{i\hat{K}t/\hbar} \, \hat{\psi}_\alpha(0) \, e^{-i\hat{K}t/\hbar} e^{i\hat{\mathbf{P}}\cdot\mathbf{x}/\hbar} \tag{31.6}$$

because $\hat{\mathbf{P}}$ commutes with $\hat{K}$. A combination of Eqs. (31.5) and (31.6) yields

$$i\bar{G}^>(\mathbf{x},t) = (2s + 1)^{-1} \text{Tr}\{e^{\beta(\Omega-\hat{K})} e^{-i\hat{\mathbf{P}}\cdot\mathbf{x}/\hbar} e^{i\hat{K}t/\hbar} \, \hat{\psi}_\alpha(0) \, e^{-i\hat{K}t/\hbar} e^{i\hat{\mathbf{P}}\cdot\mathbf{x}/\hbar} \hat{\psi}_\alpha^\dagger(0)\}$$
$$\tag{31.7}$$

where the trace can be evaluated in any basis.   A particularly convenient choice is the exact eigenstates of $\hat{H}$, $\hat{\mathbf{P}}$, and $\hat{N}$:

$$\hat{K}|m\rangle = K_m|m\rangle = (E_m - \mu N_m)|m\rangle$$

$$\hat{\mathbf{P}}|m\rangle = \mathbf{P}_m|m\rangle$$

(31.8)

and we find

$$i\bar{G}^>(\mathbf{x},t) = (2s+1)^{-1} e^{\beta\Omega} \sum_{mn} e^{-\beta K_m} e^{-i\mathbf{P}_m\cdot\mathbf{x}/\hbar} e^{iK_mt/\hbar}\langle m|\hat{\psi}_\alpha(0)|n\rangle$$

$$\times\ e^{-iK_nt/\hbar} e^{i\mathbf{P}_n\cdot\mathbf{x}/\hbar}\langle n|\hat{\psi}_\alpha^\dagger(0)|m\rangle$$

$$= (2s+1)^{-1} e^{\beta\Omega} \sum_{mn} e^{-\beta K_m} e^{i(\mathbf{P}_n-\mathbf{P}_m)\cdot\mathbf{x}/\hbar} e^{-i(K_n-K_m)t/\hbar}|\langle m|\hat{\psi}_\alpha|n\rangle|^2$$

(31.9)

In a similar way, the corresponding function for $t < 0$ becomes

$$iG^<(\mathbf{x},t) = \pm(2s+1)^{-1} e^{\beta\Omega}\,\mathrm{Tr}\,\{e^{-\beta K}\,\hat{\psi}_{K\alpha}^\dagger(0)\,\hat{\psi}_{K\alpha}(\mathbf{x}t)\}$$

$$= \pm(2s+1)^{-1} e^{\beta\Omega} \sum_{mn} e^{-\beta K_n} e^{i(\mathbf{P}_n-\mathbf{P}_m)\cdot\mathbf{x}/\hbar} e^{-i(K_n-K_m)t/\hbar}|\langle m|\hat{\psi}_\alpha|n\rangle|^2$$

(31.10)

The total Green's function is the sum of these two terms

$$\bar{G}(\mathbf{x},t) = \theta(t)\,\bar{G}^>(\mathbf{x},t) + \theta(-t)\,\bar{G}^<(\mathbf{x},t)$$

(31.11)

and its Fourier transform may be calculated exactly as in Eq. (7.54)

$$\bar{G}(\mathbf{k},\omega) = (2s+1)^{-1} e^{\beta\Omega} \sum_{mn} \Big\{(2\pi)^3\,\delta[\mathbf{k} - \hbar^{-1}(\mathbf{P}_n - \mathbf{P}_m)]|\langle m|\hat{\psi}_\alpha|n\rangle|^2$$

$$\times \Big[\frac{e^{-\beta K_m}}{\omega - \hbar^{-1}(K_n - K_m) + i\eta} \mp \frac{e^{-\beta K_n}}{\omega - \hbar^{-1}(K_n - K_m) - i\eta}\Big]\Big\}\quad(31.12)$$

Equation (31.12) shows that $\bar{G}(\mathbf{k},\omega)$ is a meromorphic function of $\hbar\omega$ with simple poles at the set of values $K_n - K_m \equiv E_n - E_m - \mu(N_n - N_m)$; the corresponding residue is proportional to $|\langle m|\hat{\psi}|n\rangle|^2$ and vanishes unless $N_n = N_m + 1$.   The ensemble average at finite temperature clearly generalizes the zero-temperature expression because both $|m\rangle$ and $|n\rangle$ can refer to excited states.   For fermions at $T = 0$, however, it is easily proved (Prob. 9.1) that

$$\bar{G}(\omega - \mu/\hbar)|_{T=0} = G(\omega)$$

(31.13)

where $G(\omega)$ is the ground-state Green's function from Chap. 3.

RETARDED AND ADVANCED FUNCTIONS

If ω is real, the real and imaginary parts of $\bar{G}(\mathbf{k},\omega)$ are readily found with Eq. (7.69):

$$
\bar{G}(\mathbf{k},\omega) = (2s+1)^{-1} e^{\beta\Omega} \sum_{mn} e^{-\beta K_m} (2\pi)^3 \delta[\mathbf{k} - \hbar^{-1}(\mathbf{P}_n - \mathbf{P}_m)] |\langle m|\hat{\psi}_\alpha|n\rangle|^2
$$

$$
\times \{\mathscr{P}[\omega - \hbar^{-1}(K_n - K_m)]^{-1} (1 \mp e^{-\beta(K_n - K_m)})
$$

$$
- i\pi\delta[\omega - \hbar^{-1}(K_n - K_m)](1 \pm e^{-\beta(K_n - K_m)})\} \quad (31.14)
$$

where $\mathscr{P}$ denotes a principal value. The imaginary part of Eq. (31.14) may be rewritten as

$$
\mathrm{Im}\,\bar{G}(\mathbf{k},\omega) = -(2s+1)^{-1} \pi e^{\beta\Omega} \sum_{mn} e^{-\beta K_m} (2\pi)^3 \delta[\mathbf{k} - \hbar^{-1}(\mathbf{P}_n - \mathbf{P}_m)]
$$

$$
\times |\langle m|\hat{\psi}_\alpha|n\rangle|^2 \delta[\omega - \hbar^{-1}(K_n - K_m)](1 \pm e^{-\beta\hbar\omega}) \quad (31.15)
$$

and it is easily verified that the real part then becomes

$$
\mathrm{Re}\,\bar{G}(\mathbf{k},\omega) = -\mathscr{P} \int_{-\infty}^{\infty} \frac{d\omega'}{\pi} \frac{\mathrm{Im}\,\bar{G}(\mathbf{k},\omega')}{\omega - \omega'} \frac{1 \mp e^{-\beta\hbar\omega'}}{1 \pm e^{-\beta\hbar\omega'}}
$$

$$
= -\mathscr{P} \int_{-\infty}^{\infty} \frac{d\omega'}{\pi} \frac{\mathrm{Im}\,\bar{G}(\mathbf{k},\omega')}{\omega - \omega'} [\tanh(\tfrac{1}{2}\beta\hbar\omega')]^{\pm 1} \quad (31.16)
$$

which was first derived by Landau.[1]

For many purposes, it is more convenient to deal with retarded or advanced real-time Green's functions [compare Eq. (7.62)]:

$$
i\bar{G}^R_{\alpha\beta}(\mathbf{x}t, \mathbf{x}'t') \equiv \theta(t-t')\,\mathrm{Tr}\{\hat{\rho}_G[\hat{\psi}_{K\alpha}(\mathbf{x}t), \hat{\psi}^\dagger_{K\beta}(\mathbf{x}'t')]_{\mp}\}
$$

$$
i\bar{G}^A_{\alpha\beta}(\mathbf{x}t, \mathbf{x}'t') \equiv -\theta(t'-t)\,\mathrm{Tr}\{\hat{\rho}_G[\hat{\psi}_{K\alpha}(\mathbf{x}t), \hat{\psi}^\dagger_{K\beta}(\mathbf{x}'t')]_{\mp}\}
$$
$$ (31.17) $$

We shall again consider only homogeneous time-independent systems with no magnetic fields. In this case $\bar{G}^R$ and $\bar{G}^A$ have the same structure as in Eq. (31.4), and their Fourier transforms are easily found to be

$$
\bar{G}^R(\mathbf{k},\omega) = (2s+1)^{-1} e^{\beta\Omega} \sum_{mn} \{e^{-\beta K_m}(2\pi)^3 \delta[\mathbf{k} - \hbar^{-1}(\mathbf{P}_n - \mathbf{P}_m)]|\langle m|\hat{\psi}_\alpha|n\rangle|^2
$$

$$
\times (1 \mp e^{-\beta(K_n - K_m)}) [\omega - \hbar^{-1}(K_n - K_m) + i\eta]^{-1}\}
$$
$$ (31.18) $$

$$
\bar{G}^A(\mathbf{k},\omega) = (2s+1)^{-1} e^{\beta\Omega} \sum_{mn} \{e^{-\beta K_m}(2\pi)^3 \delta[\mathbf{k} - \hbar^{-1}(\mathbf{P}_n - \mathbf{P}_m)]|\langle m|\hat{\psi}_\alpha|n\rangle|^2
$$

$$
\times (1 \mp e^{-\beta(K_n - K_m)}) [\omega - \hbar^{-1}(K_n - K_m) - i\eta]^{-1}\}
$$

It is evident that both $\bar{G}^R$ and $\bar{G}^A$ are meromorphic functions of ω; in addition, $\bar{G}^R(\bar{G}^A)$ is analytic in the upper (lower) half ω plane.

[1] L. D. Landau, *Sov. Phys.-JETP*, **7**:182 (1958).

The retarded and advanced Green's functions are closely related. With the definition

$$\rho(\mathbf{k},\omega) \equiv (2s+1)^{-1} e^{\beta\Omega} \sum_{mn} \{e^{-\beta K_m}(2\pi)^3 \delta[\mathbf{k} - \hbar^{-1}(\mathbf{P}_n - \mathbf{P}_m)]$$

$$\times 2\pi\delta[\omega - \hbar^{-1}(K_n - K_m)](1 \mp e^{-\beta\hbar\omega})|\langle m|\hat{\psi}_\alpha|n\rangle|^2\} \quad (31.19)$$

which depends on both T and μ, the imaginary parts of $\bar{G}^R$ and $\bar{G}^A$ may be written as

$$\text{Im } \bar{G}^R(\mathbf{k},\omega) = -\tfrac{1}{2}\rho(\mathbf{k},\omega)$$

$$\text{Im } \bar{G}^A(\mathbf{k},\omega) = \tfrac{1}{2}\rho(\mathbf{k},\omega)$$
$$(31.20)$$

Furthermore, a combination of Eqs. (31.18) and (31.19) yields the integral representations

$$\bar{G}^R(\mathbf{k},\omega) = \int_{-\infty}^{\infty} \frac{d\omega'}{2\pi} \frac{\rho(\mathbf{k},\omega')}{\omega - \omega' + i\eta}$$

$$\bar{G}^A(\mathbf{k},\omega) = \int_{-\infty}^{\infty} \frac{d\omega'}{2\pi} \frac{\rho(\mathbf{k},\omega')}{\omega - \omega' - i\eta}$$
$$(31.21)$$

whose real parts are formally identical with the dispersion relations at zero temperature [Eq. (7.70)]. If we introduce a function of a complex variable z

$$\Gamma(\mathbf{k},z) = \int_{-\infty}^{\infty} \frac{d\omega'}{2\pi} \frac{\rho(\mathbf{k},\omega')}{z - \omega'} \quad (31.22)$$

then $\bar{G}^R(\mathbf{k},\omega)$ and $\bar{G}^A(\mathbf{k},\omega)$ represent the boundary values of Γ as z approaches the real axis from above and below, respectively:

$$\bar{G}^R(\mathbf{k},\omega) = \Gamma(\mathbf{k}, \omega + i\eta)$$

$$\bar{G}^A(\mathbf{k},\omega) = \Gamma(\mathbf{k}, \omega - i\eta)$$
$$(31.23)$$

In view of the general relation between G, G^R, and G^A at $T = 0$ [Eqs. (7.67) and (7.68)] it is not surprising that $\rho(\mathbf{k},\omega)$ also determines the Fourier transform of the *time-ordered* Green's function. A straightforward calculation with Eqs. (31.14) and (31.19) shows that $\bar{G}(\mathbf{k},\omega)$ has the following alternative representations:

$$\bar{G}(\mathbf{k},\omega) = \int_{-\infty}^{\infty} \frac{d\omega'}{2\pi} \rho(\mathbf{k},\omega') \left\{ \mathscr{P}\frac{1}{\omega - \omega'} - i\pi[\tanh(\tfrac{1}{2}\beta\hbar\omega)]^{\mp 1} \delta(\omega - \omega') \right\}$$

$$= [1 \mp e^{-\beta\hbar\omega}]^{-1} \bar{G}^R(\mathbf{k},\omega) + [1 \mp e^{\beta\hbar\omega}]^{-1} \bar{G}^A(\mathbf{k},\omega) \quad (31.24)$$

For real ω, all three Green's functions have equal real parts

$$\text{Re } \bar{G}(\mathbf{k},\omega) = \text{Re } \bar{G}^R(\mathbf{k},\omega) = \text{Re } \bar{G}^A(\mathbf{k},\omega) \quad (31.25)$$

while the imaginary parts are given by Eq. (31.20) and by

$$\text{Im}\,\bar{G}(\mathbf{k},\omega) = -\tfrac{1}{2}[\tanh(\tfrac{1}{2}\beta\hbar\omega)]^{\mp 1}\rho(\mathbf{k},\omega) \tag{31.26}$$

In the special case of fermions at zero temperature, Eq. (31.24) assumes the familiar form

$$\bar{G}(\mathbf{k},\omega)|_{T=0} = \int_{-\infty}^{\infty}\frac{d\omega'}{2\pi}\rho(\mathbf{k},\omega')|_{T=0}\left[\frac{\theta(\omega)}{\omega-\omega'+i\eta} + \frac{\theta(-\omega)}{\omega-\omega'-i\eta}\right] \tag{31.27}$$

which should be compared with Eqs. (7.67) and (31.13).

The weight function $\rho(\mathbf{k},\omega)$ contains the important physical properties of the system.   Although the precise form of ρ can be evaluated only with a detailed calculation, there are certain general properties that follow directly from its defining equation (31.19).   Each term in the sum is positive if ω is positive; more generally, ρ has the following positive-definite properties:

$$(\text{sgn}\,\omega)\,\rho(\mathbf{k},\omega) \geqslant 0 \qquad \text{bosons}$$
$$\tag{31.28}$$
$$\rho(\mathbf{k},\omega) \geqslant 0 \qquad\qquad \text{fermions}$$

In addition, ρ satisfies an important sum rule, which we now derive.   Consider the following integral

$$\int_{-\infty}^{\infty}\frac{d\omega}{2\pi}i\bar{G}^{R}(\mathbf{k},\omega)\,e^{-i\omega\eta} = i\int_{-\infty}^{\infty}\int_{-\infty}^{\infty}\frac{d\omega'\,d\omega}{(2\pi)^{2}}\frac{\rho(\mathbf{k},\omega')\,e^{-i\omega\eta}}{\omega-\omega'+i\eta}$$
$$= \int_{-\infty}^{\infty}\frac{d\omega'}{2\pi}\rho(\mathbf{k},\omega') \tag{31.29}$$

where the ω integral is evaluated by closing the contour in the lower half plane. Equation (31.29) can also be computed directly from the definition [Eq. (31.17)]

$$\int_{-\infty}^{\infty}\frac{d\omega}{2\pi}i\bar{G}^{R}(\mathbf{k},\omega)\,e^{-i\omega\eta} = \int d^{3}x\,e^{-i\mathbf{k}\cdot\mathbf{x}}\,i\bar{G}^{R}(\mathbf{x},\eta)$$
$$= (2s+1)^{-1}\int d^{3}x\,e^{-i\mathbf{k}\cdot\mathbf{x}}\,\text{Tr}\{\hat{\rho}_{G}[\hat{\psi}_{K\alpha}(\mathbf{x}0),\hat{\psi}^{\dagger}_{K\alpha}(0)]_{\mp}\}$$
$$= \int d^{3}x\,e^{-i\mathbf{k}\cdot\mathbf{x}}\,\delta(\mathbf{x})\,\text{Tr}\,\hat{\rho}_{G}$$
$$= 1 \tag{31.30}$$

where the canonical commutation relations (2.3) have been used in arriving at the third line.   Comparison of Eqs. (31.29) and (31.30) immediately yields

$$\int_{-\infty}^{\infty}\frac{d\omega'}{2\pi}\rho(\mathbf{k},\omega') = 1 \tag{31.31}$$

which is correct for both bosons and fermions. This sum rule fixes the asymptotic behavior of the Green's functions for large $|\omega|$:

$$\bar{G}^R(\mathbf{k},\omega) = \bar{G}^A(\mathbf{k},\omega) \sim \frac{1}{\omega} \int_{-\infty}^{\infty} \frac{d\omega'}{2\pi} \rho(\mathbf{k},\omega') \sim \frac{1}{\omega} \qquad |\omega| \to \infty \qquad (31.32)$$

which is useful in establishing convergence properties.

TEMPERATURE GREEN'S FUNCTIONS AND ANALYTIC CONTINUATION

In the previous section, the weight function served only to determine and correlate the various real-time Green's functions. Although such relations are valuable, they would not by themselves justify our extensive discussion of the Lehmann representation at finite temperature, and we shall now prove the important result that the *same* weight function also determines the temperature Green's function $\mathscr{G}$. By this means, the Lehmann representation provides a direct connection between $\mathscr{G}$ and $\bar{G}$ and thus plays a central role in the finite-temperature formalism.

It is sufficient to consider only positive τ, and $\mathscr{G}$ then becomes

$$\begin{aligned}
\mathscr{G}(\mathbf{x}\tau) &= -(2s+1)^{-1} \operatorname{Tr}\left[\hat{\rho}_G\, \hat{\psi}_{K\alpha}(\mathbf{x}\tau)\, \hat{\psi}_{k\alpha}^{\dagger}(0)\right] \\
&= -(2s+1)^{-1} e^{\beta\Omega} \operatorname{Tr}\left[e^{-\beta\hat{K}} e^{-i\hat{\mathbf{P}}\cdot\mathbf{x}/\hbar} e^{\hat{K}\tau/\hbar} \hat{\psi}_\alpha(0)\, e^{-\hat{K}\tau/\hbar} e^{i\hat{\mathbf{P}}\cdot\mathbf{x}/\hbar} \hat{\psi}_\alpha^{\dagger}(0)\right] \\
&= -(2s+1)^{-1} e^{\beta\Omega} \sum_{mn}\left[e^{-\beta K_m} e^{i(\mathbf{P}_n - \mathbf{P}_m)\cdot\mathbf{x}/\hbar} e^{-(K_n - K_m)\tau/\hbar}\, |\langle m|\hat{\psi}_\alpha|n\rangle|^2\right]
\end{aligned}$$

$$(31.33)$$

The corresponding Fourier coefficient is given by [see Eq. (25.14)]

$$\begin{aligned}
\mathscr{G}(\mathbf{k},\omega_l) &= \int_0^{\beta\hbar} d\tau\, e^{i\omega_l\tau} \int d^3x\, e^{-i\mathbf{k}\cdot\mathbf{x}}\, \mathscr{G}(\mathbf{x}\tau) \\
&= (2s+1)^{-1} e^{\beta\Omega} \sum_{mn} \{e^{-\beta K_m}(2\pi)^3\, \delta[\mathbf{k} - \hbar^{-1}(\mathbf{P}_n - \mathbf{P}_m)]|\langle m|\hat{\psi}_\alpha|n\rangle|^2 \\
&\qquad \times (1 \mp e^{-\beta(K_n - K_m)})\,[i\omega_l - \hbar^{-1}(K_n - K_m)]^{-1}\} \quad (31.34)
\end{aligned}$$

where $\omega_l = 2l\pi/\beta\hbar$ for bosons and $(2l+1)\pi/\beta\hbar$ for fermions. Comparison with Eq. (31.19) immediately yields the important relation

$$\mathscr{G}(\mathbf{k},\omega_n) = \int_{-\infty}^{\infty} \frac{d\omega'}{2\pi} \frac{\rho(\mathbf{k},\omega')}{i\omega_n - \omega'} \qquad (31.35)$$

which shows that the function $\Gamma(\mathbf{k},z)$ [Eq. (31.22)] determines the temperature Green's function as well as $\bar{G}^R$ and $\bar{G}^A$. In any practical calculation, we first evaluate $\mathscr{G}(\mathbf{k},\omega_n)$ and therefore know $\Gamma(\mathbf{k},z)$ only at the discrete set of points $\{i\omega_n\}$. It is then necessary to perform an analytic continuation to the whole complex z plane. Without further information, such a procedure cannot be unique. Suppose that $\Gamma(\mathbf{k},z)$ is one possible continuation; for any integer p, the function $e^{2\pi p z/\omega_n}\Gamma(\mathbf{k},z)$ is another possible continuation because it also reduces to $\Gamma(\mathbf{k},i\omega_n)$ at the points $i\omega_n$. Nevertheless, these various continuations

differ from each other everywhere else in the complex z plane including the point at infinity. Since the sum rule [Eq. (31.31)] requires that $\Gamma(\mathbf{k},z) \sim z^{-1}$ as $|z| \to \infty$, we are thus able to select the proper analytic continuation, which is guaranteed to be unique.[1]

In practice, it is usually simplest to compute $\rho(\mathbf{k},\omega)$ directly from $\mathscr{G}(\mathbf{k},\omega_n)$ by formally considering $i\omega_n$ as a continuous variable. The weight function is then obtained as the limiting value

$$\rho(\mathbf{k},x) = i^{-1}[\mathscr{G}(\mathbf{k},\omega_n)|_{i\omega_n = x - i\eta} - \mathscr{G}(\mathbf{k},\omega_n)|_{i\omega_n = x + i\eta}] \tag{31.36}$$

Hence *any* approximation for $\mathscr{G}(\mathbf{k},\omega_n)$ immediately provides a corresponding $\rho(\mathbf{k},\omega)$ and thereby $\bar{G}$, $\bar{G}^R$, and $\bar{G}^A$. As a particularly simple example, consider the noninteracting temperature Green's function $\mathscr{G}^0(\mathbf{k},\omega_n) = [i\omega_n - \hbar^{-1}(\epsilon_k^0 - \mu)]^{-1}$. The noninteracting weight function ρ^0 is given by

$$\rho^0(\mathbf{k},x) = \frac{1}{i}\left[\frac{1}{x - \hbar^{-1}(\epsilon_k^0 - \mu) - i\eta} - \frac{1}{x - \hbar^{-1}(\epsilon_k^0 - \mu) + i\eta}\right]$$

$$= 2\pi\delta[x - \hbar^{-1}(\epsilon_k^0 - \mu)] \tag{31.37}$$

and some simple algebra with Eq. (31.24) gives the time-ordered function

$$\bar{G}^0(\mathbf{k},\omega) = \frac{1}{1 \mp \exp[-\beta(\epsilon_k^0 - \mu)]} \frac{1}{\omega - \hbar^{-1}(\epsilon_k^0 - \mu) + i\eta}$$

$$+ \frac{1}{1 \mp \exp[\beta(\epsilon_k^0 - \mu)]} \frac{1}{\omega - \hbar^{-1}(\epsilon_k^0 - \mu) - i\eta} \tag{31.38}$$

Equation (31.38) can also be obtained directly from the definition [Eq. (31.1)] with the relation $\mathrm{Tr}\{\hat{\rho}_G a_\mathbf{k}^\dagger a_\mathbf{k}\} = n_k^0 = \{\exp[\beta(\epsilon_k^0 - \mu)] \mp 1\}^{-1}$.

32□LINEAR RESPONSE AT FINITE TEMPERATURE

In Sec. 31 we saw how the temperature Green's function $\mathscr{G}(\mathbf{k},\omega_n)$ can be used to determine the behavior of excited states obtained by adding or subtracting one particle from a system in thermodynamic equilibrium. As noted in Chap. 5, however, there are many other kinds of excited states, the most important being those that conserve the number of particles. The theory of linear response provides a convenient basis for describing such excitations, and we shall first extend the previous theory to finite temperatures.

GENERAL THEORY

If a system is perturbed from equilibrium at $t = t_0$ by an external hamiltonian $\hat{H}^{ex}(t)$, the first-order change in an arbitrary matrix element of an operator $\hat{O}$ is

[1] G. Baym and N. D. Mermin, *J. Math. Phys.*, **2**:232 (1961).

given by Eq. (13.9). In particular, the change in a diagonal matrix element reduces to

$$\delta\langle jN|\hat{O}(t)|jN\rangle = \frac{i}{\hbar}\int_{t_0}^{t} dt'\langle jN|[\hat{H}_H^{ex}(t'),\hat{O}_H(t)]|jN\rangle \qquad t > t_0 \qquad (32.1)$$

where the subscript H denotes the Heisenberg picture with the full unperturbed hamiltonian $\hat{H}$, and $|jN\rangle$ is an exact eigenstate of $\hat{H}$ and $\hat{N}$ with eigenvalues $E_j(N)$ and N. For $t < t_0$, the system is in thermodynamic equilibrium, and the occupation of the different states $|jN\rangle$ is determined by the statistical operator $\hat{\rho}_G$. Since Eq. (32.1) is already proportional to $\hat{H}^{ex}$, the first-order change in the ensemble average of $\hat{O}$ may be evaluated by adding the contribution of each state $|jN\rangle$, weighted according to the unperturbed ensemble

$$\delta\langle\hat{O}(t)\rangle_{ex} = \sum_{jN} e^{\beta[\Omega - E_j(N) + \mu N]}\delta\langle jN|\hat{O}(t)|jN\rangle$$

$$= \frac{i}{\hbar}\int_{t_0}^{t} dt'\,\mathrm{Tr}\{\hat{\rho}_G[\hat{H}_H^{ex}(t'),\hat{O}_H(t)]\} \qquad t > t_0 \qquad (32.2)$$

This equation is a direct generalization of Eq. (13.10) at $T = 0$.

To be specific, assume that $\hat{H}^{ex}(t)$ takes the form

$$\hat{H}^{ex}(t) = \int d^3x\,\hat{O}(\mathbf{x}t)\,\Xi^{ex}(\mathbf{x}t) \qquad (32.3)$$

where $\Xi^{ex}(\mathbf{x}t)$ is a generalized c-number force that couples to the operator density $\hat{O}(\mathbf{x}t)$. The linear response of $\hat{O}(\mathbf{x}t)$ is given by

$$\delta\langle\hat{O}(\mathbf{x}t)\rangle_{ex} = -\frac{i}{\hbar}\int_{t_0}^{t} dt'\int d^3x'\,\mathrm{Tr}\{\hat{\rho}_G[\hat{O}_H(\mathbf{x}t),\hat{O}_H(\mathbf{x}'t')]\}\,\Xi^{ex}(\mathbf{x}'t')$$

$$= \frac{1}{\hbar}\int_{t_0}^{t} dt'\int d^3x'\,D^R(\mathbf{x}t,\mathbf{x}'t')\,\Xi^{ex}(\mathbf{x}'t') \qquad (32.4)$$

where D^R is a retarded correlation function

$$iD^R(\mathbf{x}t,\mathbf{x}'t') \equiv \mathrm{Tr}\{\hat{\rho}_G[\hat{O}_H(\mathbf{x}t),\hat{O}_H(\mathbf{x}'t')]\}\,\theta(t - t') \qquad (32.5)$$

evaluated in the equilibrium grand canonical ensemble. The analysis of linear response is thus reduced to the calculation of a retarded correlation function. Since the unperturbed hamiltonian is time independent, D^R takes the form $D^R(\mathbf{x},\mathbf{x}',t - t')$. Furthermore, $\hat{O}$ usually commutes with $\hat{N}$, which allows us to reinterpret the Heisenberg operators in terms of the grand canonical hamiltonian $\hat{K} = \hat{H} - \mu\hat{N}$:

$$\hat{O}_H(\mathbf{x}t) = e^{i\hat{K}t/\hbar}\,\hat{O}(\mathbf{x})\,e^{-i\hat{K}t/\hbar} \equiv \hat{O}_K(\mathbf{x}t) \qquad (32.6)$$

The Fourier transform $D^R(\mathbf{x},\mathbf{x}',\omega)$ has a simple Lehmann representation, which shows that $D^R(\mathbf{x},\mathbf{x}',\omega)$ is analytic for $\mathrm{Im}\,\omega > 0$.

It is inconvenient to calculate D^R directly; instead, we introduce a corresponding temperature function $\mathcal{D}$ that depends on the *imaginary-time* variables τ:

$$\mathcal{D}(\mathbf{x}\tau,\mathbf{x}'\,\tau') \equiv -\mathrm{Tr}\{\hat{\rho}_G\,T_\tau[\hat{O}_K(\mathbf{x}\tau)\,\hat{O}_K(\mathbf{x}'\,\tau')]\} \tag{32.7}$$

Here the Heisenberg operator is given by [compare Eq. (24.1)]

$$\hat{O}_K(\mathbf{x}\tau) = e^{\hat{K}\tau/\hbar}\,\hat{O}(\mathbf{x})\,e^{-\hat{K}\tau/\hbar} \tag{32.8}$$

Since $\mathcal{D}$ is of the form $\mathcal{D}(\mathbf{x},\mathbf{x}',\tau-\tau')$, its Fourier coefficient $\mathcal{D}(\mathbf{x},\mathbf{x}',\nu_n)$ also has a simple Lehmann representation. Just as in Sec. 31, this representation is very important because the *same* weight function determines both $D^R(\mathbf{x},\mathbf{x}',\omega)$ and $\mathcal{D}(\mathbf{x},\mathbf{x}',\nu_n)$. Furthermore, $\mathcal{D}(\mathbf{x},\mathbf{x}',\nu_n)$ can be evaluated with the Feynman rules and diagrammatic analysis of Sec. 25. An analytic continuation to the upper side of the real ω axis then allows us to calculate the retarded correlation function.

DENSITY CORRELATION FUNCTION

The precise form of the Lehmann representation depends on the particular operators involved. As an example of great interest, we now consider the particle density and carry through the preceding analytic continuation in detail. For simplicity, the system is taken as homogeneous, but the same general method applies to more complicated situations. The operator in question is the density deviation operator

$$\tilde{n}(\mathbf{x}) = \hat{n}(\mathbf{x}) - \langle\hat{n}(\mathbf{x})\rangle \tag{32.9}$$

where $\langle\hat{n}(\mathbf{x})\rangle$ is the *ensemble average* of the density operator and depends explicitly on T and μ. The retarded and temperature functions are given by

$$iD^R(\mathbf{x}t,\mathbf{x}'\,t') = \mathrm{Tr}\{\hat{\rho}_G[\tilde{n}_K(\mathbf{x}t),\tilde{n}_K(\mathbf{x}'\,t')]\}\,\theta(t-t') \tag{32.10}$$

$$\mathcal{D}(\mathbf{x}\tau,\mathbf{x}'\,\tau') = -\mathrm{Tr}\{\hat{\rho}_G\,T_\tau[\tilde{n}_K(\mathbf{x}\tau)\,\tilde{n}_K(\mathbf{x}'\,\tau')]\} \tag{32.11}$$

and have the usual Fourier representations

$$D^R(\mathbf{x}t,\mathbf{x}'\,t') = (2\pi)^{-4}\int d^3q\,d\omega\,e^{i\mathbf{q}\cdot(\mathbf{x}-\mathbf{x}')}\,e^{-i\omega(t-t')}\,D^R(\mathbf{q},\omega) \tag{32.12}$$

$$\mathcal{D}(\mathbf{x}\tau,\mathbf{x}'\,\tau') = (2\pi)^{-3}\int d^3q\,(\beta\hbar)^{-1}\sum_n e^{i\mathbf{q}\cdot(\mathbf{x}-\mathbf{x}')}\,e^{-i\nu_n(\tau-\tau')}\,\mathcal{D}(\mathbf{q},\nu_n) \tag{32.13}$$

where $\nu_n = 2n\pi/\beta\hbar$ denotes an *even* integer. It is straightforward to evaluate the Lehmann representation of each of these functions, and we find

$$D^R(\mathbf{q},\omega) = \hbar\int_{-\infty}^{\infty}\frac{d\omega'}{2\pi}\frac{\Delta(\mathbf{q},\omega')}{\omega-\omega'+i\eta} \tag{32.14}$$

$$\mathcal{D}(\mathbf{q},\nu_n) = \hbar\int_{-\infty}^{\infty}\frac{d\omega'}{2\pi}\frac{\Delta(\mathbf{q},\omega')}{i\nu_n-\omega'} \tag{32.15}$$

where

$$\hbar\Delta(\mathbf{q},\omega) = -\hbar\Delta(-\mathbf{q},-\omega)$$

$$= e^{\beta\Omega} \sum_{lm} \{e^{-\beta K_l}(2\pi)^3 \,\delta[\mathbf{q} - \hbar^{-1}(\mathbf{P}_m - \mathbf{P}_l)] \, 2\pi\delta[\omega - \hbar^{-1}(K_m - K_l)]$$

$$\times (1 - e^{-\beta\hbar\omega})|\langle l|\tilde{n}|m\rangle|^2\} \quad (32.16)$$

Equations (32.14) and (32.16) together show that $D^R(\mathbf{q},\omega)$ is a meromorphic function of ω with its poles just below the real axis.   Each pole corresponds to a possible transition between states that are connected by the density operator.

If $\mathscr{D}$ were given explicitly in spectral representation [Eq. (32.15)], then the analytic continuation would be elementary.   In practice, however, the expressions take a different form, and it is necessary to examine the perturbation expansion for $\mathscr{D}$ in more detail.   Equation (32.11) may be rewritten as

$$\mathscr{D}(\mathbf{x}\tau, \mathbf{x}'\tau') - \langle \hat{n}_K(\mathbf{x}\tau)\rangle \langle \hat{n}_K(\mathbf{x}'\tau')\rangle$$
$$= -\mathrm{Tr}\{\hat{\rho}_G \, T_\tau[\hat{\psi}_{K\alpha}^\dagger(\mathbf{x}\tau)\,\hat{\psi}_{K\alpha}(\mathbf{x}\tau)\,\hat{\psi}_{K\beta}^\dagger(\mathbf{x}'\tau')\,\hat{\psi}_{K\beta}(\mathbf{x}'\tau')]\} \quad (32.17)$$

which can be transformed to the interaction picture.   The steps are identical with those in Chap. 7, and we merely state the final result

$$\mathscr{D}(\mathbf{x}\tau, \mathbf{x}'\tau') = \langle \hat{n}_K(\mathbf{x}\tau)\rangle \langle \hat{n}_K(\mathbf{x}'\tau')\rangle - \sum_{l=0}^{\infty} \left(\frac{-1}{\hbar}\right)^l \frac{1}{l!} \int_0^{\beta\hbar} d\tau_1 \cdots \int_0^{\beta\hbar} d\tau_l$$

$$\times \mathrm{Tr}\{e^{\beta(\Omega_0 - \hat{K}_0)} \, T_\tau[\hat{K}_1(\tau_1) \cdots \hat{K}_1(\tau_l)\,\hat{\psi}_{I\alpha}^\dagger(\mathbf{x}\tau)$$

$$\times \hat{\psi}_{I\alpha}(\mathbf{x}\tau)\,\hat{\psi}_{I\beta}^\dagger(\mathbf{x}'\tau')\,\hat{\psi}_{I\beta}(\mathbf{x}'\tau')]\}_{\text{connected}} \quad (32.18)$$

where the subscript means that only connected diagrams are to be retained.

It is important to remember that a connected diagram is one in which every part is joined either to the point $\mathbf{x}\tau$ or the point $\mathbf{x}'\tau'$.   Thus both diagrams in Fig. 32.1 are considered connected.   Nevertheless, they have a quite different structure, because Fig. 32.1b itself separates into two distinct parts.   The sum of all such separable contributions is just the perturbation expansion of $-\langle \hat{n}_K(\mathbf{x}\tau)\rangle \langle \hat{n}_K(\mathbf{x}'\tau')\rangle$, and precisely cancels the first term on the right side of Eq. (32.18).   Consequently $\mathscr{D}(\mathbf{x}\tau, \mathbf{x}'\tau')$ consists of all connected diagrams in which the points $\mathbf{x}\tau$ and $\mathbf{x}'\tau'$ are joined by internal lines.   For example, the

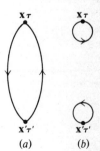

Fig. 32.1   Lowest-order contributions to (a) $\mathscr{D}(\mathbf{x}\tau, \mathbf{x}'\tau')$ (b) $\langle \hat{n}_K(\mathbf{x}\tau)\rangle \langle \hat{n}_K(\mathbf{x}'\tau')\rangle$.

only zero-order contribution is that given in Fig. 32.1a, and Wick's theorem applied to Eq. (32.18) yields

$$\mathscr{D}^0(\mathbf{x}\tau, \mathbf{x}'\,\tau') = \mp \mathscr{G}^0_{\alpha\beta}(\mathbf{x}\tau, \mathbf{x}'\,\tau')\,\mathscr{G}^0_{\beta\alpha}(\mathbf{x}'\,\tau', \mathbf{x}\tau)$$
$$= \mp (2s+1)\,\mathscr{G}^0(\mathbf{x}\tau, \mathbf{x}'\,\tau')\,\mathscr{G}^0(\mathbf{x}'\,\tau', \mathbf{x}\tau) \tag{32.19}$$

It is clear that $\mathscr{D}$ has the structure of a polarization part, and, indeed, $\mathscr{D}(1,2)$ is proportional to the total polarization $\Pi(1,2)$. An argument exactly analogous to that used in obtaining Eq. (12.14) gives

$$\mathscr{D}(1,2) = \hbar\Pi(1,2) \tag{32.20}$$

In any specific problem, it is always easier to evaluate the proper polarization $\Pi^\star$ and then to determine Π and $\mathscr{D}$ from Dyson's equation. The analysis is particularly simple for a uniform system, when the solution of Dyson's equation reduces to

$$\Pi(\mathbf{q},\nu_n) = \Pi^\star(\mathbf{q},\nu_n)\,[1 - \mathscr{V}_0(\mathbf{q},\nu_n)\,\Pi^\star(\mathbf{q},\nu_n)]^{-1}$$
$$= \Pi^\star(\mathbf{q},\nu_n)\,[1 - V(\mathbf{q})\,\Pi^\star(\mathbf{q},\nu_n)]^{-1} \tag{32.21}$$

Since $\Pi^\star(\mathbf{q},\nu_n)$ is a particular polarization insertion, its Lehmann representation must have the same form as that for $\Pi(\mathbf{q},\nu_n)$ and $\mathscr{D}(\mathbf{q},\nu_n)$:

$$\Pi^\star(\mathbf{q},\nu_n) = \int_{-\infty}^{\infty} \frac{d\omega'}{2\pi}\,\frac{\Delta^\star(\mathbf{q},\omega')}{i\nu_n - \omega'} \tag{32.22}$$

where $\Delta^\star(\mathbf{q},\omega') = -\Delta^\star(-\mathbf{q},-\omega')$ is real.

We can now perform the analytic continuation from $\mathscr{D}(\mathbf{q},\nu_n)$ to $D^R(\mathbf{q},\omega)$ [Eqs. (32.14) and (32.15)]. It is convenient to introduce a function of a complex variable z

$$F(\mathbf{q},z) = \int_{-\infty}^{\infty} \frac{d\omega'}{2\pi}\,\frac{\Delta^\star(\mathbf{q},\omega')}{z - \omega'} \tag{32.23}$$

that reduces to $\Pi^\star$ at a discrete set of values $z = i\nu_n$:

$$\Pi^\star(\mathbf{q},\nu_n) = F(\mathbf{q},i\nu_n) \tag{32.24}$$

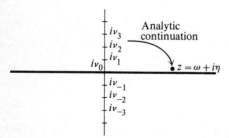

Fig. **32.2** Analytic continuation from $\Pi(\mathbf{q},\nu_n)$ to $\Pi^R(\mathbf{q},\omega + i\eta)$.

In this way, the polarization can be written as

$$\Pi(\mathbf{q},\nu_n) = \hbar^{-1} \mathcal{D}(\mathbf{q},\nu_n) = F(\mathbf{q},i\nu_n) \left[1 - V(\mathbf{q}) F(\mathbf{q},i\nu_n)\right]^{-1} \tag{32.25}$$

Since the z dependence and analytic properties of $F(\mathbf{q},z)[1 - V(\mathbf{q})F(\mathbf{q},z)]^{-1}$ are explicit in both the upper and lower z plane, this function can be immediately continued onto the real axis $z \to \omega + i\eta$ (see Fig. 32.2), where it gives the corresponding retarded functions

$$\Pi^R(\mathbf{q},\omega) = \hbar^{-1} D^R(\mathbf{q},\omega) = F(\mathbf{q}, \omega + i\eta) \left[1 - V(\mathbf{q}) F(\mathbf{q}, \omega + i\eta)\right]^{-1} \tag{32.26}$$

33□SCREENING IN AN ELECTRON GAS

As an example of this theory, we shall study the response of an electron gas to an applied scalar potential $\varphi^{ex}(\mathbf{x}t)$. The external perturbation is the same as in Eq. (13.11) (the charge on the electron is $-e$)

$$\hat{H}_H^{ex}(t) = -\int d^3x\, \hat{n}_H(\mathbf{x}t)\, e\varphi^{ex}(\mathbf{x}t) \tag{33.1}$$

where the subscript H now denotes a Heisenberg picture with respect to $\hat{K} = \hat{H} - \mu\hat{N}$, as in Eq. (32.6). For a uniform system, the induced density at wave vector $\mathbf{q}$ and frequency ω is given by [compare Eq. (13.18)]

$$\delta\langle\hat{n}(\mathbf{q},\omega)\rangle = -\hbar^{-1} D^R(\mathbf{q},\omega)\, e\varphi^{ex}(\mathbf{q},\omega) = -\Pi^R(\mathbf{q},\omega)\, e\varphi^{ex}(\mathbf{q},\omega) \tag{33.2}$$

Since $F(\mathbf{q}, \omega + i\eta)$ is the continuation of $\Pi^\star(\mathbf{q},\nu_n)$, Eqs. (32.26) and (33.2) relate the linear response of a system in thermodynamic equilibrium to the total proper polarization evaluated in the temperature formalism.

In practice, $\Pi^\star$ must be approximated by some selected set of diagrams, and we now consider the simplest choice Π^0, studied in Sec. 30. Comparison of Eqs. (30.9), (32.22), and (32.23) shows that $F^0(\mathbf{q},z)$ is given by

$$F^0(\mathbf{q},z) = -2 \int \frac{d^3p}{(2\pi)^3} \frac{n^0_{\mathbf{p}+\mathbf{q}} - n^0_{\mathbf{p}}}{\hbar z - (\epsilon^0_{\mathbf{p}+\mathbf{q}} - \epsilon^0_{\mathbf{p}})} \tag{33.3}$$

Thus the corresponding retarded function becomes

$$F^0(\mathbf{q}, \omega + i\eta) = -2 \int \frac{d^3p}{(2\pi)^3} \frac{n^0_{\mathbf{p}+\mathbf{q}} - n^0_{\mathbf{p}}}{\hbar\omega + i\eta - (\epsilon^0_{\mathbf{p}+\mathbf{q}} - \epsilon^0_{\mathbf{p}})}$$

$$= -2 \int \frac{d^3p}{(2\pi)^3} n^0_{\mathbf{p}+\frac{1}{2}\mathbf{q}} \left[\frac{1}{\hbar\omega + i\eta - \hbar^2\,\mathbf{p}\cdot\mathbf{q}/m} \right.$$

$$\left. - \frac{1}{\hbar\omega + i\eta + \hbar^2\,\mathbf{p}\cdot\mathbf{q}/m} \right] \tag{33.4}$$

where the last form is obtained with a simple change of variables. This equation applies for all T and μ and clearly reproduces the zero-temperature retarded

function $\Pi^{0R}(\mathbf{q},\omega)$ as $T \to 0$ [Eq. (15.9)]. Although a complete integration of Eq. (33.4) would be quite intricate, the expressions also become simple in the classical limit, where the distribution function reduces to a gaussian function $n_p^0 = e^{\beta\mu} e^{-\beta\hbar^2 p^2/2m}$. Equation (33.4) can then be evaluated using cylindrical polar coordinates $\mathbf{p} = \mathbf{p}_\perp + \hat{q}p_\parallel$ with $\hat{q}$ as the polar axis:

$$
\begin{aligned}
F^0(\mathbf{q}, \omega + i\eta) = &-2e^{\beta\mu} \int \frac{d^2 p_\perp}{(2\pi)^2} \exp\left(-\frac{\beta p_\perp^2 \hbar^2}{2m}\right) \\
&\times \int_{-\infty}^{\infty} \frac{dp_\parallel}{2\pi} \exp\left[\frac{-\beta(p_\parallel + \frac{1}{2}q)^2 \hbar^2}{2m}\right] \\
&\times \left(\frac{1}{\hbar\omega + i\eta - \hbar^2 p_\parallel q/m} - \frac{1}{\hbar\omega + i\eta + \hbar^2 p_\parallel q/m}\right) \\
= &-2e^{\beta\mu}\lambda^{-2} \int_{-\infty}^{\infty} \frac{dp_\parallel}{2\pi} \exp\left[\frac{-\beta(p_\parallel + \frac{1}{2}q)^2 \hbar^2}{2m}\right] \\
&\times \left(\frac{1}{\hbar\omega + i\eta - \hbar^2 p_\parallel q/m} - \frac{1}{\hbar\omega + i\eta + \hbar^2 p_\parallel q/m}\right) \quad (33.5)
\end{aligned}
$$

where $\lambda = (2\pi\beta\hbar^2/m)^{\frac{1}{2}}$ is the thermal wavelength [see Eq. (30.24)].

It is now convenient to separate Eq. (33.5) into its real and imaginary parts:

$$F^0(\mathbf{q}, \omega + i\eta) = F_1^0(\mathbf{q},\omega) + iF_2^0(\mathbf{q},\omega) \quad (33.6)$$

$$
\begin{aligned}
F_1^0(\mathbf{q},\omega) = &-2e^{\beta\mu}\lambda^{-2} \mathscr{P} \int_{-\infty}^{\infty} \frac{dp}{2\pi} \exp\left[\frac{-\beta(p + \frac{1}{2}q)^2 \hbar^2}{2m}\right] \\
&\times \left(\frac{1}{\hbar\omega - \hbar^2 pq/m} - \frac{1}{\hbar\omega + \hbar^2 pq/m}\right) \quad (33.7a)
\end{aligned}
$$

$$
\begin{aligned}
F_2^0(\mathbf{q},\omega) = &2e^{\beta\mu}\lambda^{-2} \int_{-\infty}^{\infty} dp \exp\left[\frac{-\beta(p + \frac{1}{2}q)^2 \hbar^2}{2m}\right] \\
&\times \left[\frac{1}{2}\delta\left(\hbar\omega - \frac{\hbar^2 pq}{m}\right) - \frac{1}{2}\delta\left(\hbar\omega + \frac{\hbar^2 pq}{m}\right)\right] \quad (33.7b)
\end{aligned}
$$

Furthermore, we shall use the thermodynamic relations obtained previously [Eq. (30.34)] to eliminate the chemical potential μ in favor of the density n. Since $V(\mathbf{q})F^0(\mathbf{q},\omega)$ is already of order e^2, it is permissible to retain only the leading term $e^{\beta\mu} \approx \frac{1}{2}n\lambda^3$. The imaginary part F_2^0 is easily evaluated, and we find

$$F_2^0(q,\omega) = -\frac{n\beta\omega}{q} (\tfrac{1}{2}\pi\beta m)^{\frac{1}{2}} \exp\left(-\frac{\beta m\omega^2}{2q^2} - \frac{\beta\hbar^2 q^2}{8m}\right) \frac{\sinh\left(\frac{1}{2}\beta\hbar\omega\right)}{\frac{1}{2}\beta\hbar\omega} \qquad T \to \infty \quad (33.8)$$

It is clear that F_2^0 is an odd function of ω and vanishes at $\omega = 0$, in agreement with the antisymmetry of the weight function $\Delta^\star$.

In contrast, the real part F_1^0 cannot be expressed in terms of elementary functions, but a change of variables yields

$$F_1^0(q,\omega) = -\frac{n}{\hbar q} (\tfrac{1}{2}\beta m)^{\frac{1}{2}} \left\{ \Phi\left[(\tfrac{1}{2}m\beta)^{\frac{1}{2}} \left(\frac{\omega}{q} + \frac{\hbar q}{2m} \right) \right] - \Phi\left[(\tfrac{1}{2}m\beta)^{\frac{1}{2}} \left(\frac{\omega}{q} - \frac{\hbar q}{2m} \right) \right] \right\}$$

$$T \to \infty \quad (33.9)$$

where

$$\Phi(x) = \pi^{-\frac{1}{2}} \mathscr{P} \int_{-\infty}^{\infty} dy\, \frac{e^{-y^2}}{x - y} \tag{33.10}$$

is the real part of the plasma dispersion function.[1]   If the integrand is multiplied by $(x + y)/(x + y)$, the result may be rewritten as

$$\Phi(x) = 2x\pi^{-\frac{1}{2}} \mathscr{P} \int_0^{\infty} dy\, \frac{e^{-y^2}}{x^2 - y^2} \tag{33.11}$$

which shows that $\Phi(x)$ is an odd function.   The asymptotic form is obtained by expanding the integrand for large x

$$\Phi(x) \sim x^{-1}(1 + \tfrac{1}{2}x^{-2} + \cdots) \qquad x \gg 1 \tag{33.12}$$

but the behavior for small x requires a little more effort.   Equation (33.10) shows that $\Phi(0) = 0$, because the integrand is then an odd function of y.   Differentiate Eq. (33.10) with respect to x and integrate by parts.   The resulting expression may be rearranged to yield

$$\Phi'(x) = 2 - 2x\Phi(x) \tag{33.13}$$

which has the solution

$$\Phi(x) = 2e^{-x^2} \int_0^x dy\, e^{y^2} \tag{33.14}$$

We see that $\Phi(x)$ is an entire function of x, and a direct expansion gives

$$\Phi(x) \approx 2x(1 - \tfrac{2}{3}x^2 + \cdots) \qquad x \ll 1 \tag{33.15}$$

To be specific, assume that the external perturbation is a positive point charge with potential $\varphi^{ex}(\mathbf{q},\omega) = 4\pi Zeq^{-2} 2\pi\delta(\omega)$.   We therefore need only the zero-frequency component of $D^R(q,\omega)$; a combination of Eqs. (32.26), (33.2),

---

[1] This function is tabulated in B. D. Fried and S. D. Conte, "The Plasma Dispersion Function," Academic Press, New York, 1961.

(33.8), and (33.9) yields the induced charge density

$$\delta\langle\hat{\rho}(\mathbf{x})\rangle = -e\delta\langle\hat{n}(\mathbf{x})\rangle$$

$$= Ze \int \frac{d^3q}{(2\pi)^3} e^{i\mathbf{q}\cdot\mathbf{x}} \frac{V(q)\,F_1^0(q,0)}{1 - V(q)\,F_1^0(q,0)}$$

$$= -Ze \int \frac{d^3q}{(2\pi)^3} e^{i\mathbf{q}\cdot\mathbf{x}} \frac{q_D^2\,g_1(q\lambda)}{q^2 + q_D^2\,g_1(q\lambda)} \tag{33.16}$$

where $q_D = (4\pi n e^2 \beta)^{\frac{1}{2}}$ is the reciprocal of the Debye shielding length and $\lambda = (2\pi\hbar^2\beta/m)^{\frac{1}{2}}$ is the thermal wavelength [see Eqs. (30.39) and (30.24)]. Here the function $g_1(y)$ is given by

$$g_1(y) = 2\pi^{\frac{1}{2}} y^{-1} \Phi\left(\frac{y}{4\pi^{\frac{1}{2}}}\right) \tag{33.17}$$

and has the following limiting behavior

$$g_1(y) \approx 1 + O(y^2) \qquad y \ll 1 \tag{33.18}$$

$$g_1(y) \sim 8\pi y^{-2} \qquad y \gg 1 \tag{33.19}$$

Equation (33.16) is clearly very similar to Eq. (14.14), and most of the same remarks apply.

1. The total induced charge is

$$\delta Q = \int d^3x\,\delta\langle\hat{\rho}(\mathbf{x})\rangle = -Ze \tag{33.20}$$

so that the impurity is completely screened at large distances.
2. The integrand vanishes like q^{-4} as $q \to \infty$, which ensures that $\delta\langle\hat{\rho}(\mathbf{x})\rangle$ is bounded everywhere, including $x = 0$.
3. The singular q^{-2} dependence at small q^2 is cut off at the inverse Debye screening length $q_D = (4\pi n e^2 \beta)^{\frac{1}{2}}$, which justifies our use of a cutoff $q_{\min} \propto e$ in Eq. (30.28). Since $g_1(q\lambda)$ is an entire function of $q\lambda$, it is infinitely differentiable throughout the complex q plane. The asymptotic behavior of $\delta\langle\hat{\rho}(x)\rangle$ therefore can be obtained with the approximation $g_1(q\lambda) \approx g_1(0) = 1$, because the terms neglected are of order $(q_D\lambda)^2 \propto (ne^2\beta)(\hbar^2\beta/m) = (n^{\frac{1}{3}}e^2\beta)(\hbar^2 n^{\frac{2}{3}}\beta/m) \ll 1$ [see the discussion following Eq. (30.48)]:

$$\delta\langle\hat{\rho}(x)\rangle \sim -Ze \int \frac{d^3q}{(2\pi)^3} \frac{e^{i\mathbf{q}\cdot\mathbf{x}}q_D^2}{q^2 + q_D^2}$$

$$= -Ze q_D^2 (4\pi x)^{-1} e^{-q_D x} \qquad x \to \infty \tag{33.21}$$

This expression exhibits the role of q_D^{-1} as a classical screening length and is identical with Eq. (30.41b) which describes a negatively charged impurity. At zero temperature, the sharp Fermi surface modified the asymptotic charge density by introducing additional dominant oscillatory terms [Eq. (14.26)];

no such behavior occurs in the present classical limit, because the distribution functions are smooth.

34□PLASMA OSCILLATIONS IN AN ELECTRON GAS

The present formalism also can be used to study the collective oscillations of a system in thermodynamic equilibrium, and we now examine the plasma oscillations in an electron gas. If the system is subjected to an impulsive perturbation $\varphi^{ex}(xt) = \varphi_0 e^{i\mathbf{q}\cdot\mathbf{x}} \delta(t)$, the associated induced density becomes [compare Eq. (15.7)]

$$\delta\langle\hat{n}(\mathbf{x}t)\rangle = -e\varphi_0\, e^{i\mathbf{q}\cdot\mathbf{x}} \int \frac{d\omega}{2\pi} e^{-i\omega t}\, \frac{F_1(q,\omega) + iF_2(q,\omega)}{1 - V(q)\,F_1(q,\omega) - iV(q)\,F_2(q,\omega)} \tag{34.1}$$

where $F(\mathbf{q}, \omega + i\eta)$ has been separated into its real and imaginary parts, as in Eq. (33.6). The natural oscillation frequencies are determined by the poles of the retarded density correlation function, which occur at the solutions $\Omega_q - i\gamma_q$ of the equation

$$1 - V(q)\,F_1(q, \Omega_q - i\gamma_q) - iV(q)\,F_2(q, \Omega_q - i\gamma_q) = 0 \tag{34.2}$$

This description is entirely general. If the exact proper polarization $\Pi^\star(q,\nu_n)$ is approximated by the zero-order polarization $\Pi^0(q,\nu_n)$, we obtain the finite-temperature generalization of Eq. (15.10). The theory becomes especially simple in the classical limit, when the previous expressions for F_1^0 and F_2^0 are applicable. Furthermore, we assume that the damping is small, so that the real and imaginary parts of Eq. (34.2) become

$$1 = V(q)\,F_1^0(q,\Omega_q) \tag{34.3}$$

$$\gamma_q = F_2^0(q,\Omega_q)\left[\frac{\partial F_1^0(q,\omega)}{\partial\omega}\bigg|_{\Omega_q}\right]^{-1} \tag{34.4}$$

As shown below, this is a good approximation for $q \ll q_D$, when it is possible to evaluate F_1^0 with the asymptotic form given in Eq. (33.12). A straightforward calculation yields

$$F_1^0(q,\omega) \approx \frac{nq^2}{m\omega^2}\left(1 + \frac{3q^2}{\beta m\omega^2} + \cdots\right) \qquad q \to 0 \tag{34.5}$$

Equation (34.3) then reduces to

$$1 = \frac{4\pi ne^2}{m\Omega_q^2}\left(1 + \frac{3q^2}{\beta m\Omega_q^2}\right) \tag{34.6}$$

with the approximate solution

$$\Omega_q = \pm\Omega_{pl}\left[1 + \frac{3}{2}\left(\frac{q}{q_D}\right)^2\right] \tag{34.7}$$

where Ω_{pl} and q_D are given in Eqs. (15.18) and (30.39). The collective mode again represents a plasma oscillation, and the dispersion relation has the same form as at $T = 0$ [compare Eq. (15.17)].

The finite temperature introduces one new feature, however, because these collective modes are now damped, even in the lowest-order approximation of retaining only Π^0. Since $\beta\hbar\Omega_{pl} = O(q_D\lambda) \ll 1$ at high temperatures, Eq. (33.8) may be approximated by $(q \ll q_D)$

$$F_2^0(q,\omega) \approx -\frac{n\beta\omega}{q}(\tfrac{1}{2}\pi\beta m)^{\frac{1}{2}} \exp\left(-\frac{\beta m\omega^2}{2q^2}\right) \tag{34.8}$$

The derivative of Eq. (34.5) can be combined with Eqs. (34.4) and (34.8) to give

$$\begin{aligned}
\gamma_q &= F_2^0(q,\pm\Omega_{pl})\left[\frac{\partial F_1^0(q,\omega)}{\partial\omega}\bigg|_{\omega=\pm\Omega_{pl}}\right]^{-1} \\
&= q^{-3}\,\Omega_{pl}^4(m\beta)^{\frac{3}{2}}(\tfrac{1}{8}\pi)^{\frac{1}{2}}\exp\left(-\frac{\Omega_{pl}^2\,m\beta}{2q^2}\right) \\
&= \Omega_{pl}(\tfrac{1}{8}\pi)^{\frac{1}{2}}\left(\frac{q_D}{q}\right)^3\exp\left[-\frac{1}{2}\left(\frac{q_D}{q}\right)^2\right]
\end{aligned} \tag{34.9}$$

As expected from general considerations, γ_q is positive, and both poles of D^R lie in the lower half plane at $\omega \approx \pm\Omega_{pl} - i\gamma_q$. The approximation of small damping is fully justified at long wavelengths, because $|\gamma_q/\Omega_q|$ vanishes exponentially. This weak damping is known as Landau damping,[1] because Landau was the first to note that the solutions of Eq. (34.2) are complex instead of real. It is interesting that the temperature affects both the damping and the q^2 correction to the dispersion relation, but does not alter the fundamental plasma frequency.

PROBLEMS

9.1. If $E_0(N)$ is the ground-state energy of a Fermi system with N particles, show that the grand partition function at low temperature may be written approximately as $e^{-\beta\Omega} \approx e^{-\beta[E_0(N_0)-\mu N_0]}[2\pi/\beta E_0''(N_0)]^{\frac{1}{2}}$, where $N_0(\mu)$ is defined by the relation $E_0'(N_0) = \mu$ and the primes denote differentiation with respect to N. Why can N_0 be identified as the mean number of particles? Evaluate Eq. (31.12) in the same approximation and prove that $\bar{G}(\mathbf{k}, \omega - \mu/\hbar)_{T=0} = G(\mathbf{k},\omega)$, where G is the zero-temperature function of Chap. 3.

9.2. Evaluate the weight function $\rho(\mathbf{x},\mathbf{x}',\omega)$ for the Hartree-Fock Green's function (27.8). Find the corresponding real-time Green's function $\bar{G}(\mathbf{x},\mathbf{x}',\omega)$ and the retarded and advanced functions.

[1] L. D. Landau, *J. Phys. (USSR)*, **10**:25 (1946).

9.3. (a) If the proper self-energy $\Sigma^\star(\mathbf{k},\omega_n)$ in Eq. (26.5) takes the form

$$\Sigma^\star(\mathbf{k},\omega_n) = \Sigma_0(\mathbf{k}) + \int_{-\infty}^{\infty} \frac{d\omega'}{2\pi} \frac{\sigma(\mathbf{k},\omega')}{i\omega_n - \omega'}$$

with Σ_0 and σ real, use the definition $\Sigma_1^\star(\mathbf{k},\omega) + i\Sigma_2^\star(\mathbf{k},\omega) \equiv \Sigma^\star(\mathbf{k},\omega_n)|_{i\omega_n = \omega - i\eta}$ to find the corresponding weight function $\rho(\mathbf{k},\omega)$ in Eq. (31.35).
(b) Expand $\rho(\mathbf{k},\omega)$ about the point $\omega = \omega_k$ determined by the self-consistent equation $\hbar\omega_k = \epsilon_k^0 - \mu + \hbar\Sigma_1^\star(\mathbf{k},\omega_k)$, and derive an approximate quasiparticle (lorentzian) weight function. Compute the approximate $\bar{G}_{qp}(\mathbf{k},\omega)$, and prove that the excitation energy and damping of single-particle excitations are given by $\epsilon_k = \hbar\omega_k + \mu$ and $\gamma_k = \{1 - \partial\Sigma_1^\star(\mathbf{k},\omega)/\partial\omega|_{\omega_k}\}^{-1}\Sigma_2^\star(\mathbf{k},\omega_k)$ (compare Prob. 3.14).

9.4. Repeat Prob. 5.1 for the retarded density correlation function at finite temperature $iD^R(x,x') = \theta(t-t')\,\mathrm{Tr}\,\{\hat{\rho}_G[\tilde{n}_H(x),\tilde{n}_H(x')]\}$. Consider the following equal-time limits:
(a) low temperatures ($k_B T \ll \epsilon_F$) and $|\mathbf{x} - \mathbf{x}'| \gg k_F^{-1}$,
(b) classical limit and $|\mathbf{x} - \mathbf{x}'| \gg \lambda = (2\pi\hbar^2/mk_B T)^{\frac{1}{2}}$.
Compare the discussion at the end of Sec. 14.

9.5. Use the spin-density operator $\hat{\sigma}_z(\mathbf{x}) = \hat{\psi}_\alpha^\dagger(\mathbf{x})(\sigma_z)_{\alpha\beta}\hat{\psi}_\beta(\mathbf{x})$ to construct the retarded correlation function

$$iD_\sigma^R(\mathbf{x}t,\mathbf{x}'\,t') = \mathrm{Tr}\,\{\hat{\rho}_G[\hat{\sigma}_{Hz}(\mathbf{x}t),\hat{\sigma}_{Hz}(\mathbf{x}'\,t')]\}\,\theta(t-t')$$

and the corresponding temperature Green's function

$$\mathscr{D}_\sigma(\mathbf{x}\tau,\mathbf{x}'\,\tau') = -\mathrm{Tr}\,\{\hat{\rho}_G\,T_\tau[\hat{\sigma}_{Kz}(\mathbf{x}\tau)\,\hat{\sigma}_{Kz}(\mathbf{x}'\,\tau')]\}$$

Derive the Lehmann representation for these two functions, and show that they are related through the spectral weight function as in Eqs. (32.14) and (32.15).

9.6. Study the linear response of a uniform spin-$\frac{1}{2}$ Fermi system to a weak, external magnetic field $\mathscr{H}(\mathbf{x}t)$ where the perturbing hamiltonian is given by $\hat{H}^{ex} = -\mu_0 \int d^3x\,\hat{\sigma}_z(\mathbf{x})\mathscr{H}(\mathbf{x}t)$.
(a) Show that the induced magnetization is given by

$$\langle\hat{M}_z(\mathbf{x}t)\rangle = -\mu_0^2\hbar^{-1}\int d^3x'\,dt'\,D_\sigma^R(\mathbf{x}-\mathbf{x}',t-t')\,\mathscr{H}(\mathbf{x}'\,t')$$

$$\langle\hat{M}_z(\mathbf{k},\omega)\rangle = -\mu_0^2\hbar^{-1}D_\sigma^R(\mathbf{k},\omega)\,\mathscr{H}(\mathbf{k},\omega)$$

where D_σ^R is defined in Prob. 9.5.
(b) Use Wick's theorem to evaluate $\mathscr{D}_\sigma$ for a noninteracting system, and determine D_σ^R with the results of Prob. 9.5.
(c) Find the generalized susceptibility of a noninteracting system in a static magnetic field $\chi(\mathbf{k},0) = \langle\hat{M}_z(\mathbf{k},0)\rangle/\mathscr{H}(\mathbf{k},0)$, and verify that

$$\lim_{k\to0}\chi(\mathbf{k},0) = \begin{cases} \dfrac{3\mu_0^2 n}{2\epsilon_F^0} & T = 0 \text{ (Pauli spin paramagnetism)} \\[3mm] \dfrac{\mu_0^2 n}{k_B T} & T \to \infty \text{ (Curie's law)} \end{cases}$$

9.7. Repeat the calculation of Prob. 9.6 in the zero-temperature formalism. Why does this zero-temperature calculation work, whereas that in Prob. 7.5 fails?

9.8. (a) Use Probs. 5.9 and 9.6 to show that the static susceptibility for a spin-$\frac{1}{2}$ Fermi system with spin-independent potentials is given *exactly* by $\chi(\mathbf{k},0) = -\mu_0^2 \Pi_\sigma^\star(\mathbf{k},0) = -\mu_0^2 \Pi_\sigma^\star(\mathbf{k},0)$.
(b) With the approximation used in Prob. 5.8, derive the zero-temperature magnetic susceptibility of a dilute spin-$\frac{1}{2}$ hard-sphere Fermi gas $\chi/\chi_P = (1 - 2k_F a/\pi)^{-1}$ where χ_P is the Pauli susceptibility. Compare with Prob. 4.10.

9.9. Discuss the asymptotic form of the screening cloud around an impurity in a dense electron gas at low but finite temperatures. Hence verify the discussion at the end of Sec. 14.

9.10. Show that the ring approximation to the plasma dispersion relation at all temperatures can be written to order q^2 as $\Omega_q^2 = \Omega_{pl}^2 + q^2 \langle v^2 \rangle$, where $\langle v^2 \rangle$ is the mean square velocity of particles in a noninteracting Fermi gas at temperature T. Verify that this equation reproduces Eqs. (15.17) and (34.7). Find the first low-temperature correction to Eq. (15.17). Repeat for noncondensed bosons.

9.11. Evaluate $F_2^0(q,\omega)$ [Eqs. (33.4) and (33.6)] for all T and μ and rederive Eqs. (12.41), (12.43), (12.45), and (33.8). Find the damping of plasma oscillations and zero sound at low temperature. What happens to zero sound in the classical limit?

9.12. Use the ring approximation $\Sigma^\star(\mathbf{k},\omega_n) = \Sigma_{(1)}^\star(\mathbf{k}) + \Sigma_r^\star(\mathbf{k},\omega_n)$, with $\Sigma_r^\star$ taken from Eq. (30.12), to study the single-particle excitations in a dense electron gas at zero temperature.
(a) Show that the excitation spectrum (see Prob. 9.3b) is given to order r_s by

$$\epsilon_{\mathbf{k}} = \epsilon_{\mathbf{k}}^0 - \epsilon_F^0 \frac{\alpha r_s}{\pi^2} \int d^3q \, \frac{\theta(1 - |\mathbf{K} + \mathbf{q}|)}{q^2 + 2\alpha r_s f(\hat{\mathbf{q}} \cdot \mathbf{K} + \frac{1}{2}q)}$$

where $\alpha = (4/9\pi)^{\frac{1}{3}}$, f is defined in Eq. (12.58), and $\mathbf{K} = \mathbf{k}/k_F$.‡ Hence determine the effective mass m^* (see Prob. 8.2b).
(b) Show that close to the Fermi surface the damping constant (Prob. 9.3b) is given by $\hbar \gamma_{\mathbf{k}} \approx \epsilon_F^0 (\alpha r_s)^{\frac{1}{2}} (\pi^{\frac{3}{2}}/16)(k/k_F - 1)^2$.

‡ The results for Probs. 9.12a and 9.12b were derived by J. J. Quinn and R. A. Ferrell, *Phys. Rev.*, **112**:812 (1958).

Canonical Transformations

10
Canonical Transformations

In the previous chapters, our discussion of interacting many-particle assemblies emphasized the use of quantum field theory and Green's functions. For many systems, however, the physics becomes clearer in a more direct approach, where we simplify the original second-quantized hamiltonian and obtain an approximate problem that is exactly solvable. This chapter studies a class of such problems that can be solved with a canonical transformation of the creation and destruction operators in the abstract occupation-number Hilbert space. As noted in Chap. 1, the commutation relations completely characterize the creation and destruction operators. Since, by definition, a canonical transformation does not alter these commutation relations, the transformed operators again satisfy Eqs. (1.28) in the case of bosons or Eqs. (1.50) and (1.51) for fermions. As a first example, we consider the interacting Bose gas (Sec. 35) following a treatment due to Bogoliubov,[1] and then study an interacting Fermi gas (Secs. 36 and 37).

[1] N. N. Bogoliubov, *J. Phys. (USSR)*, **11**:23 (1947).

35□INTERACTING BOSE GAS

An interacting Bose gas at zero temperature has previously been considered within the framework of quantum field theory (Chap. 6). We here treat essentially the same problem as an example of a model hamiltonian that can be diagonalized exactly, thereby yielding all the physical properties of Sec. 22 in a direct and intuitive fashion. If the assembly is dilute, then most of the particles occupy the zero-momentum state, and only two-body collisions with small momentum transfers play an important role. In Secs. 11 and 22 we have already seen that such collisions can be characterized by a single parameter a, the s-wave scattering length. For this reason, we shall introduce a model hamiltonian consisting of a kinetic-energy term and an artificial potential energy

$$\hat{H} = \sum_{\mathbf{k}} \hbar\omega_{\mathbf{k}} a_{\mathbf{k}}^{\dagger} a_{\mathbf{k}} + \frac{g}{2V} \sum_{\mathbf{k}_1 \mathbf{k}_2 \mathbf{k}_3 \mathbf{k}_4} a_{\mathbf{k}_1}^{\dagger} a_{\mathbf{k}_2}^{\dagger} a_{\mathbf{k}_3} a_{\mathbf{k}_4} \delta_{\mathbf{k}_1 + \mathbf{k}_2, \mathbf{k}_3 + \mathbf{k}_4} \tag{35.1}$$

in which the actual potential $V(\mathbf{k})$ is replaced by a *pseudopotential g*.

The constant matrix element g can be determined by requiring that $\hat{H}$ correctly reproduce the two-body scattering properties in vacuum. This problem has already been studied in Sec. 11, where it was shown that the scattering amplitude was related to the two-body potential by Eq. (11.14). In the present case, the Fourier transform $v(\mathbf{k}) \equiv mV(\mathbf{k})/\hbar^2$ is replaced by $mg/\hbar^2$, and we find

$$\mathcal{f}(\mathbf{k}',\mathbf{k}) = -4\pi f(\mathbf{k}',\mathbf{k}) = \frac{mg}{\hbar^2} + \int \frac{d^3q}{(2\pi)^3} \frac{(mg/\hbar^2)^2}{k^2 - q^2 + i\eta} + \cdots \tag{35.2}$$

The left side reduces to $4\pi a$ at long wavelengths, which yields the relation

$$\frac{4\pi a\hbar^2}{m} = g - \frac{mg^2}{\hbar^2} \int \frac{d^3q}{(2\pi)^3} \frac{1}{q^2} + \cdots \tag{35.3}$$

The first-order result

$$g = \frac{4\pi\hbar^2 a}{m} \tag{35.4}$$

is well defined. In contrast, the second-order integral diverges at large momenta. This artificial divergence arises from the substitution of g for $V(\mathbf{k})$, and we therefore cut off the integral at some large wave vector Q. We show, in the following discussion, that a similar divergence occurs in the ground-state energy, and the two expressions can be combined to yield a finite answer, even for $Q \to \infty$. We return to this question at the end of this section.

The scattering properties must be evaluated with care because the s-wave scattering length a has been defined as if the particles were distinguishable. For identical bosons, the overall wave function is symmetric, and the differential cross section is obtained from a symmetrized scattering amplitude

$$\frac{d\sigma}{d\Omega} = |f(\theta) + f(\pi - \theta)|^2 \tag{35.5}$$

Each term reduces to $-a$ in the low-energy limit, giving

$$\frac{d\sigma}{d\Omega} \to |2a|^2 \qquad k \to 0 \tag{35.6}$$

which is four times that for distinguishable particles.

The parameter g has now been related to observable quantities, and we return to the original many-particle hamiltonian, Eq. (35.1). In view of the special role of the zero-momentum state, it is again natural to replace the operators a_0 and $a_0^\dagger$ by c numbers

$$a_0, a_0^\dagger \to N_0^{\frac{1}{2}} \tag{35.7}$$

exactly as in Sec. 18. The terms of the interaction hamiltonian can be classified according to the number of times a_0 and $a_0^\dagger$ appear, and we shall retain only terms of order N_0^2 and N_0

$$\hat{H}_{int} \approx g(2V)^{-1} \{a_0^\dagger a_0^\dagger a_0 a_0 + \sum_{k}' [2(a_k^\dagger a_k u_0^\dagger a_0 + a_{-k}^\dagger a_{k} a_0^\dagger a_0)$$

$$+ a_k^\dagger a_{-k}^\dagger a_0 a_0 + a_0^\dagger a_0^\dagger a_k a_{-k}]\} \tag{35.8}$$

where the prime means to omit the terms $\mathbf{k} = 0$. This truncated hamiltonian clearly neglects the interaction of particles out of the condensate; it should provide a good approximation as long as $N - N_0 \ll N$. The validity of this assumption is examined below. It is plausible, however, that the terms omitted can only contribute to the energy in third or higher order of perturbation theory, for they involve one collision to get the particles out of the condensate, a second collision above the condensate, and a third collision to return the particles to the condensate [see the discussion following Eq. (11.22)]. A combination of Eqs. (35.7) and (35.8) gives

$$\hat{H}_{int} = g(2V)^{-1} [N_0^2 + 2N_0 \sum_{k}' (a_k^\dagger a_k + a_{-k}^\dagger a_{-k}) + N_0 \sum_{k}' (a_k^\dagger a_{-k}^\dagger + a_k a_{-k})] \tag{35.9}$$

while the number operator becomes

$$\hat{N} = N_0 + \tfrac{1}{2} \sum_{k}' (a_k^\dagger a_k + a_{-k}^\dagger a_{-k}) \tag{35.10}$$

The problem of particle nonconservation that was seen in Sec. 18 evidently occurs here as well. Although it is possible to introduce a chemical potential (Prob. 10.3), we prefer to consider $N = \langle \hat{N} \rangle$ as given and to eliminate N_0 explicitly. If only terms of order N^2 and N are kept, substitution of Eq. (35.10) into (35.9) yields our final model hamiltonian

$$\hat{H} = \tfrac{1}{2} V g n^2 + \tfrac{1}{2} \sum_{k}' [(\epsilon_k^0 + ng)(a_k^\dagger a_k + a_{-k}^\dagger a_{-k}) + ng(a_k^\dagger a_{-k}^\dagger + a_k a_{-k})] \tag{35.11}$$

where $n = N/V$ is the particle density. In obtaining this result, terms like $(\sum_{k}' a_k^\dagger a_k)^2$ have again been neglected on the assumption that $N - N_0 \ll N$.

Equation (35.11) has the important feature that it can be *solved exactly* because it is a quadratic form in the operators, and therefore can be diagonalized with a canonical transformation.

The diagonalization of $\hat{H}$ is most simply carried out by defining a new set of creation and destruction operators[1]

$$a_k = u_k \alpha_k - v_k \alpha^\dagger_{-k} \qquad a^\dagger_k = u_k \alpha^\dagger_k - v_k \alpha_{-k} \tag{35.12}$$

where the coefficients u_k and v_k are assumed to be real and spherically symmetric. The transformation is canonical if the new operators also obey the canonical commutation relations

$$[\alpha_k, \alpha^\dagger_{k'}] = \delta_{kk'} \qquad [\alpha_k, \alpha_{k'}] = [\alpha^\dagger_k, \alpha^\dagger_{k'}] = 0 \tag{35.13}$$

and it is easily seen that this condition may be satisfied by imposing the restriction

$$u_k^2 - v_k^2 = 1 \tag{35.14}$$

for each k. Equation (35.12) may be substituted into $\hat{H}$ directly, and we find

$$\hat{H} = \tfrac{1}{2} V g n^2 + \sum_k{}' [(\epsilon_k^0 + ng) v_k^2 - ng u_k v_k]$$

$$+ \tfrac{1}{2} \sum_k{}' \{[(\epsilon_k^0 + ng)(u_k^2 + v_k^2) - 2u_k v_k ng](\alpha^\dagger_k \alpha_k + \alpha^\dagger_{-k} \alpha_{-k})\}$$

$$+ \tfrac{1}{2} \sum_k{}' \{[ng(u_k^2 + v_k^2) - 2u_k v_k(\epsilon_k^0 + ng)](\alpha^\dagger_k \alpha^\dagger_{-k} + \alpha_k \alpha_{-k})\} \tag{35.15}$$

Although the parameters u_k and v_k satisfy the restriction of Eq. (35.14), their ratio is still arbitrary and can be used to simplify Eq. (35.15).   In particular, we choose to eliminate the last line of $\hat{H}$. The resulting hamiltonian is then explicitly diagonal in the *quasiparticle* number operators $\alpha^\dagger_k \alpha_k$, which allows us to determine all its eigenvectors and eigenvalues. The condition on the parameters u_k and v_k becomes

$$ng(u_k^2 + v_k^2) = 2u_k v_k(\epsilon_k^0 + ng) \tag{35.16}$$

The constraint (35.14) can be incorporated with the parametric representation

$$u_k = \cosh \varphi_k \qquad v_k = \sinh \varphi_k$$

which reduces Eq. (35.16) to

$$\tanh 2\varphi_k = \frac{ng}{\epsilon_k^0 + ng}$$

Since the left side lies between -1 and 1, this equation can be solved for all k only if the potential is repulsive ($g > 0$). The use of standard hyperbolic identities gives

$$v_k^2 = u_k^2 - 1 = \tfrac{1}{2}[E_k^{-1}(\epsilon_k^0 + ng) - 1] \tag{35.17}$$

[1] Although this step is usually known as a *Bogoliubov transformation*, it was used earlier by T. Holstein and H. Primakoff, *Phys. Rev.*, **58**:1098 (1940) in a study of magnetic systems.

where

$$E_k \equiv [(\epsilon_k^0 + ng)^2 - (ng)^2]^{\frac{1}{2}} \tag{35.18}$$

A combination of Eqs. (35.14) to (35.18) yields

$$\hat{H} = \tfrac{1}{2}Vgn^2 - \tfrac{1}{2}\sum_{k}{}' (\epsilon_k^0 + ng - E_k) + \tfrac{1}{2}\sum_{k}{}' E_k(\alpha_k^\dagger \alpha_k + \alpha_{-k}^\dagger \alpha_{-k}) \tag{35.19}$$

The operator $\alpha_k^\dagger \alpha_k$ has the eigenvalues 0, 1, 2, ... Consequently, the ground state $|O\rangle$ of $\hat{H}$ is determined by the condition

$$\alpha_k|O\rangle = 0 \qquad \text{all } k \neq 0 \tag{35.20}$$

and may be interpreted as a quasiparticle vacuum. Note that $|O\rangle$ is a complicated combination of unperturbed eigenstates, since neither a_k nor $a_k^\dagger$ annihilates it. The ground-state energy is then given by

$$E = \langle O|\hat{H}|O\rangle = \tfrac{1}{2}Vn^2 g + \tfrac{1}{2}\sum_{k}{}' (E_k - \epsilon_k^0 - ng) \tag{35.21}$$

Furthermore, all excited states correspond to various numbers of noninteracting bosons, each with an excitation energy E_k. This spectrum has the same form as that obtained in Sec. 22 for a dilute hard-core Bose gas:

$$E_k \approx \begin{cases} \left(\dfrac{ng}{m}\right)^{\frac{1}{2}} \hbar k = \left(\dfrac{4\pi anh^2}{m^2}\right)^{\frac{1}{2}} \hbar k & k \to 0 \tag{35.22a} \\[3mm] \epsilon_k^0 + \dfrac{4\pi anh^2}{m} & k \to \infty \tag{35.22b} \end{cases}$$

At long wavelengths, the interacting spectrum is characteristic of a sound wave with a velocity given by $(4\pi anh^2/m^2)^{\frac{1}{2}}$. It is again clear that these results are meaningful only for a repulsive interaction ($g > 0, a > 0$).

The distribution function in the ground state $|O\rangle$ is given by

$$n_k = \langle O|a_k^\dagger a_k|O\rangle = v_k^2 \langle O|\alpha_k \alpha_k^\dagger|O\rangle = v_k^2 \tag{35.23}$$

which varies as k^{-1} for $k \to 0$. At large wavenumbers, $v_k^2 \propto k^{-4}$, thus ensuring that the total number of particles out of the condensate remains finite. We see that the interaction removes particles from the zero-momentum condensate; indeed, there is a finite probability of finding a particle with arbitrarily high momentum. It is interesting to find the *depletion*, defined by

$$\begin{aligned} \frac{N - N_0}{N} &= \frac{1}{N}\sum_{k}{}' v_k^2 = \frac{1}{n}\int \frac{d^3k}{(2\pi)^3} v_k^2 \\ &= 4\left(\frac{2na^3}{\pi}\right)^{\frac{1}{2}} \int_0^\infty y^2\, dy \left[\frac{y^2 + 1}{(y^4 + 2y^2)^{\frac{1}{2}}} - 1\right] \\ &= \frac{8}{3}\left(\frac{na^3}{\pi}\right)^{\frac{1}{2}} \end{aligned} \tag{35.24}$$

in complete agreement with Eq. (22.14). Note that this expression is non-analytic in a (or g) and thus cannot be obtained in finite order of perturbation theory.

The ground-state energy has been found in Eq. (35.21), but the sum diverges like $\sum_{\mathbf{k}}' k^{-2}$ as $k \to \infty$. This divergence reflects the failure of perturbation theory for a Bose gas. In fact, if we evaluate the second-order term in the ground-state energy using our pseudopotential, the answer diverges in just the same way (see Prob. 1.3). Thus the divergence is not very basic, for it arises from the assumption that the potential has constant matrix elements as a function of the relative momentum. The Fourier transform of a more realistic potential falls off at high momentum, which renders the resulting expression convergent. This procedure is unnecessary, however, since the expansion for the scattering length a to order g^2 in Eq. (35.3) contains precisely the same divergence. We may therefore eliminate g entirely, which gives a convergent expression for the ground-state energy in terms of the directly measured quantity a [see Eq. (35.6)].[1] To verify these assertions, Eq. (35.21) may be rewritten by adding and subtracting the second-order energy shift

$$E = \tfrac{1}{2}Vn^2 g - \tfrac{1}{2}(ng)^2 \sum_{\mathbf{k}}' \frac{1}{\hbar^2 k^2/m} + \tfrac{1}{2}\sum_{\mathbf{k}}' \left(E_k - \epsilon_k^0 - ng + \frac{mn^2 g^2}{\hbar^2 k^2}\right)$$

It is readily seen that the last sum converges; furthermore, the first two terms are just those in the expansion of Eq. (35.3) for the scattering length a. In this way we obtain

$$\frac{E}{N} = \tfrac{1}{2}n\left(g - \frac{mg^2}{\hbar^2}\int \frac{d^3k}{(2\pi)^3}\frac{1}{k^2}\right) + \tfrac{1}{2}g\int \frac{d^3k}{(2\pi)^3}\left(\frac{E_k}{ng} - \frac{\epsilon_k^0}{ng} - 1 + \frac{ng}{2\epsilon_k^0}\right)$$

$$= \frac{2\pi a\hbar^2 n}{m}\left\{1 + 8\left(\frac{2na^3}{\pi}\right)^{\frac{1}{2}}\int_0^\infty y^2\,dy\left[(y^4 + 2y^2)^{\frac{1}{2}} - y^2 - 1 + \frac{1}{2y^2}\right]\right\}$$

$$= \frac{2\pi a\hbar^2 n}{m}\left[1 + \frac{128}{15}\left(\frac{na^3}{\pi}\right)^{\frac{1}{2}}\right] \tag{35.25}$$

which is precisely Eq. (22.19). Note that these two calculations are quite different, because we evaluated $E - \tfrac{1}{2}\mu N$ in Sec. 22, whereas here we evaluate E directly.

It is interesting to study the magnitude of typical terms omitted from Eq. (35.25). Consider first the interaction of the particles out of the condensate. As an estimate of this contribution, we multiply the strength of the interaction by the number of pairs:

$$\frac{g}{2V}\frac{1}{2}(N - N_0)^2 = \tfrac{1}{4}ngN\left[\frac{8}{3}\left(\frac{na^3}{\pi}\right)^{\frac{1}{2}}\right]^2 = N\frac{2\pi\hbar^2 an}{m}\frac{1}{2}\left[\frac{8}{3}\left(\frac{na^3}{\pi}\right)^{\frac{1}{2}}\right]^2$$

which shows that these terms represent a higher-order correction to E/N.

[1] This observation was made by K. A. Brueckner and K. Sawada, *Phys. Rev.*, **106**:1117 (1957).

Another approximation occurred in Eq. (35.11) with the substitution

$$\frac{gN_0^2}{2V} \to \frac{gN^2}{2V} - \frac{gN(N - N_0)}{V}$$

This expression omits terms of order

$$\frac{g}{2V}(N - N_0)^2 = N\frac{2\pi\hbar^2 \, an}{m}\left[\frac{8}{3}\left(\frac{na^3}{\pi}\right)^{\frac{1}{2}}\right]^2$$

which are again negligible in this approximation.   Finally, we comment on the use of Eq. (35.3) to eliminate g in favor of a.   The leading term in the energy is of the form

$$\frac{E}{N} = \frac{gN}{2V} + \cdots \tag{35.26}$$

which may be rewritten with Eq. (35.4) as

$$\frac{E}{N} = \frac{2\pi\hbar^2 \, na}{m} + \cdots \tag{35.27}$$

This term can be compared with the first-order correction for a dilute Fermi gas [Eq. (11.26)]

$$\frac{E}{N} - \tfrac{3}{5}\epsilon_F^0 = \frac{2}{3\pi}k_F \, a \frac{\hbar^2 k_F^2}{2m} = \frac{\pi\hbar^2 \, an}{m}(2 - 1) \tag{35.28}$$

where the numerical factor $(2 - 1)$ arises from the direct and exchange terms, respectively.   Apart from the different degeneracy factors, Eqs. (35.27) and (35.28) are identical, and they both can be interpreted in terms of an optical potential [see the discussion of Eq. (11.26)].   The corrections to Eq. (35.26) require the second-order terms in Eq. (35.3), as well as the additional terms in Eq. (35.21).   Once we have eliminated the divergences, however, it is then permissible to set $g = 4\pi a\hbar^2/m$ in the remaining correction terms.   Since the answer is well defined, the error introduced by this last approximation is of higher order and thus negligible in the present treatment.

The above results for the ground-state energy and depletion of the condensate reproduce those obtained in Sec. 22 with the methods of quantum field theory.   Although the canonical transformation provides a more physical picture of the ground state and excited states, it is less well suited for calculations to higher order.   In principle, of course, it is possible to retain all higher-order terms in the interaction hamiltonian (35.8); the two approaches must then lead to identical results since they are based on the same physical approximations.   Nevertheless, practical calculations have generally relied on the more systematic methods using Green's functions introduced in Chap. 6.[1]

[1] See, for example, S. T. Beliaev, *Sov. Phys.-JETP*, **7**:299 (1958).

36□COOPER PAIRS

Although the most remarkable properties of superconductors are those associated with electromagnetic fields (see Chap. 13), superconductors also exhibit striking thermodynamic effects, which played a central role in the development of the microscopic theory.   The electronic specific heat C_{el} varies exponentially at low temperatures

$$C_{el} \propto \exp\left(-\frac{\Delta}{k_B T}\right) \qquad T \to 0 \tag{36.1}$$

which is typical of an assembly with an energy gap Δ separating the ground state from the excited states.   A second important experimental observation is the isotope effect, where the transition temperature T_c of different isotopes of the same element varies with the ionic mass M as

$$T_c \propto M^{-\frac{1}{2}} \tag{36.2}$$

This result indicates that the dynamics of the ionic cores affects the superconducting state, even though the ions are not especially important in the normal state (Sec. 3).

In the present section, we study a simple model due to Cooper,[1] showing that an attractive interaction between two fermions in the Fermi sea leads to the appearance of a bound pair.   The noninteracting ground state (filled Fermi sea) thus becomes unstable with respect to pair formation, and the finite binding energy of the pair provides a qualitative explanation for the gap in the excitation spectrum.   Before Cooper's model can be considered relevant to superconductivity, however, it is necessary to show that the effective interaction between electrons is attractive, and it is here that the isotope effect gives an important clue. Although the shielded coulomb potential of Secs. 12 and 14 is repulsive, there is also a virtual electron-electron interaction arising from the exchange of phonons associated with the crystal lattice.   As first noted by Fröhlich,[2] this interaction is attractive for electrons near the Fermi surface, and it therefore gives a physical basis for the attractive interparticle potential in Cooper's model.   The electron-phonon interaction is studied in detail in Chap. 12, and we shall not attempt any further justification of Cooper's model at this point.

Consider the Schrödinger equation for two fermions *in the Fermi sea* interacting through a potential $\lambda V(\mathbf{x}_1,\mathbf{x}_2)$.   The many-particle medium affects these two particles through the exclusion principle, which restricts the allowed intermediate states, exactly as in Sec. 11.   The Schrödinger equation

$$[T_1 + T_2 + \lambda V(1,2)]\,\psi(1,2) = E\psi(1,2) \tag{36.3}$$

[1] L. N. Cooper, *Phys. Rev.*, **104**:1189 (1956).
[2] H. Fröhlich, *Phys. Rev.*, **79**:845 (1950).

can be rewritten in a slightly different form as follows:

$$\psi(1,2) = \varphi_0(1,2) + \sum_{n \neq 0} \varphi_n(1,2) \frac{1}{E - E_n} \langle \varphi_n | \lambda V | \psi(1,2) \rangle \qquad (36.4)$$

$$E - E_0 = \langle \varphi_0 | \lambda V | \psi(1,2) \rangle \qquad (36.5)$$

where the eigenstates φ_n are eigenfunctions of H_0

$$H_0 \varphi_n = (T_1 + T_2) \varphi_n = E_n \varphi_n \qquad (36.6)$$

The equivalence of these two forms can be verified by applying the operator $H_0 - E = T_1 + T_2 - E$ to Eq. (36.4) and using the completeness of the eigenstates of H_0. The remaining equation (36.5) is simply a normalization condition for ψ:

$$\langle \varphi_0 | \psi \rangle = 1 \qquad (36.7)$$

and we must naturally compute all other expectation values according to the relation $\langle O \rangle = \langle \psi | O | \psi \rangle / \langle \psi | \psi \rangle$.

If the system is confined to a large box with volume V, the unperturbed wave functions are plane waves with periodic boundary conditions

$$\varphi_{k_1 k_2}(1,2) = V^{-\frac{1}{2}} e^{ik_1 \cdot x_1} V^{-\frac{1}{2}} e^{ik_2 \cdot x_2} \qquad (36.8)$$

To simplify the discussion we shall neglect the effect of spins and treat the two initial particles as distinguishable. This is permissible if the two particles have opposite spins, while V must be spin independent. The many-body aspects of the problem are now incorporated by restricting the sum over intermediate states in Eq. (36.4) in the following way

$$\sum_n \rightarrow \sum_{k_1 k_2 > k_F} \qquad (36.9)$$

because all *other* states in the Fermi sea are already filled.

In a homogeneous medium, the total momentum of the pair will be conserved, and we therefore introduce the following definitions

$$\mathbf{P} = \mathbf{k}_1 + \mathbf{k}_2 \qquad \mathbf{k} = \tfrac{1}{2}(\mathbf{k}_1 - \mathbf{k}_2) \qquad (36.10)$$

$$\mathbf{R} = \tfrac{1}{2}(\mathbf{x}_1 + \mathbf{x}_2) \qquad \mathbf{x} = \mathbf{x}_1 - \mathbf{x}_2 \qquad (36.11)$$

$$v = mV\hbar^{-2} \qquad (36.12)$$

$$E = \hbar^2 \kappa^2 m^{-1} + \tfrac{1}{4}\hbar^2 P^2 m^{-1} \qquad (36.13)$$

The solution to the Schrödinger equation takes the form

$$\psi(1,2) = V^{-\frac{1}{2}} e^{i\mathbf{P} \cdot \mathbf{R}} V^{-\frac{1}{2}} \psi_{\mathbf{P},k}(\mathbf{x}) \qquad (36.14)$$

where the first factor contains the center-of-mass motion, while the second is the internal wave function of the interacting pair. In contrast to the Schrödinger equation in free space [Eq. (11.8)], the total momentum $\hbar\mathbf{P}$ affects the internal

wave function because the filled Fermi sea provides a preferred frame of reference. We note that P cannot exceed $2k_F$ if the particles are initially inside the Fermi sea. Substitution of Eq. (36.14) into Eqs. (36.4) and (36.5) yields

$$\psi_{\mathbf{P},\mathbf{k}}(\mathbf{x}) = e^{i\mathbf{k}\cdot\mathbf{x}} + \lambda \int_\Gamma \frac{d^3 t}{(2\pi)^3} e^{i t\cdot\mathbf{x}} \frac{1}{\kappa^2 - t^2} \langle t|v|\psi_{\mathbf{P},\mathbf{k}}\rangle \qquad (36.15)$$

$$|\tfrac{1}{2}\mathbf{P} \pm \mathbf{k}| < k_F \qquad \Gamma \equiv |\tfrac{1}{2}\mathbf{P} \pm t| > k_F$$

$$\kappa^2 - k^2 = \lambda V^{-1}\langle \mathbf{k}|v|\psi_{\mathbf{P},\mathbf{k}}\rangle \qquad (36.16)$$

which is known as the Bethe-Goldstone equation.[1]   It is simply the Schrödinger equation for two fermions in a Fermi gas, where the Pauli principle forbids the appearance of intermediate states that are already occupied by other fermions. Since the interacting pair initially lies inside the Fermi sea, it cannot make real transitions.   Nevertheless, it can make virtual transitions to all states outside the Fermi sea, as seen in the last term of Eq. (36.15), where the energy denominator never vanishes.   In consequence, the solution of this equation has momentum components corresponding to all the unfilled states as well as the original components $\tfrac{1}{2}\mathbf{P} + \mathbf{k}$ and $\tfrac{1}{2}\mathbf{P} - \mathbf{k}$.

In general, the Bethe-Goldstone equation can be solved only with numerical techniques.   Although straightforward in principle, this approach is not always sufficiently accurate to uncover the rather subtle features associated with the Fermi sea, and we shall therefore introduce a model two-particle potential that allows us to obtain an exact solution.   The concept of a potential is first generalized to include *nonlocal* potentials

$$v(\mathbf{x}) \to v(\mathbf{x},\mathbf{x}') \qquad (36.17a)$$

$$\int d^3x\, e^{-i\mathbf{k}\cdot\mathbf{x}} v(\mathbf{x})\,\psi(\mathbf{x}) \to \int d^3x\, d^3x'\, e^{-i\mathbf{k}\cdot\mathbf{x}} v(\mathbf{x},\mathbf{x}')\,\psi(\mathbf{x}') \qquad (36.17b)$$

A local potential is then obtained as the limit

$$v(\mathbf{x},\mathbf{x}') \to v(|\mathbf{x}|)\,\delta(\mathbf{x} - \mathbf{x}')$$

We now choose to consider a *nonlocal separable* potential, which takes the form

$$v(\mathbf{x},\mathbf{x}') = u(|\mathbf{x}|)\,u(|\mathbf{x}'|)^* \qquad (36.18)$$

with the Fourier transform

$$\int d^3x\, e^{-i\mathbf{k}\cdot\mathbf{x}} u(x) = u(k) \qquad (36.19)$$

It is evident that the only *local* separable potential is a delta function

$$v(\mathbf{x}) = v\,\delta(\mathbf{x})$$

but we may expect our nonlocal approximation Eq. (36.18) to provide a reasonable description of a short-range potential.

[1] H. A. Bethe and J. Goldstone, *Proc. Roy. Soc.* (*London*), **A238:**551 (1957).

With the separable potential, Eq. (36.16) becomes

$$\kappa^2 - k^2 = \lambda V^{-1} u(k) \int d^3x \, u(x)^* \psi_{\mathbf{P},\mathbf{k}}(\mathbf{x}) \tag{36.20}$$

Substitution of Eq. (36.15) in the right side then yields

$$\kappa^2 - k^2 = \frac{\lambda |u(k)|^2}{V} + \lambda \int_\Gamma \frac{d^3t}{(2\pi)^3} u(t)^* \frac{1}{\kappa^2 - t^2} u(t)(\kappa^2 - k^2) \tag{36.21}$$

which may be rearranged as follows

$$\frac{1}{\lambda} = \frac{1}{V} \frac{|u(k)|^2}{\kappa^2 - k^2} + \int_\Gamma \frac{d^3t}{(2\pi)^3} \frac{|u(t)|^2}{\kappa^2 - t^2} \equiv f(\kappa^2) \tag{36.22}$$

This equation determines the eigenvalue κ^2, and hence the energy shift per pair through the relation

$$\Delta E = \hbar^2 m^{-1}(\kappa^2 - k^2) \tag{36.23}$$

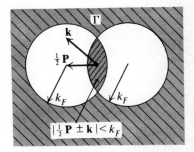

Fig. 36.1 Integration region in momentum space for Bethe-Goldstone equation.

Equation (36.22) is most easily studied graphically, and we denote the right side $f(\kappa^2)$, although it also depends parametrically on $\mathbf{P}$ and $\mathbf{k}$. The integral in $f(\kappa^2)$ decreases monotonically as κ^2 increases, becoming logarithmically singular when the denominator can first vanish. The integration region Γ is illustrated in Fig. 36.1, which shows that this divergence occurs at $\kappa^2 = k_F^2 - \frac{1}{4}P^2$. In addition, the first term of $f(\kappa^2)$ is singular at $\kappa^2 = k^2$, and it is now easy to sketch $f(\kappa^2)$ as shown in Fig. 36.2. The smooth background curve represents the integral term, which is independent of k^2. Furthermore, the first term of $f(\kappa^2)$ contributes only in the immediate vicinity of k^2, because its coefficient is proportional to V^{-1} and thus becomes small for a macroscopic system. As a result, $f(\kappa^2)$ consists of a singularity with narrow width at the variable point $\kappa^2 = k^2$, superposed on the background curve that is logarithmically singular at $\kappa^2 = k_F^2 - \frac{1}{4}P^2$.

The eigenvalue is determined by the intersection of $f(\kappa^2)$ with the horizontal line λ^{-1}. It is evident that there is only one solution for $\lambda > 0$, occurring at

$$\kappa^2 - k^2 \approx \lambda V^{-1} |u(k)|^2 + O(\lambda^2) \tag{36.24}$$

Here the integral term has been neglected, because it is finite at $\kappa^2 \approx k^2$ and contributes only to higher order in λ. We conclude that the only effect of a repulsive potential is to shift the energy of the pair by a small amount proportional to $|u(k)|^2 V^{-1}$, as expected for an interacting medium. In contrast, Fig. 36.2 shows that an attractive potential $\lambda < 0$ always leads to *two solutions* for each k^2, as long as $|\lambda|$ does not become too large. Thus an attractive interaction alters the energy spectrum in a qualitative manner. Although the ordinary solution of Eq. (36.24) still occurs, we also find a new (anomalous) solution arising directly from the logarithmic singularity of $f(\kappa^2)$. Which of the two eigenvalues lies lower depends on the relative value of k^2 and $|\lambda|$. If $|\lambda|$ is fixed, then there is a

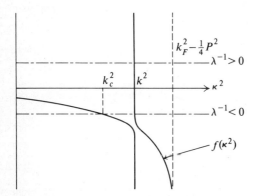

Fig. 36.2 Eigenvalue condition Eq. (36.22) for Bethe-Goldstone equation.

corresponding critical value k_c^2 such that the anomalous solution is the lower eigenvalue for all $k > k_c$, while the ordinary solution is lower for $k < k_c$. An approximate value for k_c is obtained from the solution of the equation

$$(2\pi)^{-3} \int_\Gamma d^3t \, |u(t)|^2 (k_c^2 - t^2)^{-1} = \lambda^{-1} \tag{36.25}$$

which is the intersection of the line λ^{-1} with the part of $f(\kappa^2)$ arising from the integral in Eq. (36.22). It is clear from Fig. 36.2 that the anomalous eigenvalue is essentially independent of k^2, and thus *the ground-state energy of the pair is independent of its initial relative wave vector* **k** *as long as* $k > k_c$. This behavior is very different from that of the ordinary solution (36.24), where $\kappa^2 \approx k^2$ apart from corrections of order V^{-1}.

We shall now study the anomalous eigenvalue in detail. The first term of Eq. (36.22) is negligible unless k is exactly equal to k_c, so that the eigenvalue κ is essentially equal to k_c and obeys just the same equation (36.25):

$$|\lambda|^{-1} = (2\pi)^{-3} \int_\Gamma d^3t \, |u(t)|^2 (t^2 - \kappa^2)^{-1} \tag{36.26}$$

Although this equation can be studied for all $P < 2k_F$, it is simplest to set $P = 0$, when the eigenvalue condition becomes

$$
\frac{1}{|\lambda|} = \int_{k_F}^{\infty} \frac{t^2 \, dt}{2\pi^2} \frac{|u(t)|^2}{t^2 - \kappa^2}
$$

$$
= \frac{k_F}{2\pi^2} \int_1^{\infty} x^2 \, dx \frac{|u(k_F x)|^2}{x^2 - (\kappa/k_F)^2} \tag{36.27}
$$

The logarithmic singularity of this integral can be extracted through an integration by parts

$$
\frac{1}{|\lambda|} \approx \frac{k_F}{4\pi^2} |u(k_F)|^2 \ln \frac{k_F^2}{k_F^2 - \kappa^2} \tag{36.28}
$$

In arriving at Eq. (36.28) the potential has been assumed to be a smooth function of the momentum and the remaining finite integral has been neglected. Since κ^2 is less than k_F^2, we write

$$
\kappa^2 = k_F^2 - m\Delta\hbar^{-2} \tag{36.29}
$$

and a simple rearrangement yields

$$
\Delta = \frac{\hbar^2 k_F^2}{m} \exp\left[-\frac{4\pi^2}{k_F|\lambda| |u(k_F)|^2} \right] \tag{36.30}
$$

As noted above, Eq. (36.29) determines the ground-state energy of the pair whenever $k > k_c$. The corresponding expression for Δ has several very remarkable features:

1. The energy shift of the pair $\Delta E = \hbar^2 m^{-1}(\kappa^2 - k^2) = 2(\epsilon_{k_F}^0 - \epsilon_k^0) - \Delta$ is negative near the Fermi surface and is independent of the volume.
2. Δ has an essential singularity in the coupling constant and cannot be obtained with perturbation theory.
3. $\Delta(P)$ is greatest for those pairs with $P = 0$, because the phase space where the denominator of (36.26) vanishes is then maximized. If $P = 0$, we see that t attains its minimum value everywhere on the surface of the Fermi sphere (Fig. 36.1); for finite $|\mathbf{P}|$, however, this value occurs only on a circle of radius $(k_F^2 - \frac{1}{4}P^2)^{\frac{1}{2}}$.
4. The occurrence of a bound pair for an arbitrarily weak finite-range attractive potential depends crucially on the presence of the medium; two particles in free space will not form a bound state unless the strength of the potential exceeds some critical value. This result also can be seen in Eq. (36.30), because Δ vanishes exponentially as $k_F \to 0$.

The foregoing calculation implies that two particles *with opposite momenta and spins* near the Fermi surface will form a bound pair, as long as the inter-

particle potential is attractive.[1]   In this way, the system lowers its energy by an amount Δ, and the original unperturbed ground state clearly becomes unstable.   Unfortunately, Cooper's model is restricted to two particles; it is therefore incapable of describing the new ground state, which evidently involves many bound pairs.

Nevertheless, the calculation has provided a qualitative description of the instability, and it also indicates that the new ground state cannot be obtained with a perturbation expansion.   In Sec. 37 we show how the Bogoliubov canonical transformation allows us to study the many-body ground state of such a system.

37□INTERACTING FERMI GAS

We now discuss how the formation of Cooper pairs can be incorporated into a consistent many-body theory.   The basic idea is that pairing between particles in the states $(\mathbf{k}\uparrow)$ and $(-\mathbf{k}\downarrow)$ can make the Fermi sea unstable if the interparticle potential is attractive.   In consequence, these states play a special role, and we therefore make the following canonical transformation[2]

$$\alpha_{\mathbf{k}} = u_k a_{\mathbf{k}\uparrow} - v_k a^{\dagger}_{-\mathbf{k}\downarrow} \qquad \beta_{-\mathbf{k}} = u_k a_{-\mathbf{k}\downarrow} + v_k a^{\dagger}_{\mathbf{k}\uparrow} \qquad (37.1)$$

The c-number coefficients u_k and v_k are real and depend only on $|\mathbf{k}|$.   This linear transformation is canonical if and only if the new operators obey the relations

$$\{\alpha_{\mathbf{k}},\alpha^{\dagger}_{\mathbf{k}'}\} = \{\beta_{\mathbf{k}},\beta^{\dagger}_{\mathbf{k}'}\} = \delta_{\mathbf{k}\mathbf{k}'}$$

$$(37.2)$$

All other anticommutators $= 0$

Given the original anticommutation relations

$$\{a_{\mathbf{k}\lambda},a^{\dagger}_{\mathbf{k}'\lambda'}\} = \delta_{\mathbf{k}\mathbf{k}'}\,\delta_{\lambda\lambda'} \qquad (37.3)$$

it is readily seen that Eq. (37.2) implies

$$u_k^2 + v_k^2 = 1 \qquad (37.4)$$

These equations can be inverted to give

$$a_{\mathbf{k}\uparrow} = u_k \alpha_{\mathbf{k}} + v_k \beta^{\dagger}_{-\mathbf{k}} \qquad (37.5a)$$

$$a_{-\mathbf{k}\downarrow} = u_k \beta_{-\mathbf{k}} - v_k \alpha^{\dagger}_{\mathbf{k}} \qquad (37.5b)$$

---

[1] In principle, a bound pair can also be formed by two particles with parallel spins in an antisymmetric spatial state.   To the extent that the attractive interaction is of short range, we expect the effects to be largest in (symmetric) relative s states.

[2] N. N. Bogoliubov, *Sov. Phys.-JETP*, **7**:41 (1958); J. G. Valatin, *Nuovo Cimento*, **7**:843 (1958); S. T. Beliaev, Introduction to the Bogoliubov Canonical Transformation Method, in C. DeWitt (ed.), "The Many Body Problem," p. 343, John Wiley and Sons, Inc., New York, 1959; S. T. Beliaev, *Kgl. Danske Videnskab. Selskab, Mat.-Fys. Medd*, **31**, no. 11 (1959).

As in Chap. 6, we shall consider the thermodynamic potential at zero temperature $\Omega(T = 0, V, \mu)$, which is the expectation value of [compare Eq. (18.29)]

$$\hat{K} = \hat{H} - \mu \hat{N}$$

$$= \sum_{k\lambda} a_{k\lambda}^{\dagger} a_{k\lambda}(\epsilon_k^0 - \mu) - \tfrac{1}{2} \sum_{\substack{k_1 + k_2 = k_3 + k_4 \\ \lambda_1 \lambda_2 \lambda_3 \lambda_4}} \langle k_1 \lambda_1 k_2 \lambda_2 | V | k_3 \lambda_3 k_4 \lambda_4 \rangle$$

$$\times a_{k_1 \lambda_1}^{\dagger} a_{k_2 \lambda_2}^{\dagger} a_{k_4 \lambda_4} a_{k_3 \lambda_3} \quad (37.6)$$

The use of the thermodynamic potential allows us to treat assemblies with an indefinite number of particles. In the end, of course, the chemical potential will be chosen to ensure that $\langle \hat{N} \rangle = N$. We also assume an attractive interaction potential $V > 0$.

The thermodynamic potential will now be rewritten in terms of the operators α_k and β_k, arranged in normal order with all the destruction operators to the right of all the creation operators. Although this procedure can be carried out directly, it is much simpler to use Wick's theorem. Consider the operator $a_{k\uparrow}^{\dagger} a_{k'\uparrow}$, which can be expressed as follows

$$a_{k\uparrow}^{\dagger} a_{k'\uparrow} = N(a_{k\uparrow}^{\dagger} a_{k'\uparrow}) + a_{k\uparrow}^{\dagger} a_{k'\uparrow} \quad (37.7)$$

Here N stands for normal order with respect to the operators α and β.[1] If $|O\rangle$ is the new vacuum characterized by the conditions

$$\alpha_k | O \rangle = \beta_k | O \rangle = 0 \quad (37.8)$$

the vacuum expectation value of Eq. (37.7) yields

$$a_{k\uparrow}^{\dagger} a_{k'\uparrow} = \langle O | (u_k \alpha_k^{\dagger} + v_k \beta_{-k})(u_{k'} \alpha_{k'} + v_{k'} \beta_{-k'}^{\dagger}) | O \rangle$$

$$= \delta_{k,k'} v_k^2 \quad (37.9)$$

and similarly

$$a_{-k\downarrow}^{\dagger} a_{-k'\downarrow} = \delta_{k,k'} v_k^2 \quad (37.10)$$

Thus the first term of Eq. (37.6) becomes

$$\sum_k (\epsilon_k^0 - \mu)(a_{k\uparrow}^{\dagger} a_{k\uparrow} + a_{-k\downarrow}^{\dagger} a_{-k\downarrow})$$

$$= \sum_k (\epsilon_k^0 - \mu)[2v_k^2 + N(a_{k\uparrow}^{\dagger} a_{k\uparrow}) + N(a_{-k\downarrow}^{\dagger} a_{-k\downarrow})]$$

$$= \sum_k (\epsilon_k^0 - \mu)[2v_k^2 + (u_k^2 - v_k^2)(\alpha_k^{\dagger} \alpha_k + \beta_{-k}^{\dagger} \beta_{-k}) + 2u_k v_k(\beta_{-k} \alpha_k + \alpha_k^{\dagger} \beta_{-k}^{\dagger})]$$

$$(37.11)$$

---

[1] To make the formal connection with Wick's theorem complete, we may consider these operators to be time dependent with the time of the operator on the left infinitesimally later than that on the right; however, a little reflection on the reader's part will convince him that this artifice is unnecessary.

where the normal products have been evaluated explicitly with Eq. (37.5).

The potential energy in Eq. (37.6) is more difficult. For simplicity, we assume that the potential is spin independent:

$$\langle \mathbf{k}_1 \lambda_1 \mathbf{k}_2 \lambda_2 | V | \mathbf{k}_3 \lambda_3 \mathbf{k}_4 \lambda_4 \rangle = \delta_{\lambda_1 \lambda_3} \delta_{\lambda_2 \lambda_4} \langle \mathbf{k}_1 \mathbf{k}_2 | V | \mathbf{k}_3 \mathbf{k}_4 \rangle \qquad (37.12)$$

In addition, the explicit expression

$$\langle \mathbf{k}_1 \mathbf{k}_2 | V | \mathbf{k}_3 \mathbf{k}_4 \rangle = V^{-2} \iint d^3x \, d^3y \, e^{-i(\mathbf{k}_1 \cdot \mathbf{x} + \mathbf{k}_2 \cdot \mathbf{y})} V(\mathbf{x}, \mathbf{y}) \, e^{i(\mathbf{k}_3 \cdot \mathbf{x} + \mathbf{k}_4 \cdot \mathbf{y})}$$

shows that the matrix element has the following symmetry properties:

$$\langle \mathbf{k}_1 \mathbf{k}_2 | V | \mathbf{k}_3 \mathbf{k}_4 \rangle = \langle \mathbf{k}_2 \mathbf{k}_1 | V | \mathbf{k}_4 \mathbf{k}_3 \rangle = \langle -\mathbf{k}_3 -\mathbf{k}_4 | V | -\mathbf{k}_1 -\mathbf{k}_2 \rangle$$
$$= \langle -\mathbf{k}_1 -\mathbf{k}_2 | V | -\mathbf{k}_3 -\mathbf{k}_4 \rangle \qquad (37.13)$$

where the relation $V(\mathbf{x}, \mathbf{y}) = V(-\mathbf{x}, -\mathbf{y})$ has been assumed in arriving at the last equality. The potential-energy operator can now be rewritten with Eq. (37.13) as

$$\hat{V} = \hat{V}_a + \hat{V}_b \qquad (37.14)$$

where

$$\hat{V}_a = -\tfrac{1}{2} \sum_{\mathbf{kk'q}} \langle \mathbf{kk'} | V | \mathbf{k} + \mathbf{q}, \mathbf{k}' - \mathbf{q} \rangle \, [a^\dagger_{\mathbf{k}\uparrow} a^\dagger_{\mathbf{k}'\uparrow} a_{\mathbf{k}'-\mathbf{q}\uparrow} a_{\mathbf{k}+\mathbf{q}\uparrow}$$

$$+ \, a^\dagger_{-\mathbf{k}\downarrow} a^\dagger_{-\mathbf{k}'\downarrow} a_{-\mathbf{k}'+\mathbf{q}\downarrow} a_{-\mathbf{k}-\mathbf{q}\downarrow}] \qquad (37.15a)$$

$$\hat{V}_b = -\sum_{\mathbf{kk'q}} \langle \mathbf{k} - \mathbf{k}' | V | \mathbf{k} + \mathbf{q}, -\mathbf{k}' - \mathbf{q} \rangle \, [a^\dagger_{\mathbf{k}\uparrow} a^\dagger_{-\mathbf{k}'\downarrow} a_{-\mathbf{k}'-\mathbf{q}\downarrow} a_{\mathbf{k}+\mathbf{q}\uparrow}] \qquad (37.15b)$$

The two terms of $\hat{V}_a$ differ only in the subscripts on the operators, and comparison of Eqs. (37.5a) and (37.5b) shows that the second term can be obtained from the first with the substitution ($\alpha_{\mathbf{k}} \leftrightarrow \beta_{-\mathbf{k}}$ and $v \leftrightarrow -v$). We therefore concentrate on the first term; the corresponding operator product can be rewritten with Wick's theorem

$$a^\dagger_{\mathbf{k}\uparrow} a^\dagger_{\mathbf{k}'\uparrow} a_{\mathbf{k}'-\mathbf{q}\uparrow} a_{\mathbf{k}+\mathbf{q}\uparrow} = N(a^\dagger_{\mathbf{k}\uparrow} a^\dagger_{\mathbf{k}'\uparrow} a_{\mathbf{k}'-\mathbf{q}\uparrow} a_{\mathbf{k}+\mathbf{q}\uparrow}) + \delta_{\mathbf{q},0} v^2_k N(a^\dagger_{\mathbf{k}'\uparrow} a_{\mathbf{k}'\uparrow})$$
$$+ \, \delta_{\mathbf{q},0} v^2_{k'} N(a^\dagger_{\mathbf{k}\uparrow} a_{\mathbf{k}\uparrow}) - \delta_{\mathbf{k}',\mathbf{k}+\mathbf{q}} v^2_{k'} N(a^\dagger_{\mathbf{k}\uparrow} a_{\mathbf{k}\uparrow})$$
$$- \, \delta_{\mathbf{k}',\mathbf{k}+\mathbf{q}} v^2_k N(a^\dagger_{\mathbf{k}'\uparrow} a_{\mathbf{k}'\uparrow}) + \delta_{\mathbf{q},0} v^2_k v^2_{k'} - \delta_{\mathbf{k}',\mathbf{k}+\mathbf{q}} v^2_k v^2_{k'}$$
$$(37.16)$$

where the only nonzero contractions have been evaluated with Eqs. (37.9) and (37.10). In this way, Eq. (37.15a) reduces to the following expression

$$\hat{V}_a = N(\hat{V}_a) - \tfrac{1}{2} \sum_{\mathbf{kk'}} (\langle \mathbf{kk'} | V | \mathbf{kk'} \rangle - \langle \mathbf{kk'} | V | \mathbf{k}' \mathbf{k} \rangle)$$

$$\times \, \{[v^2_k v^2_{k'} + 2v^2_{k'} N(a^\dagger_{\mathbf{k}\uparrow} a_{\mathbf{k}\uparrow})] + [\alpha_{\mathbf{k}} \leftrightarrow \beta_{-\mathbf{k}}, v \leftrightarrow -v]\}$$

which has been simplified slightly with Eq. (37.13). The normal-ordered products in the second term have already been evaluated in Eq. (37.11), and we therefore find

$$\hat{V}_a = N(\hat{V}_a) - \sum_{\mathbf{kk'}} (\langle \mathbf{kk'}|V|\mathbf{kk'}\rangle - \langle \mathbf{kk'}|V|\mathbf{k'k}\rangle) [v_k^2 v_{k'}^2 + v_{k'}^2(u_k^2 - v_k^2)$$

$$\times (\alpha_k^\dagger \alpha_k + \beta_{-k}^\dagger \beta_{-k}) + v_{k'}^2(2u_k v_k)(\alpha_k^\dagger \beta_{-k}^\dagger + \beta_{-k}\alpha_k)] \quad (37.17)$$

The remaining contribution $\hat{V}_b$ can be treated in a similar way. We need the following contractions

$$a_{\mathbf{k}\uparrow}^\dagger a_{-\mathbf{k'}\downarrow}^\dagger = a_{-\mathbf{k}\downarrow} a_{\mathbf{k'}\uparrow} = u_k v_k \delta_{\mathbf{k},\mathbf{k'}}$$

$$a_{\mathbf{k}\uparrow}^\dagger a_{-\mathbf{k'}\downarrow} = a_{-\mathbf{k}\downarrow}^\dagger a_{\mathbf{k'}\uparrow} = 0 \quad (37.18)$$

and the operator in $\hat{V}_b$ becomes

$$a_{\mathbf{k}\uparrow}^\dagger a_{-\mathbf{k'}\downarrow}^\dagger a_{-\mathbf{k'}-\mathbf{q}\downarrow} a_{\mathbf{k}+\mathbf{q}\uparrow} = N(a_{\mathbf{k}\uparrow}^\dagger a_{-\mathbf{k'}\downarrow}^\dagger a_{-\mathbf{k'}-\mathbf{q}\downarrow} a_{\mathbf{k}+\mathbf{q}\uparrow}) + \delta_{\mathbf{q},0} v_k^2 N(a_{-\mathbf{k'}\downarrow}^\dagger a_{-\mathbf{k'}\downarrow})$$

$$+ \delta_{\mathbf{q},0} v_{k'}^2 N(a_{\mathbf{k}\uparrow}^\dagger a_{\mathbf{k}\uparrow}) + \delta_{\mathbf{k},\mathbf{k'}} u_k v_k N(a_{-\mathbf{k}-\mathbf{q}\downarrow} a_{\mathbf{k}+\mathbf{q}\uparrow})$$

$$+ \delta_{\mathbf{k},\mathbf{k'}} u_{k+q} v_{k+q} N(a_{\mathbf{k}\uparrow}^\dagger a_{-\mathbf{k}\downarrow}^\dagger) + \delta_{\mathbf{q},0} v_k^2 v_{k'}^2$$

$$+ \delta_{\mathbf{k},\mathbf{k'}} u_k v_k u_{k+q} v_{k+q}$$

This last equation may be combined with Eq. (37.15b) to give

$$\hat{V}_b = N(\hat{V}_b) - \sum_{\mathbf{kk'}} \langle \mathbf{k}-\mathbf{k'}|V|\mathbf{k}-\mathbf{k'}\rangle v_{k'}^2[v_k^2 + N(a_{\mathbf{k}\uparrow}^\dagger a_{\mathbf{k}\uparrow}) + N(a_{-\mathbf{k}\downarrow}^\dagger a_{-\mathbf{k}\downarrow})]$$

$$- \sum_{\mathbf{kk'}} \langle \mathbf{k}-\mathbf{k}|V|\mathbf{k'}-\mathbf{k'}\rangle u_{k'} v_{k'}[u_k v_k + N(a_{\mathbf{k}\uparrow}^\dagger a_{-\mathbf{k}\downarrow}^\dagger) + N(a_{-\mathbf{k}\downarrow} a_{\mathbf{k}\uparrow})]$$

where we have made some simple changes of variables and used Eq. (37.13). The various normal-ordered products are readily evaluated, and we find

$$\hat{V}_b = N(\hat{V}_b) - \sum_{\mathbf{kk'}} (u_k v_k u_{k'} v_{k'}\langle \mathbf{k}-\mathbf{k}|V|\mathbf{k'}-\mathbf{k'}\rangle + v_k^2 v_{k'}^2\langle \mathbf{k}-\mathbf{k'}|V|\mathbf{k}-\mathbf{k'}\rangle)$$

$$- \sum_{\mathbf{kk'}} \{(\alpha_k^\dagger \alpha_k + \beta_{-k}^\dagger \beta_{-k}) [(u_k^2 - v_k^2) v_{k'}^2\langle \mathbf{k}-\mathbf{k'}|V|\mathbf{k}-\mathbf{k'}\rangle$$

$$- 2u_k v_k u_{k'} v_{k'}\langle \mathbf{k}-\mathbf{k}|V|\mathbf{k'}-\mathbf{k'}\rangle]\} - \sum_{\mathbf{kk'}} \{(\alpha_k^\dagger \beta_{-k}^\dagger + \beta_{-k}\alpha_k)$$

$$\times [(u_k^2 - v_k^2) u_{k'} v_{k'}\langle \mathbf{k}-\mathbf{k}|V|\mathbf{k'}-\mathbf{k'}\rangle + 2u_k v_k v_{k'}^2\langle \mathbf{k}-\mathbf{k'}|V|\mathbf{k}-\mathbf{k'}\rangle]\}$$

$$(37.19)$$

It is now possible to combine Eqs. (37.11), (37.17), and (37.19) to obtain the thermodynamic potential

$$\hat{K} = U + \hat{H}_1 + \hat{H}_2 + N(\hat{V}) \quad (37.20)$$

where

$$U = 2\sum_{\mathbf{k}} (\epsilon_k^0 - \mu) v_k^2 - \sum_{\mathbf{kk'}} \langle \mathbf{kk'}|\bar{V}|\mathbf{kk'}\rangle v_k^2 v_{k'}^2$$

$$- \sum_{\mathbf{kk'}} \langle \mathbf{k}-\mathbf{k}|V|\mathbf{k'}-\mathbf{k'}\rangle u_k v_k u_{k'} v_{k'} \quad (37.21a)$$

$$\hat{H}_1 = \sum_k (\alpha_k^\dagger \alpha_k + \beta_{-k}^\dagger \beta_{-k})\{[\epsilon_k^0 - \mu - \sum_{k'}(\langle \mathbf{kk'}|\bar{V}|\mathbf{kk'}\rangle v_{k'}^2)](u_k^2 - v_k^2)$$

$$+ 2u_k v_k \sum_{k'}(\langle \mathbf{k}-\mathbf{k}|V|\mathbf{k'}-\mathbf{k'}\rangle u_{k'} v_{k'})\} \quad (37.21b)$$

$$\hat{H}_2 = \sum_k (\alpha_k^\dagger \beta_{-k}^\dagger + \beta_{-k}\alpha_k)\{2[\epsilon_k^0 - \mu - \sum_{k'}(\langle \mathbf{kk'}|\bar{V}|\mathbf{kk'}\rangle v_{k'}^2)]u_k v_k$$

$$- (u_k^2 - v_k^2)\sum_{k'}(\langle \mathbf{k}-\mathbf{k}|V|\mathbf{k'}-\mathbf{k'}\rangle u_{k'} v_{k'})\} \quad (37.21c)$$

and we have introduced the abbreviation

$$\langle \mathbf{kk'}|\bar{V}|\mathbf{kk'}\rangle \equiv \langle \mathbf{kk'}|V|\mathbf{kk'}\rangle - \langle \mathbf{kk'}|V|\mathbf{k'k}\rangle + \langle \mathbf{k}-\mathbf{k'}|V|\mathbf{k}-\mathbf{k'}\rangle \quad (37.22)$$

It is convenient to define a new single-particle energy

$$\epsilon_k \equiv \epsilon_k^0 - \sum_{k'}\langle \mathbf{kk'}|\bar{V}|\mathbf{kk'}\rangle v_{k'}^2 \quad (37.23)$$

which will turn out to be the Hartree-Fock expression, and to measure ϵ_k from the chemical potential

$$\xi_k \equiv \epsilon_k - \mu \quad (37.24)$$

Finally, we introduce the *energy gap* by the relation

$$\Delta_k = \sum_{k'}\langle \mathbf{k}-\mathbf{k}|V|\mathbf{k'}-\mathbf{k'}\rangle u_{k'} v_{k'} \quad (37.25)$$

and the various terms of $\hat{K}$ become

$$U = 2\sum_k \xi_k v_k^2 + \sum_{kk'} v_k^2 v_{k'}^2 \langle \mathbf{kk'}|\bar{V}|\mathbf{kk'}\rangle - \sum_k u_k v_k \Delta_k \quad (37.26a)$$

$$\hat{H}_1 = \sum_k (\alpha_k^\dagger \alpha_k + \beta_{-k}^\dagger \beta_{-k})[(u_k^2 - v_k^2)\xi_k + 2u_k v_k \Delta_k] \quad (37.26b)$$

$$\hat{H}_2 = \sum_k (\alpha_k^\dagger \beta_{-k}^\dagger + \beta_{-k}\alpha_k)[2u_k v_k \xi_k - (u_k^2 - v_k^2)\Delta_k] \quad (37.26c)$$

It must be emphasized that Eqs. (37.20) and (37.26) together constitute an exact rearrangement of the original operator.

Until this point, the only restriction on u_k and v_k is that in Eq. (37.4), and we shall now impose the additional constraint

$$2\xi_k u_k v_k = \Delta_k(u_k^2 - v_k^2) \quad (37.27)$$

to make $\hat{H}_2$ vanish. The condition $u_k^2 + v_k^2 = 1$ is most easily incorporated by writing

$$u_k = \cos\chi_k \qquad v_k = \sin\chi_k \quad (37.28)$$

and Eq. (37.27) then becomes

$$\xi_k \sin 2\chi_k = \Delta_k \cos 2\chi_k \quad (37.29)$$

or

$$\tan 2\chi_k = \Delta_k \xi_k^{-1} \tag{37.30}$$

Simple trigonometry gives

$$\sin 2\chi_k = \pm\Delta_k E_k^{-1} = 2u_k v_k$$
$$\tag{37.31}$$
$$\cos 2\chi_k = \pm\xi_k E_k^{-1} = u_k^2 - v_k^2$$

where either the upper or lower signs must be taken throughout, and

$$E_k \equiv (\Delta_k^2 + \xi_k^2)^{\frac{1}{2}} \tag{37.32}$$

The term $\hat{H}_1$ may now be rewritten as

$$\hat{H}_1 = \pm\sum_k E_k(\alpha_k^\dagger \alpha_k + \beta_k^\dagger \beta_k) \tag{37.33}$$

which shows that the upper sign must be chosen to ensure that the energy is bounded from below. With this choice, Eqs. (37.31) and (37.25) become

$$u_k v_k = \frac{\Delta_k}{2E_k}$$

$$u_k^2 = \frac{1}{2}\left(1 + \frac{\xi_k}{E_k}\right) \tag{37.34}$$

$$v_k^2 = \frac{1}{2}\left(1 - \frac{\xi_k}{E_k}\right)$$

$$\Delta_k = \frac{1}{2}\sum_{k'} \langle \mathbf{k} - \mathbf{k}|V|\mathbf{k}' - \mathbf{k}'\rangle \frac{\Delta_{k'}}{E_{k'}} \tag{37.35}$$

This last relation is the *BCS gap equation*, which is a nonlinear integral equation for the gap function Δ_k.[1]

The zero-temperature thermodynamic potential $\hat{K}$ now consists of three terms $U + \hat{H}_1 + N(\hat{V})$, where U is a c number, $\hat{H}_1$ is diagonal in the quasiparticle number operators $\alpha^\dagger\alpha$ and $\beta^\dagger\beta$, and $N(\hat{V})$ is a normal-ordered product of four quasiparticle creation and destruction operators. This last term makes no contribution in the ground state of $U + \hat{H}_1$

$$\langle \mathbf{O}|N(\hat{V})|\mathbf{O}\rangle = 0 \tag{37.36}$$

and it clearly describes the interaction between quasiparticles. For many assemblies, it is a good approximation to neglect $N(\hat{V})$ entirely, in which case we obtain

$$\hat{K}_0 \equiv U + \hat{H}_1 = U + \sum_k E_k(\alpha_k^\dagger \alpha_k + \beta_k^\dagger \beta_k) \tag{37.37}$$

[1] This gap equation was first obtained by J. Bardeen, L. N. Cooper, and J. R. Schrieffer, *Phys. Rev.*, **108**:1175 (1957). The present treatment is closer to that of Bogoliubov, Valatin, and Beliaev, *loc. cit.*

Even when $N(\hat{V})$ is not negligible, the operator $\hat{K}_0$ provides a basis for a perturbation expansion, and we shall now study the properties of $\hat{K}_0$ in detail. It is evident that U is the thermodynamic potential of the ground state, while $E_k = (\Delta_k^2 + \xi_k^2)^{\frac{1}{2}}$ represents the additional contribution of each excited quasiparticle. Note that $E_k \geqslant \Delta_k$, which accounts for the name gap function because the excited states are separated from the ground state by a finite gap. The mean number of particles in the ground state is given by [compare Eq. (35.23)]

$$N = \sum_{k\lambda} \langle \mathbf{O} | a_{k\lambda}^\dagger a_{k\lambda} | \mathbf{O} \rangle$$

$$= 2 \sum_k v_k^2 = \sum_k (1 - \xi_k E_k^{-1}) \tag{37.38}$$

where Eqs. (37.9) and (37.10) have been used to evaluate the matrix elements. In a similar way, the total-momentum operator becomes

$$\hat{\mathbf{P}} = \sum_{k\lambda} \hbar \mathbf{k} a_{k\lambda}^\dagger a_{k\lambda} = \sum_k \hbar \mathbf{k} (a_{k\uparrow}^\dagger a_{k\uparrow} - a_{-k\downarrow}^\dagger a_{-k\downarrow})$$

$$= \sum_k \hbar \mathbf{k} [N(a_{k\uparrow}^\dagger a_{k\uparrow}) - N(a_{-k\downarrow}^\dagger a_{-k\downarrow})]$$

$$= \sum_k \hbar \mathbf{k} (\alpha_k^\dagger \alpha_k + \beta_k^\dagger \beta_k) \tag{37.39}$$

where Eqs. (37.9) and (37.10) have been used to obtain the second line. We see that

$$[\hat{K}_0, \hat{\mathbf{P}}] = 0 \tag{37.40}$$

so that the excited states obtained by applying quasiparticle creation operators $\alpha^\dagger$ and $\beta^\dagger$ to $|\mathbf{O}\rangle$ are eigenstates of both $\hat{K}_0$ and $\hat{\mathbf{P}}$.

Further progress depends on a detailed solution of the gap equation (37.35). Since it is a homogeneous equation, there is always the trivial solution

$$\Delta_k = 0 \qquad \text{for all } \mathbf{k} \qquad \text{normal solution} \tag{37.41}$$

which describes the normal ground state (filled Fermi sea). This identification follows immediately because Eqs. (37.32) and (37.34) then become

$$E_k = |\xi_k|$$

$$u_k v_k = 0$$

$$u_k^2 = \frac{1}{2}\left(1 + \frac{\xi_k}{|\xi_k|}\right) = \theta(\epsilon_k - \mu) \qquad \text{normal solution} \tag{37.42}$$

$$v_k^2 = \frac{1}{2}\left(1 - \frac{\xi_k}{|\xi_k|}\right) = \theta(\mu - \epsilon_k)$$

while Eq. (37.1) reproduces the canonical transformation to particles and holes [compare with Eq. (7.34)]. Furthermore, the last term of Eq. (37.26a) vanishes identically, and the thermodynamic potential in the ground state reduces to the Hartree-Fock value studied in Sec. 10.

In addition to the foregoing normal-state solution, the gap equation also has nontrivial solutions with $\Delta \neq 0$, which we shall call *superconducting solutions*. As a specific model, assume that the matrix elements of the potential are constant in the region near the Fermi surface and vanish elsewhere:

$$\langle \mathbf{k} - \mathbf{k} | V | \mathbf{l} - \mathbf{l} \rangle = g V^{-1} \theta(\hbar\omega_D - |\xi_k|) \theta(\hbar\omega_D - |\xi_l|) \tag{37.43}$$

where $\hbar\omega_D$ is a cutoff introduced to render the integrals convergent. This model is applicable to metals where the interaction with the crystal lattice can lead to an attractive interaction between electrons near the Fermi surface[1] (see Chap. 12). In this way, the potential becomes separable, and the gap equation may be solved exactly. It is readily verified that the gap function reduces to the form

$$\Delta_k = \Delta\theta(\hbar\omega_D - |\xi_k|) \tag{37.44}$$

where Δ is a constant, given as the solution of the equation

$$1 = g(2V)^{-1} \sum_k \theta(\hbar\omega_D - |\xi_k|) (\Delta^2 + \xi_k^2)^{-\frac{1}{2}}$$

$$= \tfrac{1}{2} g \int d^3k \, (2\pi)^{-3} \, \theta(\hbar\omega_D - |\xi_k|) (\Delta^2 + \xi_k^2)^{-\frac{1}{2}} \tag{37.45}$$

In all practical cases $\hbar\omega_D$ is much smaller than μ, and we may write

$$(2\pi)^{-3} d^3k = 4\pi(2\pi)^{-3} k^2 \, dk \approx N(0) \, d\xi \tag{37.46}$$

where

$$N(0) = \frac{1}{2\pi^2} \left[k^2 \frac{dk}{d\epsilon_k} \right]_{\epsilon_k = \mu} \tag{37.47}$$

is the density of states *for one spin projection* at the Fermi surface. Equation (37.45) can now be evaluated as

$$1 = \frac{gN(0)}{2} \int_{-\hbar\omega_D}^{\hbar\omega_D} \frac{d\xi}{(\Delta^2 + \xi^2)^{\frac{1}{2}}} = gN(0) \int_0^{\hbar\omega_D} \frac{d\xi}{(\Delta^2 + \xi^2)^{\frac{1}{2}}}$$

$$\approx gN(0) \ln \frac{2\hbar\omega_D}{\Delta} \tag{37.48}$$

where we have retained only the leading term for $\hbar\omega_D/\Delta \gg 1$. A simple transformation yields

$$\Delta = 2\hbar\omega_D \exp\left(-\frac{1}{N(0)g}\right) \tag{37.49}$$

which exhibits the same nonanalytic structure seen in Eq. (36.30). For typical metals, $\hbar\omega_D$ can be taken as a mean phonon energy $\hbar\omega_D \approx k_B\theta$ (the Debye energy) and $N(0)g \approx 0.2$–0.3 (see Table 51.1).

The corresponding quantities u_k^2 and v_k^2 become

$$u_k^2 = \tfrac{1}{2}[1 + \xi_k(\Delta^2 + \xi_k^2)^{-\frac{1}{2}}]$$
$$v_k^2 = \tfrac{1}{2}[1 - \xi_k(\Delta^2 + \xi_k^2)^{-\frac{1}{2}}]$$

superconducting solution $\qquad$ (37.50)

---

[1] H. Fröhlich, *loc. cit.*

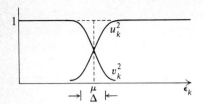

Fig. 37.1 Distribution function $v_k^2 = 1 - u_k^2$ for superconducting solution.

and are shown schematically in Fig. 37.1.   Since v_k^2 is the distribution function for quasiparticles, we see that the sharp Fermi surface of the normal state is smeared throughout a thickness Δ in energy.   Note that Eq. (37.50) is infinitely differentiable and thus can never be obtained in perturbation theory from the discontinuous step functions of Eq. (37.42).

At fixed chemical potential μ, the resulting excitation spectrum of $\hat{K}_0$ in the superconducting state is shown in Fig. 37.2, which clearly indicates the role of the gap Δ.   In the limit $\Delta \to 0$ we recover the excitation spectrum in the normal state, shown by the dotted line.   The apparent paradox that E_k is positive, even for $\epsilon_k < \mu$ in the normal state, is easily explained by remembering that all energies are here measured relative to the chemical potential or Fermi energy (recall $\hat{K} \equiv \hat{H} - \mu\hat{N}$).   Thus the ground state of $N - 1$ particles and one hole is a filled Fermi sea containing $N - 1$ particles, and the creation of a hole with $\epsilon_k < \mu$ therefore requires a minimum energy $\mu - \epsilon_k = |\xi_k| > 0$ [compare the discussion following Eq. (7.61)].[1]

It is interesting to compare the physical properties of the normal and superconducting ground states.   For fixed μ, the number of particles is determined by Eq. (37.38), and we find

$$N_s - N_n = 2 \sum_{\mathbf{k}} (v_k^2|_s - v_k^2|_n)$$

$$= V(2\pi)^{-3} \int d^3k \, \xi_k [|\xi_k|^{-1} - (\xi_k^2 + \Delta^2)^{-\frac{1}{2}}]$$

$$\approx VN(0) \int d\xi \, \xi [|\xi|^{-1} - (\xi^2 + \Delta^2)^{-\frac{1}{2}}]$$

$$= 0 \tag{37.51}$$

because the integrand is odd in ξ.   Here we note that the only contribution to

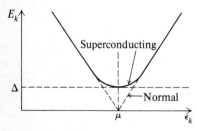

Fig. 37.2 Comparison of excitation spectrum for normal and superconducting solutions.

[1] If $\mu(N)$ is determined from Eq. (37.38) then E_k is the excitation energy at fixed N, as discussed in detail in Sec. 58.

the integral arises from the immediate vicinity of the Fermi surface, and it is therefore permissible to use Eq. (37.46). As a result, the transition from the normal to superconducting state does not alter the mean number of particles in this approximation. Alternatively, if the number of particles N is considered fixed, then the chemical potentials differ by only a very small amount $(\mu_s - \mu_n)/\mu_n = \delta$.

The quantity of direct physical interest is the change in ground-state energy at fixed N

$$E_s - E_n = U_s(\mu_s) - U_n(\mu_n) + (\mu_s - \mu_n) N$$

$$= U_s(\mu_n) - U_n(\mu_n) + \delta\mu_n \left[\left(\frac{\partial U_s}{\partial \mu} \right)_{\mu_n} + N \right] + O(\delta^2)$$

$$\approx U_s(\mu_n) - U_n(\mu_n) \tag{37.52}$$

where the linear term vanishes because of Eq. (4.9). Since δ is small, we need only compute the change in the thermodynamic potential at fixed μ [compare the derivation of Eq. (30.72)]. This expression is easily evaluated with Eqs. (37.26a), (37.34), and (37.42). Assuming that the matrix elements $\langle \mathbf{kk}' | \bar{V} | \mathbf{kk}' \rangle \equiv g/V$ are constants in the vicinity of the Fermi surface, we have

$$E_s - E_n = 2 \sum_{\mathbf{k}} \xi_k [v_k^2|_s - v_k^2|_n] - \sum_{\mathbf{k}} \Delta(u_k v_k)|_s + gV^{-1} \sum_{\mathbf{kk}'} [(v_k^2 v_{k'}^2)|_s - (v_k^2 v_{k'}^2)|_n]$$

$$= \sum_{\mathbf{k}} \left[\frac{\xi_k^2}{|\xi_k|} - \frac{\xi_k^2}{(\xi_k^2 + \Delta^2)^{\frac{1}{2}}} \right] - \frac{1}{2} \sum_{\mathbf{k}} \frac{\Delta^2}{(\xi_k^2 + \Delta^2)^{\frac{1}{2}}}$$

$$+ \frac{g}{4V} \sum_{\mathbf{kk}'} \left\{ \left[1 - \frac{\xi_k}{(\xi_k^2 + \Delta^2)^{\frac{1}{2}}} \right] \left[1 - \frac{\xi_{k'}}{(\xi_{k'}^2 + \Delta^2)^{\frac{1}{2}}} \right] \right.$$

$$\left. - \left(1 - \frac{\xi_k}{|\xi_k|} \right) \left(1 - \frac{\xi_{k'}}{|\xi_{k'}|} \right) \right\}$$

$$\approx VN(0) \int d\xi \left[\frac{\xi^2}{|\xi|} - \frac{\xi^2}{(\xi^2 + \Delta^2)^{\frac{1}{2}}} - \frac{1}{2} \frac{\Delta^2}{(\xi^2 + \Delta^2)^{\frac{1}{2}}} \right] + \frac{gV[N(0)]^2}{4}$$

$$\times \iint d\xi \, d\xi' \left\{ \left[1 - \frac{\xi}{(\xi^2 + \Delta^2)^{\frac{1}{2}}} \right] \left[1 - \frac{\xi'}{(\xi'^2 + \Delta^2)^{\frac{1}{2}}} \right] \right.$$

$$\left. - \left(1 - \frac{\xi}{|\xi|} \right) \left(1 - \frac{\xi'}{|\xi'|} \right) \right\}$$

$$= -\tfrac{1}{2} VN(0) \Delta^2 = \Omega_s - \Omega_n \tag{37.53}$$

where the double integral vanishes by symmetry.[1] Recalling our discussion of

---

[1] The thermodynamic identity of Eq. (4.3) now allows an explicit calculation of $\mu_s - \mu_n$. Assuming a single-particle spectrum $\epsilon_k \approx \epsilon_k^0$, we find $\delta = -\frac{1}{8}(\Delta/\epsilon_F^0)^2 [1 + 6(\partial \ln \Delta/\partial \ln N)]$, which justifies the omission of the δ^2 correction in Eq. (37.52). Note, however, that $N(\mu_s - \mu_n)/(E_s - E_n) = \frac{1}{3}[1 + 6(\partial \ln \Delta/\partial \ln N)]$ is comparable with one so that the separate contributions of order δ in Eq. (37.52) are not negligible. If ω_D and g are independent of N, then $6(\partial \ln \Delta/\partial \ln N)$ reduces to $2 \ln(2\hbar\omega_D/\Delta)$.

Cooper pairs, we can interpret this expression as the binding energy Δ per pair multiplied by the number of pairs $\frac{1}{2}VN(0)\Delta$ lying within the shell of thickness Δ around the Fermi surface.   It is the pairs in this shell that can lower their energy by forming the Cooper bound state.

Equation (37.53) shows that the superconducting state indeed has a lower energy and thermodynamic potential than the normal ground state, and is therefore a better approximation to the true ground state of the interacting system.   This conclusion follows from the same variational principle that determines the ground-state energy, for Eq. (37.36) shows that Ω_n and Ω_s are the expectation values of the exact operator $\hat{K}$ [Eq. (37.20)] in the normalized ground states (normal and superconducting) of $\hat{K}_0$ [Eq. (37.37)].

PROBLEMS

10.1.   Consider a Bose system with macroscopic occupation of the single mode with momentum $\hbar\mathbf{q}$.   Find the depletion of the condensate as a function of $\mathbf{v} = \hbar\mathbf{q}/m$ assuming the pseudopotential model of Eq. (35.1).   Compute the total momentum $\mathbf{P}$, and compare it with the value $N_0\hbar\mathbf{q}$ (compare Prob. 6.6).

10.2.   Consider a dense charged spinless Bose gas in a uniform incompressible background.   Using a canonical transformation, show that the depletion and ground-state energy are given by $(n - n_0)/n = 0.211r_s^{\frac{3}{2}}$ and $E_0/N = -0.803r_s^{-\frac{3}{4}}e^2/2a_0$.   In these expressions $r_s^3 = 3/4\pi na_0^3$ and $a_0 = \hbar^2/m_B e^2$, where m_B is the boson mass (compare with Prob. 6.5).

10.3.   Treat the particle nonconservation arising from the substitution $a_0 \to N_0^{\frac{1}{2}}$ by making a Legendre transformation to the thermodynamic potential at zero temperature $\hat{K} = \hat{H} - \mu\hat{N}$.   Assuming a nonsingular potential, carry out a canonical transformation; rederive Eqs. (21.5), (21.8), (21.15), and find the ground-state energy.

10.4.   (a) Solve Eq. (36.26) for $P \ll 2k_F$, and show that the binding energy $\Delta(P)$ for a pair with center of mass momentum $\hbar\mathbf{P}$ is given by $\Delta(P) \approx \Delta(0) - \hbar v_F P$, where $v_F = \hbar k_F/m$ and $\Delta(0)$ is given in Eq. (36.30).
(b) If $\Delta(0)/k_B \approx 10°$K, estimate the critical value of P where $\Delta(P)$ vanishes.

10.5.   Show that the anomalous eigenvalue corresponds to a solution of the homogeneous Bethe-Goldstone equation.
(a) Use Eqs. (36.15) and (36.18) to find the asymptotic form of the wave function $\psi_{0,\mathbf{k}}(\mathbf{x})$ for a bound pair near the Fermi surface with $\mathbf{P} = 0$; explain why it differs from the usual exponential form.
(b) Show that the form factor (Fourier transform of the density) for this state is $F(q) \approx 1 - \hbar v_F q/2\Delta$ as $q \to 0$. Interpret this result.
(c) If $\Delta/k_B \approx 10°$K, estimate the pair size and compare with the critical wavenumber derived in Prob. 10.4.

10.6. Compute the expectation value of the operator $\hat{N}^2$ in the ground state $|O\rangle$ of Eq. (37.8), and show that the fluctuations are given by

$$\frac{\langle \hat{N}^2 \rangle - \langle \hat{N} \rangle^2}{\langle \hat{N} \rangle^2} = \frac{\sum\limits_{\mathbf{k}} (u_k v_k)^2}{\left(\sum\limits_{\mathbf{k}} v_k^2 \right)^2}$$

Discuss the difference between the normal and superconducting ground states.

10.7. Compute the pairing amplitudes $F_k^* \equiv \langle O | a_{k\uparrow}^\dagger a_{-k\downarrow}^\dagger | O \rangle$ and $F_k \equiv \langle O | a_{-k\downarrow} a_{k\uparrow} | O \rangle$ in the ground state of Eq. (37.8). Sketch their behavior as a function of k, and show that they vanish in the normal ground state.

10.8. Reduce the correlation function in the superconducting ground state

$$C_{\lambda\lambda'}(\mathbf{x},\mathbf{x}') = \langle O | \tilde{n}_\lambda(\mathbf{x}) \, \tilde{n}_{\lambda'}(\mathbf{x}') | O \rangle$$

to definite integrals. Evaluate the expressions for *antiparallel* spins, and compare with the corresponding situation in the normal ground state.

10.9. The superconducting ground state was originally derived with a variational principle‡ by considering the state

$$|\varphi\rangle = \prod_{\mathbf{k}} (u_k + v_k a_{k\uparrow}^\dagger a_{-k\downarrow}^\dagger)|0\rangle$$

where the product is over all $\mathbf{k}$, and $|0\rangle$ is the no-particle state.
(a) Show that $|\varphi\rangle$ is normalized if $u_k^2 + v_k^2 = 1$.
(b) Show that the expectation value of $\hat{K}$ [Eq. (37.6)] in this state is U [Eq. (37.21a)].
(c) Varying u_k and v_k subject to the constraint $u^2 + v^2 = 1$, show that the gap equation (37.35) is the condition for minimum thermodynamic potential.
(d) Apart from normalization, verify that $a_{k\uparrow}^\dagger |\varphi\rangle$ and $a_{-k\downarrow} |\varphi\rangle$ both represent the same state which is orthogonal to $|\varphi\rangle$. Evaluate the expectation value of $\hat{K}$ in this state and show that the increase in the thermodynamic potential is E_k.

‡ J. Bardeen, L. N. Cooper, and J. R. Schrieffer, *Phys. Rev.*, **108**:1175 (1957).

Applications to Physical Systems

11
Nuclear Matter

The study of atomic nuclei represents an important application of the techniques developed in the preceding chapters. The detailed properties of finite nuclei are discussed in Chap. 15. This chapter, however, concentrates on the simpler problem of understanding the bulk properties of nuclei (nuclear matter) in terms of the interaction between two free nucleons. We introduce the discussion by giving a very brief review of the nucleon-nucleon force and by precisely defining nuclear matter.

38□NUCLEAR FORCES: A REVIEW

In this section we summarize the main empirical features of the nucleon-nucleon interaction.

1. *Attractive*: The existence of the deuteron with $J = 1$ and even parity indicates that the force between the proton and neutron is basically attractive,

at least in the spin-triplet state (that is, the $^3S_1$ state). Furthermore, the interference between coulomb and nuclear scattering in the proton-proton system shows that the nuclear force between two protons in the $^1S_0$ state is also attractive. Finally, it is clear from the existence of stable self-bound atomic nuclei that the interaction between any two nucleons is essentially attractive.

2. *Short range*: For incident nucleon energies up to ≈ 10 MeV in the center-of-momentum frame, the differential cross section for neutron-proton scattering is isotropic. We therefore conclude that scattering occurs in relative s-wave states. This result allows a rough estimate of the range of the nucleon-nucleon force from the classical limit on the maximum angular momentum $\hbar l_{max} = rp$ that can contribute to the scattering amplitude. Substituting the relation between energy and momentum gives

$$l_{max} = r \left(\frac{2m_{red} E}{\hbar^2} \right)^{\frac{1}{2}} \approx r(\text{Fermi}) \left(\frac{E}{40 \text{ MeV}} \right)^{\frac{1}{2}} \qquad (38.1)$$

where m_{red} is the reduced mass, and the following relations have been used

$$1 \text{ Fermi} = 1 \text{ F} \equiv 10^{-13} \text{ cm} \qquad (38.2)$$

$$\frac{\hbar^2}{2m} = 20.8 \text{ MeV F}^2 \qquad (38.3)$$

Equation (38.3) is a very useful result, for it sets the energy scale in nuclear physics. Since $l_{max} < 1$ for energies up to 10 MeV, it follows from Eq. (38.1) that the range of the nuclear force is

$$r \approx \text{few Fermis} \qquad (38.4)$$

3. *Spin-dependent*: The neutron-proton cross section σ_{np} is much too large at very low energies[1]

$$\sigma_{np}(0) = 20.4 \text{ barns} = 20.4 \times 10^{-24} \text{ cm}^2 \qquad (38.5)$$

to arise from a potential chosen to fit the properties of the deuteron. Since the measured neutron-proton cross section is the statistical average of the triplet and singlet cross sections

$$\sigma_{np} = \tfrac{3}{4}(^3\sigma) + \tfrac{1}{4}(^1\sigma) \qquad (38.6)$$

it follows that the singlet potential must be different from the triplet potential of the deuteron. A low-energy scattering experiment measures only two parameters of the potential. These can be taken as the scattering length a and effective range r_0 defined by

$$k \cot \delta_0 = -\frac{1}{a} + \tfrac{1}{2}r_0 k^2 \qquad (38.7)$$

[1] M. A. Preston, "Physics of the Nucleus," p. 25, Addison-Wesley Publishing Co., Reading, Mass., 1962.

where δ_0 is the s-wave phase shift.[1]   An extensive analysis of low-energy neutron-proton scattering yields the following parameters[2]:

$$^1a = -23.71 \pm 0.07 \text{ F}$$
$$^3a = 5.38 \pm 0.03 \text{ F}$$
$$^1r_0 = 2.4 \pm 0.3 \text{ F}$$
$$^3r_0 = 1.71 \pm 0.03 \text{ F}$$

(38.8)

The singlet state has a very large negative scattering length and therefore just fails to have a bound state.   (A bound state at zero energy implies $a = -\infty$.) In contrast, the triplet system has one bound state, the deuteron, with a binding energy of 2.2 MeV.   Although there is a large difference in scattering lengths and zero-energy cross sections, the singlet and triplet potentials are in fact rather similar, both essentially having a bound state at zero energy.

4. *Noncentral*: Since the deuteron has a quadrupole moment, the orbital angular momentum cannot be a constant of the motion.   In fact the ground state of the deuteron must contain both $l = 2$ and $l = 0$ to yield a nonvanishing quadrupole moment (the even parity forbids $l = 1$).   Hence the nucleon-nucleon potential cannot be invariant under rotation of the spatial coordinates alone. The most general velocity-independent potential for spin-$\frac{1}{2}$ particles that is invariant under total rotations generated by $\mathbf{J} = \mathbf{L} + \mathbf{S}$ and under spatial reflections is given by

$$V = V_0(x) + \boldsymbol{\sigma}_1 \cdot \boldsymbol{\sigma}_2 \, V_1(x) + S_{12} \, V_T(x)$$
$$\mathbf{x} \equiv \mathbf{x}_1 - \mathbf{x}_2$$

(38.9)

where the tensor operator is defined as

$$S_{12} \equiv 3(\boldsymbol{\sigma}_1 \cdot \hat{x})(\boldsymbol{\sigma}_2 \cdot \hat{x}) - \boldsymbol{\sigma}_1 \cdot \boldsymbol{\sigma}_2$$

(38.10)

Any higher powers of the spin operators can be reduced to the form of Eq. (38.9) through the properties of the Pauli matrices.   The total spin of the nucleon-nucleon system is given by $\mathbf{S} = \frac{1}{2}(\boldsymbol{\sigma}_1 + \boldsymbol{\sigma}_2)$, and the square of this relation yields

$$\boldsymbol{\sigma}_1 \cdot \boldsymbol{\sigma}_2 = \begin{cases} -3 & \text{singlet state, } S = 0 \\ +1 & \text{triplet state, } S = 1 \end{cases}$$

(38.11a)
(38.11b)

The total hamiltonian constructed with Eq. (38.9) is symmetric under the interchange of the particles' spins, which means that the wave function must be either symmetric ($S = 1$) or antisymmetric ($S = 0$) under this operation.   As a result, the total spin S is a good quantum number for the two-nucleon system.   Since the singlet wave function $^1\chi$ is annihilated by the spin operator, $\frac{1}{2}(\boldsymbol{\sigma}_1 + \boldsymbol{\sigma}_2)^1\chi = 0$,

[1] For a review of effective-range theory see L. I. Schiff, "Quantum Mechanics," 3d ed., p. 460, McGraw-Hill Book Company, New York, 1968.
[2] M. A. Preston, *op. cit.*, pp. 26–27.

it follows from Eq. (38.10) that

$$S_{12}{}^1\chi = 0 \tag{38.12}$$

Thus the tensor operator annihilates the singlet state and acts only in the triplet state.

5. *Charge independent*: The nucleon-nucleon force is charge independent, which means that any two nucleons in a given two-body state always experience the same force. The Pauli principle, however, limits the neutron-neutron and proton-proton systems to overall antisymmetric states because they are composed of two identical fermions. A complete set of state vectors for two noninteracting nucleons is obtained by specifying the momentum of each nucleon and the spin projection $|\mathbf{p}_1 s_1 \mathbf{p}_2 s_2\rangle$. In the interacting system there are still eight good quantum numbers, which can be taken to be the energy, total angular momentum, z-projection of the total angular momentum, the spin, the parity, and the three components of the center-of-mass momentum, $|EJM_J S\pi \mathbf{P}_{cm}\rangle$. The parity of the various states arises from the behavior under spatial interchange, which need not be the same as the behavior under combined spatial and spin interchange (particle interchange). These relations are shown in Table 38.1 along with the types of pairs that can exist in any of the states. Charge independence implies that the forces are equal in those states that can be occupied by all three kinds of pairs: nn, pp, and np. It is important to realize, however, that charge independence does not imply the equality of scattering amplitudes and scattering cross

Table 38.1 Low l states of the nucleon-nucleon system

States	$^1S_0$	$^1P_1$	$^1D_2$	$^3S_1 + {}^3D_1$	$^3P_0$	$^3P_1$	$^3P_2 + {}^3F_2$	$^3D_2$
Parity	$+$	$-$	$+$	$+$	$-$	$-$	$-$	$+$
Particle interchange .	$-$	$+$	$-$	$+$	$-$	$-$	$-$	$+$
Particles	nn		nn		nn	nn	nn	
	np	np	np	$np\ddagger$	np	np	np	np
	pp		pp		pp	pp	pp	

‡ Ground state of deuteron.

sections for the various pairs, since the states available are restricted by the Pauli principle. For example, at low energy we have

$$\left(\frac{d\sigma}{d\Omega}\right)_{np} = \tfrac{1}{4}|f(^1S_0)|^2 + \tfrac{3}{4}|f(^3S_1)|^2 \tag{38.13a}$$

$$\left(\frac{d\sigma}{d\Omega}\right)_{nn} = |f(^1S_0)|^2 \tag{38.13b}$$

and charge independence merely requires that

$$[f(^1S_0)]_{np} = [f(^1S_0)]_{pp} = [f(^1S_0)]_{nn} \tag{38.14}$$

6. *Exchange character*: As the energy increases, more partial waves contribute to the scattering amplitude and the analysis becomes very difficult. At sufficiently high energies, however, the Born approximation supplies a useful guide to the differential cross section

$$\left.\frac{d\sigma}{d\Omega}\right)_{cm} = \left|\frac{m}{4\pi\hbar^2} \int e^{-i\mathbf{k}_f \cdot \mathbf{x}} V(x) \psi_{\mathbf{k}_i}^{(+)}(\mathbf{x})\, d^3x\right|^2 \tag{38.15a}$$

$$\left.\frac{d\sigma}{d\Omega}\right)_{cm} \approx \left|\frac{m}{4\pi\hbar^2} \int e^{i\mathbf{q}\cdot\mathbf{x}} V(x)\, d^3x\right|^2 \tag{38.15b}$$

where

$$\mathbf{q}^2 \equiv (\mathbf{k}_i - \mathbf{k}_f)^2 = 4k^2 \sin^2\left(\tfrac{1}{2}\theta\right) \tag{38.16}$$

For large momentum transfer $\hbar q$, the integrand in Eq. (38.15b) oscillates rapidly, and the Fourier transform will tend to zero. Thus the scattering from a potential $V(x)$ should yield a differential cross section that falls off with increasing θ. In contrast, the differential cross section for neutron-proton scattering at laboratory energies up to 600 MeV is shown in Fig. 38.1. Note that there is a great deal of backward scattering; indeed, the most impressive feature of these results is the apparent symmetry about 90°. If this symmetry is exact $[f(\pi - \theta) = f(\theta)]$, then only the even l's contribute to the scattering amplitude, for odd l's will distort the cross section. To explain this behavior, the concept of an exchange force has been introduced. This exchange force depends on the

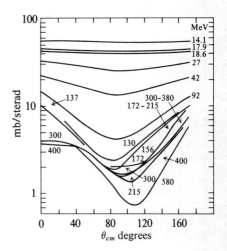

Fig. 38.1 Experimental *n-p* differential cross section in the center-of-momentum system at various laboratory energies (in MeV). (From M. A. Preston, "Physics of the Nucleus," p. 92, Addison-Wesley Publishing Co., Reading, Mass., 1962. Reprinted by permission.)

symmetry of the wave function and is written as

$$V_M = V(x) P_M \tag{38.17}$$

where P_M is the Majorana space-exchange operator defined by

$$P_M^{(ij)} \, \varphi(\mathbf{x}_i, \mathbf{x}_j) \equiv \varphi(\mathbf{x}_j, \mathbf{x}_i) \tag{38.18}$$

When operating on a state of orbital angular momentum l, we have

$$P_M \, Y_{lm}(\hat{x}) \equiv Y_{lm}(-\hat{x}) = (-1)^l \, Y_{lm}(\hat{x}) \tag{38.19}$$

and the odd l in the scattering amplitude can therefore be eliminated with a Serber force defined by

$$V \equiv V(x) \tfrac{1}{2}(1 + P_M) \tag{38.20}$$

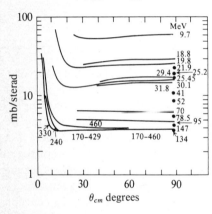

Fig. 38.2   Experimental $p\text{-}p$ differential cross section in the center-of-momentum system at various laboratory energies (in MeV). The forward peak is due to coulomb scattering. (From M. A. Preston, "Physics of the Nucleus," p. 93, Addison-Wesley Publishing Co., Reading, Mass., 1962. Reprinted by permission.)

The differential cross section for high-energy scattering from such a potential can be calculated in Born approximation

$$\left.\frac{d\sigma}{d\Omega}\right)_{cm} = \left| \frac{m}{4\pi\hbar^2} \int e^{-i\mathbf{k}_f \cdot \mathbf{x}} \, V(x) \tfrac{1}{2}(1 + P_M) e^{i\mathbf{k}_i \cdot \mathbf{x}} d^3 x \right|^2$$

$$= \left| \frac{m}{4\pi\hbar^2} \int e^{-i\mathbf{k}_f \cdot \mathbf{x}} \, V(x) \tfrac{1}{2}(e^{i\mathbf{k}_i \cdot \mathbf{x}} + e^{-i\mathbf{k}_i \cdot \mathbf{x}}) d^3 x \right|^2 \tag{38.21}$$

and is evidently symmetric about 90°. Phase shift analyses confirm that the nuclear force has roughly a Serber exchange nature and is weakly repulsive in the odd-l states.[1]

7. *Hard core*: The pp differential cross section for laboratory energies up to 500 MeV is shown in Fig. 38.2, where it is plotted only for $\theta_{cm} < \pi/2$ because

[1] See, for example, M. H. Hull, Jr., K. E. Lassila, H. M. Ruppel, F. A. McDonald, and G. Breit, *Phys. Rev.*, **122**:1606 (1961).

the identity of the particles requires

$$\frac{d\sigma(\pi - \theta))}{d\Omega}\bigg)_{cm} = \frac{d\sigma(\theta))}{d\Omega}\bigg)_{cm} \tag{38.22}$$

Although the differential cross sections for the np and pp systems look completely different, it is possible to make a charge-independent analysis of these processes.[1] The isotropy of the nuclear part of the pp cross section might suggest that only s waves contribute even up to these high energies. This conclusion can be ruled out, however, by the unitarity limit k^{-2} on the s-wave differential cross section, which is smaller than the observed 4mb/sr. The higher partial waves must therefore interfere to give a flat angular distribution. In particular, Jastrow observed that a hard core in the singlet potential would change the sign of the s-wave phase shift at higher energies. The $^1D-^1S$ interference term in pp scattering could then give a nearly uniform distribution.[2] (With a Serber force in pp scattering, the only contributing states of low l are $^1S_0$, $^1D_2$, and so forth.) Jastrow's suggestion was subsequently confirmed by detailed measurements, which show that the s-wave phase shift becomes negative at about 200 MeV and indicate that the singlet nucleon-nucleon potential has a hard core with a range

$$r_c \approx 0.4 \text{ F} \tag{38.23}$$

Further phase-shift analyses imply the existence of a similar hard core in the triplet state.[3]

8. *Spin-orbit force*: Large polarizations of scattered nucleons are observed perpendicular to the plane of scattering. These effects are difficult to explain with just central and tensor forces, and an additional spin-orbit force of the type

$$V = -V_{so} \mathbf{L} \cdot \mathbf{S} \tag{38.24}$$

is generally introduced to understand these polarizations. The spin-orbit operator can be written

$$\mathbf{L} \cdot \mathbf{S} = \tfrac{1}{2}[J(J+1) - l(l+1) - S(S+1)] \tag{38.25}$$

It is obvious that the spin-orbit force vanishes in singlet states ($S = 0$, $l = J$) and also in s states ($l = 0$, $S = J$). The usual phenomenological V_{so} has a very short range. Thus the spin-orbit force is effective only at high energy, for it vanishes in s states, and the centrifugal barrier tends to keep the high partial waves away from the potential.

In summary, our present empirical understanding of the nucleon-nucleon force is the following:

[1] *Ibid.*
[2] R. Jastrow, *Phys. Rev.*, **81**:165 (1951); see also M. A. Preston, *op. cit.*, p. 97.
[3] See, for example, R. V. Reid, Jr., *Ann. Phys. (N. Y.)*, **50**:411 (1968).

1. The experimental data can be fit up to ≈ 300 MeV with a set of potentials depending only on the spin and parity ${}^1V_c^+$, ${}^3V_c^+$, ${}^1V_c^-$, ${}^3V_c^-$, ${}^3V_T^+$, ${}^3V_T^-$, and so forth.
2. The potentials contain a hard core $r_c \approx 0.4$ to 0.5 F.
3. The forces in the odd-l states are relatively weak at low energies and on the average slightly repulsive.
4. The tensor force is necessary for the quadrupole moment of the deuteron.
5. A strong short-range spin-orbit force is necessary to explain the polarizations at high energies.

The best phenomenological nucleon-nucleon potentials are those of Hamada and Johnston,[1] the Yale group,[2] and Reid.[3]

39□NUCLEAR MATTER

Nuclear scattering of short-wavelength electrons has been studied extensively by Hofstadter and his collaborators;[4] these experiments form the basis for the current picture of the size and charge distribution of nuclei.

NUCLEAR RADII AND CHARGE DISTRIBUTIONS

A phase-shift analysis of elastic electron scattering indicates an average charge distribution of the type illustrated in Fig. 39.1 and given by $\rho = \rho_0(1 + e^{(r-R)/a})^{-1}$.

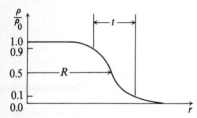

Fig. 39.1 The nuclear charge-density distribution.

Here a determines the skin thickness and R is the point where $\rho = \frac{1}{2}\rho_0$. The parameters show the following systematic behavior:

1. The central nuclear density defined by $A\rho_0/Z$ is constant from nucleus to nucleus.
2. The radius R is given by

$$R = r_0 A^{\frac{1}{3}} \qquad \text{with } r_0 \approx 1.07 \text{ F} \qquad (39.1)$$

[1] T. Hamada and I. D. Johnston, *Nucl. Phys.*, **34**:382 (1962).
[2] K. E. Lassila, M. H. Hull, Jr., H. M. Ruppel, F. A. McDonald, and G. Breit, *Phys. Rev.*, **126**:881 (1962).
[3] R. V. Reid, Jr., *loc. cit.*
[4] R. Hofstadter, *Rev. Mod. Phys.*, **28**:214 (1956); see also R. Hofstadter, "Electron Scattering and Nuclear and Nucleon Structure," W. A. Benjamin, Inc., New York, 1963.

We shall estimate the volume V of the nucleus as $4\pi R^3/3$. As an immediate consequence, the particle density in nuclear matter

$$\frac{A}{V} = \frac{3}{4\pi r_0^3} = 1.95 \times 10^{38} \text{ particles/cm}^3 \tag{39.2}$$

is a constant independent of the size of the nucleus. (This is not true in atoms, for example.)

3. The root-mean-square radius of the proton[1] is $r_p \approx 0.77$ F, while the mean interparticle distance in nuclei may be characterized by

$$\rho = l^{-3} \quad \text{with } l \approx 1.73 \text{ F} \tag{39.3}$$

Since $l > 2r_p$ (but not by very much), we may hope to understand the properties of nuclei by examining the behavior of a collection of nucleons interacting through two-body potentials. We shall certainly proceed under this assumption, but it must be remembered that all of nuclear theory depends on this very basic approximation.

4. The surface thickness $t = 2a\ln 9$, defined to be the distance over which the charge density falls from 90 to 10 percent of its value ρ_0 at the origin, is found to be

$$t \approx 2.4 \text{ F} \tag{39.4}$$

for nuclei ranging from $_{12}\text{Mg}^{24}$ to $_{82}\text{Pb}^{208}$.

We must emphasize that electron scattering measures the proton distribution or charge distribution, and the matter distribution need not be identical. The nuclear force extends outside of the charge distribution; therefore, purely nuclear measurements generally yield slightly larger mean-square radii.

THE SEMIEMPIRICAL MASS FORMULA

We next study the energy of a nucleus containing A nucleons, N neutrons, and Z protons. A first approximation, suggested by Weizsäcker,[2] is to consider the nucleus a liquid drop. If a drop contains twice as much liquid, then there will be twice as much energy of condensation, or binding energy. This result means that the nuclear energy must have a term of the form

$$E_1 = -a_1 A \tag{39.5}$$

which is known as the *bulk property of nuclear matter*. There are, of course, many other contributions to the total energy. The nucleons at the nuclear surface will be attracted only by the particles inside, leading to a surface tension

[1] E. E. Chambers and R. Hofstadter, *Phys. Rev.*, **103**:1454 (1956).
[2] C. F. von Weizsäcker, *Z. Physik*, **96**:431 (1935).

and a surface energy that decreases the binding. If σ is the surface tension, this surface energy can be written as

$$E_2 = 4\pi R^2 \sigma = 4\pi r_0^2 \sigma A^{\frac{2}{3}} \equiv a_2 A^{\frac{2}{3}} \tag{39.6}$$

which varies linearly with the surface area or $A^{\frac{2}{3}}$. There is also the coulomb interaction of Z protons, which can be calculated approximately by assuming the charges to be uniformly distributed over a sphere of radius $R_c \equiv r_{0c} A^{\frac{1}{3}}$. An elementary integration from electrostatics then yields the interaction energy of the $\frac{1}{2}Z(Z-1)$ pairs

$$E_3 = \frac{3}{5}\frac{Z(Z-1)e^2}{R_c} = \frac{3}{5}\frac{e^2}{r_{0c}}\frac{Z(Z-1)}{A^{\frac{1}{3}}} \approx a_3 \frac{Z^2}{A^{\frac{1}{3}}} \tag{39.7}$$

Some nuclear effects must now be included in the energy. First, we note empirically that nuclei tend to have equal numbers of neutrons and protons $N=Z$, and a corresponding symmetry energy E_4 will be added to the mass formula. The bulk properties of nuclear matter imply that twice as many particles with the same *ratio* of N/Z will have twice the symmetry energy. This observation suggests that E_4 is proportional to A. As a first approximation to the numerical coefficient, we shall retain only the quadratic term in an expansion about equilibrium, and we find

$$E_4 = c\left(\frac{1}{2} - \frac{Z}{N+Z}\right)^2 A = \frac{c}{4A^2}(A-2Z)^2 A$$

$$\equiv a_4 A^{-1}(A-2Z)^2 \tag{39.8}$$

Next we note empirically that nuclei tend to have even numbers of the same kinds of particles. For example, there are only four stable odd-odd nuclei $_1H^2$, $_3Li^6$, $_5B^{10}$, and $_7N^{14}$. For odd-A nuclei, there is at most one stable isobar (nucleus with a given A), while for even A there may be two or more stable isobars with even N and even Z. The experimental energy surfaces describing the situation for a series of isobars are shown in Fig. 39.2. Within such a series,

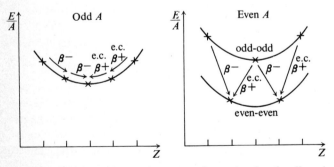

Fig. 39.2 Odd-A and even-A energy surfaces, showing the allowed β decays (e.c. stands for electron capture).

the only possible transitions are by electron or positron emission, and by electron capture. (It is a general rule, following directly from energy conservation, that of two nuclei with Z differing by 1 and the same A, at least one is β unstable.) Two adjacent even-even nuclei on the same energy surface can both be stable because the only allowed transition between them would be a double β decay, which is believed to be absent or at least extremely rare. The splitting of these energy surfaces can now be included in the mass formula by adding a *pairing energy* of the form

$$E_s = \lambda a_s A^{-\frac{3}{4}} \tag{39.9}$$

The parameter λ is defined by

$$\lambda \equiv \begin{cases} +1 & \text{odd-odd} \\ 0 & \text{odd-even} \\ -1 & \text{even-even} \end{cases} \tag{39.10}$$

while the $A^{-\frac{3}{4}}$ dependence is empirical. Combining these results leads to the Weizsäcker semiempirical mass formula

$$E = -a_1 A + a_2 A^{\frac{2}{3}} + a_3 Z^2 A^{-\frac{1}{3}} + a_4 (A - 2Z)^2 A^{-1} + \lambda a_5 A^{-\frac{3}{4}} \tag{39.11}$$

where the following best-fit parameters have been given by Green[1, 2]

$$\begin{aligned} a_1 &= 15.75 \text{ MeV} & a_4 &= 23.7 \text{ MeV} \\ a_2 &= 17.8 \text{ MeV} & a_5 &= 34 \text{ MeV} \\ a_3 &= 0.710 \text{ MeV} \end{aligned} \tag{39.12}$$

This expression has only two terms depending on Z: the coulomb energy and the symmetry energy. The stable charge Z^* can be found by differentiation, $\partial E/\partial Z)_A = 0$, which implies

$$Z^* = A\left(2 + \frac{a_3 A^{\frac{2}{3}}}{2a_4}\right)^{-1} \tag{39.13}$$

For small nuclei the equilibrium value is $Z^* \approx A/2$, which is indeed observed up to $A \approx 40$. This expression clearly does not account for local variations due to shell structure around this equilibrium value. Nevertheless, the overall fit is excellent.

Equation (39.11) is very useful in studies of fission, for it allows one to determine when the energy of two separate pieces will be less than the energy of the original excited nucleus and even to calculate the energy release in the fission process. It is also useful in predicting masses of new nuclei.

---

[1] A. E. S. Green, *Phys. Rev.*, **95**:1006 (1954); A. E. S. Green and D. F. Edwards, *Phys. Rev.*, **91** : 46 (1953).
[2] The coefficient a_3 implies that $r_{0c} = 1.22$ F [see Eq. (39.7)] in agreement with the equivalent value measured in electron scattering.

We can now define a substance known as *nuclear matter*.   If we let $A \to \infty$ in Eq. (39.11) and at the same time set $N = Z$ and turn off the electric charge, then this nuclear matter has a constant energy/particle given by

$$\frac{E}{A} \approx -15.7 \text{ MeV} \tag{39.14}$$

This value therefore represents the energy/particle of an infinite nucleus with equal numbers of neutrons and protons but with no coulomb effects.   Equations (39.14) and (39.2) exhibit the *saturation of nuclear forces*, because the binding energy per particle and the nuclear density are both constants independent of A. Nuclear matter is a uniform degenerate Fermi system and may be characterized by its Fermi wavenumber.   Since each momentum state has a degeneracy factor of 4 (neutrons, proton, spin-up, and spin-down), the particle density becomes [see Eq. (5.47)]

$$\frac{A}{V} = \frac{2}{3\pi^2} k_F^3 \tag{39.15}$$

or using Eq. (39.2)

$$k_F r_0 = \left(\frac{9\pi}{8}\right)^{\frac{1}{3}} = 1.52 \tag{39.16}$$

The experimental value of r_0 from Eq. (39.1) yields the Fermi wavenumber of nuclear matter

$$k_F \approx 1.42 \text{ F}^{-1} \tag{39.17}$$

40☐INDEPENDENT-PARTICLE (FERMI GAS) MODEL

We wish to examine the bulk properties of nuclear matter as defined above in the limit $A \to \infty$.   For a uniform system it is appropriate to use a box of volume V and apply periodic boundary conditions.   Translational invariance then implies that the single-particle eigenfunctions are plane waves

$$\varphi_{\mathbf{k}}(\mathbf{x}) = V^{-\frac{1}{2}} e^{i\mathbf{k}\cdot\mathbf{x}} \tag{40.1}$$

which are already solutions to the Hartree-Fock equations; they are the "best" single-particle wave functions that can be found (see Sec. 10).   This result accounts for the appeal and simplicity of nuclear matter.   *The starting single-particle wave functions are known and simple.*   Such is not the case, for example, with finite nuclei or atoms, where it is a very difficult calculation merely to generate the starting Hartree-Fock wave functions.[1]

The present Fermi medium consists of both protons and neutrons with spin-up and spin-down.   We know that protons and neutrons have the same

[1] We consider the theory of finite nuclei in Chap. 15.

nuclear interactions, which is the statement of charge independence. Hence it is convenient to treat them as two different charge states of a single particle, the nucleon, and to introduce the concept of isotopic spin. In this way, the nucleon acquires an additional degree of freedom that can take two values; these values indicate whether the nucleon is a proton or a neutron. Introduce the two-component isotopic-spin wave functions

$$\zeta_p = \begin{bmatrix} 1 \\ 0 \end{bmatrix} \qquad \zeta_n = \begin{bmatrix} 0 \\ 1 \end{bmatrix} \tag{40.2}$$

just as for angular momentum $\tfrac{1}{2}$. The operators in the space of these two-component column vectors will be $\mathbf{1}$ and $\boldsymbol{\tau}$, where the $\boldsymbol{\tau}$ denote the Pauli matrices. The complete single-particle wave functions can then be written as

$$\varphi_{\mathbf{k}}(\mathbf{x}) \, \eta_\lambda \, \zeta_\rho \tag{40.3}$$

where η_λ is the ordinary-spin wave function. The charge operator that distinguishes a neutron from a proton is given by

$$q = \tfrac{1}{2}(1 + \tau_3) \tag{40.4}$$

Second quantization can be introduced exactly as before, and the canonical anticommutation relations become

$$\{a_{\mathbf{k}\lambda\rho}, a^\dagger_{\mathbf{k}'\lambda'\rho'}\} = \delta_{\mathbf{k}\mathbf{k}'} \, \delta_{\lambda\lambda'} \, \delta_{\rho\rho'} \tag{40.5}$$

Here the anticommutation relations have been written in terms of a generalized Pauli principle: The state vector, or wave function, of a collection of nucleons must be antisymmetric under the interchange of all coordinates including isotopic spin. If the interaction does not cause transitions between neutrons and protons, Eq. (40.5) represents no loss of generality since it is then irrelevant whether the corresponding operators commute or anticommute. If the interaction can cause such transitions, then this choice is important, and in all the theories so far developed the anticommutation relations of Eq. (40.5) have been imposed.

The expectation value of the hamiltonian in the noninteracting Fermi system gives the first approximation to the ground-state energy of nuclear matter

$$E_0 + E_1 = \langle F | \hat{H} | F \rangle \tag{40.6}$$

The first-order calculation is also a variational calculation because the variational principle shows that

$$E \leqslant \langle F | \hat{H} | F \rangle \tag{40.7}$$

We assume initially that the potential is nonsingular, and the corresponding expectation value can be computed as

$$
E_0 + E_1 = 4 \sum_{k}^{k_F} \frac{\hbar^2 \mathbf{k}^2}{2m} + \tfrac{1}{2} \sum_{\mathbf{k}_1 \lambda_1 \rho_1} \cdots \sum_{\mathbf{k}_4 \lambda_4 \rho_4}
$$
$$
\times \langle \mathbf{k}_1 \lambda_1 \rho_1 \mathbf{k}_2 \lambda_2 \rho_2 | V | \mathbf{k}_3 \lambda_3 \rho_3 \mathbf{k}_4 \lambda_4 \rho_4 \rangle
$$
$$
\times \langle F | a^\dagger_{\mathbf{k}_1 \lambda_1 \rho_1} a^\dagger_{\mathbf{k}_2 \lambda_2 \rho_2} a_{\mathbf{k}_4 \lambda_4 \rho_4} a_{\mathbf{k}_3 \lambda_3 \rho_3} | F \rangle \tag{40.8}
$$

(We return to a discussion of the singular case shortly.)   Just as in the calculation with the electron gas, all the operators in the matrix element in Eq. (40.8) must refer to particles in the Fermi sea or the matrix element will vanish.   The matrix element of the creation and destruction operators becomes

$$\langle F|a^\dagger_{\mathbf{k}_1\,\lambda_1\,\rho_1}\,a^\dagger_{\mathbf{k}_2\,\lambda_2\,\rho_2}\,a_{\mathbf{k}_4\,\lambda_4\,\rho_4}\,a_{\mathbf{k}_3\,\lambda_3\,\rho_3}|F\rangle = [\delta_{\mathbf{k}_1\mathbf{k}_3}\,\delta_{\lambda_1\lambda_3}\,\delta_{\rho_1\rho_3}][\delta_{\mathbf{k}_2\mathbf{k}_4}\,\delta_{\lambda_2\lambda_4}\,\delta_{\rho_2\rho_4}]$$
$$- [\delta_{\mathbf{k}_1\mathbf{k}_4}\,\delta_{\lambda_1\lambda_4}\,\delta_{\rho_1\rho_4}][\delta_{\mathbf{k}_2\mathbf{k}_3}\,\delta_{\lambda_2\lambda_3}\,\delta_{\rho_2\rho_3}]$$

which gives

$$E_0 + E_1 = 4\sum_{\mathbf{k}}^{k_F}\frac{\hbar^2\mathbf{k}^2}{2m} + \tfrac{1}{2}\sum_{\mathbf{k}\lambda\rho}^{k_F}\sum_{\mathbf{k}'\lambda'\rho'}^{k_F}\{\langle \mathbf{k}\lambda\rho\mathbf{k}'\,\lambda'\,\rho'|V|\mathbf{k}\lambda\rho\mathbf{k}'\,\lambda'\,\rho'\rangle$$
$$- \langle \mathbf{k}\lambda\rho\mathbf{k}'\,\lambda'\,\rho'|V|\mathbf{k}'\,\lambda'\,\rho'\,\mathbf{k}\lambda\rho\rangle\} \quad (40.9)$$

This expression for the ground-state energy is represented by the first two Goldstone diagrams in Fig. 9.22.

As an example, consider a potential that is an arbitrary combination of an ordinary central force (Wigner force) and a Majorana space-exchange force

$$V = V(x)[a_W + a_M P_M] \quad (40.10)$$

where a_W and a_M are positive constants.   We assume that $V(x)$ is attractive, nonsingular, and—for simplicity—spin independent.   In fact, the spin dependence of the nucleon-nucleon force is quite weak; the $^1S_0$ state is just unbound and the $^3S_1$ state is just bound, as discussed in Sec. 38.   The direct matrix element (first term in E_1) then becomes

$$V_D = V^{-2}\int d^3x \int d^3y\, e^{-i\mathbf{k}\cdot\mathbf{x}}e^{-i\mathbf{k}'\cdot\mathbf{y}}\,\eta^\dagger_\lambda(1)\,\eta^\dagger_{\lambda'}(2)\,\zeta^\dagger_\rho(1)\,\zeta^\dagger_{\rho'}(2)\,V(1,2)$$
$$\times\, e^{i\mathbf{k}\cdot\mathbf{x}}e^{i\mathbf{k}'\cdot\mathbf{y}}\,\eta_\lambda(1)\,\eta_{\lambda'}(2)\,\zeta_\rho(1)\,\zeta_{\rho'}(2)$$
$$= V^{-1}[a_W\int V(z)\,d^3z + a_M\int e^{-i(\mathbf{k}-\mathbf{k}')\cdot\mathbf{z}}\,V(z)\,d^3z] \quad (40.11a)$$

and, similarly, the exchange matrix element (second term in E_1) is given by

$$V_E = V^{-2}\int d^3x \int d^3y\, e^{-i\mathbf{k}\cdot\mathbf{x}}e^{-i\mathbf{k}'\cdot\mathbf{y}}\,\eta^\dagger_\lambda(1)\,\eta^\dagger_{\lambda'}(2)\,\zeta^\dagger_\rho(1)\,\zeta^\dagger_{\rho'}(2)\,V(1,2)$$
$$\times\, e^{i\mathbf{k}'\cdot\mathbf{x}}e^{i\mathbf{k}\cdot\mathbf{y}}\,\eta_{\lambda'}(1)\,\eta_\lambda(2)\,\zeta_{\rho'}(1)\,\zeta_\rho(2)$$
$$= V^{-1}\delta_{\lambda\lambda'}\delta_{\rho\rho'}[a_W\int e^{-i(\mathbf{k}-\mathbf{k}')\cdot\mathbf{z}}\,V(z)\,d^3z + a_M\int V(z)\,d^3z] \quad (40.11b)$$

When these expressions are inserted in Eq. (40.9) and the sums are converted to integrals, the expression for the energy becomes

$$E_0 + E_1 = \frac{3}{5}\frac{\hbar^2 k_F^2}{2m}A + \frac{V}{2}\frac{1}{(2\pi)^6}\int^{k_F}d^3k\int^{k_F}d^3k'\,\{16[a_W\,V(0)$$
$$+ a_M\int e^{-i(\mathbf{k}-\mathbf{k}')\cdot\mathbf{z}}\,V(z)\,d^3z] - 4[a_M\,V(0) + a_W\int e^{-i(\mathbf{k}-\mathbf{k}')\cdot\mathbf{z}}\,V(z)\,d^3z]\}$$
$$(40.12)$$

where $V(0) \equiv V(\mathbf{k} = 0)$.   The momentum integrals can be evaluated as follows:[1]

$$\int^{k_F} d^3k \, e^{i\mathbf{k}\cdot\mathbf{x}} = 4\pi \int_0^{k_F} k^2 j_0(kx) \, dk = \frac{4\pi k_F^3}{3} \frac{3j_1(k_F x)}{k_F x} \qquad (40.13)$$

Finally, the relation between the volume and the number of particles [Eq. (39.15)] allows us to rewrite the energy

$$\frac{E_0 + E_1}{A} = \frac{3}{5}\frac{\hbar^2 k_F^2}{2m} + \frac{k_F^3}{12\pi^2}\left\{ (4a_W - a_M) \int V(z) \, d^3z \right.$$

$$\left. + (4a_M - a_W) \int \left[\frac{3j_1(k_F z)}{k_F z}\right]^2 V(z) \, d^3z \right\} \qquad (40.14)$$

As $k_F \to \infty$, the integrand in the second integral goes to zero almost everywhere, and the first term thus can be expected to dominate at high densities.   For an attractive potential, it follows that the assembly collapses, that is, the energy becomes more and more negative as k_F increases unless the coefficients of the force satisfy the inequality

$$a_M > 4a_W \qquad \text{to prevent collapse} \qquad (40.15)$$

With the present nonsingular potential, Eq. (40.15) represents a necessary condition for the exchange force to provide sufficient repulsion in the odd angular-momentum states [recall Eqs. (40.10) and (38.19)].   If this inequality is not satisfied, the potential energy will always dominate the kinetic energy at high densities, because the potential energy varies as k_F^3 while the kinetic energy varies as k_F^2.   The true ground-state energy thus becomes more and more negative as the density increases.   In particular, the experimental nucleon-nucleon force is roughly of a Serber character [see Eq. (38.20)] with

$$a_W \approx a_M \qquad \text{experiment} \qquad (40.16)$$

and it is clear that saturation cannot occur for *nonsingular* Serber forces.
   A single-particle potential can be defined in the following way:

$$U_{\lambda\rho}(\mathbf{k}) \equiv \hbar\Sigma^\star_{(1)}(\mathbf{k})$$

$$= \sum_{\mathbf{k}'\lambda'\rho'}^{k_F} \{\langle \mathbf{k}\lambda\rho\mathbf{k}'\lambda'\rho'|V|\mathbf{k}\lambda\rho\mathbf{k}'\lambda'\rho'\rangle - \langle \mathbf{k}\lambda\rho\mathbf{k}'\lambda'\rho'|V|\mathbf{k}'\lambda'\rho'\mathbf{k}\lambda\rho\rangle\} \qquad (40.17)$$

This quantity represents the first-order interaction energy of a particle in the state $|\mathbf{k}\lambda\rho\rangle$ with all the other particles in the filled Fermi sea; it is the usual Hartree-Fock potential.   It may also be interpreted as the diagonal element in both spin and isospin of the lowest-order proper self-energy for the single-particle Green's function given by the first two diagrams shown in Fig. 11.3 (see the

[1] See L. I. Schiff, *op. cit.*, p. 86.

discussion in Sec. 11). The relevant matrix elements have already been evaluated in Eq. (40.11), and we find

$$U(\mathbf{k}) = \frac{1}{(2\pi)^3} \int^{k_F} d^3k' \{4[a_W \int V(z)\,d^3z + a_M \int e^{-i(\mathbf{k}-\mathbf{k}')\cdot\mathbf{z}} V(z)\,d^3z]$$

$$- [a_M \int V(z)\,d^3z + a_W \int e^{-i(\mathbf{k}-\mathbf{k}')\cdot\mathbf{z}} V(z)\,d^3z]\} \quad (40.18)$$

which is independent of spin and isospin. The angular integrals can be carried out as before:

$$U(\mathbf{k}) = \frac{k_F^3}{6\pi^2}\left[(4a_W - a_M) \int V(z)\,d^3z + (4a_M - a_W)\right.$$

$$\left. \times \int j_0(kz)\frac{3j_1(k_F z)}{k_F z} V(z)\,d^3z\right] \quad (40.19)$$

For small momenta, the spherical Bessel function appearing in the exchange integral can be expanded $j_0(kz) = 1 - k^2 z^2/6 + \cdots$, which leads to a parabolic single-particle potential at small k

$$U(\mathbf{k}) \approx U_0 + \frac{\hbar^2 k^2}{2m} U_1 + \cdots \qquad k \to 0 \qquad (40.20)$$

This quadratic momentum dependence may be used to define an effective mass through the relation

$$\epsilon_k = \epsilon_k^0 + U(\mathbf{k}) \approx \frac{\hbar^2 k^2}{2m}(1 + U_1) + U_0 \equiv U_0 + \frac{\hbar^2 k^2}{2m^*} \qquad (40.21)$$

where

$$\frac{m}{m^*} = 1 + U_1 \qquad (40.22)$$

In the present Hartree-Fock approximation, the momentum dependence of $U(\mathbf{k})$ and effective-mass correction arise entirely from the exchange term for the direct force V_W and from the direct term for the exchange force V_M.

In the opposite limit of large k, the spherical Bessel function oscillates rapidly, and the exchange integral vanishes. As a result, the asymptotic expression for the single-particle potential becomes

$$U(\mathbf{k}) \to \frac{k_F^3}{6\pi^2}(4a_W - a_M) \int V(z)\,d^3z \qquad k \to \infty \qquad (40.23)$$

The resulting single-particle potential is sketched in Fig. 40.1. Note that $U(\mathbf{k})$ automatically includes the Pauli principle since the particle in state $|\mathbf{k}\lambda\rho\rangle$ has been antisymmetrized with all the other particles in the medium. If $k < k_F$, then $U(\mathbf{k})$ represents the interaction between nucleons actually present in the Fermi sea. In contrast, if $k > k_F$, then $U(\mathbf{k})$ represents the interaction of an

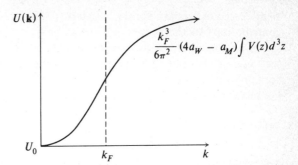

Fig. 40.1 Sketch of the single-particle potential $U(\mathbf{k})$ in Eq. (40.19). See also Eq. (40.23).

additional nucleon in nuclear matter; this quantity is just the optical potential seen by the added particle, properly including the possibility of exchange effects.

So far we have assumed a nonsingular nucleon-nucleon force of a Serber exchange nature and have calculated the ground-state energy shift to lowest order in the interaction. This result is very powerful since it gives a variational bound on the true ground-state energy and shows that the assembly is unstable against collapse with such a Serber force. We are now faced with two problems. First, how do we explain nuclear saturation? The answer is that the potential has been assumed to be nonsingular, whereas nuclear forces are actually singular. As seen in Sec. 38, there is evidence for a strong repulsion at short distances, which must be included in the calculation. The second problem is to understand the success of the independent-particle model of the nucleus. It is clear that the singular nuclear forces introduce important correlations. Nevertheless, the numerous triumphs of the single-particle shell model of the nucleus and the accurate description of scattering through a single-particle optical potential show that the independent-particle model frequently represents an excellent starting approximation in nuclear physics. In Sec. 41 we attempt to answer these questions with the *independent-pair approximation*, in which two-body correlations are treated in detail.

41☐INDEPENDENT-PAIR APPROXIMATION (BRUECKNER'S THEORY)[1,2]

The force between two nucleons is singular. This point is crucial, for it means that the nuclear potential has a fundamental effect on the two-body wave function,

[1] K. A. Brueckner, C. A. Levinson, and H. M. Mahmoud, *Phys. Rev.*, **95**:217 (1954); H. A. Bethe, *Phys. Rev.*, **103**:1353 (1956); K. A. Brueckner and J. L. Gammel, *Phys. Rev.*, **109**:1023 (1958); K. A. Brueckner, Theory of Nuclear Structure, in C. DeWitt (ed.), "The Many Body Problem," p. 47, John Wiley and Sons, Inc., New York, 1959.
[2] The present discussion of Brueckner's theory in terms of the independent-pair approximation is based on L. C. Gomes, J. D. Walecka, and V. F. Weisskopf, *Ann. Phys. (N.Y.)*, **3**:241 (1958) and J. D. Walecka and L. C. Gomes, *Ann. da Acad. Brasileira de Ciêncas*, **39**:361 (1967).

as discussed in detail in Sec. 11.   In terms of diagrams, we must retain the ladder contributions to the proper self-energy indicated in Fig. 11.3, and the corresponding contributions to the ground-state energy.   For simplicity, the present section describes the interacting pair with the Bethe-Goldstone equation, which contains all the essential physical features of the problem.   In Sec. 42 we discuss the relation to the Green's functions and the Galitskii equation of Sec. 11.

SELF-CONSISTENT BETHE-GOLDSTONE EQUATION[1]

The Bethe-Goldstone equation for two interacting nucleons in the Fermi sea was studied in Sec. 36.   The fundamental approximation was to concentrate on the two particles in question, omitting entirely the interaction of these particles

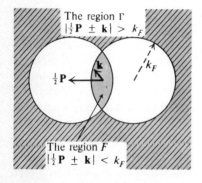

Fig. 41.1   Momentum regions in the Bethe-Goldstone equations.

with the rest of the Fermi sea.   Such a picture is clearly incomplete, and we now modify the energy of the interacting pair by including an effective single-particle potential $U(\mathbf{k})$ coming from the interaction with all the other particles.   In this way, the kinetic energy $\epsilon_{\mathbf{k}}^0$ is replaced by $\epsilon_{\mathbf{k}} = \epsilon_{\mathbf{k}}^0 + U(\mathbf{k})$, and the Bethe-Goldstone equations (36.4), (36.5), (36.15), and (36.16) become

$$\psi_{\mathbf{P},\mathbf{k}}(\mathbf{x}) = e^{i\mathbf{k}\cdot\mathbf{x}} + \int_{\Gamma} \frac{d^3 t}{(2\pi)^3} e^{i\mathbf{t}\cdot\mathbf{x}} \frac{1}{E_{\mathbf{P},\mathbf{k}} - \epsilon_{\frac{1}{2}\mathbf{P}+\mathbf{t}} - \epsilon_{\frac{1}{2}\mathbf{P}-\mathbf{t}}} \int d^3 y\, e^{-i\mathbf{t}\cdot\mathbf{y}}\, V(y)\psi_{\mathbf{P},\mathbf{k}}(\mathbf{y})$$

$$F \equiv |\tfrac{1}{2}\mathbf{P} \pm \mathbf{k}| < k_F \qquad \Gamma \equiv |\tfrac{1}{2}\mathbf{P} \pm \mathbf{t}| > k_F \tag{41.1}$$

$$\Delta\epsilon_{\mathbf{P},\mathbf{k}} \equiv E_{\mathbf{P},\mathbf{k}} - \epsilon_{\frac{1}{2}\mathbf{P}+\mathbf{k}} - \epsilon_{\frac{1}{2}\mathbf{P}-\mathbf{k}}$$

$$= V^{-1} \int d^3 x\, e^{-i\mathbf{k}\cdot\mathbf{x}}\, V(x)\psi_{\mathbf{P},\mathbf{k}}(\mathbf{x}) \tag{41.2}$$

where the excluded region in momentum space (that occupied by the other nucleons) is shown in Fig. 41.1.   These equations now contain an unknown function $U(\mathbf{k})$, which will be determined self-consistently from the interparticle potential $V(x)$ and the two-body wave function $\psi_{\mathbf{P},\mathbf{k}}(\mathbf{x})$.   The potential $V(x)$ will be taken as spin and isospin independent, but this is not an essential restriction.

[1] H. A. Bethe and J. Goldstone, *Proc. Roy. Soc.* (*London*), **A238**:551 (1957).

Consider a pair characterized by center-of-mass momentum $\hbar\mathbf{P}$ and relative momentum $\hbar\mathbf{k}$ as in Eq. (41.1). The interaction between the two nucleons mixes in two-particle states above the Fermi sea, which produces a corresponding shift in the two-particle energy given in Eq. (41.2). In the independent-pair approximation, the total energy shift of the whole system is obtained by summing over the energy shifts of all pairs of particles in the Fermi sea. (For two identical particles, for example $p\uparrow$ and $p\uparrow$, the wave function in Eq. (41.1) must, of course, be antisymmetrized.) The independent-pair approximation has the important feature that it automatically gives the energy shift of an interacting Fermi system exactly to second order in the potential. This result is evident from Fig. 9.22, since there are no other second-order terms in the ground-state energy (see the discussion in Secs. 9 and 42). In addition, the Bethe-Goldstone equation makes it possible to include the effect of the potential on the wave function to all orders. Equation (41.1) is still an integral equation for the wave function, and the potential appears only in the combination $V\psi$, which is well defined even for singular potentials.

To simplify the discussion and to gain some insight into the physical aspects of the problem, we shall assume that $U(\mathbf{k}) \approx U_0 + (\hbar^2 k^2/2m)\, U_1$ and use the effective-mass approximation. As seen in Fig. 40.1, this is a good approximation over limited regions of the spectrum, but it cannot be correct for all values of k. The single-particle energies therefore become

$$\epsilon_{\mathbf{k}} = \frac{\hbar^2 k^2}{2m} + U(\mathbf{k}) \approx \frac{\hbar^2 k^2}{2m} + U_0 + \frac{\hbar^2 k^2}{2m} U_1 \approx \frac{\hbar^2 k^2}{2m^*} + U_0 \qquad (41.3)$$

Although this approximation leads to a great simplification, it still contains an element of self-consistency, because m^* affects the two-body wave function through Eq. (41.1). It thus alters the single-particle spectrum $U(\mathbf{k})$, which is calculated as the total interaction energy of a particle in the state $|\mathbf{k}\lambda\rho\rangle$ with all the other particles. The constant potential U_0 cancels identically in Eqs. (41.1) and (41.2) because these relations only involve energy differences. In the effective-mass approximation, it follows that the self-consistent Bethe-Goldstone equations reduce to those studied in Sec. 36 [Eqs. (36.15) and (36.16)], but with the interaction potential now given by

$$v(x) = 2m_{\text{red}}^* \hbar^{-2} V(|\mathbf{x}_1 - \mathbf{x}_2|) \qquad (41.4)$$

where $m_{\text{red}}^* = m^*/2$ is the reduced effective mass.

The energy shift given by the Bethe-Goldstone equation in Eq. (41.2) varies as V^{-1}. Since $\kappa^2 - t^2$ in the denominator of Eq. (36.15) cannot vanish except close to the Fermi surface, we may make the replacement $\kappa^2 \to k^2$ in the equation for the wave function. This approximation is essentially exact for particles deep in the Fermi sea; as we have seen in the discussion of the Cooper pairs, however, it may be incorrect close to the Fermi surface. Indeed, it was

just the appearance of κ^2 in the denominator in Eq. (36.15) that led to the eigen-value equation with the exceptional (bound Cooper-pair) solution. We show in Sec. 43 that the gap Δ in nuclear matter is very small.[1]   For this reason, the possibility of bound pairs may be safely neglected in discussing the binding energy and density of nuclear matter.

We shall now examine the solutions to the Bethe-Goldstone equation. The effective-mass approximation allows us to convert the integral equation (41.1) into a differential equation by applying the operator $\nabla^2 + k^2$:

$$(\nabla^2 + k^2)\,\psi(\mathbf{x}) = \int_{\Gamma} \frac{d^3 t}{(2\pi)^3}\, e^{i\mathbf{t}\cdot\mathbf{x}} \int d^3 y\, e^{-i\mathbf{t}\cdot\mathbf{y}}\, v(y)\,\psi(\mathbf{y})$$

$$= v(x)\,\psi(\mathbf{x}) - \int_{\bar{\Gamma}} \frac{d^3 t}{(2\pi)^3}\, e^{i\mathbf{t}\cdot\mathbf{x}} \int d^3 y\, e^{-i\mathbf{t}\cdot\mathbf{y}}\, v(y)\,\psi(\mathbf{y}) \qquad (41.5)$$

where $\bar{\Gamma}$ is the complement of the region Γ in Fig. 41.1 ($\bar{\Gamma}$ is defined as the union of the regions $|\tfrac{1}{2}\mathbf{P} \pm \mathbf{t}| < k_F$).   We start by considering the simplest case ($\mathbf{P} = 0$) and look for s-wave solutions to this equation in the form

$$\psi(x) = x^{-1} u(x) \qquad (41.6)$$

The s-wave solutions are the only ones that penetrate to small relative distances where the effects of the singular potential are strongest.   Inserting Eq. (41.6) into Eq. (41.5) yields

$$\left(\frac{d^2}{dx^2} + k^2\right) u(x) = v(x)\,u(x) - \int_0^{\infty} \chi(x,y)\, v(y)\, u(y)\, dy \qquad (41.7)$$

where the kernel appearing in this s-wave Bethe-Goldstone equation is given by

$$\chi(x,y) = \frac{2xy}{\pi} \int_0^{k_F} j_0(tx)\, j_0(ty)\, t^2\, dt$$

$$= \frac{1}{\pi}\left[\frac{\sin k_F(x-y)}{x-y} - \frac{\sin k_F(x+y)}{x+y}\right] \qquad (41.8)$$

SOLUTION FOR A NONSINGULAR SQUARE-WELL POTENTIAL

As a first approximation, we shall consider a nonsingular square-well potential that fits the low-energy $^1S_0$ scattering.   Our approximate potential is sketched in Fig. 41.2.   In accordance with the previous discussion, its parameters are to

---

[1] This is similar to the situation in a metal, where $\Delta/k_B \approx 10°$K, $\epsilon_F/k_B \approx 10^4°$K.   Nevertheless, there is a fundamental distinction between the two systems, for we are here interested in an absolute determination of the bulk properties of nuclear matter, rather than the very small energy difference $E_s - E_n$ evaluated in Eq. (37.53).   This difference in attitude reflects the physical fact that the transition between a normal and superconducting metal is readily observed and studied, while there is no obvious way even to decide whether a nucleus is normal or super-conducting.

be determined from the behavior of two nucleons interacting in free space. At zero energy, the relative wave function inside the potential is given by

$$u_{in}(x) \propto \sin [(2m_{red} V_0 \hbar^{-2})^{\frac{1}{2}} x]$$

Since the $^1S_0$ potential has a bound state at essentially zero energy, there must be exactly a quarter wavelength inside the potential (see Fig. 41.2), which provides the condition

$$(2m_{red} V_0 \hbar^{-2})^{\frac{1}{2}} d = \tfrac{1}{2}\pi$$

The free-nucleon reduced mass $m_{red} = m/2$ can be used to rewrite this result as

$$V_0 = \frac{\hbar^2 \pi^2}{4md^2} \qquad\qquad (41.9)$$

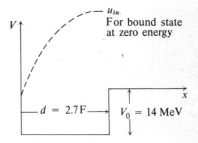

Fig. 41.2 Nonsingular square-well potential fit to low-energy $^1S_0$ scattering.

In addition, if a square well has a bound state at zero energy, then the effective range is equal to the range of the potential (see Prob. 11.1)

$$r_0 = d \qquad \text{effective range} \qquad\qquad (41.10)$$

We shall take the singlet effective range obtained from p–p scattering data[1]

$$^1r_0 = 2.7 \text{ F} \qquad\qquad (41.11)$$

and the depth of the nonsingular square-well potential becomes

$$V_0 = 14 \text{ MeV} \qquad\qquad (41.12)$$

Note that our approximate nuclear potential is *actually very weak*:

$$V_0 \ll \epsilon_F^0 = \frac{\hbar^2 k_F^2}{2m} = 42 \text{ MeV} \qquad\qquad (41.13)$$

where ϵ_F^0 is computed with the Fermi momentum appropriate to nuclear matter given in Eq. (39.17).

In the special case of the nonsingular square-well potential, it is easier to calculate the change $\Delta\psi$ in the wave function directly from Eq. (41.1) rather than

[1] M. A. Preston, *op. cit.*, p. 33.

from Eq. (41.7).   Consider the limit $k \to 0$ and assume initially that $\Delta\psi$ is small.
It is then permissible to set

$$\psi(x) = x^{-1} u(x) \approx j_0(kx) \to 1 \qquad k \to 0 \tag{41.14}$$

on the right side of Eq. (41.1); the corresponding modification of the wave function
is given by

$$\Delta\psi = \lim_{k \to 0} \left[\frac{u(x)}{x} - j_0(kx) \right] = \frac{u(x)}{x} - 1$$

$$= \frac{2v_0}{\pi} \int_{k_F}^{\infty} dt\, j_0(tx) \int_0^d j_0(ty)\, y^2 \, dy \tag{41.15}$$

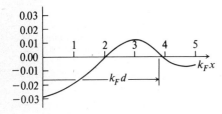

Fig. 41.3 Modification $\Delta\psi_{sw}$ [Eq. (41.17)] of
the s-wave two-body wave function caused by
the potential in Fig. 41.2. This calculation is
for a pair with $\mathbf{k} = \mathbf{P} = 0$ in nuclear matter.
(The authors wish to thank E. Moniz for
preparing this figure.)

The y integral can be evaluated explicitly

$$\int_0^d j_0(ty)\, y^2 \, dy = d^3 \frac{j_1(td)}{td} \tag{41.16}$$

Thus the modification of the wave function due to the nonsingular square-well
potential is

$$\Delta\psi_{sw} = \frac{2v_0}{\pi k_F^2} (k_F d)^2 \int_{k_F d}^{\infty} \frac{d\rho}{\rho}\, j_1(\rho)\, j_0\!\left(\rho\frac{x}{d}\right) \tag{41.17}$$

where a dimensionless integration variable has been introduced and $k_F d = 3.8$.
The dimensionless potential is given by

$$\frac{v_0}{k_F^2} = \frac{V_0}{\hbar^2 k_F^2 / 2m_{\mathrm{red}}^*} = \frac{m^*}{m} \frac{\pi^2}{4(k_F d)^2} = 0.17 \frac{m^*}{m} \approx 0.10 \tag{41.18}$$

where we have used the value $m^*/m \approx 0.6$, which is derived below.   The central
result of this calculation is that

$$\Delta\psi_{sw} \ll 1 \tag{41.19}$$

Hence *the attractive potential has almost no effect on the two-particle wave function*
$u(x)/x = 1 + \Delta\psi$ [see Eq. (41.15)].   There are two reasons for this behavior.
First, the large Fermi momentum makes it difficult for the nonsingular potential
to excite the particles out of the Fermi sea, and second $m^*/m < 1$.   The function

$\Delta\psi_{sw}$ of Eq. (41.17) is plotted in Fig. 41.3, along with the range of the square-well potential itself. We see that the correlations induced by the potential oscillate with wavenumber $\approx k_F$ and fall off for large distances like x^{-2}. In conclusion, the long-range attractive part of the nucleon-nucleon force scarcely affects the two-particle wave function; instead, the modification of the wave function arises from the hard core combined with any strong short-range attractive potential lying just outside of the hard core.[1]

SOLUTION FOR A PURE HARD-CORE POTENTIAL

The Bethe-Goldstone equation (41.7) can also be solved for a pure hard-core potential, as originally done by Bethe and Goldstone.[2] It is convenient first to rewrite Eqs. (41.7) and (41.8) in terms of dimensionless variables

$$r - k_F x \qquad r' = k_F y \qquad K = \frac{k}{k_F}$$

$$\qquad\qquad\qquad\qquad\qquad\qquad\qquad\qquad\qquad (41.20)$$

$$v(r) = \frac{v(x)}{k_F^2} = \frac{V(x)}{\hbar^2 k_F^2 / 2m_{\text{red}}^*} \qquad u(r) = k_F u(x)$$

which gives

$$\left(\frac{d^2}{dr^2} + K^2\right) u(r) = v(r) u(r) - \int_0^\infty \chi(r,r') v(r') u(r') \, dr' \qquad (41.21)$$

$$\chi(r,r') = \frac{1}{\pi}\left[\frac{\sin(r - r')}{r - r'} - \frac{\sin(r + r')}{r + r'}\right] \qquad (41.22)$$

As indicated in Fig. 41.4, the hard core introduces a discontinuity into the slope of the wave function at the (dimensionless) distance c. This result is easily verified by examining a barrier of finite height and then letting the barrier height become infinite (see Prob. 11.5). Since the wave function must vanish inside the infinite potential, the product vu can thus be written

$$v(r) u(r) = \mathscr{A}\delta(r - c) + w(r)\theta(c - r) \qquad (41.23)$$

Here the first term gives a finite discontinuity in the slope of the wave function at the core boundary, as can be seen by integrating the Bethe-Goldstone equation (41.5) across the core boundary. The remaining term $w(r)$ cannot contribute outside the core, where the potential vanishes, but it may be finite inside the core region because of the limiting process $v \to \infty$, $u \to 0$. This extra "leak" term must be chosen so that

$$u'' + K^2 u = 0 \qquad r < c \qquad (41.24)$$

---

[1] So far only the ${}^1S_0$ attractive well has been considered. In fact, this will suffice for the present analysis of nuclear matter [see the discussion following Eq. (41.39)].

[2] H. A. Bethe and J. Goldstone, *loc. cit.*

When Eq. (41.23) is combined with Eq. (41.21), the condition of Eq. (41.24) becomes

$$\mathscr{A}^{-1} w(r) = \chi(r,c) + \mathscr{A}^{-1} \int_0^c \chi(r,r') w(r') dr' \qquad r < c \tag{41.25}$$

The remaining analysis can be simplified by noting that the dimensionless constant c is small. For example, at the observed density in nuclear matter

$$c = 1.42 \text{ F}^{-1} \times 0.4 \text{ F} = 0.57 \tag{41.26}$$

where a hard core of range 0.4 F has been assumed. In the limit where both of its arguments are small, the kernel in the s-wave Bethe-Goldstone equation becomes

$$\chi(r,r') \to \frac{2rr'}{3\pi} \qquad r < c, \ r' < c \tag{41.27}$$

Equation (41.25) shows that $w(r)$ is of order c^2, while any integral over $w(r)$ will be of order c^3. Consequently, the leak in Eq. (41.23) can be neglected for small c, and a combination of Eqs. (41.21) to (41.23) yields

$$\left(\frac{d^2}{dr^2} + K^2 \right) u(r) \approx \mathscr{A} [\delta(r - c) - \chi(r,c)]$$

$$= \mathscr{A} \frac{2rc}{\pi} \int_1^\infty j_0(tr) j_0(tc) t^2 dt$$

$$\equiv F(r) \tag{41.28}$$

which defines $F(r)$. It is clear that the term $\chi(r,c)$ serves to cancel those Fourier components of $\delta(r - c)$ that lie inside the Fermi sphere [see Eq. (41.8)]. The right side of this equation is a known function of r, and the only unknown quantity is the normalization constant $\mathscr{A}$. Since $u(0) = 0$, the general solution of this equation is given by

$$u(r) = \frac{1}{K} \int_0^r \sin [K(r - s)] F(s) ds \tag{41.29}$$

for it is easily verified directly from Eq. (41.29) that

$$u''(r) + K^2 u(r) = F(r) \tag{41.30}$$

If the sine on the right side of Eq. (41.29) is expanded with trigonometric identities, the solution to the s-wave Bethe-Goldstone equation becomes

$$u(r) = \frac{\sin Kr}{K} \int_0^r \cos Ks \, F(s) ds - \frac{\cos Kr}{K} \int_0^r \sin Ks \, F(s) ds \tag{41.31}$$

where F is taken from Eq. (41.28).

We shall now prove an important result

$$\int_0^\infty \sin Ks\, F(s)\, ds = 0 \tag{41.32}$$

This follows immediately from the detailed form of $F(s)$ in Eq. (41.28):

$$\frac{1}{K}\int_0^\infty ds \sin Ks\, F(s) = \frac{2\mathscr{A}c}{\pi}\int_1^\infty dt\, t^2 j_0(tc)\int_0^\infty ds\, s^2 j_0(Ks) j_0(ts)$$

$$= \frac{2\mathscr{A}c}{\pi}\int_1^\infty dt\, t^2 j_0(tc)\frac{\pi}{2Kt}\delta(K - t)$$

$$= 0 \tag{41.33}$$

The last integral vanishes identically because t lies outside the Fermi sphere while K lies inside, as illustrated in Fig. 41.1. The foregoing derivation shows the importance of the filled Fermi sea, which removes the components $t < 1$ from the intermediate states. It is clear that this result follows quite generally from the form of the right side of Eq. (41.5). Equation (41.32) ensures that the exact solution $r^{-1}u(r)$ [Eq. (41.31)] is proportional to the unperturbed solution $j_0(Kr)$ as $r \to \infty$, so that the s-wave phase shift is zero. If the wave function is to be normalized in a box of volume V, it must approach a plane wave with unit amplitude as the relative coordinate gets large:

$$\psi(\mathbf{x}) \to e^{i\mathbf{k}\cdot\mathbf{x}} \qquad x \to \infty \tag{41.34}$$

This condition implies that $u(x)/x = u(r)/r \to j_0(Kr)$ as $r \to \infty$, and the s-wave normalization condition in Eq. (41.31) becomes

$$\int_0^\infty \cos Ks\, F(s)\, ds = 1 \tag{41.35}$$

Substituting the right side of Eq. (41.28), we obtain the overall normalization constant $\mathscr{A}$

$$\mathscr{A} = \left[\cos Kc - \int_0^\infty \cos Ks\, \chi(s,c)\, ds\right]^{-1} \tag{41.36}$$

Equations (41.28), (41.31), and (41.36) completely determine the s-wave relative wave function for a dilute collection of hard spheres. One typical case is plotted in Fig. 41.4. This result exhibits several interesting features. As

Fig. 41.4 The Bethe-Goldstone wave function [Eqs. (41.31), (41.28), and (41.36)] for an s-wave pair with $\mathbf{k} = \mathbf{P} = 0$ interacting through a hard-core potential in nuclear matter. The lower limit on the integrals in Eq. (41.31) was taken as c so that $u(c) \equiv 0$. The wave function for a noninteracting pair is shown by the dashed line and the cross-over point defines the healing distance. Also indicated are the average interparticle distance $k_F l$ [Eq. (41.38)] and the range $k_F d$ of the potential in Fig. 41.5.

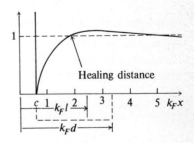

expected, the relative wave function vanishes at the hard-core surface. It then very rapidly approaches the unperturbed value of 1, crossing over that value at a "healing distance" of about

$$k_F x \approx 1.9 \qquad \text{healing distance} \tag{41.37}$$

By examining the more general expression arising from Eq. (41.5) [see Eqs. (41.7) and (41.62)], we can show that this healing distance is essentially independent of k and P.[1] Furthermore the correlation function, defined by $\Delta \psi_c = u(r)/r - j_0(Kr)$, is also nearly independent of k and P. Beyond the healing distance, the Bethe-Goldstone wave function oscillates around the unperturbed solution, approaching it with damped oscillations as $k_F x \to \infty$. The average interparticle distance l in nuclear matter, defined by the expression $1/l^3 \equiv N/V = 2k_F^3/3\pi^2$, has also been indicated in Fig. 41.4. The corresponding dimensionless parameter characterizing the interparticle distance in nuclear matter becomes

$$k_F l = \left(\frac{3\pi^2}{2}\right)^{\frac{1}{3}} = 2.46 \qquad \text{interparticle distance} \tag{41.38}$$

and we note the interesting result that the healing distance of Eq. (41.37) is less than the interparticle spacing of Eq. (41.38), as illustrated in Fig. 41.4. By the time that one of the two colliding particles has arrived at another neighboring particle, the "wound" in the wave function of the original interacting pair has healed back to its plane-wave value. For subsequent collisions, it follows that the colliding particles can again be assumed to approach each other in relative plane-wave states. This result justifies the independent-pair approximation.

   These observations also provide a simple qualitative basis for the independent-particle model of nuclear matter. The Pauli principle suppresses the correlations introduced by the hard core and restricts its effects to short distances. In particular, the hard core cannot give rise to long-range scattering because all available energy-conserving states are already occupied. Except for the short-range correlations, a nucleon may therefore be assumed to move through nuclear matter in a plane-wave state. The dominant role of the exclusion principle in explaining how an independent-particle model can describe a dilute strongly interacting Fermi system at or near its ground state was first emphasized by Weisskopf.[2]

PROPERTIES OF NUCLEAR MATTER WITH A "REALISTIC" POTENTIAL

We now combine the previous results to study a more realistic model of nuclear matter, where the two-nucleon potential consists of a hard core plus an attractive square-well potential shown in Fig. 41.5. This potential grossly oversimplifies

[1] J. D. Walecka and L. C. Gomes, *loc. cit.*
[2] V. F. Weisskopf, *Helv. Phys. Acta,* **23:**187 (1950); *Science,* **113:**101 (1951).

the actual nucleon-nucleon force discussed in Sec. 38; thus it can only provide a qualitative, or at best semiquantitative, description of the properties of nuclear matter. The model potential is given by

$$
V = \begin{cases}
+\infty & r < b \\
-V_0 \tfrac{1}{2}(1 + P_M) & b < r < b + b_w \\
0 & b + b_w < r
\end{cases}
\tag{41.39}
$$

with a hard core in all states (we shall calculate the nuclear energy both with and without a hard core in the odd-l states) and an attractive Serber force as indicated. We have here neglected the difference between the $^1S_0$ and $^3S_1$

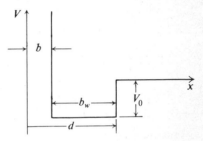

Fig. 41.5 Hard-core square-well potential.

potentials, which can be justified if this difference arises from a tensor interaction (as is true, for example, in the one-pion exchange potential). The ground-state expectation value of a tensor force with Serber exchange nature vanishes in a noninteracting Fermi gas because the spin average of the tensor operator $\tfrac{1}{4} tr_1 tr_2 S_{12}$ is zero and there are no exchange matrix elements. Thus the effect of the tensor force is much reduced in nuclear matter.

The condition that the potential in Eq. (41.39) have a bound state at zero energy is readily derived as

$$
V_0 = \frac{\hbar^2 \pi^2}{4mb_w^2}
\tag{41.40}
$$

which again ensures the correct $^1S_0$ scattering length. Furthermore, the effective range r_0 for such a potential with a zero-energy bound state is given by (see Prob. 11.1)

$$
r_0 = 2b + b_w
\tag{41.41}
$$

With a hard core of 0.4 F, the parameters of the combined hard-core square-well potential become

$$
b_w = 1.9 \text{ F} \qquad b = 0.4 \text{ F}
\tag{41.42}
$$

while the total range d of the potential is characterized by

$$
k_F(b + b_w) \equiv k_F d = 3.27
\tag{41.43}
$$

and is indicated in Fig. 41.4.   From the previous discussion, it is clear that the attractive part of this potential again has little effect on the wave function, tending to enhance its value slightly within the potential.   As a result, the correlation function $\Delta\psi$ is essentially that of the hard core alone and is of the type shown in Fig. 41.4.

To compute the interaction energy of a pair of nucleons in nuclear matter, we shall evaluate the energy shift $\Delta\epsilon_{P,k}$ with the Bethe-Goldstone equation (41.2)

$$\Delta\epsilon_{P,k} = V^{-1} \int e^{-ik\cdot x}(V_a + V_c)\,\psi_{P,k}(x)\,d^3x \tag{41.44}$$

Here V_a is the attractive part of the potential in Eq. (41.39) and V_c is the hard core.   In the independent-pair approximation, the single-particle potential and total energy of the assembly are then determined from $\Delta\epsilon_{P,k}$ by the relations

$$U(k_1\lambda_1\rho_1) = \sum_{k_2\lambda_2\rho_2}^{k_F} \Delta\epsilon_{P,k} \tag{41.45}$$

$$\Delta E = \tfrac{1}{2} \sum_{k_1\lambda_1\rho_1}^{k_F} \sum_{k_2\lambda_2\rho_2}^{k_F} \Delta\epsilon_{P,k} \tag{41.46}$$

where the sums run over the interior of the Fermi sphere.   The self-consistency of the theory is now particularly evident, because the single-particle energies $\epsilon_{\frac{1}{2}P\pm k}$ appearing in Eqs. (41.1) and (41.2) are evaluated with Eqs. (41.44) and (41.45).

Since the hard core is most important in determining the solution, it will be a good approximation to replace the exact wave function in Eq. (41.44) by that derived in the pure hard-core problem:

$$\psi \approx \psi_c \tag{41.47}$$

This substitution gives the following expression for the energy shift

$$\Delta\epsilon_{P,k} = V^{-1} \int e^{-ik\cdot x} V_c \psi_c(x)\,d^3x + V^{-1} \int e^{-ik\cdot x} V_a \psi_c(x)\,d^3x \tag{41.48}$$

For the present discussion we shall, in addition, approximate the hard-core solution in the region of the attractive well by a plane wave (Born approximation)

$$\psi_c \approx e^{ik\cdot x} \qquad \text{in attractive potential, } b < r < b + b_w \tag{41.49}$$

Although the relative wave function vanishes inside the hard core (see Fig. 41.4), it grows rapidly for $r > b$ and exceeds the plane-wave value within the range of the potential.   Since the weighting factor in the integral is $r^2 dr$, the Born approximation should provide a reasonable estimate of the attractive energy.   Note that this is true only for the very simplified potential used here. A more realistic model, including a strong attraction concentrated outside the hard core, would require a more sophisticated treatment.   For example, Eq. (41.48) could be evaluated with no further approximation or, in principle, the

coupled problem of the hard core plus nearby attraction could be solved exactly. (One tractable approach to this combined problem can be found in the work of Moszkowski and Scott.[1])

With Eqs. (41.48) and (41.49), the energy shift of an interacting pair reduces to the sum of the energy shift for a pure hard-sphere gas and an attractive contribution calculated with the independent-particle model in Born approximation

$$\Delta\epsilon_{P,k} = \Delta\epsilon_{P,k}^c + \Delta\epsilon_{P,k}^a \text{ (independent-particle model)} \tag{41.50}$$

The latter contribution has been discussed in Sec. 40, where we calculated both the energy shift of the whole assembly [Eq. (40.14)] and the single-particle potential [Eq. (40.19)] for a purely attractive interparticle potential. This last quantity is readily evaluated with the parameters appropriate for Fig. 41.5 and Eq. (41.39)

$$U^a(\mathbf{k}) = -\frac{V_0 k_F^3}{3\pi}\left[(d^3 - b^3) + \frac{9}{k_F}\int_b^d j_0(kz)\, j_1(k_F z)\, z\, dz\right] \tag{41.51}$$

because a Serber force requires $a_W = a_M = \frac{1}{2}$, and the integration runs from the hard-core range b to the outer edge of the attractive potential $b + b_w = d$ (see Fig. 41.5). It is evident that U^a is isotropic and depends only on k^2.

We are now ready to compute the contribution of the attractive interaction to the effective mass. As indicated previously, a single effective mass cannot approximate the single-particle spectrum over the whole range of k^2, and it is therefore necessary to choose the relevant region in momentum space. One possibility is to assert that the most important virtual transitions occur near the Fermi surface, choosing m^* to fit the value and slope of the single-particle spectrum at k_F (compare Sec. 29). If the single-particle potential is approximated near a general value k_0 as

$$U(k^2) \approx U(k_0^2) + \frac{\hbar^2}{2m}(k^2 - k_0^2)\, U_1 \tag{41.52}$$

then the corresponding effective mass becomes

$$\frac{m^*}{m} = \frac{1}{1 + U_1} \tag{41.53}$$

To reproduce the spectrum near the Fermi surface ($k_0 = k_F$), U_1 must be chosen as

$$U_1 = \frac{m}{\hbar^2 k_F}\frac{dU}{dk}\bigg|_{k=k_F} \tag{41.54}$$

[1] S. A. Moszkowski and B. L. Scott, *Ann. Phys.* (*N. Y.*), **11**:65 (1960).

This expression can be evaluated directly from Eq. (41.51) and we find[1]

$$U_1 = \frac{3}{2\pi} \frac{V_0}{\hbar^2 k_F^2/2m} \left[\frac{\rho^3}{2} (j_1^2(\rho) - j_0(\rho) j_2(\rho)) \right]_{k_F b}^{k_F d} \tag{41.55}$$

where the quantity in brackets is to be evaluated between the indicated limits. Numerical values for the simplified potential of Eq. (41.39) are given in Table 41.1.

Table 41.1   Effective mass at $k = k_F$ and $k = 0$ for two nuclear densities

k_F	$U_1(k_F)$‡	$(m^*/m)_{k=k_F}$	$U_1(0)$§	$(m^*/m)_{k=0}$
1.25 F^{-1}	0.54	0.65	0.96	0.51
1.48 F^{-1}	0.54	0.65	1.2	0.45

‡ See Eq. (41.55).
§ See Eq. (41.56).

Another way of choosing the effective mass is to expand the single-particle potential about $k^2 = 0$; substituting $j_0(kz) \approx 1 - k^2 z^2/6$ in Eq. (41.51) immediately yields

$$U_1 = \frac{1}{2\pi} \frac{V_0}{\hbar^2 k_F^2/2m} [\rho^3 j_2(\rho)]_{k_F b}^{k_F d} \tag{41.56}$$

Numerical values computed from this expression are also shown in Table 41.1. We note from Table 41.1 that the effective mass is rather insensitive to changes in the density about the equilibrium value, and that the effective mass at the bottom of the Fermi sea is slightly smaller than the effective mass at the Fermi surface.

So far, the hard core has been neglected entirely in evaluating m^*. To justify this omission, we recall the discussion of the Galitskii equation where the hard core does not affect the effective mass to first order in $c = k_F b$; to a good approximation, it follows that the effective mass arises solely from the attractive well and exchange nature of the interaction. In fact, Eq. (11.68) shows that the leading contribution of a hard core $c = 0.57$ to the Fermi-surface effective mass of an assembly of identical spin-$\frac{1}{2}$ particles is obtained from $\Delta U_1^c \approx -(8c^2/15\pi^2) \times (7\ln 2 - 1) = -0.067$, whereas the same hard core, if present in the p state, contributes the following amount to U_1 (Prob. 4.6) $\Delta U_1^c \approx +c^3/\pi = +0.059$.

[1] The necessary integrals of the spherical Bessel functions can be found in L. I. Schiff, op. cit., p. 86.

These contributions tend to cancel, and the correction is indeed small.[1] We shall henceforth neglect the hard core in evaluating m^*. This simplifies our present discussion of nuclear matter considerably, as the self-consistency condition is no longer a problem. The effective mass is now determined from Eqs. (41.51) to (41.54), which are *independent* of the value of m^*.

It is now possible to estimate the nuclear binding energy from Eq. (41.46). The contribution $E^{(a)}$ of the attractive well is given in Eq. (40.14); it may be evaluated just as in Eq. (41.51) and gives

$$
\frac{E^{(a)}}{A} = -\frac{V_0 k_F^3}{6\pi} \left[(d^3 - b^3) + \frac{27}{k_F^2} \int_b^d j_1^2(k_F z)\, dz \right]
$$

$$
= -\frac{V_0}{6\pi} \left[\rho^3 + 9 \left\{ \mathrm{Si}\,(2\rho) + \frac{\cos 2\rho - 3}{2\rho} + \frac{\sin 2\rho}{\rho^2} + \frac{1}{2\rho^3}(\cos 2\rho - 1) \right\} \right]_{k_F b}^{k_F d}
$$

$$
\tag{41.57}
$$

where Si denotes the sine-integral function $\mathrm{Si}(x) = \int_0^x d\lambda \sin\lambda/\lambda$. In addition, there is the original energy $E^{(f)}$ of the noninteracting Fermi assembly

$$
\frac{E^{(f)}}{A} = \frac{3}{5} \frac{\hbar^2 k_F^2}{2m}
$$

$$
\tag{41.58}
$$

Note that this expression contains m and not m^*, because m^* is merely an oversimplified way of treating the single-particle potential $U(\mathbf{k})$ that is needed in evaluating the *interaction* energy.

The final contribution to the nuclear binding energy arises from the hard core in Eq. (41.50). This quantity can be computed from the solution to the Bethe-Goldstone equation. The energy shift of a pair in the hard-core problem follows from Eq. (41.2)

$$
\Delta\epsilon_{P,k} = V^{-1} \langle \mathbf{k} | V_c | \psi_{P,k} \rangle
$$

$$
= V^{-1} \int e^{-i\mathbf{k}\cdot\mathbf{x}} V_c \psi_{P,k}(\mathbf{x})\, d^3x
$$

$$
\tag{41.59}
$$

As discussed in detail in Sec. 11, only s waves contribute to the total hard-core interaction energy $E^{(c)}$ through order c^2. For s waves, it follows from Eq. (41.23) that

$$
\frac{2m^*_{\mathrm{red}}}{\hbar^2 k_F^2} V_c u_{P,k}(r) = \mathscr{A}\delta(r - c) + w(r)
$$

$$
\approx \mathscr{A}\delta(r - c)
$$

$$
\tag{41.60}
$$

----

[1] The four *spin* degrees of freedom for nuclear matter lead to an additional factor of 3 and 5/3, respectively, in these relations. An examination of the single-particle potential [Eq. (41.45)] derived from Eq. (41.65) confirms that this correction is small for nuclear matter. When this hard-core energy is included in $U(\mathbf{k})$, the resulting effective mass at the Fermi surface is $m^*/m = 0.68$ for $k_F = 1.25$ F^{-1} (J. D. Walecka and L. C. Gomes, *loc. cit.*), which should be compared with the value $m^*/m = 0.65$ in Table 41.1 coming from the attractive well alone.

where the second line is obtained by noting that the s-wave leak contributes to the total energy only in order c^4. The overall normalization constant is given by Eq. (41.36)

$$\mathscr{A}(\mathbf{P},K) = \left[\cos Kc - \int_0^\infty \cos Ks\, \chi_P(s,c)\, ds\right]^{-1} \tag{41.61}$$

where we now consider the general case of an interacting pair with center-of-mass momentum $\mathbf{P}$ (here and henceforth in this section it is assumed that $\mathbf{P}$ is dimensionless and measured in units of k_F). It is evident from Eq. (41.5) that the generalization of Eqs. (41.8) and (41.22) to $\mathbf{P} \neq 0$ is

$$\chi_P(r,r') = \frac{2rr'}{\pi} \int_{\bar{\Gamma}} j_0(tr)\, j_0(tr')\, \frac{d\Omega_t}{4\pi}\, t^2\, dt \tag{41.62}$$

where $\bar{\Gamma}$ is the complement of Γ shown in Fig. 41.1. The angular integration in Eq. (41.62) gives

$$\int_{\bar{\Gamma}} \frac{d\Omega_t}{4\pi} = \begin{cases} 1 & \text{for } t \leqslant \left[1 - \left(\frac{P}{2}\right)^2\right]^{\frac{1}{2}} \\ 1 - \dfrac{(P/2)^2 + t^2 - 1}{Pt} & \text{for } \left[1 - \left(\frac{P}{2}\right)^2\right]^{\frac{1}{2}} \leqslant t \leqslant 1 + \dfrac{P}{2} \end{cases} \tag{41.63}$$

while the integral in Eq. (41.61) can be performed with the relation

$$\int_0^\infty \cos Ks \sin ts\, ds = \mathscr{P}\, \frac{t}{t^2 - K^2}$$

where $\mathscr{P}$ is the Cauchy principal value. Thus we find

$$\mathscr{A}(\mathbf{P},K) = \left[\cos Kc - \frac{2c}{\pi}\mathscr{P}\int_{\bar{\Gamma}} \frac{j_0(tc)}{t^2 - K^2}\, \frac{d\Omega_t}{4\pi}\, t^2\, dt\right]^{-1} \tag{41.64}$$

A combination of Eqs. (41.59), (41.60), and (41.64) yields

$$\Delta\epsilon_{\mathbf{P},\mathbf{k}}^{(l=0)} \approx \frac{4\pi c}{k_F^3 V}\, j_0(Kc)\, \mathscr{A}(\mathbf{P},K)\, \frac{\hbar^2 k_F^2}{2m_{\text{red}}^*}\,(1 - \delta_{\lambda_1 \lambda_2}\delta_{\rho_1 \rho_2}) \tag{41.65}$$

The factor $1 - \delta_{\lambda_1 \lambda_2}\delta_{\rho_1 \rho_2}$ arises from the antisymmetrization of the wave function for particles of identical spins and isospins and prevents such particles from being in relative s states. The hard-core interaction energy is therefore given by Eq. (41.46) as

$$E_{l=0}^{(c)} = \tfrac{1}{2} \sum_{\mathbf{k}_1 \lambda_1 \rho_1}^{k_F} \sum_{\mathbf{k}_2 \lambda_2 \rho_2}^{k_F} \Delta\epsilon_{\mathbf{P},\mathbf{k}}^{(l=0)} \tag{41.66}$$

Converting the sums to integrals and using Eqs. (41.65) and (39.15), we find

$$\frac{E^{(c)}_{l=0}}{A} \approx \frac{\hbar^2 k_F^2}{2m^*}\frac{2c}{\pi} \iint\limits_{(F)} \frac{d^3K_1}{(4\pi/3)}\frac{d^3K_2}{(4\pi/3)} j_0(Kc)\mathscr{A}(\mathbf{P},\mathbf{K})$$

$$= \frac{\hbar^2 k_F^2}{2m^*}\frac{2c}{\pi} \iint\limits_{(F)} \frac{d^3K}{(4\pi/3)}\frac{d^3P}{(4\pi/3)} j_0(Kc)\mathscr{A}(\mathbf{P},\mathbf{K}) \tag{41.67}$$

where F is defined by the intersection of the two Fermi spheres (compare Fig. 41.1) and $\mathscr{A}(\mathbf{P},\mathbf{K})$ by Eqs. (41.64) and (41.63). The resulting value of this definite integral obtained by numerical methods is shown in Fig. 41.6 as a function of $c = k_F b$. If Eq. (41.67) is expanded as a power series in c, the first few coefficients may be evaluated analytically. Equations (41.64) and (41.63) yield

$$\mathscr{A}(\mathbf{P},\mathbf{K}) = 1 + \frac{c}{\pi}\left[1 + \frac{P}{2} + K\ln\left(\frac{1+P/2-K}{1+P/2+K}\right) - \frac{K^2+(P/2)^2-1}{P}\right.$$

$$\left. \times \ln\frac{(1+P/2)^2-K^2}{1-(P/2)^2-K^2}\right] + O(c^2) \tag{41.68}$$

and Eq. (41.67) becomes

$$\frac{E^{(c)}}{A} = \frac{\hbar^2 k_F^2}{2m^*}[\alpha c + \beta c^2 + O(c^3)] \tag{41.69}$$

where

$$\alpha = \frac{2}{\pi} \iint\limits_{(F)} \frac{d^3K}{(4\pi/3)}\frac{d^3P}{(4\pi/3)} = \frac{2}{\pi} \tag{41.70a}$$

$$\beta = \frac{2}{\pi^2} \iint\limits_{(F)} \frac{d^3K}{(4\pi/3)}\frac{d^3P}{(4\pi/3)}\left[1 + \frac{P}{2} + K\ln\left(\frac{1+P/2-K}{1+P/2+K}\right) - \frac{K^2+(P/2)^2-1}{P}\right.$$

$$\left. \times \ln\frac{(1+P/2)^2-K^2}{1-(P/2)^2-K^2}\right]$$

$$= \frac{12}{35\pi^2}(11 - 2\ln 2) \tag{41.70b}$$

Hence the power-series expansion of Eq. (41.67) in c gives

$$\frac{E^{(c)}_{l=0}}{A} = \frac{\hbar^2 k_F^2}{2m^*}\left[\frac{2c}{\pi} + \frac{12c^2}{35\pi^2}(11 - 2\ln 2) + 0.26c^3 + \cdots\right] \tag{41.71}$$

The first two terms are exactly those obtained in the discussion of the interacting hard-sphere Fermi gas and the Galitskii equation [compare Eq. (11.72)],

generalized to include the possibility of an effective mass coming from the attractive part of the interaction. The third term, which has not been computed here, was first evaluated by DeDominicis and Martin[1] and is just that part of their result due to s-wave interactions in the independent-pair model. The power series expansion of Eq. (41.71) is also plotted in Fig. 41.6.

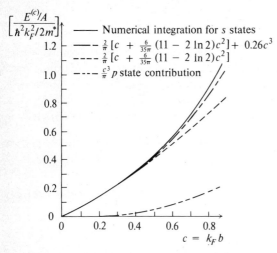

Fig. 41.6 Hard-core energy $E^{(c)}_{l=0}/A$ computed from Eq. (41.67) and the power-series approximations [Eq. (41.71)]. Also shown is the p-wave contribution $E^{(c)}_{l=1}/A$ from Eq. (41.72). (The authors wish to thank E. Moniz for preparing this figure.)

The contribution to the energy of a hard core in the p state can be obtained from an exactly analogous treatment of the p-state Bethe-Goldstone equation (see Prob. 11.7)

$$\frac{E^{(c)}_{l=1}}{A} = \frac{\hbar^2 k_F^2}{2m^*} \frac{c^3}{\pi} \tag{41.72}$$

As noted in Sec. 38, the nuclear force is relatively weak in p states but there is some evidence for an overall p-state repulsion.

The energy of nuclear matter as given by Eqs. (41.57), (41.58), and (41.67) is shown in Fig. 41.7. The results are plotted both with and without the contribution of Eq. (41.72) arising from a p-state hard core, and the effective mass at the Fermi surface has been taken from Table 41.1

$$\frac{m^*}{m} = 0.65 \tag{41.73}$$

[1] C. DeDominicis and P. C. Martin, *Phys. Rev.*, **105**:1417 (1957) and private communication.

We note several interesting features of these results.   The medium obviously saturates, which is evident from the various contributions to the energy because the hard-core repulsion will always dominate at high density.   Indeed, for close-packed hard spheres, the uncertainty principle requires that the hard-core energy become infinite.[1]   It is clear from Eq. (41.71), however, that the hard-core contribution to the energy becomes important at densities much lower than

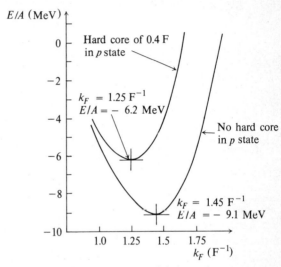

Fig. 41.7   The energy per particle in nuclear matter as a function of k_F computed from Eqs. (41.57), (41.58), (41.67), and (41.72) for the two-body potential of Eqs. (41.39) to (41.42).   The results are shown both with and without a hard core in the p state.   (The authors wish to thank E. Moniz for preparing this figure.)

that for close packing.   The hard core forces the N-body wave function to vanish whenever $|\mathbf{x}_i - \mathbf{x}_j| < b$, thereby providing extra curvature in the wave function and increasing the kinetic energy.   It is notable that this very simple picture of nuclear matter gives saturation at about the right density.   The calculated binding energy is too small; this result is to be expected because we assumed that the difference between the triplet and singlet force comes solely from the tensor force, whose effects vanish in lowest order, and used an attractive well fit only to the $^1S_0$ scattering.   The tensor force still makes a second-order contribution to the energy, however, and, like all second-order effects, these always increase the binding.[2]

The binding energy is the difference between a large attractive energy and a large repulsive energy and, as such, is very sensitive to any approximations that

[1] For a discussion of this point see R. K. Cole, Jr., *Phys. Rev.*, **155**:114 (1967).

[2] Note that a value of m^*/m closer to 1 also increases the binding.

have been made.   To demonstrate this point, we list below the various contributions to the energy at $k_F = 1.50$ F^{-1}

$$E^{(a)} A^{-1} = -76.9 \text{ MeV}$$
$$E^{(f)} A^{-1} = +28.0 \text{ MeV}$$
$$E^{(c)}_{l=0} A^{-1} = +39.9 \text{ MeV}$$
$$E^{(c)}_{l=1} A^{-1} = \quad +4.9 \text{ MeV}$$

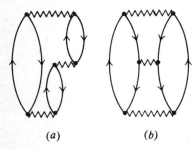

(a)   (b)

Fig. 41.8 Some typical higher-order Goldstone diagrams for nuclear matter: (a) three-body cluster, (b) hole-hole scattering.

Two features of the nuclear force tend to keep the density of nuclear matter low: the hard core and the Serber nature of the interaction, which decreases the attraction and hence also moves the minimum in Fig. 41.7 to lower densities. The resulting interparticle spacing allows enough space for the wound in the wave function to heal.   This result accounts for the success of the independent-particle model of the nucleus and justifies the independent-pair approach to the properties of nuclear matter.

The discussion in this section may be considered an over-simplified version of the theory of nuclear matter developed by Brueckner,[1] Bethe,[2] and others. Thus we have retained only the most essential physical features and made many approximations that must be improved in any more realistic treatment of nuclear matter.   For example, the present form of the independent-pair model omits a great variety of higher-order contributions, such as three-body clusters (defined to be Goldstone diagrams containing three hole lines), or contributions from hole-hole scattering, which really involve three or more particles, as seen in the discussion of the Galitskii equation.[3]   Some typical higher-order Goldstone diagrams are indicated in Fig. 41.8.   All of these processes involve the simultaneous collision of more than two particles, and the short healing length ensures that such processes are very improbable.   These many-particle cluster contributions have been analyzed in great detail by Bethe and his coworkers, who use

[1] K. A. Brueckner, *loc. cit.*
[2] H. A. Bethe, *loc. cit.*
[3] The precise relation of the present calculation to the diagrammatic analysis of $\Sigma^\star$ and the ground-state energy shift is discussed in Sec. 42.

the Fadeev equations to evaluate the three-body cluster contributions correctly.[1] The net effect of these higher-cluster contributions is to decrease the binding energy of nuclear matter by about 1 MeV.

In addition to including higher clusters, it is necessary to improve the evaluation of the two-particle contributions. For purposes of illustration and simplicity, an effective-mass approximation has been used; unfortunately, the exact answer is very sensitive to the precise value chosen for m^*. It is also true that the effective-mass approximation is not very good. A better approach is the *reference-spectrum* method of Bethe, Brandow, and Petschek,[2] which chooses the single-particle potential to minimize the higher-order contributions. As a result, particles and holes are treated differently, holes being assigned the self-consistent single-particle potential discussed here, and particles being assigned the free spectrum. In this approach, a single-particle potential is merely a calculational tool. It corresponds to the freedom of rewriting the hamiltonian as

$$H = T + \sum_i U(i) + \left[\sum_{i<j} V(ij) - \sum_i U(i) \right] \tag{41.74}$$

and then choosing the single-particle potential $U(i)$ to maximize the convergence of the expansion for the energy.

An additional problem in the study of nuclear matter is lack of knowledge of the nucleon-nucleon force in the odd angular-momentum states. This is a large effect, as can be seen from Fig. 41.7, and different potentials will give different values for the binding energy. Another question is the effect of true many-body forces, which might occur in the original hamiltonian because the meson-exchange processes between nucleons are modified by the presence of additional nucleons. Any analysis of this problem is very difficult, and the current philosophy is to calculate the best possible binding energy and density using two-body potentials fit to nucleon-nucleon scattering. Only if a discrepancy remains would we be forced to introduce many-body forces. The present situation is that the theoretical values obtained with two-body forces alone are close to the observed binding energy of -16 MeV and density $k_F = 1.4$ F^{-1}.[3]

42☐RELATION TO GREEN'S FUNCTIONS AND BETHE-SALPETER EQUATION

In the preceding sections, nuclear matter has been discussed in terms of the Bethe-Goldstone equations, and we now relate this treatment to the Galitskii equations and the Green's functions. For simplicity, we shall first neglect all

[1] See R. Rajaraman and H. A. Bethe, *Rev. Mod. Phys.*, **39**:745 (1967).
[2] H. A. Bethe, B. H. Brandow, and A. G. Petschek, *Phys. Rev.*, **129**:225 (1963).
[3] For a review of nuclear-matter calculations, see B. Day, *Rev. Mod. Phys.*, **39**:719 (1967) and R. Rajaraman and H. A. Bethe, *loc. cit.*

self-consistency in the Bethe-Goldstone equations and assume that the energy denominators contain only free-particle kinetic energies. In this way, the Bethe-Goldstone equations reduce to the simpler form studied in Sec. 36, which is more closely analogous to Galitskii's equations of Sec. 11. Recall that the Galitskii approach calculates the Green's function by summing the ladder graphs as Feynman diagrams. We first observe that if we are interested in calculating only the ground-state energy shift, the Galitskii equations can be simplified considerably. The Green's function is related to the ground-state energy shift by Eq. (9.38)

$$E - E_0 = \frac{-iV\hbar}{2(2\pi)^4} \int_0^1 \frac{d\lambda}{\lambda} \int d^4p \, \mathrm{tr} \, [\Sigma^{\star\lambda}(p) \, G^\lambda(p)] \, e^{ip_0\eta} \tag{42.1}$$

where the coupling-constant integration is still to be performed. To be consistent with the appearance of G^0 in Eq. (11.28) for $\Sigma^\star$ in the ladder approximation, we replace $G(p)$ by $G^0(p)$ in Eq. (42.1). All the ladder complexity and λ dependence is thus put into $\Sigma^\star(p)$.[1] Our starting expression for the ground-state energy shift in the Galitskii approach is therefore

$$E - E_0 = \frac{-iV\hbar}{2(2\pi)^4} \int_0^1 \frac{d\lambda}{\lambda} \int d^4p \, \mathrm{tr} \, [G^0(p) \, \Sigma^{\star\lambda}(p)] \, e^{ip_0\eta} \tag{42.2}$$

This expression now allows us to draw a set of Feynman diagrams for the ground-state energy shift. A general term in the ladder approximation is drawn in Fig. 42.1. Note that these are Feynman diagrams; consequently, only the topology of the diagrams is important, and we may draw any pair of lines as returning lines, and any pair of lines as crossed lines in the exchange diagram. Since the Feynman Green's function contains both particle and hole propagation, the different relative time orderings in these diagrams can describe very complicated processes with many particles and holes present at any instant. It was shown in Eq. (11.35), however, that any pair of particles in a ladder propagates between interactions either with both particles above the Fermi sea or with both particles below. In computing the energy shift, every pair of hole lines will lead to an extra pair of factors $\int^{k_F} d^3k' \int^{k_F} d^3k''$. At low density it is therefore meaningful to classify the contributions by the number of hole lines retained[2] (compare the discussion at the end of Sec. 11). The minimum number of holes is clearly two; *thus in the low-density limit we need keep only one intermediate pair propagating as holes and may use the particle part of the Green's function for all the other pairs.* In nth order there are n possible ways of choosing that pair which contributes as holes, and the symmetry of the diagrams shows that all these n terms are identical.

---

[1] The first correction to this approximation involves the integral $\int d^4p [\Sigma^\star(p) G^0(p)]^2$, which vanishes whenever $\Sigma^\star$ is independent of frequency. This is true of the leading terms both for a nonsingular potential [Eq. (10.21)] and for a hard-sphere gas [Eq. (11.57)].

[2] This observation was first made by N. M. Hugenholtz, *Physica*, **23**:533 (1957).

We can now carry out the coupling-constant integration for the nth-order contribution

$$\int_0^1 \frac{d\lambda}{\lambda} n\lambda^n = 1$$

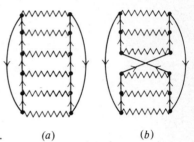

Fig. 42.1   Sixth-order ladder contribution to $E - E_0$. (a) (b)

Hence we can keep just a single graph with $n - 1$ pairs propagating as particles and one pair propagating as holes.   It is most convenient to assume that all the intermediate pairs in Γ [see Eq. (11.30)] propagate as particles, with the hole pair coming from the two extra factors of G^0 in $\Sigma^\star$ and $E - E_0$.

In this way the Galitskii equations for the ground-state energy shift in the low-density limit can be rewritten as follows.   The ground-state energy is obtained from

$$E - E_0 = -\tfrac{1}{2}iV\hbar(2\pi)^{-4} \int d^4p \, \mathrm{tr}\,[G^0(p)\,\Sigma^\star(p)]\,e^{ip_0\eta} \qquad (42.3)$$

where the coupling-constant integration has now been performed.   The corresponding proper self-energy is given by Eq. (11.49)

$$\hbar\Sigma^\star(p) = -i(2\pi)^{-4} \int d^4k \, G^0(k)\,[4\Gamma(pk;pk) - \Gamma(kp;pk)]\,e^{ik_0\eta} \qquad (42.4)$$

(see Fig. 42.2), where we have used the fourfold degeneracy of nuclear matter associated with spin and isospin.   The scattering amplitude in the medium is a

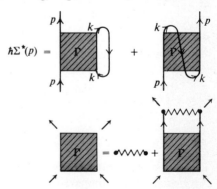

Fig. 42.2   Structure of $\Sigma^\star$ in Galitskii approach.

convolution of a *modified* Galitskii wave function χ_m with the potential [see Eq. (11.40)]

$$\Gamma(\mathbf{q}, \mathbf{q}'; P) = \hbar^2 m^{-1} (2\pi)^{-3} \int d^3 t \, v(\mathbf{t}) \chi_m(\mathbf{q} - \mathbf{t}, \mathbf{q}'; P) \tag{42.5}$$

where the variables in the scattering problem are indicated in Fig. 42.3, while

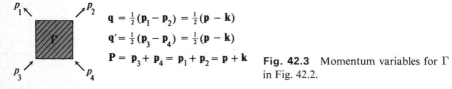

$$\mathbf{q} = \tfrac{1}{2}(\mathbf{p}_1 - \mathbf{p}_2) = \tfrac{1}{2}(\mathbf{p} - \mathbf{k})$$

$$\mathbf{q}' = \tfrac{1}{2}(\mathbf{p}_3 - \mathbf{p}_4) = \tfrac{1}{2}(\mathbf{p} - \mathbf{k})$$

$$\mathbf{P} = \mathbf{p}_3 + \mathbf{p}_4 = \mathbf{p}_1 + \mathbf{p}_2 = \mathbf{p} + \mathbf{k}$$

Fig. 42.3 Momentum variables for Γ in Fig. 42.2.

χ_m is in turn a solution to the following integral equation [compare Eq. (11.39)]

$$\chi_m(\mathbf{q}, \mathbf{q}'; P) = (2\pi)^3 \, \delta(\mathbf{q} - \mathbf{q}') + \frac{\theta(|\tfrac{1}{2}\mathbf{P} + \mathbf{q}| - k_F) \, \theta(|\tfrac{1}{2}\mathbf{P} - \mathbf{q}| - k_F)}{mE/\hbar^2 - q^2 + i\eta}$$

$$\times \int \frac{d^3 t}{(2\pi)^3} \, v(\mathbf{t}) \chi_m(\mathbf{q} - \mathbf{t}, \mathbf{q}'; P) \tag{42.6}$$

In accordance with our previous discussion, the modified Galitskii wave function satisfies an integral equation with only the particle-particle part of the Galitskii kernel. The energy appearing in the denominators is the total energy in the center-of-momentum frame, defined by Eq. (11.36)

$$E = \hbar P_0 - \frac{\hbar^2 \mathbf{P}^2}{4m} = \hbar k_0 + \hbar p_0 - \frac{\hbar^2 \mathbf{k}^2}{2m} - \frac{\hbar^2 \mathbf{p}^2}{2m} + \frac{\hbar^2 \mathbf{q}'^2}{m} \tag{42.7}$$

We shall now write the corresponding equations from our discussion of Sec. 41. If the Bethe-Goldstone equations (41.1) and (41.2) for $m^* = m$ are rewritten with a Fourier transform, the energy shift of a pair becomes

$$\Delta\epsilon(\mathbf{q}', \mathbf{q}'; P) = \hbar^2 (mV)^{-1} \int e^{-i\mathbf{q}' \cdot \mathbf{x}} \, v(\mathbf{x}) \, \psi_{\mathbf{P}, \mathbf{q}'}(\mathbf{x}) \, d^3 x$$

$$= \hbar^2 (mV)^{-1} (2\pi)^{-3} \int d^3 t \, v(\mathbf{t}) \, \psi(\mathbf{q}' - \mathbf{t}, \mathbf{q}'; P) \tag{42.8}$$

where we now use a notation similar to Eq. (42.5), while the wave function in momentum space satisfies the equation

$$\psi(\mathbf{q}, \mathbf{q}'; P) = (2\pi)^3 \, \delta(\mathbf{q} - \mathbf{q}') + \frac{\theta(|\tfrac{1}{2}\mathbf{P} + \mathbf{q}| - k_F) \, \theta(|\tfrac{1}{2}\mathbf{P} - \mathbf{q}| - k_F)}{q'^2 - q^2 + i\eta}$$

$$\times \int \frac{d^3 t}{(2\pi)^3} \, v(\mathbf{t}) \, \psi(\mathbf{q} - \mathbf{t}, \mathbf{q}'; P) \tag{42.9}$$

This is the free scattering wave equation with the Fermi sphere excluded from the virtual states [compare Eq. (11.11)]. The single-particle energy spectrum is

given in Eq. (41.45) as the sum of interaction energies of each pair

$$U(\mathbf{p}) = V(2\pi)^{-3} \int^{k_F} d^3k \, [4\Delta\epsilon(\mathbf{q'},\mathbf{q'};\mathbf{P}) - \Delta\epsilon(-\mathbf{q'},\mathbf{q'};\mathbf{P})] \qquad (42.10)$$

where the variables are defined as in Fig. 42.3. Here the second term in brackets makes explicit the exchange contribution that arises from the use of anti-symmetric wave functions for pairs in identical spin and isotopic-spin states. Finally the energy of interaction of the assembly is obtained as one half the sum of the interaction energy $U(\mathbf{p})$ for all particles in the Fermi sea [compare Eqs. (41.45) and (41.46)]

$$E - E_0 = \tfrac{1}{2}4V(2\pi)^{-3} \int^{k_F} d^3p \, U(\mathbf{p}) \qquad (42.11)$$

For simplicity, we assume spin- and isospin-independent forces.

It is now possible to prove that the Bethe-Goldstone equations (42.8) to (42.11) and the Galitskii equations (42.3) to (42.6) are *identical*. The proof is as follows. The modified Galitskii wave function χ_m in Eq. (42.6) is an analytic function in the upper half k_0 plane. (Note that this is not true of χ itself.) Since Γ in Eq. (42.5) is just a convolution of χ_m with the potential, Γ is also an analytic function in the upper-half k_0 plane. As a result, when the k_0 integral in the proper self-energy [Eq. (42.4)] is closed in the upper-half k_0 plane, the only contribution comes from the pole of $G^0(k)$ at $k_0 = \omega_k^0 = \hbar k^2/2m$. We now observe that $\Sigma^\star(p)$ is also an analytic function of p_0 in the upper-half p_0 plane; when the contour in Eq. (42.3) is also closed in the upper-half plane, the only contribution again arises from the pole of $G^0(p)$ at $p_0 = \omega_p^0 = \hbar p^2/2m$. The expression for the energy shift therefore becomes

$$E - E_0 = \tfrac{1}{2}4V(2\pi)^{-3} \int^{k_F} d^3p \, \hbar\Sigma^\star(\mathbf{p},\omega_p^0) \qquad (42.12)$$

precisely reproducing the Bethe-Goldstone results. From the preceding discussion, it is evident that the Bethe-Goldstone expression for the ground-state energy is obtained by summing the ladder contributions interpreted as *Goldstone diagrams* (see also Prob. 11.11), where the intermediate pair always propagates as particles.

In summary, we have demonstrated that the ground-state energies obtained from the Galitskii equations and from the Bethe-Goldstone equations coincide at low density. It is important to note, however, that this correspondence need not hold for other physical quantities. In particular, the proper self-energy differs from the single-particle potential $U(\mathbf{k})$ by the inclusion of hole-hole scattering.[1] Since it is $\hbar\Sigma^\star(\mathbf{k},k_0)$ that gives the correct single-particle energies, we see again that $U(\mathbf{k})$ merely represents a convenient tool for computing the ground-state energy.

[1] This point was first emphasized by N. M. Hugenholtz and L. Van Hove, *Physica*, **24**:363 (1958) and by D. J. Thouless, *Phys. Rev.*, **112**:906 (1958).

The Bethe-Goldstone theory described above still differs in principle from the Brueckner theory because the Brueckner theory relies on a self-consistent single-particle potential. In terms of Green's functions, this result can be achieved by replacing $G^0(p)$ with a $G(p)$ that includes self-energy effects associated with Γ. Furthermore, Γ must itself be determined with G and not G^0. The equations for this self-consistent theory are shown schematically in Fig. 42.4.

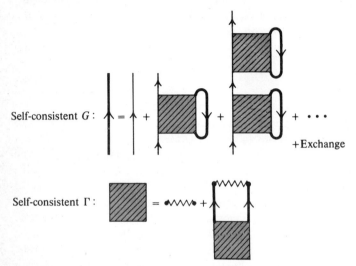

Fig. 42.4 Self-consistent theory for G and Γ.

As they stand, these equations are quite intractable because the frequency dependence of $\Sigma^\star(\mathbf{p}, p_0)$ complicates the integral equation for Γ immensely. (This difficulty is sometimes known as *propagation off the energy shell*.) The simpler Brueckner-Goldstone theory can be obtained from these equations in a series of approximations. First, the self-consistency is treated only on the average, and we use a frequency-independent self-energy $\Sigma^\star_{sc}(\mathbf{p}) \equiv \Sigma^\star(\mathbf{p}, \epsilon_\mathbf{p}/\hbar)$, obtained by setting $p_0 = \epsilon_\mathbf{p}/\hbar$, where $\epsilon_\mathbf{p}$ satisfies the self-consistent equation

$$\epsilon_\mathbf{p} = \epsilon_\mathbf{p}^0 + \hbar\Sigma^\star(\mathbf{p}, \epsilon_\mathbf{p}/\hbar) \equiv \epsilon_\mathbf{p}^0 + \hbar\Sigma^\star_{sc}(\mathbf{p}) \tag{42.13}$$

In this way, the Green's function is given approximately as

$$G_{sc}(\mathbf{p}, p_0) = \frac{\theta(|\mathbf{p}| - k_F)}{p_0 - \epsilon_\mathbf{p}/\hbar + i\eta} + \frac{\theta(k_F - |\mathbf{p}|)}{p_0 - \epsilon_\mathbf{p}/\hbar - i\eta} \tag{42.14}$$

Second, this Green's function is used to evaluate both the proper self-energy [Eq. (42.4)] and the scattering amplitude [Eqs. (42.5) and (42.6)]. We again obtain χ_m by omitting the hole-hole scattering, which is presumed small in the low-density limit. The only effect on the self-consistent wave function is to change the denominator in Eq. (42.6) from $mP_0/\hbar - \frac{1}{2}(\frac{1}{2}\mathbf{P} + \mathbf{q})^2 - \frac{1}{2}(\frac{1}{2}\mathbf{P} - \mathbf{q})^2 + i\eta$

to $(m/\hbar^2)(\hbar P_0 - \epsilon_{\frac{1}{2}\mathbf{P}+\mathbf{q}} - \epsilon_{\frac{1}{2}\mathbf{P}-\mathbf{q}}) + i\eta$. This set of equations determines the approximate self-consistent spectrum $\epsilon_{\mathbf{p}}$. Third, the ground-state energy is evaluated from Eq. (9.36) using $G_{sc}(\mathbf{p},p_0)$ and $\Sigma_{sc}^{\star}(\mathbf{p})$

$$
\begin{aligned}
E &= -4iV(2\pi)^{-4} \int d^4p\, e^{ip_0\eta} \left[\epsilon_{\mathbf{p}}^0 + \tfrac{1}{2}\hbar\Sigma_{sc}^{\star}(\mathbf{p})\right] G_{sc}(p) \\
&= 4V(2\pi)^{-3} \int d^3p \left[\epsilon_{\mathbf{p}}^0 + \tfrac{1}{2}\hbar\Sigma_{sc}^{\star}(\mathbf{p})\right] \theta(k_F - |\mathbf{p}|) \\
&= E_0 + 2V(2\pi)^{-3} \int d^3p\, \hbar\Sigma_{sc}^{\star}(\mathbf{p})\, \theta(k_F - |\mathbf{p}|)
\end{aligned}
\tag{42.15}
$$

This result is identical with that obtained by substituting $G_{sc}(\mathbf{p},p_0)$ and $\Sigma_{sc}^{\star}(\mathbf{p})$ into Eq. (42.3). We note, however, that it does *not* follow immediately from the original form of Eq. (42.1) because of the complicated λ dependence of $\Sigma_{sc}^{\star}(\mathbf{p})$ and $\epsilon_{\mathbf{p}}$.

43□THE ENERGY GAP IN NUCLEAR MATTER

As a final topic in this chapter we study the energy gap in nuclear matter. The semiempirical mass formula indicates that the last pair of like particles (*pp* or *nn*) contributes an extra amount

$$
E_{\text{pair}} = 34 \text{ MeV } A^{-\frac{3}{4}}
\tag{43.1}
$$

to the binding energy of nuclei. In addition, Bohr, Mottelson, and Pines[1] observed that the energy spectrum of even-even nuclei shows an energy gap of about 1 MeV (we shall return to this question in Chap. 15). Thus there is some empirical evidence that like nucleons tend to pair up, and it is interesting to look for an exceptional (or superconducting) solution to the gap equation in nuclear matter.

The gap is determined by Eq. (37.35)

$$
\Delta_k = \tfrac{1}{2} \sum_{\mathbf{k}'} \langle \mathbf{k} - \mathbf{k} | V | \mathbf{k}' - \mathbf{k}' \rangle \frac{\Delta_{k'}}{(\Delta_{k'}^2 + \xi_{k'}^2)^{\frac{1}{2}}}
\tag{43.2}
$$

where we now use the convention of Chap. 10 that $V > 0$ for an attractive potential. We restrict the pairing to like particles, that is, $(p\uparrow\, p\downarrow)$ or $(n\uparrow\, n\downarrow)$, and assume that V is independent of spin and isospin.[2] To obtain an explicit solution of this nonlinear integral equation, it is convenient to make the following approximations:

[1] A. Bohr, B. R. Mottelson, and D. Pines, *Phys. Rev.*, **110**:936 (1958).
[2] As discussed in detail in Chap. 15, the pairing comes from the last valence particles. In all but the lightest nuclei, the last filled states are quite different for neutrons and protons. Thus the overlap in the matrix elements of the interaction between valence neutrons and protons is generally smaller than that between like particles in the same states. This is the argument for confining our attention to pairing between like nucleons.

1. The single-particle excitation energies ξ_k measured relative to the chemical potential μ are written in the effective-mass approximation

$$\xi_k = \epsilon_k^0 - \sum_{k'} \langle \mathbf{kk'}|\bar{V}|\mathbf{kk'}\rangle v_{k'}^2 - \mu$$

$$\approx \epsilon_k^0 + U(k) - [\epsilon_{k_F}^0 + U(k_F)]$$

$$\approx \hbar^2(2m^*)^{-1}(k^2 - k_F^2) \tag{43.3}$$

2. Since the resulting gap Δ is much smaller than ϵ_F, the integrand in Eq. (43.2) is sharply peaked near $\xi = 0$, and it is then permissible to set

$$\Delta_k \approx \Delta_{k_F} \equiv \Delta \tag{43.4}$$

In this case, the gap equation becomes

$$1 = \frac{1}{2} \int \frac{d^3k}{(2\pi)^3} \int \frac{e^{-i\mathbf{k}_F \cdot \mathbf{x}} V(x) e^{i\mathbf{k} \cdot \mathbf{x}} d^3x}{\{\Delta^2 + [\hbar^2(k^2 - k_F^2)/2m^*]^2\}^{\frac{1}{2}}} \tag{43.5}$$

where $\mathbf{k}_F$ is an arbitrary wave vector lying on the Fermi surface. The angular integrations over $d\Omega_k$ and $d\Omega_x$ can now be evaluated to give

$$1 = \frac{2m^*}{\pi\hbar^2 k_F^2} \int_0^\infty k_F \, dx \sin(k_F x) \, V(x) \int_0^\infty K \, dK \frac{\sin[K(k_F x)]}{[\bar{\Delta}^2 + (K^2 - 1)^2]^{\frac{1}{2}}} \tag{43.6}$$

where the following dimensionless variables have been introduced

$$\bar{\Delta} \equiv \frac{\Delta}{\hbar^2 k_F^2/2m^*} \equiv \frac{\Delta}{\epsilon_F^*} \qquad K = \frac{k}{k_F} \tag{43.7}$$

We are interested in the limit of this expression as $\bar{\Delta} \to 0$ when the second integral in Eq. (43.6) can be evaluated as

$$\int_0^\infty K \, dK \frac{\sin[K(k_F x)]}{[\bar{\Delta}^2 + (K^2 - 1)^2]^{\frac{1}{2}}} \underset{\bar{\Delta}\to 0}{=} \left[\ln\left(\frac{8}{\bar{\Delta}}\right) - \int_0^{2k_F x} \frac{d\lambda}{\lambda}(1 - \cos\lambda)\right] \sin k_F x$$

$$+ \left(\int_{2k_F x}^\infty \frac{d\lambda}{\lambda} \sin\lambda\right) \cos k_F x \tag{43.8}$$

The finite range of the potential $V(x)$ ensures that the quantity $k_F x$ is bounded; hence the dominant behavior of Eq. (43.8) arises from the first term, and we shall write

$$\int_0^\infty K \, dK \sin[K(k_F x)] \frac{1}{[\bar{\Delta}^2 + (K^2 - 1)^2]^{\frac{1}{2}}} \underset{\bar{\Delta}\to 0}{\approx} \sin k_F x \ln\frac{8}{\bar{\Delta}} \tag{43.9}$$

For any small finite $\bar{\Delta}$, the validity of this approximation can be verified with Eq. (43.8) (see Prob. 11.12).

We can now complete the solution of Eq. (43.5). With the definition

$$k_F \int_0^\infty \sin k_F x \, V(x) \sin k_F x \, dx \equiv \langle k_F|V|\varphi_{k_F}\rangle \tag{43.10}$$

Eqs. (43.6) and (43.9) become

$$\frac{1}{\langle k_F | V | \varphi_{k_F} \rangle} \underset{\bar{\Delta} \to 0}{\approx} \frac{2m^*}{\pi \hbar^2 k_F^2} \ln \frac{8}{\bar{\Delta}} \tag{43.11}$$

The exponential of this result yields

$$\bar{\Delta} \approx 8 \exp\left(-\frac{\pi \hbar^2 k_F^2 / 2m^*}{\langle k_F | V | \varphi_{k_F} \rangle} \right) \tag{43.12}$$

and the energy gap in nuclear matter is given in usual units as

$$\Delta \approx 8 \frac{\hbar^2 k_F^2}{2m^*} \exp\left(-\frac{\pi \hbar^2 k_F^2 / 2m^*}{\langle k_F | V | \varphi_{k_F} \rangle} \right) \tag{43.13}$$

A crude estimate of this quantity can be obtained with the nonsingular square-well potential fit to $^1S_0$ scattering (Fig. 41.2):

$$\langle k_F | V | \varphi_{k_F} \rangle = V_0 \int_0^{k_F d} \sin^2 x \, dx = V_0 (\tfrac{1}{2} k_F d - \tfrac{1}{4} \sin 2 k_F d) \tag{43.14}$$

We take the value $m^*/m = 0.65$ from the discussion of nuclear matter and find the energy gap shown in Table 43.1.   Since $\epsilon_F^* = (m/m^*) \epsilon_F \approx 65$ MeV, the quantity $\bar{\Delta}$ defined in Eq. (43.7) is indeed very small.

The resulting energy gap at the equilibrium density of nuclear matter $(k_F \approx 1.42 \text{ F}^{-1})$ is very small, thus justifying our previous treatment of the bulk properties.   In particular, the calculated Δ is much smaller than both the gap observed in the spectra of even-even nuclei and the pairing energy in the semi-empirical mass formula (for the heaviest known nuclei).   It must be noted, however, that the gap has been evaluated in nuclear matter, whereas the actual pairing energy in finite nuclei arises from the nucleons in the surface region of much lower density.   Table 43.1 shows that the gap depends strongly on the density and becomes as large as 2.5 MeV at $k_F = 1.0$ F^{-1}.   This estimate is, of course, only very crude.   Emery and Sessler[1] have used the Bethe-Goldstone equation to obtain much more realistic values of $\langle k_F | V | \varphi_{k_F} \rangle$.   Nevertheless, their values for Δ are very similar to those in Table 43.1.

Table 43.1   The energy gap in nuclear matter
for two nuclear densities

k_F, F^{-1}	Δ, MeV
1.42	9.3×10^{-2}
1.00	2.5

[1] V. J. Emery and A. M. Sessler, *Phys. Rev.*, **119**:248 (1960).

PROBLEMS

11.1. (a) If a square-well potential of range d has a bound state at zero energy, use the effective-range expansion $k \cot \delta_0 = -1/a + \frac{1}{2} r_0 k^2$ to prove that $r_0 = d$. (b) If the hard-core square-well potential shown in Fig. 41.5 has a bound state at zero energy, prove that $r_0 = 2b + b_w$.

11.2. (a) Assume the nuclear interactions are equivalent to a slowly varying potential $-U(r)$. Within any small volume element, assume that the particles form a noninteracting Fermi gas with levels filled up to an energy $-B$. In equilibrium, B must be the same throughout the nucleus. From this description, derive the Thomas-Fermi expression for the nuclear density $n(r) = (2/3\pi^2) \times (2m/\hbar^2)^{\frac{3}{2}} [U(r) - B]^{\frac{3}{2}}$.
(b) Derive the results of part a by balancing the hydrostatic force $-\nabla P$ and the force from the potential $n\nabla U$.

11.3. The symmetry energy E_4/A [Eqs. (39.8) and (39.12)] may be estimated as follows. Assume the nonsingular potential of Eq. (40.10) and compute the expectation value of $\hat{H}$ in the Fermi gas model for $A = Z + N$ nucleons with $\delta \equiv (N - Z)/A \neq 0$.
(a) Use Eq. (40.9) to prove that

$$\frac{E_4}{A} = \frac{\delta^2}{3} \left\{ \frac{\hbar^2 k_F^2}{2m^*} - \frac{k_F^3}{\pi} \int_0^\infty V(z) \left[a_M + a_W j_0^2(k_F z) \right] z^2 \, dz \right\} \qquad \delta \to 0$$

where the effective mass at k_F is given by $\hbar^2 k_F/m^* = \{ d[\epsilon_k^0 + U(k)]/dk \}_{k=k_F}$ and $U(\mathbf{k})$ is defined by Eqs. (40.17) to (40.19). Discuss the physics of this result and compare with Probs. 1.6 and 1.7.
(b) With $m^* \approx 0.65$ (Table 41.1) and the potential of Fig. 41.2, show that $a_4 \approx 37$ MeV.

11.4. Prove that a two-body tensor force with Serber exchange $V = V_T S_{12} \times \frac{1}{2}(1 + P_M)$ makes no contribution to the energy of a spin-$\frac{1}{2}$ isospin-$\frac{1}{2}$ Fermi gas (i.e., nuclear matter) in lowest order.

11.5. Given a repulsive square-well potential of height V_0 and range b, if u/r is the $l = 0$ wave function, prove that $Vu \to A\delta(r - b)$ for $V_0 \to \infty$, where A is a constant that can depend on energy.

11.6. Carry out an exact partial-wave decomposition of the Bethe-Goldstone equations (41.5) and (41.2) for arbitrary $\mathbf{P}$. Show that the even-l waves are coupled, as are the odd-l waves. Estimate the lowest order (in $c = k_F a$) in which this coupling affects the ground-state energy of a hard-sphere Fermi gas.

11.7. Use the Bethe-Goldstone equation for a pure hard-core p-wave potential to prove that $E_{l=1}^{(c)}/A = (\hbar^2 k_F^2/2m)(c^3/\pi)$. Compare with Prob. 4.7$b$.

11.8. The compressibility of nuclear matter can be defined as

$$K_V^{-1} \equiv k_F^2 [d^2(E/A)/dk_F^2]_{\text{equilibrium}}$$

(a) Evaluate K_V approximately from Fig. 41.7 for the two cases shown. Relate K_V to the usual thermodynamic compressibility.

(b) Compare with the corresponding value for a noninteracting Fermi gas at the same density.

11.9. The Λ particle is a baryon with strangeness -1, and hence is distinguishable from the nucleon. Show that the energy shift due to the introduction of a hard-sphere Λ particle into a nuclear gas of hard spheres is given by

$$E_c = \frac{\hbar^2 k_F^2}{2\mu} \left\{ \frac{8 k_F a}{3\pi} + \frac{8(k_F a)^2}{\pi^2} \left[\frac{1}{3} - \frac{1}{2(1-\eta)} \left(\frac{3-\eta^2}{6\eta} - \frac{1}{3} - \frac{(\eta^2-1)^2}{4\eta^2} \ln \frac{1+\eta}{1-\eta} \right) \right] \right.$$

$$\left. + O(k_F a)^3 \right\}$$

where a is the range of the Λ-nucleon hard core (compare Fig. 11.1), $1/\mu = 1/m_N + 1/m_\Lambda$, and $\eta = (m_\Lambda - m_N)/(m_\Lambda + m_N)$.

11.10. Consider the binding energy of a Λ particle in the nucleus.

(a) If the nucleus is considered a square-well potential of depth U_0 and range $R = r_0 A^{\frac{1}{3}}$, show that the binding energy B_Λ of the Λ particle is given by the solution to the equations

$$s = (1-x)^{-\frac{1}{2}} \cot^{-1} \left[-\left(\frac{x}{1-x} \right)^{\frac{1}{2}} \right]$$

$$B_\Lambda = U_0 - \frac{\hbar^2 \pi^2}{2\mu_\Lambda R^2} \left(1 - \frac{2}{s} + \frac{3}{s^2} + \cdots \right) \qquad s \to \infty$$

where $s = [(2\mu_\Lambda R^2/\hbar^2) U_0]^{\frac{1}{2}}$, $x \equiv B_\Lambda/U_0$, and $1/\mu_\Lambda = 1/m_\Lambda + 1/A m_N$. Explain how to use these results to identify the binding energy of a Λ particle in nuclear matter.

(b) Suppose the Λ-nucleon potential is of the form shown in Fig. 41.5. Discuss the calculation of the binding energy of a Λ particle in nuclear matter within the framework of the independent-pair approximation.‡

11.11. Starting with Goldstone's theorem, show that the Bethe-Goldstone equations (42.8) to (42.11) sum that part of the ladder contributions to the ground-state energy shift where the intermediate pair always propagates as particles above the Fermi sea.

‡ For a review of this subject see A. R. Bodmer and D. M. Rote, "Proceedings of the International Conference on Hypernuclear Physics," vol. II, p. 521, Argonne National Laboratory, Argonne, Ill., 1969.

11.12. (*a*) Verify Eq. (43.8).

(*b*) Retaining all the terms in Eq. (43.8) and using the nonsingular square-well $^1S_0$ potential of Fig. 41.2, solve the gap equation (43.6). Show that the numbers in Table 43.1 are reduced by approximately a factor of 4.

12
Phonons and Electrons

Our previous discussion of the interacting electron gas treated the uniform positive background as an inert system whose sole purpose is to guarantee overall electrical neutrality. In this chapter we now investigate the dynamics of this background and the interaction between its excitation modes and the electron gas. The resulting Debye model of the background forms the starting point for a general discussion of crystals, while the model electron-phonon system provides an excellent basis for the study of metals. In real solids, of course, the ionic background forms a lattice; fortunately this discrete structure is unimportant for acoustic normal-mode excitations with a wavelength long compared to the interionic spacing (which will be true of almost all of the excitations of importance here).

44□THE NONINTERACTING PHONON SYSTEM

We approximate the background by a homogeneous, isotropic, elastic medium. It is known from the general theory of the mechanics of deformable solids[1] that such a medium can support both transverse (shear) and longitudinal (compressional) waves. Only the longitudinal mode gives rise to the changes in density that are necessary to modify the coulomb interaction between the electrons and the background. Thus for the present purposes we further simplify the model assuming that the background has no shear strength and is completely determined by the adiabatic bulk modulus

$$B \equiv -V \left(\frac{\partial P}{\partial V} \right)_s \tag{44.1}$$

just as if it were a uniform fluid. We shall assume B to be given, although it is in fact determined by the potential energy of the lattice, which depends self-consistently on both the interatomic and electrostatic interactions between the ions and on the interaction with the electrons.

The large ionic mass leads to an important simplification that allows us to treat the problem in two distinct steps. First, the small amplitude of the ions' motion means that the ions may be considered fixed at their equilibrium positions in calculating the behavior of the electrons. Second, the low-frequency ionic motion is then determined from the change in energy associated with a sequence of such stationary ionic configurations, assuming that the electrons have the wave function appropriate to the instantaneous ionic configuration. To a good approximation, it follows that the electronic system and the ionic system are decoupled.[2] As a simple example of this separation, we recall the calculation of B for a degenerate electron gas in a uniform positive background (Sec. 3). In that case, the ground-state energy $E(r_s)$ is calculated as a function of the density of the background; the bulk modulus at the equilibrium density is then proportional to the curvature of $E(r_s)$ at $(r_s)_{min} = 4.83$, and we find

$$(B)_{min} = 4.5 \times 10^{-5} \frac{e^2}{2a_0^4} = 0.66 \times 10^{10} \text{ dyne/cm}^2$$

The discussion of Sec. 16 shows that the variations in mass density $\delta\rho_m$ obey the equation of motion

$$\frac{1}{c^2} \frac{\partial^2}{\partial t^2} \delta\rho_m = \nabla^2 \delta\rho_m \tag{44.2}$$

---

[1] G. Joos, "Theoretical Physics," 2d ed., chap. VIII, Hafner Publishing Company, New York, 1950.

[2] This is the Born-Oppenheimer approximation [M. Born and J. R. Oppenheimer, *Ann. Physik*, **84**:457 (1927)], which is discussed, for example, in L. I. Schiff, "Quantum Mechanics," 3d ed., p. 446, McGraw-Hill Book Company, New York, 1968.

where

$$c^2 = \frac{B}{\rho_{m0}} = \frac{B}{Mn_0} \tag{44.3}$$

is the longitudinal speed of sound and

$$\rho_{m0} \equiv Mn_0 \tag{44.4}$$

is the mass density of the background. The solutions to this wave equation describe the longitudinal sound waves. We may again use our simple model of a degenerate electron gas at the equilibrium density to find the theoretical expression

$$c^2 = \frac{e^2}{2a_0} \frac{2}{9M} \frac{(0.916)^2}{4(2.21)}$$

For $M = 23m_p$, which is appropriate for sodium, this expression gives $c_{\text{th}} = 1.1 \times 10^5$ cm/sec, in reasonable agreement with $c_{\text{exp}} = 2.3 \times 10^5$ cm/sec, which was evaluated with the observed values for sodium[1] $B = 5.2 \times 10^{10}$ dyne/cm^2 and $\rho_{m0} = 0.97$ g/cm^3. Since the theoretical curve $E(r_s)$ [the first two terms of Eq. (3.37)] is a variational estimate that represents an upper bound on the true ground-state energy, our calculation presumably gives too small a curvature at the minimum and thus too small a value for B and c.

LAGRANGIAN AND HAMILTONIAN

A complete description of sound waves is readily obtained from the lagrangian for the system. For each point in the medium we first introduce the displacement vector $\mathbf{d}(\mathbf{x})$ that characterizes the displacement from the equilibrium position. The change in volume of the element $dx\,dy\,dz$ under deformation then can be computed to lowest order in $dx\,dy\,dz$ from

$$dV' = dx'\,dy'\,dx' = dx\,dy\,dz\left(1 + \frac{\partial d_x}{\partial x} + \frac{\partial d_y}{\partial y} + \frac{\partial d_z}{\partial z} + \cdots\right)$$

or to first order in derivatives of $\mathbf{d}$

$$dV' = dV(1 + \nabla\cdot\mathbf{d})$$

To the same order, the change in density is

$$\frac{\delta\rho_m}{\rho_{m0}} = \frac{\delta n}{n_0} = -\nabla\cdot\mathbf{d} \tag{44.5}$$

and the wave equation can therefore be written in terms of $\mathbf{d}$ as

$$\nabla\cdot\left(\frac{1}{c^2}\frac{\partial^2\mathbf{d}}{\partial t^2} - \nabla^2\mathbf{d}\right) = 0 \tag{44.6}$$

[1] "American Institute of Physics Handbook," 2d ed., pp. 2–21 and 3–89, McGraw-Hill Book Company, New York, 1963.

In an elastic medium without shear strength and vorticity, $\mathbf{d}$ satisfies the general condition

$$\oint_{\text{any path}} \mathbf{d} \cdot d\mathbf{l} = 0$$

which means

$$\nabla \times \mathbf{d} = 0 \tag{44.7}$$

Thus we conclude

$$\nabla \times \left(\frac{1}{c^2} \frac{\partial^2 \mathbf{d}}{\partial t^2} - \nabla^2 \mathbf{d} \right) = 0 \tag{44.8}$$

Both the divergence and curl in Eqs. (44.6) and (44.8) vanish everywhere, and it follows that the sound waves can be described by the pair of equations

$$\frac{1}{c^2} \frac{\partial^2 \mathbf{d}}{\partial t^2} - \nabla^2 \mathbf{d} = 0 \tag{44.9}$$

$$\nabla \times \mathbf{d} = 0 \tag{44.10}$$

It is now a simple matter to construct the lagrangian density and lagrangian that yield these equations of motion[1]

$$L_0 = T - V \tag{44.11a}$$

$$L_0 = \tfrac{1}{2} \int d^3x \left(\rho_{m0} \frac{\partial d_i}{\partial t} \frac{\partial d_i}{\partial t} - B \frac{\partial d_i}{\partial x_j} \frac{\partial d_i}{\partial x_j} \right) \tag{44.11b}$$

where repeated latin indices are summed from 1 to 3. The Euler-Lagrange equations yield Eq. (44.9), while Eq. (44.10) plays the role of a subsidiary condition guaranteeing longitudinal waves. The usual canonical procedure allows us to derive a hamiltonian, and we find

$$\boldsymbol{\pi}(\mathbf{x},t) = \rho_{m0} \frac{\partial \mathbf{d}}{\partial t} \tag{44.12}$$

$$H_0 = \tfrac{1}{2} \int d^3x \, [\rho_{m0}^{-1} \boldsymbol{\pi}^2 + B(\nabla \cdot \mathbf{d})^2] \tag{44.13}$$

where Eq. (44.10) has been substituted into the second term in Eq. (44.11b) and the result integrated twice by parts. Introduce the normal mode expansions (we work in a large box of volume V and use periodic boundary conditions)

$$\boldsymbol{\pi}(\mathbf{x},t) = \rho_{m0} \frac{\partial \mathbf{d}}{\partial t} \equiv -(Mn_0)^{\frac{1}{2}} \sum_{\mathbf{k}} \left(\frac{\hbar \omega_k}{2V} \right)^{\frac{1}{2}} \frac{\mathbf{k}}{k} (c_{\mathbf{k}} e^{i\mathbf{k} \cdot \mathbf{x} - i\omega_k t} + c_{\mathbf{k}}^{\dagger} e^{-i\mathbf{k} \cdot \mathbf{x} + i\omega_k t}) \tag{44.14}$$

---

[1] For a discussion of continuum mechanics, see H. Goldstein, "Classical Mechanics," chap. 11, Addison-Wesley Publishing Company, Inc., Reading, Mass., 1953.

$$\mathbf{d}(\mathbf{x},t) \equiv \frac{-i}{(Mn_0)^{\frac{1}{2}}} \sum_{\mathbf{k}} \left(\frac{\hbar}{2\omega_k V}\right)^{\frac{1}{2}} \frac{\mathbf{k}}{k} (c_{\mathbf{k}} e^{i\mathbf{k}\cdot\mathbf{x} - i\omega_k t} - c_{\mathbf{k}}^{\dagger} e^{-i\mathbf{k}\cdot\mathbf{x} + i\omega_k t}) \qquad (44.15)$$

$$\omega_k = ck \qquad (44.16)$$

which now explicitly incorporate the subsidiary condition $\nabla \times \mathbf{d} = 0$. After a little algebra, the hamiltonian becomes

$$H_0 = \tfrac{1}{2} \sum_{\mathbf{k}} \hbar\omega_k (c_{\mathbf{k}}^{\dagger} c_{\mathbf{k}} + c_{\mathbf{k}} c_{\mathbf{k}}^{\dagger}) \qquad (44.17)$$

which represents a system of *uncoupled harmonic oscillators*.[1] Although we can impose commutation relations on π and $\mathbf{d}$, the subsidiary condition makes this procedure quite intricate; instead, it is much more convenient to consider $c_{\mathbf{k}}$ and $c_{\mathbf{k}}^{\dagger}$ as our independent canonical variables because the subsidiary condition is then explicitly included. Thus we shall quantize by using the canonical commutation relations

$$[c_{\mathbf{k}}, c_{\mathbf{k}'}^{\dagger}] = \delta_{\mathbf{k}\mathbf{k}'} \qquad (44.18)$$

DEBYE THEORY OF THE SPECIFIC HEAT

Equation (44.17) provides a basis for investigating the thermodynamics and statistical mechanics of the free phonon system. We first observe that the chemical potential of the phonons vanishes

$$\mu_{ph} = 0 \qquad (44.19)$$

which may be seen in the following way. Consider the Helmholtz free energy computed for a fixed number of phonons $F(T,V,N_{ph})$. Since there is no restriction on the number of phonons, the equilibrium state of the assembly at fixed T and V is obtained by minimizing the Helmholtz free energy

$$\left(\frac{\partial F}{\partial N_{ph}}\right)_{TV} = 0 \qquad (44.20)$$

This expression is just the chemical potential [Eq. (4.6)], thereby verifying Eq. (44.19). The thermodynamic potential for this collection of bosons is given by [compare Eq. (5.8)]

$$\Omega_0 = -k_B T \ln \mathrm{Tr} \left[\exp\left(-\frac{\hat{H}_0}{k_B T}\right)\right] \qquad (44.21a)$$

$$\Omega_0 = k_B T \sum_{\mathbf{k}} \left\{ \ln\left[1 - \exp\left(-\frac{\hbar\omega_k}{k_B T}\right)\right] + \frac{\hbar\omega_k}{2k_B T}\right\} \qquad (44.21b)$$

where the extra term comes from the zero-point energy in the hamiltonian

$$\hat{H}_0 = \sum_{\mathbf{k}} \hbar\omega_k [c_{\mathbf{k}}^{\dagger} c_{\mathbf{k}} + \tfrac{1}{2}]$$

[1] This is the reason for choosing the particular coefficients appearing in Eqs. (44.14) and (44.15).

Since $\mu_{ph} = 0$, we immediately derive

$$\Omega_0 = -PV = E - TS = E + T\left(\frac{\partial \Omega_0}{\partial T}\right)_V$$

or

$$E = -T^2 \frac{\partial}{\partial T}\left(\frac{\Omega_0}{T}\right)_V \tag{44.22}$$

$$E = \sum_k \left\{ \hbar\omega_k \left[\exp\left(\frac{\hbar\omega_k}{k_B T}\right) - 1\right]^{-1} + \tfrac{1}{2}\hbar\omega_k \right\} \tag{44.23}$$

The sum can be converted to an integral in the usual fashion

$$\sum_k \to \int d\omega\, g(\omega) \tag{44.24a}$$

$$g(\omega) = (2\pi^2)^{-1} V c^{-3} \omega^2 \tag{44.24b}$$

$$\omega = ck \tag{44.24c}$$

In a uniform medium, the frequency ω has no upper limit. In a real crystal, however, it is clear that the wavenumber of propagation cannot exceed the reciprocal of the interparticle spacing. We can determine the maximum frequency ω_D by observing that the total number of degrees of freedom in a real crystal is $3N$, where N is the number of ions. Thus

$$3N = \int_0^{\omega_D} g(\omega)\, d\omega \tag{44.25}$$

which gives

$$g(\omega)\, d\omega = \frac{9N\omega^2\, d\omega}{\omega_D^3} \tag{44.26}$$

Defining the dimensionless variable $u = \hbar\omega/k_B T$ and the Debye temperature

$$\theta \equiv \frac{\hbar\omega_D}{k_B} \tag{44.27}$$

we find[1]

$$E = 9Nk_B T\left(\frac{T}{\theta}\right)^3 \int_0^{\theta/T} \frac{u^3\, du}{e^u - 1} + \frac{9Nk_B \theta}{8} \tag{44.28}$$

$$C_V = \left(\frac{\partial E}{\partial T}\right)_V = 9Nk_B\left(\frac{T}{\theta}\right)^3 \int_0^{\theta/T} \frac{u^4 e^u\, du}{(e^u - 1)^2} \tag{44.29}$$

which is the Debye theory of the specific heat.[2] Equation (44.29) has the following limiting values

$$C_V = 3Nk_B \qquad T \to \infty \tag{44.30a}$$

[1] Note that the only quantity depending on the volume in these expressions is ω_D.
[2] P. Debye, *Ann. Physik*, **39**:789 (1912).

$$C_V = 9Nk_B \left(\frac{T}{\theta}\right)^3 \int_0^\infty \frac{u^4 e^u \, du}{(e^u - 1)^2}$$

$$= \frac{12\pi^4}{5} Nk_B \left(\frac{T}{\theta}\right)^3 \qquad T \to 0 \qquad (44.30b)$$

The first is just the result of the classical equipartition of energy and the second is the famous Debye T^3 law. The Debye theory provides an excellent one-parameter description of the specific heats of crystals as is evident from Fig. 44.1.[1]

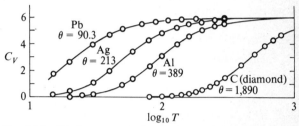

Fig. 44.1 The heat capacity in calories per degree per mole for several solid elements. The curves are the Debye function with the θ values given. (From N. Davidson, "Statistical Mechanics," p. 359, McGraw-Hill Book Company, New York, 1962, after G. N. Lewis and M. Randall, "Thermodynamics," 2d ed., revised by K. S. Pitzer and L. Brewer, p. 56, McGraw-Hill Book Company, New York, 1961. Reprinted by permission.)

In Table 44.1 we compare some values of θ determined by fitting specific heats with the values calculated from the elastic constants of the material.[2]

Table 44.1 Values of Debye temperature θ in °K obtained from thermal and elastic measurements

	Fe	Al	Cu	Pb	Ag
Thermal value	453	398	315	88	215
Elastic value (room temp.)	461	402	332	73	214
Elastic value (absolute zero)		488	344		235

Source: G. H. Wannier, "Statistical Physics," p. 277, John Wiley and Sons, Inc., New York, 1966.

[1] Metals have an additional electronic specific heat proportional to T [see Eq. (29.31)], which becomes important at very low temperatures ($\approx 1°$K).

[2] As we have pointed out, an elastic solid with shear strength can support three types of sound waves: two transverse modes and one longitudinal mode of the type considered here. The only effect on the above analysis is to replace $1/c^3$ in Eq. (44.24b) by $(2/c_t^3 + 1/c_l^3) \equiv 3/c_{av}^3$. This merely changes the relation of ω_D to the density and speed of sound [Eqs. (44.24b) and (44.26)]; Eq. (44.26) and the subsequent analysis remain unchanged.

45□THE ELECTRON-PHONON INTERACTION

Our simple model (the Debye model) for the dynamics of the uniform background allows us to investigate the *interaction* between the electrons and the collective modes of the background. The interaction hamiltonian is that of Sec. 3

$$H_{el-b} = \int d^3x \, d^3x' \frac{\rho_{el}(\mathbf{x}) \, \rho_b(\mathbf{x}')}{|\mathbf{x} - \mathbf{x}'|} \tag{45.1}$$

where $\rho_b = zen$ is the background charge density and z is the valence of the ions. With the definitions [see Eq. (44.5)]

$$\rho_b = \rho_0 + \delta\rho_b \tag{45.2}$$

$$\delta\rho_b = ze\delta n = -zen_0 \boldsymbol{\nabla} \cdot \mathbf{d} \tag{45.3}$$

Eq. (45.1) becomes

$$H_{el-b} = H_{el-b}^0 + \int d^3x \, d^3x' \frac{\rho_{el}(\mathbf{x}) \, \delta\rho_b(\mathbf{x}')}{|\mathbf{x} - \mathbf{x}'|} \tag{45.4}$$

The first term has already been included in the hamiltonian $H_{el\text{-gas}}$ of the electron gas in an inert uniformly charged background [Eq. (3.19)]; the second is the electron-phonon interaction. To examine this quantity we use Eqs. (2.8) and (45.3) and substitute the field expansions in the Schrödinger picture

$$\hat{\psi}(\mathbf{x}) = \sum_{k\lambda} V^{-\frac{1}{2}} e^{i\mathbf{k}\cdot\mathbf{x}} \eta_\lambda a_{k\lambda} \tag{45.5a}$$

$$\hat{\mathbf{d}}(\mathbf{x}) = \frac{-i}{(Mn_0)^{\frac{1}{2}}} \sum_{k} \left(\frac{\hbar}{2\omega_k V}\right)^{\frac{1}{2}} \frac{\mathbf{k}}{k} [c_k e^{i\mathbf{k}\cdot\mathbf{x}} - c_k^\dagger e^{-i\mathbf{k}\cdot\mathbf{x}}] \, \theta(\omega_D - \omega_k) \tag{45.5b}$$

where ω_D is the Debye frequency. [Note that Eq. (44.15) is in the interaction picture with respect to $\hat{H}_0$, and that the Debye model cuts off the phonon spectrum at a wave number ω_D/c.] This procedure yields

$$\hat{H}_{el-ph} \equiv \int d^3x \, d^3x' \frac{\hat{\rho}_{el}(\mathbf{x}) \, \delta\hat{\rho}_b(\mathbf{x}')}{|\mathbf{x} - \mathbf{x}'|} \tag{45.6a}$$

$$\hat{H}_{el-ph} = \frac{ze^2}{c} \left(\frac{n_0}{M}\right)^{\frac{1}{2}} \sum_{k\lambda} \sum_{q} \left(\frac{\hbar\omega_q}{2V}\right)^{\frac{1}{2}} \frac{4\pi}{\mathbf{q}^2} \theta(\omega_D - \omega_q) [a_{k+q,\lambda}^\dagger a_{k,\lambda} c_q$$

$$+ a_{k,\lambda}^\dagger a_{k+q,\lambda} c_q^\dagger] \tag{45.6b}$$

The electron-phonon coupling is proportional to the characteristic coulomb interaction

$$U_0^c(\mathbf{q}) = 4\pi e^2 \mathbf{q}^{-2} \tag{45.7}$$

Our investigations in Secs. 12 and 14 showed, however, that the effective interaction between two charges in the medium governed by $H_{el\text{-gas}}$ is modified by the dielectric constant and becomes $U^c(q) = U_0^c(q)/\kappa(q)$. In the approximation of

summing the ring diagrams with repeated coulomb interactions between the electrons (Fig. 12.4), the *effective* static coulomb interaction becomes[1] [see Eq. (12.65)]

$$U_r^c(\mathbf{q}) = \frac{4\pi e^2}{\mathbf{q}^2 + q_{TF}^2} \qquad |\mathbf{q}| \ll k_F \tag{45.8}$$

where the Thomas-Fermi wave number is given by Eqs. (12.67) and (14.13) as

$$\frac{4\pi}{q_{TF}^2} = \left(\frac{9\pi}{4}\right)^{\frac{1}{3}} \frac{\pi^2}{r_s k_F^2} = \frac{\pi^2 a_0}{k_F} \tag{45.9}$$

It is clear from this relation that q_{TF}^{-1} is of the order of the lattice spacing; since the cutoff ω_D/c in Eq. (45.6b) is of this same order, we may take

$$U_r^c(\mathbf{q}) \approx 4\pi e^2 q_{TF}^{-2} \tag{45.10}$$

for almost all phonon wavenumbers of interest.   With the substitution

$$\frac{4\pi}{\mathbf{q}^2} \to \frac{4\pi}{\mathbf{q}^2 + q_{TF}^2} \approx \frac{4\pi}{q_{TF}^2}$$

the electron-phonon interaction in Eq. (45.6) may be rewritten as

$$\hat{H}_{el-ph} = \gamma \int d^3x \, \hat{\psi}_\alpha^\dagger(\mathbf{x}) \, \hat{\psi}_\alpha(\mathbf{x}) \, \hat{\varphi}(\mathbf{x}) \tag{45.11}$$

where the following definitions have been introduced

$$\gamma \equiv \frac{ze^2}{c} \frac{4\pi}{q_{TF}^2} \left(\frac{n_0}{M}\right)^{\frac{1}{2}} = \frac{z\hbar^2 \pi^2}{mk_F} \frac{n_0}{B^{\frac{1}{2}}} \tag{45.12}$$

$$\delta\hat{n}(\mathbf{x}) = -n_0 \, \mathbf{\nabla} \cdot \hat{\mathbf{d}}(\mathbf{x}) \equiv -\frac{1}{c}\left(\frac{n_0}{M}\right)^{\frac{1}{2}} \hat{\varphi}(\mathbf{x}) \tag{45.13}$$

Note that the coupling constant γ is independent of the ion mass M and has dimensions of (energy $\times$ volume)$^{\frac{1}{2}}$.   The new phonon field $\hat{\varphi}(\mathbf{x})$ can be written in the Schrödinger picture

$$\hat{\varphi}(\mathbf{x}) = \sum_{\mathbf{k}} \left(\frac{\hbar\omega_k}{2V}\right)^{\frac{1}{2}} [c_k e^{i\mathbf{k}\cdot\mathbf{x}} + c_k^\dagger e^{-i\mathbf{k}\cdot\mathbf{x}}] \, \theta(\omega_D - \omega_k) \tag{45.14}$$

The density variations of the background also modify its own coulomb energy according to

$$H_b = \tfrac{1}{2} \int d^3x \, d^3x' \frac{\rho_b(\mathbf{x}) \rho_b(\mathbf{x}')}{|\mathbf{x} - \mathbf{x}'|} \tag{45.15a}$$

---

[1] Although this equation is strictly valid only at high densities ($r_s \ll 1$), a more general treatment merely replaces $q_{TF}^2 = 3\Omega_{pl}^2/v_F^2$ by Ω_{pl}^2/s^2, where s is the exact speed of sound in the model considered in Sec. 3 (D. Pines and P. Nozières, "The Theory of Quantum Liquids," vol. I., secs. 3.1 and 3.4, W. A. Benjamin, Inc., New York, 1966).

$$H_b = H_b^0 + \tfrac{1}{2}z^2 e^2 \int d^3x \, d^3x' \frac{\delta n(\mathbf{x}) \, \delta n(\mathbf{x}')}{|\mathbf{x} - \mathbf{x}'|} \tag{45.15b}$$

where the second result follows from $\int d^3x \, \delta n(\mathbf{x}) = 0$.   The first term on the right side of Eq. (45.15b) has already been included in $H_{el\text{-}gas}$.   Furthermore, the coulomb interaction in the integrand of the second term is again shielded at large distances, and its effects at small distances have already been included in B, which is assumed to be given.   This term therefore will be neglected.

In this way, we arrive at the (approximate) hamiltonian for the coupled electron-phonon system[1]

$$\hat{H} = \hat{H}_{el\text{-}gas} + \hat{H}_{ph} + \gamma \int d^3x \, \hat{\psi}_\alpha^\dagger(\mathbf{x}) \, \hat{\psi}_\alpha(\mathbf{x}) \, \hat{\varphi}(\mathbf{x}) \tag{45.16}$$

where $\hat{H}_{el\text{-}gas}$ was discussed in Sec. 3 and $\hat{H}_{ph}$ in Sec. 44.   Since $\hat{H}_{ph}$ describes physical phonons with the experimental long-wavelength dispersion relation, the interaction term clearly represents the coupling between electrons and physical phonons.[2]   It must be remembered, however, that the bare electron-phonon hamiltonian with $U_0^c(\mathbf{q})$ [Eq. (45.6b)] has been screened by summing the electron ring diagrams, as shown in Fig. 45.1.   The resulting effective interaction $U_r^c(\mathbf{q})$

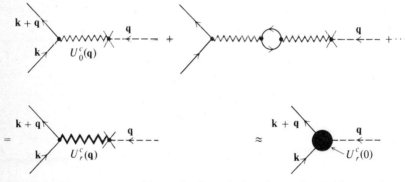

Fig. 45.1   Diagrams summed in passing from the bare interaction $U_0^c(\mathbf{q})$ (wavy line) to the shielded electron-phonon interaction $U_r^c(0)$.

[1] F. Bloch, *Z. Physik*, **52**:555 (1928); H. Fröhlich, *Phys. Rev.*, **79**:845 (1950); H. Fröhlich, *Proc. Roy. Soc.* (*London*), **215**:291 (1952).   The approach in this section essentially follows the latter paper.

[2] As an alternative approach, the ions and electrons are often considered a gas of charged particles.   The low density of the ions ($\hbar^2/Me^2 \ll n_0^{-\frac{1}{3}}$) then leads to the formation of a Wigner lattice, whose bare longitudinal phonons oscillate at the ionic plasma frequency $(4\pi n_0 z^2 e^2/M)^{\frac{1}{2}}$. The inclusion of ring diagrams screens the singular coulomb interactions, however, and yields the observed phonon spectrum.   This model also allows an improved calculation of the elastic constants, which agree quite well with experimental values.   See, for example, J. Bardeen and D. Pines, *Phys. Rev.*, **99**:1140 (1955); T. D. Schultz, "Quantum Field Theory and the Many-Body Problem," chap. IV, Gordon and Breach, Science Publishers, New York, 1964; J. R. Schrieffer, "Theory of Superconductivity," sec. 6.2, W. A. Benjamin, Inc., New York, 1964.

is then approximated by the constant $U_r^c(0)$, thus yielding the renormalized electron-phonon hamiltonian (45.11). When computing with Eq. (45.16), we must, of course, omit those diagrams already included in this renormalization procedure.

46□THE COUPLED-FIELD THEORY

To simplify the ensuing discussion, the coulomb interactions between the electrons will be treated in the Hartree-Fock approximation, and we shall examine

$$\hat{H}_{\text{model}} \equiv \sum_{k\lambda > k_F} \epsilon_k a_{k\lambda}^\dagger a_{k\lambda} - \sum_{k\lambda < k_F} \epsilon_k b_{k\lambda}^\dagger b_{k\lambda} + \sum_{k < \omega_D/c} (c_k^\dagger c_k + \tfrac{1}{2}) \hbar\omega_k$$

$$+ \gamma \int d^3x \, \hat{\psi}_\alpha^\dagger(\mathbf{x}) \, \hat{\psi}_\alpha(\mathbf{x}) \, \hat{\phi}(\mathbf{x}) \quad (46.1)$$

where ϵ_k are now the Hartree-Fock single-particle energies of the electron-gas.[1] The present treatment concentrates on the zero-temperature properties of the system, and the extension to finite temperatures is left for the problems. We now wish to examine the Green's functions for the coupled problem specified in Eq. (46.1). The motivation is the same as before; the Green's functions give the expectation value of any one-body operator, the poles of the Green's functions give the exact excitation energies of the system, and the ground-state energy shift of the interacting system can be computed from the electron Green's function according to Eq. (7.30)

$$E - E_0 = -V \int_0^\gamma \frac{d\gamma'}{\gamma'} \lim_{\eta \to 0^+} \int \frac{d^4q}{(2\pi)^4} (\hbar q_0 - \epsilon_q) \, iG_{\alpha\alpha}^{\gamma'}(q) \, e^{iq_0\eta} \quad (46.2)$$

where E_0 is the ground-state energy of the uncoupled electron-phonon system. (There is no factor of $\frac{1}{2}$ in this result since the interaction is here proportional to $\hat{\psi}^\dagger \hat{\psi}$.) In addition, the Green's functions describe the linear response of the system to an external perturbation.

FEYNMAN RULES FOR $T = 0$

The general field theory of Chap. 3 applies just as before. In the interaction picture Wick's theorem allows a decomposition into Feynman diagrams, and only connected diagrams need be considered. We shall simply state the Feynman rules in momentum space for an arbitrary process.[2]

---

[1] These energies must be appropriately smoothed at the Fermi surface to take into account the effect of summing the ring diagrams (see Prob. 8.2).

[2] Note that these Feynman rules, because of their generality, are given in a slightly different form from those in Secs. 9 and 25. To construct the Green's functions $iG_{\alpha\beta}(q)$ or $iD(q)$, an explicit factor $(2\pi)^4 \delta^{(4)}(q - q')$ must be inserted for one of the end lines (See Fig. 9.10 and accompanying discussion); for example, the lowest-order contribution to $iD(q)$ is $\int d^4q' \, i(2\pi)^{-4} D^0(q')(2\pi)^4 \delta^{(4)}(q - q') = iD^0(q)$.

1. Construct all topologically distinct Feynman diagrams, the basic vertices being the emission and absorption of a phonon by an electron as illustrated in Fig. 46.1.

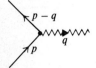

Fig. 46.1   Basic electron-phonon vertex.

2. Assign a factor $-i\gamma/\hbar$ for each order in perturbation theory.
3. Include a factor $i(2\pi)^{-4} G^0_{\alpha\beta}(q)$ for each electron line where

$$G^0_{\alpha\beta}(\mathbf{q},q_0) = \delta_{\alpha\beta}\left[\frac{\theta(|\mathbf{q}| - k_F)}{q_0 - \epsilon_{\mathbf{q}}/\hbar + i\eta} + \frac{\theta(k_F - |\mathbf{q}|)}{q_0 - \epsilon_{\mathbf{q}}/\hbar - i\eta}\right] \qquad (46.3)$$

and take the spin matrix products along the electron lines.
4. Include a factor $i(2\pi)^{-4} D^0(q)$ for each phonon line.   To compute the phonon propagator, we must examine

$$iD^0(x - x') \equiv \langle 0|T[\hat{\phi}_I(x)\,\hat{\phi}_I(x')]|0\rangle$$

$$= \begin{cases} \displaystyle\sum_{\mathbf{k}} \frac{\hbar\omega_{\mathbf{k}}}{2V} e^{i\mathbf{k}\cdot(\mathbf{x}-\mathbf{x}')-i\omega_{\mathbf{k}}(t-t')}\,\theta(\omega_D - \omega_{\mathbf{k}}) & t > t' \\[2ex] \displaystyle\sum_{\mathbf{k}} \frac{\hbar\omega_{\mathbf{k}}}{2V} e^{-i\mathbf{k}\cdot(\mathbf{x}-\mathbf{x}')+i\omega_{\mathbf{k}}(t-t')}\,\theta(\omega_D - \omega_{\mathbf{k}}) & t' > t \end{cases} \qquad (46.4)$$

and its Fourier transform

$$iD^0(x - x') \equiv (2\pi)^{-4} \int d^4q\, e^{iq\cdot(x-x')}\, iD^0(q) \qquad (46.5)$$

which can be written

$$D^0(q) = \tfrac{1}{2}\hbar\omega_{\mathbf{q}}\left(\frac{1}{q_0 - \omega_{\mathbf{q}} + i\eta} - \frac{1}{q_0 + \omega_{\mathbf{q}} - i\eta}\right)\theta(\omega_D - \omega_{\mathbf{q}})$$

$$= \hbar\frac{\omega_{\mathbf{q}}^2}{q_0^2 - (\omega_{\mathbf{q}} - i\eta)^2}\,\theta(\omega_D - \omega_{\mathbf{q}}) \qquad (46.6)$$

5. Conserve frequency and wave vector at each vertex with

$$(2\pi)^4\,\delta^{(4)}\left(\sum_i q_i\right)$$

6. Integrate over all internal lines $\int d^4q$.
7. Include a factor $(-1)^F$ where F is the number of closed fermion loops.
8. Discard all diagrams that have subunits connected to the rest of the graph by only one phonon line as in Fig. 46.2.   This result follows from momentum

conservation, which implies that the phonon line must have $q = 0$, and Eq. (46.6) shows that $D^0(q = 0) \equiv D^0(0) = 0$ for any finite η. More generally, we note that $D^0(\mathbf{q} = 0, q_0) = 0$ because the fundamental field $\hat{\varphi}$ is proportional to $\nabla \cdot \hat{\mathbf{d}}$; hence the integral of $\hat{\varphi}$ over all space vanishes identically.

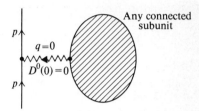

Fig. 46.2 General tadpole diagram, which vanishes.

THE EQUIVALENT ELECTRON-ELECTRON INTERACTION

These rules for phonon exchange allow us to put all the phonon-exchange Feynman diagrams for the electron Green's function in one-to-one correspondence with the Feynman diagrams of an equivalent spin-independent potential (Fig. 46.3), which is given by[1]

Fig. 46.3 Identification of the equivalent electron-electron potential in the electron-phonon problem.

$$U_0(\mathbf{q},q_0) \equiv -i\hbar^{-1} \gamma^2 \, i D^0(q) = \gamma^2 \hbar^{-1} D^0(q) \tag{46.7a}$$

$$U_0(\mathbf{q},q_0) = \gamma^2 \frac{\omega_\mathbf{q}^2}{q_0^2 - (\omega_\mathbf{q} - i\eta)^2} \theta(\omega_D - \omega_\mathbf{q}) \tag{46.7b}$$

This potential is now *frequency dependent*, even in lowest order. In the static limit, Eq. (46.7b) reduces to

$$U_0(\mathbf{q},0) = -\gamma^2 \, \theta(\omega_D - \omega_\mathbf{q}) \equiv \int d^3x \, e^{-i\mathbf{q}\cdot\mathbf{x}} V_{eq}(\mathbf{x}) \tag{46.8}$$

Since ω_D/c is comparable with k_F, the upper cutoff can be neglected in almost all cases of interest. If we assume $U_0(\mathbf{q},0) = -\gamma^2$ for all $\mathbf{q}$, then the equivalent interelectron potential becomes an *attractive delta function*.

$$V_{eq}(\mathbf{x}) = -\gamma^2 \, \delta(\mathbf{x}) \tag{46.9}$$

[1] The phonon-exchange potential between electrons was first discussed by H. Fröhlich, *Phys. Rev.*, *loc. cit.*

The consequences of an attractive interaction between particles close to the Fermi surface have been considered in Secs. 36 and 37, and they are explored in detail in Chap. 13. It is also clear from Eq. (46.7b) that $U_0(\mathbf{q},q_0)$ will cease to be attractive when the energy transfer q_0 satisfies $|q_0| > \omega_\mathbf{q}$. Since $\omega_\mathbf{q} < \omega_D$, we therefore have

$$U_0(\mathbf{q},q_0) > 0 \quad \text{if } |q_0| > \omega_D \tag{46.10}$$

In the noninteracting ground state where the electrons form a filled Fermi sea $U_0(\mathbf{q},q_0)$ can be attractive only for those electrons lying within an energy shell of thickness $\hbar\omega_D$ below the Fermi surface, because only those electrons can be excited to unoccupied levels with energy transfer less than $\hbar\omega_D$. Similarly, $U_0(\mathbf{q},q_0)$ can be attractive only when a pair is excited to unoccupied states lying within an energy shell of thickness $\hbar\omega_D$ above the Fermi surface.

VERTEX PARTS AND DYSON'S EQUATIONS

The graphical structure of the coupled-field theory can be elegantly summarized in a set of equations first derived by Dyson[1] in connection with quantum electro-dynamics.[2] These nonlinear integral equations involve the exact propagators and vertices. When iterated consistently to any given order in the coupling constant, they reproduce the Feynman-Dyson perturbation theory. Nevertheless, Dyson's equations are more than a convenient summary of perturbation theory, and their generality is often used to seek nonperturbative solutions.

The proper electron self-energy has already been discussed in Sec. 9. The proper phonon self-energy $\Pi^\star$ is introduced in an exactly analogous fashion, and leads to equations that are formally identical with those of the effective interaction propagator of Sec. 9

$$G = G^0 + G^0 \Sigma^\star G \tag{46.11}$$

$$D = D^0 + \gamma^2 \hbar^{-1} D^0 \Pi^\star D \tag{46.12}$$

where $\Pi^\star$ is computed with the effective potential of Eq. (46.7). There is one important new element, however, known as a *vertex part*, defined to be a part connected to the rest of the diagram by two fermion lines and one phonon line. Two examples are shown in Fig. 46.4. Momentum conservation implies that a

[1] F. J. Dyson, *Phys. Rev.*, **75**:486 (1949); **75**:1736 (1949).

[2] In fact, the Feynman-Dyson perturbation theory of quantum electrodynamics is formally identical with that of the electron-phonon problem, the main difference being the explicit form of the propagators. In addition, quantum electrodynamics has no diagrams with an *odd* number of photon lines connected to a closed fermion loop; such processes vanish by charge conjugation, in accordance with Furry's theorem [W. Furry, *Phys. Rev.*, **51**:125 (1937)]. For quite a different reason (see rule 8 of the Feynman rules in this section), the electron-phonon system has no closed electron loops connected to the rest of a diagram by *one* phonon line. Consequently, neither field theory has tadpole diagrams.

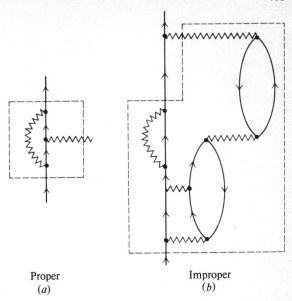

Proper   Improper
(a)   (b)

Fig. 46.4 Typical vertex parts: (a) proper, (b) improper.

vertex part depends on two independent momenta, and all spin indices may be suppressed because the interaction is spin independent. A *proper vertex part* is defined to have no self-energies on the external legs of the vertex. Thus the second diagram in Fig. 46.4 is improper, for it has self-energy insertions on both the fermion and phonon legs.

To obtain Dyson's equations, we now attempt to write the integral equations for the Green's functions in terms of the proper vertex and proper self-energy parts. Take an arbitrary Feynman diagram with any number of external legs and

1. Remove all electron self-energy insertions.
2. Remove all phonon self-energy (polarization) insertions.
3. Remove all vertex insertions.

The remainder is known as an *irreducible* or *skeleton diagram*. The irreducible diagrams for the proper self-energies and vertex parts *themselves* are defined to be those diagrams remaining after this process has been carried out *up to* the point where a further reduction would lead to a simple line or point, respectively. Some examples are shown in Fig. 46.5. The lowest-order fermion self-energy, phonon polarization part, and vertex correction are thus defined to be their own skeleton diagrams. We now claim the following:

1. For every graph there is a *unique* skeleton.
2. *All* graphs can be built up by inserting the exact Green's function G, phonon propagator D, and proper vertex part Γ in all the skeleton diagrams.

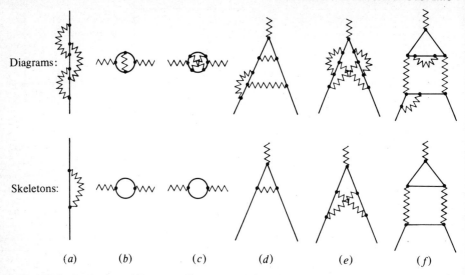

Diagrams:

Skeletons:

(a)   (b)   (c)   (d)   (e)   (f)

Fig. 46.5   Reduction of Feynman diagrams to their skeletons.

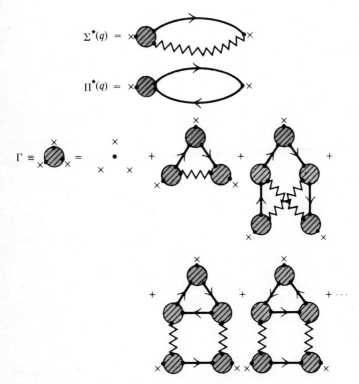

$$\Sigma^{\star}(q) =$$

$$\Pi^{\star}(q) =$$

$$\Gamma \equiv \quad = \quad + \quad + \quad +$$

$$+ \quad + \quad + \cdots$$

Fig. 46.6   Dyson's equations for the electron-phonon system.

For example, both $\Sigma^\star(q)$ and $\Pi^\star(q)$ have only one skeleton, that shown in Fig. 46.5a and b, and *all* contributions to $\Sigma^\star(q)$ and $\Pi^\star(q)$ are obtained by inserting the exact G, D, and Γ in these skeletons as indicated in Fig. 46.6. Note that the exact proper vertex must be inserted at only one end of these skeleton diagrams; otherwise some diagrams will be counted twice. For example, there is only one graph of the type shown in Fig. 46.5b, whereas this graph would appear twice if we were to insert the exact vertex in both ends in Fig. 46.6.

The remaining problem is to write an equation for the exact proper vertex. Unfortunately, this aim cannot be achieved in closed form because there is an infinite number of irreducible skeleton vertex diagrams. We must therefore resort to a series expansion and have shown the first few terms in Fig. 46.6.[1] The

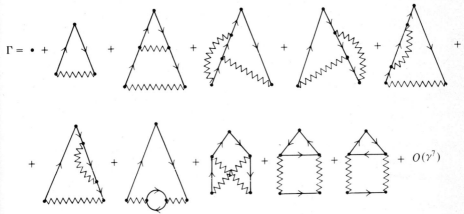

Fig. 46.7 The proper vertex Γ' to order γ^5.

lowest-order vertex, which is indicated by a point, is just γ, and the corrections become

$$\Gamma \equiv \gamma(1 + \Gamma^{(2)} + \Gamma^{(4)} + \cdots) \tag{46.13}$$

To iterate these equations through order γ^5 in the interaction strength, the propagators and vertex correction computed to order γ^2 must be inserted in the second diagram, while the lowest-order result may be inserted in the last three diagrams because they are already explicitly of order γ^5. This iteration procedure yields the expansion shown in Fig. 46.7, which contains *all* proper vertex parts through order γ^5. We can now combine these results to obtain the nonlinear coupled *Dyson integral equations* shown in Fig. 46.6. Although we have not derived them, we claim it is plausible that *a consistent iteration of the Dyson integral equations to any given order in γ reproduces the Feynman-Dyson perturbation theory.*

[1] Our convention in Fig. 46.6 is that the electron line enters from the left and exits from the right.

The components of Dyson's equations are the exact Green's functions G and D and the exact proper vertex Γ.   It is therefore possible to attempt a direct solution of these equations without resorting to perturbation theory.   For electrons in a normal metal interacting through phonon exchange, such an approach can be greatly simplified by the remarkable theorem derived by Migdal[1]

$$\Gamma = \gamma \left\{ 1 + O\left[\left(\frac{m}{M} \right)^{\frac{1}{2}} \right] \right\} \tag{46.14}$$

where m/M is the ratio of the electron mass to the ion mass.   To an excellent approximation, Eq. (46.14) allows us to *replace the vertex by the point value* γ, and the problem is thus reduced to the coupled equations for G and D.   The detailed discussion of the corresponding solutions is beyond the scope of this book, and the reader is referred to the literature for details.[2]   We shall, however, conclude this chapter with a discussion of Migdal's theorem.

47□MIGDAL'S THEOREM[3]

Migdal's theorem states that the exact vertex in the electron-phonon system satisfies Eq. (46.14), where m/M is the ratio of the electron mass to the ion mass. We shall not prove this result to all orders but merely show it to be true for the first vertex correction.   This calculation illustrates the physical ideas involved in the theorem, and the extension of the proof to higher orders requires no new principles.[4]

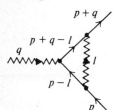

Fig. 47.1   Second-order vertex correction.

The first vertex correction, which is denoted $\Gamma^{(2)}$ in Eq. (46.13) and is shown in Fig. 47.1, can be written with the Feynman rules

$$\Gamma^{(2)}(p+q,p) = \frac{i\gamma^2 k_F^3}{\epsilon_F^0} \int \frac{d^4l}{(2\pi)^4} \frac{\omega_l^2}{l_0^2 - (\omega_l - i\eta)^2}$$

$$\times \frac{\theta(\omega_D - \omega_l)}{[p_0 - l_0 - \epsilon_{\mathbf{p}-\mathbf{l}} + i\eta S(\mathbf{p}-\mathbf{l})][p_0 + q_0 - l_0 - \epsilon_{\mathbf{p}+\mathbf{q}-\mathbf{l}} + i\eta S(\mathbf{p}+\mathbf{q}-\mathbf{l})]} \tag{47.1}$$

[1] A. B. Migdal, *Sov. Phys.-JETP*, **7**:996 (1958).
[2] See, for example, J. R. Schrieffer, *loc. cit.*; G. M. Eliashberg, *Sov. Phys.-JETP*, **16**:780 (1963).
[3] A. B. Migdal, *loc. cit.*
[4] In fact, Migdal is content to assert "It can be shown that this estimate is not changed when diagrams of a higher order are taken into account."   (A. B. Migdal, *loc. cit.*)

Here the integral is now dimensionless, all wavenumbers being measured in units of k_F and all frequencies in units of $\epsilon_F^0/\hbar = \hbar k_F^2/2m$, and

$$S(\mathbf{q}) \equiv \begin{cases} +1 & |\mathbf{q}| > 1 \\ -1 & |\mathbf{q}| < 1 \end{cases} \qquad (47.2)$$

In these units the phonon frequencies are proportional to the factor $(m/M)^{\frac{1}{2}}$

$$\omega_1 = \left(\frac{2m}{M}\right)^{\frac{1}{2}} \left(\frac{B}{n_0\,\epsilon_F^0}\right)^{\frac{1}{2}} |\mathbf{l}| \qquad (47.3)$$

and the maximum wave number $l_{max} \equiv \omega_D/c$ is a pure number [see Eqs. (44.24b) and (44.26)]

$$l_{max} = (6/z)^{\frac{1}{3}} \qquad (47.4)$$

Note that $\Gamma^{(2)}$ depends on the ion mass only through the factor ω_1 and thus through the sound velocity. In contrast, the bulk modulus B depends only on the potential-energy surface for the crystal and is independent of M. The phonon propagator has a factor of ω_1^2 in the numerator, and integrations over frequencies can reduce this at most by one power {that is, $(2\pi i)^{-1} \int dl_0\,\omega_1^2[l_0^2 - (\omega_1 - i\eta)^2]^{-1} = -\frac{1}{2}\omega_1$}; consequently, the remaining expression for the vertex correction is still linear in ω_1 and hence in $(m/M)^{\frac{1}{2}}$. This observation provides the basis for Migdal's theorem.

We now verify this result explicitly for $\Gamma^{(2)}$ by first carrying out the integral over l_0, closing the contour in either the upper or lower half of the l_0 plane. After some familiar algebra, the result can be written in the form

$$\Gamma^{(2)}(p+q,p) = \frac{\gamma^2 k_F^3}{2\epsilon_F^0} \int \frac{d^3l}{(2\pi)^3}\,\omega_1\,\theta(\omega_D - \omega_1)$$

$$\times \left\{\frac{1}{q_0 + \epsilon_{\mathbf{p}-\mathbf{l}} - \epsilon_{\mathbf{p}+\mathbf{q}-\mathbf{l}} + i\eta[S(\mathbf{p}+\mathbf{q}-\mathbf{l}) - S(\mathbf{p}-\mathbf{l})]}\right.$$

$$\times \left[\frac{1}{p_0 - \epsilon_{\mathbf{p}-\mathbf{l}} - (\omega_1 - i\eta)\,S(\mathbf{p}-\mathbf{l})}\right.$$

$$\left.\left. - \frac{1}{p_0 + q_0 - \epsilon_{\mathbf{p}+\mathbf{q}-\mathbf{l}} - (\omega_1 - i\eta)\,S(\mathbf{p}+\mathbf{q}-\mathbf{l})}\right]\right\} \qquad (47.5)$$

If the quantity in braces is denoted by $f(\omega_1)$, this expression can be rewritten

$$\Gamma^{(2)}(p+q,p) = \frac{\gamma^2 k_F^3}{2\epsilon_F^0} \int \frac{d^3l}{(2\pi)^3}\,\omega_1\,\theta(\omega_D - \omega_1)\,\{f(0) + [f(\omega_1) - f(0)]\} \qquad (47.6)$$

Provided that the integral containing $f(0)$ converges, the limiting expression for small $(m/M)^{\frac{1}{2}}$ can be obtained by neglecting the second term containing

$f(\omega_1) - f(0)$. The proof is therefore reduced to showing that the limiting expression

$$\Gamma^{(2)}(p+q,p) \approx \frac{\gamma^2 k_F^3}{2\epsilon_F^0} \left(\frac{2m}{M}\right)^{\frac{1}{2}} \left(\frac{B}{n_0\,\epsilon_F^0}\right)^{\frac{1}{2}} \int \frac{d^3 l}{(2\pi)^3} \, l\theta(l_{\max}-l)$$

$$\times \frac{1}{p_0 - \epsilon_{\mathbf{p-l}} + i\eta S(\mathbf{p-l})} \frac{1}{p_0 + q_0 - \epsilon_{\mathbf{p+q-l}} + i\eta S(\mathbf{p+q-l})} \qquad \left(\frac{m}{M}\right)^{\frac{1}{2}} \to 0 \tag{47.7}$$

is well defined, for the explicit factor $(m/M)^{\frac{1}{2}}$ in front of the dimensionless integral then gives the desired result.

The expression of Eq. (47.7), however, is as well defined as any integral over fermion Green's functions that appears in the $T = 0$ theory. The Debye cutoff limits the momentum integral to a finite region, thus removing any divergences at large l. In addition, real crystals have a smooth cutoff at the upper end of the phonon spectrum so that any logarithmic singularities caused by the sharp Debye cutoff are spurious. Furthermore, the infrared divergence of Eq. (47.7) at $q_0 = \mathbf{q} = p_0 = \mathbf{p} = 0$ [which may give rise to terms proportional to $(m/M)^{\frac{1}{2}} \ln (m/M)^{\frac{1}{2}}$] is irrelevant because the weak phonon interaction is only important for electrons near the Fermi surface where $|\mathbf{p}| \approx 1$.

The only remaining source of difficulty arises from the singularities in the integrand in Eq. (47.7). Although each one individually gives rise to a finite integral, the resulting expression may diverge when the two singularities come together. We may isolate the contribution of this region with the following series of steps.

1. The infinitesimal imaginary terms in the denominators are relevant only where the real part vanishes. Thus we may replace $S(\mathbf{p-l})$ and $S(\mathbf{p+q-l})$ with $\mathscr{I}(p_0)$ and $\mathscr{I}(p_0+q_0)$, where $\mathscr{I}(p_0)$ is defined by

$$\mathscr{I}(p_0) \equiv \begin{cases} +1 & p_0 > \epsilon_F \\ -1 & p_0 < \epsilon_F \end{cases}$$

Here $\epsilon_F \equiv \epsilon_{|\mathbf{p}|=1}$ and $\partial\epsilon_{\mathbf{p}}/\partial|\mathbf{p}|$ is assumed positive.

2. The radial part of the integrand in (47.7) contains the factor $l^3\,dl$, which weights the region $l \approx l_{\max}$ most heavily. As a simple approximation we replace one factor of l by its value at $l_{\max}$ and then transform to the new integration variable $\mathbf{t} \equiv \mathbf{p} - \mathbf{l}$. Since the remaining integral over $\mathbf{t}$ converges if $\epsilon_t \propto t^2$ at large t, we extend the $\mathbf{t}$ integration over all space.

3. The energy $\epsilon_{\mathbf{t+q}}$ in the second denominator is expanded about the value ϵ_t

$$\epsilon_{\mathbf{t+q}} \approx \epsilon_t + \mathbf{q}\cdot\hat{t}\,\frac{\partial\epsilon_t}{\partial t} + \cdots$$

After these three steps, the singular part $\Gamma_S^{(2)}$ of Eq. (47.7) becomes

$$\Gamma_S^{(2)}(p+q,p) \approx \frac{\gamma^2 k_F^3}{2\epsilon_F^0}\left[\omega_D \int \frac{d^3t}{(2\pi)^3}\frac{1}{p_0 - \epsilon_t + i\eta\mathscr{A}(p_0)}\right.$$

$$\left.\times \frac{1}{p_0 + q_0 - \epsilon_t - \mathbf{q}\cdot\hat{t}\,\partial\epsilon_t/\partial t + i\eta\mathscr{A}(p_0+q_0)}\right]$$

and the integral over angles of $\hat{t}$ can now be carried out

$$\Gamma_S^{(2)}(p+q,p) \approx \frac{\gamma^2 k_F^3}{8\pi^2 \epsilon_F^0}\left[\frac{\omega_D}{q}\int_0^\infty \frac{t^2\,dt}{p_0 - \epsilon_t + i\eta\mathscr{A}(p_0)}\left(\frac{\partial\epsilon_t}{\partial t}\right)^{-1}\right.$$

$$\left.\times \ln\frac{p_0 + q_0 - \epsilon_t + q\,\partial\epsilon_t/\partial t + i\eta\mathscr{A}(p_0+q_0)}{p_0 + q_0 - \epsilon_t - q\,\partial\epsilon_t/\partial t + i\eta\mathscr{A}(p_0+q_0)}\right] \quad (47.8)$$

4. To study the region where the singularities coalesce, we evaluate the slowly varying functions t^2 and $\partial\epsilon_t/\partial t$ at the position of the first singularity, $\epsilon_t = p_0$. With the new variable $\zeta \equiv \epsilon_t - p_0$, Eq. (47.8) reduces to

$$\Gamma_S^{(2)}(p+q,p) \approx -\frac{\gamma^2 k_F^3}{32\pi^2 \epsilon_F^0}\left[\left(\frac{\partial\epsilon_t}{\partial t^2}\right)^{-2}_{\epsilon_t=p_0}\frac{\omega_D}{q}\int_{\epsilon_0-p_0}^\infty \frac{d\zeta}{\zeta - i\eta\mathscr{A}(p_0)}\right.$$

$$\left.\times \ln\frac{\zeta - q_0 - q\,(\partial\epsilon_t/\partial t)_{\epsilon_t=p_0} - i\eta\mathscr{A}(p_0+q_0)}{\zeta - q_0 + q\,(\partial\epsilon_t/\partial t)_{\epsilon_t=p_0} - i\eta\mathscr{A}(p_0+q_0)}\right]$$

The singularity at $\zeta = i\eta\mathscr{A}(p_0)$ is important only for $p_0 > \epsilon_0$, when the integral includes the origin.   In this case, the structure of the singularities is unchanged when the integral is extended to $-\infty$ and evaluated with contour methods. If $\mathscr{A}(p_0)$ and $\mathscr{A}(p_0+q_0)$ have the same sign, the integral can clearly be closed in that half plane containing no singularities and vanishes.

5. Thus $\mathscr{A}(p_0)$ and $\mathscr{A}(p_0+q_0)$ must have opposite signs to yield a nonzero value. The integral can then be closed in that half plane containing the pole at $\zeta = i\eta\mathscr{A}(p_0)$ with the final result for $p_0 > \epsilon_0$ (reintroducing dimensional units)

$$\Gamma_S^{(2)}(p+q,p) \approx \frac{\gamma^2 \omega_D \hbar}{16\pi i q}\,\mathscr{A}(p_0)\left(\frac{\partial\epsilon_t}{\partial t^2}\right)^{-2}_{\epsilon_t=\hbar p_0}$$

$$\times \ln\frac{\hbar q_0 + q\,(\partial\epsilon_t/\partial t)_{\epsilon_t=\hbar p_0} + i\eta\mathscr{A}(p_0+q_0)}{\hbar q_0 - q\,(\partial\epsilon_t/\partial t)_{\epsilon_t=\hbar p_0} + i\eta\mathscr{A}(p_0+q_0)} \quad (47.9)$$

This expression is finite everywhere except at

$$\hbar q_0 = \pm q\left(\frac{\partial\epsilon_t}{\partial t}\right)_{\epsilon_t=\hbar p_0}$$

where it develops a logarithmic singularity.   We note the following points, however.

(a) A logarithmic singularity is generally integrable (for example, when we substitute Γ into the skeleton diagrams for $\Pi^\star$ and $\Sigma^\star$).

(b) If the electrons are on the energy shell and close to the Fermi surface, then $\hbar p_0 \approx \epsilon_F$ and $\Gamma_S^{(2)}$ is only singular when $|q_0| \approx q v_F$. Since $c \ll v_F$, this singularity is also unimportant both for real phonons with $|q_0| = qc$ and for virtual phonons with $|q_0| \leqslant qc \leqslant \omega_D$.

Thus Eq. (47.7) is well defined in most regions of interest, and we have a demonstration of Migdal's theorem to order γ^3.

Migdal's theorem also can be understood qualitatively by observing that the dimensionless ratio of the displacement of the lattice $\mathbf{d}(\mathbf{x})$ in Eq. (44.15) to the interatomic spacing $(\approx q_{TF}^{-1})$ depends on the ion mass as $(m/M)^{\frac{1}{4}}$. This quantity is small for heavy ions, explicitly verifying our remarks at the beginning of this chapter. (In fact, the small value of the ratio $(m/M)^{\frac{1}{4}}$ is just the criterion for the validity of the Born-Oppenheimer approximation.[1]) The ratio enters twice in evaluating a second-order correction as in Fig. 47.1, so that $\Gamma = \gamma\{1 + O[(m/M)^{\frac{1}{2}}]\}$. It is also true that $\Sigma^\star = O[(m/M)^{\frac{1}{2}}]$ for the same reason; as seen in Secs. 36 and 37, however, a weak interaction can still have drastic effects near the Fermi surface.

PROBLEMS

12.1. Prove that $\mu_{ph} = 0$ in the *interacting* electron-phonon system.

12.2. The exact phonon Green's function is defined in the Heisenberg picture as

$$iD(x - x') = \langle \mathbf{O} | T[\hat{\varphi}_H(x)\,\hat{\varphi}_H(x')] | \mathbf{O} \rangle$$

where $|\mathbf{O}\rangle$ is the exact normalized Heisenberg ground state of the coupled electron-phonon system. Hence derive the Lehmann representation for $iD(q)$.

12.3. Using the general relation $\partial \hat{O}/\partial t = (i/\hbar)[\hat{H},\hat{O}]$ for Heisenberg operators, show that the Heisenberg phonon field for the problem defined in Eq. (45.16) satisfies the following relations

$$[\hat{\varphi}_H(x),\hat{\varphi}_H(x')]_{t=t'} = 0$$

$$\left[\hat{\varphi}_H(x), \frac{\partial \hat{\varphi}_H(x')}{\partial t'}\right]_{t=t'} = \frac{\hbar c^2}{i}\nabla_x^2 \delta(\mathbf{x} - \mathbf{x}')$$

in the limit $\omega_D \to \infty$. Thus derive the following equation of motion

$$\left[\nabla^2 - \frac{1}{c^2}\frac{\partial^2}{\partial t^2}\right]\hat{\varphi}_H(x) = -\gamma\nabla_x^2[\hat{\psi}_{H\alpha}^\dagger(x)\,\hat{\psi}_{H\alpha}(x)]$$

How are these relations modified for finite ω_D?

[1] L. I. Schiff, *op. cit.*, p. 447.

12.4. In the limit $\omega_D \to \infty$ use the results of Prob. 12.3 to show that the phonon Green's function for the electron-phonon system satisfies

$$\left(\nabla_x^2 - \frac{1}{c^2}\frac{\partial^2}{\partial t^2}\right) iD(x - x') = \frac{\hbar}{i}\,\nabla_x^2 \delta(\mathbf{x} - \mathbf{x}')\,\delta(t - t')$$
$$- \gamma \nabla_x^2 \langle \mathbf{O}|T[\hat{\psi}_{H\alpha}^\dagger(x)\,\hat{\psi}_{H\alpha}(x)\,\hat{\varphi}_H(x')]|\mathbf{O}\rangle$$

Note that the last expression is one limit of the general vertex function. What is the corresponding result for finite ω_D?

12.5. (a) Evaluate the lowest-order contribution to $\Sigma^\star(q)$ shown in Fig. 46.6.
(b) Compute the corresponding $G(q)$ and discuss the resulting expressions for the single-particle energy and lifetime.
(c) How are the chemical potential, the specific heat, and the ground-state energy affected?

12.6. (a) Evaluate the lowest-order contribution to $\Pi^\star(q)$ shown in Fig. 46.6.
(b) Compute the corresponding phonon propagator and derive the following expressions for the renormalized phonon frequency Ω_q and inverse lifetime δ_q (neglect corrections of order c/v_F):

$$\Omega_q^2 = \omega_q^2\left[1 - 2N(0)\,\gamma^2\,g\left(\frac{q}{k_F}\right)\right]$$

$$\delta_q = \frac{\pi m \omega_q^2 \gamma^2\,N(0)}{2\hbar q k_F}\,\theta(2k_F - q)$$

Here $g(x)$ is given in Eq. (14.8) and $N(0) = mk_F/2\pi^2\hbar^2$ is the density of states for one spin projection at the Fermi surface. Note that $\partial\Omega_q/\partial q$ becomes infinite at $q = 2k_F$ (the Kohn effect‡) and that $2\delta_q/c$ is the ultrasonic attenuation constant α_n in the pure normal metal.

12.7. Write out Dyson's equations explicitly in momentum space to the order indicated in Fig. 46.6 using $G(q)$, $D(q)$ and $\Gamma(q_1,q_2)$.

12.8. Show that the energy shift in Eq. (46.2) also can be written

$$E - E_0 = \int_0^\gamma \frac{d\gamma'}{\gamma'} \int d^3x\,\langle \mathbf{O}|\gamma'\,\hat{\psi}_\alpha^\dagger(\mathbf{x})\,\hat{\psi}_\alpha(\mathbf{x})\,\hat{\varphi}(\mathbf{x})|\mathbf{O}\rangle_{\gamma'}$$

$$= -\int_0^\gamma d\gamma' \int d^3x \lim_{z \to x}\lim_{y \to x^+} \langle \mathbf{O}|T[\hat{\psi}_{H\alpha}(x)\,\hat{\psi}_{H\alpha}^\dagger(y)\,\hat{\varphi}_H(z)]|\mathbf{O}\rangle_{\gamma'}$$

where the matrix element must be calculated for all $0 \leqslant \gamma' \leqslant \gamma$. Analyze the right side of this expression in terms of Feynman diagrams and use Migdal's

‡ W. Kohn, *Phys. Rev. Letters*, **2**:393 (1959).

theorem to show that in the normal metal

$$E - E_0 \underset{(m/M)^{\frac{1}{3}} \to 0}{=} \frac{2}{\hbar} \int_0^\gamma \gamma' \, d\gamma' \int d^3x \lim_{z \to x} \lim_{y \to x^+} \int d^4r \, G^{\gamma'}(x-r) G^{\gamma'}(r-y)$$
$$\times D^{\gamma'}(r-z)$$

12.9. State the Feynman rules in momentum space for the electron and phonon propagators at finite temperature.

12.10. For the finite-temperature theory, define a vertex as in the $T = 0$ theory and write the analogs of Dyson's equations as discussed in Sec. 46.

12.11. Prove Migdal's theorem to order γ^3 in the finite-temperature theory.

12.12. Repeat Prob. 12.6 at finite temperature.

12.13. Discuss the linear response of the electron-phonon system at finite temperature to an external perturbation that couples to the lattice according to

$$H^{ex} = \int d^3x \, \tilde{V}^{ex}(\mathbf{x},t) \, \delta\hat{n}(\mathbf{x})$$
$$= \int d^3x \, V^{ex}(\mathbf{x},t) \, \hat{\varphi}(\mathbf{x})$$

(Compare, for example, Prob. 5.13.)

13
Superconductivity

In this chapter, we study the remarkable phenomenon of superconductivity.[1] Although the basic experimental facts are easily stated, the construction of a satisfactory microscopic description proved exceedingly difficult, and early theories were essentially phenomenological.   Nevertheless, these theories were surprisingly accurate and profoundly influenced the present many-body theory of superconductors.   For this reason, we consider it essential to discuss the phenomenological theories in detail, both for their intrinsic interest and as an introduction to the microscopic approach.   The latter (BCS) theory[2] represents

---

[1] Good introductory references are F. London, "Superfluids," vol. I, Dover Publications, Inc., New York, 1961; D. Shoenberg, "Superconductivity," 2d ed., Cambridge University Press, Cambridge, 1965; M. Tinkham, "Superconductivity," Gordon and Breach, Science Publishers, New York, 1965.
[2] J. Bardeen, L. N. Cooper, and J. R. Schrieffer, *Phys. Rev.*, **108**:1175 (1957).

one of the most successful applications of many-body techniques; in addition to its new predictions, it also justifies the earlier descriptions and allows an evaluation of the phenomenological constants.

48☐FUNDAMENTAL PROPERTIES OF SUPERCONDUCTORS

We start by summarizing the simplest experimental observations.   At the very least, any theory of superconductivity must account for these facts.

BASIC EXPERIMENTAL FACTS

1. *Infinite conductivity*: When any one of a large class of metallic elements or compounds is cooled to within a few degrees of absolute zero, it abruptly loses all trace of electrical resistivity at a definite critical temperature T_c.[1]   Since the transition is not accompanied by any change in structure or property of the crystal lattice, it is interpreted as an electronic transition, in which the conduction electrons enter an ordered state.   As a first approximation, we assume the usual constitutive equation (Ohm's law)

$$\mathbf{j} = \sigma\mathbf{E} \tag{48.1}$$

A combination with Maxwell's equation

$$\frac{\partial \mathbf{B}}{\partial t} = -c\,\mathrm{curl}\,\mathbf{E} \tag{48.2}$$

then implies that the flux density $\mathbf{B}$ remains constant for any medium with infinite conductivity because $\mathbf{E}$ vanishes inside the material.   In particular, consider a superconductor that is cooled below T_c in zero magnetic field.   The above result shows that $\mathbf{B}$ remains zero even if a field is subsequently applied (Fig. 48.1).

2. *Meissner effect*: Although the infinite conductivity is the most obvious characteristic, the true nature of the superconducting state appears more clearly in its magnetic effects.   Consider a normal metal in a uniform magnetic field (Fig. 48.1).   When the sample is cooled and becomes superconducting, experiments first performed by Meissner and Ochsenfeld [2] demonstrate that all magnetic flux is expelled from the interior.   Note that this result does not contradict the previous conclusion of constant $\mathbf{B}$ in the superconducting state; rather it indicates that the constant value must always be taken as zero.

3. *Critical field*: The Meissner effect occurs only for sufficiently low magnetic fields.   For simplicity, we consider a long cylinder of pure superconductor in a parallel applied field $\mathbf{H}$, where there are no demagnetizing effects.   If the sample is superconducting at temperature T in zero field, there is a unique critical field $H_c(T)$ above which the sample becomes normal.   This transition is reversible,

[1] H. K. Onnes, *Commun. Phys. Lab. Univ. Leiden, Suppl.*, **34b** (1913).

[2] W. Meissner and R. Ochsenfeld, *Naturwiss.*, **21**:787 (1933).

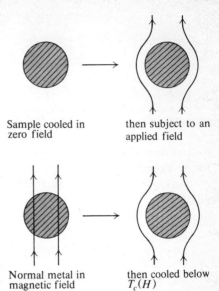

Sample cooled in   then subject to an
zero field   applied field

Fig. 48.1   Meissner effect in superconductors.   Normal metal in   then cooled below
                                                        magnetic field $T_c(H)$

for superconductivity reappears as soon as H is reduced below $H_c(T)$.   Experiments on pure superconductors show[1] that the curve $H_c(T)$ is roughly parabolic (Fig. 48.2)

$$H_c(T) = H_c(0)\left[1 - \left(\frac{T}{T_c}\right)^2\right] \qquad \text{empirical} \qquad\qquad (48.3)$$

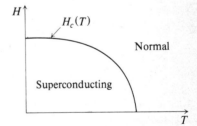

Fig. 48.2   Phase diagram in H-T plane, showing superconducting and normal regions, and the critical curve $H_c(T)$ or $T_c(H)$ between them.

4. *Persistent currents and flux quantization*: As a different example of magnetic behavior, consider a normal metallic ring placed in a magnetic field perpendicular to its plane (Fig. 48.3).   When the temperature is lowered, the metal becomes superconducting and expels the flux.   Suppose the external field

[1] It must be mentioned that many superconducting alloys exhibit a "mixed state," in which the resistivity remains zero yet flux penetrates the sample.   Although we briefly return to this question in Sec. 50, the present chapter is largely restricted to pure superconductors, where $H_c(0)$ is usually a few hundred oersteds.

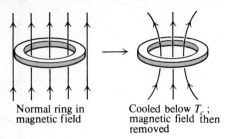

Normal ring in
magnetic field

Cooled below T_c;
magnetic field then
removed

Fig. 48.3 Flux trapping in a superconducting ring.

is then removed; no flux can pass through the superconducting metal, and the total trapped flux must remain constant, being maintained by circulating super-currents in the ring itself. Such persistent currents have been observed over long periods.[1] Furthermore, the flux trapped in sufficiently thick rings is quantized in units of[2]

$$\varphi_0 = \frac{hc}{2e} = 2.07 \times 10^{-7} \text{ gauss cm}^2 \tag{48.4}$$

5. *Specific heat*: In addition to its magnetic behavior, a typical super-conductor also has distinctive thermal properties. For zero applied field, the transition is of second order, which implies a discontinuous specific heat but no latent heat[3] (Fig. 48.4). As discussed in Secs. 5 and 29, the electronic specific

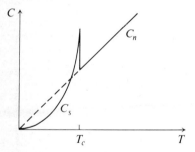

Fig. 48.4 Schematic diagram of specific heat in a superconductor.

heat C_n in the normal state varies linearly with the temperature. In the super-conducting state, however, the specific heat C_s initially exceeds C_n for $T \lesssim T_c$, but then drops below C_n and vanishes exponentially as $T \to 0$.‡

$$C_s \propto \exp \frac{-\Delta_0}{k_B T} \tag{48.5}$$

[1] Typical recent measurements are those of J. File and R. G. Mills, *Phys. Rev. Letters*, **10**:93 (1963), who find lifetimes of order 10^5 years.
[2] B. S. Deaver, Jr. and W. M. Fairbank, *Phys. Rev. Letters*, **7**:43 (1961); R. Doll and M. Näbauer, *Phys. Rev. Letters*, **7**:51 (1961).
[3] W. H. Keesom and J. A. Kok, *Commun. Phys. Lab. Univ. Leiden*, **221e**:(1932).
‡ W. S. Corak, B. B. Goodman, C. B. Satterthwaite and A. Wexler, *Phys. Rev.*, **96**:1442 (1954).

This dependence indicates the existence of a gap in the energy spectrum, separating the excited states from the ground state by an energy Δ_0.‡   For most superconducting elements, Δ_0 is somewhat less than $2k_B T_c$.

6. *Isotope effect*: A final distinctive property of superconductors is the isotope effect.   We noted that the crystallographic properties of the normal and superconducting phases are identical.   Nevertheless, careful studies of isotopically pure samples show that the ionic lattice plays an important role in superconductivity, for the transition temperature typically varies with the ionic mass[1]

$$T_c \propto M^{-\frac{1}{2}} \tag{48.6}$$

This result indicates the importance of the attractive electron-phonon interaction, which provides a mechanism for the formation of bound Cooper pairs (compare Secs. 36, 37, and 46).

THERMODYNAMIC RELATIONS

For completeness, we first review the basic equations of electrodynamics.   On a *microscopic* (atomic) scale, there are only two fundamental fields $\mathbf{e}$ and $\mathbf{b}$, defined by the equations

$$\operatorname{div} \mathbf{e} = 4\pi\rho \tag{48.7a}$$

$$\operatorname{div} \mathbf{b} = 0 \tag{48.7b}$$

$$\operatorname{curl} \mathbf{e} = -c^{-1}\frac{\partial \mathbf{b}}{\partial t} \tag{48.7c}$$

$$\operatorname{curl} \mathbf{b} = c^{-1}\frac{\partial \mathbf{e}}{\partial t} + \frac{4\pi}{c}\rho\mathbf{v} \tag{48.7d}$$

Here ρ is the total charge density and $\mathbf{v}$ is the microscopic velocity field.   The *macroscopic* fields are defined as spatial averages

$$\mathbf{E} = \langle \mathbf{e} \rangle_{\text{vol}} \qquad \mathbf{B} = \langle \mathbf{b} \rangle_{\text{vol}} \tag{48.8}$$

over a volume appropriate to the particular problem in question; they obey the conventional Maxwell equations

$$\operatorname{div} \mathbf{E} = 4\pi\langle \rho \rangle_{\text{vol}} \tag{48.9a}$$

$$\operatorname{div} \mathbf{B} = 0 \tag{48.9b}$$

$$\operatorname{curl} \mathbf{E} = -c^{-1}\frac{\partial \mathbf{B}}{\partial t} \tag{48.9c}$$

‡ Although the energy gap is a typical feature of superconductivity, it is by no means necessary, as shown by the existence of "gapless" superconductors with zero dc resistivity.

[1] H. Fröhlich, *Phys. Rev.*, **79**: 845 (1950); E. Maxwell, *Phys. Rev.*, **78**: 477 (1950); C. A. Reynolds, B. Serin, W. H. Wright, and L. B. Nesbitt, *Phys. Rev.*, **78**: 487 (1950).

$$\text{curl}\,\mathbf{B} = c^{-1}\frac{\partial \mathbf{E}}{\partial t} + \frac{4\pi}{c}\langle \rho \mathbf{v}\rangle_{\text{vol}} \tag{48.9d}$$

Although these equations are formally complete, it is customary to separate $\langle \rho \rangle_{\text{vol}}$ into a polarization density $-\text{div}\,\mathbf{P}$ and a free (externally specified) charge density ρ_f. Equation (48.9a) then becomes

$$\text{div}\,(\mathbf{E} + 4\pi\mathbf{P}) \equiv \text{div}\,\mathbf{D} = 4\pi\rho_f \tag{48.10}$$

where $\mathbf{P}$ and $\mathbf{D}$ are known as the polarization and displacement, respectively. In a similar way, the total current is separated into a magnetization current $c\,\text{curl}\,\mathbf{M}$, a polarization current $\partial\mathbf{P}/\partial t$, and a free (again externally specified) current $\mathbf{j}_f$ associated with the motion of free charges. If the magnetic field is defined as $\mathbf{H} \equiv \mathbf{B} - 4\pi\mathbf{M}$, then Eq. (48.9d) gives

$$\text{curl}\,\mathbf{H} = \frac{4\pi}{c}\mathbf{j}_f + \frac{1}{c}\frac{\partial\mathbf{D}}{\partial t} \tag{48.11}$$

The last term is generally negligible in low-frequency phenomena, and we may interpret $\text{curl}\,\mathbf{H}$ as arising solely from the free currents. When the various magnetic quantities are changed by small amounts, the work done on the system is given by $(4\pi)^{-1} \int d^3x\,\mathbf{H}\cdot d\mathbf{B}$,‡ so that the change in the Helmholtz free-energy density becomes

$$dF = -s\,dT + (4\pi)^{-1}\mathbf{H}\cdot d\mathbf{B} \tag{48.12}$$

with the corresponding differential relations

$$s = -\left(\frac{\partial F}{\partial T}\right)_{\mathbf{B}} \qquad \mathbf{H} = 4\pi\left(\frac{\partial F}{\partial \mathbf{B}}\right)_T \tag{48.13}$$

Here we assume the volume is held constant, and s is the entropy density.

The flux expulsion associated with the Meissner effect indicates that a bulk superconductor in an external magnetic field $\mathbf{H}$ is uniquely characterized by the condition $\mathbf{B} = 0$, independent of the way the state is reached (Fig. 48.1). We therefore infer that the superconductor is in true thermodynamic equilibrium and accordingly apply the techniques of macroscopic thermodynamics. For most experiments, however, it is impossible to manipulate the flux density $\mathbf{B}$ directly; instead, the external currents (in a solenoid, for example) control the magnetic field $\mathbf{H}$, and we prefer to make a Legendre transformation from the Helmholtz function $F(T,\mathbf{B})$ to a new (Gibbs) free-energy density

$$G(T,\mathbf{H}) \equiv F - (4\pi)^{-1}\mathbf{B}\cdot\mathbf{H} \tag{48.14}$$

· ‡ This result can be derived very simply by surrounding the system with a surface A in free space. Poynting's theorem shows that the energy flowing in through A in a short time dt is given by $dW_{em} = -dt(c/4\pi)\int_A d\mathbf{S}\cdot\mathbf{E}\times\mathbf{H}$. The divergence theorem and Maxwell's equations (48.9c) and (48.11) then yield $dW_{em} = (c/4\pi)\int_V d^3x[c^{-1}\mathbf{H}\cdot d\mathbf{B} + c^{-1}\mathbf{E}\cdot d\mathbf{D} + (4\pi/c)\mathbf{E}\cdot\mathbf{j}_f\,dt]$, which verifies the assertion.

with the corresponding differential relations

$$dG = -s\,dT - (4\pi)^{-1}\,\mathbf{B}\cdot d\mathbf{H} \tag{48.15}$$

$$s = -\left(\frac{\partial G}{\partial T}\right)_{\mathbf{H}}, \quad \mathbf{B} = -4\pi\left(\frac{\partial G}{\partial \mathbf{H}}\right)_{T} \tag{48.16}$$

Consider a long superconducting cylinder in a parallel magnetic field. If the field $\mathbf{H} = H\hat{z}$ is increased at constant temperature, Eq. (48.16) gives

$$G(T,H) - G(T,0) = -(4\pi)^{-1}\int_{0}^{H} B(H')\,dH' \tag{48.17}$$

To a good approximation, the normal state of most superconducting elements is nonmagnetic ($\mathbf{B} = \mathbf{H}$), and we find

$$G_n(T,H) - G_n(T,0) = -(8\pi)^{-1}\,H^2 \tag{48.18}$$

In contrast, $\mathbf{B}$ vanishes in the superconductor, which yields

$$G_s(T,H) = G_s(T,0) \tag{48.19}$$

The two phases are in thermodynamic equilibrium at the critical field H_c. This condition may be expressed by the equation

$$G_s(T,H_c) = G_n(T,H_c) \tag{48.20}$$

and a combination of Eqs. (48.18)–(48.20) immediately gives

$$G_s(T,0) = G_n(T,0) - (8\pi)^{-1}\,H_c^2 \tag{48.21}$$

$$F_s(T,0) = F_n(T,0) - (8\pi)^{-1}\,H_c^2 \tag{48.22}$$

These equations show that a negative *condensation* energy $-H_c^2/8\pi$ per unit volume accompanies the formation of the superconducting state. In addition, a simple rearrangement leads to the general result

$$G_s(T,H) - G_n(T,H) = (8\pi)^{-1}\,(H^2 - H_c^2) \tag{48.23}$$

so that the superconducting phase is the equilibrium state for all $H < H_c(T)$.

The derivative of Eq. (48.23) with respect to temperature yields the entropy difference between the two phases

$$s_s(T,H) - s_n(T,H) = (4\pi)^{-1}\,H_c(T)\frac{dH_c(T)}{dT} \tag{48.24}$$

Figure 48.2 shows that the right side is negative, so that the superconducting phase has lower entropy than the normal phase. Note that Eq. (48.24) is independent of the applied field, which also follows from the thermodynamic Maxwell relation derived from Eq. (48.15). The latent heat associated with the transition is $T(s_s - s_n)$, which vanishes at $T = 0$ and at T_c (see Fig. 48.2).

Finally, the thermodynamic identity

$$c_H = T\left(\frac{\partial s}{\partial T}\right)_H \tag{48.25}$$

gives the difference in the electronic specific heats at constant field

$$c_{sH} - c_{nH} = \frac{T}{4\pi}\left[\left(\frac{dH_c}{dT}\right)^2 + H_c \frac{d^2 H_c}{dT^2}\right] \tag{48.26}$$

In particular, the jump in the specific heat at T_c becomes

$$(c_s - c_n)_{T_c} = \frac{T_c}{4\pi}\left[\left(\frac{dH_c}{dT}\right)_{T_c}\right]^2 \tag{48.27}$$

and this relation between measurable quantities is well satisfied in practice.

49☐LONDON-PIPPARD PHENOMENOLOGICAL THEORY

The London equations[1] provided the first theoretical description of the Meissner effect. Although these equations are a pair of phenomenological constitutive relations describing the response of the supercurrent $\mathbf{j}$ to applied electric and magnetic fields, they may also be derived from the following simple model.[2]

DERIVATION OF LONDON EQUATIONS

If the superelectrons are considered an incompressible nonviscous charged fluid with velocity field $\mathbf{v}(\mathbf{x}t)$, then the supercurrent is given by

$$\mathbf{j}(\mathbf{x}t) = -n_s e\mathbf{v}(\mathbf{x}t) \tag{49.1}$$

where n_s is the superelectron number density and $-e$ is the charge on an electron. The continuity equation and Newton's second law give

$$\operatorname{div} \mathbf{j} = \operatorname{div} \mathbf{v} = 0 \tag{49.2}$$

$$\frac{d\mathbf{v}}{dt} = -\frac{e}{m}\left(\mathbf{E} + \frac{1}{c}\mathbf{v} \times \mathbf{h}\right) \tag{49.3}$$

where $d\mathbf{v}/dt$ is the total (hydrodynamic) derivative and $\mathbf{h}(\mathbf{x})$ is the fine-grained average of $\mathbf{b}(\mathbf{x})$ over a microscopic volume of dimensions large compared to atomic size but small compared to the penetration depth. In all subsequent discussion we shall refer to $\mathbf{h}(\mathbf{x})$ as the *microscopic* field.[3] The left side of Eq.

[1] F. London and H. London, *Proc. Roy. Soc. (London)*, A147:71 (1935).
[2] F. London, *op. cit.*, sec. 8.
[3] We here follow F. London, *op. cit.*, sec. 3, although the field in question is really $\mathbf{B}$, defined in Eq. (48.8). To be very explicit, the mean flux density (the coarse-grained average over the sample) is here called $\bar{B}$ instead of London's B.

(49.3) may be rewritten with standard vector identities

$$\frac{d\mathbf{v}}{dt} = \frac{\partial \mathbf{v}}{\partial t} + (\mathbf{v} \cdot \nabla) \mathbf{v} = \frac{\partial \mathbf{v}}{\partial t} + \nabla(\tfrac{1}{2}v^2) - \mathbf{v} \times \operatorname{curl} \mathbf{v} \tag{49.4}$$

and we find

$$\frac{\partial \mathbf{v}}{\partial t} + e\frac{\mathbf{E}}{m} + \nabla(\tfrac{1}{2}v^2) = \mathbf{v} \times \left(\operatorname{curl} \mathbf{v} - \frac{e\mathbf{h}}{mc}\right) \tag{49.5}$$

The curl of this equation may be combined with Maxwell's equation (48.9c) to give

$$\frac{\partial \mathbf{Q}}{\partial t} = \operatorname{curl}(\mathbf{v} \times \mathbf{Q}) \tag{49.6}$$

where

$$\mathbf{Q} \equiv \operatorname{curl} \mathbf{v} - \frac{e\mathbf{h}}{mc} \tag{49.7}$$

Consider a bulk superconductor in zero field, when $\mathbf{Q} = 0$. Equation (49.6) then implies that $\mathbf{Q}$ remains zero even when a field is subsequently applied. Since the Meissner effect shows that a superconductor in a magnetic field is in thermodynamic equilibrium, independent of how the final state is reached, we make the fundamental assumption that the equation

$$\mathbf{Q} \equiv \operatorname{curl} \mathbf{v} - \frac{e\mathbf{h}}{mc} = 0 \tag{49.8}$$

correctly describes a superconductor under all circumstances. Substitution of Eq. (49.8) into Eq. (49.5) gives

$$\frac{\partial \mathbf{v}}{\partial t} + \nabla(\tfrac{1}{2}v^2) = -\frac{e\mathbf{E}}{m} \tag{49.9}$$

Equations (49.8) and (49.9) together constitute the London equations.

SOLUTION FOR HALFSPACE AND SLAB

The implications of these phenomenological equations are most easily understood by rewriting Eq. (49.8) as

$$\mathbf{h} = -\frac{mc}{n_s e^2} \operatorname{curl} \mathbf{j} \tag{49.10}$$

A combination with the curl of Maxwell's equation (48.9d) for static fields then gives

$$\mathbf{h} = -\frac{mc}{n_s e^2} \operatorname{curl} \mathbf{j} = -\frac{mc^2}{4\pi n_s e^2} \operatorname{curl} \operatorname{curl} \mathbf{h} = \frac{mc^2}{4\pi n_s e^2} \nabla^2 \mathbf{h} \tag{49.11}$$

where the last equality follows from Eq. (48.9b). For definiteness, we study a

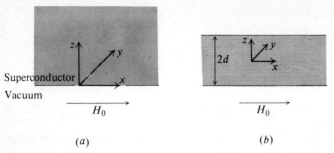

Superconductor

Vacuum

H_0

H_0

(a)   (b)

Fig. 49.1 Geometry of superconducting (a) halfspace, (b) slab in a parallel applied field H_0.

semi-infinite superconductor $(z > 0)$ in an applied field $\mathbf{H}_0 = H_0 \hat{x}$ parallel to the surface (Fig. 49.1a). The microscopic field $\mathbf{h}(z) = h(z)\hat{x}$ in the interior satisfies Eq. (49.11) with the acceptable solution

$$h(z) = H_0 \, e^{-z/\lambda_L} \tag{49.12}$$

where

$$\lambda_L = \left(\frac{mc^2}{4\pi n_s e^2}\right)^{\frac{1}{2}} \tag{49.13}$$

is known as the *London penetration depth*. Thus the magnetic field is confined to a surface layer of thickness $\approx \lambda_L$ and vanishes exponentially for $z \gg \lambda_L$. If n_s is taken as the total electron density, then λ_L is typically a few hundred angstroms (see Table 49.1).[1] Experiments indicate that the penetration depth increases

Table 49.1   Characteristic lengths for superconductors

	$\lambda_L(0)$, Å‡	ξ_0, Å	$\lambda_L(0)/\xi_0$	$\lambda(0)_{th}$, Å§	$\lambda(0)_{exp}$, Å
Al	160	16,000	0.010	530	490, 515
Sn	340	2,300	0.16	510	510
Pb	370	830	0.45	440	390

‡ $\lambda_L(0)$ is calculated by assuming $n_s = n$ at $T = 0°$K.
§ $\lambda(0)_{th}$ is the penetration depth at zero temperature, calculated with the BCS theory for diffuse scattering of electrons at the boundary.
Source: R. Meservey and B. B. Schwartz, Equilibrium Properties: Comparison of Experimental Results with Predictions of the BCS Theory, in R. D. Parks (ed.), "Superconductivity," vol. I, p. 174, Marcel Dekker, Inc., New York, 1969.

[1] This small size makes precise measurements quite difficult; typical experimental procedures are discussed in F. London, *op. cit.*, sec. 5.

with increasing temperature, and the function

$$\frac{\lambda_L(T)}{\lambda_L(0)} = \left[1 - \left(\frac{T}{T_c} \right)^4 \right]^{-\frac{1}{2}} \qquad \text{empirical} \tag{49.14}$$

provides a good fit[1] to the data for $T/T_c \gtrsim \frac{1}{2}$. Since n_s is the only variable quantity in Eq. (49.13), we infer

$$\frac{n_s(T)}{n_s(0)} = 1 - \left(\frac{T}{T_c} \right)^4 \qquad \text{empirical} \tag{49.15}$$

As a second example, consider a slab of thickness $2d$ in an applied field $H_0 \hat{x}$ parallel to its surface (Fig. 49.1b). If the origin of coordinates is located in the middle of the slab, then the appropriate solution of Eq. (49.11) is

$$h(z) = H_0 \frac{\cosh{(z/\lambda_L)}}{\cosh{(d/\lambda_L)}} \tag{49.16}$$

The mean flux density $\bar{B}$ is the spatial average of the microscopic field

$$\bar{B} = \frac{1}{2d} \int_{-d}^{d} dz \, h(z) = \frac{H_0 \lambda_L}{d} \tanh \frac{d}{\lambda_L} \tag{49.17}$$

In the limit of a thick slab, Eq. (49.17) becomes

$$\bar{B} \approx \frac{H_0 \lambda_L}{d} \qquad d \gg \lambda_L \tag{49.18}$$

and the sample exhibits a Meissner effect; in the opposite limit ($d \ll \lambda_L$) the mean flux density is essentially H_0.

CONSERVATION AND QUANTIZATION OF FLUXOID

The London equations imply a striking conservation law. For simplicity, we study only the linearized equations

$$-\frac{e\mathbf{E}}{m} = \frac{\partial \mathbf{v}}{\partial t} = -\frac{1}{n_s e} \frac{\partial \mathbf{j}}{\partial t} \tag{49.19}$$

and Eq. (49.8), but a more general treatment can also be given (Prob. 13.1). Consider a surface S bounded by a fixed closed curve C that lies wholly in the superconducting material (Fig. 49.2). Independent of whether S also lies entirely in the superconductor (Fig. 49.2a or b), we may integrate Maxwell's equation (48.9c) to obtain

$$\int d\mathbf{S} \cdot \frac{\partial \mathbf{h}}{\partial t} = -c \int d\mathbf{S} \cdot \text{curl} \, \mathbf{E} = -c \oint_C d\mathbf{l} \cdot \mathbf{E} \tag{49.20}$$

---

[1] For a comparison of the experiments with Eq. (49.14) and the theoretical prediction of the BCS theory, see, for example, A. L. Schawlow and G. E. Devlin, *Phys. Rev.*, **113**:120 (1959).

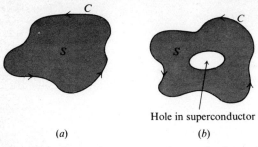

Hole in superconductor

(a)   (b)

Fig. 49.2 Integration contour for evaluation of fluxoid: (a) simply connected; (b) multiply connected.

where the right side has been transformed with Stokes' theorem. Since C lies in the superconductor, Eq. (49.19) applies at every point, giving

$$\frac{\partial}{\partial t}\left(\int d\mathbf{S}\cdot\mathbf{h} + \frac{mc}{n_s e^2}\oint_C d\mathbf{l}\cdot\mathbf{j}\right) = 0 \qquad (49.21)$$

We see that the *fluxoid*[1] defined as

$$\Phi \equiv \int d\mathbf{S}\cdot\mathbf{h} + \frac{mc}{n_s e^2}\oint_C d\mathbf{l}\cdot\mathbf{j} \qquad (49.22)$$

remains constant for all time. It is clear that Φ differs from the magnetic flux by an additional contribution arising from the induced supercurrent.

With added assumptions, it is possible to derive more specific results.

1. If C is sufficiently far from the boundaries, then $\mathbf{j}$ is exponentially small, and Φ reduces to the magnetic flux.
2. If the interior of C is wholly superconducting (Fig. 49.2a), then the other London equation (49.8) immediately implies that Φ vanishes.
3. As a corollary of the previous conclusion, Φ is the same for any path C' that can be deformed continuously into C, always remaining in the superconductor.

F. London also observed that Eq. (49.8) can be written in terms of the vector potential $\mathbf{A}$ as follows

$$\text{curl}\left(m\mathbf{v} - \frac{e\mathbf{A}}{c}\right) = 0 \qquad (49.23)$$

where

$$\mathbf{h} = \text{curl }\mathbf{A} \qquad (49.24)$$

The canonical momentum is given by

$$\mathbf{p} = m\mathbf{v} - \frac{e\mathbf{A}}{c} \qquad (49.25)$$

[1] F. London, *op. cit.*, sec. 6.

and Eq. (49.23) thus becomes

$$\text{curl } \mathbf{p} = 0 \tag{49.26}$$

which may be considered a generalized condition of irrotational flow. In addition, the fluxoid may be written as

$$\Phi = -\frac{c}{e} \oint_C d\mathbf{l} \cdot \mathbf{p} \tag{49.27}$$

This equation is reminiscent of the Bohr-Sommerfeld quantization relation, and, indeed, London suggested that the fluxoid is quantized in units of hc/e.[1] As noted in Sec. 48, this prediction was subsequently confirmed, but the observed quantum unit is $hc/2e$ [Eq. (48.4)].

PIPPARD'S GENERALIZED EQUATION

It is now convenient to choose a particular gauge (London gauge) for the vector potential

$$\text{div } \mathbf{A} = 0 \tag{49.28a}$$

$$\mathbf{A} \cdot \hat{n} = 0 \qquad \text{on boundaries} \tag{49.28b}$$

which allows us to rewrite the static London equation (49.10) as

$$\mathbf{j}(\mathbf{x}) = -\frac{n_s e^2}{mc} \mathbf{A}(\mathbf{x}) \tag{49.29}$$

This choice of gauge is always possible, because Eq. (49.28b) can be satisfied by adding the gradient of an appropriate solution of Laplace's equation. Note that the London gauge ensures that $\text{div } \mathbf{j} = 0$ and that $\mathbf{j} \cdot \hat{n} = 0$ on the boundaries. Equation (49.29) shows that the London theory assumes $\mathbf{j}(\mathbf{x})$ proportional to $\mathbf{A}(\mathbf{x})$ *at the same point*. Furthermore, the theory predicts that the penetration depth depends only on fundamental constants and n_s [Eq. (49.13)]. To test these predictions, Pippard studied the properties of superconducting Sn–In alloys.[2] Although the thermodynamic properties such as $H_c(T)$ and T_c were unaltered by rather large concentrations of the In impurities ($\lesssim 3\%$), he found that the penetration depth increased by nearly a factor of 2. Such behavior cannot be understood in the London picture, because an increased penetration depth would imply a reduced value of n_s and a corresponding modification in the free energy and other thermodynamic properties. For this and other reasons, Pippard proposed a nonlocal generalization of Eq. (49.29), in which $\mathbf{j}(\mathbf{x})$ is determined as a spatial average of $\mathbf{A}$ throughout some neighboring region of dimension r_0. For heavily doped alloys, r_0 is comparable with the electronic mean free path l in the normal metal; for pure metals, however, r_0 is not infinite,

[1] F. London, *op. cit.*, p. 152.
[2] A. B. Pippard, *Proc. Roy. Soc. (London)*, **A216**:547 (1953).

but instead tends to a characteristic length ξ_0, known as the Pippard (or BCS) coherence length.   Pippard thus made the particular choice

$$\frac{1}{r_0} = \frac{1}{\xi_0} + \frac{1}{l} \tag{49.30}$$

and assumed

$$\mathbf{j}(\mathbf{x}) = -\frac{n_s e^2}{mc} \frac{3}{4\pi\xi_0} \int d^3x' \frac{\mathbf{X}[\mathbf{X}\cdot\mathbf{A}(\mathbf{x}')]}{X^4} e^{-X/r_0} \tag{49.31}$$

where $\mathbf{X} = \mathbf{x} - \mathbf{x}'$.   An experimental fit to the measured penetration depths yielded[1]

$$\xi_0 \approx 0.15 \frac{\hbar v_F}{k_B T_c} \tag{49.32}$$

For comparison, the BCS theory of pure samples leads to a very similar nonlocal relation and identifies ξ_0 as

$$\xi_0 = 0.180 \frac{\hbar v_F}{k_B T_c} = \frac{\hbar v_F}{\pi \Delta_0} \tag{49.33}$$

where Λ_0 is the energy gap at zero temperature.   Typical values of ξ_0 are shown in Table 49.1.

The Pippard equation relates the induced supercurrent $\mathbf{j}$ to the total vector potential $\mathbf{A}$.   In the presence of an applied magnetic field, however, $\mathbf{A}$ contains contributions from the external currents as well as from $\mathbf{j}$ itself, thereby requiring a simultaneous solution of Eq. (49.31) and Maxwell's equation determining the total magnetic field.   Nevertheless, it is possible to extract the important physical features by noting the existence of two characteristic lengths.   The vector potential varies with the self-consistent temperature-dependent penetration length λ, *which need not be the same as the London penetration length* λ_L [defined in Eq. (49.13)], while the integral kernel has a *temperature-independent* range r_0, which is approximately the smaller of ξ_0 and l.   If $r_0 \ll \lambda$, then the vector potential varies slowly and can be evaluated at $\mathbf{x}' = \mathbf{x}$.   In this way, we obtain

$$j_k(\mathbf{x}) \approx -\frac{n_s e^2}{mc\xi_0} A_l(\mathbf{x}) \frac{3}{4\pi} \int d^3X \, X_k X_l \frac{e^{-X/r_0}}{X^4}$$

$$= -\frac{n_s e^2}{mc\xi_0} A_l(\mathbf{x}) \delta_{kl} \int_0^\infty dX \, e^{-X/r_0}$$

or

$$\mathbf{j}(\mathbf{x}) = -\frac{n_s e^2 \, l}{mc(l + \xi_0)} \mathbf{A}(\mathbf{x}) \qquad r_0 \ll \lambda \tag{49.34}$$

[1] T. E. Faber and A. B. Pippard, *Proc. Roy. Soc.* (*London*), **A231**:336 (1955).

Any sample that satisfies this *local* condition ($r_0 \ll \lambda$) is known as a *London superconductor*, because Eq. (49.31) then reproduces the form of the London equation (49.29) but with the coefficient reduced by a factor $(1 + \xi_0/l)^{-1}$. Comparison with Eqs. (49.10) and (49.11) immediately gives the corresponding penetration depth at zero temperature

$$\lambda(0) = \lambda_L(0) \left(\frac{l + \xi_0}{l}\right)^{\frac{1}{2}} \qquad \text{local limit}: r_0 \ll \lambda \qquad (49.35)$$

For a *pure* London superconductor ($\xi_0 \ll l$), Eq. (49.35) reduces to the previous London expression.

In practice (see Table 49.1), most superconducting elements at low temperature violate the condition for a pure London superconductor, which requires $r_0 \approx \xi_0 \ll \lambda$. Hence London superconductors are usually heavily doped alloys, where the length r_0 is determined by l instead of ξ_0, and the following inequality holds: $r_0 \approx l \ll \lambda$. In this case, Eq. (49.35) explains the observed increase in the penetration depth for dirty alloys where $l \ll \xi_0$. If a sample is a London superconductor at low temperature, Eq. (49.14) shows that it remains one for all $T < T_c$. Since the penetration depth of any superconducting material increases rapidly as $T \to T_c$, however, *all superconductors become London superconductors sufficiently close to T_c.*

It is important to emphasize that Eqs. (49.34) and (49.35) are only correct for $r_0 \ll \lambda$, and we now consider the more typical nonlocal limit ($r_0 \gg \lambda$), when the material is known as a *Pippard superconductor*. Although a general solution is very difficult, we can evaluate **j** and **h** completely for an infinite superconductor surrounding a current sheet $j_0 \hat{y} \delta(z)$ lying in the xy plane. The current sheet is a source of magnetic field, which in turn induces a supercurrent $\mathbf{j}(\mathbf{x})$. The total current is the sum of these two contributions, and Maxwell's equation (48.9d) becomes

$$\text{curl}\,\mathbf{h} = \text{curl}\,\text{curl}\,\mathbf{A} = 4\pi c^{-1}[j_0 \hat{y} \delta(z) + \mathbf{j}(\mathbf{x})] \qquad (49.36)$$

This equation must be solved along with Pippard's equation, which provides another relation between **j** and **A**.

The translational invariance makes it useful to introduce three-dimensional Fourier transforms

$$\mathbf{j}(\mathbf{x}) = (2\pi)^{-3} \int d^3q\, e^{i\mathbf{q}\cdot\mathbf{x}} \mathbf{j}(\mathbf{q}) \qquad (49.37a)$$

$$\mathbf{A}(\mathbf{x}) = (2\pi)^{-3} \int d^3q\, e^{i\mathbf{q}\cdot\mathbf{x}} \mathbf{A}(\mathbf{q}) \qquad (49.37b)$$

and the London gauge implies

$$\mathbf{q}\cdot\mathbf{A}(\mathbf{q}) = 0 \qquad (49.38)$$

It is straightforward to verify that the Fourier transform of Eq. (49.31) takes the form

$$\mathbf{j}(\mathbf{q}) = -\frac{c}{4\pi} K(q)\, \mathbf{A}(\mathbf{q}) \tag{49.39}$$

where

$$K(q) = -\frac{3n_s e^2}{mc^2 \xi_0} 4\pi \int_0^\infty \frac{dx}{x^2} e^{-x/r_0} \frac{1}{q} \frac{\partial}{\partial q} \frac{\sin qx}{qx}$$

$$= \frac{6\pi n_s e^2}{mc^2 \xi_0 q} \left\{ \frac{\arctan qr_0}{(qr_0)^2} [1 + (qr_0)^2] - \frac{1}{qr_0} \right\} \tag{49.40}$$

and the gauge condition (49.38) has been used to simplify the vector components. In addition, the Fourier transform of Eq. (49.36) is given by

$$-\mathbf{q} \times \mathbf{q} \times \mathbf{A}(\mathbf{q}) = 4\pi c^{-1} \int d^3 x\, e^{-i\mathbf{q}\cdot\mathbf{x}} [j_0\, \hat{y}\delta(z) + \mathbf{j}(\mathbf{x})]$$

$$= 4\pi c^{-1} [(2\pi)^2 j_0\, \hat{y}\delta(q_x)\,\delta(q_y) + \mathbf{j}(\mathbf{q})] \tag{49.41}$$

and the left side may be simplified with Eq. (49.38):

$$-\mathbf{q} \times \mathbf{q} \times \mathbf{A}(\mathbf{q}) = q^2\, \mathbf{A}(\mathbf{q}) - \mathbf{q}[\mathbf{q}\cdot\mathbf{A}(\mathbf{q})] = q^2\, \mathbf{A}(\mathbf{q})$$

If Eq. (49.39) is used to express $\mathbf{j}(\mathbf{q})$ in terms of $\mathbf{A}(\mathbf{q})$, the resulting algebraic equation is readily solved to yield

$$\mathbf{A}(\mathbf{q}) = \frac{4\pi}{c} \frac{(2\pi)^2 j_0\, \hat{y}\delta(q_x)\,\delta(q_y)}{q^2 + K(q)} \tag{49.42}$$

The corresponding spatial quantities become

$$\mathbf{A}(\mathbf{x}) \equiv A(z)\,\hat{y} = \frac{4\pi}{c} \int_{-\infty}^\infty \frac{dq}{2\pi} \frac{j_0\, \hat{y}\, e^{iqz}}{q^2 + K(q)} \tag{49.43a}$$

$$\mathbf{h}(\mathbf{x}) \equiv h(z)\,\hat{x} = -\frac{4\pi}{c} \int_{-\infty}^\infty \frac{dq}{2\pi} \frac{j_0\, \hat{x} iq\, e^{iqz}}{q^2 + K(q)} \tag{49.43b}$$

which provide the complete solution.

It is interesting to examine the asymptotic form of $h(z)$ as $z \to \infty$. If $q^2 + K(q)$ has no zeros on the real q axis, then the integration contour can be deformed into the upper-half q plane, showing that $h(z)$ vanishes faster than any algebraic function of z. Since this behavior is exactly that found in the Meissner effect, we obtain the general criterion

$$q^2 + K(q) \neq 0 \qquad \text{for } q \text{ real: Meissner effect} \tag{49.44}$$

In practice, Eq. (49.44) is not very convenient, because $K(q)$ is a complicated function of q, and we must instead rely on graphical methods. The Pippard kernel [Eq. (49.40)] is plotted in Fig. 49.3. It has two characteristic features:

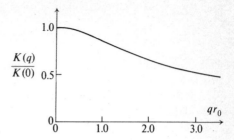

Fig. 49.3 Pippard kernel $K(q)$ [Eq. (49.40)].

$K(q)$ is positive for all q and $K(q)$ decreases monotonically. For any kernel with the first property, we may simplify Eq. (49.44) to the form

$K(0) \neq 0$ 　　Meissner effect

(49.45)

$K(0) = 0$ 　　no Meissner effect

which serves as a useful and simple criterion.[1]

The foregoing discussion considers only the asymptotic behavior of $h(z)$, which generally differs from a pure exponential. Hence we must generalize the concept of a penetration depth, and a natural choice is[2]

$$\lambda = \int_0^\infty dz \, \frac{h(z)}{h(z=0)} = \frac{A(z=0)}{h(z=0)}$$

The integral in Eq. (49.43b) converges only for $|z| \neq 0$, and $h(z=0)$ must be determined by other means. This presents no problem, however, for Ampère's law implies

$$h(z=0) = 2\pi c^{-1} j_0$$

and we find

$$\lambda = \frac{2}{\pi} \int_0^\infty dq \, \frac{1}{q^2 + K(q)}$$

(49.46)

The rather complicated form of the Pippard kernel [Eq. (49.40)] precludes an analytic evaluation of λ for all values of l and ξ_0. We note, however, that the important values of q are of order λ^{-1}. In the local limit ($\lambda \gg r_0$), Fig. 49.3 shows that we may approximate $K(q)$ by $K(0)$, and a simple integration yields the previous expression Eq. (49.35). In the opposite (nonlocal) limit, we approximate $K(q)$ by its asymptotic form as $q \to \infty$

$$K(q) \sim \frac{3\pi^2 n_s e^2}{mc^2 q \xi_0} \qquad q \to \infty$$

(49.47)

[1] M. R. Schafroth, *Helv. Phys. Acta.*, **24**:645 (1951).
[2] A. B. Pippard, *loc. cit.*

and a straightforward calculation gives the zero-temperature result[1]

$$\lambda(0) = \frac{8}{9}\left(\frac{\sqrt{3}}{2\pi}\right)^{\frac{1}{3}} [\lambda_L(0)^2\, \xi_0]^{\frac{1}{3}} \qquad \text{nonlocal limit:}\ \lambda \ll r_0 \qquad (49.48)$$

This expression is independent of the mean free path l because the spatial integration in Eq. (49.31) is limited by the penetration depth λ and not by r_0. Equations (49.35) and (49.48) constitute a central result of the Pippard theory. In addition to explaining the increased penetration depth in alloys, the theory clarifies the discrepancy of a factor ≈ 2–3 between the measured penetration depth in pure Pippard materials and the London value (see Table 49.1) because

$$\frac{\lambda(0)}{\lambda_L(0)} = \frac{8}{9}\left[\frac{\sqrt{3}\,\xi_0}{2\pi\lambda_L(0)}\right]^{\frac{1}{3}} \qquad (49.49)$$

Although the original Pippard theory does not determine the temperature dependence of $\lambda(T)$, the empirical law [Eq. (49.14)] is generally assumed for both local and nonlocal limits.

50□GINZBURG-LANDAU PHENOMENOLOGICAL THEORY

The original form of the London theory has one serious flaw, for it apparently predicts that the Meissner state in a field $H < H_c$ will break up into alternating normal and superconducting layers of thickness $d_n \ll d_s$.[2] This result is readily verified: If $d_n \ll d_s$, then the condensation-energy density remains essentially unchanged at $-H_c^2/8\pi$, while if $d_s \ll \lambda$, then the field penetration lowers the Gibbs free-energy density by $-H^2/8\pi$. F. London noted that this argument ignores the possibility of a positive surface energy associated with a normal-superconducting interface, and he used the observed stability of the Meissner state to estimate this surface-energy contribution. As a more fundamental remedy for this defect, Ginzburg and Landau[3] proposed a different phenomenological description of a superconductor, which accounts for the surface energy in a natural way.

EXPANSION OF THE FREE ENERGY

The phase transition at T_c signals the appearance of an ordered state in which the electrons are partially condensed into a frictionless superfluid. Ginzburg

---

[1] An equivalent procedure is to rewrite Eq. (49.46) in dimensionless form

$$1 = 2\pi^{-1}\int_0^\infty dt\ [t^2 + (\lambda^3/\lambda_L^2\xi_0)t^{-1}F(tr_0/\lambda)]^{-1}$$

where $F(x) = \frac{3}{2}[(x^{-2} + 1)\arctan x - x^{-1}]$. The limiting values of $F(tr_0/\lambda)$ for $r_0/\lambda \to 0$ and $r_0/\lambda \to \infty$ reproduce Eqs. (49.35) and (49.48), respectively.

[2] F. London, op. cit., pp. 125–130.

[3] V. L. Ginzburg and L. D. Landau: Zh. Eksp. Teor. Fiz, 20:1064 (1950). An English translation may be found in "Men of Physics: L. D. Landau," vol. I, p. 138, Pergamon Press, Oxford, 1965.

and Landau describe the condensate with a complex order parameter $\Psi(\mathbf{x})$. The observed second-order transition implies that Ψ vanishes for $T \geqslant T_c$, and that it increases in magnitude with increasing $T_c - T > 0$. Near T_c, the quantity $|\Psi|$ is small, and the microscopic free-energy density F_{s0} of the superconducting state in zero field is assumed to have an expansion of the form

$$F_{s0} = F_{n0} + a|\Psi|^2 + \tfrac{1}{2}b|\Psi|^4 + \cdots$$

where F_{n0} is the free-energy density of the normal state in zero magnetic field and where a and b are real temperature-dependent phenomenological constants. Since the order parameter is uniform in the absence of external fields, Ginzburg and Landau added a term proportional to $|\nabla\Psi|^2$, tending to suppress spatial variations in Ψ. In analogy with the Schrödinger equation, this term is written as

$$(2m^*)^{-1}|-i\hbar\nabla\Psi|^2$$

where m^* is an effective mass. When magnetic fields are present, this term is assumed to take the gauge-invariant form

$$(2m^*)^{-1}\left|\left(-i\hbar\nabla + \frac{e^*\mathbf{A}}{c}\right)\Psi\right|^2$$

where $-e^*$ is some integral multiple of the charge on an electron and

$$\operatorname{curl}\mathbf{A}(\mathbf{x}) = \mathbf{h}(\mathbf{x}) \tag{50.1}$$

determines the microscopic magnetic field. In this way, the total free-energy density of the superconducting state in a magnetic field becomes

$$F_s = F_{n0} + a|\Psi|^2 + \tfrac{1}{2}b|\Psi|^4 + (2m^*)^{-1}\left|\left(-i\hbar\nabla + \frac{e^*\mathbf{A}}{c}\right)\Psi\right|^2 + \frac{h^2}{8\pi} \tag{50.2}$$

where the last term represents the energy density of the magnetic field. It is conventional to choose a particular normalization for Ψ:

$$|\Psi|^2 \equiv n_s^* \tag{50.3}$$

where n_s^* defines an effective superelectron density. This choice fixes the ratio $(a/b)^2$. Experiments[1] indicate that

$$e^* = 2e \qquad m^* = 2m \tag{50.4}$$

in agreement with the pairing hypothesis of Secs. 36 and 37; we therefore identify n_s^* with the density of paired electrons and define n_s by the equation

$$n_s^* \equiv \tfrac{1}{2}n_s \tag{50.5}$$

---

[1] B. S. Deaver, Jr. and W. M. Fairbank, *loc. cit.*; R. Doll and M. Näbauer, *loc. cit.*; J. E. Zimmerman and J. E. Mercereau, *Phys. Rev. Letters*, **14**:887 (1965).

The free energy of the sample is obtained by integrating Eq. (50.2) over the total volume V. In a uniform external field $\mathbf{H}$, however, the relevant thermodynamic potential is the Gibbs free energy (compare Sec. 48), and we must consider

$$\int d^3x \, [F_s - (4\pi)^{-1} \mathbf{h} \cdot \mathbf{H}] \equiv \int d^3x \, G_s \tag{50.6}$$

where G_s is the microscopic Gibbs free-energy density. The condition of thermodynamic stability requires that Eq. (50.6) be stationary with respect to arbitrary variations of the order parameter and vector potential subject to the constraint of Eq. (50.1). A straightforward variational calculation gives the following field equations

$$(2m^*)^{-1} \left(-i\hbar\boldsymbol{\nabla} + \frac{e^* \mathbf{A}}{c} \right)^2 \Psi + a\Psi + b|\Psi|^2\Psi = 0 \tag{50.7a}$$

$$\frac{c}{4\pi} \operatorname{curl} \mathbf{h} = -\frac{e^* \hbar}{2m^* i}(\Psi^* \boldsymbol{\nabla} \Psi - \Psi\boldsymbol{\nabla}\Psi^*) - \frac{(e^*)^2}{m^* c} |\Psi|^2 \, \mathbf{A} \tag{50.7b}$$

while the remaining surface integrals vanish if $\mathbf{A}$ and Ψ satisfy the boundary conditions

$$\hat{n} \cdot \left(-i\hbar\boldsymbol{\nabla} + \frac{e^* \mathbf{A}}{c} \right) \Psi = 0 \tag{50.8a}$$

$$\hat{n} \times (\mathbf{h} - \mathbf{H}) = 0 \tag{50.8b}$$

Equations (50.7) show that Ψ obeys a nonlinear "Schrödinger" equation, while the magnetic field is determined by the supercurrent

$$\mathbf{j} = -\frac{e^* \hbar}{2m^* i}(\Psi^* \boldsymbol{\nabla} \Psi - \Psi\boldsymbol{\nabla}\Psi^*) - \frac{(e^*)^2}{m^* c} |\Psi|^2 \, \mathbf{A} \tag{50.9}$$

The boundary condition on Ψ is very different from that of the usual Schrödinger theory, however, and may be understood as guaranteeing that $\mathbf{j} \cdot \hat{n}$ vanishes at the surface of the sample. Equation (50.8b) implies that the tangential component of the magnetic field is continuous across this surface.

SOLUTION IN SIMPLE CASES

Although a complete solution of these coupled equations cannot be obtained, we can discover qualitative features by examining limiting cases. In the absence of a magnetic field ($\mathbf{A} = 0$), Eq. (50.7a) has the spatially uniform solutions

$$\Psi = 0 \qquad \text{or} \qquad |\Psi|^2 = -\frac{a}{b} \tag{50.10}$$

The first solution clearly represents the normal state because F_s then equals F_{n0}. The second solution is physically acceptable only if a/b is negative; it

represents the superconducting state with a corresponding free-energy density

$$F_{s0} = F_{n0} - \frac{1}{2}\frac{a^2}{b} \qquad \text{zero field} \tag{50.11}$$

and comparison with Eq. (48.22) yields

$$\frac{a^2}{b} = \frac{H_c(T)^2}{4\pi} \tag{50.12}$$

Equation (50.12) shows that b must be positive, which also ensures that F_s is bounded from below [see Eq. (50.2)]. Following Ginzburg and Landau, we assume that b is independent of temperature, while

$$a(T) = (T - T_c)a' \tag{50.13}$$

is negative for $T < T_c$, vanishing linearly at T_c. This choice correctly fits the linear slope of $H_c(T)$ near T_c and also predicts that $n_s^*(T) \propto (T_c - T)$ [compare Eq. (49.15)].

As a second simple case, consider a one-dimensional geometry, where Ψ varies but **h** vanishes:

$$-\frac{\hbar^2}{2m^*}\frac{d^2\Psi}{dz^2} + a\Psi + b|\Psi|^2\Psi = 0 \tag{50.14}$$

We assume that Ψ is real and introduce a dimensionless order parameter

$$f(z) = \frac{\Psi(z)}{|\Psi_\infty|} \tag{50.15}$$

where

$$|\Psi_\infty| \equiv \left(\frac{|a|}{b}\right)^{\frac{1}{2}} \tag{50.16}$$

is the magnitude of Ψ deep in the sample. A combination of Eqs. (50.14) and (50.15) gives

$$-\frac{\hbar^2}{2m^*|a|}\frac{d^2f}{dz^2} - f + f^3 = 0 \tag{50.17}$$

which defines a natural scale of length for spatial variations of the order parameter

$$\xi(T) \equiv \left[\frac{\hbar^2}{2m^*|a(T)|}\right]^{\frac{1}{2}} = \frac{\hbar}{[2m^*(T_c - T)a']^{\frac{1}{2}}} \tag{50.18}$$

This length is known as the (Ginzburg-Landau) coherence length. It becomes large as $T \to T_c$ and is thus very different from the temperature-independent parameters ξ_0 or r_0 introduced in Sec. 49.

In certain physical situations (see Fig. 50.1a) Ψ essentially vanishes at the boundary of the superconducting region ($z = 0$). Equation (50.17) can then

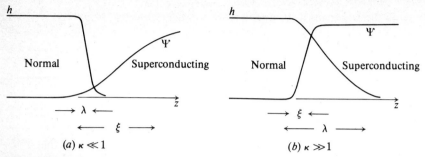

Fig. 50.1 Surface region between normal and superconducting material for (a) $\lambda \ll \xi$ ($\kappa \ll 1$) and (b) $\lambda \gg \xi$ ($\kappa \gg 1$).

be used to study how $|f|$ approaches its asymptotic value 1 at ∞. An immediate first integral is given by

$$\xi^2 \left(\frac{df}{dz}\right)^2 = \tfrac{1}{2}(1 - f^2)^2 \tag{50.19}$$

where the constant value is chosen to ensure that $f' \to 0$ as $f^2 \to 1$. If f increases with increasing z, we must take the positive square root

$$\frac{df}{dz} = \frac{1 - f^2}{\sqrt{2}\,\xi}$$

which is easily integrated to yield

$$f(z) = \tanh \frac{z}{\sqrt{2}\,\xi} \tag{50.20}$$

Just as in the electromagnetic penetration, the spatial variation of f is confined to a region $|z| \approx \xi$, because $1 - |f|$ vanishes exponentially for $|z| \gg \xi$.

For a final example, consider an applied magnetic field with an essentially uniform order parameter $\Psi = |\Psi_\infty|$ (see Fig. 50.1b). The supercurrent [Eq. (50.9)] then reduces to

$$\mathbf{j}(\mathbf{x}) = -\frac{(e^*)^2 n_s^*}{m^* c} \mathbf{A}(\mathbf{x}) = -\frac{e^2 n_s}{mc} \mathbf{A}(\mathbf{x}) \tag{50.21}$$

which takes precisely the form of the London equation (49.29). The penetration depth for magnetic fields follows immediately as

$$\lambda(T) = \left[\frac{m^* c^2}{4\pi n_s^*(T)(e^*)^2}\right]^{\frac{1}{2}}$$

or   (50.22)

$$\lambda(T) = \left[\frac{m^* c^2 b}{4\pi(e^*)^2 (T_c - T) a'}\right]^{\frac{1}{2}}$$

and is proportional to $(T_c - T)^{-\frac{1}{2}}$ for $T \to T_c$ [compare Eq. (49.14)].

It is important to emphasize that the coherence length $\xi(T)$ and penetration length $\lambda(T)$ are both phenomenological quantities defined in terms of the constants a and b. It is conventional to introduce the *Ginzburg-Landau parameter*

$$\kappa \equiv \frac{\lambda(T)}{\xi(T)} \tag{50.23}$$

which is independent of temperature near T_c. With the preceding definitions, a simple calculation yields

$$\kappa = \frac{\sqrt{2}\,e^*}{\hbar c}\, H_c(T)\,\lambda(T)^2 \qquad T \approx T_c \tag{50.24a}$$

$$\kappa = \frac{m^* c}{\hbar e^*}\left(\frac{b}{2\pi}\right)^{\frac{1}{2}} \tag{50.24b}$$

each of which is useful in applications. In particular, Eq. (50.24a) relates κ to the measurable quantities H_c and λ; it may also be rewritten as

$$H_c = \frac{\varphi_0}{2\pi\sqrt{2}\,\xi\lambda} \tag{50.25}$$

where (as shown in the following discussion)

$$\varphi_0 = \frac{hc}{e^*} \tag{50.26}$$

is the flux quantum.

FLUX QUANTIZATION

The Ginzburg-Landau expression [Eq. (50.9)] for the supercurrent allows us to verify London's prediction of a quantized fluxoid in a superconductor. The order parameter may be written as[1]

$$\Psi = |\Psi|\,e^{i\varphi} \tag{50.27}$$

where φ is real, and substitution into Eq. (50.9) gives

$$\mathbf{j} = -\frac{e^*\hbar}{m^*}|\Psi|^2\,\boldsymbol{\nabla}\varphi - \frac{(e^*)^2|\Psi|^2\,\mathbf{A}}{m^* c} \tag{50.28}$$

or

$$\mathbf{A} + \frac{\mathbf{j}m^* c}{(e^*)^2|\Psi|^2} = -\frac{\hbar c}{e^*}\boldsymbol{\nabla}\varphi \tag{50.29}$$

---

[1] This representation of Ψ is particularly useful in describing the Josephson effect, where the phase of the order parameter is of direct physical interest [see, for example, B. D. Josephson, *Advan. Phys.*, **14**:419 (1965)].

Integrate this equation around a closed path C lying wholly in the superconductor (Fig. 49.2)

$$\oint_C d\mathbf{l} \cdot \mathbf{A} + \frac{m^* c}{(e^*)^2} \oint_C \frac{d\mathbf{l} \cdot \mathbf{j}}{|\Psi|^2} = -\frac{\hbar c}{e^*} \oint_C d\mathbf{l} \cdot \nabla \varphi \tag{50.30}$$

The first term on the left may be rewritten with Stokes' theorem; if Ψ is assumed to be single valued, the integral on the right must be an integral multiple n of 2π:

$$\int d\mathbf{S} \cdot \mathbf{h} + \frac{m^* c}{(e^*)^2} \oint_C \frac{d\mathbf{l} \cdot \mathbf{j}}{|\Psi|^2} = \pm n \frac{hc}{e^*} \tag{50.31}$$

Comparison with Eq. (49.22) shows that the left side is London's fluxoid Φ generalized to nonuniform systems, and we conclude that Φ is quantized in units of $\varphi_0 = hc/e^*$. The present derivation applies only near T_c, but it is plausible to expect the same quantization for all $T < T_c$.

SURFACE ENERGY

The significance of the parameter κ is most easily understood by studying the energy associated with a surface separating normal and superconducting material (see Fig. 50.1). The boundary is mechanically stable only if the normal region has an applied field H_c parallel to the surface, since the Gibbs free energy deep in the normal region

$$G(z \to -\infty) = G_{n0} - \frac{H_c^2}{8\pi} \tag{50.32}$$

then equals that deep in the superconducting region

$$G(z \to \infty) = G_{s0} \tag{50.33}$$

[compare Eq. (48.21)]. The possibility of a surface energy arises in the following way from the occurrence of the two lengths λ and ξ. If the sample were entirely normal or entirely superconducting, the Gibbs free energy per unit area would be $\int_{-\infty}^{\infty} dz(-H_c^2/8\pi)$. In the surface region, however, the flux is expelled for $z \gtrsim \lambda$, while the condensation energy builds up for $z \gtrsim \xi$. Hence the true Gibbs free energy per unit area is given approximately as the sum of two terms

$$\approx \int_{-\infty}^{\lambda} dz \frac{-H_c^2}{8\pi} + \int_{\xi}^{\infty} dz \frac{-H_c^2}{8\pi}$$

By definition, the surface energy σ_{ns} is the difference between the actual Gibbs free energy per unit area and the value that would occur if the sample were uniformly normal or superconducting

$$\sigma_{ns} \approx -\frac{H_c^2}{8\pi} \left(\int_{-\infty}^{\lambda} dz + \int_{\xi}^{\infty} dz - \int_{-\infty}^{\infty} dz \right)$$

$$\approx (\xi - \lambda) \frac{H_c^2}{8\pi} \tag{50.34}$$

We see that σ_{ns} is positive for $\kappa \ll 1$ but negative for $\kappa \gg 1$.

The Ginzburg-Landau theory permits us to study the surface energy in greater detail. Consider a one-dimensional geometry (Fig. 50.1) with the magnetic field $\mathbf{h}(z) = h(z)\hat{x}$ and vector potential $\mathbf{A}(z) = A(z)\hat{y}$. In the present problem, Ψ may be chosen real in an appropriate gauge,[1] and the Ginzburg-Landau equations become

$$-\frac{\hbar^2}{2m^*} \Psi'' - |a|\Psi + b\Psi'^3 + (e^*)^2 \frac{A^2 \Psi}{2m^* c^2} = 0 \qquad (50.35a)$$

$$-\frac{c}{4\pi} h' = \frac{(e^*)^2 \Psi'^2 A}{m^* c} \qquad (50.35b)$$

$$A' = -h \qquad (50.35c)$$

where the primes denote differentiation with respect to z. The corresponding boundary conditions

$$\left. \begin{array}{c} \Psi = 0 \\ h = H_c \end{array} \right\} z \to -\infty \qquad \left. \begin{array}{c} \Psi = |\Psi_\infty| \\ h = 0 \end{array} \right\} z \to +\infty \qquad (50.36)$$

guarantee that Eqs. (50.32) and (50.33) are satisfied.[2] With the same definition of the surface energy, we find

$$\sigma_{ns} = \int_{-\infty}^{\infty} dz \left[G(z) - G_{n0} + \frac{H_c^2}{8\pi} \right] = \int_{-\infty}^{\infty} dz [G(z) - G_{s0}]$$

$$= \int_{-\infty}^{\infty} dz \left[F(z) - \frac{h(z) H_c}{4\pi} - F_{n0} + \frac{H_c^2}{8\pi} \right]$$

$$= \int_{-\infty}^{\infty} dz \left[a|\Psi|^2 + \tfrac{1}{2} b |\Psi|^4 + (2m^*)^{-1} \left| \left(-i\hbar \nabla + \frac{e^* \mathbf{A}}{c} \right) \Psi \right|^2 + \frac{(H_c - h)^2}{8\pi} \right]$$

$$(50.37)$$

Here the second and third lines are obtained with Eqs. (50.6) and (50.2), respectively. If Eq. (50.35a) is multiplied by Ψ^* and integrated over all z, a simple integration by parts yields

$$\int_{-\infty}^{\infty} dz \left[a|\Psi|^2 + b|\Psi|^4 + (2m^*)^{-1} \left| \left(-i\hbar \nabla + \frac{e^* \mathbf{A}}{c} \right) \Psi \right|^2 \right] = 0$$

---

[1] V. L. Ginzburg and L. D. Landau, *loc. cit.* If $|\Psi|^2$ depends only on z, the order parameter takes the form $e^{i\varphi(x,y)}\Psi(z)$. In addition, Maxwell's equation implies that $\mathbf{j}(z) = j(z)\hat{y}$. Equation (50.9) then shows that $\Psi(z)$ must be real while $\partial\varphi/\partial x$ vanishes. The remaining phase factor $\varphi(y)$ must be a linear function of y and may be absorbed with the trivial gauge transformation $A \to A - (\hbar c/e^*) \partial\varphi/\partial y$.

[2] These boundary conditions violate Eq. (50.8b) at $z = +\infty$, owing to our idealized one-dimensional geometry. A more physical configuration is a long cylinder placed in a solenoid, with a macroscopic superconducting core surrounded by a normal sheath.

Substitution into Eq. (50.37) gives the final form

$$\sigma_{ns} = \int_{-\infty}^{\infty} dz \left[-\tfrac{1}{2}b|\Psi|^4 + \frac{(H_c - h)^2}{8\pi} \right] \tag{50.38}$$

Both Eqs. (50.37) and (50.38) are exact; the former is also variationally correct while the latter, which makes use of the exact field equations, is considerably simpler.

It is conventional to characterize the surface energy with a length δ:

$$\sigma_{ns} = \frac{H_c^2}{8\pi} \delta \tag{50.39}$$

where

$$\delta \equiv \int_{-\infty}^{\infty} dz \left[-\left| \frac{\Psi}{\Psi_\infty} \right|^4 + \left(1 - \frac{h}{H_c} \right)^2 \right] \tag{50.40}$$

has been rewritten with the aid of Eqs. (50.12) and (50.16).   Although a computer solution of Eqs. (50.35) and (50.36) is needed to evaluate δ for arbitrary κ, special limiting cases have been studied analytically.   The numerical details are rather tedious, however, and we only state the results[1]

$$\delta = \begin{cases} \dfrac{4\sqrt{2}}{3}\xi \approx 1.89\xi & \kappa \ll 1 \tag{50.41a} \\[3mm] 0 & \kappa = \dfrac{1}{\sqrt{2}} \tag{50.41b} \\[3mm] -\tfrac{8}{3}(\sqrt{2} - 1)\lambda \approx -1.10\lambda & \kappa \gg 1 \tag{50.41c} \end{cases}$$

in agreement with our qualitative estimate of Eq. (50.34).

The surface energy is important in determining the behavior of a super-conductor in an applied magnetic field, and a material is conventionally classified as type I or type II according as σ_{ns} is positive or negative.   Comparison with Eq. (50.41) yields the following criterion

$$\text{Type I:} \quad \kappa < \frac{1}{\sqrt{2}} \quad \xi(T) > \sqrt{2}\lambda(T) \quad \sigma_{ns} > 0$$

$$\text{Type II:} \quad \kappa > \frac{1}{\sqrt{2}} \quad \xi(T) < \sqrt{2}\lambda(T) \quad \sigma_{ns} < 0 \tag{50.42}$$

The positive surface energy of type-I materials keeps the sample spatially homogeneous, and it exhibits a complete Meissner effect for all $H < H_c$.   In contrast, type-II materials tend to break up into microscopic domains as soon as the magnetic field exceeds a lower critical field H_{c1} (see Prob. 13.5), which is always less than H_c.   For $H > H_{c1}$, magnetic flux penetrates the sample in the form of

[1] V. L. Ginzburg and L. D. Landau, loc. cit.; D. Saint-James, G. Sarma, and E. J. Thomas, "Type-II Superconductivity," chap. II, Pergamon Press, London, 1969.

quantized flux lines, and the sample is said to be in the mixed state.   This state persists up to an upper critical field $H_{c2} = \sqrt{2}\,\kappa H_c$ (see Prob. 13.6) above which the sample becomes normal.   The possibility of type-II superconductivity was first suggested by Abrikosov,[1] who used the Ginzburg-Landau theory to study the mixed state in detail.   We regret that this vast subject cannot be included here, and we must refer the reader to other sources.[2]

51□MICROSCOPIC (BCS) THEORY

For the remainder of this chapter, we consider the microscopic model introduced by Bardeen, Cooper, and Schrieffer (BCS) in 1957.[3]   This model has had astonishing success in correlating and explaining the properties of simple super-conductors in terms of a few experimental parameters.   The ground state of the model has already been determined in Sec. 37 with a canonical transformation. Such an approach can be extended to finite temperatures, but Gorkov[4] has shown that it is preferable to reformulate the theory in terms of temperature Green's functions.   As discussed in the following paragraphs, this approximate descrip-tion represents a natural generalization of the Hartree-Fock theory of Sec. 27.

GENERAL FORMULATION

The theory starts from the following model *grand canonical hamiltonian* for an electron gas in a magnetic field

$$\hat{K} = \hat{K}_0 + \hat{V} = \int d^3x \, \hat{\psi}^\dagger_\alpha(\mathbf{x}) \left\{ \frac{1}{2m}\left[-i\hbar\boldsymbol{\nabla} + \frac{e\mathbf{A}(\mathbf{x})}{c} \right]^2 - \mu \right\} \hat{\psi}_\alpha(\mathbf{x})$$

$$-\tfrac{1}{2}g \int d^3x \, \hat{\psi}^\dagger_\alpha(\mathbf{x})\, \hat{\psi}^\dagger_\beta(\mathbf{x})\, \hat{\psi}_\beta(\mathbf{x})\, \hat{\psi}_\alpha(\mathbf{x}) \quad (51.1)$$

where $\mathbf{A}(\mathbf{x})$ is the vector potential and $-e$ is the charge on an electron.   As shown in Chap. 12, the exchange of phonons leads to an effective attraction between electrons close to the Fermi surface.   This interparticle potential has here been approximated by an attractive delta function with strength $g > 0$ [compare Eq.

[1] A. A. Abrikosov, *Sov. Phys.-JETP*, **5**:1174 (1957).

[2] See, for example, P. G. de Gennes, "Superconductivity of Metals and Alloys," chaps. 3, 6, W. A. Benjamin, Inc., New York, 1966; A. L. Fetter and P. C. Hohenberg, Theory of Type-II Superconductors, and B. Serin, Type-II Superconductors: Experiments, in R. D. Parks (ed.), "Superconductivity," vol. II, chaps. 14, 15, Marcel Dekker, Inc., New York, 1969.

[3] We have found the following books particularly useful: P. G. de Gennes, *loc. cit.*; G. Rickayzen, "Theory of Superconductivity," John Wiley and Sons, Inc., New York, 1965; J. R. Schrieffer, "Theory of Superconductivity," W. A. Benjamin, Inc., New York, 1964.   See also, A. A. Abrikosov, L. P. Gorkov, and I. E. Dzyaloshinskii, "Methods of Quantum Field Theory in Statistical Physics," chap. 7, Prentice-Hall, Inc., Englewood Cliffs, N.J., 1963.

[4] L. P. Gorkov, *Sov. Phys.-JETP*, **7**:505 (1958).

(46.9)].[1] The philosophy of the microscopic theory is then to solve this model hamiltonian as completely as possible.[2]

As an introduction to our subsequent development, we first review the Hartree-Fock theory, which may be obtained by approximating the exact interaction operator $\hat{V}$ in Eq. (51.1) as a bilinear form

$$\hat{V} \approx \hat{V}_{HF} \equiv -g \int d^3x \, [\langle \hat{\psi}_\alpha^\dagger(\mathbf{x}) \, \hat{\psi}_\alpha(\mathbf{x}) \rangle_{HF} \, \hat{\psi}_\beta^\dagger(\mathbf{x}) \, \hat{\psi}_\beta(\mathbf{x})$$
$$- \langle \hat{\psi}_\alpha^\dagger(\mathbf{x}) \, \hat{\psi}_\beta(\mathbf{x}) \rangle_{HF} \, \hat{\psi}_\beta^\dagger(\mathbf{x}) \, \hat{\psi}_\alpha(\mathbf{x})] \quad (51.2)$$

Here the angular brackets denote an ensemble average with the density operator

$$\hat{\rho}_{HF} = \frac{e^{-\beta \hat{K}_{HF}}}{\mathrm{Tr}\, e^{-\beta \hat{K}_{HF}}} \quad (51.3a)$$

and

$$\hat{K}_{HF} = \hat{K}_0 + \hat{V}_{HF} \quad (51.3b)$$

In this approach, $\hat{K}_{HF}$ is used to define a finite-temperature Heisenberg operator $\hat{\psi}_{K\gamma}(\mathbf{x}\tau) = e^{\hat{K}_{HF}\tau/\hbar} \, \hat{\psi}_\gamma(\mathbf{x}) \, e^{-\hat{K}_{HF}\tau/\hbar}$, with the equation of motion

$$\frac{\hbar \, \partial \hat{\psi}_{K\gamma}(\mathbf{x}\tau)}{\partial \tau} = -\left[\frac{1}{2m} \left(-i\hbar\boldsymbol{\nabla} + \frac{e\mathbf{A}}{c} \right)^2 - \mu \right] \hat{\psi}_{K\gamma}(\mathbf{x}\tau)$$
$$+ g\langle \hat{\psi}_\alpha^\dagger(\mathbf{x}) \, \hat{\psi}_\alpha(\mathbf{x}) \rangle_{HF} \, \hat{\psi}_{K\gamma}(\mathbf{x}\tau) - g\langle \hat{\psi}_\alpha^\dagger(\mathbf{x}) \, \hat{\psi}_\gamma(\mathbf{x}) \rangle_{HF} \, \hat{\psi}_{K\alpha}(\mathbf{x}\tau)$$

The corresponding single-particle Green's function

$$\mathcal{G}_{\alpha\beta}(\mathbf{x}\tau, \mathbf{x}'\tau') = -\langle T_\tau[\hat{\psi}_{K\alpha}(\mathbf{x}\tau) \, \hat{\psi}_{K\beta}^\dagger(\mathbf{x}'\tau')] \rangle_{HF}$$

satisfies the same self-consistent equation of motion as that derived in Prob. 8.3 and is therefore identical with the Hartree-Fock Green's function of Sec. 27 (see Prob. 13.7). The self-consistency here appears through $\hat{V}_{HF}$, which both determines and is determined by Eq. (51.3).

The precise structure of $\hat{V}_{HF}$ can be understood by seeking a linear approximation to the exact equations of motion. Since the commutator $[\hat{V}, \hat{\psi}_\alpha(\mathbf{x})]$ contains three field operators, it must be approximated by a linear form $[\hat{V}, \hat{\psi}_\alpha(\mathbf{x})] \to f_{\alpha\beta} \, \hat{\psi}_\beta(\mathbf{x})$ where the $f_{\alpha\beta}$ are c-number coefficients. This replacement has the consequence that $\{[\hat{V}, \hat{\psi}_\alpha(\mathbf{x})], \hat{\psi}_\beta^\dagger(\mathbf{y})\} \to f_{\alpha\beta} \delta(\mathbf{x} - \mathbf{y})$. In fact, the left side of this relation is still quadratic in the field operators. We therefore replace it by its ensemble average to obtain the linearized theory, which provides a prescription for determining $f_{\alpha\beta}$. The approximate form $\hat{V}_{HF}$ in Eq. (51.2) is chosen to reproduce the corresponding linear equations.

[1] The singular nature of this potential occasionally leads to spurious divergent integrals, which will be cut off at the Debye frequency in accordance with the discussion in Chap. 12.
[2] Superconducting solutions of the electron-phonon hamiltonian [Eq. (46.1)] have been studied by N. N. Bogoliubov, *Sov. Phys.-JETP*, **7**:41 (1958) and by G. M. Eliashberg, *Sov. Phys.-JETP*, **11**:696 (1960) and **12**:1000 (1961). This approach is essential for strong-coupling superconductors such as Pb (Fig. 51.2 and Table 51.1), which do not fit the usual BCS theory [see, for example, J. R. Schrieffer, *op. cit.*, chap. 7, and W. L. McMillan, *Phys. Rev.*, **167**:331 (1968)].

We may also recall the alternative derivation of the Hartree-Fock theory studied in Probs. 4.4 and 8.3. In analogy with Wick's theorem, the ensemble average of four fermion field operators is factorized as follows:

$$\langle T_\tau[\hat{\psi}^\dagger_{K\alpha}(1)\,\hat{\psi}^\dagger_{K\beta}(2)\,\hat{\psi}_{K\gamma}(3)\,\hat{\psi}_{K\delta}(4)]\rangle_{HF} = \langle T_\tau[\hat{\psi}^\dagger_{K\alpha}(1)\,\hat{\psi}_{K\delta}(4)]\rangle_{HF}$$
$$\times \langle T_\tau[\hat{\psi}^\dagger_{K\beta}(2)\,\hat{\psi}_{K\gamma}(3)]\rangle_{HF} - \langle T_\tau[\hat{\psi}^\dagger_{K\alpha}(1)\,\hat{\psi}_{K\gamma}(3)]\rangle_{HF}\,\langle T_\tau[\hat{\psi}^\dagger_{K\beta}(2)\,\hat{\psi}_{K\delta}(4)]\rangle_{HF}$$
$$(51.4)$$

This procedure immediately yields the Hartree-Fock equations for $\mathscr{G}$; it also provides a general method for dealing with the typical expressions occurring in the theory of linear response [see, for example, Eqs. (32.7) and (32.11)].

The foregoing discussion must now be generalized to include the one essentially new feature of a superconductor, namely the possibility that two electrons of opposite spins can form a self-bound Cooper pair (Secs. 36 and 37). As a model for this phenomenon, we add two extra terms representing the pairing amplitude to Eq. (51.2):

$$\hat{V} \approx \hat{V}_{HF} - \tfrac{1}{2}g \int d^3x\, [\langle\hat{\psi}^\dagger_\alpha(\mathbf{x})\,\hat{\psi}^\dagger_\beta(\mathbf{x})\rangle\,\hat{\psi}_\beta(\mathbf{x})\,\hat{\psi}_\alpha(\mathbf{x})$$
$$+ \hat{\psi}^\dagger_\alpha(\mathbf{x})\,\hat{\psi}^\dagger_\beta(\mathbf{x})\,\langle\hat{\psi}_\beta(\mathbf{x})\,\hat{\psi}_\alpha(\mathbf{x})\rangle] \quad (51.5)$$

This approximation corresponds to adding a term $g_{\alpha\beta}\hat{\psi}^\dagger_\beta(\mathbf{x})$ to the linear form $f_{\alpha\beta}\hat{\psi}_\beta(\mathbf{x})$.[1] Since the resulting linear equations of motion for $\hat{\psi}$ and $\hat{\psi}^\dagger$ are now coupled, the theory no longer conserves the number of particles. Indeed, *the condensed Cooper pairs may be considered a particle bath, in close analogy with the Bose condensation studied in Chap. 6 and Sec. 35.* For consistency, the factorization procedure of Eq. (51.4) must also be generalized to include the pairing amplitudes[2]

$$\langle T_\tau[\hat{\psi}^\dagger_{K\alpha}(1)\,\hat{\psi}^\dagger_{K\beta}(2)\,\hat{\psi}_{K\gamma}(3)\,\hat{\psi}_{K\delta}(4)]\rangle = \langle T_\tau[\hat{\psi}^\dagger_{K\alpha}(1)\,\hat{\psi}_{K\delta}(4)]\rangle\,\langle T_\tau[\hat{\psi}^\dagger_{K\beta}(2)\,\hat{\psi}_{K\gamma}(3)]\rangle$$
$$- \langle T_\tau[\hat{\psi}^\dagger_{K\alpha}(1)\,\hat{\psi}_{K\gamma}(3)]\rangle\,\langle T_\tau[\hat{\psi}^\dagger_{K\beta}(2)\,\hat{\psi}_{K\delta}(4)]\rangle$$
$$+ \langle T_\tau[\hat{\psi}^\dagger_{K\alpha}(1)\,\hat{\psi}^\dagger_{K\beta}(2)]\rangle\,\langle T_\tau[\hat{\psi}_{K\gamma}(3)\,\hat{\psi}_{K\delta}(4)]\rangle \quad (51.6)$$

Although all the terms in Eq. (51.5) can be retained, it is much simpler to omit the usual Hartree-Fock contribution $\hat{V}_{HF}$ entirely, thereby treating the normal state as a free electron gas. This approximation is based on the assumption that $\hat{V}_{HF}$ is the same in both normal and superconducting phases and does not affect the comparison between the two states (see the treatment of Sec. 37). Since the Cooper pair has spin zero, the indices α and β in Eq. (51.5) must refer to opposite spin projections, and the total effective hamiltonian becomes

$$\hat{K}_{\text{eff}} = \hat{K}_0 - g\int d^3x\, [\langle\hat{\psi}^\dagger_\downarrow(\mathbf{x})\,\hat{\psi}^\dagger_\uparrow(\mathbf{x})\rangle\,\hat{\psi}_\uparrow(\mathbf{x})\,\hat{\psi}_\downarrow(\mathbf{x})$$
$$+ \hat{\psi}^\dagger_\downarrow(\mathbf{x})\,\hat{\psi}^\dagger_\uparrow(\mathbf{x})\,\langle\hat{\psi}_\uparrow(\mathbf{x})\,\hat{\psi}_\downarrow(\mathbf{x})\rangle] \quad (51.7)$$

---

[1] P. G. de Gennes, *op. cit.*, p. 141 shows that the present choice of $f_{\alpha\beta}$ and $g_{\alpha\beta}$ minimizes the free energy.

[2] L. P. Gorkov, *loc. cit.*

which forms the basis for the BCS theory. The theory is self-consistent, because the angular brackets are interpreted as an ensemble average evaluated with $\hat{K}_{\text{eff}}$; in particular, quantities such as

$$\langle \hat{\psi}_\uparrow^\dagger(\mathbf{x}) \, \hat{\psi}_\uparrow^\dagger(\mathbf{x}) \rangle = \frac{\operatorname{Tr}\left[e^{-\beta \hat{K}_{\text{eff}}} \, \hat{\psi}_\uparrow^\dagger(\mathbf{x}) \, \hat{\psi}_\uparrow^\dagger(\mathbf{x}) \right]}{\operatorname{Tr} e^{-\beta \hat{K}_{\text{eff}}}}$$

do not vanish, because $[\hat{K}_{\text{eff}}, \hat{N}] \neq 0$.

We now introduce Heisenberg operators

$$\hat{\psi}_{K\uparrow}(\mathbf{x}\tau) = e^{\hat{K}_{\text{eff}} \, \tau / \hbar} \, \hat{\psi}_\uparrow(\mathbf{x}) \, e^{-\hat{K}_{\text{eff}} \, \tau / \hbar}$$

$$\hat{\psi}_{K\downarrow}^\dagger(\mathbf{x}\tau) = e^{\hat{K}_{\text{eff}} \, \tau / \hbar} \, \hat{\psi}_\downarrow^\dagger(\mathbf{x}) \, e^{-\hat{K}_{\text{eff}} \, \tau / \hbar}$$

(51.8)

satisfying the linear equations of motion

$$\hbar \frac{\partial \hat{\psi}_{K\uparrow}}{\partial \tau} = -\left[\frac{1}{2m} \left(-i\hbar \boldsymbol{\nabla} + \frac{e\mathbf{A}}{c} \right)^2 - \mu \right] \hat{\psi}_{K\uparrow} - g\langle \hat{\psi}_\uparrow \hat{\psi}_\downarrow \rangle \, \hat{\psi}_{K\downarrow}^\dagger$$

$$\hbar \frac{\partial \hat{\psi}_{K\downarrow}^\dagger}{\partial \tau} = \left[\frac{1}{2m} \left(i\hbar \boldsymbol{\nabla} + \frac{e\mathbf{A}}{c} \right)^2 - \mu \right] \hat{\psi}_{K\downarrow}^\dagger - g\langle \hat{\psi}_\downarrow^\dagger \hat{\psi}_\uparrow^\dagger \rangle \, \hat{\psi}_{K\uparrow}$$

(51.9)

As the final step in our formulation, we define a single-particle Green's function

$$\mathscr{G}(\mathbf{x}\tau, \mathbf{x}'\,\tau') = -\langle T_\tau[\hat{\psi}_{K\uparrow}(\mathbf{x}\tau) \, \hat{\psi}_{K\uparrow}^\dagger(\mathbf{x}'\,\tau')] \rangle \tag{51.10}$$

where a particular choice of spin indices has been made to simplify the notation. Differentiate $\mathscr{G}$ with respect to τ. The derivative acts both on the field operator and on the step functions implicit in the "time" ordering, which yields

$$\hbar \frac{\partial}{\partial \tau} \mathscr{G}(\mathbf{x}\tau, \mathbf{x}'\,\tau') = -\hbar\delta(\tau - \tau') \langle \{\hat{\psi}_{K\uparrow}(\mathbf{x}\tau), \hat{\psi}_{K\uparrow}^\dagger(\mathbf{x}'\,\tau')\} \rangle$$

$$- \left\langle T_\tau\left[\hbar \frac{\partial \hat{\psi}_{K\uparrow}(\mathbf{x}\tau)}{\partial \tau} \hat{\psi}_{K\uparrow}^\dagger(\mathbf{x}'\,\tau') \right] \right\rangle$$

$$= -\hbar\delta(\mathbf{x} - \mathbf{x}')\,\delta(\tau - \tau') - \left[\frac{1}{2m} \left(-i\hbar \boldsymbol{\nabla} + \frac{e\mathbf{A}}{c} \right)^2 - \mu \right]$$

$$\times \mathscr{G}(\mathbf{x}\tau, \mathbf{x}'\,\tau') + g\langle \hat{\psi}_\uparrow(\mathbf{x}) \, \hat{\psi}_\downarrow(\mathbf{x}) \rangle \langle T_\tau[\hat{\psi}_{K\downarrow}^\dagger(\mathbf{x}\tau) \, \hat{\psi}_{K\uparrow}^\dagger(\mathbf{x}'\,\tau')] \rangle \quad (51.11)$$

We are thus led to consider two new functions

$$\mathscr{F}(\mathbf{x}\tau, \mathbf{x}'\,\tau') \equiv -\langle T_\tau[\hat{\psi}_{K\uparrow}(\mathbf{x}\tau) \, \hat{\psi}_{K\downarrow}(\mathbf{x}'\,\tau')] \rangle \tag{51.12a}$$

$$\mathscr{F}^\dagger(\mathbf{x}\tau, \mathbf{x}'\,\tau') \equiv -\langle T_\tau[\hat{\psi}_{K\downarrow}^\dagger(\mathbf{x}\tau) \, \hat{\psi}_{K\uparrow}^\dagger(\mathbf{x}'\,\tau')] \rangle \tag{51.12b}$$

and Eq. (51.11) becomes

$$\left[-\hbar \frac{\partial}{\partial \tau} - \frac{1}{2m} \left(-i\hbar \boldsymbol{\nabla} + \frac{e\mathbf{A}}{c} \right)^2 + \mu \right] \mathscr{G}(\mathbf{x}\tau, \mathbf{x}'\,\tau') - g\langle \hat{\psi}_\uparrow(\mathbf{x}) \, \hat{\psi}_\downarrow(\mathbf{x}) \rangle \, \mathscr{F}^\dagger(\mathbf{x}\tau, \mathbf{x}'\,\tau')$$

$$= \hbar\delta(\mathbf{x} - \mathbf{x}')\,\delta(\tau - \tau') \quad (51.13)$$

In the usual case of a time-independent hamiltonian, the functions $\mathcal{G}$, $\mathcal{F}$, and $\mathcal{F}^\dagger$ depend only on the difference $\tau - \tau'$, and it is convenient to introduce the abbreviation

$$\Delta(\mathbf{x}) \equiv g\mathcal{F}(\mathbf{x}\tau^+, \mathbf{x}\tau) = -g\langle \hat{\psi}_\uparrow(\mathbf{x})\,\hat{\psi}_\downarrow(\mathbf{x})\rangle = g\langle \hat{\psi}_\downarrow(\mathbf{x})\,\hat{\psi}_\uparrow(\mathbf{x})\rangle \tag{51.14}$$

which defines the *gap function* $\Delta(\mathbf{x})$.[1]   A combination of Eqs. (51.13) and (51.14) yields

$$\left[-\hbar\frac{\partial}{\partial\tau} - \frac{1}{2m}\left(-i\hbar\boldsymbol{\nabla} + \frac{e\mathbf{A}}{c}\right)^2 + \mu\right]\mathcal{G}(\mathbf{x}\tau, \mathbf{x}'\,\tau') + \Delta(\mathbf{x})\mathcal{F}^\dagger(\mathbf{x}\tau, \mathbf{x}'\,\tau')$$
$$= \hbar\delta(\mathbf{x} - \mathbf{x}')\,\delta(\tau - \tau') \tag{51.15}$$

In a similar way, the functions $\mathcal{F}$ and $\mathcal{F}^\dagger$ are easily seen to obey the equations of motion

$$\left[-\hbar\frac{\partial}{\partial\tau} - \frac{1}{2m}\left(-i\hbar\boldsymbol{\nabla} + \frac{e\mathbf{A}}{c}\right)^2 + \mu\right]\mathcal{F}(\mathbf{x}\tau, \mathbf{x}'\,\tau')$$
$$= -g\langle \hat{\psi}_\uparrow(\mathbf{x})\,\hat{\psi}_\downarrow(\mathbf{x})\rangle\,\langle T_\tau[\hat{\psi}_{K\downarrow}^\dagger(\mathbf{x}\tau)\,\hat{\psi}_{K\downarrow}(\mathbf{x}'\,\tau')]\rangle$$
$$= \Delta(\mathbf{x})\,\mathcal{G}(\mathbf{x}'\,\tau', \mathbf{x}\tau) \tag{51.16}$$

$$\left[\hbar\frac{\partial}{\partial\tau} - \frac{1}{2m}\left(i\hbar\boldsymbol{\nabla} + \frac{e\mathbf{A}}{c}\right)^2 + \mu\right]\mathcal{F}^\dagger(\mathbf{x}\tau, \mathbf{x}'\,\tau')$$
$$= g\langle \hat{\psi}_\downarrow^\dagger(\mathbf{x})\,\hat{\psi}_\uparrow^\dagger(\mathbf{x})\rangle\,\langle T_\tau[\hat{\psi}_{K\uparrow}(\mathbf{x}\tau)\,\hat{\psi}_{K\uparrow}^\dagger(\mathbf{x}'\,\tau')]\rangle$$
$$= \Delta^*(\mathbf{x})\,\mathcal{G}(\mathbf{x}\tau, \mathbf{x}'\,\tau') \tag{51.17}$$

Typical magnetic fields of interest for superconductivity are $\lesssim 10^3$ gauss, so that the weak Pauli paramagnetism may be neglected entirely ($\mu_0 H \ll k_B T_c$).   In this limit the two spin projections are equivalent, which has been used on the right side of Eq. (51.16).

For most purposes, it is sufficient to consider Eqs. (51.15) and (51.17) as a pair of coupled equations for $\mathcal{G}$ and $\mathcal{F}^\dagger$.   Nevertheless, there are definite advantages to combining the three equations in a single matrix equation, exactly as in Sec. 20.[2]   Introduce a two-component field operator

$$\Psi_K(\mathbf{x}\tau) \equiv \begin{bmatrix} \hat{\psi}_{K\uparrow}(\mathbf{x}\tau) \\ \hat{\psi}_{K\downarrow}^\dagger(\mathbf{x}\tau) \end{bmatrix} \tag{51.18}$$

and a 2×2 matrix Green's function

$$\mathcal{G}(\mathbf{x}\tau, \mathbf{x}'\,\tau') \equiv -\langle T_\tau[\Psi_K(\mathbf{x}\tau)\,\Psi_K^\dagger(\mathbf{x}'\,\tau')]\rangle$$
$$= \begin{bmatrix} \mathcal{G}(\mathbf{x}\tau, \mathbf{x}'\,\tau') & \mathcal{F}(\mathbf{x}\tau, \mathbf{x}'\,\tau') \\ \mathcal{F}^\dagger(\mathbf{x}\tau, \mathbf{x}'\,\tau') & -\mathcal{G}(\mathbf{x}'\,\tau', \mathbf{x}\tau) \end{bmatrix} \tag{51.19}$$

---

[1] We here follow the convention of A. A. Abrikosov, L. P. Gorkov, and I. E. Dzyaloshinskii, *op. cit.*, sec. 34, but several authors (for example, P. G. de Gennes, *op. cit.*, p. 143) introduce an additional minus sign.

[2] Y. Nambu, *Phys. Rev.*, **117**:648 (1960).

The corresponding equation of motion becomes

$$\mathcal{D}_{\mathbf{x}\tau}\mathcal{G}(\mathbf{x}\tau,\mathbf{x}'\,\tau') = \hbar\mathbb{1}\delta(\mathbf{x}-\mathbf{x}')\,\delta(\tau-\tau') \tag{51.20}$$

where $\mathcal{D}_{\mathbf{x}\tau}$ is a matrix differential operator

$$\mathcal{D}_{\mathbf{x}\tau} = \begin{bmatrix} -\hbar\dfrac{\partial}{\partial\tau} - \dfrac{1}{2m}\left(-i\hbar\nabla + \dfrac{e\mathbf{A}}{c}\right)^2 + \mu & \Delta(\mathbf{x}) \\[2mm] \Delta^*(\mathbf{x}) & -\hbar\dfrac{\partial}{\partial\tau} + \dfrac{1}{2m}\left(i\hbar\nabla + \dfrac{e\mathbf{A}}{c}\right)^2 - \mu \end{bmatrix} \tag{51.21}$$

This matrix formulation has been used extensively in studies of the electron-phonon interaction in superconductors.[1] It also provides a convenient basis for a gauge-invariant treatment of electromagnetic fields.[2] Unfortunately, it is not possible to consider these questions here, and we generally rely on the original Gorkov equations (51.15) and (51.17).

SOLUTION FOR UNIFORM MEDIUM

In almost all cases of interest the hamiltonian is time independent, and the corresponding Green's functions depend only on $\tau - \tau'$. It is then useful to introduce a Fourier representation

$$\mathcal{G}(\mathbf{x}\tau,\mathbf{x}'\,\tau') = (\beta\hbar)^{-1}\sum_n e^{-i\omega_n(\tau-\tau')}\mathcal{G}(\mathbf{x},\mathbf{x}',\omega_n) \tag{51.22a}$$

$$\mathcal{F}^\dagger(\mathbf{x}\tau,\mathbf{x}'\,\tau') = (\beta\hbar)^{-1}\sum_n e^{-i\omega_n(\tau-\tau')}\mathcal{F}^\dagger(\mathbf{x},\mathbf{x}',\omega_n) \tag{51.22b}$$

where the choice $\omega_n = (2n+1)\pi/\beta\hbar$ guarantees the proper Fermi statistics. The corresponding equations of motion are

$$\left[i\hbar\omega_n - \dfrac{1}{2m}\left(-i\hbar\nabla + \dfrac{e\mathbf{A}}{c}\right)^2 + \mu\right]\mathcal{G}(\mathbf{x},\mathbf{x}',\omega_n) + \Delta(\mathbf{x})\mathcal{F}^\dagger(\mathbf{x},\mathbf{x}',\omega_n)$$
$$= \hbar\delta(\mathbf{x}-\mathbf{x}') \tag{51.23a}$$

$$\left[-i\hbar\omega_n - \dfrac{1}{2m}\left(i\hbar\nabla + \dfrac{e\mathbf{A}}{c}\right)^2 + \mu\right]\mathcal{F}^\dagger(\mathbf{x},\mathbf{x}',\omega_n) - \Delta^*(\mathbf{x})\mathcal{G}(\mathbf{x},\mathbf{x}',\omega_n) = 0 \tag{51.23b}$$

which must be solved along with the self-consistency condition

$$\Delta^*(\mathbf{x}) = -g\langle\hat\psi^\dagger_\downarrow(\mathbf{x})\,\hat\psi^\dagger_\uparrow(\mathbf{x})\rangle = g\mathcal{F}^\dagger(\mathbf{x}\tau^+,\mathbf{x}\tau)$$

$$= \dfrac{g}{\beta\hbar}\sum_n e^{-i\omega_n\eta}\mathcal{F}^\dagger(\mathbf{x},\mathbf{x},\omega_n) \tag{51.24}$$

[1] J. R. Schrieffer, op. cit., chap. 7.
[2] J. R. Schrieffer, op. cit., secs. 8-5 and 8-6.

In the most general situation, these coupled equations must be augmented by Maxwell's equation relating the microscopic magnetic field $\mathbf{h} = \text{curl} \, \mathbf{A}$ to the supercurrent $\mathbf{j}$ and any external currents used to generate the applied field. It is clear that a complete analytic solution is impossible, so that we must turn to limiting cases.   The remainder of this section is devoted to the thermodynamics of an infinite bulk superconductor in zero field.   We then examine two examples where the existence of a small parameter permits a rather complete solution: the linear response to a weak magnetic field (Sec. 52) and the behavior near T_c, where the gap function $\Delta(\mathbf{x})$ is small (Sec. 53).   These cases are particularly interesting, for they provide a microscopic justification of the London-Pippard and Ginzburg-Landau theories, respectively.

In the absence of a magnetic field, the vector potential can be set equal to zero, and Eqs. (51.23) and (51.24) assume a simple translationally invariant form

$$\left(i\hbar\omega_n + \frac{\hbar^2 \nabla^2}{2m} + \mu \right) \mathscr{G}(\mathbf{x} - \mathbf{x}', \omega_n) + \Delta\mathscr{F}^\dagger(\mathbf{x} - \mathbf{x}', \omega_n) = \hbar\delta(\mathbf{x} - \mathbf{x}') \quad (51.25a)$$

$$\left(-i\hbar\omega_n + \frac{\hbar^2 \nabla^2}{2m} + \mu \right) \mathscr{F}^\dagger(\mathbf{x} - \mathbf{x}', \omega_n) - \Delta^* \mathscr{G}(\mathbf{x} - \mathbf{x}', \omega_n) = 0 \quad (51.25b)$$

$$\Delta^* = \frac{g}{\beta\hbar} \sum_n e^{-i\omega_n \eta} \mathscr{F}^\dagger(\mathbf{x} = 0, \omega_n) \quad (51.26)$$

With the usual Fourier transforms

$$\mathscr{G}(\mathbf{x}, \omega_n) = (2\pi)^{-3} \int d^3k \, e^{i\mathbf{k} \cdot \mathbf{x}} \, \mathscr{G}(\mathbf{k}, \omega_n)$$

$$\mathscr{F}^\dagger(\mathbf{x}, \omega_n) = (2\pi)^{-3} \int d^3k \, e^{i\mathbf{k} \cdot \mathbf{x}} \, \mathscr{F}^\dagger(\mathbf{k}, \omega_n) \quad (51.27)$$

we obtain a pair of algebraic equations

$$(i\hbar\omega_n - \xi_k) \mathscr{G}(\mathbf{k}, \omega_n) + \Delta\mathscr{F}^\dagger(\mathbf{k}, \omega_n) = \hbar \quad (51.28a)$$

$$(-i\hbar\omega_n - \xi_k) \mathscr{F}^\dagger(\mathbf{k}, \omega_n) - \Delta^* \mathscr{G}(\mathbf{k}, \omega_n) = 0 \quad (51.28b)$$

where [compare Eq. (37.24)]

$$\xi_k \equiv \frac{\hbar^2 k^2}{2m} - \mu \quad (51.29)$$

These equations are readily solved to give

$$\mathscr{G}(\mathbf{k}, \omega_n) = \frac{-\hbar(i\hbar\omega_n + \xi_k)}{\hbar^2 \omega_n^2 + \xi_k^2 + |\Delta|^2} \quad (51.30a)$$

$$\mathscr{F}^\dagger(\mathbf{k}, \omega_n) = \frac{\hbar\Delta^*}{\hbar^2 \omega_n^2 + \xi_k^2 + |\Delta|^2} \quad (51.30b)$$

In the absence of an applied field, the parameter Δ may be taken as real with no loss of generality, thereby ensuring that

$$\mathscr{F}^\dagger(\mathbf{k},\omega_n) = \mathscr{F}(\mathbf{k},\omega_n) \tag{51.31}$$

which follows most simply from Eq. (51.16) for a uniform medium. Furthermore, Eq. (51.30) may be written in the form .

$$\mathscr{G}(\mathbf{k},\omega_n) = \frac{u_k^2}{i\omega_n - E_k/\hbar} + \frac{v_k^2}{i\omega_n + E_k/\hbar} \tag{51.32a}$$

$$\mathscr{F}(\mathbf{k},\omega_n) = \mathscr{F}^\dagger(\mathbf{k},\omega_n)$$
$$= -u_k v_k \left[\frac{1}{i\omega_n - E_k/\hbar} - \frac{1}{i\omega_n + E_k/\hbar} \right] \tag{51.32b}$$

where

$$E_k = (\xi_k^2 + \Delta^2)^{\frac{1}{2}} \tag{51.33}$$

and

$$u_k v_k = \frac{\Delta}{2 E_k}$$
$$v_k^2 = 1 - u_k^2 = \frac{1}{2}\left(1 - \frac{\xi_k}{E_k}\right) \tag{51.34}$$

are precisely the quantities introduced in Eqs. (37.32) and (37.34). Comparison with Eqs. (21.9) and (21.10) shows the close relation between superconductors and condensed Bose systems.

For the present uniform medium, the self-consistent equation (51.26) for Δ becomes

$$\Delta = \frac{g}{\beta\hbar} \sum_n \int \frac{d^3k}{(2\pi)^3} \frac{\hbar\Delta}{(\hbar\omega_n)^2 + E_k^2} \tag{51.35}$$

where the convergence for large $|n|$ allows us to set $\eta = 0$. The series may be summed directly with a contour integral (compare Prob. 7.6) or with the partial-fraction decomposition of Eq. (51.32b); canceling the common factor Δ, we find

$$1 = g(2\pi)^{-3} \int d^3k\, (2E_k)^{-1} \tanh\left(\tfrac{1}{2}\beta E_k\right) \tag{51.36}$$

We now introduce the approximation

$$(2\pi)^{-3} \int d^3k \cdots \approx N(0) \int d\xi \cdots$$

which will be used consistently to evaluate integrals that are peaked near the Fermi surface. The resulting gap equation is a finite-temperature generalization of Eq. (37.45). It must be cut off at $|\xi_k| = \hbar\omega_D \ll \epsilon_F$ in exactly the same way, and the symmetry of the integrand allows us to write

$$1 = gN(0) \int_0^{\hbar\omega_D} \frac{d\xi}{(\xi^2 + \Delta^2)^{\frac{1}{2}}} \tanh \frac{(\xi^2 + \Delta^2)^{\frac{1}{2}}}{2 k_B T} \tag{51.37}$$

which determines the temperature-dependent function $\Delta(T)$.   Since

$$\xi = \frac{\hbar^2 k^2}{2m} - \mu$$

in the present model, the density of states becomes

$$N(0) = \frac{mk_F}{2\pi^2 \hbar^2} \tag{51.38}$$

where μ has been expressed in terms of the Fermi wave vector k_F [compare Eq. (37.47)], and we neglect the small difference in the free energy between the normal and superconducting states.

DETERMINATION OF THE GAP FUNCTION $\Delta(T)$

It is evident that Eq. (51.37) reduces to Eq. (37.48) as $T \to 0$ and gives the same solution $\Delta_0 = 2\hbar\omega_D e^{-1/N(0)g}$.   In the opposite limit $(T \to T_c)$, the gap vanishes identically, and we find

$$1 = gN(0) \int_0^{\hbar\omega_D} \frac{d\xi}{\xi} \tanh \frac{\xi}{2k_B T_c} \tag{51.39}$$

To solve this implicit equation for T_c, it is convenient to introduce a dimensionless integration variable

$$\frac{1}{N(0)g} = \int_0^Z \frac{dz}{z} \tanh z \tag{51.40}$$

where the cutoff $Z = \hbar\omega_D/2k_B T_c$ is essential because the integral diverges logarithmically for $Z \to \infty$.   Integrate by parts:

$$\frac{1}{N(0)g} = [\ln z \tanh z]_0^Z - \int_0^Z dz \ln z \operatorname{sech}^2 z \tag{51.41}$$

In all cases of interest, the upper limit is very large (see Table 51.1) and Eq. (51.41) may be approximated as

$$\frac{1}{N(0)g} = \ln\left(\frac{\hbar\omega_D}{2k_B T_c}\right) - \int_0^\infty dz \ln z \operatorname{sech}^2 z \tag{51.42}$$

where the definite integral is given in Appendix A.   A simple rearrangement yields

$$k_B T_c = \frac{2e^\gamma}{\pi} \hbar\omega_D e^{-1/N(0)g} \approx 1.13\hbar\omega_D e^{-1/N(0)g} \tag{51.43}$$

We see that T_c and the zero-temperature gap $\Delta(T=0) \equiv \Delta_0$ [Eq. (37.49)] both depend sensitively on the parameter $N(0)g$; this dependence cancels in forming

their ratio

$$\frac{\Delta_0}{k_B T_c} = \pi e^{-\gamma} \approx 1.76 \tag{51.44}$$

which is a *universal constant* independent of the particular material.

Table 51.1   Thermodynamic properties of typical superconductors

	T_c, °K	$\theta = \hbar\omega_D/k_B$, °K	$N(0)g$‡	$\dfrac{\Delta_0}{k_B T_c}$	$H_c(0)$, Oe	$\dfrac{T_c C_n(T_c)}{H_c(0)^2 V}$	$\left.\dfrac{C_s - C_n}{C_n}\right\vert_{T_c}$
BCS				76		0.168	1.43
Cd	0.56	164	0.18	1.6	29	0.177	1.32–1.40
Al	1.2	375	0.18	1.3–2.1	106	0.171	1.45
Sn	3.75	195	0.25	1.6	305	0.161–0.164	1.60
Pb	7.22	96	0.39	2.2	805	0.134	2.71

‡ $N(0)g$ is calculated from Eq. (51.43).
Source: R. Meservey and B. B. Schwartz, Equilibrium Properties: Comparison of Experimental Results with Predictions of the BCS Theory, in R. D. Parks (ed.), "Superconductivity," vol. I, pp. 122, 141, 165, Marcel Dekker, Inc., New York, 1969; D. Shoenberg, "Superconductivity," 2d ed., p. 226, Cambridge University Press, Cambridge, 1952.

As seen in Table 51.1, this relation is quite well satisfied in practice.   For a given element, Eq. (51.43) shows that T_c is proportional to the cutoff $\omega_D \propto M^{-\frac{1}{2}}$, which therefore yields the isotope effect, discussed in Eqs. (36.2) and (48.6). The ratio $\theta/T_c = \hbar\omega_D/k_B T_c$ also determines the effective interaction $N(0)g \equiv N(0)\gamma^2$, where γ is the electron-phonon coupling constant in Eq. (45.12).   For ions with charge ze, a combination with Eq. (51.38) leads to

$$N(0)\gamma^2 = \frac{z^{\frac{5}{3}}}{2(3\pi^2)^{\frac{1}{3}}} \frac{\hbar^2 n_0^{\frac{2}{3}}}{m} \frac{\pi^2}{M c_l^2} \tag{51.45}$$

and the observed values[1] for Cd, which has the smallest valence of those in Table 51.1 ($z = 2$, $n_0 M = 8.6$ g/cm³, $c_l = 2.78 \times 10^5$ cm/sec), give $N(0)\gamma^2 \approx 0.54$. The approximate agreement with the value in Table 51.1 is evidence for the importance of phonon exchange in superconductivity.[2]

The temperature dependence of the gap parameter may be derived from Eq. (51.37).   Since its solution requires numerical methods, we shall not attempt

---

[1] See, for example, C. Kittel, "Introduction to Solid State Physics," 2d ed., pp. 100 and 259, John Wiley and Sons, Inc., New York, 1956.

[2] The comparison between theory and experiment is complicated by the repulsive coulomb interaction (see, for example, G. Rickayzen, *op. cit.*, sec. 5.7 and W. L. McMillan, *loc. cit.*).

a detailed analysis and instead merely state the limiting behavior (see Prob. 13.9)

$$\Delta(T) \approx \Delta_0 - (2\pi\Delta_0 k_B T)^{\frac{1}{2}} e^{-\Delta_0/k_B T} \qquad T \ll T_c \qquad (51.46a)$$

$$\Delta(T) \approx k_B T_c \pi \left[\frac{8}{7\zeta(3)}\right]^{\frac{1}{2}} \left(1 - \frac{T}{T_c}\right)^{\frac{1}{2}}$$

$$\approx 3.06 k_B T_c \left(1 - \frac{T}{T_c}\right)^{\frac{1}{2}} \qquad T_c - T \ll T_c \qquad (51.46b)$$

The complete function is shown in Fig. 51.1.

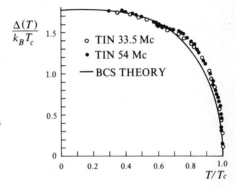

Fig. 51.1 Variation of $\Delta(T)/k_B T_c$ in Sn, measured from the relative ultrasonic attenuation in superconducting and normal states (see Prob. 13.19). [From R. W. Morse and H. V. Bohm, *Phys. Rev.*, **108**:1094 (1957). Reprinted by permission of the authors and the American Institute of Physics.]

THERMODYNAMIC FUNCTIONS

The thermodynamic potential may be determined from the basic equation (23.21). Since our model neglects the usual Hartree-Fock terms in both the normal and superconducting state, the thermodynamic potential Ω_n in the normal state is just that of a free Fermi gas Ω_0, and we find

$$\Omega_s - \Omega_n = \int_0^1 d\lambda \, \lambda^{-1} \langle \lambda \hat{H}_1 \rangle$$

$$= -\frac{1}{2} \int_0^g \frac{dg'}{g'} \int d^3x \, g' \langle \hat{\psi}_\alpha^\dagger(\mathbf{x}) \, \hat{\psi}_\beta^\dagger(\mathbf{x}) \, \hat{\psi}_\beta(\mathbf{x}) \, \hat{\psi}_\alpha(\mathbf{x}) \rangle$$

$$\approx -\int_0^g dg' \left(\frac{1}{g'}\right)^2 \int d^3x \, |\Delta(\mathbf{x})|^2 \qquad (51.47)$$

where Eqs. (51.1), (51.6), and (51.14) have been used in the second and third lines. Note that $\langle \lambda \hat{H}_1 \rangle$ differs from the ensemble average of the last term in Eq. (51.7) by a factor $\frac{1}{2}$. This factor always occurs in any Hartree-Fock theory and may be seen explicitly in Eq. (27.20).

In the present uniform system, the spatial integration merely introduces a factor V; a simple change of variables then gives

$$\Omega_s - \Omega_n = -V \int_0^g dg' \left(\frac{1}{g'}\right)^2 \Delta^2$$

$$= V \int_0^g dg' \frac{d(1/g')}{dg'} \Delta^2$$

$$= V \int_0^\Delta d\Delta' (\Delta')^2 \frac{d(1/g)}{d\Delta'} \tag{51.48}$$

This last form is particularly convenient because Eq. (51.37) expresses $1/g$ as a function of $\Delta(T)$, and direct substitution leads to

$$\frac{\Omega_s - \Omega_n}{V} = N(0) \int_0^{\hbar\omega_D} d\xi \int_0^\Delta d\Delta' (\Delta')^2 \frac{\partial}{\partial\Delta'} \frac{\tanh\left(\frac{1}{2}\beta E'\right)}{E'}$$

$$= N(0) \int_0^{\hbar\omega_D} d\xi \left[\frac{\Delta^2}{E} \tanh\left(\frac{1}{2}\beta E\right) - 2 \int_0^\Delta d\Delta' \frac{\Delta'}{E'} \tanh\left(\frac{1}{2}\beta E'\right) \right] \tag{51.49}$$

where the second line is obtained with partial integration. The first term is just the right side of the gap equation (51.37), and the second can be simplified by changing variables from Δ' to $E' = [(\Delta')^2 + \xi^2]^{\frac{1}{2}}$. In this way, we find

$$\frac{\Omega_s - \Omega_n}{V} = N(0) \Delta^2 \int_0^{\hbar\omega_D} \frac{d\xi}{E} \tanh\left(\frac{1}{2}\beta E\right) - \frac{4N(0)}{\beta} \int_0^{\hbar\omega_D} d\xi \ln \frac{\cosh\left(\frac{1}{2}\beta E\right)}{\cosh\left(\frac{1}{2}\beta \xi\right)}$$

$$= \frac{\Delta^2}{g} - \frac{4N(0)}{\beta} \int_0^{\hbar\omega_D} d\xi \left[\ln\left(1 + e^{-\beta E}\right) + \frac{1}{2}\beta(E - \xi)\right]$$

$$+ \frac{4N(0)}{\beta} \int_0^{\hbar\omega_D} d\xi \ln\left(1 + e^{-\beta\xi}\right) \tag{51.50}$$

Since $\hbar\omega_D \gg k_B T$, the last integral on the right may be extended to infinity. An easy calculation then shows that it equals the first temperature-dependent correction to the thermodynamic potential in the normal state [compare Eq. (5.53)]:

$$4\frac{N(0)V}{\beta} \int_0^\infty d\xi \ln\left(1 + e^{-\beta\xi}\right) = \frac{1}{3}N(0) V\pi^2(k_B T)^2 \approx -[\Omega_n(T) - \Omega_n(0)] \tag{51.51}$$

In addition, it is readily verified that

$$-2N(0) \int_0^{\hbar\omega_D} d\xi\, (E - \xi) \approx -N(0)\left(\frac{1}{2}\Delta^2 + \Delta^2 \ln\frac{2\hbar\omega_D}{\Delta}\right)$$

$$= -\frac{1}{2}N(0)\Delta^2 - \frac{\Delta^2}{g} - N(0)\Delta^2 \ln\frac{\Delta_0}{\Delta} \tag{51.52}$$

where Eq. (37.48) has been used to eliminate $\ln(2\hbar\omega_D/\Delta_0)$. A combination of Eqs. (51.50) to (51.52) yields

$$\frac{\Omega_s - \Omega_n}{V} = -\tfrac{1}{2}N(0)\,\Delta^2 - N(0)\,\Delta^2\ln\left(\frac{\Delta_0}{\Delta}\right)$$

$$- 4N(0)\,k_B T \int_0^{\hbar\omega_D} d\xi \ln(1 + e^{-\beta E}) + \tfrac{1}{3}\pi^2 N(0)\,(k_B T)^2 \quad (51.53)$$

where the inequalities $T \leqslant T_c \ll \theta \ll T_F$ have been assumed.

This expression correctly reduces to Eq. (37.53) at $T = 0$. It also allows us to evaluate the leading low-temperature correction, which arises solely from the normal-state contribution because $\Delta - \Delta_0$ vanishes exponentially for $T \to 0$ [Eq. (51.46a)]. A direct calculation with Eqs. (23.9) and (51.32a) shows that $N_s \approx N_n$ for all $T \leqslant T_c$ [compare Eqs. (37.51) and (37.52)], and we may therefore reinterpret Eq. (51.53) as

$$\frac{F_s - F_n}{V} \approx -\tfrac{1}{2}N(0)\,\Delta_0^2 + \tfrac{1}{3}\pi^2 N(0)\,(k_B T)^2 \qquad T \to 0 \qquad (51.54)$$

A combination with Eqs. (48.22) and (51.44) gives the low-temperature critical field

$$H_c(T) = [4\pi N(0)\,\Delta_0^2]^{\frac{1}{2}}\left[1 - \frac{e^{2\gamma}}{3}\left(\frac{T}{T_c}\right)^2\right]$$

$$\approx H_c(0)\left[1 - 1.06\left(\frac{T}{T_c}\right)^2\right] \qquad T \to 0 \qquad (51.55)$$

where

$$H_c(0) = [4\pi N(0)\,\Delta_0^2]^{\frac{1}{2}} \qquad (51.56)$$

is the critical field at $T = 0$. Since $N(0)$ determines the normal-state specific heat [compare Eqs. (5.59) and (51.38)]

$$\frac{C_n}{V} = \frac{2\pi^2}{3}N(0)\,k_B^2 T \qquad (51.57)$$

Eqs. (51.44) and (51.56) together predict a *second universal constant*

$$\frac{T_c\,C_n(T_c)}{H_c^2(0)\,V} = \frac{e^{2\gamma}}{6\pi} \approx 0.168 \qquad (51.58)$$

which is independent of the material in question. Each of these parameters is measurable, and experimental confirmation is satisfactory (Table 51.1).

It is also interesting to evaluate Ω_s itself, which may be obtained from Eqs. (51.51) and (51.53)

$$\frac{\Omega_s}{V} = \frac{\Omega_n(T=0)}{V} - \tfrac{1}{2}N(0)\,\Delta^2\left(1 + 2\ln\frac{\Delta_0}{\Delta}\right) - 4N(0)\,k_B T \int_0^{\hbar\omega_D} d\xi \ln(1 + e^{-\beta E})$$

$$(51.59)$$

In the present low-temperature limit, it is permissible to evaluate the integral by setting $\hbar\omega_D \to \infty$ and $\Delta \approx \Delta_0$; an approximate calculation yields

$$\int_0^\infty d\xi \ln\{1 + \exp[-\beta(\xi^2 + \Delta_0^2)^{\frac{1}{2}}]\} \approx \tfrac{1}{2} e^{-\beta\Delta_0} (2\pi\Delta_0 \beta^{-1})^{\frac{1}{2}}$$

which can be combined with Eqs. (51.46a) and (51.59) to give

$$\frac{\Omega_s}{V} \approx \frac{\Omega_n(T=0)}{V} - \tfrac{1}{2}N(0)\Delta_0^2 - 2N(0)\left(\frac{2\pi\Delta_0}{\beta^3}\right)^{\frac{1}{2}} e^{-\beta\Delta_0} \tag{51.60}$$

The electronic specific heat in the superconducting state can then be obtained by differentiation

$$\frac{C_s}{V} \approx 2N(0)\Delta_0 k_B(2\pi)^{\frac{1}{2}}\left(\frac{\Delta_0}{k_B T}\right)^{\frac{3}{2}} e^{-\Delta_0/k_B T} \qquad T \to 0 \tag{51.61}$$

This expression clearly exhibits the energy gap mentioned in Eqs. (36.1) and (48.5).

The preceding calculations have considered only the low-temperature behavior, where $\Delta - \Delta_0$ is exponentially small. Although a general evaluation of Eq. (51.53) for all $T < T_c$ requires numerical analysis, it is possible to derive explicit expressions near T_c, where $\beta\Delta \ll 1$ provides a small parameter. We start from the gap equation (51.35), which may be expanded in powers of Δ:

$$\frac{1}{g} = \frac{2N(0)}{\beta}\int_0^{\hbar\omega_D} d\xi \sum_n \frac{1}{(\hbar\omega_n)^2 + \xi^2 + \Delta^2}$$

$$\approx \frac{2N(0)}{\beta}\int_0^{\hbar\omega_D} d\xi \sum_n \left\{\frac{1}{(\hbar\omega_n)^2 + \xi^2} - \frac{\Delta^2}{[(\hbar\omega_n)^2 + \xi^2]^2} + \cdots\right\}$$

The derivative with respect to Δ is easily evaluated, and a combination with Eq. (51.48) gives

$$\frac{\Omega_s - \Omega_n}{V} = -\frac{N(0)\Delta^4}{\beta}\int_0^{\hbar\omega_D} d\xi \sum_n \frac{1}{[(\hbar\omega_n)^2 + \xi^2]^2} \tag{51.62}$$

Since $\hbar\omega_D \gg k_B T_c$, the integral may be extended to infinity:

$$\frac{\Omega_s - \Omega_n}{V} = -\frac{N(0)\Delta^4}{\beta}\sum_n \frac{\pi}{4}\frac{1}{|\hbar\omega_n|^3}$$

$$= -\tfrac{1}{2}N(0)\Delta^4\left(\frac{\beta}{\pi}\right)^2\sum_{n=0}^\infty \frac{1}{(2n+1)^3} = -\frac{7\zeta(3)}{8}N(0)\Delta^4\frac{\beta^2}{2\pi^2}$$

$$= -\frac{8}{7\zeta(3)}N(0)(\pi k_B T_c)^2\frac{1}{2}\left(1 - \frac{T}{T_c}\right)^2 \tag{51.63}$$

where the symmetry of the summand has been used in the second line and the explicit form of $\Delta(T)$ in Eq. (51.46b) has been used in the last line.[1]

Equation (48.22) again determines the critical field, and we find

$$H_c(T) = H_c(0)\, e^\gamma \left[\frac{8}{7\zeta(3)}\right]^{\frac{1}{2}} \left(1 - \frac{T}{T_c}\right)$$

$$\approx 1.74 H_c(0)\left(1 - \frac{T}{T_c}\right) \qquad T \to T_c \qquad\qquad (51.64)$$

where $H_c(0)$ has been taken from Eq. (51.56). Note that Eqs. (51.55) and (51.64) are very similar to the phenomenological relation (48.3). Nevertheless there are small but distinct differences (Fig. 51.2), and the BCS predictions provide a better fit for most simple superconductors. Since $H_c^2/8\pi$ is the actual difference in free-energy density between the normal and superconducting states, the excellent agreement between theory and experiment justifies our assumption that the Hartree-Fock energy is the same in both states. This assumption is extremely difficult to justify *a priori* because the condensation energy ($\approx 10^{-7}$ eV/particle) is so much smaller than the Hartree-Fock energy (≈ 1 to 10 eV/particle). Equation (51.63) also allows us to evaluate the jump in the specific heat at T_c [compare Eq. (48.27)]

$$\frac{1}{V}(C_s - C_n)\big|_{T_c} = \frac{8}{7\zeta(3)}\, N(0)\,\pi^2 k_B^2 T_c \qquad\qquad (51.65)$$

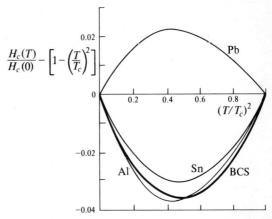

Fig. **51.2** Difference between actual critical field $H_c(T)/H_c(0)$ and the empirical curve $1 - (T/T_c)^2$. (From *I.B.M. Journal of Research and Development*, vol. 6, no. 1, Jan. 1962, front cover. Reprinted by permission.)

---

[1] An argument similar to that in Eq. (37.52) shows that $F_s(N) - F_n(N) = \Omega_s(\mu_n) - \Omega_n(\mu_n)$, apart from corrections of order $(\mu_s - \mu_n)^2/\mu_n^2$. We can therefore use Eq. (51.63) to determine $\mu_s - \mu_n$ near T_c. A simple calculation with Eqs. (51.38) and (51.44) gives

$$N(\mu_s - \mu_n)/(F_s - F_n) = \tfrac{1}{3} + 2(\partial \ln \Delta_0/\partial \ln N)\, T_c/(T_c - T).$$

and a combination with Eq. (51.57) yields

$$\left[\frac{C_s - C_n}{C_n}\right]_{T_c} = \frac{12}{7\zeta(3)} \approx 1.43 \tag{51.66}$$

in reasonable agreement with experiment (Table 51.1).

52☐LINEAR RESPONSE TO A WEAK MAGNETIC FIELD

As a further application of the microscopic theory, we now turn to the electro-dynamic behavior of a superconductor, which is probably its most striking feature. In principle, all such effects are contained in the Gorkov equations (51.15) and (51.17), but they are quite intractable in their most general form. For this reason, it is simpler to evaluate the electrodynamics of a bulk super-conductor with the general theory of linear response from Sec. 32.[1] In particular, we shall evaluate the transverse current $\mathbf{j}(\mathbf{x}t)$ induced by an applied magnetic field specified by a transverse vector potential $\mathbf{A}(\mathbf{x}t)$. Although it is possible to maintain full gauge invariance throughout the calculation,[2] the details become quite complicated and tend to obscure the simple physical results. Hence the present calculation will be carried out in the London gauge

$$\text{div}\,\mathbf{A}(\mathbf{x}t) = 0 \qquad \mathbf{q}\cdot\mathbf{A}(\mathbf{q},\omega) = 0 \tag{52.1}$$

More generally, the vector field $\mathbf{A}(\mathbf{q},\omega)$ always can be separated into its longi-tudinal and transverse parts

$$\mathbf{A}^l(\mathbf{q},\omega) = \hat{q}\,[\hat{q}\cdot\mathbf{A}(\mathbf{q},\omega)] \qquad \mathbf{A}^t(\mathbf{q},\omega) = \mathbf{A}(\mathbf{q},\omega) - \hat{q}\,[\hat{q}\cdot\mathbf{A}(\mathbf{q},\omega)] \tag{52.2a}$$

where, by definition

$$\mathbf{q} \times \mathbf{A}^l(\mathbf{q},\omega) = 0 \qquad \mathbf{q}\cdot\mathbf{A}^t(\mathbf{q},\omega) = 0 \tag{52.2b}$$

A general gauge transformation of the vector potential $\mathbf{A}$ and scalar potential φ takes the form

$$\mathbf{A}(\mathbf{q},\omega) \rightarrow \mathbf{A}(\mathbf{q},\omega) + i\mathbf{q}\Lambda(\mathbf{q},\omega)$$
$$\varphi(\mathbf{q},\omega) \rightarrow \varphi(\mathbf{q},\omega) + i\omega c^{-1}\Lambda(\mathbf{q},\omega) \tag{52.3}$$

where Λ is an arbitrary scalar function. It is evident that the gauge transforma-tion affects only the longitudinal part $(\mathbf{A}^l \rightarrow \mathbf{A}^l + i\mathbf{q}\Lambda)$, so that $\mathbf{A}^t$ is gauge invariant.

---

[1] The same results can be derived by a perturbation expansion of the Gorkov equations, as shown in A. A. Abrikosov, L. P. Gorkov, and I. E. Dzyaloshinskii, *op. cit.*, sec. 37.

[2] Careful treatments of this question may be found in P. W. Anderson, *Phys. Rev.*, **110**:827 (1958) and **112**:1900 (1958); D. Pines and P. Nozières, "The Theory of Quantum Liquids," vol. I, sec. 4.7, W. A. Benjamin, Inc., New York, 1966; G. Rickayzen, *op. cit.*, chap. 6; J. R. Schrieffer, *op. cit.*, chap. 8.

DERIVATION OF THE GENERAL KERNEL

In the presence of a vector potential, the total hamiltonian operator $\hat{H}_t$ is that given in Eq. (51.1):

$$\hat{H}_t = \hat{H} + \hat{H}_A \tag{52.4}$$

where $\hat{H}$ is the hamiltonian in zero field

$$\hat{H} = \int d^3x\, \hat{\psi}_\alpha^\dagger(\mathbf{x}) \left(-\frac{\hbar^2 \nabla^2}{2m}\right) \hat{\psi}_\alpha(\mathbf{x}) - \tfrac{1}{2}g \int d^3x\, \hat{\psi}_\alpha^\dagger(\mathbf{x})\, \hat{\psi}_\beta^\dagger(\mathbf{x})\, \hat{\psi}_\beta(\mathbf{x})\, \hat{\psi}_\alpha(\mathbf{x}) \tag{52.5}$$

and $\hat{H}_A$ is the perturbation

$$\hat{H}_A = \int d^3x \left\{ \frac{e\hbar}{2mci} [\hat{\psi}_\alpha^\dagger(\mathbf{x}) \boldsymbol{\nabla} \hat{\psi}_\alpha(\mathbf{x}) - (\boldsymbol{\nabla} \hat{\psi}_\alpha^\dagger(\mathbf{x}))\, \hat{\psi}_\alpha(\mathbf{x})] \cdot \mathbf{A}(\mathbf{x}) \right.$$

$$\left. + \frac{e^2}{2mc^2} |\mathbf{A}(\mathbf{x})|^2\, \hat{\psi}_\alpha^\dagger(\mathbf{x})\, \hat{\psi}_\alpha(\mathbf{x}) \right\} \tag{52.6}$$

As noted previously, e is a positive quantity and the charge on an electron is $-e$. For any operator $\hat{O}(\mathbf{x}t)$, the ensemble average $\langle \hat{O}(\mathbf{x}t) \rangle_A$ in the presence of the vector potential is given to lowest order by [compare Eq. (32.2)]

$$\langle \hat{O}(\mathbf{x}t) \rangle_A = \langle \hat{O}_H(\mathbf{x}t) \rangle - \frac{i}{\hbar} \int_{-\infty}^{t} dt'\, \langle [\hat{O}_H(\mathbf{x}t), \hat{H}_A(t')] \rangle \tag{52.7}$$

where the unlabeled brackets denote an average in the unperturbed but interacting ensemble. Since we shall deal with operators that conserve the number of particles, it is permissible to replace the Heisenberg picture by [compare Eq. (32.6)]

$$\hat{O}_K(\mathbf{x}t) = e^{i\hat{K}t/\hbar}\, \hat{O}(\mathbf{x})\, e^{-i\hat{K}t/\hbar} \tag{52.8}$$

defined in terms of $\hat{K} = \hat{H} - \mu\hat{N}$.

We now specialize Eq. (52.7) to the *total* electromagnetic current $\hat{\mathbf{j}}$ in the presence of $\mathbf{A}$. This operator has the intuitive form

$$\hat{\mathbf{j}} = -\tfrac{1}{2}e[\hat{\psi}_\alpha^\dagger \mathbf{v}\hat{\psi}_\alpha + (\mathbf{v}\hat{\psi}_\alpha)^\dagger \hat{\psi}_\alpha] \tag{52.9}$$

where [compare Eq. (49.25)] $\mathbf{v} = m^{-1}(-i\hbar\boldsymbol{\nabla} + e\mathbf{A}/c)$. A simple calculation leads to

$$\hat{\mathbf{j}} = -\frac{e\hbar}{2mi}[\hat{\psi}_\alpha^\dagger \boldsymbol{\nabla} \hat{\psi}_\alpha - (\boldsymbol{\nabla} \hat{\psi}_\alpha^\dagger)\, \hat{\psi}_\alpha] - \frac{e^2}{mc} \mathbf{A}\hat{\psi}_\alpha^\dagger \hat{\psi}_\alpha \tag{52.10}$$

and it can be verified from the field equations for $\hat{\psi}$ and $\hat{\psi}^\dagger$ that the second term is essential to guarantee conservation of current. A combination of Eqs. (52.7) and (52.10) yields

$$\langle \hat{\mathbf{j}}(\mathbf{x}t) \rangle_A = \langle \hat{\mathbf{j}}_K(\mathbf{x}t) \rangle - \frac{i}{\hbar} \int_{-\infty}^{t} dt'\, \langle [\hat{\mathbf{j}}_K(\mathbf{x}t), \hat{H}_A(t')] \rangle \tag{52.11}$$

The linear response is obtained by expanding to first order in $\mathbf{A}$; since the expectation value of $\hat{\mathbf{j}}$ vanishes in zero field, we find

$$\mathbf{j}(\mathbf{x}t) \equiv \langle \hat{\mathbf{j}}(\mathbf{x}t) \rangle_A$$

$$= -\frac{e^2 \, \mathbf{A}(\mathbf{x}t)}{mc} \langle \hat{\psi}_{K\alpha}^\dagger(\mathbf{x}t) \, \hat{\psi}_{K\alpha}(\mathbf{x}t) \rangle + \frac{i}{\hbar c} \int_{-\infty}^t dt' \int d^3x'$$

$$\times \langle [\hat{\mathbf{j}}_K^0(\mathbf{x}t), \hat{\mathbf{j}}_K^0(\mathbf{x}'\,t') \cdot \mathbf{A}(\mathbf{x}'\,t')] \rangle \quad (52.12)$$

where

$$\hat{\mathbf{j}}_K^0(\mathbf{x}t) = -\frac{e\hbar}{2mi} \{ \hat{\psi}_{K\alpha}^\dagger(\mathbf{x}t) \, \boldsymbol{\nabla} \hat{\psi}_{K\alpha}(\mathbf{x}t) - [\boldsymbol{\nabla} \hat{\psi}_{K\alpha}^\dagger(\mathbf{x}t)] \, \hat{\psi}_{K\alpha}(\mathbf{x}t) \} \quad (52.13)$$

is the current operator for $\mathbf{A} = 0$. It is convenient to rewrite this equation as an integral relation between the vector potential $\mathbf{A}$ and the induced supercurrent $\mathbf{j}$ [compare Eq. (49.31)]

$$j_k(\mathbf{x}t) = -\frac{c}{4\pi} \int d^3x' \, dt' \, K_{kl}(\mathbf{x}t, \mathbf{x}'\,t') A_l(\mathbf{x}'\,t') \quad (52.14)$$

where the repeated lower-case latin subscripts refer to vector components and are summed over the three spatial coordinates. The specific properties of the medium are contained in the kernel

$$K_{kl}(\mathbf{x}t, \mathbf{x}'\,t') = \frac{4\pi e^2}{mc^2} \delta(\mathbf{x} - \mathbf{x}') \delta(t - t') \delta_{kl} \langle \hat{n}_K(\mathbf{x}t) \rangle + \frac{4\pi}{\hbar c^2} P_{kl}^R(\mathbf{x}t, \mathbf{x}'\,t') \quad (52.15)$$

and the problem is thus reduced to the evaluation of a retarded current commutator in the exact unperturbed system

$$P_{kl}^R(\mathbf{x}t, \mathbf{x}'\,t') \equiv -i \langle [\hat{j}_{Kk}^0(\mathbf{x}t), \hat{j}_{Kl}^0(\mathbf{x}'\,t')] \rangle \, \theta(t - t') \quad (52.16)$$

As discussed in Chaps. 5 and 9, the retarded function is inconvenient for perturbation analysis, and we instead introduce a temperature function

$$\mathscr{P}_{kl}(\mathbf{x}\tau, \mathbf{x}'\,\tau') \equiv -\langle T_\tau [\hat{j}_{Kk}^0(\mathbf{x}\tau) \hat{j}_{Kl}^0(\mathbf{x}'\,\tau')] \rangle \quad (52.17)$$

defined in terms of the "Heisenberg" picture

$$\hat{O}_K(\mathbf{x}\tau) = e^{\hat{K}\tau/\hbar} \, \hat{O}(\mathbf{x}) \, e^{-\hat{K}\tau/\hbar} \quad (52.18)$$

The relation between Eqs. (52.16) and (52.17) is readily established with the Lehmann representation, which gives

$$P_{kl}^R(\mathbf{x}, \mathbf{x}', \omega) = \int_{-\infty}^{\infty} \frac{d\omega'}{2\pi} \frac{\rho_{kl}(\mathbf{x}, \mathbf{x}', \omega')}{\omega - \omega' + i\eta} \quad (52.19)$$

$$\mathscr{P}_{kl}(\mathbf{x}, \mathbf{x}', \nu_n) = \int_{-\infty}^{\infty} \frac{d\omega'}{2\pi} \frac{\rho_{kl}(\mathbf{x}, \mathbf{x}', \omega')}{i\nu_n - \omega'} \quad (52.20)$$

where the Fourier transforms are defined as in Eqs. (32.12) and (32.13), and $\nu_n = 2n\pi/\beta\hbar$.

The function $\mathscr{P}_{kl}$ may be rewritten as a spatial differential operator applied to a "time"-ordered product of field operators

$$\mathscr{P}_{kl}(1,1') = -\left(\frac{e\hbar}{2mi}\right)^2 \{(\nabla_1 - \nabla_2)_k (\nabla_{1'} - \nabla_{2'})_l$$

$$\times \langle T_\tau[\hat{\psi}^\dagger_{K\alpha}(2)\,\hat{\psi}_{K\alpha}(1)\,\hat{\psi}^\dagger_{K\beta}(2')\,\hat{\psi}_{K\beta}(1')]\rangle\}_{\substack{2'=1'^+\\2=1^+}} \quad (52.21)$$

where the argument 1 is an abbreviation for the variables $(\mathbf{x}_1, \tau_1)$. This equation is exact, but it is now necessary to introduce approximations. Schafroth[1] has shown to all orders in perturbation theory that an expansion in the electron phonon interaction can never yield the Meissner effect. We therefore rely on Gorkov's self-consistent factorization [Eq. (51.6)] to write

$$\langle T_\tau[\hat{\psi}^\dagger_{K\alpha}(2)\,\hat{\psi}_{K\alpha}(1)\,\hat{\psi}^\dagger_{K\beta}(2')\,\hat{\psi}_{K\beta}(1')]\rangle$$

$$\approx 4\mathscr{G}(12)\,\mathscr{G}(1'2') - 2\mathscr{G}(12')\,\mathscr{G}(1'2) + 2\mathscr{F}(11')\mathscr{F}^\dagger(2'2) \quad (52.22)$$

where $\mathscr{G}$ and $\mathscr{F}$ are the Gorkov functions, and the spin sums have been evaluated explicitly. A combination of Eqs. (52.21) and (52.22) gives

$$\mathscr{P}_{kl}(1,1') = -\left(\frac{e\hbar}{2mi}\right)^2 \{(\nabla_1 - \nabla_2)_k (\nabla_{1'} - \nabla_{2'})_l$$

$$\times [4\mathscr{G}(12)\,\mathscr{G}(1'2') - 2\mathscr{G}(12')\,\mathscr{G}(1'2) + 2\mathscr{F}(11')\mathscr{F}^\dagger(2'2)]\}_{\substack{2'=1'^+\\2=1^+}}$$

$$(52.23)$$

It is now convenient to specialize to a uniform time-independent system, where $\mathscr{P}_{kl}(\mathbf{x}\tau, \mathbf{x}'\tau') = \mathscr{P}_{kl}(\mathbf{x} - \mathbf{x}', \tau - \tau')$ may be expressed in a Fourier expansion

$$\mathscr{P}_{kl}(\mathbf{x} - \mathbf{x}', \tau - \tau') = (2\pi)^{-3} \int d^3q\, e^{i\mathbf{q}\cdot(\mathbf{x}-\mathbf{x}')}(\beta\hbar)^{-1} \sum_n e^{-i\nu_n(\tau-\tau')}\mathscr{P}_{kl}(\mathbf{q}, \nu_n)$$

$$(52.24)$$

The corresponding Fourier coefficient is easily evaluated with Eqs. (51.22) and (51.27). The first term involving $\mathscr{G}(12)\,\mathscr{G}(1'2')$ is just the product $-\langle j_k^0(\mathbf{x})\rangle \times \langle j_l^0(\mathbf{x}')\rangle$. A simple calculation shows that it vanishes identically, confirming the previous assertion that there is no supercurrent in zero field, and we obtain

$$\mathscr{P}_{kl}(\mathbf{q}, \nu_n) = 2\left(\frac{e\hbar}{m}\right)^2 \int \frac{d^3p}{(2\pi)^3} \frac{1}{\beta\hbar} \sum_{\omega_1} (\mathbf{p} + \tfrac{1}{2}\mathbf{q})_k (\mathbf{p} + \tfrac{1}{2}\mathbf{q})_l$$

$$\times [\mathscr{G}(\mathbf{p} + \mathbf{q}, \omega_1 + \nu_n)\,\mathscr{G}(\mathbf{p}, \omega_1) + \mathscr{F}(\mathbf{p} + \mathbf{q}, \omega_1 + \nu_n)\mathscr{F}(\mathbf{p}, \omega_1)] \quad (52.25)$$

---

[1] M. R. Schafroth, *loc. cit.*

Here $\mathcal{G}(\mathbf{p},\omega_1)$ and $\mathcal{F}(\mathbf{p},\omega_1)$ are given in Eqs. (51.30) and (51.31); since they depend only on $|\mathbf{p}|$, a change of variables in Eq. (52.25) $[\mathbf{p} \rightarrow -\mathbf{p} - \mathbf{q}, \ \omega_1 \rightarrow \omega_1 - \nu_n]$ shows that $\mathcal{P}_{kl}$ is an even function of ν_n, exactly as in Eq. (30.18):

$$\mathcal{P}_{kl}(\mathbf{q},\nu_n) = \mathcal{P}_{kl}(\mathbf{q},-\nu_n) \tag{52.26}$$

The evaluation of the frequency sum is lengthy but not difficult, because the partial-fraction representation in Eq. (51.32) reduces all the various terms to the form studied in Eq. (30.8). Hence we merely state the final result

$$\mathcal{P}_{kl}(\mathbf{q},\nu_n) = \left(\frac{e\hbar}{m}\right)^2 \int \frac{d^3p}{(2\pi)^3} p_k p_l \Big\{ (u_+ u_- + v_+ v_-)^2 \left[f(E_+) - f(E_-) \right]$$

$$\times \left[\frac{1}{i\nu_n - \hbar^{-1}(E_- - E_+)} - \frac{1}{i\nu_n + \hbar^{-1}(E_- - E_+)} \right]$$

$$+ (u_+ v_- - v_+ u_-)^2 \left[1 - f(E_+) - f(E_-) \right]$$

$$\times \left[\frac{1}{i\nu_n - \hbar^{-1}(E_+ + E_-)} - \frac{1}{i\nu_n + \hbar^{-1}(E_+ + E_-)} \right] \Big\} \tag{52.27}$$

where the symmetry in ν_n has been made explicit and $\mathbf{p}$ has been replaced by $\mathbf{p} - \tfrac{1}{2}\mathbf{q}$. Here the subscripts $\pm$ denote the arguments $\mathbf{p} \pm \tfrac{1}{2}\mathbf{q}$ (that is, $E_\pm = E_{\mathbf{p}\pm\frac{1}{2}\mathbf{q}}$, etc.), and

$$f(E) \equiv (e^{\beta E} + 1)^{-1} = \tfrac{1}{2}[1 - \tanh(\tfrac{1}{2}\beta E)] \tag{52.28}$$

is a modified Fermi function. Note that $f(E)$ differs from the usual distribution function even in the limit $\Delta \rightarrow 0$ (normal metal), because E then reduces to $|\xi| = |\epsilon - \mu|$. Equation (52.27) is now in the proper spectral form, and $P_{kl}^R(\mathbf{q},\omega)$ is obtained with the substitution $i\nu_n \rightarrow \omega + i\eta$. The factors involving u and v may be evaluated with Eq. (51.34), and we therefore obtain the Fourier transform of the integral kernel [Eq. (52.15)]

$$K_{kl}(\mathbf{q},\omega) = \frac{4\pi ne^2}{mc^2} \delta_{kl} + 4\pi \left(\frac{e\hbar}{mc}\right)^2 \int \frac{d^3p}{(2\pi)^3} p_k p_l \Big\{ \frac{1}{2} \left(1 + \frac{\xi_+ \xi_- + \Delta^2}{E_+ E_-} \right)$$

$$\times [f(E_+) - f(E_-)] \left[\frac{1}{\hbar\omega + i\eta - (E_- - E_+)} \right.$$

$$\left. - \frac{1}{\hbar\omega + i\eta + (E_- - E_+)} \right] + \frac{1}{2} \left(1 - \frac{\xi_+ \xi_- + \Delta^2}{E_+ E_-} \right)$$

$$\times [1 - f(E_+) - f(E_-)] \left[\frac{1}{\hbar\omega + i\eta - (E_+ + E_-)} \right.$$

$$\left. - \frac{1}{\hbar\omega + i\eta + (E_+ + E_-)} \right] \Big\} \tag{52.29}$$

which describes the general response of a uniform superconductor at temperature T to a weak applied (transverse) vector potential $\mathbf{A}$

$$j_k(\mathbf{q},\omega) = -\frac{c}{4\pi} K_{kl}(\mathbf{q},\omega) A_l(\mathbf{q},\omega) \qquad (52.30)$$

Unfortunately, this expression is complicated and unwieldy, and we henceforth consider only a static field ($\omega = 0$). As seen below, even this simpler case leads to rather long calculations, and the generalization to finite frequency does not involve any new questions of principle.

MEISSNER EFFECT

The Meissner effect can now be demonstrated by examining the limiting behavior of $K(\mathbf{q},0)$ as $q \to 0$ [compare Eq. (49.45)]. It is most convenient to evaluate the induced supercurrent itself

$$\mathbf{j}(\mathbf{q}) = -\frac{ne^2}{mc} \mathbf{A}(\mathbf{q}) - \frac{1}{c}\left(\frac{e\hbar}{m}\right)^2 \int \frac{d^3p}{(2\pi)^3} \mathbf{p}[\mathbf{p}\cdot\mathbf{A}(\mathbf{q})]$$

$$\times \left[\left(1 + \frac{\xi_+\xi_- + \Delta^2}{E_+E_-}\right)\frac{f(E_+)-f(E_-)}{E_+ - E_-} - \left(1 - \frac{\xi_+\xi_- + \Delta^2}{E_+E_-}\right)\frac{1-f(E_+)-f(E_-)}{E_+ + E_-}\right]$$

$$(52.31)$$

In the limit of small q, the quantity in square brackets reduces to

$$2\frac{f(E_+)-f(E_-)}{E_+ - E_-} \approx 2\frac{\partial f(E_p)}{\partial E_p}$$

and we find

$$\mathbf{j}(\mathbf{q}) \approx -\frac{ne^2}{mc} \mathbf{A}(\mathbf{q}) - \frac{2}{c}\left(\frac{e\hbar}{m}\right)^2 \int \frac{d^3p}{(2\pi)^3} \mathbf{p}[\mathbf{p}\cdot\mathbf{A}(\mathbf{q})]\frac{\partial f(E_p)}{\partial E_p}$$

$$= -\mathbf{A}(\mathbf{q})\frac{ne^2}{mc}\left[1 + \frac{\hbar^2}{3\pi^2 mn}\int_0^\infty dp\, p^4 \frac{\partial f(E_p)}{\partial E_p}\right]$$

$$= -\mathbf{A}(\mathbf{q})\frac{n_s(T)e^2}{mc} \qquad q \to 0 \qquad (52.32)$$

Here

$$n_s(T) \equiv n - \frac{\hbar^2}{3\pi^2 m}\int_0^\infty p^4\, dp\left[-\frac{\partial f(E_p)}{\partial E_p}\right] \qquad (52.33)$$

defines the superelectron density in the BCS theory.[1] Its limiting behavior is easily determined with the techniques developed in Sec. 51:

$$\frac{n_s(T)}{n} \approx \begin{cases} 1 - \left(\frac{2\pi\Delta_0}{k_B T}\right)^{\frac{1}{2}} e^{-\Delta_0/k_B T} & T \to 0 \qquad (52.34a) \\ 2\left(1 - \frac{T}{T_c}\right) & T \to T_c \qquad (52.34b) \end{cases}$$

and the complete function is shown in Fig. 52.1, along with the empirical function

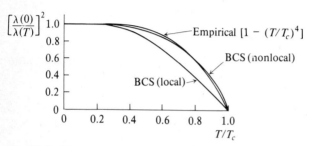

Fig. 52.1 Temperature dependence of the penetration depth in a pure superconductor. The curves BCS (local) and BCS (non-local) were plotted from Eqs. (52.33) and (52.44), respectively, using the tables computed by B. Mühlschlegel, *Z. Physik*, **155**:313 (1959). Note that the curves labeled BCS (local) and empirical also represent the corresponding ratios $n_s(T)/n$ [Eqs. (49.15) and (52.35)].

in Eq. (49.15). Since the form of Eq. (52.32) agrees with that of the London theory [Eq. (49.29)], we immediately conclude that the penetration depth for a pure London (local) superconductor is given by

$$\left[\frac{\lambda(T)}{\lambda(0)}\right]^2 = \left[\frac{\lambda(T)}{\lambda_L(0)}\right]^2 = \frac{n}{n_s(T)} \qquad \text{local limit} \qquad (52.35)$$

where the only effect of the microscopic theory is the use of Eq. (52.33) on the right side. Note that $n_s(T)$ is defined through the strength of the response to a long-wavelength perturbation and reduces to the total density n as $T \to 0$.

---

[1] The BCS single-particle excitation spectrum has a gap Δ. As shown in Sec. 54, a simple quasiparticle model then yields both Eq. (52.33) and a critical velocity $v_c \approx \Delta/\hbar k_F$ for the destruction of supercurrents. This explanation of frictionless flow must be used with care, however, for there are gapless superconductors, which have a finite order parameter $\Delta(\mathbf{x})$ but no gap in the excitation spectrum [A. A. Abrikosov and L. P. Gorkov, *Sov. Phys.-JETP*, **12**:1243 (1961); M. A. Woolf and F. Reif, *Phys. Rev.*, **137A**:557 (1965)], whereas insulating crystals also have a gap in the excitation spectrum. The correct procedure, of course, is to ask a physical question, such as the linear response to a transverse vector potential.

PENETRATION DEPTH IN PIPPARD (NONLOCAL) LIMIT

Electromagnetic effects involve wavelengths comparable with the penetration depth $\lambda(T)$, so that the previous limit $q\xi_0 \equiv q(\hbar v_F/\pi\Delta_0) \ll 1$ may be interpreted as describing the behavior of a London (local) superconductor. We now evaluate the kernel in the opposite limit $q\xi_0 \gg 1$, which will then allow us to determine the penetration depth of a pure Pippard superconductor. In addition to the above restriction, q must also satisfy the condition $q \ll k_F$, because the penetration depth is always much larger than the interatomic spacing.

It is convenient to evaluate Eq. (52.29) in spherical polar coordinates with $\hat{q}$ as the polar axis. The London gauge [Eq. (49.38)] restricts $\mathbf{p}$ to the equatorial plane, and the azimuthal integration shows that $\mathbf{j}$ takes the form of Eq. (49.39), where

$$K(|\mathbf{q}|,0) \equiv K(q) = \frac{4\pi n e^2}{mc^2} + \frac{4\pi e^2 \hbar^2}{m^2 c^2} \int_0^\infty \frac{dp}{(2\pi)^2} \frac{p^4}{2} \int_0^\pi \sin^3\theta \, d\theta$$

$$\times \left[\left(1 + \frac{\xi_+ \xi_- + \Delta^2}{E_+ E_-} \right) \frac{f(E_+) - f(E_-)}{E_+ - E_-} - \left(1 - \frac{\xi_+ \xi_- + \Delta^2}{E_+ E_-} \right) \frac{1 - f(E_+) - f(E_-)}{E_+ + E_-} \right]$$

$$(52.36)$$

This expression may be rewritten with Eqs. (51.29), (52.28), and (3.29) as

$$K(q) = \frac{4\pi n e^2}{mc^2} \left\{ 1 - \frac{3}{16} \int_{-\infty}^\infty d\xi \int_{-1}^1 dz \, (1 - z^2) \right.$$

$$\times \left[\left(1 + \frac{\xi_+ \xi_- + \Delta^2}{E_+ E_-} \right) \frac{\tanh\left(\frac{1}{2}\beta E_+\right) - \tanh\left(\frac{1}{2}\beta E_-\right)}{E_+ - E_-} \right.$$

$$\left. \left. + \left(1 - \frac{\xi_+ \xi_- + \Delta^2}{E_+ E_-} \right) \frac{\tanh\left(\frac{1}{2}\beta E_+\right) + \tanh\left(\frac{1}{2}\beta E_-\right)}{E_+ + E_-} \right] \right\} \quad (52.37)$$

where

$$\xi_\pm = \xi \pm \tfrac{1}{2}\hbar q v_F z \quad (52.38)$$

neglecting terms of order q^2/k_F^2.

We shall first consider the response in the normal state, which is obtained by setting $\Delta = 0$ and $E_\pm = |\xi_\pm|$ in Eq. (52.37). An examination of the different possible signs of ξ_+ and ξ_- yields the simple form

$$K_n(q) = \frac{4\pi n e^2}{mc^2} \left[1 - \frac{3}{8} \int_{-\infty}^\infty d\xi \int_{-1}^1 dz \, (1 - z^2) \frac{\tanh\left(\frac{1}{2}\beta\xi_+\right) - \tanh\left(\frac{1}{2}\beta\xi_-\right)}{\xi_+ - \xi_-} \right]$$

$$= \frac{4\pi n e^2}{mc^2} \left[1 - \frac{3}{8} \int_{-1}^1 dz \, (1 - z^2) \int_{-\infty}^\infty d\xi \frac{\tanh\left(\frac{1}{2}\beta\xi_+\right) - \tanh\left(\frac{1}{2}\beta\xi_-\right)}{\hbar q v_F z} \right]$$

The ξ integration can be evaluated exactly and gives

$$K_n(q) = \frac{4\pi n e^2}{mc^2} \left[1 - \frac{3}{4} \int_{-1}^1 dz \, (1 - z^2) \right] = 0 \quad (52.39)$$

This result holds for all $q \ll k_F$, thus confirming that the normal state is non-magnetic, apart from the weak Pauli paramagnetism and Landau diamagnetism, both of which are neglected in the present approximation. (See Probs. 13.17 and 13.18.)

The evaluation of the superconducting kernel may be simplified by considering the difference between Eqs. (52.37) and (52.39). After collecting the factors of $\tanh(\frac{1}{2}\beta E_{\pm})$ separately, we find[1]

$$K(q) \equiv K(q) - K_n(q) = -\frac{3\pi n e^2}{4mc^2} \int_{-\infty}^{\infty} d\xi \int_{-1}^{1} dz\,(1-z^2)$$

$$\times \left\{ \frac{4\Delta^2}{\xi_+^2 - \xi_-^2} \left[\frac{\tanh(\frac{1}{2}\beta E_+)}{E_+} - \frac{\tanh(\frac{1}{2}\beta E_-)}{E_-} \right] \right.$$

$$+ \frac{2}{\xi_+ - \xi_-} \left[\xi_+ \left(\frac{\tanh(\frac{1}{2}\beta E_+)}{E_+} - \frac{\tanh(\frac{1}{2}\beta\xi_+)}{\xi_+} \right) \right.$$

$$\left. \left. - \xi_- \left(\frac{\tanh(\frac{1}{2}\beta E_-)}{E_-} - \frac{\tanh(\frac{1}{2}\beta\xi_-)}{\xi_-} \right) \right] \right\} \qquad (52.40)$$

Since $\xi_+ - \xi_- = \hbar q v_F z$, the last term (in square brackets) contains the factor

$$\int_{-\infty}^{\infty} d\xi \left[\frac{\xi_+}{E_+} \tanh(\frac{1}{2}\beta E_+) \quad \tanh(\frac{1}{2}\beta\xi_+) \right]$$

along with another term with the subscript "$-$". It is evident that this integral converges absolutely for large $|\xi|$; it is then permissible to change variables from ξ to ξ_+, and the odd symmetry of the integrand shows that the integral vanishes. In this way, Eq. (52.40) reduces to

$$K(q) = -\frac{3\pi n e^2 \Delta^2}{2mc^2 \hbar q v_F} \int_{-1}^{1} dz \frac{1-z^2}{z} \int_{-\infty}^{\infty} \frac{d\xi}{\xi} \left[\frac{\tanh(\frac{1}{2}\beta E_+)}{E_+} - \frac{\tanh(\frac{1}{2}\beta E_-)}{E_-} \right]$$
$$(52.41)$$

Each term of the integrand separately diverges near $\xi \approx 0$, $z \approx 0$, and this region dominates the integral. We may therefore approximate the slowly varying numerators $(1-z^2)\tanh(\frac{1}{2}\beta E_{\pm})$ by their limiting values $\tanh(\frac{1}{2}\beta\Delta)$ at $\xi = 0$, $z = 0$, which yields

$$K(q) \approx -\frac{3\pi n e^2 \Delta^2 \tanh(\frac{1}{2}\beta\Delta)}{2mc^2 \hbar q v_F} \int_{-1}^{1} \frac{dz}{z} \int_{-\infty}^{\infty} \frac{d\xi}{\xi} \left(\frac{1}{E_+} - \frac{1}{E_-} \right)$$

$$= -\frac{3\pi n e^2 \Delta^2 \tanh(\frac{1}{2}\beta\Delta)}{mc^2 \hbar q v_F} \int_{-\infty}^{\infty} \frac{d\zeta}{\zeta} \int_{0}^{\infty} \frac{d\xi}{\xi}$$

$$\times \left\{ \frac{1}{[(\xi + \frac{1}{2}\zeta)^2 + \Delta^2]^{\frac{1}{2}}} - \frac{1}{[(\xi - \frac{1}{2}\zeta)^2 + \Delta^2]^{\frac{1}{2}}} \right\} \qquad (52.42)$$

---

[1] I. M. Khalatnikov and A. A. Abrikosov, *Advan. Phys.*, **8**:45 (1959).

where $\zeta = \hbar q v_F z$ and the condition $q\xi_0 = q\hbar v_F/\pi\Delta_0 \gg 1$ allows us to extend the limits to $\zeta = \pm\infty$. The remaining integrals can be reduced to $(-4/\Delta)\int_0^\infty (\sinh x)^{-1} x\, dx$ which is easily evaluated (see Appendix A) to give $-\pi^2/\Delta$, and Eq. (52.42) becomes

$$K(q) = \frac{3\pi^2}{mc^2 q\xi_0} \frac{ne^2}{\Delta_0} \frac{\Delta(T)}{\Delta_0} \tanh\left[\tfrac{1}{2}\beta\Delta(T)\right] \tag{52.43}$$

where Eq. (49.33) has been used to identify ξ_0. This expression should be compared with the corresponding nonlocal limit ($q\xi_0 \gg 1$) of the Pippard kernel [Eq. (49.47)]. The remaining calculation of the penetration depth in the Pippard limit proceeds exactly as before, and we obtain ($\lambda \gg \xi_0$)

$$\lambda(T) = \lambda(0)\left[\frac{\Delta(T)}{\Delta_0} \tanh\frac{\Delta(T)}{2k_B T}\right]^{-\frac{1}{3}} \tag{52.44}$$

where

$$\lambda(0) = \frac{8}{9}\left(\frac{\sqrt{3}}{2\pi}\right)^{\frac{1}{3}} [\xi_0\, \lambda_L^2(0)]^{\frac{1}{3}} \tag{52.45}$$

is the common zero-temperature limit of both theories. Note that the present microscopic calculation predicts a definite temperature dependence for $\lambda(T)$ in the nonlocal limit; this function is shown in Fig. 52.1 along with the empirical form Eq. (49.14) and the theoretical curve predicted for the local limit [Eq. (52.33)].

NONLOCAL INTEGRAL RELATION

As a final confirmation of the Pippard phenomenological theory, we shall transform Eq. (52.31) to coordinate space. For simplicity, the calculation will be restricted to $T = 0$, but the same approach applies for all $T < T_c$.[1] With the change of variables $\mathbf{p} + \tfrac{1}{2}\mathbf{q} \to \mathbf{k}$, $\mathbf{p} - \tfrac{1}{2}\mathbf{q} \to \mathbf{l}$, the inverse Fourier transform at $T = 0$ may be written as

$$\mathbf{j}(\mathbf{x}) = -\frac{ne^2}{mc}\mathbf{A}(\mathbf{x}) - \left(\frac{e\hbar}{m}\right)^2 \frac{1}{4c}\int d^3x' \int \frac{d^3k\, d^3l}{(2\pi)^6}$$
$$\times (\mathbf{k} + \mathbf{l})\,[(\mathbf{k} + \mathbf{l})\cdot\mathbf{A}(\mathbf{x}')]\, e^{i(\mathbf{k}-\mathbf{l})\cdot(\mathbf{x}-\mathbf{x}')}\, F(\xi_k,\xi_l) \tag{52.46}$$

where

$$F(\xi,\xi') = \frac{\xi\xi' + \Delta_0^2 - EE'}{EE'(E + E')} \tag{52.47}$$

because $f(E)$ vanishes as $T \to 0$.

To put Eq. (52.46) in the proper form, we concentrate on the second term, which contains the integral kernel

$$S_{ij}(\mathbf{x}) \equiv (2\pi)^{-6} \int d^3k\, d^3l\, (\mathbf{k} + \mathbf{l})_i\, (\mathbf{k} + \mathbf{l})_j\, e^{i(\mathbf{k}-\mathbf{l})\cdot\mathbf{x}}\, F(\xi_k,\xi_l) \tag{52.48}$$

[1] General expressions have been derived by J. Bardeen, L. N. Cooper, and J. R. Schrieffer, *op. cit.*, sec. V and appendix C.

This expression is most easily evaluated by introducing a generalized kernel

$$S_{ij}(\mathbf{x},\mathbf{x}') \equiv (2\pi)^{-6} \int d^3k\, d^3l\, (\mathbf{k}+\mathbf{l})_i\, (\mathbf{k}+\mathbf{l})_j\, e^{i(\mathbf{k}-\mathbf{l})\cdot\mathbf{x}}\, e^{i(\mathbf{k}+\mathbf{l})\cdot\mathbf{x}'}\, F(\xi_k,\xi_l)$$

which clearly reduces to $S_{ij}(\mathbf{x})$ as $\mathbf{x}' \to 0$. The vector components can now be replaced by spatial gradients with respect to $\mathbf{x}'$

$$S_{ij}(\mathbf{x},\mathbf{x}') = -\boldsymbol{\nabla}'_i \boldsymbol{\nabla}'_j (2\pi)^{-6} \int d^3k\, d^3l\, e^{i\mathbf{k}\cdot(\mathbf{x}'+\mathbf{x})}\, e^{i\mathbf{l}\cdot(\mathbf{x}'-\mathbf{x})}\, F(\xi_k,\xi_l)$$

and the angular integrals are now elementary

$$S_{ij}(\mathbf{x},\mathbf{x}') = -4(2\pi)^{-4} \int_0^\infty k^2\, dk \int_0^\infty l^2\, dl\, F(\xi_k,\xi_l)\, \boldsymbol{\nabla}'_i \boldsymbol{\nabla}'_j\, j_0(k\,|\mathbf{x}'+\mathbf{x}|)$$

$$\times j_0(l\,|\mathbf{x}'-\mathbf{x}|)$$

where $j_0(z) = (\sin z)/z$. The function $F(\xi_k,\xi_l)$ is sharply peaked near $k \approx l \approx k_F$, while the relevant spatial distances are much larger than the interparticle spacing $\approx k_F^{-1}$. Consequently, the trigonometric functions oscillate rapidly, and the variation of the denominator of j_0 may be neglected in evaluating the derivatives. A straightforward calculation gives

$$S_{ij}(\mathbf{x}) = S_{ij}(\mathbf{x},0) = 8k_F^2 \frac{x_i x_j}{x^4} \int_0^\infty \int_0^\infty \frac{k\, dk\, l\, dl}{(2\pi)^4}\, F(\xi_k,\xi_l)\cos\left[(k-l)\,x\right]$$

The convergence of the integral allows us to introduce the integration variables ξ_k and ξ_l, which yields

$$S_{ij}(\mathbf{x}) = \frac{x_i x_j}{x^4} \frac{m^2 k_F^2}{2\pi^4 \hbar^4} \int_{-\infty}^\infty \int_{-\infty}^\infty d\xi\, d\xi'\, F(\xi,\xi') \cos\left[(\xi-\xi')\frac{x}{\hbar v_F}\right]$$

The remaining double integral may be evaluated with the change of variables[1]

$$\xi = \Delta_0 \sinh(\tau+\tau') \qquad \xi' = \Delta_0 \sinh(\tau-\tau')$$

and some simple algebra gives

$$S_{ij}(\mathbf{x})$$

$$= -\frac{2\Delta_0 x_i x_j}{x^4} \frac{m^2 k_F^2}{2\pi^4 \hbar^4} \int_{-\infty}^\infty \int_{-\infty}^\infty \frac{d\tau\, d\tau'\, \cos\left[(2\Delta_0 x/\hbar v_F)\sinh\tau'\cosh\tau\right]\sinh^2\tau'}{\cosh\tau\cosh\tau'}$$

The τ' integration is easily performed with the substitution $z = \sinh\tau'$

$$S_{ij}(\mathbf{x}) = -\frac{\Delta_0\, m^2 k_F^2}{\pi^4 \hbar^4} \frac{x_i x_j}{x^4} \int_{-\infty}^\infty \frac{d\tau}{\cosh\tau}\left[2\pi\delta\left(\frac{2\Delta_0 x\cosh\tau}{\hbar v_F}\right)\right.$$

$$\left. - \pi\exp\frac{-2\Delta_0 x\cosh\tau}{\hbar v_F}\right]$$

---

[1] P. G. de Gennes, *op. cit.*, p. 168.

and the remaining expression may be rewritten as

$$S_{ij}(\mathbf{x}) = \left(\frac{mk_F}{\pi^2\hbar^2}\right)^2 \frac{x_i x_j}{x^4}[-2\pi\hbar v_F\,\delta(x) + \pi^2\,\Delta_0 J(x)]$$

(52.49)

Here the function $J(x)$ is defined by

$$J(x) \equiv \frac{2}{\pi}\int_0^\infty d\tau\,\mathrm{sech}\,\tau\exp\left(-\frac{2\Delta_0\,x\cosh\tau}{\hbar v_F}\right)$$

$$= \frac{2}{\pi}\int_{2\Delta_0 x/\hbar v_F}^\infty d\zeta\,K_0(\zeta)$$

(52.50)

and K_0 is the Bessel function of imaginary argument defined in Appendix A. Substitution of Eq. (52.49) into Eq. (52.46) shows that the one-dimensional delta function exactly cancels the first term of Eq. (52.46),[1] and we finally obtain

$$\mathbf{j}(\mathbf{x}) = -\frac{3ne^2}{4\pi mc}\frac{\pi\Delta_0}{\hbar v_F}\int d^3x'\,\frac{\mathbf{X}[\mathbf{X}\cdot\mathbf{A}(\mathbf{x}')]}{X^4}J(X)$$

(52.51)

where $\mathbf{X} = \mathbf{x} - \mathbf{x}'$. This expression is formally identical with Pippard's equation (49.31) for a pure superconductor ($r_0 = \xi_0$) at $T = 0$, apart from the appearance of $J(X)$ in place of e^{-X/ξ_0}. It is easily seen that the function $J(X)$ is very similar to the Pippard kernel for all X (Fig. 52.2), and, in particular (see Appendix A),

$$J(0) = 1$$

$$\int_0^\infty dX\,J(X) = \frac{\hbar v_F}{\pi\Delta_0}$$

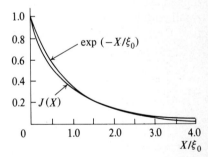

Fig. 52.2 Comparison of the BCS kernel (52.50) with the Pippard kernel e^{-X/ξ_0} for a pure superconductor at zero temperature.

which allows us to identify the Pippard coherence length

$$\xi_0 = \frac{\hbar v_F}{\pi\Delta_0}$$

(52.52)

[1] Note that $\int_0^\infty \delta(x)\,dx = \frac{1}{2}$.

in terms of the parameters of the microscopic theory.   The above microscopic calculations have been extended to finite temperatures and frequencies and to alloys with finite mean free path.   In all cases, the resulting supercurrent may be cast in the form of Pippard's original expression, thereby justifying the earlier phenomenological theory in detail.[1]

53□MICROSCOPIC DERIVATION OF GINZBURG-LANDAU EQUATIONS

The complicated and delicate self-consistency condition of the microscopic theory makes direct study of spatially inhomogeneous systems very difficult. In marked contrast, the Ginzburg-Landau theory is readily applied to non-uniform superconductors, which is probably its single most important feature. The simplicity arises from the differential structure that allows full use of the analogy with the one-body Schrödinger equation.   As discussed in Sec. 50, the original Ginzburg-Landau equations were purely phenomenological with the various constants fixed by experiment.   For our final topic in this chapter, we now present Gorkov's microscopic derivation of the Ginzburg-Landau equations.[2] This calculation determines the phenomenological constants directly in terms of the microscopic parameters; it also clarifies the range of validity of the equations and allows direct extensions to more complicated systems such as superconducting alloys.   Indeed, many microscopic calculations now proceed by deriving approximate Ginzburg-Landau equations, whose solution is considerably simpler than that of the original equations.

We start from the pair of coupled equations (51.23) for $\mathscr{G}$ and $\mathscr{F}^{\dagger}$.   Here we are interested in the effect of arbitrary magnetic fields (unlike Sec. 52), so that $\mathbf{A}$ cannot be considered small.   Instead, the calculation is restricted to the immediate vicinity of T_c, where the gap function $\Delta(\mathbf{x})$ itself provides the necessary small parameter $|\Delta(\mathbf{x})/k_B T_c| \ll 1$.   It is convenient to introduce a new temperature Green's function $\mathscr{G}^0(\mathbf{x},\mathbf{x}',\omega_n)$ that describes the normal state *in the same magnetic field*.   It satisfies the equations

$$\left\{i\hbar\omega_n + \frac{\hbar^2}{2m}\left[\nabla + \frac{ie\mathbf{A}(\mathbf{x})}{\hbar c}\right]^2 + \mu\right\} \mathscr{G}^0(\mathbf{x},\mathbf{x}',\omega_n) = \hbar\delta(\mathbf{x} - \mathbf{x}')$$

$$\left\{i\hbar\omega_n + \frac{\hbar^2}{2m}\left[\nabla - \frac{ie\mathbf{A}(\mathbf{x})}{\hbar c}\right]^2 + \mu\right\} \mathscr{G}^0(\mathbf{x}',\mathbf{x},\omega_n) = \hbar\delta(\mathbf{x} - \mathbf{x}')$$

(53.1)

obtained from Eq. (51.23a) and its analog for $\mathscr{G}(\mathbf{x}',\mathbf{x},\omega_n)$ with $\Delta = 0$.   This auxiliary function enables us to rewrite Eqs. (51.23) as the following pair of

[1] D. C. Mattis and J. Bardeen, *Phys. Rev.*, **111**:412 (1958); A. A. Abrikosov, L. P. Gorkov, and I. E. Dzyaloshinskii, *op. cit.*, secs. 37 and 39; G. Rickayzen, *op. cit.*, chap. 7; J. R. Schrieffer, *op. cit.*, sec. 8.4.
[2] L. P. Gorkov, *Sov. Phys.-JETP*, **9**:1364 (1959); A. A. Abrikosov, L. P. Gorkov, and I. E. Dzyaloshinskii, *op. cit.*, sec. 38.

coupled integral equations

$$\mathcal{G}(\mathbf{x},\mathbf{x}',\omega_n) = \mathcal{G}^0(\mathbf{x},\mathbf{x}',\omega_n) - \hbar^{-1} \int d^3y \, \mathcal{G}^0(\mathbf{x},\mathbf{y},\omega_n) \, \Delta(\mathbf{y}) \mathcal{F}^{\dagger}(\mathbf{y},\mathbf{x}',\omega_n) \quad (53.2a)$$

$$\mathcal{F}^{\dagger}(\mathbf{x},\mathbf{x}',\omega_n) = \hbar^{-1} \int d^3y \, \mathcal{G}^0(\mathbf{y},\mathbf{x},-\omega_n) \, \Delta^*(\mathbf{y}) \, \mathcal{G}(\mathbf{y},\mathbf{x}',\omega_n) \quad (53.2b)$$

which are easily verified by direct substitution into the original differential equations. Note carefully the rather complicated arguments in Eq. (53.2b); they are necessary to reproduce the structure of Eq. (51.23b). A simple manipulation of Eqs. (53.2) yields

$$\mathcal{G}(\mathbf{x},\mathbf{x}',\omega_n) = \mathcal{G}^0(\mathbf{x},\mathbf{x}',\omega_n) - \hbar^{-2} \int d^3y \, d^3z \, \mathcal{G}^0(\mathbf{x},\mathbf{y},\omega_n) \, \Delta(\mathbf{y})$$
$$\times \mathcal{G}^0(\mathbf{z},\mathbf{y},-\omega_n) \, \Delta^*(\mathbf{z}) \, \mathcal{G}(\mathbf{z},\mathbf{x}',\omega_n) \quad (53.3a)$$

$$\mathcal{F}^{\dagger}(\mathbf{x},\mathbf{x}',\omega_n) = \hbar^{-1} \int d^3y \mathcal{G}^0(\mathbf{y},\mathbf{x},-\omega_n) \, \Delta^*(\mathbf{y}) \, \mathcal{G}^0(\mathbf{y},\mathbf{x}',\omega_n) - \hbar^{-2} \int d^3y \, d^3z$$
$$\times \mathcal{G}^0(\mathbf{y},\mathbf{x},-\omega_n) \, \Delta^*(\mathbf{y}) \, \mathcal{G}^0(\mathbf{y},\mathbf{z},\omega_n) \, \Delta(\mathbf{z}) \mathcal{F}^{\dagger}(\mathbf{z},\mathbf{x}',\omega_n) \quad (53.3b)$$

which are exact integral equations for $\mathcal{G}$ and $\mathcal{F}^{\dagger}$ separately.

Further progress depends on the assumption of small Δ, and we first concentrate on Eq. (53.3b). The second term on the right becomes a small perturbation in this limit, and an expansion gives

$$\mathcal{F}^{\dagger}(\mathbf{x},\mathbf{x}',\omega_n) = \hbar^{-1} \int d^3y \, \mathcal{G}^0(\mathbf{y},\mathbf{x},-\omega_n) \, \Delta^*(\mathbf{y}) \, \mathcal{G}^0(\mathbf{y},\mathbf{x}',\omega_n) - \hbar^{-3} \int d^3y \, d^3z$$
$$\times d^3w \, \mathcal{G}^0(\mathbf{y},\mathbf{x},-\omega_n) \, \Delta^*(\mathbf{y}) \, \mathcal{G}^0(\mathbf{y},\mathbf{z},\omega_n) \, \Delta(\mathbf{z})$$
$$\times \mathcal{G}^0(\mathbf{w},\mathbf{z},-\omega_n) \, \Delta^*(\mathbf{w}) \, \mathcal{G}^0(\mathbf{w},\mathbf{x}',\omega_n) + \cdots \quad (53.4)$$

When Eq. (53.4) is combined with the self-consistent gap condition (51.24), we obtain an integral equation for the gap function itself

$$g^{-1} \Delta^*(\mathbf{x}) = \int d^3y \, Q(\mathbf{x},\mathbf{y}) \Delta^*(\mathbf{y})$$
$$+ \int d^3y \, d^3z \, d^3w \, R(\mathbf{x},\mathbf{y},\mathbf{z},\mathbf{w}) \, \Delta^*(\mathbf{y}) \, \Delta(\mathbf{z}) \, \Delta^*(\mathbf{w}) \quad (53.5)$$

where higher-order terms have been neglected. Here the kernels involve $\mathcal{G}^0$ and thus depend only on the properties of the normal metal

$$Q(\mathbf{x},\mathbf{y}) \equiv (\beta\hbar^2)^{-1} \sum_n \mathcal{G}^0(\mathbf{y},\mathbf{x},-\omega_n) \, \mathcal{G}^0(\mathbf{y},\mathbf{x},\omega_n) \quad (53.6)$$

$$R(\mathbf{x},\mathbf{y},\mathbf{z},\mathbf{w}) \equiv -(\beta\hbar^4)^{-1} \sum_n \mathcal{G}^0(\mathbf{y},\mathbf{x},-\omega_n) \, \mathcal{G}^0(\mathbf{y},\mathbf{z},\omega_n) \, \mathcal{G}^0(\mathbf{w},\mathbf{z},-\omega_n) \, \mathcal{G}^0(\mathbf{w},\mathbf{x},\omega_n)$$
$$(53.7)$$

We see that the assumption of small $|\Delta|$ only leads to a nonlinear *integral* equation. The simpler *differential* structure of the Ginzburg-Landau equations requires the additional and separate assumption $T_c - T \ll T_c$, since Δ^* and $\mathbf{A}$ then vary slowly with respect to the range of the kernels Q and R. These two conditions are physically quite distinct, for a sufficiently strong magnetic field can render Δ^* small, even at $T = 0$.

It is now necessary to examine the kernels Q and R. As a first step, we evaluate the normal-state Green's function $\mathscr{G}^0$ *in the absence of a magnetic field*. This function depends only on $\mathbf{x} - \mathbf{x}'$ and is precisely that studied in Sec. 23

$$\mathscr{G}^0(\mathbf{x},\omega_n) = \hbar(2\pi)^{-3} \int d^3k \, e^{i\mathbf{k}\cdot\mathbf{x}} (i\hbar\omega_n - \xi_k)^{-1} \tag{53.8}$$

Although the complete spatial dependence is rather complicated, the relevant lengths in Eqs. (53.5) to (53.7) are all much longer than interatomic dimensions, and it is therefore permissible to assume $k_F x \gg 1$. In addition, if the discrete frequency satisfies the restriction $|\hbar\omega_n| \ll \mu$, then the dominant contribution arises from the vicinity of the Fermi surface, and we find

$$\mathscr{G}^0(\mathbf{x},\omega_n) \approx \hbar N(0) \int \frac{d\xi}{i\hbar\omega_n - \xi} j_0(kx)$$

$$\approx \frac{\hbar N(0)}{2ik_F x} \int \frac{d\xi}{i\hbar\omega_n - \xi} \left\{ \exp\left[i\left(k_F + \frac{\xi}{\hbar v_F}\right)x\right] - \exp\left[-i\left(k_F + \frac{\xi}{\hbar v_F}\right)x\right] \right\}$$

$$= -\frac{\pi\hbar N(0)}{k_F x} \exp\left(ik_F x \operatorname{sgn}\omega_n - \frac{x|\omega_n|}{v_F}\right) \tag{53.9}$$

This last restriction ($|\hbar\omega_n| \ll \mu$) is fully justified in practice, because the terms omitted make a negligible contribution to the sum over n in Eqs. (53.6) and (53.7).

The magnetic field in Eq. (53.1) is that in the superconducting state, which varies with the natural length $\lambda(T)$. In contrast, $\mathscr{G}^0$ oscillates with a much shorter length k_F^{-1}, so that $\mathbf{A}$ can be considered locally constant over many wavelengths. Gorkov thus makes an eikonal (phase-integral) approximation, assuming that the dominant effect of the magnetic field can be included in a slowly varying envelope function φ

$$\tilde{\mathscr{G}}^0(\mathbf{x},\mathbf{x}',\omega_n) = e^{i\varphi(\mathbf{x},\mathbf{x}')} \mathscr{G}^0(\mathbf{x} - \mathbf{x}', \omega_n) \tag{53.10}$$

The contribution of $\mathbf{A}$ is negligible for $\mathbf{x} \approx \mathbf{x}'$; hence φ is chosen to satisfy

$$\varphi(\mathbf{x},\mathbf{x}) = 0 \tag{53.11}$$

Direct calculation with Eq. (53.10) gives

$$\left(\boldsymbol{\nabla} + \frac{ie\mathbf{A}}{\hbar c}\right)^2 \tilde{\mathscr{G}}^0 = e^{i\varphi} \left\{ \nabla^2 \mathscr{G}^0 + 2i\left(\boldsymbol{\nabla}\varphi + \frac{e\mathbf{A}}{\hbar c}\right) \cdot \boldsymbol{\nabla}\mathscr{G}^0 \right.$$

$$\left. + \left[i\nabla^2\varphi + \frac{ie(\boldsymbol{\nabla}\cdot\mathbf{A})}{\hbar c} - \left(\boldsymbol{\nabla}\varphi + \frac{e\mathbf{A}}{\hbar c}\right)^2\right] \mathscr{G}^0 \right\} \tag{53.12}$$

Here the terms are grouped in approximate ascending powers of $eA/\hbar c k_F$ because $\mathscr{G}^0$ varies with the characteristic length k_F^{-1}. Since A is of order λH, this parameter may be rewritten as $\lambda eH/\hbar c k_F$, which is small for all magnetic fields of

interest.   In consequence, we neglect the last term of Eq. (53.12) entirely, while φ is determined from the condition

$$\left[\nabla\varphi(\mathbf{x},\mathbf{x}') + \frac{e\mathbf{A}(\mathbf{x})}{\hbar c}\right]\cdot(\mathbf{x} - \mathbf{x}') = 0 \tag{53.13}$$

Given $\mathbf{A}(\mathbf{x})$, this first-order differential equation can always be integrated.

We now return to the kernel $Q(\mathbf{x},\mathbf{y})$.   A combination of Eqs. (53.6) and (53.10) gives

$$Q(\mathbf{x},\mathbf{y}) = (\beta\hbar^2)^{-1} \sum_n e^{2i\varphi(\mathbf{y},\mathbf{x})} \mathscr{G}^0(\mathbf{y} - \mathbf{x},-\omega_n) \mathscr{G}^0(\mathbf{y} - \mathbf{x}, \omega_n)$$

$$\equiv e^{2i\varphi(\mathbf{y},\mathbf{x})} Q^0(\mathbf{x} - \mathbf{y}) \tag{53.14}$$

which defines the kernel Q^0 in the absence of a magnetic field.   This function is readily evaluated with Eq. (53.9) and the relation $\sum_n f(|\omega_n|) = 2 \sum_{n=0}^{\infty} f(\omega_n)$:

$$Q^0(\mathbf{x}) = \left[\frac{\pi N(0)}{k_F x}\right]^2 \frac{1}{\beta} \sum_n \exp\left[-\frac{2x|\omega_n|}{v_F}\right]$$

$$= \left[\frac{\pi N(0)}{k_F x}\right]^2 \frac{1}{\beta \sinh(2\pi x/\beta\hbar v_F)} \tag{53.15}$$

Near T_c, the kernel Q^0 vanishes exponentially for $x \gg \hbar v_F/k_B T_c \approx O(\xi_0)$, and it thus has a range comparable with the (temperature-independent) Pippard coherence length.   Since ξ_0 is much shorter than the scale of variations of either the vector potential or the gap function, it is permissible to treat $\mathbf{A}$ and Δ^* as slowly varying functions.   In particular, Eq. (53.13) can be integrated explicitly

$$\varphi(\mathbf{x},\mathbf{x}') = -\frac{e}{2\hbar c}[\mathbf{A}(\mathbf{x}) + \mathbf{A}(\mathbf{x}')]\cdot(\mathbf{x} - \mathbf{x}') \tag{53.16}$$

where the symmetrized form represents a compromise between the two forms of Eq. (53.1).   Furthermore, $\mathbf{A}$ is of order $H_c(T)\lambda(T) \propto (T_c - T)^{\pm}$; the restricted range of Q^0 then means that $\varphi(\mathbf{x},\mathbf{x}')$ itself becomes small as $T \to T_c$, permitting an expansion of $e^{i\varphi}$ in powers of φ.

The above conditions allow us to evaluate the first term on the right side of Eq. (53.5).   With the definition $\mathbf{z} \equiv \mathbf{y} - \mathbf{x}$ we have

$$\int d^3y\, Q(\mathbf{x},\mathbf{y})\, \Delta^*(\mathbf{y}) = \int d^3z\, Q^0(\mathbf{z}) \exp\left\{-\frac{ie}{\hbar c}[\mathbf{A}(\mathbf{x}) + \mathbf{A}(\mathbf{x} + \mathbf{z})]\cdot\mathbf{z}\right\} \Delta^*(\mathbf{x} + \mathbf{z})$$

$$= \int d^3z\, Q^0(\mathbf{z}) \left\{1 - \frac{ie}{\hbar c}[\mathbf{A}(\mathbf{x}) + \mathbf{A}(\mathbf{x} + \mathbf{z})]\cdot\mathbf{z} - \frac{1}{2}\left(\frac{e}{\hbar c}\right)^2\right.$$

$$\left. \times\, \{[\mathbf{A}(\mathbf{x}) + \mathbf{A}(\mathbf{x} + \mathbf{z})]\cdot\mathbf{z}\}^2 + \cdots\right\} \Delta^*(\mathbf{x} + \mathbf{z}) \tag{53.17}$$

The short range of Q^0 requires that $z \lesssim \xi_0$, and the remaining functions may be expanded in a Taylor series about $z = 0$. Retaining the leading correction term, we find

$$\int d^3y\, Q(\mathbf{x},\mathbf{y})\,\Delta^*(\mathbf{y}) \approx \Delta^*(\mathbf{x}) \int d^3z\, Q^0(z) + \frac{1}{6}\left[\nabla - \frac{2ie\mathbf{A}(\mathbf{x})}{\hbar c}\right]^2 \Delta^*(\mathbf{x})$$

$$\times \int d^3z\, z^2\, Q^0(z) \quad (53.18)$$

where ∇ denotes the gradient with respect to $\mathbf{x}$ and acts only on the vector potential $\mathbf{A}(\mathbf{x})$ and the gap function $\Delta^*(\mathbf{x})$. Note that we have now reduced the original integral operator to a simpler differential one.

The properties of the normal metal appear only in the numerical coefficients of Eq. (53.18), and we first consider $\int d^3z\, Q^0(z)$, which diverges logarithmically at the origin. This singular behavior reflects the unphysical approximation of a short-range potential in Eq. (51.1). It must therefore be cut off in momentum space at $|\xi_k| = \hbar\omega_D$:

$$\int d^3z\, Q^0(z) = (\beta\hbar^2)^{-1}(2\pi)^{-3} \int d^3k \sum_n \mathcal{G}^0(\mathbf{k},\omega_n)\,\mathcal{G}^0(-\mathbf{k},-\omega_n)$$

$$= \beta^{-1}(2\pi)^{-3} \int d^3k \sum_n (\hbar^2\omega_n^2 + \xi_k^2)^{-1}$$

$$= N(0) \int_0^{\hbar\omega_D} d\xi\, \xi^{-1} \tanh\left(\tfrac{1}{2}\beta\xi\right)$$

This integral is just that considered in Eq. (51.39), and comparison with Eqs. (51.42) and (51.43) gives

$$\int d^3z\, Q^0(z) = N(0)\ln\left(2\hbar\omega_D\,\beta e^\gamma\,\pi^{-1}\right)$$

$$= N(0)\ln\left(\frac{T_c}{T}\right) + g^{-1} \approx N(0)\left(1 - \frac{T}{T_c}\right) + g^{-1} \quad (53.19)$$

The other integral in Eq. (53.18) can be evaluated directly in coordinate space using Eq. (53.15). Since this term is already the coefficient of a small correction, we set $T = T_c$ and obtain

$$\int d^3z\, z^2\, Q^0(z) \approx \frac{1}{\beta_c}\left[\frac{\pi N(0)}{k_F}\right]^2 \int d^3z\, \mathrm{csch}\,\frac{2\pi z}{\beta_c\,\hbar v_F}$$

$$= \tfrac{1}{4}N(0)\left(\frac{\beta_c\,\hbar v_F}{\pi}\right)^2 \int_0^\infty dy\,\frac{y^2}{\sinh y}$$

$$= \frac{7\zeta(3)}{8}\,N(0)\left(\frac{\hbar v_F}{\pi k_B T_c}\right)^2 \quad (53.20)$$

where Eq. (51.38) has been used.

The only other calculation is the small nonlinear correction in Eq. (53.5), which may be evaluated in lowest order by setting $\mathcal{G}^0 \approx \mathcal{G}^0$ and taking all the factors of Δ at the same point

$$\int d^3y\, d^3z\, d^3w\, R(x,y,z,w)\, \Delta^*(y)\, \Delta(z)\, \Delta^*(w)$$
$$\approx \Delta^*(x)|\Delta(x)|^2 \int d^3y\, d^3z\, d^3w\, R(x,y,z,w)$$

A straightforward calculation in momentum space gives

$$\int d^3y\, d^3z\, d^3w\, R(x,y,z,w) = -\beta_c^{-1} \sum_n (2\pi)^{-3} \int d^3k\, (\hbar^2\, \omega_n^2 + \xi_k^2)^{-2}$$

$$= -\frac{\pi N(0)}{2\beta_c} \sum_n |\hbar\omega_n|^{-3}$$

$$= -N(0)\frac{7\zeta(3)}{8}(\pi k_B T_c)^{-2} \qquad (53.21)$$

where T has again been set equal to T_c.

The final equation for $\Delta^*(x)$ is obtained by combining Eqs. (53.5), (53.18), and (53.19) to (53.21). After some rearrangement, the term $g^{-1}\Delta^*(x)$ cancels identically, and we find

$$\frac{\hbar^2}{4m}\left[\nabla - \frac{2ie\mathbf{A}(x)}{\hbar c}\right]^2 \Delta^*(x) + \frac{6\pi^2(k_B T_c)^2}{7\zeta(3)\,\epsilon_F^0}\left[\frac{T_c - T}{T_c}\Delta^*(x) - \frac{7\zeta(3)\,\Delta^*(x)|\Delta(x)|^2}{8(\pi k_B T_c)^2}\right]$$
$$= 0 \quad (53.22)$$

The relation with the Ginzburg-Landau equation can be made explicit by defining a *wave function*

$$\Psi(x) \equiv \left[\frac{7\zeta(3)\,n}{8(\pi k_B T_c)^2}\right]^{\frac{1}{2}}\Delta(x) = \left[\frac{7\zeta(3)}{8\pi^2}\right]^{\frac{1}{2}}\frac{\Delta(x)}{k_B T_c}n^{\frac{1}{2}} \qquad (53.23)$$

that satisfies the following equation (note the complex conjugation)

$$\frac{1}{4m}\left[-i\hbar\nabla + \frac{2e\mathbf{A}(x)}{c}\right]^2\Psi(x) + \frac{6\pi^2(k_B T_c)^2}{7\zeta(3)\,\epsilon_F^0}\left[-\left(1 - \frac{T}{T_c}\right)\Psi(x)\right.$$
$$\left. + n^{-1}\Psi(x)|\Psi(x)|^2\right] = 0 \quad (53.24)$$

Here n is the total electron density, and comparison with Eq. (50.7a) identifies the phenomenological parameters

$$m^* = 2m \qquad\qquad e^* = 2e$$

$$a = -\frac{6\pi^2(k_B T_c)^2}{7\zeta(3)\,\epsilon_F^0}\left(1 - \frac{T}{T_c}\right) \qquad b = \frac{6\pi^2(k_B T_c)^2}{7\zeta(3)\,\epsilon_F^0\, n} \qquad (53.25)$$

Furthermore, the characteristic lengths $\lambda(T)$ and $\xi(T)$ can be evaluated in terms of the microscopic parameters $\lambda_L(0)$ and ξ_0 [Eqs. (50.18) and (50.22)]

$$\lambda(T) = \frac{1}{\sqrt{2}} \lambda_L(0) \left(1 - \frac{T}{T_c}\right)^{-\frac{1}{2}} \qquad T \to T_c \tag{53.26a}$$

$$\xi(T) = \xi_0 \, \pi e^{-\gamma} \left[\frac{7\zeta(3)}{48}\right]^{\frac{1}{2}} \left(1 - \frac{T}{T_c}\right)^{-\frac{1}{2}}$$

$$\approx 0.739 \xi_0 \left(1 - \frac{T}{T_c}\right)^{-\frac{1}{2}} \qquad T \to T_c \tag{53.26b}$$

while the Ginzburg-Landau parameter becomes

$$\kappa \equiv \frac{\lambda(T)}{\xi(T)} \approx 0.957 \frac{\lambda_L(0)}{\xi_0} \qquad T \to T_c \tag{53.27}$$

The penetration depth agrees with that obtained with the weak-field response near T_c [compare Eqs. (52.34b) and (52.35)], but the coherence length can only be determined by including spatial variation of the gap function. In addition, the Ginzburg-Landau expressions for $n_s(T) = 2n_s^*(T)$ and $H_c(T)$ derived with Eqs. (50.12), (50.16), and (53.25) agree with Eqs. (52.34b) and (51.64). The last calculation requires the expression

$$[H_c(0)]^2 = \frac{3\pi^3 (k_B T_c)^2 \, n e^{-2\gamma}}{\epsilon_F^0}$$

obtained by combining Eqs. (51.38), (51.44), and (51.56).

The preceding derivation shows how the first Ginzburg-Landau equation emerges as an expansion of the self-consistent gap equation near T_c. We now consider the supercurrent, which can be related to spatial derivatives of the single-particle Green's function $\mathscr{G}$ [compare Eq. (52.10)]

$$\mathbf{j}(\mathbf{x}) = -\frac{e\hbar}{mi}(\nabla - \nabla') \mathscr{G}(\mathbf{x}\tau, \mathbf{x}'\,\tau^+)|_{\mathbf{x}'=\mathbf{x}} - 2\frac{e^2}{mc} \mathbf{A}(\mathbf{x}) \mathscr{G}(\mathbf{x}\tau, \mathbf{x}\tau^+) \tag{53.28}$$

Here the factor 2 arises from the spin sums. If Eq. (53.3a) is expanded as

$$\mathscr{G}(\mathbf{x}, \mathbf{x}', \omega_n) = \mathscr{G}^0(\mathbf{x}, \mathbf{x}', \omega_n) + \delta\mathscr{G}(\mathbf{x}, \mathbf{x}', \omega_n)$$

with

$$\delta\mathscr{G}(\mathbf{x}, \mathbf{x}', \omega_n) = -\hbar^{-2} \int d^3y \, d^3z \, \mathscr{G}^0(\mathbf{x}, \mathbf{y}, \omega_n) \, \mathscr{G}^0(\mathbf{z}, \mathbf{y}, -\omega_n) \, \mathscr{G}^0(\mathbf{z}, \mathbf{x}', \omega_n) \, \Delta(\mathbf{y}) \, \Delta^*(\mathbf{z}) \tag{53.29}$$

then a simple calculation with Eqs. (53.10) and (53.16) shows that the zero-order contribution vanishes

$$-\frac{e\hbar}{mi}(\nabla - \nabla') \mathscr{G}^0(\mathbf{x}\tau, \mathbf{x}'\,\tau^+)|_{\mathbf{x}'=\mathbf{x}} - \frac{2e^2}{mc} \mathbf{A}(\mathbf{x}) \mathscr{G}^0(\mathbf{x}\tau, \mathbf{x}\tau^+) = 0$$

In this way, the total supercurrent reduces to

$$\mathbf{j}(\mathbf{x}) = -\frac{e}{mi\beta} \sum_n [(\nabla - \nabla')\,\delta\mathscr{G}(\mathbf{x},\mathbf{x}',\omega_n)]_{\mathbf{x}'=\mathbf{x}} - \frac{2e^2}{mc\beta\hbar}\mathbf{A}(\mathbf{x}) \sum_n \delta\mathscr{G}(\mathbf{x},\mathbf{x},\omega_n)$$

The remaining calculation depends on the explicit form of $\delta\mathscr{G}$, and substitution of Eq. (53.29) gives

$$\mathbf{j}(\mathbf{x}) + \frac{2e^2}{mc\beta\hbar}\mathbf{A}(\mathbf{x}) \sum_n \delta\mathscr{G}(\mathbf{x},\mathbf{x},\omega_n) = \frac{e}{mi\beta\hbar^2} \sum_n \int d^3y\, d^3z\, \Delta(\mathbf{y})\,\Delta^*(\mathbf{z})$$

$$\times\, \mathscr{G}^0(\mathbf{z},\mathbf{y},-\omega_n)\,[\mathscr{G}^0(\mathbf{z},\mathbf{x},\omega_n)\nabla_{\mathbf{x}}\mathscr{G}^0(\mathbf{x},\mathbf{y},\omega_n) - \mathscr{G}^0(\mathbf{x},\mathbf{y},\omega_n)\nabla_{\mathbf{x}}\mathscr{G}^0(\mathbf{z},\mathbf{x},\omega_n)]$$

$$(53.30)$$

The spatial derivatives can be evaluated with Eqs. (53.10) and (53.16), and the result can be simplified with the slow variation of $\mathbf{A}$

$$\mathbf{j}(\mathbf{x}) + \frac{2e^2}{mc\beta\hbar}\mathbf{A}(\mathbf{x}) \sum_n \delta\mathscr{G}(\mathbf{x},\mathbf{x},\omega_n) = \frac{e}{mi\beta\hbar^2} \sum_n \int d^3y\, d^3z\, \Delta(\mathbf{y})\,\Delta^*(\mathbf{z})$$

$$\times\, \mathscr{G}^0(\mathbf{z},\mathbf{y},-\omega_n)\left\{ -\frac{2ie\mathbf{A}(\mathbf{x})}{\hbar c}\,\mathscr{G}^0(\mathbf{x},\mathbf{y},\omega_n)\,\mathscr{G}^0(\mathbf{z},\mathbf{x},\omega_n) + e^{i\varphi(\mathbf{x},\mathbf{y})}\,e^{i\varphi(\mathbf{z},\mathbf{x})} \right.$$

$$\left. \times\, [\mathscr{G}^0(\mathbf{z}-\mathbf{x},\omega_n)\nabla_{\mathbf{x}}\mathscr{G}^0(\mathbf{x}-\mathbf{y},\omega_n) - \mathscr{G}^0(\mathbf{x}-\mathbf{y},\omega_n)\nabla_{\mathbf{x}}\mathscr{G}^0(\mathbf{z}-\mathbf{x},\omega_n)] \right\}$$

The first term on the right side now cancels the second term on the left.   With the same approximations as in Eq. (53.17), the supercurrent near T_c becomes

$$\mathbf{j}(\mathbf{x}) = \frac{e}{mi\beta\hbar^2} \sum_n \int d^3y\, d^3z\, \mathscr{G}^0(\mathbf{z}-\mathbf{y},-\omega_n)\,[\mathscr{G}^0(\mathbf{z}-\mathbf{x},\omega_n)\nabla_{\mathbf{x}}\mathscr{G}^0(\mathbf{x}-\mathbf{y},\omega_n)$$

$$-\, \mathscr{G}^0(\mathbf{x}-\mathbf{y},\omega_n)\nabla_{\mathbf{x}}\mathscr{G}^0(\mathbf{z}-\mathbf{x},\omega_n)]\,[|\Delta(\mathbf{x})|^2 - |\Delta(\mathbf{x})|^2\frac{2ie}{\hbar c}$$

$$\times\, \mathbf{A}(\mathbf{x})\cdot(\mathbf{z}-\mathbf{y}) + \Delta^*(\mathbf{x})(\mathbf{y}-\mathbf{x})\cdot\nabla\Delta(\mathbf{x}) + \Delta(\mathbf{x})(\mathbf{z}-\mathbf{x})\cdot\nabla\Delta^*(\mathbf{x})]$$

$$(53.31)$$

Several terms vanish identically owing to the spherical symmetry:

$$\mathbf{j}(\mathbf{x}) = \frac{e}{mi\beta\hbar^2} \sum_n \int d^3y\, d^3z\, \mathscr{G}^0(\mathbf{z}-\mathbf{y},-\omega_n)\,[\mathscr{G}^0(\mathbf{z}-\mathbf{x},\omega_n)\nabla_{\mathbf{x}}\mathscr{G}^0(\mathbf{x}-\mathbf{y},\omega_n)$$

$$-\, \mathscr{G}^0(\mathbf{x}-\mathbf{y},\omega_n)\nabla_{\mathbf{x}}\mathscr{G}^0(\mathbf{z}-\mathbf{x},\omega_n)]$$

$$\times\left[-\frac{2ie}{\hbar c}|\Delta(\mathbf{x})|^2\,\mathbf{A}(\mathbf{x})\cdot(\mathbf{z}-\mathbf{y}) + \Delta(\mathbf{x})\nabla_{\mathbf{x}}\Delta^*(\mathbf{x})\cdot\mathbf{z} + \Delta^*(\mathbf{x})\nabla_{\mathbf{x}}\Delta(\mathbf{x})\cdot\mathbf{y} \right]$$

$$(53.32)$$

The remaining integration is most easily performed with the Fourier representation of $\mathscr{G}^0$ from Eq. (53.8), and a lengthy but straightforward calculation gives

$$\mathbf{j}(\mathbf{x}) = \frac{7\zeta(3)n}{16(\pi k_B T_c)^2}\left\{-\frac{2e\hbar}{2mi}[\Delta(\mathbf{x})^*\boldsymbol{\nabla}\Delta(\mathbf{x}) - \Delta(\mathbf{x})\boldsymbol{\nabla}\Delta^*(\mathbf{x})] - \frac{4e^2\,\mathbf{A}(\mathbf{x})}{mc}|\Delta(\mathbf{x})|^2\right\}$$

$$(53.33)$$

With the wave function in Eq. (53.23), we finally obtain

$$\mathbf{j}(\mathbf{x}) = -\frac{e\hbar}{2mi}[\Psi^*(\mathbf{x})\boldsymbol{\nabla}\Psi(\mathbf{x}) - \Psi(\mathbf{x})\boldsymbol{\nabla}\Psi^*(\mathbf{x})] - \frac{2e^2}{mc}\mathbf{A}(\mathbf{x})|\Psi(\mathbf{x})|^2 \qquad (53.34)$$

in complete agreement with Eq. (50.9).

In summary, we have derived the Ginzburg-Landau equations (50.7a) and (50.9) from the Gorkov equations under the following set of assumptions:

1. The order parameter $\Delta(\mathbf{x})$ and the vector potential $\mathbf{A}(\mathbf{x})$ are small.
2. The range of the kernels in Eqs. (53.5) and (53.30) is small compared to the characteristic length for spatial variations of $\Delta(\mathbf{x})$ (i.e., the coherence length ξ) and $\mathbf{A}(\mathbf{x})$ (i.e., the penetration length λ).
3. The eikonal approximation also requires $\lambda k_F \gg 1$ (which is generally valid).

For any superconductor, these criteria are always satisfied sufficiently close to the transition temperature T_c.

PROBLEMS

13.1. Show that Eq. (49.6) can be rewritten $\partial \mathbf{Q}/\partial t + (\mathbf{v}\cdot\boldsymbol{\nabla})\mathbf{Q} = (\mathbf{Q}\cdot\boldsymbol{\nabla})\mathbf{v}$. Hence prove the conservation of the flux $\Phi_Q \equiv \int d\mathbf{S}\cdot\mathbf{Q}$ through any closed surface bounded by a curve *that moves with the fluid.* As a corollary, conclude that the fluxoid Φ is a rigorous constant of the motion.

13.2. If $F_s(T,0)$ is the free-energy density of a superconductor in zero field, show that Eq. (49.11) is the Euler-Lagrange equation of the total Helmholtz free energy $VF_s(T,0) + \int d^3x[(8\pi)^{-1}\mathbf{h}^2 + \frac{1}{2}n_s m\mathbf{v}^2]$ for arbitrary variations of $\mathbf{h}$ subject to $\operatorname{curl}\mathbf{h} = 4\pi\mathbf{j}/c$. How does this derivation fail for a normal metal?

13.3. (a) Evaluate the mean Helmholtz free-energy density [see Prob. 13.2 and Eq. (49.16)] for a slab in a parallel applied field $H_0\hat{x}$. Use Eqs. (48.13) and (49.17) to verify that $\mathbf{H} = H_0\hat{x}$ throughout the sample, and find the magnetization $(\bar{B} - H)/4\pi$.
(b) From the corresponding Gibbs free energy, show that the sample remains superconducting up to a critical field H_c^* determined by the equation $(H_c^*/H_c)^2 = [1 - (\lambda_L/d)\tanh(d/\lambda_L)]^{-1}$, where H_c is the bulk critical field. Discuss the limiting cases $d \ll \lambda_L$ and $d \gg \lambda_L$.

13.4. Consider a semi-infinite superconductor ($z > 0$) with an external magnetic field H parallel to the surface. Use the Ginzburg-Landau theory to find $\Psi(z)$

and $h(z)$ for $\kappa \gg 1$. Show that the field-dependent penetration depth $\lambda(H)$ is given by $[\lambda(H)/\lambda(0)]^2 = 2H_c/[H_c + (H_c^2 - H^2)^{\frac{1}{2}}]$. Sketch the spatial variation of h and Ψ for various values of H. What happens for $H > H_c$? Why is it permissible to violate the boundary condition $d\Psi/dz = 0$?

13.5. (a) As a model for an extreme type-II superconductor ($\lambda \gg \xi$), solve the London equation (49.11) in the exterior of a cylindrical hole of radius ξ (see Fig. 50.1b) containing one quantum of fluxoid $\varphi_0 = hc/2e$. Discuss the spatial form of $\mathbf{h}$ and $\mathbf{j}$.
(b) Evaluate the Gibbs free energy as in Prob. 13.3 and show that the lower critical field for flux penetration is given by $H_{c1} = (\varphi_0/4\pi\lambda^2)\ln(\lambda/\xi)$.

13.6. Consider an infinite metal in a uniform applied field H that is sufficiently strong to make the sample normal. Solve the linearized Ginzburg–Landau equations, and show that a superconducting solution becomes possible below an upper critical field $H_{c2}(T) = \sqrt{2}\kappa H_c(T)$.

13.7. Use the procedure outlined below Eq. (51.3) to derive the Hartree-Fock theory at finite temperature for a potential $-g\delta(\mathbf{x} - \mathbf{x}')$.

13.8. Retain the Hartree-Fock terms in Eq. (51.5) and derive a set of generalized equations for $\mathscr{G}$ and $\mathscr{F}^\dagger$. Solve these equations for a uniform system and compare with the calculations leading to Eqs. (37.33) to (37.35). Specialize the equations to a normal system and rederive the results of Sec. 27.

13.9. (a) In the weak-coupling limit ($\Delta_0 \ll \hbar\omega_D$), show that the BCS gap equation (51.37) may be written

$$\ln\frac{\Delta_0}{\Delta} = 2\int_0^{\hbar\omega_D} \frac{d\xi}{(\xi^2 + \Delta^2)^{\frac{1}{2}}}\frac{1}{e^{\beta(\xi^2+\Delta^2)^{\frac{1}{2}}} + 1}$$

where Δ is the gap at temperature T and $\Delta_0 = \Delta(T = 0)$, and hence derive Eq. (51.46a).
(b) Near T_c, use Eq. (51.35) to prove that

$$\ln\frac{T}{T_c} = -\frac{7\zeta(3)}{8}\left(\frac{\Delta}{\pi k_B T}\right)^2 + O\left(\frac{\Delta}{k_B T}\right)^4$$

and hence prove Eq. (51.46b).

13.10. (a) In the weak-coupling limit ($\Delta_k \ll \hbar\omega_D$), use the assumption

$$\Delta_k = \begin{cases} \Delta_1 & \text{for } |\xi_k| < \hbar\omega_D \\ \Delta_2 & \text{for } \hbar\omega_D < |\xi_k| < \hbar\Omega_{pl} \\ 0 & \text{for } \hbar\Omega_{pl} < |\xi_k| \end{cases}$$

to solve Eq. (37.35) given the interparticle potential [recall the convention of Eq. (37.6) that $g > 0$ for an attractive potential]

$$\langle \mathbf{k} - \mathbf{k} | V | \mathbf{k}' - \mathbf{k}' \rangle = g_1 V^{-1} \theta(\hbar\omega_D - |\xi_k|) \theta(\hbar\omega_D - |\xi_{k'}|)$$
$$- g_2 V^{-1} \theta(\hbar\Omega_{pl} - |\xi_k|) \theta(\hbar\Omega_{pl} - |\xi_{k'}|)$$

Hence derive $1 = N(0) g_{\text{eff}} \ln(2\hbar\omega_D/\Delta_1)$ where $g_{\text{eff}} = g_1 - g_2 [1 + N(0) g_2 \times \ln(\Omega_{pl}/\omega_D)]^{-1}$ (instead of $g_1 - g_2$ as one might naively expect).
(b) If $k_B T_c = 1.13 \hbar\omega_D e^{-1/N(0) g_{\text{eff}}}$ and $\omega_D \propto M^{-\frac{1}{2}}$, show that $-d \ln T_c/d \ln M < \frac{1}{2}$, which may account for the reduced isotope effect in transition metals.[‡]

13.11. Use Eqs. (51.50) and (51.51) to show that the entropy in the super-conducting state can be written

$$S_s = -2Vk_B \sum_{\mathbf{k}} \{ f(E_k) \ln f(E_k) + [1 - f(E_k)] \ln [1 - f(E_k)] \}$$

where $f(E) = (e^{\beta E} + 1)^{-1}$. Compare with Prob. 2.1 and interpret the result.

13.12. As a model of a superconducting film, consider an infinite super-conductor carrying a uniform current, where the gap function takes the form $\Delta e^{2i\mathbf{q}\cdot\mathbf{x}}$ with Δ real [see Eqs. (53.23) and (53.34)] and $q \ll k_F$.
(a) Solve the Gorkov equations to find $\mathscr{G}$ and $\mathscr{F}^\dagger$ and show that the supercurrent is given by $\mathbf{j} \approx c v n_s(T)$, where $\mathbf{v} = \hbar\mathbf{q}/m$ [see Eq. (52.33)].
(b) Find the self-consistency condition for Δ. At $T = 0$ show that Δ is in-dependent of q for $q < q_c \approx \Delta_0/\hbar v_F$. Near T_c expand the gap equation to find

$$\left[\frac{\Delta(T)}{k_B T_c} \right]^2 \approx \frac{8\pi^2}{7\zeta(3)} \left(1 - \frac{T}{T_c} \right) - \frac{2}{3} \left(\frac{\hbar^2 k_F}{mk_B T_c} \right)^2 q^2$$

and determine the critical value of q that makes Δ vanish.[§]

13.13. Carry out the analytic continuation to obtain a real-time thermodynamic Green's function corresponding to the physical situation in Prob. 13.12. Discuss the excitation spectrum for small q.

13.14. (a) Use the analogy with Bose systems (Sec. 20) to generalize Dyson's equations for the electron-phonon system to a superconductor.
(b) Approximate the electron self-energies by the lowest-order contributions expressed in terms of $\mathscr{G}, \mathscr{F}, \mathscr{F}^\dagger$, and $\mathscr{D}$, and write out the coupled self-consistent equations for $\mathscr{G}$ and $\mathscr{F}^\dagger$ in momentum space.[¶]

[‡] N. N. Bogoliubov, V. V. Tolmachev and D. V. Shirkov, "A New Method in the Theory of Superconductivity," chap. 6, Consultants Bureau, New York, 1959.
[§] In fact, the system makes a first-order transition to the normal state at a critical value $q_c \approx 1.23(\Delta_0/\hbar v_F)[1 - (T/T_c)]^{\frac{1}{2}}$, which is smaller by a factor $1/\sqrt{3}$. See, for example, P. G. de Gennes, "Superconductivity of Metals and Alloys," pp. 182–184, W. A. Benjamin, Inc., New York, 1966.
[¶] G. M. Eliashberg, *Sov. Phys.-JETP*, **11**:696 (1960); **12**:1000 (1960).

13.15. Assume that the two functions $u(\mathbf{x})$ and $v(\mathbf{x})$ satisfy the coupled eigenvalue equations

$$\{(2m)^{-1}[-i\hbar\nabla + c^{-1}e\mathbf{A}(\mathbf{x})]^2 - \mu\}u(\mathbf{x}) - \Delta(\mathbf{x})v(\mathbf{x}) = Eu(\mathbf{x})$$

$$\{-(2m)^{-1}[i\hbar\nabla + c^{-1}e\mathbf{A}(\mathbf{x})]^2 + \mu\}v(\mathbf{x}) - \Delta^*(\mathbf{x})u(\mathbf{x}) = Ev(\mathbf{x})$$

known as the Bogoliubov equations.‡ If $u_j^{(+)}(\mathbf{x})$ and $v_j^{(+)}(\mathbf{x})$ is a solution with positive energy E_j, show that there is always a second solution $u_j^{(-)}(\mathbf{x}) = -v_j^{(+)}(\mathbf{x})^*$, $v_j^{(-)}(\mathbf{x}) = u_j^{(+)}(\mathbf{x})^*$ with energy $-E_j$. Let $\mathbf{U}$ be a two-component vector with elements u and v. With the usual definition $(\mathbf{U},\mathbf{U}) = \int d^3x(|u|^2 + |v|^2)$ show that $(\mathbf{U}_j^{(\pm)},\mathbf{U}_{j'}^{(\pm)}) = \delta_{jj'}$, while $(\mathbf{U}_j^{(\pm)},\mathbf{U}_{j'}^{(\mp)}) = 0$. Construct the eigenfunction expansion of $\mathcal{G}(\mathbf{x},\mathbf{x}',\omega_n)$ [Eq. (51.19)] and hence express $n(\mathbf{x})$ and $\Delta(\mathbf{x})$ in terms of these eigenfunctions. Why is E_j a single-particle excitation energy? Specialize to a uniform medium and rederive the results of Sec. 51.

13.16. Prove Eqs. (52.34a) and (52.34b).

13.17. (a) If $K(q)$ in Eq. (49.39) vanishes like $K(q) \approx \alpha q^2$ as $q \to 0$, use Eq. (49.43b) to show that the diamagnetic susceptibility is given by $\chi_d = \alpha/4\pi(1+\alpha) \approx -\alpha/4\pi$ if $\alpha \ll 1$.
(b) Derive a general expression for $K_n(q)$ by evaluating $\mathscr{P}_{kl}(\mathbf{q},\nu_n)$ [Eq. (52.25)] in a normal metal. Hence show that the Landau diamagnetic susceptibility χ_d of a noninteracting electron gas is given at all temperatures by $\chi_d = -\frac{1}{3}\chi_p$ where χ_p is the corresponding paramagnetic susceptibility (Prob. 7.5). (Note $\mu_0 = e\hbar/2mc$ for an electron.)

13.18. (a) Use the theory of linear response to show that the spin susceptibility χ of a superconductor is given by

$$\frac{\chi}{\chi_P} = \frac{2}{3\pi^2}\frac{\epsilon_F^0}{n}\int_0^\infty p^2\,dp\left[-\frac{\partial f(E_p)}{\partial E_p}\right]$$

where χ_P is the Pauli susceptibility of a normal metal (Prob. 7.5).
(b) Verify the following limits: $\chi = 0$ at $T = 0$ and $\chi = \chi_P$ at $T = T_c$. Interpret these results.

13.19. (a) Repeat Prob. 12.6 for a superconductor at finite temperature. Show that the approximate phonon propagator may be written

$$\mathscr{D}(q,\nu_n) = -\hbar\omega_q^2[\nu_n^2 + \omega_q^2 + \omega_q^2\gamma^2\mathscr{R}(q,\nu_n)]^{-1}\theta(\omega_D - \omega_q)$$

‡ These equations are discussed in detail in P. G. de Gennes, "Superconductivity of Metals and Alloys," chap. 5, W. A. Benjamin, Inc., New York, 1966.

where

$$\mathcal{R}(q,\nu_n) = \int \frac{d^3k}{(2\pi)^3} \Bigg\{ (u_+ u_- - v_+ v_-)^2 \, [f(E_+) - f(E_-)]$$

$$\times \left[\frac{1}{i\hbar\nu_n - (E_- - E_+)} - \frac{1}{i\hbar\nu_n + (E_- - E_+)} \right]$$

$$+ (u_+ v_- + u_- v_+)^2 \, [1 - f(E_+) - f(E_-)]$$

$$\times \left[\frac{1}{i\hbar\nu_n - (E_+ + E_-)} - \frac{1}{i\hbar\nu_n + (E_+ + E_-)} \right] \Bigg\}$$

and the notation is that of Eq. (52.27).‡

(b) Derive the retarded phonon Green's function $D^R(q,\omega)$. If $\hbar\omega \ll 2\Delta$, find the ultrasonic attenuation coefficient α_s in a superconductor and prove that $\alpha_s/\alpha_n = 2f(\Delta)$, which allows a direct measurement of $\Delta(T)$ (see Fig. 51.1).

13.20.   Derive Eq. (53.33).

‡ For a detailed comparison of ultrasonic and electromagnetic absorption, see J. R. Schrieffer, "Theory of Superconductivity," chap. 3, W. A. Benjamin, Inc., New York, 1964.

14
Superfluid Helium

The element He has two stable isotopes, He^3 (fermion) and He^4 (boson), which differ only by the addition of one neutron in the nucleus.[1]   At low pressure, both isotopes remain liquid down to absolute zero, where they solidify only under an applied pressure of ≈ 30 atm (He^3) or ≈ 25 atm (He^4) (Fig. 54.1).   Since a classical system will always crystallize at sufficiently low temperature, these substances are known as *quantum liquids*.   Their unique behavior arises from a combination of the weak interatomic attraction (owing to the closed $1s$ electron shell) and the small atomic mass, which produces large zero-point oscillations.

[1] General descriptions of the low-temperature properties of He may be found in K. R. Atkins, "Liquid Helium," Cambridge University Press, Cambridge, 1959; R. J. Donnelly, "Experimental Superfluidity," University of Chicago Press, Chicago, 1967; F. London, "Superfluids," vol. II, Dover Publications, Inc., New York, 1964; J. Wilks, "The Properties of Liquid and Solid Helium," Oxford University Press, Oxford, 1967.

As a corollary, both liquids have low density: $\rho_3 \approx 0.081$ g/cm^3 and $\rho_4 \approx 0.145$ g/cm^3.

Despite their superficial similarities, the two isotopes differ profoundly because of their quantum statistics. The Pauli principle tends to keep fermions apart, and the interparticle potential mixes in only unperturbed states with $k > k_F$. This behavior leads to a small healing length, and justifies the use of the independent-pair approximation in computing both the ground-state energy

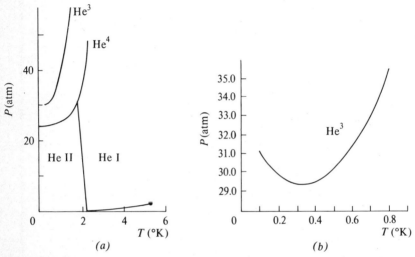

Fig. 54.1 (a) Comparison of phase diagrams of He^3 and He^4 in PT plane. (From J. DeBoer, Excitation Model for Liquid Helium II, Course XXI, Liquid Helium, Proceedings of "The International School of Physics 'Enrico Fermi'," p. 3, Academic Press, New York, 1963. Reprinted by permission.) (b) Enlarged portion of melting curve of He^3. (From D. P. Kelly and W. J. Haubach, "Comparative Properties of Helium-3 and Helium-4," AEC Research and Development Report MLM-1161, p. 18. Reprinted by permission.)

and excitation spectrum of normal Fermi systems such as nuclear matter and liquid He^3. The situation is very different for bosons because the particles tend to occupy the same single-particle state. In addition, the interparticle potential preferentially mixes in the unperturbed states that are already occupied, thus enhancing the many-body effects. For example, the success of the independent-particle model shows that the low-lying states of a normal Fermi system are generally similar to those of a free Fermi gas. This correspondence clearly fails for interacting bosons with finite mass, where the low-lying excitations usually have a collective phonon character.[1] The difference between bosons and fermions also appears in the expansions for the dilute hard-core gas. Although this system serves as a useful model for nuclear matter and He^3, the correction term in Eq. (22.19) becomes $\frac{128}{15}(na^3/\pi)^{\frac{1}{2}} \approx 2.4$ when evaluated for He^4 where

[1] R. P. Feynman, *Phys. Rev.*, **91**:1301 (1953); **94**:262 (1954).

$(na^3)^{\frac{1}{2}} \approx 0.5.$‡   As a final difference, we note that even the *free* Bose gas exhibits a complicated phase transition (compare Figs. 5.2 and 5.4).

54☐FUNDAMENTAL PROPERTIES OF He II

We first review some important features of superfluid He^4.

BASIC EXPERIMENTAL FACTS

1. λ-*point*: When liquid He^4 in contact with its vapor is cooled below $T_\lambda = 2.17°K$, it enters a new phase known as He II.   The transition is marked by a peak in the specific heat, which behaves like $\ln |T - T_\lambda|$ on both sides of the transition.[1]   This singularity is generally thought to represent the onset of Bose condensation, but no theory has yet provided a satisfactory description of the phase transition.

2. *Superfluidity and the two-fluid model*: He II has remarkable hydrodynamic properties.   It can flow through fine channels with no pressure drop, which seemingly implies that the viscosity is zero.   On the other hand, a direct measurement of the viscosity (for example, with a rotating cylinder viscometer) yields a value comparable with the viscosity of He I above T_λ.   The apparent paradox was explained by Tisza[2] and by Landau[3] with a two-fluid model, in which He II is considered a mixture of two interpenetrating components: the superfluid with density ρ_s and velocity $\mathbf{v}_s$, and the normal fluid with density ρ_n and velocity $\mathbf{v}_n$. The superfluid is assumed to be nonviscous, which accounts for the rapid flow through fine channels, and irrotational

$$\text{curl } \mathbf{v}_s = 0 \qquad\qquad (54.1)$$

The normal fluid behaves like a classical viscous fluid, which provides the measured viscosity of He II.   This two-fluid picture was strikingly confirmed by Andronikashvili[4] with a torsion pendulum of closely spaced disks suspended in He II.   The oscillating disks dragged the normal fluid and thus allowed a direct measurement of $\rho_n(T)$, which varies as T^4 for $T \ll T_\lambda$ (Fig. 54.2).

3. *Second sound*: The presence of two components gives He II an extra degree of freedom, and Landau predicted that He II would support two independent oscillation modes that differ in the relative phase of $\mathbf{v}_s$ and $\mathbf{v}_n$.   If $\mathbf{v}_n$ and $\mathbf{v}_s$ move together, the wave transmits variations in density and pressure (at constant temperature and entropy) and is known as first or ordinary sound.

‡ We follow N. M. Hugenholtz and D. Pines, *Phys. Rev.*, **116**:489 (1959), p. 505 in taking $a = 2.2$ Å.   See also F. London, *op. cit.*, p. 22.
[1] M. J. Buckingham and W. M. Fairbank, The Nature of the λ-Transition in Liquid Helium, in C. J. Gorter (ed.), "Progress in Low-Temperature Physics," vol. III, p. 80, North-Holland Publishing Company, Amsterdam, 1961.
[2] L. Tisza, *Nature*, **141**:913 (1938).
[3] L. D. Landau, *J. Phys. (USSR)*, **5**:71 (1941); **11**:91 (1947).
[4] E. L. Andronikashvili, *J. Phys. (USSR)*, **10**:201 (1946).

If v_n and v_s are opposite, however, the mode transmits periodic variations in ρ_s/ρ_n and hence represents a temperature and entropy wave (at constant density and pressure) known as second sound. The calculation is a straightforward generalization of that leading to Eq. (16.19), and we merely note that the velocity of second sound is proportional to $(\rho_s/\rho_n)^{\frac{1}{2}}$, which shows the importance of the two components.[1] Second sound was first observed by Peshkov;[2] the corresponding values of ρ_s and ρ_n agree very well with those obtained with the oscillating disk (Fig. 54.2).

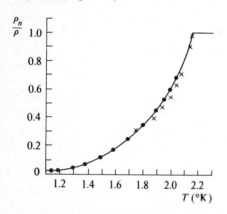

Fig. 54.2 Temperature dependence of ρ_n/ρ. The dots are obtained from the velocity of second sound; the crosses are obtained from the oscillating-disk method. [From V. P. Peshkov, *J. Phys.* (*USSR*), **10**:389 (1946), fig. 6. Reprinted by permission.]

4. *Critical velocities*: Superfluid flow cannot persist up to arbitrarily high velocities; instead, it becomes dissipative at a critical velocity v_c that depends on the width d of the channel but is independent of temperature except very near T_λ. Although the precise functional form of $v_c(d)$ is uncertain, many experiments are approximately described by a relation $v_c \approx \hbar/md$, where m is the mass of a helium atom.[3]

5. *Rotating He II and vortices*[4]: If v_s is much less than the speed of sound, it is permissible to treat the superfluid as incompressible (div $v_s = 0$). As a result, v_s is derivable from a velocity potential that satisfies Laplace's equation

$$\mathbf{v}_s = \frac{\hbar}{m}\boldsymbol{\nabla}\varphi \tag{54.2}$$

$$\nabla^2 \varphi = 0 \tag{54.3}$$

[1] L. D. Landau, *loc. cit.*

[2] V. P. Peshkov, *J. Phys.* (*USSR*), **10**:389 (1946).

[3] See, however, W. M. Van Alphen, G. J. Van Haasteren, R. De Bruyn Ouboter, and K. W. Taconis, *Phys. Letters*, **20**:474 (1966), who find $v_c = Cd^{-\frac{1}{4}}$, where C is a constant of order unity in cgs units.

[4] This subject has been reviewed by E. L. Andronikashvili and Yu. G. Mamaladze, *Rev. Mod. Phys.*, **38**:567 (1966) and by A. L. Fetter, Theory of Vortices and Rotating Helium, in K. T. Mahanthappa and W. E. Brittin (eds.), "Lectures in Theoretical Physics," vol. XI-B, p. 321, Gordon and Breach, Science Publishers, New York, 1969.

Consider a simply connected cylinder rotating about its axis with an angular velocity ω. The boundary condition $\partial \varphi / \partial n = 0$ ensures that φ is constant so that v_s vanishes for any ω. Thus Eq. (54.1) implies that the superfluid cannot participate in the rotation, and the shape of the free liquid surface should be given by the equation

$$z = \frac{\omega^2 r^2}{2g} \frac{\rho_n}{\rho} \tag{54.4}$$

where g is the acceleration due to gravity. This effect should be readily observable because ρ_n / ρ becomes very small below $1.5°K$. Equation (54.4) was first tested by Osborne,[1] who found instead that the free surface was that of a classical fluid

$$z_{cl} = \frac{\omega^2 r^2}{2g} \tag{54.5}$$

independent of temperature. To explain this discrepancy, we reexamine the cylindrically symmetric solutions of Eq. (54.1), which necessarily take the form

$$\mathbf{v}_s(\mathbf{r}) = \frac{\text{const}}{r} \hat{\theta} \tag{54.6}$$

where $\mathbf{r} = (r, \theta)$ is a vector in the xy plane. If $\text{curl} \mathbf{v}_s = 0$ everywhere (including the origin), the constant must be zero. Since this prediction contradicts (54.5), Feynman[2] suggested a less stringent condition, allowing $\text{curl} \mathbf{v}_s$ to become singular at isolated points in the fluid. The strength of the singularity may be characterized by the circulation

$$\kappa = \oint d\mathbf{l} \cdot \mathbf{v} \tag{54.7}$$

and the corresponding symmetric solution becomes

$$\mathbf{v}_s(\mathbf{r}) = \frac{\kappa}{2\pi r} \hat{\theta} \tag{54.8}$$

which is precisely the velocity of a classical rectilinear vortex parallel to the z axis. Feynman further postulated that rotating He II contains a uniform array of parallel vortices distributed with a density $2\omega/\kappa$ per unit area. On a macroscopic scale, the resulting superfluid velocity field is indistinguishable from a uniform rotation $\mathbf{v} = \boldsymbol{\omega} \times \mathbf{r}$ because both flow patterns imply the same circulation about any contour large compared with the spacing between vortices (Prob. 14.2). In addition, the superfluid now contributes to the depression of the

[1] D. V. Osborne, *Proc. Phys. Soc.*, **A63**:909 (1950).
[2] R. P. Feynman, Application of Quantum Mechanics to Liquid Helium, in C. J. Gorter (ed.), "Progress in Low-Temperature Physics," vol. I, p. 17, North-Holland Publishing Company, Amsterdam, 1955.

meniscus, thereby reconciling Osborne's experiment with the generalized condition that $\operatorname{curl} \mathbf{v}_s = 0$ almost everywhere.

6. *Quantized circulation*: Multiply Eq. (54.7) by m; the resulting equation

$$m\kappa = \oint d\mathbf{l} \cdot m\mathbf{v} = \oint d\mathbf{l} \cdot \mathbf{p} \tag{54.9}$$

is again reminiscent of the Bohr-Sommerfeld condition [compare Eqs. (49.26) and (49.27)], and Onsager[1] and Feynman[2] independently suggested that the circulation in He II was quantized in units of

$$\kappa = \frac{h}{m} = 0.997 \times 10^{-3} \text{ cm}^2/\text{sec} \tag{54.10}$$

This prediction has been confirmed both for irrotational flow in multiply connected regions[3] and for vortex rings.[4]   It is now possible to find the energy per unit length of vortex line

$$E_v = \int d^2r \, \tfrac{1}{2}\rho_s v_s^2 = \frac{\rho_s \kappa^2}{4\pi} \int \frac{dr}{r}$$

$$\approx \frac{\rho_s \kappa^2}{4\pi} \ln \frac{R}{\xi} \tag{54.11}$$

Here R is an upper cutoff that may be interpreted as the radius of the cylindrical container, while ξ is a lower cutoff representing the radius of the vortex core. Experiments[5] indicate that $\xi \approx 1$ Å, so that $E_v \approx 1.3 \times 10^5$ eV/cm for $R \approx 1$ cm.

LANDAU'S QUASIPARTICLE MODEL

At low temperatures $(T \ll T_\lambda)$, the specific heat of He II varies as T^3.   To explain this observation, Landau[6] interpreted the low-lying excited states of He II as a weakly interacting gas of phonons with the usual dispersion relation

$$\epsilon_k = \hbar c k \qquad \text{phonons} \tag{54.12}$$

where $c = 238$ m/sec is the speed of (first) sound.   More generally, he suggested that the energy spectrum has the form shown in Fig. 54.3, with a linear (phonon) region near $k = 0$ and a dip near k_0, where ϵ_k behaves like

$$\epsilon_k = \Delta + \frac{\hbar^2(k - k_0)^2}{2\mu_r} \qquad \text{rotons} \tag{54.13}$$

[1] L. Onsager, *Nuovo Cimento*, **6**, Suppl. 2, 249 (1949).
[2] R. P. Feynman, "Progress in Low-Temperature Physics," *loc. cit.*
[3] W. F. Vinen, *Proc. Roy. Soc.* (*London*), **A260**:218 (1961).
[4] G. W. Rayfield and F. Reif, *Phys. Rev.*, **136**:A1194 (1964).
[5] G. W. Rayfield and F. Reif, *loc. cit.*
[6] L. D. Landau, *loc. cit.*

Excitations with this latter dispersion relation are known as *rotons*. Landau originally determined the roton parameters by fitting the specific heat above $\approx 0.6°K$. More recently, however, the theoretical curve in Fig. 54.3 has been confirmed in great detail by inelastic neutron scattering[1] (compare Prob. 5.13),

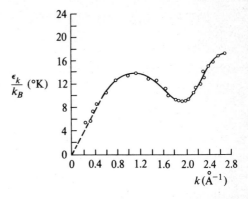

Fig. 54.3 Dispersion curve for liquid helium. The experimental points are the neutron-scattering measurements. [From D. G. Henshaw and A. D. B. Woods, *Phys. Rev.*, **121**:1266 (1961), fig. 4. Reprinted by permission of the authors and the American Institute of Physics.]

which yields an independent and more accurate measurement of the same parameters (Table 54.1).

Table 54.1 Roton parameters

	Landau (1947)‡	*Neutron scattering* (1959)§
Δ/k_B	9.6°K	8.6°K
k_0	1.95 Å⁻¹	1.91 Å⁻¹
μ_r	0.77 m_{He}	0.16 m_{He}

‡ *Source:* L. D. Landau, *J. Phys.* (*USSR*), **11**:91 (1947).
§ *Source:* D. G. Henshaw and A. D. B. Woods, *Phys. Rev.*, **121**:1266 (1961).

In Landau's model of He II, the total free energy arises from the thermally excited quasiparticles, which are treated as an ideal Bose gas.[2] Since the number of quasiparticles N_{qp} is not conserved, it must be determined by minimizing the free energy

$$\left(\frac{\partial F}{\partial N_{qp}}\right)_{TV} = 0 \qquad (54.14)$$

[1] D. G. Henshaw and A. D. B. Woods, *Phys. Rev.*, **121**:1266 (1961).
[2] An equivalent approach is to describe He II by the approximate quasiparticle hamiltonian $\hat{H}_{qp} = \sum_{\mathbf{k}} \epsilon_k a_{\mathbf{k}}^{\dagger} a_{\mathbf{k}}$, where ϵ_k is the excitation spectrum in Fig. 54.3.

and comparison with Eq. (4.6) shows that the corresponding chemical potential is zero [see the discussion of Eqs. (44.19) and (44.20)]. The thermodynamic potential Ω then reduces to the Helmholtz free energy F, and Eqs. (5.8) and (5.9) give

$$F(T,V) = k_B T V (2\pi)^{-3} \int d^3k \ln(1 - e^{-\beta\epsilon_k}) \tag{54.15}$$

$$N_{qp}(T,V) = V(2\pi)^{-3} \int d^3k \, (e^{\beta\epsilon_k} - 1)^{-1} \tag{54.16}$$

where ϵ_k is the exact dispersion relation from Fig. 54.3 and $\beta = (k_B T)^{-1}$. At low temperature, however, only the phonon and roton portions contribute significantly, and we may separate the integral over k into two independent parts

$$F = F_{ph} + F_r \tag{54.17}$$

$$N_{qp} = N_{ph} + N_r \tag{54.18}$$

As $T \to 0$, we may assume that Eqs. (54.12) and (54.13) hold separately for all k. A straightforward calculation yields

$$N_{ph} = \frac{\zeta(3)}{\pi^2} V \left(\frac{k_B T}{\hbar c}\right)^3 \tag{54.19a}$$

$$F_{ph} = -\frac{\pi^2}{90} V k_B T \left(\frac{k_B T}{\hbar c}\right)^3 \tag{54.19b}$$

$$N_r = \frac{2Vk_0^2}{\hbar(2\pi)^{\frac{3}{2}}} (\mu_r k_B T)^{\frac{1}{2}} e^{-\Delta/k_B T} \tag{54.20a}$$

$$F_r = -k_B T N_r \tag{54.20b}$$

The corresponding entropy and heat capacity are then obtained with the usual relations

$$S = -\left(\frac{\partial F}{\partial T}\right)_V, \qquad C_V = T\left(\frac{\partial S}{\partial T}\right)_V \tag{54.21}$$

It is clear that C_{Vph} varies as T^3, while C_{Vr} vanishes exponentially; both of these predictions are verified by experiments.

In addition to the foregoing thermodynamic functions, Landau's quasiparticle description justifies the two-fluid model and allows a calculation of the normal-fluid density. Consider a situation where the quasiparticles have a mean drift velocity $\mathbf{v}$ with respect to the rest frame of the superfluid. Their equilibrium distribution as seen in that rest frame[1] is $f(\epsilon_k - \hbar\mathbf{k}\cdot\mathbf{v})$, where

---

[1] This result is most easily derived in the microcanonical ensemble, where the system of quasiparticles has a fixed energy E and momentum $\mathbf{P}$. The additional constraint (fixed $\mathbf{P}$) necessitates an additional Lagrange multiplier $\mathbf{v}$, and the maximization of the entropy immediately verifies the above assertion. See, for example, F. London, op. cit., pp. 95–96, and Prob. 14.4.

$f(\epsilon) = (e^{\beta \epsilon} - 1)^{-1}$ is the usual Bose distribution function. In the same frame the total momentum carried by the quasiparticles is given by

$$\mathbf{P} = V(2\pi)^{-3} \int d^3k \, \hbar\mathbf{k} f(\epsilon_k - \hbar\mathbf{k}\cdot\mathbf{v})$$

$$\approx V(2\pi)^{-3} \int d^3k \, \hbar\mathbf{k} \left[f(\epsilon_k) - \hbar\mathbf{k}\cdot\mathbf{v}\frac{\partial f(\epsilon_k)}{\partial \epsilon_k} + \cdots \right]$$

$$\approx \frac{V\hbar^2}{6\pi^2}\mathbf{v} \int_0^\infty dk \, k^4 \left[-\frac{\partial f(\epsilon_k)}{\partial \epsilon_k} \right] \tag{54.22}$$

Thus the flow of quasiparticles is accompanied by a net momentum flux; the coefficient of proportionality *defines* the normal-fluid mass density

$$\rho_n(T) \equiv \frac{\hbar^2}{6\pi^2} \int_0^\infty dk \, k^4 \left[-\frac{\partial f(\epsilon_k)}{\partial \epsilon_k} \right] \tag{54.23}$$

while the superfluid mass density becomes

$$\rho_s(T) = \rho - \rho_n(T) \tag{54.24}$$

This result is very similar to that for the superelectron density in superconductors discussed in Sec. 52. In fact, a comparison of Eqs. (52.33) and (54.23) shows that they differ only in the statistics and spin degeneracy.

When Eq. (54.23) is separated into phonon and roton contributions, an elementary calculation gives

$$\rho_{nph} = \frac{2\pi^2 \hbar}{45c} \left(\frac{k_B T}{\hbar c} \right)^4 \tag{54.25a}$$

$$\rho_{nr} = \frac{\hbar^2 k_0^2 N_r}{3k_B TV} \tag{54.25b}$$

whose sum fits the observations within experimental error. This prediction of $\rho_n(T)$ was made before any experiments had been carried out, thus providing a particularly striking confirmation of the quasiparticle model.

Landau's description also gives a qualitative explanation of the critical velocity in He II. Consider a macroscopic object of mass M moving with velocity $\mathbf{v}$ through stationary He II at zero temperature. In this case, the momentum and energy are

$$\mathbf{P} = M\mathbf{v} \qquad E = \tfrac{1}{2}Mv^2 \tag{54.26}$$

If the object excites a quasiparticle with momentum $\mathbf{p}$ and energy ϵ, the new velocity $\mathbf{v}'$ is determined by momentum conservation

$$\mathbf{v}' = \mathbf{v} - \frac{\mathbf{p}}{M} \tag{54.27}$$

Correspondingly, the new energy E' becomes

$$E' = \tfrac{1}{2}Mv'^2 = \tfrac{1}{2}Mv^2 - \mathbf{p}\cdot\mathbf{v} + \frac{p^2}{2M}$$

$$\approx E - \mathbf{p}\cdot\mathbf{v} \tag{54.28}$$

where the recoil energy $p^2/2M$ has been neglected because M is large. At sufficiently low velocity, the process violates energy conservation

$$E - E' = \epsilon \tag{54.29}$$

As v increases, however, we eventually reach a critical velocity v_c, where $\epsilon - \mathbf{p}\cdot\mathbf{v}_c$ first vanishes. It is evident that $\mathbf{p}$ will be parallel to $\mathbf{v}_c$, and a simple rearrangement yields the Landau critical velocity

$$v_c = \left(\frac{\epsilon}{p}\right)_{\min} \tag{54.30}$$

where ϵ is taken from Fig. 54.3. If ϵ were a pure phonon spectrum, the minimum value of ϵ/p would be the speed of sound $c \approx 238$ m/sec. When rotons are included, however, v_c drops to $\approx \Delta/\hbar k_0 \approx 60$ m/sec, and such roton-limited critical velocities have been observed with ions in He II under pressure.[1]

A similar theoretical description applies to flow in channels, for a galilean transformation to the rest frame of the superfluid reproduces the previous situation, with the walls as the macroscopic object. Unfortunately, the predicted critical velocity of ≈ 60 m/sec is much too large to explain the observed breakdown of superfluid flow in channels, where v_c is instead thought to signal the creation of quantized vortices.[2]

55□WEAKLY INTERACTING BOSE GAS

The microscopic description of Chap. 6 and Sec. 35 was restricted to a stationary Bose system at $T = 0$, and we now generalize the theory to include spatially nonuniform systems at finite temperature. Although such a problem can be treated very generally,[3] the present discussion is restricted to a weakly interacting Bose gas, where the small depletion of the condensate allows us to carry through the calculations in detail. As noted previously, this model is quite unrealistic because the depletion in the ground state of He II is believed to be large (≈ 90 percent).[4] Furthermore, the model has a complicated behavior near the phase transition,[5] so that we shall study only the low-temperature properties. Never-

[1] G. W. Rayfield, *Phys. Rev. Letters*, **16**:934 (1966).

[2] See, for example, R. P. Feynman, "Progress in Low-Temperature Physics," *loc. cit.*

[3] See, for example, P. C. Hohenberg and P. C. Martin, *Ann. Phys.* (*N.Y.*), **34**:291 (1965).

[4] O. Penrose and L. Onsager, *Phys. Rev.*, **104**:576 (1956); W. L. McMillan, *Phys. Rev.*, **138**:442 (1965).

[5] K. Huang, C. N. Yang, and J. M. Luttinger, *Phys. Rev.*, **105**:776 (1957).

theless, an imperfect Bose gas contains many features of the Landau quasi-particle model and clearly illustrates the special difficulties inherent in condensed Bose systems.

GENERAL FORMULATION

Consider an assembly of bosons with the grand-canonical hamiltonian

$$\hat{K} = \int d^3x \, \hat{\psi}^\dagger(\mathbf{x}) \, [T(\mathbf{x}) - \mu] \, \hat{\psi}(\mathbf{x}) + \tfrac{1}{2} \int d^3x \, d^3x' \, \hat{\psi}^\dagger(\mathbf{x}) \, \hat{\psi}^\dagger(\mathbf{x}')$$
$$\times \, V(\mathbf{x} - \mathbf{x}') \, \hat{\psi}(\mathbf{x}') \, \hat{\psi}(\mathbf{x}) \quad (55.1)$$

where $T(\mathbf{x}) = -\hbar^2 \nabla^2/2m$ is the kinetic energy. Since Eq. (55.1) is completely general, an exact solution is clearly impossible, and we must introduce approximations appropriate to a condensed Bose system. To motivate our treatment, recall the Bogoliubov approximation $\hat{\psi}(\mathbf{x}) \to \xi_0 + \hat{\varphi}(\mathbf{x})$ used to analyze the ground state $|\mathbf{O}\rangle$ of a uniform stationary Bose system (Secs. 18 and 19). Momentum conservation further implied that $\langle \mathbf{O}|\hat{\varphi}(\mathbf{x})|\mathbf{O}\rangle = 0$ [Eq. (19.9)], and the quantity ξ_0 could therefore be interpreted as the ground-state expectation value of the field operator

$$\langle \mathbf{O}|\hat{\psi}(\mathbf{x})|\mathbf{O}\rangle = \xi_0 \qquad \text{uniform system} \qquad (55.2)$$

We now generalize the concept of Bose condensation to finite temperature and nonuniform systems, assuming that an assembly of bosons is condensed whenever the ensemble average $\langle \hat{\psi}(\mathbf{x}) \rangle$ remains finite in the thermodynamic limit. It is convenient to introduce the notation

$$\Psi(\mathbf{x}) \equiv \langle \hat{\psi}(\mathbf{x}) \rangle \qquad (55.3)$$

and the *deviation* operator

$$\hat{\varphi}(\mathbf{x}) \equiv \hat{\psi}(\mathbf{x}) - \langle \hat{\psi}(\mathbf{x}) \rangle = \hat{\psi}(\mathbf{x}) - \Psi(\mathbf{x}) \qquad (55.4)$$

The c-number function $\Psi(\mathbf{x})$ is frequently known as the *condensate wave function*; it is closely analogous to the gap function $\Delta(\mathbf{x})$ [Eq. (51.14)] in a superconductor, and, indeed, the presence of such finite anomalous amplitudes serves as a general criterion for a condensed quantum fluid.[1] Note that Eqs. (55.3) and (51.14) are merely general definitions. In any practical calculation, they must be evaluated with some approximation scheme that depends on the precise assembly considered.

In the present weakly interacting system, almost all the particles are in the condensate. Consequently, the operator $\hat{\varphi}$ may be considered a small correction

---

[1] This concept, which first appeared in V. L. Ginzburg and L. D. Landau, *Zh. Eksp. Teor. Fiz.*, **20**:1064 (1950) and in O. Penrose and L. Onsager, *loc. cit.*, is a more precise formulation of London's "long-range order" [F. London, *op. cit.*, vol. I, secs. 24–26 and vol. II, sec. 22]. See, also, C. N. Yang, *Rev. Mod. Phys.*, **34**:694 (1962).

to Ψ, and we expand $\hat{K}$ in powers of $\hat{\varphi}$ and $\hat{\varphi}^\dagger$, retaining only the linear and quadratic terms:

$$\hat{K} = K_0 + \hat{K}_l + \hat{K}' \tag{55.5}$$

where

$$K_0 = \int d^3x\,\Psi^*(\mathbf{x})\,[T(\mathbf{x}) - \mu]\Psi(\mathbf{x}) + \tfrac{1}{2} \int d^3x\,d^3x'\,V(\mathbf{x} - \mathbf{x}')|\Psi(\mathbf{x})|^2$$
$$\times\,|\Psi(\mathbf{x}')|^2 \tag{55.6}$$

$$\hat{K}_l = \int d^3x\,\hat{\varphi}^\dagger(\mathbf{x})\,[T(\mathbf{x}) - \mu + \int d^3x'\,V(\mathbf{x} - \mathbf{x}')|\Psi(\mathbf{x}')|^2]\,\Psi(\mathbf{x})$$
$$+ \int d^3x\,\{[T(\mathbf{x}) - \mu + \int d^3x'\,V(\mathbf{x} - \mathbf{x}')|\Psi(\mathbf{x}')|^2]\Psi^*(\mathbf{x})\}\,\hat{\varphi}(\mathbf{x}) \tag{55.7}$$

$$\hat{K}' = \int d^3x\,\hat{\varphi}^\dagger(\mathbf{x})\,[T(\mathbf{x}) - \mu]\,\hat{\varphi}(\mathbf{x}) + \int d^3x\,d^3x'\,V(\mathbf{x} - \mathbf{x}')$$
$$\times\,[|\Psi(\mathbf{x}')|^2\,\hat{\varphi}^\dagger(\mathbf{x})\,\hat{\varphi}(\mathbf{x}) + \Psi^*(\mathbf{x})\,\Psi(\mathbf{x}')\,\hat{\varphi}^\dagger(\mathbf{x}')\,\hat{\varphi}(\mathbf{x})$$
$$+ \tfrac{1}{2}\Psi^*(\mathbf{x})\,\Psi^*(\mathbf{x}')\,\hat{\varphi}(\mathbf{x}')\,\hat{\varphi}(\mathbf{x}) + \tfrac{1}{2}\hat{\varphi}^\dagger(\mathbf{x})\,\hat{\varphi}^\dagger(\mathbf{x}')\,\Psi(\mathbf{x}')\,\Psi(\mathbf{x})] \tag{55.8}$$

The resulting hamiltonian can be simplified by choosing Ψ to satisfy the following nonlinear field equation

$$[T(\mathbf{x}) - \mu]\Psi(\mathbf{x}) + \int d^3x'\,V(\mathbf{x} - \mathbf{x}')|\Psi(\mathbf{x}')|^2\Psi(\mathbf{x}) = 0 \tag{55.9}$$

which may be interpreted as a self-consistent Hartree equation for the condensate wave function.[1] In this way, the linear term $\hat{K}_l$ vanishes identically, giving an effective quadratic hamiltonian

$$\hat{K}_{\text{eff}} = K_0 + \hat{K}' \tag{55.10}$$

The theory can now be made self-consistent by introducing a statistical operator

$$\hat{\rho}_{\text{eff}} = \frac{e^{-\beta \hat{K}_{\text{eff}}}}{\operatorname{Tr} e^{-\beta \hat{K}_{\text{eff}}}} \tag{55.11}$$

and a corresponding ensemble average

$$\langle \cdots \rangle = \operatorname{Tr}(\hat{\rho}_{\text{eff}} \cdots) \tag{55.12}$$

Since $\hat{K}_{\text{eff}}$ does not commute with $\hat{N}$, the condensate wave function

$$\Psi(\mathbf{x}) = \operatorname{Tr}[\hat{\rho}_{\text{eff}}\,\hat{\psi}(\mathbf{x})] \tag{55.13}$$

may be finite, in contrast to the situation for a normal system.

The remaining formulation follows in direct analogy with the treatment of superconductors given in Sec. 51. We introduce Heisenberg operators

$$\hat{\varphi}_K(\mathbf{x}\tau) = e^{\hat{K}_{\text{eff}}\tau/\hbar}\,\hat{\varphi}(\mathbf{x})\,e^{-\hat{K}_{\text{eff}}\tau/\hbar}$$

$$\hat{\varphi}_K^\dagger(\mathbf{x}\tau) = e^{\hat{K}_{\text{eff}}\tau/\hbar}\,\hat{\varphi}^\dagger(\mathbf{x})\,e^{-\hat{K}_{\text{eff}}\tau/\hbar} \tag{55.14}$$

[1] E. P. Gross, *Ann. Phys. (N.Y.)*, **4**:57 (1958) and *J. Math. Phys.*, **4**:195 (1963).

which satisfy linear field equations

$$\hbar\frac{\partial}{\partial\tau}\hat{\varphi}_K(\mathbf{x}\tau) = -[T(\mathbf{x}) - \mu + \int d^3x'\, V(\mathbf{x}-\mathbf{x}')|\Psi(\mathbf{x}')|^2]\,\hat{\varphi}_K(\mathbf{x}\tau)$$

$$- \int d^3x'\, V(\mathbf{x}-\mathbf{x}')[\Psi^*(\mathbf{x}')\,\hat{\varphi}_K(\mathbf{x}'\,\tau) + \hat{\varphi}_K^\dagger(\mathbf{x}'\,\tau)\Psi(\mathbf{x}')]\Psi(\mathbf{x}) \quad (55.15a)$$

$$\hbar\frac{\partial}{\partial\tau}\hat{\varphi}_K^\dagger(\mathbf{x}\tau) = [T(\mathbf{x}) - \mu + \int d^3x'\, V(\mathbf{x}-\mathbf{x}')|\Psi(\mathbf{x}')|^2]\,\hat{\varphi}_K^\dagger(\mathbf{x}\tau)$$

$$+ \int d^3x'\, V(\mathbf{x}-\mathbf{x}')[\hat{\varphi}_K^\dagger(\mathbf{x}'\,\tau)\Psi(\mathbf{x}') + \Psi^*(\mathbf{x}')\,\hat{\varphi}_K(\mathbf{x}'\,\tau)]\Psi^*(\mathbf{x}) \quad (55.15b)$$

These field operators can be used to define a single-particle Green's function [compare Eq. (19.4)]

$$\mathcal{G}(\mathbf{x}\tau, \mathbf{x}'\,\tau') = -\langle T_\tau[\hat{\psi}_K(\mathbf{x}\tau)\,\hat{\psi}_K^\dagger(\mathbf{x}'\,\tau')]\rangle$$

$$= -\Psi(\mathbf{x})\Psi^*(\mathbf{x}') + \mathcal{G}'(\mathbf{x}\tau, \mathbf{x}'\,\tau') \quad (55.16)$$

where

$$\mathcal{G}'(\mathbf{x}\tau, \mathbf{x}'\,\tau') \equiv -\langle T_\tau[\hat{\varphi}_K(\mathbf{x}\tau)\,\hat{\varphi}_K^\dagger(\mathbf{x}'\,\tau')]\rangle \quad (55.17)$$

measures the deviation from the equilibrium values. The two terms of Eq. (55.16) refer to condensate and noncondensate, respectively, while the cross terms (linear in $\hat{\varphi}$) vanish identically owing to Eq. (55.4). As a corollary, the mean density becomes

$$n(\mathbf{x}) = n_0(\mathbf{x}) + n'(\mathbf{x}) \quad (55.18)$$

where

$$n_0(\mathbf{x}) = |\Psi(\mathbf{x})|^2 \quad (55.19)$$

$$n'(\mathbf{x}) = -\mathcal{G}'(\mathbf{x}\tau, \mathbf{x}\tau^+) \quad (55.20)$$

The equation for $\mathcal{G}'$ can be constructed from Eq. (55.15):

$$\hbar\frac{\partial}{\partial\tau}\mathcal{G}'(\mathbf{x}\tau, \mathbf{x}'\,\tau') = -\hbar\delta(\tau - \tau')\langle[\hat{\varphi}_K(\mathbf{x}\tau), \hat{\varphi}_K^\dagger(\mathbf{x}'\,\tau')]\rangle$$

$$- \left\langle T_\tau\left[\hbar\frac{\partial\hat{\varphi}_K(\mathbf{x}\tau)}{\partial\tau}\,\hat{\varphi}_K^\dagger(\mathbf{x}'\,\tau')\right]\right\rangle \quad (55.21)$$

Equation (55.4) shows that the equal-time commutator on the right side reduces to a delta function, and we readily obtain

$$\left\{-\hbar\frac{\partial}{\partial\tau} - T(\mathbf{x}) + \mu - \int d^3x''\, V(\mathbf{x}-\mathbf{x}'')|\Psi(\mathbf{x}'')|^2\right\}\mathcal{G}'(\mathbf{x}\tau, \mathbf{x}'\,\tau')$$

$$- \int d^3x''\, V(\mathbf{x}-\mathbf{x}'')\Psi(\mathbf{x})[\Psi^*(\mathbf{x}'')\,\mathcal{G}'(\mathbf{x}''\,\tau, \mathbf{x}'\,\tau') + \Psi(\mathbf{x}'')\,\mathcal{G}_{21}'(\mathbf{x}''\,\tau, \mathbf{x}'\,\tau')]$$

$$= \hbar\delta(\tau - \tau')\,\delta(\mathbf{x}-\mathbf{x}') \quad (55.22)$$

where $\mathcal{G}'_{21}$ is an anomalous Green's function [compare Eqs. (20.14b) and (51.12b)]

$$\mathcal{G}'_{21}(\mathbf{x}\tau, \mathbf{x}'\,\tau') \equiv -\langle T_\tau[\hat{\phi}_k^\dagger(\mathbf{x}\tau)\,\hat{\phi}_k^\dagger(\mathbf{x}'\,\tau')]\rangle \tag{55.23}$$

A very similar calculation gives the other equation

$$\left\{\hbar\frac{\partial}{\partial\tau} - T(\mathbf{x}) + \mu - \int d^3x''\, V(\mathbf{x}-\mathbf{x}'')|\Psi'(\mathbf{x}'')|^2\right\}\mathcal{G}'_{21}(\mathbf{x}\tau, \mathbf{x}'\,\tau')$$

$$- \int d^3x''\, V(\mathbf{x}-\mathbf{x}'')\,\Psi'^*(\mathbf{x})\,[\Psi'(\mathbf{x}'')\,\mathcal{G}'_{21}(\mathbf{x}''\,\tau, \mathbf{x}'\,\tau')$$

$$+ \Psi'^*(\mathbf{x}'')\,\mathcal{G}'(\mathbf{x}''\,\tau, \mathbf{x}'\,\tau')] = 0 \tag{55.24}$$

which completely determines the problem. Note that Ψ' appears as a coefficient in Eqs. (55.22) and (55.24). This situation is analogous to the appearance of Δ in Eqs. (51.15) and (51.17), but the self-consistency here is simpler because Ψ' satisfies an uncoupled equation (55.9) instead of the self-consistent gap equation relating Δ and $\mathcal{F}$ [Eq. (51.14)].

In the usual case of a time-independent assembly, $\mathcal{G}'$ and $\mathcal{G}'_{21}$ have a Fourier representation

$$\mathcal{G}'(\mathbf{x}\tau, \mathbf{x}'\,\tau') = (\beta\hbar)^{-1}\sum_n e^{-i\omega_n(\tau-\tau')}\,\mathcal{G}'(\mathbf{x},\mathbf{x}',\omega_n)$$

$$\mathcal{G}'_{21}(\mathbf{x}\tau, \mathbf{x}'\,\tau') = (\beta\hbar)^{-1}\sum_n e^{-i\omega_n(\tau-\tau')}\,\mathcal{G}'_{21}(\mathbf{x},\mathbf{x}',\omega_n) \tag{55.25}$$

where $\omega_n = 2\pi n/\beta\hbar$ is appropriate for bosons. The corresponding equations of motion become

$$[i\hbar\omega_n + (2m)^{-1}\hbar^2\nabla^2 + \mu - \int d^3x''\, V(\mathbf{x}-\mathbf{x}'')|\Psi'(\mathbf{x}'')|^2]\,\mathcal{G}'(\mathbf{x},\mathbf{x}',\omega_n)$$

$$- \int d^3x''\, V(\mathbf{x}-\mathbf{x}'')\,\Psi'(\mathbf{x})\,[\Psi'^*(\mathbf{x}'')\,\mathcal{G}'(\mathbf{x}'',\mathbf{x}',\omega_n)$$

$$+ \Psi'(\mathbf{x}'')\,\mathcal{G}'_{21}(\mathbf{x}'',\mathbf{x}',\omega_n)] = \hbar\delta(\mathbf{x}-\mathbf{x}') \tag{55.26a}$$

$$[-i\hbar\omega_n + (2m)^{-1}\hbar^2\nabla^2 + \mu - \int d^3x''\, V(\mathbf{x}-\mathbf{x}'')|\Psi'(\mathbf{x}'')|^2]\,\mathcal{G}'_{21}(\mathbf{x},\mathbf{x}',\omega_n)$$

$$- \int d^3x''\, V(\mathbf{x}-\mathbf{x}'')\,\Psi'^*(\mathbf{x})\,[\Psi'(\mathbf{x}'')\,\mathcal{G}'_{21}(\mathbf{x}'',\mathbf{x}',\omega_n)$$

$$+ \Psi'^*(\mathbf{x}'')\,\mathcal{G}'(\mathbf{x}'',\mathbf{x}',\omega_n)] = 0 \tag{55.26b}$$

Although these coupled equations can, in principle, be solved for any particular choice of Ψ' that satisfies Eq. (55.9), only a few simple cases have been studied in detail.

UNIFORM CONDENSATE

As a first example, we consider a stationary assembly of bosons at finite temperature, when the condensate wave function is a temperature-dependent constant

$$\Psi'(\mathbf{x}) \equiv [n_0(T)]^{\frac{1}{2}} \tag{55.27}$$

that defines $n_0(T)$. Direct substitution into Eq. (55.9) gives the following relation between the chemical potential and the condensate density

$$\mu = n_0(T) \, V(0) \tag{55.28}$$

where $V(0) \equiv V(\mathbf{k} = 0)$. Furthermore, a Fourier transform solves the coupled integrodifferential equations (55.26) because the coefficients are spatial constants. With the usual definitions

$$\mathscr{G}'(\mathbf{x} - \mathbf{x}', \omega_n) = (2\pi)^{-3} \int d^3k \, e^{i\mathbf{k}\cdot(\mathbf{x}-\mathbf{x}')} \, \mathscr{G}'(\mathbf{k},\omega_n)$$
$$\mathscr{G}'_{21}(\mathbf{x} - \mathbf{x}', \omega_n) = (2\pi)^{-3} \int d^3k \, e^{i\mathbf{k}\cdot(\mathbf{x}-\mathbf{x}')} \, \mathscr{G}'_{21}(\mathbf{k},\omega_n) \tag{55.29}$$

a simple calculation yields [compare Eq. (51.28)]

$$[i\hbar\omega_n - \epsilon_k^0 - n_0 \, V(k)] \, \mathscr{G}'(\mathbf{k},\omega_n) - n_0 \, V(k) \, \mathscr{G}'_{21}(\mathbf{k},\omega_n) = \hbar$$
$$[-i\hbar\omega_n - \epsilon_k^0 - n_0 \, V(k)] \, \mathscr{G}'_{21}(\mathbf{k},\omega_n) - n_0 \, V(k) \, \mathscr{G}'(\mathbf{k},\omega_n) = 0 \tag{55.30}$$

where $\epsilon_k^0 = \hbar^2 k^2 / 2m$ and Eq. (55.28) has been used. These algebraic equations are easily solved:

$$\mathscr{G}'(\mathbf{k},\omega_n) = \frac{-\hbar[i\hbar\omega_n + \epsilon_k^0 + n_0 \, V(k)]}{(\hbar\omega_n)^2 + E_k^2} - \frac{u_k^2}{i\omega_n - E_k/\hbar} - \frac{v_k^2}{i\omega_n + E_k/\hbar} \tag{55.31}$$

$$\mathscr{G}'_{21}(\mathbf{k},\omega_n) = \frac{\hbar n_0 \, V(k)}{(\hbar\omega_n)^2 + E_k^2} = -u_k v_k \left[\frac{1}{i\omega_n - E_k/\hbar} - \frac{1}{i\omega_n + E_k/\hbar} \right] \tag{55.32}$$

where [see Eqs. (21.7) to (21.10)]

$$E_k = \{[\epsilon_k^0 + n_0 \, V(k)]^2 - [n_0 \, V(k)]^2\}^{\frac{1}{2}} = [(\epsilon_k^0)^2 + 2n_0 \, V(k) \, \epsilon_k^0]^{\frac{1}{2}} \tag{55.33}$$

$$v_k^2 = u_k^2 - 1 = \frac{1}{2} \left[\frac{\epsilon_k^0 + n_0 \, V(k)}{E_k} - 1 \right] \tag{55.34a}$$

$$u_k v_k = \frac{n_0 \, V(k)}{2E_k} \tag{55.34b}$$

The present theory is very similar to that treated in Secs. 21 and 35, and most of the same remarks apply. In particular, the usual analytic continuation to real frequency identifies E_k as the single-particle excitation energy, and its long-wavelength behavior

$$E_k \approx \hbar c k \qquad k \to 0 \tag{55.35}$$

$$c = [n_0(T) \, V(0) \, m^{-1}]^{\frac{1}{2}} \tag{55.36}$$

shows that $V(0)$ must be positive. If, in addition, E_k is positive for all $\mathbf{k} \neq 0$, then the Landau critical velocity is finite; thus an imperfect Bose gas is superfluid, whereas an ideal Bose gas is not because c and v_c vanish identically. This is

one of the most important conclusions of Bogoliubov's original calculation,[1] for it demonstrates how the presence of repulsive interactions qualitatively alters the spectrum, leading to a linear dispersion relation as $k \to 0$.

It is interesting to study the temperature variation of the parameters n_0 and n'. A combination of Eqs. (55.20) and (55.31) gives

$$n'(T) = -\int \frac{d^3k}{(2\pi)^3} (\beta\hbar)^{-1} \sum_n \left(\frac{u_k^2}{i\omega_n - E_k/\hbar} - \frac{v_k^2}{i\omega_n + E_k/\hbar} \right) e^{i\omega_n\eta}$$

$$= \int \frac{d^3k}{(2\pi)^3} \left(\frac{u_k^2}{e^{\beta E_k} - 1} + \frac{v_k^2}{1 - e^{-\beta E_k}} \right) \tag{55.37}$$

where the sum has been evaluated with Eq. (25.38) and the parameters E_k, u_k, and v_k depend on temperature through $n_0(T)$. For low temperature and weak interactions, however, we may set $n_0(T) \approx n_0(0)$ in Eq. (55.37). A simple rearrangement yields

$$n'(T) - n'(0) \approx \int \frac{d^3k}{(2\pi)^3} \frac{(u_k^2 + v_k^2)|_{T=0}}{e^{E_k/k_B T} - 1}$$

$$\approx \frac{m}{12\hbar^3 c} (k_B T)^2 \qquad T \to 0$$

where $n'(0)$ is the noncondensate density [compare Eq. (21.15)] and $c = [n_0(0) V(0)/m]^{\frac{1}{2}}$ is the speed of sound, both at $T = 0$. Since the total density is independent of temperature, the condensate must be depleted according to the relation.[2]

$$n_0(T) = n_0(0) - \frac{m}{12\hbar^3 c} (k_B T)^2 \qquad T \to 0 \tag{55.38}$$

This equation may also be expressed in terms of the macroscopic condensate wave function

$$1 - \frac{\Psi(T)}{\Psi(0)} = \frac{m(k_B T)^2}{24\hbar^3 c n_0(0)} \qquad T \to 0 \tag{55.39}$$

showing that the temperature-dependent part of Ψ varies as T^2. In addition, we have seen that $|\Psi|^2$ is always less than n because the interparticle potential introduces higher Fourier components even at $T = 0$.

[1] N. N. Bogoliubov, *J. Phys. (USSR)*, **11**:23 (1947).
[2] If the second term on the right is multiplied by a factor $n_0(0)/n$, which is ≈ 1 in the present model [see Eqs. (21.15) and (22.14)], the resulting equation correctly describes a Bose system with an arbitrary short-range repulsive potential, as long as c is interpreted as the actual speed of sound at $T = 0$ [K. Kehr, *Z. Physik*, **221**:291 (1969)].

It is interesting to compare $|\Psi(T)|^2$ with the superfluid density $\rho_s(T)$, which can be defined through the linear response of the system to an external perturbation.   The Landau quasiparticle model predicts [see Eq. (54.25a)]

$$1 - \frac{\rho_s(T)}{\rho} = \frac{2\pi^2\hbar}{45c\rho}\left(\frac{k_B T}{\hbar c}\right)^4 \qquad T \to 0 \tag{55.40}$$

so that $\rho_s(T=0) = \rho$, with temperature-dependent corrections $\propto T^4$.[1]   It is clear that there is no direct connection between $\rho_s(T)$ and $|\Psi(T)|^2$ because these physical quantities have different temperature dependence and different values at $T = 0$ (see also Prob. 14.9).[2]   We have already discussed the measurement of $\rho_s(T)$ in Sec. 54.   The corresponding experimental determination of $n_0(T)$ is much more difficult; nevertheless it may be possible to observe anomalous quasielastic scattering (see Sec. 17) of energetic neutrons (≈ 1 eV) from He II below T_λ.[3]

NONUNIFORM CONDENSATE

We now turn to spatially nonuniform systems, where $\Psi(\mathbf{x})$ must be determined from the nonlinear integrodifferential equation (55.9).   It is often convenient to write

$$\Psi(\mathbf{x}) = F(\mathbf{x})\, e^{i\varphi(\mathbf{x})} \tag{55.41}$$

where F and φ are real.   Since the total particle current is obtained from the relation

$$\mathbf{j}(\mathbf{x}) = \frac{-\hbar}{2mi}[(\boldsymbol{\nabla} - \boldsymbol{\nabla}')\, \mathscr{G}(\mathbf{x}\tau, \mathbf{x}'\,\tau^+)]_{\mathbf{x}'=\mathbf{x}} \tag{55.42}$$

the contribution $\mathbf{j}_0(\mathbf{x})$ of the condensate becomes

$$\mathbf{j}_0(\mathbf{x}) = \frac{\hbar}{2mi}[\Psi^*(\mathbf{x})\boldsymbol{\nabla}\Psi(\mathbf{x}) - \Psi(\mathbf{x})\boldsymbol{\nabla}\Psi^*(\mathbf{x})]$$

$$= \frac{\hbar}{m}[F(\mathbf{x})]^2\,\boldsymbol{\nabla}\varphi(\mathbf{x}) = n_0(\mathbf{x})\frac{\hbar}{m}\boldsymbol{\nabla}\varphi(\mathbf{x}) \tag{55.43}$$

where $n_0 \equiv F^2$ is the condensate density.   This equation identifies the condensate velocity as [compare Eq. (54.2)]

$$\mathbf{v}_0(\mathbf{x}) = \frac{\hbar}{m}\boldsymbol{\nabla}\varphi(\mathbf{x}) \tag{55.44}$$

[1] Equation (55.40) and the phonon specific heat ($\propto T^3$) obtained from Eq. (54.19) have also been derived from the microscopic theory to all orders in perturbation theory by K. Kehr, *Physica*, **33**:620 (1967) and by W. Götze and H. Wagner, *Physica*, **31**:475 (1965), respectively.
[2] In the special case of an ideal Bose gas, these two quantities coincide; see Probs. 14.6 and 14.11.
[3] P. C. Hohenberg and P. M. Platzman, *Phys. Rev.*, **152**:198 (1966).

Note that $\mathbf{v}_0(\mathbf{x})$ is automatically irrotational [Eq. (54.1)] whenever $|\boldsymbol{\nabla}\varphi|$ is bounded, because $\mathbf{v}_0$ is proportional to the gradient of the phase of Ψ. If Ψ is assumed to be single valued, then the line integral of Eq. (55.44) around a closed path lying wholly in the condensate immediately gives the quantization of circulation in units of h/m [Eq. (54.10)], just as in Eq. (50.31).

For simplicity, we approximate the interparticle potential by a repulsive delta function

$$V(\mathbf{x}) = g\delta(\mathbf{x}) \tag{55.45}$$

and Eq. (55.9) then becomes the Gross-Pitaevskii equation[1]

$$\left(\frac{\hbar^2\,\nabla^2}{2m} + \mu\right)\Psi(\mathbf{x}) - g|\Psi(\mathbf{x})|^2\,\Psi(\mathbf{x}) = 0 \tag{55.46}$$

If Eq. (55.41) is substituted into (55.46), the imaginary and real parts can be written as

$$\boldsymbol{\nabla}\cdot\left(F^2\frac{\hbar\boldsymbol{\nabla}\varphi}{m}\right) = \boldsymbol{\nabla}\cdot\mathbf{j}_0 = 0 \tag{55.47}$$

$$\frac{\mu}{m} = \frac{F^2 g}{m} - \frac{\hbar^2}{2m^2\,F}\nabla^2 F + \frac{1}{2}\left(\frac{\hbar\boldsymbol{\nabla}\varphi}{m}\right)^2$$

$$= \frac{F^2 g}{m} - \frac{\hbar^2}{2m^2\,F}\nabla^2 F + \tfrac{1}{2}\mathbf{v}_0^2 \tag{55.48}$$

These equations are readily recognized as the continuity equation for the condensate and a quantum analog of Bernoulli's equation for steady flow.

As an example of a nonuniform system, consider a stationary condensate confined to a semi-infinite domain $(z > 0)$. The boundary condition will be taken as $\Psi = 0$ at $z = 0$ since Eq. (55.46) is similar to a one-particle Schrödinger equation. In this one-dimensional geometry, Ψ takes the form

$$\Psi(\mathbf{x}) = n_0^{\frac{1}{2}}f(z) \tag{55.49}$$

where the real function f satisfies the equation [see Eq. (55.46)]

$$\frac{\hbar^2}{2mn_0\,g}\frac{d^2f}{dz^2} + \frac{\mu}{n_0\,g}f - f^3 = 0 \tag{55.50}$$

We choose the normalization $f \to 1$ as $z \to \infty$, and the asymptotic behavior of Eq. (55.50) gives

$$\mu = n_0\,g \tag{55.51}$$

[1] This equation is *formally* identical with a Ginzburg-Landau type of field equation for $\rho_s^{\frac{1}{2}}$ valid near T_c [V. L. Ginzburg and L. P. Pitaevskii, *Sov. Phys.-JETP*, **7**:858 (1958)], but the physical interpretation is different. In the present context, Eq. (55.46) was first studied by E. P. Gross, *Nuovo Cimento*, **20**:454 (1961) and by L. P. Pitaevskii, *Sov. Phys.-JETP*, **13**:451 (1961).

just as in Eq. (55.28).   The natural scale length for spatial variation in Ψ is given by [compare Eq. (50.18)]

$$\xi = \left(\frac{\hbar^2}{2mn_0 g}\right)^{\frac{1}{2}} \tag{55.52}$$

while the proper solution of Eq. (55.50) has already been obtained in Eq. (50.20)

$$f(z) = \tanh\frac{z}{\sqrt{2}\,\xi} \tag{55.53}$$

Thus the condensate density vanishes at the wall and rises to its asymptotic value n_0 in a characteristic length ξ.   It is interesting that this same length also occurs in a uniform system with a delta-function potential [see Eq. (21.14)], for the excitation spectrum E_k changes from linear to quadratic at the value $k \approx \xi^{-1}$.

To explore the implications of Eq. (55.53), we evaluate the energy σ per unit area associated with the formation of the surface layer.   The number of condensate particles per unit area contained in a large region $0 < z < L$ is given by Eq. (55.19)[1]

$$N_0 = n_0 \int_0^L dz \tanh^2 \frac{z}{\sqrt{2}\,\xi}$$

$$= n_0 \int_0^L dz \left(1 - \text{sech}^2 \frac{z}{\sqrt{2}\,\xi}\right)$$

$$\approx n_0 L - n_0 \sqrt{2}\,\xi \tag{55.54}$$

where L is assumed to be much larger than ξ.   Similarly, the total condensate energy per unit area becomes [see Eq. (55.6)]

$$E_0 = \int_0^L dz \left(-\Psi^* \frac{\hbar^2 \nabla^2}{2m}\Psi + \tfrac{1}{2}g|\Psi|^4\right)$$

$$= \tfrac{1}{2}n_0^2 g \int_0^L dz \left(1 - \text{sech}^4 \frac{z}{\sqrt{2}\,\xi}\right)$$

$$\approx \tfrac{1}{2}n_0^2 gL - \tfrac{1}{3}n_0^2 g\xi\sqrt{2} \tag{55.55}$$

Most of this energy arises from the interparticle repulsion and also occurs for a uniform system.   We therefore define the surface energy σ as the difference between the total energy E_0 and the energy of the same number of particles

----

[1] The length L is here considered a mathematical cutoff with no physical significance, but the same calculation also describes a physical channel of width $2L \gg \xi$ since the resulting $\Psi(x)$ is symmetric.

uniformly distributed

$$\sigma = E_0 - \tfrac{1}{2} N_0^2 g L^{-1}$$

$$\approx \frac{\sqrt{2}\, \hbar^2 n_0}{3} \frac{1}{m\xi} \approx \frac{\rho \kappa c}{3\pi} \tag{55.56}$$

where we have used Eq. (55.54) for N_0 and set $mn_0 \approx mn = \rho$ in the last line. This surface energy contains both the (positive) kinetic energy associated with the curvature of the wave function and the (positive) compressional work involved in moving particles from the surface to the bulk of the fluid, where the density is slightly increased. Although the present model applies only if the surface layer is much thicker than the interparticle spacing ($n\xi^3 \gg 1$), the last form of Eq. (55.56) remains well defined even for a strongly interacting system where $n\xi^3 \approx 1$. With the numerical values appropriate for He II, we find $\sigma \approx 0.36$ erg/cm^2, in good agreement with the observed low-temperature surface tension ≈ 0.34 dyne/cm $\equiv 0.34$ erg/cm^2.

As a second example of a nonuniform system, consider an unbounded condensate of the form[1]

$$\Psi(\mathbf{x}) = n_0^{\frac{1}{2}} e^{i\theta} f(r) \tag{55.57}$$

where (r,θ) are plane-polar coordinates and $f(r)$ is real, approaching 1 as $r \to \infty$. Equation (55.44) immediately gives

$$\mathbf{v}_0(\mathbf{x}) = \frac{\hbar}{mr} \hat{\theta} \tag{55.58}$$

so that Eq. (55.57) represents a singly quantized vortex with circulation h/m [see Eq. (54.8)]. The Gross-Pitaevskii equation reduces to

$$\frac{\hbar^2}{2m}\left(\frac{1}{r}\frac{d}{dr}r\frac{d}{dr} - \frac{1}{r^2}\right)f + \mu f - n_0 g f^3 = 0 \tag{55.59}$$

whose asymptotic behavior again leads to Eq. (55.51). It is convenient to introduce the dimensionless variable $\zeta = r/\xi$:

$$\frac{d^2 f}{d\zeta^2} + \frac{1}{\zeta}\frac{df}{d\zeta} - \frac{1}{\zeta^2}f + f - f^3 = 0 \tag{55.60}$$

For small ζ, the centrifugal barrier dominates the solution, which takes the form

$$f(\zeta) = C\zeta \qquad \zeta \ll 1 \tag{55.61}$$

where C is a numerical constant. This result shows that the particle density falls to zero in a region of radius ξ, which may be interpreted as the vortex core.

---

[1] V. L. Ginzburg and L. P. Pitaevskii, *loc. cit.*; E. P. Gross, *Nuovo Cimento*, *loc. cit.*; L. P. Pitaevskii, *loc. cit.*

To clarify this result, we combine Eqs. (55.36) and (55.52) to give

$$c = \frac{\kappa}{2\pi\sqrt{2}\,\xi} \qquad (55.62)$$

showing that the core radius ξ may be interpreted as the point where the circulating superfluid velocity becomes comparable with the speed of sound [see Eq. (54.8)]. This criterion is independent of the strength of the potential; for He II, Eq. (55.62) gives $\xi \approx \frac{1}{2}$ Å, in rough agreement with the observed value ≈ 1 Å.[1]

For large ζ, an expansion in powers of ζ^{-2} yields

$$f(\zeta) \sim 1 - (2\zeta^2)^{-1} \qquad \zeta \to \infty \qquad (55.63)$$

Note that the density perturbation here vanishes algebraically rather than exponentially as was the case for a semi-infinite domain; this difference arises from the long-range circulating velocity field around the vortex. The exact solution $f(\zeta)$ must be obtained numerically (Fig. 55.1), while the corresponding

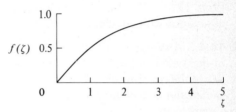

Fig. 55.1 Radial wave function for a singly quantized vortex. The curve was plotted from the numerical solution to Eq. (55.60) of M. P. Kawatra and R. K. Pathria, *Phys. Rev.*, **151**:132 (1966).

numerical calculation of the energy E_v per unit length associated with the vortex gives[2]

$$E_v = \frac{\pi\hbar^2 n_0}{m} \ln\frac{1.46R}{\xi} \approx \frac{\rho\kappa^2}{4\pi}\ln\frac{1.46R}{\xi} \qquad (55.64)$$

Here R is a cutoff at large distances that may be interpreted as the radius of the container, and we again take $n_0 \approx n$ in the last form. This expression is analogous to that for a classical vortex (54.11), but the core region is now well defined without recourse to special models. The quantity E_v determines the critical angular velocity for the formation of quantized vortices in a rotating cylinder of He II (Prob. 14.3). For $R \approx 1$ mm, experiments[3] confirm that $\ln(R/\xi) \approx 16$.

PROBLEMS

14.1. Use the Clausius-Clapeyron equation to discuss the melting curves for He³ and He⁴ in Fig. 54.1. Devise a theory of the minimum in the melting curve

[1] G. W. Rayfield and F. Reif, *loc. cit.*
[2] V. L. Ginzburg and L. P. Pitaevskii, *loc. cit.*; L. P. Pitaevskii, *loc. cit.*
[3] G. B. Hess and W. M. Fairbank, *Phys. Rev. Letters*, **19**:216 (1967).

of He^3 based on the observation that Curie's law describes the magnetic susceptibility of solid He^3 down to a few millidegrees. What happens to the melting curve as $T \to 0$?

14.2. (a) If $\mathbf{v(r)} = \omega \hat{z} \times \mathbf{r}$, prove that $\operatorname{curl} \mathbf{v} = 2\omega \hat{z}$. Hence deduce that $\oint_C d\mathbf{l} \cdot \mathbf{v} = 2\omega A$ where $A = \int d\mathbf{S} \cdot \hat{z}$ is the area enclosed by the contour C.
(b) If $\mathbf{v(r)} = (\kappa/2\pi r)\hat{\theta}$, prove that $\operatorname{curl} \mathbf{v} = \kappa \hat{z}\delta(\mathbf{r})$ where $\mathbf{r}$ is a two-dimensional vector in the xy plane. Hence prove that $\oint_C d\mathbf{l} \cdot \mathbf{v} = \kappa N_C$ where N_C is the number of vortices enclosed in C, and verify the discussion below Eq. (54.8).

14.3. Consider a system rotating at angular velocity ω.
(a) Prove that the equilibrium states are determined by minimizing the "free energy" $F - \omega L$, where L is the angular momentum and F is the Helmholtz free energy.
(b) For a superfluid in a rotating cylinder of radius R show that the critical angular velocity ω_{c1} for the creation of a single vortex is given by $\omega_{c1} = (\kappa/2\pi R^2) \times \ln(R/\xi)$ where ξ is the radius of the core. Compare your calculation with Prob. 13.5. Why can a quantized flux line in a superconductor be interpreted as a vortex with circulation $h/2m_e$?

14.4. A system of N classical particles has a total energy E and a total center-of-mass momentum $\mathbf{P}$. Maximize the entropy subject to these constraints and derive the equilibrium distribution function $f(\epsilon - \hbar \mathbf{k} \cdot \mathbf{v})$, where $f(\epsilon)$ is the usual Boltzmann distribution function and $\mathbf{v}$ is a Lagrange multiplier. Compute the ensemble average of $\partial \epsilon/\partial \mathbf{k}$ and hence identify $\mathbf{v}$.[‡]

14.5. Derive the density of phonons and rotons [Eqs. (54.19a) and (54.20a)], and find the corresponding contributions to the free energy, the specific heat, and the normal-fluid density ρ_n [Eqs. (54.25)].

14.6. Use Eq. (54.23) to show that $\rho_n = \rho$ for any noninteracting nonrelativistic gas, except for an ideal Bose gas below its transition temperature T_0, where $\rho_n = \rho(T/T_0)^{\frac{3}{2}}$.

14.7. Consider a dense charged Bose gas in a uniform background where the excitation spectrum is $\epsilon_k = [(\hbar\Omega_{pl})^2 + (\hbar^2 k^2/2m_B)^2]^{\frac{1}{2}}$ (Probs. 6.5 and 10.2). Use the Landau quasiparticle model to show that the critical velocity and the normal-fluid density at low temperature are given by

$$v_c = 1.32 r_s^{-\frac{3}{4}} \frac{e^2}{\hbar}$$

$$\frac{\rho_n}{\rho} \approx 0.360 r_s^{\frac{9}{8}} \left(\frac{2a_0 k_B T}{e^2}\right)^{\frac{1}{4}} \exp\left(-3.46 r_s^{-\frac{3}{2}} \frac{e^2}{2a_0 k_B T}\right) \qquad T \to 0$$

where $n = 3/4\pi r_s^3 a_0^3$, $a_0 = \hbar^2/m_B e^2$ is the Bohr radius, and $e^2/\hbar$ is the velocity in the lowest Bohr orbit. Discuss the numerical values involved if $m_B \approx m_{He}$.

‡ F. London, "Superfluids," vol. II, pp. 95–96, Dover Publications, Inc., New York, 1964.

14.8. (a) Show that the single-particle Green's function for a perfect Bose gas below its transition temperature is given by $\mathscr{G}^0(\mathbf{k},\omega_m) = -(2\pi)^3 \beta\hbar n_0\,\delta(\mathbf{k})\,\delta_{m0} + (i\omega_m - \epsilon_k^0/\hbar)^{-1}$.

(b) Use Eqs. (25.25) and (26.10) to rederive the results of Sec. 5.

14.9. Consider a weakly interacting Bose gas with a uniform condensate that moves with velocity **v**.

(a) Show that $\Psi(x) = n_0^{\frac{1}{2}} e^{i m \mathbf{v}\cdot\mathbf{x}/\hbar}$ and solve Eq. (55.9) for μ.

(b) Using this expression for $\Psi(x)$, solve Eqs. (55.26) for $\mathscr{G}'$ and $\mathscr{G}'_{21}$. Compare with the solution obtained in Prob. 6.6.

(c) Prove that n' is unaltered at $T = 0$ until v exceeds the Landau critical velocity for the Bogoliubov excitation spectrum E_k. At finite temperatures, show that the second term on the right side of Eq. (55.38) is multiplied by $(1 - v^2/c^2)^{-1}$.

(d) Express the total-momentum density $V^{-1}\langle\mathbf{P}\rangle$ in terms of $\mathscr{G}'$. Expand to first order in **v**, and verify that $V^{-1}\langle\mathbf{P}\rangle = [\rho - \rho_n(T)]\mathbf{v}$, where ρ_n is given by the Landau expression Eq. (54.23). Evaluate $\rho_n(T)$ for $T \to 0$ and compare with Eq. (54.25a).

(e) Repeat Prob. 13.13 for this system.

14.10. (a) Derive the remaining equations of motion [compare Eqs. (20.18), (55.22), and (55.24)] for the matrix Green's function $\mathscr{G}'(x\tau, x'\,\tau') \equiv -\langle T_\tau[\hat{\Phi}_K(x\tau) \times \hat{\Phi}_K^{\dagger}(x'\,\tau')]\rangle$ in a weakly interacting Bose gas.

(b) Repeat the calculations of Prob. 13.15 for this system and compare your results with those for a superconductor. The normalization condition must now be written $\int d^3x\,(|u_j^{(\pm)}|^2 - |v_j^{(\pm)}|^2) = \pm 1$, where $\pm$ refers to the sign of the energy eigenvalue.

14.11. Use the methods developed in Sec. 52 to study the linear response of a condensed *noninteracting* charged Bose gas to a transverse vector potential $\mathbf{A}(xt)$. In the long-wavelength static limit, show that the induced current obeys the London equation (49.29) with a temperature-dependent coefficient $n_s(T)/n = 1 - (T/T_0)^{\frac{3}{2}}$ (compare Prob. 14.6), and hence exhibit the Meissner effect.‡

14.12. (a) Generalize Prob. 14.11 to a dense *interacting* charged Bose gas in a uniform background. Use the analog of Eq. (51.6) to derive a modified London equation with a temperature-dependent coefficient

$$\frac{n_s(T)}{n} = \frac{\rho_s(T)}{\rho} = 1 - \frac{\rho_n(T)}{\rho}$$

where $\rho_n(T)/\rho$ is given in Prob. 14.7.

(b) At high density and zero temperature show that the electrodynamics is local, apart from corrections of order $r_s^{\frac{3}{4}}$.

‡ V. L. Ginzburg, *Usp. Fiz. Nauk*, **48**:25 (1952) [German translation: *Fortsch. Phys.*, **1**:101 (1953)]; M. R. Schafroth, *Phys. Rev.*, **100**:463 (1955).

14.13. Solve Eq. (55.46) for a stationary condensate in a channel of width d, and discuss the transition between the limiting cases $d \gg \xi$ and $d \ll \xi$. Compare the resulting density profile with that for an ideal Bose gas. Assume $N_0 \approx N$, which neglects the noncondensate, and take $N \propto d$.

14.14. Consider a semi-infinite domain ($z > 0$), where the condensate moves uniformly with velocity $\mathbf{v} = v\hat{x}$. Assume that the asymptotic density at infinity is given by the results of Prob. 14.9 for an infinite medium, and solve Eq. (55.46) for $\Psi'(z)$. Discuss how $n_0(z)$ varies with v.

14.15. Show that Eq. (55.46) for Ψ' can be obtained from a variational principle for the energy keeping the number of condensate particles fixed. As a particular example, consider a hard sphere of radius R in an infinite medium, where the condensate wave function takes the form $\Psi'(\mathbf{x}) = n_0^{\frac{1}{2}} f(r)$ with $f(R) = 0$ and $f(\infty) = 1$. Use the trial function $f(r) = 1 - e^{-(r-R)/l}$ and determine the effective surface thickness l. In the limit $R \to \infty$ show that $l = (6\hbar^2/11mn_0 g)^{\frac{1}{2}}$ and that the corresponding surface energy becomes $\sigma = 0.479\hbar^2 n_0/m\xi$ [compare Eq. (55.56)].

14.16. Use the variational principle from Prob. 14.15 to study a vortex in the condensate. Assume a radial function of the form $f(r) = r(r^2 + l^2)^{-\frac{1}{2}}$ and show that $l^2 = 2\xi^2$ is the best choice. Hence derive the approximate result $E_v = (\pi\hbar^2 n_0/m)\ln(1.497R/\xi)$ and compare with Eq. (55.64).

15
Applications to Finite Systems: The Atomic Nucleus

A finite interacting assembly is much more complicated than a uniform medium. Indeed, it is a major task just to generate the Hartree-Fock wave functions for a finite system, whereas in a uniform medium, translational invariance requires these wave functions to be simply plane waves (see Sec. 10).

Since the single-particle states present such a difficult problem, any practical application of many-body techniques is necessarily much less sophisticated than those discussed so far. Nevertheless, we shall see that second quantization, canonical transformations, Green's functions, and the independent-pair approximation provide powerful tools for discussing the properties of a finite many-particle assembly.

For definiteness, we concentrate on atomic nuclei, but the same techniques also apply to atoms or molecules. Hence we defer the specific problems arising

from the singular nature of the nucleon-nucleon force until the last section in this chapter.

For a finite assembly, the angular momentum plays a crucial role, and a brief review of this subject is given in Appendix B.[1]   The rotational invariance of the total hamiltonian implies that all the eigenstates can be labeled by $|JM\rangle$.[2] In addition, the eigenstates are labeled by their parity π because the invariance of the strong interactions under inversions implies that parity is also a good quantum number.

56□GENERAL CANONICAL TRANSFORMATION TO PARTICLES AND HOLES

We start by performing a general canonical transformation to particles and holes. In the first approximation, the ground state of the core (see Fig. 56.1) is assumed to be a set of completely filled single-particle levels, whose exact nature will be specified shortly.   For a spherically symmetric system, these single-particle states can always be characterized by the quantum numbers[3] $|\alpha\rangle \equiv |nlsjm_j\rangle$ with $s = \frac{1}{2}$ and $j = |l \pm \frac{1}{2}|$.   The parity of these states is $(-1)^l$.   It is convenient to make the m dependence explicit by using the notation

$$|\alpha\rangle \equiv |a,m_\alpha\rangle \tag{56.1a}$$

$$|\ \alpha\rangle \equiv |a,-m_\alpha\rangle \tag{56.1b}$$

where $\{a\}$ denotes the quantum numbers $\{nlsj\}$.   Assume the single-particle quantum numbers to be ordered with F a number that lies between the last fully occupied and first unoccupied (or partially occupied) state, as illustrated in Fig. 56.1.

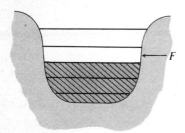

Fig. 56.1   Hartree-Fock ground state of the core.

[1] We follow the angular-momentum notation of A. R. Edmonds, "Angular Momentum in Quantum Mechanics," Princeton University Press, Princeton, N.J., 1957.

[2] The exact eigenstates can be characterized by the center-of-mass momentum $\mathbf{P}_{cm}$ and the angular momentum $|JM\rangle$ in the center-of-mass frame, but the dependence on $\mathbf{P}_{cm}$ will not be made explicit (see, however, Prob. 15.18).   We shall generally study the behavior of valence nucleons moving about a heavy inert core.   To a good approximation, the total center of mass then coincides with that of the core.

[3] For clarity, we assume initially that the system is composed of just one type of fermion.   The isotopic spin of the nucleon leads to slight modifications, which are discussed at the end of this section.

If the general fermion creation and destruction operators are denoted by $c_\alpha^\dagger$ and c_α, then the particle and hole operators can be defined by the relations

$$a_\alpha^\dagger \equiv c_\alpha^\dagger \qquad \alpha > F \tag{56.2a}$$

$$b_\alpha^\dagger \equiv S_{-\alpha} c_{-\alpha} \qquad \alpha < F \tag{56.2b}$$

where we adopt the phase convention

$$S_\alpha \equiv (-1)^{j_\alpha - m_\alpha} \tag{56.3}$$

This is clearly a canonical transformation, for it leaves the anticommutation rules unaltered

$$\{a_\alpha, a_\alpha^\dagger\} = \{b_\alpha, b_\alpha^\dagger\} = \delta_{\alpha\alpha'}$$

$$\text{All other anticommutators} = 0 \tag{56.4}$$

The m-dependent phase in Eq. (56.2b) guarantees that the operator $b_\alpha^\dagger$ creates a hole with angular momentum $|j_\alpha m_\alpha\rangle$, which may be proved by showing that $b_\alpha^\dagger$ is an irreducible tensor operator of rank j_α and component m_α. It is first necessary to construct the angular-momentum operator for the system

$$\hat{\mathbf{J}} = \sum_{\alpha\beta} c_\alpha^\dagger \langle \alpha | \mathbf{J} | \beta \rangle c_\beta$$

$$= \sum_{nljmm'>F} a_{nljm}^\dagger \langle jm | \mathbf{J} | jm' \rangle a_{nljm'}$$

$$+ \sum_{nljmm'<F} \langle jm | \mathbf{J} | jm' \rangle (-1)^{j-m} b_{nlj,\,-m} (-1)^{j-m'} b_{nlj,\,-m'}^\dagger \tag{56.5}$$

where the second line follows because the single-particle matrix elements of $\mathbf{J}$ are diagonal in $\{nlj\}$ and independent of n and l. The last two operators can be written $(-1)^{j-m} b_{nlj,\,-m} (-1)^{j-m'} b_{nlj,\,-m'}^\dagger = (-1)^{m-m'} (\delta_{mm'} - b_{nlj,\,-m'}^\dagger b_{nlj,\,-m})$, and the first term in parentheses makes no contribution to Eq. (56.5) because

$$\sum_m \langle m | \mathbf{J} | m \rangle = \hat{z} \sum_m m = 0$$

Furthermore, the Wigner-Eckart theorem shows that the matrix element of J_{1q} satisfies[1] $\langle jm | J_{1q} | jm' \rangle = (-1)^{m'-m+1} \langle j, -m' | J_{1q} | j, -m \rangle$. With the change of summation variables $(m, m' \to -m', -m)$, the angular momentum operator finally becomes

$$\hat{\mathbf{J}} = \sum_{nljmm'>F} a_{nljm}^\dagger \langle jm | \mathbf{J} | jm' \rangle a_{nljm'} + \sum_{nljmm'<F} b_{nljm}^\dagger \langle jm | \mathbf{J} | jm' \rangle b_{nljm'} \tag{56.6}$$

[1] We use the general tensor notation T_{KQ} discussed in Appendix B.

The proof that $b_\alpha^\dagger$ is a tensor operator now follows immediately from the relations

$$[\hat{\mathbf{J}}, b_{am_\alpha}^\dagger] = \sum_{\beta\gamma} \langle \beta | \mathbf{J} | \gamma \rangle \, [b_\beta^\dagger b_\gamma, b_\alpha^\dagger]$$

$$= \sum_{\beta\gamma} \langle \beta | \mathbf{J} | \gamma \rangle \, \delta_{\alpha\gamma} b_\beta^\dagger$$

$$= \sum_{m_\alpha'} \langle j_\alpha m_\alpha' | \mathbf{J} | j_\alpha m_\alpha \rangle \, b_{am_\alpha'}^\dagger \tag{56.7}$$

which serve to define such an operator.

The general canonical transformation to particles and holes can therefore be written

$$c_\gamma = \theta(\gamma - F)\, a_\gamma + \theta(F - \gamma)\, S_\gamma\, b_{-\gamma}^\dagger \tag{56.8a}$$

$$c_\gamma^\dagger = \theta(\gamma - F)\, a_\gamma^\dagger + \theta(F - \gamma)\, S_\gamma\, b_{-\gamma} \tag{56.8b}$$

and the next task is to write the total hamiltonian

$$\hat{H} = \sum_{\alpha\beta} c_\alpha^\dagger \langle \alpha | T | \beta \rangle c_\beta + \tfrac{1}{2} \sum_{\alpha\beta\gamma\delta} c_\alpha^\dagger c_\beta^\dagger \langle \alpha\beta | V | \gamma\delta \rangle c_\delta c_\gamma \tag{56.9}$$

in normal-ordered form with respect to the new particle and hole operators. Just as in Sec. 37, Wick's theorem can simplify the calculation. We write

$$N(c_\alpha^\dagger c_\beta) + c_\alpha^{\dagger\cdot} c_\beta^\cdot \equiv c_\alpha^\dagger c_\beta \tag{56.10}$$

where N now stands for the normal ordering with respect to the new operators. Take matrix elements of Eq. (56.10) with respect to the new vacuum $|0\rangle$ defined by

$$a_\alpha |0\rangle = b_\alpha |0\rangle = 0 \tag{56.11}$$

(i.e., the approximate core ground state shown in Fig. 56.1). It follows that

$$c_\alpha^{\dagger\cdot} c_\beta^\cdot = \langle 0 | c_\alpha^\dagger c_\beta | 0 \rangle = \theta(F - \alpha)\, \delta_{\alpha\beta} \tag{56.12}$$

while the other contractions vanish

$$c_\alpha^{\dagger\cdot} c_\beta^{\dagger\cdot} = c_\alpha^\cdot c_\beta^\cdot = 0 \tag{56.13}$$

The quantities appearing in Eq. (56.9) can now be evaluated with Wick's theorem

$$c_\alpha^\dagger c_\beta = \delta_{\alpha\beta}\, \theta(F - \alpha) + N(c_\alpha^\dagger c_\beta) \tag{56.14}$$

$$c_\alpha^\dagger c_\beta^\dagger c_\delta c_\gamma = (\delta_{\alpha\gamma}\delta_{\beta\delta} - \delta_{\alpha\delta}\delta_{\beta\gamma})\, \theta(F - \alpha)\, \theta(F - \beta) + 2\delta_{\alpha\gamma}\, \theta(F - \alpha)\, N(c_\beta^\dagger c_\delta)$$

$$- 2\delta_{\alpha\delta}\, \theta(F - \alpha)\, N(c_\beta^\dagger c_\gamma) + N(c_\alpha^\dagger c_\beta^\dagger c_\delta c_\gamma) \tag{56.15}$$

where the symmetry $\langle \alpha\beta | V | \gamma\delta \rangle = \langle \beta\alpha | V | \delta\gamma \rangle$ has been used to combine terms that give the same contribution when summed over the indices $\alpha\beta\gamma\delta$.

When Eqs. (56.14) and (56.15) are substituted into Eq. (56.9), the hamiltonian separates into a c-number part, a part containing $N(c^\dagger c)$, and a part containing $N(c^\dagger c^\dagger cc)$. Although this result is valid for any set of single-particle

states, we shall now choose the particular set that diagonalizes the quadratic part of the transformed hamiltonian. A simple calculation yields the condition

$$\langle \beta | T | \delta \rangle + \sum_{\alpha < F} [\langle \alpha\beta | V | \alpha\delta \rangle - \langle \alpha\beta | V | \delta\alpha \rangle] = \epsilon_\beta \delta_{\beta\delta} \tag{56.16}$$

which is just the energy-eigenvalue equation derived from the Hartree-Fock single-particle equations of Sec. 10. Consequently, if the single-particle wave functions φ satisfy[1]

$$T\varphi_\delta(2) + \sum_{\alpha < F} [\int \varphi_\alpha(1)^\dagger V(1,2) \varphi_\alpha(1) \varphi_\delta(2) d^3 x_1$$
$$- \int \varphi_\alpha(1)^\dagger V(1,2) \varphi_\delta(1) \varphi_\alpha(2) d^3 x_1] = \epsilon_\delta \varphi_\delta(2) \tag{56.17}$$

then the total hamiltonian takes the form

$$\hat{H} = H_0 + \hat{H}_1 + \hat{H}_2 \tag{56.18}$$

with

$$H_0 = \sum_{\alpha < F} (T_\alpha + \tfrac{1}{2} V_\alpha) \tag{56.19}$$

$$\hat{H}_1 = \sum_{\alpha > F} \epsilon_\alpha a_\alpha^\dagger a_\alpha - \sum_{\alpha < F} \epsilon_\alpha b_{-\alpha}^\dagger b_{-\alpha} \tag{56.20}$$

$$\hat{H}_2 = \tfrac{1}{2} \sum_{\alpha\beta\gamma\delta} \langle \alpha\beta | V | \gamma\delta \rangle N(c_\alpha^\dagger c_\beta^\dagger c_\delta c_\gamma) \tag{56.21}$$

In these equations the energy eigenvalues are given by

$$\epsilon_\alpha = T_\alpha + V_\alpha \tag{56.22}$$

where

$$T_\alpha \equiv \langle \alpha | T | \alpha \rangle \tag{56.23}$$

$$V_\alpha \equiv \sum_{\beta < F} [\langle \alpha\beta | V | \alpha\beta \rangle - \langle \alpha\beta | V | \beta\alpha \rangle] \tag{56.24}$$

This general result is not restricted to spherical systems; it applies whenever $\{\alpha\}$ denotes a set of single-particle quantum numbers specifying the solutions to the Hartree-Fock equations (56.17) and (56.22). In all the cases considered here, however, the rotational invariance of the Hartree-Fock core implies that the corresponding single-particle energies are independent of m, namely $T_\alpha = T_a$, $V_\alpha = V_a$, and $\epsilon_\alpha = \epsilon_a$.

Equations (56.18) to (56.21) are an *exact* transformation of the original hamiltonian, Eq. (56.9). For almost all purposes, $H_0 + \hat{H}_1$ provides a better starting point for many-body calculations because it already includes the average interaction of a particle with the particles in the core. The new hamiltonian has the further advantage that $H_0 + \hat{H}_1$ is explicitly diagonal and that $\langle 0 | \hat{H}_2 | 0 \rangle$ vanishes.

[1] Note that the solutions corresponding to different energies are orthogonal, whereas the degenerate states always can be orthogonalized.

The present discussion applies directly to atoms, where the coulomb interaction with the nucleus can be incorporated in the one-body operator T. For the nuclear problem, however, the preceding treatment must be generalized slightly because the nucleus consists of both protons and neutrons. In this case, the set of quantum numbers $\{\alpha\}$ simply can be expanded to include the isotopic spin of a nucleon, as discussed in Sec. 40. For spherical nuclei, we therefore define

$$|\alpha\rangle \equiv |nl\tfrac{1}{2}jm_j;\tfrac{1}{2}m_t\rangle \qquad \text{nuclei} \tag{56.25}$$

with $m_t = +\tfrac{1}{2}(-\tfrac{1}{2})$ for a proton (neutron). The phase S_α in Eq. (56.3) must also be generalized to

$$S_\alpha \equiv (-1)^{j_\alpha - m_\alpha}(-1)^{\frac{1}{2} - m_{t\alpha}} \qquad \text{nuclei} \tag{56.26}$$

so that $b_\alpha^\dagger$ is also a tensor operator of rank $\tfrac{1}{2}$ with respect to isotopic spin (the proof follows exactly as with angular momentum). With this enlarged basis, Eqs. (56.18) to (56.24) apply equally well to finite nuclei.

57□THE SINGLE-PARTICLE SHELL MODEL

The solution of the Hartree-Fock equations for a finite system is extremely difficult. Fortunately, most properties of finite nuclei can be understood with approximate, solvable, single-particle potentials, and we now discuss two specific examples.

APPROXIMATE HARTREE-FOCK WAVE FUNCTIONS AND LEVEL ORDERINGS IN A CENTRAL POTENTIAL

Consider first the simplest single-particle potential, an infinite square well shown

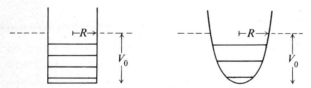

Fig. 57.1 The square-well and harmonic-oscillator approximations to the single-particle Hartree-Fock potential.

in Fig. 57.1. The solutions to the Schrödinger equation that are finite at the origin are

$$\Psi_{nlm} = N_{nl}\, j_l(kr)\, Y_{lm}(\Omega_r) \tag{57.1}$$

with energy

$$\epsilon = \frac{\hbar^2 k^2}{2m} - V_0 \tag{57.2}$$

The wave function must vanish at the boundary $j_l(kR) = 0$ giving the eigenvalue spectrum

$$k_{nl} R = X_{nl} \tag{57.3}$$

where X_{nl} is the nth zero of the lth spherical Bessel function, excluding the origin and including the zero at the boundary. The ordering of these zeros is shown on the right side of Fig. 57.2. The normalization integral can be evaluated explicitly to give[1]

$$N_{nl}^2 = \frac{2}{R^3} \frac{1}{j_{l+1}^2(X_{nl})} \tag{57.4}$$

which yields one approximate set of single-particle wave functions.

A second simple solvable potential is the harmonic oscillator. We write the potential as (see Fig. 57.1)

$$V(r) = -V_0 \left[1 - \left(\frac{r}{R} \right)^2 \right] = -V_0 + \tfrac{1}{2} m\omega^2 r^2 \tag{57.5}$$

$$\frac{V_0}{R^2} = \tfrac{1}{2} m\omega^2$$

and look for solutions to the Schrödinger equation in the form

$$\Psi_{nlm} = \frac{u_{nl}(r)}{r} Y_{lm}(\Omega_r) \tag{57.6}$$

The radial function $u_{nl}(r)$ then satisfies the equation

$$\left[-\frac{\hbar^2}{2m} \frac{d^2}{dr^2} + \tfrac{1}{2} m\omega^2 r^2 + \frac{\hbar^2}{2m} \frac{l(l+1)}{r^2} - (\epsilon_{nl} + V_0) \right] u_{nl}(r) = 0 \tag{57.7}$$

whose solutions are Laguerre polynomials[2]

$$u_{nl}(q) = N_{nl} q^{l+1} e^{-\frac{1}{2}q^2} L_{n-1}^{l+\frac{1}{2}}(q^2) \tag{57.8}$$

$$L_p^a(z) \equiv \frac{\Gamma(a+p+1)}{\Gamma(p+1)} \frac{e^z}{z^a} \frac{d^p}{dz^p} (z^{a+p} e^{-z}) \tag{57.9}$$

with[3]

$$q \equiv \frac{r}{b} \qquad \hbar\omega \equiv \frac{\hbar^2}{mb^2} \tag{57.10}$$

---

[1] This result follows from the relations in L. I. Schiff, "Quantum Mechanics," 3d ed., p. 86, McGraw-Hill Book Company, New York, 1968.
[2] P. M. Morse and H. Feshbach, "Methods of Theoretical Physics," pp. 784, 1662, McGraw-Hill Book Company, New York, 1953.
[3] A fit to mean-square nuclear radii yields the rough estimate $\hbar\omega \approx 41$ MeV/$A^{\frac{1}{3}}$.

As in the square well, n denotes the number of nodes in the radial wave function including the one at infinity and takes the values

$$n = 1, 2, \ldots, \infty \tag{57.11}$$

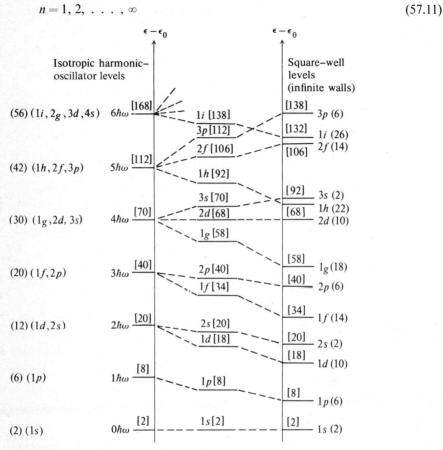

Fig. 57.2 Level system of the three-dimensional isotropic harmonic oscillator (on left) and the square well with infinitely high walls (on right). The degeneracy of each state is shown in parentheses, and the total number of levels up through a given state is in brackets. (From M. G. Mayer and J. H. D. Jensen, "Elementary Theory of Nuclear Shell Structure," p. 53, John Wiley and Sons, Inc., New York, 1955. Reprinted by permission.)

These functions can be normalized using standard formulas[1]

$$N_{nl}^2 = \frac{2(n-1)!}{b[\Gamma(n+l+\frac{1}{2})]^3} \tag{57.12}$$

[1] P. M. Morse and H. Feshbach, *op. cit.*, p. 785.

The resulting eigenvalue spectrum of the three-dimensional oscillator is well known

$$\epsilon_{nl} = \hbar\omega(N + \tfrac{3}{2}) - V_0 \tag{57.13a}$$

$$N = 2(n - 1) + l = 0, 1, 2, \ldots, \infty \tag{57.13b}$$

and is plotted on the left-hand side of Fig. 57.2.   These degenerate levels contain states of different l and are spaced a distance $\hbar\omega$ apart.   We shall refer to these as the *oscillator shells*.   In comparing the two model potentials (Fig. 57.1), the value of V_0 has been chosen so that the $1s$ levels have the same energy.

The true nuclear single-particle well has a finite depth.   Nevertheless, the low-lying levels with large binding energies are essentially unchanged by extending the walls of the potential to infinity.   For these states, at least, the real Hartree-Fock potential presumably has a shape intermediate between the square well and the oscillator, and we can easily interpolate between the two cases.   Both n and l remain good quantum numbers as the bottom edge of the square well is rounded or the bottom of the oscillator is flattened out.   The highest l states have the largest probability of being near the edge of the potential, and as indicated in Fig. 57.2, their energy will be lowered in going from the oscillator to the square well.

SPIN-ORBIT SPLITTING

It is known experimentally that certain groups of nucleons possess special stability corresponding to the closed shells of atomic physics.   These "magic numbers" are 2, 8, 20, 28, 50, 82, 126, ...   Clearly Fig. 57.2 correctly predicts only the first three of these major-shell closures.   Mayer and Jensen[1] therefore suggested that the nuclear Hartree-Fock single-particle potential also has an attractive single-particle spin-orbit term[2]

$$H' = -\alpha(r)\mathbf{l}\cdot\mathbf{s} \tag{57.14}$$

In the presence of this interaction the single-particle eigenstates can be characterized by $|nl\tfrac{1}{2}\,jm_j\rangle$, and the operator $\mathbf{l}\cdot\mathbf{s}$ has the eigenvalues

$$\mathbf{l}\cdot\mathbf{s}|nl\tfrac{1}{2}\,jm_j\rangle = \tfrac{1}{2}(\mathbf{j}^2 - \mathbf{l}^2 - \mathbf{s}^2)|nl\tfrac{1}{2}\,jm_j\rangle$$

$$= \tfrac{1}{2}[j(j+1) - l(l+1) - s(s+1)]|nl\tfrac{1}{2}\,jm_j\rangle \tag{57.15}$$

The "stretched" case ($j = l + \tfrac{1}{2}$) leads to $\mathbf{l}\cdot\mathbf{s} = l/2$, while the "jack-knifed" case

[1] See M. G. Mayer and J. H. D. Jensen, "Elementary Theory of Nuclear Shell Structure," John Wiley and Sons, Inc., New York, 1955.
[2] There is some theoretical evidence that this term arises from the spin-orbit force between two nucleons.   See, for example, K. A. Brueckner, A. M. Lockett, and M. Rotenberg, *Phys. Rev.*, **121**:255 (1961) and also B. R. Barrett, *Phys. Rev.*, **154**:955 (1967).

$(j = l - \frac{1}{2})$ leads to $\mathbf{l} \cdot \mathbf{s} = -(l+1)/2$. Thus the first-order splitting is given by

$$\epsilon_{l-\frac{1}{2}} - \epsilon_{l+\frac{1}{2}} = \alpha_{nl} \tfrac{1}{2}(2l+1) \tag{57.16}$$

$$\alpha_{nl} \equiv \int u_{nl}^2(r)\,\alpha(r)\,dr \tag{57.17}$$

For fixed l and j, the $(2j+1)$ degenerate m_j states are said to form a j shell (see Fig. 57.3).

For an attractive spin-orbit force ($\alpha_{nl} > 0$), the stretched state, or state of higher j for a given l, lies lower in energy. In addition, the state of highest l in any oscillator shell is pushed down when the bottom of the well is flattened, as illustrated in Fig. 57.2. It is therefore possible that the state of highest j and l from one oscillator shell may actually be pushed down into the next lower oscillator shell as indicated in Fig. 57.3, thus explaining the observed magic numbers. Note that the pushed-down state has the opposite parity $(-1)^l$ from the other states in the oscillator shell and has a high j. This observation has many interesting consequences; in particular, it explains the *islands of isomerism* or groupings of nuclei with low-lying excitations that decay by γ transitions to the ground state only very slowly.

SINGLE-PARTICLE MATRIX ELEMENTS

As our first description of nuclear structure, we consider the extreme single-particle shell model, which applies to nuclei with an odd number of nucleons. In this picture, the levels in Fig. 57.3 are filled in sequence, and all the properties of the nucleus are assumed to arise from the last odd nucleon. This model is extremely successful in predicting the angular momentum and parity of such nuclei. It also allows a calculation of other nuclear properties such as the electromagnetic moments.

The magnetic dipole operators for a proton and neutron are

$$\boldsymbol{\mu}_p = \mu_N(\mathbf{l} + 2\lambda_p \mathbf{s}) \tag{57.18a}$$

$$\boldsymbol{\mu}_n = \mu_N(2\lambda_n \mathbf{s}) \tag{57.18b}$$

where

$$\lambda_p = +2.793 \qquad \lambda_n = -1.913 \qquad \mu_N = \frac{e\hbar}{2m_p c} \tag{57.19}$$

The magnetic moment of a nucleus with angular momentum j is defined by[1]

$$\mu \equiv \langle j, m=j | \mu_{10} | j, m=j \rangle = \frac{\langle jj10|j1\,jj\rangle}{(2j+1)^{\frac{1}{2}}} \langle j \| \boldsymbol{\mu} \| j \rangle \tag{57.20}$$

In the extreme single-particle shell model, this quantity is computed from the matrix elements for the last nucleon, which are of the form $\langle l\frac{1}{2}j \| \mathbf{l} \| l\frac{1}{2}j \rangle$ and

---

[1] Throughout this chapter we generally suppress all quantum numbers that are not directly relevant to the discussion.

$\langle l\frac{1}{2} j \| \mathbf{s} \| l\frac{1}{2} j \rangle$. These are just reduced matrix elements of a tensor operator in a coupled scheme (see Appendix B), and we find

$$\frac{\mu}{\mu_N} = \frac{1}{2(j+1)} \{ [j(j+1) + l(l+1) - s(s+1)] + 2\lambda[j(j+1) + s(s+1) - l(l+1)] \} \quad (57.21)$$

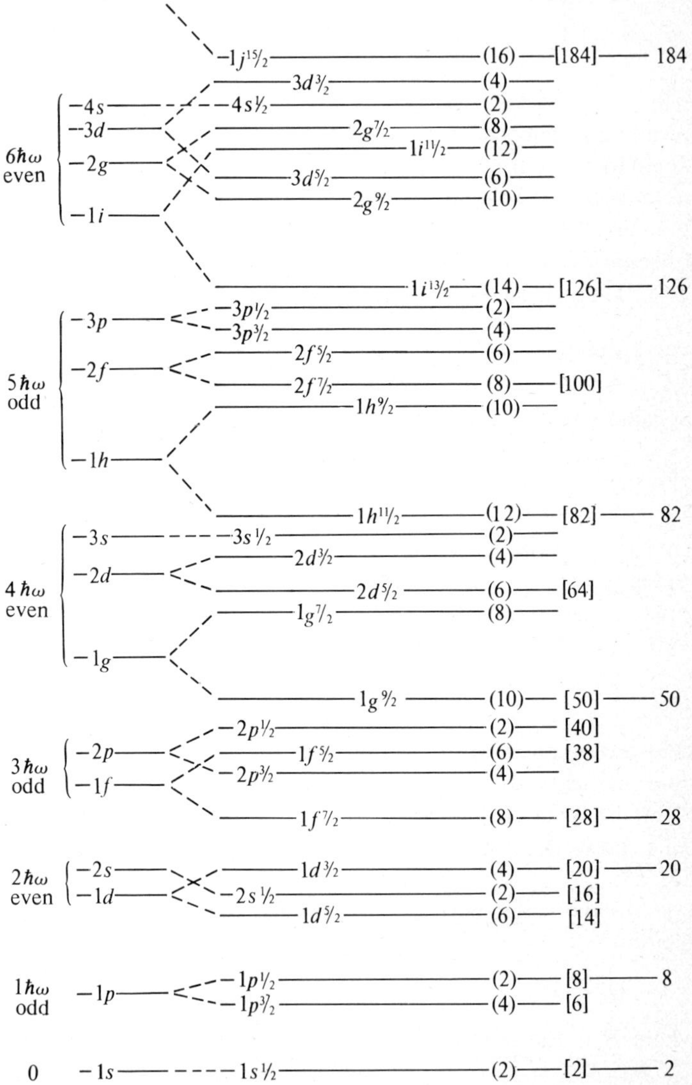

Fig. 57.3 Schematic diagram of nuclear level systems with (right) and without (left) a spin-orbit coupling $H' = -\alpha \mathbf{l} \cdot \mathbf{s}$. (From M. G. Mayer and J. H. D. Jensen, "Elementary Theory of Nuclear Shell Structure," p. 58, John Wiley and Sons, Inc., New York, 1955. Reprinted by permission.)

with $s = \frac{1}{2}$. For neutrons, only the second term (proportional to λ) contributes. Equation (57.21) is immediately recognized as that obtained from the simple *vector model* for the addition of angular momenta. The two cases $j = l \pm \frac{1}{2}$ become

$$\frac{\mu}{\mu_N} = \begin{cases} j - \frac{1}{2} + \lambda & j = l + \frac{1}{2} & \text{(57.22a)} \\ j + \dfrac{j}{j+1}(\frac{1}{2} - \lambda) & j = l - \frac{1}{2} & \text{(57.22b)} \end{cases}$$

which are the single-particle Schmidt lines for the magnetic moments.[1] These results are independent of any radial wave functions and depend only on the angular-momentum coupling. Out of 137 odd-A nuclear moments, only five lie outside the Schmidt lines. It is an interesting fact that all but 10 of these moments lie between the value given by the full moment of Eq. (57.19) and the fully *quenched* (pure Dirac) value $\lambda_p = 1$, $\lambda_n = 0$.[2]

The electric quadrupole operator for a single proton is

$$Q_{20} = 3z^2 - r^2 = 2r^2 c_{20} \tag{57.23}$$

where $c_{KQ} \equiv [4\pi/(2K+1)]^{\frac{1}{2}} Y_{KQ}$, and the quadrupole moment of the nucleus is defined by

$$Q \equiv \langle j, m = j | Q_{20} | j, m = j \rangle = \begin{pmatrix} j & 2 & j \\ -j & 0 & j \end{pmatrix} \langle j \| Q_2 \| j \rangle \tag{57.24}$$

In the single-particle shell model, the relevant matrix element is again that for the last particle $\langle nl\frac{1}{2} j \| Q_2 \| nl\frac{1}{2} j \rangle$. Evaluating the matrix element of this tensor operator in a coupled scheme yields [see Eq. (B.34a)]

$$Q = -\langle r^2 \rangle_{nl} \frac{2j-1}{2j+2} \qquad j \geqslant \frac{3}{2} \tag{57.25}$$

Odd-proton nuclei with less than half-filled shells tend to have negative quadrupole moments, as predicted by this model. If the shells are more than half filled, however, the experimental quadrupole moments tend to be positive.[3] This shows the need for a consistent many-body treatment, which is given in Sec. 58.

In the single-particle shell model, the quadrupole moment satisfies the relation

$$|Q| < R^2 \tag{57.26}$$

where R is the nuclear radius. In most cases, the experimental quadrupole

---

[1] T. Schmidt, *Z. Physik*, **106**:358 (1937).
[2] M. A. Preston, "Physics of the Nucleus," pp. 70–75, Addison-Wesley Publishing Company, Inc., Reading, Mass., 1962.
[3] M. A. Preston, *op. cit.*, p. 68.

moments are much larger, particularly away from closed shells. For example,[1] $Q(_{71}\text{Lu}^{175})/(1.2A^{\frac{1}{3}}\text{ F})^2 = +13$. Odd-neutron nuclei should have no quadrupole moments in the single-particle shell model. Experimentally, they tend to behave as if the last neutron were really a proton, and the quadrupole moment is again much larger than the model would predict even for a proton. For example,[2] $Q(\text{Er}^{167}_{99})/(1.2A^{\frac{1}{3}}\text{ F})^2 \approx +23$. The explanation for these large values is that the core is not inert, but can actually be *deformed* by the presence of the valence nucleons. Since the core has a charge Z, a small deformation has a large effect on Q.‡ Unfortunately, a description of deformed nuclei would take us outside of the scope of the present text,[3] and the remainder of this chapter concentrates on spherical nuclei, namely those in the vicinity of closed shells.

58□MANY PARTICLES IN A SHELL[4]

The previous section investigated an extreme single-particle model of the nucleus. We now take the next logical step and consider the problem of filling a j shell with interacting valence particles. Throughout this discussion, the shells already filled will be assumed to form an inert core.

TWO VALENCE PARTICLES: GENERAL INTERACTION AND $\delta(x)$ FORCE

With just one extra particle in a level, the nucleus has the angular momentum and parity of that extra nucleon. What happens when two identical nucleons are placed in the same j shell? If we confine ourselves to the subspace of a given j shell, we can use the shorthand notation $\{nljm\} \rightarrow m$. The states of definite total J for two identical particles therefore can be written

$$|j^2 JM\rangle = \frac{1}{\sqrt{2}} \sum_{m_1 m_2} \langle jm_1 \, jm_2 | jjJM \rangle \, a^{\dagger}_{m_1} a^{\dagger}_{m_2} |0\rangle \tag{58.1}$$

where the superscript 2 denotes the number of particles in the shell. Since the fermion operators anticommute, the symmetry property (B.19b) of the Clebsch-Gordan coefficient under the interchange $m_1 \rightleftarrows m_2$, together with a change of dummy variables, yields $|j^2 JM\rangle = (-1)^{2j-J+1}|j^2 JM\rangle$. We conclude that J must be even or the state vanishes; two identical valence nucleons therefore have the allowed states

$$J^{\pi} = 0^+, 2^+, 4^+, \ldots, (2j-1)^+ \tag{58.2}$$

[1] M. G. Mayer and J. H. D. Jensen, *op. cit.*, pp. 79–80.
[2] *Ibid.*
‡ J. Rainwater, *Phys. Rev.*, **79**:432 (1950).
[3] For a thorough discussion of this topic see A. Bohr and B. R. Mottelson,"Nuclear Structure," W. A. Benjamin, Inc., New York, vol. I (1969) and vols. II and III (to be published).
[4] An excellent discussion of the many-particle shell model is contained in A. de-Shalit and I. Talmi, "Nuclear Shell Theory," Academic Press, New York, 1963.

In the single-particle shell model, these states are degenerate because the core is spherically symmetric and the valence particles do not interact.

For real nuclei, this degeneracy is lifted, and it is an experimental fact that all even-even nuclei have ground states with $J^\pi = 0^+$. Furthermore, the properties of odd-A nuclei can be understood by assuming that the even group of nucleons is coupled to form $J^\pi = 0^+$ in the ground state. The question arises, can these facts be understood within the framework of the many-particle shell model? The degeneracy of the states formed from the valence nucleons can be removed only by adding an interaction between these nucleons. As an introduction, we shall use first-order perturbation theory and compute the level shifts from the first-quantized matrix elements $\langle j^2 JM | V | j^2 JM \rangle$. These matrix elements are diagonal in J and M and independent of M because the two-particle potential is invariant under rotations. They still depend on J, however, owing to the different two-particle densities.

To investigate the level ordering of two interacting particles in a j shell, we first make a multipole expansion of the general rotationally invariant interaction $V(r_1, r_2, \cos\theta_{12})$

$$V(r_1, r_2, \cos\theta_{12}) = \sum_K f_K(r_1, r_2) P_K(\cos\theta_{12}) \tag{58.3}$$

This relation is merely an expansion in a complete set of functions of $\cos\theta_{12}$, and it can be inverted with the orthogonality of the Legendre polynomials

$$f_K = \frac{2K+1}{2} \int_{-1}^{1} P_K(x) V(r_1, r_2, x) \, dx \tag{58.4}$$

Equation (58.3) can be rewritten with the expansion in spherical harmonics

$$P_K(\cos\theta_{12}) = \frac{4\pi}{2K+1} \sum_M Y_{KM}(\Omega_1) Y^*_{KM}(\Omega_2) \equiv c_K^1 \cdot c_K^2 \tag{58.5}$$

which gives

$$V(r_1, r_2, x) = \sum_K f_K(r_1, r_2) c_K^1 \cdot c_K^2 \tag{58.6}$$

For generality we evaluate the expectation value of V for two arbitrary single-particle states $\varphi_{n_1 l_1 j_1 m_1}(1)$ and $\varphi_{n_2 l_2 j_2 m_2}(2)$ coupled to form definite J and M. This matrix element follows from the relation (B.33) of Appendix B

$$\langle j_1 j_2 JM | V | j_1 j_2 JM \rangle$$

$$= \sum_K F_K (-1)^{j_1 + j_2 + J} \begin{Bmatrix} j_1 & j_2 & J \\ j_2 & j_1 & K \end{Bmatrix} \langle j_1 \| c_K \| j_1 \rangle \langle j_2 \| c_K \| j_2 \rangle \tag{58.7}$$

where the radial matrix element is defined by

$$F_K \equiv \int u^2_{n_1 l_1}(r_1) u^2_{n_2 l_2}(r_2) f_K(r_1, r_2) \, dr_1 \, dr_2 \tag{58.8}$$

All the dependence on the total angular momentum J is contained in the 6-j symbol, and all the specific nuclear properties are contained in the multipole

strengths F_K. Since[1]

$$\langle l\tfrac{1}{2}j\|c_K\|l\tfrac{1}{2}j\rangle = \begin{cases} (-1)^{j+\frac{1}{2}}(2j+1)\begin{pmatrix} j & K & j \\ \tfrac{1}{2} & 0 & -\tfrac{1}{2} \end{pmatrix} & K \text{ even} \\ 0 & K \text{ odd} \end{cases} \tag{58.9}$$

Eq. (58.7) can be written

$$\langle j_1 j_2 JM |V| j_1 j_2 JM \rangle = \sum_{\text{even } K} F_K(-1)^{J+1}\begin{Bmatrix} j_1 & j_2 & J \\ j_2 & j_1 & K \end{Bmatrix}(2j_1+1)(2j_2+1)$$

$$\times \begin{pmatrix} j_1 & K & j_1 \\ \tfrac{1}{2} & 0 & -\tfrac{1}{2} \end{pmatrix}\begin{pmatrix} j_2 & K & j_2 \\ \tfrac{1}{2} & 0 & -\tfrac{1}{2} \end{pmatrix} \tag{58.10}$$

For two identical particles with even J in a j shell, this expression reduces to

$$\langle j^2 JM |V| j^2 JM \rangle = \sum_{\text{even } K} F_K(-1)^{J+1}\begin{Bmatrix} j & j & J \\ j & j & K \end{Bmatrix}(2j+1)^2 \begin{pmatrix} j & K & j \\ \tfrac{1}{2} & 0 & -\tfrac{1}{2} \end{pmatrix}^2 \tag{58.11}$$

If all the F_K are negative, corresponding to an attractive two-nucleon force, then a detailed examination of Eq. (58.11) shows that the spectrum will be as in Fig. 58.1a. This follows since the largest 6-j symbols are generally those with $J = 0$.[‡]
    Equation (58.10) derived above also can be applied to an odd-odd nucleus with an extra proton and neutron in the shells j_1 and j_2. In this case the lowest state for an attractive interaction will have $J = |j_1 - j_2|$ and the first excited state turns out to have $J = j_1 + j_2$ (Fig. 58.1b). It is easy to see the reason for these results. The matrix element $\langle j_1 j_2 JM |V| j_1 j_2 JM \rangle$ essentially measures the

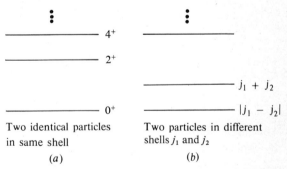

Two identical particles   Two particles in different
in same shell   shells j_1 and j_2
(a)   (b)

Fig. 58.1 Two-particle spectrum with an attractive interaction.

[1] M. Rotenberg, R. Bivens, N. Metropolis, and J. K. Wooten, Jr., "The 3-j and 6-j Symbols," p. 6, The Technology Press, Massachusetts Institute of Technology, Cambridge, Mass., 1959.
[‡] M. Rotenberg et al., *op. cit.*

overlap of the two single-particle wave functions. The best overlap always will be obtained by opposing the angular momenta and the next best by lining them up.   For example, if we write $\mathbf{L} = \mathbf{l}_1 + \mathbf{l}_2$ and take $\mathbf{l}_1 \cdot \mathbf{l}_2$ as a measure of overlap (see Fig. 58.2), then

$$\mathbf{l}_1 \cdot \mathbf{l}_2 = \tfrac{1}{2}[L(L+1) - l_1(l_1+1) - l_2(l_2+1)] = \begin{cases} l_1 l_2 & L = l_1 + l_2 \\ -(l_1+1)l_2 & L = l_1 - l_2 \geqslant 0 \end{cases}$$

(58.12)

and this overlap is larger if the angular momenta are opposed.   Two identical particles cannot be lined up because of the Pauli principle.

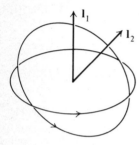

Fig. 58.2 Qualitative picture of the overlap of orbits.

These results can be seen more clearly with a simple model of the attractive interaction potential.   Assume that

$$V(1,2) = -g\delta(\mathbf{x}_1 - \mathbf{x}_2) = -\frac{g}{\pi}\delta(1 - \cos\theta_{12})\frac{\delta(r_1 - r_2)}{r_1 r_2}$$

(58.13)

with $g > 0$.   This yields

$$f_K(r_1,r_2) = -\frac{g}{4\pi}(2K+1)\frac{\delta(r_1 - r_2)}{r_1 r_2}$$

(58.14)

$$F_K = -2Ig(2K+1)$$

(58.15)

where

$$I \equiv \frac{1}{8\pi}\int u_{n_1 l_1}^2(r)\,u_{n_2 l_2}^2(r)\frac{dr}{r^2}$$

(58.16)

The energy shifts of two identical particles in the j shell can now be determined by explicitly evaluating the sum on K in Eq. (58.11).[1]   For even J, we find

$$\sum_{\text{even } K}(2K+1)\begin{Bmatrix} j & j & J \\ j & j & K \end{Bmatrix}\begin{pmatrix} j & K & j \\ \tfrac{1}{2} & 0 & -\tfrac{1}{2} \end{pmatrix}^2 = -\frac{1}{2}\begin{pmatrix} j & j & J \\ \tfrac{1}{2} & -\tfrac{1}{2} & 0 \end{pmatrix}^2$$

(58.17)

---

[1] M. Rotenberg et al., *op. cit.*, Eq. (2.19).   Note that the sum on even K can be converted to a sum on all K by inserting a factor $\tfrac{1}{2}[1 + (-1)^K]$.

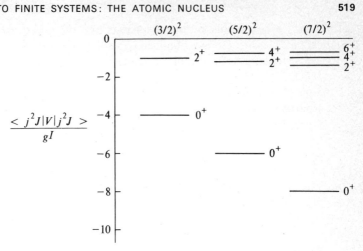

Fig. 58.3 Spectrum [Eq. (58.18)] for two identical particles in the j shell with an interaction $V(\mathbf{x}_1 - \mathbf{x}_2) = -g\delta(\mathbf{x}_1 - \mathbf{x}_2)$.

It follows that

$$\langle j^2 JM | V | j^2 JM \rangle = -Ig(2j+1)^2 \begin{pmatrix} j & j & J \\ \tfrac{1}{2} & -\tfrac{1}{2} & 0 \end{pmatrix}^2 \qquad (58.18)$$

The resulting spectrum is indicated for some simple cases in Fig. 58.3. We see that the 0^+ state indeed lies lowest and is split off from the excited states, which are nearly degenerate with this delta-function potential, by a *pairing energy*

$$\langle j^2 00 | V | j^2 00 \rangle = -(2j+1) Ig \qquad (58.19)$$

Note that this energy shift is proportional to $2j+1$ so that it may sometimes be energetically favorable to promote a pair of identical particles from the original j shell into a higher j' shell if $j' - j$ is large enough. In this lowest-order calculation [i.e., taking just the expectation value of $V(1,2)$], the relative position of these levels is a direct measure of the two-body interaction between the valence nucleons. Actual nuclear spectra show many of the features illustrated in Fig. 58.3.

SEVERAL PARTICLES: NORMAL COUPLING

For a short-range attractive interaction, we have shown explicitly that the lowest energy state of a pair of identical particles in the same j shell will be

$$| j^2 00 \rangle = \hat{\xi}_0^\dagger | 0 \rangle \qquad (58.20)$$

where we have defined a new two-particle operator by

$$\hat{\xi}_{JM}^\dagger \equiv \frac{1}{\sqrt{2}} \sum_{m_1 m_2} \langle jm_1 \, jm_2 | jjJM \rangle a_{m_1}^\dagger a_{m_2}^\dagger \qquad (58.21)$$

with $\hat{\xi}_0^\dagger \equiv \hat{\xi}_{J=0,\,M=0}^\dagger$. This argument suggests that the lowest energy state for N identical particles in a j shell is obtained by adding the maximum number of $J = 0$ pairs consistent with the Pauli principle. These states (unnormalized) are

$$
\left.\begin{aligned}
\text{3-particle state} &= a_{jm}^\dagger \hat{\xi}_0^\dagger |0\rangle \\
\text{4-particle state} &= \hat{\xi}_0^\dagger \hat{\xi}_0^\dagger |0\rangle \\
\text{5-particle state} &= a_{jm}^\dagger \hat{\xi}_0^\dagger \hat{\xi}_0^\dagger |0\rangle \\
\text{etc.}
\end{aligned}\right\} \text{Normal-coupling shell-model ground states}
$$

$$(58.22)$$

It is a fundamental assumption of the shell model that these normal-coupling states form the ground states of the multiply occupied j-shell nuclei.[1] This model correctly predicts the ground-state angular momentum and parity for most nuclei. We shall attempt a theoretical justification of this assumption shortly, but let us first briefly examine some of its additional consequences.

Probably the most useful result is that the ground-state expectation value of an arbitrary multipole operator $\hat{T}_{KQ}$ now can be computed explicitly. For an odd group of nucleons, *the normal-coupling scheme yields*[2]

$$
\langle j^N j \| \hat{T}_K \| j^N j \rangle = \begin{cases} \langle j \| T_K \| j \rangle & K \text{ odd} \qquad\qquad (58.23a) \\ \dfrac{2j+1-2N}{2j-1} \langle j \| T_K \| i \rangle & \begin{aligned} K &\text{ even} \\ K &\neq 0 \end{aligned} \qquad (58.23b) \end{cases}
$$

where N is the (odd) number of particles (for even N the model has $J = 0$). These relations express the many-particle matrix elements in the normal-coupling scheme directly in terms of the single-particle matrix elements, which in general still depend on the quantum numbers n and l. For odd moments, such as the magnetic dipole, one finds just the single-particle value. For even moments, such as the electric quadrupole, there is a *reduction* factor $(2j + 1 - 2N)/(2j - 1)$. This reduction factor vanishes at half-filled shells, $N = \frac{1}{2}(2j + 1)$, and changes sign upon going from N particles in a shell to N holes in a shell, $N \to 2j + 1 - N$. The sign change agrees with the experimental observations [see the discussion following Eq. (57.25)].

The derivation of Eqs. (58.23) illustrates the power of second quantization, so that we shall now prove these important results. The $Q = 0$ component of an arbitrary tensor operator in the subspace of the multiply occupied j shell can be written

$$
\hat{T}_{K0} = \sum_m a_m^\dagger \langle m | T_{K0} | m \rangle a_m
$$

$$
= \sum_m (-1)^{j-m} \langle jmj - m | jjK0 \rangle \frac{\langle j \| T_K \| j \rangle}{(2K+1)^{\frac{1}{2}}} \hat{n}_m
$$

$$(58.24)$$

[1] M. G. Mayer and J. H. D. Jensen, *op. cit.*, p. 241.
[2] A. de-Shalit and I. Talmi, *op. cit.*, p. 531.

where the Wigner-Eckart theorem has been used to simplify the single-particle matrix element. The many-body matrix elements of $\hat{T}_{K0}$ also can be rewritten with this theorem

$$\frac{\langle j^N j \| \hat{T}_K \| j^N j \rangle}{(2K+1)^{\frac{1}{2}}} = \sum_m (-1)^{j-m} \langle jmj - m | jjK0 \rangle \langle j^N jm | \hat{T}_{K0} | j^N jm \rangle \qquad (58.25)$$

Thus a combination of Eqs. (58.22), (58.24), and (58.25) gives

$$\frac{\langle j^N j \| \hat{T}_K \| j^N j \rangle}{\langle j \| T_K \| j \rangle} = \sum_{mp} (-1)^{j-m}(-1)^{j-p} \langle jmj - m | jjK0 \rangle \langle jpj - p | jjK0 \rangle$$

$$\times \frac{\langle 0 | \hat{\xi}_0 \cdots \hat{\xi}_0 a_m \hat{n}_p a_m^\dagger \hat{\xi}_0^\dagger \cdots \hat{\xi}_0^\dagger | 0 \rangle}{\langle 0 | \hat{\xi}_0 \cdots \hat{\xi}_0 a_q a_q^\dagger \hat{\xi}_0^\dagger \cdots \hat{\xi}_0^\dagger | 0 \rangle} \qquad (58.26)$$

where the factors $\hat{\xi}_0^\dagger$ and $\hat{\xi}_0$ appear $(N-1)/2$ times and the normalization factor in the denominator is independent of q by rotational invariance. Using the pair of identities

$$[\hat{n}_p, a_m^\dagger] = \delta_{pm} a_p^\dagger \qquad (58.27)$$

$$\sum_p (-1)^{j-p} \langle jpj - p | jjK0 \rangle [\hat{n}_p, \hat{\xi}_0^\dagger] = \frac{2}{(2j+1)^{\frac{1}{2}}} \hat{\xi}_{K0}^\dagger \qquad (58.28)$$

together with $[\hat{\xi}_{K0}^\dagger, \hat{\xi}_{JM}^\dagger] = 0$ for all J and M, we find that

$$\frac{\langle j^N j \| \hat{T}_K \| j^N j \rangle}{\langle j \| T_K \| j \rangle} = 1 + \sum_m (-1)^{j-m} \langle jmj - m | jjK0 \rangle$$

$$\times \frac{\langle 0 | \hat{\xi}_0 \cdots \hat{\xi}_0 a_m a_m^\dagger \hat{\xi}_0^\dagger \cdots \hat{\xi}_0^\dagger \hat{\xi}_{K0}^\dagger | 0 \rangle}{\langle 0 | \hat{\xi}_0 \cdots \hat{\xi}_0 a_q a_q^\dagger \hat{\xi}_0^\dagger \cdots \hat{\xi}_0^\dagger | 0 \rangle} \left[\frac{N-1}{2} \frac{2}{(2j+1)^{\frac{1}{2}}} \right] \qquad (58.29)$$

Since $\hat{\xi}_{K0}^\dagger \equiv 0$ for odd K [see the argument following Eq. (58.1)], Eq. (58.23a) is proved. For even K, we use the identity $a_m a_m^\dagger = 1 - a_m^\dagger a_m = 1 - \hat{n}_m$. The term 1 will not contribute in the numerator if $K \neq 0$, and the $-\hat{n}_m$ can be moved to the left, exactly as before. The denominator is independent of q, so that the average

$$\frac{1}{2j+1} \sum_q a_q a_q^\dagger = 1 - \frac{\hat{N}}{2j+1} \rightarrow \frac{2j+1-(N-1)}{2j+1}$$

can be taken. In this way, we obtain

$$\frac{\langle j^N j \| \hat{T}_K \| j^N j \rangle}{\langle j \| T_K \| j \rangle} = 1 - \frac{\langle 0 | \hat{\xi}_{K0} \hat{\xi}_0 \cdots \hat{\xi}_0 \hat{\xi}_0^\dagger \cdots \hat{\xi}_0^\dagger \hat{\xi}_{K0}^\dagger | 0 \rangle}{\langle 0 | \hat{\xi}_0 \hat{\xi}_0 \cdots \hat{\xi}_0 \hat{\xi}_0^\dagger \cdots \hat{\xi}_0^\dagger \hat{\xi}_0^\dagger | 0 \rangle}$$

$$\times \left(\frac{N-1}{(2j+1)^{\frac{1}{2}}} \right)^2 \frac{2j+1}{2j+2-N} \qquad (58.30)$$

With the relations

$$[\hat{\xi}_0, \hat{\xi}_0^\dagger] = \frac{2j + 1 - 2\hat{N}}{2j + 1} \tag{58.31}$$

$$[\hat{\xi}_0, \hat{\xi}_{K0}^\dagger]|0\rangle = 0 \qquad K \neq 0 \tag{58.32}$$

it is now straightforward to show that (see Prob. 15.4)

$$\frac{\langle 0|\hat{\xi}_{K0}\,\hat{\xi}_0 \cdots \hat{\xi}_0\,\hat{\xi}_0^\dagger \cdots \hat{\xi}_0^\dagger\,\hat{\xi}_{K0}^\dagger|0\rangle}{\langle 0|\hat{\xi}_0\,\hat{\xi}_0 \cdots \hat{\xi}_0\,\hat{\xi}_0^\dagger \cdots \hat{\xi}_0^\dagger\,\hat{\xi}_0^\dagger|0\rangle} = \frac{2}{N - 1}\frac{2j + 1 - (N - 1)}{2j + 1 - 2} \tag{58.33}$$

This immediately yields Eq. (58.23b).

The normal-coupling model can be extended to excited states;[1] for example, it is assumed that the low-lying states are obtained by breaking one of the $J = 0$ pairs, thus replacing $\hat{\xi}_0^\dagger$ in Eq. (58.22) by $\hat{\xi}_{JM}^\dagger$. This assumption allows us to find the energy spectrum of the many-particle system. We observe that the operator describing a general two-particle potential can be written within the j-shell subspace as

$$\hat{V} = \tfrac{1}{2} \sum_{mnpq} a_m^\dagger a_n^\dagger \langle mn|V|pq\rangle a_q a_p \tag{58.34}$$

where the two-particle matrix element has been discussed previously and only the m dependence is exhibited. The two-particle wave functions can always be expanded in a basis with given total J and M by the relation

$$\varphi_p(1)\,\varphi_q(2) \equiv \varphi_{jp}(1)\,\varphi_{jq}(2) = \sum_{JM} \langle jpjq\,|\,jjJM\rangle \Phi_{j^2 JM}(1,2) \tag{58.35}$$

In addition, the potential V is a scalar, so that its general matrix elements become

$$\langle j^2 J' M'|V|j^2 JM\rangle = \delta_{JJ'}\,\delta_{MM'}\langle j^2 J|V|j^2 J\rangle \tag{58.36}$$

with the remaining factor independent of M. Thus we obtain the general expression, valid within a j shell,

$$\hat{V} = \sum_{JM} \hat{\xi}_{JM}^\dagger \langle j^2 J|V|j^2 J\rangle \hat{\xi}_{JM} \tag{58.37}$$

where the operator $\hat{\xi}_{JM}^\dagger$ is defined in Eq. (58.21). Note that $\hat{\xi}_{JM}$ vanishes unless J is even. We may now add and subtract the expression

$$\sum_{JM} \hat{\xi}_{JM}^\dagger \langle j^2 0|V|j^2 0\rangle \hat{\xi}_{JM} = \langle j^2 0|V|j^2 0\rangle \tfrac{1}{2} \sum_{mp} a_m^\dagger a_p^\dagger a_p a_m$$

$$= \langle j^2 0|V|j^2 0\rangle \tfrac{1}{2}\hat{N}(\hat{N} - 1) \tag{58.38}$$

and the interaction potential in the j shell becomes

$$\hat{V} = \sum_{JM} \hat{\xi}_{JM}^\dagger [\langle j^2 J|V|j^2 J\rangle - \langle j^2 0|V|j^2 0\rangle]\hat{\xi}_{JM} + \langle j^2 0|V|j^2 0\rangle \tfrac{1}{2}\hat{N}(\hat{N} - 1) \tag{58.39}$$

[1] A. de-Shalit and I. Talmi, *op. cit.*, secs. 27 and 30.

When the many-particle interaction energy is calculated as the expectation value of this operator, the last term gives a constant depending only on the number of particles in the shell.   Thus the energy *differences* between the many-particle levels can be directly related to the energy *differences* between the two-particle levels.   The techniques of second quantization provide a very elegant and straightforward way of finding these relations,[1] which form the basis for a great deal of beautiful work correlating and predicting the levels of neighboring nuclei corresponding to the j^N configuration.[2]

THE PAIRING-FORCE PROBLEM

We now return to the problem of justifying the many-particle shell model.   We confine our attention to the subspace of a given j shell and assume that there is an attractive, short-range interaction between the particles in the shell.   In this case, it is evident from Fig. 58.3 that the dominant two-particle matrix element of the potential occurs when the pair is coupled to form $J = 0$.   This observation suggests that the potential in Eq. (58.37) can be written to a good approximation as

$$\hat{V} \approx \hat{\xi}_0^\dagger \langle j^2 0 | V | j^2 0 \rangle \hat{\xi}_0 \equiv -G \hat{\xi}_0^\dagger \hat{\xi}_0 \tag{58.40}$$

Such an interaction is called a pure *pairing force*.   It has the great advantage that the resulting problem can be *solved exactly*.[3]

We wish to find the spectrum of the hamiltonian

$$\hat{H} = \epsilon_0 \hat{N} + \hat{V} \tag{58.41}$$

where ϵ_0 is the single-particle Hartree-Fock energy of the particular shell and $\hat{V}$ is given in Eq. (58.40).   The calculation is most easily performed with the auxiliary operators

$$\hat{S}_+ \equiv [\tfrac{1}{2}(2j + 1)]^{\frac{1}{2}} \hat{\xi}_0^\dagger \tag{58.42a}$$

$$\hat{S}_- \equiv [\tfrac{1}{2}(2j + 1)]^{\frac{1}{2}} \hat{\xi}_0 \tag{58.42b}$$

$$\hat{S}_3 \equiv \tfrac{1}{4}[2\hat{N} - (2j + 1)] \tag{58.42c}$$

Equation (58.31) and the relation

$$[\hat{N}, \hat{\xi}_0^\dagger] = 2\hat{\xi}_0^\dagger \tag{58.43}$$

show that $\hat{S}_\pm$ and $\hat{S}_3$ obey the familiar commutation relations

$$[\hat{S}_+, \hat{S}_-] = 2\hat{S}_3 \tag{58.44a}$$

---

[1] The coefficients in these relations are known as the *coefficients of fractional parentage* (see Prob. 15.8).

[2] For a general survey see I. Talmi and I. Unna, *Ann. Rev. Nucl. Sci.*, **10**:353 (1960).

[3] G. Racah, *Phys. Rev.*, **63**:367 (1943).   The present solution is due to A. K. Kerman, *Ann. Phys. (N.Y.)*, **12**:300 (1961).   The same pseudospin technique was used earlier by P. W. Anderson, *Phys. Rev.*, **112**:1900 (1958), in a discussion of superconductivity.

$$[\hat{S}_+,\hat{S}_3] = -\hat{S}_+ \tag{58.44b}$$

$$[\hat{S}_-,\hat{S}_3] = \hat{S}_- \tag{58.44c}$$

which are just those of the angular-momentum operators. The quantity $\hat{S}^2$ can be written as

$$\hat{S}^2 \equiv \hat{S}_3^2 + \tfrac{1}{2}[\hat{S}_+\hat{S}_- + \hat{S}_-\hat{S}_+] = \hat{S}_3(\hat{S}_3 - 1) + \hat{S}_+\hat{S}_- \tag{58.45}$$

and a rearrangement yields

$$\hat{S}_+\hat{S}_- = \hat{S}^2 - \hat{S}_3(\hat{S}_3 - 1) \tag{58.46}$$

In terms of these *pseudospin* operators, the interaction hamiltonian becomes

$$\hat{V} = -\frac{2G}{2j+1}\,\hat{S}_+\hat{S}_- = -\frac{2G}{2j+1}\,[\hat{S}^2 - \hat{S}_3(\hat{S}_3 - 1)] \tag{58.47}$$

so that $\hat{H}$ is expressed entirely in terms of $\hat{S}^2$ and $\hat{S}_3$. Since the spectrum of the angular-momentum operators $\hat{J}^2$ and $\hat{J}_z$ follows solely from the commutation relations, we can immediately deduce the eigenvalue spectrum of the operators $\hat{S}^2$ and $\hat{S}_3$, which thus solves the problem.

The eigenvalues of $\hat{S}^2$ are of the form $S(S+1)$, where S is integral or half-integral. It also follows from the theory of angular momentum that $S \geqslant |S_3|$, and S_3 is fixed from Eq. (58.42c) if the number of particles $N \leqslant 2j+1$ is given. The *absolute maximum* possible value of S_3 is clearly $|S_3|_{max} = (2j+1)/4$, and the general theory of angular momentum also requires that $S \leqslant |S_3|_{max}$. Thus for fixed N, the eigenvalues S lie in the range

$$\tfrac{1}{4}(2j+1) \geqslant S \geqslant \tfrac{1}{4}|2N - (2j+1)| \tag{58.48}$$

and must be integral or half-integral depending on whether $S_3 = [2N - (2j+1)]/4$ is integral or half-integral. In either case, the allowed values of S differ by integers, suggesting the definition

$$S \equiv \tfrac{1}{4}(2j+1-2\sigma) \tag{58.49}$$

where σ is an integer known as the *seniority*.[1] It follows from Eqs. (58.48) and (58.49) that the permissible values of σ for fixed N are

$$\sigma = \begin{cases} 0, 2, 4, \ldots, N & (N \text{ even}) \\ 1, 3, 5, \ldots, N & (N \text{ odd}) \end{cases} \quad \begin{array}{l} 2N < (2j+1) \\ \text{particles} \end{array} \tag{58.50a}$$

$$\sigma = \begin{cases} 0, 2, 4, \ldots, 2j+1-N & (N \text{ even}) \\ 1, 3, 5, \ldots, 2j+1-N & (N \text{ odd}) \end{cases} \quad \begin{array}{l} 2N > (2j+1) \\ \text{holes} \end{array} \tag{58.50b}$$

The first case corresponds to a shell less than half filled, or *particles* in the shell, whereas the second refers to a shell more than half filled, or *holes* in the shell.

[1] G. Racah, *loc. cit.*

The exact spectrum of $\hat{H}$ is obtained by combining Eqs. (58.41), (58.42c), (58.47), and (58.49)

$$E_\sigma = N\epsilon_0 - G\frac{N - \sigma}{2}\frac{2j + 1 + 2 - N - \sigma}{2j + 1}$$

$$= N\left[\epsilon_0 - \frac{G}{2}\left(1 - \frac{N - 2}{2j + 1}\right)\right] + \frac{G\sigma}{2}\left(1 - \frac{\sigma - 2}{2j + 1}\right) \tag{58.51}$$

with the allowed values of σ given in Eqs. (58.50).‡

We now explicitly construct the lowest few eigenstates of $\hat{H}$ and first consider an even number of particles N. The lowest energy state clearly has $\sigma = 0$. We shall show that this state is just the normal-coupling shell-model ground state

$$|N, J = 0; \sigma = 0\rangle = \hat{\xi}_0^\dagger \cdots \hat{\xi}_0^\dagger \hat{\xi}_0^\dagger |0\rangle \tag{58.52}$$

where there are $N/2$ factors $\hat{\xi}_0^\dagger$. To prove that Eq. (58.52) is the correct eigenstate of $\hat{H}$, use the commutation relations of Eq. (58.31), replacing $\hat{N}$ by the appropriate eigenvalue at each step

$$\hat{V}\hat{\xi}_0^\dagger \cdots \hat{\xi}_0^\dagger \hat{\xi}_0^\dagger |0\rangle = -G\left[\frac{2j + 1 - 2(N - 2)}{2j + 1} + \frac{2j + 1 - 2(N - 4)}{2j + 1} + \cdots\right.$$

$$\left. + \frac{2j + 1}{2j + 1}\right]\hat{\xi}_0^\dagger \cdots \hat{\xi}_0^\dagger |0\rangle$$

$$= -G\frac{N}{2}\left(\frac{2j + 1 - N + 2}{2j + 1}\right)\hat{\xi}_0^\dagger \cdots \hat{\xi}_0^\dagger |0\rangle$$

which is the required result. It is evident from Eq. (58.51) that the first excited states have $\sigma = 2$. These states are obtained by breaking one of the $J = 0$ pairs.

$$|N, J, M; \sigma = 2\rangle = \hat{\xi}_0^\dagger \cdots \hat{\xi}_0^\dagger \hat{\xi}_{JM}^\dagger |0\rangle \qquad J = 2, 4, 6, \ldots, 2j - 1 \tag{58.53}$$

The proof goes just as before, except at the last step, where $[\hat{\xi}_0, \hat{\xi}_{JM}^\dagger]|0\rangle = 0$ for $J \neq 0$; therefore the eigenvalue of $\hat{V}$ is

$$-G\left[\frac{N}{2}\left(\frac{2j + 1 - N + 2}{2j + 1}\right) - 1\right] = -G\frac{N - 2}{2}\frac{2j + 1 - N}{2j + 1}$$

as claimed. The seniority σ is clearly the number of *unpaired* particles in these states.

‡ We do not discuss the degeneracy of the eigenstates. The enumeration of the antisymmetric states of total J in the j shell is a straightforward problem, and the answer can be found, for example, in M. G. Mayer and J. H. D. Jensen, *op. cit.*, p. 64.

For an odd number of valence nucleons, the lowest energy state can be written

$$|N, J = j, m; \sigma = 1\rangle = \hat{\xi}_0^\dagger \cdots \hat{\xi}_0^\dagger a_{jm}^\dagger |0\rangle \tag{58.54}$$

which is proved just as above using $[\hat{\xi}_0, a_{jm}^\dagger]|0\rangle = 0$. The first excited states with $\sigma = 3$ and $J \neq j$ can be written (see Prob. 15.7)

$$|N, J \neq j, M; \sigma = 3\rangle = \sum_{mn} \langle knjm|kjJM\rangle \hat{\xi}_0^\dagger \cdots \hat{\xi}_{kn}^\dagger a_{jm}^\dagger |0\rangle \tag{58.55}$$

Up through the 7/2 shell, there is only one state with $J = j$, and the states with $J \neq j$ are unique and thus independent of k in Eq. (58.55).[1]

We can now discuss the spectrum in the j^N configuration using the pairing interaction $\hat{V} = -G\hat{\xi}_0^\dagger \hat{\xi}_0$. For even N, the many-particle ground state has $J^\pi = 0^+$, and the first excited state always lies a distance G above the ground state. One can thus think of G as the energy gap, or pairing energy. In this model, all the first excited states are degenerate and consist of even angular momenta, corresponding to the possible states of a broken pair. For odd N, the normal-coupling state with $\sigma = 1$ is always the ground state, and the degenerate first excited states are separated from the ground state by a distance $G(2j - 1)/(2j + 1)$. Thus we have the important result that the *shell-model coupling rules hold for a potential of the form* $\hat{V} = -G\hat{\xi}_0^\dagger \hat{\xi}_0$. To the extent that any short-range attractive potential can also be written in this form, we have a more general theoretical justification of the many-particle shell model.

The model is quite good at predicting the ground state of nuclei and the energy gap to the first excited states, but the predicted degeneracy of the excited states is less realistic.

THE BOSON APPROXIMATION

The form of the exact commutator

$$[\hat{\xi}_0, \hat{\xi}_0^\dagger] = 1 - \frac{2\hat{N}}{2j + 1} \tag{58.56}$$

suggests a very simple approximation in the case that the given j shell has only a few particles with $N \ll 2j + 1$. We shall therefore assume the approximate commutation relations

$$[\hat{\xi}_{JM}, \hat{\xi}_{J'M'}^\dagger] \doteq \delta_{JJ'}\delta_{MM'} \tag{58.57}$$

which hold in this limit. The *exact* spectrum of the general potential

$$\hat{V} = \sum_{\lambda\mu} \hat{\xi}_{\lambda\mu}^\dagger \langle\lambda|V|\lambda\rangle \hat{\xi}_{\lambda\mu} \tag{58.58}$$

[1] M. G. Mayer and J. H. D. Jensen, *op. cit.*, p. 64.

for fixed N can then be obtained because Eq. (58.57) is just the commutation relation for bosons and $\hat{V}$ depends only on the *boson number operator*

$$\hat{V} = \sum_{\lambda\mu} \langle \lambda | V | \lambda \rangle \hat{\mathcal{N}}_{\lambda\mu} \tag{58.59}$$

$$\hat{\mathcal{N}}_{\lambda\mu} \equiv \hat{\xi}^{\dagger}_{\lambda\mu} \hat{\xi}_{\lambda\mu} \tag{58.60}$$

The corresponding eigenstates of $\hat{V}$ for even N are obtained by applying $N/2$ *boson* creation operators $\hat{\xi}^{\dagger}_{\lambda\mu}$ to the vacuum. In particular, if

$$\hat{V} = -G\hat{\xi}^{\dagger}_{0}\hat{\xi}_{0} = -G\hat{\mathcal{N}}_{0} \tag{58.61}$$

then the energy depends only on the eigenvalue of $\mathcal{N}_0$ (i.e., on the number of pairs coupled to form $J = 0$), and the spectrum is shown in Fig. 58.4. If we

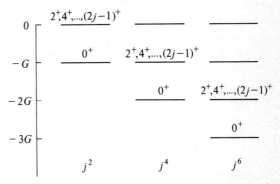

Fig. 58.4 Pairing-force spectrum in the boson approximation for the configuration j^N.

identify $N - 2\mathcal{N}_0 \equiv \sigma$, then Eq. (58.61) reproduces the exact spectrum of Eq. (58.51) in the limit $2\mathcal{N}_0 \leqslant N \ll 2j + 1$. This result justifies the use of the approximate commutation relations of Eq. (58.57) in this same limit.

THE BOGOLIUBOV TRANSFORMATION[1]

We have seen that pairing plays a very important role in nuclear spectroscopy. It is therefore of interest to include the pairing effects in a modified $\hat{H}_0$, which should then provide a better starting point for discussing nuclear spectra. This objective can be achieved with the Bogoliubov canonical transformation. Since the resulting $\hat{H}_0$ and $\hat{H} - \hat{H}_0$ will not separately conserve the number of particles, $\hat{H}_0$ will be a sensible approximate hamiltonian only if the number of particles under consideration is large and the corresponding fluctuations $(\langle \hat{N}^2 \rangle - \langle \hat{N} \rangle^2)/$

[1] S. T. Beliaev, Application of Canonical Transformation Method to Nuclei, in C. DeWitt (ed.), "The Many-Body Problem," p. 377, John Wiley and Sons, Inc., New York, 1959. For a more detailed discussion of this approach to nuclear spectroscopy see M. Baranger, *Phys. Rev.*, **120**:957 (1960) and A. M. Lane, "Nuclear Theory," W. A. Benjamin, Inc., New York, 1964.

$\langle \hat{N} \rangle^2$ negligibly small.[1]   These conditions are best satisfied in heavy nuclei, and we here consider only spherical systems.

We shall generalize our previous discussion of spectroscopy in a single j shell by working with a set of states that are completely specified by the quantum numbers $|ljm\rangle$, the radial quantum number n then being fully determined by the original choice of shells.   This set can be as large as two neighboring harmonic-oscillator shells (see the left side of Fig. 57.2).   Note that the parity of a given state is $(-1)^l$.   We again use the notation

$$|\alpha\rangle = |ljm_j\rangle \equiv |a,m_\alpha\rangle \tag{58.62a}$$

$$|-\alpha\rangle = |a,-m_\alpha\rangle \tag{58.62b}$$

where the quantum numbers $\{a\}$ denote $\{nlj\}$, with n redundant as already discussed.   For the remainder of this section, we assume that the shells are filled with just one kind of nucleon, for example, a nucleus with closed proton shells and partially filled neutron shells.

The kinetic energy is a scalar operator and hence diagonal in α, $\langle\alpha|T|\alpha'\rangle = \delta_{\alpha\alpha'} T_a$.   Consequently the thermodynamic potential at zero temperature can be written

$$\hat{K} = \hat{H} - \mu\hat{N} = \sum_\alpha (T_a - \mu)\, c_\alpha^\dagger c_\alpha - \tfrac{1}{2} \sum_{\alpha\beta\gamma\delta} \langle\alpha\beta|V|\gamma\delta\rangle\, c_\alpha^\dagger c_\beta^\dagger c_\delta c_\gamma \tag{58.63}$$

where the interaction is assumed attractive ($V > 0$) exactly as in Eq. (37.6).   We now carry out the following canonical transformation on this thermodynamic potential

$$A_\alpha^\dagger \equiv u_a c_\alpha^\dagger - v_a S_\alpha c_{-\alpha}$$

$$A_\alpha \equiv u_a c_\alpha - v_a S_\alpha c_{-\alpha}^\dagger \tag{58.64}$$

where the phase $S_\alpha = (-1)^{j_\alpha - m_\alpha}$ has again been introduced to make $A^\dagger$ an irreducible tensor operator.   The coefficients u_a and v_a are taken to be real and normalized

$$u_a^2 + v_a^2 = 1$$

so that the transformation is indeed canonical

$$\{A_\alpha, A_{\alpha'}^\dagger\} = \delta_{\alpha\alpha'} \tag{58.65}$$

---

[1] A refinement of the approach discussed in this section is to project from the eigenstates of $\hat{H}_0$ that part corresponding to a definite number of particles.   See, for example, A. K. Kerman, R. D. Lawson, and M. H. Macfarlane, *Phys. Rev.*, **124**:162 (1961).

Equations (58.64) can be inverted to give

$$c_\alpha = u_a A_\alpha + v_a S_\alpha A^\dagger_{-\alpha}$$

$$c^\dagger_\alpha = u_a A^\dagger_\alpha + v_a S_\alpha A_{-\alpha} \tag{58.66}$$

The next task is to write $\hat{K}$ in normal-ordered form with respect to the operators A and $A^\dagger$. This calculation is readily done with Wick's theorem, just as in Sec. 37, and the only nonzero contractions are

$$\overset{\cdot}{c^\dagger_\alpha} \overset{\cdot}{c_\beta} = \delta_{\alpha\beta} v_b^2$$

$$\overset{\cdot}{c^\dagger_\alpha} \overset{\cdot}{c^\dagger_\beta} = \delta_{\alpha,-\beta} v_a u_a S_\alpha$$

$$\overset{\cdot}{c_\alpha} \overset{\cdot}{c_\beta} = \delta_{\alpha,-\beta} v_a u_a S_\beta$$

The symmetry property $\langle\alpha\beta|V|\gamma\delta\rangle = \langle\beta\alpha|V|\delta\gamma\rangle$ enables us to rewrite the operators in Eq. (58.63)

$$c^\dagger_\alpha c_\beta = N(c^\dagger_\alpha c_\beta) + \delta_{\alpha\beta} v_b^2 \tag{58.67a}$$

$$c^\dagger_\alpha c^\dagger_\beta c_\delta c_\gamma = N(c^\dagger_\alpha c^\dagger_\beta c_\delta c_\gamma) + \delta_{\alpha,-\beta} S_\alpha v_a u_a N(c_\delta c_\gamma) + \delta_{\gamma,-\delta} S_\gamma v_c u_c N(c^\dagger_\alpha c^\dagger_\beta)$$
$$+ 2\delta_{\alpha\gamma} v_c^2 N(c^\dagger_\beta c_\delta) - 2\delta_{\alpha\delta} v_a^2 N(c^\dagger_\beta c_\gamma) + \delta_{\alpha,-\beta}\delta_{\gamma,-\delta} S_\alpha S_\gamma v_a u_a v_c u_c$$
$$+ (\delta_{\alpha\gamma}\delta_{\beta\delta} - \delta_{\alpha\delta}\delta_{\beta\gamma}) v_a^2 v_b^2 \tag{58.67b}$$

which is correct when summed over all indices. The resulting expression for $\hat{K}$ can be simplified considerably by using some general symmetry properties of the potential:

1. $\langle\alpha\beta|V|\gamma\delta\rangle = \langle\beta\alpha|V|\delta\gamma\rangle$ (58.68)

2. $\langle\alpha\beta|V|\gamma\delta\rangle = S_\alpha S_\beta S_\gamma S_\delta \langle-\gamma-\delta|V|-\alpha-\beta\rangle$ (58.69)

 which follows from time-reversal invariance; an explicit proof can be given in the special case where $V = V_0(x_{12}) + V_1(x_{12})\boldsymbol{\sigma}_1\cdot\boldsymbol{\sigma}_2$ (see Prob. 15.13).

3. $\langle\alpha\beta|V|\gamma\delta\rangle = \sum_{JM}\langle j_\alpha m_\alpha j_\beta m_\beta|j_\alpha j_\beta JM\rangle\langle j_\gamma m_\gamma j_\delta m_\delta|j_\gamma j_\delta JM\rangle\langle abJ|V|cdJ\rangle$

                                                                (58.70)

 which follows from the rotational invariance of V.

4. $\langle abJ|V|cdJ\rangle = \langle cdJ|V|abJ\rangle$ (58.71)

 which follows from 2 and 3 together with the symmetry properties of the Clebsch-Gordan coefficients.

The preceding expressions can be combined to yield

$$\hat{K} = U + \hat{H}_1 + \hat{H}_2 + \hat{H}_3 \tag{58.72}$$

where

$$\hat{H}_3 = -\tfrac{1}{2} \sum_{\alpha\beta\gamma\delta} \langle\alpha\beta|V|\gamma\delta\rangle N(c^\dagger_\alpha c^\dagger_\beta c_\delta c_\gamma) \tag{58.73}$$

and the other terms are those remaining in Eqs. (58.63). With the identities [see Eq. (B.20b)]

$$\sum_{m_\alpha m_\beta} \langle j_\alpha m_\alpha j_\beta m_\beta | j_\alpha j_\beta JM \rangle \langle j_\alpha m_\alpha j_\beta m_\beta | j_\alpha j_\beta JM \rangle = 1$$

and

$$\sum_{m_\alpha} \frac{S_\alpha}{(2j_\alpha + 1)^{\frac{1}{2}}} \langle j_\alpha m_\alpha j_\alpha -m_\alpha | j_\alpha j_\alpha JM \rangle$$
$$= \sum_m \langle jmj - m | jj\,00 \rangle \langle jmj - m | jjJM \rangle = \delta_{J0}\,\delta_{M0}$$

the c-number terms in Eqs. (58.63) can be written

$$U = \sum_\alpha v_a^2 (T_a - \mu + \tfrac{1}{2}V_a) - \tfrac{1}{2}\sum_\alpha v_a u_a \Delta_a \tag{58.74}$$

where the single-particle potential energy has been defined by[1]

$$V_a \equiv -\sum_b \sum_J \frac{2J+1}{2j_a+1}[\langle abJ | V | abJ \rangle - (-1)^{j_a + j_b - J} \langle abJ | V | baJ \rangle] v_b^2 \tag{58.75}$$

and the gap function by

$$\Delta_a \equiv \frac{1}{(2j_a+1)^{\frac{1}{2}}}\sum_c (2j_c + 1)^{\frac{1}{2}} \langle aa0 | V | cc0 \rangle v_c u_c \tag{58.76}$$

The terms proportional to $N(c^\dagger c)$, which give bilinear terms in A and $A^\dagger$, can be simplified with the identity

$$\sum_M \sum_{m_\alpha} \langle j_\alpha m_\alpha j_\beta m_\beta | j_\alpha j_\beta JM \rangle \langle j_\alpha m_\alpha j_\delta m_\delta | j_\alpha j_\delta JM \rangle$$

$$= \frac{2J+1}{[(2j_\beta + 1)(2j_\delta + 1)]^{\frac{1}{2}}} \sum_M \sum_{m_\alpha} \langle JMj_\alpha -m_\alpha | Jj_\alpha j_\beta m_\beta \rangle \langle JMj_\alpha -m_\alpha | Jj_\alpha j_\delta m_\delta \rangle$$

$$= \frac{2J+1}{2j_\beta + 1}\,\delta_{j_\beta j_\delta}\,\delta_{m_\beta m_\delta}$$

Furthermore, $V(1,2)$ is invariant under spatial reflections, and conservation of parity implies that $l_\beta = l_\delta$ in the matrix element $\langle abJ | V | adJ \rangle$. (The possibility $l_\beta = l_\delta \pm 2$ is ruled out by $j_\beta = j_\delta$.) *Within our subspace* of two adjacent oscillator shells we can therefore write

$$\sum_M \sum_{m_\alpha} \langle j_\alpha m_\alpha j_\beta m_\beta | j_\alpha j_\beta JM \rangle \langle j_\alpha m_\alpha j_\delta m_\delta | j_\alpha j_\delta JM \rangle = \frac{2J+1}{2j_\beta + 1}\,\delta_{\beta\delta}$$

[1] In order to emphasize that V_a and Δ_a are independent of m_α, we use the abbreviation $j_a \equiv j_\alpha$, etc.

By exactly the same argument, the terms proportional to $N(cc)$ and $N(c^\dagger c^\dagger)$ can be simplified with the respective replacements [see Eq. (B.20b)]

$$\langle j_\gamma m_\gamma j_\delta m_\delta | j_\gamma j_\delta 00 \rangle \rightarrow \frac{S_\gamma \delta_{\gamma,-\delta}}{(2j_c + 1)^{\frac{1}{2}}}$$

$$\langle j_\alpha m_\alpha j_\beta m_\beta | j_\alpha j_\beta 00 \rangle \rightarrow \frac{S_\alpha \delta_{\alpha,-\beta}}{(2j_a + 1)^{\frac{1}{2}}}$$

In this way, we obtain

$$\hat{H}_1 = \sum_\alpha [(u_a^2 - v_a^2)(\epsilon_a - \mu) + 2u_a v_a \Delta_a] \tfrac{1}{2}(A_\alpha^\dagger A_\alpha + A_{-\alpha}^\dagger A_{-\alpha}) \tag{58.77a}$$

$$\hat{H}_2 = \sum_\alpha S_\alpha [2u_a v_a(\epsilon_a - \mu) - (u_a^2 - v_a^2)\Delta_a] \tfrac{1}{2}(A_\alpha^\dagger A_{-\alpha}^\dagger + A_{-\alpha} A_\alpha) \tag{58.77b}$$

where a new single-particle energy has been defined by

$$\epsilon_a \equiv T_a + V_a \tag{58.78}$$

The analysis of these equations now proceeds exactly as in Sec. 37.   Defining the energy with respect to the chemical potential

$$\xi_a \equiv \epsilon_a - \mu \tag{58.79}$$

and choosing u and v to eliminate $\hat{H}_2$ leads to

$$\hat{K} = \hat{K}_0 - \tfrac{1}{2} \sum_{\alpha\beta\gamma\delta} \langle \alpha\beta | V | \gamma\delta \rangle N(c_\alpha^\dagger c_\beta^\dagger c_\delta c_\gamma) \tag{58.80}$$

where

$$\hat{K}_0 \equiv U + \sum_\alpha (\xi_a^2 + \Delta_a^2)^{\frac{1}{2}} A_\alpha^\dagger A_\alpha \tag{58.81}$$

and

$$\Delta_a = \frac{1}{2} \sum_c \left(\frac{2j_c + 1}{2j_a + 1} \right)^{\frac{1}{2}} \langle aa0 | V | cc0 \rangle \frac{\Delta_c}{(\Delta_c^2 + \xi_c^2)^{\frac{1}{2}}} \tag{58.82}$$

We note in passing that the normal solution to the gap equation

$$\Delta = 0 \qquad u_c = \theta(c - F) \qquad v_c = \theta(F - c) \tag{58.83}$$

reproduces the results of Sec. 56.   Within our subspace, however, we *need not assume that the single-particle wave functions satisfy the Hartree-Fock equations.* It is only necessary that the states be completely characterized by the quantum numbers $\{ljm_j\}$.[1]

---

[1] The present discussion considers only the interaction between particles in a restricted set of basis states, but it is easily generalized to include an additional inert core.   One starts with the Hartree-Fock wave functions determined by the interaction with the core [see Eqs. (56.16) to (56.24)] and then carries out the Bogoliubov transformation on the additional valence particles. If T_a is augmented by the Hartree-Fock energy of interaction with the core $T_a \rightarrow T_a + V_a^{\text{core}}$, then the results of this section correctly describe the properties of these valence particles.

The operator $\hat{K}_0$ in Eq. (58.81) is now diagonal, and its ground state $|\mathbf{O}\rangle$ satisfies

$$A_\alpha|\mathbf{O}\rangle = 0 \qquad\qquad (58.84)$$

If the exact ground state of $\hat{K}$ is approximated by the ground state of $\hat{K}_0$, then the thermodynamic potential of the system is given by

$$\Omega(T=0,V,\mu) \approx \langle\mathbf{O}|\hat{K}|\mathbf{O}\rangle = \langle\mathbf{O}|\hat{K}_0|\mathbf{O}\rangle = U(V,\mu) \qquad (58.85)$$

The expectation value of the number operator

$$\hat{N} = \sum_\alpha c_\alpha^\dagger c_\alpha = \sum_\alpha [(u_a^2 - v_a^2)\,A_\alpha^\dagger A_\alpha + u_a v_a S_\alpha (A_\alpha^\dagger A_{-\alpha}^\dagger + A_{-\alpha}A_\alpha) + v_a^2] \quad (58.86)$$

in the state $|\mathbf{O}\rangle$ is

$$N = \sum_\alpha v_a^2 = \sum_\alpha \frac{1}{2}\left[1 - \frac{\xi_a}{(\Delta_a^2 + \xi_a^2)^{\frac{1}{2}}}\right] \qquad (58.87)$$

so that the occupation number is again continuous at $\epsilon_a = \mu$. This equation can be used to eliminate μ in terms of N.

The quantity of direct interest in nuclear physics is the energy at fixed N. For the ground state of $\hat{K}_0$, this energy can be obtained from the relation

$$E(N) = \langle\mathbf{O}|\hat{K} + \mu\hat{N}|\mathbf{O}\rangle = \langle\mathbf{O}|\hat{K}_0|\mathbf{O}\rangle + \mu N = U + \mu N \qquad (58.88)$$

where $\mu(N)$ is determined from Eq. (58.87). The excited states of the system are obtained by adding quasiparticles to the ground state; they take the form $|\mathbf{n}_1 \mathbf{n}_2 \cdots\rangle = (A_1^\dagger)^{n_1}(A_2^\dagger)^{n_2} \cdots |\mathbf{O}\rangle$ with n_1 quasiparticles in the single-particle state 1, n_2 quasiparticles in the single-particle state 2, and so on. It is clear that $n_i = 0$ or 1. For fixed μ, each of these excited states has a slightly different expectation value of $\hat{N}$. We therefore consider a collection of assemblies at slightly different chemical potentials μ_{ex} such that $\langle\mathbf{n}_1 \mathbf{n}_2 \cdots |\hat{N}|\mathbf{n}_1 \mathbf{n}_2 \cdots\rangle = N$ in each case. In the present approximation, the excitation energy of these states is given by

$$\Delta E^*(N) \equiv \langle\mathbf{n}_1 \mathbf{n}_2 \cdots |\hat{K}_0 + \mu_{\text{ex}}\hat{N}|\mathbf{n}_1 \mathbf{n}_2 \cdots\rangle - \langle\mathbf{O}|\hat{K}_0 + \mu\hat{N}|\mathbf{O}\rangle$$
$$= \sum_\alpha (\xi_a^2 + \Delta_a^2)_{\text{ex}}^{\frac{1}{2}} n_\alpha + [U(\mu_{\text{ex}}) - U(\mu) + (\mu_{\text{ex}} - \mu)N] \qquad (58.89)$$

For a small number of quasiparticles, Eqs. (18.30) and (58.85) imply that the term in brackets vanishes; in addition, the coefficient of n_α can be evaluated using the μ obtained for the state $|\mathbf{O}\rangle$. Thus if $\sum_\alpha n_\alpha$ is sufficiently small, we obtain the important result that

$$\Delta E^*(N) = \sum_\alpha (\xi_a^2 + \Delta_a^2)^{\frac{1}{2}} n_\alpha \qquad (58.90)$$

where $\mu(N)$ is determined by Eq. (58.87).

These ideas can now be applied to even and odd nuclei. The ground state of $\hat{K}_0$ is identified with the ground state of an even-even $J^\pi = 0^+$ nucleus.[1] Since the state $|\alpha\rangle \equiv A_\alpha^\dagger|\mathbf{O}\rangle$ has components with the number of particles changed by one and has odd half-integral J values, it then refers to an odd nucleus. To get excitations in the original even nucleus, we must create at least two quasiparticles, and the spectrum for these excitations [Eq. (58.90)] starts at an energy greater than $2\Delta_{min}$ (the minimum value of $2\Delta_a$, $2\Delta_b$, etc.) above the ground state. *Thus the present model leads to an energy gap of $2\Delta_{min}$ in even nuclei.*

For an odd nucleus, we can repeat all the previous arguments, taking the state $|\alpha\rangle = A_\alpha^\dagger|0\rangle$ as the ground state. In this case

$$\Omega(T=0,V,\mu) \approx \langle\alpha|\hat{K}|\alpha\rangle = \langle\alpha|\hat{K}_0|\alpha\rangle = U + (\xi_a^2 + \Delta_a^2)^{\frac{1}{2}}$$

$$N = (u_a^2 - v_a^2) + \sum_\beta v_b^2 \tag{58.91}$$

$$E(N) = \langle\alpha|\hat{K} + \mu\hat{N}|\alpha\rangle = \langle\alpha|\hat{K}_0|\alpha\rangle + \mu N = U + (\xi_a^2 + \Delta_a^2)^{\frac{1}{2}} + \mu N$$

To get the excited states of an odd nucleus, we can again add pairs of quasiparticles in the j_a shell. There is, however, another class of excited states, which are obtained by simply promoting the single quasiparticle from the original j_a shell to a new j_b shell. The excitation energy of these states is given by

$$\Delta E^*(N) = (\xi_b^2 + \Delta_b^2)^{\frac{1}{2}} - (\xi_a^2 + \Delta_a^2)^{\frac{1}{2}} \tag{58.92}$$

and we conclude that *odd nuclei have no energy gap in this model.*[2] There is some evidence that this model indeed describes heavy nuclei,[3] for example, the set of Sn or Pb isotopes.[4]

The matrix elements of an arbitrary multipole operator between these low-lying (single-quasiparticle) states of an odd nucleus can be evaluated immediately. The $Q = 0$ component of a general tensor operator can be written

$$\hat{T}_{K0} = \sum_{\alpha\beta} c_\beta^\dagger\langle\beta|T_{K0}|\alpha\rangle c_\alpha$$

$$= \sum_{\alpha\beta} \langle\beta|T_{K0}|\alpha\rangle (u_b A_\beta^\dagger + v_b S_\beta A_{-\beta})(u_a A_\alpha + v_a S_\alpha A_{-\alpha}^\dagger)$$

$$= \sum_{\alpha\beta} \langle\beta|T_{K0}|\alpha\rangle [N(c_\beta^\dagger c_\alpha) + v_b^2\delta_{\beta\alpha}] \tag{58.93}$$

---

[1] One can show (see Prob. 15.14) that the state $|\mathbf{O}\rangle$ does indeed have $J^\pi = 0^+$.

[2] Typical excitation energies for spherical nuclei are about an MeV for even A and a few hundred keV for odd A.

[3] A. Bohr, B. R. Mottelson, and D. Pines, *Phys. Rev.*, **110**:936 (1958).

[4] L. S. Kisslinger and R. A. Sorenson, *Kgl. Danske Videnskab. Selskab, Mat.-Fys. Medd*, **32**, No. 9 (1960).

The expectation value of $\hat{T}_{K0}$ is given by

$$\langle\alpha|\hat{T}_{K0}|\alpha\rangle = \langle\alpha|T_{K0}|\alpha\rangle\, u_a^2 - \langle-\alpha|T_{K0}|-\alpha\rangle\, v_a^2 \qquad K \neq 0$$
$$= \langle\alpha|T_{K0}|\alpha\rangle\,[u_a^2 - (-1)^K v_a^2]$$

and we therefore find

$$\langle\alpha|\hat{T}_{K0}|\alpha\rangle = \begin{cases} \langle\alpha|T_{K0}|\alpha\rangle & K \text{ odd} \\[2mm] \dfrac{\xi_a}{(\xi_a^2 + \Delta_a^2)^{\frac{1}{2}}}\langle\alpha|T_{K0}|\alpha\rangle & \begin{array}{l} K \text{ even} \\ K \neq 0 \end{array} \end{cases}$$

$$\text{(58.94a)}$$
$$\text{(58.94b)}$$

The odd multipoles are *unchanged* by pairing, whereas the even multipoles are again *reduced* by pairing and become negative for $\epsilon < \mu$ (i.e., for holes). These results should be compared with Eqs. (58.23). A similar result holds for transition multipoles between different j shells:

$$\langle\beta|\hat{T}_{K0}|\alpha\rangle = \langle\beta|T_{K0}|\alpha\rangle\, u_b u_a - \langle-\alpha|T_{K0}|-\beta\rangle\, v_a v_b\, S_{-\alpha}\, S_{-\beta}$$

$$\langle\mathbf{j}_b\|\hat{T}_K\|\mathbf{j}_a\rangle = \langle j_b\|T_K\|j_a\rangle\, u_b u_a + (-1)^{j_a+j_b+K}\langle j_a\|T_K\|j_b\rangle\, v_b v_a$$

$$\text{(58.95)}$$

The present approach enables us to include the pairing interaction in the starting approximation. To understand the validity and implications of this approximation, consider a single j shell with N particles interacting through a pure attractive pairing force $(G > 0)$

$$\langle j^2 J|V|j^2 J\rangle = G\delta_{J0} \tag{58.96}$$

This is precisely the problem solved in the previous section, with the exact spectrum of Eq. (58.51). Since we now have only one single-particle level and v, u, Δ, and ξ are already independent of m, all subscripts can be dropped. The sum in Eq. (58.87) then becomes trivial; thus the chemical potential $\mu(N)$ is determined from the relation

$$N = (2j + 1)v^2 = (2j + 1)\frac{1}{2}\left[1 - \frac{\xi}{(\xi^2 + \Delta^2)^{\frac{1}{2}}}\right] \tag{58.97}$$

which fixes the coefficients u and v:

$$v = \left(\frac{N}{2j + 1}\right)^{\frac{1}{2}} \qquad u = \left(1 - \frac{N}{2j + 1}\right)^{\frac{1}{2}}$$

with the signs chosen as in Sec. 37. Similarly, the gap equation (58.82) reduces to the simple condition

$$(\Delta^2 + \xi^2)^{\frac{1}{2}} = \tfrac{1}{2}G \tag{58.98}$$

A combination of Eqs. (58.97) and (58.98) yields

$$\xi = \frac{G}{2}\left(1 - \frac{2N}{2j+1}\right) \tag{58.99}$$

$$\Delta = G\left(\frac{N}{2j+1}\right)^{\frac{1}{2}}\left(1 - \frac{N}{2j+1}\right)^{\frac{1}{2}} \tag{58.100}$$

and the thermodynamic potential U in Eq. (58.74) becomes

$$U = N(t - \mu + \tfrac{1}{2}V) - \tfrac{1}{2}(2j+1)uv\Delta$$

where $t \equiv T_\alpha$ is the kinetic energy of a particle in the j shell and

$$V = -\frac{2}{2j+1}\,Gv^2 = -\frac{2GN}{(2j+1)^2} \tag{58.101}$$

from Eq. (58.75). The new ground-state energy E is therefore given in terms of G and N as

$$E - Nt = U + N\mu - Nt = -\frac{G}{2}\frac{N}{2j+1}\left(1 - \frac{N}{2j+1}\right)(2j+1) - \frac{GN^2}{(2j+1)^2}$$

or

$$E - Nt = -G\frac{N}{2}\left[1 - \frac{N}{2j+1} + \frac{2N}{(2j+1)^2}\right] \qquad \text{Bogoliubov} \tag{58.102}$$

This should be compared with the exact expression, obtained from Eqs. (58.50) and (58.51)

$$E - Nt = \begin{cases} -G\dfrac{N}{2}\left(1 - \dfrac{N}{2j+1} + \dfrac{2}{2j+1}\right) & N \text{ even} \\[3mm] -G\dfrac{N}{2}\left[1 - \dfrac{N}{2j+1} + \dfrac{2}{2j+1} - \dfrac{1}{N}\left(1 + \dfrac{1}{2j+1}\right)\right] & N \text{ odd} \end{cases} \right\} \text{exact}$$

$$\tag{58.103}$$

The resulting energies per particle coincide in the limit of many available states $(2j+1 \to \infty)$ but allowing finite fractional occupation of these states $[N/(2j+1) \to \text{finite number}]$

$$\frac{E}{N} \to t - \frac{G}{2}\left(1 - \frac{N}{2j+1}\right) \tag{58.104}$$

Note that Eqs. (58.79), (58.99), and (58.101) imply that

$$\mu = t + V - \xi = t - \frac{G}{2}\left[1 - \frac{2N}{2j+1} + \frac{4N}{(2j+1)^2}\right] \tag{58.105}$$

in accordance with the thermodynamics relation $\mu = (\partial E/\partial N)$ and Eq. (58.102).

The excitation spectrum is obtained by adding quasiparticles to the single j shell. Each quasiparticle contributes an amount $(\Delta^2 + \xi^2)^{\frac{1}{2}} = \frac{1}{2}G$ to the energy at fixed N [see Eq. (58.90)] as long as the total number of quasiparticles $n_q = \sum_\alpha n_\alpha$ is small. By the previous arguments, adding one quasiparticle changes an even nucleus into an odd nucleus. Thus the spectrum of a given nucleus involves an even number n_q of quasiparticles and the excitation energy is

$$\Delta E^*(N) = \tfrac{1}{2}Gn_q \tag{58.106}$$

If we identify n_q with the seniority σ, then this spectrum *agrees with the exact spectrum of Eq. (58.51)* in the limit $n_q = \sigma \ll 2j + 1$. In addition, Eq. (58.106) is exact for $\sigma = 2$, because the first excited state of an even nucleus with a pure pairing force is separated from the ground state by precisely G. Note that this simple model has only one single-particle level available, which implies that odd nuclei also have a gap in the energy spectrum.

We have already noted that adding quasiparticles changes the expectation value of N slightly. Although this effect was treated only approximately in obtaining Eq. (58.90), the present restricted model allows us to carry through the analysis of Eq. (58.89) exactly for all n_q. The expectation value of the number operator [see Eq. (58.86)] is

$$N = \langle \mathbf{n}_q | \hat{N} | \mathbf{n}_q \rangle = (2j + 1)v^2 + (u^2 - v^2)n_q$$

Thus v^2 depends on the quasiparticle number:

$$v^2 = \frac{N - n_q}{2j + 1 - 2n_q}$$

A repetition of the above discussion with this new v^2 gives

$$U(\mu_{\mathrm{ex}}) + \mu_{\mathrm{ex}} N = N\left(t - \frac{G}{2}\right) + (2j - 1)G\frac{N - n_q}{2j + 1 - 2n_q}$$

$$\times \left(\frac{N}{2j + 1} - \frac{1}{2}\frac{N - n_q}{2j + 1 - 2n_q}\right)$$

which is valid for arbitrary n_q and reproduces Eq. (58.102) in the limit $n_q \to 0$. The excitation energy at fixed N is obtained from Eq. (58.89), and an expansion in powers of $n_q/(2j + 1)$ gives

$$\Delta E^*(N) = \frac{G}{2}n_q\left[1 - \frac{n_q}{2j + 1}\frac{2j - 1}{2j + 1}\left(\frac{2j + 1 - 2N}{2j + 1}\right)^2 + O\left(\frac{n_q}{2j + 1}\right)^2\right]$$

This result includes the first correction to Eq. (58.90) for small n_q. Assume that j is large but that the j shell is either nearly full or nearly empty, so that

$[(2j + 1 - 2N)/(2j + 1)]^2 \approx 1$.   This approximation yields

$$\Delta E^*(N) \approx \frac{G}{2} n_q \left(1 - \frac{n_q}{2j+1}\right) \tag{58.107}$$

For comparison the exact result [Eq. (58.51)] is given by

$$\Delta E^*(N) = \frac{G}{2} n_q \left(1 - \frac{n_q - 2}{2j+1}\right) \tag{58.108}$$

where we have again identified $\sigma \equiv n_q$.   These two expressions now agree up through the first correction term in the thermodynamic limit: $2j + 1 \to \infty$ with $n_q/(2j+1)$ finite.

The validity of the Bogoliubov approach to nuclear spectra can also be tested by examining the fluctuation in N (compare Prob. 10.6)

$$\langle O|\hat{N}^2|O\rangle - \langle O|\hat{N}|O\rangle^2 = \sum_{n \neq 0} |\langle n|\hat{N}|O\rangle|^2$$

$$= \tfrac{1}{2} \sum_{\alpha} |\langle \alpha - \alpha| \sum_{\beta} S_\beta u_b v_b A_\beta^\dagger A_{-\beta}^\dagger |O\rangle|^2$$

$$= 2 \sum_{\alpha} u_a^2 v_a^2$$

which leads to the general result

$$\frac{\langle \hat{N}^2\rangle - \langle \hat{N}\rangle^2}{\langle \hat{N}\rangle^2} = \frac{2 \sum\limits_{\alpha} u_a^2 v_a^2}{\left(\sum\limits_{\alpha} v_a^2\right)^2} \tag{58.109}$$

In the case of a single j shell with a pure pairing force, Eq. (58.109) can be simplified to give

$$\frac{\langle \hat{N}^2\rangle - \langle \hat{N}\rangle^2}{\langle \hat{N}\rangle^2} = \frac{2}{N}\left(1 - \frac{N}{2j+1}\right) \tag{58.110}$$

The theory makes sense only if this expression is small, which is true provided N is large enough.

In summary, we conclude that *the diagonal thermodynamic potential*

$$\hat{K}_0 = U + \sum_{\alpha} (\xi^2 + \Delta^2)^{\frac{1}{2}} A_\alpha^\dagger A_\alpha \tag{58.111}$$

correctly describes a j^N configuration with a pure pairing interaction [Eq. (58.96)] *in the limit*

$$\frac{N}{2j+1} \text{ fixed} \qquad 2j+1 \to \infty \qquad n_q \ll 2j+1 \tag{58.112}$$

59□EXCITED STATES: LINEARIZATION OF
THE EQUATIONS OF MOTION[1]

After this excursion into the theoretical foundations of the many-particle shell model, we return to the more general problem of collective excitations built on the Hartree-Fock ground state of a finite interacting assembly.   In the present section, the ground state is assumed to contain only closed shells.   If the system is excited through the single application of a one-body number-conserving operator, then the resulting states must have a single particle promoted from the ground state to a higher shell, or equivalently, must contain a particle-hole pair.   Hence we may hope to describe the strongly excited collective oscillations as some general linear combination of particle-hole states.   This procedure will now be carried out in two stages of approximation.

TAMM-DANCOFF APPROXIMATION (TDA)

We first construct the *particle-hole-pair* creation operator

$$\hat{\zeta}_{\alpha\beta}^{\dagger} \equiv a_{\alpha}^{\dagger} b_{\beta}^{\dagger} \tag{59.1}$$

which removes a particle from the filled states and promotes it to an excited state.   Consider the matrix element

$$\langle \Psi_{n}|[\hat{H},\hat{\zeta}_{\alpha\beta}^{\dagger}]|\Psi_{0}\rangle = (E_{n} - E_{0})\langle \Psi_{n}|\hat{\zeta}_{\alpha\beta}^{\dagger}|\Psi_{0}\rangle \tag{59.2}$$

where $|\Psi_{0}\rangle$ is the exact ground state of the hamiltonian $\hat{H}$ in Eq. (56.18) and $|\Psi_{n}\rangle$ is an exact excited state.   The left side can be rewritten by evaluating the commutator explicitly:

$$[H_{0},\hat{\zeta}_{\alpha\beta}^{\dagger}] = 0 \tag{59.3a}$$

$$[\hat{H}_{1},\hat{\zeta}_{\alpha\beta}^{\dagger}] = \left[\left(\sum_{\alpha>F} \epsilon_{\alpha} a_{\alpha}^{\dagger} a_{\alpha} - \sum_{\alpha<F} \epsilon_{\alpha} b_{-\alpha}^{\dagger} b_{-\alpha}\right), \hat{\zeta}_{\alpha\beta}^{\dagger}\right]$$

$$= (\epsilon_{\alpha} - \epsilon_{-\beta}) \hat{\zeta}_{\alpha\beta}^{\dagger} \tag{59.3b}$$

$$[\hat{H}_{2},\hat{\zeta}_{\alpha\beta}^{\dagger}] = \tfrac{1}{2} \sum_{\rho\sigma\mu\nu} \langle \rho\sigma|V|\mu\nu\rangle \, [N(c_{\rho}^{\dagger} c_{\sigma}^{\dagger} c_{\nu} c_{\mu}), a_{\alpha}^{\dagger} b_{\beta}^{\dagger}] \tag{59.3c}$$

where the normal ordering in the last line again refers to the particle and hole operators

$$c_{\alpha} \equiv \theta(\alpha - F) a_{\alpha} + \theta(F - \alpha) S_{\alpha} b_{-\alpha}^{\dagger} \tag{59.4}$$

The first two commutators are simple, but the last one is generally very complicated.

[1] More detailed discussions of the application of these many-body techniques to nuclear spectroscopy can be found in A. M. Lane, *loc. cit.*, M. Baranger, *loc. cit.*, and G. E. Brown, "Unified Theory of Nuclear Models," North-Holland Publishing Company, Amsterdam, 1964.

We start by evaluating Eq. (59.3c) in the Tamm-Dancoff approximation (TDA),[1] where the allowed states in Eq. (59.2) are restricted to the closed-shell Hartree-Fock ground state

$$|\Psi_0\rangle = |0\rangle \qquad a_\alpha|0\rangle = b_\alpha|0\rangle = 0 \tag{59.5}$$

and a linear combination of particle-hole states

$$|\Psi_n\rangle = \sum_{\alpha\beta} \psi_{\alpha\beta}^{(n)*}\, \hat{\zeta}_{\alpha\beta}^{\dagger}|0\rangle \tag{59.6}$$

In this case, the commutator in Eq. (59.3c) can be evaluated by retaining only those terms that yield $a^\dagger b^\dagger$ because all the other operators vanish between the states approximated as in Eqs. (59.5) and (59.6). These terms become

$$[N\{S_\mu S_\sigma a_\rho^\dagger b_{-\sigma} a_\nu b_{-\mu}^\dagger + S_\rho S_\nu b_{-\rho} a_\sigma^\dagger b_{-\nu}^\dagger a_\mu + S_\nu S_\sigma a_\rho^\dagger b_{-\sigma} b_{-\nu}^\dagger a_\mu$$

$$+ S_\nu S_\mu b_{-\rho} a_\sigma^\dagger a_\nu b_{-\mu}^\dagger\}, a_\alpha^\dagger b_\beta^\dagger]$$

$$= 2[(S_\mu S_\sigma a_\rho^\dagger b_{-\mu}^\dagger b_{-\sigma} a_\nu - S_\nu S_\sigma a_\rho^\dagger b_{-\nu}^\dagger b_{-\sigma} a_\mu), a_\alpha^\dagger b_\beta^\dagger]$$

where the symmetry $\langle \rho\sigma | V | \mu\nu \rangle = \langle \sigma\rho | V | \nu\mu \rangle$ has been used. The commutator is readily evaluated to give

$$[\hat{H}_2, \hat{\zeta}_{\alpha\beta}^\dagger] \doteq \sum_{\lambda\mu} S_{-\beta} S_{-\mu}[\langle \lambda - \beta | V | -\mu\alpha \rangle - \langle \lambda - \beta | V | \alpha - \mu \rangle] \hat{\zeta}_{\lambda\mu}^\dagger \tag{59.7}$$

where the symbol $\doteq$ means that only these terms contribute to the matrix elements under consideration. With the relation [see Eq. (59.6)]

$$\langle \Psi_n | \hat{\zeta}_{\alpha\beta}^\dagger | \Psi_0 \rangle \equiv \psi_{\alpha\beta}^{(n)} \tag{59.8}$$

Eq. (59.2) can finally be written in the TDA as a set of linear homogeneous equations for the quantities $\psi_{\lambda\mu}^{(n)}$:

$$[(E_0 + \epsilon_\alpha - \epsilon_{-\beta}) - E_n]\psi_{\alpha\beta}^{(n)} + \sum_{\lambda\mu} v_{\alpha\beta:\lambda\mu}\, \psi_{\lambda\mu}^{(n)} = 0 \tag{59.9}$$

$$v_{\alpha\beta:\lambda\mu} \equiv S_{-\beta} S_{-\mu}[\langle \lambda - \beta | V | -\mu\alpha \rangle - \langle \lambda - \beta | V | \alpha - \mu \rangle] \tag{59.10}$$

The eigenvalues E_n are obtained by setting the determinant of the coefficients equal to zero, and the corresponding solutions give the eigenvector coefficients $\psi_{\lambda\mu}^{(n)}$. In this expression, the indices $(\alpha\beta)$ and $(\lambda\mu)$ denote particle-hole pairs, while the matrix element $v_{\alpha\beta:\lambda\mu}$ represents the *particle-hole interaction potential*, related to the particle-particle interaction by Eq. (59.10). The quantity $\epsilon_\alpha - \epsilon_{-\beta}$ is just the unperturbed Hartree-Fock excitation energy for a particle-hole pair. Since the Hartree-Fock energy ϵ_α is the energy of interaction with the *filled* ground

---

[1] I. Tamm, *J. Phys. (USSR)*, **9**:449 (1945) and S. M. Dancoff, *Phys. Rev.*, **78**:382 (1950). These authors were concerned with meson-nucleon field theory and solved this problem within a truncated basis. The approach is a standard one, however, and was used earlier in many other contexts.

state [Eqs. (56.22) to (56.24)], the role of the particle-hole interaction [Eq. (59.10)] is to *subtract off* the interaction with the unoccupied state.

The excited state vectors have already been given in Eq. (59.6), and we can now use the identity

$$\langle 0|\hat{\zeta}_{\lambda\mu}\,\hat{\zeta}^{\dagger}_{\alpha\beta}|0\rangle = \delta_{\lambda\alpha}\,\delta_{\beta\mu} \tag{59.11}$$

to evaluate their inner product

$$\langle \Psi'_{n'}|\Psi'_{n}\rangle = \sum_{\alpha\beta} \psi^{(n')}_{\alpha\beta}\,\psi^{(n)*}_{\alpha\beta} = \delta_{nn'} \tag{59.12}$$

The orthogonality follows because $\psi^{(n)}_{\alpha\beta}$ is the nth eigenvector of a hermitian matrix. Furthermore, Eq. (59.9) does not determine the normalization of $\psi^{(n)}_{\alpha\beta}$, and Eq. (59.12) provides the proper prescription.

Consider next the problem of computing the transition matrix element of some multipole operator

$$\hat{T} = \sum_{\alpha\beta} c^{\dagger}_{\alpha}\langle \alpha|T|\beta\rangle\,c_{\beta} \tag{59.13}$$

between one of the collective excitations and the ground state. Within the TDA, it again follows that only the terms $a^{\dagger}b^{\dagger}$ in $\hat{T}$ contribute to $\langle \Psi_n|\hat{T}|\Psi_0\rangle$, and we find

$$\hat{T} \doteq \sum_{\alpha\beta} \langle \alpha|T|-\beta\rangle\,S_{-\beta}\,\hat{\zeta}^{\dagger}_{\alpha\beta} \tag{59.14}$$

$$\langle \Psi_n|\hat{T}|\Psi_0\rangle = \sum_{\alpha\beta} \langle \alpha|T|-\beta\rangle\,S_{-\beta}\,\psi^{(n)}_{\alpha\beta} \tag{59.15}$$

Thus the transition matrix element is a sum of single-particle matrix elements weighted with the coefficients $\psi^{(n)}_{\alpha\beta}$ determined above.

We shall discuss the TDA in more detail below (including some applications), but first we generalize the same approach.

RANDOM-PHASE APPROXIMATION (RPA)

An improved approximation can be obtained by working with a more general system of states than that considered in the TDA. In particular, we treat the ground state and the excited states more symmetrically, allowing both to have particle-hole pairs. Within this expanded basis, the equations of motion are still *linearized*. Using the same definitions

$$\hat{\zeta}^{\dagger}_{\alpha\beta} \equiv a^{\dagger}_{\alpha}b^{\dagger}_{\beta} \qquad \hat{\zeta}_{\alpha\beta} = b_{\beta}a_{\alpha} \tag{59.16}$$

we retain all matrix elements of the form

$$\psi^{(n)}_{\alpha\beta} \equiv \langle \Psi_n|\hat{\zeta}^{\dagger}_{\alpha\beta}|\Psi_0\rangle \tag{59.17a}$$

$$\varphi^{(n)}_{\alpha\beta} \equiv \langle \Psi_n|\hat{\zeta}_{\alpha\beta}|\Psi_0\rangle \tag{59.17b}$$

in the equations of motion. This condition means that the excited states can be reached either by creating or *destroying* particle-hole pairs in the ground state. For historical reasons this prescription is known as the random-phase approximation (RPA).[1]

The next section presents a physical picture of this approximation. For the present, however, we just examine the matrix elements

$$\langle \Psi_n | [\hat{H}, \hat{\zeta}^\dagger_{\alpha\beta}] | \Psi_0 \rangle = (E_n - E_0) \psi^{(n)}_{\alpha\beta} \tag{59.18a}$$

$$\langle \Psi_n | [\hat{H}, \hat{\zeta}_{\alpha\beta}] | \Psi_0 \rangle = (E_n - E_0) \varphi^{(n)}_{\alpha\beta} \tag{59.18b}$$

The commutators on the left side are written in Eqs. (59.3). [Note that $[\hat{H}, \hat{\zeta}_{\alpha\beta}]$ is obtained from the negative adjoint of Eqs. (59.3).] In contrast to the TDA, we now retain all terms in Eq. (59.3c) that yield either $a^\dagger b^\dagger$ or ba, since this procedure still gives linear equations of motion. The first contribution ($\propto a^\dagger b^\dagger$) was evaluated in the discussion of the TDA; the second requires only the single term

$$[N\{S_\rho S_\sigma b_{-\rho} b_{-\sigma} a_\nu a_\mu\}, a^\dagger_\alpha b^\dagger_\beta] \doteq 2[\delta_{\mu\alpha} \delta_{\beta,-\rho} b_{-\sigma} a_\nu - \delta_{\nu\alpha} \delta_{\beta,-\rho} b_{-\sigma} a_\mu] S_\rho S_\sigma \tag{59.19}$$

where the symmetry of the potential of Eq. (58.68) has again been used. We thus find the approximate expression

$$[\hat{H}_2, \hat{\zeta}^\dagger_{\alpha\beta}] \doteq \sum_{\lambda\mu} (v_{\alpha\beta:\lambda\mu} \hat{\zeta}^\dagger_{\lambda\mu} + u_{\alpha\beta:\lambda\mu} \hat{\zeta}_{\lambda\mu}) \tag{59.20}$$

$$u_{\alpha\beta:\lambda\mu} \equiv S_{-\beta} S_{-\mu} [\langle -\beta -\mu | V | \alpha\lambda \rangle - \langle -\beta -\mu | V | \lambda\alpha \rangle] \tag{59.21}$$

and the equations of motion (59.18) become

$$\{[E_0 + (\epsilon_\alpha - \epsilon_{-\beta})] - E_n\} \psi^{(n)}_{\alpha\beta} + \sum_{\lambda\mu} [v_{\alpha\beta:\lambda\mu} \psi^{(n)}_{\lambda\mu} + u_{\alpha\beta:\lambda\mu} \varphi^{(n)}_{\lambda\mu}] = 0 \tag{59.22a}$$

$$\{[E_0 - (\epsilon_\alpha - \epsilon_{-\beta})] - E_n\} \varphi^{(n)}_{\alpha\beta} - \sum_{\lambda\mu} [v^*_{\alpha\beta:\lambda\mu} \varphi^{(n)}_{\lambda\mu} + u^*_{\alpha\beta:\lambda\mu} \psi^{(n)}_{\lambda\mu}] = 0 \tag{59.22b}$$

which again form a linear homogeneous set of algebraic equations. If the complete set of Hartree-Fock single-particle wave functions is taken as the bound states plus the continuum states with standing-wave boundary conditions, then all the matrix elements in this expression are real[2]

$$v_{\alpha\beta:\lambda\mu} = v^*_{\alpha\beta:\lambda\mu} = v_{\lambda\mu:\alpha\beta} \tag{59.23a}$$

$$u_{\alpha\beta:\lambda\mu} = u_{\lambda\mu:\alpha\beta} = u^*_{\alpha\beta:\lambda\mu} \tag{59.23b}$$

[1] D. Bohm and D. Pines, *Phys. Rev.*, **82**:625 (1951) (see the comments in Sec. 12). The approach discussed here was originally developed for the electron gas by K. Sawada, *Phys. Rev.*, **106**:372 (1957).
[2] In our applications, the Hartree-Fock wave functions are approximated by the (bound) states of the harmonic oscillator. For a discussion of transitions to the continuum states see, for example, F. Villars and M. S. Weiss, *Phys. Letters*, **11**:318 (1964) and J. Friar, *Phys. Rev.*, **C1**:40 (1970).

In this case, the solutions corresponding to two different eigenvalues with $E_n - E_0 > 0$ satisfy the following orthogonality relation

$$\sum_{\alpha\beta} [\psi_{\alpha\beta}^{(n')*} \psi_{\alpha\beta}^{(n)} - \varphi_{\alpha\beta}^{(n')*} \varphi_{\alpha\beta}^{(n)}] = \delta_{nn'} \tag{59.24}$$

Equation (59.24) also implies a particular normalization; the justification of this choice is rather subtle, however, and now will be treated in detail.[1]

We first note that Eqs. (59.22) and (59.24) correctly reduce to Eqs. (59.9) and (59.12) as $\varphi_{\alpha\beta}^{(n)} \to 0$. A more compelling argument for Eq. (59.24) can be found within the framework of the *quasiboson approximation*.[2] So far we have approximated only the *matrix elements*, but the normalization of the coefficients requires further restrictions. Define the operator

$$\hat{Q}_n^\dagger \equiv \sum_{\alpha\beta} [\psi_{\alpha\beta}^{(n)} \hat{\zeta}_{\alpha\beta}^\dagger - \varphi_{\alpha\beta}^{(n)} \hat{\zeta}_{\alpha\beta}] \tag{59.25}$$

Then the commutator with $\hat{H}$ yields

$$[\hat{H}, \hat{Q}_n^\dagger] \doteq (E_n - E_0) \hat{Q}_n^\dagger \tag{59.26}$$

where we have used the linearization prescription that the only terms retained on the left side should be proportional to $\hat{\zeta}^\dagger$ or $\hat{\zeta}$ [Eqs. (59.3) and (59.20)] along with the equations of motion (59.22) and (59.23). Assume now that Eq. (59.26) holds as an *operator identity*, and that the interacting ground state can be defined by the condition

$$\hat{Q}_n |\Psi_0\rangle = 0 \qquad \text{all } n \tag{59.27}$$

The collective excitations can be constructed as

$$|\Psi_n\rangle = \hat{Q}_n^\dagger |\Psi_0\rangle \tag{59.28}$$

which is an eigenstate of $\hat{H}$ because of Eq. (59.26). These eigenstates must be orthonormal:

$$\langle \Psi_{n'} | \Psi_n \rangle = \delta_{nn'} = \langle \Psi_0 | [\hat{Q}_{n'}, \hat{Q}_n^\dagger] | \Psi_0 \rangle \tag{59.29}$$

Substitution of the defining relation of Eq. (59.25) then leads to the normalization condition of Eq. (59.24) provided that the replacement

$$[\hat{\zeta}_{\alpha\beta}, \hat{\zeta}_{\lambda\mu}^\dagger] \doteq \delta_{\alpha\lambda} \delta_{\beta\mu} \tag{59.30}$$

---

[1] M. Baranger, *loc. cit.*

[2] Note that the quasibosons discussed here are formed from particle-hole pairs; in Eq. (58.57), the *boson* operators contain pairs of particles.

is permissible. A direct evaluation of the commutator yields the following necessary conditions for the quasiboson description

$$\langle \Psi_0 | a_\gamma^\dagger a_\gamma | \Psi_0 \rangle \ll 1 \qquad\qquad (59.31a)$$

$$\langle \Psi_0 | b_\gamma^\dagger b_\gamma | \Psi_0 \rangle \ll 1 \qquad\qquad (59.31b)$$

To interpret these conditions, we assume that the true ground state $|\Psi_0\rangle$ consists mainly of the particle-hole vacuum $|0\rangle$ plus small admixtures of other particle-hole states with $J^\pi = 0^+$.   Since the number of particles must equal the number of holes, Eq. (59.31) really assumes that $N_h/N \ll 1$ where N is the total number of filled core states and N_h is the mean number of holes in $|\Psi_0\rangle$, for then the probability of finding a hole in the state γ is

$$\langle \Psi_0 | b_\gamma^\dagger b_\gamma | \Psi_0 \rangle \approx \frac{N_h}{N} \ll 1 \qquad\qquad (59.32)$$

Thus if the ground state does not contain too many holes, the normalization condition can be written consistently as

$$\langle \Psi_0 | [\hat{Q}_{n'}, \hat{Q}_n^\dagger] | \Psi_0 \rangle = \sum_{\alpha\beta} [\psi_{\alpha\beta}^{(n')*} \psi_{\alpha\beta}^{(n)} - \varphi_{\alpha\beta}^{(n')*} \varphi_{\alpha\beta}^{(n)}] = \delta_{nn'} \qquad\qquad (59.33)$$

The transition matrix element of a multipole operator from one of the excited states to the ground state can be immediately evaluated.   Within the RPA, only those terms of $\hat{T}$ containing $a^\dagger b^\dagger$ or ba will contribute to $\langle \Psi_n | \hat{T} | \Psi_0 \rangle$, and we find

$$\hat{T} \doteq \sum_{\alpha\beta} [\langle \alpha | T | -\beta \rangle S_{-\beta} \hat{\zeta}_{\alpha\beta}^\dagger + \langle -\beta | T | \alpha \rangle S_{-\beta} \hat{\zeta}_{\alpha\beta}] \qquad\qquad (59.34)$$

$$\langle \Psi_n | \hat{T} | \Psi_0 \rangle = \sum_{\alpha\beta} S_{-\beta} [\langle \alpha | T | -\beta \rangle \psi_{\alpha\beta}^{(n)} + \langle -\beta | T | \alpha \rangle \varphi_{\alpha\beta}^{(n)}] \qquad\qquad (59.35)$$

Equation (59.35) is again a sum of single-particle matrix elements weighted with the coefficients $(\psi_{\alpha\beta}^{(n)}, \varphi_{\alpha\beta}^{(n)})$ determined above.

REDUCTION OF THE BASIS

The dimension of the matrix equations (59.22) can be reduced considerably by noting that J is a good quantum number.   We use the rotational invariance of the system to assume that $\{\alpha\} = \{nljm_j\}$ and define

$$\hat{\zeta}^\dagger(abJM) \equiv \sum_{m_\alpha m_\beta} \langle j_\alpha m_\alpha j_\beta m_\beta | j_\alpha j_\beta JM \rangle \hat{\zeta}_{\alpha\beta}^\dagger \qquad\qquad (59.36)$$

which is an irreducible tensor operator of rank J.   In contrast, $\hat{\zeta}(abJM)$ is not an irreducible tensor operator, although we have already seen that $(-1)^{j_\alpha - m_\alpha} a_{-\alpha}$

and $(-1)^{j_\beta-m_\beta}b_{-\beta}$ are tensor operators. This defect is easily remedied with the identity

$$\langle j_\alpha m_\alpha j_\beta m_\beta | j_\alpha j_\beta JM \rangle = (-1)^{j_\alpha+j_\beta-J}\langle j_\alpha - m_\alpha j_\beta - m_\beta | j_\alpha j_\beta J - M \rangle \quad (59.37)$$
$$m_\alpha + m_\beta = M$$

which shows that $S_J \hat{\zeta}(abJ - M)$ is a tensor operator of rank J where

$$S_J \equiv (-1)^{J-M} \quad (59.38)$$

Thus we further define

$$\psi_J^{(n)}(ab) \equiv \langle \Psi_{JM}^n | \hat{\zeta}^\dagger(abJM) | \Psi_0 \rangle$$
$$= \sum_{m_\alpha m_\beta} \langle j_\alpha m_\alpha j_\beta m_\beta | j_\alpha j_\beta JM \rangle \psi_{\alpha\beta}^{(n)} \quad (59.39a)$$

$$\varphi_J^{(n)}(ab) \equiv S_J\langle \Psi_{JM}^n | \hat{\zeta}(abJ - M) | \Psi_0 \rangle$$
$$= S_J \sum_{m_\alpha m_\beta} \langle j_\alpha m_\alpha j_\beta m_\beta | j_\alpha j_\beta J - M \rangle \varphi_{\alpha\beta}^{(n)} \quad (59.39b)$$

which are independent of M by the Wigner-Eckart theorem. In this way, the general multipole operator in Eq. (59.34) can be written with the aid of the Wigner-Eckart theorem as

$$\hat{T}_{JM} \doteq \frac{1}{(2J+1)^{\frac{1}{2}}} \sum_{\alpha\beta} \{ S_{-\beta}^2 \langle j_\alpha m_\alpha j_\beta m_\beta | j_\alpha j_\beta JM \rangle \langle a\|T_J\|b \rangle \hat{\zeta}_{\alpha\beta}^\dagger$$

$$+ S_\alpha S_{-\beta}\langle j_\beta - m_\beta j_\alpha - m_\alpha | j_\beta j_\alpha JM \rangle \langle b\|T_J\|a \rangle \hat{\zeta}_{\alpha\beta} \}$$

$$\doteq \frac{1}{(2J+1)^{\frac{1}{2}}} \sum_{ab} \{ \langle a\|T_J\|b \rangle \hat{\zeta}^\dagger(abJM)$$

$$+ (-1)^{j_b-j_a-J}\langle b\|T_J\|a \rangle S_J \hat{\zeta}(abJ - M) \} \quad (59.40)$$

and it follows that

$$\langle \Psi_J^n \|\hat{T}_J\| \Psi_0 \rangle = \sum_{ab} \{ \langle a\|T_J\|b \rangle \psi_J^{(n)}(ab) + (-1)^{j_b-j_a-J}\langle b\|T_J\|a \rangle \varphi_J^{(n)}(ab) \} \quad (59.41)$$

The basis for the linear equations (59.22) can now be reduced by summing with the Clebsch-Gordan coefficients in Eqs. (59.39). For a spherical system, $\epsilon_\alpha - \epsilon_{-\beta} = \epsilon_a - \epsilon_b$ and the first terms of Eq. (59.22) immediately yield $\psi_J^{(n)}(ab)$ and $\varphi_J^{(n)}(ab)$. The interaction terms are more complicated. Since the interaction potential is invariant under rotations [compare Eq. (58.70)], we may write

$$v_{\alpha\beta;\lambda\mu} = \sum_{J'M'} S_{-\beta}S_{-\mu}\langle j_\lambda m_\lambda j_\beta - m_\beta | j_\lambda j_\beta J' M' \rangle \langle j_\mu - m_\mu j_\alpha m_\alpha | j_\mu j_\alpha J' M' \rangle$$

$$\times \{ \langle lbJ' | V | maJ' \rangle - (-1)^{j_a+j_m-J'}\langle lbJ' | V | amJ' \rangle \} \quad (59.42a)$$

$$u_{\alpha\beta;\lambda\mu} = \sum_{J'M'} S_{-\beta} S_{-\mu} \langle j_\mu - m_\mu j_\beta - m_\beta | j_\mu j_\beta J' M' \rangle \langle j_\lambda m_\lambda j_\alpha m_\alpha | j_\lambda j_\alpha J' M' \rangle$$

$$\times \{ \langle mbJ' | V | laJ' \rangle - (-1)^{j_a + j_l - J'} \langle mbJ' | V | alJ' \rangle \} \quad (59.42b)$$

In these expressions (ab) and (lm) denote the remaining quantum numbers identifying the particle-hole pair, for example $(ab) \equiv (n_a l_a j_a, n_b l_b j_b)$. When $v_{\alpha\beta;\lambda\mu}$ is summed with the Clebsch-Gordan coefficient in Eq. (59.39a), we use the relations

$$\sum_{m_\alpha m_\beta M'} \langle j_\alpha m_\alpha j_\beta m_\beta | j_\alpha j_\beta JM \rangle \langle j_\lambda m_\lambda j_\alpha m_\alpha | j_\lambda j_\alpha J' M' \rangle$$

$$\times \langle j_\mu - m_\mu j_\alpha m_\alpha | j_\mu j_\alpha J' M' \rangle S_{-\beta}$$

$$= (-1)^{J' - j_l - j_b} \left(\frac{2J' + 1}{2j_l + 1} \right)^{\frac{1}{2}} \sum_{m_\alpha m_\beta M'} \langle j_\mu - m_\mu j_\alpha m_\alpha | j_\mu j_\alpha J' M' \rangle$$

$$\times \langle J' M' j_\beta m_\beta | J' j_\beta j_\lambda m_\lambda \rangle \langle j_\alpha m_\alpha j_\beta m_\beta | j_\alpha j_\beta JM \rangle$$

$$= S_{-\mu} \langle j_\lambda m_\lambda j_\mu m_\mu | j_\lambda j_\mu JM \rangle (-1)^{j_a + j_m + J'} (2J' + 1) \begin{Bmatrix} j_m & j_a & J' \\ j_b & j_l & J \end{Bmatrix} \quad (59.43)$$

to obtain

$$\sum_{m_\alpha m_\beta} \langle j_\alpha m_\alpha j_\beta m_\beta | j_\alpha j_\beta JM \rangle v_{\alpha\beta;\lambda\mu} = v^J_{ab;lm} \langle j_\lambda m_\lambda j_\mu m_\mu | j_\lambda j_\mu JM \rangle \quad (59.44)$$

where

$$v^J_{ab;lm} \equiv - \sum_{J'} (2J' + 1) \begin{Bmatrix} j_m & j_a & J' \\ j_b & j_l & J \end{Bmatrix} [\langle lbJ' | V | amJ' \rangle$$

$$- (-1)^{j_a + j_m + J'} \langle lbJ' | V | maJ' \rangle] \quad (59.45)$$

The overall minus sign comes from interchanging the order of the two matrix elements in Eq. (59.42a).

The sum of $u_{\alpha\beta;\lambda\mu}$ with the Clebsch-Gordan coefficient in Eq. (59.39a) is immediately carried out with the help of the following identity obtained from Eq. (59.43)

$$\sum_{m_\alpha m_\beta M'} \langle j_\alpha m_\alpha j_\beta m_\beta | j_\alpha j_\beta JM \rangle \langle j_\lambda m_\lambda j_\alpha m_\alpha | j_\lambda j_\alpha J' M' \rangle$$

$$\times \langle j_\mu - m_\mu j_\beta - m_\beta | j_\mu j_\beta J' M' \rangle S_{-\beta}$$

$$= S_\lambda \langle j_\mu - m_\mu j_\lambda - m_\lambda | j_\mu j_\lambda JM \rangle (-1)^{j_a + j_l + J'} (2J' + 1) \begin{Bmatrix} j_l & j_a & J' \\ j_b & j_m & J \end{Bmatrix}$$

$$(59.46)$$

Combining the phases with the factor $S_{-\mu}$ in Eq. (59.42b), we have

$$S_\lambda S_{-\mu} (-1)^{j_a + j_l + J'} = (-1)^{j_a + j_l + J'} (-1)^{J - M} (-1)^{j_m - j_l - J}$$

The required sum is therefore given by

$$\sum_{m_\alpha m_\beta} \langle j_\alpha m_\alpha j_\beta m_\beta | j_\alpha j_\beta JM \rangle u_{\alpha\beta;\lambda\mu} = u_{ab;lm}^J \langle j_\lambda m_\lambda j_\mu m_\mu | j_\lambda j_\mu J - M \rangle S_J$$

$$(59.47)$$

where

$$u_{ab;lm}^J \equiv (-1)^{j_m - j_l - J} v_{ab;ml}^J \tag{59.48}$$

Note the interchange of the indices l and m on the right side of this relation. The recoupling relations (59.44) and (59.47) now make it possible to rewrite the linear Eqs. (59.22) as

$$\{[E_0 + (\epsilon_a - \epsilon_b)] - E_n\}\psi_J^{(n)}(ab) + \sum_{lm} [v_{ab;lm}^J \psi_J^{(n)}(lm) + u_{ab;lm}^J \varphi_J^{(n)}(lm)] = 0$$

$$(59.49a)$$

$$\{[E_0 - (\epsilon_a - \epsilon_b)] - E_n\}\varphi_J^{(n)}(ab) - \sum_{lm} [v_{ab;lm}^{J*} \varphi_J^{(n)}(lm) + u_{ab;lm}^{J*} \psi_J^{(n)}(lm)] = 0$$

$$(59.49b)$$

This calculation explicitly decouples the states of different J and demonstrates that the eigenvalues and eigenvectors are independent of M. The TDA is recovered from Eqs. (59.41) and (59.49) by setting $\varphi^{(n)} = 0$.

The equations to this point are entirely general and apply to atoms as well as nuclei.[1] In the nuclear case, however, the invariance of the interaction under rotations in isotopic-spin space can be used to reduce the basis further. With $\{\alpha\} = \{nljm_j; \tfrac{1}{2}m_t\}$ it is clear that we must merely include an isotopic-spin coupling coefficient and phase factor along with every angular-moment coupling coefficient and phase factor. From Eq. (59.41) we immediately obtain

$$\langle \Psi_{JT}^n :: \hat{T}_{JT} :: \Psi_0 \rangle$$
$$= \sum_{ab} \{\langle a :: T_{JT} :: b \rangle \psi_{JT}^{(n)}(ab) + (-1)^{\frac{1}{2} - \frac{1}{2} - T}(-1)^{j_b - j_a - J} \langle b :: T_{JT} :: a \rangle \varphi_{JT}^{(n)}(ab)\}$$

$$(59.50)$$

where the symbol $::$ denotes a reduced matrix element with respect to both angular momentum and isotopic spin. The coefficients $\psi_{JT}^{(n)}$, $\varphi_{JT}^{(n)}$ in this relation satisfy the same set of linear equations (59.49) with

$$v_{ab;lm}^{JT} = -\sum_{J'T'} (2J'+1)(2T'+1) \begin{Bmatrix} j_m & j_a & J' \\ j_b & j_l & J \end{Bmatrix} \begin{Bmatrix} \tfrac{1}{2} & \tfrac{1}{2} & T' \\ \tfrac{1}{2} & \tfrac{1}{2} & T \end{Bmatrix}$$

$$\times [\langle lbJ'T'|V|amJ'T'\rangle - (-1)^{\frac{1}{2} + \frac{1}{2} + T'}(-1)^{j_a + j_m + J'} \langle lbJ'T'|V|maJ'T'\rangle]$$

$$(59.51a)$$

$$u_{ab;lm}^{JT} = (-1)^{\frac{1}{2} - \frac{1}{2} - T}(-1)^{j_m - j_l - J} v_{ab;ml}^{JT} \tag{59.51b}$$

---

[1] For an application to atoms see P. L. Altick and A. E. Glassgold, *Phys. Rev.*, **133**:A632 (1964).

SOLUTION FOR THE [15]-DIMENSIONAL SUPERMULTIPLET WITH A $\delta(x)$ FORCE

In this section the TDA and RPA equations are solved for a specific model where the interparticle force is taken to be independent of spin and isotopic spin. The ground state of the nucleus is assumed to consist of closed shells and to have the quantum numbers $S = L = T = 0$. This model illustrates some very interesting systematic features of the particle-hole calculations. The Hartree-Fock single-particle energies now depend only on $\{nl\}$, and the single-particle levels can be characterized by

$$\{\alpha\} \equiv \{nl\tfrac{1}{2}\tfrac{1}{2}, m_l\, m_s\, m_t\} \equiv \{a, m_l\, m_s\, m_t\} \tag{59.52}$$

because both m_l and m_s are good quantum numbers for spin-independent forces. The general results derived above are written in a j–j coupling scheme appropriate for actual nuclei where the single-particle spin-orbit force is important. Although we could explicitly transform to an L–S coupling scheme appropriate for the simple spin-independent model, it is much more convenient to repeat the previous analysis from the beginning, starting with a slightly different canonical transformation

$$c_\alpha = \theta(\alpha - F)\, a_\alpha + \theta(F - \alpha)\, \mathscr{S}_\alpha\, B^\dagger_{-\alpha} \tag{59.53}$$

where[1]

$$\mathscr{S}_\alpha \equiv (-1)^{l_\alpha - m_{l\alpha}} (-1)^{\tfrac{1}{2} - m_{s\alpha}} (-1)^{\tfrac{1}{2} - m_{t\alpha}} \tag{59.54}$$

With the abbreviation $\epsilon_n \equiv E_n - E_0$, the linearized equations of motion in the TDA are now given by Eq. (59.9)

$$(\epsilon_a - \epsilon_b - \epsilon_n)\, \psi^{(n)}_{\alpha\beta} + \sum_{\lambda\mu} [\langle \lambda - \beta | V | -\mu\alpha \rangle - \langle \lambda - \beta | V | \alpha - \mu \rangle]\, \mathscr{S}_{-\beta}\, \mathscr{S}_{-\mu}\, \psi^{(n)}_{\lambda\mu}$$
$$= 0 \tag{59.55}$$

Since the interaction and single-particle energies are assumed independent of spin and isotopic spin, the basis can be reduced by introducing states of given L, S, and T, for example,

$$\psi^{(n)}_{LST}(ab) \equiv \sum_{\{\text{all } m\text{'s}\}} \langle l_a\, m_{l\alpha}\, l_b\, m_{l\beta} | l_a\, l_b\, L M_L \rangle \langle \tfrac{1}{2} m_{s\alpha}\, \tfrac{1}{2} m_{s\beta} | \tfrac{1}{2}\tfrac{1}{2} S M_s \rangle$$
$$\times \langle \tfrac{1}{2} m_{t\alpha}\, \tfrac{1}{2} m_{t\beta} | \tfrac{1}{2}\tfrac{1}{2} T M_T \rangle\, \psi^{(n)}_{\alpha\beta} \tag{59.56}$$

Furthermore, the spin and isotopic-spin dependence of the interaction matrix elements factors.[2] When Eq. (59.55) is summed with the Clebsch-Gordan coefficients in Eq. (55.56), the spin and isospin coefficients may be taken through the second term of the interaction and applied directly to the wave function.

---

[1] Note that $B^\dagger_\alpha \equiv b^\dagger_\alpha$ for $j_\alpha = l_\alpha + \tfrac{1}{2}$ and $B^\dagger_\alpha = -b^\dagger_\alpha$ for $j_\alpha = l_\alpha - \tfrac{1}{2}$ so that the two operators merely differ by an a-dependent phase.

[2] This is the advantage of the canonical transformation in Eqs. (59.53) and (59.54).

In the first term of the interaction, the spin dependence (and similarly the isospin dependence) is given by

$$\delta_{m_{s\lambda},-m_{s\mu}}\,\delta_{m_{s\beta},-m_{s\alpha}}(-1)^{\frac{1}{2}-m_{s\alpha}}(-1)^{\frac{1}{2}-m_{s\lambda}}$$

$$= (\sqrt{2})^2 \langle \tfrac{1}{2}m_{s\alpha}\tfrac{1}{2}m_{s\beta}|\tfrac{1}{2}\tfrac{1}{2}00\rangle \langle \tfrac{1}{2}m_{s\lambda}\tfrac{1}{2}m_{s\mu}|\tfrac{1}{2}\tfrac{1}{2}00\rangle$$

which contributes only for $S = T = 0$. The l dependence of the interaction matrix elements is treated exactly as in the previous section. Thus the reduced TDA equations become [compare Eq. (59.45)]

$$(\epsilon_a - \epsilon_b - \epsilon_n)\,\psi^{(n)}_{LST}(ab) + \sum_{lm} v^{LST}_{ab;lm}\,\psi^{(n)}_{LST}(lm) = 0 \qquad (59.57a)$$

$$v^{LST}_{ab;lm} = -\sum_{L'} (2L'+1) \begin{Bmatrix} l_m & l_l & L \\ l_b & l_a & L' \end{Bmatrix} [\langle l_l l_b L' |V|l_a l_m L'\rangle$$

$$- 4\delta_{S0}\,\delta_{T0}(-1)^{l_b+l_l-L'}\langle l_b l_l L'|V|l_a l_m L'\rangle] \quad (59.57b)$$

where the order of the two potential matrix elements in Eq. (59.55) has been interchanged. In these equations, the labels (ab) and (lm) again denote the remaining particle-hole quantum numbers, for example, $(ab) \equiv (n_a l_a, n_b l_b)$.

The quantum numbers S and T in Eq. (59.57) arise from coupling the spins and isotopic spins of a particle-hole pair and can take the values zero and one. We shall first concentrate on the states where either S or T differs from zero; the particle-hole interaction (59.57b) is then particularly simple because the last

Table 59.1 Degenerate states of the [15]-dimensional spin-isotopic spin supermultiplets

S	T	L	J
1	0	L	$L-1, L, L+1$
0	1	L	L
1	1	L	$L-1, L, L+1$

term proportional to $\delta_{S0}\delta_{T0}$ vanishes. As the remaining interaction is *independent of S or T*, we conclude that the 15 spin and isotopic spin states in Table 59.1 all lie at the same energy. These states therefore form a degenerate supermultiplet (the [15] supermultiplet) and must be combined with the n states of given L obtained by diagonalizing the matrix in Eq. (59.57a). The values of J in each degenerate supermultiplet (obtained by coupling L and S) are also shown in Table 59.1. The single state with $S = T = 0$ for each n and L is clearly

split off from the other states by the interaction in Eq. (59.57b), and we shall return to it at the end of this section.[1]

The problem can be further reduced by assuming that the particle-particle interaction potential is short range and attractive ($g > 0$)

$$V = -g\delta(\mathbf{x}_1 - \mathbf{x}_2) \tag{59.58}$$

In this case, the integration over d^3x_2 in the matrix element can be performed immediately. Furthermore, the identity[2]

$$\sum_{m_1 m_2} \langle l_1 m_1 l_2 m_2 | l_1 l_2 LM \rangle Y_{l_1 m_1}(\Omega) Y_{l_2 m_2}(\Omega)$$

$$= (-1)^{l_1 - l_2} \left[\frac{(2l_1 + 1)(2l_2 + 1)}{4\pi} \right]^{\frac{1}{2}} \begin{pmatrix} l_1 & l_2 & L \\ 0 & 0 & 0 \end{pmatrix} Y_{LM}(\Omega)$$

leads to the result

$$\sum_{m_a m_b m_l m_m} \langle l_l m_l l_b m_b | l_l l_b L' M' \rangle \langle l_a m_a l_m m_m | l_a l_m L' M' \rangle$$

$$\times \int Y^*_{l_l m_l} Y^*_{l_b m_b} Y_{l_a m_a} Y_{l_m m_m} d\Omega$$

$$= (-1)^{l_l - l_b + l_a - l_m} \left[\frac{(2l_a + 1)(2l_b + 1)(2l_l + 1)(2l_m + 1)}{(4\pi)^2} \right]^{\frac{1}{2}}$$

$$\times \begin{pmatrix} l_l & l_b & L' \\ 0 & 0 & 0 \end{pmatrix} \begin{pmatrix} l_a & l_m & L' \\ 0 & 0 & 0 \end{pmatrix}$$

The recoupling relation[3] (note that each of the 3-j symbols vanishes unless the sum of the l's is even)

$$\sum_{L'} (2L' + 1) \begin{Bmatrix} l_m & l_l & L \\ l_b & l_a & L' \end{Bmatrix} \begin{pmatrix} l_l & l_b & L' \\ 0 & 0 & 0 \end{pmatrix} \begin{pmatrix} l_a & l_m & L' \\ 0 & 0 & 0 \end{pmatrix}$$

$$= (-1)^{l_l + L + l_b} \begin{pmatrix} l_a & L & l_b \\ 0 & 0 & 0 \end{pmatrix} \begin{pmatrix} l_l & L & l_m \\ 0 & 0 & 0 \end{pmatrix}$$

then allows us to rewrite the particle-hole interaction for the [**15**]-supermultiplet in the very simple form

$$v^{[15]L}_{ab;lm} = \xi v^L_{ab} v^L_{lm} \tag{59.59a}$$

$$v^L_{ab} \equiv (-1)^{l_a} [(2l_a + 1)(2l_b + 1)]^{\frac{1}{2}} \begin{pmatrix} l_a & L & l_b \\ 0 & 0 & 0 \end{pmatrix} \tag{59.59b}$$

---

[1] If the forces are independent of spin and isotopic spin, the hamiltonian is invariant under the symmetry group $SU(4)$, which is Wigner's supermultiplet theory [E. P. Wigner, *Phys. Rev.*, **51**:106 (1937)]. The degenerate particle-hole states then form bases for the irreducible representations $4 \otimes \bar{4} = [1] \oplus [15]$, which is explicitly illustrated in the present calculations.

[2] A. R. Edmonds, *op. cit.*, eq. (4.6.5).

[3] A. R. Edmonds, *op. cit.*, eq. (6.2.6).

$$v_{ab}^L = \langle l_a \| c_L \| l_b \rangle \tag{59.59c}$$

where

$$\xi \equiv \frac{g}{4\pi} \int_0^\infty u_{n_l l_l} u_{n_b l_b} u_{n_a l_a} u_{n_m l_m} \frac{dr}{r^2} \tag{59.60}$$

In this expression u_{nl}/r is the radial wave function [see, for example, Eq. (57.6)]. Note that the v_{ab}^L are just the reduced matrix elements of the spherical harmonics $c_{LM} = [4\pi/(2L+1)]^{\frac{1}{2}} Y_{LM}$. Now the radial wave functions are peaked at the surface of the nucleus for particles in the first few unoccupied shells and for holes in the last few filled shells, and the overlap integral ξ will not change appreciably from one particle-hole pair to the next.[1] We shall therefore assume that ξ is a positive, state-independent constant. In this case the particle-hole interaction is *separable*. The resulting TDA equations (here, $\epsilon_{ab} = \epsilon_a - \epsilon_b$)

$$(\epsilon_{ab} - \epsilon_n) \psi_{[15]L}^{(n)}(ab) + \xi v_{ab}^L \left[\sum_{lm} v_{lm}^L \psi_{[15]L}^{(n)}(lm) \right] = 0 \tag{59.61}$$

can then be multiplied by $v_{ab}^L/(\epsilon_{ab} - \epsilon_n)$ and summed over ab to yield the eigenvalue equation

$$\frac{1}{\xi} = \sum_{ab} \frac{(v_{ab}^L)^2}{\epsilon_n - \epsilon_{ab}} \tag{59.62}$$

The solutions to this equation for a given L are indicated graphically in Fig. 59.1. If n particle-hole states are included, then $n - 1$ of the eigenvalues lie between

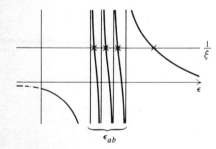

Fig. 59.1 Plot of $\sum\limits_{ab} (v_{ab}^L)^2(\epsilon - \epsilon_{ab})^{-1}$ as a function of ϵ with the eigenvalues ϵ_n of Eq. (59.62) indicated by crosses.

adjacent unperturbed energies ϵ_{ab}, and one eigenvalue ϵ_{top} is pushed up to an arbitrarily high energy depending on the quantity $1/\xi$.

To investigate further the properties of these states, we make the simplifying assumption that all the particle-hole states are initially degenerate

$$\epsilon_{ab} = \epsilon_a - \epsilon_b \equiv \epsilon_0$$

[1] See H. Noya, A. Arima, and H. Horie, *Suppl. Prog. Theor. Phys. (Kyoto)*, **8**:33 (1959), Table 2, for an explicit evaluation of these matrix elements. They are, in fact, remarkably constant.

In this case, the energy of the top supermultiplet becomes

$$\epsilon_{\text{top}} = \epsilon_0 + \xi \sum_{ab} (v_{ab}^L)^2 \qquad (59.63)$$

while Eq. (59.61) shows that $\psi_{[15]}^{\text{top}}(ab) \propto v_{ab}^L$ for these states. The normalized wave function is therefore

$$\psi_{[15]L}^{\text{top}}(ab) = \frac{v_{ab}^L}{\left[\sum_{ab} (v_{ab}^L)^2\right]^{\frac{1}{2}}} \qquad (59.64)$$

For the other $n-1$ eigenvalues, Fig. 59.1 shows that

$$\epsilon_n - \epsilon_0 = 0 \qquad \text{other } n-1 \text{ eigenvalues} \qquad (59.65)$$

and it therefore follows for *each* of these supermultiplets that

$$\sum_{lm} v_{lm}^L \psi_{[15]L}^{(n)}(lm) = 0 \qquad \text{other } n-1 \text{ supermultiplets} \qquad (59.66)$$

We may use these results to evaluate the matrix elements of the various multipoles of the charge density

$$Q_{LM} \equiv \sum_{j=1}^{A} r_j^L c_{LM}(\Omega_j) \tfrac{1}{2}[1 + \tau_3(j)] \qquad (59.67)$$

between the ground state with $T = S = L = 0$ and these excited modes. From Eq. (59.14), the transition matrix elements of a general irreducible tensor operator are given by

$$\langle \Psi_n | \hat{T} | \Psi_0 \rangle = \sum_{\alpha\beta} \langle \alpha | T | -\beta \rangle \mathscr{S}_{-\beta} \psi_{\alpha\beta}^{(n)} \qquad (59.68)$$

The spin matrix elements again factor because Q_{LM} is spin independent, and the m_s summation

$$\sum_{m_{s\alpha} m_{s\beta}} \delta_{m_{s\alpha}, -m_{s\beta}} (-1)^{\frac{1}{2}+m_{s\beta}} \psi_{m_{s\alpha} m_{s\beta}}^{(n)} = \sqrt{2}\, \psi_{S=0}^{(n)}$$

eliminates all but the $S = 0$ excited states. Within the [**15**] supermultiplet, the states with $S = 0$ must have $T = 1$ (see Table 59.1), and only the τ_3 term in Eq. (59.67) contributes to the transition matrix element. Since $\langle \tfrac{1}{2} \| \tfrac{1}{2}\tau \| \tfrac{1}{2} \rangle = \tfrac{1}{2}\sqrt{6}$, it follows that [compare Eq. (59.50)]

$$\langle \Psi_{[15]L}^{\prime n} \| \hat{Q}_L \| \Psi_0 \rangle = \sqrt{3}\, \delta_{S0} \sum_{ab} \langle l_a \| c_L \| l_b \rangle \psi_{[15]L}^{(n)}(ab) \langle r^L \rangle_{ab} \qquad (59.69)$$

If we again assume that the radial matrix elements are independent of the states (ab), the reduced matrix element can be simplified to

$$\langle \Psi_{[15]L}^{\prime n} \| \hat{Q}_L \| \Psi_0 \rangle = \sqrt{3}\, \delta_{S0} \langle r^L \rangle \left[\sum_{ab} v_{ab}^L \psi_{[15]L}^{(n)}(ab)\right] \qquad (59.70)$$

In the special case that the initial particle-hole states are degenerate, this expression becomes [see Eqs. (59.64) and (59.66)]

$$\langle \Psi_{[15]L}^{'top} \vdots \hat{Q}_L \vdots \Psi_0' \rangle = \sqrt{3}\,\delta_{S0}\langle r^L \rangle \left[\sum_{ab} (v_{ab}^L)^2 \right]^{\frac{1}{2}} \tag{59.71a}$$

$$\langle \Psi_{[15]L}^{'n} \vdots \hat{Q}_L \vdots \Psi_0' \rangle = 0 \qquad \text{other } n-1 \text{ supermultiplets} \tag{59.71b}$$

For each L, we find the following remarkable result. The one supermultiplet that is pushed up in energy carries the *entire transition strength*, whereas the remaining $n-1$ degenerate supermultiplets have *no transition strength whatever*.

It is an experimental fact that low-energy photoabsorption in nuclei is dominated by the giant resonance. This state is a few MeV wide, and its excitation energy decreases systematically from about 25 MeV in the lightest nuclei to 10 MeV in the heaviest nuclei. The dominant multipole for photons of this energy is electric dipole, and the giant resonance also systematically exhausts the dipole sum rule (see Prob. 15.17). The electric dipole operator is[1]

$$Q_{1M} = \sum_{j=1}^{A} (3/4\pi)^{\frac{1}{2}} x_{1M}(j)\tfrac{1}{2}\tau_3(j)$$

Thus the excited state must have $S-0$, $T=1$, and $L^{\pi}-J^{\pi}-1^-$ if the ground state has $S=T=0$ and $L^{\pi}=J^{\pi}=0^+$.

The simplest picture of the giant dipole resonance, due to Goldhaber and Teller,[2] is that the protons oscillate against the neutrons. The more sophisticated model presented here was originally proposed by Brown and Bolsterli.[3] The observed giant dipole resonance may be identified with the $T=1$, $S=0$ state of the top $L=1$ supermultiplet and does indeed exhibit many features of this model. It appears at an energy higher than the unperturbed configuration energies ϵ_{ab} obtained from neighboring nuclei and carries all the dipole transition strength.

For $L=1$, the present schematic model predicts a *supermultiplet* of these giant resonance states. The model also predicts other giant-resonance supermultiplets, one for each allowed L. In He^4, the simplest closed-shell nucleus

---

[1] Note that the first (isoscalar) term in Eq. (59.67) for the electric dipole operator is proportional to

$$\sum_{j=1}^{A} \mathbf{x}(j)$$

which is just the position of the center of mass. Hence this term cannot give rise to internal excitation of the system.

[2] M. Goldhaber and E. Teller, *Phys. Rev.*, **74**:1046 (1948).

[3] G. E. Brown and M. Bolsterli, *Phys. Rev. Letters*, **3**:472 (1959). (These authors were primarily concerned with the $T=1$, $J^{\pi}=1^-$ excited states of $T=0$, $J^{\pi}=0^+$ nuclei.) See also G. E. Brown, *op. cit.*, p. 29.

with four nucleons in the $1s$ oscillator shell, the first negative-parity excited states are expected to belong to the $(1p)(1s)^{-1}$ particle-hole configuration with $L = 1$. All the states of the [15] supermultiplet built on this configuration have been experimentally identified.[1] In addition, there is evidence from inelastic electron scattering that the $T = 1$, $S = 1$, $J^{\pi} = 1^{-}$ and 2^{-} components of the $L = 1$, [15] supermultiplet of giant resonances are also present in both C^{12} and O^{16}.[2]

Before considering the $S = 0$, $T = 0$ excited states, we investigate these same [15] supermultiplets within the framework of the RPA. The linearized equations are given by Eqs. (59.22) and (59.23), and the basis can again be reduced by introducing states of definite T, S, and L. Just as before, the first term in Eq. (59.21) will not contribute if either S or T differs from zero, and the Clebsch-Gordan coefficients for spin and isotopic spin may be taken through the second interaction term onto the wave function. The reduction of the l parts of the matrix elements proceeds exactly as in the previous discussion. Thus the interaction in the [15] supermultiplet becomes [compare Eq. (59.48)]

$$v_{ab;lm}^{[15]L} = \xi v_{ab}^{L} v_{lm}^{L} \tag{59.72a}$$

$$u_{ab;lm}^{[15]L} = \xi v_{ab;ml}^{[15]L}(-1)^{l_m - l_l - L}(-1)^{S+T}$$

$$= (-1)^{L+S+T} \xi v_{ab}^{L} v_{lm}^{L} \tag{59.72b}$$

With the assumption of a constant ξ, the potential is again separable, and the RPA equations can be written[3]

$$(\epsilon_{ab} - \epsilon_n)\psi_{[15]L}^{(n)}(ab) + \xi v_{ab}^{L}\left\{\sum_{lm}[v_{lm}^{L}\psi_{[15]L}^{(n)}(lm) + (-1)^{L+S+T}v_{lm}^{L}\varphi_{[15]L}^{(n)}(lm)]\right\} = 0 \tag{59.73a}$$

$$(\epsilon_{ab} + \epsilon_n)\varphi_{[15]L}^{(n)}(ab) + \xi v_{ab}^{L}\left\{\sum_{lm}[v_{lm}^{L}\varphi_{[15]}^{(n)}(lm) + (-1)^{L+S+T}v_{lm}^{L}\psi_{[15]L}^{(n)}(lm)]\right\} = 0 \tag{59.73b}$$

The eigenvalue equation follows on multiplying by $v_{ab}^{L}/(\epsilon_{ab} \mp \epsilon_n)$ and summing over (ab)

$$\frac{1}{\xi} = \sum_{ab}(v_{ab}^{L})^2\left(\frac{1}{\epsilon_n - \epsilon_{ab}} - \frac{1}{\epsilon_n + \epsilon_{ab}}\right) \tag{59.74}$$

This equation is explicitly symmetric in ϵ_n, and the excitation energies are the solutions for positive ϵ_n (indicated graphically in Fig. 59.2). Just as in the TDA,

[1] W. E. Meyerhof and T. A. Tombrello, *Nucl. Phys.*, **A109**:1 (1968).

[2] T. deForest and J. D. Walecka, Electron Scattering and Nuclear Structure, in *Advan. Phys.*, **15**:1 (1966).

[3] The explicit phase dependence on S and T can be eliminated by considering the amplitudes ψ and $(-1)^{L+S+T}\varphi$, which determine the physical quantities of interest [Eqs. (59.74) and (59.78)].

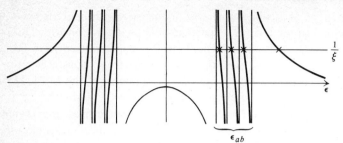

Fig. 59.2 Plot of $\sum\limits_{ab} (v_{ab}^L)^2[(\epsilon - \epsilon_{ab})^{-1} - (\epsilon + \epsilon_{ab})^{-1}]$ as a function of ϵ with the positive eigenvalues ϵ_n indicated by crosses.

$n - 1$ eigenvalues are trapped between the adjacent values ϵ_{ab} and one is pushed up, although not as far as in the TDA.

The solutions for positive ϵ_n again simplify considerably in the degenerate case where $\epsilon_{ab} = \epsilon_0$. The highest eigenvalue is given by

$$\epsilon_{\text{top}} = \epsilon_0\left[1 + \frac{2\xi}{\epsilon_0}\sum_{ab}(v_{ab}^L)^2\right]^{\frac{1}{2}} \tag{59.75}$$

For this supermultiplet it follows from the RPA equations that ψ_{ab} and φ_{ab} are both proportional to v_{ab}^L, while $\psi_{ab}/\varphi_{ab} = (-1)^{L+S+T}(\epsilon_0 + \epsilon)/(\epsilon_0 - \epsilon)$. With the normalization of Eq. (59.24), the wave function becomes

$$\varphi_{[15]L}^{\text{top}}(ab) = (-1)^{L+S+T}\frac{v_{ab}^L}{\left[\sum\limits_{ab}(v_{ab}^L)^2\right]^{\frac{1}{2}}}\left[\frac{\epsilon_0 - \epsilon_{\text{top}}}{2(\epsilon_{\text{top}}\epsilon_0)^{\frac{1}{2}}}\right] \tag{59.76a}$$

$$\psi_{[15]L}^{\text{top}}(ab) = \frac{v_{ab}^L}{\left[\sum\limits_{ab}(v_{ab}^L)^2\right]^{\frac{1}{2}}}\left[\frac{\epsilon_0 + \epsilon_{\text{top}}}{2(\epsilon_{\text{top}}\epsilon_0)^{\frac{1}{2}}}\right] \tag{59.76b}$$

The other $n - 1$ eigenvalues are unaltered, and it follows that

$$\left.\begin{array}{l}\epsilon_n = \epsilon_0 \\[4pt] \varphi_{[15]L}^{(n)}(ab) = 0 \\[4pt] \sum\limits_{ab} v_{ab}^L \psi_{[15]L}^{(n)}(ab) = 0\end{array}\right\} \text{ other } n - 1 \text{ supermultiplets} \qquad\begin{array}{l}(59.77a)\\[4pt](59.77b)\\[4pt](59.77c)\end{array}$$

The transition multipole matrix elements from the ground state are obtained from Eq. (59.35) with $S_{-\beta}$ replaced by $\mathcal{S}_{-\beta}$. For the charge multipoles of Eq. (59.67), it is again true that only the $S = 0$, $T = 1$ excited states contribute, and we find [compare Eq. (59.50)]

$$\langle\Psi_{[15]L}^n \colon\colon \hat{Q}_L \colon\colon \Psi_0^\cdot\rangle = \sqrt{3}\,\delta_{S0}\sum_{ab}\langle r^L\rangle_{ab}[v_{ab}^L\,\psi_{[15]L}^{(n)}(ab) + (-1)^{L+S+T}$$

$$\times\, v_{ab}^L\,\varphi_{[15]L}^{(n)}(ab)] \quad (59.78)$$

In the case of degenerate unperturbed configuration energies and radial matrix elements independent of (ab), this expression becomes

$$\langle \Psi^{\text{top}}_{[15]L} \| \hat{Q}_L \| \Psi_0 \rangle = \sqrt{3}\, \delta_{S0} \langle r^L \rangle \left(\frac{\epsilon_0}{\epsilon_{\text{top}}} \right)^{\frac{1}{2}} \left[\sum_{ab} (v^L_{ab})^2 \right]^{\frac{1}{2}}$$

$$\langle \Psi^n_{[15]L} \| \hat{Q}_L \| \Psi_0 \rangle = 0 \qquad \text{other } n-1 \text{ supermultiplets}$$

(59.79)

Hence the transition probability is reduced by a factor $(\epsilon_0/\epsilon)^{\frac{1}{2}}$ from the TDA result for the corresponding states. This represents an improvement because the single particle-hole TDA calculation generally puts too much strength in the top supermultiplet.[1]

Finally, we return to the $T=0$, $S=0$ states (the [1] supermultiplets), where the particle-hole interaction has additional terms. It is clear from Eq. (59.57b) and the calculation leading up to Eq. (59.59a) that the particle-hole interaction is again separable for a delta-function potential. In fact, the relevant matrix elements are given by

$$v^{[1]}_{ab;lm} = -3 v^{[15]}_{ab;lm}$$

(59.80a)

$$u^{[1]}_{ab;lm} = -3 u^{[15]}_{ab;lm}$$

(59.80b)

and therefore *change sign for the $S=T=0$ states*. All the calculations proceed exactly as before,[2] but with a new ξ' that is negative, $\xi' = -3\xi$. Figures 59.1 and 59.2 imply that the collective level is now pushed *down* in energy and is pushed *further* in the RPA than in the TDA. In addition, the $S=T=0$ collective state has a larger transition matrix element to the ground state in the RPA because $(\epsilon_0/\epsilon)^{\frac{1}{2}} > 1$, and thus becomes *more collective* than in the TDA.[3] Both of these features of the RPA generally improve the comparison with experiments.

AN APPLICATION TO NUCLEI: O^{16}

To illustrate the application of this theory to a real physical system, we summarize a calculation in the TDA of the $T=1$ negative parity states of O^{16}.‡ The relatively strong spin-orbit force in nuclei makes it appropriate to return to the single-particle states labeled with (nlj). The ground state of O^{16} is assumed to form a closed p shell, and all negative parity configurations obtained by promoting

---

[1] The RPA can be shown to preserve certain energy-weighted sum rules; see Prob. 15.16.

[2] For the [1] supermultiplet, only the isoscalar part of the charge multipoles contribute to the transition matrix elements, and the right side of Eqs. (59.69) to (59.71) and (59.78) and (59.79) must be multiplied by $1/\sqrt{3}$.

[3] For an illustration of these points, see V. Gillet and M. A. Melkanoff, *Phys. Rev.*, **133**:B1190 (1964).

‡ The first calculations of this type for O^{16} were carried out by J. P. Elliott and B. H. Flowers, *Proc. Roy. Soc. (London)*, **A242**:57 (1957) and G. E. Brown, L. Castillejo, and J. A. Evans, *Nucl. Phys.*, **22**:1 (1961). The present calculation is due to T. W. Donnelly and G. E. Walker, *Ann. Phys. (N.Y.)*, (to be published).

particles from the $1p$ oscillator shell to the next $2s$–$1d$ oscillator shell are retained (see Fig. 57.3). The resulting particle-hole states are listed in Table 59.2, together with the possible values of J^π. Table 59.2 also gives the Hartree-Fock

Table 59.2 Negative-parity particle-hole configurations in O^{16}

Configurations	$\epsilon_a - \epsilon_b$, MeV	States
$(2s_{\frac{1}{2}})(1p_{\frac{3}{2}})^{-1}$	18.55	$1^-, 2^-$
$(1d_{\frac{5}{2}})(1p_{\frac{3}{2}})^{-1}$	17.68	$1^-, 2^-, 3^-, 4^-$
$(1d_{\frac{3}{2}})(1p_{\frac{3}{2}})^{-1}$	22.76	$0^-, 1^-, 2^-, 3^-$
$(2s_{\frac{1}{2}})(1p_{\frac{1}{2}})^{-1}$	12.39	$0^-, 1^-$
$(1d_{\frac{5}{2}})(1p_{\frac{1}{2}})^{-1}$	11.52	$2^-, 3^-$
$(1d_{\frac{3}{2}})(1p_{\frac{1}{2}})^{-1}$	16.60	$1^-, 2^-$

Source: T. W. Donnelly and G. E. Walker, *Ann. Phys.*
(*N.Y.*), (to be published).

configuration energies $\epsilon_a - \epsilon_b$ of these states [see Eqs. (56.22) to (56.24)], which are obtained from neighboring nuclei with an extra neutron particle or hole.

The particle-hole interaction is computed from Eq. (59.51a). In this calculation the nucleon-nucleon potential V is taken to be of a nonsingular

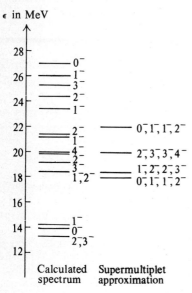

Fig. 59.3 $T = 1$ spectrum of O^{16} computed as described in the text. Also shown is the super-multiplet structure obtained when the spin-dependent forces are turned off. (The authors wish to thank G. E. Walker for preparing this figure.)

Yukawa form with Serber exchange; it is fit to low-energy nucleon-nucleon scattering:

$$V(1,2) = [^1V(r_{12})^1P + {}^3V(r_{12})^3P]\tfrac{1}{2}[1 + P_M(1,2)]$$

$$^1P = \tfrac{1}{4}(1 - \boldsymbol{\sigma}_1\cdot\boldsymbol{\sigma}_2) \qquad ^3P = \tfrac{1}{4}(3 + \boldsymbol{\sigma}_1\cdot\boldsymbol{\sigma}_2)$$

$$V(r_{12}) = V_0 \frac{e^{-\mu r_{12}}}{\mu r_{12}} \tag{59.81}$$

$$^1V_0 = -46.87 \text{ MeV} \qquad ^1\mu = 0.8547 \text{ F}^{-1}$$

$$^3V_0 = -52.13 \text{ MeV} \qquad ^3\mu = 0.7261 \text{ F}^{-1}$$

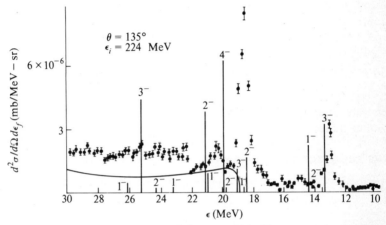

Fig. 59.4 Experimental spectrum of electrons with incident energy $\epsilon_i = 224$ MeV inelastically scattered at $\theta = 135°$ as a function of nuclear excitation energy ϵ. The calculated spectrum using the states of Fig. 59.3 is also shown (with arbitrary overall normalization; the integrated areas for the various complexes agree with the theory to approximately a factor of 2). The solid line is a calculation of the nonresonant background above the threshold for nucleon emission. [From I. Sick, E. B. Hughes, T. W. Donnelly, J. D. Walecka, and G. E. Walker, *Phys. Rev. Letters*, **23**:1117 (1969) and T. W. Donnelly and G. E. Walker, *Ann. Phys. (N.Y.)*, (to be published). Reprinted by permission of the authors and the American Institute of Physics.]

The harmonic-oscillator wave functions of Eq. (57.6) are used as approximate Hartree-Fock wave functions in computing matrix elements, and the oscillator parameter $b = 1.77 \times 10^{-13}$ cm is determined by fitting elastic electron scattering. The calculated spectrum is shown in Fig. 59.3.   These collective states may be seen, for example, through transitions excited by inelastic electron scattering, and Fig. 59.4 compares an experimental spectrum with the predicted location and relative intensities of the peaks.   The transition matrix elements are computed using the coefficients $\psi_{JT}^{(n)}(ab)$ obtained in the TDA calculation [see Eq. (59.50)]. The calculated peak locations are consistently about an MeV too high; furthermore, the experimental levels are quite broad above particle-emission threshold

(≈ 19 MeV in the present case) so that the use of simple bound states is in-adequate. Nevertheless, the general agreement is very good.

In accord with our previous model calculation, we also investigate the supermultiplet structure of these states. The appropriate particle-hole con-figurations $(n_a l_a)(n_b l_b)^{-1}$ are $(2s)(1p)^{-1}$ and $(1d)(1p)^{-1}$ with $L = 1$ (twice), 2 and 3. The supermultiplets will be degenerate only for spin-independent forces. To uncover this structure, we first "turn off" the single-particle spin-orbit force by assuming that the observed (nlj) states have been shifted from an original (nl) configuration according to Eqs. (57.14) to (57.16), and we then retain only the spin-independent part of the interaction in Eq. (59.81). The resulting $T = 1$ members of the [15] supermultiplets are shown in Fig. 59.3. The supermultiplet approximation clearly provides only a qualitative description of the actual spectrum.

60☐EXCITED STATES: GREEN'S FUNCTION METHODS[1]

In this section, we again study the collective excitations of a finite interacting assembly, but we now apply the more general and powerful techniques of quantum field theory.

THE POLARIZATION PROPAGATOR

As discussed in Sec. 13, the response of the system to a perturbation of the form

$$\hat{H}^{\text{ex}}(t) = \int \hat{\psi}^\dagger(\mathbf{x}) V^{\text{ex}}(\mathbf{x}t) \hat{\psi}(\mathbf{x}) d^3x \tag{60.1}$$

is governed by the density-correlation function, or polarization propagator. In the present context of a finite system, the polarization propagator is defined by[2]

$$i\Pi_{\lambda\mu;\alpha\beta}(t - t') \equiv \langle \Psi_0 | T[c^\dagger_{H\mu}(t) c_{H\lambda}(t) c^\dagger_{H\alpha}(t') c_{H\beta}(t')] | \Psi_0 \rangle \tag{60.2}$$

where $|\Psi_0\rangle$ is the exact (normalized) Heisenberg ground state of the hamiltonian in Eq. (56.18). The Greek subscripts now refer to the single-particle Hartree-Fock states, while $c_{H\alpha}(t)$ and $c^\dagger_{H\alpha}(t)$ are Heisenberg operators, related to the particle and hole operators by

$$c_\alpha \equiv \theta(\alpha - F) a_\alpha + \theta(F - \alpha) S_\alpha b^\dagger_{-\alpha} \tag{60.3}$$

Just as in Sec. 59, we again consider only closed-shell ground states.

---

[1] The approach in this section is largely based on D. J. Thouless, *Rep. Prog. Phys.*, **27**:53 (1964). See also W. Czyż, *Acta Phys. Polon.*, **20**:737 (1961) and G. E. Brown, Course XXIII-Nuclear Physics, in "Proc. Int. School of Physics 'Enrico Fermi,' " p. 99, Academic Press, New York, 1963.

[2] Note that here the order of the indices on Π is slightly different from that in Eq. (9.39) (compare Figs. 9.18 and 60.1). The present choice is more convenient in studying particle-hole inter-actions and allows us to write the important equations [(60.20), for example] in a particularly transparent form.

The general diagrammatic structure of $\Pi(t-t')$ is shown in Fig. (60.1). A particle-hole pair in the states $(\alpha\beta)$ is created at time t'. It then propagates to time t where it is destroyed in the states $(\lambda\mu)$. Note that the definition of Eq. (60.2) is just a piece of the full polarization propagator for the assembly defined by

$$i\Pi(x,x') = \langle\Psi_0|T[\hat{\psi}^\dagger(x)\,\hat{\psi}(x)\,\hat{\psi}^\dagger(x')\,\hat{\psi}(x')]|\Psi_0\rangle \tag{60.4a}$$

$$i\Pi(x,x') = \sum_{\alpha\beta\lambda\mu} \varphi_\mu(\mathbf{x})^\dagger\varphi_\lambda(\mathbf{x})\varphi_\alpha(\mathbf{x}')^\dagger\varphi_\beta(\mathbf{x}')\,i\Pi_{\lambda\mu;\alpha\beta}(t-t') \tag{60.4b}$$

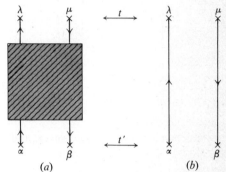

Fig. 60.1 Structure of Feynman diagrams contributing to $\Pi_{\lambda\mu;\alpha\beta}(t-t')$ in Eq. (60.2): (a) general, (b) lowest order.

where $\{\varphi\}$ denotes the Hartree-Fock wave functions [Eq. (56.17)]. $\Pi_{\lambda\mu;\alpha\beta}$ is easily shown to be a function of $t-t'$ by the methods of Chap. 3, and thus takes the form

$$\Pi_{\lambda\mu;\alpha\beta}(t-t') = (2\pi)^{-1}\int d\omega\,\Pi_{\lambda\mu;\alpha\beta}(\omega)\,e^{-i\omega(t-t')} \tag{60.5}$$

Furthermore, the Lehmann representation is derived just as in Sec. 7

$$\Pi_{\lambda\mu;\alpha\beta}(\omega) = \hbar\sum_n\left[\frac{\langle\Psi_0|c_\mu^\dagger c_\lambda|\Psi_n\rangle\langle\Psi_n|c_\alpha^\dagger c_\beta|\Psi_0\rangle}{\hbar\omega-(E_n-E_0)+i\eta}\right.$$
$$\left.-\frac{\langle\Psi_0|c_\alpha^\dagger c_\beta|\Psi_n\rangle\langle\Psi_n|c_\mu^\dagger c_\lambda|\Psi_0\rangle}{\hbar\omega+(E_n-E_0)-i\eta}\right] \tag{60.6}$$

Note that the intermediate states $|\Psi_n\rangle$ refer to an assembly of precisely N particles. The poles of the polarization propagator evidently determine the energies of the excited states that can be reached by a perturbation of the form of Eq. (60.1).

To express Π in terms of Feynman diagrams, we first go to the interaction representation and write

$$i\Pi_{\lambda\mu;\alpha\beta}(t-t')$$
$$= \sum_{n=0}^\infty \frac{(-i/\hbar)^n}{n!}\int dt_1\cdots dt_n\langle0|T[\hat{H}_2(t_1)\cdots\hat{H}_2(t_n)c_\mu^\dagger(t)c_\lambda(t)$$
$$\times c_\alpha^\dagger(t')c_\beta(t')]|0\rangle_{\text{connected}} \tag{60.7}$$

where $\hat{H}_2$ is the interaction in Eq. (56.21).   The state $|0\rangle$ is now the Hartree-Fock *vacuum* or ground state illustrated in Fig. 56.1.   When this expression is analyzed with Wick's theorem, there are no contractions *within a given* $\hat{H}_2$ because $\hat{H}_2$ is already *normal ordered*.   Thus the present theory has no Feynman diagrams of the type shown in Fig. 10.1; all these terms are explicitly summed by the canonical transformation of Sec. 56.   The polarization propagator [Eq. (60.7)] still contains disjoint graphs with the structure shown in Fig. 60.2.   Such terms

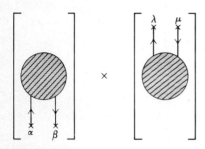

Fig. 60.2 Disjoint graphs contributing to Eq. (60.7). They contribute only at $\omega = 0$ and are therefore omitted from the subsequent analysis.

are independent of $t - t'$, however, and contribute only to the $\omega = 0$ component of $\Pi(\omega)$.   They will therefore be omitted entirely because we here confine ourselves to those components with $\omega \neq 0$.   Alternatively, we could consider a polarization propagator defined in terms of the fluctuation densities

$$\delta[c_{H\alpha}^\dagger(t')\,c_{H\beta}(t')] \equiv c_{H\alpha}^\dagger(t')\,c_{H\beta}(t') - \langle\Psi_0|c_{H\alpha}^\dagger(t')\,c_{H\beta}(t')|\Psi_0\rangle \tag{60.8}$$

as was done in Secs. 12 and 32.   The last term is a c number and can cause no transitions; it merely serves to remove the $n = 0$ terms in Eq. (60.6) so that the modified $\Pi(\omega)$ has no singularity at $\omega = 0$.   In coordinate space the corresponding c-number terms just cancel all Feynman diagrams of the type shown in Fig. 60.2.

The free single-particle propagator is defined by

$$\langle 0|T[c_\lambda(t)\,c_\alpha^\dagger(t')]|0\rangle \equiv iG_{\lambda\alpha}^0(t - t') \tag{60.9}$$

$$\langle 0|T[c_\lambda(t)\,c_\alpha^\dagger(t')]|0\rangle \equiv (2\pi)^{-1} \int d\omega\, iG_{\lambda\alpha}^0(\omega)\, e^{-i\omega(t-t')} \tag{60.10}$$

where the c's are now in the interaction representation.   A familiar calculation leads to

$$G_{\lambda\alpha}^0(\omega) = \delta_{\lambda\alpha}\left[\frac{\theta(\alpha - F)}{\omega - \omega_\alpha + i\eta} + \frac{\theta(F - \alpha)}{\omega - \omega_\alpha - i\eta}\right] \tag{60.11}$$

The one lowest-order contribution to $\mathbf{\Pi}$ is shown in Fig. 60.1b, and an application of Wick's theorem gives

$$i\Pi_{\lambda\mu;\alpha\beta}^0(t - t') = -(2\pi)^{-2} \int d\omega_1 \int d\omega_2\, iG_{\lambda\alpha}^0(\omega_1)\, iG_{\beta\mu}^0(\omega_2)\, e^{-i\omega_1(t-t')}\, e^{i\omega_2(t-t')}$$

$$\tag{60.12}$$

in coordinate space and

$$i\Pi^0_{\lambda\mu;\alpha\beta}(\omega) = -(2\pi)^{-2} \int d\omega_1 \int d\omega_2\, 2\pi\delta(\omega - \omega_1 + \omega_2)\, iG^0_{\lambda\alpha}(\omega_1)\, iG^0_{\beta\mu}(\omega_2)$$

$$(60.13a)$$

$$i\Pi^0_{\lambda\mu;\alpha\beta}(\omega) = -i^2(2\pi)^{-1} \int d\omega_1\, G^0_{\lambda\alpha}(\omega_1)\, G^0_{\beta\mu}(\omega_1 - \omega)$$

$$(60.13b)$$

$$i\Pi^0_{\lambda\mu;\alpha\beta}(\omega) = i\delta_{\lambda\alpha}\,\delta_{\beta\mu} \left[\frac{\theta(\alpha - F)\,\theta(F - \beta)}{\omega - (\omega_\alpha - \omega_\beta) + i\eta} - \frac{\theta(F - \alpha)\,\theta(\beta - F)}{\omega + (\omega_\beta - \omega_\alpha) - i\eta} \right]$$

$$(60.13c)$$

in momentum space.

It is now possible to derive the first-order corrections to the polarization propagator. The interaction hamiltonian is

$$\hat{H}_2(t - t') = \tfrac{1}{2} \sum_{\rho\sigma\eta\nu} \langle\rho\sigma|V|\eta\nu\rangle\, N[c^\dagger_\rho(t)\, c^\dagger_\sigma(t')\, c_\nu(t')\, c_\eta(t)]\,\delta(t - t') \qquad (60.14)$$

and the delta function can be written

$$\delta(t - t') = (2\pi)^{-1} \int d\omega\, e^{i\omega(t-t')}$$

Hence we find

$$i\Pi^{(1)}_{\lambda\mu;\alpha\beta}(t - t') = -i\hbar^{-1} \iint dt_1\, dt_1'\, \tfrac{1}{2} \sum_{\eta\nu\rho\sigma} \langle\rho\sigma|V|\eta\nu\rangle \int (2\pi)^{-1}$$

$$\times \exp[i\omega_5(t_1 - t_1')]\, d\omega_5 \langle 0|T\{N[c^\dagger_\rho(t_1)\, c^\dagger_\sigma(t_1')\, c_\nu(t_1')\, c_\eta(t_1)]$$

$$\times c^\dagger_\mu(t)\, c_\lambda(t)\, c^\dagger_\alpha(t')\, c_\beta(t')\}|0\rangle \quad (60.15)$$

When this expression is analyzed with Wick's theorem, there are two sets of contributions differing only by the interchange of dummy variables $\rho \rightleftharpoons \sigma$, $\eta \rightleftharpoons \nu$, and $t_1 \rightleftharpoons t_1'$. We may keep just the first set and cancel the overall factor $\tfrac{1}{2}$. Conservation of frequency at each vertex means that the variable $t - t'$ always occurs through a factor $e^{-i(\omega_1 - \omega_2)(t-t')}$, as in Eq. (60.12). Thus a factor $2\pi\delta(\omega - \omega_1 + \omega_2)$ must be included in the Fourier transform to account for the end points [compare Eq. (60.13a)]. A combination of these results yields

$$i\Pi^{(1)}_{\lambda\mu;\alpha\beta}(\omega) = \frac{-i}{\hbar} \sum_{\eta\nu\rho\sigma} \langle\rho\sigma|V|\eta\nu\rangle \int \frac{d\omega_1}{2\pi} \cdots \int \frac{d\omega_5}{2\pi}$$

$$\times \{-iG^0_{\eta\alpha}(\omega_1)\, iG^0_{\lambda\rho}(\omega_3)\, iG^0_{\nu\mu}(\omega_4)\, iG^0_{\beta\sigma}(\omega_2)\, 2\pi\delta(\omega_1 - \omega_3 - \omega_5)$$

$$\times 2\pi\delta(\omega_4 + \omega_5 - \omega_2) + iG^0_{\eta\alpha}(\omega_1)\, iG^0_{\beta\rho}(\omega_2)\, iG^0_{\nu\mu}(\omega_4)$$

$$\times iG^0_{\lambda\sigma}(\omega_3)\, 2\pi\delta(\omega_1 - \omega_2 - \omega_5)\, 2\pi\delta(\omega_4 + \omega_5 - \omega_3)\}$$

$$\times 2\pi\delta(\omega - \omega_1 + \omega_2) \qquad (60.16)$$

and the first-order Feynman diagrams are shown in Fig. 60.3. The ω_5 integration is the same in both terms, while changing dummy variables $\rho \rightleftharpoons \sigma$ in the second

term and using Eq. (60.13) gives

$$\hbar\Pi^{(1)}_{\lambda\mu;\alpha\beta}(\omega) = \sum_{\eta\nu\rho\sigma} i\Pi^0_{\lambda\mu;\rho\nu}(\omega)\left[\langle\rho\sigma|V|\eta\nu\rangle - \langle\sigma\rho|V|\eta\nu\rangle\right]i\Pi^0_{\eta\sigma;\alpha\beta}(\omega) \quad (60.17)$$

This expression can be clarified by writing

$$\Pi^{(1)}_{\lambda\mu;\alpha\beta}(\omega) = \sum_{\eta\nu\rho\sigma} \Pi^0_{\lambda\mu;\rho\nu}(\omega)\,K^\star_{(1)}(\omega)_{\rho\nu;\eta\sigma}\,\Pi^0_{\eta\sigma;\alpha\beta}(\omega) \quad\quad\quad (60.18)$$

$$\hbar K^\star_{(1)}(\omega)_{\rho\nu;\eta\sigma} \equiv -\langle\rho\sigma|V|\eta\nu\rangle + \langle\sigma\rho|V|\eta\nu\rangle \quad\quad\quad (60.19)$$

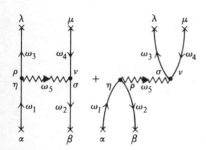

Fig. 60.3 Feynman diagrams contributing to $\Pi^{(1)}_{\lambda\mu;\alpha\beta}(\omega)$ in Eq. (60.16).

where the two matrix elements in $K^\star_{(1)}$ come from the first and second diagrams in Fig. 60.3, respectively. Note that the lowest-order proper particle-hole scattering kernel $K^\star_{(1)}$ is independent of ω. Furthermore the simple expression (60.18) arises only because the interaction potential itself is independent of the frequency ω_5, which is actually different in the two different graphs.

We next write a Bethe-Salpeter equation for particle-hole scattering. This equation iterates $\mathbf{K}^\star$ and allows a calculation of the polarization propagator $\mathbf{\Pi}$ to all orders. It takes the form

$$\Pi_{\lambda\mu;\alpha\beta}(\omega) = \Pi^0_{\lambda\mu;\alpha\beta}(\omega) + \sum_{\eta\nu\rho\sigma} \Pi^0_{\lambda\mu;\rho\nu}(\omega)\,K^\star(\omega)_{\rho\nu;\eta\sigma}\,\Pi_{\eta\sigma;\alpha\beta}(\omega) \quad (60.20)$$

corresponding to Fig. 60.4. We have here made the simplifying assumption that the kernel $\mathbf{K}^\star$ depends only on ω, as in Eq. (60.19). The most general

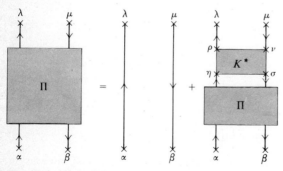

Fig. 60.4 Bethe-Salpeter equation (60.20) for $\Pi_{\lambda\mu;\alpha\beta}(\omega)$.

particle-hole Bethe-Salpeter equation will not factor as in Eq. (60.20) but instead becomes an integral equation involving an integral over frequency.[1]

Equation (60.20) is now a simple matrix equation, which can be written in the form

$$\mathbf{\Pi}(\omega) = \mathbf{\Pi}^0(\omega) + \mathbf{\Pi}^0(\omega)\, \mathbf{K}^\star(\omega)\, \mathbf{\Pi}(\omega) \tag{60.21}$$

The inverse of this matrix relation yields

$$[\mathbf{\Pi}(\omega)^{-1}]_{\lambda\mu;\alpha\beta} = [\mathbf{\Pi}^0(\omega)^{-1}]_{\lambda\mu;\alpha\beta} - K^\star(\omega)_{\lambda\mu;\alpha\beta} \tag{60.22}$$

All the matrix elements of $\mathbf{\Pi}(\omega)$ have a pole at $\hbar\omega = E_n - E_0$ unless, of course, the numerators in Eq. (60.6) vanish. For real ω close to the pole, the matrix elements satisfy the relation

$$\Pi^*_{\lambda\mu;\alpha\beta} = \Pi_{\alpha\beta;\lambda\mu} \tag{60.23}$$

Hence $\mathbf{\Pi}(\omega)$ is a hermitian matrix for real ω and can be diagonalized with a unitary transformation

$$\mathbf{U}\mathbf{\Pi}(\omega)\,\mathbf{U}^{-1} = \mathbf{\Pi}^D(\omega) \tag{60.24}$$

The inverse of this relation

$$\mathbf{U}\mathbf{\Pi}(\omega)^{-1}\,\mathbf{U}^{-1} = \mathbf{\Pi}^D(\omega)^{-1} \tag{60.25}$$

shows that the transformation $\mathbf{U}$ also diagonalizes $\mathbf{\Pi}(\omega)^{-1}$. Some of the diagonal matrix elements of $\mathbf{\Pi}^D(\omega)$ have a pole at the exact excitation energy of the assembly $\hbar\omega = E_n - E_0$, which means that the corresponding diagonal matrix elements of $\mathbf{\Pi}^D(\omega)^{-1}$ have a zero at the same point. Since these diagonal matrix elements are just the eigenvalues of $\mathbf{\Pi}(\omega)^{-1}$, we arrive at the general principle that *the zero eigenvalues of $\mathbf{\Pi}(\omega)^{-1}$ considered as a function of ω correspond to the collective energy levels of the assembly.* It is therefore necessary to solve the set of linear equations

$$\sum_{\alpha\beta} [\mathbf{\Pi}(\omega)^{-1}]_{\lambda\mu;\alpha\beta}\, C_{\alpha\beta} = \Lambda(\omega)^{-1}\, C_{\lambda\mu} \tag{60.26}$$

with

$$\Lambda(\omega)^{-1} = 0 \tag{60.27}$$

A combination with Eq. (60.22) yields the equations

$$\sum_{\alpha\beta} [\mathbf{\Pi}^0(\omega)^{-1} - K^\star(\omega)]_{\lambda\mu;\alpha\beta}\, C_{\alpha\beta} = 0 \tag{60.28}$$

which determine the eigenvalues ω and the coefficients of the corresponding state vectors $C_{\alpha\beta}$.

[1] W. Czyż, *loc. cit.*

RANDOM-PHASE APPROXIMATION

As a first approximation in Eq. (60.28), we take $\mathbf{K}^{\star} \approx \mathbf{K}^{\star}_{(1)}$, which expresses the polarization propagator as a sum of Feynman diagrams of the type shown in Fig. 60.5. These diagrams contain as a subset all the ring diagrams included in

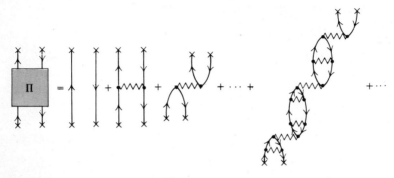

Fig. 60.5 Feynman diagrams for $\mathbf{\Pi}$ summed in the approximation $\mathbf{K}^{\star} \approx \mathbf{K}^{\star}_{(1)}$.

our discussion of the electron gas,[1] and the approximation here, as in that case, is commonly referred to as the random-phase approximation. Equation (60.28) may be written out in detail using Eqs. (60.13c) and (60.19)

$$\sum_{\alpha\beta} (\delta_{\lambda\alpha}\delta_{\beta\mu}\{\theta(\alpha - F)\,\theta(F - \beta)\,[\epsilon - (\epsilon_{\alpha} - \epsilon_{\beta})] - \theta(F - \alpha)\,\theta(\beta - F)$$

$$\times\,[\epsilon + (\epsilon_{\beta} - \epsilon_{\alpha})]\} - [-\langle\lambda\beta|V|\alpha\mu\rangle + \langle\beta\lambda|V|\alpha\mu\rangle])\,C_{\alpha\beta} = 0 \quad (60.29)$$

This set of linear, homogeneous, algebraic equations possesses solutions only for certain eigenvalues ϵ_n.

We now separate the indices in Eq. (60.29) into the regions above and below F, and change dummy indices so that α and λ always refer to particles ($\alpha,\lambda > F$), and β and μ always refer to holes ($\beta,\mu < F$)

$$(\epsilon - \epsilon_{\lambda\mu})\,C_{\lambda\mu} - \sum_{\substack{\alpha > F \\ \beta < F}} \{[-\langle\lambda\beta|V|\alpha\mu\rangle + \langle\beta\lambda|V|\alpha\mu\rangle]\,C_{\alpha\beta} + [-\langle\lambda\alpha|V|\beta\mu\rangle$$

$$+ \langle\alpha\lambda|V|\beta\mu\rangle]\,C_{\beta\alpha}\} = 0 \qquad \lambda > F, \mu < F \quad (60.30a)$$

$$-(\epsilon + \epsilon_{\lambda\mu})\,C_{\mu\lambda} - \sum_{\substack{\alpha > F \\ \beta < F}} \{[-\langle\mu\beta|V|\alpha\lambda\rangle + \langle\beta\mu|V|\alpha\lambda\rangle]\,C_{\alpha\beta} + [-\langle\mu\alpha|V|\beta\lambda\rangle$$

$$+ \langle\alpha\mu|V|\beta\lambda\rangle]\,C_{\beta\alpha}\} = 0 \qquad \lambda > F, \mu < F \quad (60.30b)$$

Define

$$C_{\alpha\beta} \equiv S_{\beta}\,\psi^{*}_{\alpha-\beta} \qquad \alpha > F,\, \beta < F \qquad\qquad\qquad (60.31a)$$

$$C_{\beta\alpha} \equiv S_{\beta}\,\varphi^{*}_{\alpha-\beta} \qquad \alpha > F,\, \beta < F \qquad\qquad\qquad (60.31b)$$

---

[1] The larger set of diagrams shown in Fig. 60.5 is just that considered in Prob. 5.8 on zero sound.

replace μ and β by $-\mu$ and $-\beta$ in the preceding equations, and multiply by $S_{-\mu}$

$$(\epsilon - \epsilon_{\lambda, -\mu}) \psi^*_{\lambda\mu} - \sum_{\alpha\beta} \{S_{-\mu} S_{-\beta}[-\langle\lambda - \beta|V|\alpha - \mu\rangle + \langle-\beta\lambda|V|\alpha - \mu\rangle] \psi^*_{\alpha\beta}$$

$$+ S_{-\mu} S_{-\beta}[-\langle\lambda\alpha|V|-\beta-\mu\rangle + \langle\alpha\lambda|V|-\beta-\mu\rangle] \varphi^*_{\alpha\beta}\} = 0 \quad (60.32a)$$

$$-(\epsilon + \epsilon_{\lambda, -\mu}) \varphi^*_{\lambda\mu} - \sum_{\alpha\beta} \{S_{-\mu} S_{-\beta}[-\langle-\mu - \beta|V|\alpha\lambda\rangle + \langle-\beta-\mu|V|\alpha\lambda\rangle] \psi^*_{\alpha\beta}$$

$$+ S_{-\mu} S_{-\beta}[-\langle-\mu\alpha|V|-\beta\lambda\rangle + \langle\alpha - \mu|V|-\beta\lambda\rangle] \varphi^*_{\alpha\beta}\} = 0 \quad (60.32b)$$

If we recall the definitions in Eqs. (59.10) and (59.21), we see that these equations can be rewritten as

$$(\epsilon_{\lambda, -\mu} - \epsilon) \psi^*_{\lambda\mu} + \sum_{\alpha\beta} (v^*_{\lambda\mu;\alpha\beta} \psi^*_{\alpha\beta} + u^*_{\lambda\mu;\alpha\beta} \varphi^*_{\alpha\beta}) = 0 \qquad (60.33a)$$

$$(\epsilon_{\lambda, -\mu} + \epsilon) \varphi^*_{\lambda\mu} + \sum_{\alpha\beta} (v_{\lambda\mu;\alpha\beta} \varphi^*_{\alpha\beta} + u_{\lambda\mu;\alpha\beta} \psi^*_{\alpha\beta}) = 0 \qquad (60.33b)$$

which are *exactly the RPA equations* (59.22) analyzed in detail in the last section. It is instructive to compare this result with that of the Tamm-Dancoff approximation.

TAMM-DANCOFF APPROXIMATION

To the extent that the positive eigenvalues $\epsilon = \epsilon_n$ of the collective excitations lie in the vicinity of the unperturbed particle-hole energies (namely, $\epsilon_n \approx \epsilon_\alpha - \epsilon_\beta$), the lowest-order polarization propagator [Eq. (60.13c)] can be replaced by

$$\Pi^0_{\lambda\mu;\alpha\beta}(\omega) \approx \delta_{\lambda\alpha} \delta_{\beta\mu} \frac{\theta(\alpha - F) \theta(F - \beta)}{\omega - (\omega_\alpha - \omega_\beta) + i\eta} \qquad (60.34)$$

In Eqs. (60.20) and (60.29) this approximation implies that the indices α and λ always refer to particles and the indices β and μ to holes. Thus Eqs. (60.33) become

$$(\epsilon_{\lambda, -\mu} - \epsilon) \psi^*_{\lambda\mu} + \sum_{\alpha\beta} v^*_{\lambda\mu;\alpha\beta} \psi^*_{\alpha\beta} = 0 \qquad (60.35)$$

which are just the TDA equations.

We can now see the relation between the RPA and TDA. Take the Fourier transform [Eq. (60.5)] of the approximate zero-order particle-hole propagator [Eq. (60.34)] used in the TDA. It is evident that this quantity only propagates forward in time. In contrast, the original zero-order particle-hole propagator in Eq. (60.13c) retains the full symmetry in ω and propagates in both time directions. Consequently the RPA sums all possible iterations of the two lowest-order diagrams for $K^\star_{(1)}$ in the sense of Feynman diagrams (Fig. 60.5), whereas the TDA sums just that subset of diagrams where all particle-hole pairs propagate forward in time. *Thus the TDA has one and only one particle-hole*

pair present at any instant of time, whereas the RPA permits any number of particle-hole pairs to be present simultaneously.

It is clear from Eqs. (60.33) that the TDA is the limiting case of the RPA when the matrix elements of the potential are small compared to the unperturbed energies, or more precisely when

$$\frac{\langle V \rangle}{\epsilon_n + (\epsilon_\lambda - \epsilon_{-\mu})} \ll 1 \tag{60.36}$$

In this case Eqs. (60.33) *uncouple*, and Eq. (60.33a) becomes just Eq. (60.35). An equivalent condition is that the true eigenvalues should lie close to the unperturbed configuration energies, namely, $\epsilon_n \approx \epsilon_\lambda - \epsilon_{-\mu}$. Hence, excited states that are strongly shifted from the unperturbed particle-hole energies (particularly those states shifted to lower energies for which $\epsilon_n \approx 0$) should be treated in the RPA rather than the TDA; these are generally the most collective states.

CONSTRUCTION OF $\Pi(\omega)$ IN THE RPA

The present results can be combined with those of Sec. 59 to construct $\Pi(\omega)$ explicitly in the RPA. Equations (60.31) and (59.17) together give

$$C_{\alpha\beta} = S_\beta \psi^*_{\alpha-\beta} = S_\beta \langle \Psi_0 | b_{-\beta} a_\alpha | \Psi_n \rangle \qquad \alpha > F, \beta < F \tag{60.37a}$$

$$C_{\alpha\beta} = S_\alpha \varphi^*_{\beta-\alpha} = S_\alpha \langle \Psi_0 | a^\dagger_\beta b^\dagger_{-\alpha} | \Psi_n \rangle \qquad \beta > F, \alpha < F \tag{60.37b}$$

These expressions can be combined with the particle-hole transformation of Eq. (59.4)

$$c^\dagger_\alpha c_\beta \doteq \theta(\alpha - F)\,\theta(F - \beta)\,a^\dagger_\alpha b^\dagger_{-\beta} S_\beta + \theta(\beta - F)\,\theta(F - \alpha)\,b_{-\alpha} a_\beta S_\alpha \qquad \text{RPA} \tag{60.38}$$

and we therefore identify

$$\langle \Psi_0 | c^\dagger_\alpha c_\beta | \Psi_n \rangle = C^{(n)}_{\beta\alpha} \qquad \text{RPA} \tag{60.39}$$

As a result the polarization propagator in the RPA can be written [see Eq. (60.6)]

$$\Pi^{\text{RPA}}_{\lambda\mu;\alpha\beta}(\omega) = \sum_n \left(\frac{C^{(n)}_{\lambda\mu} C^{(n)*}_{\alpha\beta}}{\omega - \omega_n + i\eta} - \frac{C^{(n)}_{\beta\alpha} C^{(n)*}_{\mu\lambda}}{\omega + \omega_n - i\eta} \right) \tag{60.40}$$

This expression characterizes the linear response in RPA to an external perturbation of the form of Eq. (60.1). It therefore permits us to study the excitation of nuclear states obtained by electron scattering, photon processes, weak interactions, and even high-energy nucleon scattering (to the extent that the Born approximation applies to the excitation process).

61□REALISTIC NUCLEAR FORCES[1]

So far, the discussion of finite systems has been cast in rather general terms, and the techniques apply to atoms and molecules, as well as to atomic nuclei. In this section we briefly discuss some of the specific problems arising from the singular nature of the nucleon-nucleon force. The hard core (and strong attraction just outside the core) means that the matrix elements $\langle \alpha\beta | V | \lambda\mu \rangle$ must be replaced by a sum of ladder diagrams, as in the Galitskii or Bethe-Goldstone approaches. We here use the latter framework because of its relative simplicity.

TWO NUCLEONS OUTSIDE CLOSED SHELLS: THE INDEPENDENT-PAIR APPROXIMATION

In principle, the first step in treating a finite system with singular two-body forces is to construct the Hartree-Fock single-particle wave functions for an effective two-body interaction obtained by summing the ladder diagrams. This sum, in turn, depends on the choice of single-particle wave functions. Such a self-consistent problem is clearly very difficult. As an illustration, we shall instead assume that the single-particle wave functions and energies are known from our discussion of the shell-model and consider a single interacting valence pair of neutrons or protons outside a *doubly magic* core with closed major shells (e.g., He^6, O^{18}, Ca^{42}, etc.). This simplified problem serves as a prototype for any study of a finite system with singular forces. In addition, it also allows a direct comparison with experiment, for we know from Sec. 58 that the matrix elements $\langle j^2JM | V | j^2JM \rangle$ determine the *spectrum* of such a nucleus if the interaction between the valence nucleons is nonsingular. For a singular interaction, we merely compute the corresponding matrix elements in the ladder approximation.

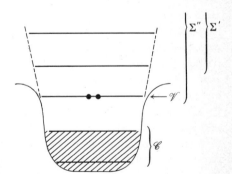

Fig. 61.1 Two nucleons outside closed shells. $\mathscr{V}$ indicates the degenerate valence levels and $\mathscr{C}$ denotes the closed-shell core.

[1] The simplified discussion in this section follows that of J. F. Dawson, I. Talmi, and J. D. Walecka, *Ann. Phys.* (*N.Y.*), **18**:339 (1962); **19**:350 (1962). For a thorough treatment of nuclear spectroscopy with realistic forces, see B. H. Brandow, *Rev. Mod. Phys.*, **39**:771 (1967) and M. H. Macfarlane, Course XL, Nuclear Structure and Nuclear Reactions, in Proceedings of "The International School of Physics 'Enrico Fermi,' " p. 457, Academic Press, New York, 1969.

The present situation is illustrated in Fig. 61.1.   Two identical valence nucleons occupy the (degenerate) set of states $\mathscr{V}$, while the core $\mathscr{C}$ consists of doubly magic closed shells.   Let the total binding energy of the nucleus with A nucleons, Z protons, and N neutrons be denoted by $_{Z}B_{N}^{A} \equiv {_{Z}E_{N}^{A}} - Zm_{p}c^{2} - Nm_{n}c^{2}$.   The ground-state binding energy $BE(2N)$ of the valence pair of neutrons, for example, can then be defined by

$$BE(2N) \equiv {_{Z}B_{N}^{A}} - {_{Z}B_{N-2}^{A-2}} - 2[{_{Z}B_{N-1}^{A-1}} - {_{Z}B_{N-2}^{A-2}}] \tag{61.1}$$

The basic problem is to compute this two-particle binding energy, as well as the excitation spectrum of the nucleus.   To achieve this aim, we assume that the inert core serves only to provide a self-consistent Hartree-Fock potential whose levels $\mathscr{C}$ are already filled.   We then work in the independent-pair approximation and write a Bethe-Goldstone equation for the valence pair that allows virtual excitation to *any states except those already occupied*.   Since this *integral equation* depends only on the combination $V\psi$, its solution is well defined even for singular potentials.

BETHE-GOLDSTONE EQUATION

The Bethe-Goldstone equation for the system illustrated in Fig. 61.1 follows directly from the discussion in Sec. 36.[1]

$$\psi_{n_1 n_2}(1,2) = \varphi_{n_1}(1)\,\varphi_{n_2}(2) + \sum_{n_1' n_2'}{}'' \frac{\varphi_{n_1'}(1)\,\varphi_{n_2'}(2)\,\langle n_1' n_2' | H_1 | \psi_{n_1 n_2}\rangle}{E_{n_1 n_2} - E_{n_1' n_2'}^{0}} \tag{61.2a}$$

$$E_{n_1 n_2} - E_{n_1 n_2}^{0} = \langle n_1 n_2 | H_1 | \psi_{n_1 n_2}\rangle \tag{61.2b}$$

Here the index n denotes the single-particle levels $\{nlm_l \tfrac{1}{2}m_s\}$ available to the valence pair, and we assume initially that the unperturbed single-particle spectrum has the form shown on the left side of Fig. 57.2.   The corresponding single-particle wave function is φ_n, and $E_{n_1 n_2}^{0}$ is the initial unperturbed energy of the pair.   The perturbation H_1 consists of the (singular) two-particle interaction and any residual one-body interaction not included in the starting approximation. In Eq. (61.2a), the sum Σ'' runs over *all unoccupied single-particle states* as indicated in Fig. 61.1.

These equations are exact within the present framework, but Eq. (61.2a) is not very useful as it stands, for Σ'' includes states that are degenerate with $\varphi_{n_1 n_2}$.   Since the corresponding exact eigenvalue $E_{n_1 n_2}$ is close to $E_{n_1 n_2}^{0}$, the energy denominator for these degenerate states becomes very small.   This difficulty can be eliminated by starting over and choosing a modified set of initial states for the valence particles in $\mathscr{V}$.   In particular, we consider a linear combination

---

[1] To simplify these equations, we suppress the antisymmetrization of the wave functions for the identical valence pair.

of these degenerate states

$$\chi_\alpha(1,2) \equiv \sum_{n_1 n_2 \subset \mathscr{V}} C^{(\alpha)}_{n_1 n_2} \varphi_{n_1}(1) \varphi_{n_2}(2) \tag{61.3}$$

requiring only that the transformation be unitary

$$\sum_\alpha C^{(\alpha)*}_{n_1 n_2} C^{(\alpha)}_{n_1' n_2'} = \delta_{n_1 n_1'} \delta_{n_2 n_2'} \tag{61.4}$$

The Bethe-Goldstone equation for the wave function $\Psi'_\alpha(1,2)$ of the two particles in $\mathscr{V}$ can now be written with these new states as

$$\Psi'_\alpha(1,2) = \chi_\alpha(1,2) + \sum_{\alpha' \neq \alpha} \frac{\chi_{\alpha'}(1,2) \langle \chi_{\alpha'} | H_1 | \Psi'_\alpha \rangle}{E_\alpha - E^0_\mathscr{V}}$$

$$+ \sum_{n_1' n_2'}{}' \frac{\varphi_{n_1'}(1) \varphi_{n_2'}(2) \langle n_1' n_2' | H_1 | \Psi'_\alpha \rangle}{E_\alpha - E^0_{n_1' n_2'}} \tag{61.5a}$$

$$E_\alpha - E^0_\mathscr{V} = \langle \chi_\alpha | H_1 | \Psi'_\alpha \rangle \tag{61.5b}$$

In these expressions the eigenvalues are now labeled by E_α, and $E^0_\mathscr{V}$ denotes the unperturbed energy of a pair in $\mathscr{V}$. The sum in Eq. (61.5a) has been split into a part coming from the other degenerate unperturbed states in $\mathscr{V}$ and a remainder Σ' containing at least one excitation to a higher shell (see Fig. 61.1). Since the small energy denominators occur only in the first sum, we shall try to choose the coefficient $C^{(\alpha)}_{n_1 n_2}$ so that the numerators in the first sum in Eq. (61.5a) vanish identically

$$\langle \chi_\alpha | H_1 | \Psi'_\beta \rangle = (E_\alpha - E^0_\mathscr{V}) \delta_{\alpha \beta} \tag{61.6}$$

In this case, only the second sum in Eq. (61.5a) remains; furthermore, all the states in Σ' involve an excitation to higher shells so that the numerators will in general be smaller than, or comparable with, the denominators.

This reformulation of the original equations (61.2) is still very difficult to solve because the exact eigenvalues appear in the denominators in Eq. (61.5a). We may now, however, observe that Σ' runs over all states where the valence particles are promoted to excited states (in the harmonic-oscillator model, valence particles must be moved an even number of oscillator spacings to mix in states of the same parity). As a result, all the energy denominators in the sum Σ' are large (at least $2\hbar\omega \approx 81$ MeV/$A^{\frac{1}{3}}$ in the oscillator model) compared to the energy shifts $E_\alpha - E^0_\mathscr{V}$ to be calculated below (a few MeV), and we may therefore replace E_α by $E^0_\mathscr{V}$ in these terms. This approximation allows us to write

$$\Psi'_\alpha(1,2) = \sum_{n_1 n_2 \subset \mathscr{V}} C^{(\alpha)}_{n_1 n_2} \psi^0_{n_1 n_2}(1,2) \tag{61.7}$$

where $\psi^0_{n_1 n_2}(1,2)$ is the solution to the linear integral equation

$$\psi^0_{n_1 n_2}(1,2) = \varphi_{n_1}(1) \varphi_{n_2}(2) + \sum_{n_1' n_2'}{}' \frac{\varphi_{n_1'}(1) \varphi_{n_2'}(2) \langle n_1' n_2' | H_1 | \psi^0_{n_1 n_2} \rangle}{E^0_\mathscr{V} - E^0_{n_1' n_2'}} \tag{61.8}$$

with a known kernel. The additional condition on the matrix elements [Eq. (61.6)] becomes

$$\sum_{n_1' n_2' \subset \mathscr{V}} [\langle n_1 n_2 | H_1 | \psi^0_{n_1' n_2'} \rangle + (E^0_{\mathscr{V}} - E_\alpha) \delta_{n_1' n_1} \delta_{n_2' n_2}] C^{(\alpha)}_{n_1' n_2'} = 0 \qquad (61.9)$$

where Eq. (61.4) has been used. This set of linear homogeneous algebraic equations determines the coefficients $C^{(\alpha)}_{n_1 n_2}$, and the vanishing of the determinant gives the eigenvalues E_α. It is clear that Eqs. (61.7) and (61.8) reproduce Eq. (61.5a) because the condition of Eq. (61.6) eliminates the first sum in Eq. (61.5a), and $E_\alpha \approx E^0_{\mathscr{V}}$ in the second sum within the present approximation. Equations (61.8) and (61.9) together form the (approximate) Bethe-Goldstone equations for a finite system with initial degenerate states.[1]

HARMONIC-OSCILLATOR APPROXIMATION

The discussion can be greatly simplified if we approximate the Hartree-Fock single-particle wave functions φ_n and energies $E^0_{n_1 n_2}$ by those of the harmonic oscillator. In this case, the perturbation becomes

$$H_1 = h_1(1) + h_1(2) + V(1,2) \qquad (61.10)$$

where $V(1,2)$ is the two-nucleon potential, and h_1 is a single-particle operator that represents the *difference* between the true Hartree-Fock potential and that of the harmonic oscillator. (To be very explicit, $h_1 = \Delta V(r) - \alpha \mathbf{l} \cdot \mathbf{s}$, where the first term is the change in the potential well leading from the spectrum on the left side of Fig. 57.2 to that on the left side of Fig. 57.3, and the second term is the spin-orbit interaction.) We shall be content to treat h_1 in first-order perturbation theory, and Eq. (61.9) becomes

$$\sum_{n_1' n_2' \subset \mathscr{V}} [\langle n_1 n_2 | V | \psi^0_{n_1' n_2'} \rangle + \langle n_1 n_2 | h_1(1) + h_1(2) | n_1' n_2' \rangle$$

$$+ (E^0_{\mathscr{V}} - E_\alpha) \delta_{n_1' n_1} \delta_{n_2' n_2}] C^{(\alpha)}_{n_1' n_2'} = 0 \quad (61.11)$$

At the end of the calculation we may introduce the single-particle states $\{nl\frac{1}{2} jm_j\}$ that diagonalize h_1, and the resulting single-particle configuration energies $E^0 + \langle h_1 \rangle + \langle h_2 \rangle \equiv \epsilon_1 + \epsilon_2$ can be determined empirically from the energies of neighboring odd nuclei.

The first step in obtaining the energy levels E_α and coefficients $C^{(\alpha)}_{n_1 n_2}$ is to solve the approximate Bethe-Goldstone equation (61.8) with $H_1 \equiv V$. The resulting wave function $\psi^0_{n_1 n_2}$ then determines the matrix elements of V appearing in Eq. (61.11). The choice of harmonic-oscillator wave functions φ_n now allows

---

[1] See in this connection H. A. Bethe, *Phys. Rev.*, **103**:1353 (1956) and C. Bloch and J. Horowitz, *Nucl. Phys.*, **8**:91 (1958). The basis for the set of Eqs. (61.9) can again be reduced in the usual manner by introducing eigenstates of the total angular momentum. We leave this as an exercise for the dedicated reader.

a very important simplification, for the two-body wave function $\varphi_{n_1} \varphi_{n_2}$ is an eigenstate of the hamiltonian

$$H_0 = \frac{\mathbf{p}_1^2}{2m} + \frac{\mathbf{p}_2^2}{2m} + \tfrac{1}{2}m\omega^2\,\mathbf{x}_1^2 + \tfrac{1}{2}m\omega^2\,\mathbf{x}_2^2 \tag{61.12}$$

With the following coordinate transformation

$$\mathbf{X} = \tfrac{1}{2}(\mathbf{x}_1 + \mathbf{x}_2) \qquad \mathbf{P} = \mathbf{p}_1 + \mathbf{p}_2$$

$$\mathbf{x} = \mathbf{x}_2 - \mathbf{x}_1 \qquad \mathbf{p} = \tfrac{1}{2}(\mathbf{p}_2 - \mathbf{p}_1) \tag{61.13}$$

H_0 can be rewritten as

$$H_0 = \frac{\mathbf{P}^2}{4m} + m\omega^2\,\mathbf{X}^2 + \frac{\mathbf{p}^2}{m} + \tfrac{1}{4}m\omega^2\,\mathbf{x}^2 \tag{61.14}$$

which separates the center-of-mass motion of the valence pair from the *relative* motion. The eigenstates of H_0 as written in Eq. (61.14) take the form $\varphi_N(\mathbf{X})\varphi_n(\mathbf{x})$, where the quantum numbers are $N \equiv \{N\mathscr{L}\mathscr{M}_{\mathscr{L}}\}$ for the center of mass and $n \equiv \{nlm_l\tfrac{1}{2}m_{s_1}\tfrac{1}{2}m_{s_2}\}$ for the relative wave function. Each of these states can be expanded as a linear combination of the original states $\varphi_{n_1}(1)\varphi_{n_2}(2)$ with the same total two-particle energy (and hence same eigenvalue of H_0) because the latter form a complete set of eigenstates of the same hamiltonian H_0. Thus we have

$$\varphi_N(\mathbf{X})\,\varphi_n(\mathbf{x}) = \sum_{n_1 n_2 \subset \mathscr{D}} \langle n_1 n_2 | Nn \rangle \, \varphi_{n_1}(1)\,\varphi_{n_2}(2) \tag{61.15}$$

where $\mathscr{D}$ *denotes all possible two-particle states degenerate with the initial state.* These orthogonal transformation brackets[1] $\langle n_1 n_2 | Nn \rangle$ have been extensively tabulated.[2] It follows from Eqs. (61.15) and (61.8) that

$$\langle n_1 n_2 | V | \psi^0_{n_1' n_2'} \rangle = \sum_{NnN'n' \subset \mathscr{D}_{\mathscr{V}}} \langle n_1 n_2 | Nn \rangle \langle N' n' | n_1' n_2' \rangle \langle Nn | V | \psi^0_{N' n'} \rangle \tag{61.16}$$

[Note that the sum on $n_1 n_2$ in Eq. (61.15) can be applied directly to the wave function $\psi^0_{n_1 n_2}$ on the right side of Eq. (61.8) since the quantity $E^0_{\mathscr{V}}$ is the same for all the degenerate states in $\mathscr{D}_{\mathscr{V}}$.]

The explicit calculation of ψ^0_{Nn} is complicated by the restricted sum Σ' in Eq. (61.8), which couples the center of mass and relative wave functions of the valence pair.   It is therefore convenient to rewrite the sum as

$$\sum_{n_1 n_2}' \equiv \sum_{n_1 n_2 \notin \mathscr{D}_{\mathscr{V}}} - \sum_{n_1 \text{ or } n_2 \subset \mathscr{C}} \tag{61.17}$$

[1] I. Talmi, *Helv. Phys. Acta.*, **25**:185 (1952).
[2] T. A. Brody and M. Moshinsky, "Tables of Transformation Brackets," Monografias Del Instituto de Fisica, Mexico City, 1960.

The first term sums over *all states with energy different from* E_{γ}^0, and the second term removes those states that violate the Pauli principle. We neglect the second term (the Pauli principle correction) for the present and return to it later in this section. If only the first term is retained, the corresponding wave function $\tilde{\psi}^0$ satisfies the equation

$$\tilde{\psi}_{Nn}^0(\mathbf{X},\mathbf{x}) = \varphi_N(\mathbf{X})\varphi_n(\mathbf{x}) + \sum_{N'\,n'\,\notin\,\mathcal{D}_{\gamma}} \frac{\varphi_{N'}(\mathbf{X})\,\varphi_{n'}(\mathbf{x})\langle N'\,n'|V|\tilde{\psi}_{Nn}^0\rangle}{E_{\gamma}^0 - E_{N'\,n'}^0} \tag{61.18}$$

obtained by combining Eqs. (61.8) and (61.15). Since V depends only on the *relative* coordinate, the matrix elements in Eqs. (61.18) and (61.16) are diagonal in N, and the solution to Eq. (61.18) takes the form

$$\tilde{\psi}_{Nn}^0(\mathbf{X},\mathbf{x}) = \varphi_N(\mathbf{X})\,\tilde{\psi}_n^0(\mathbf{x}) \tag{61.19}$$

Within the degenerate set of states $\mathcal{D}_{\gamma}$, the matrix element $\langle Nn|V|\tilde{\psi}_{Nn'}^0\rangle$ in Eq. (61.16) is also diagonal in the relative quantum numbers,[1] and Eqs. (61.16) and (61.18) take the form

$$\langle n_1\,n_2|V|\tilde{\psi}_{n_1'\,n_2'}^0\rangle = \sum_{Nn} \langle n_1\,n_2|Nn\rangle\langle Nn|n_1'\,n_2'\rangle\langle n|V|\tilde{\psi}_n^0\rangle \tag{61.20a}$$

$$\tilde{\psi}_n^0(\mathbf{x}) = \varphi_n(\mathbf{x}) + \sum_{n'\neq n} \frac{\varphi_{n'}(\mathbf{x})\langle n'|V|\tilde{\psi}_n^0\rangle}{E_n^0 - E_{n'}^0} \tag{61.20b}$$

The energy denominators in Eq. (61.20b) are again at least as large as $2\hbar\omega$; to the same degree of approximation as before, we can therefore rewrite this equation as

$$\tilde{\psi}_n(\mathbf{x}) = \varphi_n(\mathbf{x}) + \sum_{n'\neq n} \frac{\varphi_{n'}(\mathbf{x})\langle n'|V|\tilde{\psi}_n\rangle}{E_n - E_{n'}^0} \tag{61.21a}$$

where $\tilde{\psi}_n$ is the eigenfunction corresponding to the eigenvalue

$$E_n - E_n^0 \equiv \langle n|V|\tilde{\psi}_n\rangle \tag{61.21b}$$

The problem is now solved, for Eqs. (61.21) are just a rewriting of the Schrödinger equation

$$\left[-\frac{\hbar^2}{m}\nabla^2 + \tfrac{1}{4}m\omega^2\,x^2 + V(x)\right]\psi_n(x) = E_n\psi_n(x) \tag{61.22}$$

Hence the matrix elements required in Eq. (61.20a) can be obtained directly with Eq. (61.21b) from the discrete eigenvalues of the differential equation (61.22).

The unperturbed ($V = 0$) solutions to Eq. (61.22) have already been given in Eqs. (57.7) to (57.12); they are plotted in Fig. 61.2 for different values of l.

---

[1] We assume that V is diagonal in l.

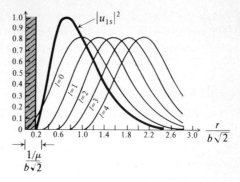

Fig. 61.2 Square of the unperturbed solutions u_{1l}^0 to Eq. (61.22) together with the square of the exact s-wave solution u_{1s} to Eq. (61.22) in the presence of the potential (61.23). The wave functions are normalized to $\int |u_{1l}|^2 \, dr = 1$. Also shown are the ranges of the hard-core and attractive interactions in Eq. (61.23). [From J. F. Dawson, I. Talmi, and J. D. Walecka, *Ann. Phys.* (*N.Y.*), **18**:339 (1962). Reprinted by permission.]

For comparison, we also give the exact (numerical) s-wave solution for a potential

$$V = \begin{cases} \infty & r < c \\ -V_0 \dfrac{e^{-\mu r}}{\mu r} & r > c \end{cases} \tag{61.23}$$

$$V_0 = 434 \text{ MeV} \qquad \mu = 1.45 \text{ F}^{-1} \qquad c = 0.4 \text{ F}$$

with the parameters determined from a fit to the $^1S_0$ nucleon-nucleon phase shift. Throughout these calculations the oscillator parameter is taken as $b = (\hbar/m\omega)^{\frac{1}{2}} = 1.70$ F, appropriate to O^{18}. It is clear that only the s waves are much affected by the potential and that the correlated and uncorrelated wave functions are very similar, the correlations being most important at small distances.

This theory has been applied to O^{18}, where the initial unperturbed configuration has two valence neutrons in the $2s$-$1d$ oscillator shell. With the Brueckner-Gammel-Thaler nucleon-nucleon potential, Eqs. (61.11), (61.20a), (61.21b), and (61.22) give the spectrum shown in Fig. 61.3.[1] This figure also

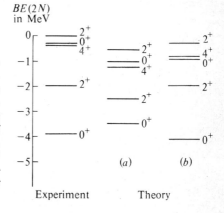

Fig. 61.3 Experimental and theoretical two-neutron binding energy and low-lying excitation spectrum of O^{18}. The theoretical results were computed using (a) the singular Brueckner-Gammel-Thaler nucleon-nucleon potential, (b) the nonsingular Serber-Yukawa potential of Eq. (59.81). [From J. F. Dawson, I. Talmi, and J. D. Walecka, *Ann. Phys.* (*N.Y.*), **18**:339 (1962); **19**:350 (1962). Reprinted by permission. The authors wish to thank G. E. Walker for preparing part (b).]

[1] J. F. Dawson et al., *loc. cit.*

shows the result obtained by using the nonsingular force given in Eq. (59.81) and replacing $\psi^0_{N'n'} \to \varphi_{N'}\varphi_{n'}$ in Eq. (61.16). In both cases the single-particle configuration energies were taken from O^{17}: $\epsilon(1d_{\frac{5}{2}}) \equiv 0$, $\epsilon(2s_{\frac{1}{2}}) = +0.871$ MeV, and $\epsilon(1d_{\frac{3}{2}}) = +5.08$ MeV.

PAULI PRINCIPLE CORRECTION

To include the effects of the Pauli principle, we define projection operators P and Q representing the first and second restricted sum on the right side of Eq. (61.17). If Eq. (61.8) with H_1 replaced by V is multiplied by V, it can be rewritten as an iterated operator equation

$$G = V + V\frac{P - Q}{E_0 - H_0}V + V\frac{P - Q}{E_0 - H_0}V\frac{P - Q}{E_0 - H_0}V + \cdots \tag{61.24}$$

where the operator G is defined by

$$G\varphi_{n_1}\varphi_{n_2} \equiv V\psi^0_{n_1 n_2} \tag{61.25}$$

Equation (61.24) can be rearranged to give

$$G = G^0 - G^0\frac{Q}{E_0 - H_0}G^0 + \cdots \tag{61.26a}$$

$$G^0 \equiv V + V\frac{P}{E_0 - H_0}V + V\frac{P}{E_0 - H_0}V\frac{P}{E_0 - H_0}V + \cdots \tag{61.26b}$$

A comparison of Eqs. (61.26b) and (61.18) shows that G^0 corresponds to the wave function we have just discussed

$$G^0\varphi_{n_1}\varphi_{n_2} \equiv V\tilde{\psi}^0_{n_1 n_2} \tag{61.27}$$

Thus the first Pauli principle correction is given by

$$\Delta G_{pp} = -G^0\frac{Q}{E_0 - H_0}G^0 \tag{61.28}$$

The matrix elements of this relation are now finite even with singular potentials. Furthermore, the denominators are again $\geqslant 2\hbar\omega$ in magnitude so that Eq. (61.28) represents a small correction to the energy levels (<0.5 MeV). This effect has been included in Fig. 61.3a.

EXTENSIONS AND CALCULATIONS OF OTHER QUANTITIES

The subject of nuclear spectroscopy with realistic forces has been developed extensively.[1] The most complete calculation is that of Kuo and Brown,[2] who also include a core-polarization term (Fig. 61.4) in the effective interaction.

[1] B. H. Brandow, *loc. cit.*; M. H. Macfarlane, *loc. cit.*
[2] T. T. S. Kuo and G. E. Brown, *Nucl. Phys.*, **85**:40 (1966); see also B. R. Barrett and M. W. Kirson, *Phys. Letters*, **27B**:544 (1968).

It is clear that the independent-pair approach also can be used to find the ground-state properties of nuclei. Eden et al. have computed the binding energy and density of O^{16} using the harmonic-oscillator framework.[1] A somewhat different procedure is to use the G matrix calculated for *nuclear matter* as an effective potential in a Hartree-Fock[2] or Thomas-Fermi theory[3] of finite nuclei.

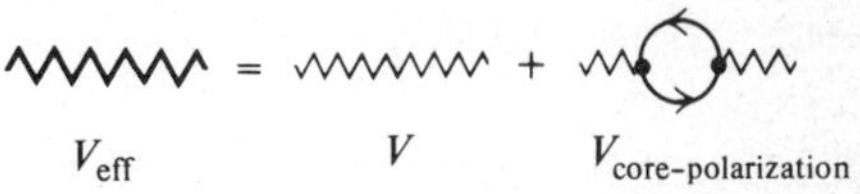

Fig. 61.4 The effective interaction of Kuo and Brown.

$$V_{\text{eff}} \qquad = \qquad V \qquad + \qquad V_{\text{core-polarization}}$$

A completely consistent calculation with the G matrix for a finite nucleus has never been carried out.

PROBLEMS

15.1. Prove the assertion that the solutions to Eq. (56.17) corresponding to different eigenvalues are orthogonal and that the degenerate states can always be orthogonalized.

15.2. Derive the Schmidt results [Eq. (57.22)] for the shell-model magnetic moments starting from Eq. (57.20).

15.3. Derive Eq. (57.25) for the quadrupole moments in the single-particle shell-model.

15.4. Prove Eq. (58.33).

15.5. Using the second-quantization techniques of Sec. 58, show that for even N

$$\frac{1}{2J+1}|\langle j^N 0; \sigma = 0 \| \hat{T}_J \| j^N J; \sigma = 2 \rangle|^2$$

$$= \frac{1}{2J+1}\left(2N \frac{2j+1-N}{2j-1}\right)\left\{\frac{1}{2j+1}|\langle j \| T_J \| j \rangle|^2\right\}$$

In the many-particle shell model, observe that this transition strength is enhanced with increasing N and reaches a maximum for a half-filled shell.

[1] R. J. Eden, V. J. Emery, and S. Sampanthar, *Proc. Roy. Soc.* (*London*), **A253**:177 (1959); **A253**:186 (1959); see also H. S. Köhler and R. J. McCarthy, *Nucl. Phys.*, **86**:611 (1966).
[2] K. A. Brueckner, A. M. Lockett, and M. Rotenberg, *loc. cit.*, which contains other references. For a review of this approach, see M. Baranger, "Proceedings of the International Nuclear Physics Conference, Gatlinburg, Tennessee," p. 659, Academic Press, New York, 1967; and Course XL, Nuclear Structure and Nuclear Reactions, in Proc. of "The International School of Physics 'Enrico Fermi'," p. 511, Academic Press, New York, 1969.
[3] H. A. Bethe, *Phys. Rev.*, **167**:879 (1968).

15.6. Consider an odd-odd nucleus with p protons in the j_1 shell and n neutrons in the j_2 shell. If both the protons and neutrons are in the normal-coupling shell-model ground state, prove that the energy *splittings* (in lowest-order perturbation theory) due to a neutron-proton potential of the type in Eq. (58.6) can be computed with the replacement

$$\langle j_1^p j_1 j_2^n j_2 J | \hat{V} | j_1^p j_1 j_2^n j_2 J \rangle \rightarrow \frac{2j_1 + 1 - 2p}{2j_1 - 1} \frac{2j_2 + 1 - 2n}{2j_2 - 1} \langle j_1 j_2 J | V | j_1 j_2 J \rangle$$

Observe that if either shell is half filled, this quantity vanishes and all the splitting comes from the spin-dependent part of the interaction.

15.7. Prove that the state in Eq. (58.55) has the quantum numbers indicated.

15.8. (a) Show that the matrix elements of the two-body potential of Eq. (58.37) in the three-particle state of Eq. (58.55) are given by

$$\langle j^3 JM | \hat{V} | j^3 JM \rangle = 3 \sum_{\lambda} |\langle j^3 J |\} j^2(\lambda) jJ \rangle|^2 \langle j^2 \lambda | V | j^2 \lambda \rangle$$

where the coefficients of fractional parentage are *defined* by the relation

$$3|\langle j^3 J |\} j^2(\lambda) jJ \rangle|^2$$

$$= N^2 \left[\delta_{\lambda k} \delta(jkJ) \delta(j^2 k) + 2[(2k + 1)(2\lambda + 1)]^{\frac{1}{2}} \begin{Bmatrix} j & j & k \\ j & J & \lambda \end{Bmatrix} \right]^2$$

$$N^{-2} = 1 + 2(2k + 1) \begin{Bmatrix} j & j & k \\ j & J & k \end{Bmatrix}$$

[The symbol $\delta(j_1 j_2 j_3)$ means that the angular momenta must add up, that is, $|j_1 - j_2| \leqslant j_3 \leqslant j_1 + j_2$.]
(b) Prove that the same relation holds for the state in Eq. (58.54) (take $k = 0$).

15.9. Assume the 0^+ (ground state), 2^+(2.00 MeV), and 4^+ (3.55 MeV) states in O^{18} belong to the $(d_{\frac{5}{2}})^2$ configuration.
(a) Prove that the only possible J^π values for three identical particles in the $(d_{\frac{5}{2}})^3$ configuration are $\frac{3}{2}^+$, $\frac{5}{2}^+$, and $\frac{9}{2}^+$. (See M. G. Mayer and J. H. D. Jensen, *op. cit.*, p. 64.)
(b) Use Eq. (58.39) and the results of Prob. 15.8 to predict the location of the states of the $(d_{\frac{5}{2}})^3$ configuration. Compare with the experimental results for O^{19}: $\frac{5}{2}^+$ (ground state), $\frac{3}{2}^+$ (.096 MeV), and $\frac{9}{2}^+$ (2.77 MeV).

15.10. Compute the matrix element in Prob. 15.5 in the boson approximation.

15.11. Compute the spectrum of the j^N configuration (N even) for an attractive delta-function potential [Eq. (58.18)] in the boson approximation.

15.12. Extend the boson approximation to an almost filled shell.

15.13.   Prove Eq. (58.69) for a potential of the form $V = V_0(x_{12}) + V_1(x_{12})\boldsymbol{\sigma}_1 \cdot \boldsymbol{\sigma}_2$. Assume real radial wave functions.

15.14.   (a) Write the angular momentum $\hat{\mathbf{J}}$ in terms of the transformed operators of Eq. (58.64).
(b) Prove that the state $|\mathbf{O}\rangle$ has $J = 0$.
(c) Prove that the state $|\mathbf{O}\rangle$ has even parity.

15.15.   Verify Eqs. (59.80).

15.16.   Let D be a sum of hermitian single-particle operators.
(a) Prove the identity

$$\langle \Psi_0 | [\hat{D}, [\hat{H}, \hat{D}]] | \Psi_0 \rangle = 2 \sum_n (E_n - E_0) |\langle \Psi_n | \hat{D} | \Psi_0 \rangle|^2$$

(b) If the right side is evaluated in the RPA, show that the result is the same as evaluating the left side in the Hartree-Fock shell-model ground state.   Whenever the double commutator is a c number (see Prob. 15.17), the RPA thus preserves this energy-weighted sum rule.‡

15.17.   (a) Show that the electric dipole moment of a nucleus measured relative to the center of mass is given by

$$\mathbf{D} = \sum_{j=1}^{A} \mathbf{x}(j) \left[\tfrac{1}{2}\tau_3(j) - \frac{1}{A} T_3 \right]$$

(b) If the interaction potential is of the form $V(x_{ij})$, derive the dipole sum rule for $N = Z$.

$$4 \sum_n (E_n - E_0) |\langle \Psi_n | \hat{\mathbf{D}} | \Psi_0 \rangle|^2 = \frac{3\hbar^2 A}{2m}$$

(c) Prove that if $N \neq Z$, the right side is multiplied by $4NZ/A^2$.

15.18.   Discuss the implications of the results of Prob. 15.16 if the operator $\hat{D}$ *commutes* with $\hat{H}$. (For example, the total momentum $\hat{\mathbf{P}}$, the total angular momentum $\hat{\mathbf{J}}$.   Note that these operators generate translations and rotations of the entire system.)§

15.19.   (a) Use the result of Eq. (60.40) for $\Pi^{\text{RPA}}_{\lambda\mu:\alpha\beta}(\omega)$ to discuss the linear response of a finite system to a perturbation of the form Eq. (60.1).
(b) Compute the cross section for inelastic electron scattering as in Sec. 17.

15.20.   Derive an expression for the core-polarization potential shown in Fig. 61.4.

‡ D. J. Thouless, *Nucl. Phys.*, **22**:78 (1961).
§ *Ibid.*

APPENDIXES

A□DEFINITE INTEGRALS[1]

The gamma function $\Gamma(z)$ and the Riemann zeta function $\zeta(z)$ are defined as follows:

$$\Gamma(z) \equiv \int_0^\infty dt\, e^{-t}\, t^{z-1} \qquad Re\ z > 0$$

$$\zeta(z) \equiv \sum_{p=1}^\infty p^{-z} \qquad Re\ z > 1$$

These definitions converge only in the specified regions of the complex z plane, but the functions can be analytically continued with the general relations

$$\Gamma(z)\,\Gamma(1-z) = \frac{\pi}{\sin \pi z}$$

$$2^{1-z}\,\Gamma(z)\,\zeta(z)\cos(\tfrac{1}{2}\pi z) = \pi^z\,\zeta(1-z)$$

[1] We here follow the notation of E. T. Whittaker and G. N. Watson, "Modern Analysis," 4th ed., Cambridge University Press, Cambridge, 1962, where most of these relations are proved.

The gamma function also satisfies the functional equation

$$\Gamma(z + 1) = z\Gamma(z)$$

and it therefore reduces to the factorial function for integral values

$$\Gamma(n + 1) = n! \qquad n \text{ integral}$$

The digamma function $\psi(z)$ is the logarithmic derivative of the gamma function

$$\psi(z) = \frac{d}{dz} \log \Gamma(z) = \frac{1}{\Gamma(z)} \frac{d\Gamma(z)}{dz}$$

At $z = 1$, it reduces to

$$\psi(1) = \int_0^\infty dt\, e^{-t} \ln t \equiv -\gamma$$

where γ is Euler's constant.   Useful numerical values are listed below

$$\zeta(0) = -\tfrac{1}{2} \qquad\qquad\qquad \Gamma(\tfrac{1}{2}) = \sqrt{\pi} \approx 1.772$$
$$\zeta(\tfrac{3}{2}) \approx 2.612 \qquad\qquad\qquad \Gamma(1) = 0! = 1$$
$$\zeta(2) = \pi^2/6 \approx 1.645 \qquad\qquad \Gamma(\tfrac{5}{4}) \approx 0.9064$$
$$\zeta(\tfrac{5}{2}) \approx 1.341 \qquad\qquad\qquad \Gamma(\tfrac{3}{2}) = \tfrac{1}{2}\sqrt{\pi} \approx 0.8862$$
$$\zeta(3) \approx 1.202 \qquad\qquad\qquad \Gamma(\tfrac{7}{4}) \approx 0.9191$$
$$\zeta(4) = \pi^4/90 \approx 1.082 \qquad\qquad\quad \gamma \approx 0.5772$$
$$\zeta'(0) = \left(\frac{d\zeta(z)}{dz}\right)_{z=0} = -\tfrac{1}{2}\ln(2\pi) \qquad e^\gamma \approx 1.781$$

Numerous series and definite integrals may be expressed in terms of the preceding functions:[1]

$$\sum_{p=0}^{\infty} \frac{1}{(2p+1)^n} = (1 - 2^{-n})\, \zeta(n) \qquad n > 1$$

$$\int_0^\infty dx\, \frac{x^{n-1}}{e^x - 1} = \Gamma(n)\, \zeta(n) \qquad n > 1$$

$$\int_0^\infty dx\, \frac{x^{n-1}}{e^x + 1} = (1 - 2^{1-n})\, \Gamma(n)\, \zeta(n) \qquad n > 0$$

$$\int_0^\infty dx\, x^{n-1} \operatorname{csch} x = \int_0^\infty dx\, \frac{x^{n-1}}{\sinh x}$$
$$= 2(1 - 2^{-n})\, \Gamma(n)\, \zeta(n) \qquad n > 1$$

---

[1] All but the last integral in this list are taken from H. B. Dwight, "Tables of Integrals and Other Mathematical Data," 4th ed., chap. 12, The Macmillan Company, New York, 1964.

$$\int_0^\infty dx\, x^{n-1}\, \mathrm{sech}\, x = \int_0^\infty dx\, \frac{x^{n-1}}{\cosh x}$$

$$= 2\Gamma(n) \sum_{p=0}^\infty (-1)^p (2p+1)^{-n} \qquad n>0$$

$$\int_0^\infty dx\, x^{n-1}\, \mathrm{sech}^2\, x = \int_0^\infty dx\, \frac{x^{n-1}}{\cosh^2 x}$$

$$= 2^{2-n}(1 - 2^{2-n})\, \Gamma(n)\, \zeta(n-1) \qquad n>0$$

$$\int_0^1 dx\, x^{m-1}(1-x)^{n-1} = \int_0^\infty dx\, \frac{x^{m-1}}{(1+x)^{m+n}} = \frac{\Gamma(m)\,\Gamma(n)}{\Gamma(m+n)}$$

$$\int_0^\infty dx\, \ln x\, \mathrm{sech}^2\, x = \left[\frac{\partial}{\partial n} \int_0^\infty dx\, x^{n-1}\, \mathrm{sech}^2\, x \right]_{n=1} = -\ln \frac{4e^\gamma}{\pi}$$

The Bessel function $K_0(x)$ may be defined by the integral representation

$$K_0(x) \equiv \int_0^\infty dt\, e^{-x \cosh t}$$

and we find

$$\int_0^\infty dx\, K_0(x) = \int_0^\infty dt\, \mathrm{sech}\, t$$

$$= 2(1 - \tfrac{1}{3} + \tfrac{1}{5} - \cdots) = 2 \arctan 1 = \frac{\pi}{2}$$

B☐REVIEW OF THE THEORY OF ANGULAR MOMENTUM[1]

BASIC COMMUTATION RELATIONS

The starting point is the fundamental set of commutation relations

$$[J_i, J_j] = i\epsilon_{ijk} J_k \tag{B.1}$$

where ϵ_{ijk} is the totally antisymmetric unit tensor and all angular momenta are measured in units of $\hbar$. Although $\mathbf{J}$ could be a first quantized operator

$$L_x = \frac{1}{i}\left(y \frac{\partial}{\partial z} - z \frac{\partial}{\partial y} \right) \qquad \text{etc.}$$

a second quantized operator

$$\hat{L}_x = \int \hat{\psi}^\dagger(\mathbf{x}) \frac{1}{i}\left(y \frac{\partial}{\partial z} - z \frac{\partial}{\partial y} \right) \hat{\psi}(\mathbf{x})\, d^3 x \qquad \text{etc.}$$

[1] This discussion is very brief. For a more detailed analysis see any basic text on quantum mechanics and especially treatises on the theory of angular momentum such as A. R. Edmonds, "Angular Momentum in Quantum Mechanics," Princeton University Press, Princeton, N.J., 1957 or M. E. Rose, "Multipole Fields," John Wiley and Sons, Inc., New York, 1955. The treatment here follows that of Edmonds very closely.

or a Pauli matrix

$$\mathbf{J} = \tfrac{1}{2}\boldsymbol{\sigma}$$

Eq. (B.1) is independent of any particular representation, and all the results depend *only on the basic commutation relations*. We define the raising and lowering operators

$$J_{\pm} \equiv J_x \pm iJ_y \tag{B.2}$$

and the square of the total angular momentum operator

$$\mathbf{J}^2 \equiv J_x^2 + J_y^2 + J_z^2 = J_z^2 + \tfrac{1}{2}[J_+J_- + J_-J_+] \tag{B.3}$$

It is then easy to verify the following commutation relations

$$[\mathbf{J}^2, J_{\pm}] = [\mathbf{J}^2, J_z] = 0$$

$$[J_z, J_{\pm}] = \pm J_{\pm} \tag{B.4}$$

The operators $\mathbf{J}^2$ and J_z can therefore be diagonalized simultaneously, and the eigenstates will be labeled by $|jm\rangle$. From the commutation relations (B.1), it is readily proved that[1]

$$J_{\pm}|jm\rangle = A(j, \mp m)|jm \pm 1\rangle \tag{B.5}$$

where

$$A(jm) = [(j + m)(j - m + 1)]^{\frac{1}{2}} \tag{B.6}$$

defines a particular choice of phases, and

$$\mathbf{J}^2|jm\rangle = j(j + 1)|jm\rangle$$

$$J_z|jm\rangle = m|jm\rangle \tag{B.7}$$

In general we deal with states $|\gamma jm\rangle$ where γ denotes the remaining set of observables and

$$[\Gamma, \mathbf{J}^2] = [\Gamma, J_z] = 0$$

COUPLING OF TWO ANGULAR MOMENTA: CLEBSCH-GORDAN COEFFICIENTS

Consider the problem of adding two commuting angular momenta

$$\mathbf{J} = \mathbf{J}_1 + \mathbf{J}_2 \quad [\mathbf{J}_1, \mathbf{J}_2] = 0 \tag{B.8}$$

where $\mathbf{J}_1$ and $\mathbf{J}_2$ can refer to different particles or operate in different spaces (for example, $\mathbf{J} = \mathbf{L} + \mathbf{S}$). We can immediately verify that

$$[\mathbf{J}, \mathbf{J}_1^2] = [\mathbf{J}, \mathbf{J}_2^2] = [\mathbf{J}, \mathbf{J}^2] = 0 \tag{B.9}$$

---

[1] See, for example, L. I. Schiff, "Quantum Mechanics," 3d ed., p. 200, McGraw-Hill Book Company, New York, 1968.

One complete set of commuting operators is therefore defined by

1. $\Gamma, \mathbf{J}_1^2, J_{1z}, \mathbf{J}_2^2, J_{2z}$

Another possible choice is

2. $\Gamma, \mathbf{J}_1^2, \mathbf{J}_2^2, \mathbf{J}^2, J_z$

Either description is complete, but the set 2 is more convenient because overall rotational invariance implies that j and m are constants of the motion. Since these bases are equivalent, they must be connected by a unitary transformation

$$|\gamma j_1 j_2 jm\rangle = \sum_{m_1 m_2} \langle j_1 m_1 j_2 m_2 | j_1 j_2 jm\rangle |\gamma j_1 m_1 j_2 m_2\rangle \tag{B.10}$$

The set of numerical coefficients are known as Clebsch-Gordan (CG) coefficients; they are independent of γ because the transformation involves only the angular parts of the wave function [this result will be shown by explicit construction; see Eq. (B.17)]. The orthogonality and completeness of the states $|\gamma j_1 j_2 jm\rangle$ and $|\gamma j_1 m_1 j_2 m_2\rangle$ imply the relations

$$\langle \gamma j_1 m_1 j_2 m_2 | \gamma j_1 m_1' j_2 m_2'\rangle = \delta_{m_1 m_1'} \delta_{m_2 m_2'}$$

$$\langle \gamma j_1 j_2 jm | \gamma j_1 j_2 j' m'\rangle = \delta_{jj'} \delta_{mm'} \tag{B.11}$$

$$\sum_{jm} |\gamma j_1 j_2 jm\rangle \langle \gamma j_1 j_2 jm| = \sum_{m_1 m_2} |\gamma j_1 m_1 j_2 m_2\rangle \langle \gamma j_1 m_1 j_2 m_2|$$

and it follows that

$$\sum_{m_1 m_2} \langle j_1 j_2 j' m' | j_1 m_1 j_2 m_2\rangle \langle j_1 m_1 j_2 m_2 | j_1 j_2 jm\rangle = \delta_{jj'} \delta_{mm'}$$

$$\sum_{jm} \langle j_1 m_1' j_2 m_2' | j_1 j_2 jm\rangle \langle j_1 j_2 jm | j_1 m_1 j_2 m_2\rangle = \delta_{m_1 m_1'} \delta_{m_2 m_2'} \tag{B.12}$$

The CG coefficients can be found by diagonalizing the operators

$$J_z = J_{1z} + J_{2z} \tag{B.13a}$$

$$\mathbf{J}^2 = \mathbf{J}_1^2 + \mathbf{J}_2^2 + 2\mathbf{J}_1 \cdot \mathbf{J}_2 \tag{B.13b}$$

in the finite basis $|\gamma j_1 m_1 j_2 m_2\rangle$. Since the operators $\mathbf{J}_1^2$ and $\mathbf{J}_2^2$ are already diagonal, it is only necessary to diagonalize J_z and $\mathbf{J}_1 \cdot \mathbf{J}_2$ where

$$2\mathbf{J}_1 \cdot \mathbf{J}_2 = J_{1+}J_{2-} + J_{1-}J_{2+} + 2J_{1z}J_{2z} \tag{B.14}$$

For the first operator, we write

$$J_z |\gamma j_1 j_2 jm\rangle = m |\gamma j_1 j_2 jm\rangle \tag{B.15}$$

and use Eqs. (B.10) and (B.13a) to conclude that $\langle j_1 m_1 j_2 m_2 | j_1 j_2 jm\rangle = 0$ if $m_1 + m_2 \neq m$. For the second operator, we combine the relation

$$2\mathbf{J}_1 \cdot \mathbf{J}_2 |\gamma j_1 j_2 jm\rangle = \alpha_J |\gamma j_1 j_2 jm\rangle$$

$$\alpha_J \equiv j(j+1) - j_1(j_1+1) - j_2(j_2+1) \tag{B.16}$$

obtained from Eq. (B.13b) with Eqs. (B.14) and (B.5) to find a set of linear homogeneous equations for the CG coefficients

$$(2m_1 m_2 - \alpha_J)\langle j_1 m_1 j_2 m_2 | j_1 j_2 jm \rangle + A(j_1, m_1 + 1) A(j_2, -m_2 + 1)$$
$$\times \langle j_1 m_1 + 1 j_2 m_2 - 1 | j_1 j_2 jm \rangle + A(j_1, -m_1 + 1)$$
$$\times A(j_2, m_2 + 1)\langle j_1 m_1 - 1 j_2 m_2 + 1 | j_1 j_2 jm \rangle = 0 \qquad \text{(B.17)}$$

This set of eigenvalue equations for α_J has a solution only if

$$|j_1 - j_2| \leqslant j \leqslant j_1 + j_2 \qquad \text{(B.18)}$$

with each value of j occurring once and only once. The resulting CG coefficients are determined only up to overall relative phases. Thus a complete specification of the CG coefficients requires an additional set of *phase conventions*; the standard choice[1] is that the CG coefficients are real and satisfy

$$\langle j_1 m_1 j_2 m_2 | j_1 j_2 jm \rangle = (-1)^{j_1 + j_2 - j} \langle j_1 - m_1 j_2 - m_2 | j_1 j_2 j - m \rangle \qquad \text{(B.19a)}$$

$$\langle j_1 m_1 j_2 m_2 | j_1 j_2 jm \rangle = (-1)^{j_1 + j_2 - j} \langle j_2 m_2 j_1 m_1 | j_2 j_1 jm \rangle \qquad \text{(B.19b)}$$

$$\langle j_1 m_1 j_2 m_2 | j_1 j_2 jm \rangle = (-1)^{j_2 + m_2} \left(\frac{2j + 1}{2j_1 + 1} \right)^{\frac{1}{2}} \langle j_2 - m_2 jm | j_2 j j_1 m_1 \rangle \qquad \text{(B.19c)}$$

Two particular CG coefficients are very useful:[2]

$$\langle j_1 m_1 00 | j_1 0 j_1 m_1 \rangle = 1 \qquad \text{(B.20a)}$$

$$\langle j_1 m_1 j_1 - m_1 | j_1 j_1 00 \rangle = (-1)^{j_1 - m_1} (2j_1 + 1)^{-\frac{1}{2}} \qquad \text{(B.20b)}$$

A more symmetric form of these coefficients is given by the Wigner 3-j symbol

$$\begin{pmatrix} j_1 & j_2 & j_3 \\ m_1 & m_2 & m_3 \end{pmatrix} \equiv (-1)^{j_1 - j_2 - m_3} (2j_3 + 1)^{-\frac{1}{2}} \langle j_1 m_1 j_2 m_2 | j_1 j_2 j_3 - m_3 \rangle \qquad \text{(B.21)}$$

which has the following properties:

1. $m_1 + m_2 + m_3 = 0$ \qquad (B.22a)

2. $\begin{pmatrix} j_1 & j_2 & j_3 \\ -m_1 & -m_2 & -m_3 \end{pmatrix} = (-1)^{j_1 + j_2 + j_3} \begin{pmatrix} j_1 & j_2 & j_3 \\ m_1 & m_2 & m_3 \end{pmatrix}$ \qquad (B.22b)

3. Any *even* permutation of the columns leaves the 3-j coefficient unchanged.

4. Any *odd* permutation of the columns gives a factor $(-1)^{j_1 + j_2 + j_3}$.

Extensive tabulations of these coefficients appear in the literature.[3]

[1] A. R. Edmonds, *op. cit.*, pp. 41–42.
[2] Note that for half-integral j: $(-1)^{j-m} = (-1)^{m-j} = -(-1)^{j+m}$.
[3] M. Rotenberg, R. Bivens, N. Metropolis, and J. K. Wooten, Jr., "The 3-j and 6-j Symbols," The Technology Press, Massachusetts Institute of Technology, Cambridge, Mass., 1959.

COUPLING OF THREE ANGULAR MOMENTA: THE 6-j COEFFICIENTS

Consider three commuting angular momenta (the index γ will now be suppressed). A basis of definite *total* angular momentum can be formed by coupling the first two to form a definite j_{12} and then coupling j_{12} and j_3 to form j

$$|(j_1 j_2) j_{12} j_3 jm\rangle = \sum_{m_1 m_2 m_3 m_{12}} |j_1 m_1 j_2 m_2 j_3 m_3\rangle \langle j_1 m_1 j_2 m_2 | j_1 j_2 j_{12} m_{12}\rangle$$

$$\times \langle j_{12} m_{12} j_3 m_3 | j_{12} j_3 jm\rangle \quad (B.23)$$

or by coupling the second and third to form j_{23} and then coupling j_1 and j_{23} to form j

$$|j_1(j_2 j_3) j_{23} jm\rangle = \sum_{m_1 m_2 m_3 m_{23}} |j_1 m_1 j_2 m_2 j_3 m_3\rangle \langle j_2 m_2 j_3 m_3 | j_2 j_3 j_{23} m_{23}\rangle$$

$$\times \langle j_1 m_1 j_{23} m_{23} | j_1 j_{23} jm\rangle \quad (B.24)$$

Either of these schemes gives a complete orthonormal basis, for the properties of the basis states $|j_1 m_1 j_2 m_2 j_3 m_3\rangle$ and the CG coefficients imply

1. $\langle (j_1 j_2) j'_{12} j_3 j' m' | (j_1 j_2) j_{12} j_3 jm\rangle = \delta_{j'_{12} j_{12}} \delta_{j' j} \delta_{m'm}$ $(B.25a)$

2. $\sum_{j_{12} jm} |(j_1 j_2) j_{12} j_3 jm\rangle \langle (j_1 j_2) j_{12} j_3 jm|$

$$= \sum_{m_1 m_2 m_3} |j_1 m_1 j_2 m_2 j_3 m_3\rangle \langle j_1 m_1 j_2 m_2 j_3 m_3| \quad (B.25b)$$

with similar relations for the second basis. As a result, the transformation from one basis to the other is again *unitary*; the 6-*j* symbols are defined in terms of these transformation coefficients by

$$\begin{Bmatrix} j_1 & j_2 & j_{12} \\ j_3 & j & j_{23} \end{Bmatrix} \equiv \frac{(-1)^{j_1+j_2+j_3+j}}{[(2j_{12}+1)(2j_{23}+1)]^{\frac{1}{2}}} \langle (j_1 j_2) j_{12} j_3 jm | j_1(j_2 j_3) j_{23} jm\rangle$$

$$= \frac{(-1)^{j_1+j_2+j_3+j}}{[(2j_{12}+1)(2j_{23}+1)]^{\frac{1}{2}}}$$

$$\times \sum_{m_1 m_2 m_3 m_{12} m_{23}} \langle j_1 m_1 j_2 m_2 | j_1 j_2 j_{12} m_{12}\rangle$$

$$\times \langle j_{12} m_{12} j_3 m_3 | j_{12} j_3 jm\rangle$$

$$\times \langle j_2 m_2 j_3 m_3 | j_2 j_3 j_{23} m_{23}\rangle \langle j_1 m_1 j_{23} m_{23} | j_1 j_{23} jm\rangle$$

$$(B.26)$$

These transformation coefficients can be proved independent of m in the following way. Consider

$$|(j_1 j_2) j_{12} j_3 jm\rangle = \sum_{j_{23}} |j_1(j_2 j_3) j_{23} jm\rangle \langle (j_1 j_2) j_{12} j_3 jm | j_1(j_2 j_3) j_{23} jm\rangle$$

$$(B.27)$$

Now operate on both sides of this equation with $J_+/A(j,-m)$. This raises the m value of the states without changing the coefficients, which still have an index m. By definition, however, the expansion coefficients of the new states have an index $m + 1$, and thus the coefficients are independent of m.

From the definition, it is seen that the 6-j symbols are invariant under (1) any permutation of the columns and under (2) the interchange of the upper and lower arguments in each of any two columns. Another very useful relation that follows from Eqs. (B.23) to (B.27) is

$$\sum_{j_{23} m_{23}} (-1)^{j_1+j_2+j_3+j} [(2j_{12}+1)(2j_{23}+1)]^{\frac{1}{2}} \begin{Bmatrix} j_1 & j_2 & j_{12} \\ j_3 & j & j_{23} \end{Bmatrix}$$

$$\times \langle j_1 m_1 j_{23} m_{23} | j_1 j_{23} jm \rangle \langle j_2 m_2 j_3 m_3 | j_2 j_3 j_{23} m_{23} \rangle$$

$$= \sum_{m_{12}} \langle j_1 m_1 j_2 m_2 | j_1 j_2 j_{12} m_{12} \rangle \langle j_{12} m_{12} j_3 m_3 | j_{12} j_3 jm \rangle \quad \text{(B.28)}$$

The 6-j coefficients also have been extensively tabulated.[1]

IRREDUCIBLE TENSOR OPERATORS AND THE WIGNER-ECKART THEOREM

An irreducible tensor operator of rank K is defined to be the set of $2K+1$ operators $T(KQ) [-K \leqslant Q \leqslant K]$ satisfying the equations

$$[J_\pm, T(KQ)] = A(K, +Q) T(K, Q \pm 1)$$
$$[J_z, T(KQ)] = QT(KQ) \quad \text{(B.29)}$$

Some examples of tensor operators are (in first quantization):

1. $f(r) Y_{LM}(\theta, \varphi)$ $(-L \leqslant M \leqslant L)$: tensor operator of rank L

2. r_q $(-1 \leqslant q \leqslant 1)$: tensor operator of rank 1

    where

    $$r_{\pm 1} \equiv \mp \frac{1}{\sqrt{2}} (x \pm iy) \qquad r_0 \equiv z$$

3. J_q $(-1 \leqslant q \leqslant 1)$: tensor operator of rank 1

    where

    $$J_{\pm 1} \equiv \mp \frac{1}{\sqrt{2}} (J_x \pm iJ_y) \qquad J_0 \equiv J_z$$

    [Note that $J_{\pm 1} = \mp \frac{1}{\sqrt{2}} J_\pm$.]

We now introduce the Wigner-Eckart theorem, which states that the m dependence of the matrix element of an irreducible tensor operator can be

[1] M. Rotenberg et al., *loc. cit.*

extracted explicitly in terms of a Clebsch-Gordan coefficient:

$$\langle \gamma' j' m' | T(KQ) | \gamma jm \rangle = (-1)^{K-j+j'} \frac{\langle KQjm | Kjj' m' \rangle}{(2j'+1)^{\frac{1}{2}}} \langle \gamma' j' \| T_K \| \gamma j \rangle \qquad (B.30)$$

Here the *reduced matrix element* $\langle \gamma' j' \| T_K \| \gamma j \rangle$ is *independent of the m values*. This powerful and useful theorem can be proved as follows:

1. Consider

$$|\Psi_{jm}\rangle \equiv \sum_{m_1 Q} \langle j_1 m_1 KQ | j_1 Kjm \rangle T(KQ) | \gamma j_1 m_1 \rangle$$

The commutation relations (B.29) between the angular momentum and $T(KQ)$ [using $\mathbf{J}^2 = \frac{1}{2}(J_+ J_- + J_- J_+) + J_z J_z$] and the set of linear equations defining the CG coefficients (B.17) show that

$$\mathbf{J}^2 |\Psi_{jm}\rangle = j(j+1)|\Psi_{jm}\rangle$$

$$J_z |\Psi_{jm}\rangle = m |\Psi_{jm}\rangle$$

2. We can therefore expand $|\Psi_{jm}\rangle$ in the basis states $|\gamma jm\rangle$

$$|\Psi_{jm}\rangle = \sum_{\gamma''} \langle \gamma'' jm | \Psi_{jm} \rangle |\gamma'' jm\rangle$$

and the coefficients $\langle \gamma'' jm | \Psi_{jm} \rangle$ are independent of m as proved following Eq. (B.27).

3. The orthogonality of the CG coefficients implies that

$$T(KQ)|\gamma j_1 m_1\rangle = \sum_{jm} \langle j_1 m_1 KQ | j_1 Kjm \rangle |\Psi_{jm}\rangle$$

4. The inner product with the state $\langle \gamma' j_2 m_2 |$ gives

$$\langle \gamma' j_2 m_2 | T(KQ) | \gamma j_1 m_1 \rangle = \langle j_1 m_1 KQ | j_1 Kj_2 m_2 \rangle \langle \gamma' j_2 | \Psi_{j_2} \rangle$$

which is just the Wigner-Eckart theorem, with the reduced matrix element defined in terms of $\langle \gamma' j_2 | \Psi_{j_2} \rangle$ through m-independent factors and signs.

TENSOR OPERATORS IN COUPLED SCHEMES

Consider two tensor operators $T(K_1 Q_1)$ and $U(K_2 Q_2)$, which we assume refer to different particles or different spaces. It is easily verified from the definition Eq. (B.29) and from the defining set of linear equations for the CG coefficients (B.17) that the quantity

$$X(KQ) \equiv \sum_{Q_1 Q_2} \langle K_1 Q_1 K_2 Q_2 | K_1 K_2 KQ \rangle T(K_1 Q_1) U(K_2 Q_2) \qquad (B.31)$$

is again an irreducible tensor operator of rank K. A special case of this result is the *scalar product* of two tensor operators

$$(2K+1)^{\frac{1}{2}} (-1)^K X(0) \equiv T(K) \cdot U(K) = \sum_Q (-1)^Q T(KQ) U(K-Q) \qquad (B.32)$$

which is a tensor operator of rank zero and therefore commutes with $\mathbf{J}$. By inserting a complete set of states, using the Wigner-Eckart theorem, and using the definition of the 6-j symbol, we can prove that

$$\langle \gamma' j_1' j_2' j' \, m' | T(K) \cdot U(K) | \gamma j_1 j_2 \, jm \rangle$$

$$= (-1)^{j_1 + j_2' + j} \delta_{jj'} \delta_{mm'} \begin{Bmatrix} j & j_2' & j_1' \\ K & j_1 & j_2 \end{Bmatrix} \sum_{\gamma''} \langle \gamma' j_1' \| T(K) \| \gamma'' j_1 \rangle \langle \gamma'' j_2' \| U(K) \| \gamma j_2 \rangle$$

$$(B.33)$$

In exactly the same fashion, the matrix element of a single operator in a coupled scheme is

$$\langle \gamma' j_1' j_2 j' \| T(K) \| \gamma j_1 j_2 j \rangle$$

$$= (-1)^{j_1' + j_2 + j + K} [(2j' + 1)(2j + 1)]^{\frac{1}{2}} \begin{Bmatrix} j_1' & j' & j_2 \\ j & j_1 & K \end{Bmatrix} \langle \gamma' j_1' \| T(K) \| \gamma j_1 \rangle$$

$$(B.34a)$$

$$\langle \gamma' j_1 j_2' j' \| U(K) \| \gamma j_1 j_2 j \rangle$$

$$= (-1)^{j_1 + j_2 + j' + K} [(2j' + 1)(2j + 1)]^{\frac{1}{2}} \begin{Bmatrix} j_2' & j' & j_1 \\ j & j_2 & K \end{Bmatrix} \langle \gamma' j_2' \| U(K) \| \gamma j_2 \rangle$$

$$(B.34b)$$

In these relations, $T(K)$ and $U(K)$ act on the first and second parts of the wave function, respectively.

INDEX†

Addition theorem for spherical harmonics, 516
Adiabatic process, 187
Adiabatic "switching on," 59–61, 289
Analytic continuation, 117p, 297–298, 302–303, 493
Angular momentum, 344, 504, 577p
  review of, 581–588
Angular-momentum operator, 505
Anomalous amplitudes, 489
Anomalous diagrams, 289
Anomalous Green's functions (bosons), 213
Anticommutation relations, 16
Atoms, 116, 121, 168p, 195p, 503, 508, 546, 567

BCS coherence length, 426, 465, 469
BCS gap equation (*see* Gap equation)
BCS theory (*see* Superconductor)
Bernoulli's equation, 496
Beta decay, 350–351
Bethe-Goldstone equation, 322, 358–366, 567
  anomalous eigenvalue, 324
  with degenerate states, 569–570
  effective-mass approximation, 359
  energy shift of pair, 371
  and Galitskii equations, 377–383
  ground-state energy of hard-sphere gas 371–374
    s-wave interactions, 371–374
    p-wave interactions, 374, 386p
    power-series expansion, 373–374
  hard-core, solution for, 363–366
  partial-wave decomposition, 386p
  s-wave, 360
  self-consistent, 358–360, 377–378
  square-well, solution for, 360–363
Bethe-Salpeter equation, 131–139, 219, 562–565
  (*See also* Galitskii's equations)
Bloch wave functions, 5
Bogoliubov equations for superconductor, 477p

Bogoliubov replacement, 200, 201, 203, 315, 489
Bogoliubov transformation, 316n, 326–336, 527–537
Bohr radius, 25
Bohr-Sommerfeld quantization relation, 425, 484
Boltzmann distribution, 39, 279
Boltzmann's constant, 36
Born approximation, 188, 197p, 219, 259, 345, 368
Born-Oppenheimer approximation, 390n, 410
Bose-Einstein condensation, 44, 198–200, 211, 481
  rigorous derivation of, 41n
  and superconductors, 441, 446, 476p
Boson approximation in shell model, 526–527, 576p
Bosons, 7, 198–223, 314–319, 479–499
  Bethe-Salpeter equation, 219
  charged, 223p, 336p, 500p, 501p
  chemical potential, 202, 206, 216, 493
  condensate, 200, 493
    at finite temperature, 492–495
    moving, 223p, 336p, 501p
    nonuniform, 495–499
  density correlation function, 223p
  distribution function, 37, 218, 317
  Dyson's equations, 211–214, 223p
  Feynman rules:
    in coordinate space, 208–209
    in momentum space, 209–210, 223p
  field operator, 200
  Green's functions, 203–215
  ground-state energy, 31p, 201, 207, 318
  hamiltonian, 200, 315
  Heisenberg picture, 204
  Hugenholtz-Pines relation, 216, 220, 222, 223p
  interaction picture, 207–208
  kinetic energy, 205
  Lehmann representation, 214–215
  momentum operator, 204

†The letter n after a page number denotes a footnote and p, a problem.

Bosons (*cont'd*):
  noninteracting (*see* Ideal Bose gas)
  number operator, 201–202
  perturbation theory, 199, 207–210
  potential energy, 200, 205–206
  proper self-energy, 211, 215, 219
  temperature Green's function, 491
  thermodynamic potential, 37, 38, 202, 207
  vacuum state, 201
  Wick's theorem, 203, 223*p*
  (*See also* Hard-sphere Bose gas; Interacting
    Bose gas)
Brueckner-Goldstone theory and thermodynamic potential, 288–289
Brueckner's theory, 116, 357–377, 382–383
Bulk modulus, 30, 390, 407
Bulk property of matter, 22, 349

Canonical ensemble, 33
Canonical momentum, 424–425
Canonical transformation to particles and
  holes, 70–71, 118*p*, 332, 504–508, 547
Charge-density operator, 188, 353
Charged Bose gas, 223*p*, 336*p*, 500*p*, 501*p*
Chemical potential, 34, 40, 75, 107, 327, 528–
  532, 535
  bosons, 202, 206, 216, 493
    hard-sphere gas, 220–222
    ideal, 39–41, 43
  classical limit, 39–40
  difference in superconducting and normal
    state, 335, 453*n*
  electron gas, 278, 284–285
  fermions:
    hard-sphere gas, 174
    ideal, 45–48, 75, 284–285
  phonons, 393, 410*p*, 485–486
  and proper self-energy, 107
Circulation, 483, 498
Clausius-Clapeyron equation, 499–500*p*
Clebsch-Gordan coefficients, 544, 582–584
Closed fermion loops, 98, 103
Coefficients of fractional parentage, 523*n*, 576*p*
Coherence length:
  BCS, 426, 465, 469
  Ginsburg-Landau theory, 433, 472
  superconductor, 422, 426, 433, 472
Collective modes, 171, 183, 193–194, 538
Collision time, 184
Commutation relations, 12, 19
Compressibility, 30, 222, 387*p*, 390–391

Condensate, 33, 200, 220, 317, 491
  in a channel, 502*p*
  ideal Bose gas, 42
  measurement of, 495
  moving, 502*p*
  and superfluid density, 495
  surface energy, 497–498
  wave function, 489, 492
    boundary condition, 496
    at finite temperature, 494–495
    Hartree equation for, 490
    spatial variation of, 497
Condensation energy of superconductor, 419,
  453
Configuration space, 7
Connected diagrams, 113, 301–302
  (*See also* Disconnected diagrams)
Constant of the motion, 59
Continuity equation, 183, 420, 496
Contractions, 87–89, 238, 327–329
Cooper pairs, 320–326, 359–360, 417, 441
  binding energy, 325, 336
  bound-state wave function, 336*p*
Core-polarization potential, 574, 577*p*
Correlation energy, 29, 155, 163–166, 169*p*,
  286–287
  and dielectric function, 154
  and polarization propagator, 152
Correlations:
  in nuclei, 362–363, 365–366, 572–573
  two-particle, 191–192
Coulomb energy of nuclei, 350
Coulomb interaction, 22, 188
  (*See also* Screening in an electron gas)
Coupling-constant integration, 70, 231–232,
  280, 379
Creation operators, 12
Critical angular velocity, 499, 500*p*
Critical current, 476*p*
Critical field, 415, 451, 453, 474*p*
Critical temperature of Bose gas, 40, 259–261
Critical velocity, 460*n*, 482, 487, 500*p*
Cross section, scattering, 189, 191, 314–315
Crystal lattice, 21, 30, 333, 389, 390, 394–396
  (*See also* Phonons)
Curie's law, 254*p*, 309*p*, 500*p*
Current operator, 455
Cyclic property of trace, 229

Damping, 81, 119*p*, 181, 195*p*, 308, 309*p*, 310*p*
Debye frequency, 333, 394, 395*n*, 396, 440*n*

Debye-Hückel theory, 278–281, 290p
Debye shielding length, 279, 306–308
Debye temperature, 394–395, 448
Debye theory of solids, 389, 393–395
Deformed nuclei, 515
Degeneracy factor, 38, 45
Delta function, 101, 246
Density:
  of free Fermi gas, 26–27
  of He^3 and He^4, 480
  of nuclear matter, 348–352
  of states, 38, 266–267, 333, 447
Density correlation function, 151, 174, 217
  300–303, 558
  analytic properties, 181n, 302–303
  for bosons, 223p
  for fermions, 194p, 302, 309p
  at finite temperature, 300–302
  Lehmann representation, 300–301
  perturbation expansion, 301–302
  and polarization, 153–154, 302
  relation to polarization propagator, 153, 302
  retarded, 173, 194p, 300–301, 307
  time-ordered, 174, 175
Density fluctuation operator, 117p, 189
Depletion, 221, 317, 488
Destruction operators, 12
Deuteron, 343
Deviation operator:
  for bosons, 489
  for density, 151, 173, 300, 560
Diagrams (see Feynman diagrams)
Diamagnetic susceptibility, 477p
Dielectric function, 111, 154, 184, 396
  ring approximation, 156, 163, 175, 180
Digamma function, 580
Dipole sum rule, 552, 577p
Direct-product state, 13, 17
Disconnected diagrams, 94–96, 111, 301, 560
  factorization of, 96
Dispersion relation(s):
  for plasma oscillations, 181–182, 310p
  for propagators, 79, 191, 294–295
  for zero sound, 183–184
Distribution function:
  for bosons, 37, 218, 317
  for fermions, 38, 46, 333–334
  for moving system, 486, 500p
Dyson's equations:
  for bosons, 211–214, 223p
  for electron-phonon system, 402–406, 411p
  at finite temperature, 250–253, 412p

Dyson's equations (cont'd):
  for Green's function, 105–111
  Hartree-Fock approximation, 122–123
  for polarization, 110–111, 119p, 252, 271
  for superconductors, 476p

Effective interaction, 155, 166–167, 252–253
Effective mass:
  electron gas, 169p, 310p
  of imperfect Bose gas, 260
  of imperfect Fermi gas, 148, 168p, 266
  in nuclear matter, 356, 369–370
  in superconductor, 431
Effective-mass approximation, 359, 384
Effective range, 342–343, 386p
Eikonal approximation, 468–469, 474
Electric quadrupole operator, 514
Electron gas:
  adiabatic bulk modulus, 390
  chemical potential, 278, 284–285
  classical limit, 275–281, 290p
  correlation energy, 29, 155, 163–166, 169p,
  286–287
  coupling to background, 389, 396–406
  degenerate, 21–31, 151–167, 281–289
  dielectric constant, 154
  dimensionless variables for, 25
  effective interaction, 155, 166–167
  effective mass, 169p, 310p
  electrical neutrality, 25
  ground-state energy, 32p, 151–154, 281–289
  hamiltonian for, 21–25
  Hartree-Fock approximation, 289p
  heat capacity, 289–290p
  Helmholtz free energy, 280, 284–285
  linear response, 175–183, 303–308
  plasma oscillations, 180–183, 307–308
  polarized, 32p
  proper self-energy, 169p, 268–271
  screening, 175–180, 195p, 303–307
  single-particle excitations, 310p
  thermodynamic potential, 268, 273–275,
  278, 284
  zero-temperature limit, 281–289
Electron-phonon system:
  chemical potential of phonons, 410p
  coupled-field theory, 399–406
    Dyson's equations, 402–406, 411p
    Feynman-Dyson perturbation theory,
    399–406
    proper electron self-energy, 402, 411p

Electron-phonon system (*cont'd*):
  proper phonon self-energy, 402, 411p
  vertex part, 402–406
  equivalent electron-electron interaction,
    401–402
  Feynman rules for $T = 0$, 399–401
  field expansions, 396–397
  finite-temperature properties, 412p
  ground-state energy shift, 399, 411p
  hamiltonian, 398
  interaction, 320, 396–399, 417
  linear response, 412p
  Migdal's theorem, 406–410
  phonon field, 410p
  phonon Green's function, 400, 402, 411p
  screened coulomb interaction, 397
  superconducting solutions, 440n, 476p
Electron scattering, 171, 188–194, 348–349,
    557, 566
Electronic mean free path, 425
Electronic specific heat, 395n
Energy gap:
  in nuclear matter, 360, 383–385, 388p
  in nuclei, 385, 526, 533
  in superconductors, 320, 330, 417, 447–449
Ensemble average, 36
Entropy, 34–35
  of He II, 486
  of ideal Fermi gas, 48
  of an ideal quantum gas, 49p
  of imperfect Fermi gas, 265–266
  of superconductor, 419, 476p
Equation of state, 187
  of electron gas, 30, 278–281
  of ideal Bose gas, 39, 42
  of ideal classical gas, 39
  of ideal Fermi gas, 45, 46, 47–48
  of ultrarelativistic ideal gas, 49p
Equations of motion, linearization, 440–441,
    538–543
Equilibrium thermodynamics and tempera-
    ture Green's function, 227, 229–232
Equipartition of energy, 394–395
Euler's constant, 580
Exchange energy, 29, 94, 126–127, 168p, 354
Excitation spectrum, 81
  interacting Bose gas, 217, 317
  in normal state, 334
  in superconductors, 334, 334n
Exclusion principle (*see* Pauli exclusion
    principle)
Extensive variables, 29, 35

External perturbation, 118p, 122, 172, 173,
    253p, 298, 303

Factorization of ensemble averages, 441, 457
Fadeev equations, 377
Fermi gas:
  interacting (*see* Hard-sphere Fermi gas;
    Interacting Fermi gas)
  noninteracting (*see* Ideal Fermi gas)
Fermi-gas model for nuclear matter, 352–357
Fermi momentum, 26
Fermi motion, 193
Fermi sea, 28, 71
Fermi surface, 179–180, 306, 334
Fermi velocity, 185
Fermi wavenumber, 27, 46
Fermions, 15–19
Fermi's "Golden Rule," 189
Ferromagnetism, 32p
Feynman diagrams, 96, 378, 399–401, 559–562
  in coordinate space, 92–100
  at finite temperature, 241–250
  in momentum space, 100–105
Feynman-Dyson perturbation theory, 112–
    113, 115, 399–406
Feynman rules:
  for bosons, 208–210, 223p
  for electron-phonon system, 399–401
  for fermions, 97–99, 102–103
  at finite temperature, 242–243, 244–248
Field operators, 19, 65, 71
  for bosons, 200
  commutation relations of, 19
  creation part, 86
  destruction part, 86
  equation of motion for, 68, 230
Finite-temperature formalism, $T = 0$ limit,
    288–289, 293, 296, 308p
First quantization, relation to second quantiza-
    tion, 15
First sound, 184, 481
Fission, 351
Fluctuations, 200, 337p, 527–528
Flux quantization, 415–416, 425, 435–436
Flux quantum, 416, 435
Fluxoid, 423–425, 474p
Forward scattering, 133
Free energy:
  Gibbs, 34
  of magnetic systems, 418
  of superconductor, 432

Free energy (*cont'd*):
Helmholtz, 34
of classical electron gas, 280
of magnetic systems, 418
of noninteracting phonons, 393
of quasiparticles in He II, 485
of superconductor, 431, 451, 453, 474*p*
Free surface in rotating He II, 483
Frequency sums, 248–250, 263, 281
Friedel oscillations, 179

Galitskii's equations, 139–146, 358, 370, 373
376, 567
and Bethe-Goldstone equations, 377–383
Gamma function, 579–580
Gap equation, 331, 492
in finite nuclei, 531, 535
normal solutions, 332, 531
in nuclear matter, 383–385
superconducting solutions, 333, 446–449,
475*p*
Gap function, 443, 466–474, 489
Gapless superconductors, 417*n*, 460*n*
Gauge invariance, 444, 454
Gell-Mann and Low theorem, 61–64, 113
208*n*
Giant dipole resonance, 552
Ginzburg-Landau parameter, 435, 472
Ginzburg-Landau theory, 430–439, 474
boundary conditions, 432
coherence length, 433, 472
determination of parameters, 471–472
field equations, 432, 496*n*
flux quantization, 435–436
microscopic derivation of, 466–474
in one dimension, 437
penetration length, 434, 472, 475*p*
supercurrent, 432
surface energy, 436–438
wave function, 471
Goldstone diagrams, 112, 118*p*, 354, 376, 381
Goldstone's theorem, 111–116, 387*p*
Gorkov equations, 444, 466
Grand canonical ensemble, 33, 228
Grand canonical hamiltonian, 228, 256
Grand partition function, 36, 228, 308*p*
Green's functions at zero temperature, 64–65,
205, 213, 228, 292, 400
advanced, 77
analytic properties, 76–79
asymptotic behavior, 79, 297

Green's functions at zero temperature (*cont'd*):
bosons, 203, 215
anomalous, 213
hard-sphere Bose gas, 220
ideal Bose gas, 208
matrix Green's function, 213–214, 501*p*
diagrammatic analysis in perturbation
theory, 92–111
for electron-phonon system, 399–406
at equal times, 94
equation of motion, 117*p*, 411*p*
Feynman rules for:
in coordinate space, 97–99
in momentum space, 102–103
at finite temperature (*see* Temperature
Green's functions)
frequency dependence of, 75
Hartree-Fock approximation, 124
for ideal Fermi gas, 70–72
for interacting Fermi gas, 145
in interaction picture, 85
matrix structure, 75–76
perturbation theory for, 83–85, 96
for phonons, 400, 402–404, 410*p*, 411*p*
physical interpretation, 79–82
real-time, at finite temperature (*see* Real-
time Green's functions)
relation to observables, 66–70
retarded, 77
as zero-temperature limit of real-time
Green's function, 293, 296, 308*p*
Gross-Pitaevskii equation, 496
Ground state in quantum-field theory, 61
Ground-state energy:
for bosons, 31*p*, 201, 207, 318
hard-sphere bose gas, 221–222
of electron gas, 25–26, 32*p*, 151–154, 281–
289
electron-phonon system, 399, 411*p*
and Green's functions, 68
of hard-sphere Fermi gas, 132, 135, 148–
149, 319, 373–374, 387*p*
Hartree-Fock approximation, 126
of ideal Fermi gas, 27, 46
of nuclear matter, 353–355, 366–377
and proper self-energy, 109
shift of, 70, 109, 111
superconducting and normal states, 335
and thermodynamic potential, 289
time-independent perturbation theory, 31*n*,
112, 118*p*
Group velocity, 183

Hamiltonian:
  first-quantized, 4
  models for physical systems:
    bosons, 200, 315
    electron gas, 21–25
    electron-phonon, 333, 391–393, 396–398
    pairing force, in finite nuclei, 523
    superconductors, 439–441
  second-quantized, 15, 18
Hard-sphere Bose gas, 218–223, 317–319, 480–481
  chemical potential, 220, 221–222
  depletion, 221, 317
  Green's function, 220
  ground-state energy, 221–222, 318–319
  other physical properties, 222
  proper self-energies, 219
Hard-sphere Fermi gas:
  chemical potential, 147
  effective mass, 148, 169p, 370–371
  effective two-body interaction, 136–137
  effective two-body wave function, 137–139
  ground-state energy, 135, 148–149, 169p, 319, 373–374, 387p, 480
  heat capacity, 148
  proper self-energy, 136, 142–146, 168p
  single-particle excitations, 146–148
  zero sound, 195p, 196p
Harmonic oscillator, 12, 393, 509–511, 569–571
Hartree equations, 127, 490
Hartree-Fock potential, 355–357, 511, 568
Hartree-Fock theory, 121–127, 167p, 168p, 399, 475p, 504–508, 575
  for bosons, 259–261
  equations, 126–127, 257–258, 507
    solution for uniform medium, 127, 258–259
  of finite nuclei, 575
  at finite temperature, 255–259, 262–267, 308p, 475p
  Green's functions, 124, 168p, 257, 308p, 440–441, 475p
  ground-state properties, 126–127, 332
  proper self-energy, 121–122, 125, 255–258
  relation to BCS theory, 439–441
  self-consistency, 121–122, 127, 258–259, 265
  single-particle energy, 127, 258, 330, 507, 510, 513, 539, 556
Hartree-Fock wave functions, 352–353, 503, 508–511, 541, 558–559, 567
"Healing distance," 366, 376

He^4, liquid (*see* He II)
He^3, liquid, 49, 116, 128, 480
  Brueckner's theory, 150
  heat capacity, 148
  zero sound, 187
He II, 44, 481–488
  critical velocity, 482, 488
  entropy, 486
  heat capacity, 44, 484, 486
  phase transition of, 44, 481
  quantized vortices, 482–484, 488
  quasiparticle model, 484–488
    phonons, 484–488
    rotons, 484–488
  surface tension, 498
  two-fluid model, 481
Heat capacity:
  Debye theory of solids, 393–395
  of electron gas, 269, 289–290p
  of hard-sphere Fermi gas, 148
  of He II, 44, 484, 486
  of ideal Bose gas, 42, 43
  of ideal Fermi gas, 48
  of imperfect Fermi gas, 261–267
  of metals:
    Hartree-Fock approximation, 269, 289p
    normal state, 295n
    superconducting state, 320, 416, 420, 451–454
Heisenberg picture, 58–59, 73, 173, 189
  for bosons, 204
  ground state, 65, 558
  modified, for finite temperatures, 228, 234
  operators, 65, 115, 213, 292
  relation to interaction picture, 83–85
High-energy nucleon-nucleus scattering, 566
Hole-hole scattering, 149–150, 381
Holes, 70–71, 504–508, 514, 520, 524, 538–543, 558–566
Homogeneous (uniform) system, 69, 190, 214, 292, 321
Hugenholtz-Pines relation, 216, 220, 222, 223p
Hydrostatic equilibrium, 50p, 177, 195p, 386p

Ideal Bose gas:
  chemical potential, 39–41, 43
  critical temperature, 40
  equation of state, 39, 42
  Green's function, 208
  heat capacity, 42, 43
  number density, 39

Ideal Bose gas (*cont'd*):
  occupation number, 37
  phase transition, 44
  statistical mechanics, 37–44
  superfluidity, 493
  temperature Green's function, 232–234, 245–246, 501p
  thermodynamic potential, 37, 38
  two-dimensional, 49p
Ideal Fermi gas:
  chemical potential, 45, 48, 75, 284–285
  density, 26–27, 45–47, 352
  entropy, 48, 266–267
  equation of state, 45, 46, 47–48
  Fermi energy, 46
  ground-state energy, 26, 46
  heat capacity, 48, 266–267
  occupation number, 38
  paramagnetic susceptibility, 49p, 254p, 309p
  statistical mechanics, 45–49
  temperature Green's function, 232–234, 245–246
  thermodynamic potential, 38, 278, 285
  two-particle correlations, 192
Imaginary-time operator, 228
Imperfect Bose gas (*see* Hard-sphere Bose gas; Interacting Bose gas)
Imperfect Fermi gas (*see* Hard-sphere Fermi gas; Interacting Fermi gas)
Impulsive perturbation, 180, 184, 307
Independent-pair approximation, 357–377, 480
  ground-state energy, 368
  justification, 376
  self-consistency, 368
  single-particle potential, 368
Independent-particle model of the nucleus, 352–357, 366
  justification, 376
Integral kernel for superconductor, 456, 458
  in Pippard limit, 463
Integrals, definite, 579–581
Intensive variables, 35
Interacting Bose gas, 215–218, 219, 314–319
  chemical potential, 216, 336p
  depletion, 218, 317
  excitation spectrum, 217, 218, 317
  ground-state energy, 318, 336p
  moving condensate, 223p, 336p, 501p
  proper self-energies, 215
  sound velocity, 217, 317
  superfluidity, 493

Interacting Bose gas (*cont'd*):
  near T_c, 259–261, 493
  (*See also* Hard-sphere Bose gas)
Interacting Fermi gas, 128–150, 261–267, 326–336
  distribution function, 333–334
  effective mass, 167p, 266
  entropy, 265–266
  ground-state energy, 27, 118p, 168p, 319
  heat capacity, 261–267
  magnetization, 32p, 169p, 310p
  proper polarization, 169p, 196p
  zero sound, 183–187, 196p
  (*See also* Hard-sphere Fermi gas)
Interaction picture, 54–58
  for bosons, 207–208
  for finite temperature, 234–236
Internal energy, 34, 247, 251
  Hartree-Fock, at finite temperature, 258
  of ideal quantum gas, 39, 46, 49p
  and temperature Green's function, 230, 247, 252
Interparticle spacing, 25, 27, 349, 366, 389, 394, 397
Irreducible diagram, 403–405
Irreducible tensor operator, 505, 508, 543, 586
Irrotational flow, 425, 481
Isotope effect, 320, 417, 448, 476p
Isotopic spin, 353, 508, 546

Josephson effect, 435n

Kinetic energy, 4, 23, 67, 205, 229
Kohn effect, 411p
Kronecker delta, 23

Ladder diagrams, 131–139, 358, 378–379, 567
Lagrange multiplier, 203, 486n, 500p
Laguerre polynomials, 509
Lambda point, 481
Landau critical velocity, 488, 493
Landau damping, 308
Landau diamagnetism, 462, 477p
Landau's Fermi liquid theory, 187
Landau's quasiparticle model, 484–488
Legendre polynomials, 516
Legendre transformation, 34, 336p
Lehmann representation:
  for bosons, 214–215
  for correlation functions, 299, 300–301, 456

Lehmann representation (*cont'd*):
  for Green's functions at zero temperature, 66, 72–79, 107
  for polarization propagator, 117p, 174, 300–301, 559
  for real-time Green's function, 293–294
  for temperature Green's function, 297
Lifetime of excitations, 81–82, 119p, 146–147, 291, 308, 309p, 310p
Linear response, 172–175
  of charged Bose gas, 501p
  of electron gas, 175–183, 303–308
  electron scattering, 188–194
  in finite nuclei, 566, 577p
  at finite temperature, 298–303
  neutron scattering, 196–197p
  of superconductor, 454–466
  to weak magnetic field, 309p, 454–466, 477p
  zero sound, 183–187
Linearization of equations of motion, 440–441, 538–543
London equations, 420–423, 425, 434, 459–460, 474p, 475p
London gauge, 425, 427, 454, 461
London penetration depth, 422
London superconductor, 427
Long-range order, 489n

Macroscopic occupation, 198, 218
Magnetic field, 309p, 418, 420
  thermodynamics, 418–420
Magnetic impurities, 179
Magnetic susceptibility, 174, 254p, 309p, 310p
Magnetization, 169p, 309p
Majorana space-exchange operator, 346, 354
Many-body forces, 377
Maxwell's equations, 417–418
Meissner effect, 414, 421, 423, 457, 459–460
  for Bose gas, 501p
  criterion for, 429
Melting curves for He, 480, 499–500p
Metallic films, 194, 476p
Metals, 21, 49, 121, 180, 188, 333, 389
Microcanonical ensemble, 486n, 500p
Migdal's theorem, 406–410
Mixed state of superconductors, 415n, 439
Molecules, 503, 567
Momentum, 24, 74, 204, 332
Multipole expansion of two-body interaction, 516

Neutron scattering, 171, 194, 196p, 485
Neutron stars, 49
Newton's second law, 183, 186, 420
Noncondensate, 491, 494–495
Nonlocal potentials, 322
Nonuniform Bose system, 488–492, 495–499
Normal-fluid density, 481, 486–487, 500p
Normal-ordered product, 87, 327
Nuclear magnetic resonance, 179
Nuclear matter, 116, 128, 348–352, 480
  binding energy of Λ particle in, 387p
  binding energy/particle, 352, 353–355, 371–377
  Brueckner's theory, 150, 357–377, 382–383
  compressibility, 387p
  correlations in, 362–363, 365–366
  density, 348–352
  effective mass, 356, 369–370
  energy gap, 330, 360, 383–385, 388p
  Fermi wavenumber, 352
  healing distance, 366
  independent-pair approximation, 357–377
  independent-particle model, 352–357, 366, 376
  many-body forces, 377
  pairing, 351, 383, 385
  with "realistic" nucleon-nucleon potential, 366–377
  reference-spectrum method, 377
  saturation, 355, 357, 375
  single-particle potential, 355–357, 381
  stability, 355
  symmetry energy, 386p
  tensor force, effect of, 367, 375, 386p
  three-body clusters, 376–377
Nuclear reactions, 171
Nucleon-nucleon interaction, 341–348, 354, 367, 504, 567
  nucleon-nucleon scattering, 342–347
  phenomenological potentials, 348, 361, 367, 557, 573
  summary of properties, 347–348
Nucleus, 49, 50p, 121, 188, 503
  Bogoliubov transformation, 316n, 326–336, 527–537
    energy at fixed N, 532
    for even and odd nuclei, 533–534
    fluctuations of $\hat{N}$, 527–528, 537
    for pairing force in the j shell, 534–537
    restricted basis, 528
    single-quasiparticle matrix elements, 533–534

Nucleus (*cont'd*):
  charge distribution, 348–349
  deformed, 515
  energy gap, 385, 526, 533
  excited states:
    application to O^{16}, 555–558
    construction of $\Pi(\omega)$ in RPA, 566
    with $\delta(\mathbf{x})$ force, 547–555
    the [15] supermultiplet, 548
    Green's function methods, 558–566
    Hartree-Fock excitation energy, 539
    the [1] supermultiplet, 555
    particle-hole interaction, 539
    quasiboson approximation, 542, 543
    random-phase approximation (RPA), 540–543, 564–565
    reduction of basis, 543–546
    relation between RPA and TDA, 565–566
    Tamm-Dancroff approximation (TDA), 538–540, 565–566
    transition matrix elements, 540, 543
  giant dipole resonance, 552
  Hartree-Fock ground state, 506, 538–539, 560
  magic numbers, 511
  many-particle shell model:
    boson approximation, 526–527
    coefficients of fractional parentage, 523*n*, 576*p*
    normal-coupling excited states, 522–523, 575*p*
    normal-coupling ground states, 520
    one-body operator in normal coupling, 520–522
    pairing-force problem, 523–526
    seniority, 524
    theoretical justification, 526
    two-body potential in *j* shell, 522–523
    two valence particles, 515–519
  odd-odd nuclei, 350, 517, 576*p*
  pairing, 351, 383, 385, 519, 523–537
  realistic forces for two nucleons outside closed shells, 567–575
    application to O^{18}, 573–574
    Bethe-Goldstone equation, 568–570
    harmonic-oscillator approximation, 570–575
    independent-pair approximation, 567–575
    Pauli principle correction, 574
    relative wave function, 572–573

Nucleus (*cont'd*):
    two-particle binding energy, 568
  single-particle matrix elements, 512–515
    magnetic moments, 514
    multipoles of the charge density, 514–515, 551
  single particle shell model, 508–515
    spin-orbit splitting, 511–512, 513
  sum rules, 577*p*
  two-body potential:
    $\delta(\mathbf{x})$ force, 518–519
    general matrix elements, 516–518
    multipole expansion, 516
Number density, 20, 66, 229, 247, 251
  comparison of superconducting and normal state, 334, 451
  of electron gas, 284
  Hartree-Fock approximation, 124, 257
  of ideal Bose gas, 39
  of ideal Fermi gas, 45
  of quasiparticles in He II, 486
Number operator, 12, 17, 20, 73, 201–202, 315

Occupation-number Hilbert space, 12, 37, 313
Occupation numbers, 7, 37, 38
Odd-odd nuclei, 350, 517, 576*p*
Operator, one-body, 20, 66, 229, 512–515
Optical potential, 135, 357
Order parameter, 431
Oscillator spacings in nuclei, 509*n*, 569

Pairing, 326, 337*p*, 351, 431, 519
Pairing force, 523–526
Parity, 344, 504, 577*p*
Particle-hole interactions, 192, 539, 562–563
Pauli exclusion principle, 15, 26, 47, 127, 134, 184, 193, 322, 344, 357, 480, 520, 572, 574
  for nucleons, 353
Pauli matrices, 75–76, 104, 119*p*, 196*p*, 343, 353
Pauli paramagnetism, 49*p*, 254*p*, 309*p*, 443, 462, 477*p*
Penetration length:
  Ginzburg-Landau theory, 434, 472, 475*p*
  superconductor (*see* Superconductor: penetration length)
Periodic boundary conditions, 21, 352, 392
Persistent currents, 415–416

Perturbation theory:
  for bosons, 199, 207–210
  for density correlation function, 301
  diagrammatic analysis, 92–116
  for finite temperatures, 234–250
  for scattering amplitude, 132–133
  for time-development operator, 56–58
Phase integral, 468–469
Phase shift for hard sphere, 129
Phase transition, 44, 259–261, 431, 481
Phonon exchange and superconductivity, 320, 439, 448
Phonons:
  Green's function, 400, 407
    Lehmann representation, 410p
    for superconductor, 477–478p
  in He II, 480, 484–488
  interaction with electrons, 320, 396–399, 417
  noninteracting, 390–395
    chemical potential, 393
    Debye theory, 393–395
    displacement vector, 391–393
    normal-mode expansion, 392
    quantization, 393
Photon processes, 566
Pictures:
  Heisenberg, 58–59
  interaction, 54–58
  Schrödinger, 53–54
Pippard coherence length, 426, 465, 469
Pippard equation, 425–430, 465
Pippard kernel, 428–429
Pippard superconductor, 427, 461–463
Plane-wave states, 21, 127, 258, 352, 392
Plasma dispersion function, 305
Plasma frequency, 180, 182, 223p, 307
Plasma oscillations, 21, 180–183, 194, 307–308
  compared to zero sound, 186
  damping, 181, 195p, 308, 310p
  dispersion relation, 181–182, 307–308, 310p
Poisson's equation, 177, 183, 279
Polarization propagator, 110, 152, 190
  analytic continuation, 302–303
  dispersion relation for, 191, 300
  in finite systems, 558, 563
    construction in RPA, 566
  at finite temperature, 252, 271
  in lowest order, 158–163, 272, 275, 282, 304–305, 561
  relation to density correlation function, 153, 302

Polarization propagator (cont'd):
  in ring approximation, 193, 307
  (See also Proper polarization)
Positron annihilation in metals, 171
Potential energy, 4, 67–68, 200, 205–206, 230
Potentials:
  core-polarization, 574, 577p
  nonlocal, 322
  separable, 322
  short range vs. long range, 127, 167–168p, 186
  spin-independent, 104–110
  symmetry properties, 328, 529
Poynting's theorem, 418n
Pressure, 30, 34–35, 222, 278
Propagation off the energy shell, 130, 382
Propagator (see Green's functions at zero temperature; Polarization propagator)
Proper polarization, 110, 154, 252–253, 302–303, 402–405
  at finite temperature, 252
  for imperfect Fermi gas, 169p, 196p
  in lowest order, 158–163, 272, 275, 282, 304–305, 561
Proper self-energy, 105–106, 355, 402
  for bosons, 211, 215, 219
  for electron gas, 169p, 268–271, 273, 402
  at finite temperature, 250–251, 264, 309p
  hard-sphere Fermi gas, 142–146
  in Hartree-Fock approximation, 121–122, 125, 256, 308p
  for phonons, 402
Proper vertex part, 403
Pseudopotential, 196p, 314
Pseudospin operators, 524

Quantized circulation, 484, 496
Quantized flux, 415–416, 425, 435–436, 438–439
Quantized vortex, 488, 498–499
Quantum fluid, 479, 489
Quantum statistics, 6
Quasiboson approximation, 542–543
Quasielastic peak, 193–194, 196p, 495
Quasiparticles, 147, 316, 317, 327, 487, 532–537
  in He II, 484–488
  in interacting Fermi gas, 332, 460n
  weight function, 309p

Random-phase approximation:
  electron gas, 156
  in nuclei, 540–543, 564–565
Real-time Green's functions at finite temperature, 292–297
  dispersion relations, 294–295
  Lehmann representation, 293–294
  for noninteracting system, 298
  relation to temperature Green's functions, 297–298
  retarded and advanced, 294–297
    relation to time-ordered, 295–296
  time-ordered, 292–293
  zero-temperature limit, 293, 296, 308p
Reduced mass, 129, 259
Retarded correlation function, 174, 299
Riemann zeta function, 579–580
Ring diagrams, 154–157, 271–273, 281, 564
Rotating He II, 482–484, 500p
Rotons, 484–488
Rydberg, 27

Scattering:
  optical theorem, 131
  phase shifts, 128–129
Scattering amplitude, 128–130, 143–146, 314
  Born series, 132, 135
Scattering cross section, 189, 191, 314–315
Scattering length, 132, 143, 218, 314, 342–343, 481n
  Born approximation, 135, 219
Scattering theory in momentum space, 130–131
Scattering wave function, 129, 138–139, 380
Schrödinger equation, 4, 54, 509, 572
  in momentum space, 130–131
  in second quantization, 15, 18
  two-particle, 129, 320–322
Schrödinger picture, 53–54, 172
Screening in an electron gas, 32p, 167, 175–180, 195p, 303–307, 310p, 397
Second quantization, 4–21, 353
Second sound, 481–482
Self-consistent approximations, 120, 358–360, 442–446, 492
Self-energy, 104, 107–108, 250
  proper (*see* Proper self-energy)
Semiempirical mass formula, 349–352
Seniority, 524, 536

Separable potential, 322
Serber force, 346, 355
Shell model of nucleus, 508–515
  boson approximation in, 526–527, 576p
  many-particle (*see* Nucleus: many-particle shell model)
  single-particle (*see* Nucleus: single-particle shell model)
Single-particle excitations, 147–148, 171, 309p, 310p, 399, 508–515
Single-particle Green's function (*see* Green's functions at zero temperature; Temperature Green's function)
Single-particle operator, 20, 66, 229, 512–515
Single-particle potential in nuclear matter, 355–357, 381
6-j symbol, 585–586
Skeleton diagram, 403–405
Slater determinants, 16
Sodium, 30, 391
Solidification of He, 479
Sound velocity, 187, 391, 407, 484
  in interacting Bose gas, 217, 222, 317, 494
Sound waves:
  classical theory, 186–187
  (*See also* Phonons; Zero sound)
Specific heat (*see* Heat capacity)
Spin density, 67, 196p, 229, 309p
Spin-orbit interaction, 511–512, 513
Spin sums, 98, 104, 189
Spin waves, 196p
Square-well potential, 360–361, 386p, 508–510
Stability against collapse, 31p, 355
Statistical mechanics, review of, 34–49
Statistical operator, 36, 228
Step function, 27, 63, 72
Structure factor, 189n
Sum rules, 191–192, 196p, 296, 577p
Sums over states replaced by integrals, 26, 38, 394
Superconductor:
  alloys, 415n, 425, 427
  Bogoliubov equations, 477p
  and Bose-Einstein condensation, 441, 446, 476p
  chemical potential, 334–335, 453n
  coherence length, 422, 426, 433, 472
  condensation energy of, 419, 453
  Cooper pairs, 320–326, 417, 441
  critical current, 460n, 476p

Superconductor (*cont'd*):
  critical field, 415, 451, 453, 474p
    lower and upper, 438, 439, 475p
  effective interaction, 448, 476p
  effective mass and charge, 431
  and electron-phonon interaction, 444, 448, 476p
    Dyson's equation, 476p
    phonon propagator, 477–478p
  energy gap, 330, 417, 447–449
  entropy, 419, 476p
  excitation spectrum, 334
  experimental facts, 414–417
  films, 474p, 476p
  flux quantization, 415–416, 425
  gap equation, 333, 446–449
  gap function, 443, 466–474, 489
  gapless, 417n, 460n
  gauge invariance, 444, 454
  Ginzburg-Landau theory (*see* Ginzburg-Landau theory)
  Gorkov equations, 444, 466
  ground-state correlation function, 337p
  ground-state energy, 335
  heat capacity, 320, 416, 420, 451–454
  Helmholtz free energy, 431, 451, 453, 474p
  isotope effect, 320, 417, 448, 476p
  local, 427
  London, 427
  matrix formulation, 443–444
  Meissner effect, 414, 421, 423, 457, 459–460
  mixed state, 415n, 439
  model hamiltonian, 441
  nonlocal, 427
  numerical values, tables, 422, 448
  order parameter, 431
  penetration length, 427, 434, 472, 475p
    general definition, 429
    local limit, 427, 429, 460
    nonlocal limit, 429–430, 460, 461–463
    table, 422
  persistent currents, 415–416
  phase transition, 431
  Pippard, 427, 461–463
  relation to Hartree-Fock theory, 439–441
  self-consistency condition, 444, 446
  spin susceptibility, 477p
  stability of Meissner state, 430
  strong-coupling, 440n
  surface energy, 430, 436–438
  temperature Green's function, 442–444

Superconductor (*cont'd*):
  thermodynamic potential, 449–454
  type I and type II, 438–439, 475p
  ultrasonic attenuation, 449, 478p
  uniform medium, 444–454
  variational calculation of ground state, 336, 337p
Supercurrent, 432, 472–474, 476p
Superelectron density, 423, 431, 459–460
Superfluid density, 481–482, 487, 495
Supermultiplets, 548, 549n, 558
Surface energy:
  in Bose system, 497–498, 502p
  of nuclei, 350
  in superconductors, 430, 436–438
Susceptibility, 174, 254p, 309p, 310p
Symmetry energy of nuclei, 350, 386p

Tadpole diagram, 108, 154
Tamm-Dancoff approximation, 565–566
Temperature, 34
Temperature correlation function, 300
Temperature Green's function, 228, 262
  analytic continuation to real-time Green's function, 297–298
  for bosons, 491
  conservation of discrete frequency, 246
  equation of motion, 253p
  Feynman rules:
    in coordinate space, 242–243
    in momentum space, 244–248
  Fourier series for, 244–245
  Hartree-Fock approximation, 257
  in interaction picture, 235–236
  Lehmann representation, 297
  for noninteracting system, 232–234, 245–246, 298
  for normal state, 468
  periodicity of, 236–237, 244–245
  and proper self-energy, 251
  relation to observables, 247, 252, 261–262
  for superconductors, 442–444
  weight function, 296–297, 309p
Tensor force in nuclear matter, 367, 375, 386p
Tensor operator, 343
Thermal wavelength, 277, 304, 306
Thermionic emission, 49p
Thermodynamic limit, 22, 75, 78, 199, 489
Thermodynamic potential, 34–35, 268–269, 274, 290p, 327

Thermodynamic potential (*cont'd*):
  for bosons, 37, 38, 202, 207
  coupling-constant integration for, 231–232
  for electron gas, 268, 273–275, 278, 284, 290*p*
  for fermions, 38, 329–332
  in finite nuclei, 528–537
  for phonons, 393
  relation:
    to Brueckner-Goldstone theory, 288–289
    to temperature Green's function, 232, 247, 252
  ring contribution, 274–275, 281–286
  of superconductor, 449–454
Thermodynamics:
  of magnetic systems, 418
  review of, 34
Thomas-Fermi theory, 177–178, 195*p*, 386*p*, 575
Thomas-Fermi wavenumber, 167, 176, 178, 182, 397
3-*j* symbol, 584
Time-development operator, 56–58
Time-ordered density correlation function, 174, 175
Time-ordered product of operators, 58, 65, 86–87
Transition matrix elements, 540, 543
Transition temperature of interacting Bose gas, 259–261, 493
Translational invariance, 73–74
Transverse part of vector field, 454
Two-fluid model, 481
Two-particle correlations, 191–192
Two-particle Green's function, 116*p*, 253*p*

Ultrasonic attenuation, 411*p*, 449, 478*p*
Uniform rotation, 483–484, 500*p*
Uniform system, 69, 190, 214, 292, 321

Vacuum state, 13, 201
Variational principle, 29, 336, 337*p*, 353, 502*p*
Vector potential, 424, 425–428, 431–433, 435–437, 454–456, 459, 465, 468
Velocity potential, 482, 495
Vertex parts, 402–406, 411*p*
Vortices in He II, 482–484, 500*p*, 502*p*
  energy/unit length, 484, 499
  vortex core, 484, 498–499

Wave functions:
  for condensate (*see* Condensate: wave function)
  Dirac, 188
  for Ginzburg-Landau theory, 471
  many-body, 5–8, 16
  scattering, 129, 138–139, 380
  single particle, 5
    Hartree-Fock, 352–353, 503, 508–511, 541, 558–559, 567
    spin and isospin, 21, 353
Weak interactions, 566
White-dwarf stars, 49, 50*p*
Wick's theorem, 83–92, 327, 399, 441, 506, 529, 560
  for bosons, 203, 223*p*
  at finite temperature, 234–241, 441
Wigner-Eckart theorem, 505, 521, 544, 586–587
Wigner force, 354
Wigner lattice, 31, 398*n*
Wigner's supermultiplet theory, 549*n*

Zero-point energy, 41, 393
Zero sound, 183–187, 195*p*, 196*p*
  compared to plasma oscillations, 186
  damping, 187, 195*p*, 310*p*
  dispersion relation, 183–184
  in liquid He^3, 187
  spin-wave analog, 196*p*
  velocity of, 185–187

2012.101